ONE LOVE

A JAMAICA HURRICANE RELIEF CHARITY ANTHOLOGY
VOLUME I

FOREWORD

On October 28, 2025, a devastatingly powerful Category 5 Hurricane Melissa slammed into the beautiful island of Jamaica. We all watched, helpless, as Jamaicans braced for the storm that destroyed countless homes and businesses and decimated the nation's infrastructure.

60 romance authors have banded together to try to make a difference by releasing this three-volume anthology with 100% of royalties going to a reputable charity helping those in affected areas. Enjoy these stories and help us support those affected by the hurricane by celebrating one love of the Jamaican people.

Wi likkle but wi tallawah.
We are small but we are mighty.

BILLIONAIRE LUMBERJACK'S BRAWN

A Lumberjacks in Love Story

Gwyn McNamee

IF THERE'S anything sexier than a bunch of burly, tattooed, muscled, bearded lumberjacks swinging an axe, I haven't seen it in this lifetime.

Thank you, Mom...

If she hadn't suggested I take a break from helping pack up the house to come check out the International Lumberjack Festival, I'd still be cooped up in there with her and Dad and a lifetime of memories going into boxes.

It's not like there is much else I could be doing in Hayes Creek to break up the monotony of wrapping knickknacks in old newspaper. In the decade I've been gone, very little has changed—except this, apparently.

The festival has ballooned since it began five years ago, and even I can admit how impressive it is. Hundreds of cars and trucks parked on the dirt lot, massive tents and food stands, and more spectators than I ever thought possible. The entire population of Hayes Creek must quadruple during these few days in July.

And I'm finally getting to see it all for the first time.

The hot summer sun beats down on the contestants in the chopping tournament, each of them swinging their axes meticulously, driving them hard into the large stumps, trying to make it deepest in the time allotted.

Sweat gleams on chiseled backs and sculpted arms.

I haven't seen this many Adonis-like men and this much plaid in my entire life.

It is fun to watch—I'll give them that.

Especially the guy on the far left, who appears to be blowing away the rest of the competition. Wood splinters fly around him, and each time his axe connects, the sheer force reverberates in my chest.

His thick, dark hair flops partially over his face as he takes another swing, but it doesn't seem to slow him down or impact his ability to see exactly what he's doing. Every muscle flexes and moves easily, accentuating his broad shoulders, bulging biceps, and tight ass in the jeans that fit him perfectly.

He slams his tool into the wood with the kind of power that sends a shiver through me despite the heat and humidity, and I fan my face to try to get myself to cool down a little bit before I pass out or jump the poor man.

"It's warm out here, huh?"

"What?" I turn toward the voice and find another woman standing next to me with a grin.

She lowers her head to peer at me over her sunglasses, then leans in with a conspiratorial smirk. The blonde inclines her head toward the competitors. "I said, 'It's hot out here, huh?'"

I chuckle at being caught. "It is *definitely* hot out here."

She grins and points to a guy on the far right. "That one's my husband."

"Oh!" I turn to watch him as he plows through his log, carving out massive chunks of wood, splinters filling the air all around him. "He's good."

A little sigh falls from her lips. "You have no idea. That man can split me any day."

Laughing, I return my attention to the dark-haired lumberjack on the left, imagining him using all that power in the bedroom instead of on the unsuspecting stump. "Lucky woman."

"Thank you." She continues to watch the rugged mountain men as the count clocks down. "What about you?"

I lean against the wooden fence surrounding the competition area and shake my head. "Not married. Not even remotely close to it."

"Are you from Hayes Creek?"

"No." I shake my head. "I mean, I *was*, but I don't live here anymore. I grew up here, but I moved to Milwaukee for college and stayed. I'm only in town to help my parents pack up their house. They just sold it."

Her blond brows rise above her sunglasses. "They're leaving town?"

I nod. "They're going to be Florida residents soon."

"Florida," she scoffs.

"Dad says he's sick of having to shovel and snowblow, and they want to spend their retirement somewhere they can enjoy a beach."

My new friend laughs. "Lake Michigan has lots of nice beaches."

I chuckle. "*I* know that, and *they* know that, but we all understand it's different, right? The freezing-cold Lake Michigan water doesn't hold a candle to the nice, warm tropical option down there."

She elbows me playfully. "But you might need that cool water after watching this, right?"

I bark out a laugh that draws the attention of a few people around us and then slap my hand over my mouth. "Shit. Sorry."

Here I am making a fool of myself my first time out of Mom and Dad's house in days...

The clock finally hits zero, and a buzzer sounds, signaling the end of the chopping competition. All six lumberjacks stop swinging their axes as the judges examine what they've done to determine a winner.

My gaze drifts back over to the man on the far left, who I haven't been able to take my eyes off since I got here. There's just something about him. The way he carries himself. The confidence. The raw sexual appeal he radiates.

Good Lord, it has been far too long if I'm sizing up this stranger...

My new friend nudges me. "I'm going to go talk to my husband. It was nice meeting you. I'm Annie, by the way."

"Oh, yeah, you, too. I'm Raelynn."

And I could really use a drink to cool off.

She gives me a little wave before darting off toward her personal lumberjack, and I make my way around the edge of the competition ring toward one of the tents set up with beer and food. The line moves up, and I order a pint and watch them pour it from the keg into a plastic Solo cup.

Classy.

I smirk as I take it and turn around to find somewhere shady to enjoy my drink and the people-watching, but my foot catches on something and I start to tumble forward. My beer splashes from my cup and onto the exposed, naked chest of a very big man already covered in sweat. His large, strong arms wrap around me and prevent me from falling face-first into the ground.

The scent of freshly chopped wood, fresh pine, and something wholly masculine fills my lungs as I struggle to catch my breath and offer an apology. "Oh, God. I'm so sorry."

He helps get me upright before I look up into his face and freeze.

Shit.

The guy from the competition—and this close, my heart flutters...

Because this man is no stranger.

A slow grin spreads across his face as he leans in. "Next time, watch where you're going instead of ogling me."

My jaw drops at both his audacity at calling me out and also at being caught.

How the hell did he know I was watching him while he was competing?

"I, I..."

He leans in slightly. "You don't have to lie, Raelynn. I caught you fair and square."

And for the second time in a decade, I am ready to turn tail and run from Jax Benton rather than die of sheer embarrassment.

His blue eyes inspect the area around us—the people milling about, chatting and eating and drinking, waiting for the next competition to start up. "The last time you were on this property, you kissed me, right over there."

I follow his pointed finger toward a wooded area to the far left of the competition rings, and dozens of memories come flooding back, threatening to drown me in a complicated mix of happiness and regret.

"Hi, Jax..."

He grins and crosses his arms over his barrel chest, making his massive biceps and pecs bulge and shimmer under the sun, covered with a sheen of sweat and my beer.

"Is this..." I scan around again, trying to place where we are after being gone for so long. "Is this your grandfather's property?"

"It's the backside. You always came up the main driveway near the house. When we started hosting the Lumberjack Festival, we decided to put it out on the back acreage, created the new turn-in and parking area. Though, I'm surprised you didn't realize where you were going. You did spend a lot of time out here. But I guess a lot has changed..."

My mind spins as I stare at the first boy I ever kissed—a very long time ago. And time has certainly changed *him*.

"Well, you certainly have"—I gulp as I allow my eyes to take in his thick mop of dark hair that he used to wear cut short to his head, chiseled powerful jawline, perfect chest and arms, and down over those jeans that fit just as perfectly in the front as they do in the back—"grown up."

Jax leans in and brushes his lips against my ear, sending a little shiver through me. "I could say the same for you, Raelynn. I heard you were back in town. Hoped we might run into each other."

"Oh, yeah?" I try to hide the way my body trembles at his proximity, but with his chest pressed almost against mine, he no doubt feels it. "Why is that?"

"Because you and I have unfinished business."

—

JAX

—

The soft hazel eyes I've dreamed about staring into for years widen slightly, and Raelynn's mouth opens and closes a few times before she swallows thickly. "What do you mean...unfinished business?"

I step closer, until my damp chest touches the swell of her breasts, and slide my hand around her lower back. Being this close to her again, seeing her after so long, has sent me spiraling back to that night as if it were just yesterday instead of over a decade ago. "That night at the bonfire..."

She trembles in my arms, hopefully for the same reason my body is vibrating.

"You walked right up to me and kissed me like you were trying to steal my breath, Rae, and then, you told me you'd always wanted to do that...and you walked the fuck away. Left the next day for college, and I've never heard from you again. I'd say we have some very *serious* unfinished business."

Her hands come up and press against my slick skin, her nails scratching lightly across my abs, making my cock twitch. "You think so?"

Fuck, yes.

I pull back and lock my eyes with her, nodding. "I do. Unless your husband would object to us going somewhere more private to discuss it?"

The corners of her lips twitch. "No husband."

"Your boyfriend, then?"

She shakes her head. "I don't have one of those, either."

Thank fuck.

If fate had dropped this woman back in my orbit only to yank her away because she's already attached, I'm not sure I could handle it. It's been hard enough not to throw her over my shoulder and take her back to my place since the moment I first laid eyes on her today.

"Good." I grab her hand and tug it gently, leading her out of the tent and onto the festival grounds. "Come on."

Her dark hair floats around her as we weave through the crowds. "Where are we going?"

"You'll see."

Rae narrows her eyes on me suspiciously but allows me to lead her through the throngs of spectators waiting for the next event to set up. She motions toward it. "Don't you need to be doing something with this?"

I wave a dismissive hand. "I'm actually not competing. I haven't in years. I was only doing the chopping because one of the guys got hurt and had to bow out." I grin over my shoulder at her. "Makes it more entertaining when there's better competition."

"Don't you need to be monitoring things?"

Her concern brings me to a stop, and I tug her up against me. "You've been here for all of thirty minutes, and you're already worried about how I operate my business…"

"Shit." She winces. "I'm sorry. I didn't mean to overstep."

I grip her chin and tilt it up. "I'm just messing with you. I appreciate the concern, but I have a really good staff who knows exactly what to do. They don't need me looking over their shoulder all the time. I'd much rather get to that unfinished business we have."

Her cheeks pinken even more than they already were from the July heat—and hopefully something else.

If seeing me affected her even *half* as much as me seeing her did today, it means all these years of wondering what could have been might have all been leading up to something other than nights spent with my cock in my hand, thinking about the one who got away.

I couldn't help but catch her watching me, feel her eyes on me the moment she stepped up to the fence and started observing the competition. From the minute I heard she was back in town, I'd hoped she'd show up, but I wasn't about to go chasing her.

It appears I didn't have to.

And that brings a grin to my lips as I brush my thumb across hers, then step back before I do something publicly I definitely shouldn't. Like kiss the ever-loving fuck out of her. "Come on."

She lets me lead her away from the competition grounds and down the cobblestone path into the thick trees. "This was where the old bonfire pit was, right?"

"Yep."

"That's where we're going?"

I grin at her. "You'll see."

The shade from the massive trees creating an arch over us helps shade the hot summer sun, but it can't cool me off—not having my hand wrapped around this woman's after so long.

We make it to the end of the path and step out into what used to be my little sanctuary growing up, where all the kids from high school would come to gather on Friday and Saturday nights for bonfires to hang out and drink and do things we absolutely should not have been.

But that is long gone.

Raelynn pulls to a stop, her eyes wide as she takes in what occupies the small clearing now. "Where did this come from?"

The log cabin sits directly in the middle, surrounded by towering firs and maples. A picturesque little postcard hidden in the woods. Smack dab on the spot Rae kissed me and broke my heart.

"I built it."

She gapes at me. "You *built* it?"

I nod and offer a slight shrug. "After high school, I went to work for my grandfather's lumber business. Learned some construction skills."

"I'd say so."

We approach the cabin, and I reach out with my free hand and twist the knob, swinging open the door to my own private refuge.

Her dark brows rise. "You don't lock it?"

I chuckle. "You've been living in Milwaukee for too long. I don't need to lock the door to my cabin in the middle of the woods in the middle of nowhere."

"Fair point."

We step inside into the slightly cooled air, and she releases a sigh. "It feels good in here."

"I put in air conditioning."

She laughs. "Do you remember growing up how so many of us didn't have it and how we'd all go hang out at Rocky's house on those sweltering days because his parents did?"

I laugh as I close the door behind us and lean against it. "I do. And if we weren't there, we were out here, enjoying those long summer nights..."

Crossing my arms over my chest, I watch her wander around the main living space of the cabin. She trails her fingers over the black leather couch placed in front of the fireplace, then makes her way over to the mantel to examine the photos lined up there.

She pauses in front of one and grabs it, bringing it closer to her face before she turns it toward me. "Was this from that night?"

That night.

Raelynn doesn't need to get more specific. We both know exactly when she's referring to. It's haunted me, my failure that night, letting her walk away and disappear from my life.

I nod slowly. "Yep."

And I have the photo memorized by heart—the eight of us. Best friends since kindergarten, all sitting around the bonfire the last night before she left, the first one of us to go off to college.

"Wow." She flutters her fingers over it. "That was a long time ago."

"It was and it wasn't."

She sets it back on the mantel, then turns toward me. "What do you mean?"

This would be a good time to keep my mouth shut, to lock away what has been buried safely for so long, but looking at that same mane of dark hair spilling over her shoulders, those hazel eyes almost the color of rich honey, it's impossible for me to lie to her.

Even if it might save my heart.

"I've missed you."

Her shoulders slump slightly, and she gives me a sad smile. "I've missed you, too."

As much as I appreciate the words, the same pain in my chest that hits me each time I think about her comes right back. "You could've called, written, emailed, sent a carrier pigeon."

Her perfect pink lips curl up slightly. "I could have. I'm sorry I didn't."

I stare down at my boots rather than at her when I say this because if she sees what a fucking sap I am, she'll probably run the out fuck of here—again. "Why'd you kiss me and then leave?"

She releases a heavy sigh, and I look up as she wanders over to the couch and lowers herself onto it. Her slender shoulders rise and fall. "Because I was a fool. Because I was seventeen, about to turn eighteen and start my new life in the big city, and I felt like if I didn't do it then, I never would."

"You should've stayed a little longer at the party."

Rae hesitates for a moment, her smile saddening. "You know what would've happened if I had."

We both do.

It's my turn to offer a shrug. "Would that have been so bad?"

Her bottom lip trembles slightly. "It would have because I might not have been able to leave if I had done what I wanted to that night."

RAELYNN

It's as much of an admission of how I've always felt about Jax as I've ever given him, and his strong, hard features soften as he takes the words in. He squeezes his eyes closed and releases a deep, heavy sigh I can feel all the way across the room before he pushes off the door and advances toward me slowly.

His skin still slick with sweat and the beer I managed to pour all over him, Jax towers over me—a massive, intimidating man full of confidence and swagger, not the boy he was all those years ago. But that shy kid still lives under it—and in his uncertain gaze.

I look away, staring down at my hands now that I've made that confession to probably the only boy I've ever *truly* loved.

He stops in front of me and lowers himself onto the coffee table—which somehow manages to support his weight—so his knees brush mine. "You know, I was in love with you since we were five."

I jerk my head up and let my eyes meet his crystal-blue ones. "What?"

He gives me a sad smile. "I always knew you were out of my league. You were the valedictorian, head cheerleader, most popular girl in school. Everyone knew you were going places. But me"—he shrugs—"I was just the dumb, skinny football player who was never going to leave Hayes Creek. That's why I never said anything, never told you."

"But—" Years of memories come flooding back: of our group of friends always hanging out together, the way Jax would slip his hand into mine and squeeze it, or give me piggyback rides or a strong hug when I needed it.

Always touching me.

Wanting to.

Always calling to make sure I made it home okay after one of our bonfires.

Constantly watching me from across the room, only to offer a shy smile when I would catch him.

I never thought anything of it. I believed we were all just friends looking out for each other. "Wow, I feel really stupid for never realizing that."

He smirks. "Don't. I intentionally hid it. I didn't want you to reject me. If I had lost you, if you had stopped being my friend because of how I felt, I don't think I could have lived with that."

Tears start to well up in my eyes, despite trying to fight them back. A thousand what-ifs I haven't let myself consider in a very long time flood my head. "I wish you had said something."

He reaches out and grabs my hand, pulling it between his. Harsh, rough calluses glide over my skin, and goosebumps break out on my arm. "You were always meant for something greater than Hayes Creek, Rae, and I was never going to be enough for you to stay. It just would have hurt both of us, even if I had known you were interested."

"Interested? I was a hell of a lot more than interested, Jax." I release a sardonic laugh, shaking my head and staring up at the beams on the ceiling. "God, Betty would have a field day with this."

"What do you mean?"

I lock my gaze with his again and smile, thinking about my childhood best friend. "All senior year, she kept telling me to go for it, that I should tell you how I feel. But—"

"But what?" He squeezes my hand between his. "Why didn't you?"

That same question has swirled through my head for so many years, and I've come up with dozens of answers—but none of them have ever seemed right.

Now that I'm sitting here with Jax, his hands on me, only one truth seems real. "I thought you would reject me. I thought you only saw me as a friend. Plus, I was leaving..."

"And you didn't want to start something you couldn't finish?"

"No." I lean forward slightly, closer to him, needing and wanting to take all of him in before I scare him away for good. "I didn't want it to finish at all, and that was the problem."

"Fuck." The word comes out on a low growl, and he squeezes my hand between his tightly. "So, we fucked it up, huh?"

I nod slowly, lowering my forehead to his. "I guess you could see it that way."

He pulls his head back and lifts his palm to my cheek, cradling it gently. "And look where we are. I'm still here in Hayes Creek, and you're off doing big things. HR, right? For the Brewers?"

"One of their many HR people." I grin. "Don't make it sound more glamorous than it is."

Pride fills his gaze, and he looks at me the way no one else ever has—full of so much devotion, even after all this time. "I bet you're great at that job, though. Everybody always loved you. I always did."

"*Did?*"

Maybe it's a stupid question, but I can't stop myself from asking it. The boy I always wanted, the one I thought I could never have, is now a man, sitting in front of me, telling me I could have had all of that back then.

I could have had him.

He could have been my first everything, but instead, it was some bumbling frat bro I met freshman year in college, whose name I can barely remember. And no one since has lived up to the feeling I had pressing my lips against Jax's that night.

"I'll always love you, Rae, but nothing has changed, right? I'm still here. You are still there."

I slip from his hold, unable to think clearly with his gentle touch and the scrape of his calluses along my skin, and I push up from the couch to pace. He watches me move back and forth through his living room, heat burning across his normally cool-blue gaze.

"I don't know what to say, Jax." I release a humorless laugh. "This is absolutely not the conversation I expected to be having when my mother insisted I come to the competition today."

His brow furrows. "That's why you came? Your mom told you to?"

The hurt and disappointment in his words slashes at my heart.

A sad smile tilts his lips. "I guess I should have figured you didn't come to see me when you didn't even realize it was on my family's property..."

I stop behind the couch and press my hands onto the back of it, thankful for something physical between us in the tight space that seems to shrink more and more the longer I'm in here with him. "I came home to help my parents, and yes, I had hoped I wouldn't run into you."

He recoils slightly. "Ouch."

"Not because I didn't want to, Jax. But because I wasn't sure what I would say, how I would react, not after I kissed you and then literally ran."

And boy, did I run that night...

I ran as fast as my legs could carry me, out of the woods, to my car, and I drove home like a bat out of hell, hoping he wouldn't come to confront me about what I had just said and done before I had to leave the next morning to start the rest of my life.

"I should have come after you." His words are so sincere, full of the heavy weight of all the years that have strung between us since that one moment in time. "I really should have."

"Why didn't you?"

He gives me a sad smile and shrugs his massive shoulders. "Because I knew the truth: that I would only hold you back. And the same is true now, right?"

I chew on my bottom lip as I contemplate his words and what they mean.

Is he saying what I think he is?

He slowly rises from the coffee table and makes his way around the couch, giving me all the time in the world to move away. Sliding in behind me, he presses his chest against my back and buries his face in my hair. "God, you still smell the same..."

"Sweaty and disgusting from being out there in the heat?"

His low, deep chuckle reverberates through me. "If anyone stinks, it's me."

"All I smell is the beer."

He laughs, the sound lightening the mood and taking me back to countless happy memories, and he wraps his arms around me and tugs me back against him. His lips find my neck, and he slowly kisses his way up to my ear, each press to my skin sending little sparks through my body. "Let me do to you what I should have all those years ago."

IT ISN'T fair of me to ask it. It isn't honorable for me to put her in this position, knowing she's going to have to leave and go home as soon as her parents finish packing up their house. It isn't right to *want* this right now.

But I'm a selfish bastard who's fantasized about having her in my arms, of having her like *this* for so long, that I don't know how I could physically let her go right now, even if I tried.

And I don't *want* to try.

Not when she sags back against me, her body trembling, my cock hardening against her lush ass, and she reaches up and runs her fingers through my hair, clutching the back of my head.

She needs this.

Needs me.

As badly as I do her.

I feather my lips along the column of her neck again, savoring the salty taste of her skin and the light floral scent that clings to her, the one I always smelled in my dreams about her over the years. Every fiber of my being wants to devour this woman, wants to take her in and never let her go. My breath flutters the hair around her ear. "Please, Rae..."

Her fingers tighten in my locks, and I slide my hand to the hem of her shirt and under it, splaying my palm across her stomach. She shudders against me again, then twists in my embrace to loop her arms around my neck and press her lips to mine.

Just like that night...everything around us fades away the moment our lips touch.

The hundreds of people milling around on my land just outside this thicket.

The ten years of time and hundreds of miles of distance between us.

All the things we never said to each other back then.

All of it vanishes as our mouths move together, as we share air and breath and the things we won't admit with words.

I grip her hips and lift her easily to wrap her legs around my waist, stepping forward to rest her ass on the back of the couch. It puts her in the perfect position to grind her core against my length.

"Fuck..." I groan, tugging her even tighter to me, wishing I could simultaneously speed this up and make it slow down to last forever.

Rae moans into my mouth, rubbing herself along me, angling her hips so the head of my cock catches along the seam of her slit. Her nails scrape on the back of my neck, and I reluctantly tear my mouth away from hers long enough to grab the hem of her shirt and tug it up and off her.

I let it fall unceremoniously to the floor, leaving her sitting in front of me, her breasts pushed up in a lacy black bra like an offering from God Himself.

Fuck me...

All the years of fantasizing about this woman were nothing compared to seeing her in the flesh. She was always stunning, even in high school, but her lush body now is the thing of every man's dreams.

I lightly drag my calloused fingertips along the edge of her bra, and goosebumps pebble across her smooth skin. The juxtaposition of my rough, worked touch against her peachy, flawless beauty robs me of words. But I still try.

"You're fucking beautiful, Rae. I should have told you that then."

She reaches up and captures my jaw in her palm, tilting my face until my eyes meet hers again. "We were young and stupid. We should stop apologizing for it."

A thousand apologies wouldn't be enough for letting her walk away from me that night, but she's right. If we keep focusing on what *didn't* happen, we won't be able to concentrate on the *now*.

I drag her to me and crash my mouth to hers again, relishing a taste that's all Rae. Everything I ever thought I needed back then and know I need now.

Need but can't keep.

A woman like Rae doesn't belong in Hayes Creek, with a rough-handed lumberjack living in a cabin in the woods. But I push away the thought of having to let her go again because if I think about it now, I'll ruin this moment, our moment, the only one we might ever have.

One Rae seems just as eager to enjoy.

She reaches between us and fumbles for my zipper. Frantic hands finally manage to get it down, and Rae uses her feet to shove my pants to my knees. My cock springs free, and she takes it in her smooth palm.

Fuuuuuuuccccccccccccccccckkkkkkk.

I issue a low groan as she strokes me slowly, sending a surge of pleasure coursing through my body, and I drop my forehead against hers.

Holy hell. I won't be able to last with her touching me like this.

This is supposed to be about me showing her how much I need her, how much she means to me, what I should have done for her the moment she pressed her lips to mine all those years ago. Not taking from her when she's already stuck between a rock and a hard place, and I'm already asking the impossible from her.

I step back out of her reach, and her eyes widen slightly, her lips parting in a gasp of surprise.

"Take off your pants, Rae."

She locks her heated gaze with mine as she slides off the edge of the couch, undoes the buttons, and slowly shimmies out of her jeans, taking her underwear with her.

"Jesus fucking Christ…"

Raelynn Hoover, naked in front of me. If I drop dead at this moment, I could die a happy man, even without ever being inside her, just seeing her like this. A true angel on earth. One I am completely unworthy of.

She kicks off her shoes and tugs her jeans free as I pull mine off, leaving us both fully exposed—in every way. The years we let pass have given both of us the benefit of losing those reservations that held us back. All that's left is to take what we want and feel, all the things we wouldn't let ourselves have back then.

I glide my fingertips up her thighs and lift her again to hug her legs around my waist. A more patient man would take her to the bedroom, but instead, I turn and push her back against the log wall of the cabin.

A little groan falls from her lips as she glides her slick core along my length. "What are you doing?"

"The bedroom's too far away." I kiss her again. "I need to taste you." Kiss. "Now." Kiss. "I need to hear and feel you come."

She frantically buries her hands in my hair, clinging to me, moving her lips over mine, desperate for the same thing I am. But I tear my mouth from hers and lift her. She issues a little yelp as I settle her thighs on my shoulders and bury my face between her legs.

"Holy fuck, Jax…"

It comes out on a gasp, and my tongue finds her core slick, hot, and ready for me.

"Fucking hell, Rae."

I probe inside her, gliding my tongue along every inch of her, devouring her arousal as she digs her nails into the back of my head and tightens her thighs around my neck.

"I'm not going to stop until you're snapping my fucking neck with these beautiful legs. You hear me?"

Rae doesn't respond, so I slap my palm against the outside of her thigh, and she jerks against me, grinding her cunt against my face even harder.

Fucking suffocate me, woman.

I grin against her wet flesh and continue to eat her like the starved man I have been for her for all these years. Her thighs tense, and her body trembles under my arm pinning her against the wall.

She's close.

My cock throbs to be buried inside her, to have this scalding heat wrapped around it, clutching at me, bringing me to release, but I want her to come down my throat more.

I slide my other hand up to slip two fingers deep inside her. She gasps as I suck her clit between my lips and probe, curling and pushing on exactly that right spot.

Her mouth falls open on a silent gasp, and she rolls her hips against my face, tightening her thighs even more around me. "Jax, I'm going to come."

"Do it," I mutter the words against her flesh and bite down on her clit, then suck hard.

She bucks her hips and twists so hard, it feels like my neck might fucking snap. And it's exactly what I wanted—her giving herself over to me the way I wish she could have that night, the way I wish she would every night since then.

Raelynn Hoover is the most beautiful and perfect woman on this fucking planet, and I let her go once. I'm not going to do it again. At least, not until I've done everything I can to prove that she belongs here with me like this.

If it takes all fucking day, this woman is going to crumble in my arms until I'm the only one who can put her back together again.

My orgasm washes over me, flooding my veins the way the waves off Lake Michigan crash into the beaches and soak the sands. It ebbs and flows. A tsunami of feelings and emotions. Of light and happiness. Utter ecstasy overtaking me in a way I've never experienced before.

And it's all because of *this* man.

I grind my hips, the wood wall behind me pressing hard into my back as my body spasms. Jax continues to suck at my clit until I can't take the overwhelming pleasure anymore. Until it threatens to consume me so completely that I won't be able to break free of it.

Gasping for breath, I push against his head. "Stop. Oh God, stop. I can't—"

He slowly lifts his face from between my legs, his scorching-hot gaze boring into mine as he licks his lips and lifts his fingers to his mouth to suck my arousal from them as well.

Good God...

Jax Benton has become a force of nature.

He was always so comfortable out here, in the woods, exploring his grandfather's land and working with his hands. Trying to learn and understand how things grew, how they worked, how to make them better. And the years have only made him stronger, more determined. With all that passion and focus directed at me, my heart threatens to burst the way my resolve did the moment his lips hit mine.

He takes a half step back and slowly allows me to slide down the wall until my unsteady feet hit the floor and his strong arms tug me firmly against his slick body. He presses his lips to mine, kissing me long and slow and sweet, the taste of my arousal still on his tongue.

"I want to do that again."

His murmured words send my heart thundering even harder than it already was, and I loop my arms around his neck and bury my face against his shoulder. He lifts me easily—the skinny boy I knew from high school, now the brawny, burley lumberjack who can throw me around like I weigh nothing.

He carries me to a door on the far side of the cabin and nudges it open with his foot, and suddenly, I'm floating before he lays me down on a soft comforter and covers my body with his.

His hard cock presses against my stomach, and I groan and wrap my legs around him, locking them and squeezing him against me tightly. He drops languid kisses across my cheeks, over my closed eyes, down my neck, to my breasts, where he tugs down my bra so he can lavish attention on each one of my taut nipples.

I twitch under him as he sucks one into his mouth hard and twists the other between his fingers. "Oh, God."

The direct line of pleasure goes straight to my clit, and I arch against him, searching for the friction where I so badly need it.

A satisfied groan vibrates from his chest through mine. "Why did we wait so long to do this?"

He moves to my other breast and gives it the same attention, sucking and nipping and twisting until I can't stop bucking wildly. A grin spreads across his face, and he looks up at me with pure contentment filling his gaze.

I score my nails over his scalp, loving the soft feel of his thick hair against my fingertips, but I can't face him when I admit this. Squeezing my eyes closed, I fight a sob threatening to slip up my throat. "Because I was scared and ran."

"I was scared, too, Rae." He kisses my chest. "To come after you." He kisses my neck. "Of what it might mean." My lips. "But I'm not anymore. Look at me, Raelynn."

I open my eyes, and the look the man gives me stops the world.

He takes my face in his palm as he positions his cock between my legs. "This was always what was meant to happen. You and me. You know that, right?"

I nod as he sinks into me slowly, his hard, wide length spreading me. He captures my gasp with his lips and stills, giving me time to adjust to his size before he draws his hips back and plunges into me again, a little deeper this time.

"Oh, God, Jax."

There are no other words.

Any I could hope to say leave me on another gasp as he rolls his hips and finally pushes himself as deeply inside me as possible.

I've never felt more at home than I do at this moment, when I'm getting ready to leave this town forever, getting ready to leave behind all the memories and the people here. The timing couldn't be worse.

Tears well in my eyes, and one slides down my temple.

Jax stills immediately. "Rae, am I hurting you?"

I shake my head and urge him to keep going, moving my hips against his, matching his slow, steady rhythm. "No, I'm just…"

Completely and utterly shattered by what's happening.

Overwhelmed.

Lost.

"Me, too." He whispers the words against my ear and buries his face in my neck as his hips begin pumping harder, pushing him deeper, driving both of us toward something we both know could change everything.

If we had allowed this to happen, if we had done what we wanted that night all those years ago, we may have had such different futures. Everything would've looked different if I hadn't run, if I'd had the guts to stand there and kiss the boy I loved and tell him I wanted him forever, not just for one night.

And now, this might be all I get.

I fight the emotion threatening to choke me as he shifts up onto his knees and adjusts my hips to give him a different position. He thrusts into me, his hand tightening at my waist, his body slamming to mine in a way that's meant to cement him there forever, as if he wasn't already there.

My best friend.

The boy who always had my back and always held my hand.

Who never asked for anything in return.

I open my eyes to watch him now, the beauty of his massive, strong body earned through hard manual labor every day since I last saw him. Jax isn't the type of guy who gives up on anything once he sets his mind to it. And he's intent now, drilling me, dragging me closer to another precipice that I'm not sure I'm ready to fall over.

The first orgasm almost killed me. And now, with him inside me, the head of his cock dragging against that perfect spot deep in my core, this one feels like it might actually finish the job.

But we roll together so perfectly, a synchronous movement, a beautiful orchestra of gasps and moans, and our sweat-slicked bodies gliding until the chords in his neck strain and every muscle in his body tightens.

He's barely holding back, ready to unleash everything into me that he's felt and wanted for the last ten years.

"Let go, Jax."

My words fill the space between us, and his eyes move from where our bodies connect to meet mine.

"I fucking love you, Rae."

In any other circumstance with anyone else like this, the words would seem hollow, fake, impossible, considering the time and distance between us, but I hear the sincerity in them.

I *know* he means them.

He isn't the type of person to throw those words around and use them as ammunition with a woman in bed, and they're exactly what I need to finally let myself go and give myself over to him fully.

This orgasm builds between my legs and slithers up my spine, coiling inside me until it breaks, releasing tension I didn't even know I was holding. I clench and spasm around his cock, and he drops his head and thrusts into me harder and faster.

"Fuck..." His fingers dig into my hips, and he tips his head back. "Rae!"

My name fills the room as he fills me and buries his face against me while my body twitches and tries to come down from the cataclysm I just experienced.

He feathers kisses along my neck, over my collarbone, and back up to my lips, where he steals what little breath I have left.

Jax Benton is a dangerous man, not because of his strength, not because of his brawn, not even because of the devilish smirk he still has and knows how to use, but because of the way he was able to reach into my chest, grab my heart, and wrap himself around it so tightly, I won't ever be able to get it back.

JAX

I FINALLY FORCE myself to roll off Raelynn, bringing her with me onto her side, needing to keep her close. My semi-hard cock still buried inside her twitches, and she squeezes around it, eliciting a low groan from deep in my chest.

Dark hair tumbles over her face, and I brush it back and use my thumbs to wipe away the tears streaming down her cheeks. "Why are you still crying?"

Given the circumstances, she has any number of reasons—all my fault.

She opens her eyes, and the haunting beauty staring back at me makes my breath hitch, just like it always did when we were young, dumb teenagers who didn't know how to handle the feelings filling our hormone-fueled bodies. "Because I want to stay."

So much uncertainty weighs on her words that guilt claws at gut. "Fuck. I'm sorry, Rae. I shouldn't have—" I squeeze my eyes closed and shake my head, dragging her more firmly against me, so there isn't even a centimeter separating us. "It wasn't fair of me to do this, to put you in this position."

"I was a *very* willing participant, Jax."

I open my eyes again to find the corners of her mouth twitching as she fights a smile.

Even with the heaviness of the topic of conversation, she still manages to find the humor in it. She waggles her eyebrows. "*Very* willing."

Despite the melancholy suddenly settling over what was, only moments ago, the best experience of my life, I return her grin because it's impossible not to appreciate life with this woman in my arms. I just need to figure out a way to keep her.

"You can stay, you know. As long as you want. Forever."

Her bottom lip quivers, and she shakes her head. "My parents are leaving. They're not coming back. This isn't my home anymore; it hasn't been for a long time. I have a job; I have friends in Milwaukee. I have a career. I have—"

"You don't have me there." As soon as the words leave my mouth, I want to take them back because her tears immediately start again. I never could stand to see her cry, and now, I'm the one causing it. "Fuck, I know it isn't fair, Rae, to even ask this, but come back to Hayes Creek. Now that I've had you like this, now that I know that everything I've ever felt was real, I can't let you go again. But...I also can't leave here."

Even I can hear how fucking selfish it sounds, and I sigh and roll onto my back, scrubbing my hands over my face, instantly regretting the loss of contact with her. But I feel like such a fucking asshole right now that I can't even look at her.

As if she can sense it, she shifts over and drapes her arms across my chest, resting her chin on my pec. "Why can't you leave? Why can't you come to Milwaukee with me?"

For the same reason I didn't chase after her that night...

"Because I belong here, Rae. This place, these woods, the people. This is always where I was meant to be. Things have happened since you've been gone that you probably don't even know about. When my grandfather passed away, the land, the lumber company, the construction company, they all went to my father and my uncle. Well, my uncle died last year, and my father took over running everything himself. Which means *I'm* running everything because he's damn near eighty years old and is going to give himself a coronary if he keeps trying to do it all."

She gives me a tight smile, and I consider how to say the next words without it sounding like arrogance or some way of bribing her to stay.

Her light fingers feather across my forehead. "What is it? Why do you have this furrowed brow?"

I lean into her touch, savoring it, wanting to memorize it in case she disappears from my life again. "The companies have gotten a lot bigger than when we were kids."

"What do you mean?"

It feels strange discussing business with her, but if she doesn't understand why it's so important, she won't understand why I can't leave. "Well, my dad and my uncle, they expanded into commercial construction instead of just residential. They got a lot of government contracts over the years. There aren't a lot of qualified companies up here that can handle the government projects."

"That's good."

"It's *very* good, Rae." I tighten my grip on her. "All the companies together, the land, the buildings, all the family-owned properties. All of it is worth billions now."

She freezes. "Billions with a *B*?"

I nod. "Yeah, with a *B*. Add the festival on top of that, and the money it brings in every year, walking away from all of this would be..."

Her kiss-swollen lips droop. "It would be stupid."

I take her face between my palms. "No, I would give it all up for you. All of it. Every single fucking penny. If it were only about me. But there are hundreds of employees who depend on me running these companies, and I still need to take care of my mom and dad. Plus, I don't know what the fuck I would do in Milwaukee." I bark out a humorless laugh. "I know how to work with my hands."

She leans up and presses a soft kiss to my lips. "You sure do."

The compliment briefly lifts my spirits, but I know what I'm asking her and how impossible it will be for her to say yes. This brief respite from the world outside and the things pulling us in opposite directions will end soon. A reality we'll both have to accept.

"I wouldn't fit in there, that place. Your life. It's not who or what I am. But up here isn't you anymore, either, Rae."

Rae considers my statement for a moment, twisting her lips as she swirls little circles with her fingertip across my chest. "I'm not so sure about that anymore."

"What do you mean?"

She sighs and rests her cheek over my heart. I let her be for a moment, thinking through whatever it is she has going on in that beautiful head of hers. This isn't the time to rush any conversations, and I want to enjoy having her in my arms for as long as possible.

"When my parents told me they were moving and asked me to come back to help them pack up the house, I didn't want to…"

"Because you didn't want to see me."

She shakes her head. "It wasn't just that. I knew it would be hard to leave again once I came up here…leave for the *final* time and cut all ties with Hayes Creek. The few times I did come home during college over holiday breaks"—she shrugs slightly—"I realized how much I missed it. I missed the town. I missed the people."

"I never saw you when you were home."

Tilting her chin up, she gives me a sad, apologetic smile. "That was inten-tional. Even years later, I felt like an idiot for kissing you like that and leaving. The thought of facing you again after that was too much for me to bear."

"It *was* pretty dumb."

She smacks me playfully on the shoulder. "Don't get me wrong, I love Milwaukee. I love my life, my friends, my job even…"

The silence hanging between us speaks volumes. Rae may not want to say the words, but I know what she's thinking—because I haven't been able to leave, either.

"But it isn't Hayes Creek."

She nods. "But it isn't Hayes Creek."

It's the opening I've been hoping for—a glimmer of hope that this might all work out. "You could come back, do HR for me, for the various companies…"

Rae pushes up on her elbows. "Are you serious?"

I nod and drag her across my body so she's fully covering me again. Her wet cunt presses over my cock, stirring it back to life. I'd give anything to plunge back into her and lose the world around us again, but this is too important to brush aside for another round right now.

"Rae, if you think there's any chance of you being happy here, really, truly being happy, I will make anything happen that needs to, in order to get you here."

Her soft brow furrows, worry lines forming. "Won't there be other people who have something to say about that?"

I shake my head. "No, I'm running everything now. I'm the boss. Which means if my girlfriend needs a job, she gets one."

Rae pulls her bottom lip between her teeth. "Your girlfriend, huh?"

"For a little while, at least." I lift her hand and brush my lips across her fingers on her left hand. "People would think it was weird if we got married right away."

Her jaw drops. "Jax, stop it. That's not even funny."

I lean up and press my lips to hers, pulling her down onto me, and rolling until she's under me again, pinning her in place. "I'm not joking, Rae. We wasted years. I don't want to waste any more time. So, you tell me, are we going to do this? Because I don't want you to resent me later if you come back home. I don't want you to wonder what would've happened if you had stayed there. I don't want you to hate me for making you come back to this place you outgrew a long time ago." I stare into her hazel eyes, imagining what it would have been like to be doing this for the last decade. "I always thought you were better than this place, that you deserved more. But goddammit, I'm selfish, Rae. And I'll take it if you'll give it to me. I'll beg you to come back."

Tears well in her eyes again, but these don't seem to hold the same uncertainty or sadness of her earlier ones. "I was never too good for Hayes Creek, Jax. I was just young and thought I wanted something that wasn't important in the end."

"What is important?"

She presses her hand over my chest where my heart beats rapidly against my rib cage, waiting for her to say what I long so badly to hear. "This. You and me figuring this out." A little laugh slips from her throat. "And to think, Mom sent me out here on a little break from packing up the house."

I grin at her. "I think your mom had other plans when she sent you over here."

Her eyes narrow on me. "What do you mean?"

My laugh floats between us, and I grin. "I ran into her at the store last week, and she told me you were coming back. I may have told her I was interested in seeing you, that I've missed you."

Rae's eyes widen. "Jax, you didn't..."

I smirk.

"So..."—a slow smile spreads across her face—"this was all a setup?"

Shrugging, I lightly drag my finger down into her bra and flick her nipple, earning a little twitch of her body under mine. "I wouldn't call it a setup, more like a happy reunion that was potentially, slightly, sort of arranged. Though, I wish you had come to see me because you *wanted* to."

Rae's light laughter fills my room and my heart. "I did want to. And Jax, my mother did *not* send me to get laid."

I shift my position to slip between her legs again, slowly pushing my cock inside her slick core on a languid slide designed to make her feel every inch. She groans and arches up into me again, clenching around me to draw me even deeper.

"Maybe not, Rae, but since you're here—and you're not going anywhere—I'm going to make use of every moment I have with you."

She scores her nails across my back, angling her hips to take me all the way to the hilt before she clamps down hard enough on me to make me gasp. "My own big, strong, determined lumberjack."

I crush my lips to hers as I pull back and plunge into her again. "You have no idea how determined I can be, Rae. This is happening. You and me. You can't kiss me and run again."

Digging her heels into my lower back, she locks us together. "I won't make that mistake again."

I hope you enjoyed *Billionaire Lumberjack's Brawn,* a short story set in my *Lumberjacks in Love Series.* Check out the full novels in the series available now at all retailers: https://www.gwynmcnamee.com/lumberjacksinlove

ABOUT THE AUTHOR

Gwyn McNamee is an attorney, writer, wife, and mother (to one human baby and two fur babies). Originally from the Midwest, Gwyn relocated to her husband's hometown of Las Vegas in 2015 and is enjoying her respite from the cold and snow. She loves to write stories with a bit of suspense and action mingled with romance and heat. When she isn't either writing or voraciously devouring any books she can get her hands on, Gwyn is busy adding to her tattoo collection, golfing, and stirring up trouble with her perfect mix of sweetness and sarcasm (usually while wearing heels).

Gwyn loves to hear from her readers. Here is where you can find her:

Website: www.gwynmcnamee.com

Shop: www.gwynmcnameeshop.com

Facebook: https://www.facebook.com/AuthorGwynMcNamee/

FB Reader Group: https://www.facebook.com/groups/1667380963540655/

Newsletter: www.gwynmcnamee.com/newsletter

Twitter: https://twitter.com/GwynMcNamee

Instagram: https://www.instagram.com/gwynmcnamee

Bookbub: https://www.bookbub.com/authors/gwynmcnamee

Tiktok: https://www.tiktok.com/@AuthorGwynMcNamee

THE BOY WHO LEFT

A St. Fleur Short Story

AJ Renee

CHAPTER ONE

"HEY!" Carolina Lawrence yelled at the mailman's retreating back. "Wait! I have something for you!"

With one foot on the truck, the man paused and glanced over his shoulder. His sunglass-clad gaze met hers at the same moment her bare foot landed on a sharp pebble. "Fudge! Owie!" she screamed and lowered to the ground. "Aw hockey sticks," she muttered as she pulled out the offending pebble and watched a drop of blood trickle from the puncture.

"Are you okay?" he asked, kneeling at her side.

The wound forgotten, she looked up at the unfamiliar deep timbre, and time stood still. He was handsome, with dark hair in need of a haircut and a neatly trimmed beard. He lifted his sunglasses to the top of his head, and his gorgeous hazel eyes drew her in. A niggling voice in the back of her mind screamed of familiarity. He pulled a tissue from a small pack in his shirt pocket and dabbed at the tender spot.

"Doesn't look too bad, but I suppose it will hurt like a bitch for the next couple of days," he said, studying her wound.

"Language!" she blurted, and heat crawled up her neck at the knee-jerk reaction.

One of his thick brows raised, and his eyes crinkled with amusement. "I'm so —wait, did you say fudge and hockey sticks?"

She smiled sheepishly. "Occupational hazard."

He cocked his head to the side, his gaze narrowing as he gave her all his attention. "Lena? Lena Butt?"

She groaned at the name and nodded as her mind caught up to why he looked familiar. "Hi, Kaleb... I had no idea you were my mailman. Wait, when did you move back to St. Fleur?" she asked, her heart racing at the mere sight of the first boy she'd ever loved. The only boy, really.

"Been here a couple of months now. The package said Carolina Lawrence. I never expected to find you still living here. I thought you'd be out traveling the world. Who was the lucky guy?" he asked, his gaze flitting behind her toward the cozy house she called home.

She shook her head. "Lawrence is Mom's maiden name. Butt was an awful surname and even worse for a grade school teacher."

"Teacher? Well, that makes more sense now." He chuckled. "Do you think you can stand yet?" he asked, offering a hand.

Placing her hand in his, the hairs on her arms stood on end. "Thank you," she muttered breathlessly. Dropping her gaze to the ground, she tested her weight on the tender spot as the smell of his cologne and sweat wafted to her nose.

As she breathed in deeply once more, her lids lowered. Her belly rolled, and her sex clenched with arousal.

Kaleb cleared his throat. "I guess I should get back to my deliveries. It was really great seeing you, Lena," he said, his voice huskier than a moment before.

"Yeah, you too," she said and cringed.

Biting down on her lower lip, she watched him step on the truck and give her a wave. Dimples she vividly remembered flashed in her direction, and she could have sworn her ovaries exploded at the sight.

Kaleb Perez.

The boy who'd been her first boyfriend. Not that it truly counted, as the most they'd ever done was hold hands. His sweet and kind ways had been burned into her memory. Without her permission, her heart had always compared every boy and man who entered her life to Kaleb. He'd given her hope that a good man existed, even if the ones she had picked cheated or treated her unkindly.

Hope was dangerous.

Turning at the sound of his truck driving away, she spotted the package she'd been trying to hand him. Kaleb had returned to her life for less than five minutes and already turned it on its axis.

He'd grown into a sexy-as-sin man. His scent alone had short-circuited her senses. There was no telling what all the years had done to the boy she'd once loved. The idea of shattering the perfect image in her mind was unimaginable. She understood that who she remembered wasn't the same man she'd just seen, but her heart couldn't bear the possibility that he would have turned into an ugly adult.

The cell phone in her back pocket vibrated, drawing her back to the present. With one last glance in the direction he'd gone, she limped inside.

Carolina peered at the package in her hand. She could drop it off after her early dinner date. "Or I can try again tomorrow..." She shook her head and sighed. Five minutes and she was making possibly stupid decisions in order to see Kaleb's handsome face once more.

"He's probably married," she muttered as she grabbed her purse and car keys.

Carolina spent the short drive into town examining the differences between her memories of Kaleb at eleven and at thirty-two years old. He'd shed the baby face, and sharp lines had formed along his jaw. He was no longer shorter than her, and lean muscles had peaked under his uniform.

Turning onto Main Street, she shelved her thoughts as a parking spot became available. In the last couple of years, it had become harder to park along the road as their small town gained more residents. Not that she was complaining. It had given her hometown the burst of renewed energy it deserved.

Looking both ways, she jogged across the street as she pressed the lock button on her key fob. She noted one police cruiser parked in front of the newly renovated sheriff's office.

Hurrying down the sidewalk toward Whiskey's Pub, the local hangout spot, Carolina waved at a few familiar faces. Nearing the big wooden door, she was thankful to not have run into any of her student's families. Not because she avoided them, which was impossible in a town its size, but because she hated making JJ, her friend and one of the town's deputies, wait any longer. With JJ's busy schedule, it had been months since the last time they'd been able to meet up for a meal.

She welcomed the blast of cool air and smiled at Jesse as his dark eyes met hers from behind the bar. The handsome, dark-skinned man grinned and nodded toward JJ, who was sitting in a booth along the wall.

"Thanks, Jesse."

He winked in reply and moved toward a customer who'd called his name.

Carolina walked between the full tables, offering smiles and hellos as she passed more familiar faces. When she reached the booth, she slid across the vinyl across from JJ. "I hope I'm not too late!"

JJ narrowed her blue eyes. "Everything okay?"

Heat crawled up her chest and settled into her cheeks. "Yeah?"

One of JJ's perfectly plucked eyebrows rose. She didn't say or ask more. She merely studied Carolina until she squirmed in her seat.

"What?" Carolina blurted before swallowing thickly. "Why are you looking at me like that?"

JJ sat forward and casually set her forearms along the edge of the table. "How am I looking at you, Carolina?"

Carolina groaned. "You never call me Carolina, and you're looking at me like you're expecting me to confess to a crime. Stop it!"

Her friend's lips twitched with amusement as she shrugged. "*Did* you commit a crime?"

"No!" Carolina's eyes rounded as dozens of pairs of eyes turned in their direction. *Sorry*, she mouthed with an apologetic smile.

Carolina dropped her head on the table and JJ's hand came to rest on top of her hand. She sucked in a deep breath, then two more before sitting back up. Concern etched around her friend's eyes, but she didn't push Carolina for more.

The two had been friends since middle school, but it wasn't until after JJ returned to St. Fleur years ago that their friendship became solid. JJ was quiet, helpful, and all too observing, while Carolina was the loud and social one of the two. They didn't need to talk on the regular, but they both knew the other would be there if they needed it.

"Do you remember Kaleb Perez?" Carolina whispered, aware their town was filled with busybodies.

JJ nodded. "Yeah."

"He's back," Carolina said.

Once again, her friend nodded. "Yeah, I helped with his fingerprints at the station. He's been back a few months now, if I remember correctly. What does he have to do with—" JJ waved a hand in her direction.

Her brows pinched. "You didn't tell me."

"No, why would I?"

Carolina blew out a breath, the wisps of hair stuck to the sides of her face releasing and flowing up.

"Hi, Ms. Lawrence!" Joanna, their waitress and one of her old students, said. She took both of their drink and food orders and moved along to the next table.

"So, Kaleb?" JJ asked.

Carolina told her about their brief exchange earlier that day. "Look, it doesn't matter. It just surprised me to see him, and he's probably happily married."

"It does matter if it's messing with your head. And for the record, he's not married. Did you two date or something? I don't really remember him," JJ said.

Carolina's heart did a little happy dance at the announcement that Kaleb wasn't married. "Kind of? I mean, as much as two eleven-year-olds can date. His family moved away before you and I became friends."

"Oh! That's who Kaleb is? Didn't you always compare other boys to him?"

A groan slipped from her lips as she covered her face and nodded. "Now I wish I never mentioned it."

JJ waved a hand. "Oh, stop it. Do you think he was interested?"

Carolina shrugged. "It was a two-minute interaction, five tops. I'm surprised he even remembered me, to be honest. I almost didn't recognize him. He's all grown up..."

"He's good looking; that's for sure."

"JJ!" Carolina chuckled.

"What? Just because Rocco and I are stupid in love doesn't mean I can't acknowledge an attractive person."

Carolina grinned. "How are things going?"

The two friends talked, teased, and listened to one another for the remainder of their meal. It didn't matter that the two rarely had this quality time together. Whenever time did allow, they soaked it up. Each visit was a continuation of the previous—neither woman upset with the other because their lives were busy.

Outside the pub, the two friends hugged before going their separate ways. Carolina crossed the road and passed her parked car before making her way to the Belles Supermarket. The automatic doors swooshed open, and Suzanne, owner of the market, lowered the paperback in her hand.

"Hi, Lena!"

"Hi!"

"Make sure you look in the special's cooler. Matt ordered some spicy cheese you may like."

"You guys are too good to me," she said and pointed the cart in the direction of said cooler. On the way she stopped to grab some fruits and veggies, her mind formulating a couple meals she could make for the coming week.

"Please, Papi!" a little voice said, making her smile.

Carolina turned to see who the voice belonged to.

"Not this time."

Startled by the familiar voice, she rammed the cart into a display of lemons. "Son of a biscuit!"

"Lena? Here, let me help," Kaleb said, kneeling to stop a few strays that attempted to roll away. "Are you okay?"

Carolina looked from Kaleb's face to his spitting image, minus the fact the little boy's eyes were green, not hazel.

"Here you go," the little boy said, his chubby fingers wrapped around a lemon.

Smiling at his sweet face she said, "Thank you."

"Milo, Ms. Lena and I used to go to school together. Lena—or is it Carolina now?"

"Lena is fine." The words sounded breathy to her ears.

"Lena, this is my son, Milo."

Carolina accepted the lemon and offered her hand. "Nice to meet you, Milo. Let me take a guess. You're four years old?"

The little boy's chest puffed out. "Almost five."

Carolina laughed. "My apologies. Five, that means you're a big boy and about to start school?"

His little head nodded so quickly, it was a wonder it didn't fall off. "Papi says I start in August!"

"Oh, I bet you're so excited!"

"Yes! I'll make friends!" he nearly yelled.

"Shh, buddy. Let's remember to use our indoor voice."

"Sorry, Papi."

Once the lemons had been gathered, they pushed to their feet. Kaleb wore a white undershirt and gray shorts, and it did things inside her belly. Her gaze moved down his body, committing to memory details she had missed the first time—like the coarse dark hair on his tanned legs, a tattoo which peeked out from under his sleeve, and strong forearms that created images of him lifting her onto a countertop.

Goose bumps formed along her skin, and her cheeks flushed at the panty-soaking imagery.

"Lena?" Kaleb said, concern etched around his eyes.

"Sorry."

"Are you okay?" he asked, dipping his head to study her.

Flustered, she laughed. "When did you grow?"

Kaleb chuckled. "I finally got the growth spurt I'd been dying for the summer after sophomore year. I forgot you'd remember puny me."

"Puny? I'd have never described you as puny."

"What would you have described me as?" he asked, his voice going husky.

For a moment she wondered what they were even talking about. She didn't really care as long as he used that voice again.

"Well, puny is not a very nice adjective," she said with her classroom voice.

His eyes darkened, but before he could reply, Milo said, "Mamá says we shouldn't name call."

Carolina tipped her head. "Mamá?"

"My mom. Milo gets to hang out with my parents while I'm at work."

Carolina lowered to Milo's level. "How lucky are you! Not a lot of people get to hang out with their grandparents. What sort of fun things do you do?"

Milo's face scrunched up. "Sometimes I help her pull weeds."

Carolina chuckled. "You don't like to pull weeds?"

His little shoulders shrugged. "It's okay, but she won't let me play with any worms I find."

Her head fell back with laughter at his words. When she calmed, she found a few townsfolk watching them closely. "Oops, I guess it was my turn to be too loud," she whispered to Milo.

Raising her gaze, she found a storm of emotions clouding Kaleb's eyes. "You okay?" she asked.

He gave her a firm nod, and his Adam's apple bobbed with a swallow. "We better not take up any more of your time. It was great seeing you, Lena."

She nervously licked her lips at the sound of her name from his mouth. The longer she was in his presence, the more he seemed to affect her, waking parts of her she'd long neglected with the small pool of available men in St. Fleur. "It was a pleasant surprise, to say the least."

CHAPTER TWO

"I LOVE YOU, PAPI!" Milo said around a loud yawn.

Kaleb grinned at his son's sleepy face. His chest squeezed tight every time he heard those words. "Night, buddy."

In the kitchen, he grabbed a beer and popped it open on his way to the patio. Sipping from the cold drink, he sat and kicked up his feet at the sounds of crickets.

Carolina "Lena" Butt—Lawrence.

His lips tipped up at the mere thought of her, images from their childhood springing to mind. Her long dark-brown hair in a single braid down her back. Glasses, too big for her oval face, perched on her nose. A light sprinkling of freckles along her nose from long days in the summer sun.

Kaleb rubbed the heel of his palm along his breastbone and sighed. Coming home to St. Fleur had been necessary after he'd found himself struggling to bounce back after his wife, Jennifer, had died. Not only had Milo needed his *abuelos*, Kaleb had desperately needed his parents, even if he couldn't find the words to tell them.

He hadn't thought of Lena in years.

Chuckling to himself, he admitted the lie as quickly as it popped into his mind. He had thought of Lena. The moment they'd arrived in St. Fleur, childhood memories had snuck their way in each time he passed a familiar spot in town.

Lena wasn't the girl he remembered. She was more beautiful than he could have ever expected. Her hair was shorter, but it was still as dark as ever. Her caramel-colored eyes popped without the glasses hiding their beauty. Gone was the girl he remembered, and in her place, a woman. The mere thought of her curvy body had him taking a long pull from his beer.

Jennifer's face pushed forward, and twinges of guilt pinched his sore heart.

Kaleb ran a hand down his face before finishing his beer. He moved through the small home, turning off lights and checking locked doors before climbing into bed.

Hours later when his alarm woke him, he stared at his morning wood. It wasn't any different than any other morning, and yet it felt heavier than he could recall from the last three years.

Lena Lawrence.

Throwing back the covers, he sat up and gripped the bedsheets at his side. He'd been celibate a long time, his desire for any sexual touch nonexistent since Jennifer's death. One—no, two short interactions with Lena, and his world had seemed to explode with vibrant colors, sounds, and now obvious desire.

And it wasn't just the sexual variety, even if his dick proclaimed otherwise. His belly stirred with nerves as he considered whether he'd run into her again.

Another glance at the clock and he snapped out of his musings. If he expected to get Milo to his parents with enough time to start his shift, he needed to get a move on.

Hours later, Kaleb stepped into his parents' home. "Hello?"

His father, Ricky Perez, popped his head from around the corner, a guilty expression disappearing at the sight of Kaleb. "Ay! Mijo! How was your day?"

Kaleb kissed his father's cheek and returned his hug. "Mami know you're sneaking ice cream?"

Ricky waved a dismissive hand. "Eh, she's gotta prove it, and you're not going to tell her."

Kaleb shook his head and looked around. "Where's Milo?"

"Maria took him down to the park," Ricky said, licking the spoon clean.

Exhausted, Kaleb ran a hand through his hair. "Come on, Pa'! I'm tired and just ready to take my boy home."

Ricky paused from washing the spoon and narrowed his eyes on him. "*Que te pasa?* Did something happen at work?"

"No, *nada paso*. It's just been a long day running packages, and I want to go home."

"Shh... sounds like there's a cranky pants in the house," his mother whisper-shouted.

Unamused by his parents, Kaleb leaned against the counter. "Papi was eating ice cream." Over his father's insult, he asked, "Hey, buddy, how was your day?"

Maria curled herself into her husband's side as Milo hugged Kaleb's hips. "Oh, he really is a cranky pants."

"What's wrong, Papi?" Milo asked.

"I'm just tired, buddy. Are you ready to go home?"

Milo looked between his abuelos and Kaleb.

"What?" he asked.

Maria shrugged. "It's the weekend, and we thought he could stay."

Milo's pleading face met his. "*Por favor*, Papi?"

"Just going to leave your old man?"

Milo's brows knit in confusion. "You're not old."

"Still young enough to meet a nice woman and—"

"Papi!" Kaleb snapped at the same time Lena's smiling face came to mind. He shot both his parents a warning look. "Milo, go see if you have everything you need."

Milo took in the adults before walking away slowly to the room his grandparents had outfitted for him.

The moment he was out of earshot, Kaleb hissed, "Please don't confuse my boy!"

Maria placed a hand over his heart, and her smile didn't reach her vibrant eyes. "Mijo, he's the one who's been asking why he doesn't have a mama. It's been years. You're young, and that boy needs a mother."

Kaleb's chest squeezed. "Ma, he has you..."

Maria's arms wrapped around his waist, hugging him tightly. "I just want both of you happy. We'll keep him tonight. Why don't you go make some friends?"

Kaleb kissed the top of his mother's pixie-cut hair. "I have friends. I have you two." Words his mother had told him all his life.

Ricky chuckled and Maria placed a hand on her hip as soon as she left Kaleb's embrace. "And you, you think I don't realize the ice cream is eating itself? If you kill yourself with your diabetes, I'm not going to your funeral," she snapped and followed the path Milo had gone.

Hungry and uninterested in cooking for one, Kaleb drove into town. The local pub hadn't been there in his youth, but it was clearly the heart of the St. Fleur community.

He heard music playing as he opened the door. Tables were being pushed aside to make room for a small dancing area. Jesse and Jaime Lynn, the owners, offered him a wave as they adjusted chairs.

Kaleb found an open seat at the bar as his name was called out.

"How are you adjusting to small-town life?" Sheriff Noah Tyler asked.

"Not much different than base living." Kaleb chuckled.

Noah, also ex-military, grinned as he nodded. "Touché. If you need anything, let one of us know. You're welcome to pull up a chair and join us," he said and pointed toward a booth in the back. "That's my wife, Sofia."

Kaleb tipped his head in greeting at the pretty woman. "Thanks, but I don't want to intrude."

Noah smiled. "Fair enough."

Minutes later, Kaleb stared into his rum and Coke.

"Penny for your thoughts?"

Cocking his head to his side, he found the woman who was occupying his free thoughts. He peered around her before allowing his gaze to sweep down her front. "Hey," he said, his voice husky and suddenly dry.

"Everything okay?" she asked as she set her small hand on his shoulder.

He offered her a smile. "Yeah, why shouldn't it be?"

Her caramel-colored eyes narrowed as she saw through his evasive question. "Where's Milo?" she asked and lowered her hand.

Missing the warmth of her hand, he bit back a sigh. "With my parents."

"Ah..."

It was his turn to narrow his gaze. "What's that supposed to mean?"

Lena shook her head, and the knot on top of her head bounced around.

"Hi, honey, were you going to eat in instead?" Jaime Lynn asked Lena, appearing before them.

Kaleb didn't miss Jaime Lynn's curious glance—or the way Lena hesitated.

"Join this pathetic dad for dinner?" His ears heated and his belly flipped with nerves he could only recall with his interactions with Carolina Butt.

"Depends…"

"On what?" he asked.

"Are you going to be a grouch?" she asked, and Jaime Lynn snickered.

"Carolina Bu—Lawrence, would you like to join me for dinner?"

She studied him for a moment before turning her attention to Jaime Lynn. "Bring it out whenever his order is ready?"

Jaime Lynn grinned. "Got it."

Lena pulled herself onto the stool and turned toward him. Kaleb did the same and his gaze dropped to their knees when they touched. Desire stirred in his groin, and he sucked in a breath. His work pants would do nothing to hide an erection if he didn't get it under control.

"I take it you don't go out much without your son?" Lena asked.

"And you don't eat in often," he observed aloud.

Lena shrugged. "I ate here yesterday."

"By yourself?"

"With my friend JJ."

He studied her a long moment as he tamped down his jealousy. "Do you eat with JJ regularly?"

Her lips twitched, and a sweet blush colored her cheeks. "Not as often as we'd like."

Kaleb lifted his glass to his lips and watched a twinkle of mischief flash in her eyes. He leaned in closer and tucked an errant strand behind her ear. "Lena, you still can't lie worth a damn."

Her giggle warmed him from the inside out. "I'm not lying, but your face is—"

Kaleb leaned in closer, the pub noises falling away as all his attention zeroed in on her. "What? My face is what?"

Her gaze dropped to his mouth, and the tip of her tongue ran along her lips. "JJ stands for Julie Jolie," she whispered.

"Muffuletta for the lady, and Cajun pasta for the gentleman," Jesse said, smothering the building tension between Lena and Kaleb with the arrival of their food.

"That was fast," Kaleb managed to say.

"What made you want to become a mail carrier?" Lena asked, wrapping her hands around the sandwich.

Kaleb chuckled. "I wanted to pay the bills. How about you? A teacher?"

"Mrs. Clifton," she said with a shrug.

Kaleb set down his fork. "Should I know that name?"

Lena laughed. "She was one of our teachers."

He shook his head slowly. "Not ringing a bell. I don't remember much from back then."

"You remembered me…"

He nodded. "I did."

She was one of the few people he remembered from his time in St. Fleur. Lena was hard to forget. The beautiful girl had stolen his heart in the sweetest of ways before he learned girls could be anything else. Growing up, he'd witnessed some become manipulative in destructive ways. Others turned ugly, mean, and vindictive.

Jennifer had been sweet and kind. One of the reasons he'd been attracted to her.

"Hey? Where did you go?" Lena asked.

Kaleb sipped from his drink, pushing back memories of his dead wife. "You never left?"

She shook her head. "Other than college and vacations, no. There's no place like St. Fleur."

One side of his mouth tipped up. "That's why my parents returned."

"And why did you return, Kaleb Perez?" she asked, her voice lowering for only his ears.

"Milo needed his abuelos," he said, studying a piece of chicken on his plate.

Lena placed her hand on his forearm. "Just Milo needed them?"

Kaleb sucked in a breath and shook his head. "No, I needed them too."

She squeezed his arm, and without a thought, he pressed a kiss to the top of her hand.

The rest of their dinner flowed easily, considering a few townsfolk stopped by to speak with the beloved teacher. He enjoyed watching her interact with them. Kindness and sincerity seemed to effortlessly flow from her.

Kaleb felt a sudden pang of jealousy for the attention the students would receive from Ms. Lawrence in the coming school year.

His childhood feelings for her gripped him, and for the first time in what seemed like forever, hope moved into his being. The concern and words from his parents came forward, and he wondered what Milo would think if Kaleb pursued Lena.

He wasn't ignorant. The woman she was today was unlike the girl he'd loved as a boy.

"Kaleb?"

"Hmm..."

"I um... was wondering if you wanted to watch a movie at my place?" Lena asked.

He shook his head.

Lena stood from the stool as her lips pulled tight. "Oh—um, okay. Well, thanks again for dinner."

Wrapping his fingers loosely around her bicep, he stopped her escape. "Would it be okay if we hang out at my place instead? I'm feeling grimy as hell after working in today's heat. Or I can come by after I cleaned up."

She took him in, and her cheeks became rosy.

His dick stirred at the sweet look.

"Oh, of course. I didn't think..."

Kaleb was aware of the curious glances directed at them as they left the pub side by side. His hand itched to hold hers, and for the first time in a while, he was excited to spend time with a woman he wasn't related to.

After walking her to her car, he gave her his address and jogged a few cars down to his own. Boyish wonder bloomed within him, in contrast to the man of thirty-two he was.

A few minutes later, Lena slipped her purse over her shoulder. Her gaze darted around the yard and the outside of the house as she walked up the driveway to where he stood waiting.

"You could have parked on the driveaway."

Lena shrugged. "Doesn't matter. The town's tongue will be wagging either way."

Kaleb paused, considering her words and their innocent actions thus far. They'd spontaneously decided on eating together, a dinner he'd insisted on paying for. They'd left the pub together, and her car was parked outside of his home.

"I can go home," she said, backing up.

Kaleb chuckled. "What's there for them to say, two childhood friends were spending time together?" A moment passed between them before he nodded toward the house. "Come inside, unless you've changed your mind."

She bit her lip, and blood rushed to his dick. He shoved his hands in his pockets and waited for her to make her decision while also attempting to hide and control his erection.

Lena nodded and passed him on her way inside. "You better have popcorn."

Kaleb laughed. "I don't, but I do have chips and queso."

"Even better!"

CHAPTER THREE

HER HEART POUNDED against her chest. Excitement and nerves warred with the desire pooling in her belly.

"Make yourself at home. Here's the queso, if you don't mind heating it up, and I'll go clean up," he said, handing her a glass jar of liquid yumminess.

Carolina did her best not to be too nosy around his place while he showered. It was a concentrated effort. Either her mind would continue spinning images of Kaleb, wet and naked in the shower, or she could peek around his warm and inviting home as she pieced together the man he'd become.

After setting the cheese to cook in the microwave, she found an unfinished drawing next to a box of crayons at the dining table. Two stick figures, a tree, and a seesaw were all labeled in an adult's handwriting. She lightly brushed her fingers along the wax and smiled.

Once the cheese was done, she wandered further into the living room. Her gaze swept over framed pictures of Kaleb with Milo, his family, and one of Kaleb's wedding day. Unable to resist, Carolina lifted the photo in the back and brought it closer.

Kaleb wore black slacks, a white button-down shirt, and tie, and his wife a cream-colored cocktail dress as she held a bouquet of roses in her hands. Simple but elegant.

"I'd gotten orders overseas, and we had to cancel the big wedding she'd wanted," Kaleb said.

Carolina gasped, her hand flying to her chest and her cheeks flaming at being caught red-handed with the picture. Her heart squeezed at the solemn expression gracing his face.

Frozen in place, she wanted to hug him badly but wasn't sure if the gesture would be welcomed.

"You guys looked happy," she whispered.

Kaleb nodded as he set the picture back. "We were." A drop of water slid from his wet hair as he faced her. "It was a lifetime ago."

"May I ask what happened?" she whispered, her voice barely audible.

"Accidental overdose after she became addicted to Percocet after her C-section."

Her arms wrapped around his waist before she could stop herself. "I'm so sorry, Kaleb."

His warmth cocooned her, and she no longer knew if she was giving or receiving comfort. It had been a bit since a man other than her father or brother-in-law had hugged her, especially a man as firm as Kaleb.

Pulling from him, she met his gaze and froze.

"It was a long time ago, but thank you." His thumb swiped along her cheek. "I'm glad to see you never stopped being sweet and big hearted."

Her heart thundered in her chest, and her stomach did somersaults. "The cheese might need to be reheated."

His lips lifted in a face-splitting grin before he moved around her. "Cold cheese won't do."

Carolina sucked in a deep breath before following him back to the kitchen. After his shower, he'd put on a snug T-shirt and a pair of shorts that fit his hips and butt better than she could have imagined.

Once they had their snacks, he guided her to the couch, where they sat a few inches apart. They talked about countries he'd been to and what made Carolina choose a career in education. If she ignored the desire pooling low in her belly, she was rather comfortable in his presence.

Years of experiences had separated them from the kids they'd been. She didn't know if he was still grieving his dead wife or if he even felt anything past nostalgia in her presence, but Kaleb Perez was still waving his magical wand over her.

"Would you like a throw? I know I keep the house cold," he said when she shivered.

"Oh, I don't know. Your couch is already really comfy; I may fall asleep."

Kaleb chuckled. "If you do, you do."

Carolina didn't know how she fell asleep with the remote under her, but when she swiped it away it wouldn't budge. It wasn't until the second time she tried to dislodge it did she realize by the simultaneous hiss and a squeeze to her side that it was no remote.

"It's attached, cariño..." Kaleb's sleepy rough voice announced.

Pushing up, she looked around the room before meeting Kaleb's amused face. "I fell asleep."

With his answering chuckle, his erection pressed into her once more. Biting her lower lip, she dropped her weight back onto him and buried her face.

He rubbed soothing circles on her back. "If it's any consolation, I fell asleep soon after you cuddled into me."

Carolina groaned with embarrassment. "I'm so sorry!"

"I'm not."

At his sincere confession she raised her face. "No?"

"I don't think I've ever slept so well," he said, cupping her cheek.

"Really?" she asked, staring at his mouth.

"Really... Lena?"

"Yeah?"

"I always regretted not kissing you..."

His lips were soft and hesitant, giving her the opportunity to object. A moment passed and he increased the pressure. He tasted salty from the chips they'd snacked on. When she moaned in pleasure, Kaleb deepened their kiss.

Tongue, lips, and little nips made up what was easily the best kiss she'd ever received in her life. Kaleb shifted her over his hips, his erection trapped between them. Carolina took ahold of his face in her hands, losing herself in Kaleb.

She may not have been with many men, but she'd kissed her share of frogs in her lifetime. No one kissed like Kaleb Perez. Maybe he'd learned along the way, or maybe he'd always kissed like his life depended on it. Carolina didn't know, but what she did know was if he'd kissed her all those years ago, he'd have broken her for all men.

There wasn't a man alive who could live up to that hell of a kiss.

Wanting—no, needing more, Carolina's hips found a rhythm. Her clit pressed against her jeans as her sex begged for him to fill her. She'd never behaved so wantonly with a man.

Kaleb's hands roamed over her thighs, hips, and sides. The closer they moved to her breasts, the heavier they felt. Her body came alive at his touch.

"Kaleb," she whimpered against his mouth.

His hazel eyes bore into hers. "*Qué?* What's wrong?"

Swiveling her hips, she pressed down on him. "You're making me nuts."

In a lightning-fast move, he flipped them so she cradled his hips between her thighs. Bringing his mouth to her ear, he whispered to her in Spanish before kissing along the tender flesh of her neck.

Before she could ask him what he said, Kaleb found and plucked one nipple. Carolina arched into his hand and slid a hand into his shorts. Taking him in hand, she squeezed gently. At his answering groan, she stroked his thick length.

Within minutes he pulled himself free and sat back on his haunches. "Keep that up and I'm going to come."

Emboldened by his words, she tugged her shirt over her head and tossed it aside. "So?" she asked as she freed her breasts from her bra.

Kaleb ran a hand down his face.

After a moment of lying bare, she whispered, "Kiss me."

CHAPTER FOUR

THE VULNERABILITY he heard tore at his heart. When he'd invited her over for a movie, he truly had only intended for two old friends to spend time together. Sure, he was attracted to her, and his dick was eager to learn more of her. He wasn't dead, after all.

Taking her face in his hands, he kissed her thoroughly.

Lena grabbed handfuls of his shirt and pulled it over his head, breaking their kiss for a brief second. Her fingertips ran up his sides, around his back, abdomen, and chest. It was second to the feel of her hand wrapped around his dick.

Taking her wrists in his hands, he pinned her arms above her head and grinned against her mouth when she whined.

"Sorry, cariño, I can't take much more, or I'll embarrass myself," he said before taking one pert nipple between his teeth.

A long, drawn-out moan filled the room and he flicked, nipped, and teased the flesh. Lena squirmed under him, and his mouth watered with the desire to taste her.

"Kaleb, please... please..."

His heart thundered against his breastbone. There hadn't been a woman since his wife. No one had interested him, not even for an evening of watching a movie. He'd questioned if his libido had died along with his wife.

"For the record, I didn't invite you over to get into your pants," he muttered along her skin.

Lena froze under him. "Oh God."

He ran his nose along hers. "Hey, what's wrong?"

"What you must think of me," she said with a shake of her head.

He released her wrists and cupped her cheek. "I think you're more beautiful than I remember. My imagination had nothing on the real thing; that's for sure."

"Oh... Thank you for not thinking too badly of me."

He quirked a brow. "There's nothing sexier than a woman who knows what she wants." Kaleb pressed his mouth to her upturned lips. This kiss was sweet and less carnal than the others. Sitting back on his haunches, he grinned at the half-naked woman on his couch. "It's clear there's still something between us. I'd like to explore it further, but how about we take a moment to cool down, and I'll make you breakfast?"

Lena pushed him backward and scrambled to her knees as he studied her with confusion.

"What did I say?" he asked.

"All the right things," she said a moment before she freed him from his shorts.

The moment her hand wrapped around his semi-erect dick and brought it to her mouth, his brain short-circuited. He became hard as a rock, his head falling back on a groan of pleasure. There was no way he'd be able to last, but by the way she sucked him off, he didn't think she wanted him to.

Kaleb gave into the sensations, and within a few strokes, he was at the brink of an orgasm. "Cariño, I'm going to come," he warned.

Lena's gaze met his, and her cheeks hollowed as he bumped the back of her throat. Giving in, Kaleb's eyes shut as his fingers became tangled in her hair. His hips bucked and his toes curled as he fell apart for what felt like forever.

When his body relaxed, Lena released him with a *pop* before pulling up his shorts. "Better?"

Kaleb moved as quickly as she had and relished her squeal of surprise when he tugged her jeans down her legs. His mouth was between her thighs in seconds, her sweet and tangy flavor on his tongue as he zeroed in on her hot spot. Determined to make her come hard and fast, he used his mouth and fingers on her sensitive flesh.

The tight bud of nerves peaked out from its hood, begging for his touch. Her body arched, and a guttural moan slipped from her lips as he flicked his tongue and curled one, then two fingers into her channel. She was tight and incredibly responsive to his touch.

His dick, the greedy bastard, stirred at the way she bowed under his atten-tion. Kaleb found one nipple and pinched hard. Lena's hips came off the couch, and he did it again to the other.

A light sheen of sweat made her skin glow, and a moment later, her thighs clamped down on his head with the force of her orgasm. Working his mouth and fingers faster, he had her coming once more before her body could recover from the first.

"Holy shit…"

"Language, Ms. Lawrence."

"Fuck that."

Kaleb laughed. "That I plan on doing another day."

Being around Lena was effortless. She brought out a part of him he'd thought the military had beat down. Seeing her naked and sated on his couch felt right but mildly scared him. Was he willing to allow another person into his heart?

CHAPTER FIVE

Was she dead?

Never had a man made her come that hard and never so quickly. She was lucky if they found her clit, let alone her G-spot. Kaleb had managed both. Maybe it was because she'd been wound so tight? After sucking him off, she was pretty sure a breeze along her clit would have had her coming.

Her heart was still racing when he kissed her mound and pulled her jeans to her thighs.

"Sorry, I'm going to need a little help here, cariño."

"You broke me," she said without moving an inch.

Stroking his ego was probably a bad idea, but she was done for. If oral sex with this man made her a pile of bones, what would sex do to her? Her toes curled at the thought of sex. It had been about two years, if she didn't count her vibrator.

"You're too good for my self-esteem." He chuckled as if he'd read her mind.

"I'll probably regret letting you know." With a sigh, she helped him dress her.

Kaleb pulled her into his arms and kissed her forehead. Her heart did a flip, and she was sure within a matter of hours she'd be halfway back in love with Kaleb Perez.

"How about I feed you now?" he said as he threaded their fingers together. "How do you feel about french toast?"

Her stomach growled on command. "Clearly my body is not shy in telling you what it wants."

He chuckled and kissed her cheek before leaving her by a stool. "Makes it a lot more fun."

They shared a few stories as she watched him move around the kitchen. It was clear he'd been on his own for a while and comfortable in his space.

Carolina, lost in her thoughts, startled when Kaleb tipped her face to meet his eyes. "Sorry?"

"Where'd you go?"

She shook her head. "Just thinking."

Kaleb reached for the two steaming plates of french toast and set one before her. "About?"

Carolina pursed her lips as she debated how much to say.

"Out with it."

She shrugged. "Honestly?" Kaleb nodded and she continued. "You've been back in my life for hours, and it feels like so much longer. I would have never done"—she tipped her head toward the living room and shook her head—"I'd never have done any of that with someone I barely knew. I've only slept with two guys in my entire life, and I was ready to make you my third."

Kaleb set down his fork and turned her to face him. "I haven't been with a woman since Jennifer. It's been almost four years."

"Nuh-uh!" she blurted.

He raised a brow, his features darkening at the suggestion.

"No, I mean... Come on! Look at you! Really? You're a great catch, Kaleb. It's just hard to believe."

Returning to his plate and cutting off the easy-going nature of their interaction, Kaleb shrugged. "I should have realized Jennifer had a problem. If I had, my son wouldn't be without a mother, Lena. So please don't put me on a pedestal."

Carolina dropped her fork with a clank. "Oh, Kaleb! I'm sorry..." She opened and closed her mouth a few times. Words formed and disappeared as quickly as they'd come. "I won't tell you how to feel, but I will say this. You can't see what others don't want you to see. Beating yourself up for things out of your control won't help you or Milo. You're human and have faults, and in time I hope you show them to me."

Pushing to her feet, she dumped the last of her food in the trash and set her dishes in the sink. She paused by Kaleb and kissed his cheek. "I'll leave you to your thoughts. You know where to find me."

CHAPTER SIX

Lena hadn't taken two steps before he'd internally acknowledged he'd been hard on her. Only, he couldn't make himself get up and follow her.

He spent a week in a dark, self-deprecating mood until his mother finally pulled his ear, both literally and figuratively. It was Milo's concerned expression that had done him in. His boy never got to know his mother, but he had Kaleb.

"Why don't we grab some ice cream in town?"

Milo's eyes grew twice their size with excitement. "Yes!"

Scoop Scoop Hooray had not been around when he was a child, but their selection of homemade ice cream flavors blew his mind every time they visited. Walking hand in hand with Milo, a familiar curvy woman caught his attention.

Without a second thought, Kaleb dropped to a knee and turned to Milo. "Do you mind if we invite Ms. Lena along?"

Milo twisted and turned until his gaze landed on her, and his free hand pointed. "Her?"

Smiling, Kaleb lowered his hand. "It's not nice to point, but yes, that's Ms. Lena. Remember her from the grocery store?"

Milo nodded. "She's nice!" he said as he turned on his heels and ran from Kaleb.

He pushed to his feet and ran a hand down his face. His mood the last week had more to do with how he'd snapped at Lena than the role he felt he played in Jennifer's death. Logically, he was aware Jennifer's addiction had gone under the radar and he was not to blame. It didn't stop the moments when guilt crept in.

"Ms. Lena!"

Lena turned around, searching for the voice calling to her before finding Milo steps away. Her brows knit in confusion as she bent at the waist to bring herself closer to eye level with Milo. The beaming smile she offered him dimmed when she spotted Kaleb's approach.

"Hi, Kaleb."

If not for the breathy way his name sounded on her lips, he would have worried she wasn't happy to see him.

"Hi, Lena."

"Do you want ice cream?" Milo blurted as he bounced on his heels.

"Ice cream?" she asked, a hesitant expression directed at Kaleb.

His heart squeezed at the guarded look in her eyes. He'd put it there, and he hoped she would give him a chance to rectify his behavior. "What Milo was supposed to say was, would you like to have ice cream with us?"

Lena stood her full height and peered from Milo to Kaleb. "I don't want to intrude."

Kaleb stepped closer and lightly grasped her elbow. "Please?"

"Please!" Milo squealed before a butterfly caught his eye as it landed on a nearby flower.

"Kaleb—" Lena whispered in warning.

"I'm sorry I was a jackass the other night. We'd really love it if you joined us."

She tucked a loose strand of hair behind her ear, a tell she'd had since a child denoting her nervousness. "I'm not sure that's a great idea. Kids are impressionable and—"

He cast his son a glance, making sure he hadn't moved from the old wine barrel, before stepping into Lena. Cupping her cheek, he ran a thumb over the soft skin he wanted to explore. "I haven't had any interest in dating until I bumped into you. There's no good excuse for how I snapped at you, but I'm sorry. I can't promise I won't do it again, but I do promise to do better. I'd really like to get to know the woman Lena Butt grew into, if you'll allow me to."

She licked her lips and gave him a small nod. "I'd like that too."

Grinning, he intertwined his fingers with hers and turned them. "Who's ready for ice cream?"

Milo's gaze zeroed in on their hands. Kaleb's breath lodged as he waited to see what his son would say. "I am!" he said after a second. Grinning, he rushed to Lena's side and grabbed her free hand.

Life had a funny way of surprising him, and Lena was the cherry topping to his banana split of a life.

THANK YOU FOR READING *THE BOY WHO LEFT*! I HOPE YOU ENJOYED LENA and Kaleb's story as much as I do! If you loved St. Fleur, head back with Widower's Aura today!

ABOUT THE AUTHOR

AJ Renee grew up in a military family and moved around until her family settled in Florida. She graduated from the University of Central Florida with a M.S. in Criminal Justice and a B.S. in Psychology. She currently resides in Virginia and spends her time with her Air Force husband, three daughters, dogs, and cat. She loves to travel and see family and friends whenever she gets a chance. She has a love of music, movies, and anything that can make her laugh. AJ believes in reading books with humor and mystery that end in a happily ever after to help ease our minds and hearts of life's daily struggles.

SHELTERING HIS DESIRE

Allyson Lindt

CHAPTER ONE

No one should be allowed to look that good in scrubs. The thought spilled into Tate's head when Alyssia walked into the office at her animal shelter, Great 'n' Small. He shook the words away, but not before trailing his gaze past her hips, up her narrow waist, and over the swell of her breasts, and landing on bright blue eyes and a face framed by long, dark hair.

That wasn't what he needed to be thinking about. Now, or ever really. He was here as a consultant, not to leer.

"Did I miss a memo?" Alyssia gave an exasperated huff. "When did it become acceptable for a guy to send a picture of his penis as a way to say 'I'm sorry, please take me back'?"

"Excuse me?" If he'd guessed a million times what she was frustrated about, dick pics wouldn't have been on the list. From Lys, he almost wasn't surprised by the blunt, ludicrous question. He'd known her for decades and very little was taboo between them anymore. This came pretty close, though.

She looked directly at him. "Sorry. But am I wrong to think this is creeptastic?" She held out her phone.

Apparently it wasn't a rhetorical question after all. He shook his head. "I'm going to take your word for it. And last time I checked it still wasn't acceptable. Care to fill in some blanks for me... Minus the visual aids?"

Her brow furrowed and she ducked her head. Her, "I suppose," was soft in the room, blending into the dogs barking in the background. "You know that guy I was talking to last week?"

"Not personally."

She stuck her tongue out. "You're funny."

He smirked. "Damn straight I am. So online distraction of the month..." He wasn't sure how he'd officially become the person she shared her dating woes with. It had started years ago. At first he participated just to make sure she wasn't hooking up with the wrong guys. She was his best friend's little sister, and looking out for her was status quo. He'd quickly realized though, that she could figure it out on her own, she just liked the sounding board.

She blew a strand of hair out of her face, sank into the chair across from him, and rested her arms on the desk. "I need to wrap my brain around how ludicrous this entire situation is first. And we have work to get done."

"If you're sure..."

She nodded. "What do you need from me?"

The conversation wasn't over, but she'd spill if and when she was ready. Besides, she was right about them being on a deadline. He was seated at her desk, using the computer to help set up a crowd-funding campaign for her animal shelter. She was one of twenty pilot groups for the application he was using to spin a new arm off his family's software company. "I've gone through the shelter's social media accounts. With the updated graphics, everything is in order. I'll write up the copy for the pledge page. You'll need to verify it. Then we just have the video left to shoot."

Normally, any computer-related favors would fall to his best friend and business associate, Jared. Or Jared's fiancée, Mikki. Both of them were scary brilliant programming geniuses.

However, this was more about sales and marketing, and proving this was a legitimate new market for them to enter. Once the crowdfunding site took off, he had several next steps, and then he'd be running the arm of the business himself. On top of that, he got to help Alyssia raise enough money for a down payment so she could buy the building her shelter was in. When it came to selling anything, Tate would rock the results like no one's business.

"Right. Video. Tomorrow night." She raked her fingers through her hair as she pulled it back, twisted it into a loose knot behind her head, and stuck a pen through it to hold it up.

Exposing her long, kissable neck—Tate mentally shook himself. Where the hell had that come from? Too long since he'd gotten laid or something.

"And recording the voice overs in office the day after—they finally confirmed your time slot." Every aspect of the project was part of an independent budget, to prove the idea was financially viable. Fortunately, he'd been able to contract most of the resources he needed from his parent company, Skriddie Bust Media. The art department was available for all the pilot groups. Marketing had a storyboard for each company's promo film. It was going to look as clean as possible out of the gate. Tate was making sure of it.

"It's just..." She fiddled with her watch. "I thought the guy was really into me. I mean, I know a lot of these men in online chat rooms are full of shit and just looking to get laid, but he actually seemed to be listening. Remembering what I said, talking to me. Interested in me and not just my boobs."

And they were back on that. "We could include those in the vid if you'd like. Draw in a new crowd." He wouldn't have made a joke like that with anyone else, but he hoped with her it would bring her out of her funk.

She looked at him, lips drawn in a thin line, expression flat. "My boobs?"

"Sure."

A smile slipped out. "You don't have to come up with excuses, you just have to ask."

Good, they were back to casual and fun. Except her teasing dragged up more mental images. Of stripping her top off, running his hands up her stomach, cupping her breasts. He needed to stop that. "But then I'd be like one of those guys online, right? I have to at least make an effort."

Her expression slipped, and her frown flew back in. "Which is where the problem started. He wanted to see me topless. I told him no. He wanted just a peek. Begged about five million times across twenty-four hours. And when I told him I was done talking to him, he sent me this—" she held up her phone, "—as a 'please forgive me' or something. I don't even know."

She sank further into her chair. "It's not like I was falling for him or anything, it was just nice... I'm about to get repetitive."

Maybe he could lighten the mood. He hated to see anyone bummed out, but especially her. He made sure to keep a teasing tone. "That's why real people are better than online people."

"Don't even start." Her mouth twisted in irritation. "The situation wouldn't have been any different if I'd met him in a bar."

He really did hate to see her like this. She deserved a guy who would give her happily ever after, not a jerk who just wanted dirty selfies. "I know, most men suck. But I promise, Lys, not all of them are bad."

Her mouth twisted in amused irritation. "What, like you?"

God, that would be a mistake. Even if he were interested—he forced himself to keep his eyes on the computer and not let them drag over her figure—she deserved better. "No. I'm an asshole. Guys not like me. Though, admittedly I've never sent anyone a picture of my junk."

"Junk. Is that the technical term?"

He liked seeing her smile. "You'd rather I called it Tate Jr.? Or George?"

"Touché. So, where do I meet this mystical man who likes me for my mind, isn't related to me, and isn't bound by some unwritten guy code not to touch me because I'm your best friend's baby sis?"

His mind stalled, and he processed her words again. Somehow, this had just become about him. "He's out there. You've got both body and mind covered when it comes to attractive, and if you were anyone else—"

"Really?" She stood so quickly it made his head spin. "If I weren't the person I am, with all the shared ties we have, you'd be interested? Or is that just lip service?"

It wasn't just lip service. Though he didn't see her as approachable, he still noticed she was equally intelligent and beautiful. Even now, he couldn't help but notice the flush in her full lips. The tinge of frustration on her cheeks. And it was all amplified by the back and forth fun of their conversation.

She moved around the desk, pushed her keyboard aside, and hopped up. She sat directly in front of him, just inches away. "Take that off the table. We're the only people in the room, right? And I know you wouldn't lie to me. If we didn't have that connection. If Jared weren't my brother, would you make a move?"

That escalated quickly. He swallowed, throat suddenly dry. Blood pounded in his ears, and his dick twitched at the thoughts of what he'd do to her if she weren't *her*. "If you were just some random woman in a bar, yes."

"Not quite what I asked, but let's go with it." She rested her stocking-covered toes near the inside of his thigh, close enough heat radiated through his slacks. "You know me as well as anyone, Tate. If there's more to me than a pair of tits, how come no one who gets to know me is interested in me *like that*? And how come no one wants to get to know me?"

His restraints were short circuiting tonight, for reasons he didn't understand. If she didn't pull her foot away in about two seconds, he might act on the impulse to find out if she tasted as good as she looked.

Except he wouldn't act on the desire. He mentally steeled himself. This was a moment of temporary insanity, on his part and hers. He'd ignore it, remind himself she was a client and his best friend's baby sister, and they could get back to work.

His cock twitched as her toes slid higher. Fuck.

⁂

ALYSSIA KNEW SHE WAS BEING A BRAT, YET SHE COULDN'T MAKE HERSELF STOP. Tate was a convenient target, and she was asking more of him than was acceptable between friends. She needed to apologize. The problem was, now that she'd nudged the edges of this boundary—this temptation that was him—she didn't want to stop. There was a reason she never pushed this line with him. What had gotten into her? Part of her brain whispered what a bad idea this was. That she needed to suck her up pride and just walk away, but the rest of her wasn't interested in backing down.

Her ego was already limping. It wasn't just him denying her now, or even that he had so long ago. It was all of it. It had been ages since she'd run into a guy who seemed to care there was a person inside her. Except Tate, and he treated her differently because of her brother. Tonight it all merged in her skull and was too much. So yeah, she was being pushy, and insecure, and bratty. And she was terrified if she stopped now—even if she backtracked and took a kinder route— she'd never find out what she needed to know. Was she only ever destined to attract, and be attracted to, the wrong guys?

Her toes slid higher on his thigh, and she paused when the landscape changed and she brushed his erection. He inhaled sharply through clenched teeth. Had she really made him hard just with a line of questions? The thought both terrified and excited her.

"The right guy is out there." His words were strained. Any of the humor that usually lined his voice was gone. "And you'll meet him, and you'll know when you do that he's different."

Of course. Just like eight years ago. Except this time, she was licking too many wounds to want to stop. His rejection back then, this bullshit online. It all jumbled into a mess, reminding her how much she normally held back around Tate, and that she'd never gotten over him. She draped her arms around his neck. "What if the right guy *is* you?"

Faster than she could blink, he grabbed her wrists, stood, and pinned her palms to the desk. He pushed her upright and slid between her legs at the same time, standing close enough heat radiated between them. Her pulse kicked into overdrive, and want slid through her. The intensity in his gaze made her mind stall.

He scraped his teeth up her neck, and she bit her tongue to hold back her whimper. Her pulse screamed for more, bringing every nerve ending to life. His warm breath on her skin was tantalizing and tempting, and she needed him to take this further. To feel his tongue explore her, his hands strip her bare. Every inch of his flesh against hers.

His whisper brushed her ear. "I promise I'm not."

"So everything you're saying is just lip service." Irritation tinged her desire, making it surge. He was so sure he knew what was best for her, and she was sick of that. She scooted closer, rubbing his erection each time she shifted her weight. He was definitely interested. What would it take to shatter his defenses?

"If we ever hooked up, it would be because you actually wanted me, not because you were hurt and wanted someone to take your frustrations out on."

That pushed another button of defiance. Heat—fury, desire, all of it mingled and seared her veins. She didn't know what to focus on, so she let it all course through her. "I do want you, and you know it."

He ducked his head closer without warning, still holding her hands captive, and crushed his mouth against hers. His groan mingled with hers when she ground against him. His tongue forced its way into her mouth. His insistent shaft pressed between her legs, making her go from damp to wet in an instant, and her nipples strained against her bra. So this was what it was like to feel sparks.

He broke away as quickly as he'd dived in, breaking all contact as he stepped back. Disappointment and longing surged inside her. His steady gaze locked on her face. "You deserve better than what I'm offering, even for just a night. Trust me."

"Goddammit, Tate." Her throat ached from just the few words. She hopped to her feet, bringing her closer to him again. She grasped at every strand of anger inside and used it to smother the overwhelming hurt making her joints ache. "I'm so tired of you telling me what I do and don't need. Do you maybe think I might know that better than you?"

She raised her hands to his shoulders to push him back, and he grabbed her wrists again, still looking her in the eye. Despite her irritation, his rough touch still spoke to the primal lust raging inside her.

"You might need to get off, but not with me. And I get as much say in the matter as you do. I can't stop you from keeping the fantasy, though."

Her face heated to red-hot. She broke free of his grasp and shoved him back. "You impossibly arrogant ass."

He opened his mouth, but a loud beep cut him off. Her heart beat against her ribcage in frustration and surprise. The tone of the speakerphone cut through the room, followed by her assistant, Sara's panicked voice. "Doctor, we need you out here."

Without thought, her fury and indignation were bundled up, shoved into a box in the back of her skull, and locked away tight, even killing her desire to tell Tate the conversation wasn't over. "On my way, what's up?"

"Mutt. Broken leg, fractured ribs, probably internal bleeding."

Alyssia's gut clenched. The stupid argument could wait. Her patient was more important. She pushed past Tate and out the door without stopping to see what he was up to. She'd care later, this was emergency time.

——————

CHAPTER TWO

——————

TATE SHOULDN'T HAVE KISSED her. That was possibly the stupidest thing he'd done in ages. His cock still ached, straining against his slacks, and he'd been seconds from telling her yes. He'd never done that before. Only partly because Jared would kill him. Largely because she deserved better than a cheap one night stand. On top of it all, she was a client. He never mixed business with pleasure.

But the conversation was apparently over. She'd gone from stubborn to professional in a flash, face hardening, and him all but ignored. Thank God for small favors.

Then again, that was one reason she was so good at running the shelter. She knew where her priorities lay. She'd started volunteering there when she was still in high school. During college, she took on more administrative tasks, along with helping the doctors and nurses, which translated into great experience for veterinary school.

She'd officially become a doctor less than a year ago. When the owner had to sell three years ago, for personal reasons, Jared had loaned her the money to purchase the business itself. Well, technically Tate had loaned her the money through Jared, but she didn't know that. Tate tried to offer, but she refused to owe him. Now she was looking to expand the place and buy the property it sat on, which meant she needed another infusion of capital. Hence the crowd-funding campaign.

He followed her out of the office, staying a few feet back for his own sanity. Getting too close to that heady scent of soap would just screw with his head again. His footsteps slowed as he reached the front lobby of the clinic. The panicked woman near the front desk was probably just a little younger than his thirty-four, and she looked painfully familiar.

He scanned the face against a list in his head. Not a business associate. Not a one night stand, or a friend of a friend. Where did he know her from?

She looked up as soon as Alyssia drew close. Her words ran together. "He's hurt, I don't know how badly, but he won't come out of the car, and he just keeps whimpering, and you have to help him, please."

Alyssia rested a hand on her arm, tone kind but firm. "We will. Show me."

He'd let them get to work. Lys had everything under control. But he couldn't help following her to the SUV near the front door. And then it clicked in his head. The woman worked for a friend of his parents. Friend was a deceptive word. Her employer was sleeping with Tate's mother. The country club's dirty little secret that everyone knew. The woman was a housekeeper. She swung the back doors open, and a low growl echoed through the dark parking lot.

"Come on, boy." Alyssia's voice was low and soothing, as she crawled inside the vehicle. A loud series of barks reverberated, and she scrambled out backwards, face pinched.

"See?" Hysteria crept into the woman's voice. "I can't get him out. I don't want him to bite me again. He already did it once when I was putting him in there. She held up a hand wrapped in gauze.

"Tranquilizer?" Sara asked.

Alyssia shook her head. "Not until I can take a look at him."

While they were conferring, Tate pushed through the small group. His chest clenched. It was the neighbor's dog. Belonged to their teenage son. Even in the dim light, it was obvious he was in pain. Tate crawled toward him slowly, murmuring random reassurances in the softest voice he could. The dog whimpered, but didn't pull away or snap. It felt like it took ages to close the distance, but it was probably less than a minute. He cradled the mutt and backed out just as slowly, trying not to jar any injuries or startle the animal.

Three faces stared back in wide-eyed surprise. Alyssia recovered first. She didn't say anything, just nodded toward the clinic. He followed without question into one of the rooms. He set the dog on the table, gently stroking his head and whispering more incoherent reassurances while Alyssia examined the dog, and then hooked him to an IV.

"Okay." Her quiet voice sounded loud and abrupt, shattering the stillness but not the tension. "Thank you. I need you out now, though."

He nodded and extracted himself from the room. He let out a long breath when he was in the hallway. "Cait," he called to the pacing woman in the lobby. "What happened?"

She tugged on her blonde braid, not meeting his gaze. "Nothing. I got clumsy cleaning his dog run. Left...something out, and, um...he got hurt."

Tate wasn't even going to point out what a bad lie that was. He stared at her a minute longer, and her shoulders slumped. "I can't tell you. I need this job. You can't even tell them it was me who brought it in. Please."

It was times like this he had no idea how Alyssia did her job without surrendering everything fun and amazing about her personality. He jammed his fists in his pockets to hide his clenched fists. "Bryce Jr.?"

Her nod was so slight it was difficult to see.

He wasn't going to yell at her. He understood where she was coming from. But it took more restraint than he thought he had to suppress his anger. If he had a reserve of self-control, he was pretty sure he'd eaten through it twice over tonight. "She's not going to let the dog go tonight regardless. You might as well go home."

"No. I have to take him back."

"Not happening," Sara broke in from her spot at the computer. "Not with injuries like that."

"But what am I supposed to tell them?" Caitlin asked.

Tate sank into a nearby chair, his verbal filters failing fast. "A better lie than you told me."

ALYSSIA DIDN'T KNOW HOW MANY HOURS HAD PASSED. SHE'D SPLINTED A broken leg, stitched up several cuts, and seen to the internal injuries before splinting most of the poor boy's frame. She was exhausted, but her patient should pull through.

Her stomach snarled. Maybe she should have taken Tate up on his offer for dinner instead of throwing herself at him like an idiot. Again. Apparently eight years was just enough time to forget the lessons of the past. Not that she would have had time to eat anyway.

She stepped into the waiting room, eyes taking a moment to adjust. They only kept half the lights on overnight. Sara looked up from behind the reception desk, and they exchanged smiles. No words were needed. They'd been working together long enough Sara would get it. The exhaustion, the stress, and the relief that the first bad part was over.

Alyssia halted in her tracks at what she saw next. Tate was seated in one of the plastic chairs, staring blankly at a magazine, not turning the pages.

"What are you still doing here?"

He jumped when she spoke, and whirled to face her. "Is the puppy okay?"

She wasn't going to acknowledge the adoration his question summoned. Especially since the dog was anything but a puppy. Tate's clothes were a wreck. Dark streaks—she assumed blood—smeared his shirt, tie, and slacks. In that brief second, any of her lingering frustration from earlier evaporated. "He'll be fine. Friend of yours?"

He gave a weak smile. "We've met. He lives near my folks."

Her stomach protested loudly, and her cheeks burned when he raised an eyebrow.

"No arguments this time." He tossed the fashion magazine aside and stood. "I'm buying you dinner."

"There's a 24-hour Mexican place around the corner," Sara offered. "I'm having two cheese enchiladas."

Tate looked between the two, pausing on Alyssia. "Chicken nachos, extra cheese?"

"It's okay. I'm fine." Alyssia didn't even believe herself. "I have cookies in my desk drawer."

Tate shook his head. "When you're not so tired, we'll work on what 'no arguments' means. I'll be back in fifteen minutes."

At least the place was drive thru, so no one would question why he was in blood-streaked clothes.

Alyssia leaned against a nearby wall for support when he vanished out the door. A glance at the clock told her it was almost midnight. She was going to need some serious coffee if she was going to make it through the rest of the night. She had her other doctors rotate night shifts. Of the four on staff, they rotated out the months and weekends they worked graveyards, and she didn't think it was fair to make them do what she wasn't willing, so she was part of that rotation. She was three weeks in, and she'd adjusted just fine, but days like today reminded her why she'd rather be asleep right now.

As if reading her mind, Sara nodded toward the kitchen. "He made a fresh pot of coffee just a little while ago."

Alyssia kicked away from her support and followed the aroma of consciousness.

"Have I mentioned yet today how sexy he is?" Sara's question followed her, carrying easily over the tile in the empty clinic.

Alyssia was too tired to roll her eyes. She didn't want to talk about Tate, because that meant thinking about him. And thinking about him meant regret, embarrassment, and a want she couldn't sate. "Not for at least six hours." She grabbed her mug from its spot near the sink, and filled it as full of coffee as she could. She followed that with generous helping of sugar and cream. Coffee threatened to escape as she stirred the mixture together. She took a long drink, not caring that it scalded her throat and tongue going down.

"Did the police say when they'd be by?" she asked as she wandered back into the lobby. She didn't have to ask if Sara had called. There was no question the dog's injuries were at least partially intentional, and that meant filing a report. Unfortunately, it didn't guarantee the felony conviction that should go along with the abuse, but it helped.

"I told them you'd be gone by seven. They said they'd be in before then."

The chairs called her name, but Alyssia couldn't sit down until she was a little more awake. "Did the girl leave a name?"

"No. But Tate really does know her and the dog. Called her Cait. She asked us not to mention her."

Alyssia rubbed her eyes as a new wave of exhaustion washed over her. That was never a good sign. Dread joined her jumbled thoughts as Tate's response about being friends with the dog floated back to mock her. Please, please, please let it not be someone powerful enough to do something like have the city change her zoning.

The front door chimed, and Sara hit the button to release the afterhours lock and let Tate in. The moment he stepped through the door, the scent of chilies and enchilada sauce nearly knocked Alyssia over. She was hungrier than she realized. She had to force herself to not tear into the food the moment he set the box in front of her. He leaned against the other side of the counter as she and Sara dug in.

"You're a heaven-sent demon," Sara told him.

"And not eating," Alyssia said once she realized it.

He shook his head. "Some of us have to sleep tonight, not tomorrow morning.

Right. She'd kept him up all night. "Thank you for everything. We're okay, now."

He still didn't move. His fingers twitched, and he stared at the wall behind her head.

Was he really making her do this? Why did he have to spoil the moment? "And earlier is in the past, right?"

"What?" He shook his head and finally looked at her. "Right. Earlier. Yeah. In the past." His brow furrowed. "The dog's name is Grim. He belongs to Thompson's kid."

Alyssia's appetite evaporated in an instant. He probably didn't have the power to get her zoning changed. Not directly anyway. But he did own a local TV network affiliate, which tended to be vocal about businesses he didn't like. He'd done editorial pieces on their place before, about how it was a waste of valuable retail space and community resources. Now she was about to potentially file criminal charges against his teenage son. She nibbled at her food, no longer tasting it. "Of course he does."

"He can't do anything other than huff and puff. I'll be back tomorrow night, we'll get your campaign up and running, and the one side of the business will never touch the other."

She ignored the reminder they would have made more headway tonight if she hadn't thrown a tantrum. The last thing she needed was to linger on the memory of the kiss. She was too busy trying to convince herself things really would be as easy as he said.

CHAPTER THREE

THE MOMENT the shelter door swung shut behind the police officer, Alyssia sank into a nearby waiting room chair. She leaned the back of her head against the wall, closed her eyes, and let the rising sun warm her face. Exhaustion rolled through every inch of her body. She was pretty sure last night had been the longest night of her life. Of course, just like the second longest night of her life, it had started with Tate, and her making a fool of herself.

She shouldn't go there. But she was too tired to hold back the unwelcome memory. Exhaustion seeped through her, dragging the memory with it. That night, eight years ago. She'd just barely turned eighteen, and her date to senior prom had canceled last minute.

When Tate found out, and asked if he could take her, she thought it was because he liked her. Teenage-her hoped he'd finally figured out she *like*-liked him, and he felt the same. She'd been in heaven the whole night. Some of her friends were dating college guys, but her, she got to show up with someone who was post-grad.

He'd been the perfect date. Sweet, attentive, a gentleman. Her friends insisted that meant he loved her. At eighteen years old, and crushing hard, that was exactly what she needed to hear.

She bit back a bitter laugh at the unwelcome rush of images and emotions. She'd thrown herself at him. Getting laid on prom night—all the movies told her that was a guarantee, and who better to lose her virginity to than the man of her dreams?

Turned out he was just that kind to everyone, and that he'd only asked her as a favor to her brother.

She sniffled and forced herself upright, shoving away the rest of the memory and the ache in her gut. Now she'd made the same mistake again.

But had she? He'd been interested, she knew it. The kind of reaction he'd had to her last night. Even before she touched him he'd been turned on.

"Ms. Tippins." A familiar voice burned away the last of her wandering thoughts, and she snapped back to the now.

Bryce Thompson. Sick dread made her insides lurch. She had a feeling he was about to become the bane of her existence. The older gentleman stood a few feet from her chair, not a single wrinkle or piece of fluff on his suit. His hands were clasped in front of him, and his dark eyes narrowed and locked on her.

"Good morning." She scrambled to her feet. Maybe this wouldn't be so bad. Sure, he'd made it clear in the past he thought her shelter was a waste of resources. That he was planning to tear the entire building to the ground to make room for retail property. On top of that, she'd just finished filling out a police report that directly involved his family.

Yeah, this was going to suck. She should have gone home as soon as she had the chance. It wouldn't have been fair to leave her staff with this burden, though.

His jaw-set expression never even twitched. "I understand you have my dog."

She could bend the truth a little. Tell him no, they didn't have anyone's dog until the animal was adopted into an actual caring family. Delaying the inevitable wouldn't make things better. "I understand the same thing."

"I'm here to retrieve him. How much do I owe you?" He pulled a checkbook from his jacket breast pocket.

This was too easy. He was being too calm. Alyssia's ill-ease grew, rolling through her and dragging more exhausted tension to the surface. "There's no charge. I can't—"

"No wonder you don't make any money here." The corner of his mouth pulled up in a sneer. "I'll take him and leave then."

Out of the corner of her eye, she saw one of the morning volunteers—the guy was as solid as a brick wall and almost as wide as he was tall, and normally a total sweetheart—step forward. She met his gaze, but didn't motion for him to stand back. Sweet disposition or not, his bulk was intimidating, and his presence made confronting Mr. Thompson that much less terrifying.

"You can't take him." She pushed the words out quickly, not talking over Thompson as effectively has he had with her, but still determined not to be interrupted again. "The new owners will pay whatever fees are associated with his care, and until then, he's not ready to be moved. He's still recovering, and will be for several more days."

"I see." He scribbled in his checkbook and tore the piece of paper out. "Then I'll be back when he can be moved."

"You can't take him home." Damn it, why wasn't he listening to her? Frustration crawled under her skin like a million ants, and she shoved her hands in her pockets to hide her clenching fists. She dragged up every ounce of forcefulness she had, and crammed it into her voice. "He belongs in a good home where he won't be hurt again."

He locked his gaze on hers, eyes hard and unyielding. "I'll be back in a few days."

He set the check on the counter, and was through the front door before she could say anything else.

A whole new wave of frustration crashed over her, mingling with everything else that had been the last twelve hours of her life, and sapping away her restraint. She had to bite the inside of her cheek to keep a string of profanities from spilling out. She grabbed the check off the counter, cringed at the four-figure amount he'd randomly chosen to write it for, a tore it into little tiny pieces.

It didn't solve anything, but the simple act made her feel a little better. A little.

"ALAN." TATE STOOD AT THE FRONT OF THE CONFERENCE ROOM. HE CAPPED the dry erase marker and set it on the tray of the white board before turning to his administrative assistant. "Do you have this?"

Alan nodded, and Tate let his attention travel around the room, scanning the remaining faces. "Any other questions or concerns?"

He was met with a series of shaking heads and smiles. He was lucky he had a solid team on this project. Technically they were all on loan from Skriddie as contractors. The lines of the new business venture were blurred, but he was close to making the crowdfunding venture its own entity.

While it was nice to get back into the technical side of things, especially getting to meld it with the marketing he loved, he'd been working directly with sales so long that a good group made the transition easier.

He turned back to Alan. "Action items?"

His assistant ran through the list, and Tate made sure everyone was ready for their test users to launch by the end of the week. Tonight with Alyssia had to be all business. Not that it would be anything else. He still didn't know what had happened yesterday. His pulse twitched at the memories—the way she tasted, the tiny gasps she made when they kissed, and the combination of frustration and desire she'd managed to overload him with.

He tried to shake the thoughts away. The meeting wrapped up, and everyone headed back to their desks. Images of Alyssia still taunted him as he made his way to his office. Damn it, why was she getting in his head now? They'd dealt with this and moved on all those years ago. Or, at least, he thought they had. She'd barely been legal when he'd offered to be her last minute date for her senior prom. She'd looked gorgeous in that dress, no longer the little girl who tagged along with them as kids. And when she'd all but thrown herself at him—both too much and nothing like last night—he'd had to tell her no.

The rambling combination of fantasy and denial skidded from his mind when he pushed open his office door. Speaking of relationships that had jaded his reality. An older woman sat in the chair across from his desk, not looking up at the soft creak. She scrolled through her phone. He personally knew her hair wasn't that shade of auburn, but not because her hairdresser had made any mistakes hiding the gray.

He hid his sigh. "Are you here for business, or personal reasons?" Her answer would determine how he addressed her. He didn't like keeping his tone so formal, but years of having it drilled into his head didn't leave him much choice. There were no favorites in his mother's business world. Especially when it came to family. Though more and more their recent run-ins made him wonder if she was pushing things in the other direction. Discounting his ideas because of their relationship. He wasn't sure if she was doing it to prove there was no favoritism, or for some other reason, but each time they talked business, he became more convinced he wasn't imagining it.

She locked her phone and returned it to her purse, never turning to look at him. "Personal."

He wasn't sure if that was a relief or not. He gave her a light kiss on the cheek before moving around his desk and dropping into his chair. "It's lovely to see you, Mother."

"Of course." Her smile was as formal as his greeting. "How are things going, darling?" Her soft southern accent slipped in, adding a layer of artificial sugar to her words. He might not see it that way, except he knew the lilting drawl vanished the moment she was in a business meeting and felt like it would make her appear anything less than intelligent and businesslike.

"Fantastic. I've been drumming. Women think it's sexy as all get out. And I'm thinking of trading in the Bentley for an F-150." He cranked his own drawl a couple of notches, poured out the clichés she saw as being 'too hick' for people like them, and never let his pleasant expression slip. "Y'all should stop by this weekend if you're free."

Her eye twitched and he knew he'd pushed the right buttons. Maybe he shouldn't have, but sometimes her sense of propriety rubbed him the wrong way.

Still, she kept smiling. "Sounds wonderful, darling. How's your little project coming along?"

He resisted the urge to snarl at the disdain in her question. She hadn't supported the idea for the crowd-funding offshoot. Had shot down his bids to rent the Skriddie's resources, saying that wasn't the industry they were in, and as COO of her husband's company, she had that kind of veto power. "I thought we weren't discussing business." His voice was flat.

"So right." Her eyes hardened, and her lips drew into a thin line. "How's Jared's baby sister doing? The one who follows you two everywhere, bless her little heart?"

That's where this was going. Please let him be wrong. Let this be something he couldn't even begin to guess at. "She hasn't done that for years."

"You're sure?"

"I'm positive. And she's fine." Wonderful, sexy, dangerously alluring. *Great, that's what I need to be thinking about right now. Not.*

"So you are on speaking terms with her. Are you personally handling her user experience for this little project of yours?"

His mother already knew all this. Frustration swelled inside. This wasn't the time to let his cool slip. "I wouldn't put it that way, but I am her contact. You're not here on business, remember?"

"Of course. Tell her to drop the charges against Bryce Jr., and give him back his dog."

She'd almost cut straight to the point. That was odd. "Why are you asking me?"

"You know her."

"Jared knows her. She's his younger sister. You're not in his office tossing passive aggressive formalities at him."

Her mouth pulled up at the corners, but her eyes were cold. "Mr. Tippins has work to do."

And Tate had the entire afternoon free? He clenched his teeth. "Why doesn't Mr. Thompson have this conversation with Alyssia himself?"

"He tried. She was unreasonable."

That almost made him smile. A hint of relief amid his mounting irritation. "I can't imagine."

"Talk to her." She stood. "Make this vanish."

"Or your boyfriend won't put out tonight?" Tate winced as soon as the words passed his lips. He'd let his guard slip for just a moment, and he shouldn't have done that. Just because everyone knew his parents had an open relationship, and his mother had spent as much time in Bryce Thompson's bed as she had her own in the last several years, didn't mean it was appropriate for anyone to talk about it. Oh well, too late to take it back. "Sorry. Gentleman caller."

Her eyes narrowed and she locked her gaze on his face for several seconds before turning away. "She won't like the alternative, and experience tells me that means you won't either."

The moment the door swung shut behind her, he clenched his hands into fists and dug his knuckles into his closed eyes. Stars danced against his eyelids. He took one deep breath and then another, struggling to find his composure again. He didn't even know where to start unraveling his fury. Had that conversation really just gone that way?

He took one more breath and tried to turn his attention back to work. It wasn't like his mother—or Bryce Thompson for that matter—was going to order a hit on Alyssia or anything so ludicrous. They were verbal bullies. His best bet was to make sure Lys got her site up and running as quickly as possible, funded her shelter expansions, and put this unfortunate coincidence behind her.

He slammed his fist into the arm of his chair. Why couldn't he believe it was going to be that simple?

CHAPTER FOUR

TATE GLANCED at his watch every few seconds as he crossed the short distance from the elevators to his car in the parking garage. Work had tied him up far longer than he'd planned, with 'just one more' phone call and email rolling in, one after another, until he had less than fifteen minutes to be at the shelter. Tate had given himself enough time to get there half an hour before the video guy who was shooting animal footage, and now he was worried it might not have been enough.

He'd sent Alyssia a text saying he might be late, but she hadn't responded. It was earlier than her overnight shift was scheduled to start, and for all he knew, she was still getting ready. Unbidden, images flashed through his thoughts of her in the shower. Tall, lean, with water cascading over her.

What was wrong with him? He dropped into his car, pulled onto the road, and turned on a local talk radio station. This time of night, they ran updates every ten minutes about the stock exchange, and he liked to hear the highlights.

Some of his tension slipped away as he navigated lighter than normal rush hour traffic. He might even make it with a few minutes to spare.

"Tonight on ABC News at seven…"

The pre-recorded commercial filtered into his thoughts, and blocked it out as standard chatter.

"You think you're taking your dog to the vet for a routine checkup, and suddenly the police are knocking on your door." The announcer's voice held a hint of threat, just enough to draw in listeners. Tate's brain froze, and then honed in on the words. "We'll tell you which local shelter may be up to no good."

Thompson's station. Please don't let this be about Lys's shelter. His gut clenched at the reminder of the scene he'd left behind the night before, and his mother's threat echoed in his head. The remaining time it took to reach his destination passed like cold molasses. Should he tell Alyssia she might want to check this story out? Keep what he'd heard to himself? She didn't need more stress, and there was no guarantee the news report was about her.

The moment he walked through the front door, Sara nodded toward Lys's office. "She said you could go right in."

He might have been worried to hear otherwise. He paused, hand on the doorknob, and spun back toward the waiting room. The TV they kept behind the counter was on, turned to the news, and a promo video for upcoming stories. Sure enough, the image on the screen was the front of the shelter. Shit. So much for figuring out whether or not he was going to tell her.

He pushed into her office, and knew immediately from the sound coming from her speakers that she was streaming the news.

She looked up from her monitor, forehead pinched, and jaw clenched. "We're so screwed."

His chest ached at the worry in her eyes. "It can't be that bad."

"No?" She raked shaky fingers through her hair. "The camera crews showed up about two hours after I told Thompson he couldn't have his dog back. I was already home asleep. The staff wouldn't tell them anything, because that's our policy. And now I see this on the commercials? How could that possibly be anything but bad?"

He forced a calm he didn't feel past his own concerns. "We'll watch; you'll deal. Life will go on."

She looked at him, eyes narrowed, and mouth flat. "That's not as placating as you may think."

ALYSSIA WASN'T GOING TO SNAP AT TATE. SHE HAD TOO MANY OTHER THINGS going on to deal with his brand of calm. He was trying to help, which was why she was biting her tongue, but sometimes he tried a little too hard. The streaming news shifted scenes, and her gut clenched. She crossed her arms. She was vaguely aware of Tate moving behind her, but her attention was focused on the news clip.

The lead-in to the story was almost the same as what she'd been hearing teased on commercials since she woke up. And then her world crumbled a little, and an insistent throb twitched behind her eye. The reporter was talking to Bryce Thompson Jr., his parents sitting next to him on the couch in a living room larger than her entire townhouse.

He frowned and sniffled as he explained how his dog had been struck in a hit and run. A growl slipped from her throat. The dog's injuries didn't coincide with that. He went on to say he hadn't known what to do. His parents were gone for the evening, but he was lucky a member of the staff was around. She took the dog in for treatment at an all-night animal hospital.

Alyssia's blood boiled hotter the longer she watched. The newsman talking about "and that's when the nightmare began." The camera and reporter trying to get into her clinic. The footage—only about three seconds compared to the truth on her own security cameras—made it look like Ricco had literally kicked them out on their asses the moment they'd walked in. "The shelter took his dog, and refuses to return the animal to its family. They declined our requests for comments. But as of now, they've kidnapped this poor child's best friend, and locked it away, cold and scared in some back room kennel."

She sank back in her chair, acid churning in her gut. A quiet, "Fuck," slipped past her lips and frustration stung her eyelids. Goddammit. What was she going to do?

She slowly became aware of Tate's hand resting on the back of her neck, his thumb kneading at the tight cord running from her shoulder to her skull. His quiet tone seeped into her thoughts. "Press release. Letter to the station. Contact Legal about slander."

His methodical list took the edge off her mounting fear and frustration, but didn't erase it. She nodded. "I should get on that." How could he sound so sure and calm right now? Everything inside her was screaming at her to do something. That this was bad. That the local news had just told the entire community that her shelter was essentially kidnapping dogs.

Nausea bubbled up again, and she swallowed it back. It didn't help. "I'll call the lawyer. And have Sara start on the press release. Someone needs to contact the station now. I should do that first. Can I counter before the ten o'clock news? We have security footage, we can show them that's not how this happened. This isn't right, we can't—"

"Stop." His voice was still low, but the single word stamped out her rambling. "Do the first two. Don't fly off in a frenzy and try and fight this war publicly. This is Thompson's TV station. Going into things half-cocked won't help."

"But he's verbally destroying the shelter." She wanted to scream. Was Tate trying to make this difficult? "He just told the entire town I'm a fucking puppy kidnapper. I have to tell them otherwise."

"Lys." Tate's gentle tone was still there but an edge lined the single syllable. "You should and you will, but not without a plan. Don't rush into this unprepared, okay?"

She ground her teeth at the condescension, but didn't have the words to argue. "Fine."

Her speaker phone buzzed, and Sara's tentative voice filled the room. "There's a camera guy here?"

Her already fractured thoughts shattered further. "They're back? What the hell? Can I go talk to them now? This is my chance, right? I can set things straight."

Her chair spun and she found herself face to face with Tate. He was half kneeling in front of her, gaze locked on hers, forehead wrinkled in concern. He rested a hand on her neck again, thumb stroking her cheek. She wanted to slap his arm away, but the shock of his touch raced through her and filled in the cracks in her thoughts with glue.

When he leaned in and kissed her, lips soft and tender, her entire world ground to a stop. Her tension was still there, struggling in the back of her mind to be heard, but she couldn't focus on it. Her attention was on the rough fingers against her skin, the tiny nips he laid along her bottom lip, the way his tongue swirled around hers.

She exhaled softly, when he broke away and rested his forehead against hers.

"Paying attention now?" The edge was gone from his voice. Was he breathless? No, she wasn't thinking straight. He was just trying to keep that infuriating calm demeanor.

She wanted to lean in for another kiss. Something more intense to chase the flutters through her veins like the night before. Instead, she nodded.

He bit his top lip for a moment, before continuing. "Good. It's Greg from the office. He's going to take video of the animals."

She swallowed, struggling with disappointment and relief, but she wasn't sure what the source of either feeling was. "Right."

"I'll hook him up with one of your volunteers. You start making phone calls about this news thing." He finally pulled away, and as he stood, she swore his hand was trembling.

"Right. Press release from Sara, and call Legal."

The moment the door closed behind him, the borders protecting her compartmentalized thoughts disintegrated. Had he really just kissed her? And why was she focused on that? Because it was an easier question that what the hell she was going to do about this possible media shitstorm. She took a few deep breaths. They had a plan, and she would follow it.

Her stomach lurched when she reached for her phone, and she pushed aside the nausea. She could do this.

Tate couldn't believe he'd kissed her. A single night of no sleep and a little stress and he was letting instinct and lust drive him? He was really off his game this week. Her taste still lingered on his lips. Stupid, stupid, stupid. But instinct had kicked in, and he'd needed to calm her down.

It was nothing more than a distraction to bring her nerves under control. Things were high stress right now. He obliterated his doubt, left the cameraman in capable hands, and pushed any tension or worry from his mind before he stepped back into Alyssia's office. He kicked the door shut behind him, only half aware he was locking it, when he registered the sight in front of him.

She was pacing and muttering to herself, not even looking up at the click of the latch. She raked trembling fingers through her hair, her feet slapping hard against the floor with each step. "I can't do this. It's not what I signed on for." Her tone grew louder and higher pitched with each word. "I can confront the abusive jackasses. I'm prepared for that. But to have to defend myself publicly, for something I didn't do, against a man who's never even wondered what it might be like to not have so many people responding to his every whim. I can't do—"

"Whoa." Tate stepped in front of her, palms on her cheeks, forcing her to look him in the eye. He couldn't watch this anymore. Her tension twisted every muscle in his body until he was sure something inside might snap if he didn't move, and her near-hysteria added a layer of something unfamiliar. If he had to name it, it was need. The need to wrap her up and protect her. The need to hold her and comfort her and let the rest of the world bounce off. The need to do something more than just gloss over things and move on.

"We'll figure it out." He kept his voice calm, despite the heat searing his palms and the nervous energy responding to her panic mingled with her soft scent. "You're not alone in this."

Her chin wrinkled, and she blinked several times. She drew in a shaky breath and then another. "It's not that easy."

He traced a thumb over her cheek. Her face was so soft against his calloused skin. Did this comfort her even half as much as it calmed him? "It's not easy at all. But it's also not unsolvable."

She covered his hand with hers, and licked her lips. A jolt of desire seared through him, ringing in his thoughts and tugging at his groin. He tried to will away his reaction. The last thing he should be doing was daydreaming about her. Even if she weren't floundering on the edge of a breaking point. She deserved—

She brushed her lips over his and all of his thoughts evaporated. Poof, gone. Her eyes searched his, wide and hopeful and terrified all at once. The kiss was so soft, rationally he wasn't sure he'd felt it. But the feather-light sensation and faint taste of bubblegum lingering on his skin snapped something inside. The tightly wound tension he'd struggled to contain broke free and shuttered open like a window shade.

He dragged one hand to the back of her head and tangled his fingers in her hair, gripping the closest thing he had to a lifeline and letting the strands bite into his palm. He couldn't ignore this. No one had that much control. He crushed his mouth to hers, years of repressed hunger roaring through him. Skin slid against teeth.

His tongue didn't meet any resistance when he pushed into her mouth and sought hers out. He couldn't think about anything except how much he wanted her. How incredible she tasted. Her gentle curves molding against his body. What it would be like to yank her scrubs to the ground, shove her onto the desk, and slide between her legs. His dick ached at the idea of being buried inside her.

Her palms rested on his chest, fingers digging into muscle. When her whimper vibrated through him, it was enough to wrap a leash around his desire, but only barely. He broke the kiss but didn't let her go. Her gaze held as much turmoil as raged in his own head.

She trailed her fingers down his chest, before drawing her nails up his back. Pleading hung heavy in her low voice. "Don't you dare stop."

This was bad. Everything he shouldn't be doing. And even knowing that, he still wanted more than anything to pin her to the desk and feel her wrapped around him. His cock strained against his slacks every time she rubbed her hip against him. His restraint almost collapsed when he spoke, but he forced his tone to stay steady. "I can't, Lys."

"Bullshit." There was a quiet fury in her response. "I want you." She slid against him again, her body taunting his erection. "You want me."

"You want happily ever after." He said the words aloud as much to reinforce them in his head as to remind her. "I can't offer that." Despite his argument, he couldn't make himself push her away.

"I want to be distracted for tonight. I'm not asking for anything beyond that. I don't expect it. Don't reject me again unless you really, honestly can't stand the thought of being with me. Please?"

The hint of pleading that leaked into her voice shattered her firm tone and the last of his restraint. A whisper in the back of his head said this was all about her. She needed him. But that was an excuse. He fucking wanted her, Goddammit.

CHAPTER FIVE

Tate yanked Alyssia's head back, and nipped her earlobe. "Just for tonight." His growl vibrated against her skin.

Every inch of her body hummed in anticipation. She shifted against him, memorizing the way his hard lines imprinted on her, from chest to groin to thigh. This was really happening, but part of her refused to process it. What if he changed his mind? Again? No, this was different. She managed to keep her hands from shaking as she undid each button on his shirt, and pushed it off his shoulders, leaving in him in an undershirt and slacks. Wow that was sexy.

She leaned her head back to expose her neck and he kissed along the soft flesh, hungry and biting. There was too much clothing between them. She needed to feel his skin on hers. She grabbed the bottom hem of her scrub top.

He wrapped his hands around her wrists, holding her captive, and broke away. A teasing smirk danced on his face. "In a hurry?"

Embarrassment joined the liquid lust heating her skin. What was she supposed to say to that?

He kissed along her fingertips, one at a time on the first hand then the second. "If we're going to do this, you're going to enjoy it."

She clenched her toes inside her shoes at the heavy promise. She was pretty sure she'd enjoy it regardless. "I'm not worried about that."

"Good." He trailed his lips down her palm, over her wrist, and then moved back to her neck. "That's my job." He pulled her top over her head with a fluid grace she didn't think she could have managed herself.

She wouldn't think about the fact that indicated what kind of practice he'd had. This was just them, and it was only for now. Nothing else existed.

He trailed his fingers down her spine, and under her bra strap. "You know." He kissed up her jaw, and nipped her earlobe, breath hot on her skin. "I've wondered for a while now what your nipples look like."

He'd spent time thinking about that? The realization sent flutters through her belly, and tingled between her thighs, making her wet. "You could have asked." Okay, that was a stupid answer.

"Not as much fun." In a single twist, he undid her bra. He dragged the straps down her arms, and tossed the garment aside. The way his gaze lingered on her chest made her desire spike. "Pink, big, and I bet a lot of fun. God, you're gorgeous." He cupped her breasts, and drew his thumbs over the already hard nubs. Each pass flooded her body with a tremor of pleasure.

When he pinched, she sucked in a sharp breath. Her frame tingled from the tug of pleasure and soft pain.

"You should know." His whisper caressed her skin. "I don't have any condoms."

Ambivalence warred inside, stealing some of her anticipation. She hated that she couldn't just say they'd be okay without. Did that mean this was only going so far? Was that his loophole? "So much for being a good boy scout." She struggled to keep the teasing in her tone.

He squeezed her breasts, rolling twin nubs between his fingers, and sucked hard on her neck. He paused long enough to reply. "There's nothing boy scout about what I'm going to do to you. I'll just have to improvise."

The promise filled her with anticipation, but her damned sense of reason wouldn't shut up. He really did expect her to be okay with it. "We can't without—"

"Give me some credit." When his gaze met hers, lust stared back at her. Heated, hungry, and unbound. She swallowed past a dry throat. He looked like he was going to devour her, and she didn't want to stop him. He kissed along her collarbone, lips vibrating against her skin. "I'm not that much of a presumptuous ass."

He wrapped his tongue around one nipple and drew it into his mouth, eliciting a gasp. It was all she could do to keep from crying out when he flicked and nibbled at the nub. Her panties had to be soaked by now. Each new nip and swipe sent another pulse of pleasure coursing through her.

He licked and sucked, alternating between each breast, until her head felt light. She almost thought she might get off just from that attention, but the need between her legs still pleaded for something more direct. She wasn't sure if he'd read her mind, or just the swaying of her hips when his affections shifted downward. He trailed over her stomach, hooked his thumbs in her waistband, and dragged her scrubs and panties to the ground.

The cool air brushed her heated skin and wet arousal. She'd never felt so exposed before, but the desire in Tate's eyes heightened the sensations. Hands on her hips, he turned, redirected her a few steps back, and nudged her onto the couch against the wall. The fake leather was a shock against her skin when it cradled her, and she gasped. Tate knelt in front of her, and kissed along the inside of her thigh, down to one knee, and up to the other.

So many sensations at once stole her reason. She'd never had a guy offer to go down on her. She'd begged a boyfriend once, and it had been so disappointing she'd never brought it up again. When Tate finally focused his attention on the aching need between her legs, a groan tore from her throat. He glided his tongue over her skin, and her breath came in short bursts.

"God, you taste amazing, Lys." His murmured appreciation tingled through her mound. With each pass, he drew closer to her clit, but never made contact. Impatience won out, and she couldn't take the teasing anymore. She tangled her fingers in his hair and pulled his head up. He closed around her swollen sex, and her entire body jolted at the contact. Her hips thrust in time with his sucking, and climax built inside.

When he shoved two fingers inside her, rough and hard, she had to bite the inside of her cheek to keep from screaming his name. She arched her back, and clenched around him when she came. He pushed harder and faster, still pumping her, until she shuddered from the pleasure.

Euphoria danced in her thoughts, and she wasn't ready for the encounter to be over. She stood, wobbling on unsure legs.

He was on his feet in an instant, steadying her. "Careful."

She used the opportunity to spin him so his back was to the couch, and press her frame against his. His erection dug into her stomach through his slacks, teasing her. She slid her fingers under the waistband of his slacks, and fumbled with his belt for a moment before finally unhooking it.

"What are you doing, Lys?" A note of warning lined his question, but he didn't move to stop her.

She undid his button and pulled down the zipper. "Returning the favor."

"You don't have to...." His words melted into a sigh when she wrapped her fingers around his shaft and freed it from his boxers.

"Nope, I don't." She fell to her knees, gaze locked on his, and flicked her tongue over the head of his cock, licking away a salty drop.

He bucked against her face, penis jerking in her hand. She stroked slowly, enjoying his every groan and sigh. When she took him into her mouth, she had to keep her hand wrapped at the base of his shaft to keep him from pushing too deep. He thrust in time with her pumping, eyes never leaving hers. The attention made her juices flow again, coating the inside of her legs. Watching him enjoy himself was turning her on all over again.

His grunts grew more frantic, and his speed increased. "Your mouth feels incredible on my cock." His stuttered breathing punctuated the words. "I'm so close."

If he meant for her to stop, or if it was supposed to be some kind of warning, she didn't care. She pumped harder, and caressed his wrinkled sac. He tensed under her touch, and a long shudder ran through him. Salty warmth hit the back of her throat in spurts, startling her. She'd never done that before, but for him she'd do it again.

No, wait. Reality was sinking back in. She wouldn't, because there was no second time for them. She'd promised.

Her thoughts evaporated again when he pulled her onto his lap. Hand on the back of her neck, he kissed her hard, claiming her mouth. That he wasn't bothered by tasting himself on her lips turned her on as much as anything. Mouth still pressed to hers, he slid his free hand between her legs. She gasped when he found her tender clit and rubbed hard and fast. He swallowed her groans, stroking and pushing her past the limits of her pleasure.

Climax tore through her, snatching away her reason. She shuddered as his touch became too much, and pulled away. She grasped his wrist, and raised it to her mouth, holding his gaze as she sucked one finger clean. His lips parted slightly as he watched her run her tongue along the pad before moving to his next finger.

She let go of him, and leaned into his chest, still struggling to catch her breath. That had been amazing, and she wasn't sure if it was just the things he'd done, or if it had as much to do with the fact it was him.

He trailed his fingers through her hair, heart hammering against her ear. This was too nice. She could get used to this. The moment the thought passed through her head, she pushed away. The last thing she could allow herself to do was get used to cuddling up to Tate. She pasted a smile on. "We're on a deadline, right?"

A flat mask passed over his face, before a pleasant expression flitted back in. "Right. Of course." He extracted himself from her couch and handed over her clothes. He turned away as she dressed, and she couldn't completely squash her disappointment at the heavy air that had settled in the room.

She straightened her clothes, skin still tingling everywhere he'd touched. That had been amazing. She struggled to pull her gaze from him as he put on his shirt. Fantasies taunted her of waking up next to him. Wandering around his house in nothing but that shirt.

She pushed the thoughts away, veins flooding with irritation at herself. She'd sated the teenager inside. The little girl who had been swooning over her older brother's best friend for as long as she could remember had gotten what she wanted. It had been incredible, but that just meant she could move on with no regrets. Right?

His eyes met hers, holding her attention captive. A wicked smile tugged up the corner of his mouth. He closed the distance between them in a few short steps, and knotted his fingers in hair again. His mouth crashed down on hers, and she yielded to the kiss without hesitation. He let her go far too soon for her liking, and stepped back. His teasing, seductive tone tickled her thoughts. "I'm feeling better. You?"

She ducked her head, heat flooding her cheeks. Was she supposed to say thank you? Tell him he was as much responsible as she was? Definitely not ask when they were doing it again. She forced confidence and professionalism to the forefront, despite the way lust kicked and clawed to maintain her attention. She was grateful her voice stayed even when she replied. "I take back anything I said yesterday. The random hookup was way better than trying to find a guy online." She plowed forward before he could reply, not sure she could maintain her mask otherwise. "We have a deadline, right?"

It would be good to stay focused. She'd keep from lingering too long on emotions she couldn't possibly unravel right now. Feelings she shouldn't have. If they dove back into work, everything could go back to what it had been before tonight. Was it last night that had been the catalyst? Or eight years ago? Or— she shook the rambling thoughts aside.

"Work. Right." He nodded at her chair. "There are storyboards and a script for you to approve." He let out a shaky breath. "You sure you're okay?"

Arrogant asshole. Irritation flared inside. Like she couldn't cope with a simple thing like a fling? A retort rushed to her lips.

He wasn't done. "With this whole Thompson thing and the news?"

Her angry comeback evaporated as her gut deflated in on itself. Right. That. The question was a more painful reminder than anything else that he'd been comforting her, and her entire world was about to crumble for more important reasons than her childhood crush didn't feel the same way about her that she did about him. She gave him a weak smile. "I'm good. If we get this done, it helps, right? Shows people the shelter is the real deal?"

"I suspect it'll help."

She focused on the sentiment, and the business of things, and dropped into her desk chair. She navigated to the files automatically. He would have placed them on their shared folder on the cloud.

A knock echoed through the room, and she jumped at the sudden banging. She giggled at her own antics. Tate gave her one more glance, furrowed his brows in concern, and smoothed down his shirt before unlocking the door. She pulled her hair back and twisted it into a knot, sticking a pen through to hold it in place. At least if it was a mess, tying it up would hide it a little. Would people be able to tell? Were her cheeks flushed? Mouth swollen and red? Her fingers twitched against the keyboard as she resisted the urge to trace her them over her lips to check.

Greg—the guy who was taking video of the animals—hovered in the doorway. She'd met him a couple of times at company parties. He was a nice guy. A little hard core when it came to his love of video, but Jared was the same about machines so it didn't faze her.

The moment her brother's name popped into her head, she dropped her face into her palms. Would Greg know what they'd been up to? Did the rest of the office know? He was going to tell her brother. Shit. She'd have to deal with another lecture about why she couldn't get involved with his colleagues, or anyone, really, as far as she could tell. Why he'd be happier if she joined a convent...

"What do you think?" Tate's question shattered her out of control thoughts, and she yanked herself back into the conversation. Greg was gone, and her office door stood wide open. Tate was on the other side of her desk, thumbs hooked in his pockets, watching her. "Do you need a couple more minutes to read?"

Right, she was approving the storyboard and script. "Yeah, give me a sec. Sorry."

She could stay as calm and collected as he was. What they'd done was meant to take the edge off her stress, and it had done that. She was going to ignore the new layer of tension that had drifted in instead. Besides, she promised Tate she didn't want more.

So she'd swallow the impulse—her preprogrammed desire to make sex into something emotional—and she'd move on, just like he was. She glanced up from her monitor, surprise filling her when she saw his fingers drumming on his leg, and his toes tapping.

She pushed the observation aside and went back to work. All she had to do was act normal and it would all be fine. Right?

CHAPTER SIX

TATE COUNTED to ten as he breathed out. Last night's 'stress relief' session with Lys had been amazing, but the world kept turning during and after. If anything, the one thing it did for him was give him a painfully erotic fantasy to slide into every time he remembered how she tasted, her scent, her soft lips wrapped around his cock.

"Did you see the news about the animal shelter?" His assistant, Alan's voice floated from the speaker phone.

Tate shook the images away. He wouldn't let the question get to him—the implication that the news report last night was anything more than an irritating splash in the media pool. There was a solution, he just had to keep his cool. He spoke into his speaker phone. "I did."

"Do we need to worry about backlash?" Alan's voice was hollow, echoing through the Tate's office. "They're not live yet. Are we sure this is a good pilot group for us? If people buy into the hype, and that spreads onto us for supporting them... We look like we're backing animal abuse."

Tate choked back a snarl. This was why he'd hired Alan. Why the guy made such a great assistant. He thought of these things, and he didn't keep the thoughts to himself. But damn it, this wasn't what Tate needed to hear right now. The bad press wouldn't be an issue. He already knew Lys would be able to stop the rumors before they became an issue, and this wasn't just business, it was a good cause. "They're going live. We won't have any problems."

"Right. I'll update the time line to show they'll be live by tomorrow night."

Tate tossed a few instructions out about meetings that afternoon, and disconnected the call. He rubbed his face, but it didn't push away his gnawing tension. He'd already ignored the email from his mother reminding him how easy it would be for Alyssia to make this go away.

He needed to step back, do his job, and let the rest roll off. He'd make sure it all worked out. This business venture, and his test user, meant too much to him to let anything go astray.

A knock drew his attention, and he dragged his gaze to the doorway.

"Lunch?" Mikki—Jared's fiancée and the company's top developer, was leaning against the frame. Her black hair had a violent blue streak through it that week, and she'd pinned the locks back from her face with butterfly-shaped barrettes. While he still struggled to understand the attraction between her chaos and his best friend's unyielding order, he knew she was the best thing to ever happen to Jared. That kind of relationship was a once in a generation kind of fluke, like a sappy movie or something.

The idea made his brain twitch. Something unfamiliar and completely unpleasant surged inside and he obliterated it, focusing on Mikki instead. "I just have to be back by two." Alyssia was coming in to record the voice-overs for her promo video. The name summoned every positive and negative emotion he'd just stuffed inside. He needed to get a handle on that before she showed up. "I'll meet you there."

"Epic." She was already spinning away. "Microbrewery off one-forty-one."

He rolled his eyes and let out a short laugh. "Got it." Almost a year in Atlanta and she didn't care to learn the names of anywhere they regularly went. Said the world was too transient for things like proper nouns on buildings.

The moment she was gone, he sank back in his chair. The two conversations had summoned the one name and image he'd been trying to keep from his mind all morning. Or rather, the memories of last night. He could still taste Alyssia, like a phantom tingle on the tip of his tongue. Every exquisite inch. The woman he'd seen almost every single day since she was a kid, and now just her name made his cock twitch.

He swallowed the lust. The inching desire to figure out what else they could get up to if there were no strings. He had lunch to get this out of his system. No big deal. He was a big boy, and flings were his specialty. He could handle this.

He finished replying to a couple more emails, suppressed any lingering fantasy from the night before, grabbed his sunglasses, and headed out the door.

Fifteen minutes later, Tate strolled through the front door of the pub. The drive had been enough to clear his head, and he felt like his mind was working again. Never pausing, he nodded at the host and cleared the corner to head into the dining area. His friends would probably be at the same table they were always at, near the back of the room.

They were exactly where he expected, but instead of three heads he counted four. He hesitated, and then forced himself to keep walking at a normal gait. Instead of the standard one table they usually sat at, two tables had been pushed together because Alyssia had joined them. No big deal; she dropped by for lunch all the time when she was working night shift.

So why were Jared and Mikki sitting across from each other, Mikki by Alyssia, and Jared by Vivian?

"I don't get the point," Jared said as Tate drew within earshot.

The table between him and Mikki was clear. She flicked a sugar packet across the smooth surface, where it glided to a stop just short of Jared's edge, half on, half off the table. "If it lands like that, you score a point." Mikki explained.

"Of course." Instead of tucking the sugar packet away, like he would have six months ago, Jared flipped it back.

Mikki met Tate's gaze for just a moment before returning her attention to the game. "Look who we found."

Tate didn't have to look. Every time he tried to pull his gaze from Lys, it drifted back to the heat and doubt in her eyes.

"I dropped by to say hi to Jared before our recording session," Alyssia said.

Of course she had. Tate hid his grimace under a wide smile. "Awesome." His skin buzzed with memories of the night before, every nerve ending dancing to life in anticipation just from the way she caught her bottom lip between her teeth. That wasn't good. Apparently his rambling thoughts weren't under control.

He took the empty seat next to Vivian, rather than continuing to stand there and gape. Vivian was the director of operations for Skriddie Bust Media, and Mikki's boss. She, Jared, and Tate had clashed when she joined the company several years ago. However, a handful of crises that pushed them together, proved the three clicked on a whole new level when it came to problem solving, and they'd become solid friends. Jared was closer to her than Tate, but Tate still had nothing but respect and admiration for her skills. And she played a mean hand of poker.

When V raised her brows in question, he scrambled for the first excuse he could find that wasn't, *"If I sit next to Lys, I'm going to spend all of lunch with a hard on."* "I have a question for you about St. Louis."

He didn't mean the city. Before they hired Mikki, her former employer, NSS had used her skill without her knowledge to violate the Skriddie corporate network. Jared and Mikki had spent several months pulling together enough information to file a civil suit for the infraction. But the violation itself had already done damage to Skriddie's public image. St Louis was their code name for the PR campaign Tate was spearheading to update their image.

"What's up?" Vivian asked.

Shit. Now he had to come up with something. A long series of questions ran through his head in a millisecond. "How often does operations re-certify developers?"

"Every six months or as operating systems update, whichever comes first."

Jared jerked his attention from the makeshift sugar-football game. "Speaking of, we got a document discover request from Vicker today about intellectual property No clue how they found out we'd even done that."

Damon Vicker was the attorney defending NSS in the civil suit Skriddie had filed against them.

Tate was good—great even—with this line of conversation. It was boring, it was dry, and it would keep him distracted. "We all know there are other ears inside the company." It was part of the reason they called their PR project St. Louis instead of Fuck-NSS-Over-Publicly.

"Send me a list of what Vicker wants, and I'll grab you the documentation this weekend." Technically, Tate was balancing two jobs. He still held his senior VP of sales job at Skriddie, but was also president of the new venture. The extra work would be worth it, though, to get his sites off the ground.

"If everyone's here, are y'all ready to order?" The waitress's pleasant southern lilt drew Tate's attention. Her nametag said she was Brittany. Large blonde curls framed her face, and her lipstick was just bright enough to draw attention without being too gaudy. Her lips didn't look as kissable as Lys's, though. And Brittany probably didn't make the same guttural moans—

He shook the thoughts away. He wouldn't compare her to Alyssia. He'd grab her number instead, to remind himself how much he enjoyed having the option of hooking up with a different woman every night.

"I'm not sure, Brittany." He met her gaze, never breaking eye contact, and let his own drawl slide in. A trick he usually either saved to irritate his mother, or to give him that boy next door sound. Even though he'd grown up in Georgia, he'd never had the accent by default. His mother had taught him. She'd said when it was used at the right time, it could shape all sorts of impressions. He never had to use it around Lys. Which didn't matter because he wasn't thinking about her.

Brittany moved to his side, and rested a hand on his arm. "What can I do for you, sugar?"

He did this all the time, so why did it feel so unnatural now? Because he was over-thinking it, that was why. "Which do you recommend? Chef's special, or catch of the day?"

She twirled a strand of hair around her finger. "Depends. Catch of the day is fresh, but chef's special is spicy. You look like you enjoy a little heat." She winked.

"Quite a bit." He handed the menu back. She was hooked, he was almost certain of it. A couple more lines, and he'd have her number. Except he couldn't force out the next line. He couldn't close.

"Me too." Vivian passed her menu between, breaking a teasing gaze about to turn awkward.

Brittany turned her attention to the rest of the table, and after one last glance at him, moved on to other customers. The conversation shifted from work, to the Memorial Day barbeque his parents were holding in just over a week. When Jared shifted his attention to his sister to ask her something about their own parents, Vivian tilted her head toward Tate.

"I'm surprised you didn't snag her number." Vivian's voice was low enough only Tate would hear.

Tate glanced at Lys, her eyes bright, a genuine smile in place as she laughed at something Jared said. "I'm off my game or something. Work, stress, blah, blah, blah."

Vivian smirked. "That's never been an issue for you before."

Irritation surged through him at the prodding. "It is now." The words snapped out sharper and louder than he intended, and everyone's heads swiveled in his direction. Why was he even upset with V? She was being friendly, teasing the way they always did. "Sorry. Like I said, stress."

Vivian pursed her lips. "Apparently so."

Again, the conversation shifted and flowed as the food arrived, and then empty plates were taken away. At some point, Brittany slipped her phone number under his hand. Tate managed to bring his rambling thoughts under control by the end of the meal. He should be fine in this afternoon's recording session with Lys, especially with the sound engineer around. Which reminded him. "We have to get back." He realized after a glance at his phone to check the time. "Recording session."

"Everyone rode with me," Jared said. "Meet you back there?"

Alyssia's eyes grew wide, and she opened her mouth, but before she could speak, Vivian cut her off. "I'm going to catch a ride with you, if you don't mind. J's back seat is cramped, and I have an idea I want to run past you." Vivian fell into step beside Tate. He tried but failed to ignore the disappointment that flashed over Alyssia's face before a smile flitted back in.

"Sounds like plan." Did V have any idea she'd just bought him another fifteen minutes by asking for a ride before Alyssia could?

Mikki and Alyssia split off toward the other side of the parking lot with Jared, and Tate let relief trickle through him. He glanced at the waitress's number one more time before crumpling it and tossing it in a nearby trashcan.

"You're going to break her heart." Vivian's comment dragged him back into the now. Exactly where he needed to stay. He'd remember that.

Which meant she was talking about the waitress, not Lys. "She served me iced tea, V. I don't think she expects a ring for that." He held the car door open for her, and waited until she was seated before taking his spot behind the wheel.

Vivian laughed. "That's good. And not who I was talking about. What do you think J's going to do when he finds out you hooked up with his sister?"

She *had* figured it out. *Fuck.* He wanted to ask if it was that obvious, but he wasn't willing to confess. "He'd probably blow a fuse. Good thing we didn't."

Vivian raised an eyebrow.

"What?" Tate didn't like the defensive mechanism kicking in. "I'm not stupid. I've known her a lot longer than you have, and I know she's not a one-time kind of girl."

Vivian shrugged. "She wouldn't look at you during lunch, she barely said two words after you showed up, and she clenched her jaw every time the waitress showed up. Something happened, at least as far as she's concerned."

He didn't want to snap at V, but the last thing he needed was her voicing every argument his mind was already tossing at him. "Were you this bad with Jared and Mikki?"

"Considering they'd hooked up, and you two *haven't*"—she made a show of clearing her throat—"I was about fifty times worse. But my reasons with Mikki were different."

Of course they were. Because no matter how much she liked Mikki, or respected Jared, she still felt like he'd betrayed her by falling in love. Tate would have bet big that Vivian had never completely gotten over Jared, but as long as the two of them were still single, she could pretend it would be that way forever. He kept the thought to himself, not interested in picking a fight. "I've known the two of them for ages, I understand what a bad idea that would be—and that doesn't even matter because there's nothing going on with Lys."

"Right." Vivian's tone was flat. "Because if there were, you'd know eventually you'd have to pick a side."

"Did that a long time ago." He just had to remember that. Jared was his best friend, and Alyssia was a client. Vivian's reminder just cemented he needed to put as much emotional distance between himself and Lys as possible.

CHAPTER SEVEN

ALYSSIA LEANED against the frame of her home office door. "It's okay, really." It was true, two days ago, she had been irritated with Jared for insisting she upgrade her home network hardware to be more secure.

Now, that seemed like an eternity ago. A flutter raced across her skin, and her gut churned at the reminder.

"If you didn't do so much work from home..." Jared sat at her desk, fingers flying across the keyboard, rarely pausing even as he spoke. "Nah, that's just an excuse. You needed the upgrade."

"Really?" She kept a teasing tone. "So you've already upgraded everything in your house, and needed someone else to techify?" Even though she was trying to keep her attention on the conversation, it kept dancing with the one name she'd been doing her best not to think of since she left the Skriddie offices that afternoon.

Not that she'd succeeded. Every unoccupied thought, and even some of the occupied ones, were interrupted with Tate. Had last night been a mistake? It had taken her this many years to get used to how he flirted without shame with pretty much every waitress, hostess, anyone. Then today at lunch, watching him with their server had almost devoured her.

Still, the memory of what she had Tate had shared, the way they'd clicked, and the things he'd done, she wouldn't give that up for anything. She would stick to her promise that what happened between them was just physical. A one-time event, and all that. Which was why, when he'd asked if she wanted him to just email the promo video to her for approval, and launch the site without her, or if she wanted to be there for all of it, she'd invited him over.

His dropping by for whatever had never been a deal in the past, and there was no reason for that to change. The faster things got back to normal between them, the better.

"Hello?" Jared's insistent voice shattered her wandering thoughts. "Earth to Alyssia. You in there?"

She shook away the mental clutter and focused on her brother, who apparently had finished what he was doing, and was watching her. "Sorry, too much going on everywhere. What?" she asked.

"You're all done." He held up a blank post-it note, then stuck it to one of the frames he'd brought back for her from a business trip. The picture frame was from Busch Gardens. The blank note was his way of letting her know what her new network password was. She did adore that he always remembered to bring her something, wherever he visited. And each new trinket had a different memory attached to it, which was why he used them for her passwords.

"Thank you." She smiled. "I really do appreciate it."

"I know you don't so much." He stood and joined her, falling into step next to her as they made their way downstairs, to the living room of her townhouse. "But I appreciate you placating me. And yes, you're right. Even Mikki doesn't think we need any more new tech in the house. But if I can show her this router works for you..."

"I'm glad I could be your guinea pig."

Jared strode toward the door. "Good luck with your launch tonight. I know you'll do awesome."

Alyssia's heart leapt, hammering in her chest, when Jared opened the door to find Tate on the other side, hand half raised to knock. Tate slid a quick smile into place, never flinching. His gaze met hers for the briefest moment, and she swore she saw heat flash in his eyes as they flicked over her.

Or that was wishful thinking on her part? Why did he have to look so good?

"You get everything squared away?" Tate turned back to Jared.

"She's set." Jared glanced back at Alyssia, and she resisted the urge to stick out her tongue. She wasn't going to fall into a childish role with her brother. Not tonight. "I'm glad you're here to take care of her, though."

Heat flooded Alyssia's face at the rush of images associated with Tate taking care of her. He certainly had last night. She shook the thoughts away, and nudged Jared forward. "You're going, right? And keeping in mind how profusely grateful you are I gave you an excuse to buy something new?"

Tate clapped Jared on the shoulder before stepping around him. "I promise any trouble she gets into will be fully supervised by me."

This time when Tate's gaze met hers, she had no doubt mischief and desire danced behind his look. Damn it, she couldn't go back to casual flirting with him so soon after.

"Glad to hear it." Jared finished saying his goodbyes and seconds later, the townhouse door closed behind him.

Alyssia summoned every last ounce of calm and cool she could find, and dragged her gaze away from Tate. She couldn't spend the whole night staring. "Should we get to work?"

He raised an eyebrow, and she hid a wince. Maybe she shouldn't have had so much ice in her tone. "Nice to see you, too." His voice was pleasant, and light.

She could be civil, no big deal. It was the meaningless innuendo she'd struggle with. "Sorry. I'm just—" What? Desperate to relegate last night to a pleasant memory, rather than intense longing? No, she'd go with a different truth. The one she'd managed to ignore in favor of more fleeting, less stressful things. "I'm just eager to get this thing online, and put more distance between the shelter and Thompson's bullshit."

Tate's left hand clenched into a fist, and he gritted his teeth. "Right. Let's get that done. Lead the way." He gestured toward the stairs, and then paused, and wrapped a loose hand around her wrist. "What's wrong with your arm?" He was looking at a large piece of gauze taped to her skin, below the elbow.

"I had a patient get a little excited, and he hadn't had his nails trimmed in a while. It's not a bad gash, but it's long."

"Are you okay?"

"Sure." She hadn't even thought about it, but his concern filled her with a soft glow. Injuries like this were status quo for her. "I'm on antibiotics just in case, but it'll be fine."

"Good. As long as you're all right." He rested a hand at the small of her back, his light touch all but searching her skin through her T-shirt. She did her best not to focus on the touch. Not to associate it with memories of his hands running over her bare skin. By the time they reached the doorway to her office, her imagination was working overtime, and her breathing shallow. She pushed aside the vivid images and tried to be subtle about pulling away from him.

"What first?" She cringed at the too-bright chirp that tore from her mouth.

"Have a seat." His tone was flat, any of the earlier teasing gone. "You do the setup, I watch and make sure it's all intuitive."

Her insides twisted in on themselves as she pulled up the admin panel for the crowd-funding site. Apparently, without the rampant fantasies of Tate, her mind was free to linger on Thompson's threats instead. The lawyer she kept on retainer had sent letters to Thompson and to the news station threatening a defamation suit if Thompson didn't retract the statements. She hadn't heard anything back, and didn't know if that was a good sign or not. But if they could get her campaign online tonight, and get promises of funding, that would help. It had to. It would be a chance for her to remind people the shelter did good things. That it was worth people's time and investment to support the animals.

She shoved aside the chaos tumbling through her head, and tried to clear her mind. "What first?"

"The art department had time to implement all your requests, so give this a look and make sure you're good with it." Tate rested his hand on her shoulder, leaned around her, and plugged a USB drive into her laptop.

His familiar scent filled her nostrils, and she inhaled deeply. His warmth radiated through her sleeve, and dragged her jumbled thoughts back to the surface. This wasn't the way to move on from last night. That would have to become her mantra if she was going to make it through the evening with her sanity and heart intact.

She leaned toward the screen, breaking the contact between them, and clicked the auto-run icon that popped up. After recording her voice-over that afternoon for the promo video, she'd sat with the art department, giving her feedback with each new tweak, so there would be as few surprises as possible tonight.

She played the video, pleased with the results. Tate told her all of the pilot groups had similar access to Skriddie's art and marketing departments, to help make the crowd-funding software launch go as well as possible. She still felt like she'd gotten a little extra attention. Not that she minded in this case.

The application was fairly easy to navigate. With only a little prompting from Tate, she finished setting everything up.

"That's it." Tate rested a hand on her shoulder, but pulled away too quickly for her liking.

Nervous energy hummed through her. Everything else aside, this project was going to take her shelter to new places. Owning the land they were on would give them new options for expansion, the opportunity to implement new projects for the animals. Her fingers twitched in anticipation. She inhaled deeply, then pressed the 'Go Live' button.

All the air escaped her lungs and she sank back in her chair, as the world continued on around them. "That was anti-climactic." She laughed at her own anxiousness. It wasn't like the world should have turned upside down just because she clicked *Go*.

Tate draped his arms over her shoulders and squeezed. "Congratulations." His breath caressed her cheek.

She wanted to sink into the hug, but forced herself to draw back. She navigated to her dashboard. "Do I take the system down if I refresh obsessively?" She forced her tone to stay light.

"No." A hint of strain lined Tate's response. "It's built for that. Refresh away."

She clicked the refresh button several times in rapid succession, just for fun, impressed when the system responded instantly each time. And then the system hung. It sat for several seconds before rendering in a jumble. "I think I broke it." She joked.

"It's a hiccup. Try again."

She did. Each time, the response took longer, until nothing was returned at all. "Nope, definitely broke it." Her teasing came out more forced than she intended.

"Can you get to other sites?"

She navigated to a couple without any issues, but still couldn't get back into her admin panel.

"Shit." Tate's curse was so soft she barely heard it. "May I?"

She stood and let him have her seat, furrowing her brow. What was going on? This shouldn't be a big deal, right? She'd been watching Tate and Jared work long enough, though, she knew something was wrong. "Do you want me to call Jared?"

Tate's fingers flew over the keyboard, new windows opening, including one with a black background and white text, and another that looked like a different computer desktop. "He and Mikki have plans." His voice was tight.

"You know he'll cancel. Is it bad?" She crossed her arms, and tapped her toes. What was going on? It was just a little glitch, right? So why did she feel like everything was about to go sideways? Her gaze drifted toward her phone, at the edge of her desk. Maybe she should call Jared anyway. Tate wouldn't let his ego get in the way of doing this right.

The high-speed clack of keys drew her attention back to what Tate was doing. Her limited understanding of what they did at Skriddie told her he was dialed into a remote computer, switching between a performance monitor and a window with text in different colors. "Fucking load balancing issue." Tate muttered a string of curses, and continued working.

Guilt joined the swirl of emotions in her head. She should have remembered, Tate had the same background as her brother, he just used it differently.

Watching Tate now, he really did shine when it came down to it. At least, she assumed he was. He never paused for more than few seconds, and as the minutes ticked away, he clicked through more things she only vaguely recognized.

The light faded outside, until the primary source of light in the room was her laptop screen. A nudge at the back of her mind told her she should turn on the light, but she was too engrossed in watching Tate work.

It seemed like eons later, but according to her clock it was less than two hours, when he leaned back in her chair with a loud exhale. "So weird." Despite his quiet tone, the sudden statement was loud in the room.

She chewed on her bottom lip, not sure what to say. "So... It's fixed?"

He stood and gestured for her to take the chair again. "Yes. You're back online."

"What happened?"

"Do you want the technical details?"

She might feel smarter if she heard them and understood them. Then again, if she described the details of neutering a dog, he wouldn't be able to keep up either. "Not really."

He gave a light laugh. "Something was wrong with the server configuration. It wasn't set up to handle as much internet traffic as it should have been."

As in, none? She had to have been the only person on the site. The clench of his jaw and way he kept glancing back at the machine made her wonder what he'd found that bothered him so much.

"It's back online now. You're good to go," he said after a final glance at the laptop.

She reached for the mouse, then paused. He'd said it was fixed, she was being silly. Still, as she clicked into her admin dashboard again, her earlier enthusiasm was missing. A whisper of disappointment mingled with the rest of her thoughts. Of course there wouldn't be any donations. The site had technically only been online for a few minutes. Still, she clicked refresh again, bracing herself for anther slowdown.

Her heart leaped, and a smile broke her face. Was that a donation? She hit refresh again. Yup, it was. It was several hundred dollars, from an anonymous source. She had no idea how it had gotten there. A voice in the back of her mind asked how that had come in so quickly. Technically they wouldn't be live until tomorrow. Advertising would go out then. The social media campaign would start up.

But it was a donation. How was that bad? "Yay." She hopped to her feet, giddiness flooding her, and spun to Tate. She tossed her arms around his neck. "It worked."

His hands rested on her back, and he squeezed. "Congratulations." He didn't let go.

Heat flooded her as the seconds ticked away. His pulse hammered a beat against her cheek, and she extracted herself from his embrace, not able to meet his gaze. She really needed to get over this.

"Hey." He placed a finger under her chin and raised her head until she was looking him in the eye. "Enough. We both had fun last night, right? I know I did."

It was okay to admit to that. Fun had been part of the point. "I did too." Alyssia felt a touch of relief being able to say it aloud.

"I don't regret it. Not in any way." His expression was soft, attention focused completely on her.

She didn't either. She just had to say so, and things would go back to the way they were. So why couldn't she say the words?

CHAPTER EIGHT

T ATE'S HEART froze for the briefest moment when Lys didn't reply.

"No regrets." Her words were a reassurance he didn't know he needed.

"Good." He intertwined his fingers with hers, and tugged her out of the room. He knew what his problem was. He'd been over-thinking everything since last night. He needed to step back, get an objective perspective, and just let instinct drive. "Let's go celebrate."

"What did you have in mind?" Lys paused by the front door long enough to slip on a pair of sandals, and grab her purse.

The one thing they always did. Something nagged at the back of his mind, asking how they had an 'always' anything. He shoved it aside. It's just the way things were between them. It didn't mean anything. "We grab a pizza and head up to the lake."

"Sounds perfect." Her grin latched onto something inside him, and send a wash of need over his skin.

Apparently he hadn't reached that objective point yet. He'd get there, though.

"You drive." She tossed him her keys.

He snagged them without missing a beat. The Bentley was nice for freeway and city driving, but Lys's ancient Suburban would handle the off-road lake paths a lot better, and he was more familiar with the route than she was.

An hour later, they'd found a quiet spot of trees, and a clearing with no one else around, and backed the SUV up several feet back from the lake. They finished the pizza and discarded the box half an hour after that, and then sat next to each other on the tailgate. Lys swung her legs in a lazy arc, and Tate leaned back, palms resting on the upholstery behind him. Once upon a time, Lake Lanier had been one of his least favorite places. His parents had a summer home that was really more of an excuse to show off than a reason to vacation. They'd sold it when the area got too crowded.

Spending time with Lys up there, though, helped him discover an appreciation for the beauty again. Especially when they could find an isolated spot of land and just unwind.

"Remember that night we came up here to study for my finals?" Her question blended into the calm of the night.

"Which time?"

She leaned into him. "Every time. I doubt I would have made it through undergrad without your help."

"I was zero help for vet school, so I guess that evens everything out. What about the time you ran away?"

"Oh, God." She scrubbed her face, laughter spilling through her fingers. "I don't even remember why I did that, but I know it was childish. I'm still grateful you never told them you found me up here."

"Right. Because I was going to tell J—anyone you hitchhiked to the lake." Tate wasn't sure why he stalled on Jared's name. Something told him he didn't want to ruin the mood that way.

She tucked one leg under the other knee, and turned to face him. "Or three years ago when I closed on the loan for the shelter."

Her eyes sparkled with amusement, holding his gaze captive. If he leaned in a few inches, he could lose himself in the soft perfume of her shampoo. His senses prickled at the idea, and he shelved the desire. "You mean the night you drank way too much champagne and almost puked in my car?"

"I don't remember it that way." She tucked a strand of hair behind her ear. His fingers itched with the desire to cover her hand. What was wrong with him tonight?

"You were wasted." He struggled to keep the conversation light, friendly, and as completely unsexy as possible. "I'm surprised you remember anything."

"I remember enough." She twisted her mouth in mock-irritation. "Was that really the last time we were up here?"

He had a feeling she knew the answer as distinctly as he did. "It was."

"Why did we stop?"

"Coming to the lake?" He was stalling. He knew exactly what she meant. "Our schedules got busy. Life got in the way." The excuse slid out without thought. It was the same one he fed himself every time he wondered why they didn't hang out more. With the question between them now, it bounced in his head.

He studied her closer. The flush of laughter on her cheeks. The smile tugged forward by the memories. Had they really spent so much time together? Up here. At home. He sifted through stacks of memories, and she was a part of so many of them.

She poked him in the arm. "What are you staring at?"

He shook away his rambling thoughts. "Just you."

Fuck it all. He was lingering too much on this one thing. Putting too much thought into a simple, physical response. She'd been open to no strings last night, would she go for it again? Once the physical wasn't taboo anymore, the tension between them would vanish, and they could go back to being casual and friendly, without the awkwardness.

ALYSSIA TRIED NOT TO NOTICE THE SUDDEN SILENCE. MAYBE SHE SHOULDN'T have brought up the celebration night. She remembered it far more vividly than she'd ever let on. She'd actually only had a couple of glasses of champagne, but had definitely enjoyed the excuse to fall asleep on Tate.

"But you know." His voice was suddenly too loud in the still. It sounded too cheerful, but strained at the same time. "That's life, right? We'll drift our separate ways, you'll meet a great guy to bring up here, and he'll be one hell of a lucky dude if you give him a chance."

But she'd already met a great guy. She bit the inside of her cheek to keep the comment from escaping. "I guess."

He hopped to the ground, and disappointment spread through her at the sudden distance between them, even though he'd only stepped a few feet away. Was the moment ruined? Was he waiting for her to say something?

"However." The strain vanished from his voice. He stepped closer, and tugged her foot so both of her legs hung over the tailgate again. "If you want a distraction until then..."

Anticipation seared her veins and her pulse kicked into overdrive. She tried to keep the teasing in her reply. "I'm not sure I know what you're suggesting."

"I'm just thinking, waiting for Mr. Right has got to get lonely sometimes." He nudged her legs apart with his knee, and pushed between her thighs. Friction built, teasing her thoughts. "And I'm guessing a battery operated boyfriend doesn't always do the trick."

Her face warmed. "I don't—" His raised brows made her pause, mid-protest. "No, it doesn't."

He glided his fingers over the backs of her hands, up her arms, and along her jaw. "I'm offering something a little more... organic, from someone you already like and trust."

Like. Such a tame word. Desire glided under her skin, focusing in her belly, then spread outward again. Could she really have casual sex? Tate didn't do long term, but he was being up front about it. She could fool around, indulge her fantasies, and then they could both step back once their needs had been met. "It sounds like a perfect arrangement." She almost stammered on the words. Where had that come from?

He cradled her face in his hands, searching her eyes. "Couldn't agree more." When he kissed her, mouth pressed to hers, palms holding her head in place, excitement squeezed her chest. She could keep things casual if it meant more of this. More of this kind of attention from Tate. Definitely.

He trailed his lips along her cheek, and down her jaw. Traipsed a line of kisses over her clavicle and to her sternum. Each new, feather-light touch sent a pleasant shudder through her. She whimpered and tilted her head back as he moved lower. His touch through fabric teased her. She shifted her weight to bring herself closer, and he lifted his head to close his mouth over hers again.

One hand found its way under her shirt, and she gasped at the barely-there sensation of his palm on her bare skin. She rested one hand at the base of his neck. The short, blond hairs tickled her fingertips as she held his head captive.

Sank into the growing hunger. She dug her fingers into his chest, memorizing each new line of definition as she grasped for something to cling to.

The desperation that had been there last night was gone, replaced with something steadier. More sensual. But need still bubbled inside her. She wanted to burn every touch into her memory to savor later. He brushed the bottom of her breast with his thumb, and a gasp tore from her throat. He dragged a path across her nipple, then back again, teasing through fabric. Dampness grew between her legs.

He kissed along the edge of her ear. "You make delicious noises when you're turned on." His voice was so quiet she felt it as much as heard it. "What kind of sounds do you make if I do this?" He dragged the cup of her bra out of the way, scraping lace and elastic over the tender skin.

She sucked in a sharp breath through her teeth. "That kind apparently." It was a struggle to find words.

"What if I do this?" He lowered his head, and flicked his tongue over the jutting pink nub. Slowly at first, but then building up speed.

She squirmed against him with a whimper. An ache called from between her thighs.

"That's good too." He blew lightly on the damp skin.

Her head felt light as the blood rushed from it. Squeaks and gasps pushed from her throat.

"I've got a better place for this." He covered her hand with his.

She managed a laugh. "Where's that?"

Palm against the back of her hand, he guided them both lower. Her fingers brushed a bulge, hard and long, outlined by denim, and he groaned. "Right there."

A new spark of desire raced through her, and she traced his erection through his jeans. Each time she brushed it from a new angle, or gripped his shaft, or caressed the head, he responded. Kissing her nipple, sucking, nipping the flesh with his teeth.

She wasn't sure how long they sat there, clothes half-out of the way, groping and kissing while she sat on the tailgate of her Suburban, him standing between her legs. But this wasn't making out with a boy at the lake. She could have more. She drew his mouth back to hers, and kissed him hard, tongues dancing around each other.

When she broke away, she met his gaze. "We should go back to my place. Or yours. Wherever."

His hungry gaze slid over her face. "What's wrong with here?"

Heat rushed to her cheeks. "We're outside." Except, did she actually mind?

He nipped at her neck with his teeth, and then her shoulder. "And no one's around. We have the area to ourselves. It's dark." He looked her in the eye again. "And tell me the idea of getting caught isn't at least a little exciting."

Her anticipation spiked. "It's more than just a little exciting."

"Good." He dragged a thumb across her nipple again. "Because I've tried. I really have. To put yesterday out of my mind." He covered her hand again, and squeezed. She followed his lead and tightened her grip on his bulge, stroking as he pressed against her hand.

He lifted her chin, holding her head in place, and locked her gaze on hers. "My best intentions have failed." His voice had dropped an octave, and the husky tone floated over her skin. His accent was back. The drawl he tried so hard to hide. The one that made her senses flare to life. "I can't stop thinking about your lips wrapped around my cock. How gorgeous you looked. How incredible it felt. But I'm dying to bury myself inside you. Knowing how tight you were, how wet you got? I want to feel your pussy squeeze around me."

He dipped his head in again, the heat from his breath hot against her cheek when he whispered, "I have condoms tonight. God, I need to fuck you, Lys."

Part of her mind snagged on the words. He'd planned to spend this evening with her. The entire night, right? But he'd stopped for protection? A smirk slid onto her face. She fumbled for the button on his jeans, and then slid down the zipper. "I like the sound of that," she said.

CHAPTER NINE

Tate was so hard, he could barely think. Every time Lys traced his cock, his entire system jerked with pleasure. When she finally freed him from his jeans, the combination of her warm palm and the cool air brushing his bare skin dragged a long groan from him. He wanted to draw this moment out, but his resistance hovered near empty.

She stroked his shaft, and he squeezed her breast harder. She made the most delicious whimpers with every touch. He made quick work of the button and zipper on her jeans, and tugged. She kicked off her sandals, and lifted her ass off the tailgate long enough for him to drag her pants down her legs. It was too dark to stop and drink her in, but her pussy—the way it looked, the way she tasted, was burned in his mind anyway. He moved a hand between her legs. When he pressed into her slit, his fingers were instantly coated.

"God, you're so wet." He dug his teeth into her shoulder, muffling his words.

"I blame you ahh—" Her teasing words faded into a gasp when he shoved two fingers inside her.

He slid in easily, pumping in and out. "You were saying?"

She shook her head, bottom lip caught between her teeth. Each time he pumped inside her, she squirmed and pushed back. He sought out her clit with his thumb. His dick throbbed in the night air, eager and waiting.

Her breathing grew more punctuated. Groans became gasps became panting. "Fuck, Tate. Oh, God."

She was close, he could tell from her rigid spine, the lilt of her sighs, and the way she clenched around his fingers. Climax rolled through her. He needed to be inside her, now. In a fluid motion, he pulled his hand away, and thrust his cock inside her.

Her fading cries peaked again, and she dug her nails into his back. He pounded her. She felt even better than he imagined. Spots danced in front of his eyes as his orgasm built. She wrapped her legs around his waist and kept the pace fast and frantic. She gripped his erection when she came again.

Every point of contact converged into a single spot in his mind. He couldn't last any longer. As much as he wanted to draw the moment out, it wasn't going to happen. He ground against her as he came, spilling hot and frantic inside her. Still driving hard until his legs were weak, and he was spent.

He rested his hands on the tailgate, on either side of her, to support his weight, and buried his head against her shoulder.

She rested her forehead on his chest, still sighing with each gasp for air as she brought her breathing under control.

He slid out as he softened, and something occurred to him. "Fuck," he muttered against her skin. What was wrong with him?

"Already?" Her laugh was light.

God damn it. He'd never done that before. Ever. "I forgot the condom."

Her frame froze beneath him, and then she pushed him back. Wide eyes met his. "You said you had one."

"I do. Still." He tried to keep his tone calm. Struggled not to let his irritation with himself leak into it. "I got caught up in the moment. I forgot..."

She lifted her clothes from the ground with her toes, and shook the dust off. The snap of denim was loud in the late evening. "Forgot."

He didn't know what bothered him more. That he'd gotten so caught up in the moment it had slipped his mind, or that he had enjoyed it so much he wanted to do it that way again. With her. "I'm sorry."

She raked her fingers through her hair. "Do you forget a lot?"

"Never." He poured all the emphasis into the word.

"So, you're clean, right?"

The question stung, but he understood her concern. If there was one thing he hadn't been for years, it was celibate. "Absolutely."

She nudged him back with her body. "I'm on birth control. We should be good."

A strange kind of ambivalence nudged his senses. What the hell? He was just a little drained. That was fantastic news. "Good. Great." He forced himself to relax.

The ride back home started quiet, but conversation eventually flowed again. Alyssia leaned back in the passenger seat, watching the passing lights, and swapping random banter with Tate. A strange moment of panic and hope had passed through when she'd said he hadn't used protection. A bubble of fantasy. Of what might happen if her birth control failed. However, she knew that wasn't his dream. The last thing she wanted was for him to feel trapped, or obligated by something like... She didn't even dare think the words. She wouldn't do that to him.

They pulled up in front of her townhouse, and she met him outside the vehicle. In the dim light, streetlights highlighting his features, he looked as handsome as he ever had. She traced a finger down his cheek. "You heading out?" She swallowed the desire to ask him directly to stay. That wasn't *no strings*.

He intertwined his fingers with hers, and led her toward her townhome. "I'm a little wired, and I don't have anywhere else to be. If you're not busy, I might stick around."

She couldn't fight her smile. "I think I could make time for that."

He unlocked the door, stepped aside for her to enter, and hooked her keys on their hook. "Movies?"

"Sure. I'll find something. I have Coke in the fridge." This was better. It was the comfortable, laid back interaction she enjoyed with Tate. It was true, thinking his name still made her blood run hot, and she didn't know if she'd ever stop daydreaming about the way he kissed. And everything he'd kissed. But at least they were acting normal again.

"I'm good." He dropped onto the couch. "Something smart?"

"Something sweet." She grabbed the remote and pulled up a list of streaming videos. Moments later, *Silver Linings Playbook* started. She wasn't worried he'd argue. For as much as Tate swore no one in real life got a happily ever after, he enjoyed the fictional version. Only guy she'd ever met who didn't mind sitting through romance movies with her.

He patted the couch next to him. No reason to overthink this now. She took the seat, and tucked her legs beneath her. He draped his arm over her shoulders, and she leaned in. This was definitely doable.

The film started, and though she'd seen it several times, she let herself be sucked into the story line. They finished one movie, and picked another. Somewhere along the way, Tate nudged her forward, lay down in the couch, and then pulled her back into him. She didn't argue when he pulled her tight, pressing her back against his chest, and draping his arm over hers.

Within a few minutes, his breathing shifted. He'd drifted off—the realization tugged something inside her. She could get used to this. That was probably a bad road for her to go down. She adjusted her thinking as she snuggled into him. It wasn't like she wanted him there every night for the rest of their lives or anything. This was just comfortable. Nothing more.

TATE STRETCHED AND TRIED TO PUSH THE LINGERING FOG OF SLEEP FROM HIS brain. He couldn't believe he'd passed out on Alyssia's couch. He had vague memories of her warm body in his arms, but maybe he'd just dreamed that. No, he was pretty sure it was real.

Something clattered from the kitchen, jarring him more awake. Might as well investigate. He paused in the doorway, and his senses roared to life. Lys had her back to him, and was grabbing something from the counter. Her damp hair hung down her back, and she only wore a T-shirt and panties.

His cock roared to life, straining against his jeans. Fuck, that was sexy. And she probably wouldn't appreciate him staring. He cleared his throat.

She let out a small squeak and whirled to face him. She blushed and crossed her arms over her chest. He tried to drag his gaze away, and finally managed. "I didn't mean to startle you." He winced at his own drawl. He must be more tired than he realized.

"It's okay." She tugged down the edges of her shirt, sighed and then stopped, looking him in the eye again. "I'm not used to waking up with someone else in the house. I guess I forgot my pants."

"I'm not complaining." His erection was starting to protest at being ignored, though. "Have you been up long?"

"My brain is still on graveyards. I haven't been to sleep yet. I was just seeing if I had any food to make. Do you want breakfast? I can cook something. Or, well, not really. I can make oatmeal—"

She was adorable when she rambled. "Stop." He wasn't sure if he was talking to her, or himself. He crossed the distance between them, and dragged a thumb over her bottom lip. His fingers tightened, wanting another touch. He tried to be subtle about smothering his rampant arousal. "We're good, right? We got past this last night?"

"I think so." She chewed on the inside of her lip, and meet his gaze. "I mean, we totally are."

"Good." He rested his hands on her hips and nudged her back until she collided with the counter. "Because you look fucking hot, and I don't think you owe anyone any apologies for that." She shifted her weight, and her hip rubbed his cock through his jeans. The blood rushed from his head, and he struggled for a moment to form words. He dipped his head, and trailed his nose along her neck, inhaling deeply. She smelled intoxicating, like lilacs. "It's too bad you already showered." He nipped at her earlobe. Her gasp burrowed into his head, short-circuiting his thoughts. "I would have asked if I could join you."

She draped her arms around his neck, and pressed her entire frame to his. Her nipples dragged over his chest, teasing him through fabric. "You're welcome to use it now, if you want."

He cupped her ass, holding her as close as possible. "I don't have any clothes here."

"No one said you had to get dressed after."

A voice whispered in the back of his head that he was playing with fire. That this was crossing a line he needed to steer far clear of. His raging desire for another chance at the woman in front of him drowned it out. "You make a good argument. I think I'm going to take you up on that."

She brushed her lips over his. "Towels are in the closet, I'll be in the bedroom."

Tate was surprised he had any restraint left, as he stripped down in her bathroom. He couldn't stop fantasizing about spending the entire day in bed with Lys. Tasting every inch of her, finding out how loud he could make her scream if she wasn't worried about someone hearing her. His dick stood at attention. He was as bad as a teenager with an inconvenient boner.

He stepped into the shower. Hot water sluiced over him, and he grabbed the body wash. Now he was going to smell Lys on his skin all day. Did he really mind that much? His cock jerked when he gripped it, hand soapy. A low groan escaped his throat. He leaned his head back, eyes closed, and focused on the sensation. Memories danced in his head as he stroked. Lys squirming against him. Her lips wrapped around him the other night. How tight she was when he buried himself inside her.

His balls tightened, and he bit the inside of his cheek until a sharp pain echoed back in protest. It ached to let go, but he forced himself to stop before he came. He definitely wanted to save that until he had her company.

He finished the rest of his shower quickly, dried off, and wrapped a towel around his waist.

There was a knock on the door so soft, he almost wasn't sure he heard it. He toed it open, to find Lys on the other side. Disappointment tried to nudge its way in when he saw she'd dressed. He pushed it aside and summoned a smile. "Hey, gorgeous. Couldn't wait?"

She grimaced, shook her head, and held up her hand. She was holding her phone. "It's for you," she said.

Shit. That couldn't be good. "Hello." Tate kept his tone chipper.

"Gorgeous, really?" Jared's irritation rolled over him. "Couldn't wait for what?"

Double shit. "Breakfast. We were going out to celebrate that her site went live last night." The lie tasted fouler than Tate expected. As if he should be bothered he had to hide what he was doing. Ridiculous. This wasn't anyone's business but his and Lys's.

"Which is why your phone's off." The edge in Jared's tone grew sharper.

Alyssia perched on the edge of her bed, eyes wide, watching Tate.

"I left it in the car, forgot to charge it, it's probably dead." Which, when Tate thought about it might be pretty close to the truth. When was the last time he'd seen his phone? Last night sounded about right.

"You just let it die?"

"Yes. Not all of us treat our electronics like additional limbs." Tate gritted his teeth. Cold air swept over him, and he shivered. Right, he was still in a towel. Though at least he wasn't as hard as he'd been a few minutes ago. "You called for a reason. And it wasn't to get pissy because I complimented your sister." Lys raised her eyebrows, and Tate shrugged. "Why did you call her looking for me?"

"I called her because we're getting a hold of everyone impacted. All of your crowdfunding sites are running slow, and since you're renting my rack space, I'm an emergency contact."

Fuck. "Let me get home. I'll call you back." Tate disconnected, and tossed Alyssia's phone on her mattress. He raked his fingers through his hair. So much for a morning with no distractions.

CHAPTER TEN

Alyssia didn't know if she was better off or not, only hearing Tate's half the conversation. Her attention drifted between Tate in just a towel, standing in her bedroom doorway, and what he was saying.

He snarled when he tossed her phone back.

So much for extending last night's play time into today. "Bad news?"

"Seems that way. Something's wrong with the crowd-funding sites. I don't have details yet." He raked his gaze over her, exhaled slowly, cheeks puffing and then deflating. "I have to get home. I really wouldn't if I had a choice."

Concern rolled over her disappointment. "My site?"

"All of them. Jared just said running slow. But it was bad enough someone called every emergency number until they got him. I'm sorry, but duty calls."

"If you're working on my stuff, I want to be in on it. Stay here."

"I get the feeling this is a more global thing." His towel slipped lower on his hips, and she couldn't keep her gaze from drifting. The corners of his mouth twitched. "I need to get dressed."

She really didn't want that, but she could compromise. "I guess." She kept the teasing in her tone. "But do the work here if you can. You've got to remote into the office even if you go home." It wasn't because she hated to see him leave. Not even close. The clench in her gut was completely and totally because the future of her shelter depended on her site working. "I'll grab your phone. Is it really in the car?"

"Probably." He gave her a half smile. "Thanks."

By the time she got back, just a moment or two later, he was already logging into a remote computer. She plugged in his phone and set it on the desk next to him. When he grabbed her wrist, a shock raced over her, sending her earlier desires tumbling through her body.

He spun in the chair, tugged her between his legs, and rested his hands on her hips. "The moment's not ruined, just delayed." With each word, his breath caressed her stomach through her shirt.

She wanted to close her eyes and sink into the moment. Drop onto his lap, and see what they could get up to. That he needed to focus was only one of several reasons that was a bad idea. She stepped out of his grasp before temptation won out. "Jared's waiting for you to call him back."

Disappointment splashed onto Tate's face before vanishing just as quickly, and he turned back to her computer. "Yes, ma'am." He fiddled with his phone.

Seconds later, Jared's voice filtered through the speaker. "What did you do, punch it to ninety to get home so fast?"

"Decided I was too impatient. I'm staying here. What's up?"

TATE FORCED HIMSELF TO CONCENTRATE ON THE CONVERSATION, AND NOT the lingering scent of lilacs that still teased him.

Jared launched into an explanation. "Someone has tweaked your server configuration so you don't have any bandwidth. Mikki is working on it. Second, we had trolls in the comments. Most of them on the shelter's site, but because of the brand, it bled into the other sites as well. We had to shut down comments."

"Mikki's not in my budget." Tate had tried to snag her, but V held onto her top talent.

"Consider it a personal favor." Some of the irritation faded from Jared's voice. "They're Skriddie services, she's Skriddie operations, so we're blurring the line."

Tate smiled, despite the situation. It was nice to have good friends. He needed to make a call on what to do next.

"What kind of comments?" Alyssia asked.

It had been a controversial decision to add comments to the campaigns, but these were meant to be social platforms to show support for the small businesses using them. Letting people interact was meant to show that, knowing they had filters in place on each site, and their assigned community managers kept an eye on what was being said.

"Nothing." Jared's response came too quickly. "Explain again why you're at her place, Tate?"

Tate rolled his eyes at the screen, glad no one was watching. "Are we talking a dozen comments? A hundred?"

"Thousands. They're hidden, but not gone from the back end."

Tate suppressed a roar of frustration. He dialed into the database server. "I'm guessing we can delete them all." Next, he loaded an admin window, and clicked into the comments. He tried not to read the details.

I could never support a shelter that kidnaps people's dogs and refuses to give them back.
What the hell is wrong with you people?
You should all rot in hell, you sick, puppy-killing fucks.

His gut sank with each new note. So much for the issue with Thompson dying quickly and quietly.

"Oh, God." Lys's soft voice dragged his attention from the vitriol. He whirled in his chair to find her leaned against the far wall, raking her fingers through her hair. "This is bad. It's so, so bad. What am I going to do?"

He was on his feet in an instant. He closed the distance between them and rested his hands on her shoulders. "Look at me. It's okay. It'll be okay. We'll fix it."

"Right now, I'm having a hard time believing that." Her voice cracked.

"Fuck. We have another problem." Jared's voice sounded tinny coming from the phone.

Tate glanced over his shoulder at the computer, then back at Lys.

"Take care of it." Resignation hung heavy in her voice.

He kept his voice low. "I'm worried about you. It will wait a minute."

She dragged in a shuddering breath, and broke free of his grasp. "I'm fine." The emotion vanished from her voice.

"Tate." Irritation swelled in Jared's voice.

"Go."

A string of foul words spilled through Tate's head as he sat back in the desk chair. "What?" He couldn't help the occasional glance over his shoulder, at Lys pacing, and tugging at her hair.

"Mikki's doing work on the structure. She says someone's been making manual donation entries in the database. She's only found the one in here so far, but since it wasn't added by the software, she's concerned there are more hiding out, and it's for a couple hundred dollars. Your development team followed security protocols, right?"

Tate risked one last glance at Alyssia, who had paused, and was watching him, brows knitted together. He didn't want her to hear this. How did they even find that? "Yes, and it's fine."

"It's not fine. It's—"

"It's not an issue." Tate barked. "I know exactly what it is. It's not a security breach." Please don't let him push the matter. Not with Lys listening. Now wasn't when he wanted to explain he'd slipped the manual donation in last night when he'd worked on her site.

"If you say so."

"Positive. Focus on the actual problems." Tate looked behind him again, but the room was empty. An invisible grip tightened around his chest. Nothing to get worked up over. "I thought you plugged all your security holes. Where's this coming from?" The dig wasn't fair, but Tate's frustration wouldn't let him hold it back. Between Jared and Mikki, they'd accounted for so many technical security holes they could fill volumes with the work they'd done. Still, someone had managed to bypass security.

"We did plug the holes. Someone's been screwing with your settings." Jared spilled off a list of details.

Right, the technical stuff. They'd done triage, it was time to step back and fix things more completely. Tate let his thoughts trip through a list of next steps. "I'll get a hold of someone to help with client and user-facing messages. We'll paint a pretty picture. Back in ten."

It was a good excuse to hang up and go check on Lys. Despite his tension, relief tickled his senses when he found her. She was in her bedroom, still completely dressed. Except she'd curled up on top of her comforter and fallen asleep. She snored softly.

Of course. She'd been up all night. He brushed her hair off her face, and the impulse to lean in and kiss her on the cheek raced through him. He banished the desire. That wasn't a casual gesture. It definitely fell outside either facet of their relationship.

After one last, ambivalent gaze in her direction, he pulled a blanket over her, and headed back into her office. He closed both doors, so he wouldn't disturb her.

He made a few calls, found someone on the Skriddie marketing team who didn't mind putting in the extra time—especially with the promise of compensation—and called Jared back. The morning melted into afternoon as they worked through configurations, strategies, handed out assignments, and monitored timelines that only had minutes of leeway depending on the task.

A hand rested on Tate's arm, and he jumped.

"Sorry." Lys's voice was soft enough only he would hear, despite the speakerphone. She set a plastic bag on the desk next to him, Chinese takeout boxes peeked out at him. The heavy scents of citrus, spice, and grease hit him, and his stomach growled in response. Maybe he should have eaten earlier. "I thought you might be hungry."

He put the phone on mute—they were in a lull anyway—and whirled in the chair to face her. "I didn't hear you get up."

"Then you didn't hear me go out, either. I snagged your keys so I could get into your apartment." She held up a second bag, and he realized it had clothes in it. His clothes. She shrugged, playful smile dancing on her face. "Wishful thinking."

The desire he'd squelched earlier rushed back. He stood, tangled his fingers in her hair, and crushed his mouth to hers. She whimpered against his lips and dug her fingers into his shoulders. His pulse roared in his veins, mingling with the desire to press her against the wall and strip her down. He subdued most of the response. "Thank you."

Pink dotted her cheeks. "How's it going?"

"Good. Getting it under control." He traced his thumb over the back of her neck, and twisted a strand of hair around one finger. "Still got a few more hours, though."

She nodded behind her, but didn't break his grip. "I'll be in the living room, watching TV."

"Do we have the new landing page?" Jared asked.

Alyssia shook her head, and stepped out of Tate's reach. "Good luck."

Tate wanted to chase her. He forced himself to unmute his phone instead. "Yeah. ETA to deploy, five minutes." He dove back into the grind, picking at his food, even after it went cold. The light outside faded, and computer clock told him it was after ten when they finally declared the day a success.

"This saved my project, and my ass today," Tate said, as he and Jared wrapped everything up.

"You're welcome. You owe me."

"Bullshit. This is you paying me back for that all-nighter in Vegas." The weekend Jared and Mikki met had led to a major crisis for the company as well. All of them had pulled an all-nighter to bring things back under control.

"Fine." Jared laughed. "You okay to make it home? Sleep in your *own* bed?"

Tate forced himself to ignore the emphasized word. "It's only ten. I'm not an old man. But now that you mention it... the couch here looks pretty comfy." A twinge in his neck reminded him he'd spent last night there, and that might not actually be true. Then again, he'd only slept a few hours, and he'd been hunched over a computer all day.

"I'm glad we got this sorted," Jared said. "And at least as glad you're not serious."

Tate ignored the lack of conviction in his best friend's voice. "Totally. Night, man." He disconnected, and leaned back in the chair. Exhaustion, combined with Jared's half-joke, summoned a doubt Tate had managed to suppress since last night. What was he doing? Carrying on like this wasn't helping either of them. He should have gone home this morning. Or last night. Whatever he was doing with Alyssia wasn't going anywhere. How had he justified it to himself?

So why did knowing that ache in his joints, and rattle uncomfortably in his head?

"How'd it go?" Lys's soft question startled him. "Sorry to interrupt. I heard you hang up."

He whirled to find her standing in the door. The way she leaned against the frame accentuated her lithe figure, and he let his gaze trip over her curves. "It's fixed. We'll put more permanent measures in place on Tuesday."

She hooked her thumbs in the belt loops of her shorts, pulling just low enough to tease. "So what now?"

She wasn't talking about work. He didn't need to clarify with her. That didn't make his answer come any easier, though. He needed to tell her he was leaving. Thank her for everything. Walk out the front door, and dial all the flirting back to zero. The words repeated in his thoughts on fast-forward until they were a scrambled mess of squeals. He was exhausted, still wearing the same clothes he'd been in yesterday, and hadn't had more than four hours of sleep any given night in the last several.

But watching Lys's chest rise and fall with each breath. The way she chewed her bottom lip. The tick of her thumbs against her bare stomach. It sent a new rush of energy through him, and the reminder they had unfinished business from this morning. He crossed the room, and rested a hand at the back of her neck. Lilacs teased him, and her warm skin against his palm jerked his senses to life. He brushed his lips over hers. "I was thinking this time, you join me in the shower."

Tomorrow. He'd walk away tomorrow.

CHAPTER ELEVEN

THEY SHED their clothes quickly between Alyssia's office, and the bathroom. When she bent over to turn on the water, Tate glided a hand up her thigh, and over her ass, cupping the cheek.

She sighed and leaned into him, pressing her bare back against his chest. She wouldn't linger on how right this all felt, just on how good. He drew his palm up her stomach, and between her breasts, though he never touched them. He rested his hand at the base of her neck, and held her tight. Every touch was another claim staked on her skin. Another searing mark holding them together.

He drew back the shower curtain and nudged her into the tub. Seconds later, he stood behind her again, as the hot water sluiced over them. She reached behind her to grab the hard length pressing into her butt.

He grabbed her wrist with a, "Tsk," and then kissed up the side of her neck, lips vibrating against her skin. "Patience."

She ground against him, satisfied when his erection jerked in response. "I'll try."

He reached over her shoulder, grabbed the body wash, and poured a generous dollop into his hand before setting the bottle back on its shelf. A shock of cold raced over her when he rested his hand on her stomach again, and she squeaked.

"Sorry." He sounded anything but. "I guess we need to warm it up." He drew his palms over her skin. Up her chest, down her thighs, everywhere but the bits of her aching to be touched. She gasped when he trailed along the back of her legs, behind the knees, and groaned when he slipped over the insides of her wrists. With her entire body begging to be touched, new erogenous zones spread everywhere. She cried out when he finally cupped her breasts, and a new spark of pleasure filled her.

"God, I love your tits." His grip slid over her skin. "Gorgeous, pink nipples. Perky." He squeezed, and she squirmed in pleasure. "Sensitive." He kept one hand on her chest, and the other slipped lower. "But this." He pushed between her folds. "What do you sound like when you're not worried about someone hearing you scream when you come?"

She swayed her hips against his touch. "You're welcome to find out."

He pulled away from her clit. "I was hoping you'd say that." He moved both hands to cup her ass, and slid a finger between her thighs. Soap slithered down her skin, pooled at her feet, and then washed down the drain.

He reached over her, and grabbed the shower head. "I've always wondered, if you get the full enjoyment out of this."

Embarrassment and a new level of arousal pulsed between her legs. She fought the desire to confess he was frequently the focus of those fantasies. "I might."

He moved the head along her skin, letting the water flow over her, and rinse away the soap. He nudged one of her legs forward with his knee, and brought the shower head to rest between her thighs. "God, I'd like to watch that sometime."

The idea of putting on a show for Tate pooled in her belly, tugging at some of her more vivid fantasies of him walking in on her. With the water pounding against her clit, his other hand still sliding between her legs from behind, and the vivid pictures in her mind, orgasm threatened her senses.

He pulled away before she climaxed. "Not yet." He whispered.

She liked this teasing. She took the showerhead from him, replaced it, and filled her own palm with soap. "Your turn." She whirled to face him.

He raised his brows. "What did you have in mind?"

"It's a shower. So, getting clean." She tried to repeat what he'd done just a few moments ago. Soaping over his chest, up his legs, everywhere but his stiff shaft.

He leaned a hand on the tile, and lowered his head until his forehead met hers. "You're killing me, Lys. I need your hands wrapped around my cock."

His groan when she obliged tickled all her senses. She kept her grip loose, stroking slowly, deliberately, sliding over every inch of his member. He lifted her chin, and crushed his lips to hers, devouring her. Driving the kiss through her. He broke away, and held her gaze. "Turn around."

"I don't—"

"Turn around." He emphasized each word.

A pleasant shudder filled her at the command in his voice, and she spun away from him. He placed his hand between her shoulder blades, and pushed. She took the hint, bending at the waist, and pressed her hand against the edge of the tub for support.

"I can't behave around you." The head of his cock slid down the crack of her ass, then nudged her pussy. She let out a loud cry when he thrust inside without any further fanfare. "Fuck, you're so tight. So slippery." His words were punctuated by groans.

He gripped her hips, fingers digging into the skin, leaving more invisible marks. Each time he pounded against her, he hit something inside. Striking the pleasure spot hard, fast, and frantic. The orgasm she'd been drawn back from rushed forward again, and she teetered on the edge.

His other hand reached around her. When he bumped her clit, climax washed away her thoughts. It rushed over her, and penetrated every inch of her mind and body. She lost herself in the hard grinding from behind, and was only vaguely aware of him coming. Grunting and filling her.

Her senses slowly drifted back in, and her legs wobbled. He helped her stand, and pulled her back into him again.

He wrapped his arms around her, and kissed her neck. "Dirtiest shower I've ever had."

She chuckled, and pulled his arms tighter, sinking into the embrace. Burning the moment into her memories.

When they caught their breath, they finished showering. This time Tate was tender as he rinsed her off, and she returned the favor. They toweled off, and she led him back into the bedroom.

He tugged her into the bed, wrapped himself around her, and pulled the blanket over them both. He didn't speak, and she didn't dare shatter the moment by saying anything. If she could only have him for right now, she was going to enjoy the moment for all it was worth. Tomorrow, when he had to leave, she'd deal with that. Right now, he was still here.

Tate extracted himself from Lys's sleeping form. She frowned in her sleep and rolled over. An ache spread inside him, knowing that he had to walk away. Which was exactly the reason he needed to leave. He shouldn't have mixed business with pleasure. He gave her one last look, resisted the urge to lean in and kiss her on the forehead, and padded into the other room for the change of clothes she'd brought him.

His brows rose, and curiosity tickled his senses when he saw what she'd grabbed. On weekends—those he wasn't working anyway—he was a board shorts and T-shirt kind of guy. She'd grabbed him a pair of jeans, and a black and white button-down shirt with a dragon wrapped around the back and shoulders. He'd completely forgotten he had it. Vivian had given it to him as a gag gift.

And it planted a tiny, rebellious idea in his head for tomorrow, at his parents' Memorial Day barbeque. He finished dressing, left Lys a note thanking her for everything—but not saying anything else—and locked the door behind him on his way out.

It was best this way. For her, probably for him, and for the lucky, future Mister Alyssia Tippins.

Alyssia shuffled through her town house, operating on autopilot. Her brain was spinning to grasp a thought, a feeling, or something just out of her reach. Waking up alone in bed left her conflicted. It wasn't a new thing, or an unexpected one, but it still drilled an empty pit into her thoughts.

She poured herself a glass of juice, struggling to make sense of what was going on in her head. This was who Tate was. For as long as she could remember, even being a girl and playing house. At the time his actions had just been those of a stupid boy who thought he was smarter than her because he was older. He'd always boasted that he was never having a wife, or a family, and that house was a dumb game for kids who thought cartoons were real life.

Even though his delivery had changed, his views hadn't much. In fact, she'd never seen Tate *date* anyone. He occasionally made a tabloid page, if he hooked up with the right celebrity, but he didn't do repeats. He was adamant about that.

Someone knocked on her front door and hope surged inside. She beat it back. It wasn't going to be Tate. What was wrong with her? She was sucking big time at this staying detached thing. She forced herself to walk at a normal pace to see who it was. Despite her mental insistence, disappointment flooded her when she saw a stranger on the other side of the peephole. She opened the door.

The guy looked up from his clipboard. "I'm looking for Lisa Tippins."

"Alyssia." She corrected him without thought. Years ago, the mistake bothered her. She was used to it now."

He handed her a stack of stapled, folded papers. "You're named as the defendant in the case of Bryce Thompson versus Alyssia Tippins and the Great 'n' Small Animal Shelter. Have a nice day."

"Thank you..." She trailed off when he turned away before she finished. His words sank in, and bile rose in her throat. Thompson was suing her now? Crap. She unfolded the complaint and scanned it. So much legalese. His lawyers probably made more writing this letter than she did in a week. Her insides knotted themselves until she couldn't breathe. She plopped into the middle of the floor, and folded her legs underneath herself. Calm down. She needed to calm down.

When the spots stopped dancing in front of her eyes, she read the letter again. It was so wordy, but as far as she could tell, he was suing her for keeping the dog after he'd brought it in for standard care, and for the slander and harassment that accompanied her calling the cops on his son.

Fuck, this was so bad. She needed help. The lawyer she kept on retainer would charge extra for a Sunday call. What was she going to do? She forced herself to her feet, and found her phone in the bedroom, on the nightstand. Her fingers were pulling up a phone number before she registered whose it was. She paused, thumb hovering over the *Dial* button, then cleared Tate's number from the screen. What was he going to do? It didn't make sense to call Jared, either. He'd be concerned, but it wasn't like he could do any more than tell her to call her attorney.

Her fingers twitched against her phone, tapping the plastic frame. What was she supposed to do? She couldn't just sit around. Waiting would devour her. She'd go to the office, catch up on some paperwork. Her mind whirred over the situation as she drove. Painting possible outcomes, making each scenario worse. Could she lose the shelter over this? What if the crowd-funding didn't pan out? What would happen to all the animals? She needed to update her list of where she could send them. What if the other local shelters didn't have room?

By the time she turned down the street for the shelter, her thoughts ran rampant, throbbing against her skull. Beating out a merciless rhythm. Her world darkened several more shades when the shelter came into view. Five people stood on the sidewalk outside the fence, holding signs.

Puppy-napper

Animal abusers like you should rot in hell

She forced herself to look away, and ignored their shouts and waved fists as she pulled into the parking lot. Fortunately, no one was near the back employee entrance.

Fuck. What was she going to do now? She settled into her desk, mind working at high speed for a solution. She needed to reply publicly. Regardless of what Tate said, these people had seen the shelter on TV, and that's where she needed to make sure people saw her rebuttal. She dialed Sara's extension. If her assistant wasn't in, she'd leave her a message.

Alyssia was surprised when she answered on the first ring. "Hey." Sara's cheery tone was strained. "I didn't think you were in today."

"Same for you." The small crowd outside must be impacting everyone. Of course, that made sense. Her employees were as dedicated to the shelter as she was. "I was just going to leave you a message, but since you're here... on Tuesday, will you call up the TV station, the same one that ran the piece on us last week, and tell them I'd like to talk to them. Clear things up?" There, that wasn't so hard.

"Actually, funny you should mention that." Sara's laugh sounded forced. "I just got off the phone with them about half an hour ago. They want the same thing, sooner rather than later, so they can air it on Wednesday night."

"That's great. Isn't it?" She didn't know if she was asking Sara, or herself.

"It seems like it, right?"

"Absolutely." Alyssia forced herself to smile, and hoped it would reflect over the line. "Tell them I'll make time, whenever they'd like between now and then." She exchanged a few more words about work and life with Sara, and then disconnected. That had gone easier than she thought. So why was her gut souring at the thought of doing the interview?

CHAPTER TWELVE

Every fucking year. Tate grabbed his ticket from the valet and made his way into the country clubhouse. He still didn't know why his parents threw this party every fucking year. He'd stopped attending in college. They invited so many people—neighbors, friends, upper and middle management from Skriddie—at the time he'd wondered what he was supposed to get out of the whole event. He'd figured it out since. It was about the networking, the meeting people, and if he managed to find the right people, enjoying Memorial Day.

He cut straight for the bar, made eye contact with the guy pouring drinks, and smiled. "Hey, man. How's it going? I'm Tate." He extended his hand.

"Gary." The bartender returned the handshake. "What can I get you?"

Tate's smile grew, and he leaned against the bar. One of the things he'd figured out was finding the right people meant being in the right place. "Whatever you're making today, I'll pay you that much more to let me slide back there and serve drinks."

Gary shook his head, easy expression never fading. "No can do. Sorry, man. I was told whatever you offered, they'd double it if I didn't let you back here."

Tate hid his irritation. Avenue number one for enjoying his afternoon, blocked by the woman in charge. One thing he enjoyed about any gathering was taking a spot behind the bar, and getting to know people that way. "They?"

Gary grabbed a glass, and polished an invisible spot. "My employers for the day."

"Right." Yup. His mother wanted him mingling, not doing *common work*. Might as well make sure the bartender made some cash for the day and strap Marge's wallet at the same time. Tate counted five one-hundred dollar bills from his billfold, and laid them on the bar top. "Keep this, and stay behind the bar. Tell Marge Foster that's how much I offered you to let me back there. Don't tell her you took my money."

"I... you're kidding, right?"

Tate nudged the bills closer to Gary. "Not at all. Enjoy the party, man." Time to search out avenue number two. Something in his chest twinged, and he breathed deep to force it away. This was nothing. There was no reason to feel bad about plan B for keeping himself occupied during this party. He scanned the room, and then outside, on the sweeping lawn. There. The redhead keeping an eye on the buffet table. Several inches shorter than he was, at least from this distance, with full curves that filled out her white polo shirt and black slacks gorgeously.

Perfect distraction for the next few hours, and great way to remind himself the weekend spent with Lys was strictly a casual thing. Her name filled his head with memories of her moans, the scent of lilac, her smooth skin pressed against his, the way she squirmed when he touched her in the right places.

He dragged in another shaky breath. That wasn't a great path to wander down. Except his racing pulse said it was a fantastic place to let his thoughts linger. He stepped out of the flow of people, and leaned against a nearby wall. He should have had Gary pour him a drink while he was at the bar.

A movement caught his attention. His mother, standing all but nose-to-nose with Bryce Thompson, laughing, and running her tongue along her upper lip. His stomach churned at the sight. They could at least try to keep that private. He forced his gaze away.

He spotted a few familiar faces in the crowd, and wove through the small clusters of chatters. Lys and Jared's parents. "Holly. Robert." He held his arms out.

"You look beautiful, as always." He gave Holly a quick hug, and peck on the cheek. She did, too. An older version of Alyssia, gray around the temples, but still with a smile for everyone. "Sir." He clasped Robert's hand and pulled him into a quick hug as well.

"You look tired." Holly's voice was lined with concern. "You're working too hard."

The genuine tone warmed Tate. "I do what the job requires." The Tippins were more like his parents than his own folks. Growing up, they'd always welcomed him at home, and treated him as well as they had their own children. Sometimes he envied Robert and Holly's relationship, but they had one of those happily ever afters that only existed in fairy tales. The lucky one in a million. And a great reminder of what Lys deserved that he couldn't offer. "How are you both doing?"

"Wishing retirement weren't so far off." Robert chuckled.

They chatted for several more minutes, before someone else called them away. As they headed off, Holly hung back. She tugged Tate aside, voice low enough he barely made out her words above the din. "Don't let them drive you into the ground. I mean it. Take care of yourself."

"Thanks." He squeezed her hand. "I'll do my best."

Time to make the rounds, meet some people, have some fun.

"What are you wearing?" A familiar voice clawed its way under his good mood.

He froze a pleasant expression in place, and spun. "Mother. I was wondering if you'd pull yourself away from Mr. Thompson long enough to say hello."

She pointed a glare at his shirt. "Did you forget to have someone pick up your laundry? Oh, for heaven's sake. What's she doing here?"

He followed his mother's gaze back to the clubhouse, and his mind checked out. Lys stood in the doorway, blue sundress stark against her pale skin, and hugging every inch of her figure. It ended a few inches above her knees, leaving her long legs on display. He struggled to pull his attention away. It was a good question, though. Her parents still came to these parties because they were friends of the family. Jared showed up because it was a work thing. But Lys... She could have opted out ages ago. Yet he couldn't remember a single year he hadn't seen her there. "I have people to talk with." He stepped in her direction.

"Yes, you do." His mother grabbed his sleeve, and redirected him. "I want you to meet someone."

A snarl bubbled in his throat, but he followed where she was pointing. And then looked again. "Who's that?"

"The young woman over there." She nodded at a girl standing just a few feet away.

Tate raised his brows. "Is she even legal?"

"She'll be twenty this fall." Marge pulled him toward the girl. "She's the Senator's daughter, and she's dying to meet you."

"She's still a kid."

"When you wait as long as you have to get married, you can't be picky." She pasted on a plastic smile as they drew within earshot. "Bonnie. This is Tate."

Irritation bubbled inside. Bonnie didn't deserve his wrath, but so help him he wanted to ask his mother why she kept doing shit like this. God, it was going to be a long day.

Lys wandered through the clubhouse, making sure she made eye contact, smiling at anyone who noticed her, and trying to keep her expression friendly. Why did she keeping coming to this thing? She should be at the shelter, catching up on work.

It had been too good a chance to pass up, though. She'd always gotten along with the guests in the past, and had several of them tell her if she ever needed any help...

This was her opportunity to mingle, shake hands, and maybe let it slip that her shelter was raising donations to buy the building they were in. Except every time she told herself that was her goal, her gut churned in nervous protest. Networking wasn't her thing. Tate was good at it.

His name added a new edge to her apprehension. She hadn't heard from him since the note he left Sunday morning. Not that she should expect to. It wasn't like he called her every day, normally. This was just how things were.

She tugged down the skirt of her dress, and scanned the crowds. So why couldn't she stop searching for his face?

Her gaze landed on someone else instead, and acid rose in her throat. Bryce Thompson Jr., taking pictures of something with his phone. She wasn't sure what. One of the girls serving drinks, possibly. Or the food. Or... she didn't even want to know. She turned her attention back anything else. Keeping her distance from him would be important today.

She found Tate, and her heart sank. He stood next to his mother, chatting up a girl who was smiling as if she'd just won the lottery. She'd giggle, and then rest her hand on Tate's arm. Twirl her hair around her finger. Lean in closer.

If she got close enough, would she see the lines around Tate's eyes that always appeared when he was wearing a mask? Or would she see the genuine expression he wore when he was picking someone up? The same look he'd had with her the night before.

Why had she thought that? Damn it. She turned back into the clubhouse, and headed for the bar. Maybe a drink would help her relax. Or she could go hunt down Jared and Mikki. Mikki's tactics for meeting people tended to be more blunt that Tate's, but she still had a gift for it.

Alyssia ordered a glass of white wine, and wandered back into the gardens. So many people wearing so many masks. This was why she liked animals. They were sweet, and accepting, and non-judgmental, and totally not intimidating.

The longer she studied the crowds, the further she drifted from them, until she lingered in a corner. The din drifted toward her, but no longer so loud it kept her from being able to think. Why had she even come to this party?

"Hey." A rough voice assaulted her ears, and she looked up to see Bryce Jr. approaching. "You're that bitch who stole my dog."

Her lungs squeezed and she forced herself to draw a breath. She stepped to the side, to move around him. "I need to see someone. They're waiting right over there." She nodded at the general area behind him.

"Not until we're done." He blocked her path. Every time he breathed on her, the stench of alcohol assaulted her senses. Who the hell had given him a drink? Though he was only seventeen, he was at least six inches taller than her, and twice as wide in the shoulders. He poked a finger in her chest, and her breast-bone winced both in pain and panic. "You're going down. You know that, right?"

"Bryce, buddy." Tate's voice cut through her spiraling panic. Bryce whirled. In a single motion, Tate grabbed his hand in what looked like a friendly grip—except Alyssia saw Tate's knuckles pale—and pushed the younger man out of her path. "I've been looking for you."

"Let go of me, queer-boy." Bryce jerked out of his grip with a growl.

Tate's smile never wavered, but Alyssia had never seen him show so many teeth. "Tell you what." The pleasantness vanished from his voice. "Why don't you walk away now, and go check out the banquet table."

Bryce stepped closer to Tate. "Why don't you leave and let me talk to the bitch?"

Tate growled, and faster than Alyssia could blink, his forearm was pressed to Bryce's throat, and he had the boy pinned to the wall. "Leave. Or I stop asking nicely."

Bryce choked out a response that might have been, "Fuck you." Tate pushed harder.

"Is everything all right?" Marge Foster joined the group.

Alyssia's head spun, and her pulse hammered in her throat. Why was her quiet corner suddenly the highest traffic area in the clubhouse?

"Everything's fine." Tate stepped back, and his expression went flat. No smile, no frown, just a blank mask. He straightened his clothes with a single shrug, and wrapped his arm around Alyssia's waist. The shock of his touch overloaded her already crowded thoughts, and she struggled with the desire to lean into him. She wasn't a helpless damsel in distress. Except right now she felt like one, and she wasn't sure she minded the possession Tate's grip conveyed.

"I was just walking Ms. Tippins to her car." Tate steered her around his mother and Bryce without hesitation. "Keep walking. Don't look at anyone." His voice was low, meant only for her ears.

He didn't say another word on the short journey to the valet, and she wasn't sure if she could manage any of her own. His flat mask never wavered. He waited by her side while the hop fetched her car, and walked her to the driver's door.

"Thank you." She managed the soft words as she slid into the vehicle.

He clenched his jaw. "Don't worry about it." Why wouldn't he look at her?

"Are you all right?"

"I'm good. You should probably get home."

She didn't like this. Cold, removed. Tate had never been like that with her. Awkward was one thing, but this cut deep, leaving gashes in her thoughts. She couldn't help trying one more time. "Are you sticking around? We could go somewhere. Hang out."

A tremor ran through the car, and she realized he was clutching the door so hard his fingers shook. He finally looked at her, and the dark cloud in his gaze dug deeper than his indifference. "Go home, Alyssia. Or, somewhere else. Just..." He inhaled through his nose. "Go."

Her full name. She forced herself to smile, despite the tears stinging her eyes. At least he was cutting her off fast and completely. No false hope or anything there. "Right. See you around. Or not."

She yanked her door shut before she could discover if he had a response. And tossed the car into gear. It was better this way. He probably knew that. She just had to convince her own heart of it.

CHAPTER THIRTEEN

TATE GRIPPED the steering wheel so hard his wrists ached. He focused on the road, and struggled to clear all the thoughts from his head. He shouldn't have gone to his parent's barbeque—the entire thing was a disaster. That girl his mother tried to hook him up with. Bryce Jr.

Alyssia. Every time her name danced through his thoughts, his pulse kicked back up, and his frustration poured in. He'd wanted to brain Bryce for cornering her. That was bad enough. But when Tate had wrapped his arm around her waist, to lead her away. The light sag against him. The hint of her weight pressing into his body.

It had taken what little control he had left not to drag her into a bathroom, lift her onto a sink, and push her skirt up to see if she was wearing anything underneath.

Except that wasn't right. He didn't want to do that there. In that horrid place filled with bad memories. He'd wanted to take her back to his place, because what they did together wasn't anyone's business but his and hers.

And when she'd turned that hurt gaze on him, next to her car. He'd almost caved. Been seconds from tossing restraint aside. The only thing that kept him from acting on the impulse was knowing he'd hold her back. The longer they pretended to be anything more than casual acquaintances, the less likely that she'd find the guy she actually deserved.

"FUCK!" He pounded the steering wheel until it creaked. He forced himself to breathe. Inhale and exhale one, two, three times.

His phone rang, and he ignored it. He couldn't get home soon enough. Even if, for reasons he couldn't explain, he was dreading going back to his own house for the first time ever. Home was sanctuary. He was in control there. But now, it was a looming, empty box.

Damn it.

Tate was pretty sure he'd never been more relieved to see a weekend come to a close. Tuesday morning was his new savior. Work was safe. He'd dive into his never ending task list and lose himself in everything he needed to do. Check on all the other crowd-funding sites, make sure they were all online, touch base with his sales team.

Today would be better than yesterday. It didn't have much of a choice.

His phone rang, and he clicked the speaker button without looking. "Yeah."

"Mr. Foster is here to see you." Alan's voice had a more formal tone than Tate was used to. Then again, it would make sense, if the company CEO was standing next to his desk.

Fortunately, Tate wasn't quite so worried about what the man thought of him. His dad didn't expect the same formality at work as his mother did. "Send him in." He looked up at the snick of his office door opening, and nodded at the chair across from his desk. "Dad."

His father closed the door, and Tate's suspicion spiked. Ben Foster took a seat, rested one ankle on the other knee, and intertwined his fingers. Tate could almost hear the seconds ticking away as he waited. The silence dragged on.

Tate suppressed a sigh. "What can I do for you?"

Ben clenched his jaw, and his gaze narrowed. "The waitresses? That's fine. I don't know if you're just trying to piss off your mother, or you genuinely like those girls, but I don't care as long as you're all having fun."

That was new. Tate waited for him to continue, despite the dread building inside. "And?"

"But you can't mix business with pleasure. Ever."

Tate choked back a retort about hypocrisy. "Great advice. Thanks." He almost managed to keep the sarcasm from his voice.

Ben drummed his fingers on his leg. "Get it out of your system now. Whatever issues you've got with my advice. Work through this, and reconsider what a stupid idea it was for you to sleep with a client."

Tate raised an eyebrow. There was no way his dad knew about that. He was shooting in the dark. He opened his mouth to ask what the man was talking about.

"Everyone." Ben cut him off before he made a sound. "Your mother, the club staff, the maids at the house—know the Tippins girl has got it bad for you. That's fine. Kids outgrow crushes, she will too someday. But that display of yours yesterday? My money says you're taking advantage of the situation. Don't. I don't care if you are already, or are just thinking about it. Stop now, and put the idea out of your head. At least while she's one of our clients. After her contract is up, I don't care what you do to her."

Tate choked on an angry retort. Taking advantage of...? Realization spread through him. Was he? He knew how Lys felt. Was he really using her? The idea sat heavy in his gut, and gnawed at his thoughts. "Nothing's happening. I know better than that. Not that it's anyone's business."

"It is, though." Ben stood. "It's my business, because it's my company."

"Really?" Tate's irritation slipped out before he considered where he was going with it. But once the word was out there, he knew exactly what he wanted to say. "You're going to come in here—you of all people—and tell me not to mix my business and personal lives? Insult Alyssia Tippins for some imagined slight, when you're guilty of the ultimate blend of company and home?"

"Excuse me?"

He didn't have these arguments with his father, because normally, the older man didn't push those buttons. But he certainly couldn't talk about it with his mother. She'd gloss over it, tell him she was right and he was wrong, and brush him off. "You're going to tell me business and pleasure don't mix when that's the entire foundation of your marriage? A contract that makes sure you both get what you want in the boardroom, and doesn't care what you do in the bedroom, as long as the world sees you as a happy couple?"

Ben knitted his brows together, and let out a long breath of air. "Do as I say, not as I do. I'd hoped you would turn out better than we did."

"I didn't mean to." The answer snapped something inside Tate. A frustration crumbling over a week-long, emotionally exhausting journey. One of Tate's driving goals had always been to keep his personal life separate. Why had he let this happen?

A frown settled onto Ben's face. "Then you already know what I'm about to say. This entire affair. The issues with the Thompson's dog, the struggling animal shelter. It's gotten too personal for you. I know you and Marge are both stubborn, and that neither of you wants to back down from this."

He met Tate's gaze, eyes soft and sad. "But you're smarter than that. You know what decisions you need to make for the business. If I didn't trust you with that, you wouldn't be in the position you're in, and you wouldn't have gotten the sign off on this project."

Tate didn't know what was worse—the accusations based on a truth he didn't want to recognize, or the underlying hint of 'don't disappoint me' in his father's voice. He didn't bother with a smile, he just turned back to his computer. "Don't worry. I know what I'm doing."

"Make sure that's true." Ben walked out and pulled the door shut behind him.

Tate tried to throw himself back into work. To immerse himself in the onslaught. But his father's words echoed in his head, jumbled and cluttered and trying to grasp at thoughts just out of his reach. About Lys, about the choices he was making.

The one thing he refused to acknowledge though, was the unspoken implication he needed to cut the shelter from the crowd-funding pilot group. That was the last thing he would do.

CHAPTER FOURTEEN

ALYSSIA PADDED from one end of her office to the other, then spun and retraced her steps. Her bare feet slapped against the cool tile. She'd stashed her heels under her desk until she really needed to wear them. They weren't conducive to pacing. She paused in front of the full-length mirror on the back of her office door. The skirt and jacket outfit were conservative, and professional looking. The perfect thing to wear in front of a camera, and tell the local news that her shelter was a good thing, instead of the spawn of some greater demon of the billionth plane of hell.

She straightened her shirt, and pushed a strand of hair back into her braid. Crap, maybe she should have worn her scrubs instead. Something that made it clear she was a doctor, and not just a girl playing a part. She squeezed her fingers together and then relaxed them. Right now she felt like a girl playing a part. This had to go well. The group of picketers outside was growing larger, instead of shrinking, and her time was running out to raise the money to keep the building.

Her phone rang, and Sara's voice followed. "Your visitors are here."

"I'll be right there." Too late to change now. Alyssia took a deep breath, and opened the door.

The interviewer gave her a warm smile, and introduced her to the small crew. Alyssia's tension ebbed as the afternoon progressed. They chatted, it was friendly, no invasive questions asked—not really. The closest it came was asking for her side of the story when it came to the Thompson's dog. She told them what she was allowed based on the pending criminal case. That the dog had come in injured, and they'd treated him, and were holding him until he found a fitting home.

She walked through the kennels with the cameraman, let a few dogs out to play.

Almost two hours later, when she saw the news crew to the front door,

Alyssia felt better about the situation than she had since that horrible news story almost a week ago. Time to change in to her scrubs and get some work done.

She strolled toward the back rooms, and a jarring crash spilled through the room. Her heart jumped into her throat, and she spun before her brain registered it was the sound of shattering glass. A large rock—twice as big as her fist at least—sat in the middle of the lobby. Fortunately the window was tempered, so most of it had rained straight down, but small shards had escaped, and littered the room.

Chants and cheers flowed in from the picketers outside. Alyssia forced her racing heart to slow. "Sara, call the police." There wasn't anyone in the waiting room besides staff—a fact she'd hated a few hours ago but was grateful for now. "Ricco, will you grab the broom? I need to change. Give me just a few and I'll help you clean up."

While she was changing, she grabbed her phone. Her thumb hesitated over Tate's number. What was he going to do? She pushed the bitter longing aside, and dialed Robert Tippins instead. "Hey, Dad. I know it's after eight, I'm sorry. But I need to board up a window at the shelter, and we don't have tools here, can you help?"

"A window? What's going on? Are you all right?"

She winced and held the phone from her ear. "I'm fine, Daddy. You still have some plywood from the remodel, right?"

"Of course, hon. I'll be right there."

She disconnected, and tossed the device back on her desk. A sob bubbled inside her, and she forced it aside. She wouldn't panic. She could handle this. Helping Ricco sweep up glass, talking to the police, making sure the window was secure once her dad got there, all of it kept her mind occupied.

When they left, her mind turned on her. Running rampant and taunting her with every fear and worry she'd swallowed that afternoon and evening. She gave Sara a weak smile, shuffled into her office, and collapsed into her chair. What was she going to do? The news interview better work out for her tomorrow. Something needed to go right.

Her fingers twitched toward her cell phone. *Call Tate*, chanted in her head. That wasn't an option. Not until she knew she could handle herself around him without caving again. She needed to get to work, instead. Bury herself in the job, and her mind would do what it needed to, just like cleaning up the mess in the lobby.

She pulled up the crowd-funding admin page. Donations spilled in slowly. A couple a day, but nowhere near what they'd need to meet their goal before their deadline. The largest donation—the anonymous one that had come in first—still sat at the top of the page. Taunting her. Something clicked in her thoughts as she studied the number. Something Jared had said the other day? Mikki had discovered...

She couldn't grasp the idea. It would come to her. Right now, she needed to concentrate on work, and not losing the shelter. The rest could wait.

Tate had a love hate relationship with short work weeks. On the one hand, taking Monday off meant all the good, obvious things like extra time away from work. On the other hand, it also meant five days of work compressed into four, and always feeling like he was a day behind. He scanned the messages waiting for him when he got into the office Wednesday morning. His eyes grew wide when he saw the newsletter from NetSafe Systems. He subscribed to all manner of industry mailing lists as part of his job, so getting the email wasn't the surprise. It was the content. *NetSafe Systems announces their newest offering—crowdfunding for your small business!*

Tate's irritation grew as he read the rest of the promo. Most of it was standard hype. It was the mentions of heightened security, twenty-four-seven community managers, and a fool-proof comment system. On top of all that, this was the first he'd heard of it.

He clenched his fist, glaring at the screen. He'd expected them to compete, it was what they did. The phrasing in the message gnawed at him, though. Heightened security. The phrase repeated in his thoughts.

Fuck. Time to take a stroll. Seconds later he stood a few doors down, in front of Vivian's office. She looked up at the knock, and gave him a half smile. "What's up?"

He took the chair across from her desk, pulled up the message on his phone, and slid it across to her. "What do you think?"

As she scanned, her lips drew into a thin line. She handed the device back to him. "So they already know what happened to you on Saturday."

"I assume. So much for non-disclosure agreements, right?" His question was flat.

"They could have seen the issues. All your sites were dragging."

Tate spit out his theory. "Could have seen, may have caused..."

She pinched the bridge of her nose. "Childish, unethical assholes," she muttered, and dialed a number on her desk phone.

"Yup?" Mikki answered.

Tate leaned in to speak. "The slowdown on Saturday. Can you take another look and see if there's anything suspicious about it."

"There was." Mikki's answer came too quickly. "Someone tried to take a bunch of websites offline that weren't doing anything but sitting out there all happy and boring like."

Tate might have laughed at the dry retort, if his suspicion and concern weren't mounting. "We're looking for more than that. A fingerprint."

"Give me ten." Mikki disconnected.

Tate leaned back in the chair, closed his eyes, and rubbed his forehead. He didn't do spite, but he still hoped if NSS was behind this, they'd left an ugly trail. Something else to crucify them with, in the upcoming civil case.

"Did you end things yet?" V asked.

Of course. She was back on the conversation from lunch last week with Lys. The last person he needed to be thinking about, and the one name constantly lingering at the back of his mind. Acknowledging her name sent a flood of memories through his thoughts, teasing him. He straightened, and met her gaze. "Pretty sure it's none of your business. But yes."

"No need to get defensive. I just missed seeing you both at the party on Monday." She said it so simply, as if it were the most innocent question ever.

"I couldn't tell you where she was." He couldn't say her name. Her voice in his head was already wreaking havoc on his senses. And it was true, he didn't know where she'd gone after she left the country club, though he still wished he could have gone with her.

Instead of replying, V looked over his shoulder, eyes focusing on something behind him.

Seconds later, Mikki claimed the chair next to him. "It's not what you think, but it is a good thing you had me look. Someone is screwing with your config, and they did it again today. Your bandwidth has been severely limited."

That didn't make sense. Tate mulled over the comment. "Someone is intentionally going in there and slowing my sites down. Over and over?"

Mikki nodded. "They've tweaked the work we did over the weekend, not as thoroughly as before, but someone's restricted access for your clients."

"Fantastic." Sarcasm dripped from Tate's voice. "Like, who?"

Mikki quirked her mouth to the side, and shrugged. "One of Jared's people. Whoever's got access to your servers, which is all of them. I'd ask if you pissed off upper management, but since you are..."

Could Marge be choking his sites, to force the crowdfunding site to fail? The thought surged into Tate's head, sounding absolutely ludicrous. This was still business, and even if she didn't like the idea, it was still surging toward successful, despite the problems.

"Do you want more?" Mikki asked.

V looked at Tate, apology in her eyes. "I'm sorry. After hours, maybe, but she's got her own work to do."

"I get it; it's fine. Thanks for looking." Tate sank lower in his seat. He needed to get to the bottom of this.

The moment Mikki was gone, V turned back to Tate. "Look, I know Alyssia is everyone's favorite baby sister. But this is business, and you need to consider shutting her down."

Tate was getting sick of hearing that. "It's not just business." The retort came out sharper than he intended. He needed to dial it back.

"It should be."

Tate rolled his eyes. "That's not what I mean. She's running an animal shelter, and they do good things. This isn't just about a bottom line. What about all those animals?"

"I'm not heartless." Vivian's expression softened. "I'll write them a check. I'm surprised you haven't done the same."

"She won't take my money. I'd fund the entire operation if I could."

Vivian raised her brows. "Strictly for the puppies?"

"Of course."

"If she won't take a perfectly legitimate donation, maybe Alyssia's the problem. I hate to say that, and I know you don't want to hear it. But if you do this emotionally, people are going to get fucked."

Tate dug his fingers into his leg, and squeezed in frustration. V was wrong. He knew it. He just couldn't figure out what was right.

CHAPTER FIFTEEN

When Tate stepped through the front door to the shelter, a painful sense of déjà vu washed over him. He shook his head to clear out the thought. The boarded up window already had his anxiety cranked to max. He'd been out since after lunch, dropping off paperwork with all their crowd-funding site pilot groups, and the shelter was last on his list. Because Lys's shift didn't start until later, of course. No other reason.

Sara's smile looked forced when she glanced up from her computer. "You might not want to go back there."

He nodded at the window. "Something I should know first?"

"That was a rock last night. Our friendly neighborhood picketers." Her usually chipper tone was flat. "But that's not the problem."

"Okay?"

"She did a rebuttal piece with the news station last night. It aired about ten minutes ago."

An invisible hand clenched around Tate's chest. "Do I want details?"

Sara just shook her head. "I heard some kind of primal-scream-type yelling. She's not answering her phone, and when I tried to check on her, she told me to go away. You should probably check on her."

Tate was already moving toward Alyssia's office, adrenaline pumping through him at a painful clip. She didn't look up when he stepped inside and closed the door behind him. Her attention was on her feet, as she traveled from one end of the office to the other, and then back.

Every impulse he'd struggled to suppress since Monday. The desire to protect her, to keep her safe, to wrap her up and never let go, flooded through him. "Lys."

She jumped and whirled to face him. Her eyes narrowed. "What?"

Not the reception he'd expected, but it was fair, all things considered. "Are you all right?"

Her laugh was bitter and sharp. "Your powers of perception are slipping if you don't already know the answer to that." She shook her head and resumed pacing. "But since it's not obvious, no. I'm not fucking all right."

Anger. He could deal with that. It meant she'd talk, and he could find a solution. "Fill me in."

"Is there something about me that screams stupid? Or gullible?"

"Absolutely not."

She finally looked him the eye. "In that case, tell me something, and be honest."

"Of course." He was losing control of the conversation, and he didn't like that. But he couldn't think of any alternative but to go along with things until he uncovered more of the situation.

"Did Sara tell you what was going on?"

The question was too easy. That couldn't be where things were going. "She gave me a brief run-down. I figured I'd get details from you."

"How many times since you walked in the front door have you told yourself you'd fix this?" Her lips twisted in irritated amusement. "How many different ways are you thinking *you'll* make this better?"

Tate didn't know what bothered him more—that she'd crawled into his head and plucked the thoughts out so succinctly, or her irritation when she asked about it. "*We'll* make it better."

She shook her head, kicked out her office chair, and dropped into it. "I did what you told me not to. I talked to the news station. That crowd outside gets larger every day, and our numbers have slumped off noticeably in the last few days. I had to do something."

Tate had to clench his jaw to keep from interrupting.

"And they slaughtered me. Took everything I said out of context. Almost all of their footage was of the people on the sidewalk. What little they showed of me was clipped to make it look like I only do this to make people suffer. I take their pets in, never give them back, and call the police on the people I don't like. They spun it that way."

It was Thompson's TV station. What had she expected? "Call your lawyer. It's slander."

She slammed her hands on the desk hard enough to shake the floor. "I know it's fucking slander. The damage is done. And so help me, if you're thinking you need to rein me in, and make me calm down, I'll have Ricco throw you out."

Once again, he was bothered she'd read him so easily. "You're not solving anything this way." He struggled to keep his tone cool and calm.

"You think?" She breathed deep. Her chin quivered, and she clenched her hands into fists several times. She scrubbed the back of her hand across her cheeks and eyes. "None of this is solving anything." The fire in her voice wilted, faded, and ended in a crack. "Your ideas aren't exactly batting one-thousand either. If the site keeps taking donations at this rate, it'll be twenty-fifty before I've raised enough for the shelter expansion."

The conversation with Vivian tickled his memory. "So let me write you a check. I can get that out of the way now, and then we can focus on the legal problems, and setting things right."

"Let you. You can get. Do you hear yourself? I don't want you to make this all vanish. Nothing gets better if you sweep your magic money wand over the entire situation."

"Where's this coming from?" He'd been cold at the party on Monday, and he owed her an apology for that, but this didn't seem even remotely related.

"You can't bail me out for the rest of my life, Tate. What happens when we grow apart?"

The question burrowed under his skin and drilled a hole into his thoughts. A wave of cold passed over him. "Why would we grow apart?" It was a stupid question. Of course they would. He'd just never thought about it before. Not seriously.

She tugged on her hair. "You keep talking about this mysterious Mister Right that I'm going to end up with. Do you think things are going to stay the same between us when he comes along? That we'll all be best buds, and our relationship won't change?"

She was just spitting his own words back at him. Reiterating the future he'd always seen for her. The one that didn't include him. But hearing her acknowledge it sank into his feet like concrete. He'd never hated an idea more.

"I'm not like you." She continued. "I don't like the idea of growing old alone. My life plan has never included not getting attached. I want kids, and a happy marriage, and a house with a big enough yard for dogs and cats. Maybe that does mean I'm stupid or gullible, but that doesn't stop me from hoping."

He couldn't think about her entire statement. Taking it in its entirety jumbled his thoughts. He zeroed in on the bits he could grasp. "I won't be alone. I'll have my friends."

"That's all fine and good. But it's not the same." She stared at him, gaze driving into his soul, as if she searched for something he was certain didn't exist. "Friends are great. But I want more."

How had this gone from being a conversation about the shelter, to the rest of their lives? He wanted to switch the conversation back to something more neutral. Bring it back to a place he understood and that didn't make him ill. Something told him that wasn't an option. Even though he'd always known her future was somewhere else, even though he'd been repeating it in his head and out loud for the last week, hearing her say it felt like betrayal. It wasn't fair to tell her that, though. Because she was right, and any other answer was selfish. "You're right. You deserve that. You deserve more."

She clenched her jaw, and her entire frame shook. Her eyes grew watery, and she sniffled. "You need to leave."

He couldn't. If he walked out now, this would never be better. But his own thoughts didn't make sense to him. He was contradicting himself, and he didn't have a response.

"Please. Leave. Have a different project manager contact me."

She was right, so why did he want to argue? He should be grateful she finally got it. This was the best solution for her, and staying was just him being selfish.

ALYSSIA DROPPED HER FACE IN HER HANDS AFTER TATE WALKED OUT THE door. She wanted to be pissed at him for just going along with what she'd said—because it was best for her. She wanted to be furious at him for making her think about it in the first place. Most of all, she wanted to get rid of the feeling it would have been smarter of her to hack off her own arm with a butter knife than to pick that fight.

But blame had bounced back and forth in her head all night. Since the news story aired. It was her fault for not listening to Tate. It was his fault for always trying to do what was best for her. It was Jared's fault for treating her like a baby for so long.

Everyone was to blame, the world sucked, and she didn't even know if happily ever after really existed. She hated Tate most of all for putting that thought in her head.

If she was going to insist on doing this on her own, she'd better get started. At least it would give her a distraction. Tate's idea hadn't worked—a glance at her crowd-funding site told her she wasn't even five percent to her goal. Her idea hadn't worked—the news story that night was proof she couldn't compete with the Thompson's connections, and he'd put her entire shelter at risk because of it. Or she had. It was time she started taking credit for her own fuck ups.

It was time to explore other options. She should have done this months ago, but it was too easy to let Tate step in. Too easy to convince herself that even though she wouldn't take his money, she was being self-sufficient by letting him do the work. She'd find an investor group, or wherever money came from when banks didn't loan it. Where to start?

Search engines were her best friend, and it was time to dig her heels in and either fund her shelter, or make sure she had contacts in other places to send the pets she wouldn't be able to take in if she couldn't expand.

Armed with a plan, she banished thoughts of Tate to the back of her mind. Just thinking his name hurt in every inch of her body, but that would lessen with time.

She didn't have a choice. She'd get over him.

CHAPTER SIXTEEN

TATE WASN'T sure how long he'd been driving. Long enough to get him all but lost in the back roads of Northern Georgia, and then turned around and heading back toward the city again.

He couldn't get the argument with Lys out of his head. Every time he managed to present himself with a logical reason to move on, his brain dragged him back to the fact he wasn't listening to himself. He didn't want to see her with another guy. That's what it came down to at every mental intersection. Thinking of her spending the rest of forever with some random guy—even if he was the nicest dude on the planet, made Tate clench his hands until it ached all the way into his fingertips.

Tate had always told himself he wasn't equipped to handle a relationship. That sat at the other end of his dilemma. His parents' marriage was a painful thing to behold. Two people bound by law for business purposes, who had only ever slept in the same bed long enough to conceive him.

So why couldn't he picture his future without Alyssia? The idea of growing old alone, of drifting away from her, of watching her fall for someone else, crushed him from the inside out.

That was what it came down to. He wanted her in his life. Needed her. Couldn't do this future thing without her. And he had to tell her.

He turned the car back toward her shelter. At least it was late, so traffic was light. Half an hour later, he pulled into the parking lot. Most of the picketers had called it a night. That was something, at least. He strode through the front door, flashed Sara a smile, and headed straight for Lys's office. He knocked, and waited.

Several seconds passed. He glanced back at Sara.

"She's in there." Sara shrugged. "Not on the phone. At least not the office lines."

Tate frowned, and knocked again.

"Hang on." Alyssia's voice sounded tiny and raw. Several more seconds passed. "It's open."

Tate nudged into her office, ill-ease growing inside. His concern spiked when he saw her in her desk chair, knees pulled to her chest, and face pale and drawn. He closed the door behind him. In just a few steps, he was next to her. "What's wrong?"

She shook her head, and her chin quivered. She opened her mouth to speak, and a sob tore out instead. Her jaw worked up and down, but nothing intelligible came out.

What the fuck? He didn't know what was going on, but it was splitting him in two. He held out a hand, and she stumbled forward and collapsed in his arms. Ear-piercing cries echoed through him, gnawing at his calm, flooding him with concern, and a desire to make this vanish, even though he didn't have a target. He rubbed her back until the sobs slowed to body-wracking, and then tiny sniffles. Her muffled whispers drifted to his ears, and he strained to hear her.

"I didn't know," she muttered. "God, what's wrong with people? I didn't..." She choked on the words.

It didn't matter what he'd come there to tell her. This was more important. "Talk to me, Lys."

She shook her head, and pressed closer into his chest. "You can't fix this. Jesus, no one can fix this. What the fuck is wrong with people?" She finally met his gaze with red-rimmed, puffy eyes. "I just wanted... I was trying to figure out what to do if the crowd funding fell through. I stumbled on a site with an article about the shelter, going on about all of the lies Thompson's told. Spewing them like they were truth. And the comments. The things people said about me, about this place..." She swallowed, and nodded at her computer.

He kept her turned away, jarred the mouse, and pulled up her web browser. It took him a moment to register what he was looking at, and when he did his lunch threatened to repeat on him. Videos were embedded in several of the comments. Of animals being tortured. Holy fuck. He closed everything, and slammed the lid shut on her laptop. No wonder she was a wreck. He led her toward the couch, and lowered them both, never letting go. He couldn't find the words to ask anything new. Everything stuck in his throat on a surge of sickness.

She curled up against him. "I know people are saying bad things about the place, but I didn't realize how malicious it had gotten." She shuddered. "I didn't expect to find... God, what's wrong with people, Tate? I couldn't stop looking, and oh fuck."

He couldn't tell her it was going to be okay. Of all the lies he could come up with, that felt like the most insulting. All he could manage was, "I don't know what's wrong with people."

He trailed his fingers through her hair, desperately searching for his own calm and not willing to let her go. He'd stay with her all night if that was what it took. It still wouldn't give him a solution, but at least they'd both have something to hold onto.

ALYSSIA'S EYES FELT LIKE THEY'D BEEN BATHED IN SAND, AND HER THROAT wasn't doing much better. She couldn't think about what she'd seen. She'd known there were sick fucks out there, but having to see it firsthand... No, she wouldn't go down that path. Digging deep, she summoned the willpower to shove the mental images aside. She sat up enough to look at Tate. "I'm sorry."

He brushed a strand of hair from her face. "You don't have to apologize for anything."

She disagreed, but didn't have the strength to say so. "Why did you come back?"

He hesitated for the briefest second. "I had a hunch." He wasn't telling her everything. She didn't care. Right now, she was just relieved he was there. "Will you be okay for a minute or two?"

She didn't know if she'd ever be okay again, but it wasn't like she could curl up in a permanent ball because she'd seen proof of how ugly the world was. "Yes."

When he returned a few minutes later, he handed her a cup of water, and a damp washcloth. She let the cold liquid slide down her throat, trying to only focus on the physical sensations, then used the towel to sap some of the heat from her cheeks.

He set everything aside. She didn't like the pity on his face. Or maybe that was just concern, and she was overreacting. Panic surged inside again, and she squashed the visuals it threatened to bring with it.

He grasped her fingers, and tugged her to her feet. "Come with me."

She didn't have any strength to protest, or even ask where they were going. She couldn't meet Sara's curious gaze when Tate led her into the lobby. He reached over the front desk and grabbed something she couldn't see, then tugged her toward the kennels.

Most of the dogs were sleeping, but a few stirred when he let them into back room. One animal barked, and seconds later the rest joined the chaos. Her soul shrank from the sound. She wouldn't react. She loved that sound. It wasn't a bad sound. She squeezed Tate's hand tighter, and followed closely behind.

They stopped in front of Grim's pen. The dog had recovered wonderfully in the week since they'd taken him in. He still couldn't do a lot of moving, but he was happy and playful as much as was possible.

Tate unlocked the pen, knelt in front of Grim, and gestured for her to do the same. He lifted her chin until he was looking her in the eyes. Even amid the barking of a dozen or so dogs, his voice was distinct, and kind. "You can't protect the world, Lys." He licked his lips. "Not any more than I can lock you away from everything bad. But what you do matters so much." He held out his hand. Grim sniffed his fingers, then ducked his head. Tate scratched him behind the ears, and under the chin, affection rolling with the loll of the dog's head.

Images from the videos spilled back into Alyssia's head, and she gasped for breath. Grim whimpered and withdrew. Tate gave her all his attention. "Don't think about it. Look at me." His voice never rose. Never wavered. "This is here, and it's just us and the dogs, which you're keeping safe."

"But, the things I saw——"

Tate brushed his lips over hers. It wasn't hungry, or demanding, just soothing. "And the animals you've already saved. Like Grim," he said. "He's not going anywhere until his doctor says it's okay, and even then, only with someone you sign off on. Right?"

She nodded, and forced herself to draw a deep breath.

Tate scooted closer to Grim, and let the dog rest its head on his leg. Fur and bits of kibble dotted Tate's slacks. If he noticed, he didn't care. He never let go of her hands, even while he scratched the dog's ears and patted its sides.

As they sat there, the din around them died, and one by one the dogs drifted off to sleep again. Watching Tate with Grim, warmth leaked back into her fractured thoughts, sealing some of the cracks. She really was falling for him.

The words jarred her thoughts as they formed and solidified. It was a relief to finally let herself admit it. She'd focused on a crush for so long, she'd ignored the actual man behind her infatuation. The realization ached and soothed her at the same time.

"Come on." She stood, and pulled on Tate's hand. "Let the dogs sleep."

He locked Grim's door, followed her into the lobby, and set the keys on the front desk.

"Everything all right?" Sara looked between them, gaze lingering on the grime on Tate's suit.

Alyssia's jaw clenched, and a response died in her throat.

"Just playing with some of the dogs." Tate flashed her a smile. Did she see the tight lines around his eyes? Or was Alyssia the only person who noticed that?

"Come on." Alyssia found her voice. "I have some scrubs you can change into. You're kind of a mess." Not only was he covered with Grim's fur, splotches of drool decorated his shirt.

Tate looked down, and his eyes widened. "Guess I wasn't paying attention."

"You know where I'll be," she said to Sara.

Back in her office, she grabbed a set of scrubs from a cupboard, and handed them to Tate. "You probably should change. I hope you didn't ruin your clothes." The normal conversation helped calm her further, and keep her in the now.

"They're pants. They're replaceable."

"I know I shouldn't ask. But, do you have anywhere to be tonight?"

He shook his head, and stroked his thumb over the back of her knuckles. "Just here."

"Are you fucking kidding me?"

Alyssia's irritated voice dragged Tate from sleep. He winced at the kink in his neck, and sat up. It took him a minute to focus his eyes. She stood in front of her computer, face contorted with fury. She wasn't back on one of those horrific sites again, was she? Tate's chest squeezed with concern.

She pointed to her screen. "What the hell is this?"

No, probably not. He climbed to his feet, to get a look at what had her so angry. It was a generic landing page from the crowd-funding site. Pretty, friendly—creative had spent weeks on the graphic. The one that said "Sorry, this campaign isn't running right now. Can we help you find something else?"

His own ire spiked. Someone had shut her down without his okay. "Son of a bitch."

She drummed her fingers on the back of her chair. "What's going on?"

"I don't know." All of the user agreements allowed the sites to be taken offline without consultation if there were legal or safety concerns. Lys's site wasn't either of those things. At this point he'd be tempted to tell her to go with another crowd-funding vendor, if there were enough time to spin her up with someone new, and get her donations in before the clock ran out. "I'll fix this."

"Of course you will." Her voice held a hard edge. She sighed. "I'm sorry. I'm not snapping at you."

"You should be. Someone needs to be reamed for this." He grabbed his phone, and dialed his mother's office line. It went straight to voice mail. Funny how it hadn't forwarded to her cell phone. She was either screening him or on the other line. "You can come with me to yell at someone, if you'd like."

She shook her head. "I don't know that I'm equipped for that this morning. Call me as soon as you have answers."

He squeezed her hand. "Of course."

He let his rage soar as he stalked to his car. He was half tempted to go into work dressed in the wrinkled scrubs Lys had loaned him, but that wouldn't help his case. If he was taking on his mother, he had to be cool, professional, and unflinching. This wasn't just about Alyssia's site, though the fact it had been shut down certainly resided at the top of his list. His mother never would have touched one of Jared's projects like this. Or Vivian's. This was about shutting his business venture down without conferring with him first. The hypocrisy that accompanied the decision infuriated him. That she thought she could do this to him because he was family.

For as long as he could remember, he'd yielded, caved, and gone along with her whim because she was his mother, and a parent should know best. It was out of respect and a sense of propriety. Her actions indicated she didn't hold him in the same regard. He was done being steamrolled, and it was time to put an end to it.

CHAPTER SEVENTEEN

Tate straightened his tie, assumed the calmest, coolest air he could summon, and strode toward his mother's office. The door was closed. He wasn't surprised. He gave her assistant, Kat his warmest smile. "Is Ms. Foster in?" He was on her turf, so he'd follow her rules of formality regardless of the unprofessional way she was approaching their relationship.

"Hey." Kat's neutral expression shifted to warm and open when she saw him. "I'd let you in if I could, but she'll be on calls on and off most of the morning. I'll tell her you stopped by. Ping you if she pokes her head out for more than a few seconds."

"Don't worry about it." He let just enough of his drawl slide in to sound polite. "You know what? I'll just hang out for a couple minutes, if that's all right. See if she frees up before the top of the hour?"

"Stay as long as you'd like." Kat's smile grew. "I'll send her a message and let her know you're out here."

He covered her hand. "Don't worry about that. I'd hate to make her hurry just to see me. I'll just hang out for a little while."

"Tate." A familiar baritone snapped through the friendly facade.

Tate ground his teeth at the sound of his father's voice, but managed to keep most of the reaction from his voice. He whirled to face the older man. "Mr. Foster." Calling him Dad in public wasn't the same taboo as referring to his mother so informally, but Tate was already in that business frame of mind.

"Can it." Ben nodded toward his office at the other end of the hall. "Let's talk."

It wasn't the conversation Tate wanted to have, but it might do. He followed, keeping his mouth shut until the door closed them off from the rest of the world. He didn't bother with sitting. "Do you have any idea what she did?" That wasn't how he'd meant to open this conversation.

"I know what she didn't do." Ben took his seat, and leaned back in his chair. "And that's shut down the shelter's crowd-funding site."

Shock filled Tate. "You? Why?"

"You made this personal; I made an executive decision. This may be your spin-off, but ultimately it still falls under the Skriddie label. Think of it as an investor getting involved."

"This isn't just about business." Tate didn't have to bullshit here, or play sweet. That was one thing he appreciated about his father. "You know what happens to that place if they can't raise the capital they need."

"It is about business. Her business is dealing with bad media. Our business is dealing with bad media for entirely different reasons. If we're seen supporting her business, ours looks worse."

Tate understood the logic. He hated himself for it, but he got it. That didn't mean he agreed. "So this is all about the bottom line."

"Yes." Ben leaned forward, fingers clasped and arms resting on his desk. "Look. I don't care what you've got going on with Alyssia Tippins. Whether it's something, or nothing, or falls somewhere in the middle. That's between you and her, and despite what your mother thinks, there's no reason to marry you to a senator's daughter who isn't even old enough to drink."

Tate bit the inside of his cheek to keep a retort from slipping out. He was curious to know where this was going.

"But that's personal, this is business. Look me in the eye and tell me you don't understand my decision."

"I get it. But I still don't agree. This isn't just about return on investment."

"That's exactly what it's about." A sharp crack lined Ben's words. "We're not a charity. The things we do, we do to make money."

Tate didn't have a retort. He knew he couldn't win, but he wasn't willing to back down or give up. "I won't be in the office the rest of the day."

"Fine." Ben turned to his computer, indicating he felt the conversation was over. "Get this out of your system. When you're back tomorrow, I expect business as usual from you."

Tate was already reaching for his phone as he stormed from the office. He didn't have a plan, or even the inklings of one, and he wasn't going to find the answers here.

A text message from Lys waited for him. *How'd it go?*

What the fuck was he going to tell her? He shoved the device back in his pocket, and headed for his car. He'd figure it out.

ALYSSIA LAY IN BED, STARING AT THE CEILING. EVERY TIME SHE DRIFTED toward sleep, horrible images flashed in her mind, muddled with a lack of solutions, and the creeping dread that she didn't have a way out of this problem. She rolled onto her side, and her gaze fell on her cell phone. She would have heard if it had gone off, but that didn't stop her from clicking the button to see if she'd missed any calls or texts.

Nothing.

"Damn it, Tate." Talking to the empty room was better than being alone with her thoughts. He was supposed to keep her updated. He'd been so kind last night, and she knew that man was still in there. She also couldn't shake the feeling he was falling into old patterns.

Sleep wasn't going to happen. She climbed from bed, and pulled on some clothes. Maybe she'd have lunch with Jared, use that as an excuse to surprise Tate. That was a stupid idea. She wasn't being that girl anymore. Jared... Something clicked in her thoughts, chinking and whirring.

She knew what to do, but she couldn't do it alone. She grabbed her phone and dialed.

"This is Mikki."

A sliver of progress wormed its way into Alyssia's thoughts. This *would* work. "Hey, it's me. I need a huge, huge favor, and then maybe you can transfer me to Tate?"

"Like, the exciting, get into trouble kind of favor?" Mikki asked.

"Probably not. But it's a challenging kind of thing, and I can't pay you."

"Then yes. But no to the second thing. Tate's not in today."

Alyssia suppressed her disappointment—and that was all it was. No irritation mingled with the feeling. "Tate told me when he set up this whole crowdfunding thing that he rented Skriddie servers because he didn't have the people to build him a setup." The way he'd phrased it, it sounded like he couldn't find the talent. He'd slipped a few times though, that hiring that kind of skill wasn't in his budget. He'd even placed the hardware orders before his investors—she'd taken that to mean his mother—pulled their funding on the IT budget. He'd sworn he would set it all up once they had the capital. "I don't even know if I'm saying this right. How long would it take you to setup and configure an entire server array for the crowdfunding sites."

Mikki laughed. "Me, personally? Thirty hours. Maybe twenty."

"So, asking you to do this means you'd be giving up your evenings for a week or two." Alyssia couldn't do that. "Never mind."

"What are you kidding? I'm totally in. Hell, I have a friend or two back in Utah who will help."

"Are you sure?"

"I might ask you to chip in on Mt. Dew funds. But yes, one hundred percent. Tell me what we're doing."

Alyssia spent the next half hour laying out her idea, and making sure Mikki had all the right information, before thanking her future sister-in-law, and disconnecting.

Tate still hadn't answered her messages. She wasn't going to waste a phone call on this; it was a conversation that needed to happen in person. She headed to her car, pulled onto the road, and pointed it in the familiar direction.

Her determination wavered when she drew within sight of his driveway, and confirmed his car was there. Maybe he was just home sick, or sleeping off too many long nights. She should wait for him to return her messages.

She summoned her resolve, and parked her car next to his. No backing down.

It was his decision if he was going to be a part of this or not, but he was going to tell her to her face, and she wasn't going to let him wrap it in excuses and faulty logic. She rang the bell, and waited, toes tapping inside her shoes.

The door jerked open more quickly than she expected, and she jumped. Tate stood there, shadows under his eyes, in a battered T-shirt and jeans, and a tired smile. "Hey. Shouldn't you be sleeping?"

He looked good, even exhausted. Concentrate. Remember the plan. Get him to sign on, or walk away. She repeated the words in her head. "I should be. I couldn't. Can we talk?"

"Absolutely." He stepped aside, and gestured toward the couch.

She hovered near the entryway. No sitting until she had a better idea of how this was going. "Did you get answers this morning?"

"Yeah, but don't worry about it. It's under control. I've got plan—"

"I am worried about it." She crossed her arms. "Do you remember yesterday afternoon? You don't get to have plans about my business without my input."

He sighed, and pinched the bridge of his nose. "I know. That's not what this is. This impacts my entire startup. I need to take care of it."

"Tate." She couldn't keep the frustration from her voice. "No. *You* don't. Is this a lack of respect? Do you not take me seriously? Maybe you think your friends are only there when you're the one taking care of them?" The words hurt, tugging at insecurities she hated to acknowledge. But she was so tired of dancing around *everything* when it came to him.

"No. Not at all." He reached for her, then dropped his hand. "I swear, that's so very far from the truth. I have so much respect for you. For everything you do. I've never met a stronger person. The things you see, every day, and the fact you still fight for something so good?"

His words flowed through her head and heart, warming her in a way she didn't want. What if it was just lip service? "Then what are we doing? You don't have to take care of everything on your own. You help me, and I do the same for you. It's who we are."

He dragged his fingers through his hair. "I want you to be happy. I want those animals to be safe. I desperately want to tell you I love you. To write you a check, to make this all go away, to move on so you don't have to deal with it. Not because you're incapable, but because no human being should have to put up with this shit, especially you."

She struggled to keep up with the conversation, but her mind was stuck on three words, skipping back to them. Replaying them over and over in her mind. "Did you just say...?" She couldn't force the question out. Already, her thoughts were working to convince her she'd imagined it.

"I did." He cupped her cheek, and her pulse threatened to burst through her heart. "I love you, Lys. For as long as I can remember. I've just never felt like I could give you what you needed. I still can't."

She pushed him back, anger and confusion mingling with the relief of the revelation. "You fucking asshole. What the hell is wrong with you? I don't even understand why you think you can't give me what I'm looking for."

He clenched his jaw, then dragged in a shaky breath before replying. "Can you really picture me being tied down?"

"I can and I do. You're already anchored here. Maybe it's easier to think that's me being delusional, and seeing things that aren't there. But you just admitted it. You're as tied to me as I am to you. You don't get to make a confession like *I love you*, and wrap it in a bullshit line like '*I know what's good for you, and it's not me.*' You don't get to dump that on me and in the same breath remove my right to tell you I feel the same.

"In fact, I'm tired of you making all sorts of these decisions without my input. Faking that first donation on my website? Okay, I convinced myself you hadn't actually done that. Loaning Jared the money years ago, so he could tell me it came from him, when I bought the shelter? I pretended I didn't know you'd done that." Her words spilled out, surprising her. How did she know that? But the look on Tate's face told her she was right. He'd been there the entire time, making sure she succeeded. Helping. Finding ways to keep her from turning him down.

He shrugged. "This is your dream, and it's a good one. You won't take the money from me."

She hadn't wanted to approach things this way. Especially not with Tate's confession—wonderful, amazing, infuriating as it may be—hanging between them. But she was laying it all on the line. "I will now." Wow, that was harder to say than she'd expected.

"What?"

She shoved her hands in her pockets to keep them from shaking. "I need a loan, Tate. Enough to move forward and make this shelter grow." Now that the words were tumbling out, it was easier. "But I need more than that."

"Of course." His shoulders relaxed, and the lines faded from his forehead. "Whatever you need."

She shook her head. "It's not about me. You need to make this idea take off. What you can do for companies like mine? It's important. These sites of yours can make a big difference and you're doing it right. So we're going to make sure your idea takes off. You, me, Mikki, and she's even going to pull in her friends. We keep failing miserably when it comes down to what I need, or what you want to do. This is about us." She hadn't meant it that way. But she liked the way it sounded.

"Slow down. I think I missed a few steps."

"Right. Sorry." She paused, dragging her thoughts together. "Everything that you've struggled with since you tried to launch these crowd funding sites—or at least a lot of it—goes away if you have your own hardware. You've said you don't have the manpower, but you have technical knowledge, and I found you people who will work for free. You do that, you keep my donation site online, and I'll make sure my expansion happens."

"You've thought this out. Thank you for that."

She felt better than she had in weeks, but she wasn't done yet. "And Tate?"

He met her gaze, eyes widened in question.

She stepped in. "I love you, too."

He grinned, and rested his hands at the small of her back.

She pushed him back playfully. "And if you ever pull this '*I know what's best for you*' bullshit on me again, we're going to have problems."

He grabbed her wrists, and pulled her in. "Yes ma'am." He cupped the back of her head, and crushed his lips to hers. Hunger, need, and security surged through her and she pressed back. She wasn't sure if their new plan was any better than any of the old ones, but this—what she had with Tate—was the one thing she wasn't worried about.

CHAPTER EIGHTEEN

Tate drew Lys into him, and trailed his fingers through her hair. God, he loved having her in his arms. Her warmth, weight, and lilac scent. And right now, he was almost as grateful she wasn't as stubborn has he was. Relief still flowed through him at her acceptance of his financial help. She'd just gotten off the phone with her contractor, letting them know she was ready to move forward with the building expansion.

Tate moved his lips against the top of her head. "When do we start work on this plan?"

"Tonight, when Mikki's done with work and before my shift starts." Her breath was hot against his skin, teasing and comforting at the same time. "Because she'll do it for the challenge instead of trying to talk me out of it for whatever reason."

Tate didn't have an argument for that. "If I might make a suggestion until then."

"What's that?"

"You should probably get some sleep."

She pulled back enough to look him in the eye, and her gaze traveled over his face. "When was the last time you slept an entire night?"

God, he wasn't even sure he remembered. "Not a clue."

"In that case, only if you join me." She pulled him toward the bedroom.

Tate shook the sleep off at the sound of his doorbell chiming. After five. He hadn't meant to sleep that long, but he felt good.

Lys watched him through lidded eyes as he climbed from bed. "What's up?" she asked.

He kissed her on the forehead. "Don't know. I'll be back." He fastened his jeans and pulled on his shirt as he crossed the house to the front door. The remaining haze of sleep evaporated when he saw Jared on his front porch. "Hey, man."

Jared was dressed as if he'd just come from the office, which made sense given the time of day. He held out a USB drive. "I wouldn't bother you at home on a sick day, but you weren't answering your phone. I need your okay on some documents by tomorrow morning."

Sick day? Right. What other reason would he have for vanishing without notice in the middle of the week? Tate grabbed the thumb drive. "No worries. Do you want input, or just an okay?"

Jared shrugged, his expression neutral. "If anything needs to be corrected, use track changes. Meeting's at eleven, so as long as I have it first thing, I'll be set."

"No problem. See you tomorrow."

Jared didn't move, and his jaw tightened.

"Something else I can do for you?" Uneasiness flitted through Tate.

"I just wanted to say hi to your guest. Where is she?"

Tate's gut sank. "Who?"

"Alyssia. Her car's in your driveway."

It was going to come out eventually, and Tate wanted to shout about their relationship to anyone who would listen, but he'd rather have this conversation with Lys's consent, and definitely not while she was half-naked in his bedroom. "Oh, she's...you know." He waved his hand vaguely toward everything behind him.

Jared crossed his arms. "I don't, actually. I can make a lot of assumptions, but my sister accuses me of jumping to conclusions, so I'm hoping I'm wrong. You're not good for her."

Was that what Tate had sounded like? No wonder she'd been pissed. "It's not your call."

Jared made a noise that landed somewhere between a growl and a bark. "Tell me I'm wrong."

"It's okay." Lys's voice greeted him from behind. Tate glanced over his shoulder to see her leaning against the far wall, hair mussed. At least she was dressed, though. "I'd rather tell him now than later."

"What are you doing, Alyssia?" Jared stepped into the house.

Tate blocked his path, and prayed he wasn't about to get socked. Not that he'd ever seen Jared hit anything, but there was a first time for everything. It's what he would do if he were in Jared's shoes. He took a deep breath. "Hear me out."

"I'm listening."

Great. So what was he supposed to say? 'But I love her' was a good start, but it didn't feel very solid. Not given his history. The words flowed into Tate's head, and he spoke without filtering them. "I know you and I have had each other's backs since we were kids," he said to Jared. "But she's my best friend. Honestly, that's the best way to put it. I can't imagine not having her there to celebrate with when things go well." He turned to Lys. It was more important she hear this than Jared. That she know how he felt when they weren't in the middle of a heated argument. "I can't imagine you not being there when I have news of any kind. It wrecks me to think I might have to share you with another man. Let alone your—"

"I get it." Jared interrupted. "Please don't give me any details."

Tate turned back to him with a shrug. "I know she's your sister. I get that you're looking out for her. Thing is, I've thought for a long time about this. Probably longer than I should've. I know what I'm doing, and what I'm saying when I tell you I love her."

Jared's expression was cold, and unyielding. "Can we do this outside?"

"Go," Lys said, before Tate could answer. "Get this out of your system, Jared."

Tate stepped onto the porch. The moment he shut the door, Jared's mask shifted, lines marring his face, brows knitted together.

The almost-calm disappeared from Jared's voice. "You've got a really pretty speech rehearsed. It's almost believable. But out of all that, you only said one thing I agree with. We have known each other since we were kids. You've never been with a woman longer than twenty-four hours. And now what? I'm supposed to just step back and tell you, knowing what I do about you, that I'm fine with you hooking up with my sister?"

A part of Tate expected this conversation to be difficult, but he hadn't lingered on the details or logistics of it. Maybe he should have thought about the repercussions a little longer. Not that it would have changed how he felt about Lys, but it may have changed his approach to the rest of it. "I'm being sincere. I don't know what else to say."

Jared clenched his jaw. "Honestly, I shouldn't make you convince me. God, it hurts to admit that. But I know you're right. You and she... I know you're close. I'm not blind. I was just hoping you wouldn't ever figure it out."

Tate ground his teeth together, measuring his response. "Because I'm not good enough for your baby sister?"

"Because she is my baby sister, and this means admitting she's grown up."

Tate almost smiled at that. He swallowed back a jab about her having grown up a long time ago. "You have to let her make her own decisions sometime."

"That doesn't mean I have to like it."

This could have gone better, but it also could have gone a lot worse. He looked at Jared. "It's not like I have a choice but to show you I mean it. I'm not going anywhere without her."

Jared stared back, jaw set. "If this goes bad, that's the point where you'd better lose my number. But I have a feeling I don't need to worry."

"Not that she needs your blessing, but I'd kind of hate to lose your friendship. So, thanks."

They exchanged a few more jabs, the tension lessening between them, and Jared left. Tate headed back inside.

Lys sat on the couch, fingers intertwined, elbows resting on her legs. "You look like that maybe went well?"

"He didn't even hit me." Tate pulled her to her feet. "Really, though, I'm glad he's not too pissed, because I'd hate to choose sides, but I wouldn't have chosen his."

She wrapped her arms around his waist, and rested her cheek on his chest. Her voice was soft. "I'm glad you don't have to. I'd hate to make you regret us."

"I don't, and I wouldn't. Not ever." He hugged her back, holding on tight. "I still meant everything I said. This doesn't change how I feel." He kissed her. "As long as you know I mean it, when I say I love you, that's what matters."

"I do." She squeezed his hand. "And I'd stay here all night and let you show me, but we have an appointment."

Right. Time to put their plan into action. "I'll meet you at the shelter?"

She nodded, and stepped away. He grasped her fingers, pulled her to him, and rested a hand on the small of her back. He kissed her, pouring everything he felt into the gesture. Memorizing each curve of her body, and the way her frame molded to his. This was what mattered. Making sure Lys had whatever it took to make her happy. He finally let her go, and the absence of her touch lingered on his skin. "See you soon."

CHAPTER NINETEEN

Mikki sat on the couch in Alyssia's office, legs crossed, and laptop balanced on her knees. She had a friend—Jaycie—on speaker, but mostly what echoed through her phone was the clacking of keys.

Alyssia scrolled through lists of supplies—purchases she needed to grow the shelter. Tate was working his contacts to find a storage facility for his hardware. So many servers had to be on and online all the time, and they needed a secure location to live in.

It was the same scene as it had been for almost two weeks, and Alyssia found it comforting. That, and—now that she was back on daytime shifts—she loved waking up next to Tate, regardless of whose place they stayed at.

Tate reached around Alyssia for a pen. He brushed his lips over her cheek before scooting away again, and going back to his pacing and whatever he was looking up on the tablet he held. Heat flooded Alyssia's face when she realized Mikki was watching, mouth twisted in amusement.

Mikki shook her head and turned back to her work. "You two are cute."

"Are they at it again?" Jaycie's teasing voice came over the phone.

Alyssia flushed at playful exchange. She needed to meet more of Mikki's friends.

"Like, non-stop." Mikki glanced at Alyssia again. "I don't know why Jared's still grumpy about it."

Alyssia tucked away the sliver of hurt at the reminder. He'd told Tate he was okay, but he still snarled when he saw the two of them together. She knew it would take time, but Jared still meant the world to her. She couldn't ask for a better older brother. "It's probably hard to get if you don't have siblings."

Mikki shrugged. "I guess. Personally, I think he's just jealous. When Holly and Robert find out, he's going to have to share the 'when are we getting grand-kids' conversations with you."

"I don't envy that," Jacyee said. "Dealing with developers is all the exposure to children that I want." She had been vague about what she did, but apparently it had to do with video games.

A nervous pit sank into Alyssia's gut. It had been there a lot lately. A hint of nausea that surged at certain times of the day, then ebbed again as she lost herself in work.

Sweet, heartfelt confessions of love were one thing, but it wasn't like they were even living together yet, let alone having a children conversation. It was true; Tate said he wanted to be her future, but they hadn't talked about things like that. And as much as she wanted kids, she wasn't sure that fell in line with his vision. She risked a glance at Tate. He stared at his tablet, his face a flat mask, and his finger tapping on the screen.

"I'm pretty sure he's not jealous." Tate finally looked up. "Really? You get the grandkids question already? You're not even married yet."

Mikki held up her left hand and wiggled her fingers. The overhead lights sparkled off diamonds. "I'm just saying, join us for Sunday dinner holding hands, instead of sitting at opposite ends of the room pretending you don't see each other, and things will change. It's not like it's a big deal, we're just running out of polite excuses."

"Kids aren't in your future?" Tate asked.

Alyssia tried not to pick apart his question. There was no reason to analyze the words, examine them for inflection. That wasn't uncertainty or disgust she heard in her voice.

"I don't know." Mikki turned her attention back to her work, typing as she talked. "Maybe. I know, he's ten years older, they've been waiting for a long time, but we're not sure if we want to do that."

Alyssia hadn't ever heard that from Jared before. Not that they spent a lot of time talking about his baby plans. Still, she'd always just assumed it was something she'd do, it was something Jared would do. "So are you saying you'll never...?"

"Maybe. Maybe not. I've still got time, and we're still having fun, you know?"

"I completely understand." Tate was making scrolling motions on the screen now, instead of random taps.

Currents of uneasiness rocked through Alyssia. "Which bit?" She tried to keep her tone casual. "The not knowing for sure, or the 'it's probably never going to happen?'"

He looked up, and his gaze met hers. "I have a press release explaining your situation with Thompson's dog. Something to help you change the perception of the shelter back to positive. Do you want to hit up the online news outlets with the information, or stick to local television stations?"

"Online too. Everyone who'll listen." She squashed her rising disappointment. She shouldn't jump to conclusions. It wasn't as if he'd said it was never going to happen. And again, it wasn't even like they had moved that far in their relationship. But she'd struggle to make things work, even with him, if kids weren't an option. Had he really thought this confession of love thing through? Had she?

She'd never kept what she wanted from her future a secret. Was she overreacting, or was this just one of many things they were about to clash over?

"So." Jaycie's voice was loud and hollow. "Speaking of media outlets, any news on Thompson?"

Tate shook his head. "Certified mail says he received the letter." They'd decided to give him one more chance to rescind the stories about the shelter, and to drop the lawsuit. To issue a public apology, and then just let the issue die. The alternative wouldn't quite be as brutal as what he'd done to the shelter, but it certainly wouldn't paint Thompson or his local TV station a good light, and Alyssia's attorney already had a counter-suit drawn up if needed. "No response. He won't take my calls, and has refused any in-person meetings."

"Bryce Thompson was not available for response," Jaycie said in chirpy voice.

Alyssia stifled a laugh when the Mikki woman flipped her hair over her shoulder, and adjusted an invisible jacket. It was Mikki and Jaycie's anchorwoman impersonation. Mikki played the face, and Jaycie provided the voice. They'd been sliding into it off and on for days.

"So, we crucify the bastard." Tate tapped out something on the screen in front of him.

"You've got one more avenue." Alyssia didn't want to bring it up. Tate would hate the idea. But she still felt like Thompson deserved a chance. His kid didn't. That sadistic fuck needed to pay, but just because his dad was delusional didn't mean he should lose the things he'd worked for.

"No, I really don't." Tate rubbed his eyes. "All right, fine. She's out of town until Friday, though. I'll talk to her then. She's not going to listen. Especially when I tell her we don't need Skriddie's hardware anymore."

"I'm missing something," Mikki said.

"His mother has certain ins with Mr. Thompson," Alyssia explained.

"They're fucking. Have been for years." Tate made himself comfortable in a nearby chair.

Mikki's brows rose. "And I thought my family was dysfunctional."

"You have no idea."

Alyssia frowned at the resignation in Tate's voice. The entire evening of conversations was just one bad reminder after another. A nudge, asking if she and Tate knew what they were doing. Or worse, reminding her this may be far more temporary than she'd like. She didn't want to think that way, but every time she banished the insistent voice in the back of her head, it pecked at her resolve until it was free again.

CHAPTER TWENTY

Alyssia stood in front of her bathroom mirror, stomach clenched in knots. Which was the entire reason she was doing this. To convince herself the nausea she felt on an almost daily basis was the stress of working so hard, and not something deeper. More... internal.

Tate. His name twisted her insides further. She looked again at the piece of plastic in her hand, and the pink plus sign in the middle. Two weeks of bliss, and everything was going to fall apart again when she told him she was pregnant. He may have made the leap to committing to her, but she couldn't imagine he was ready for a family. Not after all the protests he'd put up over the years.

She might have thought it would be all right. Maybe it would be, and she was just overreacting. But after his conversation with Mikki the other day...

She sank onto the toilet seat with a sigh. How was she going to break this to him?

As if her thoughts had summoned him, her phone rang in the other room, and the familiar song she used as his ringtone drifted toward her. She shoved the pregnancy test deep into the trash, and jogged to answer. "Hey."

"Hey, gorgeous." Tate's smile carried over the line. "You sound out of breath. Are you okay?"

Just questioning everything, from herself, to him, them. She shouldn't doubt him. Things were going well, and she was just being paranoid. "My phone wasn't in the same room as me. I had to track it down. What's up?"

"Are you free this afternoon?"

It was her day off, but she was on call. "Until someone tells me otherwise."

"Have lunch with me at that little diner in Gwinnette?"

The invitation eased her doubt. She was definitely being paranoid. "Absolutely. When?"

"One thirty, hopefully. Marge Foster pushed my appointment back to noon."

If he was calling his mom by her full name, instead of Mother, that wasn't a good sign. The full name treatment was reserved for when he was irritated with her, or trying to pretend they weren't related. "I wonder sometimes if she wishes she'd had the mailman's kid, instead of me."

"It'll be fine." Alyssia tried to keep her reassurance vague. "Say your bit, you know you'll keep your head, and I'll see you after."

"Good point. I love you, Lys."

The simple reminder helped calm her, but it didn't completely erase her doubts. "I love you, too."

TATE SAT IN ONE OF THE WAITING ROOM CHAIRS OUTSIDE HIS MOTHER'S office, doing his best not to check the time. It was almost twenty after twelve. The door never opened, but her assistant, Kat, finally looked up. "Ms. Foster will see you now. Sorry for the wait."

"It's not a problem." He gave her a warm smile, a retort surged in his throat, and he choked it back. It wasn't Kat's fault, and he was doing his best to keep his cool through this. He stepped into the smaller room, pleasant airs still painted on.

"I'm so sorry to keep you waiting." Marge's southern lilt was back. "Important people demanding my time."

"Of course." He ignored the subtle implication he wasn't part of that list. "Thanks for making room in your schedule. This won't take long."

Her eyebrows twitched up, and she nodded to the chair across from her desk. "Then let's talk business."

He made a point of closing the door before he took a seat. Keep calm, play it cool, don't let her ruffle him. That was all he had to remember. "I've been trying to get a hold of a mutual associate, and haven't been able to reach him. I'm hoping you can help me."

She muttered something that sounded like, "Of course you can't." Out loud, she said "Bless your heart. Give me their name, and I'll see what I can do."

Time to tip his hand. "I need to get a message to Bryce Thompson."

Her eye twitched, and her mask slid back into place. "I'm sorry. I was under the impression this was a business meeting. I made room in my work schedule for this."

"It is business, Ms. Foster." He leaned back in his chair, posture casual. "He's impacted a critical Skriddie Bust Media project. One that's estimated to increase our quarterly revenue by at least five percent, and that's guaranteed to challenge our strongest competitors and give us a new foothold in the market. I'd like to speak with Mr. Thompson, and see what kind of an agreement we can reach. I think his taking the time to sit down with me would be in his best interests."

"Not yours?" Her lilting accent was gone, replaced with a hard edge.

"This isn't about me, it's about the company, and Skriddie comes out on top either way. This is just a professional courtesy."

Her jaw clenched, and she leaned in. "It's a clever game, Tate. And I'm not sure what you're doing, but disguising your little friend's problems as *business* isn't going to cut it."

He stood. "I see. Then you won't help me get a hold of Mr. Thompson."

"Why don't you reach out to him yourself?"

"I tried. I haven't been able to connect with him." The conversation was going almost exactly the way Tate had expected. Disappointment welled inside. It was naive of him to think she'd cooperate, but he'd still hoped. "I'd thought maybe if you were seeing him soon. Tonight, for dinner maybe, you could drop my name."

Her upper lip pulled into a sneer. "I will, as a matter of fact. I'll pass your concerns to him, along with the opinion that my son is chasing a dream and living in a fantasy world."

The insult sliced under Tate's skin, and he forced himself to ignore it. "I appreciate it. Thank you for your time."

He started to rise, and then paused, as if he'd remembered something. "One more thing. We've discovered Skriddie is in breach of contract for the hardware they rented to the new venture."

Her brows rose and her self-satisfaction vanished. "I doubt that."

"I did at first, too." He slid her a folder. The paperwork inside was from Mikki and Jaycie—evidence that Marge had been responsible for throttling the crowdfunding sites' bandwidth and server space, he assumed to make a point about...something? He knew other companies used negotiation tactics like that, but he hadn't expected it from his own.

"If there's an issue, I'm sure we'll resolve it." Her snideness was gone, as was her pleasant tone. A mask had slid in, flat and expressionless.

"That won't be necessary. The contract has been violated, and is being terminated. Notarized documents will arrive this afternoon."

She gave him a wicked smile, eyes narrowed. "You can't bring this to life on your own. If you burn this bridge, your venture will fail."

He shrugged, not feeling nearly as casual as he was trying to look, and stood. "I'm not worried about it."

His hands shook as he strode from the office, irritation and satisfaction warring for control of his thoughts. It was true, she'd never stopped condescending while he was in there, but he hadn't flinched, or sunk to the same level.

Besides, he had a lunch date with a wonderful woman. The adrenaline racing through him ebbed as he headed toward his car. He'd be a little early, but he needed the drive and the fresh air to clear his head.

When Lys pulled into the parking lot of the diner, almost an hour later, he'd replayed the conversation in his head to the point of exhaustion. He couldn't think of a way to have handled that situation better, all things considered. But seeing Lys walking toward him, hair pulled into a loose bun, sway to her hips, erased the rambling thoughts. He met her halfway, pulled her close, and kissed her hard. She let out a tiny whimper, and leaned into him. God, he loved everything about kissing her. He intertwined his fingers with hers, and they headed toward the restaurant.

"How'd it go?" she asked.

"About like I expected."

"I'm sorry."

"Nah." He'd had enough time to make his peace with it. "We knew it probably wasn't going to happen. If Thompson is going to be an asshole about this, he can deal with the fallout. He never even considered you."

"I know. But..." She shook her head. "You're right. His choice."

The hostess led them to a table outside, and he took the seat across from Lys. "It's done and over. Did you get up to anything interesting this morning?"

She flipped the menu open and gave it her full attention. "Not really. Boring house stuff."

Doubt brushed his senses. She was just hungry. Not lying to him. "Like what?"

"Hmm?" She glanced up, but never met his gaze. Whatever she was studying seemed to have stolen her interest. "Cleaning. Laundry."

He knew he wasn't reading her wrong this time. She was keeping something from him. But what? Fuck. "What aren't you telling me?"

She finally looked him in the eye, corners of her mouth turned down. "I'm just." She pushed her menu aside. "I feel like this whole thing is going too well. There were so many road bumps to get to this point. And now it's just smooth sailing? I guess I'm just waiting for the other shoe to drop."

That was something he understood. He reached across the table and covered her hand with his. "Maybe it will, maybe it won't. We'll make arrangements for the stuff we can predict, and deal with the rest of it if it happens."

"I guess."

"Lys." He tugged her thumb. "We'll make it work. That's what we do, right?"

"Of course." Her expression relaxed. "You're right. We'll be fine. Are you coming over tonight?"

Tate still felt like he was missing something, but she said it was just stress, and after his morning, he might be overreacting. "Of course. I'll be there after work."

———

"Lys." Tate's voice drifted from the kitchen. "Are you sure you're all right?

The question filled her with an uneasiness she didn't expect. She set her glass of ice water on the table, and looked in his direction. "Not unless you know something I don't."

He wandered back into the living room, and held up an empty box. It was from her pregnancy test. Her gut sank. Why hadn't she hidden that better instead of just leaving it on top of the trash? Or maybe she should have just owned up to it right away instead of trying to hide it.

"So this was negative?" he asked.

That wasn't the way she wanted him to lead. "Would negative be better?" Not that she had planned for him finding out this way, but in a perfect, everything is going smoothly now world, he wouldn't be wearing a scowl, and he'd have asked if it was positive.

His mouth twisted in irritation. "Negative would justify the 'no there's nothing to tell you' response. I'm pretty sure positive is the kind of something you don't just dismiss."

"So what would you prefer the result was?" Alyssia knew this was childish. Coming clean was her best option, but concern twisted her from the inside out. They hadn't been together long enough for her to lose Tate.

Wait. Lose him? The phrase gnawed at her. Why would she think that? It was true, they'd had some bumps, and they hadn't officially been together for long, but even before they were a couple, he'd always been there. Since she was young, he looked out for her. And what he told Jared resonated so deeply with her. It wasn't that she always called Tate first because he was the crush she never got over. She didn't think his name first when the news was good or bad or even just mediocre because he was her brother's buddy.

He really was her best friend, and even though she'd only known about the baby for a few hours, if it had been any other news at all, she would have dialed him before anyone else, just to shout with joy and share.

The words stuck in her throat, and she forced them out. "I do have something to tell you. My birth control failed. I'm pregnant." It terrified her to say it out loud, but at the same time, it was comforting to have it off her chest. "I'm sorry."

The irritation vanished from. His face, replaced with a blank mask of nothing. "Sorry for... keeping this from me? For not trusting me with this information? For thinking... I don't know. What were you thinking, Lys?"

"I was scared. I think that's fair. This isn't something we planned for. We're still new as us. I figured the 'do you want kids' conversation was at least a few months off."

"So was the plan to keep it to yourself until you thought we were in a good place for that talk?" His mask slipped, and hurt flitted across his features.

"I haven't even known for twelve hours. I'm still adjusting to the news, and you've always made it clear a family wasn't in your future. I assumed that included kids."

"My views on my future have changed. Or did you think I was making up all everything I said about wanting you by my side? I've listened to and heard you, Lys. I know what you want out of life."

"But what do you want?" The question knocked a fear loose that she hadn't been able to name before now. Tate spent so much time worrying about her. It was sweet, but it wasn't a foundation for long term if he put his own needs aside.

He raked his fingers through his hair. "I don't know. Honestly, I haven't thought about it. The one thing I do want is what you said before. To do this together, whatever *this* entails. I know Jared doesn't believe me when I say that, and I'm sure he's not the only one. You and I have a spotty history. But you're the one who said we were doing this with each other; I thought you meant it."

Alyssia frowned. He was right. But even considering all that, "I'm still scared, Tate. And I'm still processing."

He drew his mouth into a thin line and leaned against the wall. "I get that. But..." He crossed the room, took her hand in his, and looked her in the eye. The test was positive, really?"

She nodded.

A smile cracked onto his face, and he squeezed her hand. "That's amazing."

A huge cloud she hadn't realized was haunting her lifted, and relief flooded her. She threw her arms around his neck and kissed him. This was going to be okay after all. She never should have doubted.

CHAPTER TWENTY-ONE

ALYSSIA POWERED down her work computer, and gathered her purse. Going home before the sun set, instead of as it rose, she liked that. Besides, Tate was picking her up, and she liked that even more. He was already waiting in the lobby, chatting with Sara.

The moment Alyssia stepped into the main room, his attention was on her. Her cheeks flushed at the smile that spread across his face.

"Don't keep her up too late." Sara warned. "She's got an important eight a.m."

"I'll do what I can. No promises." Tate stepped closer, wrapped an arm around Alyssia's waist and kissed her.

She moaned against his mouth. Such an amazing feeling.

Sara sighed. "So perfect," she said. Alyssia looked up just in time to see Sara snap a picture with her phone.

Alyssia held up a hand. "Delete that."

"Nope. Cutest couple of the year."

The front door slammed open, smashing into the far wall, the noise reverberating through the room. Alyssia spun, heart hammering at the abrupt interruption.

Bryce Thompson Jr. stood in the front lobby, face contorted. His cheeks were red. His mouth was twisted in a sneer. "Give me back my fucking dog."

Tate stepped in his path, fists clenched, and advanced forward. "You need to leave."

Alyssia was aware of Sara grabbing the phone, and dialing. But most of her attention was on the scene in front of her. Her stomach flipped in on itself, adrenaline spiking.

"Not until I have my dog." Bryce stepped forward and Tate met him.

Tate grabbed his arm, and pushed back. Bryce wrenched free, and let a fist fly, clipping Tate in the jaw.

"Stop." Alyssia looked for an opening. Something she could do to step in.

"Yes, we have an intruder," Sara told the person on the other end of the line. Alyssia assumed 911. "Violent. Assaulting a customer."

Tate growled, and dove his shoulder into Bryce's chest. The teenager returned the favor with a direct punch to Tate's gut. Tate grunted and doubled over.

Alyssia looked around the room for something, anything she could use to stop this. Bryce advanced on her. "Give me back my fucking dog."

She retreated as he advanced. Her pulse hammered in her ears, drowning out the background noise.

"It's not your dog." Bryce's voice was low and threatening, but a slur running through the words. "He's mine. I get to do what I want with him. If he's a bad dog, I get to beat him. I bought him. I'll buy you, too, bitch." As he got closer, a wash of alcohol on his breath hit Lys, making her eyes water.

Tate approached him from behind, hooked his arms under Bryce's and, pressed his interlocked fingers into the back of the kid's neck. He dug his knee into the back of Bryce's leg, and forced him to the ground. "Don't touch her."

"Let go." Bryce struggled against the grip, but Tate held fast.

The door swung open for the second time in as many minutes, and two officers stepped in cautiously, hands on their holstered guns.

"We got it from here," one said. Alyssia knew the man—he almost always took her reports, and had stopped by the shelter several times in the last few weeks to make sure things were going all right despite the protesters out front.

They extracted Tate and Bryce from each other, and cuffed the teenager. Relief shuddered through Alyssia, and she wrapped Tate in a hug, holding on until they both stopped shaking.

A LYSSIA GRABBED A HANDFUL OF ICE FROM THE FREEZER AND STUFFED IT inside a bag. She returned to the living room to find Tate leaned back on the couch, staring at the ceiling. Sara had canceled the 8 a.m. After spending the last several hours answering police questions, filing a report, and having a doctor tell Tate nothing was broken, but his face would look pretty nasty for a while, Alyssia knew they weren't going to be getting up early.

She knelt on the cushion next to Tate, and pressed the bag of ice to his eye. "My hero." She was only half teasing. Investing money he already had in her business was one thing, but taking a fist for her... Something she never thought she'd have to see, but she couldn't help being warmed by the gesture.

"I wasn't really thinking about being a hero." He covered her hand with his, the heat of his palm searing, where the ice bag chilled. "I was more concerned about you."

"That's what makes it heroic."

He pulled the ice pack away, and focused on her. "If you say so. Personally, I've got better things to think about."

She raised her brows. "Really? Like what?"

"Like why I'm the only one with a cold face right now."

"Because you're the guy with the black eye."

"So?" Tate plucked an ice cube from the pack. "I'd rather focus on you than that tiny purple bump on my face." He traced the frozen liquid over her bottom lip and then her top. His voice dropped an octave, gaze locked on her face. "Like how kissable your lips are."

Her mouth parted at the shock of cold and she gasped at the tease of melting water against her skin. "How long your neck is." He popped the cube onto his tongue, and lowered his head. Ice and his lips caressed a line down to her collar-bone. She arched her back and whimpered. Her nails slid up his back, and she shifted her weight to get closer.

He lowered one hand to the back of her knee. She moved her leg, until she was half wrapped around him, urging him on.

"This bit is always fun, too." His icy lips brushed her ear, and she gasped.

"That does seem like a lot to think about." Her comment was cut short when he nipped her earlobe with his teeth. Her fingers wrapped in his thick hair and she pulled him back to her, crushing her lips against his. An insistent need grew between her legs.

She covered his other hand and pushed it further up her thigh, her knee hooking on his hip. His hand moved up the back of her thigh, sliding over the curve of her hip. He traced along the waistband of her jeans, a chuckle rumbling in his chest. His mouth moved back to her neck, words tickling her skin. "Good point. I guess we'll just have to cover multiple spots."

She fumbled for a comeback, attempts failing when his teeth grazed the soft spot between her neck and shoulders, and he sucked on the sensitive flesh.

His fingers brushed her crotch through denim and she whimpered. Her nails dug into his back, holding him close. He pressed two fingers against the seam of her pants, and pressed into her slit. She squeaked and shifted her weight until her clit rested under his touch. He massaged harder, and she ground against his hand.

He pulled away abruptly, and tugged her to her feet. "We need a little more room than the couch." He led her into the bedroom, spun her to a stop, and rested his hands on her cheeks. When he pressed his lips to hers, her chest threatened to burst. His tongue pushed into her mouth, massaging and twisting with hers. Wet need throbbed between her legs, wanting more attention, and her nipples pressed against the lace of her bra.

She glided her fingers down his chest, undoing each button she encountered, then pushed his shirt off his shoulders. Hunger swelled inside, combined with the lingering adrenaline from earlier. Each touch sent fire over her skin, and his comforting scent filled her thoughts.

He broke the kiss long enough to let her yank his undershirt over his head. He gripped her hair, and she gasped at the sharp jerk when he lowered his head to the hollow at the base of her throat. Her pulse threatened to run away when he cupped her breast, and squeezed a nipple through her bra.

His strong touch coaxed every nerve ending to life. She dragged her thumb over his chest, and flicked a small brown nub, slowly at first, then faster in response to his moans. He stripped her shirt and bra off, and tossed them aside. He guided her to the bed. Her sex pulsed, wanting attention. He massaged her breast, then drew a pink button into his mouth. When he flicked his tongue back and forth at a rapid pace, she tilted her head back with a gasp. God, that felt amazing. It tugged a chord inside that ran from her nipple straight to her aching center.

He continued the motion for several minutes, switching between breasts, until her thoughts swam with so many sensations she couldn't process them.

She wanted more. To feel his entire body pressed against her. She undid his belt and slacks, and slid her hand inside his boxers. His mouth vibrated against her rigid nipple when he groaned. She worked him as free as was possible, given they were both sitting, and stroked his shaft in time with his sucking. He thrust his hips against her.

Without warning, he unsnapped her jeans, jerked the zipper down, and nudged her onto her back. He yanked her pants down her legs, then leaned over her, voice deep and gravelly. "I need to fuck you."

She nodded at the hunger in his voice, not sure she trusted herself to speak. He shed the rest of his clothing. She scooted back on the bed, already slick with anticipation. With a single thrust, he drove inside her. She arched at the sensation of being spread open, drawing him in farther. He leaned forward, hands on either side of her head, and worked his hips slowly, keeping the rhythm steady. She pushed against him, trying to increase the pace.

He dipped his head in, mouth hovering over her ear. "If you do that, I can't last long."

She smiled. "I don't mind."

He sat straight up, pushing himself deeper with a sudden thrust. "I do." He grabbed one of her knees, and drove it to her chest. With his free hand, he reached between them, and found her clit. He bumped his thumb over the button, pressing harder each time he thrust into her.

She gasped, each breath growing shorter as the combination of him hitting her G-spot and fingering her pushed her to a fast climax. She wanted to draw the moment out, though. Sink into the pleasure. She pounded against him, and this time he let her set the pace. Orgasm flowed through her. Her pussy clenched around his cock, spasming, milking him. He pulled away from her swollen sex, and pushed her other knee forward. His grunts grew more labored and thrusting more frantic. She recognized the familiar sound of him coming, and seconds later, he spilled inside her.

He continued to pound a moment longer, until the edge faded from her ecstasy. He finally slowed, then stopped and let go of her legs. Still inside her, he bent in and brushed his lips over hers. "I want this for the rest of our lives. This... everything. This us." His words were punctuated with him struggling to catch his breath.

She nodded. "Me too."

He rolled off, and they shifted on the bed until she could rest her head on his chest. She could only focus on a single thought, as they intertwined their fingers and rested their hands on his chest. This was absolutely perfect.

CHAPTER TWENTY-TWO

CONSCIOUSNESS TRICKLED into Tate's thoughts, bringing the ache of a black eye with it. He groaned and tried to ignore the throb as he forced himself to sit. He was the only one in bed. Sun shone through the window, striking his face and making him wince.

"Lys." He called through the apartment.

"Living room. You need to see this."

He couldn't tell if she sounded stressed out, or excited, or something else. He stumbled to his feet, and pulled on his clothes as he walked. For a moment he considered leaving it all behind, but with his luck Jared would be out there, or something equally as awkward.

Lys sat on the couch, wearing one of Tate's button-down shirts, and possibly not much else from the look of her bare legs tucked beneath her. She nodded at the TV. "Sara texted me. Said we made the morning news."

It wasn't Thompson's affiliate, it was the competition. And as Tate watched the clip, he understood why. It was a shaky, low quality video of the brawl last night, complete with subtitles of every abusive, arrogant comment Bryce Jr. had made.

Tate sank onto the couch, blinking back his surprise. "How'd they get this? It's not security footage."

"Sara. She said she was sorry, but not really."

"Wow." He listened to the newsman explain Bryce Thompson Jr. had been arrested. Bryce Thompson Sr. had issued a public apology for the unknowingly false reports they'd done on the shelter, and had refused any other comment.

"Thompson is going to be pissed," Tate muttered. "He won't let this drop." Not that it mattered.

Lys leaned her head against his shoulder. "We'll deal with it." Her words echoed his thoughts. "If there's backlash, we'll handle it together."

Tate held out Lys's chair for her, then slid it in as she sat, before taking his own seat across from her. It was taking a large part of his focus to keep his pulse from galloping away. He could be patient though. Only a few other diners were in the restaurant, and all sat several tables away. He'd made sure their reservations tonight would be perfect. Already discussed the meal with the chef, made sure they'd have the alcohol-free sparkling wine on hand for Lys.

The whole evening had to be just right. Though, given the company, he would have been okay with a crowded cafeteria off the interstate. Her black dress hugged her figure perfectly, flaring out at the waist, ending just above her knees. She was only seven weeks along, so she wasn't showing yet.

He'd struggled with the news of the baby. It had come as a huge shock, and he had to admit, he'd been terrified during the entire conversation with Lys. But the longer he thought about it, the more it felt right. He might not have enjoyed his childhood, and he had issues with his parents, but he'd seen other examples of amazing families all around him. Their child was going to have the same thing —a good, caring home. And he knew he didn't want it any other way.

She draped her napkin over her knees, and sipped her drink, looking everywhere but him. That was odd. He beat back a creeping smidgen of doubt. "I wanted to talk to you about something." She finally met his gaze.

His mind produced about five billion scenarios simultaneously, and he banished them all. No reason to jump to conclusions when she was sitting right there, about to finish her thought. "Sure. What's up?"

She tapped her fingers on the stem of her glass. "Now that Bryce Jr.'s preliminary hearing is over, the shelter can settle up some of our outstanding paperwork."

It hadn't been easy for her to testify when they determined whether or not the teenager should stand trial—reiterating what was wrong with Grim when he'd been brought in—but thanks to her, and Sara's video, the prosecution had a solid enough case to proceed.

She chewed on the inside of her cheek. "We need to place Grim. And I think I've found the perfect spot for him."

She would have found Grim a new home before now, but because of how public the case had become, the shelter held onto him until everything was legally finalized. Something sad tugged at Tate's chest, masking the giddy nervousness that had been there seconds earlier. He'd spent a lot of time playing with that dog during recovery. "That's fantastic." His tone came out flatter than he intended.

"The thing is, I'd like to see him with you. You've got the yard, he already loves you, and, well…"

Tate couldn't help his grin at the suggestion. He'd never even considered the idea. "I'd love to keep him. Are you sure? Am I allowed to do that?"

"Of course you are." She laughed. "There's a probationary period, but since you've spent half your free time with him, I'm not worried."

He let his joy mingle with his growing anticipation. He hadn't been sure when he wanted to do this. The meal was planned, the details were supposed to be spontaneous. Now seemed like as good a time for a segue as any. So why had his heart just paused? An unfamiliar nervousness fluttered through him "Speaking of having a lot of room..." He fumbled with a velvet box in his pocket, fingers suddenly feeling flimsy. "I want you to know, I'm so happy about the baby. And your pregnancy doesn't change how I feel about you."

She furrowed her brow, and tilted her head. "I know."

He finally grasped the box, and knelt next to her. "We've only been dating for a few months, but you've been my world for a long time. My best friend, my confidant, my everything. Alyssia Tippins, will you marry me?" He opened the box, to expose a ring with a recessed band of diamonds.

She gasped, and nodded. "Yes, and a million times over, yes."

He shouldn't have been nervous, of course she'd agree, but the reassurance didn't stop relief and joy from filling him. He slipped the ring onto her finger, stood, and brushed his lips over hers. She hooked her fingers at the back of his neck, and held him close for several more seconds, deepening the kiss.

He couldn't think of a better future. Things would only get better from here on out.

Award winning and USA Today Bestselling Author Allyson Lindt is a full-time geek and a fuller-time author. She likes her stories with sweet geekiness and heavy spice, and loves a good happily-ever-after. Because cubicle dwellers need love too. Learn more about Allyson's books, including signing up for her newsletter, by visiting http://www.allysonlindt.com.

GIANNA

Ashley Cade

Selfish. Deceitful. Manipulative. Conniving.

Evil.

I'd been called all that and worse. Sometimes by the people I loved. That was what hurt the most.

But they were right. I was all those things. I hurt a man I loved; a damn good man who treated me like a queen. And he wasn't my only victim.

Falling in love with someone else was unexpected but it happened, and in the end, I destroyed them both.

So, yeah, I deserved every barb they threw my way. I stood there and let each one land on their mark, striking me right in the heart. They cut deep, tearing me into a million little pieces. I deserved the berating, the fall from grace, and to be the lonely shell of a woman I became.

I had time to think about my mistakes, wallow in self-pity, and feel every bit of guilt and anguish I could reap from the discord I sowed. But now it was time to get back on my feet and rise from the ashes like the phoenix I was destined to become.

Because it was no longer just about me. I had something to live for now, something that made me want to be a better person. She was my entire world. With a head full of dark curls and chocolate brown eyes like her father, she restored my faith and cemented my hope for a better future. It was time to fix my crown and put my life back together.

CHAPTER ONE

Moving to Nashville was never part of the plan. I didn't care much for country music, but when a growing record label needed a publicist for an up-and-coming band, I finally had an excuse to put that public relations degree to use and take a chance to make a fresh start. It didn't matter that my father's connections most likely landed me the interview in the first place. I was getting out of this town and away from my sordid past.

No one blatantly "outed" me for what I did to Dalton, but the rumor mill started churning shortly after he and Taylor made their relationship official, and soon the whole town knew what I'd done. Or at least some version of it. Being shunned by my friends and acquaintances was damn near unbearable, but it was nothing compared to how Antonio reacted when I finally came clean to him.

He'd been upset when I told him about the pregnancy and that I was going back to Dalton because the child belonged to my ex. Later, when I confessed to him that I'd lied about it and *he* was really the baby's father, I thought he would snap. He shoved back from the table so fast, his chair tipped over when he stood. A long string of curses left his mouth as he paced, raking his fingers through his hair and tugging on the ends. It landed in a tousled mess, pooling just below his chiseled jaw. He was truly beautiful, even with hatred for me burning in his eyes.

"Why?" he growled.

I didn't want to answer. I never wanted to admit the selfish, cowardly reasons why I lied about the paternity of my baby, but it was the least I could do.

"I was scared," I admitted, my voice shaking. "My parents were already furious with me for calling off the wedding and didn't approve of my relationship with you." He winced and I immediately regretted bringing it up. "They were going to cut me off. We would've had nowhere to go and no way of supporting ourselves. You don't have a job, and I won't have access to my trust fund for another year. We would have been poor, completely destitute with a newborn. I panicked."

His face fell and shame clouded his features. "I have a job," he countered, his voice so low I barely heard him.

I let out a frustrated sigh. He had a job making art that barely sold enough to cover the gas it took to get back and forth from the studio.

"I know," I began as gently as possible. The truth was going to hurt, but it had to be said. He had to understand my reasoning, and then maybe we could work through this. Maybe he could even find it in his heart to forgive me. "But it's not enough to take care of our family." I reached for him as I spoke, gently laying my hand on his forearm.

Antonio pulled away quickly as though my touch scorched him. His nostrils flared and his lip curled in disgust. It was in that moment that I realized he would never forgive me.

I wanted to work it out. I still loved him, but I broke us. The damage was irreparable, and I couldn't blame him for how he felt. Fists balled at his sides, he made for the door, prepared to leave. He threw it open and paused, turning to speak, but didn't turn far enough around that he'd have to lay eyes on me.

"I have rights. I expect you to respect them, or I will take legal action."

When he quietly shut the door behind him, I vowed to never try to keep our child away from him again.

What I didn't know at the time was that Antonio was about to make his big break as an artist. I'd been worried about his ability to provide for us, which drove me to deceive both men into thinking the baby was Dalton's. But within a year he was making nearly six figures, and true to his word, he expected to be involved in our child's life. He was there for all the prenatal appointments, the birth of our daughter, and kept her every other weekend and sometimes during the week. Co-parenting with him was a breeze.

Wheat fields surrounded me as far as the eye could see; a weathered red barn and a white farmhouse the only permanent fixtures dotting the muted gold that blanketed the landscape. Parked several yards away were trucks and trailers with workers scurrying about, setting up equipment. It was my first day on the job and the band I'd be representing was filming a music video today, so I had to come to them. I was nervous to meet everyone. This was my first real job using a degree I never expected to need.

Peeking into the rearview mirror one last time, I checked my makeup and smoothed down my hair, ensuring every last strand was secured into my sleek, low ponytail. I was determined to present myself with an unrivaled air of professionalism, and having stripper hair and lipstick smudged on my teeth wasn't going to cut it here. This was the big leagues. Even I knew that. This band was already starting to make waves, but I would turn them into a hurricane.

I stepped onto the dirt road and headed for the largest of the buses. Surely that was where I would find who I was looking for. I reached up with a closed fist, prepared to knock on the door when a deep, southern drawl stopped me.

The sound sent a wave of awareness through my body. I could practically feel the vibrations of his baritone in my chest. *And other unmentionable places.*

"Ms. Venetti?" I turned to find deep blue, ocean eyes staring back at me. Dark brown sideburns and a long, well-kept beard framed a classically handsome face. Tan arms peppered with colorful tattoos strained the sleeves of his black tee shirt. Expertly distressed jeans hugged strong thighs, his legs ending in a pair of well-worn cowboy boots. This man wasn't at all my type, but I had to force my mouth closed to avoid looking like a stunned fish out of water. Which was exactly what I felt like at the moment.

He smirked. The man actually *smirked*. At me. Normally I would've tossed my hair over my shoulder and given him the "you wish, pal" look, but that wasn't an option here. I cleared my throat and turned to him, clutching my folders in one hand and tucking them close to my body while reaching with the other for a shake.

"Yes, that's me. Are you Mr. Fulton?" Eric Fulton was the band's manager and would be my point of contact.

His smile grew as he slid his warm hand into mine. "You can call me Eric."

That sound would be my undoing. If sex had a sound, it would be this man's voice.

I gave him a tight smile and pulled my hand from his grasp, fighting the urge to shake off the sensation he left tingling up my arm. I couldn't think about that, not here, not with someone with whom I had to work. It had simply been too long. I hadn't felt a man's touch since the ill-fated date my mom convinced me to go on when Lucia was six months old. I'd made the mistake of letting him kiss me and he took that as permission to fondle me on the ride home. I managed to keep his hands from venturing under my blouse and slammed the door shut before he could follow me out of the backseat of our Uber. After ignoring his calls for weeks, he finally stopped trying.

Before that, it had been Dalton when he believed I was carrying his child, but his heart wasn't in it. Neither was mine, if we were being honest. I craved Antonio's touch for a long time, especially when the pregnancy hormones came raging on, but he always kept me at a safe distance. Occasionally I would catch him watching me with longing in his eyes, especially when I held our newborn daughter in my arms, but he never let himself look very long. I told myself I deserved it, knowing his scorn was my cross to bear, but it didn't make it hurt any less.

"How does that sound?" Eric asked, watching me expectantly.

I'd completely zoned out. My first interaction at my new job and my mind had drifted off to left field. I'd be lucky to still have this job by the end of the day if I kept on like this.

"I'm sorry, can you repeat that?" I asked, fighting the urge to just nod and smile. I wasn't that girl anymore. This was real life. I had a daughter to feed and a roof to put over her head. I had to be all business here. A pretty face and Daddy's money wouldn't get me as far here as it did back home.

"I asked if you wanted to meet the band and get a quick rundown of how our operation works." He was fighting to keep that smirk at bay, but the corner of his lip twitched. He could tell I was uncomfortable and he was enjoying it.

"That would be great," I replied, letting out a quiet sigh of relief when he turned to lead me away.

We approached the trailer and Eric knocked on the door. It swung open and he leaned in. "You guys decent?" he called into the room. Several male voices chimed in with crude and inappropriate responses. "Watch your mouth," he warned. "There's a lady present."

Without thinking, I let out a little snort. Not many people would refer to me as a lady. He tilted his head back, one brow tipped up inquisitively. I immediately schooled my features, but my face flamed as his eyes slid down my body before returning his attention to the people in the trailer.

"Get out here and meet your new publicist." Eric stepped back and four young men emerged. "Brooks McCoy, lead guitar. Ian Black, drums. Cooper Dennison, bass. And Ethan Harris, lead vocals," Eric offered, pointing to each band member in turn.

The last man scowled at him, throwing his arms up in frustration. "Why you always gotta downplay my talent? You know I'm a kick ass guitar player, too."

"And so humble, too," Eric retorted.

Fighting back a smile, I introduced myself, assuring them that I was there to help them achieve their dreams.

"What's your favorite song of ours?" The question came from Ian.

I recognized him even before Eric introduced us, due to the extensive research I'd done on the band. I listened to their entire first album several times to get a feel for their style. And honestly, their music wasn't bad. There was a rock-n-roll edge to a lot of their songs, and they didn't overdo the steel guitar and fiddle like some of their peers.

"*What's Left of Me* or *One More Shot*. It's a toss-up. They both resonated with me, but for different reasons." I was met with stunned silence. They didn't think I'd actually listened to their music, but I had. Every last track. Several times over.

Ian's lips curved slowly until a genuine grin split his face. "Welcome to the family."

A man in a band tee shirt approached as I spoke with the guys, trying to get to know each of them better. From the corner of my eye, I noticed him talking to Eric. I always knew where the band's manager was at all times. I could feel him, his presence like a beacon I tried hard to ignore.

"Set's ready," Eric announced, putting a halt to our conversation. "Ethan, they need you in makeup. You're the last one whose nose needs powdered." That sexy smirk made its return and I looked away just in time to see Ethan's face fall, but he nodded, his jaw set in a hard line as he stalked off to another trailer.

What was that all about?

The band dispersed, leaving Eric and me to stand awkwardly across from each other. Well, *I* was standing awkwardly. He stood with an easy confidence that made me even more flustered.

"Shall we?" Eric motioned for me to join him so I stepped up to his side, letting him lead me to the house. "They'll be shooting the indoor scenes first. It's mostly just Ethan for this part. Then they'll move outside and try to get some usable footage of the band playing in that field as the sun goes down." He pointed to a section off to our left, freshly cut into a semi-circle where the band's instruments were waiting to be played. Ethan emerged from the trailer followed by a stunning, petite blonde. She looked every part the lead in any country music video with her tiny denim shorts, flowy top, and cowgirl boots. I expected her to follow him onto the set, but she ducked under a tent where refreshments were being served to grab a bottle of water.

"The makeup artist," Eric offered, noticing me watching the young woman. "She and Ethan have... a history."

Intrigued, I turned back to her, the wheels starting to spin as I envisioned what their shared connection could do for this music video.

Eric offered to let me watch them film and I eagerly agreed. We entered the house behind the director and were instructed where to stand. We watched for an hour as Ethan moped around the house, gazing longingly at an empty bed, running his fingers through his hair as he stared out the kitchen window. The crew spent a solid ten minutes filming him with his hands braced on the bathroom sink, staring at his own reflection in the mirror, the dim lighting creating a lonely, morose atmosphere.

"Cut!" the director ordered, clearly unsatisfied with the performance.

I was no expert, but what they were doing was not at all captivating. I didn't believe him. His pain was superficial, at best. The video was going to flop if something didn't change.

I hoped I wasn't overstepping and risking my job on day one, but I was willing to go out on a limb to make this band a success.

"Could I make a suggestion?" I asked, awkwardly raising my hand. The director shot a glare at me over the rim of his glasses and I let my arm fall back to my side. Eric sucked in a startled breath beside me.

"And you are?" the director asked, obviously perturbed that someone would dare question his vision.

I straightened my spine, instilling every bit of confidence into my voice as I could. My pageant training came roaring back to life as I spoke with eloquence and authority.

"This song is all about longing, yet we don't see who he's longing for." The director gripped his chin in his hand and studied me, but I refused to wither under his scrutiny. "Where is the woman he's pining after? The audience needs to see her. They at least need a few brief glimpses of her, of their time together before she left." The song was about love gone wrong and wishing things had turned out differently, but they were only showing the aftermath, not what had been lost.

"What you're suggesting would set us back weeks. We'd have to hire an actress to fill that role," he scoffed.

"I don't think you need one." A look of confusion washed over his face. Before it turned to irritation, I continued, "The makeup artist. Have you seen her? She would be perfect." A low curse left Ethan's mouth, but the director's interest had been piqued. "She wouldn't have to do much, at least nothing that would require much acting skill."

He was quiet for several heartbeats, pondering my proposal. "Bring her in," he finally said with a wave of his hand.

"What are you doing?" Eric hissed, gripping my elbow and pulling me into the empty hallway. His fingers practically seared my skin, but I ignored the electric current of attraction, allowing my irritation to slide to the forefront.

"Excuse me?"

"Do you have any idea who that is in there?"

"No," I answered defiantly, lifting my chin.

"Sonny Devlin is one of the most sought-after directors in Nashville. You can't just come in here and try to take over his shoot!"

"I didn't try to take over anything. I merely made a suggestion. And it worked." I motioned to the front door as it opened and the young woman walked in, her eyes two round pools of sapphire. She looked scared and I almost regretted bringing her into this.

"That's not the point! You're their *publicist*. This is your first day on the job. Do you even know how this industry operates?"

"I know how to do my job, Eric. Their best interest is my main concern, and this video had a first-class ticket to Suckville." *Uh, oh*. The old Gianna was rearing her ugly head. "Nobody is going to watch him mope around an empty house and then play his guitar in a wheat field. The imagery should reflect the meaning behind the lyrics. That's where *she* comes in." I motioned vaguely toward the kitchen where the young lady would most likely be by now. "So excuse me for making a tiny little suggestion to your rock star director. If he can't make changes on the fly that will make for a better music video, then he's not as great as you make him out to be."

He opened his mouth to respond, a fire burning in the raging blue depths of his eyes – eyes I could see so clearly because we'd gotten closer as we argued – when a throat cleared behind me. My head snapped up and the director's assistant had the decency to look sheepish as she nervously tucked a strand of hair behind her ear.

"They're about to start," she said.

While Eric and I were away, Sonny had brainstormed a new idea that included Tiffany, the makeup artist. When the cameras began to roll, it took Ethan and Tiffany several takes to get comfortable, but once they did, their chemistry exploded on the screen. I believed every word Ethan sang against her lips. I felt his hurt when she walked away, dropping his outstretched hand in her wake. When he cupped her face, sliding his fingers into the back of her hair, it was obvious it wasn't the first time. I was starting to understand what Eric meant by the two having a history.

When we wrapped up inside, we took a break to grab something to eat. Eric slid into the seat across from me as I bit into a crunchy pickle spear.

"I owe you an apology," he announced, framing an overflowing plate of food with his forearms on the table. I wrinkled my nose at the sight of several different dishes mixing together. If he noticed my reaction he didn't let on. "I was too harsh on you earlier and didn't trust your ability to make such a bold suggestion, but you were right. Your idea was exactly what was needed to make this video into a winner." He hung his head. "I'm sorry I doubted you."

"Apology accepted," I replied graciously. What I really wanted to do was ask if his skepticism was because I was female, or that I was at least ten years his junior, but I bit my tongue in the interest of remaining professional. He unnerved me, somehow burrowing his way under the thick skin I'd developed over the years, but I wouldn't let anything get in my way of excelling at my job… and hopefully keeping it for a while.

We wrapped up shooting just after dark. The band was set to return the next day, but I'd be meeting with the marketing team to iron out the details of their upcoming tour. I was equally disappointed and relieved that I wouldn't be seeing Eric again for a couple days. That man was dangerous, and if I knew what was good for me, I would keep my distance.

CHAPTER TWO

Since I was new to the PR firm, the band was my only assignment and all my time and energy was dedicated to them. I was able to focus solely on them and help make their careers soar. And boy, did I work my tail off to make that happen. By the second week, they had several radio and TV interviews lined up during the upcoming month. By week three, they were booked for a live performance on one of the biggest morning shows in the country, and their first album was seeing sales like they hadn't experienced. Their visibility had grown exponentially and people were starting to take notice.

For the entire first month, I tried to avoid Eric as much as I could, which wasn't nearly often enough. Luckily, I was rarely ever alone with him. Both of us were so busy making preparations and trying to keep the band members out of trouble, we mostly saw each other in passing or when we had to attend brief meetings with other members of our team present. Even then, the sexual tension between us was palpable. I just hoped nobody else noticed. Thankfully we mainly communicated via text or email and had very little time for face-to-face conversation.

Until the album release party.

Kylie Harper was quickly becoming country music's new "it" girl and was co-headlining the tour with our band. Her new album had just dropped and was heading straight for the top of the charts. Tonight was the album release party and the label was hosting a small, intimate event with some of Nashville's elite in attendance. The clout was good for the band. Kylie would bring more fans out to the shows, garnering more exposure for the guys.

"For someone whose main focus is getting her clients noticed, you try awfully hard to blend in with the crowd." Eric's deep voice and hot breath on the back of my neck sent shivers down my body. I hastily chewed the chocolate covered strawberry I'd just popped into my mouth and swallowed before turning to face him. "It's impossible, though." His lips quirked, pulling into a lopsided grin.

"Even wearing that black dress in a sea of people wearing the same color, you still manage to stand out." My cheeks warmed at his compliment, but I fought the giddy laugh bubbling up my throat.

"Looks like I'm not the only one trying to blend in." I nodded toward his monochrome ensemble. He was dressed in a black tee shirt, dark wash jeans, and black boots, the only splash of color on him the intricate tattoos covering his arms.

"I'm used to fading into the background." He shrugged. "But you, I have a feeling, are used to being front and center."

I narrowed my eyes, my lips forming a tight line. What the hell was that supposed to mean?

"I don't mean that in a bad way," he hurried to explain, holding up his hands imploringly as I glared. "But you radiate confidence and determination. You command a room. Haven't you noticed how everyone goes still and silent when you speak? Hell, you got one of the most renowned music video directors to listen to your suggestions within minutes of meeting you. Most people don't have that kind of power."

He stepped closer to me as he spoke, his eyes burning with awe and passion; cobalt blue rimmed in the shade of the night sky. His gaze was intense, but his words were what pierced the armor of my heart. No one had given me that kind of praise in years. Not Dalton, not Antonio. Not even my parents. I'd been that girl once, the one you couldn't look away from. It was how I'd excelled on my high school debate team and blew other contestants out of the water during my pageant days.

When Dalton and I got engaged, I let some of that fire fizzle out, leaving only a few smoldering embers. I was so focused on becoming the perfect trophy wife and maintaining my social standing that I lost sight of who I was.

Eric's piercing gaze pulled me back to the present and I watched as it dropped, landing on my mouth. For a moment, I thought he might kiss me, but instead he reached for the table behind me, retrieving a napkin.

"You've got a little something," he explained, lifting the cloth to my lips. "Right there."

He dabbed at my bottom lip, gently wiping away the remnants of the treat I was devouring when he approached. His eyes lifted to mine as I held my breath, trying not to react to his touch and woodsy scent filling my nostrils. My pulse thrummed as the heat of his skin seeped through the napkin.

He held my stare for a long moment, leaving me feeling unsettled and more aroused than I had any right to be around him. Dropping his hand, he took a step back and shook his head like he just realized we were in a room full of people and our interaction was growing far too intimate.

"Would you like another drink?" he drawled, motioning to my nearly empty glass of wine.

"No, thanks. I've gotta drive home."

"I can take you home," he offered. I stiffened and he cursed under his breath. "Or... I mean, there are taxis and Ubers everywhere. It's Nashville, after all," he added cheekily, misreading my discomfort.

I wasn't worried about what he'd do if we were alone in a car together. I was worried about what *I* would do. My body screamed for attention and I was terrified he'd give it to me. Imagining those strong hands with their long, deft fingers tangling in my hair and gripping my hips had my blood heating, my skin flushing in response.

"I guess one more wouldn't hurt," I blurted out, hoping he'd step away to retrieve my drink and give me a moment to collect myself. The casual setting and dark, sensuous atmosphere had all my defenses slipping away. I was letting my guard down and that was dangerous.

"What's your poison?"

"Merlot."

"Be right back."

He sidestepped me, heading toward the bar and returning a few minutes later with a drink for each of us. His was a stout, judging by the dark liquid with its foamy top filling his glass. He passed me the glass filled with the deep red I'd come to prefer over the Chardonnay I used to drink when Dalton and I were together. I shook away thoughts of my ex-fiancé, unwilling to let past regrets and wrongdoings bleed into the present.

We mingled with other partygoers and I focused on networking on behalf of the band. They played a few songs up on stage, but when they finished, I made sure to introduce them to as many people as I could, making meaningful connections we could use as their careers flourished. Eric was frequently by my side, pointing out some of the important players within the industry that I didn't already know. We worked the room, tag teaming our targets, hyping up our boys.

As the night wound down, we had a stack of business cards and promises of interviews to follow up on Monday morning. Eric and I were discussing the week ahead when I spotted one of the record label executives I hadn't officially met yet. I alerted my companion and started to head towards the man in the expensive suit, but Eric stopped me, his hand curling around my arm.

"Don't," he warned, his voice low but commanding.

His touch sent a zing of electricity up my arm and I fought back a shiver. If anyone else had done that, I probably would have wrenched away and told them where to go, but the look of concern in Eric's eyes gave me pause.

"Stay away from him." His eyes pleaded for me to take heed. He knew I wasn't the type of person to be ordered around; that much he could tell from our short time working together. "He has a bad reputation."

My gaze flicked to the man in question. He had a beautiful young lady on his arm, a svelte blonde dripping in diamonds and wearing a curve-hugging dress that showed off her ample figure. Mr. Gardner was easily twenty years her senior, but that wasn't what was unusual. It was the way he leered at the young woman carrying a tray of drinks who'd just left the group gathered around him. He sipped at his flute of champagne as his eyes raked up and down her body. It occurred to me then what Eric meant by "bad reputation".

I returned my focus to Eric. He was so close, I could feel the heat from his body and note the navy blue rimming his irises. Leaning into him would be so easy. Letting him wrap his arm around my waist and pull me close would ease a little bit of the tension building inside me. But would that satiate my hunger or make me want more? I needed to step away and put a little distance between us, but I couldn't make myself do it.

"Gianna." His voice slid over my name, smooth as honey and deep as the canyon into which I was about to plummet. If I fell, I'd never get out. There was no turning back if we crossed that line.

"Excuse me," I said in a rush, pulling away from him. He dropped my arm and stepped back, giving me some much-needed space. I didn't look at him – *couldn't* look at him – and bolted for the ladies room. The night was almost over. I only had to hold it together a little longer.

My skin was flushed and overheated when I looked into the mirror above the sink. I dabbed a cool paper towel over my chest and the back of my neck, careful not to disturb my makeup. Once I felt composed enough to return, I stepped out of the restroom to find Eric leaning against the opposite wall. He pushed off from it when he saw me, approaching me apprehensively.

"Are you okay?"

The concern etched across his face warmed me. I wanted to throw caution to the wind and act on instinct. All I could think about was wrapping my arms around his neck and digging my fingers into his dark hair as I pulled his mouth down to meet mine. I was a woman starved for affection, and he was a man whose mere touch promised explosive passion and unrivaled satisfaction.

"Yeah, I just got... overheated." Not entirely a lie. His eyes darkened at the admission and his hands flexed at his sides as though he was fighting the urge to touch me. It was a good thing he could maintain control, because if he lost it, I wouldn't stop him. I'd let him have his way with me even if it meant jeopardizing my career.

He heaved a deep breath, letting his taut muscles relax, and reached out a hand to me. "Let's find you some water." I slid my palm into his and he gently closed his fingers around mine. His touch was meant to be comforting, but it sent that same pulse of arousal through me as it had earlier.

He found me a bottle of water and handed it over. I twisted off the lid and took a couple sips. We stayed quiet for the rest of the party, enjoying the live music. When it was over, Eric offered to walk me to my car and I let him. It was late and I really didn't want to be alone. He walked with his hands shoved deep into his pockets, most likely to keep from grabbing my hand again. My disappointment was wrapped precariously in a thin shell of relief. I wouldn't let it break through, containing it deep within so it couldn't be felt. When we reached my car, he stopped several feet away and gave me a wide berth. That disappointment began to swell, threatening to crack right through that tough shell I'd built around it.

"I guess this is goodnight," he said, keeping his hands cocooned in his pockets, a soft restraint against the passion threatening to break free.

"I guess so," I replied a little mournfully.

"I'll see you Monday."

We said our goodbyes and I drove home in a daze. My mom was still up but Lucia was fast asleep in her crib. Mom had come down to visit for the weekend, as she frequently did, and was more than happy to have my baby girl all to herself for the evening.

"How was the party?" she asked as I removed my heels and rubbed my feet.

"It was good," I answered vaguely, massaging my aching arches. She had little interest in the type of work I did, but always tried to be supportive and engage in conversation regarding my job. I appreciated her effort but was too exhausted to give her more.

She gave me a goodnight hug and I escaped to my room, changing out of my dress before slipping between the sheets. I drifted off to thoughts of Eric and his deep blue, bottomless ocean eyes as they seared into me, promising more than just a friendly touch.

CHAPTER THREE

Monday morning came way too quickly. I was dragging when I rolled in at eight a.m. Eric was perky as ever, his dark hair still damp from a shower, with two cups from the local coffee shop in his hand.

"Please tell me one of those is for me," I pleaded, already reaching for the latte. He knew I always ran late on Mondays and had started grabbing an extra drink on his way to our weekly meeting. I tried not to read too much into it, though, convincing myself it was just a friendly gesture. But when his fingers brushed mine, I felt that ever growing surge of awareness spark between us and sucked in a breath. He felt it, too. I could tell by the way his fingers curled and flexed as though I'd shocked him.

Things changed between us at the release party. Our connection was undeniable, our attraction to one another growing more apparent by the day. But I couldn't give in to the temptation. I had to stay strong. Building a life and future for me and my child was priority number one, which meant getting involved with a colleague was the last thing I needed right now.

We sat down for our usual Monday meeting and went over the schedule for the week. The guys had an interview on a morning radio show Wednesday that they needed to prepare for. That was where I came in. I had the afternoon blocked off for some coaching. All the band members were straight shooters, but there was a right way and a wrong way to answer questions and I didn't want them slipping up and saying the wrong thing.

Eric sat in on our mock interview where I peppered each member with questions, encouraging Ethan to take the lead on most responses that pertained to the band as a whole. It was what an interviewer would expect from the lead singer.

By the time we wrapped up for the evening, I was ready to get out of there and head home. Eric stopped me as I slid my purse strap onto my shoulder.

"We're all going out for dinner. Wanna join us?" he asked hopefully.

"I can't," I replied apologetically. "I've gotta get home to relieve the babysitter." What I failed to mention was that my mom was watching my daughter and would understand if I called her up and told her I was going to be late, but I had to maintain some boundaries. Eric was making that increasingly difficult.

"No worries. Maybe next time," he offered with a grin. He knew I was a mom and that my daughter was just a baby. He had children from a previous marriage, but he didn't talk about them much. I got the impression it was a sore subject for him, as things didn't end well with his ex. Not wanting to pry, I avoided the subject and never asked questions. I wouldn't want someone digging into my past, so I respected his privacy.

Wednesday rolled around and I insisted the guys get an early start to prepare for their radio interview. All our hard work paid off, because they nailed it. Once it aired, the phones began ringing off the hook. More and more hosts requested interviews, but they would have to wait. Our next event was the televised interview with a big network in New York City.

We flew out on Thursday afternoon, arriving in the Big Apple just before dinner. I was a mess leaving Lucia behind, but managed to pull myself together before I arrived at the airport. She was spending a long weekend with Antonio and his family. His parents were absolutely smitten with her, just as my mom and dad were. I knew she was in good hands, but I still missed her like crazy.

We checked into our hotel and found our rooms. Eric's was right next to mine, a fact I tried to ignore as I got ready for dinner. The restaurant downstairs was no stranger to celebrities and up-and-coming artists. I was hoping to get my guys noticed. We'd be sure to post on social media where they were dining using trendy hashtags and cheeky captions.

As soon as drinks were served, a tall figure topped in a black Stetson approached the table. Ethan nearly choked on his whiskey when one of his idols walked up and shook his hand. I pulled out my phone and started snapping pictures of him with the five-time country album of the year award winner. He was a good sport, posing for pictures and even taking a shot with all of us before returning to his table.

"That was insane," Brooks gushed.

"Holy shit, my hands are shaking! Did that really just happen?" Ethan mused.

"You're damn right, it did. And I've got proof!" I handed over my phone with a huge grin. "Those are going straight to your social media profiles." He scanned through the pictures with the country superstar before passing the phone back to me. My gaze landed on Eric's and a blush crept into my cheeks. He was watching me with a mixture of pride and satisfaction.

After dinner, we decided to check out the nightlife and stopped at one of the swankier clubs. I was tired and wanted to retire for the evening, but I also wanted to keep an eye on everyone. The guys tended to get rowdy when left unsupervised. Eric was pretty good at keeping them in line, but as their publicist, I felt responsible for them and their image. So I tagged along, bringing up the rear of our little group with Eric by my side. We never let the guys stray too far from us, keeping to the periphery so they could cut loose and enjoy themselves. Occasionally someone would recognize them and ask for a picture or autograph, which they happily obliged.

"This never would've happened six months ago," Eric said, leaning in to be heard over the music. His warm breath stirred the hair tucked behind my ear and I fought back a shudder.

"What do you mean?"

"The attention," he replied, motioning to the gaggle of young women surrounding the band as they signed random objects and slips of paper. "They've never been recognized this easily, not outside Nashville, at least. This is all you."

His praise warmed me and I basked in it for a moment. My hard work and persistence was paying off.

"Come on, they deserve a little of the credit," I joked, nudging him playfully. That second beer I had was starting to go to my head, loosening my limbs and inhibitions.

Eric moved in closer, so close I had to tilt my head back to meet his gaze. I held my breath as he stared down at me, a predatory hunger darkening his eyes.

"You are so fucking adorable when you let loose like this. I wanna see more of it."

"I want to show you more," I confessed, dropping my focus to his lips.

He drew in a sharp, ragged breath, his chest brushing against mine with his inhale. I fought back a groan, wanting to beg him for more. He glanced up, finding the guys occupied with the ladies but not causing any trouble, and grabbed my hand.

"Let's dance." He led me onto the dance floor and wrapped his arms around my waist. Eric may have been country through and through, but he still knew how to move to the sensuous beat playing over the sound system. I let him pull me in close, our breaths mixing as our torsos slid against each other. My pulse skyrocketed, his touch causing gooseflesh to pebble my arms.

The song was over too soon. I wanted to stay wrapped in his arms, but I couldn't. I pulled away just as Ethan approached, dropping my gaze like I'd been caught doing something wrong.

But it didn't feel wrong.

It felt fucking amazing and I wanted more, but I didn't want my clients to think I was unprofessional.

"We're ready to head out," Ethan announced, clapping Eric on the shoulder. "Got an early start tomorrow, and I need my beauty sleep."

"Won't do you any good," Eric teased, and Ethan chuckled.

We made our way back to the hotel and Eric and I lingered in the hallway as they each went to their rooms. I was torn between inviting him in and escaping to my room to get away from his blazing intensity. I wanted him and he eyed me like he was ready to devour me whole.

I took the coward's way out and wished him goodnight, kicking myself as soon as the door shut behind me.

CHAPTER FOUR

I REMOVED my heels and dress, wondering if I was making a mistake. A tryst with Eric could be just what I needed to get out of my funk, but would it make things weird at work? Could we pretend like nothing happened, or would I imagine how his hands felt on my body while I sat across from him at our weekly meetings?

I'd just turned the water on in the shower when I heard a knock at the door. Shutting it off, I slipped on my robe and went to the door, tying the belt as I went.

Eric was standing on the other side, his hand braced against the door frame and his chest heaving. His gaze was on the floor, but when his eyes lifted, they dragged all the way up my body. My legs were bare and exposed beneath the short robe, the belt haphazardly tied in a bow.

I took a step back, silently inviting him inside. He shut the door and closed the distance between us, fingering the loop at my waist and pulling with just enough tension that I felt the tug, but not enough to untie it.

"If you don't want me to kiss you right now, tell me to leave."

I pressed my lips together in response, wanting to feel his mouth on every inch of me. In the next moment, his free hand cupped my face while the other yanked open my robe, exposing my nakedness underneath. His warm palm slid against my hip and his arm curled around me, drawing me closer as his tongue dipped inside my mouth.

I moaned into his kiss. It was euphoric and new, the culmination of weeks of stolen glances and subtle flirtation. He lifted me off my feet and I wrapped my legs around his back as he carried me to the bed. His belt buckle dug into my sensitive flesh, rubbing against me with each step he took.

He tossed me onto the bed and my robe flew open, each side pooling next to me. He swore and tilted his head back, an almost pained look crossing his features.

"You are fucking flawless," he praised, his fiery gaze meeting mine. He ripped his shirt off over his head and lowered his body over mine. His lips met mine again and I parted them, letting him inside. A growl rumbled in his chest as his hips flexed against my center. I gasped and his mouth left mine, moving to my neck and working its way down to my breasts. My back bowed off the bed the moment his tongue circled my nipple.

Flattening a hand on my stomach, he inched his way down and when his thumb connected with my clit, I let out a string of unladylike curses. His lips curved against my skin as he began circling the tender bud. My body had been neglected for far too long, so it didn't take long before an orgasm wracked my body. Legs shaking, I cried out, curling my fingers into his dark hair.

After a long moment, I finally peeled my eyes open to find him watching me reverently, but also with a hint of surprise.

"How long has it been?" He didn't have to elaborate. I knew what he was asking. It had taken less than a minute for me to reach my climax.

"A while," I admitted.

"Gianna," he began, brushing the backs of his fingers against my cheek. "If you don't want to take this any farther-"

"I do!" I barked out. "I mean, I want this. I want you."

"Glad to hear it."

His lips tipped up in a pleased, lopsided grin before he leaned in to kiss me again. I heard the unmistakable sound of a belt loosening and sliding through the loops of his jeans. My core tightened, anticipation tingling across my skin.

"Look at me," he whispered once his clothes were gone and he was sheathed with protection. I obeyed, opening my eyes to peer into his. His length nudged my entrance and I let my legs fall open a little farther, ready to welcome him inside. He held my gaze as he pressed into me inch by inch, retreating and pushing in further each time.

"Fuck, you're tight." He dropped his head to my shoulder, groaning in pleasure, and I nearly cried. It might have been silly, but I'd been so insecure about my body since having a baby. I worried that sex wouldn't feel the same, that *I* wouldn't feel the same. My stretch marks were a constant reminder of the beautiful life I brought into this world, but what if they were a turn-off for the next man I allowed into my bed?

Eric hadn't seemed to notice them, though. His eyes coursed down the length of me reverently at the first sight of my bare form, and his rough, calloused hands explored every inch of the skin I was insecure about. He made me feel beautiful and worthy.

Our lips collided and tongues tangled as he thrust into me, driving me closer to release. Every muscle in my body was strung tight as a bow string until finally, it snapped. I shouted his name as my body shuddered around his, my thighs quivering and heart pounding.

He followed shortly after with his own release and we laid there, both panting, our bodies covered in a thin sheen of perspiration. It was the most relaxed I'd been in nearly two years. Eric's lovemaking was like a drug, the euphoria and sedating effects unrivaled. I just hoped I didn't become addicted.

The next morning, I awoke to find the spot next to me empty. Had I dreamed that Eric was here last night? The lingering scent of his cologne and a long-forgotten soreness between my legs assured me that it was real. A note on the nightstand indicated he left early to avoid being caught sneaking out of my room by any of the band members.

The day went by more smoothly than I could've hoped. The band's performance on the morning show was impeccable and they interviewed like pros. They had another performance booked this evening at a historic venue where several big names had gotten their start.

The guys spent the afternoon resting up for their gig tonight, but I couldn't sit still. After video chatting with Antonio and Lucia, I decided to do a little exploring. I didn't want to go out alone in an unfamiliar city, so I decided to see if Eric wanted to join me. I knocked on his door, and when it opened a pleased grin spread over his face. He easily agreed when I proposed a little sightseeing and we hit the town.

The air was warm and the sun was bright as we strolled down the street, taking in our surroundings. Eric had been there before, but this was my first time in the city. He took me to an ice cream shop that served the most extravagant confections I'd ever laid eyes on. Though I had a stomachache by the time we left, it was totally worth it.

We talked about everything from music to our families. He told me about his kids, but quickly changed the subject when the conversation veered toward their mother. I, too, left out much of mine and Antonio's story. It was just too much, and there was no reason to share all my ugly truths with him just yet.

By the time we returned to the hotel, it was almost time for the show. I hurriedly freshened up and changed clothes, applying a little extra makeup to take my look from day to night.

The venue was nearly packed by the time the guys took the stage. They were halfway through their second song when I felt a tug on my arm. I turned to find Eric, a conspiratorial half grin tipping up one side of his mouth.

"Come on," he instructed with a jerk of his head.

"Where are we going?" I inquired, even as I allowed him to lead me away. We turned down the hallway where the dressing rooms were, and he glanced from side to side as he opened one of the doors. We slipped inside and he shut us in, nothing but the vanity light across the room to illuminate the space.

I opened my mouth to ask what we were doing in there when his kiss swallowed the sound. His hands cupped each side of my face as he devoured me, his tongue licking at the corners of my mouth. I was panting when Eric finally pulled away, dazed by his luscious lips and the fervor with which he'd kissed me.

"I've wanted to do that all day," he confessed.

"Why didn't you? We were together all day."

"I wasn't sure how you'd feel about it," he answered sheepishly. "We didn't really talk about what happened last night or whether we wanted it to happen again."

My lips turned down in disappointment. I thought he'd enjoyed himself as much as I did. It never crossed my mind that he wouldn't want to sleep with me again.

"Don't get me wrong, I definitely want it to happen again," he rushed to say. "But there are a lot of factors to consider since we work together."

"Then what was all that about just now?" I asked, waving a hand in the air between us.

"I kinda threw all my concerns out the window when I saw you this evening." He stepped back into my space, his voice low and sultry as he spoke. "I couldn't wait to get you alone so I could touch you and feel your body against mine again. I just hoped you wanted that, too."

"I do," I breathed. He kissed me again, pressing me against the door as his hand slid up my shirt.

"I want to keep doing this," he announced as his fingers plucked my nipple.

"Me too." My head fell against the door and he took his opening, his lips latching onto my neck.

"I meant even when we get back to Nashville, Gianna." He pulled away long enough to slip my shirt over my head.

"We can't tell anybody," I said, confirming my agreement as I unbuckled his belt and swiftly pulled it through the loops. It came loose with a loud snap and Eric growled, his hand tangling in my hair as he angled my mouth to his.

"Agreed."

Minutes later, I was glad the sound of the steel guitar playing overhead drowned out my screams of pleasure.

CHAPTER FIVE

RETURNING TO NASHVILLE WAS BITTERSWEET. I was glad to return to my normal routine and be with my daughter again, but I missed the layer of protection the distant locale offered my secret affair with Eric. Neither of us was ready to stop whatever it was we were doing, so we decided to see each other in secret. It was risky, but I couldn't seem to help myself when it came to him.

We agreed not to tell anyone and pretend outwardly as though nothing had changed between us while we were at work, but once we "clocked out" for the day, it was free rein. Most evenings, I had only a few minutes to spare before heading home and had to settle for nothing more than a quick make-out session. Other times, we had just enough time for a quickie at his apartment. He only came to my house when Lucia was with her father.

Our little arrangement was perfect. No strings attached. No pressure or expectations. And nobody knew about it.

Until Mr. Gardner, the record label executive with the 'bad reputation' found out.

I thought we were being careful, that we'd put on a good act for everybody, but our ruse had somehow been exposed. Apparently, the music mogul thought that if Eric had a chance with me, so did he.

He was wrong.

He learned the hard way never to put his hands on a Venetti woman without her permission the moment my knee connected with his balls.

He'd lured me into his office under false pretenses one evening. I believed I was meeting up with him and Eric to discuss the upcoming album release and tour. Turned out, he hadn't invited the band's manager at all. It was just a trick to get me alone in his office so he could proposition me. When I turned him down, he got pushy and I struck back like the old Gianna, the girl who didn't take any shit from anybody. I left him lying in a heap on the expensive Persian rug next to his desk and ran straight to Eric.

The next day, Eric stood with me as I brought the issue to the board of executives at the label, and before anyone could refute my claims, I produced some damning evidence. While I'd waited in Mr. Gardner's office, I began recording a video using an app that made me look like a puppy to show Lucia later. Luckily for me, when he entered the room, I startled and forgot to hit "stop" on the recording. It caught the whole exchange, including where I clearly asked him not to touch me again. He was immediately suspended and put under investigation.

Unfortunately, exposing him also exposed my relationship with Eric. Not only did he allude to our secret affair in the recording, but he also tried to use it to justify coming onto me. I worried there'd be repercussions, but nobody even acknowledged his claims.

Eric and I grew closer after that and decided to make our relationship official. Not much changed at work, though. We remained professional during working hours, but behind closed doors, all bets were off. When we were alone, he worshipped my body and made me feel cherished and whole, something I hadn't felt in a long time. With him, I learned to love myself again, striving to believe I wasn't this unredeemable monster, undeserving of happiness.

Once, I felt like a princess who lost her crown. Now, with Eric by my side, I felt like a queen. I was no longer the villain in someone else's story, but the hero of my own. And it felt good to finally straighten my crown.

THE END...
for now

THANK YOU SO MUCH FOR READING GIANNA! IF YOU'D LIKE TO KNOW MORE about Gianna's back story, check out Six Nights in Paradise.

For more spicy, small town romances with swoon worthy heroes and the women who tame them, check out the WILLOW BROOK FALLS series today!

ABOUT THE AUTHOR

Ashley is a USA Today Bestselling author who likes her small town romance extra spicy with a touch of angst and a splash of humor. Her swoon worthy heroes will melt your kindles (along with your undergarments). She resides in Ohio with her husband and two sons where she pens emotionally gripping love stories about imperfect people who find their happily ever after.

http://www.authorashleycade.com/

LOVING UNION

A Made Series Novella

Brooke Summers

HAYES

"Hayden will be there," Da says to his men. We're at our restaurant in downtown Chicago having our weekly meeting. The premises have been swept for bugs and made sure that we're not overheard. "Make sure that we're ready. I don't want anyone to know the plan."

He rises to his feet and I follow him out of the restaurant. My jaw is tight as I keep my head held high. Once again, I've been pushed out of the picture in favor of my younger brother. "Will you be coming with us?" Da asks, his words clipped.

He's angry, I get it, there's a lot to do in order to gain the majority control over Chicago, especially with the opposition of the Italians and the Masters. The latter are the ones putting up the biggest fight. They want The Gallaghers out of Chicago and for us to turn everything that we have built over to them. That's not going to happen and when they're interfering with our business, that affects us and my da isn't a man you want to get on the wrong side of.

I nod. "I'm coming," I say through clenched teeth. "Da, I'm your son, you don't even have to ask that question."

The man doesn't realize but he doubts me, at every turn he doubts everything that I do. It's subconscious on his level. I've seen the way that he acts toward me and the way he does with Hayden are completely different. He's already priming Hayden to take over.

It should be me. I'm the oldest son of Liam Hayes and Edwina Gallagher. I'm the one that should be second in command to my father, but I'm not. It's so fucking annoying, having to be second guessed every step of the way and he doesn't even know it. The worst thing is, I've never given him a reason to doubt me, never done a thing wrong, I've been at his side dutifully for years.

We stop by our vehicles and he turns to face me, running a hand over his face and sighs. "I'm sorry, I shouldn't have asked. I just worry about you."

"I may not be a fucking monster like Hayden, da," I snap, beyond pissed that we're having this conversation yet a-fucking-gain. "But that doesn't mean that I'm useless. I've worked my ass off for the Clann. I know who I am and what's expected of me. I do what I'm asked without question. Why do you believe that I'm not good enough?"

He stares at me for a beat. "I never said that."

I shake my head. "You didn't have to. You're training Hayden, Da, you've been training him for years to take over. You never once did that for me. So yeah, you don't have to say the actual words. I already know." I slide my hands into my pocket. "I've never given you any reason to doubt me, I've always done everything asked and then some."

His jaw slackens as he stares at me. "Son—"

"I've got to go," I say, not wanting to have this conversation, it's not only him, but the men have watched him do this and they do the same. He's unconsciously made it impossible for me to climb the ranks of the Clann. I don't hate my da, I just don't understand why he's done this.

Climbing into into my car I start my engine. I pull away from the curb and drive into the horrendous traffic. I strum my fingers against the steering wheel in frustration. Even having said this to my da, it's not going to change anything. It's too late for things to change. Hayden will become the Underboss and then go on to be the boss. I'm okay with that. My brother, even at his young age, is a monster. He will do whatever it takes to protect the family, as will I. We just go about it in different ways.

I drive around for a while, finding myself pulling up outside of a bar. It doesn't belong to us Irish, in fact, it doesn't belong to any criminal underworld family. It's a small dive bar that is run by a woman.

I step inside, and unlike when I step into a bar that we own, nobody turns to look at me. They carry on their conversation, the drink is flowing and the music is good. .

Ordering a whisky I sit down, I'm beyond pissed. My anger is simmering beneath the surface, I can feel it. Tomorrow it'll go back to how it always is. My da's a good man, he has faults like everyone else does.

"Who pissed in your wheaties?" a softly lyrical voice asks, I hear the laughter in her voice.

Lifting my gaze, I'm stunned by the brunette sitting opposite me. The woman has balls, that's for sure. "What's that?" I ask, not in the least bit trying to hide my annoyance.

She doesn't falter, instead, she smiles brightly at me. I can't help but note just how beautiful she is. Her eyes are wide and bright, she's got cute freckles that cover her nose and cheeks. "You're awfully mad, anger like that doesn't do anyone any good. Let it go."

I blink. "Let it go?" I echo.

She nods. "What good does it do? I mean, holding onto anger just destroys you, not the person who you're actually angry at."

"How would you know?" I retort.

She lifts a shoulder and shrugs, she's trying to seem nonchalant about it, but I see the pain in her eyes. "Family isn't all that it's cracked up to be. You know?"

There's a slight lilt to her words. It's barely there, almost as if she's trying to hide it.

"You're Irish?"

She flashes me a smile. "Takes one to know one," she replies. "I've lost my accent somewhat, I didn't think it was noticeable."

"It's noticeable," I tell her. "So, what's your family done?"

She waves her hand, her green eyes dull rather than with the humor they had when she first sat down. "It's been a long time since I've been home."

She's ignoring my question, which is understandable. This woman has piqued my interest. Something that hasn't happened in a while. "I'm Hayes," I tell her.

She flashes me a grin. "I know," she replies. "Everyone knows who you are. The son of the mafia man. I'm Anne-Marie."

I raise a brow. "You know who I am and yet you sat down beside me."

She grins wide. "Is that a problem?"

She's fucking crazy is what she is. "Not at all."

She flashes me that smile of hers and I know that tonight, she's mine. It's been a while since I picked up a woman at a bar. The women I've dated have been ones that have close ties to my family. The Gallaghers' marriages have always been about cementing ties with other families. To build The Clann to be the biggest and best it can be.

Anne-Marie isn't a part of this world. She's innocent. Yet, I want her.

"You want to take a walk on the wild side?" I ask.

Her laughter is husky and lyrical. "Who said anything about that? I came down to have a nice chat. Beats being alone, right?"

I can't make this woman out. She's unexpected and I like that.

"Where are you from?" I ask, wanting to keep speaking with her. I don't know what it is about her, but she has my attention.

"Originally, from Galway, but I've lived in America since I was twelve. I've been in Chicago for four years now."

I nod. "What brought you to Chicago?"

She reaches for her drink and brings it to her lips. "I'm studying law. I've got two semesters left and I'm done." She smiles widely, pride filling her words.

I lift an eyebrow. "You think it's a good idea, you sitting beside me?"

Her laughter is soft and I have a feeling it's a sound I could become addicted to. "I'd say you'd know more about the world of law than I do."

My lips twitch. "Of that I have no doubt. So you're going to become an attorney?"

"Who else is going to keep you out of prison?" she quips. "I want to help people who've been wrongly imprisoned." She looks up at me and I see the pain slice through her eyes. "But enough about me. What about you? What do you like to do outside of being Hayes Gallagher?"

I have a feeling there's a lot that she's hiding. I don't know why, but I want to uncover every little thing about her, find out who's hurt her and then kill anyone who did.

I stare at the woman that I've known for less than thirty minutes and yet, she's the first person to ask questions about me, about who I am outside of my family. No one, not one fucking person has ever asked me that question.

I want to know a fucking lot more about her. Being in this bar isn't what I want. I came here to get drunk and drown my sorrows. Now I want to spend time with the gorgeous brunette.

"You know what, Anna," I say roughly. I fucking love how her name rolls of my tongue.

"Anne-Marie," she corrects.

I give her a wide smile. "Anna," I repeat. "Let me take you to dinner and we can talk."

She pauses, her glass at her lips. I see the hesitation behind those beautiful green eyes.

"Just dinner, nothing else," I promise her. As much as I want to fuck her until she's screaming my name, I know she's not like that. So I'll bide my time, getting to know her until she's comfortable.

"Okay," she says softly. "Dinner it is."

I give her a big smile, something in my chest settles. I have no idea what, but I do know being around her is calming for me. I'm no longer feeling that anger I felt speaking with my da. Hell, I'm at ease and that's not something I've ever felt.

Anne-Marie is going to be mine. I just need her to realize that.

I SMOOTH my hands down my dress, my heart racing as I glance at myself in the mirror.

God, why on earth did I agree to go on a date? I must be losing my damn mind, that's why.

Hayes Gallagher has been someone who caught my eye a while ago. But the man has danger written all over him. He's gorgeous. I mean the man is a walking GQ model for christ sake, he's so damn sexy it makes my head spin, not only that, but he knows it. That smile of his makes my knees weak.

Agreeing to go on a date was stupid. I should never have sat down beside him. Doing so was foolish, but I couldn't help myself, there's a magnetic pull between us that I can't deny. I need to keep my head, I have a path that needs to be followed, I can't allow Pretty Boy to derail me. The cause I have is one that burns deep within me. I'm determined to become a lawyer, I'm going to finish law school and I'm going to help those that have been wrongly accused get the justice they need. I have to do it for Darragh. There's no other choice.

A knock at the door sends my pulse skyrocketing. He's here. Fuck. Am I ready for this?

I take a steadying breath and move toward the door, my apartment isn't huge, it's a studio apartment but it fits me perfectly. I've made it my own, I can't afford anything bigger, not with paying for school. Opening the door, I swallow hard. God, he really is handsome. He wears a suit really well, it's tailored to him, his white shirt crisp underneath the black blazer.

"Hey," I say once I'm able to find my voice. "You look handsome."

His gorgeous blue eyes rake up and down my body, heating with lust as they reach my face. "Anna," he says thickly. "You look divine."

"You're a smooth talker," I say with a smile, thanking myself for putting on makeup, it'll hide the fact that my cheeks heat.

"I am, but only for you," he responds quickly. "Are you ready?"

I nod. "Just need to grab my purse. Any hint as to where we're going?"

His grin is one of cockiness and secrecy. "Trust me, Anna, you're going to love the place I have chosen."

Growing up I hated being called Anna, Darragh would do it just to piss me off. No one has called me that since him and hearing Hayes do so was a shock, but I can't lie, I love that he does.

"Okay," I say softly, reaching for my purse.

I really hope we're not going anywhere too flashy, I don't think I'd be comfortable with that. Growing up we never had money, my dad worked hard to keep a roof over our heads while mam was a stay-at-home mam. We didn't have much, but what we did have was hard fought for and I've learned to pinch the pennies when things get tough. Hayes is extravagant, everything about him screams money, it's one of the very many reasons I'm hesitant to let him pursue me. While I think we have amazing chemistry, I'm not sure if we're truly compatible.

He takes the keys from my hand and locks the door behind us, once done, he pockets my keys and reaches for my hand. I'm utterly shocked by his actions, while I should demand my keys back, I'm actually loving that he does that, it's very chivalrous.

"You had a good day, Anna?" he asks as we walk down the stairs.

"Yeah, it's busy, exams are coming up soon, so I've been studying and working."

"Where are you working?" he asks, not once letting go of my hand.

"Just at a coffee shop, I needed somewhere with flexible hours," I say without giving too much away, I have no doubt if I give him the location of my job he'd show up. "How about you? How was your day?"

He lifts a shoulder. "Same shite, different day," he responds evenly.

I sigh. "I wasn't asking about your work, Hayes, I was merely curious if you did anything good or if something happened to make your day bad. It's a conversation."

He squeezes my fingers. "Shit, I'm sorry, Anna. I'm not used to this and got defensive. Talking about my job is never going to happen."

I nod. "I know, but we can talk about our days without having to delve into our jobs if need be."

His eyes soften and I know I've said the right thing. "Thanks," he says thickly. "Today wasn't the best, I'm tight with my family but fuck can they be annoying at times. There's nothing worse than feeling ganged up on at times. But I've been looking forward to this date."

My stomach flips at his words. "Have you?"

He chuckles as he clicks the button of his key fob and his car unlocks. "Let me guess, you haven't?"

I shake my head. "I guess getting involved with someone like you isn't the smartest move. I'm not sure if it's even the right thing to do."

"I get that, but now you've taken this plunge, let's see where it gets us. We'll have dinner and go from there. No pressure whatsoever."

I narrow my eyes at his seemingly innocent tone. "Now why don't I believe that?"

He chuckles. "Smart lady," he says as he climbs into the car.

———

"So?" he questions as we leave the restaurant.

Tonight has been without a doubt the best night of my life. I didn't expect it to be anywhere near as good as it was. He is the perfect gentleman and talking to him was easy and I feel so comfortable around him. It's making my decision about him a hell of a lot harder.

"Better than you thought?" he asks with a grin.

I laugh. "Definitely. I'm not going to lie, I had thought you'd take me to a pretentious restaurant, one that I'd feel uncomfortable in. But bringing me here was amazing."

It's been a very long time since I had home cooked Irish food, I think the last time was when I lived at home. It was such a comfort to eat and it brought back a lot of happy memories.

"Thank you, tonight has been amazing," I duck my head as once again my cheeks heat. Something that's happened a lot this evening.

"If you're not ready to call it a night, how about we go to my place and continue talking?"

I raise my head, my heart pounding. "Talking, is that what we're calling it?"

His laughter is rich and deep. "Sure, why not." He slides his arm around my shoulder. "Anna, baby, I'm not trying to have sex with you. If that's what you'd like, fuck, I'd be more than happy, but I'd like to get to you know you, is that so hard to believe?"

Had he said it to me last night I'd have said yes, but this evening has been magical, better than I could have ever dreamt. I saw a side to him that I hadn't expected. A side that was filled with happiness and ease. He wasn't the Mafia man, but just Hayes and I really liked what I saw.

"No, it's not. Yes, I'd love to come home with you."

He hauls me close to him and smiles, once again my knees go weak from it. Holy hell this man is lethal, especially when he pulls out the big guns.

"You have a big family?" I ask. "I don't know much about it, just what I've read in the newspapers and magazines. You and your brother are a hot commodity."

He shakes his head. "Those rags are shite, they write whatever the fuck they want, half the time it's not even true, the other half, it's exaggerated." He gives me a wink and I swear I fall so hard for him right here. "But I have one brother and one sister, I think I have a couple dozen cousins at this stage. The fuckers breed like rabbits."

I press my lips together to stop myself from laughing. "Really?" I say with a raised brow. "Not just pushing the whole Irish stereotype?"

He shakes his head, his lips twitching. "Trust me, it's a real thing." He glances down at me. "What about you? Hmm, what's your family like?"

"Ah, the usual. You know the overprotective family that wants the best for their kids so move to America in hopes of getting it."

It never works out that way though, especially for those families that aren't flush with money, we end up even poorer than when we left Ireland.

He stops up by the car, his strong hands slide into my hair, sending shivers down my spine. His deep, smooth voice fills my ears. "You're setting out to change that though, aren't you honey?" His gorgeous blue eyes lock onto mine, their intensity making it feel like he can see right through me.

"Hopefully," I say softly. "I want to give my children all the things I never had."

His gaze heats up and I can feel his desire emanating from him. My eyes dart down to his lips, slightly parted and oh so tempting. They seem closer than before and I can't tear my gaze away. My feet are rooted to the ground, anticipation building in my belly. I know what's about to happen and I want it with every fiber of my being. God, I want him to kiss me.

As if reading my thoughts, he leans in slowly, giving me a chance to pull away if I wanted to. But I don't, his lips crash onto mine with a hunger that should scare me. It's as though everything around us fades and time stands still. I lose myself in him, in the taste of his lips and the feel of his touch.

As we finally break apart, gasping for air, I realize nothing will ever be the same again. This man has got me hooked and I'm not sure if I'll be able to walk away. Glancing up at him, my chest heaving, I see his eyes they're wild and untamed. He's looking at me with such hunger in his eyes. I swallow hard, knowing that this is only the beginning for us.

I just pray it's not the end of me.

HAYES

I'M STARING at her lips, their plump and fuckable, I can almost feel them against mine again. The drive to my place was fucking excruciating. Sitting that close to her but unable to touch her. Christ.

Fuck," I hiss under my breath as I can't resist the desire to pull her closer to me. Her body pressed against mine with a low grunt escaping her lips, sending a jolt of electricity through me. My cock strains against the fabric of my pants, pleading for release, begging for a chance to dive deep inside her. I haven't been able to stop thinking about this woman since I met her yesterday.

"Hayes," she murmurs softly, her voice filled with uncertainty.

"Say the word and we stop," I assure her, not wanting to push her beyond what she's ready for. Despite my reputation, I wouldn't force her to do anything she's not ready for.

Her tongue darts out to wet her bottom lip, dilated pupils betraying her arousal as she shakes her head. "I want you," she confesses, giving in to the undeniable chemistry between us.

I can no longer resist, plunging my tongue past those luscious lips and claiming her mouth in a heated kiss that leaves us both breathless.

I skirt my hand down her body, coming to stop on her delectable ass and give it a good squeeze. She moans into my mouth and I smirk. Shit, I don't want to wait. I need to be inside her. I've never needed anyone as much as I need Anna.

I take my hands off her and unbuckle my belt, yanking down my zipper to free my cock. It's rock hard and standing to attention. "I've wanted to do this since the moment I met you," I tell her as I rip my lips from hers.

She swallows hard, her eyes hesitant but filled with desire as she reaches behind herself to unzip her dress. I watch in awe as she steps out of her dress, revealing her perfect body beneath. Her confidence is intoxicating and it only makes me want her more. My breathing deepens as she slowly removes her panties, leaving her standing before me completely naked. "You're so fucking beautiful," I growl. "So fucking perfect," I grunt as I step closer to her. I need her desperately.

Closing the distance between us, I pull her against me once again, our bodies mold together perfectly. Our lips meet in a frenzy. My hands grip onto her ass as I lift her up into the air, her legs wrapping around my waist and her arms around my neck. I line my cock up at her entrance, the heat of her pussy enticing me, I thrust hard and fast, burying myself inside of her. She lets out a strangled cry and my heart stops as I realize what has happened.

"Ah, Anna," I say hoarsely. "Why didn't you tell me?"

She shakes her head, her expression apologetic. "I'm sorry."

Without hesitation, I press my lips to hers, sealing our fate. She is mine now, and I have no intention of letting her go. As if I ever could.

"Don't apologize," I growl possessively. "Never fucking apologize, Anna. You're mine, baby. All mine."

Her smile is soft and filled with innocence, and happiness. Yeah, she's mine. Fuck.

I begin to move, slowly at first, wanting her to get used to my size. As she begins to moan, I know she's ready for more, so I grit my teeth and let go. Christ, she feels so fucking good.

My movements become methodical, thrusting in and out of her with precision and purpose. I hit deep inside of her, loving the way she throws her head back, and releases a long groan. "God," she moans.

My pace is unrelenting as I fuck her hard and fast. Never did I think it would feel so damn good, her pussy so hot and tight. A man could get fucking addicted to her. She's intoxicating. She's the drug that will have you wanting more, get you hooked and never let you go.

"Hayes," she moans, her pussy contracting around my cock. "More, please," she begs.

My fingers grip her hips possessively, leaving bruises in their wake. The thought of branding her with my touch only fuels my arousal further. I pound into her relentlessly, seeking release from the overwhelming pleasure coursing through me.

"Yes," she cries, her pussy spasming as her orgasm washes over her. "Oh Hayes," she whimpers.

I'm lost, the way her pussy squeezes my cock, suffocating it. I'm gone. I hammer into her once more, burying myself to the hilt and releasing inside of her with a groan of her name.

We're both breathing hard, none of us speak. My knees are shaking but I keep a hold of her while we both come down from our orgasms.

Christ, neither did I think I'd find my one. Until now.

Three months later

My knees tremble as I sit in the doctor's office. Glancing around I see the waiting room filled with happy couples. I'm nineteen, in my second year of studies, I can't believe this is happening. How could we be so reckless?

The automatic doors slide open with a soft hiss, and my heart stutters as I catch sight of the tall, dark, and handsome man walking towards me. Hayes. Just the sight of him sets my heart racing, and I can't help but feel giddy and nervous all at once. I never intended to fall for him, but there's something about him that I couldn't resist. Being with him feels so natural and comfortable. It's like I'm finally living, truly happy for the first time in my life. He means everything to me, and I can't imagine my world without him.

"You doing okay, Anna?" His voice pulls me out of my thoughts as he takes a seat beside me.

I nod slowly. "Yeah," I say softly. "How did you know I was here?"

He gives me a look that says it was a silly question. "Baby," he says, using the pet name that makes my heart flutter every time. "I have someone watching over you at all times. Now, why didn't you tell me about your doctor's appointment?"

I shrug, feeling a twinge of guilt in my chest. "I was scared," I admit quietly, averting my eyes to the floor. "I didn't know how you'd react."

"About what?" His voice is gentle yet demanding, and I can feel his heated gaze burning into me. "Are you sick?"

My heart pounds against my chest as I take a deep breath before blurting out the words that have been weighing on me since the moment I found out. "No, I'm not sick...I'm pregnant." The words slip out like word vomit and for a moment I wish I could take them back.

There's a long pause between us as silence fills the room. I desperately wish for him to hold me and tell me everything will be okay.

He reaches for me, intertwining his fingers with mine. "Anna," he says low. "God, baby, why didn't you tell me?"

I shake my head. "I didn't want you to be upset or hate me."

"Baby," he says thickly. "That could never happen. I love you, Anna, I fucking love you and this baby is a fucking blessing."

I turn to him, my eyes wide and filled with tears. "You're—" I swallow back the sob. "You're happy?"

His grin makes my knees go weak. "So fucking happy."

I lean against him, blinking the tears away. God, how the hell did I get so lucky?

"When we're finished here," he begins. "We're going to my parents. It's time for you to meet the family."

My body tenses up like a coiled spring. He's been talking about introducing me to his parents for weeks now, but the thought of it has always sent shivers down my spine. I've been avoiding the topic, knowing deep down that I may never be ready for such a big step. But today, he seems determined to make it happen.

"If you're sure," I manage to say, my heart racing.

"Positive, they're going to love you."

I appreciate his confidence, but in all honesty, I'm not so sure. I am nothing like the Gallaghers - they come from wealth and privilege while I come from a poor family with nothing to offer.

I can sense Hayes's eyes on me, waiting for my response. With a deep breath, I look up at him and manage a small smile. "Okay," I say, trying to sound more confident than I feel.

He presses a kiss to the side of my head. "It's all going to be okay."

I really hope he's right.

We pull up to the grand mansion, my breath catches in my throat and I feel a wave of anxiety wash over me. The Gallagher estate is even more luxurious than I had imagined. I feel like a fish out of water as we step out of the car, my palms sweaty and heart thudding loudly in my chest.

Hayes squeezes my hand gently, offering me a reassuring smile before leading me towards the front door. He doesn't knock, just opens the door and pulls me through with him.

I'm still reeling from everything that's happened today, the pregnancy and Hayes' reaction to it and now I'm here, meeting his parents. I feel like I could throw up at any moment.

"Ma, da?" he calls out and I breathe deeply, trying my hardest to push through the anxiety and fear that's threatening to grip me in a chokehold.

A woman with dark hair walks out, a dish cloth in her hands, a bright smile on her face. "Hayes," she greets with happiness but that soon dies as she glances at me. "Oh, hello."

"Hi, Mrs. Gallagher, it's a pleasure to meet you. I've heard a lot about you."

Her eyes glance over me, a flicker of distaste passes through her eyes and it takes everything in me not to step backward and hide behind Hayes. "Well I know nothing about you," she replies through clenched teeth. "Hayes, why didn't you tell me you were bringing a friend?" she questions.

I swallow back the tears. I knew this would happen, I don't know why I allowed Hayes to make me feel as though it wouldn't.

"Ma," Hayes says, the word filled with anger. "Where's da?"

"In his office with Hayden, why don't you go and get him while I bring—" she pauses, her gaze flicking to me. "What's your name?"

"Anne-Marie," I supply.

She purses her lips. "At least you're Irish," she mutters. "I'll bring Anne-Marie into the dinning room to meet your sister."

I turn to Hayes and see that he's got a dark expression on his face. "Ma," he says, his chest heaving. She waves him off and starts to move toward the room she not long exited. "Baby," he says softly as he pulls me into his embrace. "It'll be okay."

I pull in a deep breath. No matter what, I'm stuck with this family. I'm having Hayes' baby, that means I'm stuck with Cruella-De-Ville as my baby's grandma. "I'm good," I promise him as I straighten my shoulders.

I've dealt with a whole lot worse than Edwina Gallagher. Hell, I doubt she's got a fucking patch on my own ma. I'll never, not ever let someone make me feel as though I'm not good enough, to make me feel as though I don't belong in this world. I've lived through it enough, I won't let it happen again.

Walking into the dinning room, I spot an older woman sitting on a chair, her gaze firmly on me, just like Edwina, her nose turned up as she watches me. I scan the room and see Hayes' younger sister, Jade seated at the table, just like her mam, she's watching me, thankfully not with disdain.

"Hey," she greets, sounding uninterested.

"Hi," I reply warmly. As much as they don't want me here or don't like me, I have manners and I'll use them. Despite my mam being a bitch, she instilled manners in me.

"Sit Anne-Marie," Edwina practically barks at me. "Would you like something to eat?"

I shake my head as I take a seat at the table. "No thank you, Mrs. Gallagher."

"Tea?" she offers.

"If it's not too much trouble, tea would be grand. Thank you."

She humphs and storms away. Thankfully, Hayes enters with his dad and brother on his heels. They, unlike the women in the family, give me a warmer greeting.

I stay quiet letting the family interact, I just pray things get easier. I don't think I could deal with this shit for the next eighteen years.

***.

"I'm so sorry," Hayes says as he starts the engine. We're finally out of that hellhole and I'm able to breathe once again. "They're assholes, baby."

"It's okay," I say, my head pounding. I forgot how much it takes out of you having to deal with people who don't like you. "I'm used to it."

His brows practically hit his hairline. "Your family," he guesses and I nod. "Tell me about them," he says, his voice soft but there's no denying the command.

"My dad was amazing, he did everything he could for us, my mam was another story. She loved Darragh and it showed. I was the scapegoat, anything that went wrong was my fault. I couldn't do anything right, the way I dressed, the way I looked, my weight, it was never good enough for her."

"Who's Darragh?" Hayes asks, his gaze intense as he glances at me.

"My brother," I whisper. "He was my best friend."

"What happened to him?" he questions softly.

"Mam was a bitch, Hayes and it only got worse when dad passed away. Darragh's best friend got mixed up with the wrong crowd. A gang that was into a lot of illegal shit. His best friend killed someone and for some reason, Darragh was the one that got arrested. We were poor, we couldn't afford an attorney. His defense was crap, he was sentenced to life without parole." I shake my head, willing the tears not to fall. "He died in prison, was shanked by the rival gang. He didn't belong to any gang, he just had a really shitty friend."

"How old were you when he died?"

"Sixteen," I whisper. "Mam only got worse. So the moment I could, I got the hell out of there and moved here."

He reaches for my hand and presses a kiss to it. "I won't let them treat you like that again," he promises me. "No one hurts you."

I close my eyes and pray that things will work out eventually. Hayes is my world and we're having a baby. No matter what happens, as long as we have one another, I think we'll be okay.

HAYES

I'M ON EDGE, watching as Anne-Marie smiles and dances with her friend. They're surrounded by men and it pisses me off. Some are getting a little too fucking close for my liking. Her gaze finds mine and I see the happiness shining in her eyes. God, I fucking love that woman.

I fucking hate that she's alone in this world. That the only person she can rely on is me. If I ever find her mam, I'll happily put a bullet in her brain. That bitch has made my wife be so self-conscious and is the reason she has low self esteem.

My wife is happy, we got married at the weekend, the only people present were her friend, Camilla, and my closest man, Jay. I didn't inform my family, I know their stance on Anna and I won't have them treat her like she's beneath them.

Last week when I introduced her to them, I had promised her it would be okay and boy was I wrong. Christ, never, not fucking ever had I seen my ma be so rude and disrespectful to someone. Anna did nothing wrong, she was polite and sweet and ma shit all over her. Not to mention granny did too and the rest of the family didn't help matters. I'm beyond pissed at how they treated her, she's the woman I love and not one of them tried to get to know her. Fucking bullshit.

My cell buzzes in my pocket and I look at the screen. Da calling. I grit my teeth. "Da," I greet as I answer my cell.

"Son," he says sternly. "Where are you?"

"At our club, what's up? You need me?" He tends to only call when he has a job for me to do.

"No, your ma's worried, she's not heard from you all week. She's wondering if you're still with your lady friend."

Anger moves through me swiftly. "Anne-Marie is her name, Da, use it," I growl. "She's more than a lady friend, had you actually gotten to know her or even spoken to her you'd have known that."

"Son, you really like her?" he asks, his voice filled with surprise.

I don't answer him, my gaze firmly on the dance floor where a guy's getting too fucking close to my wife. I get to my feet and start to move toward them. "Get off me," I hear Anna say, her voice filled with fear.

"Hayes?" I hear da ask through the line, my cell still to my ear.

"I've gotta go," I tell him, ending the call as I move quickly to get to my wife.

"You're hurting me," Anna cries as she tries to wrench her arm from his grip.

"You heard her," I growl. "Get the fuck off her."

The fucker turns to me, his eyes filled with darkness and rage. "Yeah, what the fuck are you going to do about it?" he slurs, he's drunk as a fucking skunk.

"Take your hands off my fucking wife," I growl.

My wife, the love of my life is staring at me with big wide eyes that are filled with tears and pain. She's pregnant and this cunt is putting his hands on her.

"This whore is your wife?" he laughs. "Christ, man." He shakes his head. "I bet she's a fucking good fuck?"

"Take. Your. Hands. Off. Her," I growl, enunciating every fucking word.

"Fuck you," he shouts, as he lunges at me, his fists clenched and ready to strike. I don't hesitate; I dive forward, grabbing him by the collar and slamming him into the nearest wall. A violent crack fills the air as his nose shatters against the solid brick. He crumples to the ground, blood pouring from his face.

"Anna," I say, my voice low. "Are you okay?"

She looks at me, her face contorted with pain and fear. "I'm fine, just shaken up," she manages to say.

"Fuck Hayes," I hear my da say, Christ, I had no idea he was at the club. "You good?"

"He's not to leave," I snap and watch da raise his brow in surprise. "Da, I'm fucking serious. I'm going to fucking kill him."

"Son," Da says low. "You sure this is the road you want to go down?"

I turn to him. "He put his hands on my wife. He called her a whore, what the fuck do you think?"

He blinks, shock evident on his face. "Wife?"

"Yes, Anna's my wife." I turn to the woman I love and pull her close. "Baby, are you okay?"

"Yes," she says, her body trembling. "I'm sorry."

Christ. She did nothing wrong. Not a fucking thing. "It's going to be okay," I promise her.

"We'll take him to the warehouse," Da says, there's no missing the anger in his voice.

I have no doubt he's got a fucking hundred questions to ask me, but right now, I'm focused on Anna.

I give her my car keys. "Go straight home." I instruct. Every fucking instinct in me is telling me to take her home myself. But I know she'll want to do it herself. She's more than capable and she'll lose her mind if she thinks otherwise.

I walk her out of the club, Da right behind us, that asshole being helped out by two of da's men. I help her into my car, knowing my da's watching my every fucking move. She's shaken up, I should be with her, but I need to sort this shit first. Once it's done, I'll be home with her.

"Love you," she whispers as I close the door.

I wink at her, letting her know that I feel the same. Right now, I don't need da's bullshit. The second she drives off, I turn to my da. "Let's get this shit done."

The drive to the warehouse is quiet, I thought he'd have demanded answers, wanted some information, but no he's silent.

It doesn't take long to arrive at the warehouse. The moment da throws the fucker to the floor he starts running his mouth. "You fucking Gallaghers, you're all the same. All mouth no action."

He's goading the wrong motherfucker. I'm going to kill him and I'll enjoy every second of it.

"What were you planning on doing with my wife?" I growl, giving the cunt a swift kick to his midsection.

He releases a pained grunt and begins to cough. "I was going to fuck every fucking hole of hers."

Wrong fucking answer. The thought of this asshole touching her makes a murderous rage come over me. My family are all competent fighters, we can kill anyone with our bare hands and this cunt is going to be in for a world of hurt.

My knuckles pound his flesh over and over again. I don't tire, I'll never fucking tire. He set out to rape my wife. There's no fucking doubt that was what he planned on doing and had I not been there, he'd have succeeded. I unleash every fucking ounce of anger I have.

His screams pierce the silence, echoing through the derelict warehouse. I pay no heed to the blood dripping from my fists, feeling the adrenaline surging through me. I'll do whatever it takes to protect my family—especially my wife— and the ignorant, soulless piece of shit in front of me dared to hurt her.

Every hit I deliver is filled with every ounce of my anger, he'd have broken something in her had he had his way. That's unacceptable. He'll die for that.

He writhes on the filthy floor, blood pouring from his body, he's breathing hard, his eyes swollen shut and he's crying out for forgiveness. I reach for my knife. It's time to end this shit.

I grip his collar and haul his body to mine. My knife pressing against his throat. "Forgiveness is for losers," I snarl as I swipe my blade across his neck, severing the muscles and tendons. He's dead within seconds. I drop him to the floor, my chest heaving.

"I'm sorry son," Da says from behind me. "I never saw this side, never knew you had it in you."

"You never wanted to see it," I say, flexing out my hands, loving the crack in my knuckles.

"You've fucked up by marrying Anne-Marie, that wasn't the plan. We were to have an alliance with the Gallos."

I grit my teeth. Fucking Italians. Da's a little too chummy with the fucking boss of the Italian Mafia. "You've got another son," I say thickly. "One that's going to take over. Use him. Right now, I'm going home to my wife." I walk out of the warehouse, ignoring my da calling my name. Fuck him and fuck this bullshit.

Family is supposed to be put above all else. Well Anna is my family and this disrespect will no longer be tolerated. Marrying someone I wasn't supposed to was never going to go down well. But Anna is the woman I love and she's the only one I wanted to marry.

I'll take whatever comes my way for the decisions I've made. I know deep in my bones that marrying her was the best decision I'll ever make. Fuck what anyone else thinks.

BITTERSWEET PROMISES

Carrie Ann Ryan

CHAPTER ONE

Leif

"Not only did you convince me to somehow go on a blind date, it became a double date. How on earth did you work this magic on me, cousin?" I asked Lake as she leaned against the pillar just inside the restaurant.

Lake grinned at me, her dark hair pulled away from her face. She had on this swingy black dress and looked as if she were excited, anxious, nervous, and happy all at the same time. Considering she was bouncing on her toes when usually Lake was calm, cool, and collected, was saying something. "I asked, and you said yes. Because you love me."

"I might love you because we're family, but I still think we're making a mistake." I shook my head and pulled at my shirt sleeves. Lake had somehow convinced me to wear a button-up shirt tucked into gray pants, I even had on shiny shoes. I looked like a damn banker. But if that's what Lake wanted, that's what I would do.

Lake might technically be my cousin, even though we weren't blood-related, but we were more like brother and sister than any of my other cousins.

I had siblings, as did Lake, but with the generational gap, we were at least a decade older than all of our other cousins. That meant, despite the fact that we had lived over an hour apart for most of our lives, we'd grown up more like siblings.

I loved my three younger siblings and talked to them daily. Unlike some blended families, they *were* my brothers and sister and not like strangers or distant family members. I didn't feel a disconnect from the three of them, but Lake was still closer to me.

Probably because we were either heading into our thirties or already there, where most of our other cousins were either just now in their early twenties or still teenagers in high school. With how big we Montgomerys were as a family, it made sense that there would be such a widespread age group. That meant that Lake and I were best friends, cousins, practically siblings, and sometimes the banes of each other's existences.

We were also business owners and partners and saw each other too often these days. That was probably why she convinced me to go on a blind double date. But she had been out with Zach before. I, however, had never met May. Lake had some connection with her that I wasn't sure about, and for some reason Lake's date had said yes to this double date.

And, in the complicated way of family, I had agreed to it. I must have been tired. Or perhaps I'd had too many beers. Because I didn't do blind dates, and recently, I didn't do dates at all.

Lake scanned her phone, then looked up at me, all innocence in her smart gaze. "You shouldn't have told me you wanted to settle down in your old age."

I narrowed my eyes. "I'm still in my early thirties, jerk. Stop calling me old."

"I shouldn't call you old since you're only a few years older than me." She fluttered her eyelashes and I flipped her off, ignoring the stare from the older woman next to me. Though I was a tattoo artist, I didn't have many visible tattoos. Most of mine were on my back and legs, hidden from the world unless I wanted to show them. I hadn't figured out what I wanted on my arms beyond a few small pieces on my wrists and upper shoulders. And since tattoos were permanent, I was taking my time. If a client needed to see my skin with ink to feel comfortable, I'd show them my back. My body was a canvas, so I did what I could to set people at ease.

But I still had the eyebrow piercing and had recently taken out my nose ring. I didn't look too scary for most people. But apparently, flipping off a woman, growling, and cursing a time or two in front of strangers probably made me appear too close to the dark side.

"Yes, I want to settle down, but this will be awkward, won't it? Where the two of us are strangers, and the two of you aren't?" I wanted a life, a future, and yeah, one day to settle down with someone. I just didn't know why I'd mentioned it to Lake in the first place.

"If it helps, May doesn't know Zach, either. So it's a group of strangers, except I know everybody." She clapped her hands together and did her version of an evil laugh, and I just shook my head.

"Considering what you do for a living and how you like to manipulate things in your way, this makes sense. Are you going to be adding a matchmaking company to your conglomerate?"

Lake just fluttered her eyelashes again and laughed. Lake owned a small tech company that made a shit ton of money over the past couple of years. And because she was brilliant at what she did, innovative, and liked pushing money towards women-owned businesses, she owned more than one company at this point and was an investor in mine. I wouldn't be surprised if she found a way to open up a women-owned matchmaking company right here in town.

"It might be fun. I can call it Montgomery Links." Her eyes went wide. "Oh, my God. I have to write that down." She pulled out her phone, began to take notes, and I pinched the bridge of my nose.

"You know I trust you with my actual life, but I don't know if I trust you with my dating life."

Lake tossed her hair behind her shoulder as she continued to type. "Shut up. You love me. And once I finish setting you up, the rest of the family's next."

"Oh, really? You're going to get Daisy and Noah next?" I asked, speaking of two more of our cousins.

"Maybe. Of course, Sebastian's the only one of the younger group that seems to have a serious girlfriend."

I nodded, speaking of our other familial business partner. Sebastian was still a teenager, though in college. He had wanted to open up Montgomery Ink Legacy with me, the full title of our company. There was a legacy to it, and Sebastian had wanted in. So, though he didn't work there full-time, he was putting his future towards us. And in the ways of young love, he and his girlfriend had been together since middle school. The fact that my younger cousin was better at relationships than I was didn't make me feel great. But I was going to ignore that.

"You're not going to start up a matchmaking service, are you? Or maybe an app?"

"Dating apps are ridiculous these days, they practically want you to invest in coins to bid on dates, and that's not something I'm in the mood for. But maybe there's something I can try. I'll add it to my list."

Lake's list of inventions and tech was notorious, and knowing the brilliance of my cousin, she would one day rule the world and might eventually cross everything off that list.

"Oh, here's Zach." Lake's face brightened immediately, and she smiled up at a man with dark hair, piercing gray eyes, and an actual dimple on his cheek.

Tonight was not only about my blind date, but me getting the lay of the land when it came to Zach. I was the first step into meeting the family. Oh, if Zach passed my gauntlet, he would meet the rest of the Montgomerys, and we were mighty. All one hundred of us.

"Zach, you're here." Lake's voice went soft, and she went on her tiptoes even in her high heels as Zach pressed a soft kiss to her lips.

"Of course, I'm here. And you're early, as usual."

Lake blushed and ducked her head. "Well, you know me. I like to be early because being on time is late," she said at the same time I did, mumbling under my breath. It was a familiar refrain when it came to us.

"Zach, good to meet you," I said, holding out my hand.

The other man gripped it firmly and shook. "Nice to meet you too, Leif. I know you might be the one on a blind date soon, but I'm nervous."

I chuckled, shaking my head. "Yeah, I'm pretty nervous too. Though I'm grateful that Lake's trying to look out for me."

My cousin laughed softly. "You totally were not saying that a few minutes ago, but be suave and sophisticated now. Or just be yourself, May's on her way."

I met Zach's gaze and we both rolled our eyes. When I turned toward the door, I saw a woman of average height, with black straight hair, green eyes, and a sweet smile. I didn't know much about May, other than Lake knew her and liked her. If I was going to start dating again after taking time off to get the rest of my life together, I might as well start with someone that one of my best friends liked.

"May, I'm so glad that you're here," Lake said as she hugged the other woman tightly.

As Lake began to bounce on her heels, I realized that my cousin's cool, calm, and collected exterior was only for work. She was bouncing and happy when it came to her friends or when she was nervous. I knew that, of course, but I had forgotten how she had turned into the mogul that she was. It was good to see her relaxed and happy.

Now I just needed to figure out how to do that for myself.

May stood in front of me, and I felt like I was starting middle school all over again. A new school, a new life, and a past that didn't make much sense to anyone else.

I swallowed hard and nodded, not putting out my hand to shake, thinking that would be weird, but I also didn't want to hug her. I didn't even know this woman. Why was everything so awkward? Instead, I lifted my chin. "Hello, May. It's nice to meet you. Lake says only good things."

There, smooth. Not really. Zach began to move out of frame, with Lake at his side as the two went to speak to the hostess, leaving May and me alone.

This wasn't going to be awkward at all.

The woman just smiled at me, her eyes wide. "It's nice to meet you, too. And Lake does speak highly of you. Also, this is very awkward, so I'm so sorry if I say something stupid. I know that your cousin said that I should be set up with you which is great but I'm not great at blind dates and apparently this is a double date and now I'm going to stop talking." She said the words so quickly they all ran into one breath.

I shook my head and laughed. "We're on the same page there."

"Okay, good. It's nice to meet you, Leif Montgomery."

"And it's nice to meet you too, May."

We made our way to Lake and Zach, who had gotten our table, and we all sat down, talking about work and other things. May was in child life development, taught online classes, and was also a nanny.

"I'm actually about to start with a new family soon. I'm excited. I know that being a nanny isn't something that most people strive for, or at least that's what they tell you, but I love being able to work with children and be the person that is there when a single parent or even both parents are out in the workforce, trying to do everything."

I nodded, taking a sip of my beer. "I get you completely. With how my parents worked, I was lucky that they were able to get childcare within the buildings. Since they each owned their own businesses, they made it work. But my family worked long hours, and that's why I ended up being the babysitter a lot of the times when childcare wasn't an option." I cleared my throat. "I'm a lot older than a lot of my cousins," I added.

"Both of us are, but I'm glad that you only said yourself," Lake said, grinning. She leaned into Zach as she spoke, the four of us in a horseshoe-shaped booth. That gave May and me space since this was a first date and still awkward as hell, and so Lake and Zach could cuddle. Not that that was something I needed to be a part of.

"Oh, I'm glad that you didn't judge. The last few dates that I've been on they always gave me weird looks because I think they expected a nanny to be this old crone or someone that's looking for a different job." She shrugged and continued. "When I eventually get married and maybe even start a family, I want to continue my job. I like being there to help another family achieve their goals. And I can't believe I just said start a family on my first date. And that I mentioned that I've been on a few other dates." She let out a breath. "I'm notoriously bad at dating. Like, the worst. Just warning you."

I laughed, shaking my head. "I'm rusty at it, so don't worry." And even though I said that, I had a feeling that May felt no spark towards me, and I didn't feel anything towards her. She was nice and pleasant, and I could probably consider her a friend one day. But there wasn't any spark. May's eyes weren't dancing. She wasn't leaning forward, trying to touch my hand across the table. We were just sitting there casually, enjoying a really good steak, as Lake and Zach enjoyed their date.

By the end of dinner, I didn't want dessert, and neither did May, so we said goodbye to the other couple, who decided to stay. I walked May to her car, ignoring Lake's warning look, but I didn't know what exactly she was warning me about.

"Thanks for dinner," May said. "I could have paid. I know this is a blind date and all that, but you didn't have to pay."

I shook my head. "I paid for the four of us because I wanted to be nice. I'll make Lake pay next time."

May beamed. "Yes, I like that. You guys are a good family."

"Anyway," I said, clearing my throat as I stuck my hands in my pockets. "I guess I'll see you around."

May just looked at me, threw her head back, and laughed. "You're right. You are rusty at this."

"Sorry." Heat flushed my skin, and I resisted the urge to tug on my eyebrow ring.

"It's okay. No spark. I'm used to it. I don't spark well."

"May, I'm sorry." I cringed. "It's not you."

"Oh, God, please don't say that. 'It's not you. It's me. You're working on yourself. You're just so busy with work.' I've heard it all."

"Seriously?" I asked. May was hot. Nice, but there just wasn't a spark.

She shrugged. "It's okay. I'll probably see you around sometime because I am friends with Lake. However, I am perfectly fine having this be our one and only. You'll find your person. It's okay that it's not me." And with that, she got in the car and left, leaving me standing there.

Well then. Tonight wasn't horrible, but it wasn't great. I got in my car, and instead of heading home where I'd be alone, watching something on some streaming service while I drank a beer and pretended that I knew what I was doing with my life, I headed into Montgomery Ink Legacy.

We were the third branch of the company and the first owned by our generation. Montgomery Ink was the tattoo shop in downtown Denver. While there were open spots for some walk-ins and special circumstances, my father, aunt, and their team had years' worth of waiting lists. They worked their asses off and made sure to get in everybody that they could, but people wanted Austin Montgomery's art. Same with my aunt, Maya.

There was another tattoo shop down in Colorado Springs, owned by my parents' cousins, who I just called aunt and uncle because we were close enough that using real titles for everybody got confusing. Montgomery Ink Too was thriving down there, and they had waiting lists as well. My family could have opened more shops and gone nationwide, even global if they wanted to, but they liked keeping it how it was, in the family and those connected.

We were a branch, but our own in the making. I had gone into business with Lake, of course, and Sebastian, when he was ready, as well as Nick. Nick was my best friend. I had known him for ages, and he had wanted to be part of something as well. He might not be a Montgomery by name, but he had eaten over at my family's house enough times throughout the years that he was practically a Montgomery. And he had invested in the company as well, and so now we were nearly a year into owning the shop and trying not to fail.

I pulled into the parking lot, grateful it was still open since we didn't close until nine most nights, and greeted Nick, who was still working.

Sebastian was in the back, going over sketches with a client, and I nodded at him. He might be eighteen, but he was still in training, an apprentice, and was working his ass off to learn.

"Date sucked then?" Sebastian asked, and Nick just rolled his eyes and went back to work on a client's wrist.

"I don't want to talk about it," I groaned.

The rest of the staff was off since Nick would close up on his own. Sebastian was just there since he didn't have homework or a date with Marley.

"Was she hot at least?" Sebastian asked, and the client, a woman in her sixties, bopped him on the head with her bag gently.

"Sebastian Montgomery. Be nice."

Sebastian blushed. "Sorry, Mrs. Anderson."

I looked over at the woman and grinned. "Hi, Mrs. Anderson. It's nice to see you out of the classroom."

She narrowed her eyes at me, even though they filled with laughter. "I needed my next Jane Austen tattoo, thank you very much," the older woman said as she went back to working with Sebastian. She had been my and then Sebastian's English teacher. The fact that she was on her fifth tattoo with some literary quote told me that I had been damn lucky in most of my teachers growing up.

She was kick-ass, and I had a feeling that she would let Sebastian do the tattoo for her rather than just have him work on the design with me as we did for most of the people who came in. He had learned under my father and was working under me now. It was strange to think that he wasn't a little kid anymore. But he was in a long-term relationship, kicking ass in college, and knew what he wanted to do with his life.

I might know what I want to do with my work life, but everything else seemed a little off.

"So it didn't work out?" Nick asked as he walked up to the front desk with the clients after going over aftercare.

"Not really," I said, looking down at my phone.

The client, a woman in her mid-twenties with bright pink hair, a lip ring, and kind eyes, leaned over the desk to look at me.

"You'll find someone, Leif. Don't worry."

I looked at our regular and shook my head. "Thanks, Kim. Too bad that you don't swing this way."

I winked as I said it, a familiar refrain from both of us.

Kim was married to a woman named Sonya, and the two of them were happy and working on in vitro with donated sperm for their first kid.

"Hey, I'm sorry too that I'm a lesbian. I'll never know what it means to have Leif Montgomery. Or any Montgomery, since I found my love far too quickly. I mean, what am I ever going to do not knowing the love of a Montgomery?"

Mrs. Anderson chuckled from her chair, Sebastian held back a snort, and I just looked at Nick, who rolled his eyes and helped Kim out of the place.

I was tired, but it was okay. The date wasn't all bad. May was nice. But it felt like I didn't have much right then.

And then Nick sat in front of me, scowled, and I realized that I did have something. I had my friends and my family. I didn't need much more.

"So, you and May didn't work out?"

I raised a brow. "You knew her name? Did I tell you that?"

Nick shook his head. "Lake did."

That made sense, considering the two of them spoke as much as we did. "So, was it your idea to set me up on a blind date?"

"Fuck no. That was all Lake. I just do what she says. Like we all do."

I sighed and went through my appointments for the next day. "We're busy for the next month. That's good, right?" I asked.

"You're the business genius here. I just play with ink. But yes, that's good. Now, don't let your cousin set you up any more dates. Find them for yourself. You know what you're doing."

"So says the man who dates less than me."

"That's what you think. I'm more private about it. As it should be." I flipped him off as he stood up, then he gestured towards a stack of bills in the corner. "You have a few personal things that made their way here. Don't want you to miss out on them before you head home."

"Thanks, bro."

"No problem. I'm going to help Sebastian with his consult, and then I'll clean up. You should head home. Though you're doing it alone, so I feel sorry for you."

"Fuck you," I called out.

"Fuck you, too."

"Boys," Mrs. Anderson said, in that familiar English teacher refrain, and both Nick and I cringed before saying, "Sorry," simultaneously.

Sebastian snickered, then went back to work, and I headed towards the edge of the counter, picking up the stack of papers. Most were bills, some were random papers that needed to be filed or looked over. Some were just junk mail. But there was one letter, written in block print that didn't look familiar. Chills went up my spine and I opened it, wondering what the fuck this was. Maybe it was someone asking to buy my house. I got a lot of handwritten letters for that, but I didn't think this was going to be that. I swallowed hard, slid open the paper, and froze.

"I'll find you, boy. Oops. Looks like I already did. Be waiting. I know you miss me."

I let the paper hit the top of the counter and swallowed hard, trying to remain cool so I didn't worry anyone else.

I didn't know exactly who that was from, but I had a horrible feeling that they wouldn't wait long to tell me.

CHAPTER TWO

Brooke

"Mommy. I think I'm sick."

At those words that every mother dreaded hearing, I looked into the rearview mirror, trying to simultaneously keep one eye on the road, as Luke leaned out of the car seat that he was nearly too big for—he was nearly ready for the booster seat—but my little boy who wasn't so little anymore was currently clutching his stomach like he was ready to throw up.

"Do you need me to pull over, buddy?" I asked, hoping I didn't have to do so right now. I needed to beat the movers to the house. Thanks to a quirk of fate, a bad connection, a storm, a flood, and a water main break, I was two days late getting to our new home.

I had wanted to get everything set up for the movers. Instead, I was going to barely beat them to the house. Thankfully, my realtor was a godsend and had gotten everything ready for me, but I felt like I was behind.

I always felt like I was behind these days.

"I'm just nervous, Mommy."

I held back my look of relief at those words and swallowed hard. I knew he'd gotten the saying from me, but it sounded adorable coming out of his mouth.

"I'm nervous too, Luke. But this is exciting. A brand-new yard. A big boy's bed."

As long as the bed showed up from the furniture store the next day. Tonight we would be roughing it with sleeping bags that were currently stuffed in the back of my SUV.

"But what if I don't like school? What if school is hard?"

"Then I'm here to help you. You know I love school."

"Because you're a pro-fes-sor." He mumbled the word, sounding it out, and I was proud that he at least got that far with it. Usually, he couldn't say the word that well. But my baby boy was getting older and he was losing that little boy voice of his.

"I *am* going to be a professor. Are you excited to meet the neighbors? And your new schoolmates?"

"I just want them to like me. Because I like you, Mommy."

My heart warmed, and I wanted to reach back and grip his hand and tell him everything would be okay. Only I wasn't sure that it was because we were picking up our lives and changing everything.

I had to tell myself I could do this. I had been a single mom for my baby boy's entire existence. We were a team, a duo. We could work with anything. Face anything. Except for maybe a cross-country move with just the two of us in my SUV to a place that I hadn't lived in years.

But California and Europe were behind me. And now it was time for a whole new adventure with the love of my life.

"Does your stomach feel okay?" I asked, hoping it was just nerves and he wasn't going to throw up in the back of my car during the last few miles of the drive. We had driven all the way from California to Colorado. It hadn't been easy, and my head ached, but there was no way I could have flown with Luke and the stuff we needed. It was easier to do the drive as a team, rather than hoping my car would get to where I wanted.

"I feel better. Thank you, Mommy."

I held back a sigh of relief as I pulled into the neighborhood, looking around at the large trees, green grass, and blue skies. I loved it here in Colorado, though it had been a while since I lived here. But I did love Arvada. I had grown up in Westminster, which was only about five minutes north. The suburbs of Colorado were all tangled together, and while I lived in one burb, I was going to work in a burb about two suburbs down. It made sense to anyone who lived here, and I knew that this was the right decision. Though my family wasn't here anymore, and losing them had hurt me beyond measure, my sense of home was here. I knew this area and its roads like the back of my hand. Even with the new neighborhoods, the new businesses, and constant changes, everything still felt the same.

That's why I was coming home. That, and a job offer I couldn't refuse. So now my California baby was going to become a Colorado Rockie. And I could not wait to see how much he loved it.

His gaze had been on the mountains for most of the trip, his eyes wide as he went on and on about wanting to see bears and mountain lions and anything with park rangers. I just had to hope that none of those, including the ranger, ended up on our doorstep. Maybe when we visited the mountains, and the forest, I wouldn't mind seeing a bear.

From far, *far* away.

The neighborhood was a few years old, one of the newer developments built after I had moved to France and then California. It had been more than six years since I had lived here, after all, things were going to change rapidly. And yet things still felt the same. The roads had the same names, the people were still friendly, and the skies were still blue. That is, until the skies were no longer blue and bright, and four different seasons all happened in one day. But that was something I was used to. And that was home.

These houses were decently sized, with large yards, but not so big that you didn't get to know your neighbor or spend every weekend doing yard work until you fainted.

It was going to be a good place for me to meet other single moms and families. That way Luke wasn't lonely, and we weren't living in a far too expensive apartment while trying to do everything at once.

Our home was at the end of a cul-de-sac, surrounded by the old trees they built around and the younger saplings they planted after they finished.

I loved the look of it, the two-story home having called to me from the online listing. I had come out to see the place in person, as well as at least twenty others during my quick weekend out here. This was the place I had loved, and thankfully the previous owners had taken my offer.

The owners had loved the place, had worked with the builders personally to make it theirs, but were moving thanks to their jobs. I didn't know much about the Montgomery Builders, or Montgomery Inc., as they were called, but my realtor said that they were the best in the business. That meant the house was sturdy and nice. That was fine with me. As long as there was a place for Luke, I was happy.

We pulled in and I sighed dreamily as I looked at the place, and in relief about the fact that we had actually beaten the movers.

"We're home, Luke. What do you think?"

Luke strained in his seat and looked around. "It's beauty-ful, Mom. Is it ours?"

I sighed softly and looked back at him. "It's ours. Pretty nifty, isn't it?"

"I like nifty."

I grinned and got out of the car quickly, having pulled off to the farthest edge of the driveway so the movers could back in easily, and went to get Luke out of his seat. He had already unbuckled himself—the kid's far too smart for his own good—and I helped him out of the car before I took his hand and we looked up at our new home.

"Well, what do you think?" I asked. Luke hadn't been with me when I picked the house, though he had seen pictures and had done the online tour with me countless times.

"I love my room." He grinned up at me, and I just smiled. I knew that this was a huge change for us, but it was the only decision I could have made. Therefore, it had to be the best one.

"Okay, let's get ready for the movers."

I clapped my hands, pulled out the key that the realtor had given me that morning when I stopped by the office quickly to sign the rest of the papers, and headed into the house.

I smiled softly as I looked at the giant basket on the counter, courtesy of my realtor, a woman that I had quickly become friends with. She was a grandmother, worked her butt off, and loved what she did.

Inside the basket was food, goodies, and a present for Luke. My eyes filled with tears, and I looked around and noticed a few other welcome home gifts, including a plant that I would probably kill, but I would do my best to keep alive.

"Mommy, we have presents?"

"We do, Luke. They're welcoming us home."

His eyes went wide, confused as he looked around the open and empty space. "Home?"

My heart did that little clutch thing, wondering once again if I was ruining my son's life. I swore moms everywhere throughout history all had lists in their minds of ways that they were ruining their children's lives.

"We'll make it home. What do you say? Want to be my partner?"

"Okay!" he said, clapping his hands.

"Knock, knock," a stranger's unfamiliar voice said from the doorway. I whirled, pulling Luke behind me, my pulse racing.

A woman stood there, her dark hair flowing around her face. She had on a white blouse, comfortable gray pants, and smiled wide.

"Hello?" I said, my voice cool.

I didn't know this woman, but if she was a neighbor or something, I should probably not be a jerk and threaten her for scaring the crap out of me.

The woman's eyes widened and she held up both hands. "I'm so sorry. I did not mean to scare you. I'm your neighbor, Lake. Lake Montgomery. I saw you pull in and the door was open. I just wanted to make sure everything was okay and welcome you." She bent down and picked up a casserole dish and a bag. "Your realtor, Nancy, said that you would be here and that I should welcome you if I was home. And since I'm working from my home office today, I figured I would. I swear I didn't mean to startle you."

I let out a breath, vaguely remembering that my realtor had mentioned Lake. She lived alone next door, and her family was somehow connected to the company that built the house.

"Hi. Sorry. You did startle me, but it's been a long trip."

Luke stuck his head out from behind my legs and pulled on my jeans. "Hi. I'm Luke. Mom says not to talk to strangers, are you a stranger?"

I closed my eyes and laughed. "Hello, I am Brooke. This is my son, Luke."

Lake grinned, her hands full. "Hello, Luke and Brooke. I'm your neighbor, and I finished all my work today, so if you need help lifting anything heavy, I'm here."

I smiled, wondering if this was a sign that moving here was the right choice. "Speaking of lifting, let me help you with whatever you're holding now. And thank you. Seriously. Though you do *not* have to help with the movers."

"Oh right. Sorry." Lake laughed, her whole face brightening. "I baked a casserole. It's mostly the dreaded vegetables," she said, eyeing Luke, who just grinned.

"I like vegetables."

Lake's eyes widened. "I'm going to have to tell my mother that people actually do like vegetables. I'm shocked."

I shook my head, laughing even through the mental gymnastics of the day. "He loves his veggies, and I count it as a blessing."

Luke proudly puffed his chest. "Broccoli's the best. And brussels sprouts."

Lake nearly dropped her packages and I laughed, taking the dish from her hands.

"I know. I know. I think Luke likes the way I cook them. I roast them," I added.

Lake smiled. "I do, too, but I feel like I need to do better. Anyway, I'm off for the day, and I just need to change clothes, but I can help you. Nancy said that your movers were coming through a bunch of delays, so you have me if you need me."

I blinked at the generosity once again. "You don't have to do that. We can handle it."

"We're a team," Luke said, and I grinned down at him, ruffling his hair.

"We are a team."

"The best team ever," Lake said, grinning. "I seriously don't mind helping. The people that used to live here helped as well, although my siblings, parents, and cousins were all here to help, too. There's a lot of us."

"You said you're a Montgomery?" I asked, slowly piecing together what she'd said before. I needed some caffeine soon if I was going to be able to function the rest of the day.

"I am. You'll probably meet more of us, because a few of us do live in the neighborhood."

"I met a Montgomery from Colorado once, when I was in Paris." I hadn't meant to say that. I had no idea why I had. It wasn't like I'd thought about him.

Much.

Or at all.

Or ever.

Why had I brought it up in the first place?

Lake's eyes widened. "Really? Well, it's probably not us since it is a common name, but if you meet one in Colorado, they're more than likely to be related to me. In fact, my cousin is on his way to bum food off of me since it's my turn to feed him, so I can probably borrow his muscles to help you out, too."

"You feed him often?" I asked.

Lake nodded her head. "Yeah, we're more like siblings, and we take turns feeding each other so we're not constantly cooking for one."

"Oh, I guess that makes sense."

"We try. Anyway, do you need help?"

As soon as she asked the words again, a large truck pulled in in front of my house. My eyes widened, I looked out at my still full SUV, my kid bouncing on his toes, and sighed, giving in. "Okay. I could really use your help."

"Welcome to Colorado."

"Thank you. Now I just have to not panic when I think about everything I have to do."

"It's okay, Mom. We're a team. Lake too."

Lake just beamed. "Exactly. Let me go change. Oh, there's my cousin now. I'll tell him we're roping him in."

"You don't have to do that. He does not have to help." I already felt bad about this near stranger helping me out like this.

"Yes, he does. He's a Montgomery. It's what we do."

A man in a large gray truck got out, and I did my best not to look too hard at his jeans. At the way that he filled them out, the way that he moved, at the fact that he was very ripped.

I shook myself out of it. I might have dated a few times in the past five years, but it had been long enough for me to apparently lose my mind.

Then he moved forward and turned, and I nearly fell right off of my front step.

Lake was talking to him, but I knew that face, those eyes, those cheekbones. That jaw.

I knew those lips, those hands. I knew everything.

From when I was eighteen, in a country not my own, in a memory that didn't even feel like mine anymore.

"Ms. Adler?" a man with a gruff voice asked, and I looked towards the man in charge of the moving truck and smiled.

"That's me. We're here." The whirring in my brain got louder, and I swallowed hard, my throat suddenly dry.

"You just tell us where to unload, and we've got you. I'll get the few forms for you, but we know the drill."

"And she's got helpers," Lake added as she moved forward, the man who wasn't a stranger but apparently her cousin at her side.

I turned to them, eyes wide, as Leif Montgomery tripped and nearly fell, staring at me.

"*You*. Brooke?" he asked.

Lake looked between us, her eyes wide, and I gripped Luke's hand, looked at the mover, then back at Leif.

A blast from the past.

And apparently, the Montgomery I had met in Paris.

CHAPTER THREE

Leif

I STARED AT BROOKE, wondering if I was seeing things. I remembered that long reddish-brown hair of hers. Those hazel eyes had always captured me. She was a little below average in height. That was always a fun play against my six-foot-four frame. She was also all curves in the right places and had only grown sexier in the time we'd been apart.

Was she truly here? This blast from the past?

I let out another breath and helped move the last box into the house, doing my best to keep my eyes off the woman that had haunted my dreams for far too long.

She held the clipboard, a pen in her hair, another in her hands, a third pen attached to the cleavage on her top.

I was doing my best not to think about that particular one.

She was organized, meticulous, and had been the fantasy of my dreams for too long.

"You're staring."

I looked over at my cousin and shook my head. "I'm just in awe over here. It's spooky. I don't understand."

Lake snorted at my attempt to not sound like I'd been drooling in my own memories. "I'm the one who has questions, Leif. Not you."

"I suppose that's all right. Is she seriously your neighbor now?" I kept my voice low since Brooke was walking in, still staring at the clipboard, and I didn't want her to think I was talking about her.

Even though, *of course*, I was talking about her.

The woman I'd shared a hot and steamy couple of weeks in Paris with was now living next to my cousin. The cousin who happened to be one of my best friends.

In all the places, in all the world, she had to show up here.

After all these years, after so many unending questions because I didn't have her anymore.

She had just shown up.

I pushed those thoughts to the back of my mind and looked down at the kid who was staring up at me. I could feel his gaze boring into my side, so I tried not to act like a growly asshole.

"Hey, Luke, is it?" I asked

"That's me. Luke. Why are you so big? And why do you have something on your face?"

I held back a laugh. "I'm big because I'm a grown-up and most of the guys in my family are all this tall. I have a beard. My dad has an even *bigger* beard."

I knelt in front of him, my shoulders aching from the unexpected moving day. I'd spent the entire morning working on a client's back, bent over to get the perfect angle, so my client was comfortable. It meant that I was the one with back pain at the end of the day. One of my friends wore corsets these days to help with his stature, and I thought maybe I should try. Maybe I would force Nick to do it with me, so I wasn't alone.

I was sure my dad had even done it once before, but my dad's torso was so long that he would probably have had it custom-made.

Either way, though, I was tired and a little out of my element.

I knew kids, and one day I wanted kids of my own. I was the oldest cousin by more than a few years. Hell, I had been a grown adult when my parents adopted my two younger siblings. I had been packing for my college visit when the call came through that my parents would be parents again.

I knew how to act around kids. And although none of my generation had started the next generation yet, I knew we would soon. I helped raise my siblings and cousins, and had been their designated babysitter for years. Hell, I still was sometimes.

And yet, why did I feel so awkward around this boy?

He was cute for sure. He looked just like his mom, with dark red hair and light eyes.

A mom that I hadn't seen in years. Due to the timing, I knew this kid wasn't mine, so it wasn't like a secret baby situation, but I had still done the math just in case. It had been a shock to see Brooke standing there, her eyes wide, looking glorious and gorgeous as ever.

And here I was, kneeling in front of her son, wondering who the hell his father was and why it looked like she was here alone.

Not that I was going to do anything about it.

I couldn't do anything about it.

I was going on a dating moratorium, at least that's what I told myself. The date with May had been okay, but the lack of sparks had killed my desire to try to date again.

Especially with a woman that clearly hadn't wanted me before, no matter how hot our time together had been in Paris.

And she had enough baggage that she wasn't going to be looking at me and wanting more. I wasn't even sure why I was thinking about it.

I was just the big, bearded, tattoo artist, art-school dropout in other people's eyes. It didn't matter that the word artist was in the name. Most people didn't think of me as such.

I was fine with that. My friends and family were, too. But many of the women I had dated hadn't been.

I didn't even know what Brooke would think, but that wouldn't matter.

I was just the stranger with the beard that this kid looked curious about.

As if he had never seen a roughneck like me.

"Can I feel your beard?" Luke asked, and I shrugged.

"I guess it's okay. If it's okay with your mom." I looked up as Brooke looked down at us, something in her eyes I couldn't quite read.

She smiled and slid her hand over her son's head. "Of course, you can. If it's okay with Mr. Montgomery."

I raised a brow, wondering if I liked being called Mr. Montgomery out of a mouth that had once been wrapped around my cock. Maybe I did.

"There's a lot of Montgomerys around here, Brooke. Maybe he should call me Leif."

She cringed and I wondered what that was about.

"I guess you're right. Although, it's kind of odd if there are so many Montgomerys, I run into you here."

There was a deafening silence, and she cleared her throat while I just stared at her, wanting answers, wanting more. Knowing I couldn't have it. Again.

"Sure, Luke, honey. You can feel his beard. Just be gentle, please, and don't pull."

That reminded me of the time she had pulled because she had been tugging me closer to her pussy.

That was enough of that.

"Okay." Luke patted my beard and smiled. I lowered my head slightly, so he didn't have to reach as much. "It's soft.

"I use beard oil. It's always good to have good beard care." I winked at him, and he giggled.

"Will I have a beard?" Luke asked, his eyes wide and curious.

"When you're older, sure. I don't see why not." I looked up at Brooke again, ignoring the tightening in my gut. "What do you think? Will the kid look good with the beard?"

Brooke looked at me, blinked, and smiled. "I think you would look quite dashing with a beard, Luke. But you still have a few years to go. Remember, you are not supposed to grow up too quickly. You need to give Mommy some time to get accustomed."

"What's acc-ustomed-ed?" Luke asked, sounding out the word.

"Accustomed. Getting used to it. So you have to give your mom time before you grow up and get a huge beard." I roughed up his hair slightly and he grinned at me, smiling his mom's smile.

"I can wait. I think it will be a while until I am as big as you. But Mom's not big. Maybe I'll be like her."

"I think your mom is just the right size," I said without thinking. When I clamped my mouth shut, I stood up, stretching my back. "So, what do you think? Does everything look good? Did you empty the truck?" I asked, trying not to act as if this was awkward.

Brooke let out a soft breath. "Yes. Thank you. You honestly did not have to do all of this. I am forever grateful."

"We are always here to help," Lake put in. She had been mysteriously silent for the entire conversation, and I knew she would have questions. Of course, the other woman would have questions. If I weren't careful, she would bring those questions to the rest of the family, and then they would be a cacophony of Montgomery intrusiveness.

I loved my family. I honestly did. I loved how we were always there for each other. Only sometimes, it was almost a little bit too much. Because yes, we could keep secrets, of course we could keep secrets, yet we all wanted to help one another so much sometimes that it felt almost overwhelming.

Sometimes, despite myself, I had to remind my own mind that I was a Montgomery as well. Even after over twenty years of being immersed in this family, growing up with it and remembering that I hadn't been born into it. Maybe by blood, but not by situation.

"Seriously though, you guys have no idea how much it helped." Brooke put her hand around Luke's shoulders as the kid leaned into his mom.

It was so strange to see Brooke as a mom. She was good at it from what I could tell in the little amount of time I'd seen her at it. She had kept one eye on what she was doing, one eye on making sure that Lake and I and the movers knew where to put things, and a random third eye that must only exist for parents on her kid the whole time. Luke had been safe and secure and had snacks when he needed them.

She was a wizard, just like my mom was.

It was still just so odd to see Brooke in that situation.

"You're Lake's new neighbor. We were not going to let you do it by yourself." I nearly growled the words, and I ignored the pointed look from my cousin.

Brooke just blinked at me and shrugged. "With the timing, we ran late, and the movers were early, so I'm glad it all worked out. I would've been able to do it myself, as I did when I moved to California, but I am truly grateful. And now my house is full of boxes, and I only know for sure where my son's sheets are for his bed, but that's about it. I would offer to cook you dinner or something to say thank you, but I don't think that will happen since I don't know where my pans are. Maybe another time."

She was looking at Lake as she spoke, not looking at me at all. I had to wonder if that was on purpose. I had seen anger and surprise in her gaze when I had pulled up, but why would there be anger on her part?

She was the one who had left. Yes, because her trip had been over, but she hadn't shown up when we planned to meet.

She had decided no.

So it wasn't my fault.

But laying blame wasn't going to help this current predicament.

My cousin smiled. "Oh, you're not going to cook for us. That casserole that I brought over is for you tomorrow. That way, you don't have to cook tomorrow, either. However, I have something in the crockpot over at my house that I have been watching with the camera I have on in my kitchen, so you guys will come over and eat." Lake nodded quickly as if she were ordering soldiers and she was the general.

Brooke blinked as she stared at Lake. "You seriously don't need to do that. I just met you. You're kind, I swear. But we can order in, or indeed have that casserole."

"Think nothing of it. Let me make you a home-cooked meal and thank you for letting me help organize. You have no idea how much that helps me." My cousin winked, then stared at me as if willing me to say something.

I shrugged. "She's not lying. If she could organize the world, she would. I think she gets it from my aunt."

"Your aunt, as in her mom?" Brooke asked, looking between the two of us.

Lake and I looked at each other and laughed. "No, technically, Lake is the daughter of my father's cousin."

"I have no idea what that means," Brooke said, her voice dry. "So, you guys are like, second cousins, or first cousins once removed?"

"These are questions we do not ask," Lake said solemnly, though her eyes danced.

"Exactly. All of us in this generation are just cousins. Getting too technical hurts our heads, and we were raised practically as siblings, so it doesn't matter. But my aunt, and hers, since that's what we call her, is into planners and organizing. Lake is just like her. And is, indeed, taking over the world with her business."

"What do you do?" Luke asked, dancing on his toes.

"You see? These are things we should discuss over dinner. You can relax. And then you can sleep in your own home and get on with the rest of your lives, knowing that you have a busybody neighbor next door who is always willing to help." Lake beamed, and I just laughed, knowing that there was no way that Brooke and Luke were getting out of this.

Lake wanted to help, and frankly, I figured she wanted a friend. And I wanted answers.

"Plus, you know, we're not technically strangers. And I'm not just talking about all of the sweat and tears thrown out today. It seems you know my cousin." Lake winked at Brooke, and I cursed under my breath, trying not to be too loud since Luke was standing right next to me.

Brooke pressed her lips together while pointedly not looking at me. "Oh. Well, that was a long time ago."

"What was a long time ago, Mommy?" Luke asked, his voice curious.

There was nothing but curiosity in how Lake was looking at me as if she needed answers, and Brooke was glaring daggers at the both of us.

"Dinner sounds lovely. I guess it would be nice to catch up," Brooke said, her voice clipped.

What had I done all those years ago? Did she hate me? I sure as hell hoped not. I wasn't sure what else I was supposed to do. And fuck yes, I was going to catch up on something we should've done nearly ten years ago.

We left Brooke and Luke to make up their sleeping bags and have some alone time as I followed Lake over to her house.

Her place smelled like pulled pork and I groaned.

"Did you make the brioche rolls?" I asked, my mouth watering.

"Of course, I did. And coleslaw and baked beans. I should make a salad or something. Don't kids need vegetables?"

I just shook my head. "I think coleslaw is a vegetable."

"It's covered in sauce. I don't think that counts. You would think I would know that since we have so many kids in the family."

"This feels new, doesn't it?" I asked, feeling odd. I leaned against the counter, wondering if I should have a beer. Should I drink in front of the kid? It just reminded me that I didn't know this Brooke. I knew the eighteen-year-old Brooke, back in the day when we had been kids. Both of us had learned that wine was delicious and available in Paris.

We weren't those kids anymore, and now she was a mom, seemingly living out here on her own, and I felt like I was running in place.

"Are you going to tell me what happened?"

I shook my head. "What do you mean?"

"You know exactly what I mean, Leif. You guys knew each other. From when?"

"From a long time ago, Lake."

She cleared her throat and bit her lip. "Luke isn't yours, is he?"

I blinked at her before I scoffed. "You know exactly how I came into this family, Lake. How my birth mom hid me from my dad, and I showed up when Mom was gone, and I had no one else. Dad didn't even know I existed. He didn't ignore me, didn't push me away, didn't abandon me. I lost time with him because I didn't know who he was. Do you think I would do that to another kid? Do you think I would act the way that I did just then, trying to be as casual as fuck when it comes to her, if I thought for a second that was my kid? Jesus Christ, Lake. You know me better than that."

Lake blushed. "I'm sorry. It was just the first thing that popped into my mind when a single mom shows up at the house, and you guys look like you know each other. That was wrong of me. I didn't think that all the way through." Lake moved forward, hugged me tight. "I'm sorry."

She stepped away and went to get a bottle of wine out of the fridge, as well as the sparkling juice.

"It's okay. I did the math myself. It's been over ten years, though. Luke isn't mine."

"Wait, that means you knew her in what, Paris? Oh my God. The *Paris* girl?" Her voice got high-pitched and I saw hope in her eyes.

"Yes, it's the Paris girl. That also means she's the girl who never showed up when she was supposed to. The girl that chose another life over wanting anything more with me. That's *that* Brooke. But don't worry, things won't be weird."

"Well, that's a lie."

"What do you mean?" I asked, even though I knew what she meant.

"Because things are already weird. You should talk to her."

I took the glass of wine she handed me and shook my head. "Yes, I'm totally going to ask her why she didn't show up when she was supposed to. Why we never made a go of things, especially when she's exhausted after moving and possibly driving for who knows how many days to get here? I don't even know the whole story because I don't know her. But yes, I should totally ask these questions when she's in front of her kid and my cousin. Makes total sense."

Lake blinked slowly. "You know, I feel like you're getting more sarcastic in your old age."

"I'm not old. Watch your tone," I teased.

"Is that a gray hair in your beard? I bet you that's why the kid was so in awe of it. Because it's gray."

I scowled then froze as the doorbell rang.

"There they are. Are you ready for this?" she asked.

"I'm going to go with no. Let's do it."

Lake gave me a weird look and set her glass down. "I don't want you to get hurt, Leif. You're my best friend."

"I'm fine," I lied. "It's just a girl from the past. A girl, from the looks of it, who needs help. She said she was a single mom? Maybe she doesn't have a support system. Especially if we are the only ones that showed up to help her today, we can be her friends. I'll get over whatever the hell's going on in my mind. I promise. I always do."

"Maybe that's the problem, Leif. You're good at getting over it. I'm quite sure you know what that means."

My cousin kissed me on the cheek and then went to answer the door, Luke's laughter filling the house faster than anything I thought possible.

And I stood there, wondering if I was making a mistake. If I should just go.

But as I looked at Brooke and her wide eyes, I knew I couldn't go.

I couldn't before. I wasn't going to do it now.

CHAPTER FOUR

Brooke

I LOVED DENVER. It had been years since I had lived anywhere near the city, the mountains, the atmosphere. Yet it felt as if I had come home.

Though I had been to more than my fair share of cities, Denver always felt different to me. I could easily find my way around the city as if it had always been ingrained in my mind.

Part of me might have found that weird, but since I used to love travel, figuring out the lay of the land was usually the first thing that I did.

My home in Arvada was just now feeling comfortable, and I was as unpacked as I was going to be for a while. Today I was planning to explore the downtown area a little bit more. I would be working at the university in another suburb, so I wouldn't be in the downtown area often. But I used to like coming here for lunch, coffee, or to enjoy myself.

I loved that I could get the "city feel" and look at the Rocky Mountains all at the same time.

Luke was at kindergarten, that odd feeling of my baby growing up twisting the knife in my heart a little bit deeper. He had been in daycare and PreK since he was a baby, since I was a single mom and I needed to work, and my boy loved being with others. He loved socializing and learning and was just a joy to be around most days.

At least that's what his teachers told me.

But today was his first day of half-day kindergarten, and I was nervous.

Parents weren't allowed to stay and watch since that wasn't our job. And I needed to get used to this because even though we were in a new city and a new environment, this should be easy for him.

He had held my hand as we walked into the building and then had run off to his teacher, waving behind him after he said goodbye to me.

That knife dug a little deeper, and I told myself that this was good.

I told myself that though Luke and I were a team, it was good that he was so independent. That he was ready to face his new day and fears and was ready to leave me behind.

Alone. Because he didn't need his mommy.

I nearly kicked myself at that thought, knowing I was being overdramatic. Just because Luke could handle things on his own for a few minutes didn't mean he didn't need me.

And I was going to be working full-time, long hours, and starting a new phase of my career soon. I should be grateful that he could be so independent.

That afternoon, his new nanny and I would go and pick him up.

I had interviewed May before I moved here. We'd done online chats, and I had met with her when I came to buy the house. I liked May and figured that she and Luke would be a good team when I wasn't around.

I wasn't one of those mothers who felt that Luke gaining a relationship with his nanny or caretaker would take anything away from our relationship. I didn't believe that that could happen. Because Luke and I *were* a team, and he needed other members on that team to be a self-reliant and healthy human being.

So, this afternoon, Luke would spend the day with May, and I would head to work for a couple of meetings. This morning was all about breathing in that mountain and city air that somehow meshed well into an amalgamation that was in Denver.

There was just one street that I absolutely loved. It seemed to have nearly everything that I needed, and none of it was cookie-cutter or franchise. And every single one of my favorite places was still there.

There was a little boutique called Eden where I had bought my first pair of fancy shoes. I would probably go shopping there again as long as the merchandise felt about the same. As I walked around the tables and decorations, I smiled, knowing that I would still come back here though I was on a budget.

The woman who owned the place was gorgeous, with long, nearly auburn hair, and though it had been nearly a decade, she still looked the same to me.

"Hello there, is there anything I can do for you?"

I shook my head as I smiled at the owner. "I'm just walking around browsing today. It's been a while since I've been here. I was pleased to see that you guys are still here."

The owner grinned. "I'm glad that I'm here, too. We had a few facelifts and updates along the way since we first opened all those years ago, but I'm proud to say that Eden isn't going anywhere anytime soon."

"That's good to know. And, I'm looking at that scarf over there, I think I have to have it."

"My name is Sierra, by the way. It's nice to meet you."

"Brooke. Thank you for being so welcoming."

"I'm just glad that you're back. No matter the time between, repeat customers always make me happy."

We spoke for a little bit longer as we went over the scarf, the silk smooth on my hands.

"I love it. And I think this will be my welcome home present to me."

"So, you're moving to the area? I think that's what I got from what you were saying."

We went over to the cash register as Sierra packaged up my scarf, wrapping it in tissue paper and placing it in a gorgeous bag.

"I am. It's been a while since I lived in the Denver area, but I'm glad to be back. And though I don't need a silk scarf, I still want one."

"A girl always needs pretty things." Sierra winked as she told me the total.

I blinked. "I think you have the wrong price. I'm sorry, I thought it was a bit more."

Sierra beamed. "Aren't you an honest one? I truly appreciate that. However, you're getting the welcome home discount. Welcome back to Denver, Brooke."

She handed me the bag after I gave her my credit card, and I tried not to cry. Tears stung my eyes and I swallowed hard. I didn't have any other family. Luke was it for me. No one had said welcome home yet, although Lake and Leif had tried. They had been welcoming, sweet, and yet this just felt different.

"Thank you. Seriously. And I'll be back. I promise."

"That's exactly what I want to hear. Enjoy your day."

I said goodbye to Sierra and made my way down the street, looking at the familiar yet different places that had been here for years, scattered amongst the newer shops and cafés. There was a bookstore that I vaguely remembered had burned down at one point. But they had built it back up, and I figured that I would bring Luke here one day so that he could find a book of his own. Yes, there were probably places closer, but the street called to me.

I looked at a tattoo shop and grinned before nearly tripping over my feet because I knew that name and had to wonder if that was truly connected.

Montgomery Ink?

No, there was no way that this place was connected to all the other Montgomerys. Even though I had a feeling it was. Because Leif told me where his family worked. Spots of conversation and memories hit me again, but I told myself that I was just making things up.

There was no way, in a city as big as Denver, that my life would be this connected to a man I didn't want to think about.

This had to be another tattoo shop that just happened to have his family name on it. I didn't remember the name that he'd used for the shop, just that his last name was Montgomery.

And I was just losing my mind.

Next door was a little café called Taboo. I blinked, wondering if it was a café that was also a burlesque club for some reason, but through the windows I saw baked goods, coffee, and people milling about, enjoying their morning. Since I loved coffee, I figured I would go in and get a cup for myself. I was pretty sure I'd been here before, but then again, I hadn't remembered the name.

I had moved so many times that I seemed to have forgotten some essential things, like the fact that a Montgomery business was right next door.

No, I wasn't going to think about him or his last name.

It was just a coincidence.

A woman with bright red lips and long blond hair stood behind the counter and beamed at me.

"Welcome to Taboo. What can I get you?"

"I would love a vanilla latte. And whatever smells so good," I said with a laugh.

The woman grinned. "That could be a few things, but I did just pull some cinnamon rolls from the oven."

"Did you say cinnamon rolls, Hailey?"

I turned and looked at the open door separating the café from the building next door. A woman with striking dark hair, bright blue eyes, and full sleeves leaned against the doorway.

"I swear, as soon as I allow cinnamon into the air, you just come strolling through, Maya," Hailey said with a laugh.

"It's my curse." The tattooed woman looked at me and grimaced. "I'm sorry for cutting in line. I would say it's my prerogative since we're next door, but that still makes me a jerk. You go ahead. I'll wait in line for my cinnamon rolls."

I laughed, shaking my head. "Well, they do sound amazing, and since they seemed to have drawn you in like a moth to the flame, I'll take one."

"Two cinnamon rolls and two vanilla lattes coming up."

"She knows my drink," Maya said at my questioning look.

"That's sweet," I said, honestly. I liked the fact that this place was so welcoming.

"I'll know your drink soon, too. I always do," Hailey said as she went to work.

I held up my credit card and smiled. "I'll buy hers too. I had a good morning."

"You do *not* have to do that," Maya put in, waving me off.

"Let me. I just moved to the area, and everybody's been so nice to me. I want to be nice back."

The other woman smiled. "Well, thank you. And if you ever want a tattoo, you should come on over. We would love to have you."

"Aunt Maya, if she wants a tattoo, she's coming to me. Sorry."

I froze, that tingling sensation crawling up my spine. I told myself I would not press my thighs together, swallow hard, or react in any way. I knew that voice, that deep rumble that did things to me that I couldn't think about. Everything twisted in my brain at once as I tried to figure out exactly what happened.

I turned to see Leif standing there, a slight knowing grin on his face. He had pushed his hair back and his beard was a little scruffy. His bright blue eyes were on my face, and I tried not to lick my lips or think about exactly what effect his voice had on me in the past.

I had just had an entire afternoon and dinner with this man, his cousin, and my child. I hadn't reacted in any way then. I wasn't going to do it now. Not in public, and especially not in front of his freaking aunt.

"Oh, it's like that, is it?" Maya asked, laughter in her tone.

"It's not like anything," I blurted, and Leif raised a brow.

"Sure, Brooke. Whatever you say. Though of all the coffee places in the world, you have to walk into mine."

"Oh good, I'm delighted that I get to hear these lines," Maya said with a laugh.

"Your coffee and cinnamon rolls are ready," Hailey said from behind me. I whirled and tried not to trip on my own two feet.

"Oh. Thank you. Seriously. It smells amazing."

"No problem. But you do realize that you will have to tell us how you know our boy here." She winked as she said it, and I swallowed hard.

"Your boy?" I asked, my voice squeaking.

Leif let out a rough chuckle that did bad, bad things to me. "I told you that we Montgomerys take over the world. You just happen to be on our street."

Maya came forward and took her coffee and cinnamon roll as she raised her brow at Leif's words. "Seriously, Brooke, is it? It's nice to meet you. I'm sorry that my nephew here is being a dork and not introducing us properly."

I knew that there were other people in the café, but most weren't paying attention to us. They either had headphones on and were working, or paying attention to what was in front of them rather than the antics of whatever the hell was happening to me.

It was as if they were used to this, and knowing Leif, and how he told tales of the Montgomery family, maybe they were.

"Seriously, is everyone I'm going to bump into related to you?" I asked, my eyes wide as I looked over at Leif.

"I don't know who you've met yet. And technically, Hailey isn't related to me, but she's an honorary aunt," Leif answered.

"I am an actual aunt," Maya said as she held out her hand. "Maya Montgomery-Gallagher. It's nice to meet you."

I put my hand in hers. "Brooke Adler. It's good to meet you, too. Are you Lake's Mom?" I asked, trying to get the family tree right.

Maya raised a brow. "No, Lake is my cousin's kid. But I think of her as my niece as well. Leif over here is my brother's child. Austin, who owns the shop with me." Maya pointed behind her towards the open door of the tattoo shop. "His mom owns Eden, the boutique across the street."

I looked at the bag with my scarf in it and then up at Leif. "Your mom is that gorgeous woman with auburn hair, isn't she?" I asked, feeling like a poor gazelle surrounded by a pack of Montgomery lions.

Leif grinned. "She is. Dad's not working today because he's off with my siblings at some parent-teacher thing, but Mom is on guard at the shop. I just went to visit her, and she spoke of a lovely woman who was moving back to Denver and had bought a beautiful scarf. She also mentioned that she was pretty, and I should find her and ask her out. Because my mother is constantly trying to get me to settle down," Leif mumbled.

Maya and Hailey both leaned against the counter, staring at us and our byplay.

I let out a slow breath. "I've always loved that shop. You didn't tell me that your mom owned it."

"I want to know what's going on here, but I feel like if I ask anymore, Leif will pull you out of here and I'm never going to know." Maya laughed.

"Brooke and I go way back," Leif explained, and I was glad that was as far as he went. Because nobody else needed to know exactly how far back we went and what happened between us. I still couldn't quite believe it. "She also just moved in next door to Lake."

Maya's eyes widened and she beamed. "Oh, you bought that house, my brothers built it, and my sister did the landscaping."

I shook my head, rubbed my temple, and then took a sip of my latte.

"First, this coffee is amazing. Second, did I just step into a different realm I wasn't aware of? What do you mean your family built it? Or do I want to know?"

Leif laughed. "Some of my family own a construction business, and they just happened to have built part of the neighborhood. Seriously, it's just a coincidence. And you happen to be on the one street in all of Colorado where many of my family members own businesses. I swear you will not run into us in the grocery store or anywhere else around town. You just happened to be where we're mostly congregated."

"You mean on my favorite street in Denver," I mumbled.

"Sweet," Hailey said. She looked over at Maya. "I still have so many questions, but I think that we should leave these two kids alone."

"I guess you're right," Maya said with a sigh. "Thank you for the coffee and cinnamon roll. And I'm serious. If you don't want this big lug over there to do your ink, we would love to have you." She turned to Leif. "Say hello to my boy later, and will we see you this weekend for dinner?"

"You know it. Now I'm going to take Brooke out of here, so she doesn't run away screaming."

"I don't know if that will help," I said with a laugh. I wasn't joking either. I was just trying to keep up with everything.

Then Leif picked up his coffee, that I hadn't even seen him order, and I walked outside next to him, with him holding my bag from Eden and me nibbling on my cinnamon roll as we walked in silence.

"So, your family does own everything here. And all of my favorite spots."

"We own a lot of it. One of my aunts owns that bookshop, and a few of my aunts—that are technically second cousins or something—own places in Boulder, Fort Collins, and Colorado Springs."

I blinked. "How is that even possible?"

Leif shrugged. "I told you that my father had seven siblings, and they all needed jobs. They have lives, and nobody moved away from this area. My uncle Shep moved down to New Orleans at one point, but he moved back up here with his family later on. My cousins have moved around the United States for college and such, but we all end up coming back. This is home." He met my gaze, and I swallowed hard. "You know all about Colorado being home, right?"

"How is this even possible? I met you in Paris, Leif. *Paris*. I know we both said at the time that we were from here, but what are the odds? After all this time. How is this happening?"

I wasn't even going to touch on the fact that I was still bitter. Still angry. It had nothing to do with what happened in the past five years. Nothing to do with Luke's father, my new job, or the reason for moving.

No, it had all to do with what happened after Paris. Or rather, what hadn't happened.

"I don't know, Brooke. This is just my home. I don't know what else to think." He was standing in front of me, and I hadn't even realized his fingers were touching my skin, trailing along my jaw.

"Leave." It was the only thing I could say.

"Brooke."

"I don't know what to do."

He hadn't shown at the time, hadn't met me as we had promised.

I should be angry, push away, and forget everything that happened. But I wasn't that little girl anymore. I wasn't a teenager who thought she was an adult. I *was* an adult, a single mom, and I wanted to know him.

That was the problem with Leif Montgomery. I had always wanted to know him.

So when he lowered his head to mine and pressed a soft kiss against my lips, it was as if everything came back in a heartbeat. Memories of who we were and what we thought we wanted out of life assailed me.

"Just like I remember," he whispered.

I swallowed hard, licked my lips, and stepped back. "I'm not that person anymore, Leif. A lot of things have changed."

He studied my face and I wondered what I meant by that. What did I want? I wanted a new life, a change. That was why I moved here.

Leif might be part of my past, but he wasn't part of the past I was leaving.

I just didn't know what that meant, and since everything was so confusing, I needed to breathe first. To take things slow. To make a list, go through all of my options and then decide. That was the only way I could function.

"Welcome home, Brooke."

"To the same home you've always been," I whispered.

"I'm not going anywhere, Brooke. I never did."

"Are you sure about that?" I asked.

But he didn't answer, and I wasn't sure that he could. So we stood there on a busy street, one filled with so many memories, and yet, somehow, they were all tangled with Leif. I just hadn't known it. Once again, I stood on a precipice, waiting to fall.

Knowing the landing could only ever end in heartbreak.

CHAPTER FIVE

Brooke

I INHALED the scent of books, that familiar essence that settled me, and held back a smile. In another life, I would have been a librarian. Being surrounded by books soothed me, whether they were fiction, nonfiction, reference, or something unique.

I wasn't a librarian, though. No, as of today, I was a physics professor at Denver State University, DSU. Nuclear physics was my expertise, something I had gravitated towards in undergrad at this very university. I graduated here with my bachelor's in physics. I then had ended up at MIT for my doctorate before heading to the California Institute of Technology, also known as Caltech, for my postdoc and eventual job.

I had been a Pasadena girl for the past couple of years and enjoyed my job as a professor, researcher, and nuclear physicist, but it was nice to come home.

I had walked these hallowed halls as an undergrad, a teenager, and a young twentysomething, trying to figure out my place in the world.

And now here I was again, thirty years old, a single mom, and feeling slightly more lost than I had been when I first took the job in this tenure-track position.

"We're so happy that you're here," Patrice said as she smiled at me.

The older woman with dark hair, a kind smile, yet shrewd eyes nodded at me. "Not only is it nice to have another woman in the physics department, but your breadth of research is also quite illuminating."

I looked over at Dr. Patrice Robbins and smiled softly. "I'm glad that there is another woman in the department, as well. Whenever I work with the chemistry department, I usually get to work alongside more women, and with each passing year, there are more and more women in science, but you're right, there is a lack in most physics circles."

"Well, you're not alone here. And now it is not just me at this level, though there are many women in the associate track, postdocs, and students. We're all happy to have you." Her eye twitched for a second, and I wondered if she truly meant *everyone* was happy to have me.

Because it was my experience that not everybody liked when a younger woman stepped into such a high-powered job in academia. I was younger than most of my counterparts and had finished my degrees in fewer years than some. I was good at what I did, and I was smart. I was also very blessed with my child-care opportunities. When I lost Luke's father before Luke was even born, I hadn't been forced to put my dreams aside while caring for my infant son.

I had still somehow been able to do it all, although I don't remember sleeping those first two years.

"I'm excited to get started. I know I'm the newbie, so any help and advice you have, I'm here for it."

"I know we've been talking about lesson plans, and physics 102 you will be teaching this semester starting next week, so you're already ahead of the game on that. And the head of the department is excited to hear about it, too."

"I had a meeting with him just before this. I know he's off to speak with the President of the University for one of their board meetings, so he's a very busy man."

"He does the work of two people, but I so appreciate him. He listens to what his professors need, and more importantly, he listens to the students."

I smiled at that. "That sounds like a great place to start."

"Glad to hear it. Now, you can set up your office however you want. You know how to do office hours and what classes you will be teaching this semester. We can discuss next year's classes soon, as well. I know you are going to want to get started on your research team, any grad classes that you're working on next semester, and postdocs and graduate students you plan to take on."

I nodded, knowing the drill. I had done similar work at Caltech, though now I was in a more prominent position.

"I've been working on those plans and speaking with everyone through email and phone calls for the past three months, so I'm ready to go."

"Good, and of course, there's the social aspect of our job." She rolled her eyes and I held back a laugh, even as tension slid into me.

"Social aspect?" I asked, suddenly afraid that because we were the women in this position, we would be in charge of setting up parties and dinners for faculty.

She held up her hand. "No, not that."

"Was it all over my face?" I asked, laughing now.

"A little bit. I thought the same thing when I started here a few years ago. But you were here as an undergrad, though I was in the chemistry department then, so I don't remember teaching you. I'm sorry."

I shook my head. "I don't think we crossed paths. So, what do you mean by social?" I asked, knowing that I had a few things to do, and I wanted to get home to see Luke soon. Not to mention I was going to do my best not to think about Leif Montgomery and that kiss.

No matter what happened, I could not think about that kiss.

Even if I could still taste him on my lips, feel the tingling sensation that wouldn't go away.

No, I would not think about him.

"Our department chair wants us to be more of a 'family' than a workplace." I wasn't sure if Patrice agreed with what she said, but she wasn't rolling her eyes as she said it, so I figured it might be a good thing.

"Okay? What does that entail?"

"That means if you have a problem or need to talk to someone about anything, work, students, paperwork, anything related to that, you go to your department chair or anyone you feel comfortable with within the department. We don't want you to feel like you're all alone and new at this. We've all had a few more years of experience than you, but that doesn't mean what you bring isn't beneficial." She let out a breath. "I'm saying this all wrong because there's the party line of wanting you to feel comfortable, and me as a person telling you that I'm excited that you're here. And that if you have a problem with anyone in the department, come to me, and I'll help."

I froze, a little worried about what she was saying.

"Am I going to have a problem with someone in the department?" I asked, my voice low.

We were in my office now, a smallish rectangle of a room with bookshelves, a desk, and a couple of chairs. I would spruce it up and make it my own soon, someplace I could work, study, and bring students in, but right now it just felt like an empty box.

Patrice closed the door behind her, and trepidation filled me.

"You were the best candidate for the job, and every single one of us, bar one, is excited that you're here. You are in a tenure-track position, and this university will do great with you."

"But?" I asked, my voice a little sharper than intended.

"There is another associate professor named Landon Cunning who might make trouble."

I froze; that name sounded far too familiar for my own liking. "As in President Cunning? The former president of the university when I was a student?" I asked, pieces clicking into place.

Patrice cringed. "Yes. His son's an associate professor now and wanted your job."

I rubbed my temples. "Great. Let me guess, Landon has made it known that he wanted this job and isn't happy that I'm here?"

"Pretty much. He's very smooth about his desire for it as well. He's not going to do anything to damage your reputation or the reputation of this school. But he is going to be an asshole. Sorry for my language."

"Don't be sorry about your language. I curse more than that."

Patrice's eyes filled with laughter. "I have a feeling we could be good friends, Brooke."

"It sounds like I could use one. I have to ask though, if you don't think he will hurt my reputation or this school, why are you warning me?"

"Because he can be intimidating and a jerk. And I don't want you to be blindsided because he wanted your job and didn't get it. You were the one who was more qualified. You have the better research grants and the broader ideas for the university. You know just as well as I do that Harvard and MIT are ranked number one and two in physics in the United States. You left Caltech, which was ranked third. You could have done extraordinary things there. I know you could have. But you came here, and we are tied with Stanford at fourth in physics." Patrice gave me a grin. "It is my goal to beat Stanford, so we will no longer be tied, and maybe one day hit third while we're at it."

"That would be nice." I let out a breath. "I didn't leave Caltech because I didn't think they were as good as here or wanted greener pastures. I came here because the department gave me what I needed and will need, and this is where I grew up. I wanted to come home. Meaning I want this university to thrive with me here. And I want to thrive as well. It's good to know that I will have some bumpy roads ahead, but at least I know where they're coming from."

I didn't think it would come from the woman in front of me. She had warned me right off the bat that somebody had wanted my job, especially because this Landon was the son of the former president of the university. The president had retired because he had felt like it, rather than being pushed out for some scandal or something. So at least I counted that better than an issue that could have arisen. However, I was still worried. I had enough on my plate rather than worrying about some guy who didn't like that I got the job he wanted.

Worst case, he thought I got it just because I was a woman and I was needed to reach their "quota." Best case, he would get over it once he realized that I was a hard worker, good at what I did, and was going to bring good things to this university.

I just hoped I was given a chance.

I didn't like feeling as if I might not fit in already, and I hadn't even met the other professors, other than during my interviews and through online meetings.

Patrice left me after walking me to my lab, a place filled with a few items from the previous professor, but now I would make my own.

I rolled my shoulders back and turned as the door opened and my team walked in.

I had chosen my team without ever having met them in person. Coming in as a professor trying to build a team for papers and books and research that would help the world of nuclear physics wasn't easy. I wasn't bringing anyone with me, as some people did. My former professor had actually brought the postdoc with them as a former grad student, and at least they'd had a ready-made team with the two of them.

I was starting nearly from scratch.

"Hi there, Dr. Adler," Randall said as he set down his messenger bag. Randall was my postdoc, who had a year left under his contract before he would start looking for jobs, in the private sector, industry, or as an associate professor at some other university. He could do many things once he left this university and his place with me, but for the next year, he was my partner.

"You can call me Brooke while it's the group of us," I said as I smiled at the rest of my team.

Jennifer was a fourth-year grad student who had worked under the previous professor, and instead of moving to a group that could have accommodated her so she could finish her previous research, she decided to work with me. My research didn't follow the same path that hers had, but I was going to tailor-fit what she had been working on with what I had so that she could develop a doctoral thesis and presentation within the next two years. If she had been a fifth-year grad, I would have hoped her professor would have at least waited for her to graduate, but thankfully we didn't have to deal with that.

She and Randall would be the leaders for my team.

Randall would also be working with me for my class since it was a team effort to make sure that a GEN Ed class of introductory physics, which had over three hundred students per class, actually knew what they were doing.

The last remaining member of my team was Hannah, a second-year grad who had changed focus after the previous year.

"Hello, Jennifer and Hannah," I said, going to my laboratory desk. "I know we haven't been here that long, but I am excited that we will be working together."

"It's good to see you in person," Jennifer said as she sat down at her desk.

"I totally agree," Hannah added.

"I know I missed the introductions to the next wave of grad students that are going to be coming here in the next week, but soon they're going to be doing the rounds where we will get to put on our best faces and hope that they want to work with us in the lab."

"Of course they are going to want to work with us. We're going to kick ass," Jennifer said with a grin.

"That's what I want to hear. I know we already went over a few things that we're going to start next week, and I have about forty-five minutes before I need to head home. So, do you guys have any questions?"

"So, you don't expect us to stay too late every evening?" Hannah asked.

I shook my head. "As long as the work gets done and we are there for each other when we need to be, I don't expect you to work until one in the morning. And I'm going to be honest, all three of you know that I'm a single mom. I may have help, but I can't expect her to stay overnight so that I can get some research done that would be better served after a few hours of sleep and lots of coffee."

All three of them nodded as we went over the next steps of what we needed to do in the next couple of weeks. I was going to ensure that everybody that worked for me understood that being able to sleep during grad school led to better decisions. I didn't want my students in undergrad or grad school to be strung out, unhealthy, exhausted, and a mess to be around.

Luke was also my first priority, beyond my career or anything I was doing in the physics world. He knew that, and my team would soon know that if they hadn't already figured it out. If anybody had a problem that I was a single mom, they were going to have to deal with it.

But, so far, things were working out. We went over a checklist, and I knew I would be emailing them soon, but for now I wanted to get home and see my kiddo.

Once we were done in the lab, I followed them out to my office to gather my things. I'd spent the morning downtown, reliving my youth and memories that continued to assail me, the afternoon getting Luke from kindergarten, set up with his nanny, and getting settled at DSU. This evening I would spend time with my favorite person in the world. And not think about Leif. Apparently, I wasn't doing a very good job about that because it was all I was thinking about. Over and over and over again.

I slid my belongings into my leather bag, grabbed my purse, and headed toward my door.

A man in trim slacks, a dark Henley, and a wicked grin leaned against my doorway. His chestnut hair was longish, a lock of it trailing over his forehead. He had deep-green eyes and slight stubble over his chin.

He also did nothing for me, unlike Leif.

Well, crap.

"Brooke, correct?" the man in front of me asked, and I did my best not to stiffen. Because now I knew exactly who this was.

"Dr. Adler, yes. You must be Dr. Cunning." I held up my hand, and he looked down at it for a minute before giving me a tight and formal handshake.

"You can call me Landon if you'd like. I can call you Dr. Adler if that is what you prefer."

I grinned at him and tried not to feel weird. To be honest, he would've creeped me out just with the way he was looking at me, even without Patrice's warning. But because I had been forewarned, I wasn't going to let him get away with trying to put me off my stride.

"You know us, doctors, we spent so much time trying to get those letters, we tend to like them. But I can call you whatever you'd like. Landon or Dr. Cunning."

"I guess going by doctors works. Although if anyone asks us if we know a doctor while we're sitting in a restaurant and somebody's choking, they better not look to us, right?"

"Hazards of the job, I guess. Anyway, I'm headed out. It is so nice to meet you. I'm sure I'll see you around the halls."

He looked at my office with a proprietary gaze, and I wanted to kick him out, but I had to be better than him. I needed to show him that I was the person for this job and that he didn't have to act like a peacock strutting down the hallway. It was the only way to get things done. It was what I had learned in every situation I had ever been in when someone didn't feel like I was qualified for the place I was in.

He would learn that I was far smarter than he thought I was. And that I wasn't the bitch he wanted me to be.

"Let me take you out for a drink." He grinned, acting so smooth, as if I hadn't seen that anger in his gaze for an instant. "To welcome you to the university."

"I need to head home, but thank you. Maybe a group of us can go out for drinks soon."

There was no way I would be going out for a drink alone with this man. Ever.

"Sounds like a plan. I'll see you around, Brooke, I mean, Dr. Adler." He winked before he strolled away, going to talk with an older professor with salt-

and-pepper hair that I recognized from the chemistry department from when I was a student.

I shook my head and told myself I just imagined the hostility even though I knew I hadn't, even a little bit.

Not the perfect way to start my first day, but considering it wasn't my first full day at the university, I wasn't going to count this.

I made my way to my car and headed home, knowing that May and Luke would be waiting for me. I pulled past May's car into my garage, and practically threw myself out of my SUV, wanting to see Luke. Though I had worked long hours before, and it wasn't as if this was the first time he had ever been with a caretaker other than me, we had been spending so much time together lately. I just wanted to see my little boy. Yes, I had seen him after his half-day of school so I could hug him right as soon as he got out, but it was only for a few moments before I had had to go to work and leave him alone without me.

I missed my little boy, and I hated not being able to be with him every single moment of every single day.

But hopefully, I would get better at this.

Or at least get back into the hang of it.

"Mommy!" Luke called as he ran to me. I went down to my knees, tossed my things on the floor, and hugged him close, inhaling that little boy scent that was all my son.

He started talking a mile a minute about his afternoon with May as if I hadn't seen him a couple of hours ago. For some reason, my eyes stung, and I swallowed hard before I looked up at the woman with straight black hair, green eyes, and a sweet smile.

May waved. "Today has gone amazing. I'm so happy that we're having as much fun as we are. I can go over exactly what happened today, or maybe we can do that tomorrow? That way you can have the rest of the evening with the kiddo?"

It was as if she read my mind. Yes, I wanted to go through everything in detail because I was that anal-retentive, and I knew it would be helpful for our relationship, so we were always on the same page. But I also wanted time with my son.

So I nodded, said my goodbyes as May hugged Luke tight, and then I sat down on the floor right next to my son and heard about his day in detail once again, and knew that even though this had been a hard decision, it had been the best one.

Even though I had no family here, no connections, it was better for us to move back to Colorado.

Luke was my family, my connection.

When we heated up dinner—casserole thanks to Lake—I couldn't help but think of Leif, and the fact that Montgomerys seemed to be closing ranks around me, even though they hadn't meant to, and I hadn't even realized it was happening. Everywhere I went, I seemed to bump into a Montgomery. There were probably a couple at the university for all I knew. Either as students or professors. I would have to check into that.

Or I could just ignore it because it didn't matter.

Of course, my phone lit up at that moment, an unfamiliar number gracing the screen.

UNKNOWN NUMBER:

This is Leif. You gave me your number all those years ago, and I kept it. I hope this is still you.

I swallowed hard. I had ignored the texts between us all those years ago because I'd been so angry. And deleted his contact information.

I never blocked him.

Luke was coloring in his favorite superhero coloring book, and I knew that I only had a few minutes before I had to get him ready for bed, but I swallowed hard and picked up my phone.

ME:

It's still me.

LEIF:

You have no idea how happy I am to hear that. I was really worried I was texting a random stranger.

I don't know. It's been a few years. I feel like a stranger.

I hadn't even meant to type that, but there was no going back now. Leif Montgomery just did that to me.

LEIF:

I would like to get to know you. I know that's a line, and I could probably come up with something better, to flirt better, but I don't know. I felt the connection today. And we keep bumping into each other. That has to mean something. That's not a line. Can I take you out? I know you're busy with your new life, with Luke, but let me take you out.

I should say no. I should walk away and forget him. Just like I had been trying to forget him for ten years.

I had been doing a pretty damn good job of it too, until I moved back and met up with him again.

Not once, but twice.

There was no escaping Leif Montgomery, especially not when his cousin lived next door.

If I said no now, what would happen? Would I stop thinking about him? No, I didn't think that was possible.

So I did the only thing that made sense to me.

I let out a breath and answered.

ME:

Okay.

I hoped this time I wouldn't break when it all crashed down around me.

CHAPTER SIX

Leif

Montgomery Ink Legacy's one-year anniversary was coming up, yet it still felt like opening day had been just yesterday.

Our shop wasn't downtown, surrounded by extraordinary architecture and busy necessities. But we did have the mountains as our backdrop and trees surrounding us, though we were technically in a strip mall.

My aunt and uncle's place down in Colorado Springs was also in a strip mall right off the highway. Our legacy establishment at least had trees surrounding us. It didn't make it any easier for us to not compare ourselves to the original shop in downtown Denver, but that was something I did every day anyway, even if my family didn't.

The original Montgomery Ink had a few cosmetic changes over time. It had once been bright hot pink and black with chrome, then had gone a little more subtle, and then went back to nearly princess goth, according to my cousin.

Now it looked like a professional art-house with a similar feel to my place. Not because I wanted to emulate my parents, but because we had similar taste.

When I was younger, I tried to figure out what I wanted to be. Who I want to be. I had tried to figure out exactly *where* I wanted to find myself. I thought I'd be an artist of some sort because that's what I loved. At one point, I thought I would go to culinary school, but no, art in some fashion had been for me.

When I was trying to figure out what I wanted to do, Lake had come to me with an idea. She was an investor, a brilliant woman who had her own tech company and made a shit ton of money. She constantly put that back into other women-owned businesses but wanted something of her own that was family-driven.

So she and I decided to do something with it. I had saved and scrimped for the past ten years or so, working at my dad's shop, then down in New Orleans at my uncle's old place, and countless other sites learning art and getting experience. That's why I had gone to Paris all those years ago.

When the time came for a new branch of Montgomery Ink to open, Lake and I had come up with a plan. And then my best friend Nick had wanted in, had saved up as well, and had wanted to be a full partner.

He might not be a Montgomery, but in my heart, he was. And frankly, with how much time he spent with my family and how he'd practically lived with us when we were kids, he was a Montgomery.

Sebastian was our fourth partner, or at least he *would* be. He still needed to finish college, something he wanted to do, not just for his parents, and had a few more years of apprenticeship ahead of him, but when the time came, he was going to buy into our branch as well.

As we had come up with this plan as a group of four, we had gone to my father and aunt to discuss how we could make this happen.

That was two years ago, and now here I was today, sitting in my booth, going over sketches for my next client. All while trying not to feel like I was failing because I wasn't living up to anyone's expectations.

Not that those expectations were put on me by anyone but myself. It was complicated, and I hated that my mind kept doing this. I'd lived ten years of twisted shit in my brain before becoming a Montgomery. Those years didn't just fade away, despite trying to bury them for as long as I had.

"Okay, get it out," my best friend said from the booth beside me, and I narrowed my gaze at him.

"What?" I asked, though I knew that Nick could read my mind like no other. It should probably bother me that Nick knew me better than my siblings did, but my siblings were a lot younger than me. I loved my brothers and sister. They were everything to me. But Nick and I bonded from the moment we first met. There was no changing that bond.

The only other person I was as close to was Lake, and she hadn't come into my life until years later. My cousin and I had just clicked, and we hadn't been apart since.

"I think Nick is wondering why you are growling to yourself as you draw," Tristan clarified as he worked on a floral piece on his client's ribs.

"Maybe he's thinking about his date tonight," Taryn added, her lips twitching into a smile.

"Oh, so he finally asked her out? I missed that part." Leo ran his hands through his hair and grinned up at me. "Congrats, man."

I glared at my friends and coworkers and shook my head. "You guys know far too much about me. I don't like it."

"They just like you," Tristan's client said from where she lay face-down on the bench, her eyes closed in peace as if she wasn't getting a tattoo.

I loved that nearly every woman who came in for a tattoo either smiled, held an entire conversation, or fell asleep. It was often the big beefy guys who were assholes to us, talking about the little women who couldn't handle pain, who were usually the ones that screamed the loudest.

That always made me smile.

"What did I miss?" Sebastian asked as he walked through the door, Lake right behind him.

I shook my head, laughing now. "We're a full house here, and everybody's up in my business."

"Oh, about your date with Brooke?" Lake asked as she walked toward the back office, her high heels echoing off the walls.

We had painted the place soft cream with white trim. That way, we could add artwork and other pieces to personalize each individual station. Lake had wanted to go gold with the fixtures, with funky lighting and chandeliers to make it look elegant and yet artsy at the same time. I had gone along with it since she knew better than I did, and the guys had agreed.

We had a set of offices in the back where we did a lot of the paperwork, and Lake was there more often than I was. I had a business degree and had gotten it so I could do exactly this, but Lake enjoyed that part. Since she was the one that was a master with money and tech, I let her do it.

She leaned against the wall, slid off her high heels, let out a groan, and then slid on a pair of flats that she kept here.

"I don't understand why you wear those high heels if you just come here and take them off. Why didn't you take them off in the car? Why wear them at all?" Nick asked, grumbling.

The two were friends, business partners, and adversaries. They always rubbed each other the wrong way, and yet I knew they would do anything for each other. Just like I would for either of them.

Lake gave him her prim and proper gaze, and I held back a laugh. Nick hated when she did that. It just made me smile.

"I've been wearing heels all day, and I *can* constantly wear them, but I wasn't in the mood. I like how my legs look in them, so get over yourself, Nick."

"Ooh," Tristan, Taryn, and Leo cheered simultaneously.

I looked at Sebastian and we shook our heads before he came to sit next to me and look over what I was doing. Sebastian and I knew better than to egg the two of them on in their bickering. It wasn't like they were truly fighting. They just enjoyed the push.

Nick growled. "I was just wondering why you were hurting yourself. Far be it for me to talk about women's fashion."

"You really shouldn't be talking about women's fashion," Taryn said with a laugh.

"Fine." Nick rolled his eyes. I looked over at Sebastian.

"How was class today?" I asked, and Sebastian rubbed the back of his neck.

"Fine. I know I need a degree because I want to learn how to help take care of the business, but it's a little weird already knowing what I'm going to do for the rest of my life while a lot of my friends in college are trying to figure out where is the best place to party."

My cousin sometimes seemed older than his years, but it also made me sad because he should be able to go out to party to have fun.

"Are you going out with your girlfriend at all? Beyond your old people dates?"

"Old people dates?" Lake asked as she walked forward, looking over a stack of papers.

"He's just being a jerk. I do not go on old people dates."

"You guys went to a stamp collection *event* last week," I said dryly.

"That's a thing?" Nick asked.

Sebastian held out his hands. "I'm eighteen. I can't drink. Not that I'm sure I even want to. And Marley wanted to see if it was fun." He gave me a dry look. "It was not fun."

I laughed, shaking my head. "You love that girl something fierce."

Sebastian grinned. "I do. And one day, she's going to be my wife."

Leo coughed into his fist. "You're eighteen, man. I understand young love and all that, but have you dated anyone other than her?"

Sebastian shook his head. "No, but why should I have to date other people to know that Marley is it for me?"

"Childhood loves can be the sweetest thing," Lake put in.

"Really? How's that guy Deke that you dated in high school?" Nick asked.

In answer, Lake flipped him off. "Go to hell."

"Already there, babe."

The two went at it again. I sighed.

"They should just make out already," Sebastian grumbled, and I held back a laugh.

"I think they would kill each other if they ever dated. Plus, Lake is dating that guy. Zach."

Sebastian shook his head. "The guy from that double date?"

"Same guy. He seems good for her. Or at least she's happy. And Nick and Lake just like butting heads. Not every frenemy you have turns into something more."

"Well, if that isn't an ominous saying, I don't know what is." Sebastian grinned, then looked over my work. "You have an appointment later today?"

"Tomorrow. I'm just getting everything prepped because I'm going out with Brooke tonight."

"So, tell us about this Brooke. I hear she's the one that you dated in Paris."

I scowled over at Lake. "Did you tell everybody?

"Maybe." My cousin raised her chin. "Or maybe I just told the crew here when you weren't looking."

"Don't you dare tell my parents," I growled.

"Oh, they already know." Sebastian beamed.

I scowled over at my cousin. "What?"

"You practically claimed her in front of Aunt Maya and Hailey. Of course, the family knows. Now we're all invested in this relationship with Brooke. I'm surprised it took you this long to ask her out."

"Dear God," I grumbled.

"It's your fault for laying claim to her inside the family café," Lake warned.

"With that logic, there's no place safe in the state of Colorado when it comes to you Montgomerys," Nick complained.

"That is true. It's why I'll never date a Montgomery, and I always ask for someone's birth records before I go out with them." Leo laughed, his eyes twinkling.

I rolled my eyes. "You guys are hilarious. I'm so happy that we're sitting here discussing dating my family, not working."

"You're just salty because we're all interested in your relationship," Lake teased. "Seriously though, make this work because I want to go on a double date."

"We all know how well the double date with you worked out last time." I crossed my eyes.

"It's not my fault it didn't work. That just means you were waiting for Brooke." She rolled her eyes and went back to the office to work. I scowled at my family and friends and did the same, knowing that I needed to head home and get ready soon.

I had a date with Brooke tonight, and I knew this was my last chance.

At what?

I didn't know.

But some part of me wanted to find out.

CHAPTER SEVEN

Leif

BROOKE WANTED to meet me at the restaurant, rather than having me pick her up. Honestly, I was shocked she had even agreed to the date in the first place, so I wasn't going to be picky about it. She had a kid to worry about, and though I had been in her house, and knew where she lived, there were boundaries. And I understood them.

But I still wanted to know why.

Why she'd given up on us before we had even had a chance all those years ago.

Had she found someone else? Well, clearly, she had because she was a mom, after all. But had she found someone else right after Paris? While we were still in Paris?

Had she realized that she wanted someone different and I wasn't it?

Our time in Paris had meant something to me.

Clearly, it had meant something different to her, and maybe tonight we would actually figure out what that was.

Or we could move on from who we had been, something I was trying to do now that I wasn't a teenager or twentysomething anymore. Maybe ignoring our pasts and moving on was the best bet. She had said yes to this date, after all— that counted for something.

And I was going to make sure it did because I needed it to.

I wanted her, and I wanted to see what could happen if we finally did take that chance.

I pulled into the casual American cuisine restaurant and got out of the car, not at all surprised to see that Brooke was already there. She stood by the entrance in a pretty dress, high heels, and frowned down at her phone. That little V between her brows deepened and I wondered if she was worried about something, or if she was already regretting this.

I cleared my throat. "I should have remembered that you like to be earlier than anybody else. I'm sorry I'm late."

Brooke looked up, her eyes wide, and she slid her phone into her purse and smiled at me.

My heart sped up with that smile. I got lost in those eyes, and it was hard for me to even think.

She had always done that to me, and here she was, doing it again.

"I'm just perpetually early. My sitter and Luke were having such a grand old time, that they didn't need me to stay and interrupt their evening any longer than I was." She rolled her eyes, grinning. She wasn't worried about the sitter spending so much time with her kid that it changed her dynamic. She was self-assured when she came to being a mother; I liked that about her.

"Luke's a great kid, I could see why he gets along with everybody that he meets."

Brooke beamed as if I had told her that she just won a million dollars. "He really is the best. And he loves his nanny already. I was a little worried about starting off a whole new relationship when we moved out here, but they clicked right away, and I'm forever grateful for her."

"I'm glad that you're able to get childcare worked out."

I gestured towards the restaurant, placed my hand at the small of her back, and tried to ignore the warmth emanating off of her as she stiffened ever so slightly, before relaxing into my touch.

I counted that as a win because she hadn't pulled away. I might've surprised her, but she wasn't pulling away.

"I'm glad that I was able to work everything out as well. The school has some childcare, but not exactly what I wanted. I never want Luke to feel like a burden."

I nodded and gave my name to the hostess as she looked for our reservation. We followed the woman quickly to the table. I sat across from Brooke, trying not to get lost in her eyes, and to remember what we were talking about.

"My family decided around the time that they were all having kids to create a childcare facility for all the Montgomerys. It started off as a room in the back of the tattoo shop and turned into something a bit bigger. With so many cousins, it made sense. Now there are Montgomery family childcare services in four cities."

Brooke leaned forward, grinning. "Is it just for Montgomerys? Or do you guys have an actual business for people with Montgomery connections?"

"We're a business, in that we have all the paperwork and it is legal, but really only family and friends of the Montgomerys, and those who work for Montgomery-owned businesses can keep their kids there. We're talking about more than a dozen or so kids at a time, especially back when all my siblings were younger. I don't think they could handle much more."

Brooke's eyes widened and she shook her head. "All I have is Luke, so it's kind of unimaginable that you have so many family members. Though I felt that way when we first met. You had this huge family, and I had only had my parents."

Something crossed her features, and I wasn't sure I was ready to dive too deep into all that pain and loss. And from the way that she closed up, neither was she. I had to keep this casual at first, go slow.

As in, don't scare her with promises of forever because I wasn't sure that's what I had to offer. I had to make sure that's what either of us would want in the first place.

"I still can't believe I said yes," Brooke blurted, and I threw my head back and laughed.

I noticed a few stares our way, but I shrugged them off. I was used to people staring. I was a big guy, had tattoos and piercings, and grew up with people who had even more than I did.

Staring was the usual.

"Honestly, I'm surprised you said yes." I grinned as I said it, and she smiled right back before looking contemplative.

"What are we doing?" she asked.

I didn't have a chance to answer because our waiter was there, taking our order. By the time they were gone, Brooke was staring at me, her gaze nervous.

"I wanted to take you out to dinner, Brooke. There's something here. You can feel it, can't you?"

I wasn't good about being open like this, honest. But it felt like I had known Brooke forever, not just I had known her forever ago.

"I don't know, Leif. I'm just trying to get my life in order. Start a new career, be a good mom. I don't know if I have time for dating."

I looked around. "We have time right now. Have a delicious dinner. You tell me about your work, I'll tell you about mine. If we start talking about my family, that will take hours, and there you go, a whole date."

Brooke's brows rose. "You think a date is going to take hours?"

I smiled; I couldn't help it. "If you do it right."

"You're ridiculous, Montgomery."

"I try. No seriously, tell me about work. Luke. Anything." I paused. "Wait. What if you don't want to talk about Luke? Is he off-limits? I understand if he is. I've never actually dated a single mom before."

She gave me a small smile, playing with the edge of her water glass. "I haven't dated much as a single mom."

"Can you talk about his father?" I hadn't meant to ask that because I figured it was a touchy subject. I had just said we could talk about anything else and to keep things from getting complicated. Yet here I was, making things complicated.

"Luke's father passed away." She let out a breath as I reached forward and gripped her hand.

"I'm sorry. Let's talk about anything else. Let's talk about cheese." I blurted out the first thing that came to mind, and since I was Montgomery, of course it was cheese.

Brooke's eyes widened before she burst out laughing. "I had forgotten your love of cheese. Okay, we're not surrounded by French cheeses, so I know you must be sad, but let's talk about cheese."

I shook my head. "If that's what you want." My lips twitched, as did hers.

She met my gaze, then shrugged. "I never married Henry, Luke's father. He was an English professor, and quite a bit older than me. We had a glorious affair, that was never meant to last, and then I got pregnant." She shrugged, but I knew there's a lot more to that. "I was in my twenties, he was nearly forty."

My brows rose. "Are you serious?"

She gave me a defiant look, even though I saw the hurt in them. "I was an adult, making my own choices, but he was having a midlife crisis, and I was letting myself have fun for the first time in a long while. Either way, I got Luke out of the deal. When I was heading into my third trimester, Henry was killed in a botched robbery attempt. They found the guy. He's in jail now and will be for a long, long time. But Henry never got to meet his son, and Luke never got to meet his father." She let out a slow breath. "I was never going to marry Henry. But we would've been good friends raising him. And that is my tragic story. I'm a single mom with no parents, with no one. But I moved back to Colorado because I wanted a new chance to live life to its fullest, in a place that I used to love. In a place that I want my son to love. California worked for us before, but the job that I have now at the university is going to bring more opportunities for me and my son. And that's all that matters."

I reached out once more, gripped her hand, and squeezed. "I'm sorry. That you went through all of that, and that you have to explain all of that to random dudes you go on dates with. I'm sorry that Luke lost him. I'm sorry that you did, too."

She met my gaze again, smiling softly. "I know you lost your mom at a young age and didn't find your father until you were older, so I know you sort of have an idea what Luke is dealing with. But he is strong, and I remind him of his father as much as I can, even though they never met. I'm trying to give him everything that I possibly can. That way he never feels like he's lacking anything."

"I know you, Brooke. Or, at least, I knew you before. I'm starting to know the woman in front of me. You would never make him feel like he's missing out on anything. You're doing everything you can for him."

"You can tell that from just looking at me?" she asked, studying my face.

"Maybe. Or maybe I can just tell. Who knows." I let out a breath. "My mom was an okay mom. I know it's probably not the greatest thing to say about someone who's no longer here. But as I remember the years that I had with her, I know that she wasn't the best mom."

Perhaps this wasn't the best conversation for a first date, but Brooke knew some of it, and we had a past. A history. We weren't starting at square one here.

"Mom drank a lot, did some pot, did a few things that weren't pot. She liked what she liked, and liked who she liked, and sometimes that wasn't me."

"Leif."

I shook my head. "No, I don't mind talking about it. I spoke about it with my family and with therapists numerous times." I let out a breath, even as I gave her a self-deprecating smile.

"My mom hid my existence from my dad because she felt like it. Because she wanted the power, and she didn't want to share me. She might have made up reasons later for him, but they were lies. It didn't matter that she had been dating my dad, and even though my dad had always said that they were casual, he never would've just left me alone with her. As soon as he realized I existed, he dropped everything for me."

Brooke pressed her lips together, as if she wanted to say something, but held back.

"He went through all the legal hassles and paperwork in order to keep me, even though I had run away from CPS that day, hitching rides in order to get downtown to see him. It made no sense, and I was an idiot ten-year-old, but he took me in." I smiled at her. "So did my mom, Sierra."

"Your dad's wife?"

I shook my head. "Not at the time. They were only dating. Or, I don't even know if they were really dating then. Maybe just like one date or something. But she was there when I showed up, and she hasn't gone away since." I cringed. "I call her Mom, and most of the time I think she's a better mom to me than my mom had ever been. I know for damn sure she's a good mom to my three siblings. And I feel bad about saying that because my birth mom is gone."

My birth mom had done things that even my dad didn't know, he never needed to know. My dad had enough guilt about all that time he lost as it was. He didn't need anything else on his massive shoulders.

Brooke was quiet for a moment, as if she were trying to formulate a response. "You do have an abundance of family; I'm glad that you have them."

"I am, too. And Luke will always be happy he has you." I smiled then, thinking of my family and all they did for me. I tried to be the best son for them, to give back. I wasn't always, but I figured my track record was better than it could have been.

"You never going to answer what we're doing, are you?" she asked, after the waiter set down our food.

I looked at my plate, and then up at her, meeting her gaze. "I don't know what I'm doing. I know that you need to find your roots, to be a good mom, but you can do that while having dinner with me, Brooke. Because I want to kiss you again. I want to see you again. But if I'm going to scare you by saying things like that, you have to let me know now."

I wasn't sure why I was saying any of this. Not when I had shit to do that could crumble everything, but I had told myself I was going to try. Try to go out and have a future that wasn't just me working for hours upon hours. I tried that with my blind date, and yet here was Brooke, my past coming back with a vengeance. I didn't ask her about why she hadn't come before, after Paris. Why she was here now.

This wasn't the time for that.

It would be, soon.

"You confound me, Leif Montgomery. You make me want to say things and do things that I know I do not have time for."

I smirked. "It's what I'm best at, babe."

"Don't call me babe." Her eyes filled with laughter as she said it, though, so I grinned.

"Whatever you say, babe."

———

For the rest of our dinner, we stayed on safe topics: work, friends, and Lake.

When I walked her to her car, I slid her hair behind her ear, trying not to press her against her door and ravish her mouth. I had some standards.

Not many, but some.

"Let me take you out again."

She shook her head, and disappointment filled me. "I'm busy, Leif." She held up her hand as I started to argue. "I'm not saying no. I'm just saying I have lesson plans, new classes, and research. I have people to hire and countless other work things. I have a son, a new house, and boxes I still haven't unpacked. I'm doing so much, but I want to see you again, Leif. I don't know what that says about me, but I want to. I just don't know when."

Relief slammed into me so hard, that I knew I would have to worry about that later. Instead, I leaned down and brushed my lips against hers. "I think we can find some time to work with a few of those things. It doesn't have to be dinner and a movie, Brooke. It could be me helping you put up a shelf."

"Are you saying I can't put up a shelf by myself?" she asked, teasing.

"See, that's one of those tripwire questions that women put out that I'm not going to even try to answer."

She rolled her eyes and I kissed her again.

"Go home to your kid, get some work done if that's what you're going to do, and I'll see you soon. Because there's something here, Brooke. You know there is."

I kissed her one more time and walked away before she could say no.

It was probably wrong of me, but I'd do what I had to so I could see her again.

I was just about to start my car when my phone rang and I frowned at the readout, not recognizing the number.

"Hello?"

"Leif Montgomery?" a tired voice asked, and I froze, a sense of foreboding sliding over my body.

"This is him."

"Sorry for the late call, we've been trying to get a hold of you, but we've lost some of your paperwork."

"Who is this?"

"As you're listed here as a primary contact, we're to inform you that Roger Erickson has been released on parole."

Ice slithered into my veins and I swallowed hard. "Excuse me?

"Yes, sorry it took so long to get to you. It was three weeks ago but he is out on parole."

"How can a murderer get out on parole?" I barked.

"It was all on his paperwork and sentencing. Accidental manslaughter carries a lower sentence. We can email you more information, but as you were a primary contact, we were legally required to inform you."

The man said a few other things, but I didn't listen. Instead, I tried to calm my breathing, tried to focus.

As that letter that had come to the tattoo shop crossed my mind again, and bile filled my throat.

My stepdad was out of prison.

And it seemed the past was once again slamming full force into my life.

CHAPTER EIGHT

Brooke

I SHOULD HAVE KNOWN that once I started to believe I could get the hang of things, everything would begin to crumble.

I glared at my phone as I sat in the parking lot in my car, wondering why, once again, I was getting an email that I wanted nothing to do with.

Patrice had warned me that Landon Cunning would be coming after me somehow. I just hadn't realized it would begin with passive-aggressive emails.

Brooke,

I understand starting a new job can be difficult, so why don't I handle the next after-noon meeting so you can take your time and get your ducks in a row. I wouldn't want you to overexert yourself. Don't worry. I've done this numerous times before, and I can handle it. I'm just looking out for you.

I will talk to the head adjunct. Don't you worry.

-- Landon.

I closed my eyes and tried not to snarl.

There were so many things wrong with that brief email I didn't even know where to begin.

He might as well have told me not to worry my pretty little head over it.

With any other professor, calling me Brooke would be fine. I did not want a man I didn't know who was literally coming after me using my first name. It diminished my achievements, assuming an intimacy between us that wasn't wanted in any fashion. He was purposely taking away my doctorate, my position, and my experience, so he could drop my name as if he was talking to a middle schooler.

He then tried to take over my meeting, taking it off my hands before I had even had a chance to try to prepare for it. As if I wouldn't be able to handle setting up a meeting. A meeting, by chance, that he had requested be moved up.

It was where all of us professors would meet and discuss any upcoming items we had in our department. The physics department was quite large, but my subset of it was only a few people. And Landon was one of them.

He just wanted my tenure-track job, and I wouldn't simply back down and give it to him.

The cavalier and passive aggressiveness in his email hurt my teeth. It was as if he were so sugar-sweet, butter wouldn't melt in his mouth. He would have another think coming because I didn't bow down to anyone.

Hell, I was a woman in science with a doctorate and more than one bachelor's degree. I had done it on my own, and most of it as a single mom.

I had gotten this job on my own merits, not because of who I knew. I bet he got his because of who he knew and who his father was, not because of his accomplishments.

Because, from what I saw, he didn't do anything during the day in the name of science. What *I* wasn't going to do was lie down and let him have my job.

I shot off a quick reply, letting him know in no uncertain terms that I was fine to handle the meeting, considering all that meant was that I opened the meeting and made sure people knew where it was and what time.

That was it. I didn't need to bring damn cupcakes or something. I didn't need to make a presentation.

For this first meeting, somebody just needed to book the damn room.

And contrary to what he thought, I had already done it.

So, fuck him.

"What's wrong, Mommy?" Luke asked from the backseat, and I rubbed my temples before I set my phone back in its holder, making sure it was charging.

I turned in my seat and smiled over at him. "Just a work email that made me grumpy. But I'm fine now and all here for you. You ready to run more errands?"

"I like errands!" He beamed at me, and I fell that much more in love with my son. He was just the kindest, smartest, sweetest boy ever.

I realized that was very much something that most moms said about their kids, but it was the truth.

After making sure Luke was ready to go, I settled back into my seat, pulled out of the parking lot, and headed toward our next destination.

With my job and Luke's new school, it was hard to get everything done. Thank God for grocery delivery and May. Between those two, I was able to get most of the things I needed for my house, and my shelves were never bare.

However, there were a few things that I couldn't leave to delivery or May.

We needed to pick up a few prescriptions, and I needed a new set of sheets since an entire box of linens hadn't made it onto the moving truck somehow. I still didn't know how that had happened, since we had watched it be put on the truck, but that's what happened when you moved cross-country. Things were lost. And while insurance would cover some of it, I still needed new sheets, blankets, and a few towels.

Thankfully none of Luke's things had been lost. While he was a well-adjusted kid, the move was a big thing. And losing something that he loved, even if he only would love it for the next five minutes, would've been too hard on him. I didn't want to put any more undue pressure on him.

We went to three different stores trying to find sheets that would fit my bed and were actually in stock, and I was getting grumbly by the end of it. It shouldn't be this hard to find a nice set of white sheets, but everything seemed to be out of stock or outrageously expensive.

I also needed a few things for the house, like fake plants so I wouldn't accidentally kill them, since the one from my realtor was already barely hanging on, and a tray for the kitchen. Luke was getting tired, but I had a few more items on my list.

My brain kept going to lesson plans, wanting to check my email in case Landon emailed back, and the fact that Leif hadn't texted me. Or called me. Or contacted me in any way in the past week since our date.

I let out a breath and try not to be upset about that.

He'd said that he would be out of town for a couple of days visiting family, but I had thought all his family lived in Colorado. But what did I know about him and his family? He had a job, a business he owned. He was busy.

But he hadn't texted.

I thought he would have texted.

And now I was annoyed. Because why was I worrying so much about him when I had to get my son home, had to finish my shopping, and had a thousand other things to do that had nothing to do with that Montgomery.

The same Montgomery who hadn't wanted me before but now suddenly did.

I held back a growl and went to look for a few more things that I needed for the house. I didn't even have a damn toilet brush since mine had broken as soon as I bought it. Two weeks of cleaning, and it had snapped. Now the store I went to for the matching set was out of stock. How the hell were toilet brushes out of stock? I sighed and checked out, knowing that meant we had one more store to go to.

Luke was tired, and I knew he was hungry. So was I. I didn't know the restaurants around here, and since it was lunch hour on a Saturday, there was barely any parking anywhere.

I rubbed my temples as I put everything in my trunk, and after buckling Luke in, I looked over at my son.

"I didn't plan this well. We still have to go to another place to drop some paperwork off. I'm sorry, buddy."

Ideally all the paperwork and everything associated with moving cross-country and buying a home should have been easily organized. That was not the case for some places. Although I had all of the utilities and insurance and everything ready to go, there were still other small pieces of paperwork that had shown up out of nowhere that I needed to deal with, and I had to drop them off in person.

On a Saturday.

I still had time next week to do it if I didn't make it today, but I just wanted it to be done.

"I'm hungry, Mommy."

I looked at my kid, then leaned forward and kissed his forehead.

"Me too. I have some fish crackers if you want some, and maybe we can just head home and I will make your lunch."

"Okay. I love you, Mommy." And then he burst into tears. I rubbed my temples, knowing that I was messing things up again.

I leaned forward, unbuckled him, and held him close, rubbing his back. He was hot, tired, and had been *so* patient all day. We should have spent the day doing fun things where he could relax, and I could have mom and son bonding time. Instead, I had to be an adult and drag my kid with me. I wanted to cry right along with him.

"I'm sorry, Luke. Let's get you home, and we'll go play out in the backyard. We'll run errands another day."

"I'm sorry I'm crying. I don't know why."

Tears pricked my eyes, and I ignored the person who honked at me and wanted my spot. I was holding a crying kid who was hot, hungry, and tired.

The man flipped me off as he drove away, and I was grateful that I was holding my kid, or I would have flipped him off too.

Jerk.

"Okay, let's get you home and stop taking up space here. I could use some lunch too, kid."

"Sorry for crying. I just had a tough day."

He sounded so serious and adult-like that my eyes widened, and I just grinned. He'd probably heard that from me a time or two and had picked the phrase up. Hence why I tried not to curse around him too much since I didn't need him going to kindergarten dropping the f-bomb.

Again.

"Me too. Let's go eat something yummy."

I saw the line for a familiar fast-food restaurant behind Luke's head and figured we could sit in that line and have a greasy burger, but first I needed to buckle him in.

I did so and walked around my car and cursed under my breath as soon as I spotted it. Black dots slid over my eyes for a moment before I blinked them away, an overwhelming urge to cry along with Luke hitting me like a two-by-four.

"You have got to be kidding me."

I knelt down in front of my now flat tire and wondered how the hell that had happened so quickly. I hadn't noticed there was an issue when I'd driven earlier, but sure enough, there was a damn nail that proved to be a slow leak that hadn't stayed slow.

Luke was still in the car, and I needed to get him home, feed him, and deal with the countless other things on my list, but I couldn't because I had a damn flat tire.

In the middle of Saturday, in the middle of the parking lot, and everything that I had just bought was now piled on top of my spare.

I snarled, cursed, threatened to kick the tire, then composed myself. Then I opened the back door again. "Okay, let's get you some fish crackers because we will be a minute. Mommy has a flat tire."

Luke's eyes widened. "I didn't know you had tires."

I laughed then, mostly out of desperation. "Mommy's car has a flat tire. And hopefully, I'm going to be able to jack up this car in the parking lot."

I quickly got Luke some crackers and juice and looked at the tire again, trying to remember the last time I'd actually changed a flat. High school? Maybe.

I opened the trunk, waving off people who wanted my spot, as I pointed to the flat tire. Nobody offered to help, which was fine because I could do this on my own, but it was quite odd that not a single person even offered.

I moved everything from the back to the seat next to Luke, and then went to get out my spare, and narrowed my eyes at it.

"Okay, you and me. We can do this. It's been years since I did this, but I can."

Or I could call AAA. Though I didn't remember if I'd changed from the California AAA to the Colorado one, and now that seemed like an oversight on my part.

I shook my head, knowing I was a strong, independent woman.

I can make this happen.

I bent over the tire in the back as a familiar voice hit my ears.

"Brooke? I thought that was you. Hell, let me help."

I nearly slammed my head on the inside of the trunk as I turned to see Leif strolling towards me, jogging slightly as he sped up.

I narrowed my eyes at him and then saw where he was coming from. Behind him, on one side of the strip, was a huge sign that spelled out Montgomery Ink Legacy.

Well. I always wanted to know where he worked, and now I did.

Because fate hated me.

"Oh. That's a coincidence," I mumbled as I tried to pull out the tire.

It fought me, and I wanted to hex it. "Seriously?"

"Here, let me help. My mom has this car, and the tires are a bitch to get out." He winced. "Sorry, Luke," he called over the back seat.

Luke crawled around and waved at him. "Hi, Leif. And it's okay. Mom already cursed."

"Tattletale," I teased, even though I was sweaty, annoyed, and felt out of sorts. I was already trying not to think about *him*. About the fact that he hadn't texted, we hadn't talked at all since our date. I was a sweaty mess, stressed out, and didn't need anybody coming in and telling me how to live my life and help me when I didn't need it. I had done this all on my own for long enough that I didn't need him to step in.

I didn't need anybody to step in.

"Here, let me help. Seriously." Leif didn't shove me out of the way, but he did bump his hip against mine, grinning.

I glowered up at him. "I've got it."

"Okay," he said, studying my face.

I realized I had snapped the words, and I hated myself for it. I didn't know what to think, and it was all too much.

"I see you guys are out running errands. Getting a flat tire with all of that has got to be annoying." I knew he was speaking softly for Luke's benefit, trying to cut the tension, but I was so tired. Just annoyed.

"Thank you for your help, but I can handle it on my own." I sounded like a queen bitch, yet I didn't care. I just needed to get out of his parking lot and Leif didn't owe me anything.

"If you're sure."

"Now you're telling me I don't know my own mind?" I asked

His eyes widened.

"Okay. I was just trying to help out a friend." He let out a breath. "By the way, I'm sorry I haven't contacted you all week. I was out of town with my family, and like an idiot, I dropped my phone in the river." He smiled over at Luke. "Did you know that if you drop a phone in a river and it is underwater and hits a bunch of rocks, it won't work anymore?" he asked my son.

Luke's eyes widened. "One time, I dropped Mom's phone in the bathtub, and she was so mad. But then we put it in a rice bath thing, and it was fine. I think. Right, Mom?"

I grimaced, remembering the panic over him pulling my phone out of my shirt and into the tub. It was my fault for having it so close to him when he was so curious with his little grabby toddler hands.

"It all worked out. Don't worry."

"I have done that before, too, and I think I broke the phone, but I still used it for a few more months. I'm not great with phones. Oh, and Lake would've gone over the fence to say hi and tell you what was going on, but she was out of town for a presentation in New York. And I didn't want to send over anyone else to your house and be weird. I didn't borrow someone else's phone because I honestly didn't remember your number off hand because I don't even remember my own number most days. I'm sorry."

Well, that made sense, but I still just wanted to get home, feed my kid, and then go back out and run the four hundred other errands I had to do.

I barely had any time off these days as it was, and I knew this was my own doing, that this job, no matter the commitments that came with it, was my choice, but right now I felt like I kept making the wrong ones.

Was I losing too much time with my son because I wanted to further my career? Was I fighting with someone at work just to prove that I had bigger balls than he did?

I needed to stop making rash choices, but I also needed to just do things on my own. I was better when I was on my own.

"Do you want Luke to come into the shop and get some water while you're dealing with the tire? Let me know how to help, Brooke. I want to." He stuck his hands in his pockets, and he looked so contrite, like he was trying not to scare me or anger me.

And I didn't know what was wrong with me, but I just couldn't handle it. But I needed to.

Luke needed me to handle it.

Because nobody else would.

"I got it. I had it in Paris, and I have it here."

I hadn't meant to blurt that, and when his eyes widened, I muttered under my breath.

"What?" he asked as he leaned forward.

"I'm sorry. I'm just tired." And I knew the fastest way to get home was to let him help. Because despite the strength I had in my veins, he had more muscles than I did. So I should just let him help.

It wasn't a failure, even though I felt like it was.

"I would appreciate your help with the tire. Mostly because I can't get it out of the trunk. And it's annoying me."

"Yeah, that would be annoying." He kept studying my face as if he wanted to ask more but knew he couldn't. Not in public like this, not with Luke right there, and clearly not when I acted like the bitchiest of all bitches.

"Thank you in advance," I mumbled.

He met my gaze, nodded tightly, and helped me with the tire.

In the ways of fate and men, he had the spare on in no time, while it probably would've taken me over an hour because I was out of practice and weaker than he was.

That didn't make me feel like I was helpless or anything.

"You're all good to go."

He high-fived Luke, who had stayed in the car but had stuck his head out of the window to watch.

"Be good, buddy."

"Thank you, Leif. I'll see you soon!" Luke got back in his seat, and I quickly buckled him back in, making sure he was secure, before turning to Leif.

"Thank you. I have to head home. Things are going to start melting."

Not that I had ice cream or anything in my car, but it seemed like a good excuse. I was melting as it was.

He studied my face as if he wanted to say something, but there was nothing to say.

I had to make the right choices for my son in my own life.

And I wasn't sure the man that continually went haywire on my emotions was the right choice.

"Get home safe, Brooke," Leif said, without any hint to his emotions.

Something broke inside me, but I didn't know what it was or what it meant. So I nodded my head in thanks once again, and got into my car. When I pulled out and headed home, I refused to look in the rearview mirror at him.

Because I wasn't sure what I wanted to see.

That he was still there, waiting.

Or that he was doing what he had done before and should do now: leave.

CHAPTER NINE

Leif

I STOMPED around the front yard, sprinkling grass seed using the hand spreader. I knew Lake probably wanted me to be a little more delicate, but I wasn't in the fucking mood to care.

I wasn't in *any* mood.

I had no idea what I had done to Brooke other than be myself. I didn't know why she'd pushed me away as she had. Perhaps that was the problem. Maybe, just like before, she wanted nothing to do with me.

Oh, she might've liked that date and enjoyed that kiss, but that was it.

Because she had pushed me away.

And yet, I *had* to have done something. Brooke wasn't irrational. She was the most rational person I knew. That meant it had to be *me*.

The dumbass who kept feeling a pull to a woman who clearly didn't want me.

"Are you just going to growl at the flowers?" Nick asked from the front porch.

I flipped him off, then cringed as I looked around the neighborhood, worried that a kid had seen me do that.

"Very adult of you. I don't see any kids out, but if they're watching from the front windows, Lake will get an angry call about the big, bearded man scaring the innocent children."

"She will just have her father show up, and then the parents will swoon over Uncle Liam again." My uncle was a former model turned best-selling author. His books had been made into blockbuster movies, and most people knew his face.

Lake had been embarrassed as a kid when the parents and even some of the teenagers had swooned over her father, but now she was capitalist enough to use that to her advantage. And her father loved her enough to go with it if it meant annoying people and keeping them off Lake's lawn.

"You could just take your shirt off and do the same, you know," Nick stated, winking at me.

I scowled. "Stop hitting on me."

"You're like my brother. I would never hit on you, even though you are hot. The only other man in that house right now is Sebastian, and he's way too young for me and is practically married to that girl."

I snorted. "They do seem to be pretty serious, but he likes her, and I like Marley, too. You know there is someone else in that house. Just saying."

Nick narrowed his eyes. "I may like any gender, but I'm not going to date your cousin."

I raised a brow. "Which cousin are you talking about?" I teased.

"You are a jerk. You know I'm never going to date Lake. She's just so...*Lake*. Plus, she's taken." He practically grumbled the words.

"What do you mean by that?" Lake asked, and I cringed again as Nick stiffened and turned slowly to see Lake standing in the doorway.

"That you're taken? I thought you were dating that Zane guy." Nick raised his chin.

"His name is Zach, and yes, we are dating." She scowled before swallowing hard.

I wondered what that was about. Was it about her animosity towards Nick? Or maybe she and Zach weren't doing well. I didn't know, and it wasn't like Lake told me things when it came to dating. Oh, she might want to get all the information out of me and who I dated, but she never told me anything. Her siblings probably knew more than I did, and there was an age gap there.

But that was Lake for you. She didn't like to spill anything about herself, even though she pretended she was an open book.

"I was talking about what do you mean she's just so *Lake*. How is *Lake* an adjective?"

"You know exactly what I mean," Nick snapped before he walked past her, and she quickly darted out of the way so he wouldn't crowd her in the doorway.

She glowered at me and I raised my hands up in surrender.

"Don't glare at me. I have no idea what the hell is going on with him. And I don't know what he means by that. Other than the fact that you two do not get along, even though you guys decided to go into business with me. That's not awkward at all."

"Nick and I get along. As friends. At least, we should be. We always have been. I don't know why he gets so disgruntled whenever I'm around now."

I wasn't going to touch that with a ten-foot pole.

"Either way, thank you for reviving that part of the lawn that got screwed up with those anthills. I missed that big rain when I was out of town, and I didn't have time to worry about it myself."

"You do realize that our family has an entire landscaping division that can handle this for you." I quickly put everything away in the shed next to the house and followed Lake back inside.

"I know. I just don't like having to take up their time."

"It's not like you wouldn't pay them. They're a business. Yes, you would get the family discount, but we all decided not to do things for free for each other for things like that. Not when we didn't want to feel like we were taking advantage of anybody, even though we totally aren't."

I didn't give my family free tattoos, and I didn't get free construction work from the other arm of the family. Nor did I get free surveillance equipment from my cousins that were starting up a security firm. Yes, the discounts we got were ridiculous, and we worked at cost as much as we could because we loved each other, but we were all business people and knew that we had rules for a reason.

"I know, I know. I just like doing things myself." She shrugged, and I faltered, remembering how Brooke had said that.

"What is it with you guys? Why can't you just ask for help? I don't understand it. Yes, you can do things on your own, but it's not your responsibility to do everything on your own by pushing others away who are clearly there to help with no strings attached. It doesn't make any sense to me. You're just kicking yourself in the shin instead of actually letting someone help you."

Sebastian and Nick stared open-mouthed as Lake narrowed her gaze at me.

"I'm going to assume that has to do with somebody else, and you are not yelling at me in my own home after I allowed you to take care of the seeding even though I said I could handle it myself. You're the one who did it, and I didn't stop you. I didn't jump on your back and try to strangle you down to the ground so you wouldn't be able to do it. No, I said thank you, and I cooked dinner so that we could all eat together while discussing business. So, why don't you tell me why you're acting like such an asshole?"

I swallowed hard, then looked at Nick and Sebastian, who just shook their heads. Nick quickly took a sip of his beer while Sebastian did the same with his soda.

"Thanks for helping," I called out.

Nick snorted. "I thought I was the one digging my own grave, but it seems like you are chugging right along trying to beat me."

"You're both getting on my nerves. I'm just now remembering why I work with women-owned businesses and not with my damn cousins."

"You're not my cousin," Nick corrected Lake.

She flipped him off. "No, I'm just *Lake*. Too much of *something* for you."

Sebastian whistled between his teeth before he went to the crockpot. "Why don't I serve everybody this delicious meal that Cousin Lake made."

"Suck up," I mumbled.

"Hell yeah," Sebastian said with a laugh. "You guys are getting her all riled up."

"Oh, so I'm a woman, therefore, I get riled up?" Lake asked, even though her eyes were filled with laughter.

"Oh good, I seem to enjoy putting my foot in my mouth like the other two. At least we're consistent."

"Write this down for when you get married to Marley. When you continually eat your own foot, dig your own grave—whatever metaphor you want to use—just shut up. Say you're sorry and move on. Things are so much easier when you just admit that you're grumbly for no reason." Lake reached out and hugged Sebastian, and it surprised me that Sebastian was so much taller than her.

He was a man, no longer a kid, easily above six foot like the rest of us, and broadening out with muscle nearly every day.

There was a reason he was here with us for this business meeting. He might not have bought into the company yet, but he would. This was what he wanted with his life, and we wanted him here with us.

We went over financials and projections and made sure that our business was where it needed to be. Sebastian had input as well. He might not be a voting member yet, but we trusted him. And he was a brilliant kid.

It was the fact that he *wasn't* a kid anymore that was startling to me. Many of my cousins were now old enough to drink and start new lives. Lake and I were no longer the only Montgomery adult kids.

It was an odd transition in our lives, but I was grateful for it. No more dirty diapers, daycare, and afterschool plays. At least not until our generation started having kids.

It was such an odd thought, considering it had made up my entire life since I had joined the family, but I liked it.

Of course, that just reminded me of who lived next door.

A woman who might not have to deal with dirty diapers anymore, but she still had to deal with daycare and perhaps afterschool plays and meetings.

Things she could do all on her own because God forbid she ask for help. Or at least take help if it was offered without any strings.

"Where's your head at?" Lake asked, pointing at me with her fork.

I looked over at her and shrugged. "Probably where it shouldn't be."

"At least you're honest," she said with a laugh. "Does it have anything to do with the fact that you haven't told me how your date went with my neighbor other than *okay?*"

"It probably has more to do with him seeing her in the parking lot today and coming back inside like a lion with a thorn in his paw."

"Shut up, Nick," I growled.

"I don't believe I will." Nick turned to Lake and Sebastian and grinned. "I don't know what happened, but he saw her out there and decided to practically run to her like a kid seeing candy in the window. And then he came back in grumbling and was an asshole. He hasn't stopped being one since."

"That's it. Our friendship is over." I narrowed my eyes at my best friend.

"If that's all it took for you to lose me as a friend, I'm surprised we lasted this long." Nick laughed. "Honestly, what happened?"

"She had a flat tire and practically ripped my face off for offering to help. I don't know what I did wrong, but in the end, she let me help because it was the easiest way for me to get out of her face. Apparently."

"Oh, Leif." The sound of resignation in Lake's voice made me turn.

"What did I do?"

"Let me guess, she was out running errands, was tired, and she had a flat tire. Did you just show up and offer to help without her asking?"

"Of course I did. Even if we hadn't gone on a date, I consider her a friend. I'd do the same for someone who *could* be my friend. Or a stranger who needed help. She literally couldn't get the nuts off the tire. I wasn't telling her she couldn't do it, but she *literally* couldn't. I just don't know why she had to treat me like that."

Lake shook her head. "Of course, you do. She was embarrassed. And she's been a single mom for Luke's entire life. She has no real friends or family out here, although we will change the friends part. She's been alone and independent, doing things by herself for long enough that anybody coming into her space seems like a threat. You may not get it, but as a woman? I one hundred percent get it. I'm not saying that she is completely in the right here. But I see where she's coming from and why she reacted the way she did. It's not your fault, it's not her fault, but it still is your fault," she said, cringing.

"I hate the fact that I understood that," I grumbled.

"Hold on, I need to start taking notes," Sebastian said as he pulled out his phone.

Nick looked over Sebastian's shoulder and shrugged. "Forward that to me."

I looked at all three of them, knowing they were trying to lighten the mood, and I shook my head. "I hate that I screwed things up."

"Are you sure you screwed things up? Or perhaps you two just need to talk when you're not stressed out in a parking lot." Lake squeezed my hand.

I sighed. "I think you need to start writing a book with some of our cousins so you can explain to us idiots how women work."

"I would read it," Sebastian put in.

"I'm fine," Nick added, and Lake laughed.

"Sure you are, honey. Whatever you say."

"Don't call me honey," he growled.

"Whatever, babycakes."

"Do you call Zach those names?" Nick asked.

"I call Zach whatever he wants me to," she singsonged and went to clear off the table. Sebastian immediately began to help her as Nick went to start the dishes.

"Leif, can you go take a look at the hose out back? I think it might be melded to the house because I left it connected too long. Don't tell Dad."

I laughed and did as she asked, knowing that she could do that on her own, but she was asking for my help—probably because she knew I was stressed out over the whole situation with Brooke.

I walked out to the backyard, undid the hose from the wall, and made a note to tell Lake to get a new one.

A soft sound hit my ears, and I turned to see Brooke pacing in the backyard, a glass of wine in her hand. She stared up at the sky, then back down at the ground.

It was late enough that Luke might be in bed, but I didn't know the night-time routine of a five-year-old. I just knew that looking at Brooke under the moonlight did things to me I didn't want to name.

I walked towards the low gate in between the two homes and swallowed hard. I didn't want to startle her, so I cleared my throat as I walked. She whirled around, sloshing wine out of the glass. I winced.

"I'm sorry. I didn't mean to scare you."

Brooke looked at me then and gave a hollow laugh before she took a sip of her wine. "I was off thinking about nothing, not paying attention to my surroundings." She pulled her phone out of her pocket, checked the readout, and slid it away. "I have video alerts in Luke's room. So if he moves a certain way, I'll get a ping. Got to love technology, right? I don't think they had these things when I was a kid. At least not as motion sensitive."

"I don't even think my mom would've done something like that if the technology did exist when I was five. I know Sierra did for the twins, though."

Brooke smiled softly. "I'm glad that you have her. She was nice at the store."

"She's the best." We were silent for so long that I was afraid she would walk inside and leave my life forever, but that sounded so dramatic that I pushed the thought away. I was an adult. I could use my words. I should just fucking say what was on my mind. "What did you mean about Paris before? In the parking lot?"

She froze and studied my face. I was so afraid she wasn't going to say anything, that she would brush it off and walk away. But Paris lay between us. It always had, and it always would, no matter what we did at this moment. I needed to know what she meant, and I needed to know why. Because if I didn't, I knew that nothing would come from today or tomorrow. And part of me didn't want that, but part of me was so scared of what she might say, I didn't even know what to think.

She let out a sigh. "I came back to Colorado, you know."

I froze. Because she couldn't be saying what I thought she was.

Brooke hadn't come back to Colorado. I knew that as fact. It was the whole basis for having my heart ripped open all those years ago. She hadn't come back to Colorado to see me after Paris. That had to be the truth.

"What?"

Brooke narrowed her gaze. "You know this. You had to have known this."

"No, I don't. What the hell are you talking about?"

"I came back to Colorado. I didn't go directly to California. I came here."

The *for you* was left unsaid, but I heard it nonetheless.

"Then why didn't you meet me at Taboo?"

Because that was what the plan had been. We'd had hot and heavy nights in Paris, and I had fallen in love with the girl when I shouldn't have. We had both been young, carefree, and about to start radically different lives. I shouldn't have fallen in love with her, but I had. And she had told me she had as well. We were supposed to meet at Taboo on a certain day, at a certain time, but she had never shown.

So when I saw her at Taboo that morning years later, even after knowing she had moved back, it was like a blast from the past. I hadn't been able to stay away.

That was why I had kissed her.

And that was why I still wanted to kiss her.

She met my gaze. "I went to Taboo. On the second. I stood there and waited, acting as if my heart wasn't breaking because you didn't come." Her eyes were wet with the sheen of tears, but I stood there, shaking my head before I laughed.

I couldn't help but laugh.

"Are you laughing right now? I waited for you, Leif. And you never showed."

"I was there, you know. Every day as soon as I got back. I was there on April fourth. Just like we planned. And then I was there on the fifth. The sixth. I was there every day for a week, but you never came. I even told Hailey and the others what you looked like so they could call me and I could show up. You never showed. But it seems like I was days late."

"Are you kidding me? No, it was the second."

I leaned over the fence and cupped her face. "How did we miss out on so much because of a broken, bittersweet promise? How did I miss you for so long because we had the date wrong?"

She shook her head, her eyes wide. "Are you serious right now?"

"Apparently."

"But if I had met you there, Leif, I still would've had to go to California. At least for the year before I came back for undergraduate. And then, I needed to go to California again to go to graduate school and meet Henry. Because I needed to have Luke. It just doesn't make any sense."

"Damn it," I whispered before I leaned over and pressed my forehead to hers. "Maybe we needed to walk past one another and not realize that we had been wrong. But now we're back. So, what happens next?"

In answer, I leaned forward again and brushed my lips to hers.

And thankfully, she kissed me back.

I might have a few answers from the past and far more questions for the future, but at least I had this.

This moment. For now.

CHAPTER TEN

Brooke

THE LAST OF the incoming graduate students left my office, and I sighed as I leaned back in my chair, grateful that the door was closed.

I had known this job would be difficult, as I hadn't had an easy time of it as a graduate student myself. So being on the other side of the desk would be a different yet just as complicated experience.

I had once been the student vying for a seat with my favorite professor. There were only so many graduate students a professor could handle during a year. Not only did they have to deal with funding since we were providing their stipend, even through the school, but we also had to deal with time, desk space, and research opportunities.

I could handle three to five graduate students, and I knew that I would be getting them. I just had to try for the ones that I wanted. The large pool of incoming first-years had ideas of their own and knew where they wanted to go. Because I was the new professor, starting from the ground up, some students were eager to get a foothold. Others wanted to go to someone who had been here for years and would be able to fit into a place where there wouldn't be the extra hurdles of starting from scratch and making sure the academic world knew that you existed.

While I had connections to my previous schools and other professors and postdocs that I had worked with in the past, I was still a relative unknown. And that meant luring students to my cause wasn't easy. We had the space, and the funds, but finding the perfect student for my research wasn't an easy task.

Each student had to meet with at least five professors, and many of them met with more than that. Many students came in knowing what kind of research they wanted to do. Others had no idea, only that they wanted a higher education.

My job was to find students that worked with the personalities of Randall, Jennifer, and Hannah. They were already working for me, Randall was teaching a class for undergraduates, Jennifer was working on her thesis, at least the initial preparations for it, and Hannah was still taking classes as a second-year grad student. I wanted the full five first-year grads, I didn't think I was going to be able to get them, but three to five would be a great start to my career here and the building blocks needed for my students to thrive.

And that meant research, schmoozing, and fighting other professors for the students. Not that we actually *fought* for them. At least not so far. If anything, everybody looked like they were ready to find the students that worked for them and make sure that every student found a match.

This was in addition to the undergraduate class I was teaching, the graduate class I would be teaching next semester that I still needed to prepare for, my own research, and the day-to-day life of a professor at a university.

Sometimes I thought my life would have been easier if I had gone into industry, rather than academics, but I had taken this route for a reason. I enjoyed the connections, the research, and helping the new generation, even though sometimes I felt like I was *still* that young generation.

But it meant long nights, and my son having the patience of a saint. It didn't help that right now a feeling of inadequacy filled me.

It was after five, and I knew I would be missing dinner tonight, as meetings were planned in advance, but I still hated that May was feeding my son, cooking for him, and if I didn't get home early enough, would end up tucking him in.

This only happened once or twice a month, and I wouldn't allow for it to happen more frequently. Patrice at least understood, and I hoped the other professors would as well.

People would just have to find a way to make it work, because I needed to be there for my son like I always had, and always would be.

It was just in these moments that the little voice in my head kept telling me that I was a horrible mother.

I went through the last of my emails and made sure I was ready to go. I stood up, looking up at the door, expecting to see Randall. He was teaching an evening course, something he actually enjoyed doing because he preferred to sleep in. It was a perfect pairing since I tended to wake up early to get my day going.

But it wasn't my postdoc in my doorway. No, it was the person I least wanted to see. I rolled my shoulders back and told myself to ignore the unsettled feeling in my stomach.

"Hello there, Dr. Cunning, what can I do for you?"

"Dr. *Adler*," he said, putting an odd emphasis on my name. I knew he did that on purpose, like he wanted to call me Brooke.

He really was an asshole. I was trying not to put my preconceived notions on him, but it was hard not to when he kept acting like the asshole that he was.

He wanted my job, didn't get it, and his apparent plan was to ruin my enjoyment of it.

That wasn't going to happen. I was in a tenure-track position, and I was not going to lose my job. There was another opening coming up in a year or two, and it was all but in writing that Landon would get it. He had been second runner-up for my job, and the person who had been runner-up had taken a job at Harvard.

There was literally no reason for Landon to do this, other than he didn't want to wait until he could get a job that was handpicked for him.

It made no sense to me other than he didn't like to lose, and he wasn't used to hearing the word no.

He was going to have to get used to it because I wasn't having any of his nonsense.

"I'm just heading home. Is there anything that you needed?"

I knew better than to ask questions like that. I should've asked why he was here. But no, I had to be the helper.

I was usually better than that, but he always rattled me, and it threw me off my game. I was off my game for many things, but I wasn't going to think about that right then.

"I just wanted to see how the recruitment was going. I know it can be difficult for a new teacher. One who doesn't really have the experience that others have when it comes to bringing others to their team. I'm here if you need any advice. Or if you'd like me to speak to a few of the other professors for you. That way I can grease the wheels a bit to make sure you get who you need. I would hate for you to start the year without the right number of students. I mean, what could happen if you didn't have the research and papers that you needed in order to qualify for your next position?"

I nearly closed my eyes and told myself that beating a man senseless wasn't going to help anyone.

It might make me feel better, though.

"I have it all handled. Thank you for looking out for me. I truly appreciate it."

The sickly sweet tone escaping my lips was a little much for me, but he didn't seem to mind. Instead, something flared in his eyes, something I didn't quite recognize, and I wasn't sure I wanted to. I was tired and wanted to go home to my son, and this jerk just wouldn't go away.

And I knew if I told him to leave me alone, to stop bothering me, to walk away, he would go to all his little professor friends and say that I was a nuisance. I was the one who couldn't handle it and was bothering him. Because, after all, he was just trying to help a fellow teacher, someone new. They wouldn't hear the undertones. They wouldn't see exactly what he was doing.

So I would just have to handle this myself. Like I always did. I had dealt with people like him before, and I would again in the future. I just had to get through this one thing, and I wouldn't let Landon and his ilk bother me.

"If you're sure." He sneered as he said it, and I raised my chin.

"I'm sure. Have a good night then."

He narrowed his gaze. "Brooke."

I sighed as he closed the door behind him, and I wished there was a way to fix this. But there wouldn't be. Landon didn't want to be my friend, there was no way I could change how he felt about me. He wanted my job. He didn't think I was qualified, and he was going to do whatever he could to ensure that I was uncomfortable and unhappy.

I wasn't going to let him have that power over me.

I was stronger than that.

At least, that's what I was telling myself.

I packed my things and headed to the lab. Randall was working, his head bowed over his laptop and data.

"Everything okay?" I asked my postdoc.

He looked up, his eyes wide. Then he shook his head, that numb glaze over his eyes fading away. "Oh, I'm good. Sorry, I was deep in it, and didn't hear you come up."

I smiled. "Honestly, that's what I like to hear."

He smiled back at me. "Sounds like a good day to me. Say hi to Luke for me. That kid is pretty awesome."

I had brought Luke in a couple of days prior so he could see my office, and he had met my team. I was grateful that so far my team liked Luke. Honestly, it was easy when it came to my son. He bowled everybody over no matter who they were, or how they felt about kids. I was never going to ask one of them to babysit or watch Luke. There were boundaries, and I wasn't going to encroach. But I also wanted Luke to feel comfortable wherever I was at.

"I will tell him. And I agree. He is pretty awesome." I went over a few more things with Randall and promised I would see him after the weekend. Thankfully, we had a three-day weekend, though I knew some people would be coming onto campus to work. I would be doing mine from home, just going over papers and assignments. Randall might come in, but the rest of my team wouldn't. I trusted my team to get things done, and they knew that they could come to me with anything.

Landon was still in his office, his feet on the desk, laughing loudly over the phone as he talked with someone, and I moved quickly, hoping he didn't see me. I did not want to have to go head-to-head with him again. I just wanted to see my kid and not feel like an absolute failure because it was getting late.

Yes, he would be able to stay up a little bit later tonight because he didn't have school in the morning, but I also just missed my kid.

My schedule was a lot more flexible, and I had to keep that in mind. That was why we moved to Colorado, why I had left Caltech. At least, that was one of the reasons.

I just had to remember that I had been doing this on my own in some fashion since before Luke was born, and that wasn't going to change anytime soon. I could do this.

I had to.

I pulled into my garage, exhausted, anxious to see my boy.

I grabbed my things from my passenger seat and closed the garage door behind me, walking into the house to the smell of some form of stir-fry, the sound of my kid laughing, and May giggling.

"I told you I was going to get you!" May called out, her voice a little deeper with a fake growl.

I grinned as Luke giggled and May attacked him, the tickle monster in full force. Luke kicked his legs up in the air, and May dug her fingers into his stomach, albeit gently.

"I see that Luke has succumbed to the tickle monster again. I told him he had to be faster. We'll just have to practice."

"Mommy!" Luke called out, the sound music to my ears. In fact, it was so perfect that tears sprung to my eyes, and I swallowed hard, going down to my knees as I opened my arms. Luke slammed into me, wrapping his arms around my shoulders, as May gave me a sloppy smile.

"I missed you, buddy," I whispered, kissing Luke's cheek.

He was warm and smelled of little boy, plus sugar, and whatever he'd eaten for dinner. It was pre-bath time, but I was home, which meant I could have fun with bath time.

It was these moments I treasured.

Not those when I felt inadequate, and that I was failing.

"I missed you too, Mommy." He pulled away and spun in a circle. "May beat me in wrestling, but I'll get her. Don't worry."

I looked over at May, who rolled her eyes. "He may think he can overpower me, but he doesn't know the strength in these wee arms." May flexed her arms, and Luke clapped and shook his little butt.

The smile on my face grew. "You're probably stronger than me. Just saying."

May winked. "There is no probably about it. I'm swole."

I burst out laughing as May grinned and Luke looked at us in confusion, before he joined in laughing.

I would explain that word later.

"Thank you for staying late tonight. I appreciate it."

"No problem. It's part of the perks. I made extra dinner for you. So all you have to do is heat it up. We had honey garlic chicken with green beans and broccoli."

"Really?" I asked, surprised. I looked over at my kid. "That sounds yummy."

"It was so good. And May helped me cook."

I narrowed my gaze. "So you did the cooking?" I asked.

"May was my sous chef."

"You're going to have to teach me that recipe," I said seriously.

"No problem. I actually wrote it all down for you, and was going to email it as well. I figured if it gets us our vegetables, it's a win."

I nodded, grateful. "We like vegetables over here," I said, as I wrapped my arms around Luke again.

"I guess chocolate for tomorrow since we had vegetables today," Luke said quickly, darting his gaze from me.

I sighed, and then attacked his belly, making him giggle. "Only if you defeat tickle monster's boss."

May laughed and shook her head as Luke giggled, and I moved quickly out of the way of a flying shoe.

"Okay buddy, let's calm you down. I'm giggling at this point," I said with a laugh.

I just liked that I was in a better mood. I was happier.

Because I was here with my kid. Maybe I did do the right thing, moving him out here and changing his life completely.

After our Luke attack, we got May all packed up and headed towards the door.

"Seriously, thank you."

"You don't have to thank me for being part of your life. I love what I do. I love that you trust me enough with Luke. He is the brightest and best little boy. And I'm honored that I get to be part of this journey. I know it's not easy for you to not be here at all times of day, but I'm here. I promise. I'm not taking over anything. I'm just here to help when I can."

Once again, tears pricked my eyes, and I smiled at the other woman.

"I guess we make a pretty good team."

"Yes, we do."

The doorbell rang right as I was walking May out, and I blinked. I looked over at her. "Expecting someone?

"Well, it's six o'clock on a Thursday evening, so no," May said with a laugh.

I looked through the peephole and froze, swallowing hard. "Oh."

May's eyes filled with interest, a grin on her face.

"That sounds like a good 'oh,' I hope."

I sighed, and then steeled myself, opening the door. "Hi, Leif. I didn't know you were coming by."

May nearly dropped her bag and looked between us. "Leif?"

An odd sensation filled me. They *knew* each other. From the way the two of them were staring at one another, surprise on their faces, something happened that I wasn't sure I wanted to know about.

My stomach tightened but I forced myself to smile. "I see the two of you know each other."

Leif gave me a soft smile that actually reached his eyes. He didn't even have the grace to look guilty, even though I wasn't sure what he had to be guilty about.

"May. It's good to see you again." He turned to me. I tried not to stare at him. It was hard to do so since I always wanted to look at him.

"Brooke, May is that blind date I told you about. The one that Lake set me up with? A small world."

"Oh," I said, my eyes wide, pieces coming together slowly as I relaxed marginally.

"He told you about the date?" May asked, nervousness in her tone. "It was literally just dinner. Leif is a nice guy, and I adore Lake. But wow. The two of you? I totally have questions."

I turned to my nanny, then Leif, and swallowed hard. "No, I thought the world was small when it came to Montgomerys, I didn't realize it was also small concerning your friends and past lives," I said dryly.

"A single blind date, but it was a good dinner." Leif winked at May, who just rolled her eyes, the tension easing between all of us thankfully.

"Dinner was good. But sadly, no sparks." May shrugged. "I'm looking for sparks. I'm not great at it, but I'm looking."

I smiled then. "I wasn't looking for sparks."

Left unsaid was that the sparks came anyway. May grinned at me as Leif's eyes darkened…and I realized we were on the same wavelength.

Oops. I might as well have shouted that last part, instead of keeping it to myself. Because they both had heard it anyway.

"Anyway, I have to go," May said, before practically running out of the house to her car.

Leif looked back at her, then at me. That was when I noticed the pink box in his hands.

"I didn't know you were coming by." I hadn't meant to sound so accusatory, but Leif just shrugged.

"I stopped by Lake's to drop off paperwork, I figured I would drop off the cupcakes that I brought for you. And Luke of course, but I'm not going to mention them to him until you give me the okay."

At the sound of his deep voice, Luke came running in.

"Leif!" Luke said, as he practically ran towards the man. Leif handed me the box of cupcakes, then went to his knees and hugged Luke. Then he got up and spun Luke around on the porch as Luke laughed and talked Leif's head off.

I stood there, wondering how on earth this had happened.

I did not date. *Ever*. And I had told myself when I did start dating, I would not include Luke. That was the rule. Luke could not get attached to anyone.

Except for the fact that the two of them had met before I had a chance to keep them apart.

And with the way that Leif was talking to Luke as if the two of them were best friends, I knew there was no doing that now.

It wasn't only going to be *my* heart that broke when things fizzled out.

I had to be better. Had to not think about the worst-case scenarios. Even if it was the only thing I could think of.

"Leif brought cupcakes," I said, knowing that this much sugar tonight would be a bad idea, but then again, I was getting good at bad ideas.

"Cupcakes?" Luke looked up at Leif, his eyes wide. "Really? Thank you!"

"I did and you're welcome." Leif grinned down at my son and my heart did a little twisty thing.

Luke scrambled down and came up to me. "Can I have one?" he asked, his eyes wide. "Please?"

"Of course, you can. I wouldn't have mentioned them if you couldn't." I leaned down and kissed the top of his head. "Can you be really careful and bring the box into the kitchen? And if Leif has time, he can have some with us."

I met Leif's gaze. He smiled softly, the understanding there worrying me.

"I would love to. I have all the time in the world."

Luke cheered, and then carefully walked the pink box into the kitchen, out of sight, as I stood there in front of Leif, shaking my head.

"Apparently you not only dated my nanny, but you have also made my son fall in love with you. I'm a little worried."

"You know when you said your nanny's name was May, it honestly didn't click that it might be the same person. It should have, because that's our connection it seems, but it didn't." He leaned forward and cupped my cheek. "I didn't even kiss her, Brooke. I promise. There's been no one but you."

I swallowed hard, that familiar tight sensation shocking me. "Same here."

"You didn't kiss May?"

That twinkle in his eyes made me smile. "I didn't. She is my nanny, after all."

"I hear there are books that encourage that notion."

"Sadly, I'm not living in a romance book with May. But she is the best nanny ever. So I'm glad that you two ended on good terms."

"There was nothing to end. Just a good dinner, and I got to meet Lake's boyfriend."

My eyes widened. "You got to meet Zach? I haven't got to meet him even though I hear all about him."

"I don't hear much about him, so you should totally tell me everything, that way I can act like the big brother."

I laughed, shaking my head. "I thought she was your cousin."

"Same difference." Then he leaned down and brushed his lips up against mine. I let out a shuddering moan, even though I tried to hold it back. I parted my lips ever so slightly to slide my tongue along his.

He let out a moan then pulled away, visibly shaken. Since I was the exact same, I swallowed hard.

"Okay, enough of that, especially with your kid in the next room."

I blushed. "Thank you for that. Okay, let's go have cupcakes."

"Cupcakes sound wonderful. Thank you for inviting me, Brooke."

It's scary how his words nearly knocked me off my feet. I swallowed hard, wondering what the hell I was doing.

"Thank you for bringing them. And just, well, thank you."

Then I moved to the kitchen, knowing he was following me.

I had no idea what I was doing. And yet, it seemed like once again I couldn't stop doing it.

CHAPTER ELEVEN

Leif

TODAY WAS all about skulls and roses. I grinned as I worked on the final shading on the current skull with the rose crown.

"How is it looking?" Christy asked, and I kept silent, my focus on my work, not answering.

"You know he's not going to answer you. Not when you're nearing the end. You're just going to have to wait and be surprised," Nick said from his station.

Christy let out a breath but kept perfectly still, like she had been the entire session.

She was a trooper, didn't complain about pain, didn't bleed, and as this was her fourth tattoo with me, she knew the ins and outs of aftercare and actually listened to my instructions.

By the time I was finished and had washed off excess ink and plasma, I knew Christy was champing at the bit to get a look.

"Okay, are you ready?" I asked.

She smiled up at me. "I've been ready since you took away the mirror and didn't let me watch the progress anymore. You're a mean one, Leif Montgomery."

"I really am. The meanest. Now, take a look and tell me what you think."

My stomach twisted at that thought, waiting to see her reaction. We had gone over the sketch and incorporated the designs from her childhood. Each flower, whether blooming or wilted, was significant to her in the memories she had chosen to ink on her skin. This one piece was a small part of the growing art on her thigh. We wanted it to look like a forest that the viewer would travel through and find parts of her.

Her heart, her memories, her past, and her future.

This was the art that I loved to do most. Yes, I painted, molded clay, sketched with charcoal, among other things, and I sold what I could, and I enjoyed it.

Working with somebody else to create something that was a permanent fixture on their bodies meant something special to me. Something that couldn't be replicated on paper because the person wearing it added their own layer of… magic.

"Leif…" She let out a breath. "It looks so real. Like it's 3D and coming out of my skin. I cannot believe this is what we worked on. It's even better than I could've imagined. And I know your work, so I was already imagining perfection."

Christy, the woman who didn't cry, didn't show any emotion when it came to the pain of getting a tattoo, choked up as she spoke, and I swallowed hard.

"Glad to see it meets your approval," I said with a wink, trying to cut the tension. Christy wouldn't like anyone else knowing she cried like a human being. She liked to be stoic, sarcastic, a little bitter. She showed the world what she wanted them to see. So I was going to do my best to make sure the world saw that.

Even if it made me grin and fill with pride at the thought that she had broken just a little bit of that shell of hers because of my work.

"It more than meets my approval. It's utterly fantastic. Seriously. Thank you. I cannot wait to see what it looks like when I'm not so swollen, and it's healed. Now I'm thinking about the next piece we're going to do." She grinned up at me as I shook my head, smiling back at her.

"We can get you on the schedule. But let's make sure this heals first."

She rolled her eyes as she sat back down on my bench and I finished cleaning her up and setting her up with the Saniderm. Technology had changed a lot in the last few years, and with this and the special creams that we had, it would heal quickly.

My dad still marveled at how things had changed since he had started in this business; considering how much had changed in the years I had been doing it, I could only imagine.

"You have a lifetime canvas with me," Christy said with a laugh. "Of course, at one point we may run out of skin, so I'm just going to have to bring in friends."

"Bring in as many as you can," Nick said. "You know us, we're just trying to make a living here. We don't want to end up doing tattoos on the street in exchange for bread." He winked as he said it, and though Christy laughed, sometimes I was still afraid that's what we would end up doing.

We still had a full roster, with some time for walk-ins, but we were still new. We had made it past the first year with all the issues that had crept up, but unless we were here for at least three years, I didn't think I would ever be completely comfortable.

Of course, if you asked Nick or anyone on my team, they would tell me I would never relax fully when it came to comparing this place to the other two locations.

I needed to make my family proud.

I couldn't be the one to screw it all up.

We booked Christy for six months out, and as she left, she waved and said that she would actually be back sooner, with a friend.

I relaxed, letting out a breath as Leo walked in, a brow raised.

"Why do you look as if you want to throw up?" he asked as Nick chuckled under his breath.

"I'm glad you're the one who said it instead of me."

"I'm fine," I said, knowing I was lying. I went to clean up my station as Nick worked on the large bodybuilder next to me.

"What's up?" Leo asked, setting his sketchpad in his own station.

"Just thinking of worst-case scenarios. You know me," I said as casually as possible.

"You know, as a business owner myself, it's our job to think about worst-case scenarios, but I hope you do know how to relax."

I looked over at our other client, a large man not even looking up at us. Considering Nick was doing a piece on his back, it made sense.

"See, listen to Freddie here. He has owned his lawn and sprinkler maintenance company for twenty years. He knows what he's doing."

"Oh yeah?" I asked, honestly interested.

"Hell yeah. I've even worked with your family before," Freddie added as he turned his head slightly without moving the rest of his body, so that way he didn't screw up the tattoo. "You Montgomerys have great businesses, so it's all in the blood when it comes to you. I like it. Whenever they need extra help with sprinkler systems, they call my company. Your family does more of the planting and growing and designing, so I like it when they call on my business. Keeps everything local, and somewhat small, even though you guys are practically a corporation at this point."

I snorted, shaking my head. "Small world."

"Not when it comes to the Montgomerys," Nick grumbled, and I had to wonder what that was about. Because there was something there I couldn't quite figure out, only I wasn't about to grill my best friend in front of Leo and Freddie.

"It is true, I'm constantly bumping into one of you guys," Leo teased.

I narrowed my gaze at the other man. I liked him; he was a hard worker, a brilliant artist, and was just out of apprenticeship. "We're not that bad."

"Yes, you are. But you're good people, and you take care of those who work with you," Freddie said.

"We try," I said, looking over at Leo who shrugged.

Freddie leaned forward. "I'm taken care of, and if you're anything like your old man, you will take care of me in this business for decades."

"That's what I like to hear." Leo winked, then went back to his work as if he hadn't put more pressure on my shoulders. No, that wasn't his fault. I was the one putting pressure on my own shoulders, and I had to get used to that. I had to stop comparing myself to my father.

It just wasn't easy when my dad was the best guy I knew, and damn good at his job. I didn't want to be the one who tarnished the family name by getting their business shut down for not being able to pay the bills. Not that we were anywhere close to that, but those worst-case scenarios wouldn't go away in my head. No matter how hard I tried. And no matter how hard Nick tried to get me out of my own head.

A few more clients walked in, as did the rest of our team, and I went back to work on a few drawings. By the end of the day, I'd done two small tattoo walk-ins and prepped for my bigger project the next day. I purposely left my afternoon off to work on business things with Lake if she came in, and for any walk-ins and future drawings.

After lunch I took some charcoal to canvas, let out my feelings, just trying to see what came to mind. I would sell it to a local gallery if I felt it was worth it, so that way today didn't end up completely useless.

What the hell was wrong with me? I did good work, had made three clients very happy, and had consulted with my team on numerous projects.

I wasn't wasting my day just because I wasn't bent over a table, working until my eyes bled. I was tired of sounding whiny, so I wasn't going to be. I was better than that.

Damn it.

My phone buzzed. I looked down at it, hoping it was Brooke, but I knew it wasn't going to be her. She said she was in meetings all day, and then was going to try to rush home so she could spend time with her son. She told me point-blank that fitting a relationship into her life right now wasn't going to work, yet we were still kind of trying. Maybe I need to try harder. I brought cupcakes for her, but that wasn't enough. She had more on her plate than anyone I knew, so I needed to do more.

Only I wasn't quite sure how to do that.

One minute I was worried about work, now suddenly I was trying to woo and help a single mom. That wasn't exactly what I thought I'd be doing with my day, and yet I didn't want anything else.

My phone buzzed again, and I frowned, not recognizing the number.

Most of my team had left, Leo out front working on a sketch with Nick.

I picked up the phone, answering it even though I usually let unknown numbers go to voicemail.

"Hello."

"Boy. Good to hear that voice."

Chills skittered up my spine and I froze, that familiar voice slamming into me like a thousand shards of pain and memory that would never fade away.

"Roger."

Nick's head shot up at that. He set his notebook next to Leo, leaving the other man behind. Nick hovered over me; his arms folded over his chest as he glared at the phone.

I ignored him, as well as Leo's curious stare. I tried my best not to sound like an asshole. If I reacted in any way other than nonchalance, Roger would win. It had been that way when I was a kid, and nothing had changed since the other man had gotten out of prison. Not with the way Roger had sneered the word *boy*.

"You should call me dad. You know I like it when you call me dad."

I held back my revulsion as Nick took the phone out of my hand and set it on speaker. He gestured toward Leo, who gave us a look and went back to the office, closing the door and giving us a semblance of privacy.

I had a good team, and I was grateful. Right then I just wanted to hang up the phone and be alone.

"I hear you're out of prison. Not quite sure why you're calling me."

"I just wanted to say hi. It's been a long time, Leif."

Not long enough.

"Well, you did that. Goodbye, Roger."

"Don't hang up on me. You're not going to like it."

I hung up on him, knowing the other man had no power over me. He might have when I was a kid, but I was an adult now, and Roger had nothing to do with me.

He was my past and was no part of my present or future.

Then why did just the sound of his voice bring me back to his beatings, to the way that he would grip my shoulder, and force me to listen as he told me how worthless I was?

"He sounds like an asshole," Nick said casually, though there was nothing casual about his voice.

"He is. I don't know what he wants, but I'm pretty sure that threat performance was from him."

Nick nodded, his gaze going dark. "That note? Figured as much. You talk to your parents about it?"

I shook my head. "Roger has nothing to do with them. I don't want to worry them."

Nick met my gaze and narrowed his eyes. "You're keeping secrets. It's going to bite you in the ass."

"Maybe. But the other man can't do anything to me. And all he has done so far is call. And maybe sent that note. Hell, I just don't want my parents to worry."

"I think you're making a mistake, but it's yours to make. I'm here if you need me. Okay?"

Bile rose in my throat, but I nodded tightly as my best friend patted my shoulder in a way that reminded me of Roger. I quickly squashed that thought. I'd been hugged, touched, and roughed around before. I hadn't thought of Roger then. My real father had never hurt me, never laid a hand on me in anger. I even played football and soccer in high school and dealt with it easily.

I wouldn't flinch away when my best friend touched me in comfort.

Leo walked out then, looking between us. "The door isn't that thick, so I heard most of that, I'm sorry. I wanted to blast music or something because then you'd know I know."

I cursed under my breath. "My stepdad's out of prison. Or I should just call him my birth mom's boyfriend. Technically, she never married him."

"I'm sorry. Is there anything we can do?" Leo asked.

I shook my head. "Just ignore him. He has my phone number for some reason, and while that worries me, and I think he has the address to this place, he's an old man now. He can't hurt us." I didn't know if I was saying that more for them or myself. Probably both. "It's probably a good idea to make sure that we keep the place locked-up tight, make sure the security is on."

"We always do but will be doubly sure. You should tell your parents," Nick said again.

I sighed. "I don't want to bother them."

Leo looked between us but didn't say anything. Instead, we went back to work, and after a few moments of pretending to go back to the charcoal, I picked up my phone. I wondered if I was making mistake.

ME:

How did the day go?

BROOKE:

Long, I'm glad I'm home. How are you?

I almost told her everything. Right then and there, I almost texted it all to her. She did not need that on her shoulders. She didn't need anything else on her plate.

ME:

I got to play with art and met some interesting people.
So, I guess it's a good day.

BROOKE:

You have to show me some of your pieces. That way I
can gear up if I'm ever ready for a tattoo.

The thought of being the one to put art on her skin made me swallow hard. I wanted to be the one to do that, nobody else. Maybe that made me a territorial jerk, but I was what I was.

ME:

You say the word and I'm there.

BROOKE:

I would never trust anyone else.

My heart thumped loudly, those words doing more to me than I ever thought possible.

ME:

What do you say to dinner tomorrow?

BROOKE:

I say yes. I think I need it.

She was so quick to say that, so I knew it was true. I bit my lip and quickly made plans with her, wondering if I was making mistake.

Then again, I couldn't be. Not when it came to Brooke. Because I had made the mistake earlier, I wasn't going to do it again.

Despite my own misgivings, my own issues, I was falling for Brooke.

Too hard. Too fast.
And yet I couldn't slow down.
Not again.
Not with Brooke.

CHAPTER TWELVE

Brooke

"WHAT ABOUT THIS ONE?" Lake asked, holding up a lovely gray and silver blouse. "It'll give you great cleavage." She beamed at me, and I held back a laugh.

"Are you trying to get me to show off my boobs to your cousin? When did we cross that friendship line?" I asked.

Lake laughed and tossed me the shirt before going to my closet.

I could've found something to wear on my own. I had been doing it daily for most of my life. But it was nice getting ready for our dates together. She was heading out soon to meet Zach, and Leif would be here soon to pick me up.

Luke rushed in. "I love it, Mommy! May is letting me have cookies later after we color. Is it really okay?"

I leaned down and brushed his hair from his face. "You know it. Just make sure you try to save me one, okay?"

Luke hugged me tightly, nodded, then ran back out to the living room past a smiling May in the door. May waved at me and followed Luke.

While I had mom guilt for leaving, I knew Luke was excited to be able to eat cookies tonight. He didn't get cookies every week, so being able to go on a sugar high tonight was his reward for a good week at school and to ease my guilt for leaving him to go on a date.

I knew I needed to have a life, that dating was part of that life, and I wasn't a terrible mom for doing this. It wasn't like I went out every night or left Luke to fend for himself. But that mom guilt was trademarked for a reason.

Lake came to my side and bumped hips with me. "That is one cute kid. And by the way? Leif is not my cousin right now. He is the guy you're going on a date with. So what if I want to show off your boobs to him? They are great boobs."

I laughed and quickly changed shirts, agreeing that the silver and gray one looked nice. It was a wrapped shirt that curved in at the waist and flared out slightly at my hips. It did indeed show off my cleavage, but not so much that I would feel a draft. "Okay, you win. I like this shirt. I don't know why I don't wear it often."

"Probably because even though you just moved in, it was still stuck in the back of your closet."

"You're probably right. I try to look somewhat nice for work, but I shouldn't show off the girls there."

"You could under your lab coat." Lake grinned. "It might be fun."

I rolled my eyes as I went to finish my makeup, feeling like a giddy teen getting ready for a date rather than the single mother who worked hard and too late some nights.

"I think slacks and a button-up shirt are just fine for under my lab coat."

Lake shook her head. "Do people even call them slacks anymore?"

I flipped her off good-naturedly. "No. Maybe it's a California thing."

"You live in Colorado now, so you're going to have to get with the lingo."

"Whatever you say. Although I didn't realize Coloradans had an accent. I distinctly remember someone saying that Colorado had a lack of accent, and that's why you could always tell who is from here."

"Maybe in the past. But so many people moved here in the past couple of decades that it's not that way anymore. We say y'all just like everybody else." Lake winked as she said it and fluffed her hair in the mirror as she stood beside me. "I need to go out and meet Zach, so he's not waiting for me. I hate making him wait for me."

I looked over at her and smiled. "So, you two are doing well then?"

Lake smiled brightly, her eyes shining, that I could see the happiness there without her even having to answer. "We are. He's just so nice. And kind. And he always makes sure that I have everything I need, especially after a long day or after I've been traveling. It's just nice to have someone to lean on, you know?"

I shook my head as I picked up my purse and followed Lake out of my bedroom and towards the living room. "Not really. I've been alone for a while." I hadn't meant to say that, but it was easy to be honest with Lake.

"I would say you're not alone anymore, but I mean the fact that I'm in your life. I'm not talking about your date."

"I appreciate that. It's just a date." I let out a breath. "And I don't know a lot about dating. I'm still learning. And Luke doesn't know."

Lake nodded, an understanding look in her eyes. "You're a good mom. I don't know how I would ever be able to handle bringing up dating to my son or daughter. And I know that Leif isn't going to begrudge you for acting as if he's just your friend in front of your son. There are delicate steps to be taken, and you're traversing them well."

"I don't feel like I am."

"You are." Lake froze as she looked at her phone and winced. "And that's Zach. I'm late. I've got to go. He's waiting for me." She practically ran out of the house, and I raised my brows, wondering why she had to dash to meet him. Maybe she just wanted to be with him. I could understand that. They were still in the beginning stages of the relationship, getting to know one another, and she didn't want to spend any time without him.

It was nice. And though I would like to think I wouldn't run to go meet Leif, I figured that probably wasn't the case.

"Mommy?" Luke asked, and I turned, an odd note in his voice sending up my mom alert.

"What is it, baby?"

May rushed out, her eyes wide, as Luke bent over and vomited on my shoes.

I held back a curse, lifted Luke into my arms, and carried him into the bathroom, thankful that we made it to the toilet before he vomited again.

"I'm so sorry. He was fine, and then he wasn't. I don't think he has a fever. I just felt him." May got a washcloth and ran it under cold water before handing it to me.

Luke began to cry, and I brushed his hair back from his sweaty face, whispering sweet words to him. I lay the washcloth over his forehead and rubbed his back as he vomited again. I sat down next to him, my vomit-covered shoes next to me on the ground.

"Thank you, May. Can you get me the thermometer?"

"On it." She rushed out of the bathroom as I held my baby close, and he curled into a ball on my lap.

I was now covered in sweat and things I didn't want to think about, my pretty shirt probably ruined.

But that was fine. My baby was sick, and my mom guilt hit full force.

May came back with a thermometer, and as we took his temperature, noticed it was ninety-nine, and I sighed.

"Okay, buddy, let's keep you cleaned up and tucked into bed."

"You want me to call the pediatrician?" May asked, her eyes filled with worry but her tone steady.

I shook my head. "I can handle this. Why don't you head on home? I've got this."

"No, it's okay. I can help."

"You have a long day tomorrow, and we might have an even longer one depending on how tonight goes. You get some sleep so hopefully you don't end up sick, too." I cringed as I said it, and she nodded tightly.

"If you're sure. Let me know if you need anything. I'm just a phone call away."

I looked up at her, rubbing Luke's back. "I couldn't do this without you. Thank you, May."

"I'll clean up the mess before I go and try to do something with your shoes."

She didn't let me protest, and it wasn't like I could stop her, not with Luke in my arms, crying softly that his tummy hurt. I didn't think it would be too bad, at least I hoped not. There had been a stomach bug going through kindergarten for the last week, and I had hoped it had skipped Luke. Apparently, he was just a late bloomer.

By the time I cleaned up Luke and tucked him into bed, May had tidied up and headed home reluctantly.

I pulled off my shirt, treated it with a stain guard, and walked into my bedroom, wearing only a bra and panties. I quickly shoved on a shirt and shorts and cursed aloud as the doorbell rang.

Crap. I completely forgot I had a date.

How could I have forgotten Leif?

I walked past Luke's room, grateful he was still sleeping and looking better already, and then I ran to the front door, belatedly remembering I looked like hell.

My hair was piled on the top of my head, my makeup was probably running through sweat and tears, and I looked like I had been through the wringer.

I opened the door and cringed. Because there Leif was, looking sexy as hell in gray pants, a stone-gray button-up shirt, and those bright blue eyes of his looking far too damn good.

"Hey there. Did I get the night wrong?" he asked as he reached forward and tucked a piece of hair behind my ear.

I wanted to cry, but I knew I didn't have the right to do so. My baby was sick, and I did not have the time to break down.

"I'm sorry. Luke came down with a stomach bug, and I'm just now finished cleaning up and tucking him in. I completely forgot to text you and cancel. I'm so sorry. That must make me look like an idiot."

Leif's eyes widened and he walked in, closing the door behind him. He cupped my face and pressed his forehead to mine. "Are you okay? How is Luke? You need to take him to the doctor?"

I nearly burst into tears with how caring he was, the fact that he was so worried about Luke. Was my bar set so low for men that him just asking about my son nearly broke me?

"I'm okay. I'm just sorry to have made you come here for nothing. Luke is sleeping now, but I'm going to go in and check on him."

Leif pulled back and brushed my hair from my face again. "Why don't you go sit with him. I'll make you something to eat."

My eyes widened. "You don't want to leave? This isn't what you were expecting."

"I was expecting to spend time with you. And I can still do that, just with taking care of Luke. He's your son. Your number one priority. And he's sick. It's got to be scary and nerve-wracking. So, you take care of your kid because I want to make sure he's okay, too. I like that kid. So, let me make you dinner with whatever you have, and as long as you're okay with that, we can sit and eat together while keeping an eye on Luke."

My heart did that lurching thing, and I swallowed hard. "This wasn't what you were expecting tonight, Leif. Maybe this is all too much between work and life and family. You shouldn't be getting a single mom. You should be out there living your life, and actually be with somebody that can focus on you and only you."

Leif laughed and it made me wonder why the hell he was laughing. "I don't live in a dream world where nobody has any baggage or connections or life beyond my every whim and desire. You're a mom. I knew going into this that Luke is, and will always be, your number one priority. Sure, we could have gone out to eat tonight, and maybe I could've convinced you to kiss me, and maybe a little bit more," he said with a wink, and I laughed despite myself. "But that's not what's going to happen now. Instead, I will cook you something relatively edible, eat it maybe with some candlelight, and keep a look out all night. You do not have to worry about me, Brooke. I'm here. I'm not going anywhere."

With that, he kissed me hard on the mouth and then walked into the kitchen as if he had been doing it his whole life. I stood there, swallowed hard, and wondered why I was crying.

Because tears wet my cheeks at the thought of Leif just being nice to me and understanding, of liking my son and wanting to make sure that I was there for him. I wanted to be there for him as well.

I did not deserve Leif Montgomery. But I wanted to.

WE ENDED UP EATING BOX MACARONI AND CHEESE WITH MY OPEN BOTTLE OF rosé wine, sitting on the floor in my living room and talking quietly. I kept my video surveillance of Luke on my phone.

"His fever is already down, and he is sleeping hard. I think it was just a nasty little bug that should be over by the morning, but it scared me." I'd cleaned myself up a bit more, washing my face clear of makeup and putting my hair in a better messy bun. I still wore my bra and panties underneath a T-shirt and shorts, so it wasn't precisely date attire, but I felt comfortable.

I hadn't even slept with Leif yet, not since Paris, and yet here I was, having dinner with tea light candles lighting up the living room, and box macaroni and cheese as our gourmet meal.

It felt like home.

That should scare me, but it just felt right. I could think about everything that was wrong with it later.

"It scared me, too. I'm glad he's going to be okay."

I played with the rim of my wine glass, swallowing hard. "I know this isn't what you planned for tonight."

"I planned on spending time with you, Brooke. That's exactly what we're doing."

His eyes went dark, ever so slightly, and I bit my lip, noticing the way that his gaze went straight to the movement.

"You surprise me every day, Montgomery."

He smiled then, his gaze brightening. "I could say the same about you, Dr. Adler." He rose. "Oh, I'm going to have to call you Dr. Adler when I'm deep inside you."

I pressed my thighs together, holding back a groan. There was just something about this man. "Oh really, you're already imagining it?"

He leaned forward, brushed his lips to mine. "I imagine it every day. I'm hard enough most days that I have to begin my morning and end my night coming in my own damn hand thinking about you. And that might make me a growly asshole for daring to tell you that to your face, but I'm just going to have to lay it all out there. I want you to come on my cock. I want you to ride my face. I want to remember exactly what you look like when you orgasm. Even if it takes another year to get there, I want to know it all."

I swallowed, memories hitting me hard of what we had done in the past and what he put into such descriptive words.

I honestly could not think of a reason to wait.

So I wouldn't.

"It will not take another year," I said as I watched his throat work and swallow hard. "In fact, if you promise to keep quiet, it won't take another minute."

Then I leaned forward and kissed him harder. He groaned, the tension in the room shifting into something hot, primal.

He slid his hand over my hair, taking it out of its bun. It tumbled down my shoulders. He wrapped it around his fist, tugging ever so slightly.

I parted my lips, letting his tongue slide along mine as he deepened the kiss. I slid my hands up his back, over his shirt, and gently scratched my nails down the linen covering his muscled arm.

"Are you sure?" he asked, his voice a guttural moan.

"As sure as I'm ever going to be," I whispered. Probably not the best answer, but the truthful one. When he pulled back and looked at my face, I saw him searching, needing to know. But this was the moment. The only moment.

So I pulled away, noting the curiosity in his gaze and how I stood up and pulled him with me. "Be quiet, very quiet," I whispered, winking.

He grinned and followed me to the bedroom. The bedroom was still slightly messy from getting ready with Lake, but it wasn't as bad as it could've been. But in the end, it didn't even look like he studied my room. Instead, he cupped my face again and deepened the kiss. The door was closed behind us, my phone in my hand. He took the phone from me, put it on the bedside table, and gently lifted me by my hips. My eyes widened at the show of his strength, subtle as it was, before he set me on the bed and kissed me harder. This time there was a sense of urgency as if we both knew if we weren't quick enough, if we didn't touch each other in the need that we held, this moment would shatter.

So I pulled at his buttons, undoing his shirt clumsily. We laughed as we both pulled away and he helped me undo the rest of his shirt. He tossed it to the floor, leaving him naked above the waist with nothing but ink.

I slid my hands down his chest, unable to hold myself back anymore. His skin seared mine, all hot and hard over sleek muscle. I sucked in a breath as I looked up at him, his eyes nearly glowing with need.

"Touch me, Brooke. I love when you touch me." He leaned forward, brushed his finger along my jaw. "I need you to touch me."

"Only if you touch me," I whispered, far more brazen than I thought possible. I knew we needed to be quiet, oh so quiet, so when he leaned down and gently lifted my shirt up over my head, I had to press my lips together so I wouldn't moan aloud.

I couldn't think then as he leaned down and kissed me, his hands on my breasts over the lace of my bra, then down my sides and over my hips. I pushed back onto the bed, needing him as I pulled him on top of me. He obliged, hovering over me and between my legs, and he kissed me in long, sure motions as if he had all the time in the world and he wasn't burning up from the inside out like I was.

Waiting.

Needing.

Aching.

Then his hand was between my legs over the thin cotton of my shorts, and I felt as if I were on fire. I arched into him, silently demanding more as he rubbed me over my shorts. When he finally, *finally*, slid his hands under the band to cup me, I nearly shot off the bed. It was only the fact his mouth was on mine that kept my moan contained.

This was so familiar, as if the two of us hadn't spent a decade apart, and yet it was all new and needy and everything I wanted and craved.

"That's it, Brooke. Ride my hand. Let me look at those pretty eyes as you drench my palm."

At the deep growl of his words, I nearly came. "Leif."

"It's just you and me." Then he slid his thick fingers deep inside me and curled them, my wetness making me so slick that he eased in without any resistance. "Fuck. You're so fucking wet, Brooke. Did I do that to you? Did I make this pretty pussy all wet and eager for me?" He began to work his fingers deep inside me, stretching me carefully. The sounds of my slickness over his hand nearly made me blush, but then he flicked my clit with his thumb, and it was hard for me to think.

I came on his hand as he worked me, his gaze greedy and pleased as I whispered his name, trying to keep quiet.

"That's it, Brooke. You're so pretty when you come. I need you to do it again. Can you do that for me, baby? Can you come on my hand?"

I shook my head, and he quirked a brow.

"Oh?"

"I want to come on your face," I said boldly, my cheeks so bright red they flamed.

He looked at me, his eyes wide, then he laughed before crushing his mouth to mine. I hadn't meant to say the words, but I couldn't help but imagine his face between my legs, the roughness of his beard along the inner silk of my thighs. Everything ached, and my pussy pulsated, needing more, needing him.

He moved us both, sliding off my shorts fully, then my bra.

He did the same to his pants and I swallowed hard, finally seeing all of him for the first time in years.

"When did you get your dick pierced?" I squeaked, my eyes going wide.

He looked down at himself, his cock hard, long, and thick with a barbell at the tip. "I've had it for a few years. I forgot that you haven't seen me since Paris." He met my gaze and stroked himself, once, twice.

I nearly came right then.

"Did it hurt?"

"A little, but not too badly. It'll feel good, Brooke. And I have condoms with me that are made for the piercing, so you don't have to worry about it breaking over it. I had it with me just in case. I promise I didn't think tonight would end like this."

I bit my lip, not realizing I was cupping my breasts and staring at his dick until he stroked himself again.

"You ready, Brooke?"

I nodded, licking my lips. "Always."

Then he was over me again, and his mouth was between my legs. I arched off the bed, slamming my hand over my mouth as he licked my pussy, sliding his tongue between my folds as he dove deeper. He spread me, blowing cool air over my heated flesh before he was licking and sucking and nearly sending me over the edge. When he shook his head slightly, humming along my clit and holding my thighs apart, feasting as if a man starved, I slid my free hand over his head, keeping him in place as I came, holding back another moan in case I shook the house with my screams.

Leif was over me then, as if I'd blacked out at that moment, his mouth on mine. I could taste myself on his lips, and I nearly came again. Instead, I wrapped my legs around him, needing him.

He pulled back, shaking his head before he moved to grab the condom I hadn't realized he'd placed near us.

I let out short, choppy breaths as he slid the condom over his length, his gaze never leaving mine.

"Brooke. You're gorgeous when you come. You're all pink and rosy. I can't wait to fuck you hard into this mattress. Do you think you can be quiet, baby? For me? Can you be quiet when I pound hard into you and make you come around my dick?"

I spread my thighs, slowly playing with my folds. "I think if you don't move and make good on those promises, I'm going to make myself come and never touch your cock. As it is, you've been selfish and haven't let me...play."

Again, I didn't know this Brooke. She sounded like the girl she had been in Paris, not the single mom she was now.

But that was what Leif did to me, and I didn't care.

Not now, and maybe not ever.

And then Leif was between my legs and slowly, oh so slowly, sliding inside me. He was big, bigger than I remembered as he kissed me and slid deep inside me. He stretched me, the burn and ache, perfection. And when he was seated, I could feel the piercing within me, and the sensation was new, dangerous, and everything I hadn't known I'd wanted. Everything I hadn't known I'd needed.

And when he moved, taking his time, and not going hard and fast as he'd said, I knew this was rightness.

We crested over the abyss together, his hands and mouth on me as he shifted, so I was over him, riding him and rocking my hips. When he came, he held me close, kissing me as if there were no tomorrow, no yesterday, and only this moment forever.

I hadn't realized I was crying until he kissed my tears away and rubbed my back.

I looked at him then, and there were no words.

There didn't need to be.
I was falling for Leif Montgomery.
Again.
And I wasn't sure I could stop myself even if I wanted to try.

CHAPTER THIRTEEN

Brooke

SOMEHOW, in the month since Leif and I had taken that next step in our relationship, I only got to see him in stolen moments. We were both busy between our jobs and families.

I wished there were more moments where we could just be calm together. And I knew that would be easier once I introduced Luke to Leif as my boyfriend rather than just a friend. That would have to be soon because I wanted to spend as much time as possible with my son and Leif.

I hadn't realized that I would want to be in a relationship as quickly as it had come about, but there was no turning back. Because we were trying to find our happy middle, whatever that was.

However, none of that was important at the moment because I needed to finish getting ready for work and had to head to class. I had to teach, and then I had a meeting with a few advisors, and then there was research. Some professors didn't enjoy the teaching aspect and only wanted to do research. While for others, it was the opposite. I enjoyed both, which surprised me, but it added work to my already overloaded plate. I felt like I was doing a million things at once. But I juggled it.

It was like what Nora Roberts, one of my favorite romance authors, had once said. You can juggle as many balls as you want. Just remember which balls are glass and which are plastic. The glass ones will shatter, so you don't want to drop them. So that would be Luke and maybe Leif—which was a terrifying thought.

The plastic ones, though, could bounce. And I wasn't saying that was my career, but if I let my postdoc and team work on items like they were supposed to rather than micromanaging them, that was okay.

"Mommy, you look pretty."

I looked to see Luke standing in the doorway, his smile bright, his dark hair falling over his eyes.

"Why, thank you. We need to get you a haircut."

"I was just putting that on the list," May put in, a bright smile on her face. "Only because it's getting in front of his eyes. I kind of like it long in the back."

"Yes, because mullets are so in," I said with a laugh.

"I don't know. I'm starting to see kids with mullets. They could be in fashion. On trend, if you will."

I shuddered. "Okay. Whatever makes everybody happy. We do need to cut those bangs, buddy," I said as I knelt and hugged Luke tightly.

"It's okay. I like spiky hair."

"We could do spiky hair."

"What about the mohawk?"

I shook my head, laughing along with May. "I don't think so, Luke. Maybe a faux-hawk. Are those in?" I asked May.

"I have no idea. I think I will do some research today when he's in school before I pick him up."

May and Luke had an early day today thanks to teacher meetings. I liked being able to drop him off at school, and sometimes pick him up depending on my schedule, today was not going to be one of those days, but it was okay. We were making it work, and I wouldn't be able to do it without May. If it weren't for the fact that I had gotten a settlement from Luke's father and life insurance from my parents, I wouldn't be able to afford it, even with my good job. So I had to count what blessings I had.

I kissed the top of his head again and said goodbye as May and Luke went off to finish breakfast.

My car was parked in the driveway because we had an art project drying in the garage, so I walked out the front door and paused at the sight of Leif standing in my neighbor's yard, frowning at something.

"I didn't know you were going to be here."

I tried not to sound flushed or giggly. But it was hard to do with him around. Whenever I was near him, I wanted to touch, kiss, or just hear him laugh. I knew I was falling, and I had to be smarter about that. If nobody was around, nobody would know.

Except for the fact that we were in my front yard, and everyone would know.

Leif looked up at me, surprise etched on his features. "Hey, I would've stopped by, but I thought you would already be on your way to work. I know it's Luke's half-day, so I didn't want to confuse him by showing up early."

I smiled at that, loving the fact that he remembered. My heart did that wanting thing, and I pushed it away. I had to slow down. It would be smart to slow down.

"I'm heading to work now. I don't have class until later this morning."

I stood next to him on the driveway and tilted my head up as he kissed me, gripping my chin, just a soft good-morning kiss.

It felt...*everything*. That was probably the wrong thing to think, but I wasn't going to think about anything else right then.

"Anyway, I'm here because Lake needed me to water her plants, and I'm on my way to work. She should be back in town soon, but she asked me to come over."

"I could handle that. She shouldn't have to ask you."

"I know, but I think she just wanted me to come over just in case I could see you. My cousin is sly like that."

I laughed; I couldn't help it. "That sounds like Lake. If you need to water the plants, why are you outside?"

"Because I don't know if she wanted me to water these new roses, even though the sprinklers are on a timer. They look fine, but my aunts and uncles are way better at the whole gardening thing than I am."

"I'm honestly not great at it, but the flowers look fine. Nothing looks wilted, so maybe just the indoor plants?"

"Good to know that neither one of us has the green thumb in this relationship. We will have to hire someone in the future for our lawn needs. Because I don't think it will be either one of us."

He continued to talk about something else, and I listened with only half an ear. Because he had just casually mentioned the future, as if it was certain we would be living together, dealing with gardening together. Or maybe he was thinking of two separate homes like we were doing now.

I didn't need to think too deep about his words. Not when I was trying to rein myself in as I was.

"I need to go to work."

"No worries. Have fun." He kissed me softly and I held back a moan.

"I'm going to try. I have to deal with Grouchy Dude again today, not in the mood."

He narrowed his eyes. "Grouchy Dude? Why haven't you mentioned him before?"

I winced. I had been good about not bringing home that part of work before, mostly because I didn't want to deal with Landon outside of the office, but there was no taking it back.

"It's just a normal man and science thing. He gets annoying because he wanted my job."

"Idiot man," Leif said with a laugh, and I grinned. "How can you not like a woman in science? At least my woman in science. Makes me all tingly." He leaned forward and kissed me again, and I laughed against his lips.

"Thank you for that." I rolled my eyes, and I knew he was thinking about Landon. Leif wasn't going to handle it for me, he trusted me enough to know my own worth and process, but I also knew he was all growly because he wanted to handle things for me.

We were trying to figure out a balance, but I also knew it wasn't his problem.

We said our goodbyes, and I tried not to watch him as I drove away, knowing that we hadn't been careful then. Anyone could've seen us kiss, which was fine because it wasn't like I was hiding my relationship, except that my son could've looked outside at any moment and seen me kiss Leif. And that was something that I needed to deal with. Because I didn't want to lie to Luke. And I didn't want to hide Leif. Leif was worth more than that. It just meant things were going to get complicated. I had never brought a man home before. And though I had brought Leif home multiple times, it was never in the context of Luke knowing exactly what was going on.

I knew there were countless blogs and books about how to go about this, but those situations weren't my situation. I was going to have to figure out what to do. That was, of course, after my long day.

I enjoyed the drive, even in traffic, because though the mountains were behind me, Denver was still such a gorgeous city. Soon the light rail would be out here, and I would be able to take mass transit rather than driving. I was looking forward to that, although I did love the drive itself.

I pulled into my spot and walked into the physics department, nodding at a few people, and saw Patrice walking down the hall.

"Hey there," the older woman said, grinning at me. "I saw your latest proposal. It looks great."

My heart kicked up a beat. "Really? Okay, good. I swear I feel like a first-year sometimes with those."

Patrice laughed. "Same here. But you're not alone. And it looks great. I actually have a proposal for you that I want you to look at because I think we can work together on this latest thing." She looked at her phone. "I have to head to class, and I know you have one at ten a.m. But I do want to talk to you."

Everything just clicked. I had a work friend. She wanted to work together. It didn't feel like we were in competition. Well, that was a fantastic way to start the day.

"That sounds wonderful. And yes, we should meet up and talk. I would love to work together. I'm excited."

"I'm excited too. I was thrilled when they hired you on. I loved your work out at Caltech and even referenced it in my own papers."

I laughed, pleased. "I feel all proud right now. Seriously."

Patrice grinned, then headed off to class while I made my way to my office.

Things just felt right. I was making headway with my research. I had built my team, and my students were doing well. Yes, classes were difficult just with the grant scope, but I was getting the hang of it. And yes, I could probably sleep more if I didn't have so many papers to grade along with my TA, but it was fine. I was making do.

And maybe the next night, I would invite Leif over and we would have dinner with Luke. The three of us. When I didn't just have my friend over for dinner.

As if he were thinking about me, Leif texted, and I picked up my phone as I closed my office door behind me.

LEIF:

Just thinking of you.

Well then, that wasn't kismet or anything.

ME:

Hi.

That was great—a great way to start off a texting conversation.

LEIF:

Do you want to go to the farmers' market this
weekend? Luke will love it.

I bit my lip, now wondering if it was too quick. Yes, I'd just thought about bringing him over to dinner, but going out as a family seemed like too far. Or maybe I was thinking too deeply. It was just a farmers' market. It wasn't like I was asking him to move in. I needed to stop being indecisive and let things go with the flow. Damn it.

I swallowed hard, my palms going clammy.

ME:

That sounds great. I have a busy weekend coming up.
Errands and haircuts.

LEIF:

I can help with errands. I work in the evenings both
nights since I'm covering for Nick. But I can help.

ME:

You don't have to help with errands. You have your own
life.

LEIF:

I want to be part of yours. Luke knows I'm your friend.
That's not going to change, Brooke. I'm not going to
scare him.

I swallowed hard, knowing that he was right. And our thoughts were going in the right direction. Just because he thought as I did, didn't mean I had to be scared.

ME:

Okay. Let's work on timing. And if you're not busy
tonight, you should come to dinner.

I practically threw my phone on the desk as I said that, knowing that that was taking a leap.

LEIF:

See you tonight. I'll bring dessert if Luke is allowed to
have sugar.

ME:

Okay. You can just bring yourself, but I like dessert, too.

LEIF:

I have to go to work now, and I can't have a hard-on. So
I'm not going to think about exactly how you can be a
dessert for me.

I rolled my eyes and set my phone down, shaking my head. He was just too much, yet he was still the same person he had been in Paris. The person that made me smile and always put others first. He was kind and talented and a little growly. But I liked that about him.

But I couldn't think about him when I needed to focus on work.

I picked up my things to head to class and just opened the door to find Landon standing there. For some reason my pulse jumped. It was just Landon. And yet there was something off about him when he narrowed his gaze at me.

"We need to talk."

He practically shoved me into my office and slammed the door behind him.

"Excuse me? What do you think you're doing?" My pulse sped up, and my mouth went dry. This was bad. Oh, so bad. My phone was still on my desk because I hadn't picked it up when I picked up my things, and he closed the damn door, locking us inside. I could call out for help, but everybody was either at their morning classes or not in yet. This was so stupid. I just had to calm him down. But he had pushed me. This could go only a few ways, and I didn't like any of them.

"I'm doing what I should've done to begin with. I should've had your job. But no, they had to go in and hire a woman because we don't have enough pussy here."

I held back a flinch at his tone, not wanting to show weakness.

"Landon, you're going to want to leave my office right now. This is highly inappropriate, you shouldn't be in here, and you should not talk to me that way." I was doing my best to sound professional, but inside I was screaming, wondering what the hell I was supposed to do.

"Bitch." He moved quickly, wrapping his hand around my throat and shoving me sideways into the door. My eyes widened and I sucked in a breath, only barely catching up to what he had just done. It took me a moment to figure out exactly what the hell was going on, and in that moment of being too slow, he got the upper hand.

"This is supposed to be my job. I was supposed to be on the tenure-track. Instead, they brought you in because they only had little Patrice. She's too old and fat for any of the professors to want. So they brought in this hot young thing to take my job. Well, screw that. You don't get to take what's mine. So I'm going to take what's yours." He slapped me then, shocking me. Red-hot pain slid up my face, my eyes watering.

"You stupid cunt." He slammed my shoulders against the door, his hand on my throat, the other gripping my shoulder so hard I knew I would bruise.

It took too long for my brain to catch up as he hit me again, but then I finally focused, taking the deepest breath I could with him still holding my throat. My hands were free, so I scratched at his face and lifted my knee, using that moment of distraction to knee him right in the balls. I pushed him down to the ground and tried to open the door. He scrambled up and gripped my hips, so I kicked back, elbowing him in the chest.

I opened the door and nearly fell out into the hallway, shouting for help.

"Help! Somebody help me! Landon has lost his mind. Help!"

I never yelled, I never asked for help, but my own pride would not stand in my way. I saw Patrice there, her eyes wide as she ran to me, phone in hand.

"Brooke? Oh my God."

Landon threw himself through the door and looked ready to kick me before he saw other people coming out of their offices, all coming towards us.

I knew what this looked like, me practically on the ground, shaking, blood seeping from a cut to my lip. I knew my eyes were wild, my hair askew.

Landon looked like he'd stopped mid rage, his face nearly purple.

Then Patrice was on the phone, talking with 911. A few professors I couldn't name at the moment and Randall were holding Landon back, students ready to jump in.

Patrice was in front of me, holding my hand, asking me what happened, and I tried to catch up, try to let my brain unfreeze.

Everything went dark for a minute, and I swayed, and then Jennifer and Hannah were there, both holding me tight, keeping me steady. I tried to lift my chin and did my best to look as if I hadn't just been attacked in my own office. As if I wasn't bleeding or scared.

Because I would not be weak.

I could not be weak.

And then the tears came, and I let the women of the physics department hold me, and I tried to tell myself everything would be okay.

Even though I knew nothing would ever be okay again.

CHAPTER FOURTEEN

Leif

ANGER ROLLED off me in waves, and I did my best to rein it in. Yelling at anybody in my path wasn't going to help anything. But it was all I could do not to see red and find this damn Landon person and beat the shit out of him. Violence had already come into her life. I wasn't going to add to it.

I fisted my hands at my side and took in a deep breath.

"She's fine, son. She's okay."

We sat in the waiting room in the hospital, something that we had done countless times when I was a kid, through various things with my aunts and uncles and parents. You would think I would be used to this by now, since we basically had our own Montgomery wing, and yet nothing felt right.

"I should be back there," I whispered.

My dad squeezed my shoulder and I let out a breath. "You will be. You know how it is, HIPAA restrictions and all that. As soon as you are able, I know you will be back there."

I looked at my dad, his big beard always comforted me. My dad had been through hell and back, a lot of it having to do with me. But he'd always been there for me—just like he had always been there for my siblings and my mom.

Sierra, not my birth mom. I tried not to think about my birth mom, but it was hard not to these days when my so-called stepdad/birth-mom's-boyfriend was back in the picture. Not that I was going to tell my dad about that. No, adding that on top of everything else wouldn't help anyone.

"I want to be there now. I want to know what's going on."

"You will know soon." My dad turned and I followed his gaze. "Good, here's your mom and Luke."

I stood up, practically scrambling to Luke.

May had met us at the hospital, Luke in tow, when we had heard about the incident at the university. I wanted to rush behind the nurse's counter and find Brooke, but I wasn't family and wasn't on her emergency contact list. Apparently, nobody was. That was going to have to change soon.

But May had left shortly after dropping off Luke, the right side of her face swollen from a badly needed root canal that popped up out of nowhere. Nick, of all people, had driven her to the dentist under protest. She hadn't wanted to go, had wanted to stay there with Luke to wait to hear more about Brooke, but we had all pushed her into leaving.

That meant Luke was with us in the waiting room, and I was thankful that my parents had come. Any one of my siblings, cousins, or numerous other family members would be here. But I hadn't wanted to overwhelm Brooke, considering she hadn't even officially met my family.

We had been dating for a few weeks now, and it seemed odd that I hadn't had her and Luke over for family dinner. Then again, Luke didn't even know we were dating. He just thought I was Brooke's friend.

Things were going to change after this. As soon as I made sure she was okay, she would have to realize how important she was to me.

I hadn't even realized the words rang true until they were practically spewing out of me. I only held it in because Luke was in front of me now, and I went to my knees, holding my arms out. Luke ran to me and nearly strangled me as he hugged me tightly.

"Is Mommy okay?"

I stood up, set Luke on my hip, and pushed his hair back from his face.

"She's going to be just fine." I hoped I was not lying. But if it was bad, she would've told me. She would've sent somebody out to tell me.

I hated not knowing. I hated not being her emergency contact. Because she was all alone back there, and here I was, holding Luke, and I didn't know what to say. I wasn't good at this. I wasn't a dad.

That thought made my mouth go dry.

I would do anything for her and Luke. I just had to figure out what all that meant. The fact that this was coming at me all at once nearly took the words from me, and it was hard for me to speak. Because I hadn't been prepared for this. I hadn't been prepared for her or Luke. I wasn't sure what the hell I was supposed to be doing.

"Luke enjoyed our little walk, and now he promised to go play with the puzzles in the back with me."

I looked up at my mom, and she smiled at me. There was such kindness in her gaze, even with worry. It reminded me of the first time she had been in the hospital when she had been hurt when I was a kid. But she was okay now, strong.

Brooke was just as strong. I had to remember that.

"I like puzzles," Luke said shyly as he looked over at Sierra. She smiled at him, and I knew that Luke was a goner. My mom had that way with kids. After all, I had fallen for her just like my dad had. I wanted her in my life, even before I knew that my dad wanted her, too. I was forever grateful that Sierra was my mom. That she had stood up and said her vows to my dad, holding my hand and making me promises as well.

That had been so long ago, yet I could still remember that day, the tears running down her face as she had promised to be the best mom she could be for me. And then she had cried again when the adoption papers had come through, and she was my mom in truth.

Luke looked over at her with that same knowledge, that same love.

"Let's go play puzzles while Leif and Austin go see what we can do about seeing your mom."

Luke buried his face into my neck, sighing. "I want my mommy to be okay."

My heart clutched, and I rubbed my hand on his back. "I want her to be okay, too." I pressed my lips together, knowing that probably was the best thing to say. "And she will be okay. We will figure out when we can see her, and then we will take her home. Then you and I get to have the fun job of ensuring that she's all tucked in and comfortable. What do you say?"

"And then we can all sleep in Mommy's bed and make sure she is safe?"

I did my best not to look at my parents as they met each other's gazes, holding back a laugh.

"We can make that happen." I kissed the top of Luke's head, then set him down as he went off to the children's area with my mom.

My dad gestured towards the nurse's station, but before I could go and harass them, albeit nicely, a woman in scrubs walked out and looked over at me.

"Leif Montgomery?"

My heart did double-time, and I swallowed hard. "That's me. Is it Brooke? Can I see her?"

She held up a hand, looking very serious. The floor fell out from beneath my feet, and I swayed. My dad squeezed my shoulder tight. He grounded me as always, and I swallowed hard.

"Just tell me."

The woman smiled, looking slightly tired. "She'll see you now, and she can tell you how she's doing."

I didn't know what to make of that, but maybe it was in the rules that because I wasn't Brooke's emergency contact, I wasn't allowed to know anything about how she was doing. I wasn't sure how I felt about that, but it didn't matter in the end. All that mattered was that Brooke would be fine, Luke and I would definitely talk her into resting, and make sure that she was safe and wrapped in bubble wrap.

And that I could find this Landon and beat the crap out of him.

My dad gave me a tight nod, squeezed my shoulder again, and then let go to walk over to where my mom and Luke were playing. I was glad for it. They would keep Luke occupied while I talked with Brooke.

I hated the fact that she was alone. But she wouldn't be for long. Damn it.

The doctor gestured towards a curtained-off room, and I nodded in thanks as I saw Brooke lying there, my body nearly failing me.

She looked so small, so fragile. Brooke never looked small. She always looked as if she could take on the world and did so every day. She was brilliant, a freaking doctor. She was an actual nuclear physicist who could take over the world. But she looked so fragile I was afraid that a stiff breeze could break her.

A bruise marred the side of her jaw, and at the narrowing of her gaze, I had a feeling she knew exactly where my thoughts were. She wouldn't want me to think she was fragile.

But I was so pissed off I couldn't even breathe. I wanted to shout and scream and make sure that she was okay. But that wasn't helpful.

Vengeance, my anger, it didn't matter what I was feeling.

"Brooke? Are you okay?" I blurted, my voice coming out with a growl. The nurse walking by gave me a look. I sucked in a breath and exhaled through my nose, telling myself to calm down.

"May said you had Luke." She held up her phone. "I'm sorry. I'm so sorry. You shouldn't have to take care of him. Just...you know, thank you."

I moved to her and reached out to touch her hand. She didn't flinch, didn't move away, but I saw the bruising on her throat, the cut on her forehead, on her lip. And I wanted to scream. But that wouldn't help.

I closed my eyes, counted to five, and opened them as I leaned forward. Her hair was pushed back from her face. She just looked so frail, and I hated that. I wasn't going to let myself think that. Not when she needed me to be strong. And yet it was all I could do not to growl.

"Luke is with my parents in the waiting room. He's fine. Worried about you, and he wants to see you."

Her eyes widened, her mouth parting. "He's with your parents? He's just alone with your parents."

My brows raised. "Lake is out of town, May is having oral surgery, and my parents have raised four kids. I trust them with my life."

"I don't know them." She closed her eyes and cursed. "I'm sorry. I've met your mother, she was lovely. Even though I didn't know she was your mother at the time, and it was only for a few minutes. I just can't believe they're putting everything aside to watch my son. I need to get out of here, need to go and see him."

"You will. As soon as you tell me what's going on."

"Don't tell me what to do, Leif. You're not my husband."

My eyes widened and that rage came right back. "Oh, so we're going to do this right now?"

"Do what?" she snapped.

"I might not be your husband, but we're together. You're mine just like I'm yours. And beyond all that, we are friends, Brooke. You know that."

"I am doing just fine on my own. I always have."

I sighed and pushed back the rage threatening to overtake me. "Yeah, you did just fine on your own. And you always will. But you do not *have to*. What would happen to Luke right now if my parents weren't out there? Where would you want him to go?"

"Stop it."

"Stop what?" I asked, exasperated. "Stop caring about you? That's not going to happen, Brooke. It can't."

"That has nothing to do with the situation. I got hurt. I'm fine. And thank you. Thank you for taking care of Luke. They will discharge me soon, and I can handle this."

I was quickly losing control of this conversation, and I needed to get us back on track before either one of us said something we regretted.

"What happened? Let's start there, and then we can go back to what you're yelling at me about. What I'm about to yell at you for."

"Don't go off on me."

"You're the one going off on me. I'm not being a jerk, Brooke. I am your friend. Your fucking boyfriend. Let me help." Tears filled her eyes, and I felt like an ass. "Brooke."

She shook her head. "I'm sorry. That guy at work got weird." She let out a rough laugh, and I understood because "weird" was the understatement of the year. "Apparently, he was drunk and he attacked me." She went into detail about everything that had happened, about her coworkers holding him and calling 911. How she'd already spoken to the authorities twice, all while thinking May could take care of Luke. And then May had called me. Not Brooke.

That hurt, but I understood. I did. Brooke was so used to doing everything on her own, so it made sense that she wouldn't reach out.

But things were going to have to change.

I was falling for her, and I damn well knew she was falling for me, too. So we couldn't pull away from each other. She had to rely on me, to lean on me, because if she didn't, what was the damn point?

"I want to kill him." I whispered the words I hadn't even realized I was saying until they were already out.

"The authorities will handle him. I don't want to make it a big deal. As it is, I have to go to work, to that same office where everybody will know that somebody hurt me. I have to be *that woman* with them. I don't want to be *that woman* with you."

The way that she emphasized *that woman* told me it was a whole other thing that she needed to deal with. I didn't know if I was the right person to help. Maybe my mom would be able to help. Maybe Lake. I would bring it up later, but first, I needed to touch her.

I leaned forward and cupped her bruised cheek. "You scared me, Brooke. You scared me so damn much."

Her eyes watered, and thankfully she leaned into my touch. Leaned in and didn't back away. I had to count that as a good sign.

"I was scared, too. I don't want Luke to see me like this."

I nodded, looking down at her hospital gown. "When are we breaking out of here?" I asked.

Her lips twitched, and she winced since one of them was cut. I held back a curse. "They said it would be another hour. I don't know what to do, Leif. I always know what to do."

I sat down next to her and gripped her hand. "Okay. Why don't my parents take Luke home?" She opened her mouth to argue, and I held up my hand. "May can't help right now, and it's understandable. She feels bad about that, by the way, so make sure you know that she tried her hardest to help. Nick had to practically drag her out."

Brooke's eyes widened. "She was in that much pain?"

"She tried to hide it from you because she was scared. For you and for herself, I think. But she's okay. She's going to be okay. Lake is touching down at the airport any minute now, and we have that transportation handled, but how about this? My parents take Luke home, give him a fun evening, and then you can video call him later. That way, he doesn't feel as scared. Then later, after we get you settled at home, we can bring Luke back, after dinner, after he gets spoiled by my parents, and see what happens then."

"I guess you have it all handled." She paused and frowned. "I'm not good at letting other people handle me, Leif. I've never been good at that."

I let out a rough chuckle. "I know. But it's okay. Because you're going to let me do this. You let me take care of you. I already promised Luke that I would help talk you into letting us take care of you." I raised a brow. "He also asked if we could all sleep together in your big bed to make sure you're okay." She sputtered, and I grinned. "Smart kid there."

"I don't know what to do, Leif. I was so scared. But I'm okay now. I'm going to be okay. I don't have a concussion. I didn't even need to get stitches. I am just a little banged up. And it took a while to get through the emergency room because of a pile up on the highway and then dealing with the authorities."

"You're going to be okay," I repeated, primarily for myself. "Luke and I will take care of you because we're your guys. It's what we do."

"Leif... I don't know what to say."

I sat up, leaned forward, and brushed my lips against hers. "Don't say anything. Just be okay, Brooke. Let us be there for you."

I kissed the tears away from her cheek and then held her hand as we waited. I needed her to lean on me. I just needed her.

But even as I thought the words, the fear of what happened to her hit me. Something so inconspicuous, something I hadn't even realized was a threat to her, hurt her.

And my own secrets, my own past, were still waiting.

I knew that if I didn't deal with it soon, the danger that blurred between us both wouldn't end here.

I just didn't know where that end would be.

CHAPTER FIFTEEN

Leif

I FINISHED RINGING up my final customer of the day and looked over at my dad leaning against the wall, arms folded over his chest as he stared at me.

I knew that he wasn't judging me or staring at me to ensure that I did everything right. That was just the way that my dad leaned. He was big like I was, so we tended to take up room. To look intimidating without even trying. And yet, even as his son, I wasn't sure how I was supposed to not feel intimidated.

"I just love it, Leif. I can't wait to be able to show it off to the world."

I looked at Kathleen and grinned. "Just don't get arrested for indecent exposure when showing it off," I teased.

Kathleen rolled her eyes. "I may have gotten a bouquet of flowers in between my breasts, but I can still show it off with the right top. I promise not to flash random strangers on the street. But I'll tell them I got it at Montgomery Ink Legacy if I do. I'll be your billboard." She winked and then waved at us with her fingers before strolling out of the place, singing a song to herself.

I shook my head, laughing softly as my dad joined in.

"That is good for business, a nice walking billboard."

"How many women have flashed you, Austin Montgomery?" Mom asked as she came up from the back, my portfolio in her hands. She had been in the office, on the phone with one of her suppliers while looking over my work.

"I plead the fifth," Dad said as he wrapped his arm around his wife's shoulders. "I don't want to incriminate myself."

"Pleading the fifth only works in the court of law, not my court." She went to her tiptoes and kissed his cheek. "I'm sure you did lovely work, even as you were touching other women's breasts."

"I don't think I need to be here for this conversation." I shuddered as they looked at me before we all burst out laughing.

"What did I miss?" Sebastian asked as he walked in, phone in hand as he practically bounced.

"Just talking about boobs," Mom said dryly.

Sebastian blushed. "Aunt Sierra, really?

"You asked," she said with a laugh. Then she moved around the counter and hugged Sebastian tight. "Why are you all bouncy?"

Sebastian wrapped his arms around her, looking down. I hadn't realized that my cousin was now taller than my mom. I should have, it was jarring.

From the way that my mom looked up, she felt it too.

"I had a good day. I got an A on my exam, thought of a kickass tattoo for later, and have a date with Marley tonight."

"I just love that girl. I know your parents do, too." Mom moved away and went back to my portfolio, keeping her attention on the group of us.

"I love her, too. One day soon, I'm going to marry her." Sebastian practically beamed, and I shook my head.

"Soon? As in how soon?"

My dad let out a sigh. "Give my brother some time to get used to the fact that his kids are grown before you go out and get married." And then Dad looked at me. "Of course, you have been grown for a while now. When are you going to ask Brooke?"

I choked on air and looked over at my dad. "What?"

"I love how his voice gets all high-pitched like that," Sebastian said. "And Marley and I want to wait until after college to get married. We can pay for the wedding ourselves and not beg my parents for money."

I noticed he hadn't mentioned Marley's parents. Marley's parents didn't like to spend money, didn't like parties, and didn't like Sebastian. Mainly because their baby girl was precious to them, and nobody would be good enough for her.

But that wasn't my problem. At least not until they hurt my cousin. Then I would make it my problem.

"That sounds like a plan," I said, being honest. "And as for Brooke and me, we're doing good. Taking it slow, but I like her. And Luke."

"I just hope that we get to meet her in a circumstance of our own choosing." Mom gave me a look, and I winced.

It had been a few weeks since the attack, physically Brooke had healed, and found her way. I knew she still needed to talk about it with someone else, to recover fully, but she was doing better.

The three of us were.

"I told you we're taking it slow." Even though I didn't believe that we were taking it too slow. Because we saw each other nearly every day, and I slept over at her house more often than not. She had yet to sleep at my house, and I understood. We hadn't wanted to leave Luke overnight, and while I had a guest room, I didn't have a room for Luke. I didn't think we were ready for that, and honestly, the complications made it too difficult. So I was fine sleeping at her place.

As long as she let me, I would sleep there as much as possible.

But marriage? I needed to make sure we were both ready.

"Anyway, so I don't stress you out about Brooke anymore, I was looking over your latest drawings for the art show. I love them. Have you shown your uncles?" Mom asked, speaking of my uncles who worked in art outside of the tattoo world.

"Uncle Alex and Uncle Jake both looked at them. I know that the gallery was interested in one. I'm fine with it as long as it hits the bank." I shrugged. "I love drawing, but I love what I'm doing here more. I'm doing okay."

"You're doing more than okay." Mom reached up and kissed my cheek, then cursed as she looked down at her ringing phone. "I need to take that."

"And I need to go look at my next project," Sebastian added as he gave us a two-finger salute and headed back to his station.

That left me alone with my dad while I waited for Nick to come in and start his shift and take care of any walk-ins.

"While the others are away, want to tell me why you're so stressed?" Dad asked.

I looked up at him, confused. "Why do you say that?"

He gave me a look that told me he once again could read me like no other. "Is it Brooke?"

Honestly, Brooke was the one thing in my life that was making sense. But I didn't need to tell my dad that. Maybe I did. Maybe I just needed to tell him what was going on. Only I saw the worry in my dad's gaze, saw the stress.

I knew that Gideon and Jamie took up most of their time these days outside of the business. They were fifteen now and ready to take over the world. Colin was twenty-one, finishing college soon. My parents stressed about a lot of things.

Roger calling me like he had that one time almost two months ago shouldn't be a problem. It shouldn't be something on my dad's shoulders, so I wouldn't mention it. I could handle it. I always had been able to handle those memories, and I would handle them in the future. But there was one thing I could mention. Because it was something I knew I needed to get over.

"Is it weird that I opened a tattoo shop just like you? Following in your footsteps even though I didn't mean to?"

Dad's eyes widened, looking honestly surprised. Hell, I was surprised I'd even said the words. "Is that what you think? That you have to live up to our expectations? Because that's not it. I thought you wanted to open up this place. To have your own business and not work with me or for me. Did I push you in a direction you didn't want? Fuck, Leif."

I shook my head and ran my hands through my hair. "I'm not saying it right."

"Then tell me. Did we do something to force you into this? I know your mom is just talking about your other art because she loves your talent. Same as I do. Drawing and clay and other media like you do never appealed to me as an artist, never did. But you have always been so talented with it all. You didn't have to follow in my footsteps. Not that I thought you would."

I shook my head. "I don't know. I'm the oldest cousin. I always felt like living up to what Montgomery Ink is, could be a little daunting." I let out a sigh. "I know it's stupid."

My dad shook his head and squeezed my shoulder. "Look at all you've accomplished on your own. *And* with family. I had my family. I might've tried to forget that when I was your age, but in the end, you and I are both blessed with this big damn family. You are your own man. You always have been. You've grown into someone that I will always admire and trust. Breathe, okay? This place has its own reputation outside of the place Maya and I made with our friends. One day we will retire, a long ways away, boy, which means we will have a place for every Montgomery who wants to join us. Or do whatever they want. You have always been who you wanted to be. I admire the man you've become, and the art you create, on canvas or on skin. You have the talent, the drive, and the trust. Don't worry about what we think but know that we think the world of you."

My throat tightened, and I tried not to react to every single word my father had just said.

"What the hell is wrong with me?" I said after a moment, laughing. "I know you guys are proud of me. You guys have never once pushed me in any direction I didn't feel comfortable with. And as for Brooke, by the way, you're not going to be able to force her into a Montgomery dinner."

"I might the next time we see her. Only because it's been long enough. But it's not like we found where she worked and asked her there," Dad said after a minute.

I laughed. "I need to invite her to a family dinner. She's just been busy, and well, we wanted time."

"I get you." Dad ran a hand over his beard. "You're at a crossroads. With your woman. Your new life. Of course, you will be filled with doubt. But you have your friends. Your family. Lean on us. It's okay to lean."

I smiled and reached out to hug my dad hard. There were many things to say about Austin Montgomery, but he always gave good hugs.

"I love you, kid. Just saying."

"Can I get a hug, too?" Sebastian asked, and I rolled my eyes and turned, pulling my cousin into the hug.

Sebastian laughed, then pushed away. "I meant from Uncle Austin. You're fine, but your hugs need work."

I push at his shoulder, laughing, as the three of us roughhoused playfully.

My mom came out of the back office and rolled her eyes. "Seriously, I leave the three of you alone for five minutes, and now you're fighting."

"You love me," my dad said, and Mom laughed as the bell above the door jingled, and the woman who took my breath away walked in.

I swallowed hard, trying to get my thoughts in order so I wouldn't drool. But that was really hard to do when Brooke was there, looking sunny and amazing, with her hand in Luke's.

"Oh, my," Brooke said, her eyes wide.

"Leif," Luke called out and ran towards me. Brooke reached for him but missed, so I went around the counter and scooped Luke up in my arms.

"Hey there, buddy. You're looking smooth in that sweater."

Luke beamed. "Mom picked it out."

"She did a good job." I looked over Luke's head at Brooke. "Hi."

"Hi." She clutched her hands in front of her, nervous. She looked behind me at my family, who was staring, grins on their faces.

I cleared my throat and knew it was time to stop hiding her in our bliss and confusion. "You know everybody here, but let me do introductions anyway," I said as I kissed the top of her head, holding her close.

"Okay, Luke, that is my mom, and dad, and my cousin Sebastian. Everybody, this is Luke and Brooke. You've mostly all already met, but now it's not in a stressful situation."

My chest filled with pride as Luke waved to everybody and then scrambled down so he could go and say hello to Sebastian. Sebastian picked the kid up, settled him on his hip, and proceeded to hear all about Luke's day.

Brooke just laughed and came forward. "Well, we see where we place in terms of hierarchy here," she said dryly.

"It's the Montgomery boys. You just can't help it." Mom came out from behind the counter along with Dad, and she hugged Brooke tightly.

"It's good to see you. I was trying to give you space because I didn't want to overwhelm you. We Montgomerys tend to do that." She winked, and Brooke laughed. "However, we're ready for the next phase, so here it goes."

"Now I'm worried," Brooke said, her eyes wide as she looked at me.

Mom waved her off. "Don't be. We're just inviting you to a Montgomery dinner."

Sebastian whistled between his teeth, and I narrowed my gaze at him as I looked over at Brooke. "It won't be all the Montgomerys. Not even close. Literally just my immediate family. No extra cousins, aunts, and uncles."

"Hey, that's not nice," Sebastian whined.

"That's what I was thinking," Sierra said dryly. "I was thrust into the lion's den of Austin's seven siblings. Since Leif only has three siblings, you are getting off easy here."

Austin Montgomery snorted. "I feel like I should apologize for that, but I can't. I like my family. And I promise my parents won't be there either, even though they want to meet you."

Brooke's eyes widened, and she laughed, looking at all of us. "I know that Nick told Leif that he needs to get me a family tree so I can get all the names right. I thought he was kidding."

"You'll be fine. I still mess up," Mom said with a laugh.

Brooke rolled her shoulders back. "Okay, dinner sounds good. I wanted to invite you guys over for dinner at my place anyway, just to say thank you."

The reasons why were left unsaid, and I knew it was because Luke was there and probably because nobody wanted to mention the subject.

"We can do your place next. This is fun. I can't wait. You'll have to tell me any allergies you have." Then my mom went still. "And if you like cheese. These are things I need to know."

Brooke threw her head back and laughed. I just grinned as Luke clapped and Sebastian chuckled. "Oh, I know all about the Montgomerys and cheese. I hear that, along with tattoos, are your favorite vices."

"Guilty," Dad said, deadpan.

"I love cheese. As does Luke. Right, buddy?"

Luke smacked his lips together. "Cheese is the best."

"That's what I like to hear," my dad said as he held up a hand. Luke looked at it curiously before he high-fived it, and my dad grinned.

As Mom and Brooke talked a bit more, I went over to listen to Sebastian and my dad joke around with Luke. I stayed quiet, watching them, and swallowed hard.

This felt right, like a family. I didn't want anything to break it. I couldn't. That meant I needed to deal with one last thing before I could take that next step. Only I wasn't sure exactly how to do that.

My parents left before too long, Brooke and Luke leaving soon after, which left me alone with Sebastian while we waited for Nick to show up to work.

"I hear there's a Montgomery dinner in order," Nick put in as he set his stuff down at his station.

I glared over at Sebastian. "It's been like ten minutes."

Sebastian shrugged. "I only texted Lake. She texted the rest of the family group chats."

I pulled out my phone and cursed at the twenty-nine notifications. "My God."

"It's a big thing, bringing a girl and her kid over for dinner," Sebastian said sagely.

"My family is going to give me gray hair," I said with a laugh and then froze as someone else walked into the shop.

He looked different, and yet the same. Twenty years had passed, but I had looked up his picture once I was notified of his release so I would be able to recognize him. Gray hair, strong jaw, thick nose. He was big now because he had used the prison yard to stay in shape. He still looked mean and smarmy and like the man who had made my life hell when I was a kid.

And then he was taken away, and Mom died, and I ended up with Austin. In the end, it all worked out, but I never wanted to think about him.

Or fucking look at him.

"What are you doing here?" I asked as both Nick and Sebastian stood up. They both had clients, regulars who looked up and narrowed their eyes, noticing the tension. This was my place of business, and I didn't want this to be a big thing, but I wasn't sure what else to do.

"I just wanted to see where my kid worked."

"I'm not your kid. Mom never married you. You're just some guy she was with. Then you were in prison. You need to go now. This is my place of business, and I don't want you here."

Did I sound calm? Because I didn't feel calm.

"I just thought you owed me. Don't you think you owe me? You have all of this while I was sent to prison. Doesn't really seem fair."

"You were sent to prison for your own actions and decisions that had nothing to do with me."

"Yet you have such a good life, but where would you be without me?"

"You have nothing to do with who I am. You need to go."

"Maybe I should go see that girl, the one that just left here with the pretty hair and eyes. What about that little kid? Your mom was about that age when I met her. You were about that kid's age, too. Brings back memories."

I moved forward, my fist flying out without even thinking. But then Nick was there, holding me back.

"This is just what he wants," Nick whispered in my ear.

"Got yourself a boyfriend holding you back, too? Well, I knew things got weird in your family. I didn't realize that you were one of them."

I pushed forward, but Nick held firm. "Get your hate speech and dickishness out of here."

"That's just fine. If you're not going to help me, maybe she will. She looks rich. I'll see what she wants to do to help a poor man."

"Stay away from her."

"Maybe I will, maybe I won't. She reminds me of your mom. Be nice to see her."

Then Roger walked out, and I sucked in a breath, my gaze going fuzzy.

"You need to call the family," Nick whispered as their clients got up and came forward.

Brett, a big man and construction worker that worked with my family, narrowed his gaze. "You need to call your parents. Seriously, at least let them know. And the cops."

"Brett's right," Jared put in. He was a fireman, worked long hours, and was one of Nick's regulars.

"I'm fine. I can handle it." Even as I said the words, I knew they were a lie. I ran my hands over my hair, then growled. "I need to go."

"Are you going to go talk to your dad?" Nick asked, anger in his gaze.

"I will. When I see them. I need to go find Brooke first."

"Make sure she's safe," Sebastian said, his voice quiet.

"You want me to talk to one of my friends down at the precinct?" Jared asked.

"I'll figure something out."

"Leif," Nick said, the disappointment and anger in that one word evident.

I let out a breath, the clock ticking loudly in my head. "Fine, I should talk to the authorities. So they at least know he's harassing me. But I need to talk to Brooke."

"We can do that. Come on, I'll go with you," Jared said.

I shook my head. "No, I can do this."

"And I'm going with you," Nick said.

"Well, our tattoo artists are going, it looks like I'm coming, too," Brett put in.

"I'll stay here and hold down the fort." Sebastian put in.

"I'm taking up your days," I said, shame crawling up my spine.

"No, that man came in and harassed you, and from what it sounds like, he's probably on parole. So let's see what we can do to keep your family safe." Jared nodded tightly before getting his things.

"What the hell does he want from me?" I asked as Nick glared.

"He wants everything he couldn't have before because he's a bully. And I know all about bullies, Leif. We'll fix this. But you have to stop trying to handle it on your own. You have to stop trying to hide the stress from your family."

"I just don't want to hurt them," I said, my voice breaking.

"Then don't. But you're not going to get hurt because of that asshole. So come on. Let's go."

I let my best friend, and two men I hardly knew, walk me out the door and right back into my past.

It was my present that kept echoing in my head.

I needed to keep Brooke safe.

Even if I made the wrong choice in the end. The only choice I could.

CHAPTER SIXTEEN

Brooke

"IT ALWAYS STUNS me that I know a real, live, nuclear physicist," May stated as she sipped her drink.

I laughed as Lake clapped her hands. "Isn't she brilliant? I mean, she's a physicist, so I knew she was brilliant, but the way that she can casually just discuss radioactive materials, silicates, and chemical leaching without anyone the wiser just makes me grin."

"That was for my graduate degree. I don't work with that branch anymore. At least not in detail."

The girls went on to ask more questions about physics, and I did my best to answer them. I didn't do the same type of research I had back in California or even in graduate school. Instead, my research went in a slightly different direction. I wasn't a rocket scientist like Leif called me at one point, but I was close to it. At least in some aspects.

I ate a bite of my cupcake, then sipped my champagne as the three of us enjoyed our girl time. Luke snuggled into my side and I kissed the top of his head. He might not understand all of the physics explanations I was going into, but he enjoyed being part of the group. And I loved the fact that while I was slowly making friends, Luke was part of everything. He was my everything. I might be finding myself in a serious relationship with Leif, somehow slowly finding my footing at work again, but no matter what, Luke was mine. My everything.

"I want to be a tattoo artist," Luke said suddenly, and Lake gave me a knowing look.

Luke had been looking at Leif these days as if he were my little boy's hero, and I was a little worried about that. What happened when Leif left? When things didn't work out? It was hard to find the balance, and I wasn't sure I was doing it right.

"Do you want to show us what tattoo you would make? Your crayons are right here," I said, pointing towards the coffee table where Luke and May had played with coloring books earlier.

"Okay, Mommy," Luke said as he scrambled down off the couch and knelt in front of the coffee table.

He bit his lip, then tapped his chin with his pointer finger as he studied the crayons, and then reached for a blue one before starting his outline.

"You're going with blue?" I asked

"I need to sharpen the purple one because purple is what you outline with." He nodded tightly and then went back to his drawings.

I widened my gaze, trying to think when he would have learned something like that.

"I think I remembered Leif saying that he and Luke had talked about tattoos before when you were making dinner a couple of nights ago," Lake said, as if she had known where my brain had gone.

I nodded as May and Lake continued to speak, watching Luke draw.

I needed to sit down with my son and have a long conversation about what it meant for Mommy to be dating. He knew that Leif was my friend and was honestly so great with him.

I hadn't meant to begin a serious relationship before Leif, but this happy accident had turned into something I wanted to trust.

I just needed to learn to trust again.

We had dinner with his family coming up in a couple of days, and Luke was coming, too. It scared me to think that I was taking all these serious steps, but I felt like I was also just getting started. I had known Leif for longer than anyone else in the state. I was friends with his cousins, his family, and him.

And I trusted him.

"You look like you just had a revelation," Lake whispered as she leaned toward me.

May smiled over at me, winked, then looked down at Luke's drawing.

"I'm just thinking," I answered.

"About?" Lake prodded.

I looked over at the other woman as she tugged on her long sleeve. She had her hair piled up on the top of her head and was wearing foundation but no other makeup. It seemed out of place for her since Lake was usually so put together.

"The fact that I'm falling for your cousin," I whispered, barely more than a breath.

May heard, though, and gave me a thumbs-up as Lake clapped her hands.

"I knew it. I like to think that I had something to do with this, but knowing my cousin, he would always find a way into your life."

We were being quiet as we watched Luke draw.

"I just have to take things slow. Be careful."

Lake nodded. "Because you're a good person, and an even better mom."

I smiled at her as the doorbell rang and I frowned, wondering who it could be.

I got off the couch, waving May down, as she and Lake went to help Luke with his drawing, each of my friends adding their tattoos to the paper.

I looked through the peephole, and warmth spread through me, my toes curling as I opened the door to see Leif standing there.

He had his hands in his pockets as he rocked back, a serious expression on his face.

I studied his eyes, the darkness in them, and dread filled my stomach even as I told myself I was just reading too much into it.

He opened his mouth to speak and then shook his head as if he were trying to figure out what to say.

Alarmed, I stepped out on the porch, closing the door behind me. "What is it?" I asked.

"I don't think I can do this anymore," he said after a minute, shocking me. I pressed my back against the door, my eyes wide. "What? You can't do what anymore?"

He pulled his hand out of his pocket and gestured between the two of us. "This. It's not working out. I have to go. You're safer here."

"Safer? What the hell are you talking about? Are you breaking up with me out of the blue and not telling me why? What is going on, Leif?"

"It's over, Brooke. This was nice. But I can't do this."

Then he turned on his heel and left. That's when I realized that he hadn't even driven here. He'd walked from his place on the other side of the neighborhood, and I just stood there, shaking.

Lake opened the door after what seemed like an hour, or possibly ten minutes, and frowned. "I heard someone shout, but it wasn't my cousin, right? Why are you standing there? Why are you so pale?"

I turned at her, my eyes widening. "I have to go figure out what the hell just happened."

"What is wrong, Mommy?" Luke asked and my heart twisted.

I had just told myself that I was trusting Leif. That I was falling for him. And Leif showed up, leaving us, leaving Luke. Well damn it. I was not going to let that happen. No matter what, I would not let him hurt my son.

Or myself.

I moved past Lake to kneel in front of Luke. I pushed his hair away from his face, realizing he needed another haircut, and kissed his forehead. "I need to go talk to a friend. Do you think you can stay with May and Lake for a little bit? You can have another cupcake."

Yes, I was bribing my son, trying to make him feel better because he could sense the nervousness wafting off me.

"I like cupcakes." Then he leaned forward and kissed the tip of my nose and I nearly burst into tears. "Don't be sad, Mommy. You'll fix it. You fix everything."

I knew my son had no idea what he was talking about, but I wanted to be that strong. To be the protector who could fix things. I just had no idea how I was going to fix this.

"What happened?" Lake asked, concern etched on her features.

I swallowed hard. "I think Leif just broke up with me." My voice broke, but I refused to cry. I did not have time to break down. I had to fix this and let my anger take over because I would be damned if Leif walked away like this. Not when something else had to be going on.

He had been the one to hold me, to get angry with me over what had happened at work. He had been the one to start this relationship with me when I wasn't sure I had the time or strength to do so. And yet he could just walk away?

Lake's eyes widened, and she nearly staggered back.

"Anything you need. We're here. Something must have happened because I saw the way he looks at you. He loves you."

My heart stopped for a moment, and everything went cold. "I don't know about that, but I thought he at least respected me enough to tell me what's on his mind."

May was watching us, but she kept her attention on Luke, and for that, I was grateful. They would take care of my son while I figured this out. I trusted them, and I had to believe in that trust. Because if I allowed myself to break down after just thinking I could trust Leif with everything, I was not going to make it for long.

I said goodbye to them, and since I'd had two glasses of wine, I walked toward Leif's house rather than getting behind the wheel.

It might be after dark, but the streetlights were on and there was a full moon. I would only need a few more minutes outside to make it to his place. I'd always found it comforting that we lived so close, even as I resisted starting a relationship, and yet he had just walked away. From me, from everything.

Damn it. I couldn't let him do this.

At least not without answers.

I stormed up to his porch and banged on the front door, ringing the doorbell a couple of times for good measure. The light in his living room was on, so he had to be home, even though his car was probably parked in the garage. We'd barely spent any time at his place, mainly because Luke had everything at my place. It was just easier.

Was that the problem? Was it because he felt like I wasn't taking this serious enough, putting enough effort in?

I swallowed hard, a single notion of worry sliding into anger. Maybe I didn't put in as much effort as I needed to. He was always the one setting up dates and taking me out when we had time. But the three of us did things together. Although not as much as Leif probably would like. I was taking things slow, trying not to hurt Luke or get his hopes up.

Or rather, my own hopes.

That was the truth. I didn't want to hurt myself, so maybe I had hurt Leif in the process.

Leif answered the door, his hair disheveled as if he'd been running his hands through it, his eyes wide. I'd only been a few minutes behind him, and yet he looked even worse now than he had on my porch. "Brooke? Why are you here?"

I ignored the knife in my heart at that and pushed past him.

"You better be alone in here and not cheating on me. Because if that's why you broke up with me, you will have to answer for a lot more."

Leif's eyes widened, the hurt on his face slicing into me. But I had to be numb. Had to ignore it. "There is no one else, Brooke. Why would you think that of me?"

"Why else? You broke up with me out of the blue. What else am I supposed to think? What is wrong?" I let out a breath, shaking. "What is *wrong*, Leif? Because you can't have had a personality change this drastic in the hours since we last spoke. What happened?"

"Nothing, everything. Brooke. It is better for you if I'm not around. Better for Luke."

"No, you don't get to bring up my son after walking away. You invited us to the damn farmers' market. You wanted us to go out and enjoy it as a family. Like a damn *family*, and here you are, walking away? You said it wasn't safe before. What do you mean by that? If you want to break up with me like this, I need answers. It's what I do for a living. Find answers. So give them to me. Now."

My voice rose with each sentence as I moved forward, pressing my finger against his chest. "Talk to me."

"Brooke," he said, his voice barely above a whisper.

"Tell me what's wrong. Don't walk away from me. You made me believe in you, Leif. Trust you. Don't break that trust. Don't break me."

Now I was crying, my anger bursting like a bubble as I just wanted to know why.

"It's to keep you safe," he said, pressing his forehead to mine.

"I'm going to need a better answer than that." My hands shook and I stepped back, wiping away my tears as I stared at him. "I deserve better than that, Leif. And so do you. I left my son with Lake and May, and I walked here. I need to know what I did wrong."

I hadn't meant to say that, and my voice broke at the words. Leif cursed under his breath and began to pace. "You didn't do anything wrong. I promise you. I'm just trying to keep you safe."

I threw my hands in the air. "What do you mean by that? What on earth could I be in danger from? Just tell me. Tell me. I deserve that. You don't get to make my choices for me."

"Brooke, Roger threatened you."

I blinked at him, confused. "Roger?"

"Fuck. I need to start at the beginning."

"Yes. You do."

"You didn't do anything wrong. I promise you. I love being with you. I love seeing you and spending time with you. I love spending time with Luke. You coming back into my life the way you did changed everything. I would never take that for granted."

"You were just going to walk away without a second thought."

"There were a lot of thoughts, Brooke."

"Then tell me," I whispered, my voice breaking. "Tell me."

Leif met my gaze, the agony in his eyes breaking me. "My birth mom had a lot of boyfriends when I was younger. You know that when she got pregnant, she hid it from my dad, Austin. She said it was because she thought she could be a better mom, that she and my birth dad weren't too close and so that's why she did it. And maybe my dad believes that. Or maybe he just hid his anger from losing ten years of my life for me so well. I don't know because all I remember is that my mom tried her best at the beginning and then quit trying. But when she started doing drugs, started dating men that hated her, and hit her, I had always thought, looking back on it, that she would've died from something else if she hadn't gotten sick."

I didn't have any words for this. I couldn't even imagine putting Luke in the situation Leif had been in, and my heart hurt. "I'm so sorry."

"I am, too. I know she tried sometimes, but not always. And while I told my therapist this, I didn't really tell my parents too much about it. I didn't want them to feel guilty about not being there for the first ten years of my life. And they *shouldn't* feel guilty. It wasn't my dad's fault that he didn't know I existed. The moment he knew I existed, he took me in. Sierra was barely even dating Austin at the time and took me in. They *are* my parents."

"And how is Roger connected?" I asked, confused, trying to keep up. I wanted to reach out and hold him, but he kept pacing, and I knew he needed space to tell me these things.

"He was my mom's boyfriend. My mom never married him. He went to jail before my mom died. So he wasn't even around when I was thrust into the system. They tried to figure out where I would go. I don't remember a lot of the legal part of that, about how hard my dad fought, or even if the will stated where custody went. I don't know the legal stuff. But the man my mother was dating before she died was a horrible person. He was in prison for a long time, longer than I ever thought possible, because of what he did while he was behind bars. But now he's out."

I looked up and then, my eyes wide. "When did he get out?"

"Right about the time you moved in. When we started to be together, he sent a threatening note. Because he wants money or to scare me like he did when I was a kid."

"Oh, Leif. I am so sorry. Why didn't you tell me this?" I asked.

He pushed his hair from his face, and I wanted to hold him and tell him everything was going to be okay. "I didn't want to worry you. I realize that that's stupid. The only people that know are Nick and Sebastian. One of the only reasons they even know is because Roger showed up."

"He showed up? At your house?"

He shook his head. "No, at Montgomery Ink Legacy. That's also where he sent the note. I don't think he knows where I live, but now that I've talked to the authorities, they are going to keep an eye on him. Roger is out on parole, so they will talk to his parole officer. But there's no real evidence other than him coming by. I don't have a restraining order against the man. Why would I?"

"Leif...I am so sorry."

He moved forward and cupped my face. I wanted to move away, unsure what I felt, but I didn't. He needed me just as much as I needed him. Maybe that realization told me that he had pushed me away for a reason. But we needed to be better than that.

"He came in today, and he threatened you and Luke. He saw you leaving my place, and he threatened you. I was going to tell you about that so that you could be on alert. The cops will want to talk to you, too. I had this whole speech planned out to tell you, then I saw you, and I heard Luke laughing, and I just needed to end it to keep you safe."

I push back, my eyes wild. "He threatened my son?"

Leif nodded. "Yes. I'm never going to let him hurt Luke. Or you. I'll do whatever I can."

"You were just going to walk away."

"To protect you."

I snarled. "That's idiotic. If he's going to threaten us, he will do so even if we are no longer together. Nobody hurts my son, Leif."

"Damn straight. Nobody will hurt you or your son."

"No one will hurt you either, damn it," I practically screamed. "Don't hurt *us* by walking away."

"The authorities are going to talk to you tomorrow. I promise you I was going to tell you everything. Only I saw you, and everything went blank. I wanted to keep you safe. So I ran."

"That's stupid," I blurted.

Leif raised his brows. "What?"

"That's stupid. No, you don't get to break up with me. I didn't break up with you, and you acted like the alpha asshole after my attack. We will work through this together because if someone is threatening you, then we need to keep *you* safe. You will tell the girls and your family about what's going on, so everybody is safe. Keeping this all bundled up and trying to take care of everything by yourself doesn't work. No one is going to hurt this family. But you need to tell me when you're in pain, or when you're scared. Because I don't know how to keep us safe if you don't tell me things."

He leaned forward and kissed me then, hard and fast, before he stepped away, breathing hard. "Brooke."

"Tell everyone. But don't leave me." I hadn't meant to say that. I pressed my lips together, annoyed that I'd once again left myself so open. When he nodded tightly and kissed me again, my thoughts began to whirl.

It was hard to think with Leif Montgomery around.

"I just wanted to keep you safe."

"Then be by my side and do it. Be open. No more secrets."

"I'm sorry. I'm sorry for hurting you. For acting like an idiot."

He kissed me again, and I stepped away as my phone buzzed.

"I'm sorry for yelling back at you. One second."

> LAKE:
>
> Everything okay?

I looked up at Leif, at the hunger and seriousness in his gaze, and swallowed hard. I needed him. I knew we needed to talk more. But right then? I needed him.

ME:

Yes. Finally. Give me an hour?

LAKE:

smiley emoji Take your time. We've got Luke. And cupcakes.

I laughed, then set my phone on the table beside me.

"Since you scared me, I think it's time you make it up to me." Leif's eyes widened for a minute before he grinned.

"Oh, I think I can do that."

And then his lips were on me, and I sighed, wrapping my arms around his neck.

He gripped my ass, then lifted me. I wrapped my legs around his hips, continuing to kiss him as we thrust against one another. And then he was walking, taking me to the dining room.

"Leif?"

"There is something that I've wanted to do for a while now."

He set me on the dining room table and then slid his hands over my body and then up my chest, caressing my breasts before cupping my face again.

"I will never hurt you again."

"Just talk to me. That's all we need."

"I think I might give you a little more than that," he said with a wink, and then my shirt was over my head and his lips were on my breasts.

I tried to keep up, tried not to breathe too quickly or to make too many moaning sounds. But it was hard to focus on anything for too long when he was there, touching me, kissing me. Then my bra was off, and he was pulling at my leggings.

Somehow, I was ripping off his clothes, and then we were both naked in his dining room. He knelt in front of me, my legs spread wide.

"Hands on the table, keep your legs spread."

"Leif."

"Now, Brooke," he ordered, and then he was licking me, sucking on my clit, spreading my lower folds. I groaned, riding his face as he continued to suck and lick and eat me out right on the dining table.

He hummed along my clit before he twisted his lips slightly, and I came, my body going tight and then relaxed against his face. He licked, and he sucked, and then he moved back, licking my juices from his lips. His beard was wet, and I wanted to blush, but I couldn't, not with all the heat and warmth sending shockwaves through my body.

He gripped his cock, slid his thumb over the piercing at the end. Then he thrust into his palm before I finally gathered my strength and slithered down the table to my knees. I gripped his thighs, digging my nails into his skin, and he smiled down at me, sliding his hand through my hair.

"Look at you on your knees in front of me. I like that look."

I spread my thighs and slid my hand between my legs, sliding over my swollen clit. "I want you."

"I'm going to come right on those pretty breasts if you keep touching yourself like that."

I grinned before I took him in one hand and swallowed him whole. He hit the back of my throat and groaned. He tugged on my hair and I swallowed, my throat closing around the tip of his dick.

I continued to play with myself, sliding my fingers in and out of my wet heat as I bobbed along his cock, hollowing my throat as I relaxed, letting him slide down deeper.

He thrust his hips, practically fucking my face as I did the same with my fingers. I knew I was wet, literally dripping on the floor, as he pulled back and then gripped me again. Somehow, I was in his arms, wrapped around him, his cock sliding between my folds and over my stomach as he moved me to the table again. He set my feet on the floor then twisted me, putting my ass in the air as he slid his length between my cheeks.

"I need a condom," he whispered before pressing a quick kiss to my shoulder and moving to the other side of the room. I kept playing with myself, moaning, before he came back and slid right into me in one thrust.

I could barely breathe, standing on my tiptoes, as he began to work in and out of me, hard, fast, needy.

When he slid his finger along my ass, spreading me, playing with me in a way he hadn't before, I groaned and moved so he could go deeper.

"That's my girl. My dirty, dirty girl."

"Make me come already," I ordered, my voice low, throaty.

He laughed roughly before he slid his hands over my breasts and then in my hair, pulling me back for a deep kiss that sent me over the edge.

I came over him, shaking, my knees going weak as he came too, holding me close.

Somehow we were both on the floor, wrapped in one another as we continued to move through our orgasms.

I couldn't breathe, couldn't think.

But this was Leif. He was taking care of me, even though was hard and fast, it was what we both needed.

And I made a vow right then and there.

I would never let anyone hurt him.

Not even myself.

CHAPTER SEVENTEEN

Brooke

"Don't be nervous. You know them already. You don't have to be scared."

I narrowed my gaze at Leif. "So says the man who is about to take me to a Montgomery family dinner, as if it's not a daunting task."

"It's not going to be too daunting. I promise you."

"I'm excited. Will there be cheese?" Luke asked, and my lips twitched as Leif took a staggered step back, his hand over his chest. "Will there be cheese? It's like you don't even know me, kid. Of course, there's going to be cheese. It's a Montgomery dinner."

"What if somebody doesn't like cheese comes to visit, would they be kicked out?"

Leif lifted Luke into his arms as my son began to laugh, and I ignored that little clutch of my belly at the sight. We were walking up the long driveway to Austin and Sierra's house, and from the cars already parked in the driveway, we were possibly the last ones there.

I didn't like being late, but I'd had a morning meeting with a few advisors that hadn't been able to be postponed. Leif understood, and he told me his family would as well, but I still felt bad about it.

"If someone does not like cheese, then they are forever ostracized."

"What does ostrich-sized mean?"

"What that means it's a big bird," Leif said, laughing at his own joke as I rolled my eyes. "But ostracize means that they are forever kicked out of the family." At Luke's wide eyes, Leif tapped Luke on the nose. "But I was only kidding. If somebody doesn't like cheese, that just means more cheese for us.

However, if you bring in any processed or fake cheese into the house, you are forever gone. That is a fon-don't, not a fondue. It must be gouda to be good."

I rolled my eyes. "How many cheese jokes do you have for this?"

"I have amassed a countless supply of cheese, dairy, and cow jokes from a long life of cheese-related humor. Just know that this will not be the first time you hear them, nor the last. It's sort of what you're forced into since you're with me."

He took my hand and my heart sped. Here I was, meeting the family, about to go to an actual dinner, and bringing my son. This was a big step. A scary one.

Leif's parents lived less than twenty minutes away, in the suburb just north of ours. They had a large house that I knew was Montgomery built. It was a two-story place with beautiful corbels under the eaves.

It looked like a home, welcoming, and with the backdrop of the Rocky Mountains, it was gorgeous. Leif told me that there was a huge deck on the back, one where he and his family had eaten countless dinners. Tonight, we would be eating inside since the mosquitoes were terrible.

"This home is beautiful. It's like something out of my childhood dreams."

"Well, that's a nice thing to hear when I walk outside," Sierra said as she opened the door and beamed at me.

I blushed, not having realized that she was there. "Oh, well, I love the house."

"So do I. Austin had it built before we were married, and I moved in and never left. We have done some renovations to keep it updated and the like, but the Montgomerys know how to build."

"That's what I like to hear," Austin said as he came up behind Sierra and put his hand on her shoulder. He was a full head taller than her, his big beard flecked with slight to moderate granite. They looked happy and in love and as if they had been made for each other.

That was what I wanted. That settled happiness still seemed to thrive even after four children and countless changes. Could I have that with Leif? I wasn't sure. I wasn't sure if I could trust myself enough for that, but maybe I should try.

Luke scrambled down out of Leif's hold and practically ran toward Sierra.

My eyes widened as Leif's mom bent down and lifted Luke up to her waist.

"Hello there," she said, laughing.

"It is good to see you again. Thank you for welcoming us into your home." Luke said it slowly, reciting everything I had told him, and Sierra beamed as Austin rubbed his mouth, holding back a smile.

"We're trying," Leif said, and once again, my heart did that pit-pat thing.

Because he said *we*.

We were trying. Together.

I was in love with Leif Montgomery, and I needed to come to terms with that.

"Come on inside. We'll get you all situated with the Montgomerys," Austin said as Sierra moved into the house, Luke in her arms as the two of them talked.

I bit my lip, walked inside, and handed over the bottle of wine I had brought.

"Like Luke said, thank you for welcoming us into your home."

"Thank you for bringing this stranger with you, since I never get to see him these days." Austin took the bottle from my hand and then held me close, giving me a big bear hug.

I swallowed hard, tears stinging my eyes.

What was with me?

Leif hugged his dad and then gestured towards the living room.

"And here is the rest of my immediate family. There's Colin." He pointed to a tall man with dark hair and thick-rimmed glasses perched on the bridge of his nose. I knew that Colin was finishing up his last year of college. He grinned as he came toward us.

"Finally, the woman that tamed the beast."

"Colin," Leif growled, but Leif's little brother waved him off, picked me up around the waist and twirled me around the living room.

"Welcome to the Montgomerys."

I sputtered and laughed. "He said you were going to be the one that made a scene."

"At least I'm living up to my expectation."

"Okay, hands off my woman," Leif growled as he pulled me back.

"Seriously? You decide to go with *my woman*?" I asked, laughing.

"I've got to claim my territory. There are a lot of freaking Montgomerys out there. This is why it's just the immediate family today, rather than all of the cousins and aunts and uncles. I don't think you're ready for that kind of dinner."

"Nobody is," a young woman said from the couch as she stood up, her twin brother beside her.

"Gideon, Jamie, this is Brooke. And over there, in Mom's arms, is Luke." My son waved from Sierra's arms, and I had to wonder if I was ever going to hold my son again tonight, because he looked mighty comfortable in Sierra's arms. Of course, that just made me smile.

"It's nice to meet you," Gideon said, grinning. "Will you drive us around? Or let us drive your car?"

"Gideon Montgomery," Austin growled, though I could hear the laughter in his tone.

"What am I missing?" I asked as Leif pinched the bridge of his nose.

"The twins are trying to get their driver's licenses, which means they need adults who are suckers enough to let them drive their cars. Do not touch Brooke's car. She has Luke to drive around, so if you wreck it, then Luke won't have a car."

"Well, that's a leap of logic," Jamie said with a teenage roll of her eyes. "We'll be careful, and it is not like Luke would be in the car as we drove."

I held up my hands in surrender. "I'm not getting in the middle of this, but I bet you Leif could help. He is the big brother, and he's nice."

"Brooke," he growled, but his eyes were filled with laughter.

"Oh, we already like you. You're going to fit nicely," Austin said as he squeezed my shoulders and led me to the sitting room.

"We all helped cook, so Sierra didn't have to do it all on her own, but she's still the best cook of us all."

"I'm catching up," Colin said, his chin raised.

"Yes, you are," Sierra said, grinning. "Now, what can we get you to drink?"

"Milk?" Luke asked as he came practically barreling towards my legs.

I laughed, thankful that Leif kept me standing upright.

"We do have milk, as long as it's okay with your mom," Sierra answered.

I nodded. "Milk is good, but you also need to have water. Okay?"

"Okay."

"Come on. I have the perfect cup for you. It used to be Leif's. I don't throw anything away."

Austin rolled his eyes, much as his teenage daughter had. "I don't know why she said that. She's constantly cleaning out the house so we don't end up like hoarders." he grumbled.

"Let me guess. She finally threw away those old shorts that were more holes than cloth." Leif grinned.

"They were fine."

"Dad, you used to have to wear shorts underneath them so you didn't get arrested for indecent exposure." Jamie added with a huff, her eyes dancing.

Austin growled though it was halfhearted. "I swear, I'm outnumbered by all of you."

"I don't know. I seem to be the one surrounded by Montgomerys. I think Luke and I are the ones outnumbered."

"Okay, fine. I guess that counts." Austin winked. "Come on, let's get you that drink, now that Luke is taken care of."

Soon, I found myself laughing over barbecue ribs and fajitas, two foods that Leif loved, and they hadn't been able to choose which one to eat. There was pico de gallo and cilantro, beans and a fruit salad, macaroni and cheese, and coleslaw. Somehow it was the perfect amount of food for everybody though, without anyone feeling like they had to overeat. Everything was delicious, and I knew I needed a recipe or two for the sauce at least.

"Are these tortillas homemade?" I asked, after Luke and I shared a final one.

Sierra grinned. "Yes, one of my nieces went down to San Antonio for school for a while and learned how to make them from her roommate's family."

"I'm jealous."

"I can teach you. It's fun. I bet Luke would have fun making them, too."

Luke grinned, his mouth closed but full of tortilla.

"I'm going to take that as a yes," I said with a laugh.

"I know you only wanted immediate family here," Austin said after a moment, looking at Leif. "But I wanted to invite Lake, as I need to meet this man of hers."

"You know, I haven't met Zach either," I said with a frown. "That's weird, right?"

"They are both constantly out of town, and when they are in town, they want to spend time together. I guess it makes sense." Leif said as he shrugged. "I met him on that double date. Remember?"

"Oh yes, when you went on a date with my nanny," I teased.

The table broke out into laughs and hoots as Luke's eyes widened.

"You and May?"

"I just went out to dinner with May. She's nice. But you know, I have a thing for your mom."

Everybody laughed louder as I shook my head, blushing.

"Of course you like Mom. She's the best," Luke said, as if that was everything in the world, and went back to his tortilla.

"Well then," Austin said, clearing his throat even though he was still laughing. "I still want to meet him. I know that my cousin Liam, Lake's father, can handle it, but since she lives near us, I feel a sense of responsibility for my generation."

"I'm sure Lake can handle everything on her own," Sierra said, admonishing her husband. "But if we happen to invite her over for dinner just because, maybe with a few of the nieces, she can bring her boyfriend. Then we can meet him and interrogate him."

"I'm going to have to take notes on how you think," I said with a laugh.

"Before you know it, your kids are asking to go to school dances, go on dates, to drive. Then it's college, starting their own business, and bringing home a lovely woman that we adore, along with her amazing son." Sierra winked, and I blushed even harder as Leif let out a sigh.

"Subtle, Mom."

"You know I try."

"Speaking of dates, we saw Sebastian and Marley out at the Connolly Brewery for dinner yesterday."

I turned to the twins, frowning. "Marley is Sebastian's girlfriend, right?" I asked.

"Yep, and I keep waiting for him to propose already," Jamie said, that teenage winsome note in her voice.

"They're too young to get married," Sierra said before she stiffened. "Great, now I sound like an uppity mother from a TV show. But they are only eighteen."

"Sebastian's nearly nineteen," Leif corrected.

"And they do love each other. I just still think of them as babies. And that's on me." She narrowed her eyes at the twins. "You two are fifteen. So don't even start thinking about it."

"I'm just saying they're adorable," Jamie said.

"Don't worry. I'm looking to get married once I'm old, like thirty." Gideon grinned as he said it, and Leif rolled his eyes.

"You're lucky there's a kid here."

"You are lucky that I'm here," Luke said as he beamed, and I cackled, the rest joining me.

By the time we cleaned up and headed out to the porch for the evening, Leif cleared his throat and whispered something to Jamie. She gave him an odd look and then nodded before holding out her hand.

"Hey, Luke, do you want to see our playroom? It's changed over the years, but there might be a couple of toys to show you."

Gideon stepped right up as if the twins had mind-reading abilities. "Yeah, come on, kiddo."

Luke looked at me and I nodded, knowing why Leif wanted Luke out of the room along with his youngest siblings.

The three walked away, and Austin gave us a worried look before clearing his throat. "What is it that you want to tell us that you didn't want little ears around for?" he asked, his voice soft.

Colin, I noticed, had been allowed to stay, but considering he was an adult, that made sense. Sierra slid her hand into Austin's while I did the same to Leif's.

"I have to tell you something, and you're going to get mad, but let me get through it."

I squeezed his hand again, and Leif let out a breath before explaining the entire situation about Roger.

As expected, Austin growled and threw his hands in the air. "Why the hell didn't you tell us?"

"Austin, let him finish," Sierra put in, even as she glared at her son. "Once you're finished, then we can yell at you."

"Damn straight," Colin added.

Leif ran his hand through his hair and went through every detail, sparing no feelings, and even mentioned how he had broken up with me for those few short minutes.

Colin reached out and smacked the back of Leif's head, but nobody admonished him for it. Instead, they continued to listen to Leif. When he finished, I hugged him tightly and moved back so Sierra could hold her son. Colin began to rant, repeatedly going over what happened and asking questions. Leif answered systematically, and I knew this was hard for him.

Then Austin spoke, and everyone quieted. "All this time. All this fucking time, Leif. You never told me. I don't know why."

Because Sierra was holding her son, Colin came up to me and hugged me tightly. It was as if I was part of the family already, and tears slid down my cheeks. I looked over and saw Sierra was crying, too.

Austin sighed. "I wish you would've told me all those years ago about everything that happened to you. I thought I knew, I thought you would have told me, but you didn't. We're going to have to work through that, but the thing is...we're family, Leif."

"I know that, Dad, I promise you. I'm sorry."

"We're a family, meaning we're going to handle this together. I know you thought you had to handle this on your own because you're the oldest and because you feel like everybody is trying to lean on you. We talked about this. We've all got you. People younger than you, older than you, all of us. So, we're going to deal with this as a family." Austin Montgomery looked at me then, his eyes directly on mine. "And that means you too, Brooke. You and Luke. We're all a family in this. So we will protect each other, and we will keep that man out of our lives. Just like we should've done all those years ago. Come here, son," Austin growled as he moved forward and opened his arms. Leif went straight into them, as did Sierra. Colin tugged on me, and suddenly the five of us were hugging, laughing, and crying.

In that moment, I knew I truly loved Leif. His family loved him so much that while they were angry that he had hidden this, they loved him more than that anger. They cared for him and wanted to keep him safe. And they wanted to keep my son safe.

I had fallen in love with Leif Montgomery.

And I was truly scared I could lose him if we didn't protect him.

But right then and there, I let the Montgomerys hold me, and I imagined what it would mean to have a family like this.

And what it could mean if this was truly mine.

CHAPTER EIGHTEEN

Leif

"I HEAR that the meeting of the parents went well," Sebastian said as he leaned against the wall.

I sipped my beer and nodded. "Brooke's met them a couple of times now, but dinner? Yeah, it went well."

Everybody in this room already knew about Roger and the threats. The authorities knew, so there was nothing to do other than be on alert and try to live our lives.

Brooke was at home grading papers and having Luke time. She had almost finished by the time I had left after dinner, and now she just wanted time alone with her son. If I hadn't had this guys' night already planned, I would've been able to stay as well. As if we were a family.

That hit me like a ton of bricks to the chest and I swallowed hard, thinking about us as a family. I had almost run because I was too scared.

I was still worried about what Roger would do. He thought I had money that I didn't have, or maybe he just wanted retribution for being in jail when I had my own life, but I had nothing to do with that. And maybe once the man understood that, or once the cops talked to him, things would be better.

Until that happened, the doors were locked, Brooke was behind the security system that my family's company had put in, and I was trying not to be overwhelmed by the fact that they were being threatened because of my past. A past that had nothing directly to do with me, but that didn't help me sleep at night.

"Earth to Leif. What's up with you?" Leo asked.

I looked at my fellow tattoo artist, then Tristan, Nick, and Sebastian, and tried my best to push away all thoughts of the man who haunted my nightmares and focus on what was in front of me.

"Sorry, just thinking."

"You better not be thinking about that asshole," Nick warned, ever the best friend.

"If it helps, my thoughts started with Brooke."

"That's always good," Leo said, grinning. "She seems nice... You know, I'm real nice. She have a sister? It would be killer to find a woman who doesn't mind the ink and my job."

"She doesn't have a sister, but I know you can find someone. I didn't realize you were looking." I took another sip of my beer.

"I don't know if I'm looking for forever actively, but I'm not *not* looking."

Tristan rolled his eyes. "What my cohort over here is saying is that love looks good on you."

Everyone was silent for a minute when I didn't spit out my beer, and Nick's eyes widened. "Well then. *Love*. Does Brooke know that?"

I shrugged and played with the label on my bottle. "Probably. I just haven't actually told her."

"You know, as the resident love expert here, I do have to say telling her is the first step. The most important step. Just like we men joke that we can't read women's minds. They, in turn, cannot read ours."

Both Tristan and Leo glared at Sebastian while Nick and I burst out laughing.

"The thing is, of all of us, the hatchling knows what he's talking about. It is not even a little contrived."

Sebastian shrugged, though there was something in his eyes I couldn't quite read. "I may be young, but I know things. I have responsibilities. And I know I love Marley. That's all that matters, you know?"

"I know," I said. I cleared my throat. "I'm going to tell her. I just don't know how to do it."

"Start with the words," Nick said with a shrug. "What do I know? I'm not in a serious relationship. Not like the kid here."

"Excuse me. I'm your business partner, not just a kid." Sebastian raised his chin, his eyes filled with laughter.

"That is true. But until you can buy me a beer, I don't know if I can stop making fun of you."

"So, is that the age that you finally treat me like a grown-up?" he teased.

"No, I'll just keep moving the finish line. Then it will be renting a car. And then the age where we have to go to bed early because life sucks. Which is thirty, by the way," Nick added.

"You're not kidding about the whole thirty thing. I thought people were joking when they said once you turn thirty, your body starts to give out, but I was picking up Luke the other day, and my back twinged." I shook my head in disgust as everybody else jeered. "I would be annoyed that you're laughing at me about my sad state of affairs, but honestly, I'm not an old man or anything, but I am thirty now. I guess this means I should start taking control of what I want."

"Hear hear," Leo put in. "Tell that woman that you love her. That you want to be with her and that Luke means everything in the world to you. Do it all. Then tell us exactly how to do it so I can take notes for when I find my lady love.”

“Okay, first off, don't use the term 'lady love,'” Tristan said with a laugh.

Nick smiled. “Ever, seriously. And more power to both of you for finding relationships and making them work. When I get to your age, though? I don't see me falling like the rest of you. No, thank you. Relationships aren't worth the headache. I'm good just like I am. Getting Montgomery Ink Legacy off the ground, making sure Leif doesn't make any more stupid decisions, watching all of you Montgomerys and friends fall. That's not for me.”

“Well, doesn't that sound like a challenge,” Leo mumbled, and I held back a smile. No, I didn't think my best friend would appreciate me grinning just then, even though it did indeed sound like a challenge to the gods of fate.

Although I had eaten dinner earlier, I still had a couple of wings that Sebastian had brought over, saying he had a nervous stomach, and I just sighed at the eighteen, nearly nineteen-year-old who could gorge himself on wings and root beer as if he wasn't going to have heartburn later.

Leo and Tristan headed out, having dates, which I found ironic considering that Leo wanted me to hook him up with someone. He was going to have to slow down on the serial dating if he wanted something serious, but I wasn't going to be the one to tell him that. It had taken me long enough to figure it out.

Nick headed out next, saying he had an early morning, and left it at that. Knowing how Nick was growly over the idea of dating, I figured he was actually going home, but I didn't pressure him to say anything more.

That left Sebastian and me, and I knew he would be heading out soon because he had exams coming up, and I wanted to get back to Brooke. Although I had guys' night tonight, I would be spending the night in her bed. Exactly where I needed to be. It still surprised me how quickly everything had changed. I was going to stop trying to look for every fault there was.

“Hey, do you have a minute?” Sebastian asked as we were cleaning up the last of the dishes.

I frowned at the worried note in Sebastian's voice and nodded.

“Of course. What's up?” I asked, sliding the final plate into the dishwasher.

“I don't know how to start.”

Tension slid up my spine and I swallowed hard, reaching out to grip Sebastian's shoulder. “Anything you have to say to me will stay between us. You know that's always the case with us. We're cousins. Family. Although, wait.” I paused. “Except for Brooke. I feel weird about keeping secrets from her.”

Sebastian's eyes widened, then he nodded. “Yeah, you're right. I wouldn't keep secrets from Marley, especially after everything that just happened with Brooke. You shouldn't keep secrets from her.” He let out a breath. “Hell. I should just say it.”

My eyes widened. “Did you ask Marley to marry you? Is that what you're worried about? Because you know your parents love her. We all might think you guys are young, but you guys have been together forever.”

Sebastian shook his head. “No, it's not that. I mean, I am going to marry Marley. I love her. She is my future. I know that. Damn it.” He cursed a few more times, then looked me straight in the eyes. “Marley is pregnant.”

I nearly dropped when I was holding and stared at my cousin. My teenage cousin. He might be an adult, might pay his own way, might soon own part of the business. He was in college and going towards his future.

But he was still only nearly nineteen.

"I don't know what to say."

Sebastian ran his hand through his hair, then began to pace through my kitchen. "We didn't mean for this to happen. She was on birth control until her parents found out, and yes, she's an adult, but her dad kept throwing it away. So we used a condom. Every time. We even used spermicide, and anything else we could've possibly done with her not being on birth control."

"Hold on. Her dad threw away her birth control?" I asked, practically shouting.

Sebastian held up his hand. "Her parents are ultraconservative. To the point that they didn't even want her dating me. I thought I had won them over. But it didn't matter that Marley was in college, nearly nineteen. They didn't want their daughter to have sex, so they didn't let her have birth control. In their mind, that made sense. She was just getting on a new prescription, and she was going to hide it at my house when, well, apparently, condoms aren't one hundred percent effective."

My mind went in a thousand different directions as I tried to catch up. "I have so much to say to that. To begin with, I'm so sorry for Marley. For what her parents did because I feel like that's illegal."

Sebastian shook his head. "I don't know. *I don't know.* But it doesn't matter, does it? It's not like I can go back and add birth control. We never had a condom break, not to my knowledge, and were very careful. We've always been careful. There wasn't one slip up, one accidental 'oh, we can go back and fix it.' We were always careful. But she's pregnant. Marley is pregnant. We're going to keep it."

I reached forward and gripped his shoulders. "Okay. What do you need from me?" I asked softly.

Sebastian relaxed marginally before he pulled away and swallowed hard. "I'm an adult. I'm going to tell Mom and Dad. Because they deserve to know, because somehow my parents will be grandparents, and I have no idea how that's going to go."

I blinked and held back a laugh even though nothing was funny about the situation. But Grandpa Alex and Grandma Tabby had a certain ring to it.

"Her parents are not going to be okay with this. I don't know what they're going to do, but I'm going to take responsibility, and so will Marley. If we have to get married, we'll get married early. I know everyone joked that we were going to get married young, but we were going to wait till after college. We had *plans*. And this throws a wrench in it, but I don't want Marley to have to quit school. I don't want to quit school, either. I don't know. I just need to figure things out."

"I'm here when you need me. And you're going to need me. You'll need all of us. But that's what we Montgomerys do. We take care of each other. I know this is unexpected and so not the right time, but it's okay. We're going to figure this out. You and Marley are not alone." Then I smiled, even though my stomach twisted at the thought of my baby cousin being a dad. "Well then, Daddy. It looks like you have to learn how to change diapers," I teased.

Sebastian cursed under his breath before he laughed, though I didn't hear much humor in it. "I'm so not ready for this."

"I don't think you're supposed to be ready for parenthood. Even when you think you will be. So you'll figure it out. Hell, you guys are helping me figure out how to keep Brooke and Luke safe. So, we will help you and Marley. You are not alone. You don't get kicked out of our family for having sex and dealing with the consequences. And now I feel like a jerk for calling a baby a consequence."

"I'm pretty sure I nearly did." Sebastian let out a breath. "I can figure something out. I don't know. But I just don't want Marley to be scared. Or feel like she's alone. Because her parents? They're not going to be understanding about this."

From the way that her parents sounded, no, I didn't think they were going to be understanding about it at all. And while I knew with certainty that every single one of our family members would understand, some would still grumble at the thought because it was a scary and monumental event.

I calmed Sebastian down a bit and then made sure he headed home. He would talk with his family in the morning, and then the rest of the Montgomerys would hear about it soon and be on board to do what they could. I just had to hope that in all of our numbers, we would be enough to help when Marley's parents made things difficult.

And from how Sebastian sounded, the fear he had, I had a feeling that was an actual worry.

I packed up my things and headed to Brooke's, wondering what else would change. Because Lake seemed to be in a serious relationship, Sebastian was about to be a dad, and here I was, finding myself with a seemingly ready-made family. It was scary as hell, and yet, I was ready for this. Scared but ready.

I knocked on Brooke's front door as I got there, and she opened it quickly, a smile on her face. "I saw you pull up. Would it be weird if I gave you a key?" she asked, tumbling over her words.

I grinned, my heart squeezing. "I was thinking I should give you a key to my place."

"Oh? That would be nice. Though I feel bad that we always do things at your house because Luke's here, and all his things are here. But then I end up feeling Luke and I are taking advantage of you."

I shook my head. "You are not. I like your place. And you're right, Luke's things are here."

"Maybe we can do better about taking turns. I don't know, but we can try."

I smiled. I leaned down and took her lips with mine. She groaned and I smiled, setting my bag down near the front door. "We can do whatever you want. I'm easy. A key sounds good, though. It would make things easier to help out around here more."

"Oh?" The fire flared back into her voice.

"Only because I want to. You were just saying that you needed somebody to help with the air filter because you can't reach it, even on a ladder. I'm a foot taller than you. I can help."

"I can reach if I jump," she said with a laugh.

"It's like we were both just now saying, you don't have to do things on your own, and we can try to help each other out. You have been doing most of the cooking because you like it, but I can help with other things. I don't know, Brooke. I'll be honest. I've never had a serious relationship like this before. I'm not good at it. So you're going to have to be patient with me as I figure out what we're supposed to do."

"I'm going to try to accept help. You're going to try to figure out what we're supposed to do. Because I don't know about serious relationships either, remember? I'm just as lost as you."

I raised a brow. "I didn't use the word lost."

She rolled her eyes and then led me back to the house as we tiptoed past Luke's room. "You didn't have to use the word. I got it in context."

I smiled and followed her back to her bedroom.

"Did you get your work done?" I asked as we got ready for the night. I didn't comment that this felt more like we were living together, a married couple, than anything I had ever felt in my life, because I didn't want to scare her away. But, hell, I was pretty scared too.

She piled her hair on the top of her head and then headed to her closet, probably to change into her pajamas.

I shrugged and then stripped down, keeping on my boxer shorts. Neither one of us slept naked in case Luke came in, though I had noticed that Brooke had locked the door.

She only locked the door if we wanted to keep Luke out.

And that was only for a certain reason.

My cock pressed through my boxer briefs, and I looked down, groaning. "Behave."

The door opened, and Brooke stood in short shorts and a tank top that barely held her generous breasts.

"Or don't behave." I blinked.

"Our faces are washed, your beard is clean, our teeth are brushed. I guess you just want to go and read in bed."

"Maybe. But it has been a long day. And I could use some tension relief." In more ways than one, I stood at attention. I swallowed hard. And then I was moving, cupping her face, and crushing my mouth to hers.

She tasted of mint and Brooke.

My dick slid against her belly and I licked her lips, then mine, before thrusting slightly against her.

"Those boxer briefs do not contain you at all," she teased, sliding her hand between us to squeeze.

My eyes nearly crossed and I groaned before picking her up and carrying her to the bedroom. She wrapped her arms around my neck as she held back a squeal.

"We have to be quiet. Luke will be able to hear us."

"I'm just saying if one of us wants to do some renovations to either one of our homes, soundproofing this bedroom will have to be number one." I tossed her on the bed, and she bounced, laughing.

"Oh, that was so sexy." She rolled her eyes, and I fell that much more in love.

Then I was over her, taking her shorts down, my mouth on her cunt before she could take her next breath. She put her hand over her mouth and arched, cupping her breast with her free hand as I licked her, spreading her, tasting her.

She was sweet and tart and everything that I craved. I was practically humping the bed as I went down on her, eating her out.

She came on my mouth in a silent scream, wet and hot and nearly sending me over the edge. We moved quickly, stripping each other, knowing each other more now than we ever had before. We had been hot and heavy all those years ago in Paris. We had quickly learned each other's bodies then.

But it was nothing like now. Our bodies had changed, we had changed, but this moment? We were more together now than we ever had been before.

When she rose above me and slid down, over my length, both of us groaned.

She rode me, cupping herself as I played with her nipples and her clit, both of us taking our time, knowing that even though the world might come down around us soon, this was our moment. And when she came, she clamped down around me, and I pulled her by her hair to my mouth. I took her mouth, kissing her hard, before I slid out of her and moved just as she was pressed against the bed. I pulled her hips, ass in the air, before I pounded into her, both of us groaning, trying to be quiet.

But there was nothing quiet about the heavy breaths, the sound of flesh against flesh, heat against heat.

And then I came, filling the condom, as I held back my groan.

I loved this woman.

I didn't want to wait any longer.

While still in her, I lay down behind her, holding her close.

"I love you, Brooke. I've loved you for far longer than this moment. But I can't hold it back anymore."

Brooke stiffened, and I was afraid I'd said the wrong thing. She looked over her shoulder, tears sliding down her cheeks.

"I love you, too, Leif. Now turn me around so I can see your face."

I laughed softly before I slid out of her, careful with the condom before I kissed her again.

"I love you," I whispered. I kissed her lips, a sweet touch of promise. "I love you."

"Love you, too."

She held me, and I knew that, no matter what happened next, no matter who came at us, no matter what pressures came forward, I loved Brooke.

She was mine. And I couldn't wait to tell the world.

CHAPTER NINETEEN

Brooke

I SLID out of my lab coat and headed out of the lab, waving at my students as they finished up their work. I started early that morning, far earlier than I usually did, because I wanted to head home and meet with Leif and Luke for dinner. It was nice thinking that I had someone to come home to. It was a whole other dynamic that I was still getting used to.

I walked down the hallway towards my office and rolled my shoulders back, letting out a breath.

In the weeks since the attack, I had spoken with my therapist, the school board, and countless other administrative people. Honestly, I was tired of the politics behind it because everybody was so afraid that I would sue the school.

I just wanted to get past it, to get over it.

Because while they had created the environment that Landon had thrived in, nobody else had hurt me.

His father wasn't the president of the University anymore. The old guard would soon be leaving. The new guard consisted of people who trusted women, and my team were all people who were going to be safe because of the faculty in place.

Nobody had ever treated me like Landon had. In fact, everybody had always treated me with respect. And had continued to do so.

After the incident, I'd been afraid that they would think differently of me because I hadn't been strong enough to fend off the attack. But I had been. I'd gotten out of the office and called for help, and people had come to me. Nobody had taken Landon's side or blamed me.

Every single person believed me and had pushed Landon back.

The physics department at our university trusted women. They trusted who we were as scientists and people.

"You're looking introspective today," Patrice said as she came out of her office, books in tow.

"I was just thinking that our department is strong. And worthy. I guess." I rolled my eyes at my words, but Patrice grinned.

"You're right. When I first started at the university, it was a boys' club with nearly no women. Now there are more and more coming every year. We are a diverse group, and we are brilliant. All of us."

I laughed, even though I believed her. "We are brilliant."

"I don't talk about my personal life often, mostly because it's not anybody's business, but I admire you, Brooke."

I froze, looking at the other woman who was slowly becoming my friend.

"When I first started here, I was a young academic, who eventually became a single mother."

I blinked. "Really? How did I not know that?"

Patrice gave me a wry smile. "I had to keep my own secrets and personal life for so long, it's hard for me to change that. But when I first started here as an associate professor, I was a single mom. Eventually, I got married and kept my last name because it was hard to explain to the boys of the department why I would want to change it." She rolled her eyes and I laughed.

"I can only imagine."

"My kids, all of them, added my name to my husband's. My husband's is even hyphenated. It was easier for everybody involved, even though their names went a little long. Now I'm about to be a grandmother, and I'm looking towards the future. Knowing that while there may be bumps in the road, women in science have a future because of people like you. So, one day when you're not rushing home to be with your baby, we should have a drink. I think my kids would love to meet you as well. My youngest daughter wants to be a physicist too, and it just makes me grin."

I nearly wanted to cry, knowing that this move out here had been the best choice for me. Landon had tried to take it from me, but in the end, he didn't matter. It was everybody left behind that did. Making the choice to come out here, to change everything, had been the best one.

I had this department, my team, and I was making a family.

I smiled to myself as I packed up my belongings and headed home, knowing that I had an early day tomorrow. Research was going well, but it still took hours of my life just to untangle the data. While some professors might just let their students take over, that wasn't me. I loved to be in the thick of it.

I pulled into the driveway, the garage door was closed, but I knew it was full of kitchen cabinets. Leif and some of his family had come over the day before to help me sand them down because we were going to paint them. They needed to be refinished, and since I was dating somebody who had family with an actual homebuilding business who knew what they were doing, I wanted to use my resources.

It was also nice that I could lean on someone, and ask for help, and know that there were talented individuals who would help, no matter what.

I got out of the car and waved at Lake, who pulled a hoodie over her head.

It was warm out, so I wondered why she was wearing a hoodie rather than her usual dressy outfit, but she just waved at me and then headed to her car without saying anything.

It was weird, but maybe she had places to go. I shook my head, headed inside, and grinned at the sight of Leif and Luke running around the house.

They were playing with some Nerf gun that Nick of all people had gotten them, and I laughed.

"Well, this is a sight to see."

"Mommy! Be on my team!" Luke said as he ran towards me. I threw my arms open and he jumped into them before I turned and blocked him from Leif's aim.

"I see how it is, two against one? I can take those odds."

"Where's May?" I asked.

"I finished with my client early, and Nick and the rest of the team had the shop covered, so I headed here. I let her go. That okay?" he asked, tentatively.

I grinned, my heart growing two sizes. "That's more than okay. She knows that you're allowed to be here anytime that you want, and you're also on my emergency contact list with the school. Everything's great, Leif."

It was the truth. Everything was great.

I was happy. My son was happy.

And I was in love with a man who loved me and my son.

Nothing could go wrong.

I put Luke down, picked up the spare Nerf gun, and winked.

"Okay, the battle is on."

Luke giggled, the laugh melting any ice that could have been lingering on my heart over any doubts I was doing the right thing, and then the battle was on.

In the end, Luke and I won, because of course we did. Leif made us a wonderful chicken piccata for dinner that made my mouth water, and we settled onto the couch to watch a kid show before bed. I snuggled into my son as Leif slid his arm over my shoulders.

"Love you," he whispered, and I grinned before leaning over Luke's head to kiss him gently.

"I like when you kiss," Luke said, and I looked down at him.

"You do?"

"It means you love each other. And I love you both." And then he settled back into the couch and focused on his TV show.

My throat tightened slightly, making it hard to swallow as Leif looked at me, his eyes watery.

That big man, with his beard, piercings, and tattoos, nearly crying over that, made my heart swell four sizes.

This was it. This was exactly what I wanted.

What exactly I thought I would never have after losing Luke's father all those years ago. He had never had a chance to meet Luke.

We had never had a chance to figure out how to co-parent without being in a relationship.

I missed him, in the sense that I missed the man he had been, but I had never loved that man.

But I loved who he gave me. Our son.

Now Leif was here. There was no going back.

Glass shattered behind us, and I threw myself over Luke as Leif did over both of us.

"Mommy?" Luke asked, and I scrambled off the couch, Luke in my arms.

"Quiet, baby," I whispered, holding him close.

Leif was in front of us, cursing under his breath.

"Roger. What are you doing here?"

I stood behind Leif, Luke in my arms, my eyes wide.

This was the man harassing Leif. This was the man who dated Leif's mother all those years ago. The man who had gone to prison and should still be there.

Apparently, the authorities hadn't convinced him to leave us alone.

And he knew where I lived. Where my son lived. My entire body was ice cold.

"I told you that I was going to find your girl and get what I wanted," the other man slurred.

He was drunk, that was for sure, and maybe on something else. Fear coated my tongue, and I held Luke tightly, hiding his face from this strange man. I didn't want my son to be scared, but it was hard for him not to be when I was terrified.

"I'm not sure what you want, but let's talk about it outside. You know this isn't the place to do this, Roger," Leif said, his voice oh so calm. But I heard the rage beneath his words. The fear. The same things that were within me.

"I want what I should've had. Your mom is the one that sent me to prison. Did you know that? She's the one that forced me to go. If she hadn't, I could've had this family. I could've had so much more. But now here you are, with Montgomery money, acting as if you're better than me? You're nothing." The other man tossed something at my lamp, shattering it.

That's when I realized he had a knife in one hand.

I looked down at the coffee table, where our phones were. I wanted to reach out, to call for help. Roger followed my gaze.

"You move towards that phone, and I stab this man in front of me. This piece of trash. And then I'll come after you and that little boy. All I want is a few bucks to get me going. I have places to be. I've retribution coming to me. Places to be…"

"I can give you money, Roger. To get out of here, but if you stay here, the cops are going to come here. They're going to know you were here, and there's no going back from that. I'm sorry that my mother sent you to jail," Leif blatantly lied. "But we can't do anything for you here. I'm just a tattoo artist. I barely make rent."

Another lie.

"Brooke is a struggling single mom, we're trying, but we don't have the money that you want. None of my family does. We're blue-collar."

"You still think you're better than me."

"I'm sorry that you went to prison," I said, and Leif stiffened. He might not want me to speak, but I wasn't just going to stand by while we waited for Roger to do something. "I'm sorry," I repeated. "But coming here isn't going to help you. It can't. So why don't you leave, and we won't do anything."

"You're lying," he snarled, before he swayed.

Leif moved and I reached out, wanting to scream, but instead I held Luke back, shielding his eyes, trying to cover his ears.

Leif moved as if he had been born for this, as if he had fought strange, drunk men with knives all his life.

He took Roger's wrist, twisted as the man screamed.

When the knife dropped, I reached for the phone and quickly dialed 911.

Leif moved quickly, punching Roger in the face, and then knelt down over him, pinning his arms behind his back.

Roger was out, either drunk, or knocked out from the punch, and my knees shook as I listened to the 911 operator.

"Yes, ma'am, we received an alert from your security company, and people are on the way. Are you safe?"

I looked at Leif, at the way that he held Roger down, and at Luke as he held me tightly, but didn't cry, just trusted us to keep him safe.

"For now. Please hurry."

"Luke, you okay?" Leif asked, his eyes wide as he began to shake, even as he pinned Roger down.

I pushed Luke's hair back from his face and pressed my forehead to his.

"Are you okay, buddy?

"Of course, I am. I had you and Leif."

I nearly burst out crying, and only stopped because it would scare my son. I held myself back, clutching the phone, keeping Luke away from Roger. I wanted to hurt the man for daring to threaten my family, but I had to keep Luke safe.

Just like Leif had kept us safe.

"I love you," I gasped.

Leif gave me a small smile, even as guilt filled his gaze. "I love you, too."

"Don't blame yourself. This isn't your fault. It's his," I said, gesturing towards the unconscious man.

Leif's jaw tightened and he nodded as the sirens came. I let out a breath.

Things moved quickly then, the police entering my house, going through everything.

They checked over Luke, although he was perfectly fine according to the paramedics. I would take him to his pediatrician the next day, just in case. As well as find a child psychologist.

We stood in the front lawn, as the neighbors came outside to see what was going on, and Leif held me close, waiting.

"I love you," he whispered.

"I love you too. You better not blame yourself for this."

We were whispering now as Luke was passed out on my shoulder, sleeping hard after the adrenaline rush.

Leif moved, taking Luke in his arms, doing his best not to jostle him. I was grateful that I didn't have to carry my son for much longer since my arm was asleep, and I wrapped myself around them both, needing their touch.

"Roger's going away for a long time," I said, my voice low. "He came here because he had nowhere else to go, not because it's your fault. This is on him. Just like I don't get to blame myself for Landon's actions. You don't get to blame yourself for Roger's."

"I'm not quite sure I like you throwing my words back at me," he whispered before he kissed the top of my head. "I love you. I don't blame myself. But I am so fucking angry." He looked over my head and let out a soft laugh.

The fact that he was laughing at all told me that we were at least going in the right direction.

"The cavalry is here. Be prepared. The Montgomerys are on their way."

I turned and saw countless people that I knew, some that I didn't, but they all looked so much like Leif that I knew they had to be related.

The Montgomerys were coming in full force.

Family was coming in full force.

As the authorities let Leif's family come past the roped-off area, I let them hold me.

For once, I knew I would never be alone.

This wasn't just Luke and me facing the world.

I had a man that I loved. The family we were making. An extended family that was far larger than I had ever once thought possible.

I had fallen for a Montgomery. That meant I would face the future with them, too.

I made a promise to myself when I was younger, that I would try to fight the darkness and face the world even if I was on my own.

But now, I would get to break that promise because I would never be alone.

I would never have to be.

CHAPTER TWENTY

Leif

I HAD MADE a promise while on the Eiffel Tower, like any young man who fell in love and lust with a young woman that he couldn't have.

The fact that we had broken our promises left a bittersweet taste on my tongue, but in the end, we had grown into the people that we needed to be.

I was Leif Montgomery, son, brother, cousin, friend, and, one day husband and father.

All of those words wrapped up into an enigma of who I was, a complicated man who was trying to find his way. At least, that's what Brooke told me. And I always listen to what she said, with a yes ma'am, a gleam in my eye, and a kiss on her lips.

"Are you ready for this?" I asked as I looked over at Brooke, with Luke standing between us, holding each of our hands.

"It's not going to be that bad," she said and I laughed. Luke joined me, and then the door opened, the noise chaotic and brilliant.

It was my mother's birthday, and while it would've been fun to get all of the family together, not everybody could make it. They had decided to hold the festivities with just the family in this part of the branch rather than everyone in the area. It got a little insane if you went past those numbers and we wouldn't fit in the house.

"You're here!" Colin grinned, and my brother came forward and picked Luke up. He spun the kid around and then ran into the house with him, leaving us behind.

Brooke blinked. "Well, nice to see you, too, Colin."

"Look how I feel. I'm related to the kid," I said with a laugh, before I gripped my mother's present firmly in one hand, took Brooke's hand with my other, and made my way inside.

My aunts and uncles and most of their teenage and adult children were in the house, laughing, talking about cheese boards, presents, and an upcoming football game.

My dad stood near the front window, laughing at something my uncle Alex said. Sebastian stood between them, weariness in his gaze. I knew he told his parents and other members of the family about the pregnancy. I didn't know what would happen next or how he would handle it, but he would. Because my cousin was intelligent, responsible, and strong, and so was his girlfriend. They would figure it out.

And we would be there if they needed us.

"There you are," my dad said as he came forward, a smile on his face. "We were afraid you got lost."

"That was my fault," Brooke said as she hugged my dad back. "I had a last-minute meeting with one of my students. She has her huge presentation next week and had a slight panic attack."

Austin nodded, his eyes full of understanding. "I know how that feels. Not that I went to college or grad school, but presentations were never my thing."

"I find that hilarious considering all you do is talk and tell us what to do," Uncle Alex said with a wink.

Even as my dad scowled, I laughed, and Brooke wrapped her arm around my waist.

In the week since the attack and break-in, we had been dealing. Trying to figure out our path and how to heal. We stayed at my house more than hers because of the cleanup and memories. But we had yet to spend the night apart, and Luke was okay with it, and we were finding our routine.

Soon we would have to decide where to live, because I wasn't letting my new family out of my sight.

My lips twisted into a grin at the word family, and Brooke gave me a look.

"What?" she asked.

"Just thinking that I love you."

"Well, isn't that nauseating," Noah, another one of my cousins, said as he came up and hugged Brooke. "I can't believe he found you first. I'm sad."

Brooke snorted. "I'm nearly a decade older than you, darling. I don't think you could handle this."

Everybody whistled, and Noah just took it in stride. "Oh, I'm going to have fun finding a woman like you when my time comes. I'm going to take my time though. I'm not like Sebastian here, jumping the gun."

Sebastian flipped him off as everyone laughed. "I can't help it. I found the love of my life early."

I looked down at Brooke. "So did I. It just took me a little bit longer to find her again."

Brooke blushed and my dad cleared his throat. "Is that a present for your mom? We have the table over there. That way, you don't have to hold it this whole time."

"I want to hand this to her. Is that okay?" I asked.

"You don't have to ask me, son." My dad squeezed my shoulder and went back into conversation with the others. I took Brooke's hand and led her towards the back, where my mother held court with a few of my aunts. Aunt Maya grinned at me and waved at Brooke before I leaned down and kissed the top of my mom's head.

"Happy birthday, Mom."

"We're not going to mention what year it is. While I am grateful for growing into this age of not giving a fuck, I don't need the number."

I chuckled as Brooke and my mother fist-bumped.

"That sounds like a plan. Here you go. I wanted to give this to you rather than wait for you to open it later." I knew nerves were apparent in my voice. Brooke squeezed my hand.

My mom seemed to sense it because she quickly set down her drink and opened up the bag.

Maya leaned forward, wanting a look, and my mom waved her off, laughing.

"Oh, Leif," she whispered, opening the sketchbook.

"I have been working on it for the past couple of years, not quite sure what I would do with it when I was done. You can work out a few pages if you want to frame them, throw them away, or do whatever you want. But I don't know, it just felt right."

Tears were streaming down my mother's face as she turned the pages of the hand-drawn sketches I had made over the past year. Sketches of my parents, my brothers, sister, Brooke, and Luke. Nick laughing, Lake going over the books with that brilliant smile of hers. Sebastian and Marley dancing. It was the people in my life who had brought me here.

I was a tattooist, an artist, son, brother, cousin—all of those labels I had been given before, and they were all encompassed in that sketchbook.

My mom stood up and cupped my face. I leaned down so she could kiss my cheek. "You are a brilliant, wonderful, talented man. Thank you for letting me be your mother."

I swallowed the hard lump in my throat. "Thank you for being my mother. Thank you for taking me in."

Others around us were sniffling now as Mom held me close. "I love you, Montgomery. All of you."

"And that's it for me," Brooke said as she pulled a tissue out of her purse, handing one to Maya before wiping her face.

"You're stuck with us now, girl," Maya said with a laugh, and she held Brooke close.

As I looked over my mother's head at Brooke, at how my family had taken to her, as I heard Luke's laughter in the back, I knew that these were the promises I had made. The promises I would keep.

I was a Montgomery. And that pretty much said everything.

CHAPTER TWENTY-ONE

Lake

"What is the point of spending all this money on concealers when they don't work?" My voice shook as I stood in front of the mirror, my hands unsteady. I had fourteen tubes, pots, and other containers of concealers strewn about on my counter.

Zach would hate the mess. He would tell me to clean it up. And then he would force me to clean it over and over again until it was exactly how he wanted.

And I would do it. Because I wanted to make him happy.

I looked at the different shades of pink, cream, and beige on my counter and gripped the edge of the marble, trying to suck in a breath.

Everything hurt. How could this have happened?

This was on me.

I wasn't someone who got hurt like this. I was smarter than this. It was my fault, because I hadn't seen the signs even though I worked with people who did it daily.

It was my fault that I had allowed this to happen.

I was going to fix it because it wouldn't happen again.

I picked up the final tube of concealer in hopes that this one would work. That it would be the correct shade to cover up the bruising.

Tears bit at my eyes. My lip ached from the cut in its flesh.

I could see his hand marks on my neck. The width of his fingers with every achingly slow squeeze of his hand as he looked at me and told me I was nothing.

I could trace his thumb along my throat, his fingertip brushing my chin.

I could see the edge of the bruising already forming after such a short time on my neck, down to my shoulders. I could see where he had tried to choke me, to end me because I had said no.

My lip still had a cut that had finally stopped bleeding, and the bruise around my eye would eventually fade. The concealer did a better job of hiding that, but not as good a job as I needed it to.

I needed to hide it so the others couldn't see. So I could fix this on my own.

I was Lake Montgomery. I had been pulled out of my own hell once before and been blessed into this family. I couldn't shame them by telling them I had made a mistake. A mistake that would cost me everything.

I could not cry, I could not weep, I could not break. Because none of that would help. Nothing could help. But all the money spent on concealers in the world was not going to hide these bruises.

Nothing would hide these bruises.

With a cry, I shoved the concealers into the sink, the act of violence causing bile to rise in my throat. I needed to breathe, needing to do anything but stand here and feel sorry for myself.

Other people had it much worse than I did. They were living paycheck to paycheck, living out of their cars, needing help when I didn't. I helped others.

I didn't *need* help.

I pressed my hand to my side, the sharp pain making it harder to breathe.

I met my gaze in the mirror, the blue faded.

When had that happened? When had my eyes changed color?

I swallowed hard, my throat dry. It hurt to think, it hurt to breathe.

If I didn't need help, why was I putting concealer on my neck at seven p.m.?

If no one was going to see me, why was I trying to hide it?

I stood there, my thoughts going in a chaotic swirl as I tried to remember everything that happened and what I needed to do. I needed to leave, to stay away. I needed to hide. I needed to run. I need to do anything but stand here and wonder why I didn't have the perfect shade of pink concealer to cover up Zach's handprints on my neck.

"I need help," I whispered, the words broken, shattered remnants of the person I had been.

I was Lake Montgomery. A millionaire who was brilliant in tech and could form a business that helped others. Who *constantly* helped others.

I was not the woman in the mirror. The shadowed reflection of a wraith.

I closed my eyes, trying to find a semblance of composure. But there was nothing.

My phone was broken, my purse long gone. He had taken everything.

He had taken me.

I stumbled out of the bathroom, through my bedroom, and down the hallway. I moved past the broken lamp, the upturned chair. I kept walking over the glass shards, ignoring the searing pain in my feet. Then I opened the door and kept moving. I just kept moving.

Although Leif and Brooke would be moving soon, I knew they would be over there. Because Luke still lived there. *That little boy.*

I hoped it was late enough that he was sleeping because I didn't want him to see me. I didn't want anyone to see me.

I needed something. I just couldn't remember what it was. My head hurt, and I felt as if I saw double every other time I blinked. Things weren't making sense, and I had a hard time keeping my thoughts in order.

I moved across the grass achingly slow, ignoring the piercing shards of pain in my feet and down my sides.

I just needed Leif. My cousin would help.

He always helped. He wouldn't hate me. I didn't want him to hate me.

I moved up the porch, sucking in a breath as I tried to move one foot in front of another. I wanted to sleep. If I slept, things would be better. I would be able to breathe, and nothing would hurt anymore.

I needed my cousin. He would know what to do.

The door swung open before I could knock, and I saw the one person I didn't want to see. I would rather see anyone other than him.

No, that was a lie. I didn't want to see my parents, not now. They couldn't see this.

And I couldn't see Zach.

It became harder and harder to breathe. I knew I was hyperventilating. I had to be stronger than this.

I *was* stronger than this.

"Lake? What the hell, baby?" His voice was so soft. So unlike the Nick I knew. Maybe this wasn't him? Maybe it was Zach pretending to be him. Alarm shot through me. I needed to run.

And then Nick was there, coming closer. I cringed instinctively, my body stiffening.

I saw the storm echo over his face before he cooled his features, looking as if he hadn't wanted to break down the walls around us, to tear through anything between us.

This was Nick. My cousin's best friend, my family's friend.

My friend. A business partner.

My jokingly fake nemesis.

And I didn't want him to see me like this.

"Lake. Baby. What happened?"

"Nick?" I croaked, my voice hurt. Everything hurt.

Why was he here? I thought that Leif would be here, not Nick. Nick didn't live here. I knew that. Why was I telling myself these things that were true and yet not relevant? Why was everything taking so long to think through?

I wanted to hide. I wanted to go away. I wanted to pretend this never happened. But I had been doing that for far too long. I had nowhere else to go.

So I said the one thing I didn't want to, but the only thing that I knew would change everything. Because this was next, if my cousin wasn't here, then Nick would be there. Because he always was. *Always.*

"I need help."

My knees gave out and Nick caught me, saying words I didn't understand. I knew that everything would be okay because Nick was here.

Even if nothing was ever okay again.

***

NEXT IN THE MONTGOMERY INK LEGACY SERIES:
Lake and Nick take a chance in AT FIRST MEET.

IF YOU'D LIKE TO READ A BONUS SCENE FROM **LEIF & BROOKE:**
CHECK OUT THIS SPECIAL EPILOGUE!

ABOUT THE AUTHOR

Carrie Ann Ryan is the New York Times and USA Today bestselling author of contemporary, paranormal, and young adult romance. Her works include the Montgomery Ink, Redwood Pack, Fractured Connections, and Elements of Five series, which have sold over 3.0 million books worldwide. She started writing while in graduate school for her advanced degree in chemistry and hasn't stopped since. Carrie Ann has written over seventy-five novels and novellas with more in the works. When she's not losing herself in her emotional and action-packed worlds, she's reading as much as she can while wrangling her clowder of cats who have more followers than she does.

www.CarrieAnnRyan.com

LOVE IN THE CLUB

DL Gallie

LINC

It's the first Tuesday of the month and like I do on every first Tuesday of the month, I head to Cedar Valley to pick up Grandma and her best friend, Bonnie, and together, the three of us head off to the local library for book club. Yep, Lincoln Schofield is a reader, but not just any reader. I'm a spicy, smutty romance reader. All thanks to my grandma. Kelly Schofield may look sweet and innocent, but underneath her cardigans and silver hair is a dirty, dirty minx. I mean, would you expect anything else from an ex-Vegas showgirl dancer? For ninety-two, she's still a spring chicken, and I reckon between her life in Vegas and Hollywood, she could pen a bestseller with all the things she's seen … and done.

For as long as I can remember, Grandma and I have read together. She and I may have started off with Dr. Seuss and Roald Dahl, but as I got older, our material changed. In high school, it was Danielle Steele and Jackie Collins with Stephen King and Patricia Cornwell thrown in for variety. Now that I'm a sometimes-mature thirty-something adult, it's Rebecca Barber and her cowboys, E.L. James and her red room of pain, and Dean Koontz with his thrillers that blend elements of horror, fantasy, science fiction, mystery, and satire into one juicy novel. To this day, his novel *Intensity* is my all-time favorite book.

"How's my favorite grandson?" Grandma says when I walk into her room.

"As your only grandson, I'm great."

"Marshall did well on the weekend."

"He did yes."

"That girl did wonders for him." Grandma is referring to Marshall's wife, Eloise. She came into his life right when the stubborn asshole needed her, and well, she needed him too, but that's a whole other story. "When are you going to find a girl and settle down?"

"I just haven't met her yet, Grandma."

"Bonnie says Nikki is single again." Grandma is always trying to set me up but, no offense to her, the people she knows, their kids and kids' friends are—how do I put this nicely?—fucking crazy.

"Grandma, we all know Nikki is single again because she's a—"

"Druggie whore," Bonnie interrupts from the doorway. She shuffles into the room and stares daggers at Grandma. "Why would you even suggest that a lovely man like Linc here date my granddaughter?"

"Because maybe she just needs the right man to keep her clean."

"That may be true, but I can tell you, it's not Linc. Now, let's get to book club. I can't wait to discuss this week's book, *Obsessive Addiction* by K.L. Donn because Crux Malcom is—"

"Unhinged, but in a good way," Grandma interrupts Bonnie.

"I wouldn't mind him being obsessed with me," Bonnie adds, and I just laugh. I hope when I'm as old as these two that I still have the love for life they do.

"Ohhh, yes," Grandma agrees, fanning herself. "I loved it when, well, you'll just have to wait till we discuss it to find out, but I heard from the social face-thingie it's K.L.'s personal fave."

"I can see why," Bonnie coos, then she looks to me. "You're awfully quiet, Mr. Schofield."

"Like you, I'm waiting for book club, but I can say, I loved Farren. Even though she's broken, she has a strength about her, which is why Crux was so gaga for her."

"You're going to make some gal lucky one day," Grandma says with a smile, then morosely adds, "I just hope I'm around to see it."

"You will be, Grandma." *I hope.* "We never know when she's going to appear. Now, let's go get our book on."

TAYLOR

Sitting in my car, I stare up at the building before me, willing myself to walk into the library for my first book club in LA. When I moved here, I made a promise to myself that I'd do more than just sit at home and read after work. I vowed I'd get out and start to live life, so when I saw the poster for book club, I thought "why not?" It's technically still reading, BUT it's getting OUT to read. The reading point is moot because I'll be meeting new people and mingling, while reading.

Knowing I need a pep talk, I call my best friend and sister from another mister, Asher King—no relation, even though we share the same last name.

"Hey, stranger," she says in greeting.

"Hey-hey, how's things?" I ask in reply.

"Don't ask," she huffs, and I shake my head.

"What did Bonnie and Clyde do this time?"

"Nothing."

"Nothing?" I question.

"Yep, nothing, meaning they haven't done anything and that in itself is scary. I thought they would have been on the first plane here so they could be at the front of the line to pull the plug." Asher's grandfather is a real estate and sports mogul. He owns the Colorado Dragons, most of the high-rise buildings in downtown Denver and a cattle station in Australia because Australian beef is far superior to American beef. Papa King is currently in hospice. His cancer finally caught up with him and he only has a few days left. Asher is going to be devastated when he passes. Her parents are less than stellar people. Luckily for her, she had Papa King. Even while running his empire, he also raised my best friend, with a little help from my parents.

"Maybe your mom is upset her dad is dying."

"Please, that woman doesn't have a heart inside her chest."

I snort but she's right, her parents are deplorable people but, luckily for her, we moved to town, and Mrs. Dawn seated us next to each other in second grade. We became besties right away, and I got the sister I always wanted.

Asher and I became inseparable from that first moment. Me relocating to LA is the first time we've ever been apart. And I mean ever. After school, we got an apartment together that was close to the arena for her and college for me. She's the equipment manager for the Colorado Dragons, and she's bloody good at her job. She knows what the players need, sometimes even before they do. She knows what each of them likes, and no one can sharpen a blade like Asher, no one. You wouldn't think her job is all that important, but she's just as important as anyone else on the team.

When I told her about my new job with Blackstone Publishing and having to move, she didn't talk to me for three days, and that was hard, since we lived together. But like always when we have a tiff, she came around and told me, in no uncertain terms, if I turned into a stuck-up Californian, she'd whack me around the head with a hockey stick.

"I still maintain you were adopted."

"I sometimes wonder that myself, but then I look at Papa and know I'm not."

"This is true. How's he doing?"

"Holding on."

Papa King is a stubborn man, but he has a heart of gold. He won't want to leave Asher alone, and I have a feeling me being here is playing into that. I feel guilty that I'm not there but I also know, if I went back, he'd be angry since I just started. He loves me, just as much as he loves Asher.

"And back to my original question, how are YOU doing?" I emphasize the "you" part because Asher always focuses on everyone else. Apart from me and Papa King, she has no one. And right now, being so far away sucks donkey dick.

"I'm getting there. Storm..." She drifts off.

"Is there a storm coming in?"

"Ummm..."

"Asher," I probe, "what aren't you telling me?"

"I, umm, well, shit, fuck."

Suddenly my brain kicks into gear and I sit up in my seat. "No freakin' way, you and Storm Cromwell?"

"Keep your voice down," she hisses.

"I'm in my car, alone, and even if I wasn't, who cares? Now, spill the deets."

"There's nothing to tell."

"Bullshit! Don't lie to me. Did you go all cougar on that sexy-as-sin center?"

"Yes," she barely whispers.

"Asher King, I'm sooo proud of you for putting yourself out there. Can he wield his stick just as good off the ice?"

"Oh My God, I'm not answering that."

"I'll take that as a yes."

"Speaking of putting out." She's totally ignoring me right now, and that means it's something. If anyone deserves to be happy, it's her. So I'll wait until she's ready to spill the beans on her and Storm. "Are you getting out there?"

"For your information, I'm in my car, about to go into book club."

"I'm so proud of you... even if it's book related."

"I'm getting out to read, it's totally different."

"Mmmhmpf, but for the record, I'm proud you're putting yourself out there. There's more to life than work."

She has a point there. I focused so hard on my studies and trying to get a job that I lost my spark, but when the Blackstone offer came, I leaped without thinking. Something I never do, just like her and Storm. Never did I think she'd go for a player.

A lull falls between us, and I wrap the call up before reminding her, "If it's not on, it's not on," because I'm too young to be an aunty ... even if she and Storm would make the cutest babies.

Climbing out of my car, I walk up the stairs and into the library, ready to put myself out there.

Pushing open the door, I step inside the old building, and a calm instantly washes over me. I don't know what it is about books, but they just make me happy. Glancing around the place, I find myself grinning. Inside these walls there are many stories of love and happiness and gore.

"Come on," a sultry voice purrs. "You know you want to."

Turning my head to where the voice came from, I see a woman and a man chatting. A ridiculously attractive man. She's flirting, hard, and he looks like he'd rather be anywhere else. He looks up and our gaze catches across the room. Everything around me fades into the background. It's just him and me. He's pleading with his eyes for help, and before I know what's happening, I'm putting one foot in front of the other and heading over to them. Reaching them, I slide my arm around his waist, look up into his gorgeous hazel eyes, and murmur, "Hey, baby."

EVERY WEEK it's the same thing, and every week, I turn Eve down. She just doesn't get the hint. I'm. Not. Interested. Sure, Eve is nice … ish, but there's something about her that irritates me … like her not taking no for an answer

The hairs on my neck prickle, and when I look up, I see the most beautiful woman in the world. She's wearing dark-washed jeans and a pale purple tank. Her honey-blond locks are up in a high pony, but it's her eyes that capture me. They're the most vivid shade of blue. I've never seen anything like them before.

Eve starts talking again, and I reluctantly turn my attention back to her. I'm thinking about how to let her down, again, when a hand slides around my waist. When I look down, I see the angel from moments ago beside me.

"Hey, baby," she utters, and it takes me a few seconds to realize what's happening.

"Hey," I gruffly reply, sliding my arm around her waist and placing a kiss on her temple. "You made it."

"I did. Sorry I'm late, I'm still not used to this LA traffic." She turns to Eve. "Hi, I'm Taylor." She offers Eve her hand, but Eve just looks at it. Shock and anger mar her face as she flicks her gaze from Taylor to me.

"I didn't realize you were dating someone," Eve snaps.

"It's new," Taylor and I both say at the same time. She giggles and, normally, a woman giggling like that irks me, but this time it's cute and leaves me feeling all warm and fuzzy.

"Jinx," she says, digging me in the ribs.

Offering her a shrug, I gaze into her eyes. It feels like I can see into her soul. Apart from a handful of words, I know nothing about this woman but at the same time, I feel like I've known her forever.

"And where did you two meet?" Eve hisses. There's a sour look on her face, and panic starts to build within because this is all fake and, right now, my mind is empty.

"It was your cliché meet-cute in the grocery store," Taylor begins. "We were both reaching for the last bag of—"

"Coffee beans," I interrupt.

"I insisted he have it, but..." She hesitates because she doesn't know my name, but fate steps in in the form of my grandma, and she calls my name out. I wave, and Taylor continues with our faux meeting. "...Linc insisted I could have it, so I invited him over for coffee and, well, here we are."

"Really? Sounds like something from a romance novel," Eve spits at us. I can tell she doesn't believe Taylor and I are a couple but, to be honest, I don't care what she thinks.

"What's something from a romance novel?" Grandma asks as she joins us.

"Taylor and your grandson apparently met over the last bag of coffee beans."

"So she is real," Grandma teases, playing along with our ruse. "When you told me you'd met someone, I thought you were just trying to avoid the date I was trying to set up for you."

"I'd never lie when it comes to dating," I state. As soon as the words pass through my lips, I hate it because I am, in fact, lying.

Without another word, Eve turns and storms off, leaving Grandma, Taylor, and me alone. That is until Grandma speaks, "So, you two are dating, huh?"

Taylor's eyes widen at Grandma's statement, and she pulls away. Immediately, I miss the feeling of her next to me. "I ... I'm sorry I did that, I hope you don't mind."

"Not at all, but I feel like I nee—" Before I can ask her out to say thanks for saving me from Eve, Glenda calls out for everyone to take their seats. Taylor smiles at me and walks off to grab her seat. I go to follow but Grandma pulls on my arm. When I look back to her, she's grinning like a carnival clown.

Tapping me on the cheek, she murmurs quietly, "She's the one." Then she turns and walks over to the group ... taking a seat next to Taylor.

Standing here, I watch her and Grandma together and start to wonder if she's right. Is Taylor "the one"?

TAYLOR

My mind was a mess all through book club, I can only imagine what these people must think of me. All I kept thinking about was the feeling of being in Linc's arms, and his scent—smoky and sweet. It was very manly and rugged. I know nothing about him, but the way he is with his grandma and her friend, Bonnie, makes me think he's one of the good ones. The last few guys I dated were duds, hence, why I'm still single and cautious when it comes to the opposite sex.

I still don't know what compelled me to waltz over to a stranger, a sexy as hell stranger, and do what I did. But with his dark hair, hazel eyes, and lips that looked ohh so kissable, I was drawn to him like a good girl to a bad boy ... not that I'm getting bad boy vibes from this man. When I told Asher I was going to do things that push my boundaries, I didn't think I'd be doing anything like this. But I have to say, pretty sure I smashed said boundaries. She will never believe I did this, and I can imagine her now. She's going to say, "Photos or it didn't happen." She'll want proof, but how do I prove I fake dated a guy for all of fifteen seconds?

Book club has finished—and I think I had a great time—but Bonnie, Kelly, and a few other ladies are still discussing the FMC from this week's book, and the way they are reacting to the possessive hero has me wanting to read it too. Quickly logging into my book account, I download it so I can see what they are excitedly chatting about.

Pocketing my phone, I look up and see Eve still scowling at me. She looks like she sucked a super sour lemon. Clearly, she's pissed Linc is with me. Going by the way she and her friend are animatedly talking, I'm guessing I'm the topic of conversation. Mean girls piss me off, but then again, so do people who can't take the hint. Doesn't matter if you're male, female, or a penguin, no means no.

Linc garners my attention so I walk over to him. "It seems I've made an enemy of Eve."

"I'm sorry about that."

Shaking my head, I rest my hand on his arm and a spark jolts from him to me. My breath hitches in the back of my throat. That's never happened before. "Don't be sorry. I'm the one who initiated the pretend dating charade."

"And I thank you from the bottom of my heart for that. I've been thwarting her advances for weeks now, but no matter how many times I say no, she just doesn't get the hint." He opens his mouth to say more but stops himself. A silence develops between us, but it's interrupted when the she-devil herself walks over to join us.

"So, what are you two love birds up to after this?"

"I'm heading home for an early night," Linc tells her. Then adds, "I'm going out of town tomorrow."

Internally I deflate that he's going away, but then I internally slap myself because what he does is none of my business. "I'm heading home too, I—"

But Eve interrupts me. "Linc, I can give you a lift to the airport, if you like?"

"Thanks, but I've got it sorted." He turns his attention to me, alluding that it's me sorting him. I know this is petty, but the incredulous look on Eve's face at his dismissal is priceless. She's genuinely shocked he turned her offer down. "Can I walk you out?" he asks me.

Nodding, I smile. "I'd love that." Linking my arm through his, we bid a scowling Eve farewell and head toward the exit.

Pushing the door open, we step outside, and I look to the sky. The sun is just about to set and the sky is a kaleidoscope of color. "So pretty," I mutter.

"I agree," Linc says, and when I look over at him, he's staring at me.

"Call me," he says, breaking the silence.

"Maybe."

"Well, how about I call you?"

Like before, I reply with a smile and a timid, "I'd love that."

Handing me his phone, I enter my number and hand it back to him. "Have a good trip," I tell him, and then I start walking backward.

"I'll call you soon," he sings out, and I smile at the gorgeous man as I back away. Throwing him a wink, I spin around and head toward my car when my pocket begins to vibrate. Pulling it out, I stare at the screen. I don't recognize the number, but something is telling me to answer. Hitting the green button, I bring the device to my ear. "Hello."

"Hey, it's Linc."

Spinning back around, I stop and stare at my caller and can't help but smile. "Ohh, hey, long time no speak."

He laughs, and it's a deep chuckle that vibrates through me. "So this is me calling you."

"I see, and why are you calling me?"

"Well, since we're fake dating, I was wondering if I could take you out on a date?"

"Would this date be of the fake kind?"

"It can be whatever kind you like."

"And what if I want it to be real?" Waiting for him to answer is killing me, even though it's literally only a few seconds.

"Then I guess it'll be a real date." Nodding at his words, I stare over at Linc, the phone still to my ear when he says, "I'll pick you up Friday at seven."

"You don't know where I live?"

"Text your address to me and then I'll know where you live."

"What if you're a serial killer?"

"I'm not," he tries to assure me.

"That's exactly what a serial killer would say."

"Just text me your address."

"So bossy," I tease.

"You ain't seen nothing yet, baby."

"Mmmhmpf," I reply but he's right, I can't wait to see what happens. Or just how bossy he is. This man oozes sex appeal. It's no wonder skanky Eve was hitting on him.

"So, you gonna text me your address?"

"Maybe," I throw back at him but before he can utter another word, I quickly add, "I'll see you Friday at seven. Don't be late."

"Wouldn't dream of it."

We disconnect our call, just as Kelly and Bonnie join him. The two of them are talking loudly about penis piercings. He takes their potty mouths in stride, and I have to say, he gives as good as he gets. It must run in the family genes. For elderly ladies, those two sure are vivacious, and I hope—when I get to their age—I'm just as spritely and sexually adventurous.

Standing here, I watch Linc with his grandma and her friend. It's adorable seeing him with them, especially when Bonnie asks him if he has a penis piercing. I can't help but chuckle, but from where I'm standing, I can't hear his response. Whatever he said, it has Bonnie doubling over in laughter.

My cheeks are hurting from grinning at the scene before me.

Just before Linc climbs into his SUV, he looks over his shoulder and winks at me. I feel that little eye twitch deep in my soul and, for the first time ever, I have a feeling that I've met "the one." I haven't felt a connection like this ever before. Linc and I may have only spoken for a few brief minutes when I rescued him from the clutches of Eve and on the phone just now, but I feel something—and it's not the heebie-jeebie creepy feeling I usually get. This is like something from the books I read and, dare I say it, I have Eve to thank. Had she not cornered Linc and made him feel uncomfortable, I'm not sure I would have had the courage to speak to him. But when I saw the look of fear in his eyes, I knew I had to act. I'm glad I did because now I have a date on Friday.

Seems this move to LA has been good for me professionally and personally. The world is my oyster, and I cannot wait to see what happens next.

TAYLOR

Friday finally rolls around and to say I'm nervous is the understatement of the century. I don't think I've ever been this anxious before a date. I spilled coffee all over myself in the monthly staff meeting, and it was even more embarrassing because the owner, Bastian Blackstone, was in attendance. Thankfully, he didn't seem to mind, but it doesn't show a good impression of me, the head of the LA office. I'm already nervous enough as it is. I applied for this job as a joke. Never in my wildest dreams did I think I'd be the head of the LA office. Apparently, Kerrie and Bastian saw something in me, but earlier today, I bet he was regretting his decision.

When I arrive home from the office, I run a bath and jump back into this week's book club book, *Pen Pal* by J.T. Geissinger. I got so sucked into the story. FYI, I did not see that twist coming, it was chef's kiss amazing. Due to me finishing the book, I was running late but, somehow, I managed to be ready on time.

Linc and I have been messaging all week and from the text banter, I think I can see something developing between us. He's funny, crass at times, but he's also caring and friendly. But I already knew that after seeing him with his grandma at book club. As it turns out, we both live in Malibu, not too far from one another.

There's a knock at my door, and those nerves I had managed to calm down take flight once again. Walking over to the door, I open it, and when I see what Linc is wearing, I burst out laughing. We're both in jeans, black tops, mine a spaghetti strap blouse and his, a tee that hugs his muscular arms and showcases his pecs. On his feet are Chucks, black, just like mine. "Do you have cameras in here or is this," I flick my finger between us, "just a stroke of luck?"

"Considering jeans and a tee are my staple, I have to ask if *you're* spying on me?"

"You wish I was spying," I cheekily throw back at him. "But when I'm not in the office, I'm a jeans and a tee kind of gal."

"Seems like we have something in common then."

"Seems so. Let me grab my jacket, and we can go."

"It's seventy-five degrees outside. It's not going to get any colder, you won't need a jacket."

Nodding, I toss my jacket aside, grab my purse, and walk back to the door. As I lock it, I say, "I'm not used to weather like this. In Denver, you always take a jacket with you."

"Why did you move to LA?"

"Work," I tell him, as we head to his car. "I applied on a whim and somehow managed to get the position." We stop when we reach a flashy-looking sports car. "Fancy," I coo, taking in the machine in front of me.

"Thanks, it's a McLaren GT."

"That means nothing to me. Is it a Toyota?"

He fakes being hurt, clutching at his chest. "You wound me, Tay."

"Sorry, cars are not really my thing, but I'm guessing they're yours since the other night at book club you were in an SUV."

He laughs, a deep belly chuckle. "You could say that. I, umm, own a racing team."

"You own a racing team?"

"Yep. Have you heard of Schofield Racing?" I nod. "Well, I'm Lincoln Schofield."

Processing his words, it finally hits me. He's *the* Schofield in Schofield Racing. "Holy shit," I hiss, "that's amazing." Then my eyes widen. "Didn't one of your drivers recently have a really bad accident?"

"Yeah, that was Marshall Kerr. He fractured his hip. It was a tough, slow-going recovery because his head was up his ass, but he finally pulled it out, and once again, I saw the gung-ho driver I hired. It's great having him back in the driver's seat."

"That's good, I can't wait to watch him race."

"Thought you weren't into cars?" he asks, opening my door for me.

"I'm not, but I couldn't imagine not being able to do what I love and to see someone overcome so much, it will be thrilling to see."

"I wouldn't be surprised if fuel ran through his veins in lieu of blood."

"Why do I feel the same is true for you too?"

He shrugs in reply, and I climb into my seat. Like a gentleman, he closes my door, and I watch him walk around the hood. Those nerves from earlier are gone and excitement has taken up residence within my body. I can't wait for my date and to see where the night leads.

LINC

When she said she wasn't into cars after asking if my baby was a Toyota, I thought our night was over before it began. But I was wrong. W-R-O-N-G, wrong.

Taylor and I dined at a favorite beachside restaurant of mine in Zuma Beach, and the evening has been amazing. It's what all first dates should be like. Conversation flowed. There were no awkward silences and lots of laughing. Boy, did we laugh.

Taylor King has a warped sense of humor and a wicked tongue. She and Grandma are going to get along like a house on fire. That thought doesn't scare me, but then again, I shouldn't be surprised after the conversation I had with Grandma the other day. We were having a cup of tea—well, I was having tea, Grandma was having tea-quila, as she likes to call it—and she put the spotlight on me, and my love life...

..."I'm not getting any younger, Linc."

"And neither am I," I throw back at her.

"Don't sass me, boy. What I mean is, I'm not getting any younger and all I want to see is you settled down. I've seen you thrive in the racing world, and I couldn't be prouder of you, but now, I want to see you happy and in love."

"When the right woman comes along—"

"Are you shitting me?" Grandma interrupts, her eyebrows raised.

"Language, Grandma," I scold her.

She waves me off, sips her tea-quila and continues. "Ohh, Linc, you fool, you've already met her."

"Grandma, Eve is not the one for me."

"I'm not talking about that skanky ho, I'm talking about your fake girlfriend."

"I don't have a fake girlfriend," I refute.

"So you really are dating that lovely girl then?"

"Well, I don't know, but Tay and I are going out Friday night when I get back from Chicago."

"You have a nickname for her already, that's cute." She pauses and thinks hard. "Would your couple name be Lincor? Or would be Taycoln?"

"How about just Linc and Taylor?"

"Pffft, that's boring. When Jason Statham leaves what's her face for me, he and I will become Kelson because Jasly just sounds stupid."

"This whole nickname conversation is stupid."

"Hush your mouth," she admonishes. "Finding love is not stupid." She places her teacup down, reaches over, and takes my hand in hers. "Lincoln, my dear boy, you have a heart of gold and I want to see you happy."

"I am happy, Grandma."

"I know you are, but I want to see you in-love happy. There is no greater feeling than being in love." Grandma gets a wistful look on her face, and I know she's remembering her one true love, my grandfather, Michael Schofield. He was the love of her life, even though their love affair was brief—he was killed in a robbery when Grandma was eight months pregnant with Mom. Pop-Pop died saving Grandma when a shootout between the robbers and the police started. A stray bullet hit him in the back, and he died. After losing Pop-Pop, she gave up on love. She once told me, "Your pop-pop loved me more than life itself. I always felt cherished, and I'd never been happier than when I was with him. He died protecting me and your mom, there is no greater sacrifice than that. No one will ever live up to that, so why tarnish it? Besides, they will only di,e and I can't go through that again. Micheal Schofield is my one and only love. The other men are just footnotes and someone to scratch that itch."

That's not a thought I want but creepy images aside, I know she's right. "But, Grandma, how do you know you've met 'the one'?"

"You just know, my boy, you just know."

As I sit across from Taylor, I realize, Grandma is right—shhh, don't tell her I said that. When you know you know, and I have a feeling about Taylor. When the waitress clears away our plates, I decide I don't want the evening to end, so I brazenly ask her a kind of forward question.

"Would you like to spend the night with me?"

His question shocks me, but at the same time, it doesn't, because secretly, I was hoping it would end this way. Reaching across the table, I place my hands down, palms up. He places his on top of mine, and I stare into his hazel eyes, which in this light are more green than brown. They're sparkling and full of hunger.

Inhaling deeply, I breathlessly pant, "Take me home, Linc."

"Are you sure?"

The fact he's asking is so sweet and confirms he's one of the good guys. My head begins to move up and down like a bobblehead. "I'm sure."

"Your place or mine?"

"I don't care," I honestly tell him. "As long as you and I are together and naked, I'll be happy."

"This is not how I was picturing tonight ending but I do have to say, I like your ending better."

"Less talking and more leaving."

"So bossy," he teases.

"You ain't seen nothing yet, Mr. Schofield, now, let's get going."

Without another word, he throws a wad of cash down on the table and stands up. He offers me his hand, and when I place mine in his, he links our fingers, and we exit the restaurant.

Hand in hand, we walk around the side of the restaurant and back to the car. The need to kiss him washes over me, so I do just that. I tug on his hand, halting him. He turns to face me, I drop his hand, grip his cheeks in my palms, and kiss him. My tongue licks along the seam of his lips before I push into his mouth. His tongue duels with mine, and when he covers my hands with his, it's game on.

On the sidewalk in Zuma Beach, with the waves crashing into the shore behind us, Linc and I kiss each other as if our lives depend on it. His lips press against mine, and just like I thought when I first saw him in the library, they *are* soft and ohh so kissable. Breaking the connection, I rest my forehead against his, panting. I stare into his eyes and lose myself. I've never felt a connection like this with anyone before, and I want to explore things further. I want this, and him, like I need my next breath.

Without another word, he takes my hand in his, and we continue over to his car. Stopping near it, he spins me around, slides his hand around my waist, and begins to kiss me again. Backing me up against the restaurant building, he attacks my mouth. Lifting my leg, I hook it around his thigh, and I unabashedly begin to grind myself on him. My hearts starts thumping. The Earth begins to shake, well, I begin to shake. "Please," I beg against his lips.

Breaking our kiss, he reaches up and cups my cheek. "I want to, but I'm not about to fuck you in some dark and dingy corner of a parking lot. I'm going to take you back to my place, and as soon as the door clicks closed behind us, you're mine."

"Bring it," I challenge, and from the look in his eye, I'm in for a banging good night.

LINC

HAVE you ever tried to drive with a hard-on? I have and, let me tell you, it's not fun ... at all. But the pain will totally be worth it once I get Tay inside, naked and writhing beneath me.

Parking my McLaren in the garage, I turn the engine off and climb out. Meeting Tay on her side of the car, I slide my hand around her waist and tug her closer. Pressing my lips to hers, I kiss her deeply, earning myself a moan that heads straight to my already straining dick. Quickly, I break the kiss because I don't want to injure my dick before I get to have any fun. "I'm tempted to take you here and now on the hood of my car."

"I'm game, but I have a feeling, even though it would be amazing to take me here, the thought of possibly denting your precious baby is probably just as painful as that." She points at my crotch.

A chuckle escapes me because she's right. As much as that would be fun, I don't want to damage my baby. I'd dreamed of owning a car like this since I watched my first race when I was a kid. Ever since that moment, I was obsessed with racing and hot cars. "How do you know me so well already?"

She shrugs and lifts her eyebrows in a "beats me" kind of way.

She leans into me, her hot breath tickles the skin of my neck. I need to get her inside before I give in to temptation. As if she's in my mind, she huskily murmurs, "How about we head inside so I can fix this?" She reaches out and rubs my dick through my jeans. The feeling of her hand on me causes me to groan, and when she squeezes my shaft, it almost has me coming in my boxers like thir-teen-year-old Linc.

Grabbing her hand, I remove it from my cock and bring it to my lips. Placing a kiss on her knuckles, I stare intently at her, and before she knows what's happening, I throw her over my shoulder, slap her on the ass, and head inside. Stalking across the open-plan living, dining, and kitchen area, I aim for my bedroom.

"What, no tour?"

"My tongue is about to tour your body, I'll give you a tour of the house tomorrow."

"I like the sound of that, as long as I can tour your body with my tongue too?"

"Deal."

Placing her down on her feet, I take a step back and rake my eyes over her. From top to bottom, I peruse the stunning creature before me. "You are fucking gorgeous," I honestly tell her.

"You're not too bad yourself, stud muffin, but we seem to have a problem."

"We do, do we?" She nods and bites her bottom lip. "And what may the problem be?"

Lifting her hand, she traces her fingertip along the neckline of her tee. "Well, we both have too many clothes on."

"That's easy to fix," I tell her.

Stepping toward her, I grab the hem of her tee and lift it up and over her head, dropping it to the carpet beside us. Tay stands there in nothing but her jeans and bra. "I've never seen a more beautiful sight," I whisper.

Leaning down, I suck on her nipple through the lace of her bra. Her head drops back, and she moans in a sexy and seductive way. Reaching behind her back, I unclasp her bra. She wiggles out of it and when I pull back, I swallow deeply. "Okay, I was mistaken, *now* I've never seen a more beautiful sight."

"Well, I like what I see before me too, but you're still overdressed."

"And you still have pants on," I toss back at her.

Quicker than The Flash, she kicks off her shoes and removes her jeans. She stands before me naked, except for a pair of barely-there lace panties. "I'm going to tear them off your body with my teeth," I matter-of-factly inform her.

"I'll allow it, once you lose your clothes."

"As you wish," I tell her.

Gripping the hem of my shirt, I lift it up and over my head, dropping it to the carpet next to her discarded clothes. Stepping into my personal space, she rests one hand on my hip, and the other traces over my abs and pecs. She circles my nipple with the tip of her finger, and like I did to her, she leans forward and sucks.

"Fuuuuuck," I hiss. No one has done that to me before, and I have to say, I'm not opposed to it.

She kisses and nibbles her way down my chest and abs, dropping to her knees. She stares up at me, and with her eyes locked on mine, she makes quick work of flipping open the button on my jeans and lowering my fly. The pressure relief on my dick is instant. She hooks her fingers into the waistband of my jeans and my boxers and, in one fell swoop, pushes them down my thighs to my ankles. My dick springs free, and it almost slaps her in the face.

"Holy shit, that's the biggest dick I've ever seen."

"Why thank you," I say, nodding my head in thanks. "And may I say, you have the prettiest tits I've ever seen, and I cannot wait to get acquainted with them."

"Well, how about we talk less with our mouths and let our mouths get acquainted with one another?"

WHO IS THIS VIXEN? I've never been so brazen with a partner before, but Linc brings out a side of me I never knew existed.

"I like the way you think, Ms. King." He offers me his hand, placing mine in his, he pulls me up and immediately presses his lips to mine. With our lips fused, he shuffles us backward and awkwardly kicks off his shoes and pants as we go. He drops down to the end of the bed and rakes his gaze all over my body. My body thrums with desire, want, and need. He furrows his brows and growls, "Why do you still have panties on?"

"You said you were going to tear them off with your teeth."

"That I did." And without another word, he slips off the end of the bed, grips the back of my thighs, and pulls me to him. He presses his face into my crotch and inhales.

"Why is that so hot?" I pant like a wanton hussy.

"Because it's me doing it. Now shush, I have a job to do."

He sticks his tongue out and licks me from taint to clit and gently bites my clit through the material of my panties. Like he said, he takes the waistband between his teeth and tugs but when he lets go, they flip back up. He grunts in frustration but not one to give up, he goes back to the task at hand. Finally, he gets into a rhythm and eventually my panties are off.

Standing before him naked, I reach out and run my hands through his hair. Tugging on the strands, I guide his head forward and without any prompting, he licks and nibbles me in the most exquisite way.

Lifting my hands, I tug on my nipples. Pleasure begins to simmer low in my belly. My head drops back, I close my eyes, and I focus on his tongue sliding between my folds. When he pushes his fingers into me, my inner porn star comes out, and I moan, but unlike in a porno, there's nothing fake about the sounds coming out of me.

My eyes fly open, and my head snaps upright when I feel a pressure on my ass. Dropping my gaze, even though his face is pressed between my thighs, I can feel him smirking at me. Not-ready-to-combust me would say something about where his finger is, but ready-to-combust me goes back to playing with her boobs. Never have I felt this alive from oral before. I'm about to crash over the edge, and I'm here for it.

"Yes," I pant. Who knew a finger in the ass could be so ... so, amazing. Now, it has me wondering what a dick in there would feel like.

Linc is lapping at me like a starved man. The things this man can do with his tongue should be illegal, and I cannot wait to see what he does with his dick.

Out of nowhere, my orgasm crashes into me, and I cry out. Wave after wave after wave of pleasure ripples through my body. If he didn't have hold of me, I'd be a crumpled mess on the carpet next to our clothes.

My body relaxes, and with a gentle push, I fall back to the mattress. Lying here, I stare up at the ceiling, panting as I come back to Earth.

Linc rises to his feet, his chin glistens with my arousal. I'm embarrassed with how wet his face is, but that embarrassment flies away when I see him grab his dick and begin to stroke himself.

Even though I just came, that sight has me ready to go again.

With our gazes locked, I slip my finger between my folds and slide it in and out. My finger isn't enough. I need him so I remove my hand from between my legs and beckon him to me with my index finger. He climbs onto the bed and like a predator, stalks up my body. Cocooning me under him, he leans down and kisses me. I can taste myself on his lips, and never has anything tasted so sweet. Sliding my hands over his shoulders, I pull him closer to me, deepening the kiss and connection between us. His cock presses into my thigh, but I don't want it in my thigh. I need him inside of me, and I need that now. "Please fuck me," I mumble against his lips.

"I'd love nothing more," he replies, and I find myself smiling that we're on the same page.

He lifts himself up and I mourn the loss, but when I see him reach for his side table, I realize what he's doing. I'm glad someone is thinking clearly.

Intently I watch as he tears open the foil packet and sheaths his cock. With his eyes back on me, he lines himself up with my entrance and with a flick of his hips, he presses inside. The feeling of him entering me is mind-blowing, but when he starts to thrust in and out, I have no words.

"Kiss me," I command.

With a nod of his head, he leans down and does just as I ask. His tongue plunges into my mouth in sync with what's happening below. Once again, that feeling begins to develop deep within, and before I know it, I'm crying out his name as my second orgasm for the evening detonates.

My release sets him off and moments after I crash over the edge, I feel his body stiffen as he empties himself into the condom.

He pulls out, removes the condom, and throws it to the side before he collapses onto the mattress next to me. This is not how I pictured our night going, but I'm not going to complain one bit.

This man is perfect in every way and I cannot wait to see what happens next.

"Wow," I mutter when I finally catch my breath.

"I ... that ... wow, indeed," Tay replies, her voice husky from screaming my name as she came.

We turn our heads to face one another, silently staring at each other. She rolls to her side and rests her head on her palm. Reaching out, I brush a tendril of hair off her face, tucking it behind her ear. I trace my fingertip along her jawline before gently running the pad of my finger over her kiss-swollen lips. She nips at my finger playfully.

"Where have you been all my life?" The question slips out before my mouth-to-brain filter kicks in.

"Denver," she nonchalantly replies. "I could ask you the same question?"

"California ... and the occasional summer in Vegas with my grandma."

"I love the relationship you have with your grandma, it's very ..."

"Manly," I offer.

"I was going to say—" I open my mouth to interrupt, but she presses her finger to my lips shushing me. "Cute."

"Cute," I mumble against her finger, "I'll show you cute."

Grabbing her wrist, I pull her toward me and slam my lips to hers. She climbs on top, her hair falls down around us like a golden curtain. Brushing her hair back, I grip her cheeks and pull her in for another kiss. It starts out soft and slow, but it quickly turns heated.

Flipping her onto her back, I stare down at the angel beneath me. "You really think I'm cute?" She nods. "Cute, really?"

"You're cute in a manly, rugged way."

"That's better, but I think we can come up with a better adjective than that."

"Like?"

"Well, for starters, dazzling or handsome or my favorite pulchritudinous."

"Pulcha-what-nous?"

"Pulchritudinous. It means having great physical beauty, and going by the 'ohh Gods' and 'Liiiiinc's' you shouted earlier, I exceed expectations in the physical department."

"You can also add modest to your list of traits," she teases with a giggle. "But for the record, yes, you are pulchritudinous. Now, show me the physical side of that again, and then I want to snuggle with you all night long."

"You have yourself a deal, foxy lady."

She scoffs, "I think you mean pulchritudinous lady."

We both burst out laughing, and then I show her just how physical I am, and in the early hours of the morning, like she requested, we drift off to sleep, wrapped in each other's embrace.

Morning comes and when I wake, I feel happy and content. Something I haven't felt in a very long time. Reaching out, I pat the mattress next to me and furrow my brows when all I feel is a cold sheet. I was hoping to feel a naked and pulchritudinous woman.

Sitting up, I look around and my heart sinks when I see her clothes from last night are gone. "Well, this sucks," I mutter to myself.

Throwing the sheet off, I climb out of bed and head into my en suite to take a piss. I really thought we had something, but I guess I was wrong.

Washing my hands, I grab my toothbrush and squeeze out some paste and begin to brush my teeth. My mind drifts to last night and the connection I felt with Tay. Maybe I was just caught up in the moment since she's not here. Rinsing my mouth, I grab a pair of workout shorts and a Schofield racing shirt and get dressed for the day.

After dressing, I head to the kitchen in search of coffee and when I step out of the hallway, I pause mid-step because there, in my kitchen, in one of my Schofield racing tees is Taylor, and she's making breakfast. Her hair is up on her head in a messy bun, and she's bopping along to A-Ha's "Take on Me."

Leaning against the wall, I watch her. Seeing her so carefree and at home in my kitchen causes my heart to stutter, and that feeling of contentment slams back into me. She looks up, and our gaze connects across the room.

"Morning, sleepyhead. I hope you don't mind, but I'm making us pancakes."

"I don't mind at all," I tell her, pushing off the wall and walking over to her. "I have to admit, seeing you in my team shirt and kitchen is a great sight. And I really hope you're naked under that shirt."

She shrugs but from the seductive glint in her eye, I think she is. "This shirt, it's comfy AF and cooking in your kitchen is amazeballs. This is like my dream kitchen."

You're my dream girl, I think to myself.

"I was going to make coffee too but that machine of yours," she head nods toward my coffee station, "needs a doctorate to operate."

Chuckling, I stop next to her and rest my hand on her lower back and press myself into her side. Her body melts into mine, and I'm positive I hear her sigh. She looks up at me and smiles. "Think you can make coffee while I finish up?"

"I can do that," I tell her.

She nods and turns her attention back to the pancake batter. Leaning over, I place a kiss on the side of her head. Squeezing her hip, I turn away from her to make our coffees ... on the machine that is *not* complicated.

I've just placed her coffee next to her when there's a knock at the front door. Walking over, I swing it open. My eyes widen when I see my grandma standing there. "Grandma, what are you doing here?"

"It's Saturday. We moved our pancake date forward since you're off to who knows where for the next race." She leans in and kisses me on the cheek

Shit, I internally hiss. I totally forgot we swapped our breakfast date, but before I can say anything, she sniffs the air. "Are those pancakes I smell?"

Without waiting for my reply, she steps around me and walks inside. I know the moment she spies Tay in my kitchen because she lets out an excited squeak. "Taylor, what are you doing here?" She flicks her gaze to me and her eyes widen. "Oh My God, did you two have a sleepover?"

"Grandma," I groan, while Taylor grins and her cheeks darken.

"Morning, Mrs. Schofield. Would you like to join us for breakfast?"

"Ohhh, I couldn't intrude," Grandma tells her but I can tell from the tone of her voice, there is no way she's leaving.

"Please," Taylor begs, "we insist."

"Well, if you insist," Grandma replies quickly. She climbs onto a stool at the island bench and watches Taylor intently. She's beaming right now, and I love seeing my grandma so happy.

"Can Linc get you a coffee?"

"A mimosa goes with brunch."

"Then, can Linc get you a mimosa?"

"Of course he can." Grandma turns to me. "Three mimosas, young man."

"Yes, ma'am." I salute her and go about making three mimosas.

Taylor and Grandma start chatting, and the two of them are getting along like a house on fire. While Taylor finishes cooking the pancakes, the three of us chat and laugh. Boy do we laugh. We discuss books, politics, celebrity gossip, and everything in between.

Taylor excuses herself to use the bathroom, and I can't help myself, I swat her ass as she walks past. She playfully scowls at me, and I blow her a kiss, earning myself a headshake.

The door to my room clicks, and Grandma pounces. "My boy found love in the club," she coos. "Is that not like the most perfect love story ever?"

"Grandma," I say, rolling my eyes. "It's been one date."

"When you know you know, Lincoln—"

"Ohhh, you full named me."

"Don't sass an old woman. That girl in there," she points toward my room, "is your penguin. Don't fuck it up, I like her."

"I like her too," I tell her.

"I know you do. Now make an old lady happy and get her another mimosa, and maybe a grandbaby too."

Shaking my head, I chuckle at her request but do as I'm told—in the first request. I grab the empty glasses and head into the kitchen. As I'm pouring our drinks, I think Grandma might be right. I have found my penguin. I'm not in love yet, but I can totally see myself falling in love with Taylor King.

EPILOGUE

Taylor

... One month later

Sitting in my car, I stare at the library, and unlike the first time I was here and apprehensive to head inside, this time I can't freakin' wait. Linc and his grandma will be inside, and I'm excited to see my man. He's been away for the past five days with the team. FaceTime through a screen isn't the same as in person face time.

Grabbing my bag, I climb out of my car and head inside. Entering, I find Linc off to the side and, once again, Eve has him pinned down. Putting one foot in front of the other, I walk over to them and do exactly what I did last time.

Sliding in next to him, I slip my arm around his waist and look up at him. "Hi, boyfriend."

"Hi, girlfriend," he replies, leaning in and kissing my temple.

"Really, you two are still going with the 'we're dating' ruse?" She air quotes "we're dating" and sneers at the two of us, well, me.

"There's no ruse," I tell her. "Linc and I are a couple."

"Bullshit," she growls. "What's his favorite color?"

"Green," I answer confidently but then again, since his team's color is green, that wasn't a hard one.

"Favorite book?"

"*Intensity* by Dean Koontz."

"Wroooong," she singsongs. "It's *Fallen* by Rebecca Barber, because the hero, Zach, is living the life he would have lived if he didn't do what he does."

"I did say that," Linc agrees with her, and she give me a "ha" look, but that look is wiped off her skanky face when he adds, "But I never said it was my all-time favorite. That title goes to *Intensity*."

"Bullshit," she snaps. "Why are you playing along with this hussy?"

"Watch your mouth, Eve. I won't have anyone disrespect my girlfriend. Tay and I are dating and—"

"They're gonna make me a great-grandma," Linc's grandma interjects with a beaming smile as she joins us.

"You're pregnant?" Eve hisses, shock and outrage marring her face.

"N—"

Kelly interrupts me, "Well, maybe. She's always there for pancakes and mimosas on Sunday, but I guess since she's drinking, she's not pregnant … yet … but she will be."

"Grandma," Linc warns her.

"What? I'm just stating facts, and I cannot wait for the day it happens."

"As much as talking about babies is fun, I'm not pregnant." I look to Kelly and offer, "Sorry," with a shrug. Then I look back to Eve. "Linc and I are dating. We may have embellished things the other week, but now we really are dating, and if that upsets you, I'm sorry. But I love Linc, and I'm not going anywhere."

"You love me?" he asks from beside me, and then I realize what just slipped out.

Looking up at him, I nod. "Yeah, I do. You're an amazing man, Lincoln Schofield. How could I not love you?"

"Well, you, Taylor King, are an amazing woman, and I love you too."

"Kiss her," Bonnie sings out, and when I turn toward the sound of her voice, I realize we have an audience. Everyone is grinning. Well, almost everyone. But Eve's facial expression is moot because Linc loves me, and I love him.

"Guess we better give them what they want," Linc says, and I can't help but laugh.

"You just want an excuse to kiss me."

"I don't need an excuse, Tay. You're my girlfriend and I love you, therefore, I can kiss you anytime I want."

"Then what are you waiting for?"

"Nothing." Turning to face me, he grips my cheeks in his palms and in the middle of the library, he kisses me. I can feel this kiss deep in my soul because it's one filled with love, hope, happiness, and all the other descriptive words for being in love.

Since moving to LA, my life has been a whirlwind but in the most amazing way. Who knew putting myself out there would lead to finding my penguin. I guess you could say, I found love in the club. Well, I found love at book club.

THE END!

ABOUT THE AUTHOR

DL Gallie is from Queensland, Australia, but she's lived in many different places all over the world. She currently resides in Central Queensland with her husband and two teenagers. She and her husband have been together since she was sixteen, and although they drive each other crazy at times, she couldn't imagine her life without him.

Shortly after her son was born, DL began reading again. With encouragement from her husband, she picked up the pen and started writing. Fifty books later and the voices in her head won't shut up.

DL enjoys listening to music, drinking white wine in the summer, red wine in the winter, and beer all year round. She's also never been known to turn down a cocktail, especially a margarita.

Want to know more about DL Gallie, you can on her website: http://www.dlgallieauthor.com

CATCHING UP WITH MR. B

Indie Sparks

CHAPTER ONE

I DON'T KNOW if it's possible to die from the off-gassed fumes of furniture polish and cologne, but I feel like I'm hanging on by a thread in this lawyer's office.

The business at hand is settling my father's estate, and it's a good thing there's an expansive desk between me and the custom-suited asshole who handled his legal affairs because I might actually resent him as much as I did my father.

"Well," the attorney says, his manicured, fat fingers tapping the mountain of documents he had me sign until my hand cramped. "I think that does it. You are a very fortunate woman, Ms. Alexander."

"Again, it's Ms. Carrigan. As I explained when I arrived, I took my mother's name after she rescued me. I wouldn't think it would be so hard to remember that, given the number of times you've watched me sign that name this evening."

"Or when she stole you, depending on perspective." Before I can launch myself over the desk to rip out his jugular, he says, "At any rate, you are a very wealthy young woman now, Jewel. May I call you Jewel and forgo the issue of your rightful last name versus your chosen one?"

"Doesn't really matter what you call me at this point. I can't imagine we'll ever need to speak again." I stand and take my coat from the back of the stiff chair.

"Like I said, I will be happy to remain the registered agent for the corporation and continue to manage the assets." He gets up and starts around the desk. "There are quite a few. . . well, intricately structured entities in the portfolio."

"I'm sure I can find someone smart enough to sort the details for me. Selling it all first chance I get, anyway, so there won't be anything left to manage soon."

"That could get complicated."

"My whole life's been complicated. If any questions come up, I'll be in touch."

"I'll be waiting."

Don't hold your breath.

I walk quickly through his office and past the firm's receptionist, hoping he won't follow. He doesn't, but I still frantically press the button for the elevator like I'm the next victim in a horror movie.

Inside the steel box, I take my first full breath in hours. It's done. My evil father is truly gone, and I'm about to liquidate everything he worked so hard for, to erase his name from the only things that ever mattered to him: property and possessions.

Two years too late for my mom to see it. She should've outlived him. So much about her life should've been different.

I blink away tears. As someone who believed her mother was dead until I was sixteen, losing her for real at twenty-four had felt like grieving her second death. And that was twice as many times as I should've had to feel that pain.

So, where Donovan Alexander is concerned, I'm all grieved out. If anyone deserved to die more than once, it was that bastard, not her.

I realize I'm white-knuckling the folder filled with my copies of all the documents I spent the last three hours discussing and signing, and I'm besieged by the same thought I had when I walked up to this building: *Does Gareth Branson still have his office here?*

I'd ignored the directory in the lobby when I arrived because if I'd found his company listed, there's no way I would've been able to concentrate during the meeting with my father's henchman attorney, but the pull to look before I leave is too strong to ignore.

There it is. BRANSON ARCHITECTURAL & ENGINEERING CO.— not only still in the building, but still in Suite 300, where I'd once tagged along with Shandy and her mom to bring him something he'd forgotten at home.

I glance back at the elevator, tell myself not to do it.

The last time I saw Mr. B was when the Bransons dropped me off after my final night at their lake house. That night had been the first and only time he'd ever touched me like that. The night he abruptly pulled his hands out of my shorts and sent me to bed, leaving me to fantasize about what might've come next for ten years and counting.

I understand why he stopped, of course. He came to his senses. Reality intervened and slapped him hard with the realization he had his fingers buried in the pussy of an almost-but-not-quite-eighteen-year-old girl, and no desire to destroy his family.

Not that I'd have told anyone about it. I never have.

I rode home the next morning in the backseat next to my best friend, Shandy, hoping I wasn't telegraphing any clues about what had happened between me and her dad the night before, and wishing I could ask him all the questions screaming in my mind.

A caravan of Feds lined the street in front of my father's house. Black sedans and SUVs, just like in the movies.

Agents whisked me away as soon as I stepped out of the car. The most terrifying moment of my life. I thought I was being kidnapped. My mind was still reeling from my encounter with Mr. Branson, but then someone said my mom's name—and that they were taking me to her.

I kept trying to tell them my mom was dead, and they were making a huge mistake, they had the wrong girl . . . but no one would listen to me.

The ground spun out from under my feet. Trauma on trauma.

I tell myself as I stand in this lobby that if the elevator doesn't come by the time I count to ten, I'll go. That will be my sign that our reunion wasn't meant to be.

The doors open when I get to nine. My feet make the decision before my brain can weigh in, and my stomach barely has time to flip before the doors open again on the third floor.

This is it: my opportunity to ask him if he's thought of me as often as I have him over the past decade. I try to imagine his expression when he sees me, but all that comes to mind is the way he looked at me and whispered my name like it was a holy incantation as I panted in his arms against the kitchen counter of his lake house nearly a decade ago.

I was a trembling, confused seventeen-year-old, who had just come all over the hand of the man she'd once thought of as more of a father than her own. But somewhere along the way that summer, my thoughts about Mr. B had shifted. He'd obviously been thinking of me in a whole new way, too.

It never should've happened, but for the life of me, I've never been able to make myself regret it.

He may not remember that night the same way I do; he may not remember it at all. Regardless of his memories, he may not be able, or willing to tell me what I want to hear.

But I've never needed to be fucked into oblivion more than I do right now. My thoughts of him have been twisted and tangled for so long.

Fuck me, Gareth. Unravel me. Yeah, maybe I won't lead with those exact words . . . what the hell am I going to say to him?

My mind is still struggling to come up with something reasonable as I approach the door. The woman rushing out is obviously thinking of something else as well. We collide and end up clutching each other and apologizing in surround sound.

"I'm here to see Gareth Branson," I manage to say, though I can't hear myself over the thudding of my heartbeat in my ears. "Has he left for the day?"

"No, he's still here. I didn't realize he had a late appointment scheduled."

"Oh, he's not expecting me right now." *Great. Just introduce yourself as a stalker.* "My flight got delayed so we rescheduled, but traffic was better than I expected, so I thought I'd run over and see if I could catch him."

"Well, you're in luck. His office is to the right, in the corner."

"I remember." My eyes follow the path that leads to him. "Thank you."

She locks us in and heads for the elevator. No turning back now. It's time to catch up with Mr. B, for better or worse.

CHAPTER TWO

His office door is closed. I should turn around while I still can. Maybe I don't need a key to get out? As hard as I'm willing myself to turn and go, I keep moving forward.

The hallway isn't long. The half-closed blinds lining the windows to his office are visible from here. I spy movement between the slats and swallow hard. Gareth Branson is right there, so close, moving around, doing important work, not expecting me to barge in after-hours like this, or at any time.

I'm going to take him by surprise and I'm not sure if that's fair. Or sane. But my knuckles meet the wood just below his title. President. I turn the knob and let myself in before he has a chance to cross the room and open the door.

"Well, hello there, Mr. B Still a workaholic, I see."

He blinks as if he thinks he might be hallucinating. "Oh, my God. Jewel Alexander."

"It's Carrigan now." My smile is unyielding, like the corners of my mouth have been yanked up and super glued. He looks happy to see me. Unless I'm the one hallucinating.

"Congratulations."

"Oh, no. I'm not married. Carrigan was my mom's name. My birth name, the real one."

"Right. I'm sorry. Please, come in." He stands and motions toward the leather sofa under the mounted sailfish. It strikes me that his eyes are the same deep blue of the fish's scales, and I can't help but look back and forth between them again.

I'd forgotten the depths of his eyes, but his voice is exactly as I remember it, even with the nervous energy I've infused into it.

"I'm in town to finalize my father's estate. His attorney is in the building, so I thought I'd pop in and say hello. Hope I'm not interrupting anything important."

"No. Of course not. Seriously, sit. I'm going to have a drink. Can I make you one?"

"Sure. Whatever you're having." I sink into the worn leather cushions and am overcome with the desire to kick off my shoes and pull my legs up under me, make myself comfortable.

"Make yourself comfortable," he says, as he plinks ice cubes into whiskey glasses.

Damn. Hope he can't read all my thoughts.

"Have you seen Shandy?" he asks as he walks toward me, his eyes studying me. I'm not sure if he's suspicious or simply cataloguing my changes since we last saw each other.

My fingers graze his when I take the drink, and I swear that scant second of contact sizzles the air between us.

"No," I say. "I haven't kept up with anyone, so I didn't reach out. It's been so long."

"I bet she'd still like to hear from you. You two were like sisters."

"We were, but my life was very different after . . ."

I let my voice trail off, the gravity of his likening Shandy and me to sisters weighs too heavy on my chest to say more.

"Your lives are probably pretty different now, too. She's married, three kids. Soccer mom."

The high-dollar whiskey I'm attempting to swallow burbles back up from my throat. "I'm sorry. Did you just say Shandy has kids old enough to play soccer?"

"Her oldest is seven. She got pregnant in college, quit and married Connor. His office is right down the hall. I always imagined she'd be the one working here someday, not her husband."

"Yeah, that was definitely her plan when I knew her." I don't mean to rub salt in a wound, and judging from his expression, this truth hurts. "But people grow up and change, I guess."

"That they do. How about you? What are you doing these days?"

"Designing commercial kitchens. Started out in culinary school. Took me a year and a half to realize cooking wasn't my passion, but I knew what worked in a kitchen, and I had a good eye for design so, here I am. I get to travel to restaurants all over the country and work with owners and chefs. Spend a lot more time mediating arguments and egos than I ever would've imagined, but I like the challenges. Predictability never really appealed to me."

"Good for you. You made smart changes, didn't throw your life away."

"Is Shandy not happy?"

"Can't imagine how she could be, but she was always closer to her mom. When we divorced, Shandy was a pregnant college dropout. I didn't hide my opinions on the subject too well. I'd be the last person she'd confide in at this point."

"For what it's worth, I think your opinions were probably justified."

He shrugs. "Sharing them didn't help. Didn't change the situation."

I sip from my glass and try not to let my true reaction to his failed marriage show. "I didn't realize you and Allison had gotten divorced. I'm sorry to hear that."

"Don't be. We were no better matched than Shandy and Connor. But you can't stop your kids from repeating your mistakes."

I'd always known the Bransons were younger than most of the other parents, but it never occurred to me how much younger. I see it clearly now. His hair is barely starting to gray at the temples, his jawline still tight, like the rest of him unless that white button down has muscled padding built into it.

My fingers unconsciously tap against my thigh like they're working over a keyboard in slow motion, but what they're itching to work is his buttons, to open that pressed shirt and trail through the curls on his chest, clutch a fistful of it to pull him closer.

"You made some damn good choices, too, not just mistakes. I mean, look around. You've done pretty well."

"Yeah," he says solemnly. "But I definitely made my share of mistakes."

God, those stormy-night eyes of his are destroying me. "I hope you don't think of me as a mistake."

"I was wondering if that's why you came. To confront me."

He remembers.

"No, not to confront you. It is why I came, but only because I've never been able to get over it."

"I am so sorry, Jewel. I had no right—"

"No, you've got it all wrong. I'm not here for an apology, Gareth."

"That's the first time you've ever called me anything other than Mr. B."

"Mr. B is what I called you when I was a girl. I'm a woman now. And you star in more of my fantasies than I should be willing to admit. The only hand that had gotten me off before yours was my own. I'd been fingered before, fucked, too. But they were boys with no idea what they were doing, all stabbing in the dark. Literally." I pause to laugh, watching his beautiful mouth break into a smile. "I barely remember their names. But I remember your kiss tasted like spiced rum and coke, your shirt smelled like smoke from the steaks you'd grilled for dinner, and when I buried my face in it and you whispered my name into my hair, I wanted to freeze time so you could hold me like that forever. No one had ever made me feel like that. And no one has since."

"Jesus, Jewel. You've put me on a pedestal I don't deserve. And if I were a better man, I'd send you out of here right now before I make another mistake."

"Please don't remember me as a mistake, Gareth." I walk to him, position his knee between my legs. "Besides, I'm not that girl anymore. I'm a grown woman now. Any mistakes I make are my own."

He sets his glass on the floor and I shiver when his cold hand meets my thigh under my skirt. His stare sends an electric current up my spine.

"My actual desires run a little darker than your innocent memories, sweet girl."

"And I'm not as innocent as you remember, but I'll be your sweet girl. Teach me, Daddy."

CHAPTER THREE

As soon as I call him Daddy, Gareth's eyes darken, and his gentle touch on my thigh becomes a tight grip. It's a moment shot through with uncertainty; I'm not sure if I've angered him or thrown open the gates to those darker desires that he's just warned me about.

To make my position unflinchingly clear, I say, "I didn't come here to heed warnings. And I'm not scared of the dark."

I thread my fingers into his hair.

"Jesus fuck, Jewel." He shoves my skirt higher, and his fingers trace the lace band at the top of my thigh highs. "You always dress so sexy to meet with attorneys?"

"There's nothing sexy about my outfit, only what's underneath. And he didn't get to see what was under my clothes." I pull my shirt over my head to show Gareth more of my black lace. "What can I say? I have a weakness for lingerie."

"That makes two of us." His lips meet the swell of my breast, and the heat coming off his mouth sends a chill through me.

"I bet we like a lot of the same things," I say, running my fingers through his thick, dark waves. "Let's pick up where we left off and find out."

"We left off with your insanely tight little pussy clenching my fingers and your panties soaked. Are your pretty little panties wet right now?"

"You tell me." I reach back and lower the zipper on my skirt, letting it fall below my hips. The fabric rests on his wrists for a few seconds before he pulls his hands away from my legs and his gaze follows it to the floor.

His eyes roam back up over my body, taking in every inch of me, but stopping short of meeting my stare. He runs his hands up my arms and his thumbs curl at my shoulders, hook under my bra straps, and yank them down my arms, pulling the cups away from my skin until my breasts are fully exposed to him.

"Gorgeous tits." He immediately pinches and pulls on my nipples. "Can they handle rough play like this?"

My voice catches in my throat when I try to respond. I nod mid-gasp and that's enough confirmation for him to keep going.

"Big, perky nipples like these should be pierced," he says. "Why aren't they?"

"Almost did it in college," I say. "Chickened out at the last minute." I squirm between his arms but he doesn't release my nipples.

"Is that what you're going to do here? Chicken out on me at the last minute?"

"No. I'm not going anywhere until you're done with me." He closes his mouth over my left nipple and his tongue teases the peak for a bit before he begins to suck, working it forcefully with his mouth while his finger and thumb continue to test my limits on the right.

His free hand slips inside my thong, and he groans when he feels how incredibly wet he's already made me.

He doesn't give my pussy any warmup play, goes straight to reaming me and pressing hard circles over my clit. My orgasm hits too soon, denies my desire to slowly rediscover the joy of his hand, to savor every sensation of his touch after all these years.

Gareth withdraws his fingers from inside me before I'm done trembling and brings them to my lips, prying my mouth open. I suck on them the way I know he wants me to. His eyes hood and his breaths turn ragged, intensifying until they practically echoes around us.

"My turn to taste it," he says, lying back on the sofa, stretching his legs long on the cushions, his head resting flat. "Get up here and make a mess on my face."

Oh, God. Definitely should've asked for another drink before I came on to him. With my bra still twisted around my waist, I step next to him. His hands grab my hips and lift me until I have no choice but to climb aboard, my knees sinking into the leather above his shoulders.

He moves the crotch of my thong aside with two fingers and stretches his tongue to flicker at my opening. His hand presses at the small of my back to bring me closer to him.

God, he looks incredible beneath me like this. When he finds me watching, he bites gently along my labia and smiles up at me. He makes several firm strokes through my seam with his tongue like he's licking thick frosting off a cupcake, coating his tongue with my arousal.

Then he lifts his head while simultaneously pulling me further onto his mouth and eats me out like a man starved, ensuring that mess he asked for, and obliterating my self-conscious hesitation about sitting on his face.

By the time I come, I'm riding his mouth. There is nothing within reach to brace myself, no headboard to press against to keep from flying apart when my fuses all blow. I fist my hair at the scalp and pull hard, seeking balance in the tension as I attempt to lift off him to ease the intensity, but he chases me up to maintain contact and pulls me right back down, forcing me to expel the scream I'm trying to swallow, and leaving me no choice but to endure the electrical current zinging across my nerve endings at maximum wattage.

Tears involuntarily stream from my eyes as if my body needs every possible outlet for this release. It's all I can do to keep from collapsing on him.

He's exorcised every ounce of stress that's haunted me for weeks, all the terror of coming back here to face the memories is now melted all over his face.

I could curl onto his chest and sleep until morning, but he grabs my ass with both hands and says, "I'm about to do things to you that are going to knock me right off that pedestal, sweet girl. If you want to tap out, now is the time."

"I'm all in. Go ahead, make me hate you."

Please. Because I have adored you for too damn long.

CHAPTER FOUR

"I don't need you to hate me or love me or anything in between," Gareth says, sitting up and narrowing his deep ocean eyes at me. "I only need you to obey me. To be a good girl for me."

"I'll do my best, Daddy." With that he pushes my hips back from his face, and I climb off him. He stands and helps me up.

I make quick work of his shirt buttons, revealing his manscaped but not bare chest. My fingers skate through the trimmed, dark curls that remain. When I slide the shirt over his shoulders and down his arms, my palms map his muscles, and I want to touch every inch of him.

He unbuckles his belt and whips it free from the loops, doubles it over and snaps the leather against itself once. "Turn around and put your hands behind your back."

I can't think of any other man I'd allow to do what he's about to do to me, but I comply with his command. He binds my wrists with the belt, knotting it until it's tight.

Keeping my smile turned toward the carpet, I relish the truth that I could probably break free of this if I really wanted, and I think he knows it, too. This binding is symbolic as much as it is physical.

He needs to know I will allow him to restrain me, that I will relinquish control to him.

If he only knew that he's held a crucial piece of me in bondage since the first time he touched me, when he came up behind me in the kitchen in the middle of the night and the heat of his words against my neck made me quiver in his arms.

But I didn't try to get away from him then either. Far from it.

That's it. Lean back into me, let me explore this sweet little pussy. I'm going to make you feel good, baby girl. I promise.

He did more than make me come that night; he rewired me. I think I sensed even then there was something dark about him, and I know it awakened something within me that I didn't understand. But he abruptly denied me any further knowledge of him, sent me back to bed full of questions and wonder.

I've been playing out what-if scenes in my head for so long. Tonight, I finally get to know what comes after with Mr. B.

I will do anything he asks of me.

"Face me and drop to your knees." His voice is raspy and heavy, and I am spellbound.

He unzips his pants and shoves them and his underwear down to his thighs, bringing his erection to my lips. I look up to meet his eyes as I circle the tip with my tongue, and then I open wider to let him push it inside. He doesn't grab the back of my head or pull my hair, just holds there, looking down at me.

"I knew your pretty red lips would look good stretched around my cock. Show me what you can do with that painted mouth."

I lean forward to slide down his full length and retreat slowly, twisting my head from side to side to create friction, sucking in my cheeks with increasing pressure. His groan of approval is feral.

Keeping only the tip inside, I repeat the same moves several times, expecting him to take my head and shove it at a faster pace any second, but he doesn't.

Gareth basks in the attention I'm lavishing on him, enjoying my performance. He told me to show him what I could do, and now he's watching, not directing, as I kneel before him with my wrists bound, acting on his original cue.

He swells in my mouth, and I register the twitch that lets me know he's not going to be able to retain control if I keep doing what I'm doing for much longer.

That's when he slides his hands into my hair and takes over, moving me off him, extracting his glistening dick from my lips. He pulls me to my feet and crushes his mouth against mine as he walks me back to his desk.

"Turn," he says when he breaks our kiss, and I obey the word. My shoulders relax in relief as he undoes the knotted belt, but when he tells me to plant my hands on his desk and bend over, I shoot a panicked look back at him.

I love having my ass slapped by a man, but no man has ever hit me with a belt, not with anything other than his hand.

"Dirty little sluts get their asses striped," he says. "And then they take the rest of their punishment. But you can stand up and walk right out that door if you've had enough." His eyes are swirling with lust, but brimming with challenge, too. "Or you can give me your safe word and bow your head."

This is a test. And I'll be damned if I'll walk out of here now with my thighs slick and my legs weak, but not having felt his dick buried inside me yet.

"My safe word is Viking."

His laughter tumbles out like the beginnings of an avalanche.

"Well, that might sound like a compliment in the right moment."

"Like the kitchen appliances," I clarify with my head still turned to look at him. "The first time I was asked for my safe word, I didn't have one, but I desperately wanted the chef behind me to unleash whatever beast he was holding back and he wouldn't keep going until I gave him a word. We were in the middle of the kitchen I was remodeling for him so I spit out the first word I saw. Viking."

I flash a coy smile and turn my face back toward the windows.

The sting of the first lash takes my breath.

"Don't ever talk to me about another man fucking you unless I've asked. Do you understand?"

"Yes, Daddy." I lower my head, press hard against the polished surface under my hands.

"That's my good girl." He delivers two more lashes and stops, tosses the belt aside. "There we go. That beautiful ass looks good with pink stripes across it."

He rubs over the rising welts, and I feel my juices gush at the alternating current of pleasure and pain, the sting that subsides when he caresses my skin, but rushes back the moment he moves his hand away and the cool air replaces his heat.

"Stand up." He steps in close behind me, wraps his arms around my waist and presses his body against my back, letting one hand slide down and between my legs. A replay of how he approached me and cupped me inside my sleep shorts when I got up for a drink of water, not knowing he was sitting at that table in the dark, drinking the spiced rum I still taste in my dreams.

"I bet the chef has excellent memories of you every time he enters that kitchen. I still get a hard-on whenever I walk into the kitchen at my lake house, still stand there and wish every time that you'd been a few years older and my divorce had already been final, so I could've known how it felt to replace my fingers with my dick. God, I wanted to fuck you sore, and I hated myself for it. Have ever since. I've thought a dozen times about selling the place to try to escape the guilt, but I can never bring myself to make the call."

"Maybe you just need to have the kitchen remodeled. I know a girl."

"That's not a bad idea." His fingers probe deeper and he bites my shoulder. "Or maybe I just need to finally ravage you in it to complete the fantasy."

"Mmm, that's another viable option."

"How long are you in town?"

"Undecided. Only booked a one-way flight in case a job came up and I needed to go in a different direction when I was done here." I lean harder into him, tilt my hips to give him better access as he inserts another finger. "Just packed a heavy bag and got on a plane."

"Still a free-spirit, wild and unbroken. I love it." He claims my clit between his thumb and index finger, pinches and rolls until I flinch. Then he eases to a firm massage under the pad of his thumb.

"I wouldn't say unbroken."

"Everybody is broken in some way, Jewel. Hold still." He steps away to retrieve his belt from the floor, stretches it in front of my face, brings it to my mouth. "Bite down on it and resume the position you were in when I spanked you. Show me that pretty pink pussy, let me see how ready it is to be punished."

He holds both sides of the belt in one hand behind my head, pulling it taut like a gag to keep my neck extended while I bend over his desk again. I couldn't lower my head this time if I wanted. My back arches, and he gets the view he's requested.

His hips thrust with force from the first stroke. I've never been wetter, but his stiff cock stretching my tight walls still abrades my tender skin within minutes and ignites a burning sensation that lights me up in exactly the way I need.

My teeth sink into his leather belt.

Fuck, yes. Make it hurt.

I've never been able to fuck the pain away. But a better pain replacing a worse one always works as a temporary fix.

Tomorrow will be another day where I feel no sorrow for my latest dead parent, only another level of resurfacing anger, but I will be physically sore and bruised. And that will be enough to get me through whatever stage of grief I should feel next, but won't.

And my curiosity about Gareth will be sated. I'll finally know, and I can let him go. My last tie to this place will be severed.

He yanks on the belt and my head snaps back. When he simultaneously pinches my nipple like a clamp, I yelp at the additional twinge of torment, and he erupts like a volcano. I clutch at the desk, and my thoughts spin like a roulette wheel.

My delicate silk and lace lingerie is twisted and shoved askew on my body. A sheen of sweat coats my back, and my neck feels like I have whiplash from a head-on collision. But it wasn't enough.

I look back at him still panting from his orgasm. He smiles, and my rage surges. No, we're not done here.

"Spank me again," I say. "Use your hand this time but longer. Don't stop hitting me until my ass is covered in your handprints, until I beg, until I safe-word out—"

"No."

"What do you mean, no?"

"You don't get to decide when or how I punish you, sweet girl. That's not how it works."

"Fuck you!" I straighten and turn on him. "Fuck you, Gareth. Oh, I'm sorry. Mr. B! Is that better? Am I too grown for you now or what?"

The lights blur, and I launch myself at him, slapping and clawing at his chest and his face. I'm flailing blind, no idea where my assault is landing, and I don't care. I can't stop.

His voice is loud, until it's not.

Until he has my arms trapped in his, holding me pinned against his chest, and I'm shaking like I'm having a goddamn seizure and my vision is still blurred so I can't see his face. I can't move to hit him. I can't stop shaking. I can't get free. I can't breathe.

I'm sobbing but not breathing, and shaking and shaking and shaking...

When the room comes back into focus, I'm wrapped in his arms on the sofa. He's holding me, rocking me, telling me it's okay, I'm okay, everything is going to be okay. I try to apologize, but he shushes me with his fingers against my lips, kisses me softly. Blood trails from a deep scratch on his cheek.

"I did that to your face? Oh, God. I'm leaving. No more psycho outbursts, I swear. Just let me up, and I'll get out of here."

He holds me tighter. "The only place you're going tonight is my house."

CHAPTER FIVE

WAKING up in Gareth Branson's bed was not part of my plan. The flashbacks of how I got here? Not good.

At least I don't have to roll over and face him. He's in the shower, and the sound of the water rushing through the pipes could lull me right back to sleep in no time, if that were an option. Not to mention the soft early morning light breaking through his bedroom windows.

God knows this is my favorite time to sleep, but I need to get the hell out of here.

I'm stumbling around in nothing but my thigh high stockings, searching for my bra when he emerges from the bathroom with a towel around his waist.

"Oh, good. You're up." He lifts my bra from his nightstand on his way to the closet. "Looking for this?"

He tosses it on the bed.

"Yeah, thanks." The headrush when I stand straight makes me sway like I've just stepped off a boat. "We drank a little when we got back here last night, right?"

Everything after being bent over his desk is fragmented. Like video clips being played out of order. And out of focus. I sit on the bed to keep from toppling onto the rug.

"Sure. Let's go with a little." He walks out of his closet already wearing pants and pulling on a crisp dress shirt. Light blue, and fuck if it doesn't make his eyes look like morning glories in contrast.

How is he so bright-eyed? I can't even open mine all the way.

Then again, he isn't the one who had a breakdown last night.

"I'm really sorry. I don't know what came over me—"

"How many times do I have to tell you it's fine? You're dealing with a lot, Jewel. Your father just died."

"Please, I barely knew him. He had nannies raise me until I was thirteen.

After that, it was just me. He was never around, always gone for work. Christ, I don't even know what he actually did for a living."

I manage to hook my bra, despite my shaking hands. The rest of my clothes are easier to find, lying in a rumpled heap like I dropped them where I stood before I climbed into his bed.

"Why don't you get some more sleep?" He knots a royal blue tie and, Jesus, he's going to ruin every shade of blue for me. "I'll come back at lunch and take you to your car."

Shit. My car is still parked in front of his office.

"Don't worry about it. I'll get a ride."

"I'd rather you didn't." He pulls his wallet and keys from a wooden box on his dresser, takes a business card from a slim holder, and sets it on the nightstand. "My office number and my cell are on here. Let me know if you decide not to wait for me. But for now, will you please go back to bed?"

"Okay. I'll be gone before lunch though. It was good to see you again."

"You, too, Jewel."

"Liar."

"Not at all." He kisses me on the forehead before he goes. "Don't leave, sweet girl. Wait for me."

His freshly showered scent lingers over me as I burrow into his sumptuous sheets and pillows.

When I wake again, the sun is bright, and it's less of a struggle to open my eyes, but I need coffee. And a sauna to sweat out the rest of last night's alcohol.

His shower looks like something out of a magazine, more jets and controls than a carwash, and big enough to accommodate a truck. There are motion sensors on the faucets at the counter. Lights embedded into the mirrors that can be dimmed or brightened with the same touchpad on the wall that controls the overhead fixtures. The whole bathroom is designed to stroke the male ego. Sleek. Powerful. Excessive.

I get the psychology behind the design. I've applied the same concepts to dozens of kitchens. Five minutes into meeting with a new client, I know if I'm going to need to play up the bells and whistles or keep it simple and classic. Gareth is apparently a bells and whistles guy.

Nothing simple about Mr. B.

He was such a mystery to me before I walked into his office yesterday, and now I'm standing naked in his bathroom looking inside his brain, spying through a window he doesn't even know he's left open. They never know.

I tell myself I'll use the same towel he used this morning to keep from adding more laundry for the housekeeper I'm certain he has, but I know the real reason, and the disappointing truth before I even wrap it around my body.

It's a poor substitution for his skin against mine, but it's the closest thing I can give myself as a parting gift. One last touch.

Walking back into his bedroom wearing only his towel feels entirely too comfortable. This isn't the house my best friend grew up in. It shouldn't feel familiar to me at all, but I am so at home in his space. And I need to get the hell out of here right now.

I got the answers I came for. It's time to go, to drive away and never look back.

When I drop the towel to his bedroom floor, a wolf whistle sounds at my back, and I freeze, until I recognize the gravelly laughter trailing it.

"I thought you weren't coming back until lunch," I say without turning to face him.

"How careless do you think I am, sweet girl?" His cologne snakes through the air behind me, the smell preceding his touch as it slithers over my shoulders, before it coils up from my waist as his arms encircle me, positioning us like the portrait burned in my memory.

"I had to take a meeting, sign off on some prints, but I was never going to wait that long to come back for you."

He brushes my damp hair aside, and his teeth leave tracks down my neck. "No way would I let you leave here feeling like you did something wrong. All you deserve to feel is satisfied. And sore."

His fingers press inside me. "I want this creamy little cunt tender and bruised, cock-shy but still burning for it. Fuck, sweet girl, I want you addicted to the things I do to you, the way I make you feel. And shameless in the face of it. What do you want?"

"All of that. Everything you just said. Use me, Daddy."

He spins me to face him, shoves me so I fall back onto his mattress, clutches my legs, and yanks my ass to the edge. "Grab your ankles. Hold them up and show me what's mine. Keep them there until I'm done with you."

"Is this what you were thinking about in your meeting?" I ask as he rams his hard dick inside me.

"You know it's exactly what I was thinking about. I couldn't get back here fast enough. Did you make yourself come in my shower?"

"No."

"Did you play with your pussy in my bed?"

"No."

"You will." He takes my right ankle from my grasp so we each have hold of one. "Do it now. Touch your clit."

I trace it with my fingertip, enjoying the gentle sensation, careful to circumnavigate the most sensitive center, but when he thrusts his erection fully inside me, it forces my touch across the lightning switch and sends a flash through my core too soon.

I'm not ready for that much stimulation yet; it agitates, stings. I move my hand to my breasts, try to draw his attention upward, but he's not having it.

"Put your hand back where it was. Work your clit while I watch."

"It's too soon."

Without warning, he pinches my clit, rolls it between his thumb and forefinger the way he plays rough with my nipples. I lift my hips, seeking relief but his hand follows, his fingers continuing to knead and squeeze.

"Please," I pant. "Let go. It's too much."

"Relax." He releases the pressure in increments that match the lowering of my hips. His dick is still seated to the hilt. When my back is flat on the mattress again, he lets go of my clit like I've asked.

"Reach back up here." He returns my second ankle to my hand. "Spread wider, open all the way for me."

I can't imagine how much more open I could be, but I pull my legs farther apart. The harder he fucks me, the more my body slides toward him. My ass is fully over the edge, but he isn't slowing to reposition me. Grasping for purchase on the comforter, I fist the material and press my shoulders into the mattress. By the time his fuse blows, I'm nearly jack-knifed, my knees practically kissing my shoulders.

Gareth slides his arms under me and lifts me back onto the bed before he pulls his spent cock out of me. "Hold your legs there. I'll get a towel."

"Hurry. I'm not actually a contortionist."

He drags the tip of the towel over my stomach teasingly. "I've not even begun to contort you into all the positions I have planned."

"I don't think I'm going to be in town long enough to check off your whole list."

"You'll have to come back soon then. Or maybe I'll come to you next time."

There can't be a next time. I should be gone already. I'm fucking this up nine ways from Sunday. And the longer I stay, the more fucked up I'll be when I leave.

He climbs onto the bed next to me. "Sit up against the headboard." I slide back and stretch out my legs, and he hands me a pillow. For what? To cover myself? Seeing the confusion in my eyes, he moves it where he wants it: over my arm just above my waist. A pillow for his head. My arm positioned to cradle him there.

"It's not just your pussy I want sore when you leave me." He stretches across my lap and squeezes my breasts together. "I want these gumdrop nipples raw, throbbing under your clothes, keeping me on your mind."

"I could be here for weeks still. Never said when I was leaving town."

"That flight reflex is lit up like neon in your eyes, sweet girl. Just want to be sure you think of me after you're gone."

God, I shouldn't love this, holding him against me while he does things to me with the singular intention of making me hurt in the end. It hurts now, even as his warm soft tongue rolls over my nipple in between the nibbling and fervent sucking, but I don't want him to stop. Not yet.

I look down at him with my nipple in his mouth and his jaw moving as he sucks on me as if I'm actually nursing him, and I know how sore I'm going to be when he pulls off, but I still don't want him to stop.

Letting my head fall back, I close my eyes, try to imprint this moment somewhere it will stay forever. As if I'd ever be able to forget him touching me in any way.

When Gareth is satisfied that he's left a lasting impression on my nipples (and he has—he definitely has), I dress, and let him drive me to my car.

He asks for my number as if he's some guy I just met. This is all so strange, but I give him my number, and then he kisses me like we're ending a date.

"If you have clothes with you, you can come in and change in the bathroom in the lobby. It's private, no multiple stalls."

"No, everything's in my hotel room."

"Where are you staying?"

"The Monarch."

"Do me a favor? Go see Shandy this afternoon. I'll text you her address."

"Gareth, we literally haven't seen each other since I moved away."

"Please. I really think it would do her good to see you."

"Send me her phone number, too. I'm not going to show up on her doorstep out of the blue."

"Thank you." He kisses me again, and so help me, I would attempt to negotiate with terrorists if he asked me to.

"What am I supposed to say when she asks where I ran into you?"

"Tell her the truth, Jewel. In the building where you had to meet with your father's attorney."

I sit behind the wheel of my car with cold air blowing on my face and watch him go inside, wondering if I can really do what he's asked. Gareth makes it sound so easy, so logical. Of course, I should go see Shandy while I'm in town. Why wouldn't I?

Everything I've done with him since last night plays out in my head like a movie. And now I'm supposed to go be his daughter's long-lost best friend? Sit at her kitchen table and meet her kids? Pet her dog? Drink her wine?

Fuck. I do want to meet her kids. And pet her dog. And I could really use a glass of wine with an old friend. If only I could roll back time and do all those things before I sat on her dad's face, let him tie my hands behind my back and shove his dick in my mouth, felt his belt across my ass, attacked him, spent the night in his bed, fucked him again, and then engaged in a little breastfeeding kink to put the cherry on top of the whole batshit banana split. Christ on a corn chip, I should probably be seeing a whole team of psychiatrists for even considering this.

I send the text before I chicken out. She responds right away. Gareth was right. She'd love to see me, says I should come straight over. I pull out of the parking lot and head back to my hotel room to change clothes and do something with my hair—to brush my teeth, rinse and spit the taste of her father out of my mouth.

SHANDY OPENS the door with a baby girl on her hip and two little boys peeking out from behind her legs. "Jewel the Fool on my doorstep. Oh, my God! Why do you look the exact same?" She mouths "bitch" so her little ones can't hear it and I laugh. This feels right. Feels like coming home to a sister I haven't seen in far too long.

Damn if Gareth wasn't right.

Until my mom found me, Shandy felt more like family than anyone.

Jewel the Fool. Only she ever called me that. Not an insult, but a term of endearment earned by my wild, foolish antics. I was a reckless girl. We both were. But I was the fool. Some things don't change.

She ushers me inside and introduces her brood. "This is Maclaren. He's seven and has recently decided he goes by Mac because when you are seven, you can name yourself." She winks and turns to the younger boy. "This is Sterling. He just turned three and is making excellent progress in teaching the cat to talk." Another wink. With a hoist of the chubby babe on her hip, she says, "And this is Arden, the baby sister of the bunch and the last of her kind. We. Are. Done."

"Wow, such grown-up sounding names for such little people."

"Yeah, well, when they're actual grown-ups they can thank me for giving them dignified names, unlike Shandy." She motions for me to follow her beyond the foyer.

"Aw, I still love your name."

"Easy for you to say with a name like Jewel." She says my name all breathy, and if I didn't know Shandy and her sarcastic nature, I might think there was a hint of actual resentment in her voice.

"The fool," I add, following her into the kitchen. We both laugh.

She gives the boys each a snack bar of some kind and directs them to the sun porch. I watch them happily skip off through French doors to a miniature table and chairs where they sit obediently. No hesitation, no considering even for a moment that they could do something other than exactly what they were told. It doesn't seem natural for kids to obey so instinctually.

They must get it from their father because their mother would've dashed outside, cartwheeled across the yard and into the pool just to prove that she could. Snack bar be damned.

I catch myself redesigning her kitchen in my head. It's not efficient, no triangle between the stove, fridge, and sink. "Who was your builder?" I ask.

It's opportunistic but they could use some design input, and I'm never without a business card. I could drop one off while I'm in town, maybe charm my way into a meeting. This neighborhood is all custom builds, and how any high-end builder would offer this ridiculous kitchen plan, I don't understand.

Anyone who would put a dishwasher on the opposite wall from the sink needs me. Desperately.

Shandy beams when she realizes I'm taking in the layout. "Well, Hargrove built it, but I redesigned the kitchen. A perk of being the wife and daughter of architects. I knew a couple of guys." She laughs. "Anyway, I didn't want my house to be so cookie-cutter, you know? Especially not the kitchen. Go ahead, give me your professional opinion. I've stalked you a little over the years."

She shrugs. "This is your thing, right?"

"It's got your name all over it. Unique, for sure." I force a smile.

"My dad hates it. I think Connor does, too, but this house was a condition of our staying married at that point, so I got whatever I wanted. Power of the pussy and all. You want wine?"

At this point, I'm not sure if she's winking or has a nervous tic that causes her eye to spasm. If having a pussy is the only power she has in her marriage . . . I shake my head to clear the pity that's rising like smoke.

Granted, I haven't met Connor, but I'm sure he's aware all women have that attribute. "Yeah, wine would be great."

She passes Arden to me as if it's the most natural thing in the world. I reach to take her and try not to grimace. She's a beautiful baby, but I don't do kids. They can sense it, too. This baby is definitely going to start bawling the moment Shandy turns her back.

I brace for the screams. But she doesn't cry, just clamps her little dimpled hand around my necklace and examines it with wide eyes. She doesn't yank on it or pull my hair. Oh, God, she's sweet.

If Shandy had to have a whole passel of kids before she hit thirty, at least she got good ones, I guess.

When the glass hits the table in front of me, I try not to cringe. It's a sparkling rosé. As far as wines go, this is like finding black licorice in a box of truffles for me. And my stomach is completely empty. No good can come of this. Shandy lifts her glass to toast, and I raise mine as well. Not the first time I've toasted a terrible idea.

"To girls like us," she says.

Well, fuck. Now I have to drink it. That was our toast way back when—careless girls too damn young to be toasting with anything other than juice or soda. But alcohol was readily available in both our houses, and we had plenty of unsupervised time to drink as much of it as we wanted.

Vodka was our drink of choice back then. Pour some out, replace it with water. Repeat as the opportunity presents itself. Jesus, we thought we were so smart. We had one thing right: we were the same kind of girl.

Not anymore though. Our lives couldn't be more different.

"We were such idiots," I say after taking my first sip. "It's a wonder we made it to adulthood."

"I wasn't so wild after you left," she says. "My mom was thrilled to be proven right."

"Right about what?"

"That you were a bad influence."

Yeah, well, I fucked her ex this morning. He doesn't say hi.

"I never knew your mom felt that way. She was always so nice to me."

"To your face. She felt sorry for you because your mom was dead, or so we thought at the time, anyway."

"Yeah, we did think that. For what it's worth, I wasn't so wild after I left either. Maybe we were bad influences on each other."

"I missed you like crazy for sooo long," Shandy says with a wistful tone in her voice, which seems odd, delivered so hot-on-the-heels of the coldhearted shit she just divulged about her mother's opinion of me.

I was a kid. A neglected kid, who looked at that woman like a surrogate mom. I loved her. I'm feeling a lot less guilty all of a sudden about her husband's hand between my legs while she slept off her Ambien down the hall.

"My whole life felt like a bad reality TV show for a long time after I left here, but my mom was the absolute best. She got me therapy, loved me through it, taught me how to survive life's nasty curve balls. I should've never been taken from her and lied to, but I am so damn lucky I got to have her back in my life. She was an amazing mom, a genuinely good person, nothing fake about her. What she showed the world was who she truly was."

Dig intended.

"Was? Is she dead for real now?"

I nearly choke on my wine. "Yeah. For real now."

"Shit. I'm sorry. I didn't mean to be insensitive." She takes Arden back, and snuggles her as if holding her baby will somehow soften her, atone for her callousness. "I'm sorry about your dad, too. His death, I knew about."

"His death would've been hard to miss around here, I'm sure. Mr. Big Shot."

"What did his company actually do? I never knew."

"That makes two of us."

"Whatever it was made plenty of money. You must be set for life now. Not that you weren't always."

"I don't care about his money. Or his death. My mom died in debt, still trying to pay off what she spent looking for me. The world's a better place without Donovan Alexander in it. Cheers to the sorry fucker's cold corpse."

I down a gulp of the sweet, fizzy wine.

Shandy covers Arden's ears.

Oh, please. She's like six months old.

"Sorry. I'm not used to being around kids."

"It's hard to believe you're not married. Jewel Alexander, most beautiful, most charming, most enchanting smile, prettiest eyes. Was there a superlative you didn't win?"

It hits me that maybe this isn't Shandy's first glass of wine today. "None of those were actual awards. I won Friendliest Classmate in the tenth grade. That was it. And it's Jewel Carrigan now."

"Oh, you were friendly all right." She laughs and winks. I kind of want to pluck her eye out at this point. "Hell, we were all just jealous. You had everything anybody could ever want *and* you got all the attention? It was a lot to take. That's why everybody always talked so much shit about you."

"I had nothing, Shandy. My entire life was a lie. Who talked shit about me?"

"Alexa, Teagen, Kara, pretty much every girl in our class. I took up for you as much as I could, but sometimes you were hard to defend. Christ, you had Luis Vuitton luggage in middle school, Jewel!"

"Because my dad decided that's what his daughter should have. I didn't even know what Luis Vuitton meant. I wanted Hello Kitty. Did everyone who I thought was my friend back then actually hate me?"

"No one hated you. We all wanted to *be* you."

"No, you didn't. Trust me. I was alone in the world, Shandy. My friends were all I had. Or thought I had."

"Sure, us and boys. So many boys. I guess the quality of dick has probably improved with age, huh? Still plenty of variety though, am I right?"

She doesn't bother to cover Arden's ears for any of that. Hell, she dings the kid's head with the base of her wine glass as she brings it to her mouth.

"Actually yeah, I've had some incredibly high-quality dick recently." I down the last of my wine. "It's been great catching up, but I have to go."

"No, don't leave. I didn't mean to be an ass. Come on. Have another glass. Tell me about your life."

"I really can't. Thanks for the wine. You have beautiful children, but you should consider a nanny. Seems like you could use some help."

"Whoa, that sounded bitter. Are you a little jealous of me now?"

"No, Shandy. Jealousy is not at all what I'm feeling. And your kitchen's a fucking travesty."

I see myself out, and blink away tears as I back off the driveway and turn up my music. Loud, I need it loud.

My emotions are tangled and my stomach is in knots. Even the few things I thought were sincere about my life here were lies. A speed limit sign flashes a warning at me as I exit Shandy's ostentatious neighborhood.

Sure, like driving twelve miles over the limit is what I most need to be cautioned about right now. Lucifer himself couldn't warn me off what I'm about to do. The accelerator submits under my foot.

Gareth looks up, startled when I burst into his office. He's not alone. And that won't do.

"Jewel, hi. Um, this is my son-in-law, Connor."

My stomach settles a bit. *This* is Shandy's husband? Dad bod, premature balding he thinks he's covering with that shitty combover, and I don't need to guess what he's compensating for with that blinged-out watch. *Dazzle them with diamonds.*

Compared to her father, her husband is a basset hound standing next to a wolf.

"Hi," I say. "It's nice to meet you, Connor."

"Ah, the infamous Jewel. The pleasure's all mine." He eye-fucks me on the way out of Gareth's office, but I know he's going to text Shandy to let her know I'm here the moment he's in the hall.

Good boy, Connor. Go fetch your wife's attention however you can.

Gareth's expression is wary. "How was your visit with Shandy?"

I stare at him without answering.

"She's miserable, isn't she?"

"Entirely." I reach back to lock the door.

"No. Not here. Too many eyes and ears, but I know what you need, sweet girl." He grabs his jacket from the back of his chair. "Let's go."

CHAPTER SEVEN

I SNEAK a glance into Connor's office as Gareth pauses in the hallway to answer a question for a baby-faced young man, who I assume is an intern.

That's really Shandy's husband. Wow.

If someone had shown me a lineup of eleven guys, and asked me to guess which one she'd married, the one I'm looking at right now wouldn't have even ranked in my top ten choices.

He's talking on his cell phone, huddled over it like he's whispering. In his own office. Behind a closed door. He looks up and catches me watching him.

I narrow my eyes into what I'm sure must be a piercing stare, one I'm sure he'll return when he sees Gareth.

I'm clearly leaving the office in the middle of the day with his boss. Who also happens to be his father-in-law. His livelihood currently depends on the man at my back. Connor should probably tread carefully.

I, on the other hand, can throw caution to the wind, which is something I haven't done in a very long time. Well, prior to yesterday, anyway. I didn't realize how much I've missed Jewel the Fool.

She might not be good for responsible times, but she's been responsible for plenty of good times.

Gareth starts walking again, and I follow him to the elevator. An elderly couple shuffles aside to make room for us when the doors open, and I notice the man is holding a folder emblazoned with the logo of my father's attorney's office.

I want to tell them they should entrust their legal affairs to someone more scrupulous, but with my luck, that sleazebag lawyer is probably related to one of them, so I keep my mouth shut. I've stirred up enough familial drama for one day.

Not that I have any interest in backing away from Gareth to keep from creating any further family strife for him, but what we do when we leave here will stay between us.

EXCITEMENT SIZZLES DOWN MY SPINE WHEN HE TAKES THE EXIT THAT LEADS to the lake. He's taking me back to where this all began—to finish what we left undone ten years ago.

My pussy gets wet just imagining what it will feel like to walk back into that house. Warmth settles over my shoulders like fate has dropped a blanket on them.

Of course, we should do this. We have to. Not going back there together would leave loose ends for both of us.

We need to fuck at the lake house to write the ending to that eternal fantasy, but God help me, I know I'm going to be almost-but-not-quite-eighteen again the moment we walk through the front door.

And still-seventeen-year-old Jewel was a mess.

But maybe that's who I'm meant to be in this scenario. I'm not sure he's changed much since that night. I've gotten a glimpse behind the façade of Mr. B and seen the real Gareth Branson now.

He is absolutely the man I met in that dark kitchen, through and through. My pussy clenches, and I realize that I want it to be exactly like it was back then, to relive it in all its depravity, but see it through this time.

Why does the lake have to be two hours away? I shift uncomfortably in my seat, craving his fingers inside me, his hot breath on my neck, and his raspy voice tickling my ear as he tells me what a good girl I am.

I reach for the volume on the stereo and turn it up so I can hear something other than the throbbing of my pulse.

He takes a strange exit. It's too soon, and this isn't the way.

According to the time, we should still be about thirty minutes out from the lake. Unless this is a new shortcut, I may have misjudged his intentions entirely.

My breath catches in my chest, and I've never wanted to be wrong so badly in my life. Neither of us has talked much since we left his office, and the nervous energy in his car could fuel a nuclear reactor.

As if he has a radar sensor for my anxiety, he looks over and smiles, takes my hand, and says, "We're still going there, but I thought maybe we could both use a drink first."

And just like that, he's put me at ease. Or as at ease as I can be around him while I'm jonesing to be back in the only kitchen I never think about changing, to let it take us back in time while he does dirty, bad things to me—a wild young girl who thinks she's far more worldly than she is.

Me, not knowing what I don't know. Him, experienced and knowing what he's doing is wrong, but not giving a damn because all he can think about is sinking his mature cock into my tight little taboo pussy. Jesus, my nails are leaving crescent moons in his soft leather covering door handle, but I can't unfurl my fingers. A drink could only help right now.

How does he intuit another person's needs like that? Is it just with me or is he this perceptive with all women?

After he exits, he takes a side street and winds through an industrial park, pulls into a spot near a detached building at the very back. Every other structure looks the same: beige stone with a glass entrance door and garage bay doors on the same side. But they're all attached in sets of four to six, except this lone smaller one.

This one faces a different direction as well. It sits at an angle, a position that shields most of the parking spots near it. The entry faces a greenbelt and the door is steel. No windows. No garage doors.

"This is a bar?" I ask.

"It's a private club." He cuts the engine and unbuckles his seatbelt. "But yes, they have alcohol."

My fingers go slack and fall from the door handle. Gareth didn't just bring me to a strip club, did he? I mean, I've been to a few, but never one in such a strange location. One with no sign.

"What the hell goes on in a club with no sign?"

"Things no one inside wants advertised."

He says it in that domineering tone that makes me quiver, but right now, it also makes me hesitant to get out of the car.

"We can leave anytime you want, sweet girl. But I think you might like it here."

I unbuckle my seatbelt because I need to find out what's inside, and I know he isn't going to tell me. If I want to know, I'll have to enter and see it for myself.

It's dark inside, but surprisingly well appointed, like walking into a different world. Dark wooden floors with deep burgundy velvet curtains that soften the hard walls. There is a reception area behind glass, but no one sits in the chair, probably no need at this time of day. There is a sign-in kiosk on this side of the partition.

I step up to the screen, but hesitate, not sure I want to document my visit. This could be some sort of private jazz lounge based on the décor so far, but it could also be anything else at all.

Gareth taps in *Sapphire*. I smile. He knows how to navigate this. After my alias he signs himself in as *Viking*. My smile widens, but falters as quickly. Is that a friendly jab at my safe word or a warning of what I'm walking into?

Is this. . .?

No, it's the middle of the day. In the middle of nowhere.

Polished ornate, double wooden doors block us from going any further. Gareth presses *enter* and a new screen comes up requesting a membership access code. He types *GB 4008* in the first space, tabs to the second one and taps out *Happy Hour*.

A buzzer sounds, and I hear the locking mechanism release the doors.

"If you have a membership, why did you sign in with an alias?"

He steps past me to hold the door open, but before he introduces me to the rest of the club, he holds me in his gaze for a beat. His sailfish eyes are vibrant even in this dim light.

"Those are our names for today's visit."

My knees soften, but I accept his invitation to enter, savoring the reassuring warmth of his hand at the small of my back. The interior boasts more velvet, dark wood, and dim light.

Leather booths line the walls, all facing a circular empty stage in the center of the room, a small lamp with a beaded lampshade on every tabletop. There are no other people.

Where are the dancers or musicians or whoever performs here? Where is anyone? Gareth presses me forward.

Another set of double doors leads us into a long hallway that runs the length of the building. Seven single doors greet us from the back wall. They're all painted a glossy cream color and adorned with a small black placard featuring curlicue script, each one flanked by flickering sconces like a scene from a Gilded Age hotel.

Gareth leads me to the middle door and presses a gold button located below the placard.

I read the script: *Happy Hour.*

A guy who looks like he could do bicep curls using train cars opens the door and announces us. "Viking and Sapphire have joined the party."

I'll take that drink now, thanks.

As if she read my mind, a gorgeous pony-tailed brunette wearing lingerie I'd like to steal appears in front of me with a martini. I take the drink and whisper, "Thanks." She nods and begins unbuttoning my top.

I don't bother protesting because it's apparent from the state of undress around me that taking another step fully clothed isn't an option for me.

Gareth sips his own martini, watching this woman undress me and carefully place my shirt and jeans on a hanger. She has me step out of my sandals and stores all my belongings in a huge armoire in the corner.

I attempt a sip from my glass but gulp instead. Thank goodness sexy underwear is my default because there are three other women in the room, and they all got the memo.

The men remain fully dressed. All they've shed is their shoes, neatly resting on a rack like soldiers in formation.

One of the suited men steps toward me and brazenly trails his fingers over the swell of my breast before reaching underneath to feel the weight of it.

The bouncer guarding the door says, "This room is now closed. The party is full."

Everyone else seems to know exactly what this announcement means. They break away from their partners and start to mingle—which entails a lot more communicating via touch than words. The man in front of me circles my nipple through my lace bra with the pad of his thumb.

"You are exquisite."

The woman whispers something into Gareth's ear, steps back, and bites her bottom lip in anticipation of his response. He cocks his head at me. "You good with this?"

I'm not sure what he's asking me. Am I good with that woman blowing in his ear or this guy groping me? And then it hits me.

It's both. People are pairing off, and nobody is looking to dance with the one who brung 'em. I've had a threesome, more than one. But this is beyond that. This is a room of four couples all swapped out in full view of everyone else. But there are no beds. How does this even work?

Gareth raises his eyebrows. "We can go if you'd rather."

"Exactly what happens if we stay? Exactly, Gareth."

"We adjourn to other rooms, some more private, some less. In this case, we would all four go to another room together. I'm not leaving you."

That makes me feel better, but I'm still not certain I want this. I look at the guy marveling at how hard he's made my nipple. He is attractive, a little younger than Gareth. Fit. He isn't unappealing, but this is so far from what I was expecting.

So far from the lake house.

Why did he bring us here?

Is it a message? *Don't get attached.*

I went to his office yesterday to fuck him and get over him. But fucking him had a different effect. He knows. This is a layer of protection for us both.

"Yeah," I say. "Why not?"

We make our formal introductions. The deft hand on my tit belongs to "Damien," and the lithe legs itching to wrap around Gareth belong to "Athena." The goddess smiles and takes Gareth by the hand. We all walk back into the hallway, and everyone but me seems to know exactly which room we're meant to enter next.

I float along with them, numb. Until the next door opens.

Oh. This room is. . .equipped.

CHAPTER EIGHT

DAMIEN TAKES my hand and leads me to a padded bench with grips on the sides and cushioned lengths to support my knees and lower legs, should I choose to bend over this thing, to rest my weight on it and let him punish me. A spanking bench.

This may be my first visit to a sex club, but some things are self-explanatory. He watches my face for a reaction, his own expression questioning.

If I were to bend over, it's not him I'd want behind me. But there's no way I'm letting him handcuff me to the wall either, and I don't even know how to begin to climb into that suspended mass of ropes and restraints in the corner.

Gareth is watching me, his expression as curious as Damien's. He isn't asking Athena which apparatus she'd like to engage with. She's on her knees in front of him, unbuttoning his pants, preparing to suck his dick.

I give Damien a gentle shake of my head and he doesn't ask why or attempt to coax me into trying the bench.

"I just don't want another man to spank me right now," I blurt.

"Then I won't spank you," he says. His smirk is a little too arrogant for any setting other than this one, but I wouldn't find him attractive here if he weren't giving off such dominant vibes.

With Gareth so close, I know I don't have anything to fear.

I'll be safe if I drape my body over this bench and let this sexy stranger do things to me while Gareth watches. While we watch each other.

Oh, fuck. This is twisted, but the sudden rush of warmth between my legs is all the encouragement I need to give in to it.

I reach back and unhook my bra, let the straps fall down my arms, and drop it to the floor. Damien's smile heats up. He steps closer and lowers his head to kiss the nipple he played with earlier. When he draws it into his mouth, I draw in a pronounced breath and weave my fingers into his hair.

I'm still sore there from Gareth.

Damien releases my nipple and kisses his way back up my chest and neck until he's facing me. He nods at the bench, his expression questioning if I'd like to try it, anyway.

It doesn't take much imagination at all to realization the bench can be used for much more than spanking.

I mount the narrow, padded supports, lie down, and hold on to the handles, keeping my eyes on Gareth and Athena. She's sliding her mouth slowly up and down his erection, and his eyes are glazed like any man's when he's having his dick sucked like that, but they're fixed on me.

The bench has a slight forward angle that leaves me no choice but to arch my lower back and jut my ass upward. Damien's hand massages my cheeks, and I remember the bruises there. All the more reason for him not to spank me.

He lowers his hand and cups my pussy before he begins toying with my thong, pulling it aside and letting the backs of his fingers graze my swollen tenderness. His hand skates feather-light figure eights over my seam, and I desperately want him to part it and slip his fingers inside me.

My trickling juices coat his skin, and he spreads them over me, creating an effortless glide when friction is what I want. I rock my hips, but he denies my attempts to increase his pressure.

Gareth's eyes are blue flames. The glimpse of his engorged cock when Athena pulls off and teases the head with her pink tongue stokes my burning need to feel it inside me. His cock, her tongue, Damien's fingers—fuck, anything would be better than this torture.

When I thrust my pelvis back to increase Damien's access, he slowly slides two fingers into me and begins to leisurely probe, knowing that's not how I want it, teasing me, no doubt savoring the torture he's inflicting.

God, he could spank me at this point, anything to light up my sensors. Some form of actual relief. Athena is throating Gareth's perfect dick right now, and I need Damien to take a fucking cue already, to give me more, too.

He takes his hand away completely, and I want to cry out, but he drops to his knees and replaces it with his hot mouth. And then he gives me his fingers again, faster and harder this time while his tongue teases my clit.

I relax into the contrasting sensations, and he sucks on my clit to bring me back into a heightened state of tension.

My eyes meet Gareth's, and I can see how close he is to coming inside Athena's beautiful lips while her partner's strong tongue ignites my nerves and sets me teetering on a narrow edge. Our gazes lock and we come together on the mouths of strangers.

And I am so done with this man on his knees between my legs. I want to push him off me like shedding a jacket when the sun comes out. Gareth walks toward me, and Athena and Damien connect as if they couldn't care less that we no longer want anything to do with them.

"I don't think they need us anymore," Gareth says as he helps me up from the bench, making it clear he isn't going to fuck me here.

We're going back to the car, to the lake house to finish a more crucial scene. He picks my bra up off the floor and hands it to me. I stumble into my jeans while he refastens his. My shirt buttons don't seem right. I think I've missed one somewhere but it doesn't matter. I'm dressed enough to walk out of here.

If it was truly his plan to have this place put a layer of distance between us, it didn't work. Not for me, anyway. I've never felt a deeper connection to any man than I do to him right now.

But I'm not kidding myself; I know exactly what this is. And I'll walk away clean when we're done. We're just not done yet.

I turn the music up loud in his car, and he doesn't object. He drives fast, and my heart beats faster. Everything is up-tempo and pounding.

My misaligned buttons don't slow Gareth down once he slams the front door behind us. He rips my shirt open, sending more than one of the plastic discs flying, ensuring this shirt will never be buttoned correctly again.

The shirt follows its buttons to the floor, and my bra lands on top of it. I kick off my shoes, and he peels my jeans down my legs before he walks away from me and sits at the kitchen table.

It's still daylight out but all the lights inside are off.

Showtime. I understand.

I walk softly into the kitchen, keeping my eyes averted as if I don't know he's there, watching me, drinking in my bare legs and the curve of my ass as I reach for a glass, the silhouette of my hardening nipples—not even covered by thin fabric this time—when my hand touches the cold metal of the faucet handle.

His heat shrouds me as cool water spills over my lips, the first sip nearly drowning me when his arms encircle my waist and his hand glides inside my panties. We slip so easily into the roles of our past trespassing selves, our moral compasses recalibrated by trepidation and raw lust.

He gasps when he finds me waxed bare and wet, increasingly wet as his fingers move inside me. I hold the glass suspended in mid-air, forget my thirst in the wake of his touch.

No words pass between us for fear the spell will be broken. I'm her again, no need to act. All I have to do is close my eyes and the room goes dark. It's late at night. We are quiet. I am quivering. He is everything.

I come on his hand, swallowing the moans and whimpers that want to escape, the sounds that could get us caught and ruin everything, staying silent like the good girl I was for him back then.

Except this time, he doesn't yank his hand away like my clit has become a lit candle, doesn't let a flurry of shame swirl between us until we're both cloaked in it and scurrying in different directions—him back to his drink, and me down the hall to the twin bed where I won't sleep, not for the remainder of that night or ever again.

But this is the juncture where the fantasy pivots, and we don't have to worry about anyone else because we are all alone this time.

This is where the past meets the present and he is allowed to fuck me and I know how to fuck him, but proceeding right now won't erase the history that binds us.

I had it all wrong in my head. We can't rewrite the past, can't pick up where we left off because that ended for us before it ever began.

That ended . . . because that was never anything more than a moment in time.

But this, what we're doing with each other now, it's not a continuation of that. It's something else entirely.

As if he can read my mind, he picks me up and carries me toward the hallway.

"You're not the ghost of that girl anymore, Jewel. She's haunted me here for a long time, but it's you, this grown woman in my arms that I need to fuck in this house, not her."

"I know. But I was her again, for a little while. For long enough. If you carry me out of this kitchen, I promise it won't be her fucking you, and I won't see you as him. Take me to bed, Daddy."

I grab the doorjamb as he attempts to carry me into his room. "No," I say. "I used to fantasize about being in your bed here, but I was lying in a smaller one while I did it."

I jerk my head down the hall, toward the twin beds of Shandy's room.

"We relived our defining moment in this house, Gareth, and if I'm ever back here again, we'll fuck in your bed. Hell, maybe we'll go for round two in here today, but first, I need you to take me there. I'm not asking you to pretend I'm her. I very much want it to be me enjoying what she never got."

"Jewel, I don't know if I—"

I twirl a curl on his chest between my thumb and forefinger, turning my eyes up to him. "Look at me and tell me you never thought about sneaking down this hall and slipping into that bed with me."

"Thank God you grew up and came back around." He changes course.

"Second chances are a fucking gift."

"Goddamn right."

He lowers me to the bed, and tears his clothes off. I lie with my legs open, thrumming with desire for him, fully me in the present tense, but there are whispers of the girl I left here ten years ago, lingering in the stale air of this room.

This is where we fuck away the last vestiges of her.

His hesitation is gone entirely when he lowers his body over mine and sinks his full length deep into my hot wet heat. I clench to hold him inside a second longer, and he groans as he withdraws, his strength overpowering mine.

I moan at the pressure when he buries his cock in me again. And then he picks up his pace, creating that hot friction I crave, despite the fact that I'm flooding the sheet beneath us. He grasps both my wrists in one of his hands and pins them above my head.

"You are such a good little cockslut. Tell me what you are."

"Daddy's dirty little cockslut."

"Fuck yes. Pull your knees up, sweet girl. Show me that tight ass."

He doesn't release my hands, so I bend my knees and rock my hips forward to lift my legs for him. His thumb pulls my arousal down to coat my asshole and circles a few times. I anticipate the initial sting of his thumb stretching me there, but instead, he presses two fingers inside at once.

The fullness is overwhelming. I shudder beneath him, and he shifts his weight to drag his cock along my clit, shortening his strokes to rub against it continuously. His grin is wickedly self-assured, and entirely justified.

There is nothing quiet about this orgasm for either of us.

I have to fight not to doze off with my head on his chest. He tugs a section of my hair as if he knows I'm drifting.

"Let's take a shower and grab an early dinner before we head back," he says. "I skipped lunch. I assume you did as well."

"I did. But I need to lie here for a while longer. Shower without me."

"I'll start without you. You've got two minutes."

I wait for him to get in the shower before I climb out of bed and cross the room. The white paint inside the frame of the closet door still bears our stats. Two columns, one crowned with an S and the other with a J, both boasting a series of hashmarks to tally our lake hookups. We always used the same pink pen.

The gel ink has dulled and turned darker, giving the illusion of rust around the edges. I take a thin marker from the desk and increase the count on my side. Blue ink. Vibrant and distinct.

Gareth calls out for me to join him. He says I better hurry, so I drop the marker back in the plastic cup, but I leave the closet door ajar. It's the closest I can come to telling her.

Someday she'll notice the new entry and wonder. Maybe she'll think one of her kids made the mark, not realizing what they were adding to.

I will always know exactly what's been altered. And I'll never regret a moment of it.

"Jewel! If I have to call your name a third time, you're going to regret it!"

Never.

CHAPTER NINE

I'm seriously struggling to stay awake on the ride back from the lake house, full from dinner and exhausted from the emotional and physical releases this day has ripped from my body.

Part of me wishes we'd stayed the night at the lake, but Gareth probably has to be in the office early tomorrow, and I definitely need to get back to my hotel room and refocus on reality.

My head lolls against the headrest, and I replay the last forty-eight hours. How did I ever believe having him touch me again would help me get over him? How did I not know exactly what would happen?

I guess I never really thought I'd get the chance to find out. There's safety in fantasies.

"What are you thinking about?" he asks.

"How totally off the rails everything has gone since I came back here."

"You really think so?"

My phone buzzes, and when I pull it from my purse, the name on the screen makes me forget Gareth's question. "Jerry, hi. How are you?"

The words I hear on the other end wake me up completely, bring me back to reality in an instant.

"Yeah, sounds great. I'll get a flight out tomorrow." One glance at Gareth and I know he's not pleased about what I've just said. "Sure. See you then."

"Tomorrow, huh?"

"That was a restaurant owner I've been trying to work with for months. I thought they'd gone with someone else. But the job's mine, apparently. I've got to fly to Philadelphia for a few days. Shit, this is short notice. I don't even have time to go home and repack."

"Book your flight and then see where you're at. Maybe you'll have time to do some shopping in the morning. But for what it's worth, it seems like what you've worn the last few days would be fine. If you need to wash clothes, you can do it at my place."

"That would be great, actually. Thank you."

"Anything to keep you close a bit longer."

He drives to The Monarch instead of his office so I can pick up my car. "Grab your stuff and check out. You're spending your last night in town in my bed."

As much as I pride myself on being independent and living by my own rules, his tone when he speaks to me like that, as if he has the ultimate say, liquifies my strength. And nothing within me wants to change that.

"Okay. I'll just be a few minutes."

"I'll be right here." His grin is self-assured in a way that should infuriate me, and it does to some degree. But it's really myself I'm mad at, not him. I should've never gotten in the elevator and gone up to his office, should've never played out that *what if* because there was another one right behind it, and another and another. . .it's like living inside a set of nesting dolls with him.

What lies inside this scenario, and what will happen after that one, and then what comes after this one? I can't imagine it ever reaching an end. Every shell reveals a center more intricate and interesting than the last, and I need to force an end to it.

I will. It will be easier once I'm gone. This job came along at exactly the right time. I'm just a flight away from returning to normalcy, or my version of it, anyway.

Housekeeping has left my hotel room pristine. The bed is ready for the next guest. When I checked in, I was anxious and bitter. Checking out, the bitterness is subdued, but the anxiety has just found a new catalyst. Progress?

Gareth steps out of the car when he sees me returning. He puts my suitcase in his trunk, and then he kisses me like we've been apart for days.

Is this what it would be like if I came back here instead of going home? We are out in the open for anyone to see, and he doesn't care, just keeps kissing me like he wants to devour me right here in this parking lot, like he can't get enough.

We.

Like we can't get enough.

Jesus, what is wrong with me? Coming back here is not an option. I should've never deviated from my original plan: tie up loose ends and walk away clean.

I break the kiss, struggle against his effort to keep my mouth on his.

"That pedestal might be higher than you thought," I say. "Take me to your place and let's burn it the fuck down and end this for both of us."

"Oh, sweet girl. We can't fuck this away. In fact, every time I fuck you, it's going to have the exact opposite effect."

"Why are you so goddamn arrogant?"

"Because I'm right. Get in the car. Let's go home."

HIS KITCHEN GLOWS AS WE STEP IN FROM THE GARAGE. THE SOFT UNDER-cabinet lighting is soothing. In the living room, a floor lamp emits an amber halo over a leather chair in the corner. It's a perfect chair for reading, or napping.

"You like that chair?" Gareth asks.

"Yeah, it has a welcoming vibe. Your whole house does, actually."

"Good, because you are most definitely welcome here. Take your clothes off and put them in the wash."

"I was just going to wash the ones in my bag."

"Are you disobeying me?" His eyes hood, but his jaw tightens and his shoulders draw back.

I bite the inside of my bottom lip and tell myself not to play along, to break this bond that's intensifying way too fast, right here and now. Deny him.

He unbuckles his belt and whips it free of his pants, folds it over and snaps it taut. The crack of the leather makes my decision for me.

I walk back from the laundry room naked. He's still holding the belt. My nipples harden when he nods at the chair in the corner. I move to the chair with my back to him, expecting to kneel on the cushion, but he stops me and turns me around, pushes me to sit down in the chair instead.

"Lean back and put your arms over your head."

I do as he says, and he climbs onto the chair with me, his knees caging my legs. He pushes my hands back farther behind my head, weaves the belt between my wrists until it's tight and secures them around the lamp pole. This binding isn't symbolic.

I can't get out of this one.

"I'll be right back. Don't go anywhere."

His wink in the dim light sparks goosebumps over my body as if he's tossed them onto me like confetti. His open-concept floorplan provides a clear view into the kitchen, so it's no surprise when he returns holding a cup of ice in one hand, and a taper candle and lighter in the other.

But watching him approach holding those items has me squirming already.

"Relax, sweet girl."

"I don't think you actually want me relaxed."

His laugh is ominous. "You always were smart."

He sets everything on the side table to free his hands, and touches an ice cube to my bottom lip, traces my mouth with it.

"And gorgeous. Your hot mouth is melting this ice on contact."

Cold water drips down my chin.

"You want to play, don't you?"

I lick the ice cube. "Yes, Daddy."

He slips the ice inside my mouth, and I hold it on my tongue while I watch him light the wick.

"You look so pretty in candlelight," he says, bringing the candle close to my face. Water trickles from my mouth, and I shiver as it drops to my chest.

"Was that cold?" he asks, tipping the candle to let a thin drip of hot liquid follow. The wax forms a soft bead when it meets the cold water on my skin. Gareth rights the candle to let more wax liquify.

I take a deep breath in anticipation of where he'll spill it next.

My spine undulates like a wave, and he presses his palm flat between my ribs.

"Are you nervous?" he teases. "Lie still like a good girl. You know I'm not going to hurt you. Don't you?"

I nod, keeping my eyes on the wax quivering at the lip of the candle. His gaze follows mine, and he twirls the taper, letting a tiny trail of wax run down the sides to his fingers.

And then he pours the rest over my left nipple. My pussy clenches along with my jaw.

"Relax, Jewel."

He rubs ice over the wax to harden it for a few seconds, and then he pours again, starting higher this time so it meets unprotected skin before it joins the first layer. The melting ice cube slides down my body and comes to rest between my legs.

Gareth looks at what remains of it and smiles. He bends down to take the ice into his mouth, and a bit of wax splashes between my breasts.

His cold mouth closes over my bare nipple. He peels the wax off the other as he sucks on this one. Then he pulls his mouth away and coats the nipple he's just chilled with hot wax. The one he's freed from the wax stings in the open air.

They're both still sore from all the attention he's already given them, but this is a different kind of discomfort, so fleeting, and the desire to feel it again is immediate, to determine which is better (or worse): the ice or the heat.

He recoats my nipple and lets the residual melted wax dribble between my ribs, creating a sparse trail down my abdomen.

"Open your legs."

He repositions himself between my knees so I can't close them.

The ice on my pussy is intense, a cold burn, and knowing the level of heat that will follow causes my legs to shake. He teases my clit with the ice before running it back and forth between my seam to let it melt more rapidly.

Holding what's left of the cube against my clit, he stares into my eyes. I'm not sure how much longer I can take this cryo-torture, but I keep my eyes wide open and fixed on his. It's impossible to be completely still.

A spritz of wax hits my stomach when I shiver. My spine bows in response and sinks me deeper into the chair, but there is no escape, not with my wrists restrained above my head. I'm defenseless, aside from the word I'm not ready to say.

He would definitely take it as a compliment right now. I'm unclaimed territory, and this is him, conquering me, but I can't relent completely.

The challenging look in my eyes is all I have to throw back at him right now, but I'm sending it with all the obstinate resolve I possess.

You can't break me.

Hot wax engulfs my clit, and fire and ice duel across my nerve endings as it runs down over my tender skin. My spine reverses and arches, my body rising up in search of relief—or something more.

Gareth blows out the candle and sets it on the table. He peels the wax from my nipples, off my torso, and moves down to roll it gently off my pussy, leaving my clit encased and throbbing.

He knows what I want, but I arch my back again, anyway.

"What's wrong, sweet girl? Does it ache, having your clit trapped, so it can't swell and harden like it needs to?"

I nod.

"Do you need me to free that, too?"

I know he isn't going to do it yet, but I nod again, fast and desperate, my back still arched.

"Relax for me," he says.

My spine slowly unfurls and reconnects with the leather, one vertebra at a time. I spread my legs wider and Gareth nods.

"That's a good girl." He retrieves the candle from the table and holds it sideways with the wick facing him. I think he's going to light it and let the wax fall onto me as it melts this time, but he doesn't reach for the lighter.

He places the base of the candle at my opening and presses it inside me. It isn't large but the cold hardness of it makes my muscles tighten around it.

"You trying to take that away from me?" he teases. "This hungry little snatch will latch onto anything, won't it? You're so eager to be fucked, aren't you, sweet girl?"

I feel my face flush, and suddenly, I'm her again. He's undone me and rewound time, found territory that's unfamiliar to me, something new he can be the first to do to me. For the love of fire, he's fucking me with a candle, and I can't stop rocking my hips to aid the effort.

"Take the wax off. Please, Daddy."

His teeth scrape away the soft cocoon and graze my sensitive skin. He spits the wax aside, and brings his mouth back to my warm clit.

I can sense how hard it is under his soft tongue. I'm far too wet now for the thin candle to provide any friction, and I desperately need to feel more. Gareth pulls the taper free of my pussy and drops it to the floor. He replaces it with his fingers and sucks hard on my clit.

Shocks jolt through my body as if it's pulling electricity from the lamp. But it's all him. He's the reason every receptor in my body is twinkling like Christmas lights as my orgasm ebbs.

I'm his. And there's not a damn thing I can do to refute it. He unbuckles the belt, frees my wrists, and carries me to his bed.

I wake to Gareth's hand sliding between my thighs. "Rise and shine, sweet girl."

He presses his erection against my thigh.

"Feels like one of us has already risen," I say.

"I told you I always want you sore when you leave me."

He rolls on top of me, and his hard cock slips inside my pussy with no resistance. But the expanse of him provides plenty of friction. I'm already sore, and his strokes sting, but my juices rush at the burning memory of last night's fire and ice session.

"There's Daddy's dirty little cockslut." His hot breath tickles my ear and sends a chill down the back of my neck. "You like it when it hurts don't you, sweet girl?"

"Yes." Oh, God. I've never been fucked this hard in my life. "Harder, Daddy. Hurt me. Fuck me sore so nobody else can touch me."

He erupts into an orgasm that locks his entire body, and the he collapses on my chest, panting and laughing.

"Oh, you wicked, dirty-sweet girl."

I play with his hair at his temple. "Just the way you like me."

"There is no denying that, for either one of us. What time's your flight?"

"One."

"I'll put your clothes in the dryer while you shower."

"So domestic."

"I have my moments. But don't tell anybody."

"Actually, I got up after you fell asleep last night and put some stuff in the dryer and hung up the things that needed to air dry. But if you want to fold it all up for me, that would be great."

"I'll make coffee." He kisses me on his way out of the bed, and I watch him walk away. I'm afraid this is going to hurt one day. Bad.

And in a whole different way than it's hurt for the past ten years. I try not to catastrophize, but old habits are hard to break.

I direct Gareth to my rental car and he parks right next to it, even though he has his own parking spot much closer to the door.

"I'd take you to breakfast if I didn't have to be available to sign off on so much stuff this morning. Come up with me, and I'll order food. We can eat in between interruptions."

"I don't want to be in the way while you're trying to work."

"You won't be. I want to look at you until the last possible minute. Indulge me."

The blinds to his office are closed, so we can't see beyond them to what awaits us inside. Gareth opens the door and gestures for me to enter before him.

I see her first.

Shandy stares at us from behind her father's desk.

"You fucking whore," she says. "Did you honestly think you were going to get away with it after Connor saw you here? Or was that the point?"

Gareth slams the door behind us.

"This is not your husband's office. It's mine. This whole goddamn company is mine. And who visits me here, or anywhere else is none of your business. Get the fuck out of here. Now!"

"How long has it been going on?" she yells. "How long have you been fucking my father, Jewel!"

She spins in the chair to focus on Gareth. "Is she the reason you and Mom split up?"

"My marriage to your mother and the dissolution thereof are none of your business. And my relationship with Jewel damn sure isn't. Take your hysteria and your paranoia and go home."

Shandy stands and swipes her forearm across her father's desk, sending plans and pens flying.

"I fucking hate you!"

She launches the stapler at her father's head. It sails past him and through the glass between him and the hallway, hangs trapped in the now broken blinds.

I stand frozen in horror.

Veins bulge on the side of Gareth's neck. He charges at Shandy and drags her from his office by her wrist, marching her down the hall to Connor's like an insolent child being corralled after a public meltdown.

There is more yelling, but I can't make out the words because my hearing is as blurry as my vision. Everything is spinning. Oh, God. Again, I should've never come up to his office. None of this ever had to happen.

People mill around in the hallway, whispering and stealing glances at me. They all disburse suddenly, so I know Gareth is heading back to his office.

He holds me close, one hand pressing between my shoulder blades as if to shield me, and the other massaging the back of my neck like he can knead the last five minutes from existence. His fingers are clenched just tight enough to create a sensory memory that will still be squeezing my subconscious when my plane lands in five hours.

Phantom palpations spread to other parts of my body like his touch carries an echo. "Sit down. I'll order breakfast."

"Gareth, no. I can't stay."

"I understand. I will make this up to you, Jewel, I promise. Let me know when you're safe in your hotel room."

"I will."

"This will all blow over," he says with the conviction of a man accustomed to creating his own reality.

"It won't, but that's okay. I don't actually care what anyone else thinks, not even her."

His goodbye kiss is a scorcher, and if I could afford to miss this flight, I'd already be naked, maybe just to spite Shandy.

She wants to know about my relationship with her father? Oh, I'd love to let her hear distinct details right about now. I pull away from him and stare into his eyes for a moment, absorb the searing heat. That, along with the memories of the past few days, will sustain me for the next few.

And I will most definitely be back. Maybe I am still a foolish girl at heart.

I feel his gaze on me as I walk away, slip through his door, and close it behind me, loving that he watched me go. The hallway is clear. Everyone is tucked away in their own offices, but they're probably all actively texting each other about the morning's drama.

Connor's door is closed, but his blinds are open. Shandy sits on his lap with her head down in despair. He's nodding along to whatever she's saying.

Keep walking. Just keep walking. Let it go. Don't do it. Do not. . .

I gently turn the knob and push the door open, step one foot inside his office, just far enough to get their attention and say, "Your dad loves you, and I'm sorry for the way this makes you feel, but I'm not sorry about anything that has happened between me and him. You can hate me over that for as long as you need to, but don't start believing it's the reason you're miserable. I won't own that, and I wouldn't want him to, either. Face your shit. For once in your life, stop being a follower and blaming other people when you don't end up where you want to be. Save yourself, Shandy."

I'm calmer and more in control of my emotions than I've been in two years as I slide behind the wheel of my rental. No lingering anger at all. Gareth wrecks me and puts me back together stronger.

This is how obsession grows, I think, but then, no.

The obsession has been growing for a decade; this is where I meld it into armor, learn to keep myself on the safe side where the arrows can't land.

CHAPTER TEN

After a full flight with a crying baby in front of me, a panting dog behind me, and an overly friendly woman in the seat right next to me, who absolutely would not shut up no matter how curt my responses, I'm drained.

I skip the long line at the car rental counter and order a ride. The driver doesn't ask any questions about my two requested stops before the hotel: a liquor store and a drugstore.

Thankfully, he isn't chatty at all. The only question he asks is what kind of music I prefer. When I half-jokingly suggest anything loud and angry, he smiles and nods.

"Been there," he says, and then he cranks up the volume. I make sure his tip reflects my gratitude.

My room smells fresh, and everything seems new, even the mattress. After this day, a recently remodeled hotel room feels like a gift.

Shandy has sent me half a dozen text messages. Her tone has become less threatening and more desperate in the last few. I can't give her what she wants, though.

She can ask why and how all night long, but I'm never going to be able to answer those questions.

I open the bottle of wine from the liquor store with the cheap folding corkscrew the clerk threw in for free, followed by the bag of chocolate chips from Walgreens with my teeth.

Dinner of champions.

I text Gareth like I promised. He calls in response. Because he's one of those people.

"Hey," I say through a mouthful of melting chocolate. A swish of wine between my cheeks like mouthwash enables me to go on. "How are you doing?"

"Am I interrupting your dinner?"

"It's fine. I can talk and eat."

"I assume Shandy has probably been sending you messages, too."

"A few. Now that I've had a chance to calm down, I kind of get where she was coming from. In all fairness, she was expecting to confront you alone. But then I walked into your office, and she lost it."

"Doesn't excuse her behavior."

"No, but it's understandable why she freaked out."

"She's not a child. What time is your meeting tomorrow?"

"Nine. Picking my car up at eight."

"You didn't rent a car tonight?"

"Too tired to drive."

"I guess I shouldn't have sent you off so exhausted. How was the flight?"

"Not the best."

"Okay, I'm going to let you get some sleep. I want you well rested when you come home."

"That place hasn't been home for me in a very long time."

"Things change. Sleep well, sweet girl."

"Goodnight."

I turn on the TV, and search for the worst trash-fire reality show I can find. The wine gets better with the second glass, and I remember I have a protein bar in my purse that I'd intended to eat on my flight.

This night's looking up.

Shandy sends a new text: *Please just go away and never come back. You're fucking toxic. You always were. My dad deserves better.*

Time heals. She's obviously going to need a while longer to process this.

A FEW DAYS OF WORK IS EXACTLY WHAT I'VE NEEDED. THIS IS MY REAL LIFE, staying busy has saved me more than once. Measurements, floorplans, material samples, ordering, arguing, thinking on my feet—proving myself. Exceeding expectations. Outpacing demons.

I *absofuckinglutely* love every minute of it. But there is not enough coffee in the world to clear my head this morning. Thank goodness for digital boarding passes because I have no idea what happened to the paper one the kiosk spit at me when I checked my bags.

"Cart coming through!" The driver beeps his horn as he yells the warning to part the shuffling crowd.

Oh well, I was probably going to spill coffee on myself at some point today, anyway. That's what I get for thinking I could wear a white sweater in an airport.

All I want right now is to get on the plane and sleep for three hours. My phone buzzes, and I fish it out of my purse without breaking stride, knowing the text will be from Gareth before I even see his name.

Gareth: Are you at the airport?

Me: Headed to the gate. Spilling coffee with every step.

Gareth: See you at baggage claim.

Me: You really don't have to pick me up. And you definitely don't have to come inside.

Gareth: But I am. We're going to the lake for the weekend. See you soon.

I should protest, tell him I need to get back to my apartment, take some time alone to sort things out. But the second I read "the lake," my core heats up, and my shoulders melt like wax.

Mmm, wax. The memory of him and that candle is going to burn forever. With nothing more than two words in a text, he's got me hot and dripping like a walking, breathing candle, though I'm not exactly mastering either task at the moment—more like a stumbling, winded candle.

Shit, I should've hopped on that cart. I drop my phone back into my purse and take another gulp of coffee.

The pilot's voice is deep and soothing, possibly more so because I'm barely awake, but I swear he should narrate audio books. Dirty, dirty audio books.

"We've got clear skies ahead, folks. Sit back, relax, and enjoy the flight." I lower the window shade and follow captain's orders.

T minus two hours and forty-eight minutes to Mr. B. Dirty, dirty Mr. B.

THE MIRRORS IN AIRPORT BATHROOMS ARE FROM HELL. OR MAYBE IT'S THE lighting. It's got to be one of those things because I can look fine before I leave for a trip, but as soon as I look into a mirror in an airport bathroom, I look like I just clawed my way out of a grave.

I take a deep breath and remind myself it's always like this. That haggard corpse in the mirror is not what Gareth will see. God, if he knew I was giving myself this silent pep talk right now, he'd die laughing.

The urge to grab another coffee is strong, but I resist it. Gareth is probably waiting, and I stared at myself in the bathroom mirror long enough that my bag might be on the carousel already.

Why am I so nervous? It's only been a few days since we've seen each other, and I've been fine. Busy. Working.

Not obsessing over him. Much.

I see him before he sees me. Damn, he looks good.

This feels good, coming home to him.

Home.

Fuck.

CHAPTER ELEVEN

SOMEHOW, I manage not to hit the floor when the word "home" invades my psyche the moment I see him standing at baggage claim. My steps settle, but my thoughts scatter. His broad shoulders fill out that shirt like it was custom made for him.

Maybe it was—how would I know? That's just it. I don't know him. Not really. I only know the man I've built him up to be in my mind over the past ten years.

That man was created from a fantasy.

I mean, granted, I know some things quite well: how he fucks, how he speaks, how he kisses, how he feels, how he smells, how he tastes, how he teases. . .how he commands. Dozens of women probably know him like that.

It doesn't make sense to trust him the way I do, but yet. . .

My whole body seizes, and I can't take another step. I don't trust *anyone*. And it's batshit backwards to trust someone you don't truly know. But I guess he and I have never done anything the traditionally *right* way.

He turns his head toward me as if my realization has beckoned his attention. He smiles, and I want to know everything about this man.

My feet move again, and it's all I can do not to run to him.

His arms lock around my waist, and my feet abandon the floor at the intensity of his hug. I feel like he could crush me, but I know he won't. My pussy clenches when I breathe in the first whiff of his cologne or aftershave or shampoo, whatever creates that alluring combination of warm spices and fresh air.

"Welcome home," he whispers, his voice tickling my ear. "Let's grab your bag and get on the road. I'm very much looking forward to doing depraved things to you for the next forty-eight hours."

"You have no idea how good that sounds to me."

"I'm going to find out when we get to the car." With that, he walks toward the tumbling bags on the conveyor and grabs mine without me having to point it out. He pays attention to details I never notice him noticing.

He's parked in the garage near the end of an aisle. There are closer spaces. I assume he chose this spot to avoid door dings from other cars. He quickly disabuses me of that innocent assumption.

We're barely inside the car before he says, "Show me how wet you are."

"Not here."

"Right here. Right now. Undo your pants and coat your fingers with your sweet pussy juices. We're not leaving this parking garage until I've tasted you."

The things he says would hit different coming from anyone else's mouth, and I might literally hit them for saying it. But his voice and those eyes . . . all I want to do is obey, be his sweet girl.

I unbutton my pants, slide the zipper down, and slip two fingers inside my pussy and slide them in and out a few times for him before I bring them up and rotate them so he can see how they glisten.

He taps his lips with two of his own fingertips. "Bring them to me."

His hot mouth claims my fingers, and his playful tongue makes me shift again, roll my shoulders.

"I love when you're needy," he says. "Take your pants off."

An objection materializes in my head, but it fizzles. This is harmless fun. My sweater is long enough to cover my underwear. To anyone looking into the car, I could be wearing shorts under it. All they'd see would be bare legs.

I kick off my shoes and shimmy out of my jeans.

"You don't really think I'm going to let you keep your panties, do you, sweet girl?"

He holds out his hand and I squirm.

"If you don't want to comply, I have no problem taking them forcibly, but that spanking you've already got coming won't wait for the lake house if I have to do that. You either slip those pretty panties down your beautiful legs and give them to me, or I'm getting out of this car and walking around to your side. And once I open that door, your dignity won't be taken into consideration."

I don't really think he'd physically humiliate me in public like that, but I absolutely believe he knows how much the threat unnerves me, and turns me on. He takes my peach lace thong and hangs it from his rearview mirror.

"Classy," I tease.

"Pull that sweater up and put your fingers back in your pussy. Play with yourself where I can see."

"Anyone can see."

"Lucky them if they do."

"After we're out of the garage."

"You are feeling awfully brave today. Challenge me again, and I'll take the sweater and the bra that I already know matches these."

His fingers twirl my dangling panties and I want those fingers inside me, not my own.

And he's right. I am feeling brave today. "You finger me first. And if you do a good job, I'll do what you want for the rest of the ride."

He laughs. "You know I'm going to punish you later for challenging me like this. But if that's what you want."

I'd only meant for him to reach his hand over the console but he leans his entire upper body across it instead and stares into my eyes, making us much more conspicuous than a couple sitting in their respective seats, possibly just having a conversation.

No, now it's glaringly obvious we are doing something more than talking. Though his filthy mouth is definitely delivering as he parts my seam and strokes me, taunts me, but refuses to plunge a finger inside and give me all of what I want.

"Mmm, this tight, tasty little pussy is sopping. Did you think of me while you fingered yourself in your hotel room?"

"Yes."

"Did you think of anyone else?"

I hesitate, swallow, and try not to look away from him.

His laugh rolls out with a sinister satisfaction. "For such a bold girl, you get shy quick. How many men do you fantasize about at once? What's the number that hits your sweet spot, sweet girl?"

"Three."

His smirk is skeptical as he pushes his fingers inside me. "Three, huh? That's your number? You want three?"

These three fingers, yes. Fuck, yes. I nod and close my eyes. His thumb circles my clit and the twitch in my core becomes the epicenter of a quake. I gush on his hand, and when I open my eyes, his are stormy, just the way I love them.

"God, I want to pull you out of this car, bend you over the hood, and fuck you for the whole world to watch. You're lucky the possibility of children walking through here has occurred to me."

"Not to mention the possibility of security seeing us."

"That show would be the highlight of their day." He presses his fingers to my mouth. "Clean my fingers so I can drive us out of here."

When I'm done, he hands me napkins from the console. "Sorry, this is all I've got. Unless you want me to use my mouth to clean you, too."

"I most definitely want you to use your mouth, but not here. I'll make do."

I reach for my panties when I'm done, and he gently slaps my hand away.

"You know better."

When I pull my sweater down to cover my bottom, he shakes his head. "No, not that either. Sit your bare ass on my seat."

My sweater bunches at my lap and falls around my hips, anyway. It doesn't matter that I've pulled the hem up this high. No one can see anything. When we reach the highway, he takes his cock out and tells me it's my turn to lean across the console.

As a teenager, the thrill of maybe getting caught was the catalyst for a lot of things I probably shouldn't have done. Not everything changes about a girl when she grows up. I'm not down to fuck in a busy parking garage, but *head on the highway*?

Yeah, that's a thrill I'm still willing to chase.

I get on my knees, facing him, and lean down to lick the precum from his tip, grateful my sweater is long enough to cover my ass so no one gets the money shot through the passenger window. Until Gareth grabs a fistful of it and yanks it up to my midback. If I protest, I know he'll make good on his earlier threat to take it all the way off.

And the truth is I don't hate this, the not knowing if anyone is watching and how much they can see. I swirl my tongue as I sink my mouth down over his cock. He groans, and I say a quick prayer he keeps us between the lines.

His dick pulses in my mouth, and I know he's close, but then the car slows, and I feel us exit the highway.

Please tell me we are not being pulled over.

I attempt to lift my head, but his hand forces it back down. The car changes direction again, and then once more before we abruptly come to a stop. Gareth pulls me up by my hair. All I see are trees on either side of a narrow, unpaved road.

"Where are we?" I ask.

"Somebody's private property would be my best guess."

"You're going to get us shot."

"No." He grins. "They might shoot me, but they'll keep you."

"Way to be reassuring."

"Get out."

"No way."

"The longer you delay, the greater the chance we'll get caught."

"I'm not bending over the hood out here."

"Because I care, I'll give you the option to climb over the seat. Make your choice by the time I get to your side. Whichever seat you're in will determine which door I open and where we go from there, but I can't wait any longer to fuck you."

He gets out and starts walking.

The door opens and cool air rushes over my bare skin. He shoves his pants and underwear down his thighs. As soon as he frees it, his erection lurches like it's dowsing for pussy.

"When was the last time you got fucked in the backseat of a car?"

"So long. Before I moved away."

He pushes me onto my back and spreads my legs with his knee, leaving the door wide open behind him. "Sounds like too long to me."

His first thrust is hard enough that we both gasp. Every stroke that follows is hard, too. Backseat sex. Just like I remembered it, but with the added bonus of an orgasm.

"Hey," I say between uneven breaths. "You wanna know the first time I came in the backseat of a car?"

"You trying to flatter me?"

"No, just being honest."

He laughs. "Honesty's good."

His face clouds as soon as he's said it, but he tries to cover it with another smile. My own smile falters and he sits up, reaches for the console and brings out more napkins. His movements are methodical.

"We're going to go to the club for a while. I want you to see it on a Friday night. It's a whole different place on the weekend."

"Okay, sure."

He feels so far away all of a sudden. I want to know why he retreated like that, but I know he won't tell me, or won't tell me the truth, anyway.

I take my panties from the mirror when I get back in the front seat, and he doesn't say anything. He starts the car and all the intimacy we've just shared is swept into the past.

No matter what happens at the club, there is nothing that'll make me forget the way his face changed at the word honesty. I tell myself I'm making too much of it.

There is nothing he could've lied to me about because I haven't asked anything of him.

GARETH PUTS THE CAR IN PARK, BUT HE DOESN'T KILL THE ENGINE.

"Jewel," he says, my name rolling off his tongue too slowly and in a guarded tone, as if he's about to say something I might not want to hear. All I can think is if he's about to end things between us, this is a weird fucking choice of locations.

"Have you looked over all the paperwork for your dad's holdings?"

"No. I sent everything to my attorney. She said she'd be in touch next week sometime. Why?"

"We need to talk about one of them. Gardon, LLC."

"What's Garden, LLC?"

"Not garden. Gar. Don." He stares through the windshield, straight at the front of the club.

"You cannot be saying what I think you're saying." I shake my head, never taking my eyes off him, waiting for him to clarify before I get carried away. But he doesn't say anything, so I swallow hard and ask the question outright.

"Is Gardon an acronym from Gareth and Donovan? Please tell me I'm jumping to conclusions here and you and my father were not goddamn business partners, Gareth!"

"Only in this venture. Nothing else." He makes direct eye contact, but his hypnotic blues are caged in cold gray steel right now.

"What is it? What exactly does Gardon do?"

He looks puzzled, like I've spoken in a language he's never heard before, and then his gaze flits from my face to the building and back again, and I get it. That's why he looked toward the door before. He was trying to tell me without having to say it. This.

This is what it is.

I grip the door handle. "You're telling me I own this place?"

"No, sweet girl. I'm telling you *we* own this place."

CHAPTER TWELVE

"Say something, Jewel." Gareth's tone is soft and cautious, and I hate it.

"Viking."

"Something else."

"Buy me out. I'll have my attorney work on Gardon first. We can communicate through her, and I'll sign as soon as the docs are ready."

"Do you at least want to know how much money this place makes before you bail on it?"

"There isn't a number high enough." My eyes burn, but there are no tears verging. They ache like I've been walking through the desert for a week with no sunglasses. Like I've stared directly into the sun.

"How long were you partners?"

"The club is only two years old. We'd never worked together before. There was a need for a place like this here. We saw a void in the marketplace, and we filled it. It was a risk that paid off, and it keeps paying. And I'm not sorry."

"Didn't ask for an apology."

"You and I would work well together, Jewel. And you deserve this."

"To be kept in the dark? Lied to? That's what I deserve?"

"I never lied to you. Stability and security. That's what you deserve, and this place can provide it."

"My job provides plenty."

"Not like this, sweet girl."

Don't you fucking dare call me that right now.

"I thought you brought me here the other day to put a layer of distance between us, because we were getting too close too fast, but that wasn't it at all, was it?"

"No, I don't want distance between us. I brought you here because I wanted to tell you before you saw it in black and white, but I couldn't make myself do it. I was afraid you'd walk away, and I wasn't ready to let you go. I'm still not, but I couldn't keep being a coward about it. When you first stepped into my office, I thought this was why you'd come. To confront me about being partners with him. When I realized you'd come for an entirely different reason—."

"That's what you thought? When you looked at me and said you thought I'd come to confront you, I thought you meant about what happened in your kitchen when I was seventeen. If I'd known about this, I'd have never come to see you."

"Christ, I thought you were going to confront me about all of it, Jewel."

He runs his hand through his hair like he might pull it out by the fistful.

"We're here. Might as well go inside. If you still want nothing to do with it after you see the club on a Friday night, I'll buy you out."

"Why him, Gareth? How?"

"I ran into him in a similar place in Vegas. What are the odds, huh?"

I think that was an attempt at a joke but I'm not laughing. I glare at him, and he sighs before he goes on.

"Obviously, we recognized each other. A few weeks later, I got a phone call. He requested a meeting, showed up with market research, numbers, and projections. He'd done his homework, or had it done for him, but the information was solid. It made sense from a purely business perspective. We were not friends."

"He didn't have friends. All he cared about was owning and earning, and I was just another possession. His dirty fucking money protected him from every consequence he should've paid for taking me, for what he put my mom through all those years, for the trauma I suffered when the truth came out."

"I know. This is a legitimate business. I promise."

"Seems to me like I'm going to be a rich woman when the ink dries, regardless. Why would I want to keep this place and deal with the headaches of owning a swingers' club? Fetish club? Sex club? What's the preferred term, Gareth?"

"Maybe you'd like owning this place. Maybe you'd have good ideas about how to improve and expand it."

"Or maybe it's in trouble financially. Maybe you can't actually afford to buy me out."

"I understand why you'd be skeptical, but you have access to all the financials. And I can absolutely afford to buy you out. I just think you should know the potential here before you make that decision."

"Fine. Fuck it. Let's go in."

He follows close behind me, but I make sure to stay a few steps ahead, too far away for him to rest his hand on my neck or at the small of my back.

The tension in my body is unlike any I've ever dealt with before.

No better place to find a release than this one, right? He wants me to enjoy the club, I will.

There is a woman behind the glass checking guests in tonight. Two guys who look like bouncers stand behind her, and one is posted at the second door.

Dear God, the level of testosterone is stifling in this small space. Gareth's hand brushes my hip, and I flinch. The woman behind the glass recognizes him, smiles and calls him sir.

Sir Lying Shithead.

A woman and man in front of me have to sign a waiver of some sort before they're given a keycard.

When the inner door opens, I catch a glimpse of a woman on the circular stage. She's bound to something, but I can't tell what it is before the door sweeps closed again. The bouncer reopens it as soon as Gareth steps forward.

No words are spoken but respectful nods are exchanged between them. Exactly the way people treated my father.

The bondage show has a pretty full audience, and they all seem to be enjoying it, but seeing a woman wearing a blindfold only exacerbates my anger. I know she's wearing it willingly, and it's not keeping her from knowing that the man who is touching her is harboring a giant fucking secret that would knock her whole world off its axis, but it still feels like a personal taunt.

I want to climb onto the stage and unmask her eyes. And then shove it down Gareth's throat until he chokes on it.

We don't go through the same door we took last time. He leads me to the back corner of the room and through a door that is camouflaged with wallpaper to look like a continuation of the wall.

It requires a keycard but the woman up front didn't give him one; he already had it in his wallet. The door opens into another room, smaller and without a stage. There is a bar along one wall and couches and chairs grouped throughout, some hosting people already engaged in sex acts.

I walk to the bar and order a Gordons and tonic. Gareth walks up behind me and his reflection in the mirror nods at the bartender. An answer to a question I've missed.

"What was that?" I ask. "Did he just ask you for permission to serve me? Like you fucking own me, and I can't have a drink unless you say so?"

"I'm the owner. He was checking to see if I wanted my usual. That's all."

"Well, apparently, I'm an owner, too. Maybe someone should let your boy know that a dry G&T is my usual."

"Hey," Gareth's tone loses all softness. "You want to be a brat to me right now, that's fine. But you will be polite to the people who work here. He's doing his job. If you'd like me to announce your role, I'd be glad to introduce you."

"No. There is no point in making things complicated for your employees."

"*Our* employees."

"Stop."

A silver fox sidles up next to me, and even if I wasn't spoiling to piss Gareth off, this guy would've pulled my attention. Close-cropped hair and beard, broad chest, Superman arms, and tight abs under a black tee. Tight ass under black jeans, too. Ex-military, I'd bet anything.

Not really my type, but he'll do nicely for my purposes tonight.

Hello, Daddy.

Gareth leans in closer. "You're a grown woman. If you want to fuck him, go for it."

"Are you testing me?"

"Who's testing who, Jewel?"

I step closer to the stranger, touch his bicep and trail lightly over his pirate ship tattoo.

"Hi," I say. "I'm Jewel."

Gareth's grimace doesn't go unnoticed in the mirror.

Black t-shirt guy sizes me up, and nods like I'll do for his purposes as well. "Apache."

Shit. I forgot people don't use their real names in here.

"Let me guess, helicopter pilot?"

He smiles. "Clever girl."

Right, like that was a hard code to crack.

"Should we sit?" I ask.

"We should do something."

Before I take a step, Gareth has a hold of my upper arm, and he's pulling me away.

"Get your hands off me." I try to twist out of his grasp but he's too strong.

He pushes me through another door, and we are alone in a short, narrow hallway. His body presses me into the wall, and his hands pin my wrists above my head. His eyes blaze, and he opens his mouth like he's about to yell but he stops before the words fly. Kisses me instead.

It's an aggressive, angry kiss, and he's hurting me everywhere he's touching me. I hold stone-still, refuse to kiss him back, act as if he's having no effect on me at all.

"You want to hate-fuck me?" I ask. "Is that what you want?"

"I'd be out of luck if I did, seeing as how I don't hate you."

"That's okay. I hate you enough for both of us."

"No, you don't. You might wish you did, but you don't hate me, sweet girl. And if you're going to try to fuck away your emotions right now, it's not going to be with somebody else."

"I'm a grown woman, remember?"

"Oh, I am well aware."

"We're business partners." I attempt to push him away. "This is unprofessional."

"File a complaint with HR."

He picks me up, tosses me over his shoulder, and carries me to the end of the hall where he yanks open another door that takes us into a stairwell. The door slams behind us.

As soon as he sets my feet on the ground, I try the doorknob but it's locked. "Are we trapped in here?"

He shrugs.

I start up the stairs.

"Where are you going?" he asks.

"To the next level so I can get out of here."

He follows me, laughs when I try the second-floor door and find it locked, too. "Huh," he says. "I guess we are trapped in here,"

"Use your card."

"On what? You see a reader anywhere?"

"I'm not going to spend the rest of the night arguing with you in a goddamn stairwell, Gareth."

"That's not at all what I had in mind." He closes the space between us in two steps and presses his forearms against the wall, caging me between them.

His face is inches from mine, and the heat waves radiating off his body are practically vibrating the air.

"Look, it's been a hell of a week," I say. "But it's over. I'm over all of it. Over you, finally."

"Is that right?" He lowers a hand and slips it under my sweater. His palm feels like a hot coal when he presses it flat between my ribs. He bites my bottom lip as his scorching hand roams under my bra, and my traitorous nipples knot at the proximity of his touch. When his thumb grazes one, I grit my teeth and lock my jaw.

Jesus fuck, that was way too much of a reaction for a woman who is unbothered by him. Not like he didn't already know I was bluffing, but damn.

He nuzzles my neck, and his husky whisper sends a shiver all the way to my core.

"You have the most perfect nipples I've ever seen. Ever touched." He pinches hard, and I reflexively shoot up onto my toes. "Ever sucked. We both know what happens when I suck on them, don't we, sweet girl?"

His other hand cups my pussy through my jeans. "So warm. Is it already happening? Are you already soaking your panties for me?"

I squeeze my eyes shut and refuse to play along. He pushes my sweater up and lowers his mouth to my nipple. My hands are free, and my fingers want so badly to weave into his hair, to pull him closer.

I truly hate him now. Hate him for making me want him. Hate him for being able to play my body like an instrument he's mastered. "I hate you," I say through gritted teeth.

"There is nothing about you that I hate," he says. "I don't hate looking at you. I don't hate the way you smell." He inhales against my chest. "And I damn sure don't hate the way you taste. You wanna end this? Let's bring it full circle then, end it like it started."

I don't put up a fight when he takes my jeans off, but when he starts to take my panties off, I shove hard on his shoulders. "What are you doing?"

"Removing these so I can lick your pussy one last time since you're so hell-bent on running away. Do you want me to kneel or do you want to ride my face to make it authentically the same as the night you came to my office?"

"That's not how this all began." I turn and put my hands on the wall. "You stood behind me and fingered me. Just like at the lake house ten years ago, you got me off with your fingers first."

"No. I was behind you all those years ago at the lake, but you were facing me in my office. Your gorgeous tits were bared to me. Take off your sweater." I want this too badly to care about being angry at him.

I've got the rest of my life to be pissed off. Right now, his eyes are slicing through me, and I want to feel everything with him one last time so I can burn every second of it in my memory.

The moment my sweater hits the floor, his thumbs hook under my bra straps, and he yanks them down.

"My memory doesn't falter where you're concerned," he says. "I remember every detail."

Oh, God. He's right. This is exactly how we were in his office. He pushes my thong aside and strokes me.

He groans into my hair, and tears leak from my eyes.

"Be rough with me, just like you were then. Make it hurt."

He pushes two fingers inside me, but he isn't rough. His fingers sink deeper, and he takes his time, sliding them back and forth until my hips are thrusting in time to his rhythm, seeking more.

When he finally touches my clit, I gasp.

"Stop being so gentle. I don't like it like this."

"Yes, you do," he says. "But you've convinced yourself pain maintains distance. He inserts another finger and starts to ream me harder like I've asked. My fingernails curl into the skin at his shoulders

"What you've not yet realized is when the pain is delivered by the right hand, it obliterates distance. It fuses desires, unlocks secrets, creates a bond that running away won't break. You'll feel me in your dreams. The sting of my hand-print on your ass, the clamp of my fingers pinching your nipples after I've sucked them raw, the bruising of my teeth leaving tracks on your skin, the pressure of my cock stretching your tight needy cunt."

My orgasm sweeps my feet out from under me like a riptide. Gareth holds me tighter and closer than ever as I come down, whimpering and panting on his shoulder. Until my vision blurs and I lose control completely.

There is no screaming this time, no hitting him. I don't have enough strength to even lift my arms. All I can do is cry uncontrollably on his shoulder. Sob until I can barely breathe.

He holds on. Rubs circles between my shoulders.

"Let it all go, sweet girl. I've got you. I'm right here, and I've got you."

When I'm able to stand on my own again, he helps me get dressed. He kisses my tear-stained cheek.

"You don't have to see anything here tonight, but I want you to come back. To see what the club has to offer and talk to me about what we could add and where we could take it. Will you do that for me?"

I nod. He puts his arm around my shoulders and sends a text message. My vision is still too blurry to read it, but I hear the door unlock behind us.

We walk through the smaller room with the couches, and skirt the perimeter of the larger room on our way out. There is no one on the stage now. People are dancing and we have to weave through a group before we reach the door.

I look around before we walk outside.

My father left me a sex club. I've been chasing normal my whole life. But I wouldn't know what to do with it if I caught it.

———

GARETH DRIVES LIKE HE'S HEADING TO PUT OUT A FIRE AS WE MAKE THE LAST part of the trip to the lake house.

He flips on the lights when we walk inside, and the kitchen comes into view. I can't help but stare at the sink.

His arms are warm around my waist. "I'm thinking of selling the firm and moving out here full-time."

"You'll just run the club and that's it?"

"Renovating this place would keep me busy for a while." He brushes my hair aside and kisses my neck. "So, what do you think? Got any ideas for the kitchen?"

"Are you looking to add square footage?"

"Double."

"I could work with that."

"I think you and I are going to work very well together, Ms. Carrigan."

"Don't get ahead of yourself, Mr. Branson. You haven't seen my bid yet."

"Shoot high. I am excellent at negotiating."

I stare through the window over the sink. She's gone for good. Banished to adulthood. But right back in his arms.

Destiny, I guess. If you believe in shit like that.

"It isn't just the offerings of the club you want me to see, is it? I'm going to learn things about you there, too, aren't I?"

"Do you want to know more about me?"

"I want to know everything there is to know about you, Daddy."

"I'm an open book for you, sweet girl."

And this is how our next chapter begins, right back where we started, but with nothing to hide.

Indie Sparks lives just outside Austin, Texas where she spends her days arguing with her dog about whether or not he really needs to go outside again, and writing strong heroines whose knees go weak for cinnamon roll heroes with dirty mouths and the skills to walk the talk.

She believes steamy rom-coms are the answer. The question is irrelevant.

But before she found her footing in the witty banter world of rom-coms, she wrote things that were less humorous, and sometimes, a tad forbidden. Catching Up With Mr. B was borne of that era, and though she has long since unpublished it, and now even rewritten sections of it, Jewel and Gareth remain one of her favorite couples.

You can find all her current work and news of upcoming titles and events at: https://indiesparks.net

HANDS OFF

A Trophy Doms New York Story

Kate Hawthorne

CHAPTER ONE

NIKO

"Have a good trip," I said, fake smile plastered across my face as I closed the door to Christian and Kale's over the top brownstone home. Though, over the top was subjective, considering before Christian had hauled me halfway around the world we'd both lived and worked in an actual palace. Or rather, he'd lived in the palace and I'd worked there, hired by his oldest brother and heir to the throne, Prince Phillip. Christian was the youngest of three boys and like most last borns, had a flair for the dramatic. What had started with a daring escape from his security detail at the opera during one visit to the city had ended with a ring on his finger and everything I owned tucked into three large suitcases.

Christian had fallen in love with Kale from the start, and I knew long before either of them that our end would be in America. It wasn't the worst place to live, but I missed the smell of the air at home, like lemons and sage on the breeze. New York was smog and gasoline, and it wasn't all bad. I knew there were people who loved the city, but I'd yet to find myself in their ranks.

For Kale, falling in love with royalty had brough its own fair share of bumps in the road, me being the biggest one. It was one thing to get Christian out of the country, it was another entirely to do so without security. Hence...my relocation.

Normally, at the end of the day I would have been home in the sprawling apartment Kale had rented to keep me close but not underfoot. Tonight was different, because the two of them had gone out of town for the weekend and essentially suggested I house sit in their absence. Neither had given me much of a choice, but I quickly grew bored without my things to entertain me.

My instructions hadn't required that I stay at their place twenty four hours a day, so I made a quick check of my pockets for my keys, wallet, and phone, then twisted the knob back open. There wasn't any harm in going back to my apartment for a little while. Just enough to grab some books and some more comfortable clothes. But when I stepped onto the stoop, I ran smack into the last person I'd expected to see in New York, especially with Kale and Christian being out of town.

"Parrish," I muttered, yanking the door closed behind me and leaving us chest to chest and almost eye to eye.

"If it's not my favorite little plaything," Parrish practically purred at me, not moving away. If anything, he moved closer until my shoulder blades hit the door.

"What are you doing here?"

"I came to visit my best friend, Niko. Why else would I be in this disgusting and overcrowded city?"

I snorted, rolling my eyes and side stepping away so I could breathe.

"Well, your best friend and the American have gone upstate for the weekend," I said with a disapproving frown, "to a farm."

"A what?"

"Do you really need me to define it for you?" I asked.

The corners of his mouth turned into a gleefully sadistic smirk. "I miss spanking that attitude right out of you, did you know that?"

My cheeks burned, and I took the steps two at a time to get down to the sidewalk and away from the last man I wanted to see. The last man I'd gotten into bed with. My bosses very best friend, Parrish Bernadotte. Our relationship, or lack of, had always been contentious. Parrish came from the kind of money that only rivaled the wealth Christian had grown up with, and he had the attitude to match. He was cocksure and arrogant, never willing to back down when he felt like the outcome would be either entertaining or at the very least, fun for a while.

He'd set his sights on me before I knew a single thing about him, and it hadn't taken long for me to end up on my knees for him, tucked into the shadows of a palace alcove with a mouthful of cock and a throat painted with cum. Everything happened quickly after that, a slippery slope that often ended with the kind of teasing that should have made me mad, but only made me hard.

"I'm sure you do," I muttered.

Parrish followed me down the steps. "If Christian is gone, where are you off to?"

"Does it matter?"

"I didn't come all this way for nothing," he pouted.

"You came all this way for him," I said.

"And he's not here, so you'll have to do." Parrish slung his arm over my shoulder, and I swallowed, keeping my eyes on the cracked sidewalk instead of his stupidly handsome face.

"I was going home to get some clean clothes," I grumbled.

He knocked his head into mine, a stupid grin on his face. "That sounds terribly boring, Niko."

"Well." I shrugged.

"Has Christian ever taken you to a dirty little club out here called The Black Door?"

My cheeks burned, and I was grateful Parrish was beside me and not facing me head on. I'd been to The Black Door on more than one occasion, and I'd seen the things him and Kale did there just as many times. Kale had talked to me months ago about the kinds of things the two of them did together, the kinds of things I'd see…I appreciated he wanted my consent, that he wanted to understand how far was too far to go when I was around.

And truth be told, I didn't mind watching.

Even if sometimes watching them made me hard and I didn't have anyone to touch me…the pain of the unfondled cock sometimes felt like pleasure, and…

"It's been so long, Niko," Parrish crooned in my ear. "I haven't fucked anyone since you, and you know that pretty shade of pink you used to turn when I called you a whore? No one else looks as perfect as you do when they cry, sweetheart."

I balled my hand into a fist at my side, cursing Parrish, Christian, Kale, and the whole world under my breath.

"Come to The Black Door with me, Niko. Get on your knees for me again."

I'd never been able to tell Parrish no. I'd never *wanted* to tell him no, and I knew myself well enough to know I wasn't going to start now.

"Fine," I agreed. "We'll go to The Black Door."

CHAPTER TWO

PARRISH

TURNS OUT, the club had Niko's name on the list already and it was easy enough to get myself in on a guest pass. They did have impressive security, and I appreciated the attention to detail that would mean even if anyone behind the door saw Niko choking on my cock, they weren't going to say anything about it.

It had been so long since I'd been with a man. It felt like a lifetime since Christian had left home and taken my favorite little fuck toy with him. Sure, I liked to let Niko think I didn't care about his company, wanted him to believe I'd come across an ocean for Christian, when in reality, I would never. I loved Christian like a brother, but video chats were fine.

Niko was the one I was after. Niko and his swollen lips and round ass and his strong hands. Niko and the way he sucked my cock like we had all the time in the world, no secrets between us, just skin and sweat.

"I have to be honest." I flung my arm over his shoulders after we were inside. "I'm already hard. Can I fuck you before we get a drink."

"You're the same as you've always been," he muttered, reaching down to adjust his cock.

"You begged me not to change. Or did you forget?"

The last time Niko and I had gotten naked together, I'd said insufferably cruel and spoiled things to him. Each jab and taunt making his cock leak more and more until cum had spurted across both our stomachs.

He was so easy, so delicious.

After his senses returned, he buried his face in my neck. He didn't want to leave, not with things just finally getting started between us, but life had dealt us a blow that not even my father's rank or bank account could get us out of.

"What's your favorite thing about this club?" I asked, heading toward the bar because even though I was more than ready, Niko often needed a round to loosen up a little. It was too easy for him to get lost in his head once I started talking to him if he hadn't prepped himself with a little liquid courage.

"The drinks are strong," he said.

"Perfect."

I led him to the bar and snatched a framed menu toward us. Niko pressed in close, staring down at the piece of acrylic in my hand, a preemptively stressed out grunt leaving his throat.

"What's this?" he asked.

"Looks like a sex menu," I said, flipping it over to look on the back and finding a list of utterly indecent sex acts that had my own cock twitching to life in my pants.

"It's Naughty November," he read aloud, "Find a friend and try something new."

"Thirty things in thirty days," I said, tracing my finger down the rows of kinks the club had so thoughtfully provided. "Too bad we only have tonight."

"What?" Niko moved so quickly he almost knocked me over. I tightened my grip on the sign and grabbed his face with my other hand.

"What *what*?" I asked, pinching my finger and thumb into his chin.

"You're leaving tomorrow?"

Arousal flared hot and low at the base of my spine.

I'd really been apart from him too long. I'd nearly forgotten how responsive he was, how much he *wanted*.

"It's a guest pass," I reminded him. "One night *here*."

His shoulders sagged, embarrassment coloring his face. I released his chin and tapped my palm a little harder than he deserved against his warm cheek.

"Pick one," he rasped, tearing himself away from me and shoving the plastic menu into my chest. He flagged down a bartender and got himself a whiskey, his posture so tense I could have tied someone *to* him and he could have kept them standing tall through a good lashing.

God, I loved Niko.

Loved the way he hated himself for the things he liked.

It made things so much more fun for me.

"This one," I said after he swallowed down a shot of whiskey. He glanced over and followed my finger to where it pointed in the middle of the third row.

"Of course." He ordered a second whiskey, this time with water. He knew me and my rules well.

I propped my chin on his shoulder, lips grazing over his earlobe. "I do love to degrade you, sweetheart."

The shivered against me, leaning back so slightly that if I hadn't felt the change in his body heat, I wouldn't have noticed.

"I want another one of these, too," I said, dragging my finger toward the line that called for a hands free orgasm. "I know you can do it, in fact I jerk off at least once a week thinking about the last time it happened."

"I wish you'd never come to New York," he lied.

"Not yet, you don't," I promised, sinking my teeth into the thin skin at the base of his neck. "But you will soon."

____

CHAPTER THREE

____

NIKO

PARRISH TOOK the whiskey out of my hand, sipping at the overpriced liquor while he watched me with a fiery and dangerous expression. He'd never been anything less than trouble, taunting me and teasing me from the first day we'd met. Sometimes I wondered if taking a job at the palace had been the biggest blessing or curse in my life, and when Parrish's lush mouth burned hot against my skin, I didn't see the difference between the two options.

My affair with Parrish had started off the same as most, I imagined. And not unlike Christian and Kale's own relationship, against a wall under the cover of shadows. He'd spent weeks pushing my buttons, poking at me, calling me names and diminishing me over my job. And every night I'd gone home horny and frustrated, turned on beyond belief from all the things Parrish had spent the day spewing into my ears.

Finally, once I'd had enough, I shoved him against a wall, my forearm pressed hard against his Adam's apple and instead of fighting me off, he moaned. The asshole moaned at me, bucked his hips forward and pushed his erection into my thigh. Before I could get away, he reached down and took my own hardening length into his hand, spun us both so it was *my* back against the wall, then he made me come in my pants with nothing more than his fingers.

The next morning, he'd deliberately spilled his coffee on me and ordered me to clean up the mess he'd left on the floor. I could have called a maid, should have, but he already had the towel in his hand and he was pushing me to my knees before I could argue. Whereas he'd spent weeks talking down to me, once I kneeled at his feet, wet rag in hand, Parrish bent low to my ear and called me a good boy, the *best* boy.

I'd almost come in my pants a second time.

After I finished cleaning up the mess, he'd sent me on my way. He'd given me a two hour reprieve until he caught me in the same corridor, the same afternoon shadows, and his hand was down my pants again, fist hot and tight around my cock. Parrish whispered all sorts of names into my ear, slut being his favorite by far. Though sometimes he called me sweetheart instead and the synapses in my brain misfired completely.

We carried on like that for months until Christian fell in love and decided to move to America. Phillip sent me with him, and everything had been in a state of upheaval ever since. Christian and Kale were kinkier than half the guest list at The Black Door, and I'd ended up with an eyeful—or earful—on more than one occasion. I wasn't a stranger to the things that went on in a place like this, even if my personal understanding of it wasn't up to par with their own lived experience. Every night I had to tail them to The Black Door, I found myself resentful of my job, my status, my rank. All the things Parrish had taunted me over, the things he'd made into sticking points with the intent to get me off, they burned. Real life reminders that I couldn't have the things I wanted for myself.

I could have my apartment and my paycheck.

The rest would have to wait.

Parrish wrapped his arm around my midsection, a warm banded reminder that my time to wait was, at least temporarily, over.

"Before I make you come, Niko, I want to know why you haven't called me since you moved," he said, pulling me away from the bar and toward a small over-stuffed chair in the corner. He landed on the cushion and pulled me down onto his lap, using his feet to spread my legs apart and his arm to press my back against his chest.

"I've been working."

"You worked before," he said, "you'll work again."

"I don't know, Parrish." I closed my eyes and leaned against him, relaxing into the familiar yet somehow still cruel heat of him.

"Is it because you didn't know better?"

"What do you mean?" I asked.

"Because you left so soon, so rushed. I didn't have time to explain what I expected of you."

I curled my fingers over the top of his forearm, but he wasn't going anywhere. For as slight as Parrish was in stature, he was just as strong as me, even though I towered over him. I had more height, more muscle, my cock was thicker and longer, but it had never stopped him from dominating me in every possible way.

Sometimes, he liked to remind me of that, too.

"Look how pathetic you are," he had said to me one night, minutes after sunset. My tongue licked him from his ankle to the back of knee and he told me, *"bested by a man half your size."*

"What did you expect?"

"Do," he corrected, dragging one of his hands to the inside of my thigh. The touch was delicate and tender, and then he gouged his nails in, pinching the most sensitive skin he could find through the expensive wool of my slacks.

My instinct was to fight him, but he kept me pinned on his lap, fingers twisting the small piece of skin they'd managed to latch onto.

"I wasn't ready for things with you to end, Niko," he said it so simply, so out of context for everything our relationship had been up to that moment. I didn't know how to process the meaning, so I asked him the only five words that my brain could make sense of.

"What *do* you expect, Parrish?"

CHAPTER FOUR

I didn't have an answer.

The things I expected from Niko at home were not things he could give me with an ocean between us. Even before...we hadn't talked about any of the things we did. We just *acted,* like I'd just acted by chartering a flight halfway around the globe when I knew Christian was going to be incapacitated because I wanted Niko off duty so I could get him back into my bed.

"We can talk about that later," I told him, cupping my hand around his burning hot and hard cock. "For now there's two items on that to-do list we need to take care of."

"Then you should probably take your hand off me," he rasped.

I tightened my hold on him. "Who are you to tell me what to touch, Niko? You're nobody, right?"

"Nobody," he repeated, hips bucking off my lap.

"Nobody who matters, at least. Isn't that right?" I pulled my hand off his lap and reached for the watered down whiskey he'd ordered at the bar. Raising the glass to his mouth, I let him take another drink, then I had a swallow for myself.

He licked his lips. "Right."

I finished the rest of the whiskey so he didn't have a chance to get at it. I wanted him buzzed, not out of his mind drunk.

"Go get us some water," I told him, setting the glass back down onto the table and giving him a shove off my lap.

Niko stumbled forward, standing up and moving to adjust his erection, but I stopped him with a quiet tsking noise against the roof of my mouth.

"No," I said simply before flicking my fingers toward the bar. "Let them see how being my errand boy gives you an erection. In fact, make sure they all know."

"How would I do that, Parrish?" he asked, mouth pulled into a frown.

"I don't know." I grinned at him and folded one leg over the other, ankle resting on the opposite knee. "Why don't you tell them?"

I could see the fight in his eyes. He wanted to argue with me, but he also wanted me to get him off, and he couldn't have both. I didn't ask for much from him besides everything, and a protest was as good as a safeword for me. I watched him as he worked his jaw, then he stalked away from me toward the bar. He leaned over to order a drink, and I watched with rapt attention as he leaned closer and kept talking. Niko gestured between his legs and the bartender shook his head, giving Niko the slightest eye roll in return. I didn't imagine he was unused to that sort of thing happening. The Black Door had a clearly stated open door policy, and the staff were no exception to the blanket consent rule.

Niko returned, red faced, cock even harder than before, with a soda in one hand and a water in the other. I pointed to the ground and he went right to his knees. We might have been out of practice, but the muscle memory was real. He hadn't yet forgotten where he belonged. Where I wanted him the most. And I thought again, what do I expect of him? Of this?

"Take it out, Niko," I said, dropping my foot to the floor so he could move between my spread legs.

He set the drinks on the table and moved to my belt, undoing the leather quicker than he ever had before. Then both his hands were in my pants, desperate and eager while he fished my dick out from behind the waistband of my black briefs.

"Good boy," I praised him, his fingers gripping me tighter before loosening again. "Now suck. Do you remember how I like it?"

"Yes," he whispered, bowing his head and dragging the edge of his tongue through the already soaking wet slit of my dick.

"Then make yourself useful."

He sealed his lips around the flared head of my cock, welling up enough spit in his mouth until it felt like my cock was drowning in it. I threaded my fingers through his hair and urged him down farther. Spit trickled out from the seal of his lips, racing down my shaft and pooling in my balls, and Niko tried to move faster, using his tongue to lick me as he went.

I liked sloppy blow jobs.

Wet blow jobs.

Loud blow jobs.

Niko was hitting two of the three, and a quick twist at the root of his hair reminded him of the third. He made a show of moaning loudly when I pulled his mouth off my cock, and then couple at the table against the wall looked up from their drinks with curiosity in their eyes. Before Niko could get distracted, I pushed him back down around my cock.

"Make sure everyone here knows what a slut you are, Niko. Make sure they know how much you get off on sucking cock," I said.

And he did.

With years of having Christian as a friend, I'd done my fair share of watching, but I was oddly new to exhibitionism. The couple who'd looked up at Niko's slutty little moan both had their cocks in hand. I could make out the movement from the corner of my eye, but it was impossible to care what they were doing when Niko was swallowing down my shaft like both our lives depended on it.

"You're the best cock sucker, Niko. Fuck." I lifted off the chair, pushing my shaft into his mouth until his throat was filled with the tip of my cock. He gagged and sputtered, spit flying down his chin and over my thighs. I held myself as deep inside his mouth as I could manage without him blacking out, and right as I was ready to come, I pulled out.

I jerked my shaft once to send me the rest of the way over the edge, even though his mouth had done a more than suitable job in getting me there, and with a muffled grunt, I sprayed my load across his face. Cum splattered his cheek, his mouth, his eyelid and eyelashes. There was so much cum on his face he looked like he'd gone bobbing for apples in a bucket of it by the time I finished with him. My cock still pulsed in time with my heartbeat, and I used my leaking dick to smear my release into his pores, hand still held tight in his hair until my muscles relaxed enough for me to let go.

CHAPTER FIVE

NIKO

I'D BEEN to The Black Door at least half a dozen times, but I'd always lurked in corners. Not because I was ashamed of being there, but because I was trying to avoid being seen. I was there to keep an eye on Christian, nothing more and nothing less. Being there with Parrish, on my knees with his cock in my mouth and his cum on my cheeks, it was another experience entirely.

"You're good, Niko," Parrish praised, stroking my hair back from my face, "but not good enough to deserve my load in your mouth."

"How can I be?" I whispered.

This was the crux of all the games Parrish and I played with each other. I was the best hole, the best cock sucker, but it still wasn't good enough. Our relationship had started with his rude taunts and my bitter jabs, but even after we'd fallen into bed together, the cruelty had remained. I wasn't mad about it. The things Parrish said made me unbelievably hard. It made me sometimes wonder if there was something wrong with me, but after spending as many nights at the club as I had since moving to America, I knew it wasn't the case.

There was a couple in the corner who'd stroked each other off while I sucked Parrish's cock. There was nothing wrong with them. There were people down the hallway in the private rooms doing far more depraved things, and there was nothing wrong with them, either. There was nothing wrong with him and nothing wrong with me, and it didn't matter that I got turned on when he was mean to me. The only thing that mattered was the way his eyes sparkled when he looked at me, like even though his mouth said one thing, his body said another.

"You can start by thanking me." Parrish crossed one slim leg over the other, kicking my arm as he went. He gave his foot a little shake, and I knew what he wanted.

I shifted back, pressing my mouth against the tip of his shoe.

"Thank you for putting up with me," I said, looking up in time to see him pick up the water from the table and take a long swallow. His throat worked, and I wanted to kiss him there next. Lick him and bite him and suck him.

He hummed in response, and I kissed the side of his shoe, then worked my way toward the laces. Cum smeared off my cheeks and all over the expensive black leather, and he jerked his foot away from my lips and pressed the pointed toe beneath my chin.

"These shoes cost more than you make in a month, Niko. Don't get them dirty."

I nodded quickly, using my tongue to clean up the cum I'd tracked over the leather. From his perch on the chair, Parrish stared down the length of his nose at me, moving his other foot between my legs. My cock was so hard already it hurt, and the pressure of his foot against my shaft did nothing to ease the ache.

"You're doing great with the degrading, sweetheart, but I know you and you're nowhere near coming without your hands," he said, twisting the cap back onto the water bottle and setting it down.

There was the edge of threat in his voice, but I tried to ignore it and focused my attention on the taste of leather against my tongue, the burning press of his foot against my cock and balls.

"Take it out," he said next, giving his foot a shake. "I want to see it."

I glanced up at him, heat burning in my cheeks as he moved his foot out of the way. I fussed with my belt and my fly, then pulled my cock out from behind the waistband of my underwear. My balls were beyond sensitive, my own hands almost too much for me to bear. Parrish was quick with his movement, getting the toe of his shoe behind my sac. He leaned forward, leveraging himself off the seat and pressing a shocking amount of pressure into his foot, pushing all of it down onto the very sensitive spot behind my balls and in front of my hole.

I tumbled backward, catching myself before I fell, with my hands behind me. My legs came out from under me, splayed out like a starfish, and I wanted more than anything to cover my face in embarrassment. I was spread out on the floor of the most exclusive club in New York City, my cock was out of my pants, jutting toward the ceiling and spurting precum like a geyser. There were at least two people jerking off while they watched me, three if I wanted to count the way Parrish reached down and took longer than necessary to adjust himself back into his own pants.

Parrish walked around and squatted down beside me, close enough that I could hear him over the hum of conversation that filled the room when he said, "They're all watching you."

I swallowed, letting myself fall into the ground entirely.

"They all know that even if I wanted to give it to you tonight, you're not good enough to swallow my cum, Niko." Parrish's mouth quirked up into a cruel grin. "Everyone sees you here, cleaning up my shoes with your tongue like the worthless nobody you are."

My muscles tightened, contracting and releasing, and contracting again until I was sure my bones would snap from the tension.

"The problem is I really want to come inside of you. Maybe more than I've ever wanted anything in my life," he said softly. "But if I did, it would just leak right out of that loose asshole of yours after we were finished. It would run down your legs and stick to the hairs on the inside of your thighs. And for what, Niko?"

"No." I shook my head.

"No," he mimicked me, then he laughed. "You'd waste my cum, I know you would. It would ooze right out of you because you don't know how to have nice things, Niko. Do you? You don't know how to take care of things of value."

I screwed my eyes closed, grimacing when Parrish put his palm against my forehead and pushed me against the ground. He covered my body with his, knee pressing into the spot he'd been toying with earlier.

"I have value, Niko," he whispered into my ear, breath hot and moist. "And you're nothing."

My orgasm came with a whimper, a hot burst of semen against my shirt, my back arched off the floor, body giving into Parrish's cruelty like he'd planned all along.

Like *I'd* wanted all along.

CHAPTER SIX

PARRISH

Debasing Niko offered me some of the best orgasms of my life, and I'd truly missed him since he'd left for New York with Christian. Losing my best friend and my favorite fuck toy in one fell swoop had made for the worst day of my life, and for the first time since they're departure, I found myself smiling and sated.

I gave Niko another shove onto the ground for good measure before relaxing back into my seat. Niko's chest heaved, the cum splattered across his stomach like confetti at the end of a race. His eyes were closed, and I kicked the toe of my shoe against his ribs when he held his breath too long for my liking.

"Go on," he murmured, flinging an arm over his eyes. "Say it."

"Say what, Niko?"

"You know."

"Do you want me to tell you that you came hands free because you're a bitch?" I asked, reaching for my whiskey and taking a drink.

He swallowed, whole face flushed.

I leaned down, resting my elbows on my knees and bringing my face closer to his.

"Or did you want me to tell you how much I love it?" I brushed his hair back, my own heart swelling as I spoke. "How when I can't sleep at night, I think about the way you come for me and then everything makes sense?"

Niko slid his arm away to reveal his eyes, wide open with his pupils still shot from arousal.

"Sometimes," he said quietly, barely audible over the chatter of the club, "I come thinking about you."

"Only sometimes?"

Niko huffed, cock still hard.

"Sometimes I don't let myself come."

"Why not?" I asked.

"Because it feels too easy."

"You like to work for it? Is that what you're saying?"

"I like when you *make* me work for it."

I hummed, grabbing him by the collar of his shirt and yanking him onto his knees. He settled easily again between my legs, all disheveled and spent and desperate for more. It was a curious thing, the way Niko made me feel. For as long as I could remember, I'd always been best friends with Christian, and having a best friend who was actual royalty came with its own unique set of challenges.

There was no instance in my entire upbringing where I'd ever had a chance to come before Christian. Even when it came to my own family, the needs of the Spencers always came first. But with Niko, when he got onto his knees for me, his back, when he came for me...there was nobody in his world that mattered more than I did. The power was heady and dangerous, and I hadn't realized how addicted I'd become to it until he'd left for America.

"Tell me more," I prompted, swirling the ice around my glass and waiting for him to explain.

Instead, his throat flushed a dark pink that matched the color of his erection.

"Tell me more, Niko," I said again, using that tone he loved so much.

He shivered, flicking a stare at me through the dark fan of his lashes. He was still covered in cum, but I wasn't sure he remembered. Niko was always so concerned about other people's perception of him, and for a moment with me, he cast all that to the side to live in the moment. It was more intoxicating than the most expensive whiskey.

"In detail," I added.

For good measure.

"I use a toy," he whispered, his cheeks turning the same color as his throat and his dick. "I fuck myself with it."

"A toy doesn't tell you how sloppy your hole is."

Niko shivered. "I know."

"A toy doesn't remind you that you're just a useless little cock sleeve, waiting for a load, does it?"

He screwed his eyes closed, sinking back onto his heels and resting the backs of his hands against the tops of his thighs. Niko turned himself into the perfect picture of submission, and I loved it.

I loved *him*.

"You've missed me," I whispered, the realization of my own feelings dawning in the same breath.

Niko missed me as much as I'd missed him, and as fun as our little escapades were, there was a part of us both that needed the exchange. I needed to be first for once, and Niko...he needed to put me there. That wasn't for me to explain or understand, beyond the fact that we worked together in all of the right ways, and his relocation to New York had left us both sad and horny.

"I'm sorry if that's—"

"Don't you dare." I swallowed the rest of my whiskey and clamped my hand over his mouth to stop him from uttering one more wrong word. His nostrils flared, breath puffing hot against the side of my finger as he exhaled. "Don't you dare apologize for the way you are."

He swallowed, Adam's apple bobbing, lips flush against my palm.

"This is more than we thought, isn't it?" I asked.

A quick nod.

I shifted my hand from a gag to a hook, pressing my fingers into his cheeks and yanking him up off the floor and onto my lap. He came easily—in multiple ways—landing against my chest with a startled exhale and his arms braced on my shoulders to stop himself from falling. The position made him taller than me, and I tilted my head back to gaze up at him, the cum on his face and the stubble and the sweat.

"I'm desperate to fuck you," I whispered, wrapping my arms around his back and pulling him down closer. "It's been so long since I've been inside that gaping asshole of yours, I don't know what to do with myself. Is that what you want, too? Do you want me to make you gape and leak like the fuck toy you are?"

His reply came soft and scratchy, "I've missed you so much."

"Is that a yes?"

His lashes fluttered and I pulled him the rest of the way down to me, slanting our mouths together just in time to swallow down his answer.

"Yes."

CHAPTER SEVEN

NIKO

Wʜᴀᴛ.

The.

Fuck.

Things with Parrish were suddenly more real than they had been before, and I'd barely gotten him back to my apartment before he was on me again. His hands tearing off my clothes, his tongue, plundering my mouth. Sex with Parrish was always good, but this was something different.

Something more.

"I want to see you come again," he said, breaking away from the kiss long enough to get both of our shirts off. "Where is your bedroom?"

I laughed, fingers scrabbling at his fly.

"The only room that isn't the bathroom," I told him.

"You think Christian and his millionaire boyfriend could have gotten you a bigger place."

"I don't need much room," I said.

Parrish hummed, walking us both down the short hall to my bedroom. He flicked on the lights and shoved me down onto the bed. My pants were half off, one leg free, the other still tangled around my ankle.

"Where is that toy you use? Get it out."

I rolled onto my stomach and went for the small drawer in my nightstand, pulling out the eight-inch dildo and a half-used bottle of lube. Parrish arched a brow at the size of the toy, but didn't say anything about it.

"Show me how you do it," he said, leaning against the wall and taking his cock in hand.

"I don't want to fuck it," I whined, "I want to fuck you."

"You haven't earned the right."

A shiver tore through me, his cruelty as much of an aphrodisiac as his affection.

With minimal reluctance, I arranged myself onto my back, planting my feet on the mattress and spreading my legs wide to give him a view.

"Closer to the edge," he rasped.

I obeyed.

"Start with your fingers," he said next. "I wouldn't want you to hurt yourself."

Heat exploded out from the base of my spine, and I poured lube into my hand, slicking the entire thing up before reaching between my legs and pushing two slippery fingers inside of me. Lifting off the bed, my back arched and my cock sprang back to life. It was embarrassing how hard Parrish made me, but the loud groan of approval from across the room was enough to help me forget.

"Just like that," he whispered, voice almost a growl. "It doesn't take much to open you up, does it?"

I added a third finger, whimpering at the stretch.

"No wonder you don't always come," Parrish said from his perch against the wall. "You're nowhere near as good at fucking yourself as I am."

"Arrogant prick," I muttered.

"Foul mouthed fleshlight," he shot back. "Fuck yourself like you mean it Niko or stop wasting my time."

Without asking, I pulled my fingers out and switched to the dildo. If he wanted me to fuck myself, I was going to do it. With a lot more anger than I really had, I slammed the suction base of the toy against my headboard and threw the pillow and sheets out of the way.

"Right where you sleep," he said under his breath while I shifted my positioning and lined my stretched hole up with the long and thick toy.

I took the whole length in one thrust, leveraging one foot against the nightstand in the awkward arrangement I'd spent months perfecting.

"I have to admit I'm glad you told me about this toy," Parrish drawled.

I turned my head to the side and watched him stalk toward the bed. He climbed on beside my head, straddling my face and digging his knees into my biceps. Parrish dragged his asshole across my mouth, then his balls, before lifting and pushing his cock against my tongue.

"The only way your asshole will be tight enough to get me off is if you're double stuffed," he said on a groan, sinking his cock into the back of my throat. Falling forward onto his hands and knees, he fucked my mouth with short snaps of his hips and I fucked the dildo on my headboard the same way.

His face was inches away from my cock. I could feel the hot puffs of his exhales dance across the swollen and stretched skin of my shaft, but Parrish never made a move to lean down and take me into his mouth. Something about the proximity and the denial wrapped around me like a drug, drawing my balls tight against my body. The promise of another orgasm was just within reach, even as it became increasingly hard to breathe with Parrish's dick in my mouth.

The thought alone had my erection twitching against my stomach, and instead of licking or sucking at me, Parrish spit on me. A thick glob of spit landed against the tip of my dick and he called me a good for nothing fuck toy, and that was all it took. One more slide of his cock into the back of my throat, my asshole swelling around the thickest part of the toy and I was neck deep in the throes of another hands-free orgasm.

Parrish laughed as I came, climbing off of me so fast the sudden rush of air into my lungs almost made me black out. I cried and thrashed against my headboard, spurts of cum jetting wildly across my stomach as I rode through the roughness of the very unexpected orgasm.

"Fuck, I want you," he said, leaning over and popping the dildo off the headboard. With the toy still inside of me, Parrish spun me back around and teased the tip of his cock around my rim.

"It won't fit," I gasped, trying to swat the dildo out of me to make room for the one thing I wanted.

Him.

CHAPTER EIGHT

PARRISH

"If you want my cum inside of you, Niko, you're going to make it fit so quit whining and relax," I said, pouring lube down Niko's balls. He was wet and the bedding was ruined, the mattress was probably soaked, but I didn't care. The only thing that mattered was getting inside of Niko and never leaving.

I slid two fingers into him, around the girth of the dildo, sliding them around until there was room for me to get a third in there. Beneath me, Niko sweated and panted, mumbling lots of four letter words that had no real place between us, and yet...

And yet.

"Want you," he whispered, arching toward me. "Need you. Oh god, please."

"I thought it wouldn't fit," I teased, pushing my pinky finger in next. Inside of him, I curled my fingers around the dildo, fucking him from the inside as best I could without getting my whole hand in there.

That was a lofty goal for another day.

"I'm so fucking loose, Parrish," he said next, eyes screwed shut like he was in pain. "Need you to fill me up, please."

"Loose indeed," I agreed, even though his muscles were actively trying to amputate my fingers for how tight he was. The degradation was all part of our game and if the throbbing heat of my cock was any indication, I liked it as much as he did. If not more. Shifting my hips, I notched the head of my cock beneath the toy and with a slow thrust forward, replaced my fingers with my dick. "Gotta plug you up with all the cocks to keep my cum inside of you. Isn't that right, Niko?"

His mouth parted, no sound coming out until he loosed a gasping and shuddering breath.

"It hurts," he choked out, fingers scrabbling for purchase around my arms, my ribs, my stomach, anywhere he could reach. "It hurts. Oh fuck, it's too much."

"Shut up," I warned, but it was near impossible to speak when the only thing my body wanted to do was explode and drown Niko in cum. "Shut up, shut up. Stop fucking talking."

Falling forward, I pressed our foreheads together, taking a pause to catch my breath so I didn't finish myself off before even having a chance to get started. Though admittedly, things with Niko had started a long time ago. And even though there was an ocean between us now, I didn't see an end to it. Niko and the fucked up way we played was the best part of my life, and there was no going back from that. If it meant I had to leave home, follow him to New York, then that was what I would do.

"Parrish."

My name sounded like a plea. I smoothed Niko's hair away from his face, a rough grip on his forehead holding him down to the bed because if he so much as breathed the wrong way, I was going to come.

"I know," I told him, withdrawing no more than an inch before easing back in.

Gooseflesh peppered his arms, and he slid them around me with ease. Digging his nails into my back, Niko spread his legs wider and then wrapped them around my waist. The shift added more pressure, clamping his hole around the dildo and my cock at the same time.

"I'm going to come," I warned him, going still again.

"I want you to," he said, words breathy against my mouth. "I need it. Oh..."

I started to move and Niko trailed off, returning to the place of mindless muttering and the kind of nonsense I'd only ever dreamed about hearing from his gorgeous mouth.

"I know you have another orgasm in you," I said, pulling back enough to slide my palm beneath his erection. I didn't grip him or move him. Only held the weight of him in my hand, feeling the slick strings of precum leak against my fingers with every pump of my hips.

I finally managed to set a slow and steady pace, enough to drive Niko mad and bring me close enough to the edge I could hold off until I was ready. Though, I wasn't sure I ever would be ready. Being so deep inside of him, covered in him, *surrounded* by him...the thought of pulling out, of getting dressed, of getting on a plane and going home?

Leaving Niko was no longer an option.

"What if I stayed?" I asked, teeth nipping against his ear lobe. "What if you spent your days with Christian and your nights with me?"

"What are you saying?"

I licked my lips.

I licked his jaw.

"What if I pumped you full of cum every morning and plugged your slutty, gaping hole before sending you to work?" I gritted my teeth together, balls churning. The orgasm was too close to avoid, so I stopped trying. "Just imagine trying to do your job with my cum sloshing down your thigh with every step."

"Parrish."

My name again.

A whisper.

A prayer.

"I have a secret," I whispered, thrusting into him one last time before my body went rigid, shockwaves from my orgasm tearing through me like a storm. It was as if all the blood in my body rushed between my legs, centralizing in my cock to pump my cum deeper into Niko's body than I'd ever shot before. My vision went black around the edges and I threw my head back, crying out his name as I came.

Niko reached between us and pulled the dildo out of him. A cool rush of air washed across my shaft while his hole gaped and puckered before clamping down hard and milking another wave of cum out of my balls. His heels dug into my thigh so hard it gave me a cramp, and I collapsed on top of him, stomach smearing against the mess he'd already made of himself. Judging by the sounds coming from Niko's mouth, he'd managed another orgasm after all, which was honestly beyond impressive.

I wasn't sure he had it in him.

"What's the secret?" he asked after I pulled my still-hard cock out of him.

I flopped onto my back and let out a long and shuddering breath, turning my head to the side so I could face him.

Niko looked as well fucked as I felt, his cheeks permanently flushed and cum from earlier in the night caked in the stubble across his cheeks. Brushing the hair back from his face, I gave him the softest smile I had in me, and then he started to cry.

———

CHAPTER NINE

———

NIKO

I ROLLED AWAY from Parrish just in time to narrowly avoid his searching grasp. Sitting on the edge of the bed, I gave myself two seconds to comb my fingers through my hair and then I was up, padding barefoot to the bathroom with cum dripping out of my ass and down my thigh. Parrish jumped out of bed, but I was in the bathroom with the door closed before he could get to me.

I locked the door and slid down onto the floor, propping my forearms on my knees and letting my head hang down low. The sight of lube and cum spilling out of my ass onto the tiled white floor offered me no relief, and I bit my lips between my teeth to stifle another cry.

"What's wrong, Niko? Did I say the wrong thing?" Parrish sounded near frantic on the other side of the door. "Did I go too far?"

"It's fine," I said. "I'm fine."

"You're a lot of things, but you're not a liar."

I let out a derisive snort, head banging against the door. On the other side, I heard Parrish slide down and land against the floor with a quiet thump.

"I'm fine," I said again, hoping it sounded more convincing.

"Well." He laughed under his breath. "I'm not."

"Did you go too far?" I asked.

"Open the door and I'll tell you."

I dragged my tongue across the front of my teeth. "What was the secret?"

"Open the door and I'll tell you everything."

I didn't want to open the door, but my legs and arms and hands moved of their own volition. The door opened and there he was, sitting on the floor in the hallway of my rented New York apartment, buck naked with his cock soft and wet against his thigh. I returned to my place on the floor in the bathroom, stretching my legs as far as the cramped space would allow.

"The door is open," I told him.

"I went too far with you," he said gently, mouth twisted into a grimace.

Licking my lips, I nodded, blinking back tears.

The situation was absurd, I wasn't a crier. I never had been, and yet I was freshly fucked and debased, sitting on my floor with cum leaking out of my ass and tears out of my eyes and I couldn't stop. Scrubbing a hand down my face, I turned my attention to the ceiling so I didn't have to see the apology on Parrish's face.

"I went too far," he said again, as if the first time wasn't enough, "and I fell in love with you."

My eyebrows shot up and I jerked my head in his direction, pulse stuttering in my neck.

"What did you say?"

He reached out tentatively, hand hovering over my thigh before he slowly lowered it and brought us back into contact. His hand was warm, grip broad around my trembling muscle.

"I'm in love with you." Parrish shifted onto his knees, then forced himself into my small bathroom and straddled my lap, taking my face into his hands. "I fell in love with you."

"Why?" I asked.

"Does it matter?"

My eyes rolled on their own volition, and Parrish leaned in, slanting our mouths together and licking past my lips with a patience and kindness he'd never shown me before that moment. I whimpered, going pliant beneath him and reluctantly resting my hands on the swell of his hips.

"Why did you start crying?" he asked, peppering the corner of my mouth with gentle kisses, a far cry from the way he normally touched and handled me.

"Because I'm in love with you, too," I admitted, pressing my forehead against his.

Parrish's fingers against my cheeks dug in deeper, and he jerked my head until I was forced to look him in the eye.

"Say it again."

"I'm in love with you." I blinked hard, tears falling. "I love you, and you're not here, you're going to leave, and—"

He cut me off, crashing our mouths together and kissing me until I was hard again. Kissing me until I was hard and his hips gyrated against me, moans slipping past his lips and onto my tongue.

"If you want me to stay, I'll stay."

"It's not that easy."

"Isn't it?" Parrish reared back, brows scrunched in confusion.

"Your life is in Chance Island."

"So was yours."

I swallowed, letting my head fall back against the bathroom wall, but Parrish made an unhappy noise in the back of his throat, pulling me close to him again.

"Don't do that," he chided, no real heat or warning in it. "Don't...go."

"This is absurd."

The corner of his mouth twitched into a wry smile. "I have to admit that I find it absolutely endearing that you find everything else we've done together tolerable, but the idea of me loving you and wanting to stay with you is the absurdity."

"The other things…"

"Are not absurd either," he said before I could demean the way we liked to fuck. "You're allowed to like what you like. And so am I. You're also allowed to love what you love…*who* you love…"

Parrish trailed off again, leaning close and brushing his mouth over mine. It was less of a kiss and more of a question, which I answered by sliding my hands up the curve of his back and spearing my tongue into his mouth. He groaned, pumping his hips down over mine and changing the angle of my head so he could kiss me the way he wanted.

That was the thing about Parrish. I'd realized long ago it was his way or no way, and it was only by some fate that we were cut from the same cloth.

"God, I want you again," he moaned into my mouth, reaching between us and curling his fingers around both of our cocks. "I want you more than I want to breathe."

"I don't think I can come again," I warned, bucking off the floor so rough he almost fell right into the toilet.

Still close, he smiled against my lips.

"Those are dangerous words, Niko, because to me, that sounds like a challenge."

He flicked his wrist, tightening the pressure around the middle of our cocks and I cried out, another fresh wave of tears rolling down my cheeks. I loved Parrish and he loved me, and I wanted to come for him more than anything, but I didn't know if I could.

"Make me," I rasped, screwing my eyes closed against the pain of his touch. "Make me come."

CHAPTER TEN

PARRISH

It took me two months to tie up all my loose ends at home and get all the paperwork sorted to allow my move to America. It would have been a longer process, but thankfully money talked and I had plenty of it. I'd spoken to Niko every day since he told me he loved me, but I hadn't been entirely honest with him.

I hadn't told him I was ready to move.

That I already had.

Christian knew, but I'd sworn him to secrecy. He'd been beyond pleased to find out I'd been fucking his bodyguard behind his back, but I think that was just because he knew I'd keep Niko's attention where it *really* belonged.

On me.

It was through Christian I'd found out Kale had planned them a date night to The Black Door, where I'd watched Niko sulk through their dinner, his attention only slightly perking up when the trio got to the club. They checked in and I tailed them inside, close enough to keep my eyes on them but far enough back to not be seen. At the bar, Kale exchanged some hushed words with Niko, then took Christian to a private room.

Niko frowned down at his water with lemon, pulling his phone out of his pocket. Two seconds later, my phone buzzed in my pocket and I was helpless to stop myself from smiling.

Niko: Are you up?

I waited a minute to reply.

Me: I am.

Niko: It's late where you are.

Me: Not so bad.

I grinned, snaking my way around the perimeter of the room until I found an empty seat in the corner.

Me: Where are you?

Niko: The Black Door.

Me: Remember the last time I was there with you?"

Even across the room, I could see the flush that raced up Niko's freshly shaven cheeks.

Niko: Vividly.

Me: Me too, but to be honest, I think you look better tonight. The all black thing suits you well.

I huffed a laugh, watching Niko fumble his drink and his phone at the same time before both things landed on the bar. He reached for his phone first, re-reading my message before scanning the room with wide and frantic eyes. It only took him one pass to find me in the corner, and I stood as he approached. Niko crashed into me, his larger frame knocking the wind out of me as he crashed our mouths together in a blistering kiss.

"What are you doing here?" he asked, breaking away enough for air but not enough for me to reply.

I humored him, because even though I knew I'd missed him, I hadn't realized just how much until I had him back in front of me where I could touch him and tease him.

"In New York?" I asked, nipping at his bottom lip. "I live here."

"What?"

His eyes were wide, shocked and pleased and welling with tears again. Preemptively, I traced the edge of my knuckle beneath his lash line, catching the first one that escaped.

"I live here," I said again.

His mouth twitched into a smile, falling away before settling back into place like it was an expression he was going to wear for the rest of his life. It was too beautiful to bare, and I slanted our mouths back together until I was confident his expression had morphed into something far more lustful than before.

"Needy thing," I whispered, wanting him more than I ever had before and beyond ready to resume our relationship properly. I fisted the placket of his shirt in my hand and shoved him off of me. "The distance has made you forgetful."

He opened his mouth to protest, but realization dawned and he snapped his already kiss swollen lips closed.

"You haven't earned the right to kiss me like that," I said, sinking back down into my seat. "But I'm open to suggestions if you wanted to try."

He sucked in a breath, then another, and another, shoulders heaving with every inhale.

"It's been a long time since I watched you come," I lied.

I'd made him jerk off for me two days before, with that fake cock shoved all the way up his ass he'd shot his load so hard it streaked across the dip in his throat, all the way up to his chin. But watching over the phone and seeing it in person were two separate things entirely.

"I'll come for you," he whispered.

I curled my foot around the back of his leg, kicking his calf hard enough to knock him off balance. He went to his knees with a whimper and I rubbed the toe of my shoe against the quickly growing bulge between his legs.

"You know the rules, Niko," I said, sliding my cell phone back into my pocket and giving him my full attention. "No hands or it doesn't count."

"I missed you so much," he said, fingers working furiously at his fly. And then it was down, underwear along with it and that hard cock of his that I loved to torture was out between us, leaking and pulsing in time with his heartbeat.

"I believe you," I whispered, bending forward and brushing his gelled hair back from his forehead. I kissed his temple, then leaned back in my seat, giving him my leg as a humping post. "But prove it to me anyway."

(FOR)EVER MINE

Katrina Marie

$$\overline{\qquad}$$

CHAPTER ONE

$$\overline{\qquad}$$

CORINNE

I'M LATE. My brother is going to kill me. I'm zipping through traffic as fast as I can while still being safe. To be fair, if he wanted me there by a specific time, he should have told me to be there an hour earlier. Maybe then I wouldn't be rushing through Austin to get to his house.

There isn't much I miss about living in a small-town. But no traffic is definitely one of them. A tractor driving down the road, or a cow being loose, are the only things that bring cars to a dead stop back home. And the place we're going for the weekend is barely above that.

I'm excited, though. I had a blast photographing Stella's wedding. Her house is stunning and we're all staying there. A quick glance at the passenger seat is all the confirmation I need. My camera bag sits buckled in the seatbelt. Justin makes fun of me for taking the extra precaution, but that thing is my baby. It's how I earn a living and I'll be damned if it gets messed up because I have to slam on my brakes trying to get through this city.

Two miles until my exit, and I slide over into the right lane. A honk meets my ears and a car zooms by me on the other side, giving me the finger. There wasn't a car when I got over. That's the other thing I miss about small-town life. People wave when you pass them. They don't give you the one-finger salute.

Taking the exit, I slow down to make sure I can get over so I'm not honked at again. Where is all this smalltown melancholy coming from? I couldn't get out of there fast enough, that long ago. Now, I long for it more than I thought I would.

Finally, the street to my brother's house is in sight. I glance at the clock to see how late I am. Only thirty minutes. That's actually good timing for me.

I park on the curb and head toward the door. It swings open before I lift my hand up to knock.

"Would it kill you to be on time?"

"What a nice way to welcome your sister to your house." I push past him and head straight for the living room. Audrey is sitting on the couch, shaking her head. "Hey Audrey, sorry to keep you waiting."

"Oh, you're fine." She laughs. "I don't know why he thought we'd leave on time. Or why he picked this time to head to Asheville. He knows what this highway is like right now."

"That ain't no lie," I mutter.

Justin storms into the living. "Seriously, Corinne. Do you treat your clients with this level of respect?"

"Hold up," I face him and put my hand in the air. Stopping him from saying whatever he's going to come at me with. "At work I'm a professional. I mark gigs an hour before I need to be there, so I have plenty of time to set up. This isn't a job. So, calm the hell down before you blow a gasket."

He takes a deep breath and lets it out. "You're right, I'm sorry." He opens his arms and takes two steps toward me. Ready to make up. It's something we did when our parents got together. Why? No clue. It's not like we've ever been able to stay mad at each other for long.

"It's all good." I take a step toward my brother and wrap him in a hug.

Audrey puts her arms around both of us and laughs. "Group hug!" She squeezes tight before letting go and we all pull apart. "Now, let's get the car loaded. Cori, where are your bags?"

"In the car," I point toward the door. "But um, there's a lot."

"We're only going to be gone for a weekend. What could you possibly be bringing?"

"I want to take some photos while we're there. Stella's place is gorgeous, and you never know when inspiration is going to hit." I wave his frustration away as I walk to the door. "Besides, it's not like it can't sit in the back seat with me. There's plenty of room."

It goes silent and I have a feeling I'm about to hear something I don't want to hear.

"About that—" Justin trails off.

Pulling the door open, I attempt stepping outside. But I run into something solid. I look up and this can't be happening. "What's he doing here?"

"Well, hello to you, too." Carter grins at me, and I want to smack the smug smile off his face.

CHAPTER TWO

CARTER

I KNEW she wouldn't be excited to see me. Not after the way things ended with us, which wasn't exactly my fault. Not completely.

"Seriously, Justin," Corinne turns toward her step-brother, "what is he doing here?"

"I'm here for the trip, Rin." I shake my head as if she's being ridiculous. "What other reason would I be standing in this room?"

Justin tries to answer, but she doesn't give him the chance. "Absolutely not. There's no way in hell I'm going on this trip with him. It's supposed to be a stress-free weekend getaway. How is that supposed to happen when your wingman is out causing trouble?"

Wingman? I can't be one of those when he's practically married. If anything, he's mine. "Why am I classified as a troublemaker?"

Three sets of eyes fall on me, eyebrows lifted in question. Audrey finally speaks up. "No offense, Carter, but you tend to go ham when we go out. And where we're going isn't exactly used to that. Everyone knows everyone in this town."

"Are you saying I'm going to embarrass you and your cousins?" I should be offended, but she's not completely wrong. I can get out of hand. Justin usually pulls me back when I've gone too far, but he's not around as much. Then it was Corinne. Until I pissed her off.

So maybe it was partly my fault, and I don't blame her. But, geez, I don't think it warrants the frosty tone everyone is giving me.

"Yes," Corinne answers. "Maybe I'll take my own car. I won't have to worry about my camera being thrown around in the back."

I almost offer to stay behind after all, but Justin comes to the rescue. "That's dumb. We can all ride in one car. I'm sure the two of you can get along during the four-hour drive."

"Doubtful," Corinne mutters, "but fine. I'll go grab my stuff out of my car. Do I need to move it in the driveway?"

"Most likely," her brother says. "Especially if you don't want it dinged up."

"I can help." I start to follow her out of the house. But she raises a hand to keep me at bay, and that's all the answer I need. I wasn't even supposed to come on this trip. I worked my way into it so I could see Corinne. To try and patch things up between us. Maybe even win her back. She's kept her distance since we broke up and this will be the first I'm around her for any length of time. It looks like I have my work cut out for me. She's not going to make this easy.

THANK GOD JUSTIN HAS AN SUV. THE RIDE IN A CAR WOULD BE ALMOST unbearable. Not because of the size, but from the vibe coming from Corinne. She has gone as far as putting her camera bag in the seat between us, leaving me with very little room to spread my legs. My only saving grace is Audrey is sitting in front of me. Had it been Justin, I would be miserable. Audrey offered to sit in the back, but I couldn't make her do that. Besides, if that were the case, I wouldn't be this close to Corinne.

"We're making a bathroom and food stop," Justin says as he takes the next exit. He pulls into a parking spot, and kills the engine.

Him and Audrey get out of the car, but Corinne makes no move to exit. Okay, that's weird. She loves food from this particular gas station. "Do you want anything?" She shakes her head and doesn't say a word. The silent treatment is already getting old and we're not even close to being done with this weekend. "You have to talk to me eventually."

She turns toward the window, acting as if I don't exist. I honestly don't know why I bother at this point. At this rate, she's never going to give me a chance to make my past mistakes up to her. Sighing, I open the door and get out of the car.

Entering the store, I go straight to the food counter. They have sausage sandwiches wrapped in foil packing under heat lamps. I grab two before heading off to find some chocolate and get a couple of drinks.

I beat both Audrey and Justin to the car, though they aren't far behind me. Once I'm settled in the backseat, I pull my purchases out of the bag. I place a sandwich, chocolate bar, and root beer on top of the camera bag. My peace offering to the woman on the other side.

It takes her a few moments to look down, but when she sees the items between us, a small smile tugs at her lips. It's not monumental, but it's progress. I'll take that any day of the week.

CHAPTER THREE

After four long hours, Stella's house finally comes into view. It's a welcome sight after being stuck in the backseat with Carter.

Not that he's been annoying or anything. It's being this close to him and knowing I can't have him. I can't be with him the way I want. Or, well, wanted. That ship sailed long ago.

My brother slows down and puts the car in park. There is no hesitation as I open the door and hop out. Dramatic? Maybe, but I've never been a great car rider, and I haven't outgrown it.

"Dang, girl, where's the fire?" Tiffany laughs as she comes down the porch steps. Out of Audrey and her cousins, I think Tiffany is the person I connect with most.

"Just ready to be out of the car," I grin. "It's been forever. How have you been?"

"Good, just trying to keep Stella from going overboard on the wedding planning. Also, looking for a house down here."

"What? You're moving?" Audrey never mentioned this to me.

"Yeah. Spencer and I kind of fell in love with this town when we were trapped in that snowstorm," she shrugs, "and if I'm being honest, I miss the whole small-town vibe."

She isn't the only one. I've been feeling the pull to a small town again. I hated it growing up, but I'm just not cut out for the speed of life in the city. I think I enjoy being city adjacent. "Awesome. Since we're all in the same place this weekend, you want to get some engagement photos with Spencer? I brought my camera."

"I'd love to. We've been trying to work out a time to get them done, but both of our schedules have been nuts."

"Good deal. I should probably grab my bags."

"I don't think you'll need to. It seems like Carter is doing a good job of getting it all on his own." She cocks her head to the side like a confused puppy. "I didn't even know he was coming."

"You and me both." I'm not sure what I would have done had I known, but it definitely puts a strain on the entire weekend.

"I guess things are still not great with y'all." She's the only person who knew we were dating at the time. I couldn't exactly hide it from her when she caught us making out at a concert.

"Nope." And I doubt they ever will be. "My plan for the weekend now includes avoiding him as much as possible."

"That might be a problem." She doesn't stick around to explain why. Instead, she hightails it inside. Most likely looking for Stella.

Carter makes his way to me with his bag over his shoulder and my suitcases in each hand. The only thing he doesn't have is my camera bag. "You didn't have to get my stuff."

He shrugs and his bag strap falls down his shoulder. He can't adjust it, so I lift it back on his shoulder. He relaxes at my touch and I pull my hand back. "I know, but I wanted to. All that's left is your camera, and I didn't want to try to grab that with my hands full."

"Smart man," I smirk.

"Sometimes." His eyes lock on mine and it's hard not to feel the pull between us. I'm not sure why he's here, or what game he's playing at, but whatever it is...it will not work.

"Well, I better grab my camera." I rush back toward the car and leave him behind me. This may prove harder than I imagined. Especially if I keep getting lost in his gaze.

<hr>

With my camera bag in tow, I stop in the living room. Everyone is gathered in a huddle and looks worried. "What did I miss?"

"Well," Audrey is wringing her hands, "nobody told Stella that Carter was coming along. And there aren't enough rooms."

Before I have a chance to speak, the man causing all the fuss does. "I can get a hotel room. It's no problem."

"That's nonsense," Stella says. "The couch is available."

Tiffany laughs. "You and Johnny are morning people, unlike the rest of us. You're likely to wake him up coming down the stairs."

"I can make the couch work," Carter glances at it, knowing full well it's not going to be comfortable. He's also not a morning person. That I can attest to because I'm not either.

I could be the bigger person, or let him fold himself onto the too small couch. A part of me wants to make him suffer, but the other part. The part that locked eyes with him on the front porch, and could feel the way old times were, she's the one who wins.

"He can stay in my room."

"Absolutely not," my brother yells. Little does he know I've spent many times with his best friend in a bedroom.

"We'll buy an air mattress," I roll my eyes. "He can sleep there. I'm not giving up my bed for anyone."

"Fine," Justin scoffs. He turns toward Carter and points his finger at him. "You know the rules. No flirting or messing with my sister."

It's kind of him to think he can make that threat. That ship has sailed for us. But I can do this. I can resist whatever pull I still feel toward the man I thought I loved. Everything will be fine. It's not like I'll be in the room for anything else but sleep. Project stay away from Carter is still in effect.

CHAPTER FOUR

ALL THE LADIES went to the store. No doubt trying to find an air mattress. It's not exactly what I wanted to happen. It beats sleeping on the tiny couch or floor. So, there's that. "Do you know which room we're going to be in?"

"I don't know that I like the way you say *we*," Justin shakes his head and sighs, "please don't think anything is going to come out of this. I know you flirt with Corinne...a lot, but please don't make me regret this. I've told you from the beginning that dating her is off limits. And it still is."

He acts like I need it repeated constantly. I don't. He's told me that since the day I met Corinne. The only problem is we haven't exactly listened to him. Which in turn is what bit me in the ass. She wanted to tell him, but I didn't. It may be a little selfish, I can admit that. Him being on my ass is the only reason I was against it. Also, the fact he most likely won't think I'm good enough for her. I'd like to avoid that bit of rejection at all costs. It hurt enough coming from the woman I was falling in love with. I can't take it from my best friend, too.

"I know, Justin." Every time he brings it up it gets more annoying. "I'll be on the air mattress. Besides, I don't think she's all that warm and cuddly toward me. You saw her reaction when I showed up at your house."

"Good." He nods and points toward the stairs. "I'll show you to the room y'all are staying in. I swear if I hear anything I shouldn't, I'll make you sleep with me."

"Gross," I scoff. "No offense, dude, but you snore."

"So does my sister."

"Not like a freight train."

"You have a point." He grabs their bags, and leads the way up the stairs. "We'd normally fight with Tiffany over who gets the bigger room, but since you'll need it for the mattress, Spencer already moved their stuff to another room. After we get settled, we can grab a beer."

This house is massive. It looks big on the outside, but that's nothing compared to the inside. I didn't think this much space could fit inside the frame. I was wrong. Justin stops at a door next to the bathroom. "I guess this is me?"

"Yep." He points to the door two doors down. "That's me. Meet you in the kitchen in a bit. With any luck Johnny will be home and we can really kick this weekend off."

I nod and open the door. Anything to put some distance between us. I'm not really annoyed, but he tends to suck the fun out of the room when he's harping on me. I throw my bag on the bed and roll Corinne's suitcase to the dresser. I have no idea where she wants her stuff, and I'm definitely not the type to look through a woman's things. She'd also probably murder me.

Glancing around the room, I scope out the best spot for the mattress. There will only be about two feet of space between the bed and where I'm sleeping. Temptation will be hard to resist. But I can do it, I think. Well...at least for one night.

Sitting on the bed, I pull my clothes out of the bag and set them on top of the dresser. They won't get put up until I know where Rinne is putting her things. I don't want to take up the space she's going to use. I'm trying to get on her good side, and hogging everything won't accomplish that.

With my bag empty, I roll it up and set it inside the closet. Hopefully, Stella and Johnny have some blankets I can put over the mattress. The texture isn't great for sleeping on it bare. I search the closet and come up with one.

I close the door at the same time the bedroom door opens. What does Justin need now? "I'll be down there in just a sec."

"Down where?" I drop the blanket on the floor at the sound of Corinne's voice. "We just got back with this thing." She lifts the box with a huge grin. I don't know how to feel about that. She looks like she's planting some sort of trap. Or happy I'll be uncomfortable most of the time we're here.

"Oh, sorry." Bending down, I pick up the blanket and set it on the bed. "Your brother told me to meet him downstairs once I was done getting settled." This is one of those awkward moments where I don't know what to do with my hands. Do I get the box out of her hands and set up the bed? Or do I excuse myself? In all honesty, I don't want to do either. I want to stay here with her and figure out a way to fix things between us.

"Oh yeah, they are getting dinner together and pulling out the liquor bottles." She hooks her thumb over her shoulder. "Sounds like your kind of time. Better hurry down there."

She's snarky now. At least she's talking to me, even though this is totally her style, too. "I'll set that up later," I point to the box. "And help with whatever they need since I crashed the weekend."

"That you did," she bites back, but her eyes betray the statement. They haven't left me since she entered the room. I don't know if she's lying to me or herself, but there's still something there between us. Even if she's denying it.

I move toward the door. She moves to make room for me, but it's the same way I was going and we're face to face. The box holding the mattress is the only thing between us. A piece of hair has fallen from her bun, and I push it behind her ear. My fingers a soft touch against her skin. Her breath hitches. She moves closer, and I lean down, my lips inches from hers. She's not stopping me, and I close the distance between us.

She jumps back at the sound of a throat clearing and steps aside.

———————

CHAPTER FIVE

———————

CORINNE

I can't believe I almost let him kiss me. What the hell was I thinking? Tiffany is standing in the hallway, hands in her pocket, swaying back and forth on the balls of her feet.

"What are you two doing?" She smirks, and I can't blame her. We were in a compromising position.

"Absolutely nothing." I move away from the door and Carter slips past me. But not before letting his hand graze my waist. The shiver that runs through my body has nothing to do with the touch. It's the air conditioning, and nothing else. "Want to help me set this up?"

"Not really, but I have a feeling you won't let me go downstairs until I do."

"And this is why I love you." I set the box on the floor and rip the tape off. Within minutes, I have the mattress out of the box and on the floor. "Do you have outfits for pictures?"

Tiffany unrolls the mattress and makes sure the plug is next to her on the wall. "Yeah. It's nothing fancy, but we're not really dressed up sort of people."

"Please tell me y'all brought costumes. I would love to photograph y'all cosplaying. And it would totally work because it's who y'all are. That's what we want to show everyone."

Tiffany falls over laughing. "No, we didn't bring costumes, but there's a convention coming up soon. We'll have to get together when we're dressed up so you can take some photos." She gathers her composure and plugs the air mattress into the outlet and turns the knob until air begins filling it. "I also think Stella would die if our official engagement photos were us cosplaying. When we suggested adding some comic fun to the wedding, she lost her shit."

"You do know it's your wedding, right?" Opening the bottom drawer of the dresser, I pull out one of the fitted sheets Stella keeps in there. Carter may be a pain in the ass, but I'm not going to let him sleep on that scratchy felt that covers the mattress. "You can do whatever you want. You don't have to let her bulldoze over you because that's what she usually does."

"You're one to talk." She grabs a pillow off the bed and throws it at me. "When are you going to stop letting your brother tell you who you can and can't see?"

"He doesn't."

"Yes, he does." Tiff checks the firmness of the air mattress. "You and Carter could be happy together if he wasn't always throwing hints about y'all being a bad idea."

"That's not the only problem between us."

"I know. But admit it, you still have feelings for him." She flutters her lashes and makes kissing sounds.

"Not so loud. You are literally the only person who knows. I can't let my brother overhear." I glance at the door to make sure nobody is nearby. "He'll lose his shit and I'll be stuck sleeping on this mattress in his room."

Tiffany bites her bottom lip before turning toward the wall to pull the plug out now that the mattress is full. "Well, I'm not the *only* person."

"What do you mean?"

"I may have told Spencer." She faces me again. "But you don't have to worry, he's not going to say anything to anyone."

Shit. I have to get downstairs. If guys talk like girls do, one of them is bound to slip. Never mind the fact they have alcohol added to the equation. Our secret will be out in the open and I'll have to break up a fight. "Help me get this bed made. Then we can head downstairs to make sure nobody says a word."

"Fine," she grunts. "I'll help, but you also didn't deny having feelings for him."

"Shut up." I grab the pillow she threw at me and toss it back at her. She's quick and dodges without a problem, but the damn thing hits the lamp. It teeters from side to side and I think it's going to fall, but Tiff comes to the rescue again and moves it back into place.

"You better be happy I stopped that. I'm almost certain the lamp is an antique."

"Let's not add murder to the weekend agenda." I laugh.

We make quick work of putting the sheet down and the blanket on top of it. I'm not even sure why I'm going through all this trouble. We aren't dating. Not anymore.

But I can't push aside the gratitude I felt when he brought me snacks from the gas station. After the way I treated him, he didn't have to bring me anything. He did, though. And if the closeness between us a few moments ago is any indication, we both have some desire still hiding beneath the surface. But we shouldn't be. Not after everything that went down between us.

"You okay?" Tiffany asks.

Shaking my head to clear away the thoughts, I nod. "Yep. Let's get downstairs. I think I need a margarita."

"You're speaking to my heart," she grins and helps me off the floor. "Though you better be careful with the alcohol, or Carter might be sharing your bed."

Rolling my eyes, I follow her out of the room, closing the door behind us. "I don't think so. That'll never happen, and if my brother found out. He'd be pissed. That would be a long, uncomfortable drive back to Austin. I'm definitely not ready for that."

"Not ready for what?" My brother is making his way toward us. Holy shit. Talk about a close call.

"To get completely drunk." I shrug. "If that happens, I'll be worthless tomorrow, and how am I supposed to take photos of the bride to be if I'm still in bed?"

"Okay," he drawls out, eyeing me as if I'm not telling him something. I'm not, but he doesn't need to know that. As long as he's in the dark, everything is good. Well, other than these old feelings creeping up despite me trying to bury them with little success.

"We'll see you downstairs." I grin.

"Yeah," Tiff adds. "I'm going to look for the cards. I think a game of spoons is on the table for tonight."

"Dear God, no." Justin runs his hand down his face as he passes us. "This is not good."

"What's he talking about?" We make our way down the stairs.

"I have no idea." I don't miss the gleam in her eyes, though. There's something she's definitely not telling me, and I think I'm about to find out what it is.

CHAPTER SIX

CARTER

"YOU HAVE TO BE CHEATING," Justin yells. Everyone in the kitchen is laughing. The type where you hold your stomach because you can't control it. Except Justin. He's staring at the table in utter disbelief. "There's no way in hell you made it clear across the table to get the spoon without me noticing."

"You have to be paying attention," Tiffany sing-songs, "you shouldn't be surprised, though. I haven't changed since we were kids. You know damn well I'm ruthless."

"And that is why I admire you, Tiff," I say before taking a sip of my beer, "anyone who can knock Mr. Perfect down a peg, is pretty amazing if you ask me."

"Hey," my best friend scoffs, "I'm not perfect."

Corinne shakes her head. Stella and Johnny are between us, and I wish like hell she would have picked the seat beside me. I don't blame her, though. Not completely. Especially after that almost kiss. Maybe I took it too far. She didn't exactly back down, and that's enough to give me hope.

"Are y'all ready for another round?" Tiffany holds her hand out for all the spoons, "except you, Justin. You're officially out of the game."

"I hate this stupid game." He gets up and walks to the fridge. "We are grown ass adults. We should be playing something like poker."

"Except that isn't any fun." I add to the smack talk. "I'm pretty sure I won't be far behind you, buddy. I barely got the last spoon, and I think Tiff is going to knock us all out before it's said and done."

"Literally," Corinne snickers. "I thought this was supposed to be a non-violent game?"

"Clearly, you've never played with these three," Justin points toward the table. "They get downright dirty. When we were teens, I saw Tiffany pull Stella across the table until she held the last spoon in her hand."

"Damn, that's brutal." I shake my head. "You are definitely not someone to mess with."

"It got pretty intense when we were on the ski trip, too." Johnny groans. "I played football in high school, and I'm not exactly tiny. She ripped that spoon out of my hand like she had super powers." He shivers and I can't comprehend this small redhead besting Johnny. He's definitely not small.

"How do you know I don't? I mean, there's a reason other than my stunning looks that Spencer fell for me." Tiffany pours herself another margarita and sits down at the table. "Now, who is ready to lose?"

Spencer mutters something under his breath, but I can't make it out. I don't miss the smack on his shoulder, though. It must have been pretty bad. Everyone gets ready for the next round. There's no telling how this is going to turn out, but I'm almost certain Tiffany will come out on top.

One after one, people leave the table. First, it's Stella, then Johnny. Audrey has to leave the table next. Spencer holds out until close to the end, but now there are only three of us left. Me, Corinne and Tiffany.

We all had to move close together so we could be equal distance from the two spoons on the table. One of us has to get Tiffany off the leaderboard. There's no way she's winning the whole thing. Corinne gets antsy in her chair. The anticipation is too much for her to bear.

Her leg brushes against mine, and I lose all focus. My hand reaches under the table, wondering if she did it on purpose. Her leg is still against mine, and I can't think. I make it seem like I'm brushing a crumb off my pants. Anything to hide my true intentions. My pinky gliding across her knee. It has to be subtle. Everyone is looking this way, trying to see who the victor is going to be.

That distraction cost me. I look down and both spoons are gone. "You cheated," I whisper to Corinne.

"No, sweetie, I distracted you. There's a difference." She winks and then hands me the spoon. "It's time for you to join the loser's circle."

Damn, and I thought Tiffany was ruthless. Corinne knows how to knock a man down. Not that I didn't know that before. "Fine. But for that, I'll be cheering for her." I point the spoon at Tiffany.

"I don't need your cheering, Carter. I have practiced skills." She beams at me. "Now, run along and refill our drinks, please."

"If I didn't know better, I'd think you're trying to get me drunk." Corinne laughs. "You realize I can drink just as much as you and still keep up with the game, right?"

Tiffany shrugs. "It's worth a shot."

While Tiffany shuffles the cards, I grab their glasses and fill them with the last of the margaritas. After setting them in front of the two women, I join the *losers' circle*. All of our attention is on the table. I'm pretty sure most of us are hoping Tiffany will lose.

Tiffany deals the cards, and Corinne is studying them like it's a final exam. In a way, I guess it is since she's trying to knock her off her high horse. The game begins as Tiffany picks up a card and passes another along. This game is as much about bullshitting the person you're playing against as it is about quick reaction times. The only caveat, you can't let them know you're going for the spoon. Otherwise, a war ensues. At least, that's been the case playing against Tiffany.

All of us have our eyes glued to the table as we watch cards being passed, but not one person going for a spoon. Tiffany is showing signs of frustration, and a quick peek over Corinne's shoulder tells me why. Tiffany keeps discarding numbers she most likely could have used. Corinne has four of a kind, and she's biding her time. While Tiffany's focus is on her cards, Corinne's hand slowly goes toward the center of the table, and lifts the spoon, before quietly bringing it in front of her.

Holy shit, how did Tiffany not notice that. Maybe the alcohol consumption helped in Corinne's favor this time around. After a few seconds of discarding, Tiffany reaches for the middle of the table and realizes the spoon is gone. "What the fuck?"

Corinne shows her cards and the spoon with a wide grin. "Read 'em and weep." She sticks her tongue out at Tiffany and jumps out of the chair. "Victory is mine!"

"You must have used some type of magic, there's no way I would have missed the spoon leaving the table."

"Except you did." Justin laughs. "Now's not the time to be a sore loser."

"Whatever," she rolls her eyes. "I think I'm going to bed."

Her cousins laugh and shake their heads. I'm guessing this is normal behavior for her. Though the thought of falling asleep does sound appealing. "I think I'm going to hit the hay as well. I have a feeling I'll need the energy for tomorrow."

"Why? What are we doing tomorrow?" Corinne sets the spoon on the counter and leans against it.

"According to Johnny, cooking out with some of their friends here and playing cornhole." I head toward the stairs. "That is a game I can definitely win."

"In your dreams, buddy," Justin follows behind me. "You're going down."

He's the one dreaming. Out of all the years we've been friends and played at various events, he's always lost against me.

I wave goodnight to him as I enter the room I'm sharing with his sister. Turning the light on, I'm slightly shocked. The air mattress is up and Corinne made the bed up for me. I lift the corner of the blanket and see a fitted sheet covering the mattress. For someone who claims she despises me so much, she went through the trouble of doing this for me.

It's the little things that give me hope we can have a future together. All these things are adding up and it's proof I'm not as out of her mind as she claims I am. I kick off my shoes and undress. Grabbing the basketball shorts off the dresser, I slide them on before turning off the light.

I flop on the air mattress and immediately regret it. I can't remember the last time I slept on one of these, but it's not comfortable. Maybe the couch would have been a better idea. This bed is stiff and squeaks with every move I make. I hear the knob turn and go still under the blanket. Maybe she'll think I'm asleep when she comes in.

CHAPTER SEVEN

CORINNE

WELL, that was a stressful game. I remember playing spoons when I was younger, but not at the level Tiffany and her cousins play it. It's more intense than it should be. All I want now is to change into my jammies and fall into a deep sleep. I know Stella and Johnny have a day full of stuff planned for us tomorrow, but I'll also need time to slip away from the group to take pictures of Tiffany and Spencer. It can always wait until we get back to Austin, but the scenery around here is absolutely gorgeous.

The light is off when I enter the room. That's one thing about Carter. He's quick to fall asleep once he's in bed. I only hope he appreciates me making his bed for him, considering it wasn't something I *had* to do. I pull my phone out of my back pocket and use the dim light to find my suitcase. I didn't even unpack everything earlier and will probably wake up Carter while looking for my stuff.

I unzip the suitcase as slowly as possible to minimize the noise. Present me is grateful that I put my jammies on the top. Not that it's anything special. T-shirts and shorts are the fanciest I get. With the clothes in hand, I debate going to the bathroom to change on the off-chance Carter is actually awake. I shine my phone in his direction, but his eyes are closed. I think that's safe enough. I pull my shirt off and replace it with my sleep shirt. Next is the pants and I'm ready for bed. Crap my bra. I unfasten it and pull it through the sleeves of my shirt. Tossing it on my suitcase, I turn back toward the bed. I don't bother plugging my phone in. I don't have the energy to find the cord and the alarm isn't needed.

Sliding between the sheets, I get comfortable. My eyes are drifting closed when I hear the air mattress move. The plastic squeaking is annoying as fuck. I don't know if I'll be able to sleep if he keeps flopping like a fish and making that noise. After a few moments he settles and the noise stops. Finally, I can fall asleep.

Closing my eyes, I turn to my side and start drifting into a dream filled oblivion. Moments away from deep sleep the mattress squeaks again, and I sit up, sighing. "Carter." He doesn't answer so I scoot to the side of the bed the air mattress is on and lean over. "Carter," I whisper yell. Still nothing. I reach out and shake his arm and say his name again. This time louder, "Carter."

He sits up and I can't tell because the only light in here is coming from the moon, but it doesn't look like he's been asleep at all. "Yeah." He rubs his hands over his eyes, but he's not fooling me.

"Can you please stop moving around? The mattress is keeping me from sleeping."

"I can move to the couch." He looks toward the door, but I know he wouldn't be comfortable with that, either. "Sorry I'm keeping you awake."

He could always sleep in the bed with me. I mean it's not the first time we've done that, but also not ideal with my brother a couple of doors down. "It's okay." Now's the time to decide. If he sleeps on the couch, he'll end up back on that damn air mattress when everyone goes downstairs, and I'll still get woken up. But if he sleeps on the bed...both of us will actually get some sleep. "Look, we're both adults. And even though we have a past, I feel like we can share this bed without things getting weird."

"Are you sure?" Carter cocks his head to the side, "I have no problem sleeping on the couch."

"Nope," I shake my head, "I'm not sure at all. But I need some sleep or else I'm going to have a massive hangover in the morning. This is the easiest way to solve the problem." I scoot back to my side of the bed and wait for him to get in. I grab all the decorative pillows from the bottom of the bed and put them between us. "There. This should keep us away from each other and temptation."

"I don't think all this is necessary." He points toward the wall of pillows. "I'm perfectly capable of keeping my hands to myself."

Little does he know, it's not him I'm worried about. While I did brush my leg against his as a distraction during the game, I also wanted to see how he would react. Everything he's done today signals that he wants to build something between us again. But I don't know if I can. What tore us apart last time was not being on the same page, and I refuse to let that be the case in the future. "It'll make me feel better, okay?"

"Okay." Wow, that was easy. I expected an argument. The bed shifts and I assume he's laying on his side, facing the opposite direction. To make me feel better? Maybe, but most likely to keep temptation at bay. Especially after that almost kiss earlier. He's quiet for a few moments, and I think he's gone to sleep but then just above a whisper he speaks. "Rinne?"

It takes everything in me not to groan. I just want to go to sleep. "Yeah."

"Do you think there could ever be an us again?"

Seriously? He wants to talk about this now? He's had so many opportunities over the last six months to talk to me. But he didn't. Not that I would have answered the phone, and I have been avoiding him at all costs. So, the opportunity wasn't really there. "I don't know, Carter. We had fun when we were together, but I can't be in a relationship in secret. It's not fair to me."

"I understand that." The bed shifts again. I'm not sure which way he's facing because I'm scared to look. Scared to see what might be written all over his face. The fact we're having this conversation in the dark with only the light of the moon makes it feel heavy and intimate. Both things I don't know that I'm ready to feel right now.

"I'm going to sleep now." I fluff my pillow and pull the blanket tighter around me. A safe little cocoon to ward off the feelings bubbling up once again.

"One more question." Ugh, he just won't stop. "If I were to remedy the secret part, would you consider giving us another go?"

In all honesty, I never wanted to end things with him. Not really. Even when my step-brother warned me against him. I imagined a future with him, but he was too scared to tell Justin we were together. How was I supposed to build a life with him, or possibly start a family with him, if I had to hide it all from the people who mean everything to me? "I don't know, Carter. Maybe? But it would have to be something we tell everyone from the beginning. No more secrets. It felt wrong to hide our relationship, and it feels even worse that you are the one that pushed for that so hard."

The bed moves one last time and I'm certain the conversation is over. "Goodnight, Corinne."

"Goodnight." As much as I want to sleep, at least that is out in the open now. He knows how I feel and he can do whatever he wants with the information. Sleep comes quickly once the night stills.

Weight on my waist jostles me from my sleep. I glance over my shoulder and the pillows are squished between me and Carter. His arm is slung over my waist and his hand's gripping my shirt. A clear sign he's not quite ready to let me go. Despite my protests, I'm not ready to let him go, either. I should push his arm off me. I know that, but for now I'm going to sink in the comfort of him being with me. Tomorrow, we'll have to have a conversation. One that is long overdue. And most importantly, if I continue to let him hold me like this. Like his life depends on it. We need to be on the same page.

CHAPTER EIGHT

A SOFT TAP on the door catches my attention. Why are these people waking me up? Then I remember last night. The truths Corinne and I whispered to each other in the cover of darkness. The truth of how I made her feel, and it was never my intention. Hurting her isn't something I wanted to do, and I did without even really knowing.

The pillows she put between us last night are gone. Her back is to my chest, where she belongs, and my arm wrapped tight around her. The knob turns, and I yank my hand back. Shit. This isn't going to look good to anyone on the other side. I hope like hell it's Tiffany.

My hopes are dashed. The door swings wide open and Justin comes into view. "What the fuck?"

Corinne jumps up, wide awake at the sound of her brother's voice. "What are you doing here?"

He blinks twice, opens his mouth, closes it, and opens it again. "What am I doing here? You didn't answer your phone when I called. I was coming to ask if you needed anything from the store. But this? I told both of you to stay away from each other. Just because you had a few drinks last night doesn't excuse this."

Corinne jumps out of the bed and points a finger in Justin's face. "I'm a grown fucking woman. I know you don't think I can handle myself, but I'm capable of making decisions on my own. And *nothing* happened. The air mattress made noises every time he moved and I told him he could sleep in the bed. And if you-"

I cut her off. She doesn't need to go to battle for me sleeping in the bed. I can also take care of myself. "She's right. Nothing happened. At least, not last night." Corinne glances at me eyes wide. She shakes her head slightly, a warning to keep me from saying what I'm about to say. But I don't care. She was right last night when we were talking.

I never should have kept our relationship a secret. I should have had the guts to tell her brother the way I feel about her.

"What do you mean not last night?" Justin's nostrils are flaring and his hands are balled into fists. There's a good chance he's going to hit me, I know it.

Deep breath. Here goes nothing. I only hope this is enough to show Corinne I'm serious this time. "I dated Corinne for a few months until about six months ago. The whole reason I came on this trip is so I can try to win her back. I love her, and you being pissed about it isn't going to stop how I feel about her."

He laughs, but it's not full of joy. It's dark and scary. I've never seen this side of my friend. "You? You love my sister? You flirt with anything that walks by. There's no way in hell I'm taking that declaration seriously."

Well, now I know what my best friend truly thinks about me. I'm good enough to hang out with him and his family, but not good enough to possibly be his brother-in-law. Talk about kicking me when I'm down.

"You can think whatever you want. I don't really care. The only person whose opinion I value is hers." I point toward Corinne. Her mouth is hanging wide open. "If she'll take me back, I'll go gladly. With or without your approval."

Justin opens his mouth to speak, but Corinne cuts him off. "You love me?"

My heart sinks because her words are wrapped in disbelief. Before I stuck my foot in my mouth last time, I was sure she knew exactly how I felt about her. I'm such a dumb ass. If only I'd done as she asked the first go around, we wouldn't be having this showdown now. Maybe then Justin wouldn't be so mad about it now. So much heartache and anger could have been avoided. "Of course, I do. I did then. Even more now since you told me how you really felt. It was wrong keeping our relationship from him," I wave my hand in Justin's direction "you're it for me. I've known for years before anything ever happened between us. Why do you think I pursued you so hard?"

She climbs over the bed and into my arms. Her arms fly around my neck, and I have to fight to keep my balance. That was unexpected. "I guess there's no way to really hide our relationship now, is there?"

"Pretty sure that ship sailed," I whisper in her ear.

"Really," Justin grunts, and we both turn toward him. "You're going to act like I'm not even here? Just because you two seem okay with this. I don't think I am. But I can't stay in this room any longer. When I get back, the three of us are going to have a talk."

"Why?" Corinne asks before he leaves the room. "What Carter and I do isn't really any of your business."

Without another word, Justin turns and leaves the room. The door slams hard enough behind him to rattle the frames on the wall. He's not going to let this go. If anything, he's going to be even more pissed that we had a relationship before and didn't tell him about it.

"I think you made him madder than he was." I laugh and rest my forehead against Corinne's.

She laughs, and the pure joy in the sound makes me happier than I ever thought I could be. "Do you honestly think I care? This was all I wanted six months ago. Why the hell would I push the issue so hard if I didn't love you? I can't share every aspect of my life with you if I was hidden like a dirty little secret. Do you have any idea how hard it was to know we were together and have to act like we weren't all those months?"

"That part I understand. I think it may have been just as hard for me not making eye contact with you in case Justin noticed." I pull her as close to me as possible. "Luckily, that's something we don't have to worry about anymore."

The door downstairs closes and a car starts before pulling away. "What are the odds everyone went but us?"

"Probably not great." I mutter. "Why?"

She lets go of me and walks to the door, locking it. Then she goes to the window and closes the blinds. "Because now that everything's out in the open, we can do this."

She pulls her shirt over her head and takes her shorts off, throwing them on the floor. She can't be serious. "What if other people are still here?"

"I guess we'll just have to be quiet." She climbs on the bed and makes her way to me. Within seconds she has my shorts pushed down and pulls me toward her. "You have no idea how torturous the last six months have been."

Leaning her back until she's lying on the bed, I hover over her. "I guess I have some time to make up for."

"Yes, you do." She pulls me down and her lips meet mine. The kiss is straight passion and hunger. Her tongue mingles with mine before she pulls away from the kiss, and pushes me down. "A lot of making up to do."

I know when to do what I'm told. I press a trail of kisses down her chest, stomach, and stop when I get to her pussy. "God, I've missed this."

She laughs, and my tongue dances over her clit until she stops. Her breathing is already heavy and she's squirming. It's good to know after all this time she wasn't with anyone else. Neither was I, which makes this all the sweeter. We don't have a lot of time before people come looking for us, and I'll have to take my time with her when we're home.

Her fingers tangle in my hair and she pulls hard. As much as I want her to come with my mouth, I understand the need she feels. The need to be inside her and have her wrapped around me. I move over her and slide inside of her. Her breath hitches and I lean down until our bodies are flush. Her arms hooked under my shoulders and I have one hand wrapped around her. I don't know what I was thinking before because this...this feels right. Feels like home and exactly where I should be.

Before long she's coming, and it takes everything in me to hold off. It hits me then that I didn't even bother with a condom. She's on birth control, but it's still not worth the risk when we're rekindling our relationship. I pull out and finish. Before rolling off her and lying beside her. "That was incredible."

"Just think what we could do with more time." She laughs and sits up. "I'm going to go get cleaned up and take a shower before they get back."

"I could always take one with you."

"Let's not press our luck. We still have to smooth things over with Justin."

"You're right." I sit up and kiss her. "I'll clean up in here before I get my shower in."

I watch her get dressed, gather her things, and slip out. I'm not ready for Justin to get back, and I know she thinks it'll be an easy task. I know him and it's going to be anything but.

CHAPTER NINE

CORINNE

IT FEELS nice being able to walk around holding Carter's hand. Letting everyone know we are together. This didn't happen the last time we were together. Back then it was stolen glances and keeping as far away from each other as we could. My brother hasn't talked to me all day. I half expected that, but it still hurts. If anything, he should want nothing but happiness for me. Instead, he's acting like a child and refusing to acknowledge my existence. Well, too bad for him. I already talked to Audrey and we're going to get a friendly game of cornhole going. We're just waiting for the current game to end.

Tiffany and Spencer purposefully lose their game against Audrey and Justin. Winner plays the next team, and I know it kills Tiff to not be the victor. I'm only happy she's willing to do this for me. It'll force Justin to talk to me. Maybe I can smooth things over between him and Carter.

I grab a couple of beers out of the ice chest and stand next to him. Carter walks to the other board next to Audrey. I hold one of the beers out to him, and he grabs it without a thank you. "Are you kidding me right now?"

"What? You don't like the fact you're about to have your ass handed to you?"

"You know exactly what I'm talking about. There's a reason I've been avoiding your love fest all day."

I roll my eyes. Ugh, he's such a man child. "And this is the only way I could force you to talk to me. I can drag this game out as long as I need to."

"Fine," he grunts. He grabs one of the bags and tosses it. It almost hits Carter and is nowhere near the board. "What do you want me to say?"

I grab my bag and toss it. It lands on the board. One point for me. "First of all, I'd like you to stop trying to take out my boyfriend with bean bags. And I want you to say you're happy for us."

"I don't know if I can, Rinne." Another bean bag flies through the air. This time he hits the board. Bastard. "I told the two of you not to get involved. What if things don't work out in the long run. That puts me in the middle."

"Considering we've already broken up once, I think everything will be just fine." I throw another bag and this time it goes in the hole. I'm up again. "I know you think we're wrong for each other, but we're not. We are actually very much alike. We're compatible, and love each other. What more could you want for me?"

"I don't know. Maybe for you to be with someone who isn't my best friend." He tosses the bag and misses the board completely. At least he didn't aim for Carter again.

"That's not good enough, Justin. There has to be another reason."

"There really isn't. I don't want to be put in the middle of your squabbles. And if you do one day break up, I will have to choose. My sister or best friend. It's not fair to me."

I toss another bag and make it on the board. "The proof of what happened between me and Carter before should make those fears less than they are. We avoided each other for the most part. That has to account for something."

"Maybe." He shrugs. He throws his last bean bag and I throw mine.

Silence sits between us as we wait for Audrey and Carter to take their turns. I'm still up after they are finished. "How are you feeling about your odds?"

"I need to switch sides," he grumbles and walks to the other board.

Audrey looks shocked but comes to stand by me. "I'm not sure that was a good idea."

"You aren't the only one." I sigh.

We both take our turns with our eyes on the two men at the other end of the yard. For a while, neither of them says a word to each other. This doesn't bode well at all, but I'm going to see how it plays out.

After each turn, they seem to be talking more and more. Each time a chance for them to speak to each other instead of yelling like what happened in the room this morning.

Carter and I are winning, and it's down to the last point. If I make this, we're golden. I throw the bean bag and it lands on the board. Audrey misses all of her shots and it's a victory for us. Audrey doesn't look disappointed, though. She points in the direction of the guys. They shake hands and do that weird bro hug.

They walk toward us and Justin stands next to Audrey while Carter comes to my side and puts an arm around my waist. "You two have my blessing." I'm seconds from jumping for joy, but he continues, "just please don't be all kissy face in front of me. It's weird."

"I'm not making any promises," I grin and turn to kiss Carter. I hear my brother groan, but I don't care. He approves, not that I needed it. Things are just easier when we're not on the outs. "You can have the next game. I need to grab my camera."

"I'll get it," Carter says and bounds off toward the house.

"Hey, Tiff," I call out. "Are you and Spencer ready to get those pictures taken before we're all too buzzed to do it."

"Damn, that would be funny," Tiffany answers. "But yeah, we're in." She pulls Spencer by the hand and we wait for Carter to come back with the camera.

I had my doubts about how this weekend would turn out, but it may be one of the best ones I've had in a long time. After all this time, I can call Carter mine without having to worry about any sort of blow back from the people I love.

SECOND CHANCE CHRISTMAS LOVER

Lore Townsend

CHAPTER ONE

Mateo

HOME SWEET FUCKING HOME.

I close the heavy front door behind me and walk into the grand entryway.

"Hello?" The words echo through the room.

I frown at the continued silence. It's unlikely there's no one home in a place this size. I did park right at the front door, without having to weave between a handful of haphazardly parked cars, but it's possible that the valet lined them up in the detached garage for the holiday weekend.

There's a storm in the forecast, after all.

I walk across the wooden parquet floor toward the sitting room, my shoes tapping out my steps as I go. The sound is deafening in the quiet house.

Tossing my duffel on a side chair, I shake my head in confusion. It's not exactly the homecoming I expected after eight years away. Eight long years of excuses and invented work obligations to avoid holidays. Eight years of trying to think about anything but this house, this island—and the years I spent here.

A noise in the kitchen draws my attention so I head down the hallway. No sooner have I raised my hand to push open the swinging door, than the door swings back in my direction. Hard.

I fail to react quickly enough to keep the wood from slamming right into my face.

"Ah, goddammit," I sputter out as I hunch over, holding my face in my hands.

The door swings back the other way and a woman appears. I don't even need to look up to know who's standing before me.

Sylvia Caitlin McAll.

"Mateo," she cries, kneeling before me and reaching up to touch my face, which is still held tightly in my hands.

The shock of being hit with the door is nothing compared to the shock of finding her here. Of being in her presence again. My heart wants to leap with joy but I quickly stomp it down.

I turn away and head back down the hallway, needing to escape the pain and the confrontation.

The woman—who's now trailing me into the sitting room—is the real reason I haven't been to our family's estate in so many years.

The woman who may have just broken my nose...also broke my heart.

CHAPTER TWO

Sylvia

SHIT.

Mateo wasn't supposed to arrive for hours. I would have been long gone by then.

Now there's going to be hell to pay.

I wonder briefly if I could beg him to keep this a secret and still sneak out before his family gets back from the mainland.

But I know that's not going to work.

This is the last man on the planet who would do me any favors.

"Are you okay?" I ask as he collapses on the couch. I approach hesitantly. There's nothing I want more than to touch him, but I know I can't.

"I'm fine. Thank you," he responds in his calm, even baritone. Always good under pressure, that's Mateo. Never flustered. Never rattled. That's how I know he'll make an amazing doctor. I wish I could see him in his white coat, working in the clinic.

"Can I get you a towel or some ice or..." I trail off as he lowers his hand from his bloody nose enough to pin me with those piercing green eyes.

The breath leaves my lungs in a rush as I struggle to stay upright on my weak knees. All my terrified thoughts from moments before about the consequences of us being in the same room melt from my mind like ice cream at the beach.

I'm actually here with Mateo. He looks good. A bit older, but mostly the same. His hair is shorter than it was when I last saw him. His dark stubble has been replaced by a clean shave. After all this time, I want so badly to run my hand over the smooth skin of his cheek.

"I'll take a towel and ice. Thank you." His voice is cold, as if he's speaking to a stranger.

The words hit my chest like stones, snapping me out of my fantasy. I bite my lip and nod, hurrying to the kitchen to make up the ice pack.

As I head back down the hall to the sitting room, I repeat the plan to myself in my mind. Give Mateo the ice, go get my bag, and take one of the maintenance golf carts down to the dock to catch a boat to one of the larger islands.

I already have the keys in my pocket.

Even taking this moment to bring him the ice is a risk, but it's one I have to take. I owe this man so much more than an ice pack. I'll never be able to give him closure for what I did, but I can give him this small comfort. I mean...I am the one who hit him with a door.

"Here you go."

Mateo takes the makeshift ice pack from me with a nod. I can see as soon as he removes his hand to bring the ice to his face that the bleeding hasn't stopped.

"Mateo, we may need to get you to the clinic. The bleeding looks bad."

"Thank you for your concern. I'm perfectly qualified to tend to my own bloody nose. I'll be fine, I'm just tired from a long day of traveling."

"I could—"

"You've done enough, Cat. More than enough."

The use of my old nickname nearly buckles my knees. As if he notices and wants to finish the job, he speaks again.

"What are you even doing here? I know you don't still live here with your mother. You can't possibly work here." His voice sounds both curious and dismissive. He wants to know, but would prefer anyone besides me tell him.

I let out a sigh. "No, I don't work here. I dropped off some gifts and helped my mother with her holiday cards. I'm staying in town, not here at the estate. I'll...I'll be out of your hair soon."

He glances around the room as if just remembering where we are. "Where is everyone?"

"Your father went to the mainland for some last-minute shopping, and the staff is in town running errands. There's a storm coming. Everyone's planning to stay here for at least the holiday weekend, maybe longer." As I glance up through one of the massive windows, I can see the sky darkening, raindrops already starting to fall.

But when I glance back down, Matteo has slumped over, eyes closed.

"Mateo," I cry out, kneeling next to him on the couch and leaning over his slack body.

My shiny new college degree might only be in hospitality management, but I know enough to be able to check his pulse and breathing. He's okay, just passed out. At least he's still sitting upright, the last thing he needs to do is lie down with a bloody nose.

I twist up some tissues to place inside his nose, but the bleeding seems to have stopped for the most part. He really must have been exhausted from his trip. I figure it's about thirteen hours from Chicago to the airport on the mainland. Goodness knows how many connections and layovers he suffered through before even starting his boat journey to the island.

With a frustrated sigh, I flop back on the couch next to him, my perfectly laid plan officially gone up in smoke. I wonder briefly if his father would be more angry to find me here...or to find out that I left him like this.

The answer doesn't matter anyway. I could no sooner leave this man alone here, passed out, than I could stop the earth's rotation.

I take the opportunity to examine his face, now that his hand has fallen to his side. It doesn't look as bad as I feared. I'd even venture to say it isn't broken. I fetch a warm, wet cloth and clean him up, situating him even more upright with a pile of pillows behind his head to keep it from flopping backward.

I remove his shoes and run my hand up his calf, the fabric of his dark jeans adding enough friction to my palm to make me gasp.

I can't believe I'm touching Mateo again, after all these years. Sure, he's passed out. Sure, my little family will lose everything if I'm caught doing it. But still.

He's here, and for a moment, I let myself pretend.

But then I remember.

I'm on my feet in an instant and heading back down the hallway. He may have thought he was fine, but he did just pass out from blood loss and a possible concussion—I'm calling the island medics. I don't care if he's pissed when he finally comes to.

I've gotten very used to knowing that the love of my life thinks I make terrible choices.

When I reach my mother's room, the small suite that we shared for so many years, I fumble through my duffel until I locate my phone.

No service.

It's not unusual to lose reception out here, hell we only just started getting cell service at all the year I left for college. I lift the receiver on the landline and find that dead as well.

With a shake of my head, I walk to the window. Rain is falling steadily, but it seems unlikely that it's caused so many problems yet. Maybe a tree took out a power line. Whatever the reason, there's one thing I know for sure. Mateo is alone out there and I'm the only one who can help him.

I head back to the sofa and curl up at the far end of the couch where he still sleeps. I want to lay my head on his lap like I always used to, but I know my touch wouldn't be welcome. I can't bring myself to violate his wishes, even though my heart longs to be near him.

The house is silent, with nothing to watch but the rain falling from the sky. His family will be back anytime now, and I'll have to offer an explanation as to why I'm here. I hope my reason for staying will be good enough to keep my mother's job—and her home here at the estate—safe.

CHAPTER THREE

Mateo

WHEN I OPEN MY EYES, the room is dark. I'm stiff from sitting up, but grateful that I didn't end up laying down while unconscious. I use my hand to examine my nose, which has finally stopped bleeding. I actually feel alright, all things considered. I guess all I needed after my long flight was a nap.

Movement at the other end of the sofa draws my attention and I find my nemesis curled up there, head resting against the arm as she sleeps.

Cat.

What the hell is she doing here?

I never would have come home for Christmas if I thought there was any chance I'd see her. Everyone assured me that she was long gone. Off to college somewhere and rarely back to visit.

But here she is, asleep just inches from me.

And why isn't my family back yet?

I look around the dim room. It's dark enough in here, and outside, for me to be able to see right through the large window.

And what I see makes me actually laugh.

The sound wakes Cat and she sits up, glancing around nervously. I don't know what she has to be anxious about, but I avoid her gaze anyway. Just in case she's nervous to be here with me.

"I can't believe I fell asleep. I was supposed to be watching over you," she says softly.

Her voice brings back a rush of memories, each one a dagger straight to my heart.

"I'm fine," I manage.

She's on her feet, smoothing her green dress before fixing her long, strawberry blonde hair. "Yeah, but I didn't know that. You were bleeding like crazy and then you just passed out."

"Nice of you to think of me." I want my tone to convey how much I would have liked her to care so much eight years ago, when she left me alone on that train platform.

I'm pretty sure I succeed because her worried eyes fall to the floor. "I'm sorry that it didn't work out between us."

I don't want to get into this, so I try to deflect. "It's fine, Cat. Ancient history."

"It's not fine—"

"Yes," I interrupt sternly, "it is. What happened happened. We were kids. It was probably for the best." I don't believe my own words, and I don't know if she will either.

"How can you say—"

"I'm going to head up to my room."

"Oh." Her fiery gaze, which had been pointed at me, drifts away. "Yeah. I should probably head out."

"Fat chance of that."

Her eyes meet mine, confusion painted over her features. I gesture toward the window with my head, holding her gaze.

When she walks over to the large picture window, she gasps. And then laughs out loud just like I did.

The sound pains me more than my nearly broken nose ever could. Hell, more than any broken bone at all. It's soft and sweet, melodic. Suddenly, it's as if we're right back to the time before I left for Chicago—alone. The good times, when we were growing up, getting closer and closer. Falling in love.

Or, I was falling in love anyway. I'm not sure what she was doing.

I shake it off and turn to where she's still at the window. "I must have been out for a while. That much water would have taken hours to accumulate. The drains must be blocked."

She glances over her shoulder at me. "Must be why no one came back to the island." Concern furrows her brow, and her smile fades. "I hope they're okay."

I grind my teeth as I consider the implications of her statement and our situation.

The house is empty—except for the two of us. And now a freak December tropical storm threatens to keep us trapped here, alone, for days.

I sigh. Why me? What did I do to deserve this kind of torture?

"Do we have food?" I ask, needing to say something to still the war raging in my mind.

"Yes, of course. I mean, not the full feast the staff was planning, but they've been shopping for weeks in preparation. My guess is they just went in today for produce and bread from the bakery."

I nod. "Okay, well...I guess I'll be seeing you around the house, then."

I turn and prepare to leave the room. To walk away from the only woman I've ever loved. The one who still haunts my dreams. The one who betrayed me beyond forgiveness.

When her voice stops me, the feeling that rushes over me can only be described as relief.

"Mateo."

I pause in the doorway but don't turn. I know what I want her to say, but somewhere deep down, I'm sure she's not going to.

"I'm sorry. I'm sorry about how it all happened. If I could explain—"

I turn too quickly and have to steady myself with a hand on the doorframe. "Go ahead. Explain."

The overhead lights in the foyer behind me cast enough light on her face for me to see the anguish there. The tears.

What does she have to be so upset about?

She's the one who ruined everything.

"I can't," she finally manages to get out.

My confusion and pent-up emotions all boil into anger. "What do you mean you can't? You left me there, alone, waiting for you. You never answered a single one of my calls or texts. And you have no explanation for why you did it? Why, Cat? What did I do that was so terrible that you would cut me out like that?"

She's full on crying now, pushing her tears to the side with her hands as she tries to keep holding my gaze. She always was the strong one.

"If I could tell you, I would, Mateo, I swear to you—"

I've heard enough. My journey back from a broken heart over the last eight years was long and painful. The last thing I need to do is tear the damn thing back open again.

I hear her steps behind me as I head for the stairs. I'm dreading the moment when she catches up, but I'm still not steady enough to run.

If I could, I would. I would run right out the front door into the storm. I would run anywhere to avoid what I know is coming.

Her hand touches down on mine with what feels like an electric shock. I snatch my hand back quickly. Roughly.

Cat watches me recoil from her touch. A fresh river of tears starts down her cheeks and I have to look away.

"You have to understand..." she starts, but I have no patience for this.

"No, Cat. I don't have to understand anything. You could make me understand. You could speak the words and tell me why. Maybe then I'd understand."

She says nothing, her gaze dropping to the floor, shoulders curling in.

"But you're not going to. So, I'm just going to go upstairs and keep not understanding."

This time, when her soft, warm hand snakes its way up my arm, I don't pull away. The warmth of her touch seeps into my skin and my eyes fall closed.

I feel her take a step closer as I stand frozen to the spot. My mind screams at me to flee, but my body refuses to obey.

I keep my eyes closed as she climbs another step, bringing us to an even height. I could cry now myself, as the memories of us standing this way so many times, in this very spot, wash over me.

I know what comes next, but somehow, I'm still not prepared for the kiss.

Her lips touch down on mine so softly, timidly, waiting for me to push her away.

Why am I not pushing her away?

Instead, I find myself leaning into it, allowing her hand to travel further up my arm, around my shoulder.

My own hand reaches out to touch her, landing on her waist and moving to her lower back, even though I don't remember telling it to.

Cat presses her lips more firmly, and I feel them part slightly in offering. The logical part of my brain seems to have checked out, because I open for her, allowing her to deepen the kiss.

It feels light, soft, warm, and so fucking perfect. Just like it was before. She and I have always fit together like puzzle pieces.

I can't reconcile this woman with the one who made promises that she didn't keep. The one who helped me create a dream world and then smashed it all down. What is she doing standing here, on the stairs, allowing her lips to tell me a different tale?

Is this really the touch of someone who hates me enough to break my heart?

But she did.

Anything I'm feeling right now...is all in my head.

I break away and take a step backward. I try to look anywhere other than into those familiar green eyes, but her gaze catches mine long enough for me to see the longing there. The hope. It's almost as if she's waiting for me to save her.

Maybe I have a concussion after all, because there's no way she needs saving.

Right?

I take a deep, steadying breath and shake my head.

Sidestepping where she still stands on the step above me, I head up the stairs without another word.

CHAPTER FOUR

Sylvia

I PULL the light blanket off my mom's bed and set a small, battery powered fan on the nightstand. As of now, the power is still on, and the temperature hasn't risen too much. It's only a matter of time, though, before we lose power like we always do in storms like this.

I'm dying to check on Mateo, make sure he has fans ready for when the house gets hot, make sure he finds something to eat, but I manage to keep myself in my room. He's a grown man, perfectly capable of feeding himself and making his own bed.

As always, my mind drifts to thoughts of what his life must be like now. I know from social media and bits of gossip my mother manages to pass on that he has a job at a community clinic in Chicago. He must have an apartment there in the city. I wonder what his couch looks like, what kind of dishes he picked out for himself, what his bedroom looks like…and who shares it with him.

Stop, Sylvia.

I force my mind back to safer territory. The last thing I need to do right now is go into a full doom spiral with the man actually under the same roof as me.

Something that was never, ever supposed to happen.

I know going through the speech I've prepared isn't going to make me feel better, but it's necessary. It's only a matter of time before the road clears enough for the family to come home.

For *him* to come home and find me here with his son.

Maybe it would be better to hide. To run, even. There are plenty of raincoats and boots in the garage. I could leave at first light, make my way into town, and find somewhere to ride out the worst of the winds and flooding.

But it's no use. Mr. Ricci's words from eight years ago echo through my mind as if he'd only spoken them yesterday.

"You can't run or hide. Wherever you go, I will find you. The choice is yours, Sylvia."

Think of your mother, he'd said. Think of her job, her visa, her livelihood, the home she enjoys at the estate.

I try to think of my mother now, how worried she must be, trapped in town, knowing I'm here at the estate.

But I can't make myself.

There's only one person my traitorous mind is willing to conjure up images of, and it's the man sleeping just upstairs from me. The shape of his muscular chest under my fingers as I ran my hand over it. The smile he always had waiting for me, even after the harshest of his father's criticism. The secret future we planned during those late nights when he would sneak me up to his room.

The future he's now living...without me.

The lamp goes dark beside me, but I'm not surprised.

I should get up and pull the drapes closed, but I can't muster up the energy to move just yet.

When the crash comes, I barely have time to shield my face before the whole world becomes a blur of wind and wet, flying objects.

CHAPTER FIVE

Mateo

I'm NOT surprised when the lights go out. It was just a matter of time.

The estate is miles from the new construction of town, isolated and enormous. A wood and coral stone relic of island history.

My bedroom is on the second floor, at the end of the east hallway. It's a massive room, with an attached sitting room and ensuite. I was only allowed to claim it for myself because no one wanted it due to the lack of natural light. There's only one small, stained glass window, so any sunlight that comes in colors the room red.

A vampire's lair, my mother called it.

When I was a kid, I pretended that the sunlight would burn my skin. I'd hide in my lair for hours on the weekends, reading and drawing. When a new housekeeper moved in the summer I turned nine, bringing along her daughter, I finally had a friend. Someone who understood me in ways that my much older siblings never could. Ways that my parents never even tried.

I lost my mother that winter, and Cat became my lifeline. She was the only one I would talk to for months after we buried my mother, tasked with bringing up all of my meals and staying with me while I studied. Our friendship blossomed into so much more, and we had our life all planned.

Or I thought we did.

Turns out, I knew nothing.

I'm halfway to the closet to grab a lighter sheet and a fan when I hear the crash.

I don't think before I'm out the door and rushing down the stairs. I pause at the foot, listening for any indication of where the noise came from. The muffled cry I hear from down the east hallway on the main floor sends chills through my entire body.

Cat.

"Cat, where are you?"

"Mmmsmm," is the muffled reply.

I rush down the hallway only to be stopped in my tracks. Whatever took out the windows on this side of the house also let in enough water and debris to block the entire hallway. "Shit. I can't get through this way. Are you okay?"

There's no reply.

"Cat, say something!"

There's still no answer from the end of the hall. All I hear is the raging wind and the sound of the water rushing in as I stand there.

Terror sends a rush of adrenaline through my system, and I briefly consider plowing right through the mess to get to her.

But my common sense prevails. I can't help her if I hurt myself.

I turn and run back the way I came, up the stairs and into my room. I can't let myself think about what I'm about to do—otherwise I might not have the strength to go through with it.

I pull aside a heavy antique dresser, one I moved to this exact location the one time I visited home since leaving for college.

Since Cat left me.

The doorway behind is dusty and draped in cobwebs, but the handle turns easily. With a deep breath, I plunge down into the darkness.

I can follow the familiar stairs with my eyes closed, which is lucky, since not a speck of light reaches this secret staircase. Down, down, down I run, my mind focused on getting to the woman at the bottom...not allowing in thoughts of the many wonderful years she and I spent sneaking up and down these very stairs to visit each other.

There's no time for that now.

The door at the bottom won't budge, and it takes a mighty heave to push whatever's blocking it far enough into the room to get the door open.

When I emerge, the scene in front of me does nothing to calm my nerves.

The window is demolished, a large branch impaling the house from where a large tree has fallen. The floor is strewn with leaves, glass, and splintered wood. The bed is—

Oh my god.

Cat.

I rush to her and drop to my knees beside the bed. Using one hand, I brush her hair from her face, while my other hand moves expertly to her neck to check for the pulse I know will be there. I don't allow myself to even entertain other possibilities.

It's slow, but she's still with me.

It's all I can do not to gather her into my arms right then and there, but I'm afraid to hurt her even more. I have to check for spinal injuries first. I have no idea what happened here, whether she was struck by the tree or collapsed from the heat or shock.

My quick but thorough physical examination shows no signs of injury. I finally dare to move her a bit, to try to rouse her.

"Cat, can you hear me?"

Her eyes remain closed. I'm sure I heard her cry out not ten minutes before, but now she's unresponsive.

Out cold.

With the power out and the window smashed in, the whole east side of the ground floor is filling with water. It's very windy and wet in here.

I brush aside a few palm fronds and gather her up in my arms, making my way back to the hidden staircase. I shift her carefully so I can close the door behind me and block out some of the wind as I climb. I'll have to come back and figure out what to do about the house later.

Back up in my bedroom, I lay her on the bed and get the blankets from the large wardrobe. She's sopping wet, but I'm not sure if changing her is the appropriate thing to do.

When I take one of her hands in my own, however, the decision is made. Her fingers are clammy and cold.

I gather some soft, warm clothes from my own closet and set to work pulling off her soaked ones as detached and clinically as I can. She's just another patient who needs my lifesaving attention.

Once Cat is dry and cool under the sheet of my bed, I pull on my raincoat, and head back down the staircase to the ruined first-floor bedroom. I don't have the tools or materials I need to board up the windows, and there's no way I'm going to make it out to the detached garage in this weather. I'll just have to do the best I can.

Cat's mother's room is halfway filled with water and broken plant matter now, obscuring almost the entire bed. Dread melts over me at the thought of what might have happened if I hadn't come to get her out of this room.

It's almost as if her look from earlier, where her eyes seemed to beg me to save her, foreshadowed this tragic event.

If only I had a similar gift of seeing the future, then I might have been able to save myself from the heartbreak of putting myself on the line for the girl I loved only to have her turn her back on me.

But even as I think it, I know it would never have worked. I was thoroughly, foolishly, blindly in love with Cat on the day I waited for her to catch the train to Chicago—to our new life.

And I still am.

I spot her duffel bag and phone on a side table luckily not already covered with water. I unzip the bag to toss the phone in and something catches my eye. It's a photograph of her and I, posing in one of the trees on my family's property. I can't help but smile at the memory of that day. We'd climbed up to pick mangoes and ended up spending the whole day up there, munching on fruit and making up stories about how it was going to be when we were grown up.

I am loath to snoop, but I can't help but see another picture sticking out of the side of a leatherbound journal. And another. I shake the book and our whole childhood falls out—at least a dozen snapshots of the two of us together. I flip through them one by one, smiling to myself at the happy memories. Memories I've tried so hard to block out of my mind the last Eight years.

Why is she carrying these pictures around with her? It doesn't make any sense. The woman washed her hands of me years ago, and yet...

I burn with the desire to unwrap the soft leather cord and open the journal—just to see if there are any clues as to what is going on here...but I can't. Even though she violated my trust, I can't bring myself to return the favor.

I will, however, be demanding some answers as soon as she wakes up. Her behavior earlier—her hesitancy to offer even a single reason for abandoning me—felt dismissive at the time, but faced with this new evidence...it almost feels suspicious.

Growing up in a family like mine, where money and power are valued above all else, I'm used to hearing stories of people being bought off or "disappeared" when they didn't fit the correct narrative.

Could that have been what happened with Sylvia?

I shake my head, not wanting to even consider that my Father could be cold hearted enough to take from me the person who kept me alive after my mother's untimely death. The person who shined the light into my darkness.

The explanation must be something else. I vow to get to the bottom of it as soon as Cat wakes up.

I gather up everything that looks like it might belong to Cat, including her shoes and coat, and drag the dressers, wardrobe, and secretary desk to the far wall, away from the broken window. It might not be enough to save all of Cat's mother's belongings from water damage, but it's the best I can do with the hallway blocked by debris.

Back up in my room, I check her breathing and pulse once more before crossing the room to shed my damp layers and pull on dry clothes. Then I stand next to the bed like an idiot.

Do I get in? Lay on top? Fucking hell.

I finally crawl beside her and pull another sheet over myself, deciding she might not want me to crawl under the covers with her.

But after that kiss? And the photographs I found? The mystery of it all is astounding.

The truth is, I don't know much about the woman lying beside me. She could be married. She could have a family waiting for her. It's very possible that she knows what I'm doing with my life now. I've made sure to keep social accounts up to date on the slim chance that she wants to reach out someday, but she doesn't have a single profile. And believe me, I've looked.

My anger over what she did sometimes flares up, but for the most part it's mellowed into a dull ache of sadness. She doesn't want to be with me, but I made myself believe there's a reason.

Now that I know she still cares about me, I'm even more curious about what that reason could be.

With the storm still raging outside, I take what comfort I can from the love of my life finally asleep beside me and drift off to sleep.

CHAPTER SIX

Sylvia

I WAKE IN A WARM BED, and I don't even need to open my eyes to know Mateo is beside me. I'm still a little fuzzy as to what happened after the window blew out, but one thing's for sure. I feel safe.

For now.

I can't think about what will happen when Mr. Fuentes returns home and finds us. That will be the end of all the safety and security I've enjoyed in my life. It will be the end of my mother's trust in me. The end of my budding career and bright future.

But I can't worry about that right now. Because at this moment, I have everything I've ever wanted.

Mateo opens his eyes as I watch and suddenly, we're just two sets of green eyes locked in the intimate stare of soul mates. How many times have I laid just like this, in this very bed, allowing those very eyes to look into my soul? Too many to count.

I should move. I should roll over or at the very least squeeze my eyes closed, but I don't. And neither does Mateo.

The silence stretches for so long I think it might strangle me. Finally, his whisper cuts through the darkness.

"I've missed you."

I can't respond, but my eyes well up with tears as I continue to hold his gaze. I hope it's enough.

"All I ever wanted was this. We wanted this...we talked about it so often. Whatever changed that for you, we could have figured it out together," he goes on softly.

It's amazing, in this day and age, that a secret like the one I hold managed to stay secret. I guess it's because he more or less never came back here after that day. If he had come home, and trusted his family enough to share his story of heartbreak with them, it would only have been a matter of time before someone told him the truth.

"I think about you every second of every day," he whispers.

"I..." What? What on earth can I possibly say to this man? "I miss you, too."

His eyes close as my words strike him.

"Why?" he asks, eyes still closed.

I snake my hands out of the covers and find his. For a moment, I think he's going to pull away, but he doesn't.

He pulls me closer.

"Can we just pretend it's before for a little while?" I ask softly, fully prepared for anger to explode out of him for my cruel, unfair words.

His mouth opens slightly, but his eyes stay closed. I don't dare breathe. After a moment so long that I nearly suffocate, he nods.

There's no stopping my tears now and they rush out of me in silent sobs. Mateo pulls me so close that I'm enveloped in his scent, his warmth. He holds me until my crying wanes and I go still in his strong arms.

When I lift my tearstained face up to meet his, he places a soft kiss on one cheek. And then the other.

He kisses down my jawbone and across my chin. When I realize he's kissing away my tears, they start all over again and he kisses each drop as it falls.

When I can't stand to wait a second longer, I chase his lips with my own, locking us in a kiss that turns passionate so quickly, it sweeps me away. I squeeze my eyes closed and allow myself to go back. Back before everything went wrong. Before I knew the harshness of the real world.

I can tell Mateo went back in time with me. He's pressing my lips open with his tongue, invading deep into my mouth as I surrender to him. No thought. No questions. Just feeling like we did back then. He's up on one elbow, his other hand reaching up to cradle the side of my face as he kisses me like a man who needs saving and I'm his lifeline.

Maybe it's true.

It's only when he pushes the blankets away and runs his hand down my torso that I realize I'm dressed in his clothes. The thought of him undressing me while I slept turns the budding heat between my legs into an inferno.

Did he look at my body as he undressed me? Did he want me even then?

I shouldn't be having these thoughts, shouldn't be doing any of this, but it's a lost cause. With Mateo and I together again all is right in the world.

Even if it's just pretend.

"Cat, I'm going to take this off." His hand is on the hem of the large sweat-shirt he dressed me in.

"It seems like you already did." I can hear the lightness, the humor in my voice and I know Mateo can, too.

He grins at me and it takes everything I have not to break out in tears again. That beautiful, devilish grin. It used to be mine.

"I changed you, but I was very respectful. I found you wet and freezing."

"Will you be less respectful now?" The daringness of my words shocks me, but in the best possible way.

"If that's what you want," Mateo replies, already lifting the sweater up to expose my breasts.

"You know exactly what I want, Matty, you always did." I'm asking for trouble throwing his nickname out like that, conjuring up memories of the many, many times we were in compromising positions in this very bed.

And trouble is exactly what I get.

As soon as the sweater hits the floor, Mateo captures my nipples with his teeth, one at a time, offering sharp little nips followed by the smooth caress of his tongue. I cry out with each jolt of pain, sinking deeper into him with each offering of pleasure. I've never forgotten how this man touches me—and I've never allowed another man to even come close.

I'm dying for more contact, so I pull his own shirt over his head and toss it off the bed. I run the pads of my fingers down his gorgeous, muscular chest.

"Hmm, eager, are you?" Mateo teases, gathering my breasts up with both hands, giving my nipples another soft bite.

"Yes," I moan, arching my back.

"What are you so eager for, my little kitty?"

"You," I offer bravely, baring my heart with no regard for its safety.

He could so easily leave me cold and wanting, just like I once did to him, but I have a feeling he's not going to.

I'm immediately glad I trusted my instincts.

Mateo's lips are back on mine, his tongue exploring my mouth as I reach up with my own to do the same. I want to do everything with this man, be everything. Connected as one just like we were before. I can't get enough of him, and I can't get it quickly enough. My fingers graze down his stomach and hook in the waistband of his pants.

I feel him smile against my lips.

"Not so fast there, kitty." He lifts up to kneeling and my hands fall away. There isn't time for fear or disappointment, because he's got his own fingers in the waistband of my sweats and pulls them down with one sharp tug.

The too large pants come easily off my body and land on the floor beside the bed.

"I'll give you a taste, but first, I need to taste you," he says.

The desire that smolders in his eyes can't be a lie. My mouth sags open and I struggle to take a full breath with his gaze running up my legs and over my bare stomach and breasts. I've been hiding myself away for so long, and never thought I would be here...nearly naked with Mateo. The feeling is electric, joyous, and devastatingly familiar.

I allow my full weight to rest back on the soft pillows as Mateo begins his descent. Down my neck his lips go, tongue flicking out to taste me as his hot breath leaves chills in its path. When he reaches my navel, my most ticklish spot, he stops to trace a slow circle. I laugh and squirm, but his strong hands hold me steady, making me endure the torture until I'm breathless.

With a soft laugh of his own, he moves on. I know he saw my panties earlier when he changed my clothes, but I can't help my shyness when his teeth latch onto the lacy rim.

I would have dressed up if I'd known, put on something fancier than the simple lace trimmed cotton panties I chose this morning.

Before my shame can overtake me, he has them on the floor with the rest of my clothes.

I'm now fully bared for him.

Maybe I should want to hide, but I don't. Maybe I should be ashamed of the blatant desire waiting for him between my legs, but I'm not. My knees fall open and the growl of approval that escapes Mateo's lips sinks deep into my chest.

When his tongue touches down softly at my entrance, slipping inside my body like it has so many times before, I finally let all apprehension melt away.

Everything will look different in the morning, but for now, I'm going to let myself have this. Have him.

The tension that's been building since the moment I woke up beside him finally has an outlet, and I find myself approaching the edge quickly. Soft, long swipes of his tongue around my swollen clit, slowly and then quicker has my breath quickening and my legs shaking.

I try to slow my mounting pleasure, dying to feel his fingers inside me when I climax. I could ask him to touch me, but I don't want to. I want Mateo to set the pace. I want to follow him down this road to pleasure.

He doesn't let me down.

Just when I think I won't be able to hold on a second longer, I feel him slide his fingers inside me, curling just right while pumping in and out.

I gasp and trap the air inside my lungs, the swell of ecstasy starts where his fingertips connect with my flesh and radiates out like a song.

One I know by heart.

My orgasm crashes through me, leaving me breathless and shaking. Mateo doesn't let up, continuing the pump of his fingers and the delicious slide of his tongue as I quiver and grasp at the sheets beside me.

"Mateo," I cry out when I'm finally too sensitive, needing a respite from his touch. "Matty, please."

He looks up from between my legs, smiling at me and licking his lips. "Had enough, little kitty?"

"Yes. That was…" I'm still shaking, my mind floating a foot over my body, unable to string together coherent thoughts. "Incredible," I manage.

"You're incredible. I can't believe it's been so long since I licked your sweet pussy."

I don't want to think about how long it's been. I only want to live in this moment. "Fuck me, Matty."

He always liked when I talked dirty. It's all I have to fall back on now.

His lips curl up into a snarl and I know I've said the right thing. "Are you going to be a good little kitty?"

I shake my head like I know I'm supposed to.

His answering mischievous smile is a prize I tuck away in the depths of my mind for later.

"You're going to be a bad kitty?"

I nod.

"Do bad kitties really deserve to get fucked?"

I nod, earning me another little smile.

"Oh? And why is that?"

I sit up and bring myself to my hands and knees, crawling away from him toward the headboard. I toss a sultry look back over my shoulder and find his green eyes blazing. "Because bad kitties know just what you want." I give my ass a little shake.

It has the desired effect. No sooner have I wagged my naked ass in his face than he has me roughly in his hands, pulling my back up to meet his chest with a fistful of my long hair, his stiff erection pressed against my body through his jeans.

"You know just how to get to me, you know that?" he growls right into my ear.

I nod, the action sending a thrill of pain through my scalp where he still holds my hair.

"Yeah, I guess you do, don't you."

He releases my hair and I fall back to my hands on the mattress.

For a second, I wonder if I ruined it all, if he's going to get up and leave me there, naked and kneeling for him.

But he doesn't.

I hear the familiar sound of his pants being discarded, but I don't dare to look back. With my breath held, I wait patiently for him to touch me again.

Mateo's fingers enter me without warning and I gasp in surprise.

"Tsk, tsk. Don't pretend you're a virgin, little kitty. We both know that's not the case."

"I..." I'm terrified to tell him the truth, but I feel like he should know. "It's just been a while."

"How long?"

"Since...well, since you."

His fingers stop dead, still buried deep in my pussy. "You haven't been with anyone since me?"

I shake my head, still not brave enough to look back and see what expression he wears as he speaks the words.

"Why?"

I shake my head again, letting it hang a bit lower. The real reason is too close to the truth—and the truth will only get me in trouble.

"I shouldn't like that as much as I do." His hand starts moving again, this time his pace and depth could only be described as punishing. I suppose it's what I deserve. "But the thought of your pussy waiting for me...the thought of no other man ever being here..."

When his massive cock plunges inside me, straight to the hilt on the first thrust, I cry out. It's pain, it's pleasure, it's relief. It's a cry of celebration.

I collapse down to my elbows, opening my body further to the exquisite stretch of him. Mateo responds by grabbing my hips with both hands, pulling me closer, driving himself deeper.

"It's been so long. Too long," he laments, and although I can't speak, I agree with a whimper. "Where have you been? You should have been with me." Whatever emotion drives the words from his mouth also makes him drive his cock into me more swiftly. I clench down on him in response.

For a few long, enchanted moments, there are no words, just the sound of our bodies, our breathing merging together in passionate gasps.

I start climbing back up the hill toward climax—the rocking of our hips, the emotion of it all too much for me to hold on. I'm about to reach for his hand, demand his touch just where I need it, but he pulls out suddenly.

Before I can react, I'm flipped over to my back, looking up into the lustful eyes of my one and only. He kneels over me, mad with desire, his glistening cock pointing at me like a beacon.

"Mateo, I—"

"Don't." He cuts me off with one word, crashing down on me, claiming my mouth with his.

I'm still lost in the depths of his kiss when he enters me, gently at first, both hands cradling my face. It's such a departure from the maniac taking me from behind just moments before, it takes me a full beat to relax into it.

Into being loved by him again, rather than just fucked.

This is far more terrifying. I can already feel myself sinking into him. It's only a matter of time before I'm lost.

My legs grip his back as he rocks his hips, pressing his cock deep into my body and then pulling it out, slowly, tenderly.

When his mouth touches down on my breast, licking around my nipple, sucking the tight bud into his mouth, I come again, my body clenching down on his as I moan in pleasure.

"Fuck, kitty, you're going to make me come. Is that what you want?"

"Yes," I manage to get out through my blissful spasms. It's my consent, my surrender, and a prayer, all wrapped into one tiny word.

Mateo thrusts hard into my tight pussy, my orgasm still milking him as he fills me. The contrast of pleasure and pain—the orgasm and the stretch, the love and the betrayal—leave me breathless.

He lets out a bellow as he finishes inside me. I don't have the strength left to even consider the implications of what we've done—or where we'll go from here.

All I can do is accept him, all of him, as his core clenches and he fills me. When he finally stills, he doesn't pull out, but his eyes open and he pins me with that stare.

The one I used to know meant he would love me forever.

Now, I have no idea what it means.

We stay locked in the stare for too long. My legs ache and I'm nearly on the verge of tears again when he finally speaks.

"You trust me enough to let me fuck you like this when you haven't let anyone else fuck you."

It's not a question, but I nod anyway.

"You trust me?" he asks.

I nod again.

"I love you, do you know that? I never stopped loving you." His voice starts as a whisper, but gains strength as he finishes.

The tears that were threatening before well in my eyes. I nod again, holding his gaze.

"Do you love me?"

I squeeze my eyes closed as I nod, the tears carving hot rivers down my cheeks.

"Why, Cat?"

"Matty, I can't—"

He pulls out suddenly and sits up, pulling me up by my shoulders and shaking me, holding me up to face him. "Yes, you can. You say you love me, that you trust me, so trust me now. Tell me why."

I know it's a lost cause. I've never been very good at denying this man, especially not in the face of his passionate determination. I put up one last half-hearted fight. "You have to promise not to freak out."

His forehead creases and his hands relax, letting my shoulders free. I've surprised him with my demand. Possibly even scared him. He thought he was ready for my reasons, but now he's hesitating.

"I promise," he finally offers, and I have no choice but to believe him.

CHAPTER SEVEN

Mateo

I CAN'T BREATHE for the full moment it takes Cat to start speaking, terrified of what she's going to say. All these years, I thought it would be something so simple, so stupid, that if I ever got this chance, I'd be able to hear her reasons and go on with my life.

But now I'm not so sure. The look on her face isn't shame, or embarrassment. It's fear.

"Your...your father found out."

It's all she needs to say. My eyes fall closed and my heart breaks all over again. But this time, it's not her betrayal breaking it—it's mine.

Even when I found the pictures in her bag that proved she still loves me, I refused to allow myself to imagine for a second that my father could have had something to do with her sudden change of heart.

What a damn fool I've been.

"He...he told me I could never speak to you again. He threatened my mother's job, her visa." She pauses, waiting for me to speak, but the words stay trapped below the shattered remains of my heart.

She goes on, and I can hear the panic enter her voice now. "I was scared, Matty, you have to understand. I was young. I didn't know any better. And then I went to college, and the more time that went by without hearing from you, the more I started to think maybe it was for the best. I mean, you were going to find someone better, someone from a good family, just like he wanted. I..."

"He sent you to college?" I don't know why I ask, there are more pressing questions I need the answers to.

Cat's face crumples and another wave of tears pours from her mournful eyes. "Yeah. He bought me off. Threatened me and bought me off. And I went along with it." She waits, but I'm still processing and can't speak. "Can you ever forgive me?"

The soft plea, straight from the mouth of the only woman I've ever loved, finally breaks more words free. "Jesus, Cat. It's not me who needs to forgive you. Can you ever forgive me?"

Because the truth is, I should have realized. I know damn well who my father is. I know he wanted someone different for me. When this woman, who I love and trust with my life, disappeared off the face of the planet, I should have known to ask him...blame him.

"What do you mean?" she asks.

I look back up from my hands to find her face stricken with confusion. "I should have known. I just believed him when he told me you'd run off. That you didn't want me. I never should have lost faith in you. I let eight whole years go by. Eight wasted years that we could have been together. I should have found you, no matter where you were. Oh, Cat. How can I ever make this up to you?"

I watch the relief on her face turn back to sadness and cold dread crashes over me.

"You have to let me go. Even though you know the truth, you still have to let me go. Be a doctor and find the perfect society wife and live your life."

"What? Fuck no. No way that's happening. No way I'm letting you go again."

I reach for her but she scoots away.

"Mateo, your father's threat still stands. I need my mother to be safe, to have her job here. I need to find a job that can support us both by the time she's too old to work. I can't risk her future, my future. He's too powerful, too vindictive."

Her words hold weight. I, too, know just how far the man will go to get what he wants. But this time, he's come up against a far more formidable enemy than an immigrant housekeeper and her daughter.

I won't be intimidated so easily.

"It's not you who's going to be taking risks this time, kitty. It's me. I'm going to protect you like I should have been doing all along. No one will ever threaten you or your mother again. And no one will ever touch you. Not when you have me."

Even if my words aren't enough to convince her to stay here in bed with me, the storm will buy us at least another day before my promises have to be put to the test.

And by then, I'll have a plan.

"I want to believe you," she says, voice unsure but hopeful.

"That's good enough for now. Let's get some sleep. This will all look brighter in the morning."

I curl her into my arms and pull the blankets over us. Cat falls asleep quickly, the peaceful look on her face setting at least part of my mind at ease.

She's going to trust me. She's going to allow me to take control and fix this situation so we can finally have our happily ever after.

I just hope I'm strong enough to pull it off.

CHAPTER EIGHT

I'M JUST FINISHING LAYING the table for breakfast when Mateo appears.

We worked together earlier to get the doors to the east hallways closed off and with the storm surge receding enough to pull the water out of the house, things feel almost normal. Thank goodness for the old island estate, built to withstand these storms and drain water when needed.

He managed to save my clothes and shoes from my mom's room last night, something I was very grateful for this morning. Getting dressed in my own clothes brings a level of comfort I need right now.

We've still got at least a few hours before any boat captain will risk the crossing, and they'll be lucky to find one willing to work on Christmas morning. When the family and staff arrive, I'm hoping the crisis of the fallen tree and house full of debris will overshadow the fact that Mateo and I have been here, alone, for so long.

I'm grateful for the time, and for our apparent reconciliation, but the situation is far from settled. The conversations we still need to have are going to be difficult, but I'm hopeful that we'll be able to figure things out. To be together at last.

I'm nervous about what will happen when his father finds out I went back on our agreement, but less terrified now that I have Mateo on my side. I should have contacted him right away. Of course he would have helped me. I'm trying to forgive myself at the same time I'm coming to terms with this enormous life change—it's a lot to handle at once.

"Morning," Mateo crosses the kitchen and pulls me into his arms for an embrace that lasts a deliciously long moment.

It feels so good, so right, I melt into his heat and inhale the scent of him. "Morning. Merry Christmas."

"Merry Christmas, love. You've been busy, I see," he says, stepping back to admire the spread I've laid out for our holiday meal.

I smile bashfully. I couldn't cook anything, but I sliced fruit and layed out pastries the cook prepared the previous morning. "I just got excited. It's the first real Christmas I've had in a while."

"For me, too."

I look up from the place setting and cock my head at him. "What do you mean?" I know from stories my mother told me that the estate still puts on the big holiday celebration every year. She hadn't mentioned Mateo, of course, but I just assumed she wanted to spare my feelings.

"It wasn't the same without you. Christmas was always our day. The last few years I've signed up for holiday rotations in the clinic and stayed in Chicago."

The thought of him spending Christmas alone breaks my heart, but then I remember it's how I've spent the last eight years as well.

We could have been together if I'd only been brave enough to reach out. My gaze falls as I try once again to hold back a rush of emotion and the tears that come with it.

Mateo is at my side in an instant, pulling me close. "No, no. No more sadness. Not anymore. It's been a long few years for us both, but we have each other now. Everything's going to be fine."

I want to believe him, but the old fear, the fear that's protected me and my mother for years, still sits in the back of my mind. When I glance out the dining room window, however, I decide to set those worries aside for now. The rain has lightened up, but it's still falling, and the wind makes it crash against the picture window.

"I know you just set the table in here, but I've got the curtains open to the ocean view in the living room. It's pretty spectacular with the dark skies. Want to take our plates in there?"

I smile up at him and nod. It's how we spent every Christmas morning since I first came to this house with my mother. The adults would all either be working to set the meal, or eating in the dining room, but us kids were allowed to eat around the Christmas tree in the living room. The mountain of presents in there were never for me, but I still enjoyed the magic of shaking boxes and dreaming about what could be inside with the other kids.

Mateo wasn't kidding about the view. The dramatic grays and purples of the storm clouds contrasting with the bright spots where the sun is trying to peek through, all framed by thrashing palms in the enormous picture window.

The Christmas tree looks just as I remembered it, albeit with less gifts underneath now that all the kids have grown up and moved out. We can't turn the lights on, but we still settle on the sofa closest to the glittering tree and pretend.

Snuggled up next to him on the sofa, all thoughts of breakfast quickly fall away. I can eat anytime, but to have Mateo here in my arms? This is the only sustenance I need to survive.

"You know, Matty..." I start, feeling a bit bashful about what I'm about to say. "You told me last night that I could taste you. But you never let me."

A playful smile tugs up the corners of his lips as he sets his own plate aside. "I made you wait all this time, did I?"

I nod, trying to play serious and offer him a little pout. It's insane to be instigating something like this here, so close to the front door, where anyone could walk in and see us.

Well, if it wasn't for the foot of water outside.

Mateo stands and pulls me into his arms. "Here's a little taste."

His lips press against mine and I push up to my tiptoes to get more of the kiss. I open for him and he rushes in, his hand holding firmly on my lower back.

I pull away and lock eyes with him. "That's not exactly what I had in mind."

Mateo laughs and scoops me up like a baby, tossing me over his shoulder. "Oh, really? My kisses aren't enough for you, huh?" His voice is filled with laughter and it sets my heart free.

It really feels like we're going to make it. Like everything's going to be okay.

I squeal and squirm, laughing uncontrollable as he slaps my ass and plops me down to sit on the sofa. When I look up, however, the dark desire in his eyes makes my breath catch.

How many years have I been imagining him looking at me like that again? How many nights have I lain awake dreaming of being able to touch him?

For that sad, lonely girl, who never thought she'd ever get this opportunity, I reach out and grasp Mateo by the belt loops, pulling him close. His eyes aren't the only place where desire is evident—the outline of his erection greets me as the seam of his jeans connects with my lips. I open my mouth and bite down gently on the bulge.

Mateo growls his approval and I look up at him from under my lashes.

"You're in charge," he says, setting me free.

I slide down to my knees and unhook his belt, slipping down the zipper of his pants. When I pull down the elastic of his boxer briefs, his cock jumps out and hits his stomach with a soft slap.

I laugh and take it in both hands. "Who's eager now, huh?"

"You have no idea, kitty," he whispers as he winds both hands into my hair.

When my tongue touches down gently on his tip and glides down his long shaft, his hands clench into fists, holding my head tightly in place. I could free myself, demand that he give back the control he just told me was mine, but I don't mind letting him guide me. Letting him use me.

As a matter of fact, I can't imagine a better Christmas gift.

I slide him into my mouth and moan at the fullness he brings. The taste of him. The feeling of having him inside me once more. My hands grip his base as I slide him in and out, working him deeper and deeper with every thrust.

When I finally feel relaxed enough, I let my hands drop to his thighs and look up at him. Mateo's evil grin spreads over his lips as he takes the hint.

He moves slowly at first, holding my head and rocking his hips, sliding his tip down my tongue and then back to my lips. I suck and nibble at him when I can, focusing on keeping my breathing calm when he's too far back for me to do much else.

My heart pounds in anticipation of the moment I know is coming, the moment I worked up to with this very man in this very house. As I feel his tip start to breach the top of my throat, I resist the natural urge to pull away and repeat the affirmation he gave me all those years ago silently in my own mind.

Good kitty…

My eyes swell with tears as he starts to pump a little faster, pressing the tip of his cock further down my throat and holding for just a second before sliding it back into my mouth. The next time, he presses it further and holds it just a bit longer.

Good Kitty…good kitty…good kitty…

The overwhelming feeling of his invasion starts to go to my head—and between my legs. I can feel the heat pooling there as his thrusts swing quickly from pleasure to the brink of pain.

"You're doing so good, little kitty. Do you like taking my cock so deep?" Mateo coos at me in his dirty talking voice, the sound of it nearly pushing me over the edge just.

I nod and make a strangled noise of affirmation—the action makes him moan in pleasure.

"Fucking hell," he groans, pumping faster, taking my throat harder.

There's always an edge, right around this point, where I think I won't be able to take it anymore. Where I think I'll have to tap out by giving the signal on his thigh. I feel myself reaching that point and try to calm back down.

Good kitty.

Mateo must sense my agitation because he pulls his tip into my mouth and keeps it there for a few thrusts, allowing me to catch my breath. "Good kitty," he whispers as he strokes his hand down my jaw in a tender caress.

But the hand doesn't stop there.

I squeeze my eyes closed as his fingers descend to wrap around my neck. When he has a nice, firm grip, he offers a word of warning—and encouragement. "You're doing so good, kitty. Are you ready to finish me off?"

As excited as I am to feel the heady rush of Mateo cutting off my airway as he pounds his orgasm into my throat, I'm also nervous.

Luckily—or unluckily, perhaps—I don't get a chance to answer.

He knows damn well that I have my signal to use if I need him to stop. He trusts me to use it just as much as I trust him not to kill me.

The first thrust is a shock to my system, sliding deep so quickly I don't have time to prepare. I can hear myself whimpering. I can feel the hot tears running down my cheeks, but it's almost like it's happening to someone else.

There's nothing quite like a throat fuck to trigger an out of body experience.

"Good kitty. God, fuck, that feels so good."

He's deep in me now, his stomach pressing against my forehead as he tilts my head up and drives his cock further down. Every three or four thrusts he pulls out a bit further and I gasp for air, choking and crying, but then he's right back inside me.

Before long, the lack of constant airflow coupled with the adrenaline in my bloodstream starts to make me feel like I've taken some kind of drug. I'm seeing stars with a full body high. It's magical and terrifying and so, so fucking erotic. My clit pulses between my legs to my own heartbeat. I take that as a good sign— it means I'm still alive.

I snake one hand between my legs, chasing the drumbeat of my own arousal.

"Yeah, kitty. Touch yourself. Are you going to come with me?"

I'm not sure, all I know is that I have to relieve some of the pressure between my legs. When my finger finds my swollen clit, I can't help but moan—just as Mateo forces his tip back into my throat.

"Fuck yes, that feels so good."

I'm on fire with the pleasure from my fingers and the unbearably sexy knowledge of just how much I'm pleasing him. I flick my finger over my clit and slide another into my dripping pussy. Mateo's fist is so tight in my hair, his hand gripping my neck, his cock wedged inside me, pausing there as he sucks in a deep breath.

It's over for me then, my orgasm exploding out of me in a strangled moan. Mateo loses his control as well, pulsing down my throat with a mighty roar. When he pulls out I gasp for air.

When he releases my hair, my head falls forward, mouth hanging open. Most of the liquid falls from my mouth onto my bare thighs, as my throat spasms through swallow after swallow, trying to convince itself that the danger has passed.

When I finally calm down enough to look up, Mateo is watching me with his cock in his hand, his eyes dark with desire. "You are unbelievably sexy, you know that?"

I swallow again, running my damp hands through my hair in a half assed attempt to straighten it.

Mateo grabs my wrists and pulls my hands to the sides, tossing them into my lap. "Don't ruin it. You look perfect. Perfectly fucked."

I can't help but smile at that.

"I felt you come, little kitty. Does that mean there's a mess down there waiting for me to clean it up?"

I nod and move back so I'm sitting on my butt, leaning back against the sofa. I let my knees fall to the side.

"Up," he commands, sitting back on his heels.

I obey, climbing shakily to my feet.

"Strip."

My mouth falls open as I glance nervously around. "Here?"

Mateo shrugs. "No one's getting through that storm anytime soon, Kitty. It's just you and me."

I know he's right, but I can't help but glance at the window as I start to pull off my sweater. The air has a chill to it that feels good against my hot body as I slip down my jeans and panties. I sit on the edge of the couch and spread my knees for him once more, the lust in his dark eyes giving me the boost of confidence I need to let my fear go completely.

"Mmm, yes, I see," he says, crawling toward me to press my legs wider. "You've made quite a mess down here, haven't you?"

There's no need for me to answer.

Mateo dives into my pussy face first, lapping at the sensitive flesh as I squeal and cry out. It doesn't take long, however, before his touch turns from overwhelming to pure pleasure.

His tongue knows just how to move in my folds, just how to find the perfect spot to flick and rub. I feel him enter me with his finger, and it quickly becomes two fingers and then three. Four. He stretches me open as I lay my head back and moan.

"Greedy little kitty always did like getting her pussy stretched."

It's true. The soreness from taking his cock just hours before in bed weaves into the feeling of his fingers hitting my g-spot over and over, giving me just the right mix of pleasure and tingling pain. "Yes, Matty, just like that."

He murmurs his agreement and tongues me faster, harder. I come quickly, the blinding pleasure overtaking me as his fingers continue to pump in and out. He's lapping me up, drinking me like his favorite cocktail. I pour myself into him, letting the sound of my ecstasy escape my lips in sharp, happy cries.

When he finally pulls away, the heat from my drenched pussy keeps my fire stoked. I lift my head from where it fell back on the sofa and watch as he works himself, hardening cock clenched tightly in his fist.

"I'm about to fuck you right here in front of the Christmas tree, would you like that, kitty?"

I smile and nod, glancing up at the glittering decoration briefly before bringing my eyes back to the carnal need in Mateo's eyes as he firmly jerks his cock.

"Why don't you get yourself in whatever position you want."

I look around, trying to pick the perfect spot.

On the sofa looking out at the storm?

Standing against the hearth with the stockings rubbing against my stiff nipples?

On my back looking up at the mistletoe?

I decide I want them all but start by crawling to my hands and knees until my face is just inches from the tree. I can smell the fragrant pine as I hear Mateo getting in position behind me.

"Dirty girl, always wants it from behind."

"I'm the sleigh," I say, glancing over my shoulder bashfully. "And you're riding me to Christmas."

"Jeez, am I Santa in this little fantasy?"

I nod and Mateo laughs, the sound resonating down to my bones.

"Not happening. How about you're the naughty little girl who isn't going to get any presents unless she takes my cock and likes it."

"That sounds good, too."

"And because I know you're still down there pretending I'm Santa, we're going to start this off with a spanking."

The man knows me so well.

He lands a few sharp smacks on my ass and I cry out—but I know he's just warming up.

When he comes around to my side and takes a handful of my hair, pulling my neck taut, I know it's time to settle in for my punishment.

At the first slap, I squeeze my eyes closed. I can't hide my face with my head held up like this, so whatever I'm feeling will be on display for Mateo to see.

Just how he likes it.

I moan and whimper as he spanks me, letting tears of joy and pain run down my cheeks.

Mateo licks them off my cheeks in two long, slow swipes as he holds my head up.

When he lets my hair go, I drop down to my elbows, needing a rest, but also wanting to open my pussy up to him further. A brand-new rush of desire swells between my legs.

He moves around behind me and rubs his palms over my sore ass. "You're really getting the full gamut, aren't you? All the old tricks coming out of the bag."

"Like Santa," I offer, my face still pressed into the carpet, muffling my words.

I know Mateo hears them because he lands one last slap on my sore ass, harder than ever. I squeal in surprise and protest, but wag my ass at him anyway.

I'm rewarded with the mind numbingly delicious sensation of Mateo filling me. He does it slowly this time, pressing his tip into my body in one long, leisurely stroke.

"So wet for me," he murmurs as he drags himself back out just as slowly.

When he starts another slide, just as slow as the last, I moan with impatience. "Matty, I can't take it."

"Can't take it, huh? You want me to fuck you hard so you can forget," he says as he does just that, gripping my hips and offering a few punishingly hard, fast thrusts.

But then he slows once more. "But I don't want you to forget, Cat. I want you to remember."

His words bring tears to my eyes, even in the face of overwhelming pleasure. "You want to punish me?"

He scoffs out a dark laugh. "No, I think there's been enough punishment today. And for the last eight years."

His pace starts to pick back up gradually. "But I want to remember. I want you to remember. What we had, what we almost lost, and how it feels to be back together like this. I don't want us to forget what's at stake here."

I can't speak through my mixture of happy tears—and mournful ones. As Mateo slowly, lovingly, massages my insides with the tip of his cock, I do remember. I remember everything we promised each other. All the plans we made for our future together.

I remember exactly how much we have to fight for.

And I finally get enough courage to try.

"I remember, Matty. I'll never let anyone keep us apart again."

My words are the magic spell that sets us both free.

With a growl, he pumps me harder, reaching down to slip his finger over my clit. I bite my lip and ride the mounting wave of bliss as he rocks me back and forth. I can hear his breathing start to catch and quickly suck in one of my own, desperate to feel the moment of climax together with my love.

I get there just as he comes inside me. As I clench and spasm, I look up into the branches of the decorated tree and smile. I really couldn't have asked for a better Christmas.

Mateo carries me up to his room to shower, tenderly washing my body in the last of the lukewarm water from the rapidly cooling water heater. When we're finally snuggled back on the couch, I can hardly make myself look away. The reality of him being here with me is almost too good to be true.

Mateo seems to agree.

"I can't believe we're finally here together. I hate to admit it, but after eight years, I'd almost given up hope that you were ever going to contact me," Mateo says, setting his empty plate on a side table.

I shake my head and look down at my barely touched plate of sliced fruit and pastries. "I wasn't going to contact you. I couldn't."

He sighs and pulls me toward him. "It should have been me who found you. I never should have let you go like that. What a damn fool I was to just think you'd abandon me after all we'd been through. I should have known something was wrong."

It's my turn to sigh. "Something is still wrong, Mateo."

"I know. And if I could have stormed into his room last night and confronted him about it, I would have. We don't have to put up with this, Cat. We're adults now, we can make our own choices. I decided to go into medicine rather than join the family business, so he can't hold my career over my head. My portion of the family fortune is already in my name, set up by my grandfather's will. He doesn't have any actual power over us."

"My mother."

"She'll come live with us. I'm only back right now because I'm taking a job on Faraday Island. Some guys bought the old White Sands and turned it into an upscale, destination resort. They hired me to be the full-time in-house doctor."

His plan sounds perfect, especially the idea of getting to live in the islands again, but the uncertainty still hovers over me. "You're sure you want to saddle yourself with me and my eighty year old mother?"

Mateo laughs. "Well, now that you mention it..." He stands and fumbles around in the pockets of his sweater until he finds what he's looking for.

When he drops to his knee, my hand flies to my mouth as I gasp.

"Cat, Sylvia, my love. My one and only. The sun and stars in my sky. Will you marry me?"

Until this moment, I hadn't realized this was the confirmation I so desperately wanted. The last layer of security. I wanted to risk everything, leave my life behind, for this man. But I needed this promise from him to be sure.

"Yes, Matty. Of course." I get the words out before emotion cracks my voice.

Mateo slips the diamond on my finger and places a gentle kiss on my knuckles. When I take my hand back, the most beautiful ring I've ever seen adorns my finger.

It's a simple gold band with round solitaire and two small opals to either side. It's absolutely perfect.

"It was my grandmother's ring. My mother wore it for the first few years of marriage, before my father bought her the big one. It's always been meant for my wife. I used to carry it with me. It was in my pocket when I left for Chicago." He pulls my hand back to his and gives it one more kiss. "The one time I came home after I moved, it was to bring the ring back here for safe keeping."

The sadness of what we nearly lost threatens to overtake the moment. "Oh, Matty..."

"No, no. No sadness. We made it back here and the ring was waiting for us to pick up where we left off. And wouldn't you know, it's the perfect fit."

It really is. I give the band a spin on my finger as happiness swells inside me.

I finish my cold breakfast before we curl up together on the couch. Mateo pulls a soft throw over us and I allow the heat from his body to seep down to my bones. I'm not sure how long I lay in his arms before I drift off or how long I sleep, but when I'm startled awake, our peaceful little bubble bursts.

We should have escaped when we had the chance.

CHAPTER NINE

Mateo

I leap from the couch as the front door opens with a bang.

"Mateo," I hear my father's stern voice call.

Tossing a reassuring glance down at Cat, who's looking like her whole world is caving in on her, I make my way to the foyer. My whole family is piling in, peeling off their jackets and looking a bit haggard. I guess a night at a hotel in a tropical storm will do that to you. I can only imagine how harrowing the journey home was on still choppy waters.

"What on earth happened to the house?"

It takes me a moment to answer, the collapsed east wing having fully slipped my mind in all the excitement of having Cat back. "A tree fell in the wind last night, took out a few windows. The hallway and a few of the rooms flooded, but the water's gone now. We've been safe and relatively dry."

"Why didn't you call?" he demands.

"The power's been out for hours. The storm must have taken out a cell tower because my phone hasn't worked either. Do yours work?"

My sister Samantha steps forward and nods, holding her phone up. "We've been trying to call you since yesterday. And did I hear you say we?"

My heart sinks. I hoped that little slip of the tongue would go unnoticed. No sooner has my father's glare returned to me than he's looking over my shoulder toward the living room. I don't need to turn around to know who appeared there.

"Sylvia," he says, tone flat. Her beautiful name on his lips enrages me. "What are you doing here?"

"I...got caught in the storm—"

I step protectively in front of her. "She's with me. And she's going to be with me forever." I hold up her left hand as I pull her into my side. "I learned the truth about what you did, father." I'm brimming with anger, but I keep my cool. There's no point in allowing this to come to blows. The only thing on my mind is getting this woman, and her mother, out of this house safely. "But that's a discussion for another time. If you all made it home, that means the waters are calm enough to cross."

"We found a boat willing to make the crossing. Dad paid them a fortune to take us on Christmas," my sister offers from over my father's shoulder.

He glares back at her before turning that harsh gaze on me and my brand new fiancé. "Your girlfriend and I made a deal, or didn't she tell you?"

Divide and conquer. His signature move.

Too bad it's not going to work this time.

"She told me everything. Honestly, I can't believe I didn't guess that's what happened all those years ago. You convinced me that she just left, and you let me think that this whole time. You're unbelievable."

"I did what I had to do for this family. It's bad enough that your older brother ran off to be a damn musician, I couldn't have you throwing your future away as well. There's power in marrying someone from the right family, son. You have to understand that I did what I did with your best interests in mind."

"Like I said, this is a conversation for another time. Right now, Cat and I are leaving, and we're taking her mother with us."

"You're making a mistake," he says defiantly, but I can hear the resignation in his voice. Other than manipulation and blackmail, he doesn't hold any real power over us.

Thank goodness my grandfather knew the man well enough not to put the future of his legacy in my father's hands.

"The only mistake I made was believing that I could trust you. I can't even imagine what else you've been lying about over the years." I turn to face my sister, who's cowering in the corner. "Are you paying attention, Samantha? This is what he's capable of. Lying, deceit, anything he has to do to get his way."

She's not going to speak against the man with him glowering down at her, and I can't blame her for that. "If you need anything, Sam, you call me, okay?"

She gives the faintest nod before freezing once more into a statue under our father's icy glare.

Benjamin, the house manager and driver, steps into the foyer loaded with shopping bags. He must feel the tension of the moment because he stops short and looks around.

I seize the moment. "Ben, where's Ms. McAll?"

"I'm right here." Cat's mom steps over the threshold, clutching her raincoat around her body. Her face is troubled, and I wonder how much of that she heard.

"Perfect," I say, turning back to Cat. "You ready?"

She glances at her mother momentarily before nodding. I nod in return, reaching for her hand. We're going to be leaving a few things behind. It's the price we have to pay to get out of here safely. I won't risk one more minute in this house, not for things that we can easily replace.

Her mother's room, containing all of the woman's worldly possessions, is another story. It was hard to tell how much will be salvageable after the storm damage, but I know for certain we're going to need to come back for whatever we can get.

"I'm going to have one of my high school buddies drive out tomorrow to pick up Ms. Mcall's things. He'll box them up himself if they aren't already."

My father says nothing, just glares at me with his arms crossed.

"Go wait in the car, okay?" I say to Cat, passing her my keys. She takes them and leaves the house without another word, her mother's hand clasped tightly in hers.

I cross the foyer to my sister and pull her into an embrace.

"You're ruining Christmas, you know?" she teases into my chest as I give her a squeeze.

I laugh softly. "I know. Sorry about that."

"It's fine. I'm used to it. We haven't had a proper celebration since you stopped coming home."

I hold her at arm's length and give her a warm smile. "You okay?"

She nods and I believe her. Samantha is strong and independent. She's going to be just fine.

I dare one last glance at my father, but he's still waiting for me to leave, unwavering disapproval painted across his features.

"Bye, Dad."

I don't wait for an answer.

CHAPTER TEN

Sylvia

My mom and I are quiet until we get to the car. I click the button to unlock the doors and hold one open for her.

Turning to face me, her face spreads into a loving smile. "Oh, Sylvia." She pulls me into an embrace. "I was so worried when I couldn't get a hold of you."

I help her get seated in the backseat. "I'm alright, mom, but neither of us are safe here anymore. We have to go."

"I heard everything." Her face is clouded with worry. "Where will we go?"

"We're going to Faraday. Matteo has a job as the doctor at a new resort, and I'll be able to get a job there as well. You won't have to work anymore, okay?"

Her eyes are wide with surprise as she takes in my words, but it's not long before they narrow with concern. "But Mr. Ricci...he'll ruin us."

"He's not the one calling the shots anymore, mom."

"I trust you, but...this is my home."

"We're going to make a new home together."

She bites her lip and crinkles her forehead as she considers. Finally, she gives me a confident nod. "Okay. That's what we'll do. This old house is too drafty, anyway. And so many bathrooms to clean."

Grateful tears prick at the corners of my eyes as I laugh and lean down to hug her once more.

Mateo jogs down to us as best he can through the scattered palm fronds. "You ladies ready to go?"

We both look at my mother.

"Hell yes. Let's go," she says fiercely, shaking her fist in the air.

Mateo and I share a moment of silent laugher as we buckle ourselves in the front seats.

The damp palms glisten in the afternoon sunlight as we make our way down the long driveway toward town.

Toward the mysterious future.

Toward the vast, wide open world of possibilities.

Toward the life I thought I'd never have.

"How you holding up over there, love?" Mateo asks, braving a split second to look away from the road and over at me.

I reach for the hand not holding the wheel and pull it into my lap. "I've never been happier to be yours."

THE END

RACING TO FALL

Michelle Moncrieff

CHAPTER ONE

"Hurry up, they're here!" Sophia called over her shoulder, running toward the other side of the property, her long red hair trailing behind her. Lydia St. James had known her best friend since high school. They were called the 'chess set' because they were inseparable, and Lydia's dark features contrasted with Sophia's very pale Irish ones. The temperate day gave them an excuse to show off a little extra skin in their halter tops, their motivations being on opposite sides of Lydia's Aunt Gladys' estate.

Every inch of the St. James' one hundred acres in the suburbs of Washington, D.C., was utilized for the annual fall festival to benefit mental health awareness charities. A warm breeze carried the aroma of cinnamon, apples, and freshly baked goods across the grounds. The meadow, trimmed short, was covered with dark green and white striped tents in various sizes, but Sophia dashed around them with the skill of a gazelle on a mission to the stage.

"I'm supposed to be at the booth. You know Auntie is still mad at me because of the reunion, and there will be hell to pay if I'm not at my post when we open," Lydia whined, dragging her feet over the already trampled grass. She didn't dare tell anyone her true destination, knowing she would only incur more criticism.

The festival opened in a couple of hours, and the entire St. James clan was required to participate enthusiastically. Lydia was surprised that she hadn't been relegated to following the hayride around to pick up horse crap, considering how she had behaved a few months earlier.

"I can't help it if you were a bitch to Dahlia and your brother. Besides, this will only take a minute." Sophia's voice dropped to a whisper, and her pace slowed to a strut as she caught sight of her prey. Her current obsession, Crushing Clover, was a new alternative music group that Sophia was so sure was going to be the next big thing, she created a fan group and blog called 'Dear Future Rockstar'.

"You know that's not true," Lydia huffed to herself. Sophia was already lost in a mutual admiration contest, surrounded by the bandmates. "I'll catch you later, I guess."

Determined not to let jealousy get the better of her again, Lydia set off to check on her own preoccupation. Circumventing the bustling center of preparations, she cut through the manicured pumpkin patch where paths had been cleared between rows of the enormous orange gourds in anticipation of the droves of families who would be searching for the perfect jack-o-lantern. At the edge of the tree line was what Aunt Glady called the carriage house, but Lydia knew it as the garage—although that was an understatement for the space that could hold a dozen cars. Even so, family members parked on the gravel drive surrounding the stone building that matched the other structures on the expansive estate.

Ignoring the side door, Lydia took advantage of the open bay to observe the object of her desire: Joseph Caruso, better known as Joey to her. She was sometimes surprised there wasn't an imprint of her feet in the corner of the garage, considering how often she stood in the exact spot, leaning against the frame to watch Aunt Gladys' chauffeur unobserved. Lydia's short-curvy stature barely made it to his broad shoulders. Charcoal gray coveralls stretched tight across his back as he leaned across the motor of the late 1950s Cadillac he was restoring for Aunt Gladys. The taut fabric didn't show off his assets as well as his favorite jeans, but it didn't make him any less appealing.

Standing upright, he stretched his arms wide before slowly lowering the zipper down the front of the coveralls. She covered her mouth to avoid making a sound as she gaped at the toned chest and carved abs covered in tattoos. Her eyes followed the zipper to the thin trail of hair appearing below his belly button, her neck craning to see more than the dark space shadowed by the cloth

"Did you see enough, or was there something more you wanted?" His soft, velvety accent echoed off the walls, disrupting her gawking, as he slid the jumpsuit off his shoulders and tied the arms around his waist. She wondered if he knew it was her, or if he just knew that someone was there. He had always been flirtatious with her when they were alone, but she assumed it was just how Spanish men were. He turned it off quickly when someone else was around, so she had made it a point to find reasons to be alone with him.

"Lydia," her name danced across his tongue with a sigh. "You're the only one who hasn't come for their festival cash box and that…" His voice trailed off as he raked his hands through his tousled curls, away from his aquiline face. It was a new style for him. She liked to pretend he changed from his slick-back look because she commented on how much she admired his curls, but knew it was probably just easier for him to maintain.

"I was just tying my boot," she lied, standing in the entry.

"Uh-huh. This car isn't going to fix itself. Are you going to make yourself useful, or have you forgotten what a carburetor is?" He held out a wrench, knowing her competitive side needed to be vindicated, even if he was just baiting her.

When he had first come to work for Aunt Gladys, Lydia didn't know anything about the inner workings of an engine, but since it was the only thing he seemed willing to talk about, she took every class or workshop she could until she could work alongside him. While it may not have impressed him, it proved advantageous by leading her to a new career path.

"Fine, but I'm supposed to be at my booth."

"Not for another hour, princess. And I know you well enough that everything is in place already."

"Don't call me that. And you don't know anything about me except that I can fix this car, probably better than you can." She stalked over to him, grabbed the wrench, and stared under the hood. She was tired of everyone thinking she was just some airhead that wasn't going to amount to anything. It's one of the reasons she didn't tell anyone she was pursuing a PhD and was waitressing to help fund it, rather than spinning her wheels at the administrative job they all seemed to think was the best she could do.

"You think I don't know you?" He crowded behind her, the heat of him burning through her t-shirt, his body curving to hers. "I know the way your lips quirk when you think you have a secret. I hear how your breath quickens when you're watching me. I can tell that you're not working the desk job you proclaim. And I know you've been snooping around my workshop. So tell me why, princess. What are you really up to?" His arms braced on either side of the car frame, caging her in. The heady scent of musk and spice made her as dizzy as his touch did.

"I...HOW...WHAT makes you think that?" Lydia stuttered, goosebumps appearing the length of her arm, just like they always did when he got too close.

Joey was only slightly ashamed of taking advantage of how his nearness seemed to confuse her just to elicit a confession. He inhaled deeply, letting his senses consume her and making his blood surge in a primal scream. His cock hardened at the feel of being nestled in her backside. There was no question of their intense attraction that had only burned stronger over time. Eight years her senior, he had worked hard to keep his distance from her. She had proved relentless in finding ways to sneak into his thoughts and feelings. If it wasn't for his suspicions that she was spying on him for his former mentor, he would give in to his incessant need for her.

"I always take notice of your moods, especially what makes you happy. The stains on your fingers," he said, lifting her hand to his lips, "give away that you are working with food, not ink. And that unmistakable spicy vanilla scent of yours is everywhere. It puts me in a chokehold, stealing my mind, and telling me to devour you like a creme brulee." He ran the tip of his tongue up her dark, slender neck, realizing too late that it only made him salivate for more.

"You never tell me anything about you," she murmured, leaning her head against his chest. He spun her around, searching for the truth in her golden eyes. "I only wanted to know you better." There wasn't anything in the garage to give her any insight into his past, and she hadn't found a way into his small apartment over the garage.

"Why? Why me? You could have any man your age. Am I just some exotic curiosity to you?" Her statement had seemed sincere, but there were reasons he had avoided any entanglements, and he wasn't ready to risk everything for a fling. When she got what she wanted, and his eccentricities became flaws that could be used against him, would he survive the fallout?

"You claim to know me, but after all these years, you still have no idea?" she yelled, pushing her way out of his hold and walking toward the bay door. "Sure, when I was eighteen, you were my tall, dark, and dangerous crush. Believe it or not, I've grown up since then. We've spent hours hunched over various engines, talking about life and our dreams. I thought we had become close, and maybe we could be more to each other. I guess I misunderstood." Her voice trailed off into a whisper before she disappeared around the corner.

He should run after her. Tell her that she wasn't wrong. Berate himself for being so insensitive. Proclaim…. what? He wasn't sure how he felt. If her words were anything to go by, she didn't care if he was just a mechanic or a chauffeur, but he couldn't start a relationship with her until he could be honest, and there were still too many questions he needed to answer for himself.

Closing the bay door, he glanced around the space and realized she hadn't taken the cash box for her booth. He doubted her stubborn temperament would let her come back for it, so he would take it to her, but it would have to wait until later, when he had to fill his shift at the festival.

At the stairs to his living space, he opened the multiple locks on the door he had installed when he'd first noticed signs of an intruder. A large shoe print and familiar heavy cologne had pointed to one of his old adversaries. The entrance to his apartment was similarly guarded, with the addition of cameras concealed throughout the building. With all of the security measures back in place, he dropped his overalls onto the floor, his still erect cock bouncing against his stomach as he walked across the simply furnished space to the second bedroom.

Leaning against the window frame, he could see the preparations for the festival in the distance, but with the one-way film on the windows, he was confident no one could view him in his natural state. He missed the cooler temperatures of his home, cradled between the mountains and the bay. Even in the mid-70 degrees Fahrenheit, like it was for the festival, it was warmer than the hottest summer day in Oviedo. His thoughts turned back to Lydia, as they increasingly seemed to do. He stroked himself, imagining her standing by the waterside, the breeze plastering her dress against her curvaceous body and her long dark curls. How would she react if he lay her down in the wildflowers on the rolling hills and made love to her? Love? Yeah, it was time to admit what this was with her and figure out how to move forward.

Opening a large carved wooden armoire, he unfolded the shelves into a long table and spread his papers out. An old, discolored news article stood out against the rest of the clean white pages, reminding him of his why for so many things, including his need for anonymity. He traced his finger over the picture, thinking it might be time to start over somewhere else. The ache in his chest at the idea of losing Lydia argued that he needed to share his story with her. What would she think of the teenagers kart racing through the streets, like he did when he was younger, and the noises echoing off the medieval buildings? Would she feel the thrill of it, like she did when they got an ancient motor to come back to life?

The alarm on his phone, sounding from the floor by the front door, reminded him to get ready. It amused him that Gladys had assigned him to the only driving task in the festival. It might not be cars, but the horses and customers would help distract him for a little while. Before he could do that, he would relieve some stress by indulging in one of his favorite fantasies of Lydia pressed up against his shower wall, begging him for more.

CHAPTER THREE

"Sir, as I've stated several times, the noise-canceling headphones are free for anyone to use. I just need credit card information from you to ensure they are returned by the time we close." Lydia smiled sweetly, gritting her teeth and pulling the zipper of her jacket up to her neck. The stocky man who had been standing at her booth for the last twenty minutes asked a lot of questions about the festival and how she was involved. It wasn't so much what he had asked but how he leered at her chest as if he was groping her with his eyes.

"Why don't you just let me back there and get a sampling for myself?" He licked his lips as if the idea made him drool. Obviously, he was done being polite and indirect.

"I'm sorry, sir. If you don't need a set of headphones, please proceed to the festival, so I can take care of the other attendees."

"There's no one around, sweet cheeks. Just me." His Cheshire cat grin had her internally cringing.

"Hey, Lyds! Everything ok here?" At the sound of her brother's voice, she closed her eyes in a small prayer of thanks.

"Yeah, the chick was just going to give me a special tour of her palace, if you know what I mean."

Lydia's skin crawled at the idea.

"Excuse me?" Remy seethed, getting in the man's face.

"Hey, hot head, I was here first. But I'll give you dibs on that sweet ass when I'm done with it."

"Remy, you brought my cash box. Thank you so much. Maybe you could help me get it set up." She hoped her brother saw through her thinly veiled plea. Clutching the man's collar, Remy looked at her and back at the stranger.

"That's my sister you're harassing. But even if she weren't, it wouldn't make it ok. Now apologize and get out of here. If I see you bothering her again, I'll have security after you." Remy hissed, dropping his hand with a slight shove to the man's chest.

"Dumb bitch isn't worth my time anyway," the aggressor, needing the last word, called out.

"Are you ok? Why are you alone? Isn't Kim supposed to be here with you?"

"She was. But she and Jeff got into another fight, and they ran off."

"I hate to think about where they're making up. Hopefully, they waited until they got to the house."

"I'll be fine. It's only a couple of hours until Auggie and Birdie take over until later this afternoon."

"Sure. That's why you forgot to get the cashbox, and Joey asked me to bring it to you. And that's why a sleazebag was r..." Remy went on, but she was stuck on his comment that Joey wouldn't come see her himself. It only seemed to confirm that he didn't think of her the same way. She didn't doubt his attraction. She could feel its evidence. But she didn't want just a hook-up with him. Her family and friends were tired of listening to her lament the relationship. They all told her to get him out of her system and move on. Did they not think that in the six years she'd known him, she hadn't tried to date other people? There was just something about him, especially when he seemed to understand her better than she did herself.

"Did you hear me?"

"What? Sure..."

"I said, I'll send one of the cousins over to help you, but make sure you don't walk around alone. I don't think that guy is going to take 'no' so easily. Where's Sofia?"

"She's helping the band."

"Maybe you should too, when you're done here."

"Yes, sir," she saluted him in jest and was rewarded with his contagious laugh. "Hey, Remy, thanks for your help. I'm glad we're good again."

"I'm always here for you, Lyds. And we were never not good. You were just being a jealous brat. I'm glad to have you back to yourself." If he only knew how untrue that was. She might not be jealous of him and Dahlia anymore, but she was feeling broken inside. Worse, she was mad at herself for letting herself crumble over a man who wasn't deserving of her. She resolved to let it go, to focus on her career and make a new life for herself.

As if he read her mind, the hayride turned the corner to the main strip of tents. Dressed in a leather jacket and blue jeans, he looked like a movie star filling in for someone in a Western at the helm of a horse-drawn cart, reins relaxed in his large, strong hands. Even his usually soft melodic tone was harsher as he emphasized his Rs and rounded his vowels, at a jarring volume that could be heard not only by the passengers but everyone in the vicinity.

"If you're looking for something less stimulating, there's yoga and art therapy at the gazebo and noise-canceling headphones..." She waved and smiled at the mention of her stall. His passengers responded excitedly, but he didn't make eye contact with her.

"Hey, you look so familiar. Weren't you that Formula One guy from way back?" An older man on the ride leaned across the seats to get a closer look at Joey.

"I get that a lot, but I'm afraid you have the wrong person." They were so close to her, she could practically feel him bristle at the man's words.

"No way. There's no mistaking that face and accent. The girls were all gaga about you. Well, until you just vanished."

"It was nice meeting you all." Joey jumped down from his perch, far from where the drop-off was supposed to be. "The festival will officially kick off in a few minutes at the main stage." He helped each of his passengers down, until the man who was determined that Joey was someone else.

"Joey Cruz! Yeah, that's the name. How about an autograph and a selfie before I go? Come on, Joey!" The man's rowdiness was drawing attention that seemed to make Joey more uncomfortable as he averted his gaze and pulled a ball cap out of his jacket pocket, angling it low over his forehead.

"I'm really sorry, but I don't know anyone by that name." Joey rushed back into his seat and flicked the reins for the horses to move before he finished his sentence. Joey could dodge her questions with ease. A wink and a question to redirect her rarely failed. Nothing ever seemed to rattle him. There had to be more to this.

"What was that about?" Great Aunt Althea tiptoed to the booth to keep her spiky heels from getting stuck in the ground.

"Do you know anything about Formula One or a guy named Joey Cruz?"

"The only Joey I know is that gorgeous chauffeur. I know he's fast, but not as fast as me," Althea cackled, thumbing toward the direction Joey had already disappeared.

"Will you be ok if I take a quick break?"

"If you've got a place for me to rest these old gams, I'm ready to take on the men of Washington." Resting on the stool provided, Althea smacked her thigh with a loud guffaw.

Lydia loved spending time with her outspoken, confident aunt, but she needed to do some digging for information. She started walking aimlessly, fingers flying across her phone screen, until she heard the familiar snarl of the lecherous man from earlier. Turning quickly, Lydia escaped into the baking contest tent. The appetizing scents mingled, making her stomach growl, but she stayed focused on her phone and hid in a corner out of the way.

Now that she had a name, page after page of stats and pictures of her Joey appeared. There was no mistaking the visage that she had stared at so often. His life unfolded before her, from his youth in the small Medieval town near the coast to learning to race and traveling the world. He was mentioned in so many articles, it was hard to understand what might have caused him to go into hiding. Her mind spun with the possible trouble that had driven him to disappear, and what the dangers were to her family. She had to figure out a plan. Did her aunt know about Joey's history, or was Lydia the only one in the dark? Who did she confront first?

CHAPTER FOUR

It had been a long time since Joey had encountered such a fervent fan. He had forgotten how intense, to the point of aggressive, they could be. Back in the day, he would have basked in the adoration and posed for as many pictures as they wanted. While life seemed quiet and peaceful now, the noise and chaos from the past still roared like a thousand speeding race cars in his head.

Joey's phone buzzed on his couch, where he had thrown it with his jacket when he'd returned to his apartment earlier. He had let the avid admirer rattle him and break his calm, controlled facade. After calling in sick, he paced his apartment, trying to calm the panic, reasoning through his fight or flight response to the situation.

Most attendees wouldn't take notice, but Lydia would, and who knew if the person belonging to the large shoe print might have also been lurking. That shortened his timeline to share his story with Lydia, if it wasn't already too late. Knowing her attention to detail, she probably already had a dossier on him with colored tabs and sticky notes. He would find out soon enough.

He grabbed his phone as it continued to vibrate, absentmindedly looking at the alert about movement on the perimeter. It was probably the volunteers bringing their cashboxes to him to lock up in the garage safe. Lost in his thoughts, he hadn't noticed it had gotten dark. He threw on a clean pair of over-alls and rushed downstairs.

As each person came by, Joey greeted them with an attempt at his usual laid-back persona. Scrolling through the internet looking for any sign that his story had hit the news, another alert from his security system flashed on the screen. It had been twenty minutes since the last box had been handed over, yet Lydia's was still missing. He felt a sense of relief that she was ok.

After closing the small vault, he switched apps on his phone to the surveillance feed from the cameras around the building. Toggling through the views, the lanterns on the side door only showed a silhouette with light bouncing toward the far side of the garage. He illuminated the floodlights on the roof from his phone. On his screen, he saw Lydia, clutching her cashbox, shielding her eyes from the glare, but she didn't slow down. Then came the man following her, who froze like an animal facing a speeding car. When the shock wore off, he ran to catch up with her.

"Hey, I was talking to you!" Joey heard the burly man shout through his speaker. The scratchy voice was oddly familiar.

"Why can't you just leave me alone?" Lydia picked up her pace, and Joey had to switch to another camera view to keep up.

"You've been teasing me all day, ya little hussy. It's time to pay up."

"Security threw you out hours ago. How did you get back on site?"

"I have my ways." Her aggressor rubbed his fingers on one hand together. It was a common enough gesture for money, but combined with the accent of home, Joey felt a chill run through him.

Fuck! Not now. Not here. Joey zoomed in to examine the man's face more closely.

"You are going to regret this," Lydia stated, digging into her pocket and facing the trespasser.

"The lady told you to leave her alone." Opening the side door, Joey took a step in front of Lydia.

"Why don't you go back where you belong, kid?" Emilio Perez, Joey's former mentor, flashed a menacing smile.

"I'm not going anywhere unless she tells me to." Joey looked to Lydia, who was still pointing a small can towards the other man.

"I'm just having a little fun. You always did take things so seriously, Joey."

"Get out of here and leave her alone." He folded his arms across his chest, blocking Emilio's view of Lydia.

"Like you're going to stop me from getting what I want. You never had it in you, and you still don't." The words pierced Joey harder than he'd like to admit.

"I'm not the man you remember. I won't fail to protect the people I care about ever again."

"What the hell, Joey? I could have handled this, and I don't need you pretending I can't." Lydia scolded. She put her box in the garage and stomped off into the night.

"Looks like you let her down anyway. Funny how history repeats itself." Leaning against the wall, Emilio acted like they were just having a friendly chat.

"What the hell are you doing here?"

"I just wanted to catch up."

"I have nothing to say to you that I haven't already said."

"And when the anniversary of the accident comes next week? You're going to keep your mouth shut, right? You owe me that much."

"I don't owe you a fucking thing. I know what you did, even though I don't have proof. And you're the one who's going to have to live with that on your conscience."

"Yeah, I'll cry about it on my yacht."

"You goddamn son-of-a-bitch!" Rage pulsed through Joey as his hand closed around Emilio's throat and pinned him to the wall.

"Tsk, tsk, Joey. You're going to get yourself kicked out of this cushy setup you've got."

"How the hell did you find me anyway?" He dropped his grip and stepped back.

"Don't you know by now? I've got friends in high and low places. People see things and help me out. For instance, a man who didn't want the press to pursue him like the rabid animals they are would share with me his latest project, so I didn't accidentally tell anyone his location." Emilio jabbed a finger into Joey's chest to emphasize his point, reiterating all of Joey's fears from the past.

"I don't know what you're talking about," Joey lied, keeping his body relaxed and maintaining direct eye contact. He wasn't going to let Emilio have the upper hand ever again. His days of hiding were over.

"Heh, like you could ever be content with driving some old lady around and fixing her car. Although that Studebaker you restored was a beauty." Of course, Emilio had to stick it to Joey, that he'd been in his space so easily. But it obviously wasn't recently, since he didn't seem to know about the new security measures.

"It's time for you to leave. For good this time. I have plenty of pictures and videos of you from this evening if you should be brave enough to show your face around here again." Joey marched towards Emilio, forcing the man backward towards the parking lot.

"You'll regret this. Mark my words." Flashlights and gruff shouts sounded as the festival security personnel wrangled Emilio to the ground with his arms behind him. From beyond the melee, Gladys and Remy waved to him. Thankful for this family having his back, he signaled his gratitude with a salute before turning back toward the garage.

"Lydia!" he called out, hands cupped around his mouth, loud enough that even people in the next town could hear him. He didn't actually expect a response, but the flicker of a phone going dark in the pumpkin patch was enough to put him in the right direction. Being on the receiving end of Lydia's fury was not how he had hoped this would go, but letting her brood about his betrayal wouldn't help his case.

CHAPTER FIVE

"Leeee-deeee-yaaaa!" As angry as she was with Joey, he made her name sound like a melodic song.

The pumpkin patch had been the closest option without having to walk past that sleazebag again. She huddled against the 1000-pound prize pumpkin to shield herself from the cold wind that crept in with the setting sun. She wasn't ready to talk to him. Her thoughts and feelings were all over the place, and she would just come across as an immature, emotional wreck. Lights blazed to life around her. Contemplating whether to run, there was a scuffing of the ground near her, followed by a thump against the giant gourd.

"You ok, princess?" Reaching around the pumpkin, his fingertips brush against hers.

"Don't call me that! I'm not some damsel in distress that needs a knight in shining armor."

"I never doubted it, but that guy…"

"You've never given me a second thought. Why interfere now?"

"You haunt me. In my dreams, asleep and awake, you are always there. I wonder at the taste of your mouth and the softness of your skin." He locked his fingers with hers, pulling her closer.

"But you act like I'm not there," she whispered.

"I want to know every part of you, but when you're near, my mind can only think of all the things I fantasize about doing with you."

"Hmm?" Her body hummed at the memory of him pressed against her, his heat igniting her desire.

"I crave the sight of your full lips wrapped around my cock. I need to know the sounds you make when I go down on you. And I want to cause you to scream my name every time you come." A tug on her hand encouraged her to move to him.

"What's changed, Joey?" He pulled her across his lap, her legs straddling him.

"At first, I thought if it were only a crush, you'd move on." He tucked a strand of hair behind her ear.

"I just wanted to spend time with you. But that doesn't explain why now." She leaned into his touch as he smoothed his hand down her neck.

"Someone was snooping around my place. I was afraid you were spying for a new job or a project. Not only did you tell me your true feelings, but also the actual culprit was caught." Unzipping her jacket, his breath caught as he stared at each inch of skin being revealed around the small halter top she was still wearing.

"I didn't tell anyone that I went back to school. I've been working at the diner to help pay for it." His fingers combed through her hair, and he pulled her closer.

"I'm sure your aunt would be happy to help." His face was so near, she could feel his breath on her cheek.

"Maybe," she sighed, closing the space between them and brushing her lips against his. He pressed her to him, intensifying the kiss. Their mouths melded together, tongues exploring each other. His large calloused hands traced her exposed midriff. Rubbing the bare skin on her back, his touch was like fire everywhere it landed, but she needed more. She began lowering the zipper on his overalls.

"Wait. Not yet, princess. I want this with you, but it has to be right." He clasped his hands over hers. It felt like a slap in the face, reminding her of why she had run from him in the first place. She pulled away with a gasp, realizing that he was teasing her again.

"Why do you insist on calling me that?" It felt like he was intentionally provoking her. It was stupid to believe his pretty words. She moved to stand up, but his fingers gripped her hips, holding her in place.

"One day, you'll see yourself the way I do. Gorgeous. Smart. Witty. Strong." He shifted her across his hardened bulge. "When that time comes, you'll be a queen. And if I'm lucky enough to convince you to stop doubting my sincerity, you'll be mine." He wiped at a tear she hadn't realized had escaped.

"Please don't make me want what I can't have." If he didn't let her go soon, she might fall apart right there.

"Why can't you accept that this is real and always has been?"

"You're saying all the right things, but you also suspected me of sabotage until you caught someone else."

"I distanced myself from everyone, not just you. It may seem paranoid, but some reasons seemed valid at the time."

"I know who you really are, but I don't know what danger you brought to my family. How could you do this to my aunt, after all she's done for you?"

"Gladys knows everything. Even today, after that guy recognized me, she was the first person I called. I wouldn't put her or your family at risk."

"What is it then? How can you expect me to believe your lovely declarations but not trust me with the truth?"

"It's difficult for me to confide in anyone. But I do trust you," he stated, unzipping his overalls to his waist.

"I'm not sure you can give me more mixed signals." She attempted to rise, finding his arms wrapping around her waist, stopping her again.

"Give me a minute to explain. This tattoo..." he pointed to a quaint scene near his left shoulder.

"Is that your race car?"

"Technically, it's referred to as a kart, with a 'k'. This is where I grew up and learned kart racing with my best friend, Pedro. Our mentor was from the same town near the coast."

"It looks a lot like here with the meadows and trees."

"There are some similarities, I think you would like. This other one," he gestured to his other shoulder.

"That's the Formula One car I saw on your profile."

"I drove many cars for different sponsors. But this was ours. Pedro was the brains behind it. Any advances in the industry to make the car faster, he absorbed faster than water. Our mentor was the money."

"And you were the driver?"

"Pedro was actually a better driver than I ever was, but he preferred to create the tech and materials. I learned a lot from him, but, yeah, I usually drove."

"I get the feeling this doesn't have a happy ending."

"That man earlier, the one harassing you... if it had been anyone else, I know you could have handled it, but I believed your life was at risk. He's immoral, ruthless, and used to be my mentor."

"He was after me all day. How did you finally get rid of him?"

"Gladys and Remy called the police."

"Was it a coincidence that he found you?"

"No. Which brings me to this," he stated, laying his hand in the middle of his chest, across a dove in flight holding a scroll of paper with dates on it.

"What happened?" she whispered reverently.

"Emilio, that's his name, my former mentor. He insisted the car was ready to race. I knew it wasn't and refused to drive it. He bullied me in every way he could think of, but I wouldn't back down. I don't know how he convinced Pedro to do the test drive..." His voice cracked, and she grasped his hand in both of hers. "The first date...is the day Pedro succumbed to his injuries after losing control and careening over the cliffside."

"Oh! That had to be so difficult. I'm almost afraid to ask about the other dates?"

"My family." He wrapped his arms around her and held her tightly to his chest.

"You were married?" She lifted her head to look at him.

"No, princess, you are the only one to hold that possibility." His lips quirked in a small smile while stroking her back under her jacket as if she were the one needing soothing. "When the paparazzi couldn't access me for interrogation, they came for my parents and sister."

CHAPTER SIX

"I don't understand. You did all of this so the press couldn't hound you?" Lydia laid across his chest, her soulful eyes encouraging him to continue.

"They're much more aggressive in parts of Europe. I had joined a new team and was on the circuit in the States. My sister was at university when the press decided to come after her. Her friends tried to help her escape, but the paps were relentless. They all perished in a multi-car accident."

"Oh my god, Joey, I'm so sorry. You don't have to go on if it's too difficult." Her arms tightened around him, giving him comfort. Even talking about such a difficult part of his life was easier with Lydia. Lying together under the night sky felt like something they had done a hundred times, but wthey ould never tire of the closeness.

"I need you to know why I was deceptive, but I love you too much to let you get hurt by anyone, even me." It felt good to finally admit it, even if her only acknowledgment of his statement was a slight movement on his chest.

"Have you been home since then?"

"My parents asked me not to. They felt my presence would turn my sister's funeral into a media frenzy. They said the same when they fell ill during the pandemic. I never got to say goodbye to any of them."

"Joey! I don't know what to say. My heart is breaking for you," she exclaimed, sitting up abruptly.

"I don't want you or anyone to feel sorry for me." Holding her hands, he tried to reassure her that the devastation he had once felt had faded to an ache.

"The anniversary of your friend's death is soon; is that the reason for the big change? Is Joey Cruz coming back?" He tried to read her expressive face as she stared at the dates on his tattoo when he felt a drop of rain fall on his chest.

"No, he doesn't exist anymore, but I'm not going to keep hiding. I thought disappearing would protect the people I cared about, but it didn't. It just let the tyrants believe they'd won and come back for more. So, there may be a lot of press asking questions in the next few weeks." A light mist was gathering on Lydia's jacket, but she didn't seem to notice.

"I'm sure Auntie has it all handled already," she joked.

"They may want to talk to you, too." He hinted more overtly at his objective.

"Me? Why on earth would they have any interest in me?"

"It depends on what you decide about us." Large droplets seemed to splash around them.

"There's an 'us'?" Her voice softened to a whisper.

"If you want there to be…" It was as far as he got when a deluge of icy rain poured down on them. He jumped up and ran with her in his arms. Wrapping herself around him, she laughed, letting her head fall back and reveling in the moment.

At the garage door, he was thankful he had installed a fingerprint lock, so he didn't have to let go of Lydia while he fumbled for his keys. He crossed the bays quickly, noticing she had started to shiver.

"Go ahead up," he stated, after he had unlocked the door to the stairs.

"I need the code for your door," she shouted down to him.

"It's your birthday, " he called back to her, securing the downstairs.

"What?" she yelled, not realizing he was behind her. She danced in place, rubbing her hands over her limbs.

"Your birthday." He reached around her to tap in the numbers, then waited for the sound of the mechanism to release before pushing the door open. "You should take a hot shower. Bathroom's to your right. I'll get you some of my sweats to wear." He reviewed his app to ensure that the lights were out, everything was locked, and security was on.

"When did you get that lock? None of them were here when you came." He looked up to find her staring at him. She had hung her jacket on the corner of a chair and crossed her arms across her chest, accentuating her cleavage more than usual.

"I told you there were signs someone had been searching the place. I updated the security after that," he explained casually.

"When you thought it was me. So why did you use my birthday?" She strode toward him until he was backed against the wall. He found her even more alluring when she was bossy.

"Princess, there was no way you would wear a horrendous cologne like that. I much prefer your vanilla sweetness." He watched a drop of water trail down her neck and disappear between her breasts.

"Still with the princess? Just tell me about the code."

"You haven't earned queen yet," he winked at her, hoping she remembered his profession. "What do you remember of your twenty-first birthday?"

"I went clubbing with my friends and had many first legal drinks."

"That's it?" He tried not to let his disappointment show.

"Oh, did you mean how I called you when they all ditched me and you took me to the adorable French bistro that was open late? You ordered a Rioja, and we talked well past closing time. It almost felt like a real date, the way you treated me like a princ—" Her hands grasped the sides of his face, her lips capturing his in a fierce kiss, their tongues dueling. He couldn't catch his breath, and he didn't care, knowing that she finally understood what he'd been telling her all night. Trying to press closer together while their hands roamed each other's bodies, they were teetering across the room. He scooped her up in her arms, not breaking the kiss, and carried her to his room.

Setting her on the bed, he kneeled on the floor, lifting one of her feet at a time, and he removed her boots.

"I've dreamed of you being here so often, this doesn't seem real." He gazed over her body, eager to explore and wanting the moment to last forever.

"I have also. I don't want to wait another minute." She kissed down his neck while lowering his zipper. Her hands eased up his torso, pushing the cloth off his shoulders and letting it fall to the floor. Leaning back, she ogled his naked form with his erection reaching his belly. She licked her lips.

"Your turn," he insisted.

She reached behind her neck, pulling the strings that let her top fall. He stroked the side of her chest and was rewarded with goosebumps erupting down her arm. Cupping one of her breasts, he brushed his thumb over her nipple before bringing it to his mouth. He lavished the other side with attention, a hand rubbing over her jeans between her legs.

"Mmm, Joey," she sighed.

"I need more of you, princess." He unfastened her jeans and slid them off with her panties. "You are so much more than I could have ever imagined." Scanning her body, he spread her legs wider for a better view. He inhaled her unique scent of vanilla and musk before running the flat of his tongue up to her clit. Giving her a smile and a wink when she gasped, he rubbed the bundle of nerves while licking her folds.

"I... I..." When she started to writhe, he lifted her hips, giving him a better angle to thrust his tongue into her. He listened for every sound she made to understand what increased her pleasure more. She cried out with her release.

"Joey, I need you." He was tempted to elicit another orgasm with his mouth until she grasped his hair and pulled him toward her face. Her hand enclosed around his erection and stroked him while he reached for a condom in his side drawer.

"That feels too good, princess. I'm not going to last long if you keep doing that." Kneeling between her legs, he held the foil square between them. When she reached for it, he snagged it away.

"What's going on, Joey? You have that look like when a repair is going right."

"I forget how well you can read me sometimes. It's just ... I told you things tonight I've never told anyone. I feel like I laid out my heart and soul to you..."

"Ah. I get it." She shifted to kneeling and aligned her body with his, her arms around his waist. "Joey Caruso, you have been in my heart and mind for so long, I barely remember a time without you there. I am honored that you shared your history with me. While I'm not thrilled that it took you so long to trust me, I do understand."

"Thank you. I guess I needed some reassurance—"

"I'm not done yet. You don't ever have to hide from me, and you don't have to face the world alone. I want to be there with you, through all the good and bad, even if the press hounds me for being with you. I love you too, Joey Caruso." Holding his face in her hands, her lips tenderly pressed against his. She pulled him with her down to the bed, wrapped around each other. He relished the warmth and softness of her in his arms. His cock, having a mind of its own, rubbed between her legs, drawing more delicious noises from her.

He rolled the condom down his shaft and positioned himself at her center. Sliding into her heat felt like coming home from a long winter's travel. They shared a moan and then found a rhythm of give and take as they joined together, trying to give the other more pleasure. He ground against her clit and the nerves along her channel each time he thrust deep inside of her. Feeling her muscles tighten around him, he increased his pace, chasing after her orgasm.

"Joey!" she screamed. She came hard, pulling his release with her. He came with a growl, still holding her through her aftershocks. He discarded the condom and pulled the covers over them.

"Sleep now, my queen. We have more to come." He smirked at his pun.

"You can't scare me off with your cheesiness, but you have a lifetime to try."

BRASSY BIGWIG

Murphy Wallace

PROLOGUE

Carley

WHEN MY EYES OPEN, the last thing I expect to see is the taut, tanned length of muscular back in bed with me. As my brain struggles to remember where I am and how I got here, my eyes travel across a set of broad shoulders and down an arched spine, stopping when they reach the white sheet covering up the bottom half of the masterpiece of man in front of me.

A quick lift of the soft, high thread count sheets uncovers one of the most glorious sights I've ever seen. The ass belonging to the man beside me is so perfect, it looks fake. It's round and smooth and tanned, just like his back. The perfect compliment to the rest of him.

Believing I'm still dreaming, I squeeze my eyes shut before opening them once again.

Nope. The hunk of hotness is still there.

I drop the sheet as the memory of the carnal, lascivious sex I took part in the previous evening seeps back into my brain, and the shock causes my eyes to grow wide. I remember his burning touch, licking flames along my skin as his hands roamed my body. I remember the feeling of him inside of me. His size was intimidating at first, but once he entered me, it was as though we were made for one another.

A perfect fit.

I have to cover my mouth to keep my loud gasp from escaping. I look around the room slowly, desperate to find my clothing.

I spot my thong immediately, laying on the floor right next to the bed. I vaguely remember him removing it before throwing it across the room last night. I guess this is where it landed. My dress is draped over the back of the sofa, and that's when I remember him tearing it from my body the moment we walked through the door. I hope I'll be able to wrap it around me long enough to make it back to my room. If not, I'll just take the robe from the bathroom.

On the end table next to the sofa, I catch the white dress shirt the masterpiece wore last night, barely hanging onto the shade of the lamp. I see one of the obnoxiously tall stiletto heels Saylor made me wear over by the bedroom door. I can't see the other one from my place in bed, and if I can't find it quickly once I crawl out from underneath these covers, I'll just have to buy Saylor a new pair. I'm not going to chance him waking up and being forced in to an awkward morning-after conversation.

I don't think I have enough courage in me to face him in the light of day. Not after everything we did last night. It's astounding how easily a few drinks, a sexy dress, and the desire-filled stare from a deviously handsome stranger can make you feel so liberated. Last night, I felt empowered and sexy. This morning, however, I feel like the shy girl who first arrived at the Santa Marina Resort in Mykonos.

If I'm being perfectly honest, I'm scared he's going to wake up and regret everything that happened. I'm terrified he's going to look at me and see nothing more than an easy slut who isn't worth his time.

That being said, I don't regret my actions. It was the best sex I've ever had with one of the most gorgeous men I've ever laid my eyes on. But the girl I was last night was a one-time-only thing. I'm headed back to New York today, and I'll once again fall into the rigid routine and life of Carley Garrettson.

However, if there's any time and place to become someone else, it's in a foreign country where you'll never have to see the people you meet ever again.

CHAPTER ONE

Carley

WHEN MY BEST FRIEND, Saylor, came up with the idea to go to Greece before starting my new job, I'll admit, I wasn't sure about tagging along. I'm a planner, and committing to something this huge last-minute sends my anxiety into a tailspin. However, I just busted my ass through grad school, got my master's in business management, and landed a job at the largest private equity firm in the country. Saylor told me I deserve a break and to let loose before I start next Monday, so I agreed to go.

Now that I'm sitting poolside with an ice-cold drink in my hand and plenty of eye candy to stare at, I can't believe I nearly passed this up. Even better is the fact that we settled into a cabana which happens to be directly across from one of the sexiest men I have ever seen. He's large and muscular with tanned skin. He has a tattoo of a compass over his heart which has something written around it. His head is covered in thick, dark hair and he's got a beard I'd love to feel tickle my skin. I catch a glimmer of silver at his temples from the light of the sun as he moves his head.

He catches my eye when he turns, and I thank God for dark sunglasses because they're the only thing hiding the fact that I was ogling the shit out of him. Despite having cover, I still tear my eyes from his. Staring at him causes my stomach to churn, although not in a bad way. His tempting stare conjures a heat deep down inside that I've rarely felt before.

"Holy hell, would you get a look at Captain Colossal over there?" Saylor exclaims, a little too loud for my taste.

"*Saylor*," I hiss through gritted teeth. "He probably heard you."

"Good, maybe he'll come over here then," she laughs and wiggles her eyebrows playfully.

My eye roll contradicts the voice in my head which agrees with her.

I spy a slight lift of the left corner of his mouth, as though he's amused by our conversation, but he quickly continues perusing the rest of the guests on the pool deck. He must have been reacting to something his equally hot friend said.

"Quick, perk up your boobs or something," Saylor commands. "Get his attention back over here."

"Perk up your own damn boobs. You're just as single as I am," I counter.

"But yours are bigger than mine," she explains.

"Bigger isn't always better, you know."

Saylor rolls her eyes, irritated I'm not playing along and throwing myself at a guy I don't even know just so she can have an opportunity to talk to him.

"Besides, this is supposed to be a girls' trip. We didn't come here to meet guys."

"Speak for yourself," Saylor laughs, but I know she isn't joking.

She's the most boy crazy girl I've ever met. I love her to death, but sometimes she lets her mission to find a man get in the way of an otherwise fun, relaxing time.

"Besides, look at the girl they're with. She's absolutely breathtaking," I admit, envious of her near perfect everything.

I say girl, but she's all woman. Remarkable raven hair, perfectly round, perky boobs, a tanned and toned body, legs for days.

"Way out of our league," I add once I finish assessing her.

The same goes for the guy Saylor has her eye on. Everything about him screams wealth and status. Saylor and I both grew up with wealthy parents. We can recognize it in others, easily. But this guy exudes money and power as though he belongs in his own tax bracket. There's no way a man of his stature would ever be interested in me—*I mean Saylor*.

"And the guy, he looks like a Greek god who's been carved from stone. He also looks closer to our parents' age than ours. He'd never be interested in us."

"Mmm..." Saylor practically salivates as she gawks at the poor, devilishly handsome man.

I've always had a thing for older guys, but those I've dated have only been a couple years older than me. Still very immature for my taste. I've never considered dating a man more than five years older than me, but damn...

Maybe I should.

The heat deep within me, which had started to dissipate slightly, fires up once more. As I shift in my seat, my thighs clench, applying mild pressure to my clit. I close my eyes briefly and let myself imagine for a split second it's his thumb tracing light circles over it.

Speaking of immature boys, before I have a chance to get pulled too far under, I'm jolted back to reality by a group of three guys cannonballing into the pool like children. They appear to be roughly the same age as Saylor and me. Definitely not older and more refined like the devastatingly handsome god across the pool.

It's probably for the best. I shouldn't waste my time fantasizing about someone who would never even notice me. Before I can get sucked too far into my pit of self-deprecation, our server comes by with a fresh round of drinks for us.

"Strawberry daiquiri and a Cosmo." I reach out for my drink when he hands it to me. "Can I get you ladies anything else at the moment?"

He stares at Saylor for a few seconds longer than is comfortable. Well, I would be uncomfortable anyway. Saylor's eating it up, though.

"I think we're … *satisfied* … for now," she flirts, cocking her eyebrow at him.

Jesus, help her.

I take off my sunglasses and stare pointedly at her as she watches the server walk away from us. When she finally breaks her connection from his retreating ass, she turns back to me and shoots me a questioning look.

"What?"

"We're *satisfied* for now?" I repeat her desperate words back to her.

"Oh, leave me alone. Just because you're not trying to get laid on this vacation doesn't mean I have to go without."

"As long as you don't bring them back to our room," I declare, mildly disgusted.

"Well, I'll do my best, but if you see the scrunchie on the doorknob, you know what that means."

"Ew," I snicker.

I can't help but laugh. We may not see eye-to-eye on everything, but that's what makes our friendship so exciting. We bring out different parts of each other and challenge one another to try things we normally wouldn't.

She rolls her eyes playfully as I shake my head.

"But seriously," I start again, "if you fuck a stranger on my bed, I'm leaving your ass in Greece."

CHAPTER TWO

Dimos

SCANNING the aquamarine sea over the tops of my feet, I yearn to be on the water in my yacht instead of on a beach surrounded by obnoxious twenty-somethings. I told Ez I would sail us out here, but he couldn't be away from work for that long. It would take more than a month to get from Hermosa Beach, California to Mykonos and back, not to mention the week-long stay at the Santa Marina Resort they booked.

My yacht, The Cerulean, is where I feel most at home.

I should have sailed out here by myself and met them on the island.

Oh well. Now that I'm here, I supposed I better make the most of it.

I let my compass guide me in every aspect of my life—faith, love, family—as well as on the open sea. It's why I have a compass tattooed over my heart. Even when it seems like it's not working, I have to have faith in it. Like when it led me to Emma. I don't think it was wrong; I just think I needed to be with her so I know what I'm *not* looking for in life.

Which is why I'm even here in the first place.

It's not every day you finalize your divorce. What a shitshow it was. That circus finally coming to an end is more than enough reason to celebrate.

Laying back in my chaise lounge, I take a swig of my beer as I try to cast off the secondhand embarrassment I feel for these young guys out here. They're laying the compliments and pick-up lines on thick. Now that I'm single, is this really what I have to look forward to?

Fuck that.

I'm not planning on getting back into a relationship anytime soon anyway. Maybe never again.

I down the rest of my beer and look for the server who has been floating around here. When I spot him, he's busy flirting with the friend of the captivating girl I locked eyes on at the pool a few days ago. But *she's* nowhere in sight.

Where is she?

Théa mou. My goddess.

My mouth pulls up at the corner, recalling when I first laid eyes on her.

As I scan the clientele on the pool deck of the resort, my eyes lock onto one of the most alluring girls I've ever seen. Her long brown hair is in waves down to the swell of her breasts. Her sunglasses, which are blocking my view of her eyes, sit atop a thin nose. Her skin is perfectly sun-kissed.

My eyes roam over the rest of her body, taking in the sight of her laying back against the cushion under the cabana in her lavender bikini, and my cock hardens instantly. She's much younger than any other girl I've been attracted to before. Unless she showed a fake ID at check-in, she's at least twenty-one, which is how old you need to be to reserve a room here.

At least I know she isn't jailbait.

I think that as though I'm actually considering pursuing her, which is absurd.

I watch as she tries to hide behind her sunglasses, but it's fruitless. I may not be able to see her eyes, but make no mistake, there's no missing the way I'm affecting her.

It doesn't appear she realizes the way her shoulders are pushed backward, arching her back slightly so her tits protrude out a little more than they were a moment earlier.

But I did.

She also may not notice her thighs rubbing together the longer she pretends not to stare at me. I ache to know how strongly her clit is throbbing.

I JOLT BACK TO THE PRESENT BEFORE MY COCK GETS TOO UNCOMFORTABLY hard. The girls left not long after that, and it killed me to watch her go. My eyes hadn't had their fill of her beauty yet.

What did she do when she left? Did she forget about me? Did she go back to her room and rub herself off to thoughts of me? Did she make herself come, pretending it was my fingers that were rousing her orgasm?

I tear my eyes from her friend. I can't have these thoughts here. Not when I am in public. Not with Ez and Eliana right next to me. Not when *théa mou* isn't in my sights.

Where is *she?*

Irritated I can't find her, I take another swig of my beer, forgetting it was empty. Not knowing how long the server is going to be shamelessly flirting, I decide to go to the bar myself to get another round.

"I gotta take a leak and get another beer. Either of you want anything?" I inquire.

"Sure, I'll take one," Ez speaks up. "El?"

"Yeah. Thanks," Eliana responds.

I pretend to take one final sip of my beer as I silently plead with my erection to die down, so I'm able to stand. I sneak another look at Ez who glances strangely at me. Not wanting to explain myself, I get up and rearrange my cock as discreetly as possible. Walking away from the shining sea, I head to the building—a hut, really—just outside of the access trail from the resort to their private beach, where the bar and bathrooms are located.

I place our order then tell the bartender I'll be right back to pick them up.

Heading around the end of the bar to the bathrooms, I take a deep breath. I need to chill out where this girl is concerned.

The ink on my divorce papers is barely dry, and the last thing I want or need is to get involved with someone else right now. That's partly how I got myself into this mess anyway. As I round the corner past the bar, I run head-on into someone else.

"Ma Kala den prosexeis!" Watch out!

This *théa* has me so riled up, I'm about to lose my shit on this person when I'm just as much to blame. My irritation is very short-lived as a light, floral scent fills my nose, and my eyes latch onto the sparkling, blue stare of none other than *théa mou.*

Her eyes are the color of the sea, and they run just as deep. My mind is momentarily paralyzed by her beauty, whereas my body reacts like that of a sixteen-year-old boy.

"I'm so sorry!" she exclaims.

Her eyes catch on mine, and I watch as her pupils dilate when she realizes who she's run into.

"No, please," I protest. "The fault was all mine, *théa.*"

I lift the corner of my mouth slightly as I use the nickname she doesn't know I've given her. She narrows her eyes at me, barely, but it's noticeable. Nodding her head slightly, she tucks her hair behind her ear and walks around me, back toward the chair where her friend is still flirting with the waiter. Watching her tanned, bikini-clad ass sashay away from me for the second time this week, it's getting harder to let her go.

My cock agrees with me.

Today, she has on a black bikini with some type of cream-colored, crocheted sarong tied around her waist that looks more like a fishing net than a cover-up. Her suit isn't cut high or too revealing like the suits some of the other girls out here are wearing, but that's just fine by me. It leaves a little more to the imagination.

It takes me longer than I'd care to admit to use the restroom because I had to wait for my erection to die down before I could go. I would have been fine if not for running into her, but you'll never hear me complain about that. Once I'm finished, I wash my hands, grab our drinks from the bar, and return to my seat.

"Here you go," I grab Ez's attention and hand him his and Eliana's drinks.

"Thanks, man."

"So, D," Eliana chimes in, "Ez and I are thinking about heading up to Little Venice tonight for some drinks and dancing. Are you in?"

In an effort to delay my "no", I take a drink of my beer. The cold, crisp taste of hops and citrus slide down my hot, parched throat.

"I might let you crazy kids go out by yourselves tonight," I respond after a few moments. "I'm not sure I'm up for it."

I laugh inwardly. Ez and Eliana are older than I am, but *I* feel like the old man at the moment.

"You know what you need, don't you?" Ez encourages.

"What's that, Ez?"

This ought to be good.

"You need to get laid, my friend."

A dry laugh escapes my mouth. "I think that's what got me in to the mess I'm in."

"D. How many times do I have to tell you? Your... *mishap* wasn't what killed your marriage. You checked out a few years ago when Emma's grip on your balls began to tighten. Way before what happened between you and Kati. Christ, for all you know, Emma was fucking whatever his name is long before Kati got her claws in to you."

"Gary. And thank you for that thought, Ez," I mutter sarcastically, tipping my beer in his direction.

"Look, all I'm saying is now that your divorce is final, Emma and her games are out of your life for good. I know it's been a long and tiring journey for you. I just think it's time you begin your new life as a born-again bachelor."

As glad as I am about having Emma and all of her bullshit behind me, as much as I would love to sink my cock inside of another woman and try to forget about the past year—*fuck, the past ten years*—I just don't think I'm ready for it.

My eyes shoot to *théa* again. She's currently in a fit of laughter over something, and I desperately want to know what it is. More than that, I need to know why this girl is holding so much of my attention hostage.

Maybe I could be ready for something if it were with the right person...

Or maybe it's just because it's been too long since I've had any kind of meaningful sexual encounter. My cock doesn't know what the fuck it wants, but it has a stronger pull than my heart and my brain combined at the moment.

"I'll think about tonight, but I wouldn't count on my being there."

"Fair enough," Ez replies.

I shoot him a smile, knowing he has my best interests at heart.

I met Ez and Eliana nine years ago when I moved to New York temporarily while getting Okeanós' New York City office up and running. Just after opening, I was visited by someone from the NYC Business Owner's Association, who wanted to welcome me to town. I hadn't had any interest in going to the luncheon they'd invited me to, but I thought at the very least I would be able to start a good rapport with other business owners in the new and unfamiliar city.

Sitting at Ez and Eliana's table was the one good thing to come out of it. We quickly learned they only asked us all there to get donations out of us. They were trying to create a program for college-aged kids who wanted to start their own business. About halfway through, Ez mentioned the fact that they would have gotten more money out of us if they would have plied us with alcohol instead of boring us to death. To which I picked up my water and hooted, *"Opa."*

That's when I found out Eliana is Greek as well, and we got to talking. Ez mentioned he was the CEO of Martinique Enterprises, and he talked me in to meeting with him the following week to discuss some of my investments. Eliana suggested we meet at their place over dinner instead of the office, and the rest is history. We've been like family ever since.

It's tough living three thousand miles away from them sometimes, but I try to get back to the big city once a month to ensure the east coast office is running just as smoothly as the one back home in Torrance.

At least, I used to, before Kati.

Now I see to it that my assistants work out of the New York office exclusively, keeping me at a three-thousand-mile distance from them at all times. I haven't been back there in nearly a year.

Sensing their eyes on me, I feel antsy, like I need to move around.

"I'm going to go cool off," I tell them.

I take a long pull of the ice-cold liquid in the bottle I'm holding before I hop up out of my seat.

"Enjoy," Eliana calls from behind me in a wistful tone.

I know she wishes there was something she could do to help me. I'm not sure there's anything that can be done, but, *fuck...* If there was, I'd take it. The mistake I made with Kati was just one of the many unfortunate events that occurred during my marriage. I know we weren't perfect. Ez was right about Emma. For years she's berated me, talked down to me, and made me feel like less of a man.

But that doesn't make what I did okay.

The fact that Emma was cheating as well also doesn't make what I did okay.

My head is jumbled. My heart is heavy. My cock has a fucking mind of its own. I chance a glance at *théa*, briefly, once more as I walk toward the water.

The sea is calling me, and it's the only place that will calm me and offer my mind and body the peace it's looking for.

CHAPTER THREE

Carley

"Who are you looking for?"

Saylor breaks me from my trance as I search through the crowd of people on the pool deck, hoping to catch a glimpse of Captain Colossal, as she referred to him.

I groan, unhappy that I've become accustomed to calling him by that ridiculous nickname.

"Hmm?" I question, turning to look at her. "Did you say something?"

"My, my ... he's got you wound tight, and you haven't even spoken to him yet," Saylor taunts.

"What on *earth* are you talking about?" I play dumb, knowing she isn't going to buy it.

"You've got it bad for Big Daddy Zeus."

I roll my eyes at the new nickname.

"That might be the worst nickname you've ever come up with. And I do not, I'm just looking around at the selection of men in which to choose from," I counter.

"Oh? So you've finally decided to join me in finding some action on this trip?"

The same waiter we had at the pool our first day was our waiter again at the beach two days ago. Saylor invited him over that evening while I enjoyed a quiet dinner by myself followed by a solo walk on the beach. It was wonderful and exactly what I needed.

I love Saylor to death, but everyone needs a little time to themselves.

"Well, I was thinking about it," I lie.

I'm fully aware nothing will ever happen with the hot Greek god, but a girl can dream, right? At least, I think he's Greek. He looks like he is. I wonder if he lives here or is just vacationing. I've tried keeping him out of my thoughts ever since leaving the pool that first day, with little luck. I was hoping we would run into one another again, but *actually* running into him was not quite what I'd had in mind.

The moment I realized who he was, a flush covered my body, and my clit began to throb. It was as if it knew he was close by. I was a little shaken when he screamed at me in whatever language it was he spoke.

Was it Greek?

I have no clue, but it sounded like it could be.

Once he'd realized it was me, his hard face softened. The scent of clary sage and citrus that floated off of him in waves was enough to do me in. And, when my eyes met his intense silver stare, it made my knees weak.

Théa, he'd called me when he apologized. I need to know what it means. Maybe I'll take a trip to the business center later and see if I can Google it. My dumb phone doesn't have service here, despite the international plan I'm paying extra for this week, so I haven't been able to look it up yet. It's driving me crazy.

"Atta girl," Saylor breaks me from my inner thoughts once again. "You can stop looking now, though."

"What do you mean?"

She nods at something to my right, and I turn my head just in time to spy the drop-dead gorgeous hottie himself walking down the stone steps leading from the upper deck of the hotel to the pool deck. Seeing him again causes the air in my lungs to leave me in a single whoosh.

How is it he looks even more enchanting than he did the last time I saw him?

He's with the same two people I'd seen him with previously. I swear, the three of them are cut from the same striking cloth. Looking that good is so unfair to the rest of us. The girl points to an open cabana at the end of the row.

No, not there.

I silently pray they choose a seat across from us again so I'm able to watch him from behind my sunglasses without getting caught. The other guy with them says something, and they all laugh. Then he points to a few chairs on the other side of the pool and thankfully, they sit there instead.

Once they're seated, I relax slightly and take a large sip of my strawberry daiquiri. As he settles into his chair, I swear I can see the corner of his lips perk up a little. I can't see his eyes, but the way my heartbeat accelerates, the heat that blooms deep within me, I know he's looking at me.

I think.

I hope.

My god, I'm ridiculous.

I roll my eyes from beneath my shades, irritated I can't get the thought of this stranger off my mind. I force my eyes from him, pull the book I brought with me from my bag, and try to distract myself with someone else's love life.

A little while later, Saylor forces me to get into the pool with her. I love sitting by the pool and lounging on the sand at the beach, but I've never been one to enjoy being in the water. Today is hot enough, though, and the cool water is more refreshing than I expected it to be.

Saylor, doing what she does best, pretends to swim into a guy not too far from where I'm hanging out at the edge. When they begin striking up a conversation, I decide to get out and go back to the cabana. Before I get the chance, I freeze, noticing *his* shimmering eyes are locked directly on me. I stare back for a few seconds before remembering my sunglasses are laying on my chair.

My eyes grow wide as I feel the heat spread across my cheeks, embarrassed about getting caught. Swallowing nervously, I turn around and climb the steps out of the pool. As soon as I get to our cabana, I wrap myself in a towel and put my sunglasses back in place. Feeling safe and unseen once again, I lay my chair flat and rest for a little while.

It feels as though I've barely closed my eyes before I'm awoken suddenly by a ruckus next to my chair and cold drops of water dripping onto my skin. When I finally get a chance to see what's happening, I realize Saylor has invited the group of guys she was hanging out with in the pool to do shots in the cabana.

I roll my eyes, irritated at the intrusion.

Luckily, the majority of them go back into the pool after that, but two linger behind. Saylor sits on her chair with one of them, and they're lip-locked, instantly.

Ew.

The other guy who stayed is looking at me awkwardly, as though he's expecting me to pull him in for a slobber fest of our own. Without being asked, he takes a seat on the end of my chaise.

"What's your name?"

I'm so shocked he sat down, I can't come up with something quick enough to get him to leave.

"Gianna," I state sternly, crossing my arms and legs.

Anytime I meet a guy, I give him my mother's name until I get a chance to feel him out. They don't need to know my real name until I feel like they're someone who I'd like to keep around for a while. Some of them have ended up as just friends, others turned into relationships, but none of them have been the man I've needed them to be.

This guy? He'll never know my real name.

"Carley," Saylor slurs, having broken the sloppy kiss between her and whoever the hell he is.

"I thought you said your name is Gianna," the clueless guy interrupts.

"It *is*," I assert.

"I don't think—"

"What, Saylor?" I glare at her so she knows just how unhappy I am.

"They're having a bonfire on the beach tonight. We're *so* going," she insists.

"You have fun, I'll have to skip it," I explain.

"Aww come on, it will be fun," Clueless whines.

Like a toddler.

"She can't make it."

A sexy timbre breaks through the conversation, and that's when I turn my head to find *him* standing on the other side of my chair with drinks in hand. A beer, a strawberry daiquiri, and a Cosmo.

"Who are *you*?" Clueless asks. "Her dad?"

Oh my god, what an asshole. Before I get a chance to tell him off, the dreamy one speaks up.

He gives the dumbass a smug grin, completely unaffected by the dad comment and not taking his eyes off mine. "She can't make it because she's accompanying me to dinner this evening."

He places the drinks down on the table between mine and Saylor's chairs, and we both stare at him in utter surprise. Leaving his beer, he picks up the daiquiri and the Cosmo and hands them to us. Then he turns to Clueless.

"You mind?" he asks.

"What?" Clueless responds.

"You're in my seat."

Clueless stands up and mutters something that sounds like "whatever" under his breath as he walks away. His friend, the one who just had his tongue down Saylor's throat, follows him.

The handsome slab of chiseled marble sits on the end of my chair, staring at me as he takes a sip of his beer. Saylor is so shell-shocked, she doesn't even notice tongue guy is gone.

"Tha—" My voice gets caught in my throat. Clearing it, I continue. "Thank you. For the drinks as well as scaring them away."

"It was my pleasure. It was pretty uncomfortable watching from afar. I figured it was even more regrettable over here."

"Definitely," I agree.

"What?" Saylor finally snaps out of it. "Speak for yourself. I was having fun."

"No one is stopping you, Say. Have at it. Just be careful, please."

"I have my phone if you need me," she squeals excitedly as she runs after the two of them.

Realizing too late her leaving means I'm alone with him, I swallow a ball of nerves stuck in the back of my throat. As he takes his seat at the end of my chair, I struggle to figure out what to say next.

"I'm Nick. Nick Evans," he sticks his hand out in greeting.

The moment our fingers touch, my skin tingles like a spark of electricity is shooting through me. When my eyes meet his, the fire in his eyes tells me he was affected by the same energy.

"Gianna Manford, nice to meet you."

Everything in me wanted to tell him my real name, but I couldn't do it. No matter what happens here, we're leaving tomorrow, and I'll never see him again.

It's pointless.

"A sexy name for a sexy girl," he states earnestly before bringing my hand to his lips and whispering a kiss along my knuckles.

His words and actions make me melt where I sit, and I wish like hell I would have told him my real name. I can't tell him now, though. I'd look as crazy as I feel. My eyes shift, focusing on different areas of the pool deck because I can't let him see how badly he's affecting me. I don't know him. I don't need him thinking I'm some stage-5 clinger he needs to steer clear of. I certainly don't want him thinking he can win me over with his charm so easily.

"Are you enjoying your stay?" He relinquishes his hold on my hand and brings my attention back to him.

"Yes," I admit, flipping my hair behind my shoulder. "One last hurrah before I start my new job on Monday."

He nods his head in approval. My eyes flit to the tic of the muscle in his jaw.

Why is he so tense? When I catch his gaze once more, I realize he was staring at my boobs. Was the tense tic of his jaw him trying to hold back from tackling me? From sucking my nipple into his mouth and not stopping until I'm dripping wet with desire?

What if we were vacationing here together? I picture us cuddling close on the chaise lounge. Enjoying drinks at the bar. Skinny dipping in the ocean at night.

Oh my god, Carley. Get a fucking grip.

Bringing myself back to reality, I continue the conversation before he starts thinking I don't know how to carry myself.

"What about you?" I question. "Do you live here? In Greece, I mean."

"My parents used to live in Athens, but they moved to the States before they had me. Florida, to be specific."

"I love Florida," I smile. "It's one of my favorite places to visit."

"Well, who wouldn't love the Sunshine State?" When he flashes me his pearly whites, my smile grows, and the fluttering of butterflies in my stomach quickens.

"Which part do you live in? I've been to a few different places, but my favorite is Islamorada."

"I grew up in Miami, but I live in Southern California now. Hermosa Beach."

"So you're a beach bum?" I joke.

"Born and raised," he confirms. "What about you? Where do you live?"

"New York," I answer.

Just as he opens his mouth to say something else, his friend calls him from the other side of the pool.

"Hey, D!"

D?

How do you get "D" from Nick Evans? Maybe his middle name begins with a D? While I'm left to wonder, they continue their conversation.

"We're going to grab some lunch. You coming?"

"Yeah," he shouts back. "I'll be right there."

Damn it.

I haven't gotten my fill of speaking to him, but I'm not sure I ever would if given the chance. I offer him a smile when he turns back to face me.

"Well, Gianna. It was wonderful meeting you."

"Same to you, Nick."

I feel like an idiot when my heart clenches as he begins to walk away. I put my sunglasses back in place to hide the sadness I know is in my eyes. I'm so stupid, why am I acting like this? Before I'm able to get too upset by the light-ning fast ending to my shortest, make-believe relationship, he pivots and takes hold of my attention once more.

"So I was thinking." He walks a few steps back toward me.

"You were, were you?" I answer coyly. He smiles before pulling his lip between his teeth.

"We should probably keep our dinner plans for tonight," he continues. "In the event you run in to that kid again. I wouldn't want you to get caught in a lie or anything."

"You bring up a very good point." I play along. "I *do* hate a liar, and I wouldn't dream of being labeled as one."

I'm not sure which of us is working harder to come up with these bullshit excuses, but I welcome them all.

"I'll meet you in the lobby at eight, then?"

"It's a date," I confirm.

Quickly, I wonder if calling it a date was too much, but his wink and half smile tell me he isn't bothered by it. He may even like the idea.

I try holding in my big, goofy grin, but I can't.

"Looking forward to it, Gianna Manford." He flashes me his killer smile before turning and walking away again.

Same here, Nick Evans. Same here.

CHAPTER FOUR

Dimos

I can't remember the last time I was this nervous, and I hate it. This is *barely* a date. It's one night and I'll never see this girl again.

I ignore the tightness in my chest as those words bounce around in my head.

These feelings are as irksome as they are a relief. I'm glad I'm not so jaded I can't feel emotion for another woman anymore, but feeling something this soon after Emma is unwelcome. I need a break from it all. I don't want to want someone else right now. I need to spend some time alone.

"Here's to our last night in paradise, my friend."

Ez breaks me from my thoughts as he walks out onto the balcony of the suite where he and Eliana are staying. He hands me a highball glass with a couple of fingers of whiskey in it. They were headed back to Little Venice tonight, but at the last minute decided they were going to stay at the resort.

To spy on me, I'm sure.

"Oh, I don't know. I'm thinking about sticking around for a while," I joke.

Kind of.

I finger the smooth surface of the glass, and it reminds me of Gianna's silky, tanned legs.

Stop it, D.

"I know you would stay if you could."

"There isn't anything for me to return to, Ez. I can work from anywhere. Emma's gone, *finally*." I ponder the possibilities for a moment. "I *would* miss my yacht, though. Someone would have to sail it out here for me."

We clink our glasses together, and I take a sizeable gulp of the warm amber liquid. I relish the burn as it coats my throat. A brief period of silence follows before Ez speaks again.

"I know you were thinking of making the move from the West Coast to the Big Apple. Now that you're no longer tethered, have you given it any more thought?"

Ez and Eliana have been trying to get me to move to New York City for the past few years. We have a blast when I'm out there, and I know I would enjoy it. But I haven't been able to take the leap yet. I blamed it on Emma a lot of the time, but the truth is, I don't know if I'm ready. I love my house on the Strand in Hermosa. It's beachfront, serene both inside and out, and the marina is so close, I could walk if I wanted to.

However, hearing the words I just uttered to Ez out loud, that I have nothing to return home to, does make me a little sad. I've dreamt about the day Emma would finally be out of there, that she would stop sucking the air out of every room she walked into. By no means would I want to go back to that life, and I never would, but...

I don't want to go home to nothing.

The vision of Gianna sitting on the chaise lounge by the pool earlier flashes through my mind. She had on a cream-colored bathing suit today, the outline of which was covered in turquoise stones. Her perfectly tanned skin seemed to glow beneath it. Then the image shifts to her sitting on the sundeck at my house in Hermosa. Sprawled out on a bed of cushions, topless, lying on her stomach with a thin piece of gauzy fabric covering her bottom half.

I can picture myself going home to *her*. To *théa*.

"I'm still not sure I'm ready to make that move just yet," I finally answer.

"Fair enough," he nods.

I down the rest of my drink in one swallow, and within five minutes, we're entering the elevator from the hallway outside of our door. When we step inside, I speak, needing to make a request.

"I have to ask something before we get downstairs. Gianna lives in New York, too. I don't know if she's in the city or upstate or what, but I'd prefer it if she didn't find out you guys live there or that I have ties there."

"You got it," Ez agrees easily.

"I'm assuming she knows you as Nick." Eliana states rather than asks as she shoots me some serious side-eye.

It's my go-to fake name when I don't want to give out my real one. My full first name is Dimosthenis. My parents used to call me Nick when I was a young boy because of the "nis" at the end. And Evanos is my middle name, so it's not *exactly* a lie. Before I'm able to admit or attempt to deny it, the elevator doors open, and we step from the car into the lobby.

"Saved by the bell," I joke as I walk.

Ez and Eliana are eating at the main restaurant this evening, while I've made plans for Gianna and myself to dine privately in a more intimate setting. But when we get to the lobby, I realize I'm a little early.

"You guys go ahead, I'll wait here for her," I point to the sofa in the grand lobby area.

I sure could use a drink while I'm waiting.

"We were planning on stopping by the bar for a few drinks first, D. Why don't you join us?" Eliana suggests.

I swear, it's like we're connected somehow, as if she's my long-lost sister or something like that. We joke around that it's the pull of the Greek inside of us. She can tell exactly what I'm thinking and feeling, sometimes even before I do. I think about it for a second, worried I won't notice when Gianna arrives. But before I'm able to answer, I hear the familiar click of high heels echoing down the hallway behind me.

It's like a universal siren for the male species. We all know it when we hear it, and it's usually followed by the strut of a sexy woman. It's too early for it to be her, but that doesn't keep me from pivoting toward the noise.

When I turn around, I lock eyes on a sultry woman marching down the hallway toward me. She's one of the sexiest creatures I've ever seen, and my dick twitches thinking about bending her over the concierge's desk and having my way with her. I begin to feel guilty for having sordid thoughts of one girl while waiting on another, but then I realize exactly who it is I'm practically drooling over.

Théa.

I struggle to swallow the lump in my throat, and I pull on my tie, loosening it slightly. Everything seems to slow down as she continues to strut across the marble floor.

Does she even know how gorgeous she is?

She's dressed in a low-cut, black, lace dress that barely covers the sacred place between her long legs. The same place I've been itching to get a taste of since the moment I laid eyes on her. The thin straps helping to hold her ample tits in place look like they could snap at any moment under the weight of them.

God help me if they do.

Her hair is done up in large curls which are pinned to the side with a crystal-studded bow barrette. The strappy, black stiletto shoes she has on make her already svelte legs look even more elegant. They add several inches to her shorter height, bringing the top of her head to the level of my eyes.

She flashes me a shy smile that contradicts the confident sway of her hips.

"*Sweet Jesus,*" I mutter under my breath, forgetting where I am and that there are other people around. I don't even care who heard me.

"Gianna ... hi." I can barely get my words out.

"Hello," she greets me before looking at Ez and Eliana.

Her angelic voice practically does me in.

"You look ..."

My eyes trace every inch of her body while I try to think of a word strong enough to convey my feelings. From her gorgeous, chocolate tresses to her piercing blue stare that's locked on me from beneath lids hooded with what I hope is lust. Over the swell of her tits, following the curve of her hips, down to the bottom of her dress. I stop momentarily when my eyes meet the hem.

What I wouldn't give to run my hand up the length of her silky legs. Starting from her fuck-me heels, over her toned calves and thighs, right to her warm center ... If *I'm* thinking it, surely countless others who feast eyes on her tonight will, too.

What was she thinking, wearing such a tight, tiny, poor excuse for a dress like that out of the hotel room anyway? If I had the power to take my eyes off her, I'm sure I would find every other man within eyesight staring at *théa mou*. The beast within me, a raging bull I haven't felt stir in years, comes out, and I fight my instincts to tell her to go back upstairs and change into something less revealing. Something that looks less like a negligee and more like a cocktail dress.

But I won't do that to her. I take a calming breath, needing to control both my beast as well as my dick. I don't want to ruin my chance with her, but more importantly, I don't want to embarrass her. Besides, she has every right to wear whatever she wants. Plus, it wouldn't be the worst thing in the world to show up to dinner with her on my arm. To have every woman we pass along the way wishing they were her, every man wishing they had her. The envy on their faces would be a fair trade.

"...breathtaking," I finally finish my sentence and pray my pause wasn't actually as long as it felt.

"Hi, I'm Eliana," Eliana offers Gianna her hand, breaking me from my trance and once again proving she knows what I need.

"It's very nice to meet you, I'm Gianna."

"Oh, I know," Eliana answers, smirking at me.

I watch as pink tints Gianna's cheeks, and her posture stiffens. She's embarrassed, and it's adorable.

I roll my eyes at Eliana before introducing her to Ez.

"Nice to meet you as well," Gianna smiles, correcting her reaction quickly and taking Ez's hand when he offers it to her.

"We were just going to grab a drink before dinner," Eliana explains. "Do you guys want to join us? I know you're early for your reservation."

I look to Gianna to weigh her response before I answer.

"That sounds wonderful," she states.

She appears relieved, and I wonder if she needs a drink to help her relax as much as I do. As Eliana and Ez turn toward the bar, I place my hand on the small of Gianna's back and guide her across the lobby. I can feel her skin heat through the thin, lacy material, and I'm reminded of the searing heat emanating from her when I kissed her hand at the pool earlier.

I need my lips on her skin again.

As we enter the bar area, I maneuver Gianna in front of me and use the opportunity to adjust my cock. It's stiff and pushing against the waistband of my boxer briefs, trying like hell to overpower my conscious thought and dictate how this evening will play out.

As much as I want to let him take over, as much as I want this fiery hot sex kitten in my bed tonight, I need to keep it together. I don't think I will be able to caveman Gianna into coming back to my room. She's classy. She both commands and deserves more gentlemanly wooing.

"Kalispera." *Good evening.*

As we're greeted by the bartender, I watch as his eyes fall on Gianna's cleavage, taking in her attire. I can see the wanting gleam in his stare, and while I can't blame him, it makes me want to tear his head off.

"What can I get for you this evening?"

"Another strawberry daiquiri?" I ask, turning to Gianna.

My hand settled on the middle of her back, and I can't help but run my thumb up and down along her spine. If she's bothered by my touch, she isn't showing it.

"Actually, I'd love a vodka soda with a lemon, please," she requests.

"In addition to that, we'll have two McCallan's and a Merlot, please."

As the bartender busies himself making our drinks, both Ez and I pull out a stool for each of the girls to sit on. I notice Gianna mirror Eliana's posture as they sit, facing one another. I catch sight of something black and silky between her legs as she crosses one over the other. I didn't mean to look, but...

Who am I trying to kid? Maybe I'm more okay with this dress than I'd thought. Easy access is never a problem.

Before I can think of something to talk about, Eliana starts in on her questioning.

"So, Gianna, what brings you to Mykonos?"

"I just finished grad school, and I'm starting a new job on Monday. So my best friend convinced me to get away for the week before jumping back into the real world."

"Smart girl," Eliana answers. "What will you be doing?"

I shoot Eliana a knowing look from my spot next to Gianna's stool. She needs to stop with the career questions. The reason I don't tell girls my real name is because I don't want them finding out who I am and how much I'm worth. I don't know Gianna yet, and while I may want to fuck her, it doesn't mean she's stable enough not to try and trap me into something if she knows too much about my business.

"An office assistant. Nothing too glamorous. I'm just starting out and haven't *made it* quite yet."

As much as hearing the term "assistant" puts a bitter taste in my mouth, I don't like the idea of her thinking of herself as less than anyone else.

"You shouldn't be so modest. Good assistants are oftentimes the cement that holds the castle together, so to speak." I wink at her, and the way she smiles and bites on her lower lip nearly kills me. "Everyone needs to start somewhere."

The fire that erupts in my gaze as I'm reminded of Kati—my previous dirty, lying, blackmailing, whore of an assistant—forces me to look away from Gianna, even when it's difficult taking my eyes off her.

I drift to Eliana and Ez; they know why. They know what the bitterness in my stare looks like whenever I'm reminded of her. And they're the ones who picked me up after she swept through my life like a hurricane. One look at them is all I need to dispel these unwanted emotions. This isn't the time or the place. I swallow it all down. She's out of my life for good. Gianna is here now, and I don't want her to think the violence in my gaze was meant for her.

"Here we are."

The bartender's timing is impeccable, as he puts our drinks down just before the silence has a chance to stretch to the point of being awkward.

"Can I get you anything else at the moment?" he inquires.

"Just the check? You can charge this round to room forty-seven eighty-nine."

"Yes, sir," he nods before returning to the register to print the room charge receipt for me to sign.

"Thank you for the drink," Gianna offers with a grateful smile and another bite of her bottom lip.

That seems to be her tell when she's feeling shy. My only response is a sly smile and a wink.

"Where did you go to school?" Ez interrupts, breaking her stare from mine, causing me to miss it already.

I'll let my friends grill her for a little while longer, but then I'll have to put a stop to it. I know they only want what's best for me, but again, it's not like this is going further than the property lines of this resort. They can save the Spanish inquisition for my next future ex-wife.

"Wharton Business School in New York City. My dad went there, so I didn't have much of a choice in the matter," she laughs.

"Oh? I've heard that's a really nice school," Eliana states.

I have to hold in a laugh, knowing Eliana attended the school herself but she's unable to say anything more because of the promise her and Ez made to me in the elevator. I clear my throat to keep my chuckle concealed.

Just then, there is a commotion in the lobby as a group of people enter it. At once, we all turn our attention to it as we see Gianna's friend and a group of boys passing by.

"Oh my god," Gianna sighs under her breath.

I watch as she tries to shield her face and stay hidden, but when her friend happens to lock eyes on me from across the lobby, the group of rowdy beach party-goers detours to the bar. I don't miss the glare of the boy who vied for Gianna's attention earlier today. He's angry she's with me and not him, and I love how that makes me feel.

"Hey, guys," the best friend practically shouts, grabbing the attention of everyone else in the bar.

"Shh..." Gianna commands, though she's smiling.

It seems as though she may have a love-hate relationship with her friend's bubbly, vivacious personality.

"Everyone, this is Saylor, my best friend. Saylor, this is Nick, Ez, and Eliana."

I have to admit, Saylor seems like a blast to hang out with, but perhaps in small doses.

"I can't believe you're going to miss out on all the fun tonight. Won't you reconsider?" Saylor pleads with Gianna before locking eyes on the rest of us. "You can all come, you know..."

"Okay, yeah," Gianna answers, surprising me. Earlier she had no interest in going. "We'll be there as soon as dinner is over."

That's the *last* place I want to go after dinner, but if she really wants to make an appearance, then I'll deal with it.

"Oh my god, yay!" Saylor squeals, hugging her friend. "Have fun at dinner. See you all later!"

"Bye," Gianna sings as her friend walks away. When she turns her attention back to me, she says, "We're so not going, that was just the quickest way to get rid of her."

With a shrug of her shoulders and wide eyes, she picks up her drink and downs the rest. Her expression pulls a genuine belly laugh from me, and a light feeling ripples through my body for the first time in a very long while.

She's adorable.

"Well, on that note," I pause to finish my own drink. "Shall we?"

I hold my arm out, and she hops down from the stool, linking her arm through mine.

"We shall."

"See you guys tomorrow," I say to Ez and Eliana.

"It was wonderful to meet you both," Gianna says to them over her shoulder as we walk away.

They respond back, letting her know the feeling is mutual. When Gianna looks up at me with dilated pupils and a cock of her left eyebrow, I wonder if it has more to do with the alcohol, or if she's also curious where the night will lead us.

CHAPTER FIVE

Carley

THE FINAL GULP of the drink I slammed before we left the bar is doing exactly what I need it to. The heat in Nick's stare helps too, of course. As we walk across the lobby toward our dining destination, I can feel the strut in my step intensify. The sway of my hips becomes a little more dramatic. I raise my chin a little higher instead of keeping my eyes trained on the ground ahead of me.

I feel sexy.

I've never been the type of girl to want all eyes on me, to be the center of attention. But whether people are staring because I'm with Nick or if I'm turning heads all on my own, I'm relishing it. Being next to him—especially in *this* dress—is doing things to me. It's as though the confident air about him is expanding and wrapping me up in its clutches.

"I debated taking you somewhere in Little Venice, but I thought we'd stay here at the resort instead."

He wants a quick getaway should the evening go south.

I didn't mean to think it, but my anxiety broke through the thick cloud of confidence that enveloped me a moment ago.

"I'm happy with anything. I'm fairly easy to please."

Oh, shit.

As soon as the words left my mouth, my body tensed with unease. As a flush of embarrassment paints my cheeks red, I chance a glance at Nick. He practically knocks me dead with a seductive grin, and the action sends flames licking through my body, straight to my core. I know nothing about this man, but the smile that's been taunting me all week is a quality of his I already can't get enough of.

"Duly noted," he quips with a wink.

His eyes hold mine for longer than is usually comfortable, but I can't look away.

No, not I can't. I don't want to.

I wrinkle my nose with unease and bite my bottom lip. Before I finally look away, I see a fire in his eyes that makes me nervous. I'm not a virgin, but I'm far from experienced. I'm sure Nick has been around the block more than I have, and I know exactly what that look means.

He doesn't have to say the words, the promise in his sultry stare reveals his intentions for me this evening.

As moisture pools at my core, I know I will be taking a page out of Saylor's book tonight.

"Are we eating in the main dining room?" I ask him, trying to change the subject as we exit the lobby to the upper deck at the back of the resort.

The sun setting over the water catches my attention and takes my breath away. Before Nick has a chance to answer my question, my feet stop of their own accord. I gaze out over the vast, turquoise Aegean Sea.

"Oh ..." I drift off. "The view is absolutely stunning."

"It is," he agrees. "Especially with a woman as captivating as you in the foreground."

With blushing cheeks, I face him once more and expect to see an insincere or phony look on his face. But his expression is far from it. I smile through the shock of receiving such a genuine compliment for once. The boys who usually toss them my way say things merely because they believe it will lead me into bed.

"To answer your question, no. We aren't eating in the main dining room. I opted for something a little more private," he begins. "I hope you don't mind."

He nods his head toward the water, and that's when I see the glow of candlelight on the dock surrounding what looks to be a table set for two with a bottle of wine already sitting beside it. A waiter in a tux with a white towel over his arm is standing to the side, patiently waiting for us.

When I realize Nick opted for private elegance to public distraction, I immediately feel bad for thinking he tried to plan something that allowed for a quick getaway. He actually put thought in to this evening.

"It's wonderful. No, of course I don't mind," I offer him a smile.

When he smiles back at me, I can see the relief in his eyes, however slight it may be.

Is he as nervous as I am?

It doesn't seem possible. He holds himself with such an air of confidence, I never would have thought he'd be anything but.

He places his hand on the small of my back, and again, his touch is like a shock of electricity. I allow him to guide me to the stone steps that lead down to the pool deck. We cross the deck and walk down the final staircase to the sandy beach area below.

As I struggle to walk through the sand in the five-inch tall, strappy, leather monstrosities Saylor made me wear, he must realize my struggle.

"Here, let me help you," he says.

Without warning, he whisks me into his arms like a prince rescuing a princess. I squeal briefly but quickly wrap my arms around his neck, gripping my hands together tightly as he carries me across the remaining stretch of beach.

Whether it be from close proximity or not wanting to fall, my entire body tenses up.

"You do *not* need to carry me ... oh my goodness, this is embarrassing."

"Don't be embarrassed. It's a good excuse for me to come to your rescue. Let me bask in the glory of being a hero."

His cocky smile does me in, and I relax immediately.

"Well, if it makes you feel better, then by all means."

I allow my body to relax slightly, and the devious grin I receive in return sends another rush of warmth through my stomach.

When we reach the dock, I expect him to put me down immediately, but he doesn't. He pauses for a moment and looks into my eyes. His head twitches in my direction at the same time as my neck cranes slightly toward him.

I lick my lips in anticipation of the kiss, but the longer we stare at each other, the quicker the moment passes.

I feel terrible when he puts me down, and I notice the look of disappointment on his face. Was he expecting me to lead? Was he waiting for a clearer sign that I yearn for his lips on mine? Once again, he puts his hand on the small of my back and leads me to the end of the dock over the water.

"*Kalispera*. Good evening," the waiter greets us as we approach him. "My name is Markos, and I'll be serving you this evening."

"*Kalispera*," Nick responds to him in what sounds like perfect Greek compared to the way our waiter spoke. He impresses me even more than I already was. Whatever it was he called me the other day, *théa*, it must have been Greek he was speaking. I know it's a saying of admiration, and I'm making it my mission to find out exactly what it means tonight if it kills me.

Markos pulls my chair out for me. Before I have a chance to sit, I don't miss how Nick casually forces him out of the way and takes his place. Another brownie point for him.

Taking the wine from the stand, Markos pours a small amount into Nick's glass. After he samples it and approves, Markos fills my glass halfway before pouring more into Nick's. With his attention on the wine, I use this time to slip out of my death heels. I'll carry them back when dinner is over.

"The chef has prepared a wonderful feast for you this evening. Enjoy the wine. I will be back with your first course shortly."

"*Efxaristo*," Nick answers.

I wonder what he said.

"This is so nice, but I hope you didn't go to too much trouble."

What I really wanted to say is, I hope this isn't costing you an arm and a leg.

"No trouble at all," Nick winks at me.

He picks his wine glass up at the same time as me, and before I can take a sip, he speaks.

"How about a toast?"

"To what?" I inquire.

He looks at me intensely, as he continues.

"*Se afto to omofo vrady me afto to apolafstiko fagito kai stin igeia tis omorfis kopelas pu exo tin xara na dipno mazi tis.*"

He could very well have told me I'm an ugly hag, but I would still be practically drooling over the enchanting words. They give me chills and make my heart swell.

What girl doesn't want a hot guy toasting her in their native tongue?

"That's lovely. What does it mean?" I ask.

"To a fabulous evening, delicious food, and the most breathtaking girl I've ever had the pleasure of dining with."

His words leave me speechless. All I can do is blink and smile before lifting my glass and taking a large sip of the burgundy liquid.

"I'm sure that's not true," I challenge once I've swallowed the delicious wine. "A handsome man such as yourself. You probably have gorgeous women throwing themselves at you all the time."

"A few, here and there, but none of them grabbed my attention as completely as you did the first time I saw you."

I try to blame the heat rushing through me on the wine, but it's the promise that has returned to his stare that's making me melt where I sit. I'm thankful for the skimpy dress and slight breeze coming off the ocean we're sitting over.

As if knowing I needed something, some touch to let me know I'm not dreaming, Nick reaches his hand across the table and places his fingers over mine. I swallow the thick lust that's caught in my throat and keep my eyes trained on his.

Fuck dinner.

I would give anything to take him back to my room and let him tell me how stunning he thinks I am until the sun comes up. With a knowing smile, Nick breaks the tension. "So how long are you visiting?"

I take another large sip of wine before answering. It might be the only thing keeping me sane until dinner is over. "We're leaving tomorrow, unfortunately. I'm not ready to return to the real world."

"I feel the same. We're due to check out tomorrow as well."

"At least you get to live at the beach. I get to go back to the concrete jungle."

"Which part of New York are you in?"

"The city; the Upper West Side."

"Swanky," he laughs.

"I'm sure my apartment couldn't hold a candle to your beach house."

"Oh, I don't know. The Upper West Side isn't exactly the slums."

"True," I answer. And then, before I chicken out, I throw in, "What does *théa* mean?"

The finger that was just tracing his chiseled jawline stops abruptly. I've caught him off guard. I watch his eyes as he contemplates whether to tell me or not. It's either really bad or really good, but I get the feeling he isn't going to translate it for me.

"I'll tell you later. After dinner ... maybe." He puts on that smirk that causes the butterflies in my stomach to flit around in a frenzy.

Our eyes continue to communicate as we each take another sip of our wine. A silence falls between us, but it's not awkward. Far from it. It's full of unspoken desires and promises. Whether from the wine, the atmosphere, or Saylor's words ringing in my ears to let go and have fun, I swing my foot out until it connects with the expensive fabric of his custom-tailored suit underneath the table. The moment I find his leg, his eyes light up like a kid in a candy shop.

I don't know what I expected to happen next, but what came spilling out of his mouth wasn't it.

"Gianna, I didn't have any expectations for this evening. Hopes, yes," he smirks, but his expression is more serious than light. "But I'm only going to say this once."

Now with a serious tone to match, he has my full attention.

"I've thought up over a dozen different ways to fuck you since the first moment I laid eyes on you. On the chaise lounge in your cabana, over the bar down by the beach. Most recently, bent over the arm of the sofa in the lobby when you showed up in that negligee you call a dress and those fuck-me shoes."

My eyes widen, and I'm struggling desperately to swallow, but I can't. I freeze in my spot, and before I have a chance to let my leg fall back to the ground, Nick reaches under the table and grabs a hold of my ankle. Running his thumbnail from my instep to the arch of my foot sends powerful shockwaves through my stomach. My eyes close of their own volition, and I relax into my seat.

"Currently, I'm debating whether or not to lay you down on this tabletop and indulge in my dessert before my dinner."

My eyes shoot open again, and just like that, it's as though Niagara Falls found a new home ... *between my legs.*

"If you're giving me the green light to act out any or all of my various fantasies with you this evening, then I suggest you hold off on the advances until after the main course. We're going to need to gather as much energy as possible for what I have planned."

CHAPTER SIX

Dimos

THE REST of dinner was the worst torture I've ever been made to endure. At the same time, the anticipation of what was to come kept the intensity of our feelings piqued and roaring to go when the time came.

When the waiter came back with our salads, I asked him to bring the main course out as soon as possible, as we had somewhere else we needed to be. I wanted to make sure we got some food in our stomachs before the alcohol overtook us, and we got sloppy. I also wanted to make sure Gianna had a healthy helping of protein because we have a long night ahead of us. I meant every single word I said to her earlier. I want to take her in every position, on every surface of my room.

I have a feeling I may not get my security deposit back.

Not that I care.

Even though her shoes are off, I still insisted on carrying her. Placing Gianna onto her feet once we're clear of the sand, my hand finds the small of her back again, but this time I let it fall over the swell of her ass. I've waited desperately to caress her body since the moment I saw her. She looks up at me through her long eyelashes, and I can't hold back any longer.

Crushing her against the stone wall next to the steps, my mouth finally connects with her wine-stained lips. Nothing I've ever eaten before tastes as exquisite as she does. It feels like lava is racing through my veins as my dick hardens, and I grind against her stomach.

I shouldn't be doing this to her here. She deserves privacy ... intimacy. She deserves to be devoured by a gentleman, not by a heathen out in the open for all to see. But I can't stop myself. Not yet.

I pull her hands up over her head and hold them hostage in one of my own. Spreading kisses down her neck, I wander across her slender collarbone and nibble my way to her exposed shoulder. Her smooth skin is left glistening from the specks of saliva I'm leaving behind.

Leaving my scent on her. Marking her as mine.

No other woman has ever elicited this type of possession from me. Not Emma. Definitely not Kati.

No. Stop thinking about them.

Letting the image of Gianna in that black bikini on the beach permeate my mind, my free hand covers her breast over the thin lace. She's not wearing a bra, and it's turning me into a crazed lunatic. With barely any material to cover her, it wouldn't take more than a quick tug to rip it off so I can finally get a look at what I've craved for the past week. I'll have to find out where she bought it so I can replace it for her when all is said and done.

No. Forget that. I don't want her wearing something like this for anyone but me.

I tear my lips from her finally, wanting to get to my room as quickly as possible before I shred her dress to pieces here and now. It takes her a moment to open her eyes, and when she finally does, she pants my name.

"Nick..." The look of unbridled lust in them nearly sends me over the edge.

No one has ever looked at me the way she is right now. I stop for a moment and study her gaze. She's not looking at me like this because of the booze. It's not because of my money. Not because I'm Dimos Anastos.

She's attracted to me for me.

No, she's attracted to Nick.

Fuck. I would give anything to hear my real name leave those swollen, pouty lips of hers. Before I beg her to call me Dimos and have to explain why I gave her a fake name, I close my mouth and swallow down my feelings. Not letting that thought ruin this moment, I take her by the hand.

"Come," I command, and her nostrils flare as she pushes her body off the wall.

I lead her back up the steps we walked down to get here and across the lobby. When I glance over to the bar, I catch Ez's eyes. He shakes his head in disbelief and shoots me a knowing smile as I walk by. I return his look with a wink just before turning the corner and out of his sight.

The elevator is taking its time getting to us, delivering another wave of torture. I stand behind her while we wait and pull her body against mine. I know the moment she feels my erection on her back. Watching her eyes grow large in the reflection of the elevator doors makes my dick twitch.

I rub my palms over her slender shoulders and down to her perfect tits. She lets her head fall back against my chest as I grip them in my palms, feeling her nipples pebble underneath the lace. I tighten my hold on them, trying not to squeeze too hard, and take her nipples between the thumb and forefinger on each of my hands.

Her sharp intake of breath at the pressure nearly makes me lose it. I'm thankful for the elevator doors shooting open just then, forcing me to remove my hands and keeping me from exploding prematurely.

The couple in the elevator take their time exiting, and I impatiently guide Gianna in and press the door close button before the guy's back foot even hits the floor of the hallway. The door nearly closes on his leg, but he gets it out just in time.

Even though the ride to the fourth floor is short, it doesn't stop my hand from roaming her body. Her eyes close as I find my way between her legs. I practically drool over the heat I feel emanating from her core. One swipe of my long, middle finger, and I collect some of her arousal on my fingertip.

She groans and opens her eyes as I remove my hand and bring the glistening tip of my finger closer to my mouth. Before I lick the taste of her from it, I ask her a question.

"Have you ever tasted yourself, Gianna?"

She can't speak, but she shakes her head, letting me know she hasn't.

I run my finger along my tongue, my saliva thickening upon tasting her sweet musk. Then, I place my mouth on hers once again and press the tip of my tongue against her lips. She parts them slightly, enough for me to slip it inside of her mouth and give her a taste. A wide, sly smile spreads across my face when I hear the moan sound in the back of her throat.

When we get to the second floor, I take her by the hand again and lead her down the hallway to my suite. Before I unlock the door, I turn and face her. Placing a hand on either side of her neck, my thumbs rub along the bones of her jaw.

"This is your last chance to back out. Once we enter that room, I'm going to devour every last inch of your gorgeous body. I won't be able to stop myself once I get started."

"No," she whispers and my heart skips a beat, thinking she's changed her mind. "I'm not backing out now."

Relief washes over me, and I flash her a grin as I slide the key card into the lock and open the door. The second it closes, I drop the key to the floor and fist the material of her dress with both hands. With not so much as an "I'm sorry," I rip it in two and let it float to the floor at her feet. I've never seen someone more captivating than her.

"I théa mou einai akoma pio omorfi apo oti boursa pote na fadasto." My goddess is even more beautiful than I could have ever imagined.

I'm hardly able to tear my eyes from her, but now that I am finally basking in the glory of her perfection, I can't hold back any longer. I take advantage of her surprise and lift her from the floor, carrying her to the sofa. She barely gets her arms around my neck before I lay her down across the back of it and drop to my knees in front of her. Pulling her black lace thong to the side, I slide my nose and tongue through her silky, wet folds, inhaling the scent I've craved.

"Fuck, Gianna ..."

I remove my mouth from her just long enough to coat two of my fingers with my saliva. Then I lock my lips on her clit and indulge in the sound of the raspy moan that escapes her slender throat. The sound of her pleasure is something I will miss hearing when this night is over. Sucking on her gently, I insert my fingers inside and twist them around, curling them upward and making her pant with need.

"Oh, fuuuck ..." she moans, arching her back off the sofa.

I curl my free arm around her thigh, keeping her from falling as well as pulling away from me. I switch between sucking and flicking her clit, all while continuing to massage her from the inside.

"*Nick* ... oh god, Nick ... I'm gonna come ..."

Ready to taste more of her, I suck harder and massage faster, removing my lips only so I can command her to come.

"Come, Gianna. Come for me, *théa*."

The second my lips latch onto her clit again, she comes undone. I never would have taken her for a screamer, but then again, I wouldn't have ever pictured her in a dress like the one she had on, either. She's a different girl tonight than she has been the rest of the week, and I am not sure which version of her I like more.

Feeling the warmth trickle from her pussy and down my chin has me ready to come myself. I remove my fingers from her and lick them clean before working my belt open and unbuttoning my pants, lapping up her dripping juices as I go.

When I stand, I take off my shoes before placing myself between her legs. Then I look down at her as her hands cover her face.

"Are you okay?"

"Yes," Her answer muffled beneath her hands.

"What's wrong?" I force her hands away from her face so I can see and hear her clearly.

"Nothing," she pants, almost unable to get the word out, "I've just never done that before."

I can't stop the smile spreading over my face.

"You've never had someone go down on you?"

"No, not that part ... the *other* part ..."

"You've never come before? Or you've never squirted?"

This time she nods her head instead of speaking, and I assume she means she's never done either.

"Well, I hope you liked it, because I plan on making you come at least nine more times tonight."

When her eyes go wide, I pull her into a sitting position with her legs hanging free. Grabbing her cheeks, I gently place my lips on hers. Again, she moans when she tastes herself on me. Taking hold of her bottom lip with my teeth, I give it a soft tug as my hands begin to roam her body once more.

She surprises me when I feel her hand tracing a path along my side, dipping into my open pants and flirting with the elastic band of my boxer briefs. I open my eyes briefly and watch her without her knowing. I can't get over how utterly exquisite she is. My chest grows tight thinking about leaving and never being able to see her again. Tomorrow morning, over breakfast, I think I'll tell her who I really am. Maybe we can keep in touch, and I can resume my trips to New York, here and there, to see her. Hell, I've been looking for a good reason to leave Hermosa Beach and start over fresh. Maybe she'll be the final push I need to do it.

My thoughts are interrupted when her hand slides beneath the fabric of my underwear and her fist locks around my dick. Now I'm the one to moan. With her free hand, she pushes me backward, and I step out of my pants. Hopping down, she directs me around the arm of the sofa and guides me until the backs of my legs hit the cushion. Before I can sit, she grips the sides of my boxer briefs and tugs them down until they fall to the floor on their own.

Giving me a little push, I sit down on the sofa and watch as this gorgeous girl, my *théa*, lowers herself to her knees in front of me. She offers me a small smile, and I can tell she's nervous. Taking her cheek in my hand, I whisper to her gently.

"Only do what you're comfortable with, *théa*."

She nods softly. Not letting go of my cock, she relaxes into a more comfortable position before covering my dick with her swollen lips. The warmth of her mouth feels incredible.

"*Téleio*," I moan. *Amazing.*

I comb my fingers through her hair so it doesn't hang in her way. Keeping my hand on her head, I gently massage her scalp, urging her to continue. I don't know what she was nervous about. The way she's twisting her hand as she pumps her fist up and down my shaft, the way her tongue licks at the underside of my cock as she bobs up and down … fuck … everything she's doing is making my balls clench with the threat of emptying themselves inside of her perfect mouth.

"Fuck, Gianna…" I place my finger under her chin and reluctantly lift her mouth from around my dick.

"I'm so sorry, I've never really done this before, either. I'm not even sure what I'm doing."

"No, no. Stop. It was perfect. *You* are perfect. But if you would have kept going, then I would have come in that pretty mouth of yours. It's too soon for that, and I still have many more orgasms to deliver to you."

I lean forward and plant a kiss on her lips, reassuring her she's done nothing wrong. Then, I pull her on top of me so she is straddling my lap. Gripping the skimpy thong she's still wearing, I rip the slight piece of fabric from her and toss it behind me, not knowing or caring where it lands. Wrapping her in my arms, I take one of her pebbled nipples into my mouth and reach down between her legs to make sure she's still wet and ready to go. I'm very pleased when my fingers slide through her opening with ease.

I grab my cock and place it at her entrance. Without letting her nipple go, I look up into her eyes and wait for her to let me know she's ready. When she gives me a slight nod, I don't wait. I grab her hips and guide her down over my cock until I'm deep inside of her.

"*Gamáto*." *Fuck.* "You feel so fucking good, Gianna."

I relish the sight of her eyes rolling back into her head from pleasure. She places her hands on my shoulders and dips her head, planting her lips on mine. Not losing traction, I lift her body a little and pull her back down onto my cock over and over again until she screams out another orgasm, and her muscles contract around me.

I don't give her any time to relax before I pound into her from below like a jackhammer. Hard and fast. She's going to feel it tomorrow, and I hope she thinks of me with every twinge of pain.

After savoring the sight of her coming undone once more. I pick her up and walk over to the desk in the room. I remove myself from her just long enough to turn her around and bend her over the surface of the desk. Reaching around the front of her, I take her clit between my fingers and gently rub it as I begin to thrust into her again.

"Shit! Nick, I can't. It's too much. Oh, shit ..."

Leaning over her body, I slowly drag her hair to the other side of her neck before seductively whispering in her ear.

"You can do it, come for me again, *théa.*"

My words are her final undoing. After covering my dick with her delicious juices, her eyes flutter, opening and closing as though she could fall asleep while still bent over, my cock still deep inside of her. I rub her back gently before lifting her up and carrying her over to the bed. I pull back the covers and lay her down on the expensive cotton sheets.

"I'll let you sleep for a little while, *théa mou*, but I've still got six more orgasms in store for you tonight," I promise her.

I lay down next to her, gently stroking her arm, running my fingers through her hair, and basking in the sound of her ragged breaths relaxing into a deep sleep. Once she's completely out, I sneak out of bed and go into the bathroom.

A cold shower is in order before we get started on round two.

CHAPTER SEVEN

Carley

ONE MONTH LATER

THE PAST MONTH has been *hell*.

I was so excited to start this new job, but it's kicking my ass. Well, my new boss is the one doing the kicking. I wasn't even hired for this position. I was interviewed for the role of executive assistant to the director of human resources, so imagine my surprise when I get there, and I'm told they think I would be a better fit as the assistant to the CEO. I was ecstatic—it felt like I got a promotion on my first day—and so were my parents, but I honestly don't know if I'm cut out for it.

Dimos Anastos is very smart and extremely successful. He was a self-made millionaire by the time he was thirty, when he first started Okeanós. Now, fifteen years later, he's worth over fifteen billion dollars.

Unfortunately, he's also an arrogant, standoffish prick. So much so, I'm already on the hunt for a new job. I called the firms I turned down initially and asked if they would still consider me, but they've already filled their open positions. I managed to get an interview at two other companies, however, which take place next week.

"Oh, come *on*, Carley!" Saylor screeches at me as I flop down on our sofa.

She is itching to go out and hell-bent on dragging me along with her.

"All you've done since we got home from Greece is sulk. Let's go out and find you a new guy. Someone to get your mind off Mr. Golden Dick."

And then there's that...

My shoulders slump farther at the mention of Nick. The worst thing I ever could have done besides having a one-night stand—a blazing hot, multiple orgasms from a drop-dead gorgeous, tall, dark, and handsome stranger one-night stand—was leave his bed in the morning without even a goodbye.

If I stayed, who knows what would have happened. Maybe we would have exchanged phone numbers so we could keep in contact with one another. But when I woke up that morning, I was too nervous to face him. If I'm honest, I was scared he was going to wake up regretting what happened. That he would realize he made a mistake. So I left without taking into consideration that no one else I meet in this lifetime will ever measure up to him.

They'll never measure up to Nick Evans.

"I'm really tired, Say. It's been a long week."

"I *know*! All the more reason to go out and blow off some steam."

I can't keep up with Saylor on a social level even on a good week. While I don't want to go, maybe it *would* help if I got back out there and tried to find someone to get my mind off him. It would keep me from another pointless Google search for Nick Evans from Hermosa Beach.

There isn't a Nick Evans in Hermosa Beach, by the way.

I try to believe he didn't lie to me about his name or where he lived, but even if he did, I have no business getting mad at him about it, right? Perhaps he was also trying to keep a low profile in Greece? As much sense as it makes, and as much as I have no right to be upset with him, I am. I begin to stew in my anger as Saylor continues her plea.

"We can grab drinks at The Lounge and then head over to Lush after that. I told you Rocky just started working the door over there. We won't have to wait in line, *and* we'll have access to the VIP area."

The more I think about being lied to, the angrier I get. At Nick. At myself. At that jackass Dimos Anastos.

I take a deep, soothing breath, and something inside of me stirs. Whether it be reminiscent feelings from Greece I would die to feel again, or the desire to drink away the stress caused by my overbearing boss, I finally cave.

"Fine, I'll go," I tell Saylor.

She claps her hands together and jumps up onto the sofa in celebration.

"But no more drunken, slutty one-night stands for me. *Ever*. Okay?"

"Whatever you say," Saylor answers with a mischievous smile.

THE LOUNGE WAS FAIRLY QUIET FOR A FRIDAY NIGHT. SOMETHING I WAS more than okay with because we were actually able to find seats, which is usually impossible. Saylor called some of our other friends to join us, including Brittany, much to my dismay. She's just like Saylor in the sense that she is a rich socialite with zero real-life responsibilities and more money than she knows what to do with. Although unlike Saylor, she thinks she's God's gift to the world, and everyone should worship at her feet.

Brittany and I have been *frenemies* for the better part of our entire lives. We each know how the other ticks, we invite each other to parties and other events, but we don't exactly like one another. It's stupid, really.

"Carley, that guy over there can't keep his eyes off of you."

I look over at Brittany, ignoring her eye roll, as she nods her head toward a chair across the room. When I turn to see who she's talking about, I lock eyes on a handsome blond with rosy cheeks and dark eyes. After a slight smile, I return to the group of girls around me.

"Meh," I shrug. "He's not my type."

"And what's your type?" Brittany asks with attitude in her tone.

Nick flashes into my mind, and I close my eyes.

"Just … not that," I explain, opening my eyes once again as the image of Nick vanishes.

I feel my phone vibrate in my clutch, and I fish it out. Checking the notifications, I see I have an email from Mr. Anastos.

Don't look at it. It can wait until Monday.

But I can't help myself. I have to know what short, nasty put-down he has for me this time. I swear, it gets worse with each email.

CARLEY—

HE *NEVER* SAYS HI.

I WAS JUST LOOKING OVER THE OFFICE EXPENDITURES REPORT YOU SENT THIS afternoon. The margins are off and there should be an additional space between each line. Furthermore, the total is off by seventy-three cents.

I'll need this fixed and sent back to me by lunchtime tomorrow.

—D.A.

"TOMORROW?" I SHOUT. "YOU'VE GOT TO BE KIDDING ME."

"Carley, what's wrong?" Saylor asks.

"That bastard wants me to work tomorrow."

Brittany looks at me like I have two heads, and she forgets I have a job.

"Mr. Anastos. You know, my *boss*. He just sent me an email saying he needs me to fix a report and have it to him by lunchtime tomorrow."

"Can't you just tell him you're sick? Or save it until Monday? Maybe he forgot what day of the week it is."

"No, *Brittany*, I can't just blow off my boss. You'd understand if you worked a day in your life."

"Okay, look," Saylor interrupts our spat before it escalates. "Carley, put your phone away and worry about the reports tomorrow. You have to remember, you don't work at your father's company anymore. You're in the real world now. People aren't going to cater to you."

I try not to let my hurt feelings show at her words. She's absolutely correct, but it still hurts hearing it. Socialite party-girl or not, Saylor definitely has a handle on the workings of the real world.

"Right now, you have a hot blond who can't take his eyes off of you."

Saylor takes my cell phone from my hand and nods in the direction of the guy across the room.

"Go," she commands.

If for nothing other than to get away from the shit-eating grin on Brittany's face, I get up and walk over to the boy. Yes, *boy*. I spend thirty minutes speaking with him—which was about twenty-nine minutes too long—before I excuse myself to the restroom, make sure he's not looking, grab my purse, and then tell Saylor I'll see her at home later.

The boy was nice. He was friendly and smart. But he just wasn't who I wanted.

He wasn't Nick.

When I awaken, my eyelids are almost too heavy to lift. Until I feel something burrowing between my legs, slipping in between the swollen folds of my pussy. My breath hitches, and I'm frightened for a moment before I remember where I am.

I'm in Nick's suite.

In Nick's bed.

"Are you ready for round two, théa?"

His voice filters over my shoulder from behind me, his body melded to mine. His front against my back, his long arm curled around my body as his fingers wreak havoc between my legs for the thousandth time this evening.

I barely remember falling asleep after he ...

I can feel the fire burn my cheeks as I recall the way he balanced me across the back of the sofa, holding me steady so I wouldn't fall, and licking me until I came undone.

Holy hell.

The way he fucked me as he had me bent over on the surface of the desk. It was the most pleasurable sex I've ever had. My blood feels like it's rushing to my core, throbbing intensely over my clit as another orgasm begins to rocket through me.

"Oh my god."

Rolling me over, he climbs on top of me as my orgasm begins to dissipate. As I gaze into Nick's eyes, I see a darkness I haven't seen in them before.

It's possessive. It's hungry. It's feral.

He makes a show of licking my arousal off his fingers before pushing them inside of me again.

"Nick..." I cry out just as his mouth covers mine, swallowing the sound of my pleasure before it's able to echo off the walls of his suite.

Keeping me just on the edge, he removes his fingers and brings them to my nipple. He traces a damp path around each before reaching between us once more and lining his cock up to the entrance of my pussy again.

"Nick, I don't think I have anything left in me."

"But I promised you five more orgasms tonight. I never break a promise."

Thrusting his hips, he enters me fiercely as my eyes roll into the back of my head. He scoots his knees under him so he's kneeling before me, spreading my legs open wide on either side of him. Fucking me savagely, he grabs my clit between his fingers and tears leak from my eyelids as I reach the euphoric place only Nick can send me to, once again.

. . .

GASPING FOR AIR, I SIT UP AS I REALIZE I'M BACK IN MY OWN BED. ON THE Upper West Side. I'm not in Greece. I'm not getting fucked relentlessly by Nick until I'm no more than a floppy rag doll.

I am, however, throbbing between my legs at the memory my subconscious likes to remind me of so often.

I fling myself back onto my pillow and wallow in my bitterness for a little while. Several minutes pass without any reprieve from the pulsating feeling of desire flowing straight to my core. My clit feels like it's as large as a damn marble. As hard as one, too.

Fuck, I need relief.

I've been making a habit out of this. Wild sex dreams starring Nick and me. Waking up panting. Desperately in need of relief. I have to put a stop to this madness.

Tomorrow.

Unable to stop myself, I reach between my sweaty thighs and connect with my clit. As I pull the image of us in his bed back to the forefront of my mind, I rub myself faster and faster until I cry his name as quietly as I can into my empty room.

I thought the memory of him would fade the longer I went without seeing or speaking to him. Seems I was incredibly wrong about that.

As I come down off my high, the realization hits me.

I screwed myself in Greece when I left Nick's room without saying goodbye, and because of my stupidity, I've been stuck screwing myself ever since.

CHAPTER EIGHT

Carley

WHEN I WOKE up on Saturday morning, I was more tired than I ever remember being. My head hurt, and my body felt like I'd run a marathon.

It felt just like it did the morning I woke up in Nick's bed.

I got my coffee and began to fix the report Mr. Anastos needed so badly, he had me working on a Saturday. It was a simple mathematical error that needed to be fixed, and the margins weren't off. Not even by a millimeter.

I think he was just looking for something else to criticize me over. When I sent it back to him, almost immediately he responded with:

CARLEY—

I already fixed that one. It couldn't wait any longer. Send me the hours report from the past two months.

—D.A.

NO PLEASE. NO THANK YOU. JUST ONE HUNDRED PERCENT PURE ASSHOLE.

I got him the reports he needed and logged off before he could send me another task. I even went so far as to shut off the notifications for the email app on my phone. Luckily, he was quiet for the rest of the weekend anyhow.

Just as I'm settling into my work after getting back from lunch, I hear the elevator ding. I pick my head up, and my eyes meet the sliding doors about seventy-five feet in front of my desk. My heart drops into my stomach when I spot Ez, Nick's best friend, walking toward my desk with Ronald from finance.

Is this for real?

Do he and Eliana live in the city? I'd assumed they lived in California, like Nick.

"Ez?" I practically squeak with shock and excitement. "What are you doing here?"

"Gianna?" I see his eyes lock onto the nameplate on my desk, and I panic.

My palms are covered in sweat instantly, and I can feel my body temperature rise at the same time as my blood pressure. My throat is suddenly very dry, and it's hard to swallow.

"Um. It's Carley, actually." I wait for his response apprehensively.

"Huh." Is all he gives me.

The questioning look on his face has me fighting to get my words out quickly, to try and explain to him why I lied before he has a chance to accuse me of being a horrible person.

"I'll meet you in the boardroom whenever you're ready," Ronald looks suspiciously from Ez to me before walking away.

"I don't usually give my real name out to random guys. At least, not until I get to know them better. I had a bad experience once and ..."

I stop blabbering and take a deep breath. I'm about to speak again, but Ez beats me to it.

"I can understand that." he smiles.

"I've been wishing I could take it back since the moment it happened. I should have given Nick my real name."

"Well, sometimes things happen for a reason," Ez explains.

"Wait." Something just clicked in my head. "*You're* Ezra Treuth? Of Martinique Enterprises?"

"The one and only," he smiles, performing a slight bow.

"How crazy is that? How do you know Mr. Anastos?"

Ez puckers his lips and squints, as though he's choosing his words carefully. A weird feeling creeps up my spine as I watch him. His reaction seems odd, but I know some of the business Mr. Anastos conducts is confidential.

"It's okay if you can't answer. I know some things can't be discussed publicly." I try letting him off the hook.

Ez sucks in a breath before answering, "Yeah, it's ... a bit of a confidential, financial, partnership."

"Understood," I nod.

"Well, I better get going—"

"Ez—"

I speak up at the same time as him.

"Oh, yeah. Definitely. I don't want to be the reason you're late. Mr. Anastos would *not* approve. Not that he approves of much of anything I do, but—oh god. Please don't tell him I said that."

"It's fine. I won't tell him." He smiles at me as though he finds me entertaining. "So I take it the new job hasn't been going smoothly?"

Carley, this is not the time for honesty.

But what if Ez takes pity on me and offers to pass along a message to Nick? Or even Mr. Anastos? He could tell Nick I miss him. Or he can let Mr. Anastos know I seem unhappy?

Oh my god, I'm pathetic.

Saylor was right, this is the real world. I can't expect people to coddle me because I'm upset. But I'm planning on leaving anyway, so what could it hurt to tell Ez how I feel? Maybe it will get back to Mr. Anastos. At least, then he might be nicer to his next assistant.

"Honestly, Mr. Anastos is kind of a dick."

Judging by the laugh that just escaped his nose, Ez wasn't expecting that.

"I'm sorry, I shouldn't have said that. It's just ... sometimes he has very unrealistic expectations. He's snippy, he never tells me I'm doing a good job. He refuses to speak to me on the phone, only through email. It's *absurd*. If he's so unhappy with my performance, why doesn't he just fire me, you know?"

Ez is leaning against my desk now, his chin propped up on his fist, listening intently as if it's one of the most fascinating conversations he's ever been a part of. He doesn't, however, offer any advice. He probably feels like he can't speak against Mr. Anastos because of their partnership. He wouldn't want anything he says to get back to him. I can understand that.

"Anyway, it doesn't really matter. I have two interviews next week for a new position with different companies. Hopefully, I'll be out of here by the end of the month."

"Oh, really?" Ez seems surprised by this and slightly concerned.

It's sweet he's worried, but I'll be fine. Offering him a smile, I debate asking him to give Nick a message for me. I shouldn't. He's already late as it is. Also, I don't want to seem clingy. My eyes meet his and he looks like he wants to tell me something as badly as I want to say something to him.

Is it about Nick? Has Nick been talking about me? Has he been trying to find me, too? I take a deep breath, deciding I would regret not saying something just as much as I regret leaving Nick the morning after our dinner without a word.

"Ez? Would you..." I pause. "Would it be possible for you to relay a message to Nick for me?"

"Of course," he agrees, and the relief I feel is palpable.

"Can you tell him I'm sorry for leaving without saying goodbye?"

That's not all you want to say, Carley.

If you're going to do it, then *do it*.

"Also," I continue, my heart feels like it's going to beat out of my chest.

Grabbing a sticky note and a pen, I jot down my real name and my phone number.

"Tell him I've been able to think of little else, other than him, for the past month. He's consumed my thoughts and my dreams. I know he lives three thousand miles away from here, and a relationship between us would never work ..." I pause briefly as I begin to get choked up. "But in the event he's been going through the same agony I've been going through, and he'd like to reach out, tell him I would love to hear from him."

Ez studies me carefully, like he's trying to determine whether I'm being sincere or not. Biting my lip, my nerves kick in, thinking he isn't going to take the small, square piece of paper I am holding out. That he won't deliver my message to Nick, and I've blown the only chance I have at contacting him.

He removes his fist from under his chin and tugs the pink square from my hand gently.

"I'd be glad to," he smiles. "I think he would be happy to hear from you, too."

My hand lands on my stomach as my breath leaves me in a relieved sigh.

"Thank you so much, Ez, really. It means everything to me."

"You're very welcome, *Carley*."

With a final nod, Ez tucks my information into the inside pocket of his suit and walks around my desk and into the boardroom across from Mr. Anastos's office.

I watch him with a smile, recalling how much fun it was, the four of us at the bar that last night in Greece. What I wouldn't give to be back there right now.

Back in Nick's bed, curled around his hard, chiseled body. To have him deep inside of me again. Not knowing how he felt when he woke to find me gone, I take a deep breath and pray he even wants to have anything to do with me anymore.

"SAYLOR, YOU'RE NEVER GOING TO BELIEVE WHO I RAN INTO TODAY," I squeal to the empty living room as I walk through the door of our apartment later that evening.

I cross the living room and turn the corner to find Saylor in the kitchen, cooking dinner ... And the blond boy from the bar on Friday night sitting at our kitchen island.

"Woah," I stop dead in my tracks.

"Carley, you remember Ren, right?"

"Um, yeah. Hi."

"Hey, it's the ghost," he laughs, tipping his beer bottle in greeting.

Saylor told me they ended up making out almost all night after I left the bar. He even followed them to the club afterward, but I did *not* see this coming. The only time she has guys over is usually between the hours of two and four in the morning.

"Sorry about that. I wasn't feeling very well on Friday night."

"Yeah, she was having big *D* problems, if you know what I mean." She winks at him, and he laughs lightly.

I close my eyes in embarrassment at Saylor's reference to Dimos Anastos. Or did she mean dick problems? Not that it matters, either one would have been correct.

"Don't listen to her. My boss just ... Well, he's an asshole, and I'm looking for a new job. But anyway. Say, guess who came into the office today?"

"No idea."

"*Ez!*"

"Who?" She scrunches her nose and furrows the skin between her brows.

"Nick's friend. The one who was with him in Greece," I remind her.

"Ohhhh! What was he doing there?"

"A business meeting. Side note, he's a business associate of Mr. Anastos. How *weird* is that?"

"Super weird ..." she cocks one eyebrow high. "Like ... very, very weird."

"I know, right? Small world. Anyway, we got to talking, and he's going to pass a message, as well as my number, along to Nick for me!"

"OHEMGEE!"

Saylor and I jump up and down with excitement in the kitchen like we're twelve all over again, completely forgetting Ren is here.

"Oh, okay. I see why you ghosted me. You have a boyfriend," Ren jokes.

"Yeah, right," Saylor jokes. "She wishes."

"We ... connected in Greece, and I was an idiot and left without getting his number or email or anything. The more time that goes by, the more I miss him."

I don't know why I'm explaining this to Ren as though he's a friend. I don't know this kid. I quickly turn my attention back to Saylor.

"God, I really hope he calls, texts ... anything at this point."

"Me too," she winks at me.

"Well, dinner smells amazing. Let me go get changed, and I'll be back out to help in a minute."

CHAPTER NINE

Dimos

LONG DAYS at the office are nothing new for me. I've been working crazy hours since the moment I became my own boss fifteen years ago. However, the days have seemed longer still these past few weeks. I've been trying to train my new assistant via email, which is far from efficient. It's not the way I prefer to run things, but after Kati ... I don't want to leave anything to chance.

I'm not the cheating kind. At least, I never wanted to be. But Kati had this allure to her. This magnetism. She captured the eyes of everyone in the room, men and women alike.

Just like Gianna. In that fucking *dress.*

My cock gets hard like it does every time I think about her.

Unlike Kati, Gianna actually has class. Kati only got attention because she's a man-eating whore.

And I'm the poor asshole she chewed up and spit back out.

Day by day, she wore me down. She knew when Emma and I would have a fight or when she would make me feel like less of a man. Kati could read me like a book, so finally, I opened up to her. Little by little, she weaseled her way under my skin.

First it started with little smirks across the table during meetings. The way she would nibble on the end of her pen while she stared at me, eyes hooded with lust like she could crawl across the table and into my lap at any moment. We'd toss sexy, suggestive banter back and forth with each other when no one else was around.

Then she began to stay late when I did. We would order dinner in and end up talking instead of working. That's when it turned physical. We would fuck here most of the time—there isn't one surface in this office her naked body didn't touch—but occasionally we would go to her apartment.

My stomach rolls just thinking about it.

She made me feel powerful again. Like I was the smart, strong, and capable man I used to be before Emma got her claws into me and started wearing me down. It continued several months before it came crashing to a halt.

One day she didn't show up for work. I got a call from her just before lunchtime. She was crying and told me she needed me to come to her apartment right away. I thought she was pregnant, and it made me sick to my stomach. I knew sleeping with her was a bad idea. It was wrong and immoral, and my values have always been much stronger than that. But I couldn't help myself. I went over how I was going to break the news to Emma in my head the entire time I raced to Kati's.

Only, when I got there, she seemed perfectly fine. She'd even invited two friends over. Two large, muscular, mean looking Russian men who stood over me as she spoke.

She handed me a large envelope. Inside of it were pictures of us in her bed, on her sofa, the kitchen island. There was also a tape recorder. My stomach dropped when I realized what was going on. She played the recording for me. It was from the night she talked me into acting out a rape fantasy of hers.

I didn't feel right about it the entire time it was happening, but I did it anyway. It's shameful how tight her grip was on my balls. She really wasn't much different from Emma. Fury rages through me as I close my eyes and think back to that day.

"This is what's going to happen next, Dimos. You and I are going to take a little trip to the bank, and you're going to request a transfer of five-million dollars into my account."

I was dumbstruck. I couldn't believe what was happening.

"As soon as it's complete, you'll receive the only other copy of this recording as well as the thumb drive containing all the pictures. If you don't comply, I'll release the tape to the media and have you arrested for rape."

Not much of a choice there. We went straight to the bank and initiated the transfer. As soon as we stepped outside of the building, she handed everything over to me.

"At least you'll have something to remember me by," she joked before turning on her heel and walking out of my life.

A couple weeks later, Emma hit me with divorce papers. Not because of Kati but because she found someone else. I didn't know it at the time, but she'd been cheating on me for longer than I cheated on her. Unfortunately, I ended up having to pay big time in both cases.

Since Kati, I've had a revolving door of executive assistants working for me remotely in my New York office. I refuse to hire one to work with me here in Torrance. Furthermore, I never speak to them on the phone. Communicating with them via email means everything is in writing. There can be no he said, she said. I'll never get myself into that kind of shit show ever again.

I do feel bad for the people HR has hired for the position since then. I guess you could say I haven't been the nicest boss in the world. But I need to be firm so no one can take something I've said and make it out to be anything other than business.

I hear my cell phone vibrate seconds before it starts dancing along the surface of my desk. Looking down at the screen, I see Ez's name and pick it up.

It's 11 P.M. in the big apple.

"Ezra, is everything okay?"

"Yeah, man. Why?"

"It's late for you. Just wanted to make sure."

"Oh, yeah. No, everything is good, I had a business dinner and am just now getting home. How's it going, man?"

"Can't complain too much. Just sitting at my desk, trying to get some work done," I explain.

I leave out the fact that I get depressed going home to an empty house every night, which is another reason why I work late.

"My new assistant finally seems to be getting the hang of how I like things to be run."

"That's actually why I called. I ran into your new assistant today when I was there for my meeting."

His voice sounds off, like there's something wrong.

"What's the matter? Did something happen?"

"No, not exactly, but…"

But? Come on, Ez. Spit it out.

"There's no easy way to say this, but Gianna *is* your new assistant."

My heartbeat increases at the sound of her name, but Ez must be mistaken.

"What? No. Her name is Carley. Carley Garrettson."

"Gianna *is* Carley, D."

Now it feels like my heart has stopped. There's no way.

"I took her picture when she wasn't paying attention. I'm sending it to you now," he explains when I can't come up with a response to the bomb he's just dropped on me.

I pull the phone away from my ear and wait for the picture to come through. When it does, the biggest smile crosses my face. She's leaning over her desk, reaching for something off camera, in a tight black pencil skirt and blue blouse that matches her eyes.

I've found her.

I tried looking her up a few times since Greece, but with no luck. My gratification is short-lived, however, when I realize what this means.

I fucked my assistant. Again.

"Did you talk to her? Did she see you?"

I feel like a fourteen-year-old boy all over again, asking my buddy if the girl I liked said anything about me.

"Yeah, we talked."

"What did she say?"

"She told me she felt bad for not giving you her real name. She said she doesn't give it out to random guys—"

"*Random* guys? Now I'm just a random guy?" I'm fuming.

"She did it to protect herself, D. She mentioned she had a bad experience in the past, so she only gives her real name once she gets to know someone better."

"Well, we got to know one another pretty fucking well that night, if you ask me."

"Look, you know I'll always have your back, but you really don't have a right to be angry with her, *Nick Evans*."

Damn it. I hate it when he's right.

"But she also said leaving your bed the next morning was one of the worst mistakes she's ever made. She can't stop thinking about you, and she gave me her number to pass along."

"Well ... shit. This isn't what I was expecting when I saw you calling," I laugh.

"There's ... something else, too," Ez adds slowly, and it worries me.

"Which is?"

"She *hates* you, Dimos Anastos, with a passion, and she's going to quit. She has two interviews next week. You have a very small window of opportunity here, D. I think you need to get on the phone ASAP and come clean with her."

"Yeah ..." I say, as another realization hits me. *Hard.*

She's known the dickhead me for longer than the me I showed her in Greece. Once she finds out, what if she can't look past the way I've been treating her?

Fuck.

"I'm sending her number through to you now."

"Thanks, Ez. I appreciate it."

"You're welcome, man. Good luck and let me know how it goes."

"I will. Goodnight."

As I hang up the call, I think about everything Ez just told me. I do have a small window to connect with her and make things right. And I *want* to make things right with her.

I pull up the photo I took of her wrapped in a sheet in my bed on the night we spent together. She's asleep, her hair is like a messy halo around her head. She looks sated and absolutely the most radiant thing I've ever seen in my entire life.

A phone call doesn't feel like the right way to handle this situation. She needs more. She deserves more. Placing my phone back on my desk, I stand and walk to the small bar on the other side of my office. As I pour myself a couple fingers of bourbon, I look out toward the sea. I never thought I would want to leave Hermosa Beach, but Ez was right. I'm incredibly lonely out here by myself.

I think about seeing Gianna—*Carley*—again and my heart races. I'd be lying if I said I wasn't hurt when I woke up in an empty bed the morning after our date. The only trace of her she'd left behind was the smell of her perfume on my sheets and her decadent, aromatic desire on my fingers.

I've been toying with the idea of moving to New York for quite some time, especially after Kati, but I couldn't picture myself packing up and leaving the beach behind. With this latest bit of news, however ...

Yes.

Yes, I think it *is* time for a change of scenery.

I can take my jet and have Captain Percival follow behind with The Cerulean.

Walking back to my desk, I place my highball glass down and pull up my email.

CARLEY—

    I need to take the rest of the week off. Reschedule all my meetings for next week.
    —D.A.

PART OF ME WANTS TO CHANGE HER NAME TO GIANNA AND MAKE HER SWEAT for the next few days, but I won't do that. I'd rather see the look on her face when she realizes who I am. Will she look past the asshole I've been and see the man I was in Greece? Or have I pushed myself past the point of redemption?

I don't know what's going to happen, but one thing is for certain.

I'm not going to let her run from me twice.

CHAPTER TEN

Carley

THIS PAST WEEK has been bliss.

Except for the fact that Nick still *hasn't called.*

Dinner on Monday night was more fun than I'd expected it to be. I wasn't sure how I felt about having Ren around because Saylor doesn't have the greatest track record with men. However, he's funny, sweet, and *really* into her—he's even slept at over the majority of the nights this week. The guys she tends to flock to are dicks who push her away at the first sign of commitment. Ren seems ... different.

For starters, he's not a trust fund baby, which I think makes a huge difference. Also, he does *actual* manual labor, installing residential and commercial security systems. I think Ren will be really good for Saylor, I just hope she doesn't lose interest in him if she's not forced to chase him around for a while longer.

When I woke up on Tuesday and saw Mr. Anastos's email telling me he was going to be out of the office the rest of the week, it was like Christmas had come early. The past couple of days have been quiet instead of filled with disrespectful emails from the cranky boss man.

I've been using the time to practice some interview questions. Interviews are the worst. I can sit and have a conversation with ease any time, any day. But these forced, almost fake conversations always feel so awkward.

The other reason I've been consuming myself with them is so I don't obsess over why Nick hasn't reached out to me. I'm trying so hard not to think about it. I can't lie, I'm worried I blew my chances. Did Ez actually pass my message along? I like to think he did. He seemed so sincere when we were talking.

But if that's true it means Nick doesn't want to speak to me. Or it could also mean I was right to leave because he doesn't feel the same way about me as I do him. I can feel my heart begin to crack, but I quickly return to my sheet of questions and answers before it breaks completely.

Another thirty minutes goes by before I hear the ding from the elevator arriving. My head flies up when it sounds. It's the first time anyone has arrived since I saw Ez walk through it on Monday. I'm curious who it is. There are no appointments and no reason anyone else should be up here when Mr. Anastos is out of the office.

When the doors slide open and my eyes land on the one person I thought I would never see again, shockwaves soar through me, causing goose bumps to break out over my skin. If I thought he was hot half-naked in a bathing suit … If I thought he looked like a statue sculpted from marble in bed next to me …

Okay, both of those are totally still true.

But the way Nick Evans wears a suit should be illegal.

Fuck. Me.

Literally. Bend me over my fucking desk and take me. I beg you.

As heat I haven't felt in a month blooms within me, I stand, unsure if my legs will be able to hold me upright. As though I'm watching a movie, he seems to walk toward me in slow motion. One hand in his pocket, the other straightening the gold tie around his neck. His eyes are locked on mine, and they look as dark and possessive as I remember them looking just before he fucked me for the umpteenth time that night. It's a long, slow path he's taking, and it feels like he will never reach my desk.

I sure as hell can't move, or else I'd help him bridge the gap.

Finally, he approaches me, and my mouth falls open, but no words come out. With a final glance, he passes by me and walks right into Mr. Anastos's office as though he owns the place.

What is he doing?

The odd maneuver is enough to break me from my spell, and I follow him inside just as he's making himself comfortable behind Mr. Anastos's desk.

"Ni—Nick? What are you doing here? You can't be in here, I'll get fired."

This time when he looks at me, it's dangerous, and I feel my goose bumps return.

"But I thought you hated this job? I thought you were quitting anyway."

Why would he seem so angry about that? It has nothing to do with him.

"I *do* hate this job. I don't really know why Ez chose to tell you that part of our conversation, but I hope he told you the most important part."

I gaze at him with hopeful eyes as he leans back in his chair and rests his ankle on the knee of his other leg. He runs his hand over his sexy as fuck beard as he appears to think about what I just said. Before answering, he opens Mr. Anastos's bottom drawer, pulls out his laptop, and turns it on.

"*Nick!* What are you doing?"

"I thought today was a good day for your probationary period review."

He stands up and gestures to the chair across from Mr. Anastos's desk, and that's when the final piece falls into place.

Oh. Fuck.

I start to hyperventilate, and I feel like I'm going to be sick.

Nick is Mr. Anastos. Mr. Anastos is Nick.

The only reason I take a seat at his request is because I feel like I'll faint if I don't. This is why Ez was acting weird when I saw him. This is why Ez couldn't—

didn't—tell me how he knows Mr. Anastos. He knew ... he knows ... oh god. Nick —I mean Mr. Anastos—knows how I feel about him.

Oh my god, I called him a dick.

"Okay, let's get started," he says.

He's going to fire me and kick me out of his life at the same time.

"I'll start out by asking you some questions. After that, I'll tell you the things I've observed, and then you'll have a chance to make any statements you feel necessary."

He doesn't look at me until the last sentence. I really feel like I'm going to lose my lunch at any moment.

"First question. Did you know who I was when we met in Greece?"

This question shocks me. One, because *no* I had no idea who he was. Two, what does this have to do with my job?

"No," I clear my throat as I struggle to speak. "No, I had no idea who you were."

He studies me carefully, looking like he's not sure I'm telling him the truth. I want to know where he's going with this. My unease begins to morph into anger.

"Why did you take a position with Okeanós?"

I furrow my brow with confusion at his question.

"Because I needed a job, and they offered me one. Ni—*Mr. Anastos*, what is this about? With all due respect, which *frankly* I'm not sure you deserve anymore, what's with this line of questioning?"

His nostrils flare as I speak.

"I told you, *Ms. Garrettson*, you will have a chance to make a statement at the conclusion of the review."

With that, my unease is gone. I can feel my blood pressure rise as he *puts me in my place.*

"Did you take this position with the intention of seducing and blackmailing me?"

What? The fuck?

I shake my head in disbelief. This is exactly why I don't give random people my name and why I don't have meaningless sex with strangers. Because I never know when one of them is a closeted *psychopath.*

It sure didn't feel meaningless, though.

I guess that feeling wasn't mutual.

"This is unbelievable. I've never been so insulted in my entire life."

I stand up, furious, shaking-mad, and storm off. But then I realize I have more to say. A lot more.

"You know what?" I rear back around. "*Fuck* you."

I point my finger at him as though it's a knife I want to slice through his heart. All the anger I've had toward Mr. Anastos this past month flows through me. He doesn't move, and he doesn't try to stop me so he can continue his ridiculous questioning.

"I thought the biggest mistake I made was leaving your bed without saying goodbye. I thought I ruined any chance at happiness and you were out of my life forever. And you know what? It fucking *killed* me inside. I've done nothing but lie around, bitching, moaning, and complaining that I'll never find someone as ... as ... *spectacular* as you!"

I didn't want to admit that last fact but fuck it.

"It turns out the mistake was actually crawling into your bed in the first place. *God,* I'm so fucking stupid."

With that, I turn on my heel and march out of his office. I fight back the tears that are threatening to fall because I'll be damned if I let this asshole see me cry.

"Carley, wait," I hear him call after me, but I'm not turning back.

I've waited so long to hear him utter my real name. But instead of it warming my heart, it hurts. I don't care what he has to say, no apology will be good enough. As I open the bottom drawer of my desk and pull out my purse, I feel him behind me. His arm snakes around my waist, and his warm breath is in my ear.

"I'm sorry. I'm so fucking sorry. This isn't how I wanted this to go down. Please don't leave."

He spins me in his arms and pierces me with a sorrowful, hopeful gaze. I push him away from me and take a deep breath to calm myself down. Slinging my purse over my shoulder, I cross my arms and wait for him to speak again.

"Will you please come back into my office?"

I shouldn't do it. I should *not* go back in there. He doesn't deserve a second chance, but ... what if I hurt him by leaving without saying goodbye that morning? Maybe this is his way of getting back at me?

It's not very nice, regardless.

I'm sure there's a lot both of us would like to say. If I can get the reason for this cruel and insensitive interrogation, that would be a good start.

"One condition."

"Anything."

"Tell me why you're acting like this?"

He sighs and looks down. His large hands fall onto his hips, and the vision of them as he thrust into me over and over again forces its way to the forefront of my mind.

Not now, Carley.

"I will, please come sit down."

He waves his hand toward his office again. Rolling my eyes, I take a deep breath and march back into the room. Flopping down into the chair, like a toddler who doesn't want to sit in time out, I wait for him to take his seat again.

But he doesn't. He turns the chair I'm sitting in so it faces the one next to it. Then he sits in that chair so we're nearly knee to knee.

I cross my arms and legs at the same time and wait for him to speak. With his eyes glued to mine, he leans forward and rests his elbows on his knees.

"About a year ago, I had an assistant that I ... started a physical relationship with. Long story short, she blackmailed me with photos and an audio recording that painted a bad picture of me. It took a lot of money to make it go away, and I regret everything that ever happened between the two of us."

Um, red flag alert...

I don't know what to say to that. Was it consensual? Do I work for a monster? What the hell do *I* have to do with any of this?

"When Ez called me on Monday and told me you were my new assistant, I was ecstatic. I'd been trying to find you ever since you *fled*, and I was happy I finally knew who you were."

My heart speeds up when I realize he's been looking for me, too.

"But when I got to thinking about it more, it all seemed like too big of a coincidence. And finding out you gave me a fake name, I thought it was happening all over again. That you were like *her* and were going to try and set me up for something I didn't do in exchange for money."

"I mean, I know we don't know one another, but after the connection we had in Greece ... Do you *really* think so little of me?"

"No."

His quick answer stuns me. If he didn't actually think it, then why go through all of this?

"If you recall, *you* were the one who asked *me* out on a date," I remind him. "Also, *Nick Evans*, I'm not the only one who wasn't truthful about their name."

"I know. And I know I've been incredibly unfair to you today, but I didn't think *she* was that kind of person, either. At least, not in the beginning."

"And what kind of person are you, Mr.—"

"Dimos. Please, call me Dimos."

"Which version of you is more accurate, Dimos?"

His eyes light up when his name rolls off my lips.

"Are you the romantic gentleman who rescued me by the poolside? The generous lover whose bed I shared? Or the arrogant asshole who has been making my life a living hell the past month?"

Tension tics in his jaw as I spit those final words at him. Does he know who he is? Is he afraid to tell me? Afraid it will drive me away? I'm halfway gone already, so it might not matter anyhow.

"I guess you could say all of them are different parts of me."

I wasn't expecting that. I thought he'd try to excuse his way out of his behavior the past month.

"The reason for my brash behavior as your boss has nothing to do with you. Ever since ... my mistake ... I've kept my distance from my assistants. They only work out of this office, instead of with me in California. I only communicate through email so everything is in writing. I'm short with them so nothing I say will come off as flirtatious or anything other than professional."

He takes a deep breath and runs his hand over his chin.

"And I don't give out my real name because when people know who I am, they don't see me. They see dollar signs. It's really hard getting to know someone when you're wondering if they're with you for you or for your money."

There's a reason I don't give my real name to people also. It was because of a guy I met at a bar once. Things started out great, but he got more and more clingy as the night went on. He ended up finding out where I lived and stalking me. Saylor and I had to move twice before he ended up getting arrested for something unrelated. I haven't heard from him since, thankfully.

"Safety reasons." I don't want to delve into the details with him just yet, so that's as much of a reason as he's getting. "It's why I gave you the wrong name. And regardless of why *you did the same thing*, that still doesn't give you the right to come in here and treat me like shit."

"I know, and I'm sorry. I'd like to start over, if you'll let me."

He places a hand gently on my knee, and I know I'm in trouble. Suddenly, all I can think about is climbing into his lap and telling him I forgive him.

But I can't.

CHAPTER ELEVEN

Dimos

I've dug quite a hole for myself. I didn't intend to completely blow shit out of the water the way I did. I planned to come in here and gradually work my questions into the conversation in a way that wasn't clearly accusatory. When the elevator doors opened and I saw her again, I lost it. The memories of that night came back to me. The agony I felt when I woke up and realized she was gone was back with a vengeance.

I was excited and ready for this move after deciding it was time. When I woke up on Tuesday, though, the coincidence of it all hit me like a Mack truck. I flew out of bed and ran straight into the bathroom, emptying my stomach of what little was in it. It couldn't be as simple as fate. It was happening again, but this time I was going to be one step ahead of her.

"I don't know if that's something I can do," she answers, breaking my heart. "I don't know if I can forgive and forget how easily you went off on me without even attempting to have an adult conversation first."

"I meant to. That's why I came here. That's why I packed up my entire life and moved to New York. Because I liked the idea that a relationship between us was possible. When those doors opened and I first saw you, I wanted to let it all go. I didn't want to believe you could be the same as her. But the closer I got to you, the more I was reminded of what happened in the past. The angrier I became. And the quicker I lost control."

I really wanted to bend her over the desk and angry fuck the answers I needed out of her, but it's probably best I keep that to myself.

"I haven't let my guard down around anyone since then. I haven't wanted to *be* with anyone until I saw you sitting across the pool in Greece."

"You can't sweet-talk your way out of this."

"I know, I'm just trying to tell the truth."

"I won't sleep with my boss," she insists.

"And I don't want to sleep with my assistant ever again."

"So where do we go from here?"

"I don't know, but I don't want you to quit. If you promise not to be a black-mailing whore, I promise not to be an arrogant asshole." I smile, letting her know I was joking, but it's not returned.

"If you don't want me to quit, then I guess you'd rather have me as an assistant than a girlfriend."

"That couldn't be further from the truth, but I think we have a prime oppor-tunity to get to know one another. We'd get to spend more time together this way."

"That's a pretty big reach. You realize that, don't you?" Her smirk tells me she's fighting hard to keep the smile from her face.

"I know," I admit.

"I don't know what I want to do. A lot has happened in such a short period of time. We've, essentially, only known one another for a week—a *day*, really—and I feel like we've gone through the entire gamut of emotions. I need to sort through them all."

"I understand," I tell her.

"Is there anything else you feel I should know about you before making my decision?"

Fuck.

"No," I tell her.

The fact that I cheated on my ex-wife—or that I have an ex-wife to begin with—has nothing to do with this. Would telling her help her make a decision? Maybe. But I don't know if she would be won over by my honesty, or if it would only push her further away.

"I'm going to take the rest of the day off. All your meetings were rescheduled, per your email, so it should be a quiet afternoon for you."

"I'm still on vacation. How about you take the afternoon off—paid—and have lunch with me?"

"I already ate lunch. But thank you for the paid time off."

With that, she stands from her seat and marches back toward her desk.

"Carley?"

She turns and looks at me but doesn't speak. I stand and meet her in the doorway of my office.

"You have until Monday to decide. I'll see you then."

Her eyes narrow slightly, and I wait for her to respond with a snide remark that I know will make my dick hard. Surprisingly, she only responds with a fake smile before strolling across the lobby to the elevator. Once the doors close, I pull out my cell phone and call downstairs to Izaak, my driver.

"Yes, sir," he answers.

"A girl in a cream-colored skirt and black button up blouse will be exiting the building any minute."

"Yes, sir?"

"Follow her, but don't get out of the car."

"Yes, sir."

Izaak is very tall and very noticeable. I don't need Carley catching on to someone tailing her. He's not a man of many words, but he does as he's asked, and he's loyal as fuck. He follows me wherever I go. I believed Carley when she said she wasn't out to get me, but I'd like to keep tabs on her while she's deciding what she wants to do. I was serious when I said I wasn't going to let her get away twice.

I want Carley, and I won't take no for an answer.

———————

IT WASN'T LONG BEFORE I GOT MY FIRST REPORT FROM IZAAK. CARLEY HAD hailed a cab, which dropped her off at her apartment. I told him to wait nearby and see if she leaves to go anywhere. That was almost seven hours ago. Since then, they've left the apartment and gone for dinner somewhere on Columbus Avenue, which is where they've been for the past hour and a half. I wanted to join him in the stakeout, but I decided to wait it out at my penthouse in the Financial District instead. I still have a lot of unpacking to do, and it will help keep my mind off what she may be doing or thinking.

The walk from the office to my building was nice. I forgot how much I like the city. It's no Hermosa Beach, but Hermosa Beach doesn't have Carley.

Neither do you.

Was I completely crazy to make the move out here not knowing if things were going to work out?

No. I don't want to second guess my decision. I've rarely done it in the past, and my intuition has a fairly good track record.

Except with women.

I finish hanging the shirt I'm holding and head to the study for a glass of whiskey. A *tall* glass of whiskey. I take a sizeable swig as I pull my phone from my pocket and check Izaak's location.

Again.

This time, my limo is still on Columbus, but he's no longer parked.

Where is she headed?

Izaak knows to call me when they get wherever it is they're going. So I'll wait as patiently as I can until I hear from him.

I take my drink back into my room and continue emptying my suitcases. The penthouse came fully furnished, but I hired a staging company to bring in some additional pieces that were more my taste. My Hermosa house is all light wood with teal and navy accents, courtesy of Emma. I wanted my penthouse to have an entirely different feel, so I ordered several pieces of furniture in black or gray leather.

There is something I find soothing about hanging and folding my clothes and putting everything away just right. Call it OCD or whatever you want to call it. But that, and this whiskey, are the only two things keeping me from going after Carley and forcing her to make a decision right now.

Best case scenario, she shows up for work on Monday and tells me she's forgiven me and is ready to move forward. That she wants to get to know me better and would like the chance to do so by working for me. Once we know if we're ready for a relationship, she can find a new job somewhere. Hell, I'll even help her. I'm sure Ez would hire her in a heartbeat.

Worst case scenario, she doesn't show up. Doesn't call. Doesn't write. Strips every memory of me from her mind and moves on. A new job. A new man. A new life that doesn't include me in it.

That's not going to work for me.

I check my watch and wonder if they're headed home from dinner. It's ten o'clock. Apparently, that's dinner hour in New York City time. As if he knew I was thinking about them, I get a call from Izaak right then.

"Yeah?"

"They were just dropped off at the SMR nightclub."

Fuck.

"Okay, thanks."

As I end the call, I ball my hands into fists and squeeze.

A nightclub?

I haven't been to one since I was in my early thirties, but I'm sure they haven't changed much. Crowded dance floor. Sweat soaked skin sliding across the people around you as you gyrate against your dance partner. I can't imagine Carley at a dance club. She seems too sophisticated for that type of venue.

But I would kill to see her on the dance floor. To watch her move her body the way she did as she straddled my lap on the sofa in my hotel room. To feel her skin against mine. To smell her on my clothes when the night is over.

I look at my watch one more time, though I don't know why. It's only been two minutes since the last time I checked. Taking a deep breath, I down the rest of my whiskey and change into the closest thing to club attire I own.

———

SMR ISN'T TOO FAR FROM MY PENTHOUSE, SO I TEXTED IZAAK TO COME PICK me up and take me there. I've been here for thirty minutes, and I still haven't found Carley. There are so many fucking people. And they all look like jailbait.

I'm too fucking old for this shit. Why am I here?

The second I think the question, she comes into view.

Her.

Théa mou.

She's why I'm here.

She's sitting in the VIP area with a group of mostly girls and one guy. Thankfully, he's lip-locked with Saylor and not paying attention to Carley. She looks incredible, as always, in a dress I can't tell the color of because of the lights in this place.

But she looks sad. I watch her gaze over at Saylor and the guy she's with. If I would've handled myself better today, she could be at my penthouse right now. We could have been the ones who went out to dinner. I could be the one sitting next to her on that sofa.

Suddenly, her eyes meet mine, and I duck my head into the crowd because I don't want her to know I'm here. I make my way to the bar. Giving it a few minutes before I chance a glance at her again, I signal a bartender and order a beer. Then I find her once more across the room. I watch as she laughs about something with Saylor just before lifting a shot glass into the air and downing it in one gulp. Then the two of them make their way to the dance floor with the boy in tow.

Luckily, I have a pretty good spot where I am. I can see her but also remain unseen. I watch as her and Saylor dance together, the boy swaying behind Saylor the entire time. Briefly, I wonder if they just met tonight or if they've been an item for longer. I seem to remember Saylor locking lips with several men throughout the course of the week in Greece.

The sight of Carley making eyes at someone across the dance floor pulls my attention quickly. Moving my head, I try to see around the crowd to find out who she's looking at. And if they're looking back at her.

The moment I see a tall guy approaching her, strutting across the dance floor, I know he's the one she's looking at. The one she's invited over to dance with her. To rub her body against.

Fury rolls through me at the sight of it. I want to go over there and punch him right in the face. I want to throw her over my shoulder and into my car. Take her home with me and fuck her until I'm the only guy she wants to think about.

But I won't do that to her. It takes every ounce of strength I have to stay put, drink my beer, and watch her.

With him.

A couple of songs later, she gestures toward the back of the club and leaves the guy alone on the dance floor while Saylor walks back to the sofa. Just before Carley walks down the back hallway, she looks behind her.

Is she looking for me?

No. She couldn't have seen me earlier when I thought she did. Otherwise, I'm certain she would have confronted me. Walking along the perimeter of the room, I head to the same hallway she just went down and push the door to the ladies' room open.

I don't care who sees me.

CHAPTER TWELVE

Carley

EARLIER THAT DAY

I CAN'T REMEMBER a time when I was angrier than I am right now. Maybe when I found out the real reason my parents split was because my mom cheated on my dad and then hid me from him until I was sixteen. But this may even top that.

How *dare* Nick—ugh, *Dimos*—come at me with his accusations and insinuations. I get he had a shitty thing happen to him, but who the hell does he think he is, acting like that?

"Taxi," I scream when I get to the curb outside of the building.

Thankfully, one comes fairly quickly, seeing as how it's three o'clock in the afternoon and not five o'clock in the evening. As I get situated in the back seat, I pull out my cell phone and shoot off a message to Saylor.

ME

Get the wine out. Do I have a story for you!

SAYLOR

!!!What???

ME

This is not something I can tell you over text, girl. It's going to require lots of alcohol and curse words. Maybe even a re-enactment.

SAYLOR

Uh-Oh. The Brassy Bigwig?

Saylor and her nicknames... I swear.

ME

Yes.

I think about my answer for a second. Is this more a Mr. Anastos problem or more of a Nick Evans problem?

ME

And also no.

SAYLOR

I'm confused.

ME

Same. Wine.

ME

And maybe ice cream, too.

ME

I'm in a cab now. Be home soon.

SAYLOR

See you then.

I'm home in record time, also due to the early hour in which I left work. I could get used to this. As I ride the elevator to the eighth floor, I laugh to myself. I still can't believe everything that just happened.

"Un. Real." I say to no one.

When the doors open, I walk to mine and Saylor's apartment. No sooner do I unlock the door, Saylor is nearly attacking me, begging for details.

"What happened?"

"Wine first. And I need to change into some comfy clothes."

"Ugh. Fine," Saylor pouts.

I'm dressed in sweats and my Wharton College T-shirt and sitting on the sofa in no time as Saylor hands me a large glass of Pinot Grigio.

"Okay, you have the wine and your comfy clothes. Now spill."

I take a large gulp before placing my glass on the coffee table and standing up.

"So I was sitting at my desk earlier, minding my own business, when the elevator dings. I was a little confused because Mr. Anastos is on vacation, and there was no reason for anyone to come up to his floor."

"Uh-huh," Saylor answers impatiently.

"I look up. And you'll never guess who I lock eyes with."

"Bradley Cooper."

"What? No." I roll my eyes at her.

"Oh. Um, I don't know then."

A huge, goofy grin breaks out on my face when I remember laying eyes on him again. I think about the excitement I felt that he was here to profess his undying love for me and whisk me away back to Greece.

"Nick."

I watch as Saylor's eyes grow wide with surprise.

"Shut. Up. Are you fucking serious right now?"

"Dead. Fucking. Serious. But that's just the tip of the iceberg."

"Oh lord."

She takes another sip of wine at the same time as me.

"So I'm freaking out, I feel like I might faint, I can't believe this is happening, right? He's walking toward me, and I'm just waiting for him to crush me up against the wall and make out with me or something."

"Oh my god, please tell me that's what happened."

"No. *That* didn't happen. He didn't even say hello. He just waltzed right past me like the fucking King of England and takes a seat behind Mr. Anastos's desk."

"What? Why?" Saylor's eyebrows furrow with confusion.

I stare at her for a few moments as I grab my glass off the table again. Cocking my eyebrow as I take a sip, a realization hits her.

"No. Fucking. Way," she gasps in shock.

"Yup."

"No!"

"Yes."

"Holy shit."

"I know. But wait, there's more. He tells me to take a seat so we can 'go over my probationary period review' as though it's a normal day. As though the man I had a *crazy* night of *redonkulous* sex with didn't just walk through the door after a month of no contact."

Saylor's only response is a series of rapid blinking. It's incredibly rare to shock Saylor speechless.

"Then he starts asking me the most absurd questions."

"Like what?"

"Like, did I know who he was before we met in Greece? Why did I start working for Okeanós? And—wait for it—did I accept my position with the intention of *seducing and blackmailing* him?"

If I thought she was speechless before, I don't know what to call the face she's making right now.

"That *motherfucker*!"

I lean over and pick up my glass again, downing the rest of it. Saylor doesn't skip a beat and fills it again in seconds flat.

"So what did you say?"

"I told him I've never been so insulted before. And then I told him to fuck off."

"Good for you!"

"I told him I'd thought my mistake was leaving without saying goodbye, when in actuality it was crawling into bed with him in the first place. Then I stormed out."

"Fuck yeah! I'm so proud of you. Man, I would have loved to see the look on his face when you walked out."

I try to avoid her eyes as I take another sip of wine.

"What else happened?" She narrows her eyes at me.

Taking my wine glass with me, I sit with my legs folded underneath me on the sofa again.

"When I walked out, he followed me. He wrapped me in his arms and told me he was sorry. He said that's not how he meant for the meeting to go, and he asked me not to leave."

"But then you left anyway, *right*?"

"Not right away. I sat and listened to his sob story about why he's been acting like a fucking asshole."

"Oh, right. And you actually believe him?"

"Yeah, I kind of do. It's really messed up, Say. He slept with his former assistant—something he said he greatly regrets—and she turned around and blackmailed him for a lot of money. She had pictures of them, and apparently, an audio recording with some pretty incriminating stuff on it."

"Okay, yeah, I get that's messed up. But that's no reason to treat you the way he did."

"I know, and I told him so. He asked me if we could start over, but I told him I wasn't sure it would be possible. I made it clear that I would *not* be sleeping with him if he was my boss. He agreed, obviously."

"So ... where does that leave things?"

"I told him I needed to think about it. He agreed, but as I started walking away ..." I take another sip of wine because I'm about to get mad all over again. "He told me I have the weekend to decide, but then he said 'I'll see you Monday' as though he knows I'm going to come crawling back to him."

I'm fuming.

"How dare he drop this bomb on me. Telling me I have such a limited time to think about it and then basically making my decision for me as though I don't know what's best for myself."

"Okay, here's what we're going to do." Saylor excitedly and animatedly holds her hands in the air, as though stopping this moment in time.

Oh, I don't like the sound of that.

"We're going to call in an emergency to Steffi at La Beauté Naturelle and have her come here. You're going to have your hair and nails done, then we're going out for a night on the town."

"I really don't—"

"*No!*" Saylor yells at me. "You don't get to decide. You need to just let loose, Carley. Forget about that asshole."

If one more person tells me what I *need* today ... I take another large sip of wine.

"Let me work some magic. I might even be able to grab a table at Vine."

She squeals and jumps off the sofa, leaving me alone with my wine and my thoughts.

Let's take away the fact that Dimos basically told me what I was going to do, completely disregarding my own feelings. That leaves me with his proposal of working for him while we get to know one another.

It's not the most conventional courtship I've ever had, but our *relationship* didn't start down a conventional path anyway. On the plus side, he still wants to be with me. I could see it in his eyes when he first got off the elevator. I could feel it in his touch when he wrapped his arms around me. And I could hear it in his voice when he told me he was 'so fucking sorry.'

He moved across the country because he thought something between us could work.

Do I give him another chance?

I shouldn't.

On the other hand, I've been whining like a baby—and aching for his touch —for weeks. I've dreamt about finding him. Now that I have, and he's the polar opposite of the person I fell for in Greece, I realize my fantasies over the last month were solely based on only one facet of many that make up Dimos Anastos.

Do I want to stick around to find out if any of his other facets are as bad as—or worse —than the one I saw today?

I'd be lying if I said I wasn't scared.

I'm scared he's going to turn out to be a horrible person. I'm scared he's going to break my heart. I'm scared to walk away, never knowing what could have been if I'd only given him another chance.

I'm scared of losing myself. I'm scared of finding myself.

But mostly, I'm scared of living day-to-day, never feeling the passion he ignited inside of me ever again.

OKAY, I HAVE TO HAND IT TO SAYLOR. SHE MAY HAVE BEEN RIGHT. I FEEL LIKE a fucking queen tonight. Steffi worked magic only she can perform. My hair and nails look incredible, and the dress Saylor had delivered—last minute from Bergdorf's—is stunning.

I don't know how she pulls things together like this all the time, but she doesn't get hounded by bars, clubs, restaurants, designers, celebrities, and the like, who pay her to show up at their events, for no reason. This girl knows every in and out of the New York City social scene.

After we finished primping and getting gussied up, it was time for dinner at Vine, the biggest up-and-coming restaurant in the city. With a waitlist two-months long, I don't even know what Saylor had to do or say to get us in there.

But I was totally okay with whatever it was.

We finish the bottle of Moët & Chandon Imperial just as our driver pulls the limo alongside the curb in front of SMR. I'll admit, I've had more to drink than I usually do, but Saylor keeps pouring me more. She's been right about every other aspect of this evening, so bottoms up.

Ren is waiting outside for us when we pull up, and Saylor runs to him. They're lip-locked in no time, and a part of me thinks our fun night has reached its peak. I didn't know he was coming out with us tonight. I thought it was just going to be the two of us.

I don't let myself wallow in disappointment for long. As soon as they break their kiss, he awkwardly waves to me, and the bouncer lets us through. I secretly smile at the sound of groans from the crowd who have been waiting to get in for hours, I'm sure.

The hostess leads us to the VIP section as soon as she sees Saylor. She presses the button on the radio in her ear as she walks, speaking to whoever is on the other end. When we get to the VIP area, our cocktail waitress meets us at the sofa in the back where we'll be sitting with a bottle of Absolut Pinstripe Black. I've never had it. I don't think I'd be able to tell the difference between that and regular Absolut, but apparently, this is 'top notch' according to Saylor.

About an hour in, we're surrounded by a ton of other people Saylor invited, unbeknownst to me. Models, socialites, entourages ... Our girls' night out is quickly being invaded by strangers. I know Saylor means well, and I'm trying not to be ungrateful, but the more people who join us, the less fun I'm having.

Watching Saylor making out with Ren, I start to think about Dimos again. It might be the alcohol talking—okay, I'm sure it's the alcohol talking—but I *miss* him. I think part of the reason I was so angry with him today is because deep down, even I know I'm going to show up to the office on Monday.

As I look out into the crowd, I swear I see him there. Watching me.

No fucking way.

I look through the crowd, trying to find his eyes again, but he's nowhere to be found. I know it's not the alcohol talking now. Right? *Is* he really here?

Ugh, I don't know.

But I *do* know I can't sit here and watch them make out any longer.

"Saylor, let's go dance," I request.

She detaches herself from Ren and turns to me.

"Yes! But first, tootskies!" Saylor reaches for the bottle of vodka and pours each of us one.

Yes, Saylor even has a nickname for shots.

We cheers to one another again before downing the smooth, clear liquid and making our way to the dance floor as Ren follows us. I try to keep an eye out without making it obvious I am looking around for *him*.

After a few minutes, I see a random guy on the edge of the dance floor making eyes at me.

Please don't come over here.

But he does. I don't dismiss him right off the bat, though I want to.

"Hi," he screams over the loud music. "Want to dance?"

I don't say yes, but I don't turn him away. I just offer him a small, awkward smile and shrug my shoulders. Apparently, that's as good as a yes to him, because he starts swaying along to the music behind me. The smile on Saylor's face as she sees this all go down makes me roll my eyes.

The four of us dance as another two songs go by, before I'm past the point of being comfortable.

"Hey, I'm going to use the ladies' room. I'll meet you back at the sofa in a minute."

Saylor flashes me two thumbs up as I excuse myself from the guy behind me. Just before I enter the back hallway, I turn around to see where he wandered off to, and I am happy to see it's *not* to the sofa with Saylor and Ren.

Thankfully, the bathroom is empty when I get in there. I run some cold water over my hands and pat my cheeks with them.

No more alcohol for me. The room is beginning to spin.

I think I'll tell Saylor I want to go home. She can stay and—

Suddenly, the bathroom door opens, and I see Dimos's reflection staring back at me.

I knew I saw him.

"Are you following me now?" I turn and glare at him with an accusatory stare.

He doesn't answer me. His only response is to lock the door to the bathroom behind him so no one else can get in.

"What are you doing?" My voice goes from stern to shaky in a heartbeat.

Still, he doesn't answer me, but he no longer needs to. The look in his eyes. The jealousy and possession that burns beneath them is radiating outward, and I can feel the heat from here.

"Dim—" I don't get a chance to finish panting his name before his lips are on mine.

CHAPTER THIRTEEN

Dimos

As my lips finally grace hers again, I feel like a horny teenager who's lost all sense of restraint. My hands find the hem of her dress, and I lift it to gain better access to her. Her hands dive into my hair, and she pulls tightly, as though she desperately needs something to hold onto. I fist the hair at the nape of her neck, getting better control over her, as my other hand dips beneath the lace stretched across her hips.

I can feel the rapid beating of her heart against my chest as I slide my fingers through her already dripping wet slit and deep inside of her. Swallowing her sweet moan, I can taste the alcohol on her breath, and I know I should stop this.

God, but that's the last thing on earth I want to do right now.

With every ounce of willpower I have inside of me, I stop the onslaught from my fingers as I reluctantly break our kiss. I watch as her eyes shoot open, and a whine escapes her mouth.

"Are you drunk?"

"What?"

Her sluggish blink tells me everything I need to know. She's had a lot more than the one shot I saw her take a moment ago.

Fuck.

I take a deep breath as I remove my fingers from inside of her. Not wanting to waste this small moment, I make a show of licking them clean before I pull her dress back into place.

"What are you doing?"

Rubbing a hand over my mouth and down my chin, I think about my next move. There's no way she can go back out there. She'll only get more drunk, and who knows what could happen to her.

"We're leaving, let's go." I take her by the hand.

"You don't get to tell me what to do!"

She tears her palm away from mine instantly. After what just almost happened, I thought she'd come willingly. Then an idea hits me.

"Tell me you don't want to go home with me, and I'll leave you here. With that little boy you were just grinding your ass all over."

"I was *not*."

A sly smile crosses my face.

"Were you thinking about me while you were dancing with him?"

She swallows nervously but doesn't answer. I step toward her, eliminating the space between us once again. Placing my hand—the one that was just three knuckles deep inside of her sweet pussy—against her cheek, she closes her eyes, relaxing into it.

"You were, weren't you?"

I press my body against hers, and I know she can feel my rock hard erection against her stomach. She still doesn't answer, but the feeble moan that escapes her throat is telling.

"Come home with me tonight, Carley. No strings. No expectations. I just want to take care of you."

Finally, her eyes open, giving me the answer I've been aching for.

SAYLOR TRIED TO GET HER TO STAY. SHE SLURRED SOME NOT VERY NICE things at me across the table when we went to say goodbye.

I deserved every one of them, but I wasn't going to tell her that.

Finally, the guy she was with told her that Carley is an adult and can make her own decisions.

Maybe she's actually found a smart guy for once.

Carley was quiet on the ride home. She sat next to me, staring out the window with her arms and legs crossed. It's her defensive position. It's the same one she had earlier today in my office, and it's the same one she had when that idiot tried to invite her to the bonfire in Greece.

It's the same way she's sitting in the chair in my living room when I bring her a bottle of water.

"Here, drink this."

She looks at me almost like she wants to tell me off again, but she says nothing.

"I mean, *if* you want to. I'm not telling you what to do. Only suggesting."

I take the chair next to hers.

"Then maybe you should phrase your sentence as a suggestion and not a command."

I love her smart mouth. Even when every other word is slurred from a drunk tongue.

"Would you like some water, Carley?"

I hold the bottle out for her to take, which she does this time. I'm relieved to see a slight smirk on her face as she takes it, too. I turn my body so I'm facing her with my arm resting along the seat back.

She's actually here.

I was beginning to think she was merely a figment of my imagination.

"What?" she asks softly.

"I just can't believe you're sitting here."

"You didn't give me much choice," she scoffs.

"There's always a choice, Carley."

"You blur the line between choice and coercion pretty well."

"Only when I know you need help admitting what it is you want."

She narrows her eyes at me again, but both she and I know I'm right.

"How do you feel?" I inquire.

I really do want to know the truth. Because I'd like to talk to her, get to know her more. Have the conversation we never had in Greece before we tore into one another like starving hyenas.

"Fine." She shrugs her shoulders.

"Are you up for talking?"

She takes a deep breath before she answers.

"I honestly don't know if I have the mental capacity to discuss what happened this afternoon and where to go from here, Dimos."

"I don't want to talk about that either, I just meant maybe we can get to know one another a little better."

"Oh." Her eyebrows shoot up in surprise. "Okay."

She rotates in her seat so her body mirrors my own. Her elbow resting on the back of the chair and her head gently laying on her closed fist.

"I'll go first this time. I know you struggle with easing into a conversation." She smirks again, making light of the vicious way I began questioning her earlier today.

"That's fair." The corner of my mouth raises slightly. "Ask me anything. I'm an open book."

"Do you have any siblings?"

"I have a younger brother, Enrikos."

"Are you close?"

"Very. We don't talk nearly as much as we used to, as we're both busy with our businesses, but when we need each other, we're always there."

"That's really nice," she smiles.

"What about you? Any siblings?"

"I have a half-brother named Elias who is twelve years younger than me."

"What about your parents. What are they like?"

She narrows her eyes at me and takes another deep breath followed by guzzling a lot of water, giving me the sense I've already breached a touchy subject.

"Wow, I'm sensing a little tension," I laugh sarcastically. "You don't have to tell me if you don't want to."

"No, it's okay. I get along great with my dad. But my mom and I aren't really close anymore. I'll tell you as long as you can keep up." She closes one eye and cocks the brow of the other as she slurs another sentence.

"My mother," she wrinkles her nose before continuing. "Gianna—"

"Wait a minute. Hold on … Change of subject for a second. Are you telling me the whole time we were … together … I was moaning your *mother's* name?"

"Unfortunately," she cringes.

"I bet that was awkward for you," I laugh. "Out of *all* of the names you could have chosen, why on earth did you settle on that one?"

She starts cracking up, and it's one of the most endearing things I've ever seen. To see the joy on her face, knowing she's experiencing it as a result of a conversation we're having, means more than I ever thought it could.

"Well, *first of all*, I didn't expect we would end up doing even a fraction of what we did that night. Second of all, it's the name I give out all the time to strangers. I've never jumped into bed as quickly as I did with you. And I honestly didn't think I would ever see you again, so I didn't think telling you my real name actually mattered."

"I remember you mentioned that earlier today, about not giving your real name to strangers. What happened, if you don't mind me asking?"

"I met this guy once, who ended up being a total creeper." The casual way she brushes off what happens doesn't fool me. My thoughts immediately turn dark, and I'm ready to go out and find the asshole who hurt her.

"Nothing super bad happened, thankfully," she explains.

She must have sensed the air around me shifting.

"But he did stalk me for a little while. Eventually, he got arrested, and I haven't seen him since."

"My god. Is he still in jail?"

"I honestly don't know. Saylor and I have moved since then. I think I'm safe."

I don't like knowing there is a possibility that someone is out there who could hurt Carley. I'm going to need to look into this guy, but for now, I want to continue our conversation.

"So I'm sorry. You were telling me about your family before I interrupted you."

"Right ... okay, in a nutshell ..." She takes a deep breath, filling her lungs completely with air. "My mom cheated on my dad with her life-long best friend. My mom never told George—my dad—she was pregnant, and he thought I was just the lovechild that developed as a result of the affair. When I was sixteen, the man I was raised thinking was my father, Lucas, died in a car accident. My mom, wanting my dad back now that she was alone again, finally told him about me."

She explains it all in one breath before stopping, and I honestly don't know how she got it all out without tripping on her words from the alcohol.

"Were you able to follow that?" she giggles.

"I think so," I nod my head slowly.

"Not to mention, at Lucas's funeral, I also found out that he'd been cheating on my mother with his assistant. My mother had known about it for a few years and, instead of leaving him, decided to blackmail him for control of his company in lieu of public disgrace. I was infuriated at Lucas, but there wasn't much I could do about my anger ... But, that's when I stopped trusting anything that came out of my mother's mouth *and* how I developed my deep-rooted hatred for liars and cheaters. My relationship with my mother has never recovered."

Now it's my turn to swallow nervously, but I try my best not to let my unease be known. I'm torn between relief I didn't tell her about what happened with Emma and grief.

Whether I would have told her or not, either way I'm both a liar and *a cheater.*

Unable to think of what to say, I ask her for more details about her parents.

"So what does your dad do?"

"He owns Manford Financial Holdings."

"Your father is George Manford?"

"You know my father?" she deadpans.

"No, not personally. But he and Ez haven't always gotten along. They've become rivals in their industry."

"Actually, now that you mention it, I have heard my dad grumbling about the *nefarious dealings* of Martinique Enterprises before," she jokes, cupping her chin and tapping her lips with her finger.

The way her eyes flash and her nose flares as she speaks makes my dick twitch.

"Well, anyway," she continues, "what about your parents? Hopefully you get along better with them than I do with mine."

"Yeah, we've always been close. Not geographically—they still live in Miami. They own a mom-and-pop grocery store and deli."

"Oh, that's neat."

"Yeah, they sell a bunch of different Greek dishes and desserts. It's small, but they've found a lot of success there, which is all I could ask for."

Sincerity in her smile at my statement sends warmth through me, and I hope she's able to see the compassion I *do* possess.

"We grew up dirt poor, and they brought us to America with the hope that we would find whatever it was we were looking for here."

Before I continue, I think about all the hardships we overcame in the years after getting here.

"And did you? Find everything you were looking for, I mean."

She looks at me through her thick lashes. Her hair is still slightly a mess from our brief encounter in the bathroom at the club. She's breathtaking no matter if she's pristinely put together or a disheveled disaster.

"Yeah, I did."

I stare deep into her striking blue eyes as I utter the words. I found her, and she is everything I've ever wanted.

Her eyelids are getting heavier the longer we sit here.

"Good," she whispers, finally shutting them and letting the alcohol and fatigue pull her under.

I carefully lift her from her chair and carry her down the hallway to the guest bedroom. Pulling back the comforter, I lay her down gently before removing her shoes. When she's free of them, I cover her up and stare down at the beauty she is.

There isn't one thing about her that screams deviant, and for the second time today, I realize how utterly and truly stupid I was for even thinking she'd be capable of doing what Kati did.

She's the epitome of innocence, and I pray to God when she wakes up tomorrow morning, she doesn't regret coming here tonight.

CHAPTER FOURTEEN

Carley

THE NEXT MORNING, I wake up to the delicious aroma of coffee.

There's no way Saylor is up before me. That never happens.

Opening my eyes, I expect to find the clock on my side table I always see first thing in the morning. But I don't. My eyes widen further as I remember where I am. Quickly, I pull back the covers to see if I'm naked, and I'm relieved to find I'm still in the dress I had on last night. I turn over, wondering if Dimos is in bed next to me, but it's empty. The pillow lays untouched, and that entire side of the bed is still made.

I breathe a sigh of relief knowing I slept alone last night, however, it's short lived before I start cursing myself for coming here at all. I vaguely remember being accosted by him in the bathroom at the club. My clit throbs as I recall the way his fingers burrowed deep within me after a month-long absence. I groan as my head flops back down on the pillow.

What am I doing here?

After several minutes of not being able to answer my own question, I swing my legs over the side of the bed, steadying myself as I sit up too fast. My head feels like it's full of concrete, and I want nothing more than to crash back into my pillow, but I can't. Nature is calling, and I would kill for a toothbrush.

I walk into the connecting bathroom and do my business. After that, I snoop through the cabinets, hoping to find something to freshen my breath. I don't find any toothpaste, but there is a small bottle of mouthwash which I open and swish around.

When I'm finished, I slowly exit the bedroom, letting the smell of rich coffee lead the way. As soon as my feet hit the hallway, I'm distracted by the sweeping view of the city below us. It's mesmerizing. Just as much as the inside of Dimos's seventy-sixth floor penthouse, something I failed to notice in my inebriated state last night. I only remember bits and pieces of our conversation, and I'm hoping I didn't say anything stupid or embarrassing.

Hopefully, I didn't profess my undying love for him.

I timidly peer into different rooms as I search for the kitchen, looking for Dimos. All the furniture and finishings in his penthouse are high-class and high dollar. It's chic with just the right amount of masculinity, so it's clear a man lives here. Just before I make it to the great room where we were sitting last night, I feel a presence behind me. I spin on my heel quickly and am suddenly face-to-face with him.

"Good morning, *théa*. You look as ravishing as ever."

God, his voice.

I want to ask him what it means—I still don't know and I tried so hard not to think about it after Greece—but I can barely form words. That and I'm fighting to keep a moan from escaping me.

"Good morning, Dimos," I'm finally able to get out.

"You can call me D if you'd like."

I remember Ez calling him D when we were by the pool one day. I thought it was a nickname of sorts, but it makes perfect sense now.

"D." I smile nervously at him and tuck my hair behind my ear.

He returns my smile with a dashing—*and devious*—one of his own. It makes me feel things I'm having a harder and harder time controlling.

"Can I get you some coffee?" he offers.

"Yes, please. Thank you."

"I'll be right back. Feel free to make yourself at home."

I walk closer to the window, wondering if I can brave a look straight down, as D heads into the kitchen. Aside from the Empire State Building, I've never been in a building this high before. I feel like I'm on a cloud. Once I'm about five feet away, a slight feeling of dizziness takes over and keeps me from getting any closer. Instead, I take the chair I was seated in last night and curl my legs beneath me as I wait for D to come back.

"Do you take any cream or sugar?" he calls from the kitchen.

"Cream only, please. Thank you."

As I answer, I spot my clutch on the table across the room.

My phone. Saylor.

She's probably worried about me. Hopping out of the chair, I grab it from the table quickly and take my seat once again. I'm almost nervous to pull my phone out and check my messages. She was very brutal toward D when we left last night—though nothing she said wasn't true—and I am hoping her animosity didn't transfer to me for not being strong and sticking to my guns about not seeing him. Maybe she was too drunk to text anything after we left. Probably wishful thinking. When I pull my phone out, the first thing I do is check the time.

Ten o'clock?

I never sleep this late. I must have been a lot more intoxicated than I thought I was. I should have already picked up on that by the massive pounding in my head, but it seems my hangover has left me both physically and mentally sluggish. I'm shocked to find I only have two text messages since last night and even more surprised just one of them is from Saylor. Unlocking my phone, I pull up my messaging app and open them, starting with the one from Saylor at two-thirty this morning.

SAYLOR

Ren told me I should apologize for being such a dick.
But I'm not really that sorry about it. I don't like when
people hurt my best friend. I just want you to be careful.

I smile softly at my best friend's words. Saylor is goofy and sarcastic ninety-nine percent of the time, but every now and again, she says something meaningful, straight to the point, and exactly what I need to hear.

ME

I know you do, and I love you for it. I'll be home in a bit.

The second text was from my mother. I groan as soon as I see her name.

MOTHER

Hi, sweetheart. I wanted to see if you'd like to grab
some lunch with me today? It's been a while since
we've gotten together, and I miss you.

I take a deep breath and try not to roll my eyes. I can only take her in small doses. I have a love-hate relationship with her. Maybe that's too strong of a phrase. I'm confused about my feelings toward her at best. I grew up thinking she was an incredible person. Therefore, a daughter's love is rooted inside of me for her. But once I found out who she really was ... I can't stand being around her. She's right, however. It has been a while since we've seen one another. If I don't meet up with her, she'll only keep begging. I give it some thought and come to the conclusion I am in no shape to deal with her today, but I respond with an alternative option.

ME

I can't today. Plans with Saylor. What about brunch
tomorrow?

Immediately, I see the three dots appear at the bottom of the screen.

MOTHER

That sounds wonderful. I'll call around today and make
us a reservation somewhere. 10:00?

ME

See you then.

As I hear footsteps approaching, I put my phone back into my clutch and tuck the bag in between my leg and the chair.

D puts a tray down on the table between my chair and the one next to it. As he does so, in addition to coffee, I also see a bottle of water and some pain medication. The thought he's putting into taking care of me right now is very sweet. *This* is the guy I met in Greece.

"I brought you some ibuprofen, in case you needed it."

"Yes, *please*. I don't know what possessed me to drink as much as I did last night. It was stupid."

Really? You can't think of one *reason?*

"I think I have a bit of an idea why. And I am sorry, again, for the way I treated you yesterday."

"I really appreciate that," I admit. "But I need to take some of the responsibility, too. Plus, Saylor is also somewhat to blame."

We both laugh, knowing the wild party girl she is.

"How did you sleep?"

"Fine," I confirm. "Um, thanks for … putting me to bed."

I scrunch my nose, hating that I had to be taken care of. I pick up the bottle of water and pain medication as he speaks.

"It was my pleasure. I thoroughly enjoyed sleeping under the same roof last night. I'm hoping we can do it again sometime. Soon, perhaps?"

I nearly choke on the water as I swallow the pills down. The dark and dangerous look in his stare is back, making me squirm in my seat. My breathing increases, and I can feel the blood in my veins warming up as it flows to the place between my legs I've fantasized about him touching over and over again for the past month.

The corner of his mouth curves upward, and I know he knows if he were to touch me down there right now, he would find I'm nearly drenched already.

"There's … still a lot I need to think about," I explain, placing the bottle of water back onto the tray and picking up my coffee.

"Mmhmm."

He rubs his hand over his chin. Distracted by his fingers, all I can think about is us in the bathroom last night. For the first time, it hits me that *he* stopped it. *Not me.* Nor did I have any intention of stopping it. If it weren't for the strength of his willpower, I probably would have let him fuck me over the bathroom sink.

Oh my god, how hot would that have been?

Clearing both my throat and my mind, I speak again.

"I also want to thank you for what you did for me at the club last night. If it weren't for that, there's a possibility I would have woken up regretting it or feeling used. That's the last thing I want to feel where you're concerned."

"But you told me you regretted getting into bed with me in Greece. Do you still feel that way?"

Do I?

I think about it for a minute before I realize I don't regret it.

"I'm partly to blame for the mishap that occurred yesterday. I'm not going to sit here and say I deserved it, but I wasn't honest with you just as much as you weren't honest with me. I really am sorry I left without saying goodbye and without telling you my real name."

"Why *did* you leave?"

Shaking my head slightly, I smile at him, still in disbelief about what occurred in his suite that night.

"The girl you were with that night is *not* who I am. I morphed into someone who I don't recognize to this day. While it was wild and freeing, she scares me a little bit." I turn away from him, thinking about it, ashamed of my behavior all over again. "When I woke up the next morning, I couldn't believe half of what happened the night before. Not that I didn't enjoy it. But I was also worried you'd already lost interest or would wake up with regrets. Or worse, you'd think I was just some floozy who will jump into bed easily with anyone she meets."

I can feel his eyes burning into me, but I still can't look at him. After a moment, he gets up and squats down in front of my chair. One hand grips my knee, and the other grazes my chin, finally making me lift my gaze.

"Let me be clear about a few things here and now, okay? First, yesterday had nothing to do with you and everything to do with me and the mistakes of my past. Second, I regret nothing about that night with you. Not a damn thing, Carley. It was the best night of my life. When I woke up and you weren't there, I felt the closest thing to heartbreak I've ever felt before."

This is what I've been looking for. *Begging for*. A real man who knows what he wants and is mature enough to say exactly what he's feeling. And *fuck*, I want to kiss him so bad it hurts. Then the devious gleam in his stare returns, and I fight to swallow the ball of nerves stuck in my throat.

"Third, I believe you *are* the girl I was with that night. She is the part of you you're afraid to embrace, but she's also the part of you that will set you free. Mark my words, I *will* be meeting her again. I'm going to draw her from you, little by little, for as long as it takes until you need her as much as you need your next breath."

CHAPTER FIFTEEN

Dimos

I WENT the rest of the weekend without seeing or talking to Carley. After I made my promise to her—*and I meant every word*—she told me she wasn't sure what she wanted to do about the situation at work and would think more about it over the weekend. I have a good feeling she's going to show up today, but if not, it won't be the first time she's shocked me.

I don't know if the suggestion to work together while we get to know one another was stupid or genius. But I *do* know we're walking on shaky ground. I can see the desire in Carley's eyes every time she looks at me, even though she's hell-bent on fighting it.

I hear the ding of the elevator as it arrives on my floor. I want to know if it's Carley, but I don't want to appear too needy, so I keep my seat. The echoing click of high heels hitting the marble floors is a good sign. The sound brings me back to Greece again, and suddenly, she's there, walking toward me in that little black dress. I hear the clicking get closer to my office door, but it stops before I can see who it is. When I hear a desk drawer open and close, I know it's her.

Thank God.

Once she's through putting her things away, I see her angelic face appear in the doorway to my office.

"You're here early."

"Yeah, I wanted to get in and take care of a few things before the day started."

"I'm going to have to get used to having another person up here all the time. It was nice being alone all day. But I think I'll be able to deal with having you around," she admits with a coy smile.

I can't stop my smile as I take in her meaning. I meant what I said to her on Friday, I don't want to fuck my assistant ever again. However, being near her as often as I will with her working for me is much better than finding time to see her in the middle of my jam-packed work week. And definitely better than only seeing her on weekends.

I may need to make an exception to my own rule.

"I brought you coffee."

She walks the full distance to my desk and places the cup on its surface.

"Oh. Thank you. You didn't have to do that."

"I know," she smiles. "I wanted to. I was getting some for myself anyway."

I smile at her.

"I'm going to go start up my computer. Let me know if you need anything."

I nod as she turns and walks out of my office, and I'm both pained and enraptured with each step she takes. Turning my attention back to my email, I try to keep myself distracted by going through my ever-growing inbox and separating the junk emails from the important ones.

A little while later, my phone begins buzzing on my desk. Picking it up, my stomach churns when I see *Unknown* scroll across the screen.

Fuck.

Every time this happens or I get a call from a number I'm not familiar with, my stomach gets twisted up in knots. I'm waiting for the day when Kati calls me to let me know she's not happy with the five million she's already received from me.

"Is everything okay?" Carley breaks my concentration.

"Huh? Oh, yes, it's fine," I answer, declining the call.

"I went ahead and printed the discrepancy report from last week for you rather than emailing it. I figured you'd print it out anyway. But let me know if you'd rather I do it differently from now on."

"This is perfect, thank you," I confirm.

She smiles awkwardly before leaving once again. The last thing I thought we would deal with in the office together is awkwardness, but I guess I was naive to believe there wouldn't be any. I need to think of something to get us past this part of our boss-employee-lover relationship.

I need to get her underneath me again. Soon.

After completing a few more hours of work, my body is stiff and in dire need of a walk. I make a few laps around the perimeter of my office before my stomach rumbles. I look down at my watch. 11:00 A.M. My feet point their way toward the lobby, and I walk to Carley's desk.

"Are you hungry? Do you have any lunch plans today?" I inquire.

"No, no plans. But yes, I could eat."

"Okay, I'll order something in for us."

"Thank you."

"This is one of the best Greek salads I think I've ever had," Carley insists. "Although, to you I suppose it's just called *salad*." Her laugh is infectious.

She's sitting on the sofa in my office, next to me. Close enough for me to smell her intoxicating perfume but still just out of reach.

"You haven't had my mom's *salad*. I don't even have to taste yours to know hers is better."

Our food got here a little while ago, and we've been enjoying one another's company in my office while eating.

"Well, next time I'm in Miami, I'll have to look them up."

"Or I can just take you there," I suggest.

She doesn't answer but offers me a smile between two flushed cheeks.

"So tell me more about your brother," she requests.

"Well, Rikos is five years younger than me. He owns a successful real-estate company in Miami."

"You said you were close growing up, right?" she asks.

"Yeah. I think the age difference helped. But we've always been best friends."

"That's awesome. I always thought it would be fun to have a sister, but that never happened. I love my brother, though."

"Family is really important. I don't know what I would do without mine. Actually, Rikos almost died when he was ten."

If I want to get to know Carley better, I need to offer up some of my own history.

"Oh my god, that's terrible. What happened, if you don't mind me asking?"

"Of course not," I offer her a smile. I place my to-go box on the table in front of us before turning to face her. "He collapsed playing basketball one day. He was rushed to the hospital, and the doctor found a heart murmur. The surgery for that, way back then, was very invasive and really expensive. Rikos needed it desperately, but my family didn't have the money."

"How awful." She looks genuinely upset about my past situation, and I can feel empathy rolling off her. "So what happened?"

"My mom and dad told the doctor to go ahead with it, and we would deal with the bills somehow. My parents got our family through it, but not without a lot of sacrifice. That's actually what made me go into business for myself. I knew I wanted to make a lot of money so I, and my family, never had to go without or worry about finances ever again."

"That's incredible. I'm so glad it all worked out for Enrikos. And for you. I went to Wharton because I want to start my own business one day."

"What do you want to do?" I prompt.

"You're going to think I'm stupid," she responds, putting her own food down now.

"I would never think that about you."

"Honestly? I don't know what I want to do. It's a weird feeling. I want to be someone, I want to make a difference, but I don't know how or what."

"That's not stupid. You just haven't found your niche yet. I lucked out and found mine at a young age, but that's not usual. Don't let not knowing stand in your way of pursuing your dream. I mean, Henry Ford was forty-five when he created the Model T. Julia Child was fifty when she published her first cookbook."

The smile that spreads across her face is the one I've pictured in my mind over and over again for the past month.

"There it is," I tell her.

"What?"

"That smile I've been missing."

I love watching her cheeks flush when she gets bashful.

"Anytime I had a bad day, and believe me there were a lot, I would picture that smile, and it would ease my stress in an instant."

I'll leave out the fact that I would picture her staring up at me through her thick lashes while she sucked my cock when I needed to rub one off.

She swallows nervously then.

"Your eyes are very telling, D."

"What are they telling you?" I solicit.

She takes a sip of her water, as though her mouth is too dry to speak.

"They're telling me I should finish my lunch back at my desk."

As she reaches for her food, I place my hand on hers.

"Wait, please don't go. I'm sorry. I can't help the thoughts that pop into my head when I'm around you."

She looks down and takes a moment before she responds.

"I—I know what you mean."

When she looks up at me again, I can see the lust swirling around in her gaze. My cock hardens, and I have to fight every instinct in my body not to shut and lock my office door. Clearing my throat, I check my watch. We still have a little more time to talk before the staff meeting at one.

"So how did the rest of your weekend go?" I seek.

She laughs slightly before responding.

"Well, when I finally made it home on Saturday, Saylor was awake and waiting for details of our *sleepover*."

"I can imagine how happy she was. Honestly, I wasn't expecting her to try to keep you from leaving with me. In Greece she seemed gung-ho about you having a good time."

"She's just protective of me. She has been ever since we met in middle school. She was one of the most popular girls in our class. When a few other girls started picking on me, she stood up for me. She ended up getting suspended for cutting one of the girl's braids off. It was then I realized it would be safer to stay on her good side," she giggles. "No, I'm joking. She just ... as ditsy as she seems, she really is a smart, compassionate person."

"Wait, you're joking about the braid?" I inquire.

"Oh, no. That actually happened. I meant me being friends with her to stay on her good side."

"Got it," I laugh. "Hopefully, I can find my way back into her good graces."

"Well, once I got home, I told her what happened in the bathroom and that you were the one to put a stop to it. I also told her an abbreviated account of what we talked about Saturday morning. I don't think you have too much to worry about anymore."

"Does that mean another sleepover is in order soon?"

Her face drops slightly at my question.

"You don't have to answer that. I was half joking anyway."

"It's not that I don't want to. I remember what you told me the other morning. About the part of me I'm afraid to embrace."

"What about her?"

I'm trying not to get my hopes up, but I want her to realize she can be both. She can have it both ways with me. The sweet and meek as well as the sultry and seductive parts of her.

She keeps her eyes trained on her nails, which she's fiddling with in her lap. When she finally looks up at me, both my heart and my dick feel like they could explode.

"I want to be more like her ..."

"But ...?"

No, Carley. No buts.

"But I don't know how."

Keep going. Ask me what you're dying to ask me, théa.

I lick my lips and lean in slightly. Placing my hand on her knee, I can feel her shaking beneath my touch.

"Don't be scared. You don't need to feel embarrassed in front of me. Ever. Understand?"

She nods her head in response.

"I need your help," she finally admits, lightly dragging her teeth along her bottom lip.

I can imagine the devious smile she sees forming on my face as she looks at me.

"I want to help you. I want you to trust that you can be your full, authentic self around me without fear. Can you do that?"

Taking a final, nervous swallow, she answers.

"Yes."

"You're a good girl, *théa mou.*"

"What does that mean? You never did tell me after dinner in Greece."

Moving closer to her, I can't help myself any longer. I gently place my finger under her chin and lift her lips to mine.

"It means *my goddess.*"

Her pupils dilate, and I close my lips over hers. I breathe easy when she doesn't pull away. She isn't just my assistant, and she never will be. She's so much more than that. Cupping her cheek in my palm, she lets out a tiny moan. Fisting the front of my shirt, she pulls me in closer to her still.

Uh-oh.

I'm getting dangerously close to the point of no return. Just when I'm about to make the decision to push the staff meeting back, I hear the ding from the elevator in the lobby, signaling someone's arrival.

I'm so fucking glad that elevator is as far away as it is. It gives us plenty of time to pull away from one another and act like all we're doing here is eating. I hear several voices echo through the lobby and a set of heels clicking closer and closer to my office door. A moment later, I see the face of Carol, the head of human resources, appear in my doorway. That's the *last* person I need to catch us making out.

"Hey D, are we still meeting at one?" She checks her watch to make sure she's not early or late.

"Yeah. We're just about through here."

"Great. See you in a few."

"I can get this, if you need to get in there," Carley offers.

"No, I don't want you cleaning up after me. Plus, I'd like you to attend the meeting. If you want to run your own business someday, it will be helpful for you to see how a successful business runs."

"That's incredible. I don't mean for this to sound harsh, but I was feeling as though my skills were going to waste behind that desk. I'd love the opportunity to be more involved in the day-to-day life of the business."

The shocked look on her face makes me feel guilty for treating her so badly before realizing who she was.

"I really am sorry for the way I treated you for the past month. To be perfectly honest, I didn't have a genuine issue with any of the tasks you completed for me. It was just my asshole way of keeping you at a distance."

I watch as a grateful smile crosses her face, and I know she's accepted my apology.

"I would love to attend. Thank you so much."

We finish cleaning up and walk out to the lobby together.

"I'm going to grab a mint and some paper to take notes on. I'll be right in."

"Okay," I agree, but I wait for her.

She grabs her things, and I follow her into the boardroom.

"Hello, everyone." Carley walks to the back corner and takes a seat. "Carley, please feel free to take a spot at the table with everyone else. Have you all had the chance to meet my new assistant?"

I glance around the room to several people nodding their heads. A couple of them wave to her casually. Ronald, my head of finance, looks at her for a little too long, and it takes all the power in my body not to react too noticeably to him.

It was tough to keep my attention on my staff as we went through our agenda with Carley sitting at the other end of the table. The knowing looks we shared reminded me of our night together and had me visualizing all the places in this room I wanted to lay her down and claim her over and over again as mine.

She showed up today. A small part of me was terrified she wouldn't. That she would realize what a schmuck I am and that she's too good for me. I'm sure she does know that; she's a smart girl. But she's here anyway, *and* she admitted she wants me to help her be comfortable enough to let loose and be the girl she was in Greece.

This has all the potential to turn into one regrettable disaster. But I didn't pick up my entire life and move three-thousand miles to play it safe.

If we're going to do this, we're going all in.

CHAPTER SIXTEEN

Carley

IT'S ALMOST the end of my first week of knowingly working with D. I can't believe the difference between this man and the one I dealt with via email. We've gone over almost every aspect of Okeanós, and I already feel like I know his company inside and out. D told me I was a quick study. He's been so supportive, even going as far as asking my opinion on a few business decisions. I don't know if he went with my ideas or not, but the fact that he was genuinely interested in my point of view speaks volumes.

Unfortunately, that's where our conversations have ended. There's been no more talk of sleepovers at his place. No question of whether he or I still want to pursue anything further with each other.

Don't get me wrong, there have been many looks exchanged over the past few days. Slight brushes, skin grazes as we've exchanged folders, papers, or a pen. That time he stood right behind my chair at my desk, leaning over my shoulder to explain something to me—don't ask me to tell you what it was now because I'd never remember. I silently begged him to take me on the desktop, then and there.

I barely recognize the person I've become this week.

But, I've been waiting for him to take me. Like he did that night in Greece. After both of our recent talks, I figured I'd given him the greenlight to act on his wants. That I was open to being the girl he'd masterfully taken in Greece. If he's waiting for me to make the next first move, I don't know if I can do it. I need him to lead.

The sexual tension between us is *thick.* I would be shocked if someone hasn't picked up on it, but I sincerely hope they don't. For D's sake more than mine. I don't know who on his staff knows about the incident with his previous assistant, but he doesn't need someone finding out about us regardless.

And, *god,* the dreams I've had this week ... Now that I know Nick is actually D, they've been getting even more depraved.

D is like a forbidden fruit, and I'm aching for a taste.

Last night, Saylor had to wake me up because she thought I was having a nightmare. She could hear me panting all the way from her room. It wasn't until she turned the light on that she realized I was humping my pillow instead of trying to fight off the boogeyman.

I feel like I could come just from him looking at me. I don't know what's happening to me, I've never felt this out of control before. It's scary, but I also kind of like it. When I got here on Monday, my clit started throbbing and didn't stop until I got into the cab that afternoon. Tuesday, it was more of the same, but that's the night my sex dreams really started ramping up. Yesterday, I woke up hornier than a frat boy, and nothing I did or thought about could help me quell the feeling. It still hasn't stopped, and we're nearing the end of the day again. I'm so wound up I could scream.

"Carley," D says from the doorway to his office, pulling me from my pent up, desire-filled trance. "I need to finish reviewing these semi-annual reports, but you can feel free to head home if you'd like."

"No," I answer, almost too quickly. "Um, I'll stay and help so you can finish quicker."

Quick finish, huh?

I swallow my lust and hope he can't see the fire burning in my stare. Or maybe I hope he does. I don't know.

"I'm not going to turn away your help, but I don't want you to feel obligated."

The way he rubs his hand over his chin, his five o'clock shadow scraping against his palm ... I picture us together, back in Greece. His beard is scratching the skin between my thighs as he eats my pussy like it's his last meal. The memory sends a gush of moisture to the silk between my legs. Taking a deep breath, I try to form words.

"I want," I clear my throat, dislodging my voice that's caught there. "I want to help. I'll stay."

"Okay." He smiles.

He turns and walks back into his office. I haven't seen that dangerous gleam in his eye since Monday.

He knows.

Or has it been there, but I've been too preoccupied to notice? No, I would have noticed it *more* feeling the way I have been. I stand and straighten my skirt before following him into his office.

"What can I do?" I inquire.

"Have a seat," he commands.

I take a seat on the sofa and cross my legs. The pressure it puts on my clit has me uncrossing and recrossing them at the ankle instead.

I watch him at his desk, pushing papers around, looking for something. Finally, he picks up a stack of papers and brings them to me.

"Okay, if the number in column B of this sheet is greater than the number in column D on this one, just highlight it for me. This means the department didn't stay within the budget they proposed at the end of last year."

"Got it. Let me go grab a highlighter, and I'll be right back."

I hop up off the sofa, but I don't make it far before D grabs my hand and spins me back around into his arms. His lips crash into mine, and I feel like I'm going to come undone. His hands roam my body over my clothing, and I relish every second they're on me. After another lip-locked moment, he finally pulls away from me, and we're both able to catch some air.

"I want you so fucking bad it hurts," he confesses.

"Me too. I've been so worked up these past few days. It's crazy. I've never felt this way before."

"I know you have. I've enjoyed watching your body movements immensely."

"You have? I've been waiting for you to make a move like you did in Greece. I hope no one else noticed."

"I know. It's been agony waiting, but I wanted to give you the chance to first. And, no. No one else noticed. They don't know you the way I know you," I assure her.

"Are you an expert on me already, Mr. Anastos?"

I watch as his eyes roll into the back of his head. When they meet mine again, there is a storm brewing inside of them that captivates me. Like rough waves in the middle of the ocean, I want them to pull me under and swallow me whole.

"We can't do this here," he begins. Thinking quickly, he speaks again, "I'm going to send out an email that I'm working from home tomorrow. Then Izaak will drive us to your house. I want you to pack a bag and spend the weekend with me. We can lock ourselves away in my penthouse and only come up for air to eat. We'll need the energy."

He stops talking only to kiss me again. But it's short-lived before he tears his lips from mine once more.

"I don't know if I can wait that long. I feel like a dog who's gone too long without a bone to devour. Fuck packing a bag. I'll send Izaak out for any essentials you may need."

His lips crash against mine again. This time, he doesn't back away to speak. He asks his question with his lips still firmly planted on mine.

"Are you wet?"

"Yes."

"If I lifted your skirt right now, would I find a wet spot on your panties?"

"Yes," I pant as his lips trace a path down my neck.

He pulls my blouse to the side and continues his kisses over my collarbone. I feel him rifling through his pocket for something, and for a moment, I wonder if he's touching himself. Until I realize he's trying to get his phone out.

He removes his lips from me and presses a couple buttons on his screen. Then he holds the phone up to his ear and pierces me with his gaze.

"Izaak, I need to get home ASAP. Are you close?"

Is he asking me that or Izaak?

Either way, I know my eyes tell him I am close.

So. Fucking. Close.

Close to losing all control and begging him to take me, here and now. Close to telling him I don't care who catches us. I don't care if it ends with me losing my job. I would suffer any and all consequences just for him to plant his cock inside of me and take me back to that night in Greece.

"Excellent, we're coming down now."

He ends the call.

"Get your things," he barks.

If this were any other situation, any other person, I wouldn't appreciate being commanded like that, but at the moment, I love it. I love his dominance over me. It's new and exciting, and it's something I've never experienced before.

I'm not thinking straight. I have plans this weekend, but right now, I couldn't care less about any of them. It feels like this relationship is clouding all the good judgment I have and is about to take over my entire life.

When I get to my desk, the phone starts to ring.

In my lust-filled daze, I barely hear it. D struts out of his office as I reach for it and places his hand on my ass. Luckily, the lobby camera's view is obstructed by the height of my desk.

"If you pick that phone up, I'll finger your pussy until you're about to come and then send you home without release." My head snaps to the left and my eyes find his. The threat in his stare culls more moisture from me, and I abandon my reach for the phone. "You go down before me. Izaak will be there with the limo, and he will let you in. I am going out the East entrance so no one sees us leaving together. Tell Izaak to meet me there. I'll be down in a few minutes."

"Okay," I respond, grabbing my purse and heading toward the elevator.

By the time D made it down to the car, he had already sent an email out to his staff letting them know I would be taking a vacation day tomorrow, and he would be working from home. He works very fast.

"Hello, Ms. Garrettson," Izaak greets me.

Am I really surprised he already knows my name?

"Hello. Mr. Anastos would like for you to pick him up on the other side of the building."

"Yes, ma'am. Thank you."

We drive around the block, and I see D waiting at the curb on the East side of the building.

As soon as he gets in, he practically attacks me. You would have thought we'd gone another entire month without seeing each other. I'm relieved D's car has a partition separating us from Izaak. I'm not convinced he wouldn't try something even if there weren't one. He kneels in front of me and mumbles something about being thankful for summer because there are less layers of clothing to go through.

My breathing gets heavier again as he wraps his hands around my legs, at the back of the knee. Pulling me forward until my ass is lined up with the edge of the seat, he pushes my skirt up my thighs and out of his way. I know the moment he spies the wet spot on the red silk between my legs because the hunger in his eyes intensifies.

"I can't wait until we get home. I need to taste you now."

Throwing my legs over his shoulders, he rips the soaked fabric from my body and tucks it into the inside pocket of his suit coat before his tongue dives through my wet slit. The groan he makes as he tastes me draws more moisture to my core. He sucks on my clit with heated fervor, and I can feel my orgasm building already. My clit is throbbing, and a heat I haven't felt in a month seeps into my skin.

"D, I'm not going to take long, and I don't want to make a mess in your car."

But he doesn't stop what he's doing. Ever since our night in Greece, I've squirted every time I've come to the thought of him. It's not something I've ever been able to do before. It goes hand in hand with the part of me he unlocked that night.

"I don't give a fuck about this car. I want to taste you, *théa*. All of you. Don't hold back."

He breaks his hold just long enough to tell me that, and then he's right back on my clit with his relentless pull. He can sense when I'm about to come because he pulls me farther off the seat and pushes my skirt all the way up so he can see me better. Thank God the fabric is black. At least it won't show if it gets wet.

He replaces his mouth with his hand as he holds me in place with his other arm. Rubbing his fingers rapidly over my clit, he doesn't stop until I'm screaming his name and spraying my release into his awaiting mouth.

Seems silly to have worried about the partition now, I'm *certain* Izaak heard me.

Drinking it all in, he helps me back onto the seat and leans in for a kiss again. Just before our lips meet, I notice a drop of my cum rolling down his chin, getting ready to fall. My tongue connects with it, and I lick a path up his chin to his lips. I nibble a little on his bottom lip before sliding my tongue back into his mouth. Again, the taste of me on him is different yet surprisingly intoxicating.

"I don't know which surface I want to fuck you on first," he explains when we break our kiss again. "I don't even know if I'm going to be able to wait until we get inside."

"Thankfully, we won't have to wait long."

I nod toward the oddly shaped steel building towering over us as Izaak pulls up under the porte-cochère off Spruce Street. Without speaking, D exits the car when it comes to a halt. He takes me by the hand, and I barely latch onto my purse before he's pulling me out of the car.

"Good afternoon, Mr. Anastos," the doorman greets him before pulling the door open for us.

"Colin," D nods stiffly toward him as we walk through the door.

He releases my hand for just a moment, only long enough to pull his access card from his wallet. When we're in the elevator, he scans his card and presses "P" as we begin the long journey to the seventy-sixth floor.

He shoves his card into his pocket and pushes me against the wall of the elevator. Gripping my blouse in both hands, buttons go flying as he rips the material open swiftly and unapologetically.

Seizing my breasts, I wait for him to try and rip my bra from my body like he did my panties. But he doesn't. Squeezing them, he hoists them upward, and I watch as desire flashes in his eyes. He buries his face in my cleavage before snaking his hand down my body and grasping the hem of my skirt again. Pulling it up until I'm completely exposed, he leaves me feeling both nervous as well as aroused.

At any moment, the elevator could stop, and someone could walk in and catch us. It's a feeling I both fear and invite.

"*Théa*," he moans as he runs his fingers through my soaking wet slit. I watch his eyes roll back, and I can feel his erection poking into my hip. "*Anipomono na bo xana mesa su*. I can't wait to be inside of you again."

I practically salivate over his words as the ding of the elevator sounds. Reluctantly, D pushes my skirt back down, and we exit the car into the penthouse lobby. There are two units, each taking up half of the top story. It's incredible to think about how large this floor is as a whole. You can fit two of my apartments inside of D's penthouse alone. Maybe even three.

Turning right out of the elevator, D places his hand on the small of my back as he leads me on shaky legs to his front door. Sliding his key into the lock quickly, he turns the knob, and we nearly fall over one another into the entrance-way. As soon as the door is shut and locked, he tosses my purse onto the table by the door then tears the rest of my shirt from my body before slowly unzipping the side zipper of my black pencil skirt.

Pushing it to the floor, he takes my hand and helps me walk out of it. Suddenly, he whips me around and smacks my bare ass. An act I never would have thought I'd be excited by. He reaches around the front of me with one hand and latches onto my clit as he unfastens my bra with the other one. I hold out my arms and let it fall to the floor before he turns me to face him once again. As I reach down to pull my heels off, he stops me.

"No. The heels stay on."

Naked, while he is still fully clothed, I'm led down the length of his hallway and into the great room. The room comes to a point straight ahead, one of the many corners of this peculiarly constructed building. D stops me in the center of the room and walks in a circle around my body until he's directly in front of me.

I want to cover myself all of a sudden. The balance of power feels incredibly skewed with him still in his clothing and me in nothing more than my favorite pair of Louboutins. As I wrap my arms around myself, he pulls off his sport coat and tosses it onto the floor. Next, he works his shoes off. Then his belt followed by his pants. I have to say, I'm enjoying his little strip tease very much. His indecent stare never leaves mine as he continues undressing until he's down to his boxers only.

Finally, he closes the small distance between us and reclaims my lips with his. As his hands roam my body, I gently cup him in my palm.

"*Gamáto*," he utters, closing his eyes with pleasure.

"D, I..." I'm too scared to say what I want.

"What? Tell me, *théa*. You don't have to be shy around me."

I swallow my nerves and take his dick in my other hand. My lust gives me just as much courage as alcohol would.

"I ... I want to suck your cock."

I look up at him through my lashes and give him the best sexy, yet innocent, porn-star look I can come up with. I pray I don't look like an idiot. I must have done something right because in seconds flat, he gently guides me to the floor at his feet.

Using my nails, I lightly scratch my way up his inner thighs and underneath the fabric of his boxers. He shudders the farther up I go, and I don't miss the dick twitch my actions elicit. Wrapping my fist around his erection, I work it up and down a few times before I tug on his boxers, pulling them down his legs.

Once they're out of the way, I sit back on my heels and take in his entire body. He's an absolutely gorgeous man. Toned and tan with dark features. He's muscular without looking like a bodybuilder. I refamiliarize myself with his compass tattoo. I take him in my hand once more, and he reaches forward, rubbing a thumb down my cheek.

"*Eisai panemorfi.*"

I want to know what he said, but at the same time, nothing in English will sound as irresistible coming from his mouth. The soulful look in his eyes tells me whatever he said came from the heart. With that, I lean in and wrap my lips around the tip of him. While his dick is rigid beneath the surface, his skin is soft and warm against my tongue. I swish it back and forth along the underside of his cock as my head moves farther, taking even more of him inside of me. I want to take it all for him. I want to make it feel so good I bring him to his knees.

Moving my head in and out, I run my lips along his erection, creating a soft friction I can tell he's enjoying. He lets out a low groan, and I can feel him tense up inside of me. I didn't think he could get any stiffer than he already was.

"*Théa, théa,*" he moans. "*O, thee mu.* You're incredible."

He runs his hands through my hair, turning me on every time he fists a section and helps guide my mouth over him.

"Are you still wet, Carley?" he asks suddenly.

I stop moving and look up at him. When I try pulling my mouth away from him to answer, he stops me.

"No. Answer me with my cock in your mouth. Are you wet?"

"Yes," I admit, struggling to say the word around his length.

"Touch yourself. I want you to reach between your legs, gather some moisture, and use it to massage your clit."

My eyes grow wide. I've never touched myself in front of anyone before.

"I love watching your cheeks bloom red when you're embarrassed. But you don't need to be." He cups my chin, staring me straight in the eyes. "Touch yourself while you're sucking my cock."

Slowly, I reach between my legs until I feel the wet warmth covering the entrance to my pussy. Driving my fingers through my opening, I gather up some of the thick, sticky fluid that has built there. Then I gently cover my clit with my index and middle fingers, and I begin rubbing small circles over it. It doesn't take long until a soft moan builds within me.

"That's it, *théa*. I want you to rub harder now. I want you to make yourself come while my cock is in your sweet mouth."

D takes control by holding my head in place and thrusting himself in and out of my mouth. I'm grateful for his help because I am not coordinated to do both things at once. That leaves me better able to concentrate on my movements. As I feel myself getting close, my eyes close.

"Eyes open, *théa*. I want to see the fire ignite in them the moment your pleasure rips through you, and you come all over my floor."

His words are my undoing. I moan around his dick as my orgasm roars through me like a freight train. He pulls himself from my mouth and takes a step back so he can get a better look at me. I can only imagine what I look like through his eyes.

Kneeling in front of him, legs wide open, fingers rubbing my clit furiously. Moisture flowing from my body, dripping onto the marble floors beneath me. He fists his cock as he watches me. I can see the flames of passion burning in his eyes, reflected off mine.

It was one of the strongest orgasms I've ever had, but it's still not enough. It won't be enough until D is inside of me.

"D," I whine.

"What is it?"

"I need you."

He reaches down and grabs my hand, helping me up. Then he nudges me toward the window of his penthouse. My fear from the other day returns.

"No, it's too high. I'm scared," I protest.

"You can trust me, *théa*."

He reaches around my body and tugs on my nipple at the same time as his fingers burrow between my legs and locate my sensitive clit.

"I'll never let you fall."

The combination of his touch, his words, and my lack of strength after that last orgasm have me in an almost hypnotic state. Until he pushes my body up against the chilled, floor-to-ceiling glass in front of me.

My fear comes back, but before I can move, D is there. He gently nudges my legs open with his foot before reaching between them again, this time from the back. Starting at my clit, he massages my worries away as I remain against the glass, *nine-hundred feet in the air.*

"I'm going to fuck you up against this glass, Carley." I squish my cheek against the cold surface so I'm not looking straight down. D lightly brushes my hair away from my neck and plants kisses there. He moves his hand around to the front of my body and finds my clit again, gently circling it. "Concentrate on your pleasure. Mix that with the adrenaline from your fear of heights, and you're in for one hell of a ride."

Before his words even sink in, he thrusts into me from behind and doesn't stop until he's rooted inside of me. A gasp escapes my throat as I take in the pleasure I feel. I've wanted him inside of me again for so long.

Now that he is, I never want this moment to end.

CHAPTER SEVENTEEN

Dimos

THIS IS what I've been craving for far too long. Not a lot about us makes sense right now. She's only twenty-five, fifteen years younger than me. She's my assistant. The whole cheating thing is hanging over my head, reminding me I'm the type of person she hates. But *none* of that matters right now because when we're together—*especially when I am balls deep inside of her*—everything feels right in the world.

"Oh my god, D ..." she pants as my body crashes into hers from behind.

"Tell me, Carley. Does it feel good?"

"If feels ... *So. Fucking. Good.*"

"Are you afraid? Do you want me to stop fucking you up against the window?" I goad her.

"No, *god.* No, please don't stop, D."

I drill into her harder until we're both about to come, and that's when I stop. I don't want this to end yet.

"*No,*" she whines when I pull out of her.

"Don't worry, *théa*, I'm far from done with you," I whisper into her ear.

Taking her by the hand, I lead her over to the sofa. Helping her up onto the back of it, I lay her down across the thick stretch of black leather, just like I did in Greece. I want to bring some of that night back to us, here and now. I push through her but don't move yet. I want to keep her on the brink until I start moving inside of her again. Then I look down at her, and I utter the same words I did that evening.

"*I théa mou einai akoma pio omorfi apo oti boursa pote na fadasto.*"

Her pupils dilate as I slowly circle my hips, wiggling myself inside of her.

"Do you remember me saying that to you that night in Greece, *théa?*"

Nodding her head, it makes me happy that she can recall the events of that night as well as I can.

"My goddess is even more beautiful than I could have ever imagined. It was true then, and it's even more true now. I didn't think you'd ever look more striking than you did that night, but there isn't a dress in this world that can hold a candle to the sight of you naked and laid out for me to devour."

"Devour me, D," she pleads in a voice strangled by lust.

I pull back and thrust deep inside of her again, forcing a pleasurable cry from her lips. Harder and harder, I drill into her. I plan to make love to her tonight, but right now? This is about reclaiming what I lost, marking her as my own, and reminding her of everything she left behind in the hope she'll never want to leave me again.

"How are your drunken noodles?" I ask her.

We're lounging on a blanket on the floor in front of the main window in my great room—the same window I fucked her up against. After we both came, I took Carley into the shower in my room, and we cleaned one another off. I called Izaak and had him pick up some things she will need while she's here. Toothbrush, toothpaste ... more underwear for me to rip from her body.

I also called over to Bloomingdales and requested they send over a couple casual outfits for her to wear. Not while she's here, of course—I'm thinking of instituting a no-clothing rule—but she will need something to travel home in.

"So good, I'm famished." She smiles at me, and my entire body warms in the heat of her stare. "How is your pho? I've never had that before."

"Why don't you come over here and have a taste?"

She doesn't miss a beat—*or my lewd innuendo*—and her reaction to my indecent proposal couldn't be more arousing. My cock jumps to attention beneath my black boxer briefs as she pulls herself up onto all fours and crawls the short distance to where I'm sitting.

She insisted on wearing one of my dress shirts when we got out of the shower, despite my objection. I have to say, though, the way it came down just to the curve of her ass once she put it on is pure perfection. She only has a couple of buttons secured in place, and as gravity grips the fabric and pulls it toward the ground, I can see all the way through her cleavage to that sweet spot between her legs.

She hits me with a sultry stare as she stalks toward me like a wild animal on the hunt.

"*Léaina...*" I pant.

"You know, one of these days I'm going to make you translate all of these wonderful things you're saying to me."

"I called you a lioness. The way you're prowling over here, like you're ready to pounce."

"I *am* ready to pounce, D."

A hunger flashes in her eyes, but just when I'm about to put my food down and give her what she's looking for, she speaks again.

"Because I really, *really* want a taste ... of your soup."

I can feel the features of my face fall at her words as a storm brews beneath my body's surface. I've been teased before by both Emma and Kati.

They were vicious in their teasing, though, and used it to both shame and manipulate me.

If I didn't agree with Emma about something, she would flaunt herself in front of me for days, denying each and every advance I made toward her. When, and only when, I finally caved in did she allow me to touch her, to fuck her. The entire time, she would tell me how much of a pervert I was. That it was shameful how I was unable to restrain myself and my desires, and how easy it was for her to control me with her body.

It was the same with Kati. She would use Emma and the way I was being treated against me. I would stupidly open up to Kati about it, and she would turn around and tell me she would never control me like that. I felt weak and less of a man throughout my marriage because I let Emma walk all over me. Kati made me feel strong again, but she was the one with all the power.

But the way Carley is acting right now, it's different. *She's* different. When I look into her eyes, I see the same desire I feel for her shining through. It's not controlling. It's not manipulative. It's simply a passionate fervor we share for one another. I can feel a low growl beginning deep in the back of my throat before the sound actually hits my ears.

Let's play, léaina.

"Carley." She stops crawling, and the look on her face goes from seductive to nervous. "You're making me feel things that leave me fighting for control over my own body. I'm going to give you a three second head start before I come after you. I suggest you run, because I won't be able to stop myself from ravaging you once I start. And I can't be held accountable for what kind of shape you're in when I'm done."

She's frozen in place. Unsure of whether to run or even if she's able to.

"Or you can stay put and give up easily. Either way, I can't fight the savage urge soaring through me that wants to hunt you down and eat you alive."

Her eyes shoot between mine, and I know she's having a hard time choosing which she wants to happen more.

"Three."

Her eyes widen as I begin my countdown, and she realizes how serious I really am.

"Two."

She sits back on her heels, and I think she's decided to stay put in hopes of dealing with a gentler version of me.

"One."

Her eyes appear content with her decision until they shift toward the hallway that leads to the rest of my penthouse. Suddenly, she jumps up from the floor and takes off running. I reach out for her ankle as she leaps over our dinner. My fingers flirt with her skin, but I'm unable to grasp onto her.

I give her one more second to get to where she's going before I stand and stalk through my house, searching for my prize. I stop and listen to see if I can hear anything, any small noise that will give away her position. Her footsteps didn't last long before they quieted, so the first room I decide to check is the primary suite. It's the first door on the right headed down the hall toward my front door.

Turning on my bathroom light, I peek my head in quickly but don't see her. There's nowhere to hide here so I don't waste a lot of time looking. I turn the light back off and walk farther into my room. If I go straight, I'll enter my closet and dressing area, but I decide to make a left and search the bedroom first. I check both sides of my king-sized bed. Then I look under it, but she's not there. I can see straight through to the chaise on the other side of my bed, and she isn't there, either.

Standing up again, I slowly walk into my dressing area. There is a rectangular dresser in the middle of the space, and my walk-in closet is to the right. I peer over the dresser as much as I can before walking into the closet. When I'm busy checking in between my hanging clothes, I hear her dart out from behind the dresser and flee the room.

She turns right, away from the great room, and makes a sudden left, sprinting through the kitchen. She chances a look back, which allows me to gain a little speed on her, and she squeals in fright, but she has a grin on her face from ear to ear. She runs through the dining room, turning left down the main hallway again, but this time she runs past my room and farther down the hall, into the bedroom where I laid her down to sleep last Friday night.

Perfect.

I enter the room moments after her, and I see her standing at the foot of the bed, panting from overexertion.

Or lust.

My body crashes into hers. There's nothing gentle about the way I lift her and throw her onto the bed, but I warned her my animalistic side was coming out to play. I quickly remove my boxer briefs and crawl on top of her. She lets out a small yelp as I straddle her, pinning her arms to her sides with my knees.

In what's turning out to be my signature move, I rip her shirt open, buttons fly through the air in all directions. My fingers lock onto her pert, pink nipples, and I give them a tug.

"*Oh ...*" she moans beneath me.

Scooting down her body, I set her arms free, and she uses them to push her upper body up off the bed.

"D," she pants.

But I don't answer her. I push her back down onto the mattress before pulling her legs apart and reaching my hand in between them to make sure she's good and wet. When I feel her arousal coating my fingers, I lift them to my lips and lick her stickiness from them. Lining my dick up with her entrance, I push myself through hard and fast, forcing a cry from her. I notice a lone tear cascading from the corner of her eye, and it halts my movements immediately. I lean over her and wipe the tear away with my thumb.

"Did I hurt you, *théa?*"

"No. It's just *so* much. It feels so good. Please don't stop."

I shoot her a wicked grin before sitting up again. Gripping her legs hard, I rocket into her over and over again.

"Oh, *fuck!*" she cries, and I feel her muscles contract around my cock.

"Are you coming, Carley?"

She can't speak, but the way she's gripping the blanket beneath her, like she's desperately holding on for dear life, tells me. I move inside of her until the wave she's riding has finished crashing down on her. Pulling out, I flip her over onto her stomach quickly. Tugging on her hips, I pull her ass up into the air. Holding back only a little, I smack her perfect, round ass, and she yelps as I watch her tan skin grow pink where my palm landed.

Then I dive back inside of her, pounding away with reckless abandon. There's no way she won't be sore after this. I can't wait to watch her walk through the halls of my penthouse, stark naked and limping from the onslaught of my dick.

Time barely passes before she's moaning again. This time, as soon as she clenches around me, I pull out of her, allowing her arousal to run down both of our legs. I might need a new mattress when all is said and done here tonight, but it will be money well spent.

Without giving her time to recover after that last orgasm, I'm back inside of her. This time, I don't stop until I'm ready to come. I don't want to drag this out like I did earlier. There will be many opportunities for us to take things slow this weekend, but this isn't going to be one of them.

I thrust into her through one more orgasm, never stopping to let her catch her breath. When I feel my own orgasm building, it only spurs me on. Driving into her faster than before, she screams her release into the mattress. I don't stop until every ounce of cum has left my balls, and I'm completely and utterly spent.

CHAPTER EIGHTEEN

Carley

HE SNATCHES me up as I run like hell to get away from him. The fire in his eyes makes me nervous, but his touch calms me. Spinning me around, he bends me over and thrusts into me. The pleasure he's delivering is like nothing I've ever felt before...

My eyes open slowly as I'm pulled from my current, delicious sex dream starring Dimos Anastos. It's still dark in the room where he fucked me earlier. After he came, we both collapsed onto the bed and passed out. I really need to buy D some clocks. I hate not knowing what time it is.

I hear ringing echoing through the hallway outside of the bedroom. That must have been what woke me. D's heavy arm is holding me close to him and keeping me from being able to scoot off the bed with ease. Carefully, I lift it and place it onto the mattress before I slowly roll away from him.

I'm still naked, and it makes me a little uncomfortable. But I tell myself there is no one else here and not to worry about it. I think this is something I will need to get used to if I'm going to be spending more time with D. I walk out into the hallway, and I realize the ringing is coming from my purse which is still sitting on the table in the entryway of the penthouse.

Shit. What time is it?

I grab it and walk quickly to the great room so I don't wake up D. The ringing stops as I spot our now cold dinner still sitting on the blanket on the floor. I rifle through my bag, finally latching onto my phone, and my stomach drops when I look at the screen.

Shit. It's nearly midnight, and I have eight missed calls from Saylor. How did I miss her calling me eight times?

Uhh ... the running through the penthouse? The feral way in which D wrung every drop of moisture from your body and hung you out to dry?

Yeah, that'll do it.

She's going to kill me. I told her I'd be home in time for dinner tonight. I don't think she'll care that I missed it, but she'll be livid for making her worry. I can't talk to her yet, I'm too nervous. I know she's going to give me an earful. I don't want to listen to her messages either, but at least that way I'll get an idea of her mood before I call her back.

Pulling up my voicemail, I see she's only left three messages. I pull the throw off the back of D's sofa and wrap myself in it, then I take a seat. Clicking on the earliest message, from six o'clock this evening, I hold the phone up to my ear and prepare for Saylor's wrath.

"Hey, biatch. It's about six o'clock, and you aren't home yet. I tried calling your office, but you didn't answer there, either. Maybe you left late and took the subway, for some god-awful reason, and you don't have service. Anyway, I just wanted to make sure you were still going to be here for dinner tonight? Ren is making his specialty: tossed salad."

"Don't tell her that!"

I hear Ren yell from the background. Saylor laughs just before the recording cuts out.

There are two more missed calls between six-thirty and eight o'clock. The first of which must have come through when we were in the shower. Then, another message at eight-fifteen which was well after we were into our surprisingly arousing game of cat and mouse.

"Umm, okay, so I'm trying not to freak out. Ren said you probably went out for happy hour with your office people. Which is great, I hope that's where you are. It's just really unlike you not to call or text if you're going to be late. Please, when you get this, just let me know you're safe. I love you, jerk face."

I smile at the nickname Saylor uses because it's one I haven't heard since we were in eighth grade. We had gotten into a tiff about something I can't even remember—Saylor would know, though. One afternoon, she came to my house, and when I opened the door, she was standing there with a plate of cookies.

"I'm sorry, and I love you, jerk face," was all she had to say, and we made up then and there. I remember it like it was yesterday.

The last message from her was just before this most recent missed call. She's pissed, and I can't say I blame her. Usually, the tables are turned, and I'm the one freaking out when she goes missing.

"You'd better be dead when I find you. If not, I'm going to kill you myself."

Another message came through as I was listening to the last one. I'm scared to listen to it, but I do it anyway.

"Carley, I'm sorry, I really hope you're not dead. Please, please, please call me, and let me know you're okay."

She's bawling her eyes out, and I feel like the worst person in the entire world. I get out of my messages and pull up my missed calls. Clicking on Saylor's name, the phone barely rings before she answers.

"Carley?" she screams into the receiver.

"Hey," I speak quietly, not wanting to wake D up.

"Are you okay? Why are you whispering?"

"I'm fine. I'm so sorry I didn't call. I've been ... occupied."

The line goes silent.

"If you're about to tell me you haven't called because you've been getting laid for the past *six* hours ... then I may be able to forgive you. If it's anything other than that, then I'm still mad."

"I've been getting laid for the past six hours."

A shrill scream sounds through the phone, and I pull it away from my ear before I go deaf.

"So wait. Why are you whispering?"

"D is asleep. I just woke up when I heard my phone ringing. Saylor ... *Oh. My. God.* What we did tonight makes what we did in Greece feel like child's play."

"Spill!" she demands.

"Okay, but just the gist. We can get into more details when I see you on Sunday."

"Wait. Sunday?"

"D wants me to stay with him all weekend. Including tomorrow. He told everyone I'm taking a vacation day and he's going to work from home."

I had plans with Saylor initially this weekend. With me starting this job, it's been a while since we've been able to spend the entire day together like we used to. So I'd told her we could do lunch and shopping on Saturday.

"I'm sorry, I know we were going to go out." My whisper has risen slightly. "This was completely unplanned, though. D is kind of ... persuasive, if you know what I mean."

"Yeah, I think I have an idea." There is a sadness in her tone that kills me.

"But next weekend, I'm all yours," I promise her.

"You better be. Also, we're heading to 2-1-2 tomorrow night for drinks and then maybe a club after that if you and *D-bag* want to tag along."

"Okay, I'm vetoing that nickname here and now. You can be mad at me all you want, but he had no idea we had plans this weekend. And I'll let you know about tomorrow. We can't exactly parade around the city together. Someone from the office might see us, and that would create a shitstorm he doesn't need right now."

I think about what happened with his former assistant.

"It wouldn't bode well for you, either. Don't think for one second you wouldn't be painted as a ladder-climbing harlot."

"No, I know. It would be bad all-around. Listen, I really am sorry. If nothing else, maybe I can slip away by myself tomorrow night for a little while."

I don't know how D would feel about that, but I don't think he's going to want to go with me, either.

"I would love that, bestie. I miss you." The smile in her voice has returned a bit, and I make a silent promise to make D understand why I need to go tomorrow.

"Me too," I pause. "Hey, I'm still pretty tired, so I am going to go back to bed, but I love you, I'm so sorry again for making you worry, and I'll hopefully see you tomorrow."

"You better. Love you, too. Good night."

I take a deep breath when the line goes dead, letting it ease my nerves a little.

"Is everything okay?"

D startles me, and I jump, turning in my seat to look at him.

"Sorry, I didn't mean to scare you." He leans over the back of the sofa and presses his lips to mine. "I woke up, and you were gone. I panicked that you'd left me again."

He circles the sofa and takes a seat next to me, yawning.

"I'm not planning on going anywhere anytime soon," I tell him as he pulls me back against him.

"I know you're not. Besides, I wouldn't let you even if you tried. I'd follow you to the bottom of the deep blue sea if I had to."

I've never been one to feel aroused by threats and the idea of being held hostage by a crazy, obsessive man. Especially not after having an *actual* stalker. But it's different with D. Even though I don't *really* know him yet, the idea that he wants me so badly is exhilarating.

He speaks again as he begins to run his fingers up and down my arm, forcing goose bumps to the surface.

"I didn't mean to listen in on your conversation, but when I came looking for you, I overheard what you said. I didn't take into consideration that you may already have plans this weekend. I'm sorry about that."

"It's okay, I can go to lunch with Saylor any time."

"I know you can. As much as I want you all to myself, I don't want to come between you two, either."

"That's sweet of you."

I lean my head back so I'm looking up at him. He peers down at me before pressing his lips to mine again.

"Where were you planning on going?"

"I don't know for sure. We were going to go shopping and have lunch somewhere. Why?"

"Just curious. And you mentioned something about tomorrow night?"

"Yeah, Saylor said her, Ren, and whoever else are going to Bar 2-1-2 and maybe to a club after that. She invited us."

"We can go if you want to go."

I sit up and turn toward him so we're face-to-face.

"Aren't you worried someone is going to see us together?"

"It's a concern, yes. But we can cross that bridge when we get to it. I don't want to miss out on anything because we need to hide what we have from anyone. I want it all with you, Carley. The last thing I want is to have an office romance. However, I can't imagine not spending all day with you again. I don't want to be that cliche, but I also don't want to leave your side."

I want to say something, but I can't speak through the big, goofy smile on my face.

"As stupid as this sounds, I think we should go all in until we get caught. If and when that time comes, then we can tell people you're quitting so we can be together."

My smile drops slightly at the thought of leaving Okeanós.

"What's wrong?" he asks me.

"It's silly, considering I was preparing for interviews with other companies when you walked through the lobby last Friday."

He hits me with a look of disapproval.

"I cancelled them, don't worry," I laugh. "I want both, too. I don't want to leave the company, but I also don't want to stop seeing you. I don't know if we're meant to be, but I'd like to see how it plays out."

Leaning forward, he pulls me in for another kiss. I can feel the heat building within me again as his tongue dances with mine.

Seriously? Haven't you had your fill yet?

When he pulls away from me, I immediately miss his lips.

"How about this? Call Saylor back and ask if you can move your girl's day to tomorrow. Enjoy the day—on me. Izaak will drive you girls wherever you want to go. Shopping, lunch. Hell, hit up the spa if you want to. I really do have to finish reviewing the semiannual report, in addition to a few other important items, so I'll do that while you're out. Go home, get ready, and I'll meet you at the bar tomorrow night."

The big, goofy grin is back on my face at his generosity and desire for me to keep my promise to Saylor.

"Are you sure?" I question.

"Well, I was going to have you *entertain me* while I work tomorrow, but there will be plenty more opportunities for that in the future."

Saliva pours into my mouth at the thought of sitting under his desk, sucking off one of the most powerful men I've ever met while he runs his empire. My eyes go wide, and my breath quickens.

"Only one stipulation." He cocks his eyebrow as the side of his mouth rises the way I like.

"Anything." I answer, biting my bottom lip flirtatiously.

"You leave with me, and we finish our naked weekend."

"Sounds perfect."

This time I move. Standing up on the sofa, I let the throw fall from my body. I don't recognize myself right now, but I'm loving everything about the girl I am when I'm with D. I'm in love with the look that materializes on his face when I straddle him and kneel down over his lap. Reaching beneath me, I wrap my fist around his dick and line it up with my entrance. His hands immediately land on my breasts, his thumbs already rubbing over my pebbled nipples.

"I need you again, D."

"You have me, *théa*. You have *all* of me."

Gently, I lower myself down, letting his dick fill me once again. It hurts. He's rubbed me raw inside from all our activity today, but I love every twinge of pain.

It reminds me of his passion for me.

It tells me what we have is real.

It obliterates any doubt I had about Dimos, and I am ready to give *all* of myself to him in return.

CHAPTER NINETEEN
Carley

THIS MIGHT BE THE BEST GIRLS' day Saylor and I have ever had. Made perfect mostly by D, and it has nothing to do with the fact that he's footing the bill. The confidence I have when I am with him hasn't wavered once since I left him this morning to pick up Saylor. Even she can sense the difference.

"If you don't get that dress, I'm going to smack you."

I smile at Saylor's threat as I twirl around in front of the large mirror outside of the dressing rooms of Alexander McQueen on Madison Avenue. I found a very short, very tight, red cocktail dress adorned with intricate beadwork.

It's sexy, it's not something I would normally wear, and D is going to die when he sees me in it.

"Oh, I'm *totally* getting this dress. I think I'll wear it tonight, too."

"Who are you, and what have you done with my conservative, stick-in-the-mud best friend?"

I stop staring at myself and turn to face her.

"I have no idea. I thought I left her back in Greece. Being with D again, I feel like he has awoken this primal seductress inside of me. I'm telling you, Say. I think he's good for me."

"I'll say," she smiles, but it doesn't reach her eyes.

"What?" I urge her to tell me what she's not saying.

"I don't know," she shrugs. "Don't get me wrong, I like this version of you. She doesn't have a stick up her ass, but I don't want you to change everything for this guy. You've *known* of each other for over a month, yes, but you still don't *know* him."

"No, you're right. I don't want to change who I am because of D, and I'm not. I promise. Not fully anyway. I do like that I feel more relaxed around him. It's nice giving someone else control for once."

"You're right about that. Ren is quiet on the surface, but he's completely *take-charge* in the bedroom, and let me just say, *c'est manifique*."

She finishes her thought by kissing her fingertips, like a chef might do when they nail the flavor of their dish.

"Really? I never would have thought that. I know I've only spoken to him a handful of times, but he seems so ... introverted."

"It threw me for a loop at first, too. But yeah, he's surprisingly domineering, telling me which position he wants me in, talking dirty with me ... damn. I need to stop or else I'll have to cut our day short to go fuck his brains out."

I smile at her and realize I wouldn't be upset about that. It would allow me to go do the same.

"I'm starving," I tell her, as I unzip the dress I have on. "Where do you want to go eat?"

"What about Delray? I'm kind of in the mood for seafood, and I don't want to eat anything too heavy."

"Okay, I'll text D and let him know."

D asked that I give him a heads up of our whereabouts so he can contact each place and give them his credit card information so Saylor and I don't have to pay for anything. When I pull out my phone, I see I have another text waiting from him. He's had my number since Ez gave it to him, but he finally gave me his in return this morning. We've been texting back and forth all morning, sending crude messages and talking about how much we miss one another.

DIMOS

Feel free to send me a picture or two of the outfits you're buying. Or one while you're undressed ... in front of the mirror ... hand between your legs ...

My cheeks heat, and my clit starts throbbing again.

ME

You're making it harder and harder to continue girls' day. I'd rather have your hand between my legs.

DIMOS

That can be arranged ...

ME

It'll have to wait until tonight, but I wouldn't mind going round two in the bathroom with you.

DIMOS

Don't tempt me. This time, there will be no stopping it, no matter how much you've had to drink.

ME

Promise?

DIMOS

Stin timi mu.

ME

I'm assuming that means yes?

DIMOS

On my honor.

ME

I'm holding you to it. In the meantime, Saylor and I are almost finished at Alexander McQueen, and we're heading to Delray for lunch.

DIMOS

Did you find something you like there?

ME

Yes, actually. A sexy little number I'm planning on wearing tonight.

DIMOS

Can I have a sneak peek?

A sly smile stretches across my face as I consider his request.

"I'm going to go change so we can pay and get out of here," I inform Saylor.

Not waiting for her response, I walk back into the dressing room and take another look at myself in the mirror. Pulling the dress up a little, I let a sliver of my baby blue thong—courtesy of D's clothing delivery—show. I flip my phone around and point it at the fabric between my legs, making sure to get just a hint of the dress fabric in, too.

I pull the pic up from my library and make sure it looks okay. You can see a lot of the dress from the angle I took it at, so I crop most of it out, making sure D will still be able to identify what he's looking at. Then I send it off to him in another text message.

ME

Until tonight ...

I don't wait for him to respond before tossing my phone back into my purse and slipping out of the dress. Once I'm fully clothed again, I walk out into the store.

"All set?" Saylor asks.

"Yes, let's go eat. I'm starving."

DIMOS

I'm pulling up out front now.

ME

I can't wait to see you.

DIMOS

You too, théa.

"Is he here?" Saylor questions as I slip my phone back into my clutch and place it on the table in front of us.

"Yes!" I squeal. "I can't wait for him to see me in this dress."

"You'll be lucky if you make it out of here without him tearing it off of you."

"Seriously, though. What's up with that? I'm not going to say I don't like it, but at the rate he's going, I'm going to run out of clothing."

I take a sip of my drink and watch as Ren places his arm around Saylor. I'm really happy for them. Saylor deserves a nice guy for once.

"Ren, do you like to do that?" I ask him to get a guy's perspective.

"Do what?"

"Rip Saylor's clothes off in the heat of passion?" I giggle.

His eyes dilate slightly, and I can tell he's thinking about it. He turns away to hide his reaction but re-enters the conversation pretty smoothly.

"There's never any time. You know how quickly she can strip out of her clothing."

"Touché, Ren," I laugh. "Touché."

"Hey, don't hate. You've never complained about the rate at which I get naked for you."

Suddenly, my eyes catch sight of someone across the room. He looks vaguely familiar, and a feeling of unease settles over me. As he turns toward me a little more, the light cascades over him, and I see his full face.

Oh, fuck.

My hand flies to Saylor's, and I squeeze it hard from freight the moment his eyes lock on mine.

"Oh my god, Saylor. We need to get out of here right now."

"Why? What—"

"*Théa.*"

D's husky, lustful voice breaks my concentration on the man across the room. When I look at him, he catches the fear in my eyes, and his bewitched stare turns lucid.

"What's the matter?"

He squats in front of me and cups my cheek in his hand. I want to feel the immediate relief he usually brings me, but I can't.

"She's white as a ghost," I hear D tell Saylor. "Did she drink something?"

Unable to concentrate on D, I gaze out into the crowd of people so I can get another look at the man. Maybe it was my eyes playing tricks on me. Maybe it wasn't him at all.

"Carley? What is it?" Saylor asks, everyone now looking in the direction that I was.

But he isn't there anymore.

"I could have sworn ..."

"What's the matter, *théa*? Excuse me." D gets the attention of a nearby cocktail waitress. "Can you please bring her some water immediately?"

"Yes, sir," she complies.

"I'm sorry, I thought I saw him."

"Who?" Saylor and D inquire at the same time.

"Blaine." My eyes find Saylor's as I answer, and her face turns to shock.

"Who the *fuck* is Blaine?" D demands.

"The psycho who stalked her for two years."

At that, D looks around the bar for him, even though he has no idea *who* he's looking for.

"I'm sorry, I thought it was him, but—"

Then I see him again, walking through the crowd and heading straight for me. My eyes widen in fear as Blaine gets closer. Saylor, Ren, and D all follow my gaze. D stands up and puts his arm out, stopping Blaine's forward movement.

"Get the fuck away from her," D orders him, his fists clenched and ready to strike if necessary.

Blaine puts both of his arms up and takes a step back.

"I'm not here to cause you harm. I didn't even know you were going to be here tonight. I happened to see you from across the room when you walked in, and it's taken me the past twenty minutes to gather up the courage to tell you what I need to tell you."

"Get out of here before I pound your fucking face in," D threatens.

"I'm in therapy, Carley," Blaine says, ignoring D. I knew he wasn't bright, but he's downright stupid to ignore D, looking as furious as he does right now. "I've learned a lot about why I was the way I was, and I just wanted to come and say I'm sorry. I—it's part of the twelve step program. To make amends. That's all I'm trying to do."

"You've said it, now *go*." D commands him.

"I'm leaving," he backs away some more. "I'm sorry, Carley. For everything."

I don't look at him as he walks away. I'm fighting to keep the tears at bay. I don't want to make any more of a scene than Blaine just did. But I need to get out of here. Once he's gone, D squats down in front of me again.

"Are you okay?" he questions.

"No. Get me out of here," I mutter, trembling.

D takes his sport coat off and lays it over my shoulders as he speaks to Saylor.

"You're welcome to leave with us, and Izaak can take you home after he drops us off."

"Let's do that, Say. I don't really feel like hanging out anymore," Ren chimes in.

"Yeah, of course. Let's get out of here," Saylor agrees.

The four of us ride to D's penthouse in complete silence. When Izaak stops the limo outside of the building, Saylor grabs me in a hug and gives me a big kiss on the cheek.

"Are you sure you're okay?"

"Yes, I'm feeling a little better already. I just needed to get out of there. I'll be okay."

"Okay, but call me if you need anything," Saylor insists.

"Will do. Love you."

"Love you, too."

D grabs my hand as Izaak closes the car door behind me. Silently, we walk across the lobby and get into an awaiting elevator. D scans his access card, and we begin the climb to his penthouse.

"Are you sure you're okay?"

"I'm sure. Like I told you, he never hurt me before. He just gives me the creeps, and seeing him brought up some unpleasant history, that's all."

"I'm really sorry I wasn't there sooner." He runs the backs of his strong fingers across my cheek, soothing me.

"You're fine. You were there, you kept him away from me. You were perfect."

"I'm far from perfect. Do you know how badly I wanted to punch that motherfucker in the face?"

"You're so good to me. Thank you for everything today. Saylor and I had a great time."

"You have no idea how much it means to me to hear you say that."

He leans in for a kiss, which I return with a little less passion than normal.

"How about this? When we get inside, I'll run you a bath. Then we can pop some popcorn and watch a movie. Just take it easy. Does that sound good to you?"

"That sounds wonderful," I admit, completely enamored at the fact that D knows exactly what I need right now.

D wraps his arms around me and holds me tight the rest of the ride to his floor. When we get inside, we do everything he said we were going to do.

After that we went to bed.

Where he held me, safely in his arms, all night long.

CHAPTER TWENTY

Dimos

While Carley was in the bath, I texted Izaak and asked that he tell Saylor to message me. I was planning on looking into this *Blaine* eventually, but that's when I thought he was no longer a threat. Now that he's made contact with her again, it's time to move him to the top of my to-do list.

I'm even more pissed because I made a promise to myself to tell Carley about Emma tonight, before our weekend went any further. But I can't bring it up now. The last thing Carley needs is another bomb to go off and more stress added to her plate.

While waiting for a response, I change out of my dress clothes and into a pair of gray sweatpants. I was hoping Saylor would text me before Carley got out, but I hear the water draining out of the tub, and there's been no message from her.

I watch as my *théa* walks out of my bathroom, wrapped up in a towel. I ache to see her, to touch her, but this isn't the time. I'm livid the little prick ruined her night. From the texts I'd gotten throughout the day, it seemed like the girls were having an incredible time.

Then, when I walked into the bar and saw her in that fucking dress...

O, thee mu. Oh my god.

It was all I could do to keep myself from dragging her into the bathroom or the back of my limo and having my way with her. She was stunning. Even more so than in the black number she had on in Greece.

But the fear I saw in her face when she spotted him nearly gutted me. I'll do whatever it takes to make sure I never see that look on her face again.

"How was your bath, *théa*?"

"It was really nice, thank you. Those oils you used, what were they?"

"It's a blend of olive oil, lavender, and almond."

"It smells wonderful, and my skin feels like it just got a body polish."

She sidles up to me and leans into my chest. My heart warms as I wrap her in my arms. It feels like they were made to hold her close. I rub my hand over her back reassuringly.

"You're safe here, *théa*," I ensure her softly as I lay a kiss on the crown of her head.

"I know," she whispers.

"Here." Taking her by the hand, I lead her into my dressing area. I grab an undershirt from my drawer and hand it to her. "You can wear this until we get you some pajamas to keep here."

"Thank you, D. For everything."

I give her a wink.

"Go ahead and get dressed. I'll start on the popcorn."

She smiles sweetly before I turn away from her and leave the room. I feel my phone vibrate in my pocket, and I pull it out to see an unknown number has sent me a message.

212-555-9187

Hey, it's Saylor. Lurch said you wanted me to text you.
Is Carley okay?

ME

Lurch? Yes, Carley is fine.

212-555-9187

Your tall-ass driver. He's giving off serious creepy, silent
guy vibes.

ME

Oh. He's harmless. Did you guys make it home okay?

While I wait for her next reply, I add her number to my contact list.

SAYLOR

Yes, thank you for the ride. What did you need?

ME

I wanted to get some more information on this Blaine
asshole, but I didn't want to involve Carley in it. Do you
know his last name or anything else about him?

I watch as three dots appear as she types out her response. They stay there, blinking over and over for several minutes, so I put my phone back in my pocket and start the popcorn. When it's all finished and my penthouse smells like a movie theater, I take the bowl and some water out to the great room and place it on the coffee table in front of the sofa.

I get a brief flash of taking Carley on the back of the sofa last night, and it causes my dick to twitch. Before I allow myself to reminisce about it too much, my phone vibrates in my pocket again.

SAYLOR

His name is Blaine Markson. Carley met him at a bar
about two years ago. He seemed normal at first, but
Carley wasn't into him enough to want to pursue
anything further. After that night, they kept "bumping
into one another." But really, he had looked her up, got
ahold of our address, her school schedule, where she
worked. He tried to convince her it was fate that they
kept meeting and that she should give him a shot. She
was too nice to him and continued letting him down
gently.

I suddenly feel even worse about accusing her of working for me with the
intent of blackmailing me. If this is the reason she gives random guys a fake
name, I don't blame her one bit.

I'm such a fucking dickhead.

SAYLOR

Finally, I told her he was never going to get the hint if
she wasn't firm with him. When she finally told him
enough was enough, he went crazy. Trashed the coffee
shop they were in. Cops were called, etc. After that, he
would call us and hang up all the time. Then he started
showing up at our apartment. He would wait out front of
our building for Carley to come or go. He showed up in
a few of her classes. He never really did anything, just
stood around, being creepy as fuck. Until he somehow
broke in and ended up spending the night in Carley's
closet. She didn't realize he was there until the next
morning when she went to get dressed.

ME

Jesus. She didn't mention that.

I'm so furious I could kill someone. Now I really wish I had punched that
asshole back at the bar.

SAYLOR

We moved after that, and Carley got a restraining order.
She even got a new job, but he still found us. Finally,
she went to work for her father so he could keep a close
eye on her. We moved again, but we didn't put her
name on the lease this time. We hoped that would make
it harder for him to find her. We got a call from a
detective about a month after our second move. He told
us Blaine had been arrested on charges unrelated to
Carley's order of protection.

SAYLOR

I guess he's out now …

Yeah, I guess so.

ME

Thank you for the info. I'm going to get a guy on him. I
don't trust that he won't try anything again.

SAYLOR

Ren works for a security company. He is going to install
an expensive home security system in the apartment
for us.

That makes me feel a little better. Although they don't deter some people like they should. I don't believe for one second this psychopath has turned over a new leaf. And I don't believe he was at that bar tonight by chance.

ME

Does Ren's company do any sort of cell phone tracing?
Anything where we can hack into this shithead's phone
and see what he's up to?

ME

Also, I've been in the market for a security system for
my new place. I'd like to interview Ren and see what
packages his company offers. Can you give him my
number and have him call me next week to set up an
appointment?

SAYLOR

Sure. Ren said he can't legally hack into his cell phone
…

I recognize that Saylor is hinting toward Ren being able to hack it illegally. Before I pursue that avenue, I change my mind. I can get a PI to do it, and that will alleviate any risk of Ren getting caught.

ME

Okay. Don't worry about it. I'll talk to Ren next week.
Thanks Saylor.

SAYLOR

Back atcha, Zeus.

I stare at the screen and can't stop a hint of a smile at the nickname. I don't know whether to be flattered or offended.

"I hope you don't mind," Carley breaks my concentration. "My feet were cold, so I went looking for a pair of socks."

As she comes around the edge of the couch in nothing more than my white t-shirt, a pair of pink underwear, and white crew socks, I realize it's going to be even harder than I thought to keep my hands off her tonight.

"Of course not. My socks are your socks."

She giggles before climbing onto the sofa and curling her body next to mine.

"What would you like to watch?" I inquire.

"It honestly doesn't matter," she yawns. "The bath kind of took a lot out of me. I don't know how long I'll last."

I run my hand up and down her arm, consoling her once again. She knows it's the shock of tonight's events that are making her tired. She's trying to minimize its effect on her by blaming it on the bath. I know she's doing it for my benefit, and as much as I don't want her to ever have to feel that way, I admire her wanting to set my mind at ease.

THE REST OF THE WEEKEND WAS PURE BLISS. WE NEVER LEFT THE PENTHOUSE. We watched movies. She introduced me to the *Pitch Perfect* franchise. That's not something I thought I'd ever see in my lifetime, but I actually found myself tapping my foot and nodding along to the acapella beats.

I sent Izaak on a field trip to the toy store, and he came back with some board games and a few decks of cards, which ultimately ended with us playing strip poker. We even turned Yahtzee into a lively game of dirty dice.

I was *almost* excited when Carley would put clothes back on, because I knew taking them off again was going to be even more enjoyable than the last. I can't remember a time when I was more engrossed in what was going on around me than I was with making sure my company was still running smoothly. It was incredible not to touch my cell phone, check my work email, or even think about Okeanós for an entire forty-eight hours.

There was no shortage of fun and excitement with Carley under my roof. Unfortunately, it's already Sunday afternoon, and she's getting ready to leave. Izaak just pulled the car around, and I'm trying my best to pretend like I don't want to beg her to stay forever.

"I'm going to miss you, D."

Carley has her arms wrapped around my neck as I hold her body close to mine.

"I already miss you, *théa*. I'll see you at work tomorrow, okay?"

"Okay," she smiles sweetly, and I lean in for a kiss.

"Text me when you get home so I know you're safe."

"I will. Promise."

"*Antio, agapi mia.*" *Goodbye, my love.*

Biting her bottom lip, she leans into the car and takes her seat. I stare at her with longing as I close her in. Taking a deep breath, I tap on the roof of the car, signaling to Izaak that he's free to drive away. As he pulls out onto Spruce Street, I'm already fantasizing about when I'll see her again. I debate firing her the moment she gets off the elevator tomorrow morning, just so I can fuck her on my desk. As visions of her, skin flushed, eyes dilated, me thrusting in and out fill my head, I'm interrupted by my cell phone vibrating in my pocket.

It's from a local number I don't recognize, so I let it go to voicemail. By the time I make it back upstairs, I have a message from Ren wanting to figure out a time to meet up and talk about the security system for my penthouse. I call him back immediately.

"Ren, hi. Thanks for calling."

"Hello Mr. Anastos—"

"Please, call me D."

"D. Saylor told me you're interested in a security system for your home?"

"Yeah, when can you come by to take a look and so we can discuss plan options?"

"I'm booked all of this week, but I'm sure after what happened the other night you're anxious to get something in place soon. I can come over this evening to show you what we offer, and if you're interested, I can work on the installation outside of my normal work hours this week."

"That would be fantastic. I'll pay you extra for overtime. Whatever the cost."

"Great. I'll call you when I get to your building."

"Thanks, Ren. See you soon."

CHAPTER TWENTY-ONE

Carley

REN AND SAYLOR are snuggled on the couch watching television when I walk through the door. I think Saylor is slowly moving him into our apartment. He's here nearly every weeknight and usually every weekend, too.

"Hey!" Saylor calls.

"Hey," I answer, locking the door behind me.

I pull out my phone and open up my messages. Typing out a quick message to D, I let him know I am home.

"How was your weekend?" Saylor prompts.

"Jeez ... why don't you let her get settled before you start in with the questions?" Ren laughs, looking at Saylor as though he forgot how overbearing she can be.

"Um," Saylor's eyebrows raise with both shock and annoyance. "Because I'm not wired to wait. Duh."

"Have you met your girlfriend?" I tease.

"Good point," he points to me and clicks his tongue.

"It's fine, I'm used to it," I over exaggerate my exhale in a joking manner. "My weekend was great, but I will save the details for when Ren isn't around. I'm sure the last thing he wants to hear about is ... well ... any of it."

Saylor scoffs and rolls her eyes.

"Whatever. So Ren installed a security system while you were having naked fun all weekend."

"Really?"

A small amount of relief washes over me, hearing that we're going to have a way to monitor what goes on in our apartment when we're not around. I don't need Blaine showing up in my closet again. A chill rolls through me as I remember back to that morning.

I had just gotten out of the shower, and I was still wrapped in my towel. I grabbed my undergarments and then went to the closet to choose the outfit I was going to wear that day. The moment I opened the door, there *he* was. I was frozen in place, completely paralyzed. I couldn't even call for help. His leering stare still haunts me from time to time.

Saylor was out all night, but thankfully got home right around the time this happened. She came into my room to say good morning just as Blaine was trying to pin me down on the bed. She jumped on his back, pulled his hair, and was scratching at his face until the two of them ended up on the floor. He got up and ran off after that.

I don't know why he didn't attack me in the middle of the night when I was asleep. He had to have known Saylor wasn't there. But I don't like to question it, and I can't think about what would have happened if she hadn't gotten there when she did. I picture him standing over me as I slept, and another ice-cold chill pierces me from the inside out. I filed a police report that day, but I never heard from him after that.

Until Friday night.

"Hey, are you okay?" Ren thankfully breaks me from my inner thoughts.

"Yeah, no. I'm good. Thanks."

I'm grateful for the sincere, concerned look in his eye.

"So," Saylor interrupts, "go get settled, and then we can show you how it all works. It's pretty cool."

"Okay, I'm going to take a quick shower, and then I'll be out."

I take my purse and what's left of the clothing I was wearing on Thursday into my room. Looking around, I immediately miss being at D's place. I feel safe with him. Not that I don't feel safe here. Well, I did up until Blaine came back into the picture.

And that *apology* he offered me? No fucking way do I think it was sincere. The look in his eyes on Friday night varied greatly from the one that stared back at me that morning. He appeared almost innocent, harmless, kind of like he did the night I met him. Which is exactly why I don't trust him or believe he's changed.

Closing and locking the door to my room, I get undressed and throw all my clothes into the hamper in the bathroom. Turning the knobs in the shower, I let the water start heating up. Looking at myself in the mirror, I think about all the crazy fun I had with D the past few days. I run a hand through my hair and catch a whiff of D's cologne on my thin, chocolate strands. Holding my locks up to my nose, I inhale deeply, breathing him in and exhaling with a sigh.

I won't go so far to say that I'm in love with him. It's still too early for that. But I *can* say I'm falling.

Hard.

Into love? Lust?

Perhaps both.

I got comfy in my Wharton sweatpants and a thin T-shirt when I finished showering. I can hear Saylor telling me to, "move my ass" from the living room as I comb my hair. Rolling my eyes, I place the comb on my dresser and walk to my bedroom door.

When I open it, I come face-to-face with Ren, and I gasp loudly.

"Oh, my god you scared the shit out of me!"

"Sorry, I didn't mean to scare you. This camera needed to be adjusted a little."

He points to the upper corner of the hallway. That's when I notice a chair situated underneath a brand-new camera, installed in the ceiling. I take deep breath with my hand still on my chest as I try to control my breathing.

"It's okay. Not your fault. I'm just still a little shaken up from Friday night."

"Yeah, that ... that was weird," he mutters. "I'm sorry that happened to you."

"Thanks," I reply. "And thank you for installing these so quickly. And over the weekend? I hope you still had time to relax."

"Eh, it's okay. It helps that I like my job."

"For once, I can actually relate to that," I smile.

Work doesn't seem like work when you enjoy what you do.

Or when you're fucking your boss.

"Anyway, sorry again. If you want, I can show you how everything works now."

"That would be great, thanks."

I follow Ren as he walks the chair back into the kitchen, then he leads me to the living room.

"Jesus, finally," Saylor says from the sofa when we enter.

"Can I see the remote?" Ren asks, and Saylor hands it over.

"Okay, so when you turn on your TV, hit the 'Source' button on the remote to toggle through all the devices that are hooked up to it. You have Live TV, which is your cable. HDMI1 is your Blu-ray player. HDMI2 is going to be where you can view your security footage."

Ren clicks on HDMI2, and the screen is suddenly split into four sections. One shows the hallway outside of the door into our apartment, another shows the living room. I see the kitchen in a third square. In the last one, I can see perfectly down the hallway from the camera Ren was adjusting a moment ago.

"Wow, I didn't even notice one outside the door."

"It's small, you'd have to look really hard to see. Technically, you're not allowed to put cameras out there, but I thought it would be best for you to have one."

"Yeah, I think you're right."

"All the footage gets downloaded to a thumb drive which is plugged into the back of the TV."

"Does it record twenty-four-seven?" I ask.

"Yep."

"Won't it run out of memory quickly? Do we need to change it every so often?"

"Not very. The one I put in can hold up to two terabytes worth of data."

"Is that a lot?"

Saylor laughs out loud from the sofa, and I look over at her quizzically.

"Sorry. It's just that I asked him the same exact question when he told me that. Anyway ... continue."

"Yes, that's a lot. Since it's video, and the files are much larger, it will fill up quicker than if you were using it for pictures or documents. But still, it's ... a lot."

"Okay," I take another deep breath, slightly overwhelmed we even needed to install cameras in the first place. "Well, great. Thank you again."

"No problem." Ren offers me a kind smile before speaking again. "Well, I need to get going so I can get over to D's place."

"Wait, what?"

"*Ren!* You weren't supposed to say anything," Saylor yells.

"I thought we just weren't supposed to tell her about *the guy?*"

"No, no, no ... we're not playing that game. What's going on?"

"Look, it's nothing bad," Ren explains. "D asked Saylor to text him the other night after we left the bar. He wanted to know more about that dude who approached you."

"Yeah, it's nothing," Saylor interrupts. "I gave him a little background, and he said he has *a guy* he's going to pay to keep an eye on Blaine. That's all."

"Well, why didn't he tell me this?"

"I don't think he was trying to keep anything from you," Saylor explains. "He probably will tell you eventually, but he didn't want to hound you with upsetting questions about your psycho-stalker. He was trying to be thoughtful."

"He *is* very sweet," I gush.

"Anyway," Ren interrupts, "he asked me to come over and give him pricing for a system. I'm booked all week, so I told him I would squeeze him in tonight."

"Aww, that's so nice of you."

"Isn't he the greatest?" Saylor squeals, causing Ren to roll his eyes.

"I need to get going. You can finally have your girl talk." Ren seems eager to get out of the apartment, but I think he's just reacting to Saylor's playfully, over-enthusiastic reactions toward him.

I actually feel jealous he's going to see D right now, and I'm not.

Calm yourself, Carley.

I definitely need to take a chill pill. The last thing I want is to become a clingy girlfriend or push D away by not giving him his space.

I GOT TO WORK A LITTLE EARLY THIS MORNING. I WANTED TO GET CAUGHT UP on the things that were left sitting on Friday while I was out with Saylor. I'm certain D would tell me not to stress over it, but I don't want to fall into a bad habit of neglecting my work just because I'm dating the boss. I know if people were to find out we're sleeping together, they would think I'm doing it for advancement. I want to be able to show everyone I'm still doing my job well despite having an outside relationship with D.

When the ding of the elevator sounds, it brings a smile to my face knowing D is on the other side of the doors. It's only been a little over twelve hours, but I miss him. I miss having his eyes on me. I miss his smell. I miss being wrapped in his arms.

I miss his dick buried deep inside of me.

I swallow as the doors open revealing D, looking as dashing as ever in a tailored suit. I smile as he walks toward my desk.

"Good morning, *théa*."

"Good morning, Mr. Anastos."

His eyes flare with desire when I call him that.

"Would you meet me in my office in a minute? I'd like a word."

My face drops slightly, and anxiety creeps in. Did I do something wrong? Is D having second thoughts about being with me? Maybe it wasn't desire I thought I saw? But then why would he call me *théa*?

I give D a moment to get situated before I get up from my chair and straighten my skirt, getting out the wrinkles in the back from sitting down. I walk into his office but stop just over the threshold when I don't see him at his desk. Almost immediately, something grabs hold of my wrist and pulls me to the left of the doorway. I squeal as I'm spun around, and in seconds flat, D has my back up against the wall and his lips on mine.

"You're going to get tired of me, but I can't help it. I had to talk myself out of coming to your apartment several times since you left yesterday just so I could see you. I don't like being away from you for so long."

"I highly doubt I'll ever get tired of you, and I missed you, too. Next time you get the urge to come see me, you should do it."

"I'll keep that in mind."

He brings his lips to mine once more, and his velvet-soft tongue darts out into my mouth. The feel of it takes me back to this weekend again. The countless times he traced my body with it. I think about the *many* times it found its way between my legs. The way he flicked the tip of it against my clit.

He catches my soft moan in his mouth, and I feel his cock harden against my stomach.

"Do you know how badly I wish we were working from my penthouse today?" He tears his lips from mine. "No ... even better. I would give anything to work remotely with you for the next three months from my yacht as we sail from island to island with no clear destination in mind. I want to fuck you on every continent, Carley."

"You can do that?"

"Fuck you on every continent? You better fucking believe it," he explains, rubbing his hands up and down my ribcage.

"No, I mean work from a yacht in the middle of the ocean."

"I worked from my yacht about seventy-five percent of the time when I was still in California."

"That sounds ... incredible."

Just then, the ding of the elevator echoes through the lobby.

"I swear to God, I'll strangle whoever it is that's about to interrupt us."

D walks away quickly, as I hurry to the couch in the middle of the room. Picking up the pad of paper, I realize there's no pen or pencil around for me to pretend like I'm doing something constructive. I don't have any time to think about it, though. D begins speaking right before a knock sounds on his open office door.

"After that, I need you to—Ronald, good morning."

"Sorry, I didn't mean to interrupt," his eyes flit from me to D and back.

Shit, can he tell we were just making out? Are our lips swollen?

"Not a problem. Carley, I'll catch up with you in a little while," D says, dismissing me from his office.

I'm more than happy to leave. That was a close call, and I'm still not convinced our behavior isn't blatantly obvious to everyone around us.

I have a feeling this secret relationship of ours isn't as secret as we think it is.

CHAPTER TWENTY-TWO

Dimos

AROUND LUNCHTIME, I poke my head out of my office and watch as Carley works away at her computer. I love the way she's concentrating on the words on her screen, pen between her teeth, her left leg tucked under her body on her chair.

"You know, that posture will lead to back and neck problems," I inform her. "But I'll have no issue rubbing your sore muscles later. Stay the night with me again, Carley."

She drops the pen from her mouth as her head snaps toward me, and she bites that bottom lip of hers the way she always does. It has my cock at attention in no time.

"I'm going to need you to stop doing that at times when I can't act on my desires, *théa.*"

When a look of confusion appears on her pretty face, I explain.

"When you bite your lip like that, it makes my dick hard." I feel my nostrils flare as she immediately releases her bottom lip from the clutches of her pearly white teeth.

"Sorry," she smiles, but her smirk tells me she isn't fully apologetic.

And I'm glad.

It means that girl from Greece I spent all weekend luring out of her hasn't retreated back into the confines of her mind.

"What are you in the mood for?"

I realize immediately I didn't phrase my question the way I'd intended to. I can see the desire pool in her eyes as she silently tells me exactly what she's in the mood for at the moment.

"For lunch, you horny lech," my half smile crinkles the corner of my eye.

She recovers quickly, too quickly.

"I knew what you meant," she winks. "I don't know. I've kind of been craving

Asian food ever since our dinner was disrupted by your predilection for hunting your prey last Thursday night.

I wipe a hand down my face, recalling chasing her around my penthouse.

"Yes, a game I'm looking forward to playing again very soon. Asian it is. Anything in particular?"

"You know what I like."

With that, she goes back to biting her lip, and I have to remind myself we're in view of the lobby camera. My eyes bore into hers before I pivot and stalk back into my office. Grabbing my phone from my desktop, I see a missed call notification flashing on my screen, and it's like a splash of ice-cold water on my libido.

Emma. What the hell does she want?

I don't have anything to say to her, and my alimony checks arrive on time. There's no reason why she should be calling.

I clear the notification and check my voicemail, but she hasn't left a message. Maybe she called by accident?

Wishful thinking.

I take a deep breath and try to forget I had a missed call in the first place before she completely ruins my day.

I pull up the app for the food delivery service I usually use, then I order the same two items we got on Thursday night, drunken noodles and pho. She never did get to sample a taste.

I was too busy tasting her.

WE ENJOYED A PLEASANT LUNCH WITH ONE ANOTHER. CARLEY FINALLY GOT to sample my pho, which she loved. The delightful sound she made the moment the broth hit her taste buds had me ready to pounce. Just as we finish cleaning up, I hear the elevator signal the arrival of someone on our floor.

"*Damn*," I exclaim. "Who the hell is that, interrupting us before I've gotten my dessert?"

I cock an eyebrow at her and she gets my meaning immediately.

"Perhaps we can have dessert after you chase whoever that is away?" she suggests, and I would like nothing more.

We head out to the lobby, and I see the young man from the mailroom halfway across the large space as I approach the trash can. I cast a sideways glance at him as he places the mail on the ledge of Carley's desk.

"Hey, Carley," he smiles at her, and it makes me want to rip his throat out.

"Hi, Sid, how are you today?"

She regards him sweetly and casually looks over at me. I know the moment she notices my reaction because the smile melts off her face. Without missing a beat, she turns her attention back to *Sid* and picks up the stack of mail he left.

"Good, thanks. Enjoy the rest of your day."

"You too," she offers as she takes her seat.

I don't move until *Sid* is back in the elevator and out of sight.

"A friend of yours?" I inquire.

"No, not really."

Carley grabs her water bottle from her desk and takes a sip.

"Why? You jealous?" she challenges when she's finished drinking.

Balling my hand into a fist, I squeeze it tightly as the need to claim her begins to take over. She smiles from ear-to-ear as she flips through the stack of envelopes that was delivered. The skin on her forehead puckers as she regards one in particular. She opens the envelope carefully as I get closer to her desk.

As she pulls the letter out and unfolds it, I notice bold lines shining through the other side of the paper, illuminated by the light overhead. Her eyes grow wide, and she turns white as a ghost which causes me to quicken my pace.

"What's wrong? What is that?"

She doesn't answer me, and she doesn't hand it over, either. She just sits there, trembling, frozen in fear. Tearing it from her hands, I read the note written in scraggly handwriting:

I CANT WAIT TO SEE YOU AGAIN

"What the fuck?" I pick up the envelope from Carley's desk to inspect it.

There's nothing identifying where it came from. It's blank, other than her name. No stamp, no return address at all, which means someone must have delivered it to the building by hand.

"*Fuck*." I drop to my knees in front of Carley and force her eyes on mine. "You're okay, *théa*. No one is going to set foot near you while I'm around. Do you understand?"

She barely nods.

I take a deep breath.

"I'm going to go down to the mailroom and see if I can find out where this came from."

"N—no, no. Don't leave me here, D. *Please*." The terror in her voice absolutely crushes me.

"Okay, okay. I won't leave you. Here, come into my office with me. I'll call down there instead. Okay?"

As a lone tear crawls down her cheek, she gives me a weak nod. Helping her out of her chair, I wrap my arm around her shoulders, trying to comfort her as we walk. I direct her toward the sofa in my office, and she takes a seat. Removing her shoes, she tucks her legs underneath her.

I place the letter on the table before walking to my desk to make the call. Grabbing the receiver of my phone, I punch in the extension to the mailroom. After four rings, someone finally picks up on the other end.

"Mailroom."

"This is Dimos Anastos. Who am I speaking to?"

My eyes stay locked on Carley as I speak. I'm absolutely furious this asshole is contacting her again.

"This is Ray. I'm the manager."

"Ray, Sid just delivered a stack of mail to my assistant. In it was a letter addressed to her. I need to know who it came from."

"Uh, sure ... just one second while I grab the log."

Carley finally looks up at me, and I offer her a slight smile while I wait.

"Okay, got it. What is her name?"

"Carley Garrettson."

"It says here it's from Rapid Flyers Courier Service, but that's it. No other information was provided."

Fuck.

"Does it say the date and time it came in?"

"Yeah, this morning at seven after ten."

"Thanks, Ray."

"You got it."

I place the phone back on the receiver and think. I need to get a hold of the courier company and find out if they have a record of who dropped the letter off to them.

"Carley, how long was your order of protection good for?"

"Only for one year. It expired while he was in jail."

Damn it.

"Okay, let's do this. Why don't you call Saylor and have her bring you some work clothes for tomorrow? I'd like for you to stay the night tonight. Actually, invite her to stay for dinner. Ren will be there, too."

When she looks at me with confusion, I explain why.

"I hired him to install a security system for the penthouse. He's coming over tonight to begin installation."

"Oh. Okay, good," she agrees, but when she doesn't move, I approach her.

Sitting on the sofa I wrap her in my arms, and she begins to sob.

"I thought this was all over and done with."

"I know, *théa.*"

"No, no you don't," she sits up straight and backs away from me so she can look me right in the eyes. "If Saylor hadn't stopped him ... if she hadn't come home at that moment ..."

Large, terrified tears leak from her eyelids, and it's tearing me apart. She told me he didn't hurt her. But I had no idea he'd attempted to or that he was damn near successful. I pull her to me again and wrap her in my arms. Rubbing soothing circles over her back, I repeat the same words to her that I told her on Friday night.

"You're safe with me, *théa.* I'll never let anything happen to you."

The moment I get Carley back into the safety of my penthouse, I'm putting out a call to my PI. I want to know every last detail about this motherfucker. I want to know when he got out of jail and what he's been up to since. I want to know where he lives, where he hangs out, who he talks to.

Everyfuckingthing.

And then I'm going to find him, and I'm going kill him.

CHAPTER TWENTY-THREE

Carley

I can't believe this is happening again.

I knew I was right not to trust what Blaine said on Friday night. How coincidental that we *run into* one another, much like we used to back when he first started stalking me. And now I get a letter from him. That's a new one. He never used to send letters before.

"I want to call the police," I tell D, wiping the overflowing tears from my cheeks. "Get another order of protection in place. I want to take charge and cut him off before things go too far this time. I refuse to sit around crying like a weak, scared little girl."

"It's okay to be scared, Carley. That doesn't make you weak. I think it's a great idea to get in touch with the police." D checks his watch. "Let's head out early today, okay? Get you back to my place. You can call the police from there, and they can send someone out to take your statement."

"But what if someone sees us?" I wonder.

"Fuck it. I don't care anymore." He leans in and cups my cheeks with his palms. "You are more important to me than the opinions of the people on my staff."

The warmth of his words wrap me up like a blanket and quiets my shaking. But it's short lived when I spot the letter sitting on the table in front of us. I close my eyes as D brings his lips to mine, laying a gentle kiss upon them.

When he pulls away from me, he tucks a strand of hair behind my ear and rubs my cheek reassuringly. I'm lucky to have D this time around if shit gets ugly like it did before. I just hope he doesn't change his mind about being with me once he realizes how much work this relationship could amount to. I think about how long it took to get Blaine to leave me alone last time. It was two long, dark years. He never actually stopped, he just got caught for doing whatever dumb shit it was that got him locked up.

Now that he's out, he's back to finish what he started.

"I'm going to shut down. Why don't you go gather your things, and we'll get out of here?"

"Okay," I agree, wiping a leftover tear from my eyelashes.

I grab my shoes, but I don't put them back on. Carrying them out to my desk, I drop them back onto the floor before fishing my purse from my bottom drawer. My stomach drops, thinking if Blaine already knows where I work, then he probably has all my other information now, too. I wonder if he sent anything to the apartment, yet.

"All set?" D asks as he exits his office.

Nodding lightly, I let him lead me across the lobby. With his hand still on the small of my back, I think about the declaration he just made. He was sincere when he said he didn't care if anyone finds out about us, but I hope they don't. It's not like either of us would get into trouble, it's D's company after all, but I don't want anyone looking at or thinking of us differently because of it.

Thankfully, we were able to ride down to the ground floor of the building without running into anyone we knew. Izaak is waiting for us at the curb with the back door to the limo already open. We enter the car quickly, and Izaak shuts us in. I retrieve my phone from my purse as soon as I feel the car pull into traffic. Opening my messages, I click on my conversion with Saylor.

"I'm going to check with Saylor to see if anything came in the mail today."

"That's a good idea. Remember, you can invite her over tonight," D reminds me.

"Thank you," I offer him a grateful smile.

ME

Did I receive any letters or packages today?

SAYLOR

I don't know. I haven't checked the mail yet.

ME

Can you take a look now? It's important. D and I just left work, and we're headed to his penthouse.

SAYLOR

You guys can't keep your hands off one another, can you?

ME

No, it's not that. I got a letter delivered to me at work today.

ME

From Blaine.

SAYLOR

Oh, fuck. Throwing shoes on now so I can check the mail.

ME

Thank you.

A few minutes go by, more than enough time for Saylor to go downstairs, check the mail, and tell me if I got anything. I'm not sure whether to be relieved or stressed by the lack of response.

ME

Anything there?

SAYLOR

Sorry, Ren called me, and I got sidetracked. Checking now.

I don't have patience for unfocused Saylor right now.

SAYLOR

No, nothing but junk and bills.

I inhale a deep breath and relax a little bit.

ME

Okay, thank you for checking.

"Saylor said nothing came to the apartment today," I inform D. "That's great news," he responds.
Yeah. But I know it's just a waiting game.

ME

Also, you're invited to dinner at D's place tonight. Ren is going to be there installing a security system.

SAYLOR

Yeah, that's actually why he just called. I'll be there.

ME

Can you bring me some work clothes when you come? I'm going to spend the night.

SAYLOR

Sure

"She'll bring me some clothes for tomorrow."
"That's if we make it in. I was just thinking it may not be a bad idea to take a few days. We can work from my office at the penthouse."
"I hate changing my life because of him. I don't want him to affect my behavior."
"I know, but at least he doesn't know where I live. He can't reach you there."
"D, you don't understand. I have no doubt in my mind he already knows everything there is to know about you."
As D struggles to hide his shock, I put my phone back into my purse. I should tell my parents, but I'm not ready to do that yet. The last thing I need right now is them forcing their way into my everyday life and trying to control

what I do like last time. I know this is a serious situation, but I've never felt safer than I do when I'm with D.

Colin opens the back door of the limo when we pull up to D's building. D takes my hand and doesn't let go the entire way up to his penthouse.

———

WHEN WE GOT UPSTAIRS, I CALLED OFFICER HARRISON, THE POLICE OFFICER I worked with the last time I filed a report on Blaine. He came by the penthouse within an hour and took my statement as well as a copy of the letter Blaine sent. Unfortunately, I'll need proof that Blaine is the one behind it, and then I have to go through the entire court process again to get another order of protection filed. It took a lot out of me the first time around, but D assured me he would be with me every step of the way. As grateful as I am, I'm still worried that, at some point, he's going to get tired of all the drama he's about to be pulled into.

"What's the matter, *théa?*" D asks, breaking me from my thoughts

"Hmm? Oh, it's nothing," I assure him.

It's been several hours since we got here, and Saylor and Ren have since joined us. Ren picked up dinner for all of us on his way over, and the three of them are chowing down on chicken parmesan and lasagna from Cibo. I, however, have been pushing my food around my plate for the last thirty minutes, trying to make it seem like I'm eating and not going crazy inside.

D drops it, but he definitely has more to say.

"I'm going to get started," Ren speaks up.

I shoot him a smile as he gets up from the table and takes his plate into the kitchen. Apparently, he's giving D a deal on their most expensive system. Even though he could price gouge the shit out of D because he's loaded, Ren is only charging him cost not labor. D even offered to pay him for dinner, but he wouldn't accept that, either. Ren really is one of the good ones. For the smallest moment, I think if I would have met him before going to Greece, I may have given him a chance. My mind was too consumed by D by the time we met, though.

Not that I'm complaining.

I take a deep breath and think about where I would be if Ez hadn't come in for a meeting that day. I can feel my pulse quicken at the thought of not being here with D right now. My heart aches as I think about everything I've experienced with him over the past two weeks.

What if I stuck to my guns and never went to Greece with Saylor at all? I tense up, panicking over the idea of being without D and having never known him in the first place.

"Hey, what's wrong?" D places his hand on my leg.

"Can I talk to you for a second? In your room?"

"Of course," he answers.

"What's going on, Car?" Saylor asks.

"Nothing, I'm fine. I just need to talk to D about something."

Saylor is visibly upset that I am keeping something from her. I will explain it to her later, but I just *have* to be with D right now. It feels like my life depends on it.

I take him by the hand and lead us both into his bedroom. The moment he clears the doorway, I close and lock the door behind him.

"What's—"

He doesn't get a chance to finish his question before I leap into his arms and wrap myself around him. His hands fly under my ass, holding me up as he takes me over to the bed, and we collapse onto the mattress. As I attack his lips, my hands roam his body while attempting to pull him closer still. My lips plead with him as I deepen our kiss.

I feel a lone tear drop from the corner of my eye as my heart swells for the man on top of me. His eyes open as I sniffle, and he pulls away.

"Are you okay, Carley?" He cups my cheeks in his strong hands, concern in his voice.

"I'm okay, I just need you so bad right now." Recognition of my intentions with him cause his pupils to dance with desire.

No more words are spoken. His lips move across mine again as his hands fly to his waist. Quickly, he has his belt off and his pants unfastened as I fight to lift my skirt and pull my panties down my legs with him still on top of me.

"See why I prefer to rip them from your body, *théa*? Much easier that way."

My smile turns into a moan as he lines himself up with me and thrusts deep inside. I cry out, a noise he swallows with another kiss. He doesn't take his time, and that's exactly what I need right now. This isn't about making love. This isn't about seeing how long we can last. This is about displacing fear and rising above the terror caused by an unhinged psychopath.

As I feel my orgasm build, D looks deep into my eyes. His tell me, with everything he has, he will protect me. He will keep me safe. He tells me he will be here for me, for the long haul, no matter what. I see the affection I feel for him mirrored in his stare.

I come undone moments before D does. He rolls over onto his side, bringing me with him. My legs are still curled around him, his dick still in place inside of me. We stay like that for several minutes, gently kissing one another, my fingers combing through his hair. I have an almost uncontrollable urge to tell him I love him, but I fight it. I need to make sure that's actually how I feel before just blurting it out.

I'm sure it's true. I don't fall quickly for just anyone, but I also don't want to say anything until I know he feels the same. I doubt it would chase him away, but nothing is certain. He's forty and has never been married. D hasn't given me any reason to think he's afraid of commitment, but maybe he's one of those guys who is afraid of love.

I try to get my mind to switch gears so I think about anything other than the possibility that D may never love me. It's ridiculous, and I don't need another thing to worry about right now. Besides, everything he's done for me since the moment he followed me into that bathroom—hell, since the moment he moved three-thousand miles to be with me—has shown me how he feels.

Actions speak louder than words.

"As much as I would love to fall asleep like this tonight, I can't keep Saylor waiting much longer. Don't think for a moment she won't waltz her ass in here to make sure we're *okay*."

"I don't doubt that for a second," D laughs. "I wouldn't put anything past Saylor."

Slowly, D pulls out of me and rolls off my leg that's pinned underneath him. Carefully, I hop out of bed and scurry into the bathroom to get cleaned up. After that, I quickly change into a pair of leggings and a t-shirt D bought me.

"As soon as they leave, I'm tearing those off your body."

"You have a problem, you know that, right?" I giggle.

"And I don't intend to get help for it anytime soon," D kisses me. "I'm going to get cleaned up, and I'll be right out."

Saylor is sitting on the sofa watching television when I enter the great room. Ren is on a tall ladder at the far side of the room mounting a camera to the wall that looks out over the space.

"Ohh, I get it now," Saylor winks, taking in my outfit change.

"What? I had to talk to D, and then I wanted to get changed so I was more comfortable."

"Mmhmm..." Saylor hits me with an eye roll.

Silently, I place my finger to my lips to quiet her. Then I jerk my thumb in Ren's direction to tell her to knock it off because Ren doesn't need to know D and I were in the other room having a quickie while he was out here hard at work.

"Anyway ... your phone was blowing up while you were *getting comfortable*."

I pivot before taking a seat on the sofa to grab my purse off the bar against the wall between the great room and the dining room. Before I collect it, I realize mine and D's plates are still on the table. Picking them up, I'm stopped by D, who has finished getting dressed.

"I'll take care of that. Go hang with Saylor."

"Are you sure? I don't mind helping."

"I'm fine, go." D winks at me.

I flash a smile at him before grabbing my purse and walking back to the sofa. Thankfully, I'm already sitting when I pull my phone out, because I'm not prepared for what's waiting for me. After his letter today, I should have expected it wouldn't end there, but that doesn't make this any less terrifying.

212-555-1212

DID YOU GET MY LETTERS CARLEY

212-555-1212

IVE THOUGHT ABOUT YOU IN THAT RED DRESS
EVER SINCE I SAW YOU AT THE BAR THE OTHER
NIGHT

212-555-1212

DID YOU WEAR IT FOR ME CARLEY

212-555-1212

I CANT WAIT UNTIL WERE ALONE TOGETHER

212-555-1212

THAT BITCH WONT BE ABLE TO INTERRUPT US
AGAIN ILL MAKE SURE OF IT

My hands start to shake as I read the messages, causing my phone to clatter to the ground.

"What is it, Carley?" Saylor inquires from her spot next to me.

D speeds out of the kitchen, presumably from hearing my cell phone connecting with the hard marble floor and the echo of Saylor's concern bouncing off the walls of his penthouse.

I take a deep breath as Saylor picks my phone up off the floor.

"That *motherfucker*!" she spits, looking at the messages on the screen before handing it over to D.

"What time did he send these?" he wonders.

I see Ren in my peripheral sight climb down from the ladder and join us, worried about what's happening.

"When you guys were in the other room," Saylor answers. "It was one right after the other."

"What's going on?" Ren questions.

D continues hitting buttons on my phone as Saylor explains to Ren about the letter I received at work today in addition to the text messages. That's when it hits me.

"Wait a minute," I state.

Everyone turns their attention toward me.

"He said letters. Plural. Saylor, are you sure I didn't get anything from him today?"

"I'm positive," she assures me.

I look up at D then.

"Where is your mailbox?"

"There's a mailroom in the lobby," he informs me.

"Get your keys," I demand, walking to the front door.

D listens to me, and he and I journey down to the lobby to check his mail.

"Good evening, Mr. Anastos." One of the guys at the security desk nods his head in D's direction as we pass by.

"Carl," D acknowledges stiffly.

When we enter the mailroom, thankfully no one else is in there. D opens his box and pulls out the mail for today. Shuffling through several envelopes, he stops when his eyes land on what I was expecting to find. Throwing everything else onto a nearby counter, he tears open the envelope with the same scraggly handwriting that was on the letter back at the office.

There's no name, only D's address. I stand next to him as he reads it, scared yet desperately needing to know what it says.

HE WILL NEVER LOVE YOU LIKE I LOVE YOU

CHAPTER TWENTY-FOUR

Dimos

THE PAST WEEK has been one of the most stressful weeks of my life. It's agony, watching Carley worry, and not being able to make this pathetic piece of shit go away. We haven't received any more communication from Blaine, and honestly, I think Carley would feel better if we had. She's been jumpy and on edge, waiting for the other shoe to drop ever since we found that letter in my mailbox.

I've been communicating with a PI named Travis who was recommended to me by several business partners. Supposedly, he's the best at what he does. I sent him all the information I have on Blaine so far, which really isn't much. Unfortunately, he's wrapped up in the middle of another assignment and hasn't gotten back to me with anything yet.

The owner of Rapid Flyers wasn't any help, either. I asked for a copy of the courier request and whether or not he had camera footage I could view. He didn't care that his company was responsible for sending threatening letters from a known, violent stalker. His only response was some bullshit about respecting the privacy of his clients. I think it's obvious why Blaine chose to work with this particular company. Carley had to talk me down from going over there and beating him senseless.

I don't like when Carley goes home each evening. I'm left in fear for her and wondering if that nut job is going to break into her apartment again. The only thing that brings me any peace of mind is knowing they have the cameras in place.

I would drop everything to move her into the penthouse with me this second, but I can't in good conscience ask her to do that before she knows about Emma. I need to figure out what I'm going to say to Carley. And I need to put a stop to Emma's calls before shit gets out, and Carley finds out about her before I'm able to explain.

The ding of the elevator pulls me from my spiral. Glancing at my watch, I realize what time it is.

1:13 P.M.

Mail time.

Every day since the first letter was delivered, I've made sure I was the one to receive the mail. Carley has assured me over and over she can handle it, and I know she can, but the protector in me has been unleashed. Until we get this motherfucker out of our lives for good, I want to be the first line of defense, protecting Carley from any and all dangers to her. Physically, mentally, or otherwise.

Exiting my office, I cut Sid off on his path to Carley's desk.

"I'll take the mail." I stand in the way of the cart as he tries to pass by.

He looks over my shoulder toward Carley as I squeeze my hand into a fist, trying to quell the annoyance he brings me.

"Sure, Mr. Anastos." He hands me the stack of envelopes and junk mail before speaking again. "Hi, Carley."

"Hi, Sid. Have a nice day." She dismisses him knowing the longer he's here, the more I begin to lose control of my anger.

It's selfish of me to make her worry about my actions, but I am who I am, and there's no changing that at this point in my life.

"You too," he smiles before turning his cart around and walking back to the elevator.

As I walk toward Carley's desk, my eyes meet hers. Her cocked eyebrow is all I need to see to know I'm not hiding my irritation very well.

"He's harmless," she quietly tells me.

"Well, I'm not. Especially not while there is a psycho out there threatening you. I don't trust anyone. Nor do I want anyone anywhere near you."

After pinning her with my stare, I begin to sort through the stack of mail in my hands. When my eyes land on a white envelope with "Carley Garrettson" written in the same scraggly handwriting on it as the first two, I see red. Letting everything else drop to the ground at my feet, I tear open the offending letter.

"What does it say?" Carley stands from her chair immediately and joins me at my side.

I MISS THE SWEET SMELL OF YOUR SKIN
AND THE WARMTH OF YOUR GAZE
YOUR EYES BELONG ON ME CARLEY
NOT HIM
DO YOU THINK OF ME WHEN YOU FUCK HIM
IT MAKES ME ANGRY EVEN THINKING ABOUT IT
SOMETIMES I GET VIOLENT
ILL FORGIVE YOU IF YOU FORGIVE ME
IVE BEEN FUCKING SOMEONE TOO
I DONT WANT TO BUT I HAVE URGES THAT NEED TO BE MET
UNCONTROLLABLE URGES
DONT WORRY THOUGH
YOURE THE ONLY ONE I THINK ABOUT

WHEN IM VICIOUSLY FUCKING HER
SOON IT WILL BE YOU CARLEY
JUST ME AND YOU

I can feel the fear emanating from her as she reads the newest message from this sadistic fuck. Fire burns me from the inside out, and I'm finding it more and more difficult to channel my rage. I want to—*no, I need to*—find this motherfucker.

Slowly, Carley walks the few steps back to her desk and takes a seat. Removing my phone from my pocket, I type out a quick email to Travis, asking him to call me as soon as possible. I need answers. Something. *Anything.*

I'm honestly at a loss here. There has never been a time in my adult life where I didn't feel like I had complete control over a situation. I busted my ass from the moment I entered college so I would never feel this way again.

Fuck waiting. This unhinged lunatic isn't going to let a few cameras stop him, and his latest demented *love letter* has accelerated my timeline. I'll need to deal with Emma as soon as possible now. I refuse to let that conniving bloodsucker come between Carley and me.

"I think you should move in with me."

Carley's eyes snap to mine, her shock evident in her features.

Before she's able to speak, I feel my phone buzzing in my pocket. Swiftly I pull it out thinking it might be the PI, but it's not.

Emma.

It's as though the universe is warning me shit is going to blow up in my face the longer I wait to tell Carley the truth.

Why is she reaching out to me now? I was over her before the ink was dry on our divorce papers. I moved on. She moved on. What is this about? Part of me wants to tell her to fuck off, but the other masochistic part of me wants to know what she wants.

My eyes shift back to Carley's, still looking like a deer in headlights, and I decline Emma's call for the second time in a week.

"What?" she finally questions, still looking at me as if I have three heads.

I walk to Carley and drop down onto the floor in front of her. Her eyes grow wider still as she inhales a sharp breath. Suddenly, I realize what I must look like.

"No, no. It's not that. I just, I want you to know that I care about you deeply. I don't want anything to happen to you, and I think the best way to do that is for you to stay with me. At least until Blaine is well and truly gone from our lives."

She lets go of the breath she was holding on to, and a rush of air floats over me.

"Look, I want nothing more than for you to move in with me, not because of Blaine, but because..."

I stop suddenly, realizing I almost told her I love her. It's true. One hundred percent totally and emphatically true. But it's too soon, and there is too much that hasn't been said yet.

"Because of our relationship. I hate that he's messed up the way in which I would have preferred asking. I had several other ideas in mind, each way more romantic than springing it on you in the middle of the office. But nothing is more important to me than you and your safety. Your well-being supersedes romance any day of the week."

I watch as tears pool in her eyes, and her lips form the widest smile I've ever seen grace her face before.

"You may not see this as romantic, but I do. I see it in your worry. In your desperation to protect me. The fact that you didn't hit the pavement running when things got hairy."

"Believe me when I tell you there isn't anything that would make me want to leave you. Especially now that we have a second chance. And don't worry, I plan to ask you again, the correct way when the time is right."

"I don't need a redo. Nothing tells me you care about me more than everything you're doing to keep me safe."

"I would lay my life down to make sure nothing happens to you. Swim to the—"

"... bottom of the deep blue sea," she smiles, finishing the promise I've made to her numerous times over the past two weeks.

"If it meant you were safe." I return her smile.

Standing up from the ground, I grab her hand and whisk her into my office. Unable to control myself one moment longer, I shut my doors, press her up against the hardwood, and kiss her like it's the first time all over again.

"Is this the last of it?"

I grab one of two Michael Kors suitcases from Carley as she wheels them out of her building to my waiting limo. I'm loading them up while Izaak grabs some lunch from a street vendor around the corner. There are three suitcases already inside, and I'm trying to make room for more.

"No, there is one more up there."

"I may as well hire a moving company to come get the rest of your things at this rate. We can make this more of a permanent arrangement."

Before she gets a chance to protest, and before I actually follow through with it, I pull her in for a kiss. She wraps her arms around my neck as I comb my fingers through her wavy hair. She smells so fucking good, and the feeling of her tongue on mine makes my dick twitch.

I run my other hand down her side, stopping when I get to her denim clad ass. Grabbing a palmful of her perfectly round cheek, I allow both my hands and lips to linger a while longer.

"I'll go up and grab it for you," I offer, finally breaking our kiss.

"It's okay. I promised Saylor I would go back up one more time to say good-bye. She told me she wouldn't come down here to see me off. I think she's half joking, but it's her way of showing her disapproval of our plan."

Carley rolls her eyes and shakes her head gently at her best friend's behavior.

"She'll come around," I promise her, but I honestly don't care if she does or not. Of course, I don't want to cause a rift between the two of them, but if

Saylor can't see that this is our best option to keep that maniac away from Carley, then that's her problem. I know she's going to miss her friend, but it's not like they won't ever see one another again.

"You know, it may not be under the most desirable circumstances, but I'm ridiculously happy that you'll be under the same roof as me for the foreseeable future."

Carley giggles and whispers another kiss to my cheek.

"I'll be back down in a minute."

As I watch her walk back into the building, I can't help but feel like everything is coming together. I'll call Emma sometime this week to try and get that situation under control.

I make a firm, silent promise to Carley that I will come clean tonight, and tell her everything I've been too afraid to say.

"Still fucking your staff members, I see. I guess it's true what they say. That old habits die hard."

As if Satan took over as the universe's puppeteer, my blood runs cold when the icy shrill I've grown to loathe over the past ten years fills my ears.

Emma.

It takes me a moment to realize I'm not imagining this. She's here. Emma is in New York City. At Carley's fucking *apartment building.*

Fuck.

"You sure do like them young, Dimi. Once a predator, always a predator, I suppose. Is that child whore the reason you won't return my calls?"

She's always insisted on calling me Dimi. No one, not even my parents, has ever called me that. She thought she was special, like she gave me an exotic nickname only she was good enough to use.

I fucking abhor it.

But my blood boils more from her referring to Carley as a whore. The last thing I want to do is turn around and acknowledge her presence, but I know she won't leave without getting to speak with me first.

"What the fuck are you doing here?" I spit through gritted teeth once I'm facing her where she sits in the back of a Town Car.

"Is there somewhere *private* where we can talk?"

I hate the sexual connotation she uses as she utters the word *private.* It's how she used to speak to me when she wanted something and was going to use sex in order to get it from me.

"No. Why are you here?" I refuse to look at her as I question her again.

"You're not taking my calls. I had to do something to get you to talk to me."

"I don't want you here." This time, I lean down and stare straight into her cold eyes, enunciating each word as it leaves my lips. "*Go. Home.*"

"I want you back, D."

"That's *never* going to happen," I laugh in her face.

"We'll see." She purses her lips as she looks me up and down. "I'll expect a phone call from you this week, letting me know when and where you're taking me for dinner. We have a lot to discuss."

"I have nothing to say to you."

"I would hate for your little plaything to find out she's merely a habit you can't quit. She probably thinks she's special," she mocks, clicking her tongue. "Poor girl. If you refuse to meet with me, then I'll hunt her down and tell her all about your adventures with the slut who screwed you over in Torrance."

Red paints my vision as I think about Emma getting anywhere near Carley. I don't need to tell her that Carley is already well aware of Kati, but that wouldn't stop Emma from going after her anyway.

"At least she was smart and wasn't afraid to go after what she wanted. That one there..." she nods her head toward the doorway Carley walked through only seconds earlier. She pauses as she thinks about what she is trying to say. No doubt whatever comes out of her mouth will be vicious and spiteful. "She seems ... simple. Plain. Of no consequence whatsoever."

I ball my hands into fists and squeeze tightly to keep myself from reacting to Emma. That's what she wants, and I refuse to let her feel any amount of satisfaction at Carley's expense.

"Once she realizes she's no longer *unique*, hopefully she'll have enough self-respect to leave you. Although, how much does she really have to begin with to be sleeping with her boss? Come to think of it, maybe I won't even bother with *Plain Jane*. She doesn't seem like much fun to play with anyway. Maybe I'll go to your board of trustees and tell them how worried I am about your pattern of destructive behavior. Maybe I'll send an anonymous tip to the news outlets that hints toward foul play within Okeanós. The possibilities are endless, D."

I don't doubt she would spark a news story and then stand by my side, attempting to play the role of supportive wife while she watches my empire burn. That's exactly the kind of narcissistic sociopath she is.

I feel frozen. Stuck. Completely worthless and weak, just like I did when we were married. When I don't respond, she speaks again.

"I expect a call this week, Dimi. Otherwise ..." she cocks an eyebrow before winding her window up.

Finally, as her car pulls away from the curb, the fire I felt when I first laid eyes on her returns. Quickly, I rush inside, pulling my phone from my pocket as I make my way to the elevator. I pull up my messages and slam my thumbs down on the screen, frantically typing out a message to Ez and Eliana. If there's anyone in the world who can give me the advice I need right now, it's them.

ME

911!

EZRA TREUTH

What's up, man?

ME

Are you home right now? I really need to talk to you.

ELIANA TREUTH

What's wrong? Are you okay?

ME

Yes and no. I'll explain it to you when I get there. I need
a few minutes to finish getting Carley's things loaded
into the car. After that I'll come over.

EZRA TREUTH

Okay, see you soon.

Pocketing my phone once again, I exit the elevator and walk toward the girls' apartment. I overhear them talking once I step inside and close the door. Their conversation is like a complete one-eighty to the one I just had with Emma.

"... just never felt this way before. Say, I'm falling in love with him."

My heart stops for the second time in five minutes. This time, though, I welcome it. Hearing Carley say she's falling in love with me stokes a different fire within. I hear some sniffling coming from the kitchen, but I don't know which girl it's coming from. Perhaps both.

"I really am happy for you. You know that, right?"

"Of course, I do," Carley reassures a sobbing Saylor.

"I'm glad you have D, Carley," Ren adds. "He seems like a decent guy. But make sure you're not falling for him for the wrong reasons. It's natural to develop feelings for someone who is protecting you. Especially when you're as vulnerable as you are right now."

"Ren, what the fuck?" Saylor questions, and I wholeheartedly agree with her.

"I don't mean to sound like a dick. All I'm saying is, make sure your feelings are genuine. Are they based on actual affection, or are they rooted in your fear of Blaine?"

Jesus. Thanks a lot, Ren.

But what if he's right? What if Carley only feels like this because she's scared? I can't think about that right now. One crisis at a time.

"Uhh ... okay, Dr. Phil," Saylor jumps in again. "No more daytime TV for you."

I walk back to the front door and open it as quietly as I can before shutting it a little louder than I did before. Casually, I walk into the kitchen, pretending like I wasn't just eavesdropping.

"How's everything going up here?" I ask, staring pointedly at Ren for a little longer than necessary. "All right, Say?"

She nods her head as she wipes a tear from her cheek.

"You just make sure you take care of her, or else we're going to have a problem, got it?"

"I would lay my life down for her."

My eyes latch onto Carley's as I say the words, and I can see the love in them. She *does* love me, and as I gaze deeper into her eyes as blue as the sea, I *know* it doesn't have anything to do with her fear.

I can feel it.

"We better go. I need to stop by the office on the way home, but I'm going to have Izaak take you straight to the penthouse."

"On a Saturday? I'll come with you," Carley insists.

"How about this," I lay a kiss on her lips before continuing. "You go get started unpacking. Colin will help you bring your things upstairs. When I'm finished doing what I need to do, I'll have Izaak come get me and grab takeout on the way home—drunken noodles and pho, perhaps."

Her eyes dilate when I mention *which* food I'll be bringing home. And I know she's picturing the events that occurred the last time we had this meal at the penthouse. I feel bad using the promise of good food and even better sex to manipulate her, but I need her to change her mind.

"O—okay," she breathes.

"Clearly we've missed something here," Saylor interrupts, pulling Carley from her lust-filled reverie. "Promise me we can all have dinner again soon."

"Promise," Carley agrees.

"Saylor," I nod then turn to Ren and hold my hand out. "Ren."

With a firm shake, we finish our goodbyes and are out the door. When Carley is settled into the back of the limo, I walk to the driver's door with Izaak.

"Keep an eye out for a blacked-out Lincoln Continental following you."

"That's the majority of the cars in the city, other than cabs."

"I know, but maybe take a different route home than you normally do. If you notice you're being followed, do *not* go to the penthouse until you lose them. Got it?"

"Yes, sir. Anything I need to be worried about?"

I look him dead in the eye. "Emma is here."

"Understood."

"Thanks, Izaak."

Once the limo is out of sight, I hail a taxi. As I'm entering the back seat, I feel my phone vibrate. Pulling it from my pocket, I see I have a text message from Emma.

EMMA

One week, Dimi. I'm not playing around.

Without responding to her, I pull up my message with Ez and Eliana.

ME

Emma is in the city. I'm on my way.

CHAPTER TWENTY-FIVE

Dimos

THE MOMENT EZ opens the front door, he shoves a highball glass filled with three fingers of whiskey into my hand.

"Come on in, man."

Ez shuts the door behind me as I walk into their home. Taking a large swig, I make my way into the living room. Eliana is already sitting on the sofa, glass of red wine in hand.

"What happened?" she asks, not wanting to waste time with small talk.

"She showed up at Carley's apartment as we were loading some of her things into my car. Literally seconds after Carley walked inside. Purposefully, of course. If she wanted Carley to know she was there, she wouldn't have waited."

I take another large sip of whiskey, and the fire that remains within me grows hotter.

"She told me she wants to get back together."

"Ew." Both Ez and Eliana scoff at the same time.

I place my glass down on the coffee table and lean forward with my elbows on my knees and my head in my hands.

"I've really made a mess of things. One that keeps growing the longer I go without telling Carley about Emma."

"Wait, Carley doesn't know about Emma yet?"

Picking up my head, I look Eliana in the eyes and let my reaction answer her question. Standing, I pace the living room.

"Carley's mother cheated on her father with her best friend. She didn't even know her biological father—who happens to be George Manford, by the way," I look over at Ez and catch his shock at this revelation, "until she was sixteen years old. Her mother had moved on with the best friend, until he died in a car accident. It turned out he was cheating, too. Get this ... with his assistant."

I watch as both Ez and Eliana try to put together everything I just told them.

"She *hates* liars and cheaters. She made that very clear to me, and I don't blame her one bit. But I'm *both*. I should have told her when I first got into town, before things started heating up between us again. But I honestly didn't think it was relevant to anything. Then when I finally decided I was going to tell her, this shit with that motherfucking psycho stalker started. It didn't feel right to lay this on her, too."

"D, this bomb is going to blow up in your face if you don't diffuse it ASAP."

"You don't think I know that? I wanted to tell her tonight after she got settled in, but that was when I thought Emma was still in California with Gary. And now I find out Carley's falling in love with me—"

"She told you that?" Eliana interrupts. The smile on her face is priceless.

"No. I overheard her telling her friend Saylor. And I feel the same way about her, but I'm terrified I've waited too long to tell her about Emma, and my love won't matter to her enough to be able to forgive my omission."

"Listen," Ez speaks up. "I believe you and Carley have what it takes to get through whatever pain this omission could cause her. But if *you* don't tell her and she finds out on her own—*which she will*—I don't know if you can come back from that."

"I know," I agree.

Still, the thought of telling her makes me want to throw up.

"So what else did that bitch Emma have to say?"

I scoff, thinking back to our conversation.

"She's a fucking piece of work. She told me I have one week to call her with a date and time we can meet for dinner so we can talk. If not, she said she's going to go to the board of trustees and tell them about my *pattern of destructive behavior* in reference to sleeping with my assistants. And also, she will write to whatever fucking news outlets to tell them about the *sexual corruption* taking place within Okeanós."

I take my seat once more and rub my hand down my face, still in disbelief of my earlier run-in. Grabbing my glass from the table, I down the rest of my whiskey.

"Another?"

"No, no," I decline. "I told Carley I was going to the office for something. Another fucking lie. I can't come home smelling like a bar."

"D, I honestly think everything will be okay. Carley is a smart girl, and she doesn't seem like the type to react without getting all of the facts. But you need to let her know."

"I know. I'll tell her."

After I deal with Emma.

MY PENTHOUSE ALREADY SMELLS LIKE CARLEY WHEN I WALK THROUGH THE door, and it makes my knees weak. I nearly toss the food back out in the hallway because I know it's only a matter of time before it overpowers her floral scent.

"Carley, I'm home," I give a shout as I lock the door behind me.

Fuck, both my heart and my dick love hearing those words. When she doesn't answer, I figure she's in the shower and can't hear me. Passing my bedroom, I decide to get dinner out on the table and then see what she's up to. Maybe join her for a shower before we eat.

When I get to the end of the hallway and make a left into the dining room, my dick nearly leaps out of my pants. There at the end of the table is Carley, scantily clad in the sexiest fucking lacy black lingerie I've ever seen in my entire life.

With her feet flat on the table and her legs relaxed to the sides, her pussy is wide open and completely on display. She looks at me as I drop the food on the floor and stalk toward her.

"I thought you might like your dessert before dinner tonight."

That's what I said to her at dinner in Greece. But the way she says it, so sweet and innocent, it's as though she's served me a piece of cake instead of an entire mouthwatering pie.

"*Théa...*"

I don't think I can form a coherent thought at the moment, but this doesn't require thinking anyway. I drop into the chair at the head of the table and curl my arms around her slender thighs, pulling her closer to the edge.

My tongue dives between her thighs, and she wraps her legs around my neck, pulling me in close. Using my thumb and index finger, I hold her open, exposing her clit so I can tease it while my other hand breaches her opening and burrows in, knuckle deep.

Carley's sharp intake of breath tells me I've hit her spot. Both my fingers and the tip of my tongue work feverishly to bring her the pleasure she deserves. The pleasure I never want to stop bringing her for as long as I live.

Soon, she begins to arch her back off of the table, and I know it won't be long until I get to drink her all up.

"Oh, *shit*," she releases in a breathy whisper. "Right there! Don't stop, D."

And I have no intention of stopping. I moan as I suck on her clit, letting the vibration of my voice aid in her pleasure. My fingers move within her, faster than I think they've ever moved before.

That's when I feel it. The hot rush of her arousal, beginning to pour out of her. As my fingers still dance inside of her, she writhes on the table in front of me. Needing to taste even more of her, I dip my head and open my mouth wide, catching as much of her sweetness as I can.

Once I've gotten all that she's given me, I remove my belt and unfasten my pants quickly. Pulling her into a sitting position, my lips seek hers out as my cock finds her entrance, and I push inside of her. She cries out when I'm seated all the way in. Curling her legs around my waist, like she did to my neck a moment ago, she holds on as I lunge forward.

Moving swiftly, I grip her tightly. I fist her hair at the nape of her neck with my other arm curled around her lower back for more support. For more leverage. Because I need more. I'm as far inside of her as I can get, but it's still not enough.

With Carley, it will never be enough.

CHAPTER TWENTY-SIX

Carley

THE SOUND of my phone vibrating breaks me from my concentration. I've been working my way through emails since nine this morning, barely stopping for a break. Glancing at my phone's screen, I see a message from Saylor waiting. She's been messaging me nonstop since I moved out. It's hardly been a week, and I do miss seeing her regularly, but falling asleep and waking up next to D every day is the kind of heaven I wasn't sure I'd ever find.

I already knew we had a lot in common, but you don't really get to know someone until you live with them. So far, there aren't any red flags I need to worry about. He works the majority of the time, sometimes even through breakfast and dinner. He's always very apologetic, but I honestly don't mind. I love watching him work. It's like a weird type of foreplay I've never experienced before.

Outside of work, he's a bit of a homebody, much like myself, which works out especially well at the moment.

There's nothing like a stalker to keep you from wanting to go outside.

I'm more than okay with staying in while we're not at the office. I know my time at Okeanós is limited, and while I would love to stay, leaving means D and I can be free to have the kind of relationship we deserve.

I sigh because I know that can never happen with Blaine still in the picture.

There are times, like right now, when I'm more angry than frightened where I want to seek him out and tell him he is insignificant. Tell him he doesn't scare me anymore. It would be a lie, but that's the point in my life where I wish I was. I don't want to live in fear any longer.

Grabbing my phone, I unlock the screen and read Saylor's latest message.

SAYLOR

Did you know studies have shown you can gain up to
seventeen pounds during the first year of a new
relationship?

Her message makes me smile and shake my head. These are the types of things we would normally talk about at home, and I love her for not wanting to let that go.

ME

No, I didn't know that.

SAYLOR

It's true. So I'm switching to black coffee to help shed
the couple pounds I've gained since meeting Ren.
Trying to nip it in the bud before it becomes an issue.

Now I shake my head at her for a different reason. She gets this way all the time, even though she barely has one ounce of fat on her bones. She isn't sickeningly skinny, but she definitely doesn't need to lose any weight.

ME

Well, you have to do whatever you think is best for your
body.

You can't just tell Saylor not to do something. In all the years we've been friends, I've learned she is going to do whatever she's determined to do.
Even if it's stupid.
The more you fight her on a topic, the more obsessed she gets. If you don't entertain her ridiculous ideas, she gets bored of them fairly quick.

SAYLOR

Do you want to meet up for lunch today?

ME

D and I have a lunch meeting with some prospective
clients, or else I would. Maybe tomorrow?

SAYLOR

Boo, you whore!

ME

Calm down, Regina.

SAYLOR

Okay, tomorrow it is. I'm holding you to it.

ME

It's a date.

D pops out of his office just as I put my phone down. I still feel guilty when I have it out while I'm supposed to be working. The other day, he told me he could take me into his office and spank me for using it if that would make me feel better.

Thinking back to our conversation now, I don't think I would mind one bit. Maybe I'll test him later.

As my thighs begin to clench, D speaks.

"Any thoughts on lunch?" he asks me.

"It doesn't matter to me. I could go for anything."

His eyes glimmer with lust, and his tongue darts out over his lower lip at my response.

"Be careful what you wish for, *théa*."

"You're insatiable."

He stalks toward me, his eyes glued to mine. I see a promise in them, like he wants to prove to me just how insatiable he actually is. Just before he stops at my desk, the phone rings. I have to clear my throat, breaking free of his lustful spell in order to speak.

"Dimos Anastos's office," I answer.

"Emma Kersey for Dimi." The woman on the other end is short and almost hostile in her response.

Covering the receiver, I whisper to D, "Emma Kersey for Dimi? Is that you?"

The lust vanishes from D's face immediately before he responds.

"I'll call her back."

I'm thrown off by the weird name the caller used, but I don't think much of it.

"He's unavailable at the moment, but I will leave him a message."

There's no response on the other end. I don't hear any background noise, either.

"Hello?" I check to see if she's still there, but I don't receive a response.

Placing the receiver into the cradle, I turn back to D.

"She hung up," I shrug. "Weird, she called you Dimi."

"I'm sure it wasn't important anyway. I'll order in from Delray." Winking, he turns on his heel and saunters back into his office.

After our prospective clients leave, and as I help D clean up lunch in the board room, I hear the sound of high heels clamoring across the marble floor in the lobby just outside. Both mine and D's heads snap toward the sound.

"I'll go see who it is," I tell D.

"No I—" he begins to protest, but I'm already out the door.

As soon as I step into the hallway, my anxiety shoots through the roof. I watch her as she sashays her way across the marble floor, dressed impeccably as always, but she's about as welcome as a case of measles.

"Mom? What are you doing here?"

"Well, it's lovely to see you too, Carley."

"Sorry, I just didn't expect you to be here. Is everything okay?"

"Well, I should ask you the same quest—" something behind me cuts her off, and I know exactly what it is.

She may be my mother, but the amount of rage I feel toward her at the moment is completely warranted. Her eyes practically glow when they land on D. I feel his presence as he walks behind me and stands to the side of my desk.

"Hello, Gianna Martin. You must be Dimos Anastos."

She approaches him, offering him her hand like she's the Queen of fucking England, and he should fall at her feet.

She's unbelievable.

Taking it in a firm shake, and without validating her shameless flirting, he nods to her.

"Very nice to meet you, Ms. Martin."

"Please, call me Gianna."

Please don't.

"Mom. I wish you would have called first. You can't just show up here like this."

"Well, I just wanted to make sure you were okay. You know, since you moved out of the apartment and all."

Panic.

How the hell does she— *Saylor!* I'm going to kill her.

"I shouldn't have to hear about your life from Saylor's flavor of the week, dear." She turns her attention back to D and lays the *loving mother* act on thick. "She never tells me anything. I swear, it's like she's trying to punish me for caring about her."

"Wait, *what?*" *Ren* told her?

"You've been dodging my calls, so I decided to show up to your apartment last night. That boy said you moved in with your boyfriend. I didn't even know you were dating anyone."

I fidget uncomfortably while I try to think of what to tell her. I don't want her knowing I've gone and shacked up with my boss. That can wait until ... *never* ... or at least until I find a new job. But my mother is like a CIA operative. There isn't much that gets past her.

"Well, are you going to tell me about him?"

"Not right *now*. Not when I'm trying to work."

"Well, I'm *sure* your *boss* won't mind if we catch up for a little, right?" It's the wink she gives me that tells me she already knows exactly who my boyfriend is. "Saylor was quite inebriated when I stopped by. She was rather loose-lipped, although there's not really much about her that *isn't* loose. By the way, is she going through a phase? The new boy she's with seemed a little *ragey*. Angry."

As quickly as she makes the statement, she shrugs her shoulders and waves the entire idea off.

Saylor. Is. Dead.

What the fuck was she thinking, telling my mom about me and D?

"Don't you think you'd have more fun with someone your *own* age? Someone with more experience?"

Are you fucking kidding me right now?

"You are completely out of line, Mother. It's time to leave."

"I'm just trying to get to know your boyfriend a little more, Carley." She runs her fingers over the long, gold chain that dips in between her cleavage.

"No, you're throwing yourself at him like a desperate hooker."

"Carley, do *not* take that tone with me," she scolds, as though I were a child. "Do you honestly think you can hold his attention for very long? You're so young, so inexperienced. This office fling is going to be over and done with before you know it. Then you will be out of a job and out on your ass. I've been down this road before, darling. It never ends well."

I refuse to have her come to my place of work and treat me like a child in front of D. Let alone eye-fuck the shit out of him. Before I'm able to tell her off, D comes to my rescue.

"I'd like to make something very clear, Ms. Martin. What I feel for your daughter is, quite frankly, none of your fucking business. However, since you seem to be overly interested in my intentions with her, I'm happy to tell you I have incredibly deep feelings for your daughter. Feelings that make it impossible to look at or think of another woman as anything more than an annoyance. It didn't start as an office fling nor will it end as one. As far as I'm concerned, I don't see an end to our relationship at any time in the near, or far, future."

My mother looks like she just got slapped across the face. If I wasn't still seething with animosity, I think I'd be smiling.

"I know your type. You go for young, insecure girls who would do anything to get your attention. You pay them compliments as a form of foreplay and use their vulnerability to get into their pants. Right before you drop them like a bad habit. Gaslight them to make them think you didn't do anything wrong. Make them think they're crazy and bring too much drama into your life. Make them believe they're too much of a liability, so you have to cut them loose."

"I'm sorry for whatever happened to you in the past, but it sounds to me like you put your faith in the wrong person a time or two. You sound like a bitter woman who lost the only man she ever truly loved—if you were ever capable of love in the first place—and is hell bent on making the rest of us pay for your mistakes."

Now both my mother and I are speechless. My heart is thrumming faster than it ever has before. Adrenaline and anxiety rip through my body as heat seeps from my pores, and a sheen of sweat covers my skin. I've never heard anyone speak to my mother this way—except my father a couple of times. Usually, men kiss the ground she walks on.

"I would never do anything to hurt Carley. I think it's time you leave."

With her head held high, my mother looks from D back to me before turning on her heel and marching out of the office. As soon as the elevator doors close her in, I lunge at D, cameras be damned.

He catches me and carries me into his office, kicking his doors closed along the way.

"Oh my god," I pant against his lips. "No one has ever spoken to her like that before."

"I'm sorry—"

"Don't be. It was so fucking hot."

D walks us over to the sofa and lays me down. I lift my skirt up and pull my underwear down before D gets a chance to rip them from me. That's how badly I want to fuck him right now. I'm moving faster than he is for once.

In a flash, his belt is open, his pants are unzipped, and he's pushing himself into me. I cry out loudly, unable to keep quiet and not giving a fuck anyway. If someone were to catch us and today is the last day I work here, what a fucking way to go.

Within two minutes, we're both wrung dry. We may as well call it a day because we look like we just ran a marathon. There will be no hiding what we just did if someone were to catch our appearances now.

Barely able to lift myself from the sofa, I slip into D's office bathroom to try and make myself look presentable enough to leave the building. When he's finished getting his pants back on, I hear the doors to his office open. I watch as he ducks his head out to see if anyone is out in the lobby.

"All clear," he assures.

Just then, the ding of the elevator sounds, and I rush out of his bathroom, thinking my mother has come back for more. But it's just Sid with the mail. I watch as he hands the stack over to D. In it is a large manilla envelope that looks awfully suspicious.

My stomach drops.

D tosses everything other than the envelope onto my desk and opens it. After pulling out a piece of paper, he digs back into the package and pulls out a cell phone. Bile rises in my throat as I stand next to D to try and see what was sent.

> DONT THINK FOR ONE SECOND THAT
> HE CAN KEEP YOU FROM ME FOREVER
> WE BELONG TOGETHER CARLEY
> I KNOW IT
> YOU KNOW IT
> THE UNIVERSE KNOWS IT
>
> LEAVE HIM OR THIS GETS LEAKED

D drops the letter onto my desk and powers on the cell phone. When it's on, there is a video waiting to be played, already queued up. D clicks play, and I'm shocked to realize the video isn't of us, but of Saylor and Ren.

"Here." D averts his eyes immediately, paying respect to Saylor even when she isn't here to witness it.

He takes a seat at my desk and busies himself on my computer, further affirming the amazing person he is and shoving away all of the ideas my mother just tried to plant in my head.

Though I've heard countless stories of Saylor's sexcapades, it's something else entirely to watch it unfold with your own eyes. The video is a compilation of them having sex on the island in the kitchen. On the sofa. Of Saylor tied to a chair while Ren plays with her. While he pinches and bites her nipples until she cries out. At first, I think he's hurting her on purpose, but when he asks her if she wants more, she begs him for it.

The next clip is of Saylor bent over the kitchen table with Ren's hand clutching tightly onto the back of her neck. He's pounding into her so hard that the table is sliding across the floor with each thrust.

I know Saylor likes it rough sometimes, but I didn't know she liked it *that* rough. I remember her telling me that Ren, while quiet on the outside, has a very domineering personality behind closed doors.

I'll fucking say...

"It's footage from the security system in the apartment," I state. "If Blaine was able to hack in to ours, then there's no way he won't be able to hack in to yours, too."

After seeing this, suddenly I'm not as angry with Saylor for spilling the beans about moving in with D to my mother.

"I have to call her and tell her about this."

"Yeah, of course," D stands again and walks to my side.

"Blaine knows I will protect Saylor with everything I have. Which, I'm sure, is why he sent me a video of her and not myself."

"Carley," D pulls me to him and places his hands on either side of my neck. "I don't care what that letter says or who is in that video, you're not going anywhere."

"No. I'm not."

CHAPTER TWENTY-SEVEN

Dimos

I TRIED to get Carley to leave after the package arrived earlier, but she said she was fine. I think she is, for the most part. But I also know she's trying to be strong for the people around her. She wanted to wait and tell Saylor about the videos in person, so she invited her and Ren over for dinner tonight.

"Almost ready to go?" We're finally leaving for the evening, and I can't wait to get her home.

"*God, yes*. Shutting down now. I'm going to text Saylor and tell her to come over."

"Okay, I'll be right out."

I have my own text message to send.

Pulling Emma up in my contacts, I start a new message.

ME

Tomorrow 8 P.M. Meet me at Angelo's Coffee House.

EMMA

I said dinner, Dimi.

ME

You want to talk? This is where we're doing it.

EMMA

Pick me up at 8:30 at The St. Regis Hotel.

EMMA

Don't be late.

I shove my phone in my pocket without responding.

Whatever.

I'll just do what she wants and get it over and done with. The quicker I can get her out of our lives the better.

"What do you feel like doing for dinner?" I ask Carley once I reenter the lobby.

"I'm not very hungry, so whatever you're in the mood for is fine by me."

The elevator doors close as she speaks, and I get a flashback of her laying on the dining room table the other day.

"That's a dangerous statement, *théa*."

A smile tugs at the corner of my mouth as I watch her blush.

"As wonderful as that sounds, honestly, I'm completely worn out. I can't remember the last time I was this tired."

I wrap my arm around her, and she rests her head on my shoulder.

"We'll go to bed early tonight. Maybe we can work from home tomorrow."

"Sounds wonderful," she responds. "You know, I would bet money people have figured out there is something going on between us by now."

"I'm sure you're right, but I can't bring myself to care about what they think."

"I know. I don't, either. I just don't want it to look bad on you, that's all."

I know it bothers her. She's very proud, as she should be. She's great at what she does, and she puts her heart in to her work. I don't want people thinking poorly of her any more than she wants them thinking poorly of me. But there will always be assholes out there who are jealous and won't see it that way.

Kissing her on the top of her head, we ride the rest of the way to the ground floor in silence.

As the four of us chow down our dinner from Katz's Delicatessen, Carley and I exchange nervous glances back and forth with one another. She doesn't want to be the one to tell Saylor about the video we found any more than I do.

"What gives, lovebirds?" Saylor calls out as she watches us from across the table. "You've been shifty eye-fucking the shit out of each other since we got here."

"Nothing—" I begin before Carley cuts me off.

"No, it's okay," she assures me. "I have something to show you and Ren, Saylor. I'll be right back."

As she walks into the bedroom to retrieve the letter and phone from her purse, Saylor pins me with a glare.

"Is she pregnant?"

"What? *No.*" I answer quickly.

"You're both acting very weird."

"Just ... wait until she shows you what she needs to show you."

A moment later, Carley reappears from the hallway with the phone and letter in hand.

"I got this at the office today. I didn't want to tell you over the phone."

Both Saylor and Ren have matching grim expressions on their faces as Carley hands the phone to Saylor.

"He said if I didn't leave D, he would leak this on to the internet. Don't worry, I'm the only one who's seen it."

Ren rests his arm on the back of Saylor's chair as she presses play. Together, they watch in horror as I hear the same audio I heard earlier today. Moans, grunting, thrashing, cries of pain and pleasure. There's no denying what's on that tape, and it could ruin Saylor if it got out. Ren would probably get a pat on the back and an *atta boy* or two for his role.

This is the longest amount of time Saylor has gone without speaking around me. When the recording has finished, she places it on the table and looks from me to Carley.

"That was hot. Can you send me a copy?"

"*Saylor!*" Carley exclaims.

"What? I look good. Let him share it, I don't care." Saylor rolls her eyes and shrugs it off.

Believing her actions can only be a defense mechanism, I turn my attention to Ren who has a look of disbelief on his face.

"You okay, Ren?"

"Uhh…" He pinches the bridge of his nose before looking at me. "I don't … I don't even know. I'm pissed he was able to get this footage. It makes me wonder what else he has on us. He had to have gotten through the Wi-Fi at the apartment in order to get access to the footage. That's the only thing I can think of."

"Wouldn't that mean he'd have to be close by to figure out which network was yours?"

"Yeah, he'd have to get really close. Like in the hallway. Saylor, can I borrow your phone to check the footage real quick?"

Carley speaks up again as Saylor hands her phone off to Ren.

"If Blaine needed to hack the apartment's feed from the hallway, I would assume he would need to do the same from outside the penthouse door?"

"Yeah, I would think so. But there's no way he can access the penthouse lobby outside without making it through security and obtaining an access card."

"That only makes me feel a little better. He is tenacious, D. If he wants it badly enough, he *will* find a way. Saylor, you guys need to change your Wi-Fi password or something. Maybe get one of those systems that randomly changes it every day or hour or whatever."

"You may as well be speaking Spanish to me. I don't understand techie. Talk to this guy." She juts her thumb at Ren.

"I'll change it as soon as possible and get a VPN set up, too," he agrees. "*Fuck.* Here, look at this."

Ren places Saylor's phone on the table and presses play on the video he pulled up. Carley and I both stretch as far across the table as we can in order to see. On the screen, I catch a glimpse of a man walking up and down the hallway outside of the apartment door holding an electronic tablet. He's wearing a hoodie, pulled low over his eyes. It casts a shadow almost to the bottom of his chin.

The sight of the person on the screen causes goose bumps to break out over Carley's skin. I wrap my arm around her shoulders and pull her close to me.

"I'm assuming that's him? That's Blaine?" I ask.

"I can't be one hundred percent sure without seeing the rest of his face, but it sure does look like him. And who else would be lurking outside of the apartment?"

"What's the time and date stamp from the video?" I ask Ren.

"Midday, two days ago."

"Anyway, like hell are you leaving D because of this," Saylor completely changes the subject, addressing Carley. "I mean, nobody's life is in danger here. Frankly, it feels like Blaine may be losing his touch."

"The letters and texts are confusing me," Carley adds.

"How so?" I inquire.

"It's just ... not Blaine's style. He never cared about violating the restraining order when I had one. Not that I'm complaining, but why is he keeping his distance this time?"

"Well, maybe he doesn't want to get sent back to prison?" Ren offers. "Or maybe it's because you have someone else in your life to protect you this time around. Before it was just you and Saylor, right?"

"My dad had one run-in with him. But, yes, basically it was just Saylor and I."

"And now Saylor has Ren," I add. "So that's double the amount of protection than you girls had before."

"Yeah, I guess you're right."

"Hey, listen to me." I take my seat again and pull Carley onto my lap. I take her chin in my grip and force her eyes on mine. "I'm not going to let anything happen to you. I won't let you out of my sight. You're going to get sick of me by the time this asshole is out of your life for good."

"Somehow I doubt that."

Wrapping her arms around my neck, she leans in for a kiss.

"I'm going to call it a night. Get back to the apartment and try to update the Wi-Fi." Ren pulls Carley's attention from my lips, and she stands up to say goodbye.

"Do you guys have a ride back? Izaak can drive you if you'd like."

"Nah, we're good," Ren confirms, shaking my hand as Saylor and Carley hug one another.

With one final goodbye, they're out the door.

"Would you like me to run you a bath?"

"No, I'm thinking about brushing my teeth and watching a show from bed. Maybe get to sleep a little early tonight."

"I'll get dinner cleaned up. You go relax," I suggest.

"Thank you, D. For everything." Rising up onto her tiptoes, she plants a kiss on my lips.

I can't wait to crawl into bed next to her tonight.

LESS THAN THIRTY MINUTES LATER, CARLEY'S CELL PHONE ECHOES THROUGH the room from the table next to her side of the bed. She rolls over to grab it, and the chill in the air licks my side where she was just curled up.

"It's Saylor," she informs me before answering the call. "Hello?"

I can't hear what she is saying, but it must not be good. Carley's face drops, and she puts the phone on speaker.

"Wait, wait. Hold on. Say that again so D can hear you."

"I got a package today, too. Same as you, only it's a video of you guys, and my letter says, 'Break them up or this gets leaked.'"

FOR THE THOUSANDTH TIME, I PRESS PLAY ON THE VIDEO SAYLOR RECEIVED last night. I sent Izaak to her apartment to retrieve it as soon as she called us. Carley hasn't been able to eat anything today, she's so upset. As soon as we finished watching it for the first time last night, she ran into the bathroom and got sick.

If I wasn't so irate from that motherfucker getting a peek in to our private life, I think I'd be turned on. The video is like a highlight reel of some of our most intimate moments since the cameras were installed, ending with the way Carley was sprawled out on the dining room table waiting for me the first night she moved in.

I shift in my seat to take some pressure off my hardening cock and chide myself for being such a dirtbag. I shouldn't get any pleasure out of this. It's despicable and such a gross violation of our privacy.

Just then my cell phone rings, bringing me back to the present. My own stomach churns this time, thinking it's Emma. She texted me earlier, letting me know she got reservations at Boku—some swanky sushi restaurant—and reminded me not to be late picking her up. I don't intend to.

Well, Izaak won't be late anyway.

I'm sending him to pick her up while I take a cab. I want to limit the amount of time we're together, and I especially don't want to spend any of it in close quarters with her.

But she isn't the one calling me. It's the security desk from downstairs. I asked them to pull the footage from the penthouse lobby from the last week and check to see if there are any suspicious people who could have gotten past all of the security measures to get up here.

"Dimos Anastos."

"Mr. Anastos, it's Carl from the desk downstairs."

"Carl, hi. What did you find?"

"Nothing out of the ordinary, sir. Only you and Ms. Garrettson. And another couple who I've cross-checked with the guest logs, a Ms. Saylor Wright and Mr. Ren Wilson. In addition to the four of you, I only saw owners and approved guests from Penthouse B."

How the fuck was he able to get on to our network without being within range of the Wi-Fi?.

Then an idea occurs to me. The range of a Wi-Fi signal doesn't stop just outside of someone's door. He could have gotten access from one of the floors beneath us.

"Can you check the hallway footage from floors sixty and up? Again, we're looking for a loiterer. Someone who you don't recognize. He could be in one of the common sitting areas, or he could be camped out in a dark corner. Check everywhere."

"Sure thing, Mr. Anastos. I'll review the footage as quickly as possible, but it will probably take me a week or two to get through all of it."

"That's okay, just let me know what you find out. I'll pay you handsomely for the extra work you're putting in. Thanks, Carl."

Tossing my phone back down on the desk in my study, my fingertips find my temples and rub gentle circles over them in an effort to relieve the tension building in my head.

"D, I appreciate everything you're doing, but is it really important that we find him on tape in our building? That's not going to stop the letters from coming."

I look up to find Carley leaning against the doorframe. I nod my head for her to come closer.

"I know, but if we have that footage, at least we can use it to help our case against him. Remember, Officer Harrison said the letters and messages aren't enough to go after him. We need visual proof Blaine is the one behind all of this."

Carley nods her head in agreement as she leans against my desk.

"Is your stomach any better now than it was earlier?"

"Not really."

"I'll go make you some soup. I think I have some in the cabinet."

"Thanks, but what are you going to eat for dinner?"

Anxiety nearly cripples me upon hearing her question. I haven't told her I have a meeting tonight, yet. I don't want to lie to her, but I remind myself I will come clean about everything once I can confirm Emma is gone and not a threat.

"Actually, I have a last-minute dinner meeting tonight."

"With a client?"

"Someone who isn't going to be in town for very long but wants to meet in person."

She looks at me as I speak, and I hold my breath, ready for an onslaught of questions.

"D, I ..." *Shit.* Here it comes. "Are you meeting with your *guy* tonight?"

"My *guy*?" I'm genuinely confused now.

"I know you're trying to keep some details from me, and I appreciate the lengths you're going to in order to protect me. But Saylor told me you mentioned you have a *guy* tailing Blaine to see what he's up to."

Oh.

I consider my options here. I haven't exactly lied about having a meeting with someone. Emma does want to meet in person, and I'm going to see to it she leaves town immediately when our conversation is over.

However, letting Carley believe I'm meeting with Travis is a blatant lie. I'd be leaving the gray area I've been in since not telling her about Emma from the start. As much as it kills me, for now, I need to make her believe what she thinks is true.

I *will* get information from Travis. Emma *will* leave town.

Once she's gone, I'll sit Carley down and explain everything. She's a smart girl. She may not be happy about it, but she will see reason why I did what I did.

"Yes, we haven't been able to meet in person yet as he lives in another state."

"Thank you, D. At every turn, you've proven how much you care about me, and I can't tell you how grateful I am for you. The month we went without one another was awful. I kicked myself every single day for walking out without saying goodbye. I'm so glad the universe has given us another chance."

"Me too, *théa*." I pause for a minute, running my thumb over her bottom lip. "Carley ... I—"

I'm feeling so many different things right now, but the one that stands out the most is love. I love her. I love her, and I just lied to her. I want nothing more than to tell her exactly how I feel, take her into our bed, and make love to her all night long. She's looking straight into my eyes, the window to my soul, and I know she can see what I'm feeling for her.

"What is it, D?"

I can't tell her yet. I can't lie to her one second and then profess my love for her the next. The timing isn't right. It will have to wait until I come clean about Emma.

"I'm ... going to go heat up your soup."

Planting a kiss on the top of her head, I walk around her and out into the hallway.

I love you, théa.

I've made a mess of things. One Carley doesn't even know about yet. I feel like I'm digging a hole for myself. I just hope Carley will see I did it because the only other alternative was losing her.

And I'll do whatever it takes to make sure I never lose her again.

CHAPTER TWENTY-EIGHT

Dimos

I'm already sitting down in the restaurant, completely uninterested in being here and ready to get home to Carley by the time Emma arrives. I'm not doing her any favors by waiting out front for her like a gentleman, either. I want to make it perfectly clear to her where I stand. The waiter is already pissed because I told him we only needed one menu since I won't be eating.

"Here you are, madame."

I look up from my phone to find a pristinely dressed, narrow-eyed, pucker-lipped Emma standing next to the chair across from me, waiting for someone to pull it out for her to sit in.

It won't fucking be me.

The host, having already left, leaves her standing alone amongst a sea of occupied tables. When she realizes I'm not getting up to greet her, she shoots daggers at me as she pulls her own chair out.

I lean back in my chair, trying to put as much space between us as possible while also making myself appear unaffected and indifferent.

"Dimi," she starts, and I already have to keep my eye from twitching. "I thought we agreed you were going to pick me up."

"You were picked up, but that doesn't mean I needed to be in the car with you. We're at dinner, now what the fuck do you want?"

"Everything is business with you, D. Always has been, always will be."

"Yeah, and my time is precious, so start talking, or I'm leaving. You have ten minutes."

"Fine," she clears her throat. "You know it's not easy for me to admit I was wrong, or to grovel—which I'm *not* doing. But I've been thinking about our marriage for a while and where we went wrong."

Unbelievable. She's deranged if she thinks I believe she feels as though she was wrong.

"You mean you're finally ready to admit you're a controlling, narcissistic bitch?"

Damn that felt good.

"No," she deadpans.

"What then?"

"It's just that I had so many hopes and dreams for us, but you were always caught up in your work. You never made me a priority."

Her comments rile me up to the point where my blood starts to boil. For years, I stood by her side while she chaired this committee and organized that charity banquet. I *tried* to be with her. There was a brief period of time when I remember feeling for Emma a fraction of what I now feel for Carley. But every time I would disagree with her, she would lash out at me. She would tell me I'm an idiot, tell me I know nothing, that I embarrass her in front of her friends.

Her fake friends. I don't think any one of them genuinely liked the other.

"I'm not dignifying that with a response. You and I both know that's not true. You killed our marriage, Emma. Let's not pretend you didn't. You take and take and take from everyone until there's nothing left for them to give you, then you toss them aside. Is that what happened with Gary? Did you bleed him dry already?"

I've shocked her. Never in the course of our marriage did I speak to her this way. I don't miss a glimmer of something flash in her eye when I mention Gary.

"No, that's not it." Suddenly, I realize why she's here. "*He* left *you*, didn't he?"

The look on her face is priceless. She's pissed I was able to figure out why she's here, and especially as quickly as I did.

"That's it, isn't it? And now you've come crawling back because, what? You need money? As if I don't give you enough every month in the disgusting amount of court-ordered alimony you were granted. No ... You're trying to make people believe you left him. That it was your decision, and you were gracious enough to let me back into your life?"

Her affronted look brings me more satisfaction than I ever thought I would feel upon seeing her again.

"You're not capable of love, Emma. It took me a little while to understand that. Now that I have, I realize very little of what happened during our marriage was my fault. Unlike that bullshit you just tried to feed me, I have the ability to admit when I've wronged someone and *actually* mean it."

"Don't try to tell me how I feel."

I wait for her to continue, but she seems to have lost some of the gumption she had when she arrived.

"I—don't presume to think you still know who I am. It's been over a year since I left you. An entire year is a lot of time for ... for ..."

Nothing she says is going to make me believe she's different. That she's changed in just a year's time. That she's not the same exact cold-hearted bitch she was when she left. Even if she *has*, that ship has sailed. Carley is my life now. My anchor. I used to think it was Emma, but boy was wrong.

Carley keeps me grounded, whereas Emma was trying to drown me.

"You can't even pretend to be sorry. A narcissist can't admit when they're at fault because they truly don't believe they have any."

"*Stop that,*" she reprimands, catching the attention of the people at the table next to us. "You're causing a scene."

"You're exactly the same miserable, insufferable, cunt you've always been. You'll never change because you don't want to. And for the first time, being around you doesn't make me feel sorry for myself. It makes me feel sorry for you."

She looks like I slapped her across the face.

"Listen, you've already taken up significantly more time than I wanted to sacrifice for you. You want to blackmail me because you're a petty bitch? Go right ahead. Say whatever you want to say to whoever you think will listen. I know and trust in my truth. Can you say the same?"

With a final piercing glance, I stand up from the table and walk away, leaving Emma and her manipulative games behind.

For good.

CARLEY IS ASLEEP WHEN I GET HOME. I TAKE A QUICK SHOWER BEFORE crawling into bed next to her. The moment my body relaxes, she curls herself up against me, her ass to my dick.

So much for being relaxed.

My cock stiffens as her ass grazes it through my boxer briefs. I look around the shadowed room and debate whether to wake her up or not. Deciding to test the waters, I wrap my arm around her and gently place my hand on her stomach. I run my fingers over her warm skin, down toward the area where her thighs meet, waiting to make contact with the fabric of her panties so I can slide underneath. But I never do.

Because she isn't wearing any.

Inching my fingers farther, the heat intensifies as I reach her core. I dip one finger through her slit and am pleased to find she's not entirely dry. A barely audible moan catches in her throat as my fingertip connects with her clit. Slowly and gently, I move the tip of my finger back and forth, waiting for her reaction.

When she doesn't wake up or make any more noises, I run my finger through her slit once more. I'm a little less careful this time around, hoping she will wake up and join me. My cock twitches as the beginning of another moan sounds. I run my finger along her slit several more times, gathering additional moisture and circling her clit each time. Then her hips begin to shift forward and backward.

"Carley," I whisper in her ear, knowing she may not be able to hear me. "I want to make you come in your sleep. I want you to wake up moaning, writhing, coming all over my fingers."

Her only answer is increased hip movement. It urges me on.

This time, I dip my fingers inside of her. Swirling them around, I feel more arousal building, waiting for its turn to slither out between her legs and seep into the cotton sheets. I hear her breathing increase, and she squeezes her legs together, compressing my fingers inside of her. I use the added pressure and increase my motions.

This time, a loud, unmistakable moan escapes her lips. Her hips gather more speed, and before long, I'm no longer finger-fucking her pussy. Instead, she's fucking my fingers of her own accord. As I begin to wonder if she's awake now, I hear a strangled whisper.

"D..."

She reaches down and clamps her hand around my wrist, as though she's afraid I'm going to pull out of her.

"Fuck my fingers, Carley. Make yourself come."

Not missing a beat, she thrusts her hips faster as she guides my hand in and out of her pussy. I know the moment she's about to come because I feel her inner walls clenching my fingers tight once again. A second later, my hand is coated in warmth as her orgasm bursts out of her.

Slowly, I remove my fingers, and she rolls over onto her back. Now adjusted to the darkness, my eyes catch hers, and I see need gleaming in them. I place my hand between her legs again, but this time she stops me.

"What is it, *théa?*"

"I ... I want ..."

"Don't be afraid to tell me what you need. Whatever it is, I'll give it to you."

My words give her the confidence she needs. She sits up and pushes me down onto the mattress. It's then I realize she's not asking me for something, she's telling me. Her confidence makes my cock ache.

Removing the pillow from underneath my head, she straddles my chest, and I realize what's about to happen. Scooting her body forward, she doesn't stop until her pussy is lined up with my mouth.

"I want to ride your tongue," she says boldly. "And come in your mouth."

Licking her slit, I taste the arousal that still clings to her. She lowers herself down over my tongue, and it slides inside of her. Rising and falling, she takes what she wants from me. When she changes direction and her hips begin to buck forward and back, I remove my tongue from her. My lips cover her clit, and I suck it into my mouth.

Holding her still, I ravage her bundle of nerves until she cries out and succumbs to another orgasm. Drinking all that she gives me, I quickly roll over and pin her to the mattress beneath me.

"Se xreiazomai perissotero apo otidipote allo sti zoi mu, *théa.*"

I need you like I've never needed anything else in all my life.

"Stunning words from an irresistible man," she answers. "I have no idea what you said, but I think I know you well enough by now to guess. Take me, D. Take me however you want, however you need. All day, every day. I'm yours. And there's no one else I'd rather be with than you."

Her words cause my heart—as well as my cock—to swell. Balancing myself on one forearm, I quickly remove my boxers. Then I line my cock up and push inside.

"S' agapo, *théa.*"

I love you.

CHAPTER TWENTY-NINE

Carley

I WAKE UP WITH A MIGRAINE.

It hurts so bad it almost makes me forget about how D woke me up last night and all the fun we had. I'm getting more and more comfortable with asking for or telling D what it is I want and need, but sometimes I still require a little nudge.

As I lay in bed, my eyes land on my phone on the nightstand, and the text message I received before going to bed last night flashes into my mind.

HE ISNT WHO YOU THINK HE IS

It makes me angry that Blaine is so hell-bent on trying to break us up. There's nothing he can do or send that will make me give up on what I have with D.

Speaking of D, when I roll over, his side of the bed is empty. The smell of coffee brewing tells me he's in the kitchen, but the last thing I feel like doing is getting out of bed. I can't remember a time my head hurt this bad. But caffeine will likely help, so I pull the covers back and sit up.

As soon as my feet hit the floor, I catch D walking into the bedroom with a steaming mug of coffee in his hand.

"Good morning, *théa*. I made you coffee."

"How did you know that's exactly what I need right now?"

"I make it my business to know what you desire at all times."

A smile breaks out on my face, but it shoots pain into my head, and I wince.

"What's wrong?" D asks, placing the mug on the nightstand.

"I woke up with a migraine," I tell him, rubbing the side of my head, "but it's nothing a little caffeine can't fix."

"Why don't you go back to sleep? Take the day off and relax."

"No, I'm sure I'll be fine with coffee and a shower."

"Carley."

He stuns me with a glance, and I know I won't be going into work today.

"Or I can lay back down."

D winks at me as I tuck my legs back under the blankets and get comfortable. I stay sitting up so I can still drink my coffee. He's looking at me the same way he did last night, and it makes my heart race. I want to tell him I love him. I think—I *know*—he feels the same. I see it in the way he looks at me sometimes. As though he can't believe this is true. That it must be a dream.

I know, because that's exactly how I feel, too.

I inhale a deep breath, ready to finally spit it out and tell him how I feel, but he speaks first.

"Carley, there's something I need to talk to you about. But it deserves more than a quick morning conversation before I rush off to work. Maybe I can cook us a special dinner tonight, and we can talk about it then."

Goose bumps scatter down my arms at his proposal.

"That sounds wonderful. Looking forward to it."

D leans forward and kisses my head gently.

"Enjoy your day, and I hope you feel better soon, *théa*."

"I'll miss you," I tell him.

"You too."

I watch D's sexy ass walk out of the room, and I actually think the sight of it alleviates some of my headache. I laugh to myself as I take another sip of the delicious caffeine in my hands. As soon as his figure is out of sight, I put my coffee on the table and lay down again. In no time, I'm back to sleep.

It only felt as though a second went by when I'm awoken again. This time from a notification pinging on my phone. The last thing I need right now is to look at a bright screen, but when I peer over and see Saylor's name, I pick it up.

I glance at the clock first.

8:50 A.M.

Even with another hour of sleep, my headache still feels the same.

I turn my screen's brightness down as far as it can go before checking out what Saylor wants. That takes a bit of strain off my eyes and doesn't make my brain hurt quite as much. When I open up my messages, I click on Saylor's name and read what she sent me.

SAYLOR

So do you and D have a plan for the videos yet?

ME

Good morning. What do you mean?

SAYLOR

Morning. I mean, are you going to ignore the asshole's threats?

ME

> Of course. I don't like the idea of them getting out there,
> but at the same time, they aren't crystal clear videos.
> We know it's us because they're from our cameras, but
> if they're put on the internet, you can't really see who
> we are clearly. Same with you and Ren.

SAYLOR

> Good. That delicious Greek may have taken you away
> from me, but I kind of like him. And I think he's really
> good for you, too.

I think about the brief conversation D and I had before he left earlier, and butterflies swirl around in my stomach all over again.

ME

> I think he's going to tell me he loves me tonight.

Before she responds, my phone rings, and I see Saylor's face covering my screen.

"Hello?"

"That's *awesome!* What makes you think he's going to say it?"

"You're ridiculous," I laugh. "I can see it in his eyes whenever he looks at me. It's like my own feelings are being reflected. This morning before he left for work, he mentioned he had something he needed to tell me tonight. He even said he wanted to cook me dinner, which he's never done."

"Morning, boyfriend," Saylor says taking her mouth away from the receiver. I hear her make a kiss noise before speaking to Ren again. "You got in late last night. Sorry, Car. Ren just woke up."

"That's okay, want to talk later?"

"No, it's fine. Now why aren't you going to work today? Playing hooky? Can we do lunch?"

"I woke up with a migraine, so D told me to stay home and get some rest."

"Oh, man, that sucks. So is that a no to lunch? Wait, you're leaving already?" Saylor asks Ren again. It's hard enough keeping up with her conversations under normal conditions, I'm not even going to try when my head hurts as much as it does. "Oh. Okay then. I'll see you tonight."

"Sorry, so lunch, yes?"

"No, Saylor. Focus. I don't feel good, so I am going to stay in bed all day."

"Oh. Want me to bring lunch to you, then?"

"Um, maybe. Can I let you know?"

"Sure, but if I don't hear from you by eleven, I'm coming over, deal?"

"Deal," I concede. Sometimes it's just easier that way. "I'm going to go back to bed now."

"Okay, get some rest, and I'll see you soon."

"See you later."

My head hurts even more by the time I hang up the phone. I walk to the kitchen and grab an ice pack from the freezer. Taking it back to bed with me, I put it over my eyes and fall back to sleep.

THE NEXT TIME I WAKE UP, IT'S DUE TO THE TELEPHONE RINGING throughout the penthouse. It's not a regular landline telephone. It's only there for the security staff to ring us when guests are here to visit or if we have a package waiting that can't fit in our mailbox. Otherwise I would just ignore it.

I glance at the time on my phone when I open my eyes.

12:33 P.M.

That's sure to be Saylor.

Slowly crawling out from under the covers, I notice my head feels a lot better than it did earlier when I went back to sleep. There is still a mild ache, but that extra sleep was exactly what I needed.

I pad out into the hallway, crossing over to the kitchen where the phone is.

"Hello?"

"Hi, Ms. Garrettson, this is Carl from the desk downstairs. I have a Ms. Wright here to see you."

"Thank you, Carl. Please send her up."

"You also just received a package. Would you like me to have her bring it to you?"

My stomach drops. I can't deal with another bomb like the last one Blaine sent us.

"Please," I tell him reluctantly.

"Thank you, ma'am."

I hang up the phone and walk to the front door. Opening it, I lean against the door jamb to wait for Saylor to get here. A couple minutes later, I watch the elevator door open, and Saylor walks off with a bag of delicious smelling food in one hand and a manilla envelope in the other.

"Are you feeling better?" she asks. "I brought you your favorite soup."

She holds up a bag from the Chinese restaurant that makes the best hot and sour soup I've ever tasted. It's my ultimate comfort food.

"Thank you, you didn't have to do that."

"I know," Saylor turns and flashes me a bright smile.

"You're the best, *ever*. And yes, I *was* feeling better until I heard another package was delivered."

"Yeah, and judging by the looks of it, I don't think we're going to like what's inside."

"Ugh. Don't tell me that."

Saylor walks through the doorway and into the penthouse as I close and lock the door behind her.

"Why don't you put the soup in the kitchen. I'm going to shower real quick, and then I'll eat."

"What about this?" She holds the package up.

"I can't even think about that right now. I'll deal with it when I get out."

"Okay, I'm going to find some shitty daytime talk show to watch while I'm waiting."

I leave Saylor in the hallway as I reenter the bedroom and head straight for the shower. I'm in and out in a few minutes, and I feel even better than I did when I got out of bed.

"Okay, I'm back, and I'm starving," I tell her as I walk into the kitchen and grab the food. There is only one container in the bag.

"Aren't you eating?" I ask when I get into the great room.

"I already ate."

"You haven't started one of those ridiculous fad diets again, have you?"

"Hell no," she promises. "Don't you want to know what's in here?"

She holds the envelope up so I know what she's talking about.

"I need food in my stomach first. I have a feeling I'm going to lose my appetite once I see what's in it."

"You're probably right," she agrees as I get comfy on the sofa. "Hurry up and eat. I want to know what it is."

I roll my eyes at her.

"So what have you been up to lately?" I ask. I feel like I haven't gotten a good chance to talk to her in a while. Other than when we've spoken about all things stalker related.

"Not too much. Ren has been working a lot. He's got some huge project going on right now. He's not around as much as he was before. He didn't even get home until like two this morning, and he was out the door around nine again."

"Well, making money isn't a bad thing." I pry the lid off the bowl of soup and dig in.

"Yeah, but it's more than that. I think all this shit with Blaine is causing a rift between us."

My heart clenches for my friend.

"I'm so sorry. If it wasn't for me then none of this would be happening."

"Um, no. If it wasn't for that psycho asshole, this wouldn't be happening. You didn't do anything wrong."

"I'm lucky to have a friend like you who doesn't get sick of me when my life takes a dramatic turn. It's more than anyone should have to put up with."

"I'm your best friend. It's going to take a lot more than this to get rid of me."

I smile at Saylor before my eyes move to the envelope on the table. I eat a few more spoonfuls before I can't take it anymore.

"Okay, give me," I put my soup down. "I need to know what he sent this time."

"*God,* finally," Saylor grabs the envelope from the table and tosses it at me.

I tear it open and look inside. There is a whole stack of things to look at. I take the paper out first.

I TOLD YOU SO

What the hell does that mean?

Saylor takes the letter from me and reads it as I pull the rest of the items from the envelope. My heart plummets into my stomach as I realize what it is

I'm looking at. And the text message I received last night, as well as this letter, begins to make sense. It's a series of photographs of D and another woman at a restaurant.

These can't be recent, right?

But my eye catches another detail in the bottom right corner of each image, and my body goes rigid. A series of numbers on each image. A date and time stamp.

Yesterday's date. 9:02. 9:07. 9:15.

"What the *fuck*?" I exclaim.

"What is it?"

I ignore Saylor's question. *This* was the dinner he had last night? I don't know if I'm more angry or sad, but the feeling of complete betrayal immediately has me questioning everything D has ever said to me.

"That lying son of a bitch."

"*Carley*, what's happening?" she screams.

"D told me he had a dinner with his *guy* last night. You know, the one you told me about when all this shit started happening?"

"Yeah?"

"Look at these pictures. Look at the date and time in the corner. These were taken *last night*."

The photos shock even Saylor silent for a moment.

"Maybe there is a perfectly good explanation."

"I hope so because I'm so upset I'm ready to move all of my shit out of here today."

"Okay, but before you go doing all of that, why don't you talk to him?"

I hop up from the sofa and storm into the bedroom as Saylor calls out from behind me.

"Where are you going?" she asks.

"I'm getting dressed and going into the office. I want answers, and I'm not waiting until he gets home from work to get them."

CHAPTER THIRTY

Carley

I WAS DRESSED and out of the penthouse within fifteen minutes. Colin hailed me a cab when I got out front, and I managed to make it to the office in decent time. As I make my way to D's floor, I try to take a few deep breaths and clear my head.

It almost works, but then I feel the heavy envelope in my hand, and I remember what's in it. And the anger seeps back in. The agony bleeds into my heart. When the elevator doors open, I march across the lobby and don't falter one step before I make it to his office.

"You *fucking asshole!*" I shout.

Unfortunately, I didn't realize he was in a meeting with two other colleagues until it was too late.

Fuck.

The room is blanketed in silence for a few awkward moments before D speaks.

"Uh, Ronald, Lyle, do you mind if we pick this up later?"

"Uhh, ye—yeah," Ronald can barely get his words out. "That works."

I move to the side as the two of them walk toward the door to leave. I can't look at them, so I keep my eyes trained on the floor the whole time.

"Carley?"

When I look up, I'm face-to-face with a very serene looking D. Either he has no idea why I could be this angry or he doesn't care.

"Do you care to explain this to me?"

I throw the envelope of pictures on the ground at his feet. His confusion is quickly overtaken by the shock of my actions. He reaches down and picks it up. Opening it, he looks at the pictures, stunned.

"Look at the timestamp. You told me you were meeting with your *guy*. Sure doesn't look like a guy to me."

D takes a deep breath and rubs his forehead. Anger sears me from within.

"It's not what it looks like."

"Tell me what it *is* then. Who is she?"

"My ex-wife."

"Your—your *what?*"

His ex-wife?

All this time, I thought he'd never been married. I didn't ask him, but he also never mentioned it. I told him everything about me. My family, my history.

"My ex. Emma."

As realization hits, I understand her shitty attitude on the phone now. As well as that dumb nickname she used for him.

"Emma. Emma Kersey is your ... Oh my god." I need to sit down. I feel like I'm going to be sick. Clutching my stomach, I walk the two steps to his sofa and take a seat.

"Carley," D sits next to me and puts his hand on my back.

"*Don't* touch me." I pull away from him.

For the first time ever, I can't stand the feel of his hands on me.

"The day you showed up here, I asked you if there was anything else I should know before making a decision to give us a chance or not. You said *no*. Don't you think this is something you should have told me then?"

He looks at me but doesn't say anything.

"*Why* didn't you tell me?"

D shouts, "Because I love you."

Knowing how much I cared for him until now, hearing him say the words I've been thinking, hits me hard. There have been a few times recently, like this morning, when I felt like he was going to say it. Like he ached to say it, but something was holding him back.

Is this it?

The fact that he's chosen *this* moment to tell me is fucking bullshit. I don't know whether or not to believe him. Is he only saying it because he thinks I'll get over him going to dinner with another woman—*no ... his fucking ex-wife?* Or does he genuinely mean it?

"You're unbelievable. Did fucking your assistant have something to do with your divorce?"

"No."

"I don't believe you. Do you lie to everyone you *love...?*"

"I'm telling you the truth. She left me for someone else. There's a lot more to the story than you know, Carley."

"I can't *imagine* why she would want to leave you, D."

"She was cheating on me, too. Our whole marriage was a fucking disaster. We were completely wrong for one another."

"*I don't care!* I sat in front of you the night you followed me to the club and told you exactly how I felt about liars and cheaters. And you didn't say one word. You sat there acting like a fucking saint who would never do anything like that."

"I didn't. This is what I wanted to talk to you about tonight. I wanted to tell you before something like this happened, but I was scared. Carley, I'm a stupid fucking coward who is terrified of losing you forever. The whole week in Greece, I couldn't keep my eyes off of you. I wanted to know you, to spend time with you. At dinner, I fell in love with your personality. The night we spent together was one of the greatest nights of my life. When I woke up and you were gone, it felt like my heart had been ripped from my chest."

Yeah ... he's told me this story before. The first time I heard it, I practically melted into the marble floor. This time, I still want to melt, but my icy exterior is keeping me in place.

"When Ez called me and told me he found you and who you were, it took me less than thirty minutes to realize I wanted to pick up my entire life and move here so we could be together. I knew then I would do anything to keep you from leaving me again."

God, why is this so fucking hard? He *lied*. I've been sitting here, listening to him for longer than I should have already. I have a firm no liars and no cheaters policy.

D is both.

My heart is burning, threatening to destroy my resolve. But fortunately, my brain is putting up a tougher fight.

"Well, your plan failed. I don't ever want to see you again. Consider this my resignation."

"No! Carley, stop."

His words cause me to halt, but I don't turn around and look at him. I can't.

"Please don't do this. Don't leave like this."

He's right behind me. I can feel his breath on the back of my neck. I can hear the pain in his voice as tears start to pool in my eyes.

"Carley, please ... please don't give up on us. I was going to tell you tonight, I just wanted to get rid of her and make sure she was gone for good this time."

I honestly don't know what to say to him. I deserved the truth when I asked for it. It may not have been a flat-out lie, but a lie by omission stings just as much.

"Carley—"

"Goodbye, Dimos." I whisper to him over my shoulder with tears in my eyes and a painful crack in my heart.

"This isn't over, Carley," I hear him shout just before the elevator doors close, and I leave D's office for the last time. Hailing a cab, I hop in and pull out my phone to text Saylor. I'm reminded of the last time I felt this way, which was also caused by D.

ME

I'm on my way home. To the APARTMENT. Get out the wine. One bottle won't be enough.

I ride the entire way home in both silence and disbelief.

"*His ex-wife?*" Saylor shrieks.

I just walked in the door, and the moment I laid eyes on her the words practically fell out of my mouth.

"His ex-fucking-wife."

"Holy shit, you really do need some wine."

I follow Saylor into the kitchen and sit at the island while she grabs the glasses. With my head in my hands, I close my eyes and try to keep it from spinning. My migraine is back in full force.

"Oh my god," I scoff. "I should have gone straight back to the penthouse before coming here. I have all my shit there."

Fuck.

"I'll help you get it tomorrow while D is at work if you want."

"Thanks."

When I hear the front door open, I think it's D coming to take me back for a moment. I'm stupidly let down when I realize it's Ren.

"Hey," Saylor says to him. "I thought you were working."

She approaches him and plants a kiss on his cheek.

"I've been busting my ass for a while now. I told them I was taking a little time off."

That's random and weird. Especially after what Saylor just said about him pulling away from her. But maybe she was wrong, and he really has just been very busy.

"Besides, when you told me Carley was moving back in, I thought you girls would probably need some of this."

Jesus, Saylor moves fast. But she has to. She keeps up with the gossip in this town like no one I've ever seen before. People rely on her for it. He holds up the bag in his hand, and I can make out the Ben and Jerry's label on two pints of ice cream inside of it.

"I didn't say she was moving back in—I mean, I think maybe she might be—but that's very sweet of you. Thanks for thinking of us."

"Yeah, thanks, Ren."

"Sorry to hear things aren't going to work out for you and D. He was a pretty cool guy."

I offer Ren a tiny smile.

"Here's your wine." Saylor places a glass on the counter in front of me, but I don't even want it anymore.

"I'm sorry, I think I'm just going to go lay down. My migraine is back."

I hop off the stool and walk into my old room, which makes me feel claustrophobic compared to what I was used to at D's place. Shutting the door behind me, I crawl into bed and sob. I hold my pillow to my face to keep the noise from drifting down the hall and into the kitchen. I don't want them to know I'm in here, crumbling to pieces. That my heart hurts so badly, I don't know if I'll ever be able to love again.

I hear Saylor softly enter the room and shut the door behind her. She crawls into bed and wraps her arms around me.

That's all I needed to let go and allow my tears to flow freely. For the rest of the day and the entire night that followed, she held me while I sobbed.

CHAPTER THIRTY-ONE

Dimos

One Week Later

I never should have let her walk out.

It was one of the hardest things I've ever had to do, but I told myself not to make her stay. To give her time to get her anger out and by doing so, she would contact me when she was ready. But that backfired, and she's been going strong for seven days.

It's been the most agonizing week of my life.

I haven't left the penthouse in days. I told the staff Carley had to take some time off, and I was going to work from home.

Carol reached out to me to let me know there has been a lot of talk circulating around the office. Ronald and Lyle approached her not long after Carley broke up our meeting. She could see there was something between Carley and I the moment she saw us together for the first time.

She never said anything because Carley was great at her job, and she started long before I even moved to New York. I gave her a brief explanation of how Carley and I met in Greece and hit it off, but we fell out of touch. She couldn't believe how big a coincidence it was that she began working for me without knowing it. She promised me she would quiet any and all rumors floating around and see to it that Carley will be protected if she ever decides to return.

I pray every day she does.

When I got home from work the day after she left, I realized a number of her things were missing. I pulled up the security footage for that day and watched as she and Saylor collected her belongings. The sight of it hurt almost worse than watching her walk away.

I've sent countless bouquets of flowers to her, apologizing in each and every one. Begging for her to give me another chance. To see my only fault was trying to hide a dark part of my past. A side of me that died before she and I ever met.

When it felt to me like flowers were getting old, I switched to food deliveries. I sent her drunken noodles, her favorite sandwich from Katz's, chicken parmesan from the Italian place up the street that she likes, hot and sour soup.

I've texted, called, and showed up at her door only to have Saylor or Ren tell me she doesn't want to see me.

Not only do I miss her, but I'm scared Blaine is going to get to her. Carl hasn't finished searching through all the footage I asked him to review. If I can get a shot of Blaine on any of the floors of my building, I may be able to get him arrested for trespassing.

But there is a part of me that's even worried to do that now. If I fail in having him arrested, he could go after Carley because of it. And I'm not there to protect her from him anymore.

Walking through the penthouse is depressing. It's almost like living with a ghost. The cup of coffee I made for her that morning sits in my sink, unwashed. Her lip gloss has long since hardened to the ceramic.

A few nights after our run in with Blaine at the bar, Carley told me she was upset we never got to dance together that evening. So I put on some music, and we danced around the penthouse, talking and laughing for hours.

Now as I walk through the space, I can hear the echo of the music that played that night. I can see Carley in her red dress, hair and makeup done, and the biggest smile on her face. Holding on tightly as I spun her around and around. I can picture her naked body pressed up against the window in the great room while I fucked her from behind that first day we left the office.

I walk to the bar and pour myself a double bourbon. The warm, amber liquid burns going down, and the heat spreads into my arms and legs, somewhat relaxing me. Taking to the sofa, I remove my phone from my pocket and sit down. I pull up my messages and scroll through what I've sent Carley since last week.

ME

> Carley, please talk to me. I need you to understand that I had plans to tell you the entire time. I wanted to tell you as soon as she approached me, but things aren't that easy when Emma is involved. She's a vulture, and I wanted to get her out of the city and away from you as quickly as possible.

ME

> I was going to tell you tonight over dinner. After that, I wanted to tell you and show you just how much I love you. Because I do, Carley. I love you so damn much.

Then nothing for a few more days. I didn't want to bombard her.

ME

> Good morning, théa. I know you're still angry with me, but I'm not giving up on us. I haven't given up since the moment I woke up in an empty bed in Greece …

Then from just a couple days ago.

ME

You not being here tears me in two. Please just let me know if you're okay.

ME

He must still be watching us somehow. I added additional measures of security to the Wi-Fi to keep him out, but I haven't received any more letters. He knows you're gone, Carley. Away from me and the safe haven I tried to build for you. That scares me more than the thought of never seeing you again.

I close my messages to Carley and open a new one to Saylor. For a week, she's also been ignoring me, which I completely understand, but I still try. I need to know what's going on.

ME

How is she today?

This time, I see the three dots pop up on the screen. For the first time in a week, is one of them actually going to answer me?

After ten minutes, she finally responds.

SAYLOR

Not good. You really messed up.

If I can get Saylor on my side at least a little bit, then there's a chance she can help Carley realize how much she misses me. Maybe then she'll at least start talking to me again.

ME

I was just trying to protect her. My ex is a vicious, cunning bitch, and she would have chewed Carley up and spit her out.

SAYLOR

I understand, but that's pretty much you saying Carley isn't tough enough to handle her. Do you even know Carley? She's one of the toughest people I've ever met.

I know that, too.

ME

I do know that. I didn't for one second think she couldn't handle Emma. But with all the shit going on with Blaine, I didn't want to add to her plate.

ME

Can you please help me? Can you ask her to text me? Call me? Come by the penthouse? Anything?

SAYLOR

I shouldn't be telling you this. If Carley ever finds out
she'll kick my ass for real and probably not talk to me
for a long time.

ME

Please, tell me.

SAYLOR

I think you and Carley are the real deal. I believe you're
meant to be together. She's hurt, and she needs to work
through her feelings, but if you give her a little more time
and space, I think it will work to your benefit.

For the first time in a week, I can feel my heart start to beat again. It's faint,
but Saylor just gave me the little glimmer of hope that I needed.

SAYLOR

And by space, I mean stop texting her. No more
deliveries. Cut her off. Absence makes the heart grow
fonder and all that bullshit. Got it?

ME

Got it. Thank you, Saylor. Thank you so much.

SAYLOR

You're welcome. I'm deleting these messages and
putting my phone down now.

SAYLOR

Radio silence, bossman.

ME

Understood. Goodbye.

Placing my phone on the table, a small smile breaks through the melancholy
exterior I've displayed since Carley walked out of my office. I pick up my glass
and down the rest of the bourbon in a silent cheer to Saylor. What she just said
to me gives me the strength I need to make a promise to myself that I won't try
to contact Carley again. That I'll let her come to me when she's ready.

THE NEXT MORNING, I'M AWOKEN EARLY BY A PHONE CALL. THINKING IT
could be Carley, I answer it, still half asleep, without even checking the caller ID.
"Hello?"
"Mr. Anastos. It's Travis. I apologize it's taken me so long to get back to you."
Tell me about it.
The only reason I haven't fired him yet is because everyone who recom-
mended him to me tells me this is how he works. He goes dark while he's investi-

gating, and you won't hear from him unless there is something he thinks you need to hear.

"It's fine, do you have anything for me?"

"Well, that's the thing. I've dug as far as I can, and there is not much on Blaine Markson past his prison stint last year. Since he got out, he's been the poster child of the perfect parolee."

That's not what I wanted to hear.

"He's never missed a meeting with his parole officer. He attends his therapy and group sessions regularly, only missing one for an illness that he was able to obtain a doctor's note for."

There's no way.

"Are you sure? I mean, how easy is it to make others believe you've changed, and you're meeting all of the requirements?"

"It's not very easy, actually. I've been trailing him for a week, and he hasn't made one misstep. Nothing to cause any alarm or to make me think he's up to anything other than exactly what he's supposed to be doing."

"You've only been on him for the past week?"

The week that Carley has been out of my life. The week where the threatening letters have stopped. Of course, he's been good this week, he got what he wanted.

"Yes, it was the first opportunity I've had to fly into town."

"I need you to stay on him for a while. I'll pay whatever you need me to pay you. But here's the thing, he's been sending us threatening letters telling Carley he will leak personal photos and videos if she doesn't leave me."

"My personal opinion is to continue living your life as you would if he weren't in the picture."

"Yeah, I would except he sent her photos of a dinner meeting I had with my ex-wife. My ex-wife who Carley wasn't aware of yet. So she moved out. *A week ago.* He got what he wanted, so I'm guessing that's why he's been *good* this week."

"Oh, I see. Okay, I'll extend my trip and keep an eye on him."

"Thank you," I say, but he's already gone.

CHAPTER THIRTY-TWO

Carley

One Week Later

IT'S BEEN ALMOST a week since D last texted me. I haven't received any more flowers or food deliveries, either.

Has he already given up on me? What if I'm making a huge mistake?

So much for following me to the bottom of the deep blue sea.

As each day passes, I'm increasingly consumed by thoughts of him. Touching him. Fucking him. My agonizing sex dreams have returned with a vengeance. It's a thousand times worse than after I got home from Greece. Sometimes I think my pride is at fault. Usually staying firm to my values and beliefs gives me a sense of fulfillment. Right now, however, I just feel empty.

Also absent recently are the letters and text messages from Blaine. He must have found a way around Ren's additional security measure because he obviously knows I moved out.

Just like that motherfucker wanted.

"Carley," Saylor calls my name from the living room. "Food is here."

I'm not hungry, but I know I should eat. Groaning, I roll out of bed and drag my feet down the hallway to the living room. Saylor and Ren are laying the food out on the table in front of the television.

I curl up into a ball on the sofa and pull my baggy t-shirt over my knees for extra comfort.

"Here you go," Saylor hands me a container of kung pao chicken, which I take but set back down on the table. This earns me an overexaggerated sigh from Saylor.

"Knock it off, okay? I feel too lousy to eat."

"Listen," Saylor begins, and I know she's about to say something that will piss me off. "I get that you're sad, and you have every right to be. I was angry at him at first, too."

"At first? Meaning you're not anymore?"

"You know I'll always be *angry* with him as long as you are."

I don't miss the sarcasm in her tone when she says the word *angry*.

"As you should," I reply.

"*Should* he have told you? Yes. He should have had the balls and the intelligence to know the truth may have been hard for you to hear, but ultimately you would have respected him more for being upfront about it."

I think about that for a minute. If D would have told me in his office that day, or later that night when he brought me back to his penthouse when I was drunk, would I have given him—*us*—another chance?

Why do I even have to think about it? I *know* I would have. Just like when I left his office the first day I realized who he was, *knowing* I would be back the following Monday.

"But at the end of the day, *you* aren't the one he cheated on."

"But he still lied to her," Ren interjects. "And he blatantly told her he was going to a meeting with a *guy*."

"Who's fucking side are you on?" Saylor shoots back at him.

"I'm on Carley's side," he shrugs, and I like knowing he has my back.

But once again, Saylor is right.

"Since the moment you laid eyes on him in Greece, there hasn't been one second of one day that he hasn't taken up space in your mind and in your heart. If I thought it was truly over with you guys, then I would be stuffing my face with crab rangoon and chicken in garlic sauce instead of trying to beat it into your head that you need to give him a chance to explain, and then work things out with him."

"Say, you know what happened with my parents. The lying. The cheating. What if Lucas never died? I don't think I ever would have met my real father, and I can't imagine a life without him in it. I don't want to go through that. It's why I told him outright those are hard limits for me. Whether he lied or just omitted the truth, what's to say he won't do it again?"

I watch as Saylor shakes her disappointed head at me.

"I just really don't think lying and cheating come natural to him. Your mother? Yes. D? No. Sometimes people lie to protect those they care about."

Yeah, or to protect themselves.

"I love you, Say. And I really appreciate the advice and everything you're trying to do. But I can't be with someone who is afraid to tell me their whole truth. No matter the reason. I'm a big girl, and I can handle it."

At that, I stand from the sofa and take a deep breath. I know what I need to do.

"I'm going to get dressed and go to the office. D should be gone by now, and I'll finally be able to get my things that are still there. When I wake up tomorrow, I am going to go out and look for a new job. It's time I start to put all of this behind me and move on."

I don't stick around to wait for Saylor's look of disapproval. When I get to my room, I change into jeans and a t-shirt, straighten my hair, and throw on some mascara and lip gloss. As painful as it's going to be, I need to say goodbye in order to move on.

IT'S ABOUT 7:45 WHEN I GET TO THE OFFICE. I DON'T SEE ANY REASON WHY D should still be here, but just to be safe, I hang out outside of the building until 8 P.M. When I finally make it upstairs, I move quickly across the lobby toward my *former* desk. As I get closer, the sight of D's office door cracked open and light streaming out of it stops me in my tracks.

I stand, frozen to the spot.

Did he hear the elevator? I walk to the wall next to his office and listen carefully for any indication he's approaching his door. That's when I hear the unmistakable sound of moaning coming from inside the office.

What the fuck?

Does he have another girl in there? Is it Emma? Someone else? Another colleague? I want to march right in there and catch him in the act. Let him know he's just proven to me everything I needed to know about him.

What the hell did I think I was getting in to with a man who is practically a stranger? I don't *really* know a whole lot about him. Obviously, or else I at least would have known he has an ex-wife.

Instead of barging in there, I take a deep breath and try to calm myself down a little bit. Deep down, I *know* at the heart, D is a good person. He just chose to make a dumb choice. Now I need to check and see if he's in the middle of making another one.

Pushing the door open, I peek my head inside slowly, until I know which way his attention is focused. When my eyes land on him, his back is to me, and I can see the top of his head resting on the back of the chair.

Another moan hits my ears, and based on his positioning, I'm having a hard time not visualizing a woman on her knees between his legs at this very moment. But I can't see past his desk to confirm that theory. The sound of him, though, has my stomach stirring in a way only D can conjure. I close my eyes and try to control my own breathing.

Before I have a moment to obsess over the maybe woman sucking his dick, he moans again. But this moan is a little different.

"Carley ..." My eyes fly open, thinking he's spotted me, but he hasn't.

He's turned his chair toward the door slightly. Enough for me to see he's controlling his own pleasure at the moment. With his fist hugging his dick and my name on his lips, he's jerking off to thoughts of me.

Me.

Now that the terror of him being with someone else has worn off, this suddenly feels very inappropriate. Like I'm some kind of sick voyeur. Before I have a chance to leave, he reaches for the pile of tissues on the top of his desk and uses them to cover the tip of his dick.

"Fuck," he's breathing even harder now. *"Carley ..."*

He moans my name loudly as his orgasm rips through his body. With several more pants and a lot of shaky breathing, I watch him as he wipes off his tip and throws the tissues into the trash can under his desk.

I need to leave. I shouldn't have come. As I turn to go, my elbow slams into the door, and you'd have to be deaf not to have heard it.

Damn it!

"Carley?" D's voice is filled with shock.

I flee the doorway just as I hear him shouting behind me.

"*No!* Carley wait!"

But I'm already halfway across the lobby by that point. I make it to the elevators and press the button just as I feel D's hand clamp around my bicep.

"Wait, *please.* I'm begging you, Carley."

He swings me around and gently pushes me up against the marble wall next to the elevator. Boxing me in with his arms, there's nowhere for me to go. But the pleading look in his eyes is what keeps me there. His head falls as though weighed down by anguish. The second I open my mouth to tell him to let me go, his gaze finds mine again, rendering me speechless.

His eyes speak to me, saying everything I've wanted to hear from him for the past two weeks.

He's sorry. He was an idiot. He should have had faith in me. He knows he fucked up, and he will have to earn back my trust.

Then his gaze turns dark, and he removes his hands from the wall, gripping my shirt in both of his fists. My breathing increases as my heart beats faster than it ever has before. I no longer want to run. I don't want to cast D from my life. I lose my hold on the barricade around my heart I have struggled to keep in place over the last two weeks, and it comes crashing down.

"I fucking love you, *théa.*"

The ferocity in his voice heats me from within. There is a fire in his eyes I've only seen once before, when he chased me around his penthouse before completely and thoroughly ravaging my body in ways I never thought were possible.

"I protect what's mine, and I will never apologize for that. That's all I was trying to do for you. I'm not always going to make the right choices, but my actions will *never* be against you. Everything I do, I do it with you in mind. With our *future* in mind. Because we *will* have a future together, Carley."

My heart swells at the thought of a future with D. It always has. Saylor was right, from the first moment I laid eyes on him, I knew. He *is* my future, and nothing else will ever compare to him.

"There's no way in hell I'm letting you go again. I don't care if I have to tie you to the bed in my penthouse and fuck you until you forget why you were angry in the first place. I'll do it. I'll fuck this insane notion of you leaving me right out of your head. I'll—"

"D," I interrupt his monologue, and he stops, his eyes never leaving mine. "I fucking love you back."

A split second later, D has me in his arms. I drop my purse to the floor and curl myself around his muscular body, my flip-flops flying to the ground. With a kiss more passionate than any we've shared before, he carries me back across the lobby toward his office. He kicks the door closed behind us and turns the lock into place.

He walks us to his desk and sits me down on its surface. With one quick motion, he sends everything on it crashing to the floor. None of it is important.

The only thing that matters right now is him and I and reconciling our feelings in the only way we know how.

D takes the hem of my shirt and pulls it over my head quickly. As he begins to unhook my bra, I reach for the button of his pants. His belt is still undone from a moment ago. I can't believe he's even ready to go again. But when I unzip his pants and they fall to the floor, the outline of his dick through his boxer briefs confirms he's rock hard and more than ready for round two. I reach between his legs and cup his fabric covered balls, delighting in the moan that escapes his lips.

When my bra is off, D gently pushes me backward so I'm laying across the surface of his desk. Once he removes his own shirt, his hands fly to the button of my jeans, and he pulls the loose denim and my underwear down my legs in one swift motion. The last thing to come off is his boxers. Once he's free of them, he grabs my legs around the backs of my knees and pulls me forward.

"Carley, I've been so lost without you the past two weeks. I've dreamt of you every day and night. Dreamt of holding you, fucking you, tasting you."

"Me too. I need you so bad right now."

He places his index and middle fingers into his mouth and lathers them up with his saliva. It's completely unnecessary as I'm already sopping wet for him, but it's hot as hell to watch him, so I don't say anything.

He reaches in between our bodies and plunges his fingers through my opening.

"*Fuck*, you're already so wet."

"It was so painful without you, D. See what you do to me?"

Removing his fingers, he replaces them with his dick. The pleasurable pain I feel as he fills me after two long weeks is staggering. Completely unimaginable. He drives his hips back and forth, giving me little time to get used to the size of him all over again. But I don't care. I need it. I crave it. I wrap my legs around his torso as he lays his body over mine. Cupping my cheeks, he holds my stare as he continues pounding into me over and over again.

I can feel my first orgasm build within me quickly. Placing my hand on his cheek, I pull him toward me and kiss him like my life depends on it. As he pushes me higher, my breathing grows heavier. I break away from his lips, gasping for air.

"D, *fuck*. Don't stop," I moan.

"Never, *théa*. I'll never stop."

"I've missed hearing you call me that."

My admission spurs on his thrusting. I didn't think he could move any faster than he already was. When he leans down and sucks my bottom lip between his teeth, it feels like electricity jolts through my body until it homes in on my core, and my orgasm tears through me.

D groans as I clench around his dick. He holds his breath as the added friction pushes him toward the edge. One more thrust and he's coming inside of me, spewing like a geyser. With one final exhale, his body collapses onto mine. I feel him trembling, and I wonder if that's the biggest orgasm he's ever had before. Mine certainly felt like it.

"Come here," he pants, lifting me from the desk and carrying me to the sofa.

He lays me down, and the leather helps to cool my feverish body. When D pulls out of me, I can feel our joint warmth leaking out from my core.

"I'll be right back. Don't move," he orders me.

I admire his taut back and ass as he walks behind his desk and picks something up before returning to the sofa holding a box of tissues.

"These are getting a lot of use tonight."

The corner of his mouth lifts with his smile, and the sight of it wins me over once again. Just like it did in Greece. Rubbing the soft cloth between my legs, he cleans up any evidence of our pleasure from my body as well as the sofa before tossing the used wad onto the floor.

His gaze flits from between my legs to my eyes before he speaks again.

"I think I missed a spot, but it's not something I'll be able to clean with a tissue."

I don't understand what he means at first. But when he slowly lowers himself onto the seat of the couch and curls his arms around my thighs, his message becomes crystal clear. Before I've fully recovered from my last orgasm, D's tongue attacks me. He plunges it inside of me, lapping up any remaining arousal that was left behind while also creating more. His thumb presses on my clit as his tongue continues to dance inside of me.

As another orgasm threatens to detonate, D's eyes shoot to mine. Not letting go, he holds my stare the entire time he's devouring my pussy as though it's the sweetest dessert he's ever tasted. Removing his tongue from inside of me, he moves his mouth up to my clit. With one hand, he holds me open so he has better access to it. With the other, he curls his fingers inside and moves them around until he finds that sweet spot he knows is there.

"*Ohh* ..." I moan. "D ... it feels so good."

He stretches me wider as he deepens his reach inside of me. With one final nibble on my clit, I come undone. D, always infatuated with my arousal, moans at the taste and feeling of the moisture flowing from me.

Once he's had his fill, he covers my body with his again.

"I'm still not done. You have no idea how hard it's been without you for the past two weeks. I haven't been this horny since I was in college."

"I do know," I tell him. "Because it was hard for me, too. I thought about you constantly. I tried to take care of myself, but nothing compares to your touch."

"Carley, the thought of you touching yourself does exhilarating things to my body."

I laugh gently, but then I feel his dick hardening against my stomach. My eyes grow wide when I realize he's already ready to go again.

"You're ... ready *again*?"

"I told you I was horny. I'm not quite there yet, but I know a way to speed it up."

"Oh, yeah? What's that?"

He sits back on his heels and places a hand on each of my knees. Pulling my legs open wide so he can see me, I watch as his eyes glisten.

"I want to watch you play with yourself, *théa*."

The idea of him watching causes moisture to pool at my core immediately. Even though I'm already wet, I make a show of sticking out my tongue and running my fingers through my saliva. I push them inside of my mouth and close my lips around them, pulling them in and out, mimicking the actions I take when giving D a blow job.

His stare turns severe, and I know he's mad at me for teasing him.

Removing my fingers from my mouth, I shoot him a devilish grin as I slide my hand over my chest, down my stomach, and in between my legs. I gather additional moisture from below and spread it over my clit, making it easy to rub over the already sensitive area.

I give him a light moan the second I touch myself there. I think about all the times over the past two weeks when I've sat in my bed, rubbing myself to thoughts and mental images of D. Of him and I together. Thinking about his hands on me. His dick inside of me. All the times he went down on me. When he fucked me against the window in the great room. For two weeks I was barely able to get off.

Now, with D here in front of me, having just had him inside of me, it's exactly what I needed. In seconds, I already feel like I could come. My legs close of their own accord as my muscles clench, preparing for another orgasm to take me over. But D doesn't like that. He grips my knees again and forces them back open wide.

"Open, *théa*."

"Sorry," I can barely whisper.

My breathing is erratic, and I know when I do orgasm, it's going to be explosive and uncontrolled.

"You have nothing to be sorry for. Now come for me, *théa*."

As though his words were a switch, a euphoric feeling overpowers me and sends pins and needles through my veins, piercing me from the inside out.

I cry out as my release splatters across the leather beneath me. Just before my eyes are forced closed with pleasure, I get a good look at D. His eyes are dilated, focused on my pussy. His hand is wrapped around his dick, pumping up and down rapidly. He's hard as a rock and looking like he could blow again at any moment.

He's the epitome of imperfect perfection.

And I am deeply, madly in love with him.

AFTER MY SELF-IMPOSED ORGASM, D MADE LOVE TO ME ON THE SOFA FOR what felt like hours. We didn't talk. All we did was feel. It was healing, cathartic, and one of the best moments of my entire life.

Now that both of us have come down from multiple, mind-blowing orgasms, the elephant in the room has appeared. But right now, it's the last conversation I feel like having. I don't want to ruin the moment.

"D?"

"Yes, *théa*?" He runs the back of his hand over my arm again.

"Tonight was wonderful, but it doesn't erase what happened. I'm still hurting, but I want to work through it with you."

We're completely naked, laying back to front on his sofa. He has me wrapped in his arms, and things feel almost perfect between us again.

Almost.

"I think there's still several things we need to talk about. I'm not going to go so far as to say this was a mistake, but I would have preferred discussing what happened with you first."

"I agree with you. I know I fucked up and risked losing you. And I know I'm the luckiest bastard in the world to get another chance."

"You are," I chuckle. "But our discussion will have to wait until tomorrow. You've thoroughly exhausted me, and I need sleep."

I try sitting up, but suddenly his arm feels like it weighs about a hundred pounds.

"D ... I need to go."

Reluctantly, he lets me up but grabs my wrist before I have a moment to gather my clothes.

"Come back to the penthouse. You can sleep there," D suggests.

"I think we both know neither of us will get any sleep if I go back to your penthouse tonight."

Again, he lets me go but he doesn't like doing it. His annoyed, displeased stare tells me so.

"Okay, fine. But meet me for lunch tomorrow. We can talk it over then. Please, Carley."

I don't answer him as I pull my clothing back onto my body. Once I'm all dressed, my eyes find his. The pleading look in them that held me hostage against the wall next to the elevator earlier is back.

"Okay," I tell him, pretending I'm giving in. "I'll text you in the morning."

Finally accepting of the plan, D stands and gets dressed as well.

"How did you get here?" he asks.

"I took a cab."

I don't miss his look of annoyance at my choice of transportation.

"I'll call Izaak. He can take you home. There are a few things I need to finish now that I'm taking tomorrow afternoon off."

"You don't need the whole afternoon. It's just lunch."

"Carley, once I make you realize you want me back, I plan on taking you home—to *our* home, at the penthouse—and we won't see daylight again for at least three days."

All I can do is smile.

Because I would love nothing more.

CHAPTER THIRTY-THREE

Carley

I can't remember the last time I felt this hungover.

My head is thumping, and the light streaming in through the windows feels like a knife to my eyeballs. I don't know if it's because of the mind-blowing sex or the celebratory wine Saylor and I had when I got home. The last thing I remember is walking in the door and telling Saylor what happened. We accidentally woke Ren up with our squealing, and then she asked him to get us some wine before he went back to sleep.

When I throw my legs over the side of the bed, they feel like they have cement in them. I glance at the clock on my bedside table and have to rub my eyes to see it right. I thought it said 11:23 A.M.

When I look again, I realize I wasn't seeing things. It's actually that late.

Holy shit.

What the fuck?

I can hear Saylor now. As soon as I get to the kitchen and she sees how late I slept, she's going to say something ridiculous, like D really dicked you good or something else just as ludicrous. I tap my phone screen, and I notice a couple of notifications. Unlocking it, I see a text from Saylor, and I realize D has also texted me a few times this morning. I open D's messages first.

The first one at 8:33.

DIMOS

Good morning, beautiful.

Next, at 9:17.

DIMOS

Last night was mind-blowing. I can't wait to see you today. Let me know where you want to eat and when, and I'll make the arrangements.

Then at 10:04.

DIMOS

I hope everything is okay and you aren't having second thoughts. I went ahead and made reservations for Il Forno 12:30. Looking forward to seeing you, théa.

Finally, at 10:59.

DIMOS

Okay, I'm officially worried. Please text me, Carley. I love you.

Shit. I hate that I made him worry, and I respond immediately.

ME

Hey! Good morning. I'm so sorry I made you worry. When I got home last night, I told Saylor what happened (not everything that happened) and we celebrated with a little wine.

ME

At least, I think it was a little. But this morning it feels like a lot more than I may have originally thought.

ME

Anyway, Il Forno at 12:30 sounds great. Looking forward to it.

I'll have to move quickly if I want to make it there in an hour. I shoot D one final message before I get ready.

ME

And I love you, too.

After that, I put my phone down and head into the kitchen for some much-needed coffee. My head is so foggy, and this may be the only thing that will help. The apartment is suspiciously quiet. Once my mug is full of delicious, hot caffeine, I head back down the hallway and poke my head into Saylor's room before going into my own. It's empty.

I'm sure Ren is working, but where the hell is she? That's when I remember I also had a text from her that I completely forgot about. When I get back to my room, I place my mug on the bedside table and pick up my phone again. I see another message from D waiting.

DIMOS

You should wear that red dress for me …

ME

Don't you think that's a little fancy for lunch?

DIMOS

Never.

ME

I think I'll stick with shorts, but maybe I'll pack it in my overnight bag.

DIMOS

Okay, deal. See you soon.

ME

Can't wait!

After that, I pull up my conversation with Saylor and finally read her waiting message.

SAYLOR

I know you said D was a generous lover, but he must have generously fucked you the fuck up last night. You were dead halfway through one glass of wine.

I can't help but laugh at her message. She's not wrong.

SAYLOR

Anyway, Ren surprised me with breakfast followed by a full spa day today. Massage, facial, hair, nails … the works. And he's getting us a limo to the club tonight. He told me he got a promotion at work and wanted to splurge by spoiling me. So I won't be available most of the day. I hope you have a blast with D, and I can't wait to hear all the details!

That's so adorable. I think Ren feels inadequate sometimes, compared to Saylor. She makes substantially more than he does, almost without trying. He works so hard, and he's good at what he does. If anyone deserves a promotion, it's him.

ME

Wow! Have a great time!!! I doubt I'll be reachable once I meet up with D. He was pretty adamant about not coming up for air for a while once we talked through everything.

ME

> I promise to call or text as soon as I can, though. Thank you so much for being on OUR side and not just mine. As always, you knew exactly what I needed to hear.

ME

> I love you, jerk face. And tell Ren I said congratulations!

Once the message is sent, I take another swig of my coffee before heading into the bathroom to shower. That should help clear my head, but I also want to make sure I'm completely cleanly shaven and smooth for D.

When my hair is knot free and I'm happy with the silkiness of my skin, I turn the water off and grab a towel from the hook outside of the shower door. I wrap it around my body and then grab another one for my hair.

Before I exit the bathroom, I brush my teeth and apply some moisturizer to my face. Finally, once I'm back out in my room, I grab a pair of shorts out of my dresser. I toss them onto the bed and turn back around to grab a pair of underwear from my drawer, but something stops me, and I give further thought to my wardrobe choice.

It'll be sexier if I wear a skirt.

And D isn't expecting it. Quickly, I drop my shorts back onto my bed and go into my closet. I grab a tight black pencil skirt and a bright red blouse and take them back out into my room. I select a sexy black thong out of my underwear drawer, and I pull it on before zipping the skirt into place and tucking in the blouse.

As I look at myself in the mirror, I hear my phone vibrate again. Before I check it, I flash myself an excited grin. I haven't felt this giddy or nervous since my first date with D back in Greece.

Walking to my bed, I take another sip of coffee, careful not to spill it. Then I pick up my phone, but when I pull up my messages, I nearly drop it.

There's a text from Blaine.

I haven't heard from him in two weeks, and the moment I meet up with D again, he's back? What the fuck?

Against my better judgement, I open the message and nearly throw up as soon as I see what he sent. Staring back at me is Saylor. Tied to a chair with duct tape over her mouth and tears streaming down her face. She looks absolutely terrified, and it crushes me. Next to her in another chair is Ren. At least it looks like him, but I can only see the top of his head and part of one side of his face. I think there is duct tape over his mouth too, but I can't make it out. He has blood dripping out of his ear, and the way his head is hanging, he looks unconscious.

"Oh my god," I cry to the empty room as hot tears roll down my cheeks.

What the fuck do I do? Where are they? Saylor just said her and Ren were out to breakfast. How could this be?

Opening my conversation with Saylor once more, I type out a quick message.

ME

> Saylor, please message me back ASAP. Something
> happened, and I need to know you're okay!

I double check the time she sent her first message. It was a while ago at 9:34. *Fuck.*

That's plenty of time for Blaine to have gotten ahold of them and taken them somewhere. But how? And where?

I feel my phone vibrate in my hand again, and I look down to see another message from Blaine has come through.

> 212-555-1212
>
> REN DIDNT MAKE IT
>
> 212-555-1212
>
> UNLESS YOU WANT SAYLOR TO SUFFER THE SAME
> FATE MEET ME AT 8293 72ND STREET BROOKLYN
>
> 212-555-1212
>
> COME ALONE AND DONT TELL ANYONE WHERE
> YOURE GOING OR ILL FUCKING KILL HER
>
> 212-555-1212
>
> ILL KNOW IF YOU DO

My phone drops from my hands as I read the new messages from Blaine. I can't believe this is happening.

Fuck.

What do I do? He can hack in to our security system, so why wouldn't he be able to hack in to my cell phone, too? Did he track me to the office last night? Maybe he realized how long I was there? Or that Izaak drove me home instead of me taking another cab?

I want to call D so bad and tell him what's going on, but I'm scared Blaine will find out and hurt Saylor because of me. I can't let that happen. My head still feels like it's stuffed full of cotton, but I can't let that slow me down. I only allow myself to linger in the apartment long enough to change into the shorts on my bed and a t-shirt before flying down the eight flights of stairs to the street and hailing a cab. As soon as I'm seated, I shout the address and tell him to step on it.

The drive through the city and into Brooklyn feels like it takes forever. My heart lurches when we pass the street Il Forno is on. I look at the time and wonder briefly if D is already there. It's 12:00. I'm sure he is, because he wouldn't have been able to focus on work anyway. He's probably sitting in front of the restaurant in the limo, wasting time, waiting for me to arrive. I try to control my breathing while also reminding the driver I'm in a hurry. Though I'm terrified to get to my destination. I want to save Saylor more than anything, but I don't know if I can take on Blaine by myself.

And Ren. Poor Ren didn't deserve to get dragged in to this. He's so innocent in all of it. My heart breaks at the fact that he's gone. And it's all my fault. I wipe away more tears as we exit the Queens Midtown Tunnel. We're that much closer to wherever it is that Blaine has Saylor.

Why did I have to drink wine last night? If I hadn't, maybe I would have been awake in enough time to go to breakfast with Saylor and Ren. We all would have been together when Blaine contacted them or attacked them or whatever he did to get them where they are now.

I feel the taxi driver's eyes on me as I let out a sob I was trying to hold in.

"Are you okay, miss?" he inquires.

"Yes, I'm fine. Thanks," I try to offer him a tiny smile, but I can't.

Not wanting to draw any more attention to myself, I wipe my eyes and try to think about what I can do to get Saylor out of there and away from that sick fuck.

Before I'm ready, the cab pulls up in front of a strip of rowhomes. Right in front of me is 8293. I throw a hundred-dollar bill at the driver and get out of the car. Running up the front steps, I feel the effects of the wine still in my system. Something is wrong; wine has never done this to me before. I chalk it up to my anxiety and take a deep breath, trying to convince myself I'm strong enough to handle the situation I am about to walk into.

I have to be. Saylor's life depends on it.

Wrapping my fingers around the door handle, I turn it to try and open the door, but it's locked. I make a fist to knock on the door, but it flies open before I get a chance to make contact. A hand reaches out and grabs me, and the shock of it takes away my ability to see him clearly. Once I'm in his grasp, he pulls me inside and backs me up against the wall.

His face doesn't register properly at first, and I feel the same way I did when I woke up this morning and looked at the clock. Whether it's my eyes or my brain playing tricks on me, Blaine looks a little different than I remember. It was dark in the bar when I saw him weeks ago, and it was almost a year before that when I saw him last. Surely he's changed a bit over the past nine months.

As he speaks, I can feel his hot, acrid breath on my skin.

"Hello, Carley."

CHAPTER THIRTY-FOUR

Dimos

I EXIT the limo at 12:25. As soon as I got here, I realized I should have sent Izaak to pick Carley up. That would have been the gentlemanly thing to do, but I was so preoccupied with thoughts of last night, it didn't even cross my mind. It's just one more thing I'm looking forward to apologizing for as I feast on Carley's delicious body when I get her back to the penthouse after this.

As my eyes scan the street, my heart leaps at every cab that turns down it, thinking Carley has finally arrived. But as the minutes tick by, I begin to get worried she isn't going to show. Only barely an hour ago she told me she was looking forward to it. So that doesn't make any sense.

At 12:40, I pull up our conversation and type out a text to her.

ME

> I'm sure you're just running a few minutes late, but I wanted to check in on you to make sure everything's okay?

Several minutes go by with no response.

ME

> I'm worried about you. I hope you're not having second thoughts. Even if you are, please respond so I know you're okay. It's not like you to be late.

After that, I pull up Saylor's number and shoot her a text, too. She's likely to answer me and might be able to put my worries to rest.

ME

> Hey, Carley was supposed to meet me for lunch. Do you know if she's left the apartment yet?

A couple minutes later and I feel my phone vibrate in my hand as a phone call comes through. I quickly answer it, thinking it's Carley.

"Carley?"

"No, Mr. Anastos. It's Carl."

"Oh, hi, Carl. Listen, this isn't the best time—"

"I finally finished going through the footage from the building like you requested. Sorry it took so long. But I wanted to tell you there was no sign of anyone suspicious on the tapes. The only people I saw were owners and their guests."

Fuck.

"Okay, thanks Carl. I'll drop off some money to you at the desk next time I swing by."

"I appreciate it, sir. Thank you."

I end the call, and a terrifying feeling creeps up my spine as I continue looking up and down the street for any sign of Carley. How the hell would Blaine be able to get access to our security system without being on our network?

I unlock my phone again and give Travis a call.

"Travis."

"You're good with computers and back doors and all that, right?" I ask as I pace the sidewalk outside of Il Forno.

"Yes. I'm an elite hacker."

"So tell me, how would Blaine be able to get on to our network or view our security footage without gaining access to our Wi-Fi first?"

"He'd have to be some kind of high-level hacker in order to pull something like that off. I mean, either that or work for the security company who installed the system.

His words cause my feet to stop moving, like they're stuck in cement as a horrible thought enters my mind.

Ren.

No. That can't be right. Ren has been nothing but supportive and helpful this entire time. He offered to install the system outside of ... regular business hours. He initiated the installation and said it would be good to get it set up as soon as possible. He's been living with Saylor this whole time. He's been to the penthouse and around Carley for months. Surely, one of us would have noticed something was off about him, right?

Suddenly, I feel like I'm going to be sick.

"Forget about Blaine Markson. I need you to look in to someone else."

"Who?"

"Ren Wilson. I don't have much else on him other than he works at Guardian Elite Security. I need an address, anything you can get quick. I can't get ahold of Carley, and now I have a really bad feeling *he's* the one behind it all."

"I'm on it. I'll call back as soon as I can."

I end the call and pull up Ren's number, but the call goes straight to voicemail.

Shit.

Opening the internet browser on my phone, I search for the local branch of

Guardian Elite here in the city. I click on their number and pray someone answers.

"Guardian Elite," a man answers after the third ring.

"Hi, I need to talk to a manager or someone with decision making abilities about a current employee of yours."

"Uhh ... okay, just one second."

He puts me on hold, and my blood boils hotter with each second that passes before someone comes back on the line. I end up having to wait several agonizing minutes.

"This is Benton."

"Benton, my name is Dimos Anastos. I'm calling in reference to an employee of yours. Ren Wilson."

"I'm sorry, but we don't have anyone here by that name."

My heart plummets into my stomach.

"You're sure? Because I had someone by that name, with your uniform and all your marketing materials, install a system in my home several weeks ago."

"We did have someone by the name of Ren who worked here, but his last name was Butler. He was let go a couple of weeks ago, though."

"I know you're probably not at liberty to tell me why, but I'm going to ask anyway. I'm having an issue currently where I believe he may have been spying on my girlfriend and I through our camera system."

The line is silent on the other end.

"Are you still there?"

"Yes, sir. And uhh ... I can confirm he was let go for something of that nature. We tracked recordings of two different systems over the course of a couple weeks, each leading back to his login credentials."

The fire that started in my veins a moment ago is now a raging inferno.

"And you didn't think it was worth a phone call to make me aware there had been a security breach on my account?"

Again, there's silence.

"Hello?"

But there's no response. I check my phone screen and see the call has been disconnected.

Motherfucker.

I quickly call Travis back.

"Yeah," he answers.

"Butler. His last name isn't Wilson, it's Butler."

I hear a lot of typing going on in the background before he speaks again.

"What's the name of the company he works for again?"

"Worked. He was fired a couple weeks ago. And it's Guardian Elite."

Again, more typing.

"Got him."

"What do you mean you got him?"

"I was able to get into the company's North American employee database, and I pulled up his file. Ren Wilson Butler. Address is 1736 E 23rd Street, downtown."

"Can you text that address to me?"

"Sure thing."

"And let me know if you find anything else out. Thanks, Travis."

"You got it."

I climb into the back of the limo and shout the address Travis gave me to Izaak, telling him to step on it.

I have a bad feeling I might find Carley there.

And an even worse feeling I won't.

CHAPTER THIRTY-FIVE

Carley

*"R*EN*?"*

I have no idea what's happening.

"I thought you were dead? *Saylor!*" I shout, as I sluggishly run up the stairs behind the door.

I don't hear any movement when I get to the top of the steps.

What the hell is going on?

"Where's Saylor?" I lock eyes on Ren as he slowly climbs the stairs.

"I don't know. Off doing whatever idiotic thing she does. It was getting really hard to put up with her after a while. She almost didn't make it."

What is he saying? Why is he talking about her like that?

"She's not here?"

"Uhh, no."

"I'm so confused. Blaine texted me with a horrifying picture with the two of you in it."

"My roommate is a design major. I asked him to make it look brutal. He delivered."

"It was fake? Wait, is Blaine here?"

"Oh, Carley. You're usually *much* smarter than this. I think I slipped a little too much Rohypnol into your wine last night."

The more I try to make sense of things, the less things make sense. I take a deep breath and shake my head to try and break through the fog. Rohypnol?

"You drugged me?"

"I had to. I couldn't listen to one more goddamn word about you and D fucking for hours."

The realization of what exactly is going on finally hits me then.

"*Oh my god.* You're the stalker ..." I whisper more to myself than to Ren.

My entire body is trembling. I want to run, but he's blocking my way to the stairs.

"Yes, you're finally getting it," he confirms, breathing a sigh of relief.

"Where is Saylor?"

"I'll answer whatever questions you have, but I want you to sit down first."

He waves his hand toward the doorway to my right. In the room I see a bed and a dresser, and there is also a chair set up in front of a television set. There's no way in hell I'm going into a bedroom with him.

I shake my head, "I don't want to sit."

His eyes narrow slightly, and I can tell he doesn't like being told no.

"I'll only ask nicely one more time, Carley."

He takes an intimidating step toward me. His frame towers over me, and he's never seemed taller than he does right now.

I look toward the room again, but I also take note of a large gap between Ren and the wall. It gives me an idea. A *stupid* idea, but I have to try.

I take a step in the direction of the bedroom, and as quickly as I can, I try to lunge at the gap to get past him and back downstairs.

"Oh, no you don't," he grunts as he grabs onto the back of my t-shirt. My feet slip, and I begin to fall down the steps. Ren's hold on my shirt keeps me from sliding down them, but the force of gravity pulls on my body. The neckline of my shirt stretches over my throat, cutting off my supply of oxygen. I have a hard time breathing as he drags me by the shirt into the bedroom he just ordered me into.

"*No!*" I'm barely able to get my words out.

I manage to get my feet underneath me, and I rise to a standing position again. Reaching out for Ren, I scratch at his arms and face, doing whatever I can to loosen his grip. That's when he swings me around and lets go of my shirt, causing me to fly across the room and land on the bed.

My head makes contact with the wooden bedpost, and pain radiates through my skull. The last thing I see before my vision goes black is Ren advancing on me quickly with his arms outstretched and a look of pure rage on his face.

When I come to, the first thing I see is my lap. My head bobs slightly as I try to get my bearings and figure out where the fuck I am. The last thing I remember is Ren attacking me on the bed. My vision clears as my head snaps up, and I'm staring Ren in the face.

"There you are." He's crouched down on the floor in front of me. When he places his hand on my chin, I quickly snatch it from his grasp in disgust. "I thought I may have lost you for a second. You hit your head pretty hard."

I can't move my arms or legs. They're taped to the chair I'm sitting on. The same chair Ren told me to sit on before our struggle began. I also have duct tape stretched tightly over my mouth. I try to say something, but nothing more than a few small noises come out.

"If you remember before you went crazy, I offered you the opportunity to ask questions. All you had to do was come in here and sit down. Unfortunately, you didn't follow directions, so you lost that privilege."

He cups my cheek and runs his fingers through my hair in the same way D has done in the past when he wants to be affectionate. It makes me want to hurl.

"Let me fill you in, Carley. It's kind of a long story, but I'll do my best to explain everything to you. The night we met, I couldn't take my eyes off of you. As soon as you walked through the door, I knew you were special. I had to know you. You surprised me when you approached me first. The combination of your sapphire eyes and delicious perfume was like an aphrodisiac. I couldn't get enough. You gave me hope that night, Carley. That's something I haven't felt in a very long time. But then you left. You told me you needed to use the restroom, when in actuality you snuck out and snatched away all traces of the hope you had just given me."

Why do I attract the crazy ones?

"I knew I wasn't finished with you, however. I thought if I got close to your friend, I would still have the chance of seeing you. Of getting to know you. When I found out Saylor was your roommate, the plan practically fell at my feet. I knew then what I had to do."

He stands and backs up before turning the chair so I'm still facing him and taking a seat on the bed. The blankets are all disheveled, and my shorts lay in a crumpled heap at the end of it. I didn't even realize I wasn't wearing them any longer until now. A tear rolls down my face, not knowing what he did to me while I was unconscious.

"I've never been good at flirting, but luckily Saylor is an attention-hungry slut. She ate it right up."

"Don't talk about her like that!" I scream, but my words are only decipherable in my mind.

"It doesn't take much to get *her* into bed, am I right? So I followed her around that night, made sure to get her number and text the appropriate number of times a guy should when he's interested in a girl. By the following Monday, she invited me over for dinner. I made sure to bring an overnight bag with me. I knew I was staying the night even before she did."

With each word that comes out of his mouth, I get more and more nauseated.

"I waited forever for you to get home that night. I couldn't wait to see you again. I needed to smell you. When you came in, you barely gave me any notice before talking about *him*. That's all you wanted to talk about, ever. It made me angry. I knew then I would have to do whatever it would take to keep him out of your life. We went on with dinner, but the best part of my night, Carley, was yet to come. That was the first time I watched you sleep. You looked like an angel."

My stomach lurches, and for a second, I think I'm going to be sick. Then his smile disappears as he begins speaking again.

"Every night I stayed over since then, I would sneak into your room and watch you. A couple times, I would lie down next to you as carefully as I could so I didn't wake you up. That would have been bad. You would have sent me away."

My body trembles again as his words sink in. He's been in my bed with me, unknowingly, while I've slept. More tears stream down my face the longer I think about it.

"Don't cry, Carley."

Ren gets up from the bed and places his thumbs on my cheeks beneath my eyes. I try to shake him off, but his grip tightens. Slowly, he wipes away my tears before returning to the bed.

"Anyway, this went on for almost two weeks. The whole time, the only thing you talked about was him. Dimos this and Dimos that. That was enough to piss me off, but then ..." he scoffs, "then there was the night you never came home."

He's angry again.

"I waited around with Saylor, pretending to be the perfect guy who cared about her and was supportive of your friendship. She's exhausting. I don't know how you've remained friends with her for so long. But it was a small price to pay to be near you. She was so worried about you, and the longer you took to get home, the angrier I got. I knew *exactly* where you were."

His breathing increases before he continues.

"You were with *him*. That's when I knew I needed to step up my game. I wasn't sure exactly how I was going to play it until the next night at the club when that Blaine kid came up to you. You were terrified. After reading the text messages Saylor sent to D, explaining who he was and what he did, everything became clear."

I almost feel bad for Blaine at this point. I've held so much anger toward him, and rightfully so, but this time he really *didn't* do anything. Meanwhile, I've been *living with* my latest stalker. No wonder the letters stopped when I moved back in.

"It was the perfect cover up. Make it seem like it was him and no one would ever suspect me. Soon after, I started sending the letters. I knew I couldn't go the same route Blaine did. Besides, my way was smarter. Some letters here, a few carefully scheduled text messages there. I made sure they would be delivered when I was going to be in the same room as you. You wouldn't see me sending anything. *And* I was able to watch every single move you made, too."

Oh god. The security tapes. How long was he watching us for?

"Only, my plan backfired when you *moved in* with that fucker. I didn't know what I could do to make you leave. Then, after watching one of your more provocative sexual encounters where you were on the dining room table—you'll never believe how much I came watching that one, Carley. It was impressive. I'm getting hard again just thinking about it."

As his eyes roll backward into his head, I dry heave so hard I can taste stomach acid in the back of my throat. I have to get this tape off of me before I choke on my own throw up.

"Unfortunately, my manager was alerted soon after to my unauthorized access, and I was fired. Thankfully, I'd been planting additional hidden cameras all over D's penthouse every time we came for a visit. I needed more angles, Carley. I became obsessed with watching every move you made. Don't worry, I put them all over the apartment, too. Especially in your room and bathroom."

My breathing increases, and my mouth turns with disgust the longer I look at him.

"Back to the video. It may have gotten me fired, but it gave me a great idea. Blackmail. At that time, I was pretty sure you'd be more willing to act for

Saylor's benefit than your own. But then you had us over for dinner, and you made it clear the video wasn't enough for you to leave him. Luckily, I already had another package waiting with your video in it. But still, you stuck to your guns."

The only positive to come out of this is knowing neither of those videos will actually make it onto the internet.

"That's when I knew I needed to kick it up a notch. Now that I was no longer employed, it left me with more time to follow D. He puts on a pretty good act, but no one is *that* perfect. I knew I would catch him doing something incriminating eventually. I *never* anticipated he had a secret ex-wife though. Watching him sit across from her at dinner was like finding buried treasure."

I vaguely remember Saylor saying Ren was working the night D went out to dinner with Emma. That he didn't get home until late.

"I scoured the city for a photo lab that was open late until I found one. I wanted to send those pictures out to you as soon as possible. But I had to wait until you were by yourself. I couldn't have him getting to them first. So when I heard you weren't going into work the next morning, I hurried to the courier and put a rush delivery on the package to make sure it got to you within a few hours. I thought for sure you'd be angry, but I never expected you to come home to me that night."

My mind, whether because of the effects of the Rohypnol, from hitting my head against the bed earlier, or from being forced to sit here as Ren details his sick obsession with me, is aching. I'm getting tired and suddenly I feel like I could fall asleep.

"Ah, ah, Carley." Ren smacks my cheeks to get my attention. "I can't have you falling asleep yet, and risk getting a concussion. It would throw a huge wrench in our travel plans."

Travel plans?

The thought of going anywhere with him brings on another wave of tears.

"I'm almost finished, I promise. Then, I have a video I want to show you. After that, I can let you rest. We have a big day tomorrow."

What the fuck does he have planned?

"Where was I? Oh. How could I forget ...? You'd returned to me. Yeah, you were sad. Your red-rimmed eyes made the blue in them pop, though, and made you even more desirable in my opinion. I watched you all day from my phone. At night, while Saylor was asleep, I would pull up your live feed and watch you. You struggled so much to make yourself come. You were so sexually frustrated. One night, I nearly came in to give you a hand, but then Saylor woke up to use the bathroom and ruined everything. After that, all I could do was jerk off while I watched you."

I don't care about getting a concussion, I pray for sleep to steal away my consciousness. I can't handle hearing anymore. It's literally killing me inside. With every word that leaves his mouth, I feel another part of me die.

"Anyway, everything was going along smoothly, and I was beginning to formulate an exit strategy for us. Until you came home last night talking about your little *reconciliation*. I couldn't let that happen, Carley. I knew there would come a time when I would need to take you with me, but I thought it would be a little longer before you jumped into bed with someone again. When you proved me wrong, I had to act fast. I called the spa manager this morning and told her I needed her to clear the schedule for Saylor. You know how people jump when they hear her name, so she was happy to do it. I needed her away from you for as long as possible, without access to her phone so she wouldn't cause any issues."

Screaming as loud as I can through the tape, I thrash my head back and forth. But the pain from hitting my head earlier starts throbbing even more, and I have to stop. I relax the muscles in my neck, letting my head fall forward as I try to shake the tape loose from around my mouth. I need him to stop talking. I can't listen to any more of this. Finally, I lick my way through my lips and manage to push on the duct tape covering my mouth enough to cause one of the corners to detach itself from my face. That little corner is all I need to work more of it from my lips.

"*Shut up!*" I scream. "You're a crazy psychopath, and I will never go anywhere with you. *Ever!* D is going to find me, and once he does, he's going to kill you, you son of a bitch!"

I don't have time to react before hot pain shoots through the right side of my face. My head flies to the side with the force of Ren's backhand. My vision begins to fail again, but before I pass out, it comes back. My head bobs a few more times and my eyes roll around like they have a mind of their own. Finally, I'm able to get enough control over myself to pick my head back up. Ren stands over me with a vicious, cold look in his eye.

"Carley, don't ruin this day before we get to the best part. We haven't watched the movie I have planned yet."

Gripping the back of my chair, he tilts it backward so I feel like I'm falling. Turning it on one leg, he places me upright again, directly in front of the television. When he's finished, he pulls a knife out from the waistband of his jeans and cuts the duct tape off my right wrist, releasing it from the armrest, but he maintains a tight grip around it. He shows me the knife and delivers a warning.

"I don't want to hurt you, Carley, but I will if I have to. Leave your hand on the arm rest until we're ready to use it. I don't think it will take long."

With that, he turns the television on and presses play. That's when I realize him telling me the story of how he pulled all of this off was nothing compared to what I was about to endure.

He drops down on one knee next to my chair with the knife in his left hand. With his right hand, he gently moves my hair off my neck and over my other shoulder.

"I love watching you play with yourself on camera, Carley. But I've been dying to see it in person. Touch yourself. Slide your hand beneath your panties and play with your pussy for me. I want you to mimic the actions you're making on the screen."

As my body trembles, I can't see myself on the television any longer. My tears are too thick. Ren runs the tip of the knife over the fabric of my shirt. Tracing one nipple, then the other. When he grips my shirt in the middle, and cuts through the fabric before ripping it open altogether, I pray D finds me before it's too late.

Wherever you are, please, *please* come to me. Follow me to the bottom of the deep blue sea. I can feel the weight of my situation crushing my body as I sink deeper into its depths. The longer Ren forces me to watch this horror movie, the closer to death I become.

CHAPTER THIRTY-SIX

Dimos

I JUMP out of the limo before it stops along the curb in front of Ren's apartment building. A couple exits as I approach the entrance and I duck through the front door before it shuts with Izaak close on my heels. Running up four flights of stairs, we stop in front of Unit 4F.

Without knocking, I kick the door open on my first try. I have so much adrenaline pumping through my veins right now, I think I could lift a city bus if I tried.

I listen for any sign of life inside before the two of us quietly search the unit. No one is here, and I have a feeling Ren is smarter than I'd like him to be in order to pull off a successful abduction. There are two back bedrooms, and I enter the first one I come to.

"Check in that one, and let me know if you find anything of interest," I direct Izaak.

The room I enter is messy. There are empty bags of chips and candy bar wrappers all over the place, littered in with empty 20 oz bottles of Mountain Dew. The screensaver is floating around the computer screen. I give the mouse a little nudge, and the monitor comes to life once again. The Photoshop application is open, and there is a jumble of different sea creatures being placed onto a sand dune in the middle of outer space.

I click on the downloads folder and search through the images inside of it. There are several of Ren and Saylor. One where Saylor is tied to a chair, smiling seductively at the camera. There are more of her laughing. One of her pretending to cry—at least I think she's pretending. Her face looks sad, but I don't see any real tears.

I also see pictures of Ren sitting in a chair with his hands behind his back. He's bent over, and he looks like he may be sleeping. There are a few more in the series, but this is the only one where he isn't looking at the camera.

After that, I sort through the pile of papers scattered over the desk, and my eye catches on a very disturbing image. It's one of the images of Saylor I just saw in the downloads folder, only in this version, she's tied to a chair with tape over her mouth. Her cheeks are wet with tears, and she looks like she's scared out of her mind.

Is it digitally enhanced, or did this actually happen?

Rifling through a few more papers, I find an identical image of Saylor crying in the chair, only this time the image of Ren with his head hanging down is next to her. But in this image, he has blood coming out of his ear and what appears to be duct tape on his mouth.

What the hell?

"Excuse me? *Hey!*"

The voice behind me belongs to a stocky kid with glasses wearing a back-pack. He looks like he just got home from school. Izaak has him in a chokehold with no intention of letting him go.

"What do you think you're doing in here?" he questions.

I wave Izaak off.

"I'm looking for someone. Ren Butler. Do you know where I might find him?"

He rolls his shoulder once he's out of Izaak's grasp and shoots him a death stare. Then he looks back to me, but his eyes quickly shift to the images in my hands.

"No."

"What do you know about these pictures?" I hold up the stack in my hands, showing him the one of Saylor. "This one here. Do you know if Ren hurt her before taking it? Or was it photoshopped?"

I point to the computer screen.

"I edited it."

I breathe a small sigh of relief.

"Why?" I ask.

"Ren asked me to. What is this about?"

"How well do you know Ren?"

"I know him a little. We've only lived together for about six months."

"I think he abducted someone very special to me. Do you happen to know where he might have taken her?"

He's looking at me like he wants to ask a question, but he's almost afraid of the answer he might get.

"Does this have to do with Carley?" he nods his head toward the picture of Saylor in my hand.

I hold up the picture and look more closely. No, that's definitely Saylor.

"This girl's name is Saylor. She's Carley's best friend. What do you know about Carley?"

The boy takes a deep breath and puts his backpack down.

"About six weeks ago, he comes home from the club acting strange. I asked him what was going on, and he tells me he's met the girl of his dreams. I didn't think much of it, and we both went to sleep. After that, he started staying at her house more often. He would come home from time to time, but not for long. But then, he started getting ... weird. Every time I saw him he would say things like 'he's trying to take what's mine', or 'I need to take her far away from here and save her.' I kept asking him who 'he' was, but that made him angry. Like, violently angry. I don't know, things just didn't seem right."

Before I'm able to speak, he starts again.

"I've been searching for a new place for about two weeks now. He's been really unstable lately, and I'm scared to be under the same roof as him. Don't tell him I told you that, though!"

"I won't. Promise. *I'm* the 'he' Ren was talking about. And Carley is *my* girlfriend, and he's been stalking her since the night they met. I need you to think. Has he ever mentioned family or friends? Maybe someone out of state where he can stay off the radar for a while?"

"Umm..." I try to be patient while he's thinking, but the longer I wait, the more hopeless I feel. Finally, he speaks. "The only thing I remember him saying is he grew up somewhere in Brooklyn."

"Brooklyn. That's great. Anything else? A street? A neighborhood?"

"No, I'm sorry. He didn't mention it."

"That's okay, you've been a big help ..." I just realized I never got his name.

"Alec."

"Thank you, Alec. I really appreciate it. I'll send you money to repair the door I broke."

Exiting his room, I pull out my phone and call Travis, with Izaak on my heels.

"Travis."

"See if you can find anything linking him to Brooklyn."

"On it."

Izaak and I make it to the ground floor of the apartment building before Travis comes back with any information. Just as I'm about to tell him to call me back, he speaks up.

"Got something here. He lists some references on his resume. Walter Butler, 8293 72nd Street, Brooklyn. And Grace Wilson, 5236 64th Street Brooklyn.

"Thanks, keep digging. In the meantime, Izaak and I will go and check it out."

I TOLD IZAAK TO GO TO VISIT GRACE WILSON WHILE I CHECKED OUT Walter Butler's house. With both Wilson and Butler in Ren's name, I'm assuming these two are his mother and father. If I'm right in my assumption that he would take Carley somewhere familiar, then I'm hoping she's at one of these locations.

She fucking has to be.

I called Officer Harrison from the cab on the drive from downtown to Brooklyn. I explained Blaine isn't the one who has been sending the letters this time. When I gave him Ren's name and the addresses Izaak and I are each headed to, he put a call out to the nearest precinct. After telling me someone would be out as soon as possible, he instructed me to wait outside until they got there.

Like fucking hell I'm waiting.

I toss whatever bills are in my wallet to the cab driver before practically throwing myself from the car and running to the front door. For the second time today, I kick the door open in search of the woman I love.

"*Carley!*" I shout.

I listen for noise, and I hear what sounds like muffled screams coming from up the stairs. I take them two at a time, running directly into Ren on the landing between the two floors.

I don't miss the large knife in his hand before I throw him back against the wall into a picture frame. It crashes to the floor and shatters into a thousand pieces. His hands circle my neck, the knife dangerously close to my face, and he pushes me backward so I lose my grip on him. I swing my fist and land a right hook to the side of his face, causing him to lose his footing just long enough to push him to the side and run up the remaining steps.

Before I can get out of his reach, he grabs a hold of my ankle and stops my progress. I roll over so I can pry him off me. Kicking my foot out, I try to connect with his fist so he'll drop the knife, but I'm not successful. He brings the knife down, nearly hitting me in the chest. I'm able to twist at the waist, rolling the top half of my body away from the incoming blade and knocking him off balance.

I stand up, but Ren roundhouse kicks, knocking my leg out from underneath me before I can get my footing on the steps. When I go down, my back cracks against the wooden step, and it knocks the wind out of me.

"I'm going to enjoy this..." Ren utters with a maniacal smile on his face as he lunges for me.

When he lands on my stomach, it hurts more than it should have. I try lifting my arm to fight him off, but I can't. I can barely move at all. And that's when I feel the fire licking its way through my abdomen. Slowly, Ren gets off, but I still can't move. Trying as hard as I can, I look down at my stomach and watch as crimson paints my white dress shirt red.

Ren reaches down and grabs my shirt with both hands, dragging me up the rest of the way upstairs.

The last thing I picture before my world goes black is Carley, standing in front of the sunset, overlooking the Aegean Sea.

She's never looked more beautiful than she did that night.

CHAPTER THIRTY-SEVEN

Carley

A FEW MINUTES EARLIER

WITH MY SOUL crushed beyond repair, Ren cuts me loose. I don't know how long he had me in that chair, forcing me to do the things he made me do. I tried to go to a happy place in the middle of it all.

I tried to go back to the night D and I spent together in Greece.

"Don't try anything crazy like running again, Carley."

Taking a strong hold on my bicep, Ren helps me up from the chair and walks me to the bed. I would be an idiot to think he's going to leave me alone and let me go to sleep.

"Get into bed, Carley." He points to the mattress using his knife.

I watch him carefully as I sit down. With the knife still at the ready, he reaches into the drawer of the nightstand and pulls out two pairs of handcuffs, tossing them onto the mattress.

"Please don't," I beg. "I'll do whatever you want, just please don't use those on me."

"Carley, I think you and I both know you're not going to do what I say. It was like pulling teeth to get you to sit in a fucking chair. Then, once the movie began, you repeatedly disobeyed me. I didn't *want* to threaten you, Carley, really I didn't. But you left me no choice."

I open my mouth to protest, but he rips a length of duct tape from the roll and places it over my mouth again. This time, he reinforces it with two more pieces, making it almost impossible to get off without using my hands.

"It's a shame I had to do that," he curls my hair behind my ear as he speaks. "I wanted the chance to kiss you while we make love, but I can wait until you're more compliant."

You'll have to kill me first.

"Take these and place one on each of your wrists." He tosses me the handcuffs and raises his knife again. "Make sure they're tight. I can't have you getting away."

Reluctantly, I do as he says. When I've secured each pair around my wrists, he pushes down on the metal, squeezing them so they're excruciatingly tight.

I moan in pain, but he ignores me.

When he's satisfied they're tight, he pushes me back onto the bed and lifts my legs onto the mattress. I fight the urge to be sick again as I hear him securing the handcuffs to the bedposts above my head. Although choking on my own vomit sounds more appealing than spending one more moment at Ren's mercy.

"Finally," Ren breathes as he straddles my body.

The moment he reaches for the hem of my shirt, there is a loud crash somewhere on the floor below us. That's when I hear him.

"*Carley!*"

D. He found me.

I begin to scream as loudly as I can, and I thrash around violently, no longer caring about the knife laying next to me on the bed. D is here, and no weapon will be able to stop him from saving me.

"Ahh!" Ren shouts, irritated he was interrupted. He grabs the knife and holds it to my throat. "I'm going to slice him open and make you watch while he takes his last breath."

"*No!*" I scream, knowing even if he could understand me, there's nothing stopping him now.

I watch as he exits the room and stalks out of sight. Hearing the sounds of the fight and not knowing which one of them is on the receiving end of each attack kills me. I pull at my restraints with no luck. The only thing that does is cut into my skin even more, causing me to bleed.

There is a loud crash as glass breaks and clatters to the ground. Then a few more grunts and bangs before it goes silent for a moment. I hear nothing other than my heart beating as blood pumps rapidly through my veins. That's when I see him again. Ren. Walking backwards into the room. But D is with him, too.

The sight of him getting dragged across the carpet by Ren, blood gushing from his stomach, is one I'll never forget. Painful sobs wrack my body as I cry harder than I've ever cried before. There's no way he's dead.

Wake up, D, please. I need you! I can't live without you.

With one final drag, Ren picks his body up off the floor and throws him half onto the bed. Holding him in place by his shirt, he smacks his cheeks, trying to wake him up.

"Come on, old man. Don't die on us yet. I promised Carley she would get to watch that part."

D got him pretty good. Ren has a black eye and a bloody nose, but it wasn't enough.

Come on, D. Wake up.

But even if he does, there is a trail of blood across the floor, and he's losing more as each second passes.

Ren continues smacking him, harder each time, and finally I see one of his eyes crack open.

"Carley …" I can hardly make out what he's saying, his voice is so weak.

"There you are, that's it." Ren turns D's head so we're looking at each other.

"I'm sorry … S'—S' agapo, *théa*," he mumbles, barely audible, but I can hear it as if he whispered it in my ear.

I love you, too …

His eyes close again after that, and I scream in agony behind the tape once more.

Ren lets go of D's body, and he falls to the floor with a loud thud. The moment I hear the sound, my body goes numb. Then everything moves in slow motion. I see Ren's mouth moving, but I can't hear what he's saying. I watch him walk to the window and look out of it. His face is angry, but I don't know why.

He got exactly what he wanted.

Then he climbs back onto the bed and straddles me again. Just like I can't hear him speak, I can't feel the weight of his body on mine, either. I wait for him to remove the rest of my clothing, but he doesn't. Instead, he raises his knife high into the air.

Do it. Send me home to be with D.

The anger in Ren's face no longer scares me. The fear I felt vanished the moment D took his last breath. I watch as Ren swings the knife down, aimed directly at my heart. I watch my blood splatter everywhere as the knife slices through me.

The moment it makes contact, my eyes close, and I take one final breath.

I'm ready to be with D. He's my entire world.

In this life and the next.

CHAPTER THIRTY-EIGHT

Carley

AGONY.

Complete and utter agony is the only way to describe how I feel when I regain consciousness.

But I can't remember why.

What happened? Where am I?

Slowly, I'm able to open my eyes. The bright lights are blinding and I close them again.

D.

I open my eyes once more and try to sit up, but I can't. Searing pain coming from my left shoulder stops me immediately, and I cry out.

"*Carley.*" I hear someone say.

As my vision comes into focus, I see a room full of people scattered around me.

I search from left to right, taking in each of their faces.

Saylor. My mother. Daddy, Sheila, and Elias. They all look so incredibly sad.

"Carley ... thank god." My mother sighs with relief.

Where is D?

"D ..." I mumble.

My head throbs with a sudden *boom boom boom.*

Memories appear in my mind like someone turning a flashlight on and off in quick succession.

Ren. Chair. Knife.

My heart starts pumping faster as I remember a little bit more.

D. Floor. Blood.

"D," I say a little louder as I recall how Ren dragged him across the floor of the bedroom. A trail of blood in his wake. D told me he loved me before he...

"No," I sob. "*D, no!*"

"Carley," Saylor comes to my bedside and wraps my shaking body in her arms.

My shoulder burns with pain as she holds me tight, but I don't care.

"He's dead ... I saw ..." I can't get the words out. "I saw ..."

"Shh ... It's okay, Carley," My father tries to comfort me, but nothing will ever be able to take away the pain of watching D die in front of me while I was powerless to help him.

"No, it's not okay. It's not okay. He's *gone!*" I sob.

"He's not, Carley." Saylor gently lets me go and holds my head in place so she has my attention. "He's not dead."

"*What?*" I look around the room, and there isn't one dry eye. "Don't lie to me."

"I would never lie to you. It's me, Carley."

And I know what she says is true. Saylor would never tell me a lie, especially not one so cruel.

"Where is he? I want to see him. I *have* to see him."

"He's downstairs in the ICU. He has a punctured lung, and he lost a lot of blood. He needed surgery to repair it."

I need to go to him.

Throwing the covers back as best I can with one arm, I ungracefully swing my legs out of my bed and try to stand as everyone screams at me.

Big mistake.

I fall back down onto the bed.

"Carley, stop! You're going to bust through your stitches," I hear my mother say from across the room.

"Yes, and the nurse has to check you out, take your vitals. And there is also a police officer outside who needs to speak with you," my father adds.

"I'm not doing or saying *anything* until someone takes me to see D."

Saylor is the first to move. She marches out in the hallway, and I hear her speaking with someone. A moment later, she comes back into the room with a nurse in tow.

"Ms. Garrettson, so lovely to see you awake."

"Take me to see Dimos Anastos, *now.*"

I've never been mean to anyone in my entire life, and I don't like who I am right now, but until they let me see him, this is who they're going to get.

"I'll make you a deal," the nurse begins. "I'll radio for a wheelchair for your transport, and while we're waiting on it, you let me give you a once over."

I stare at her, breathing heavily with exasperation through narrow eyes as I consider her offer.

"*Fine.*"

After calling for my transport, she takes my blood pressure, which I'm sure is through the roof. Then she checks my eyes and vision before changing the dressing on my shoulder wound.

"What happened?" I ask Saylor as the nurse works.

With tears in her eyes, she tells me the story one of the officers told her and my parents.

"*Thankfully,* D called Officer Harrison on his way to you. When the cops got to the house, they said Ren was straddling you on the bed, shouting that if he couldn't have you, no one could. When he tried to stab you, the officer shot him, and he died instantly. The force of the shot pushed him forward, which is how you got stabbed in the shoulder and not the heart."

"I saw the blood splatter, but I thought it was mine," I tell them. "And D?"

"They found a very faint pulse. By the time the paramedics arrived ..." she swallows nervously, "he was moments from death."

"Okay, I'm finished here, Carley. Let me go check on that wheelchair for you," the nurse says.

"Thank you," I tell her.

"Oh, Carley," my mother sobs as she comes forward. "I'm so glad you're okay, sweetheart."

"Yeah, you really had us worried sick there." I want to give my father a reassuring smile, but I just can't.

"Okay, your ride is here," the nurse comes into the room with a wheelchair.

Once she locks it into place, she helps me down off my bed before hooking my IV to the metal pole sticking out of the back of the chair.

"Would you like me to come with you?" my mother asks.

"*No*," I answer quickly. "Thank you, but I need to go alone."

I don't want anyone standing around, waiting for me. No one knows this yet, but once I get into D's room, I won't be leaving until he's ready to leave the hospital. I'd like to see them try to remove me.

We take the elevator down one floor, then my nurse leads me into the intensive care unit. She pushes me through the hall, taking so many turns I don't think I'll ever be able to find my way back.

Not that I'll need to.

"Here we are." She knocks on the door to D's room, and when it opens, I see the melancholy face of Eliana staring back at me. Ez is here too, and he looks just as downtrodden as I feel.

"Oh, *Carley*," she leans down and hugs me gently. "I'm so sorry."

"I need to see him," I beg.

"Of course, come on in."

They *must* know who D is because his room is the size of about five of my rooms put together. I'm wheeled in, and as she parks me next to D's bed, I lose it. I begin sobbing all over again as I slowly climb from the wheelchair.

I walk to the side of D's bed and collapse onto it. I grab his hand and rest my head on his chest gently.

"D, I'm so sorry," I cry. "This is all my fault. I should have called you. But I was so scared ... Please wake up, D." I place my hand on his cheek and lay a kiss on his cold, unmoving lips. "You have to be okay. I can't live without you."

I stay like that until I've cried all of the tears I can cry.

"Why don't you take a seat, Carley?" the nurse suggests. I had no idea she was still here. "I can take you back to your room to rest."

"No, I'm not going anywhere. You're welcome to wheel my bed down here, there's more than enough room, but I'm not leaving, and there's nothing you can do to make me."

She exchanges a glance with both Ez and Eliana, who look at her with sympathy, but offer no assistance.

"I'll give you some more time, but I can't permit you to stay in this room. It's against hospital policy."

"We'll see about that," I spit at her.

Watch what happens when they try and take me from this room. Stab wound or not, they will force a side of me to come out that even I'm scared to meet. I can feel the rage simmering beneath the surface as I look at her.

My nurse looks around the room uncomfortably once more before finally leaving. When she's gone, I call upstairs to my father and ask him and Saylor to meet me down here. I'm seated in the chair at D's bedside when they walk through the door.

"What's going on?" my father asks.

"Daddy, I think you know Ezra Treuth. He's D's best friend."

My father looks across the room at Ez, and I watch carefully to see if there is going to be an issue. I remember what D told me a while ago about the two of them not getting along.

But I didn't have anything to worry about.

"George," Ez nods to my father.

"Ezra. I'm so sorry for ..." he doesn't know what to say, but he gestures toward D.

"Thank you, that means a lot."

"You guys—Daddy, Ez, and D—are three of the most powerful and influential men in this city. Now, I'm not leaving this room until D does, and there must be something one of you can do to see to it this hospital accommodates my demand. I want to spend the duration of my stay with the man I love. The man, without whom I wouldn't be here right now." I start to cry again. "The man who is fighting for his life because of me."

Through my tears, I look back and forth between Ez and my father and wait for one of them to say something. I catch Eliana's expression as she stands just behind the two of them. She winks and offers me a nod, giving me all the silent support that I need. Saylor comes to my side and places her hand on my good shoulder.

"We'll talk to someone, Carley. We'll get it taken care of." Ez promises.

"Thank you."

"We'll be back in a little while," my father adds.

The two of them exit the room, leaving me, Eliana, and Saylor behind.

"Are you in any pain, Carley?" Saylor asks me as I turn back to face D.

As I look at him, I feel an immense amount of pain. But it has nothing to do with my shoulder. I'm in pain, agonizing over what happened to D. Terrified he's never going to wake up. That I'll never again get to look into his striking, gray eyes. I'm frightened I'll never be able to feel him against me while we sleep. I'll never be able to taste another one of his kisses.

"Yes, the pain is immeasurable," I answer without looking at her. "And I won't get any relief until D opens his eyes."

DADDY AND EZ CAME BACK WITHIN THE HOUR WITH GOOD NEWS.

Very expensive good news.

It took quite a large donation, but the CEO agreed to have a bed placed next to D's as well as a separate staff of doctors and nurses to handle our care. Daddy stayed for a little while longer before Sheila and Elias came looking for him. When they left, I begged him to take my mother home when he leaves. I can't be around her right now.

Ez and Eliana left shortly after that but told me they would be back tomorrow. I promised to call with any change in D's status until they return.

"Can you help me with this pillow?" I ask Saylor.

She is staying the night tonight. The nurse brought her a plush chair that folds out into a bed for her to sleep on, but she's currently laying in my bed with me.

"Sure. Can you lean forward a little, or do you need help?"

"No, I've got it," I tell her as she fluffs up my pillow, helping to raise my head off the bed a little more. "That's better, thank you."

She lays back down and rolls onto her side so she's facing me. When I turn my head to look at her, I see shiny, unshed tears in her eyes.

"Say ..." my voice fades away as I take her hand in mine.

"I'm so sorry, Carley. This is all my fault. I should have done something sooner. I could have put a stop to all of this before it got so out of hand."

"Saylor, he was obsessed with me before the two of you even met. From the get-go at the bar that night. Nothing you did contributed to his behavior."

"I know, but there were ... things. Things I should have picked up on but brushed them off because I thought *I* was crazy."

"What do you mean?" I inquire.

"Well, there were little things, like flashes of anger I would notice in his eyes from time to time. Sometimes it was during sex, other times it would happen when I mentioned you and D. I asked him about it once, and he swore I was imagining it."

I think back to when my mother came to the office and told me Ren seemed *ragey*. Saylor is lucky that he didn't take his anger out on her. At least not seriously. I know he did when they were having sex. He was too rough not to be.

"And then there was the way he acted when we were having sex."

"I was just thinking about that. The video he sent us of you guys was *brutal*, Say. Some parts you *seemed* to enjoy, but others ...?"

"I enjoyed sex with him in the beginning. But as our relationship progressed, things got ... a little scary. And then, there was ..."

She stops talking and closes her eyes.

"There was what?"

"Oh, god. I'm too embarrassed to say it," she admits, looking at me again.

"Saylor, it's me."

"I know, and that makes it harder."

She's scaring me a little bit. Finally, she covers her eyes with her hand and speaks again.

"A few days ago, he woke me up in the middle of the night because he was horny, and he wanted to roleplay. It wasn't unlike him to do this, but this time was very different." She stops talking and exhales loudly.

"Different how?" I encourage her to continue.

"Ren wanted me to pretend I was you."

What?

"Are you joking?" I *know* she's not. I don't know why I asked her that.

"It was so weird, and I didn't want to, but he got that look in his eye again. Only this time, it was more than just anger. He was terrifying, Carley."

"Saylor, I'm so sorry any of this happened to you. *Why* didn't you say anything? I would have helped you get rid of him."

Knowing now what Ren was capable of, I'm not certain I *would* have been able to help Saylor get away from him. But I would have at least tried. For my best friend, I would have fought with everything I had.

"I was scared," she whispered, as more tears roll down her face. "It took everything in my power to pretend I was okay. And I tried to be."

"My god," I cry. "How self-absorbed was I that I didn't notice this going on?"

"No, he put on such a good act, Car. He even had me fooled a few times. I knew something wasn't right yesterday when he woke me up and surprised me with breakfast and a spa day. But I wanted to believe everything was fine, so I went with it."

To see my strong and confident best friend doubting herself so severely because of that asshole, makes me angry. I have to remind myself he's dead to feel even the slightest bit better.

"What happened in that house, Carley?" She gives me a sorrowful look. "You don't have to tell me if you don't want to."

I still don't remember everything that happened, but I remember enough. I just don't know if I can talk about it yet.

"I want to tell you, Say. But I just can't yet."

She brings her hand to my cheek as more tears come.

"I love you, jerk face," she smiles as she cries harder. "And I'm so happy you're okay."

"I love you, back," I tell her.

But I am far from being okay.

CHAPTER THIRTY-NINE

Carley

WHEN I WAKE up the next morning, Saylor is sitting in her chair across the room, scrolling through her phone. Shortly after our talk last night, I fell asleep. But my dreams were vicious and kept me up half the night, trying to sob quietly into my pillow so I wouldn't wake her up. Eventually, I turned my body in D's direction as much as I could, and I watched him as he lay there, fighting for his life. I begged him to wake up. I prayed harder than I've ever prayed for anything in my entire life.

"Good morning," Saylor breaks my concentration, and my eyes shift from D to her.

"Morning," I respond.

"I was thinking about running home and taking a shower, but I'll come back after that. Do you need me to bring you anything when I do?"

I shake my head gently. The only thing I need is D. And she can't bring him back to me. He has to be the one to do that.

"Can I grab you a coffee before I leave?"

I nod my head, just because I know she wants to do something to feel useful right now.

When she's gone, I try my hardest to get out of bed so I can sit in the chair at D's bedside. But I can't. I can barely get the top half of my body off the mattress, even though I'm already mostly upright. The strain to my shoulder is too painful.

I lay back down and close my eyes until Saylor returns. I've already lost what strength I gained through the night. A few minutes later, I hear someone walk into the room. When I open my eyes, I see Saylor approaching the bed with two cups of coffee in hand.

"Here you go," she offers.

"Thank you."

"Can I do anything else for you before I leave?" she asks.

"Actually, yes. Can you help me up? I want to sit in the chair."

I point to the chair beside D's bed.

"Yes, of course."

Once I'm situated, she brings me a pillow and a blanket before leaving.

I don't know how long I sit there, watching the shallow rise and fall of D's chest, before my nurse comes in to check on me, but my coffee is ice cold.

"Good morning, Carley," she practically sings as she walks to the monitors next to my bed and starts pressing buttons. "How are you feeling today?"

Empty.

I don't speak, nor do I look at her.

She's smart. Other than asking me if she can get me anything, she keeps quiet as she checks my blood pressure and monitors my concussion. I don't mean to be so standoffish, but I can't bear the thought of making small talk while desperately trying to told myself together at the same time. As soon as she's done redressing my wound, she leaves, and I'm finally alone with D once again.

That's when the tears come back. They form so quickly I can barely see in front of me as I pull myself to the edge of my seat with my good arm. I place my coffee cup on the floor, and on shaky legs, I stand and take one step before I collapse onto the side of his bed.

I can't remember the last time I cried this hard. My sobs are painful, causing my body to shake and my bad shoulder to throb. But that pain will never match the pain I hold in my heart.

"I'm so sorry D," I cry in a strangled whisper. I grab his hand in mine before I place my forehead on his chest. "I'm begging you, if you can hear me, please wake up. I promise I'll never leave your side ever again. I'll do anything if you just come back to me."

I wipe away the tears with the back of my hand, but my eyes are full of them again in a second.

"Do you remember that night, at your penthouse, when we danced for hours? I finally got to wear that red dress for you." I sniffle, trying to control my runny nose in between whimpers. "You put on a fancy suit and romantic jazz blared throughout the entire house. When we get out of here, I want to do that again."

I pick my head up and look at his handsome face. Exchanging hands, I grip his hand tightly with my left while I run my right hand through his hair, gently.

"And don't forget you promised to sail me around the world on your yacht. You wanted to fuck me on every continent, remember? That's exactly what we're going to do when we get out of here, and you're all better."

I squeeze my eyes closed as more tears run over onto my cheeks. I know full well there is a chance he's not leaving this hospital alive.

"Don't worry, D. If you go, I go." Sobs wrack my body, and my speech is barely audible. "I'd follow you ... t—to ..."

I begin to make the same declaration he's made to me before, but I can't get the rest out. The mere thought of him not making it is too much for me to bear. I'm not strong enough to go on without him. I squeeze his hand, probably too hard as I need something to hold onto. It feels like the ground is crumbling beneath my feet, and I'm about to get sucked into the abyss.

"... bot—bot ... tom ...

Now I'm hearing things.

I can hear your voice in my head, D. It's calling out to me, and I want to run to you, to save you. To bring you back to me so we can find our happily ever after.

"... to the bottom ... of the deep blue sea ..." a voice sounds somewhere in the room, followed by an exhale you'd make after over-exerting yourself.

My head snaps up, and I don't believe my eyes as I latch on to his.

His eyes.

D's alluring, wonderful gray eyes.

"D? Oh, my god."

"*Théa*," he whispers again.

"You're *awake*, you're *okay*."

Quicker than I've moved in the last twenty-four hours, I plant my lips on D's and just about die when I feel them move against mine. Standing over him, I shake my head, still in disbelief.

"How are you? Can I get you anything? Oh my god, let me call the doctor in here."

"Wait," he requests.

I remember how everyone acted when I first woke up and how much I hated it, so I try to take it down a notch.

"Don't leave. I just ... want to hold you."

"I'm here, D. And I'm not going anywhere ever again."

TWO WEEKS LATER

D WAS IN THE HOSPITAL FOR A WEEK BEFORE HIS DOCTOR WOULD RELEASE HIM. In the week since, his parents were here, and we also had many visits from friends and work colleagues who came by to give D their well wishes in person.

I got along with his mother, Camilla, very well. She's one of the sweetest people I've ever met. She insisted on cooking all of our meals, and I don't think I'll ever taste anything as good as her food so long as I live. I tried to help out and pick up a few tips, but she shooed me out of the kitchen every time.

His father, Estevan, is just as handsome and charming as D is. Enrikos even flew up for a quick two-night stay but needed to get back home to close out a business deal. D's family wanted to stay in a hotel down the street, but we insisted they utilize the guest rooms here in the penthouse.

Before they left earlier, they thanked me for making their son happy. The way Camilla held both of my hands in hers and stared pointedly into my eyes, I could tell how grateful she was that her son has someone in his life who truly cares about him.

Now that everyone is gone, D and I finally have the penthouse to ourselves again. As I walk toward the great room, I can't help but feel thankful to be back here. It took two weeks longer than we planned, but finally, D and I are alone together again. I'm almost nervous about it. We haven't talked about what happened yet, but with the pain and sadness in D's stare every time he looks at me, I know it's inevitable.

"How are you?" I inquire as I sit on the sofa next to D.

I take off my sling as he slowly turns his body to face me. He still has quite a bit of healing to do.

"You're here and you're safe," he answers with a slight smile that doesn't meet his eyes.

He combs his fingers through my hair. My gaze stays on his as he takes a deep breath, and his eyes gloss over with tears.

"D ..." I put my hand on his cheek, trying to comfort him.

"Carley, I was so scared when you didn't show up at the restaurant. I knew something awful had happened. I was terrified I wasn't going to find you in time."

"But you did, just in the nick of time," I smile.

"No, I didn't. He—he had you on that bed. I'll never forget that sight. Some-times, when I can't sleep at night, I lie awake, wishing he was still alive just so I'd have the opportunity to kill him myself."

I scoot in as close to D as I can get without squishing his wound.

"I know, but we have to be thankful he's out of our lives forever."

"Part of me never wants to find out, but there's another part of me that *has* to know what he put you through. Did he ... touch you?"

How much does D really *need* to know? I put myself in his shoes. If things were flipped, I would want to know everything, too. I think about the fact that he tried to protect me from Emma before telling me about her, and look what happened.

Not that this was D's fault, not by a longshot. Ren was completely unhinged. But we made a promise to one another those first few nights in the hospital to never keep anything from each other ever again.

"No, he didn't touch me, exactly."

I look down at my hands and fiddle with the skin around my nails. D hooks a finger under my chin and forces me to look at him again.

"He ... made me do things. To myself. While he watched. He told me he enjoyed watching me on camera, but he wanted to see me do them ... in person."

"*Gamo to kerato mu, gamo, théa.*" It kills me to watch him cry. "I'm so fucking sorry."

His head falls into his hands, but I don't miss the pain and the anger on his face before it's hidden.

"*Gamo tin panagia mu, gamo,*" he mumbles under his breath, and I want to know what he's saying.

"It's not your fault, D. Look at me." Guiding his gaze back to mine, my hands cover his cheeks. "I'm fine. And do you want to know why I'm fine?"

"Why?"

"Because you're here. And I'm here. And after everything that happened, we fought our way back to one another."

His tongue darts out as he licks his dry lips. Then he takes my face in his hands and pulls me close.

"I would go to hell and back for you, Carley."

I nod my head.

"I know you would. All the way to the ..." My eyes glisten as I stare at him.

"... bottom of the deep blue sea."

$$\overline{\qquad}$$

EPILOGUE

$$\overline{\qquad}$$

Dimos

THREE MONTHS LATER

THE SUN STREAMS down from the bright blue sky, bathing us in its golden beauty as I move within Carley. Three months ago, I thought my chances of making love to her again were over.

I should have known better.

Nothing can keep me from her. Not a vengeful ex-wife. Not a certifiable nutcase. Not even a severe, life-threatening stab wound that punctured my lung and caused me to bleed out until I was moments from death.

There isn't anything the universe can throw at us that could keep us apart.

"*Théa.*" As passion contorts her face, I cup her cheek in the palm of my hand. "*I ómorfi gynaíka mou.*" *My beautiful wife.*

Carley and I set out on our private adventure as soon as the doctor cleared me to travel. We only had one destination in mind.

Mykonos.

The two of us were wed at the end of the pier where we shared our first meal together, in a ceremony where the only witness was Stavros, from the registration desk. Captain Percival officiated. When it was over, we spent two equally mind-blowing and breathtaking nights in the same bed we shared together five months ago.

We plan to have a reception when we return to New York—*if we return*—but we didn't want to have to focus on anyone but us for right now. I'll never forget the night we decided we were going to get married. It was the best moment of my life right up until the second we said, "I do."

. . .

I stare down at Carley, who is resting her chin on my chest, tracing my tattoo with her finger.

"What does this say? I've never asked, but I've always been curious."

I put my hand over my heart and point to each word, slowly, as I translate it for her.

"Agapi means love. Písti means faith. Oikogéneia means family. And the compass is not just because I love to sail, but because these are the three things in my life that guide me. The only three things I trust."

She smiles up at me.

"That's beautiful."

"Eisai omorfos, théa. You are beautiful."

"I don't ever want to leave this spot, D. Your arms. Your bed. Your life."

"So don't," I tell her.

As my eyes burrow into hers, I take her hand in mine and kiss the back of it.

"Theleis na gineis diki mu gia pada? Will you be mine, forever Carley?"

I've seen her smile big before, but none could compete with the one on her face at this moment. As tears shine in her eyes, she speaks.

"Are you asking me to marry you?"

"I can get down on one knee, but you just told me you never want to leave my arms. And besides, I can't officially ask without a ring anyway."

She hops up into a kneeling position and throws her arms around my neck. It hurts near my incision, but nothing could keep me from letting her hold me tight right now.

"Yes! Yes, of course, I will marry you and be yours forever. S' agapo, Dimos."

AND *I* LOVE HER. WITH EVERY FIBER OF MY BEING.

"*O ómorfos syzygos mou.*" *My handsome husband,* she responds.

I've been teaching her a little Greek along the way.

I push and pull, in and out of her, leading both of us closer to the pleasure we seek. With a final thrust, we dive off the cliff together, and I swallow her delicious moan as I come inside of her.

We're in the middle of the Indian Ocean, headed toward the private villa I rented in the Maldives for a week. We have to stay mostly clothed while we're on board The Cerulean because of the captain and crew members. Although, with just one word from me, they'll busy themselves on the opposite side of the yacht whenever the desire to devour my wife hits.

Which is quite often.

But we're not planning on taking very many articles of clothing with us to the villa. I told her I'm reinstating the naked weekend rules that I created what feels like 5 years ago, but it will extend for the entire week-long duration we're on the island.

She doesn't mind, though. I saw her eyes as I told her I wanted her primed and accessible to me whenever and wherever the mood should strike. To which she dropped to her knees and wrapped her pouty lips around my cock. When she was finished, she told me the mood had struck her, and she couldn't help herself.

I promised her once I would fuck her on every continent, and I wasn't joking. The Maldives is the home to continent number three, which is far too close to seven. I don't care that it will take months for us to sail between the other four. I already know the day I fulfil my promise to her will come too soon.

Not to mention the fact that we'll probably have to make our Antarctica encounter a quickie.

When I'm done, we'll have to sail back to New York City and face real life once again. Start another leg of our adventure together. But no matter where in the world we are—feet firmly planted on solid ground or dancing in the waves of the unpredictable ocean—I'll be content as long as *théa mou* is by my side.

Carley.

My goddess. My everything.

ABOUT MURPHY WALLACE

Murphy Wallace is an International Bestselling Author with works in several different genres. She tends to write darker romance, but enjoys the time she spends between the light and the dark.

When Murphy is not writing, she enjoys listening to music, reading, and spending time with family.

She currently resides in a small Eastern Florida town with her husband, who doubles as her best friend, and their two boys.

She has a cat named Maisy who is her constant writing partner.

BOUNDARIES

Sadie Rose

CHAPTER ONE

San Francisco

Pitch black.

My eyes are wide open and adjusting to the darkness of night, but all I can see is blackness. I rub my eyes in an attempt to get them to adjust to the darkness. There's no light coming through the windows, and my clock is off; it's not even flashing the annoying 12:00 a.m. due to the breaker tripping. Was it a noise that woke me up? I can't figure out where the noise came from, and I don't even know if there really was a noise because I'm still half asleep and not for sure if it was a dream. I reach for my phone and the lock screen tips me off that something isn't right. Instead of the time and my normal background image, I've got a not connected to the network message. *I'm always connected to the network.*

I sit up and then stumble out of bed and walk to the window. Moving my drapes back, I can see my reflection in the glass thanks to the moonlight I look tired with my thick hair hanging half out of its top knot, sweatshirt crumpled and sweatpants pushed up to my knees. I'm so pale that I look like a ghost in the darkness surrounding me. The solar lights on my sidewalk are the only glow that I can see on my street. My house sits on an angle which affords me a view of the bay, a tiny view but a view none the lessWhen I look down into the San Francisco Bay, all I see is darkness. Sporadic lights dot here and there but nothing like the usual nightlights of the city.

I pull my drapes closed, and I make my way around the dark house to the kitchen so I can get a different view out my back window. I can see the south tower of the Golden Gate Bridge from the window above my sink. It's then that I realize I'm staring at more blackness in the night.I become increasingly alarmed. January has brought heavy rainstorms and high winds to the area. Maybe that's what caused the power to go out? I use the light on my phone to walk back to the front of the house to find the television remote. The news will tell me what's going on in the city. I'm banking it's been a windstorm or the usual low-grade earthquake that will wreak havoc on all our day. Now that I think of it, maybe that's what woke me up to begin with.

I press the power button on the remote and nothing happens. I turn the remote over, pop the backing off and roll the batteries. I press the power button again and nothing. I huff out a frustrated sigh, pointing the remote to the television one last time and having it do nothing in return. I'm tired, cold and intrigued about the status of my lights and my phone. I walk to the breaker box and check my fuses. They are all in working order, nothing amiss so I decide it's got to be a power outage debate going back to bed, but I know I won't fall asleep. I'll just end up laying there staring at the ceiling. I go to my kitchen counter where I left my watch the night before, and it tells me it's 4:44 a.m. *At least something is still working around here.*

Making my way over to my desk, I try my laptop, and find that it too has no connection to the network. With no options of entertainment in the house, I put on my running clothes and lace up my shoes. I'll start this year off productive by working out, actually accomplish one of the resolutions that I set out to do this year- get fit I'll even impress my family when I tell them I got up to do an early run before today's predicted rain. They might surprise me and even cheer on my enthusiasm. One thing is for certain, they'll all be shocked that I was up before dawn. I shut my front door and lock it behind me. I secure my house key around my wrist and draw my hood tight around my head. The wind is strong and already threatening to blow it off.

I start to run downhill and as I do I realize all the houses in my neighborhood are dark. Apparently, all of Russian Hill has lost their lights and power. I start making my way around the streets in search of a better view of the bridge. Surely they wouldn't have drivers going across it in this darkness. In my short time living here, I've never seen the bridge's lights off. But then again, I don't just sit around and stare at it either. I'm sure they have a backup generator for storms and earthquakes- some contingency plan for power outtages and earthquakes

As I run towards a better view, I think about the first few runs that I did here. Each run helping me learn the layout of my neighborhood and new city. Runs exactly like his early morning help me learn the city and surrounding neighborhoods when the streets are empty and I can take it all in with little distractionsWhen my parents bought me the house, I was overwhelmed. I had never lived on my own before, and here I was moving across the country, out of the Dome, to the west coast. I had just turned eighteen years old and it was only my second time to my new city, my new hometown when I unlocked the door to my new home. My parents told me it would be a *learning* experience. A good place to spend my year of self-reflection. They told me I would be safe here and that I'd meet new people and could figure out what I wanted to do with my life since I had decided not to go to college. I flew straight into the city and arrived a day before my things. The first night I slept on the hard wood floor. It felt like camping...or at least what I think camping feels like since I've never actually camped.

Looking back now, it's hard to believe that was six months ago. Half my year of reflection is gone, and I'm no closer to understanding what I'd like to do or who I want to be in this world. You should have seen the way my parents rushed me out the door and onto the plane. It was as if I was a criminal seeking asylum. I'd only left the Dome a few times growing up; it was always on Government sponsored trips from my parents work and usually to only surrounding areas on the east coast.

As much as I hate to admit it, my parents were right though about it being a learning experience. I've learned a lot about myself the last six months. For one, I'm a loner. I'm one of those people that never want to leave their house for anything. Ihave everything shipped or delivered into me. I don't want to interact with people that I don't know and since I know no one out here, that would be everyone. On my first solo outing into the city, everyone could tell I wasn't from here. I stuck out like a sore thumb. From the way I dressed and the way I talked and interacted with people. Most people thought I was a tourist and the other half seemed annoyed with me once I opened my mouth to speak with my accent quickly giving me away. I think I answered twenty times in a day the question*where are you from?* When I'd respond to them the Dome, I'd get looks of disgust, get turned away, even screamed at I quickly learned to lie or not answer at all. I still get the questions if I venture outbut not on these runs. No one bothers you when you're running. Plus there's usually no one else out to bother me at this time.

I turn another corner and get my first real look of the bridge. It stops me dead in my tracks, my arms falling to my sides and my mouth gapping open in shockHalf of the bridge is gone, sinking into the bay and the other half is jutting out of the water. Car after car is piled up on the bridge, slowly sinking and falling into the water The lights coming from the cars and the flames are the only things that illuminate the scene. I hear an explosion off in the distance, and the blast makes me jump. I see a giant fireball climbs the sky. Then a car catches on fire, the fuel leaving a fire trail in the water. For a split second after the blast, I can see more of the bridge in front of me. I wonder where are the police or the fire fighters? I don't know if I should keep running or turn around. The bridge looks close, but it is far away. I wouldn't be of any help, even if I ran all the way down to it.

I take off running as fast as I can getting further around the block, the sound of another blast has my ears ringing, making my mind up for me I turn and run towards my house. I must get home because something horrendous has happened for the iconic bridge to be in such a state with no signs of help. I look at my watch for a time check. It's 5:15 a.m., and the sun won't start coming up for at least another full hour. I begin to run as fast as I can toward home...my safe haven.

I continue running, and continue to hear more explosions, and the ground shakes beneath my feet. I'm running up hill as fast as I can, sweat pouring down my face matting my hair against my forehead. Pure adrenaline is what's keeping my legs going. They're tired, and I'm trying to cover too much distance in a short time. I can see my house, up the hill in the distance, which gives me some comfort. *I'm so close but so far.* I sprint to my front door and pull the keychain from around my wrist. It's then that I realize my hands are shaking as I try to get the key into my lock. I have to try to get the key in not once but twice before I step inside and lock the door behind me. I feel safer now that I'm indoors. I know that I might not *really* be safe but it gives me enough of an illusion that I'm able to calm down my racing heart. I need to find out what's happening. This feels like a nightmare.

I find mymy phone, and the message is still on display: *Network Not Connected.* I try the television and my computer once more. No luck, nothing is working. I'm racking my brain, trying to figure out what to do. I have no access to any outside news. I have no clue what is going on and I know that something is definitely happening. Sunlight is starting to slowly creep up on the city so the house isn't in complete darkness. What little safety I felt being inside is starting to disappear with the tremors from the ground and the loud explosions going off in the distance. The television pops on with the emergency broadcast beacon scaring the shit out of me. Illuminating the room in a yellow hue coming from the screen background. The beacon continues to beep, and the screen reads:

EMERGENCY: DEVASTATION SWEEPS AMERICA.

Residents encouraged to seek shelter and remain calm.

That's all the screen contains and before I can read it again the screen goes black and the power goes off. The ground shakes so hard, photographs on my wall begin to crash to the ground shattering the glass on contact. Screw the message there is no calm. I bet everyone in the neighborhood is awake now. How can anyone remain calm through the tremors, let alone after reading that message? I need to get a hold of my mom or my dad or just anyone that I know but if I can get ahold of my mother shehe can tell me what the hell is going on. How can I reach her with no phone or internet?

CHAPTER TWO

As I stand in my kitchen looking out the window, I rack my brain thinking of ways to get ahold of someone I know. There's no power so anything with electronics is out. While I've been standing there trying to come up with a plan the sun has risen and I can finally see my neighborhood clearly and down into the bay. I feel like I'm going to faint, my nerves on edge and the adrenaline wearing off. I look out onto the bay, and fires are everywhere. Houses are collapsed and fire hydrants are shooting water straight up to the sky. I do a double take out the window When I think it's starting to snow which I know for a fact is impossible here. I lean over my sink trying to get a closer look at the falling pieces and realize it's some type of grey ash falling from the sky. My body starts to involuntarily shake. Now I'm completely coming unglued. There aren't any volcanoes here either What can this be?

I eye the fires in the bay, and they are burning wildly with no signs of help coming their way. I don't understand where the police could be. Where are the firefighters? I've got to figure out what to do on my own. The fires are getting closer to my house. If the wind picks up or if they are left untamed, they will eventually arrive here. *If only my phone or internet was working!*

I sit down at my kitchen table and rest my head against the cool table top. Then the memory pops into my head and I swing back up, getting up from the table and going back to my bedroom. Two months after I moved into my house in San Fran, I found a sealed letter at the bottom of one of my suitcases. It had a burgundy pouch attached to it and was addressed to me in my mother's handwriting. On the front of the black envelope written in silver ink it read: *Only to be opened in an Emergency. You will know the right time, Love Mom.* I wanted to open it right then out of curiosity but knew not to. I knew to follow her instructions. Now, remembering it, I know this is definitely the time to open it. I can feel it in my gut and, as the letter said, I would know when the time was right to open it.

I'm scared, alone and thousands of miles away from my parents and friends. *Yep, ripping into that one.*

! I go into my bedroom, fling the doors open on my closet and grab my suitcase. I've kept the letter and pouch there since the day I discovered them. *Out of sight, out of mind* I told myself. I drop to my knees and run the zipper around the length of the bag, flip open the lid and pull out the letter. I lay the pouch to my side. I break the heavy wax seal on the black envelope and begin to read the letter inside.

Asmita,

If you are reading this letter, then we are in the new state of our world. We knew this day would come and wanted to try to keep you safe as possible on the other side of the country. We tried to do the right thing. Now is the time for you to be strong. You must get yourself to a safe place. Get out of the city and head inland. Go someplace that has always made you happy, think about this place and the perfect spot will come to you Take only essentials. Pack anything you have that's expensive like jewelry and things you can barter and trade with. Get out of town as fast as possible and don't trust or drink the water. Use the pills we have enclosed on water at all times. Do not trust anyone no matter what they may say or do to persuade you. The only person you can trust now is yourself. Remember your father and I love you. We will one day see each other again.

Love, Mama

I stare at the letter, not believing what I'm reading but trying to understand. I'm in shock. I have to read the letter a second time. . How did they know this could happen and why would they send me so far away from them? What jewelry? The necklace they gave me? It's only a small gold heart and wouldn't bring much from a jeweler let alone on the street. I wear it every day and never take it off. I unzip the pouch and shake its content out onto the ground beside me. The light from the window hits the small mound of diamonds momentarily blinding me. Well, I guess this is what she meant by jewelry. The pouch is full of loose diamonds in various shapes and sizes, heavy bracelets and rings mixed among them. None of it looks familiar from my mother's so it must be things that she gave me specifically for whatever this situation is.

Underneath the jewels are small bottles of tiny orange pills. The pills are so small that they are maybe one fourth the size of a dime. There's got to be several hundred of them since they are so tiny. I read the small print on the bottle: one pill per ten ounces. Shake and wait 30 seconds before drinking. Whatever my parents may or may not have known , they knew it wouldn't be safe to drink the water now. I sit on the floor until my legs feel numb. What had my parents never told me? And what else have they been keeping from me? It takes me awhile but I snap out of my disbelief and get to my feet.

I skip a much-needed shower because I'm unsure now about the water. The letter didn't explicitly say anything about using the water only drinking it but at this point, I'm not going to chance it. I change out of my running gear and into a pair of jeans and a sweater. I leave my running shoes on and comb my hair and pull it back into a tiny nub of a ponytail. Packing a small backpack with the pouch and the letter from my mother, I keep the pills in the pouch and grab a water bottle from the kitchen and some protein bars. I take a frame from my bed side that holds a family photo and an extra day of clothing. I have no idea how I'm going to get out of the city, but I must. My cell phone is useless, but I take it anyway and power it off to save what battery I have. I take one last look around at my house and lock the door behind me.

Outside, the smell of smoke is strong. The ash is coming down hard and reminds me of the beginning of a blizzard I remember experiencing growing up. My garage door won't open so I have to manually pull it open using the cord hanging in the center of my garage. I throw my backpack into the front passenger seat and start my car up. I've got almost a full tank of gas and, since it's a hybrid, can also use the electric it's got stored. I've only driven my car or any car for that matter a handful of times so hopefully I can get out of the city. I back my car out of the garage and get out, pulling the garage door down behind me. I don't see any of my neighbors out of their homes. I wonder if they are inside accounting for the damage or trying to find a way to get news. How many people were awake to see the announcement? Either way, I'm going to follow my mother's instructions. I'm trying to get somewhere safe out of the city.

I start driving in the opposite direction of the Golden Gate. There is no way across that bridge, and my other closest option out of the city is the Bay Bridge; that will get me out of San Fran and access to mainland California the fastest. I speed down the hill and can see the damage done so far. Houses are on fire, and pieces of cement and drywall are all over the sides of the road. I'm paying careful attention to power lines as some look like they could fall to the ground any minute. Wires are down in places, and I throw all caution to the wind and plow through the red lights. I've only seen a few other cars on the road which is extremely rare for the city.

People are starting to flood the sidewalks and spill out into the roads as I further away from my residential area . As I start getting closer to the Bay Bridge, I can see that it appears crossable.. The bridge spans farther than I can see so I take the chance and get on. I can't go back, I have to keep moving forward. Traffic is nonexistent on the bridge, with onlya few abandoned cars sitting in lanes. Out of the five lanes, most are free to drive in. Some people have stopped and are on the side of the bridge while others are stopped in random spots causing me to have to weave in out of the lanes.

I'm trying to cross the bridge as fast as I can. I don't know if it's the wind or another earthquake, but I can feel the bridge moving as I drive. I'm almost to the end when I can see a section of the bridge is missing. Cars have stopped in three lanes, and people are out of their cars staring out into the dark water. Two lanes on the right side are still intact, but no one is driving across them. If I stay here, who knows what could happen. My gut tells me to gofor it. I lay on my horn as I barrel down on the people. I'm getting out of here one way or another. I weave in and out of more cars parked trying to watch both the road and the bystanders. I can see heads turning toward me as I come up on them. My car is flying now, no longer going anywhere near the speed limit.

I force my car all the way to the right side of the bridge. I'm so close to the barrier wall that I hit my mirror on the concrete. As I drive over the falling concrete, I can see cars down in the water. It's a mess of steel and concrete. They must have gone down with the initial tremors. I feel bad for them, but I'm too scared for myself to keep my mind on the scene. I get my eyes back on the road and get back onto the section of bridge that's still intact.

That was the most exciting trip to Oakland I've ever had. Actually, it's my only trip to Oakland. Once I'm across the bridge, I realize that traffic is going to be my enemy. I've made it a few miles, but the freeway is flooded with stopped cars, abandoned or involved in some state of an accident. Grey ash is still falling from the sky, and it's coming down at a rate my wiper blades can't keep up with. The wind is so strong, it's attempting to blow my car into the other lanes. The normally flashing billboards along the ides of the road normally showing ads are now black. I make it several miles before I have to come to a complete stop. As I look over at the drivers around me, the look on people's faces is a mixture of confusion and horror. Panic has set in, and everyone is trying to figure out how to react to the insane amount of ash falling or the lack of information in the emergency broadcast.

My thoughts are to just keep moving. I pull my car off the road and power on my phone. It shines back at me the now familiar message, *Network Not Connected*. I sit there and stare at the phone for a few minutes, not knowing what to do with myself. If I can't call or get information on my phone, then I'm really on my own. I've got to get myself to somewhere safe like my mother's instructions said. Only one major problem so far... where the hell am I supposed to go? It's time to get out of the car. I won't make it anywhere on this congested road, and I'm only killing daylight by sitting here. I have no other choice but to get out and walk.

CHAPTER THREE

I'M WALKING beside the highway, and people are everywhere; they look lost and confused. I hear some groups of people talking and saying they can't get the radio on in their car. I hear others saying their cell phones aren't working and that they haven't heard any news. I can hear people screaming over the wind smacking against my face. The ash is still falling hard, and I wrap my scarf around my face to stop the ash from getting into my nose and mouth. I don't know where the ash is coming from, but it can't be good. I pull my coat sleeve back to check my watch; it's almost one o'clock in the afternoon, and I've only made it to the outskirts of the nearest big city. I need to get out of major cities, but I'm not sure where to go.

I sit down on the hard ground to rest. My feet aren't used to this much walking and running in one day. I remove a bottle of water from my backpack and take a drink. I know the bottled water I have with me is safe but once I run out, I'll have to figure out where to find water and use the pills my mother left me. I think about what to do next. I'm racking my brain, thinking of any clues my parents may have mentioned in the last few weeks during our phone and video chats. I don't get why they didn't warn me this could happen. I take out the note and carefully reread it. They sent me here to be safer, but they knew this was going to happen. Is it worse on the east coast? What is happening? I have more questions than answers. I stuff the letter and water into my bag and pick myself up off the ground.

I start walking north and off to the freeway side. I need to get away from the crowds before they turn violent or start looting. I haven't seen any police this entire day, which is odd. The Dome would already have police on every corner assuring citizens that everything will return to order shortly. Once I'm off the freeway side, I find a concrete side road to walk down. The wind is at my back now, giving my face a rest. I can hear a car coming so I move to the side. The car gets closer and slows. It's a young woman with a baby in the backseat. She slows down to pass me but doesn't stop. This road must connect to the surrounding farms and houses because it isn't polluted with abandoned cars or people. I stay on it for as long as I can. I can see up ahead the road meets another road. It has a green mile marker sign at the end.

I search my mind for any hint of today that my parents might have given me, and then it hits me. My mom kept mentioning it would be wonderful to go skiing this winter in Salt Lake City. I remember the conversation exactly. I thought it was so odd for my mother to say. In my whole life, I've never known her to ski or have any interest in it. She hates the cold. I remember her exact words. "Asmita, I just love skiing, and Salt Lake City is the perfect place! You should go since you're closer. We could stop by and see Antelope Island. I've heard amazing things about it and that it's life changing!" I laughed at her and, when I pointed out the fact that she never skis, she stopped talking and changed the subject. I didn't think anything of it at the time, but now that I'm replaying all of our conversations in my head, that's the one that sticks out. My mother hasn't left the Dome in years. This conversation was my clue.

I know where to go now... Utah and specifically, Antelope Island.

CHAPTER 4

Jesse

THIS MUST BE what hell feels like. We all live in hell now.

I can feel the sun burning my skin, literally burning my skin as I walk. My arms are covered by my long sleeve shirt, but the sun is relentless. It's strong and coming through the threads of my shirt. The sun is starting to set and should be down soon. I've travelled a few miles now, and I know I should have waited to move till it was completely dark, but I just couldn't wait. I haven't been able to cover as much ground since the riots started. In the three months that have passed since the disaster, the world we all knew has changed.

It took some time in the beginning before people really began to get out of control, when they realized no one was coming to help them and that things wouldn't go back to normal. The electric wasn't coming back on, the water wasn't safe to drink in the cities and no one had any answers... that's when the rioting and outrage started. That's when the people started fighting back against the government and amongst themselves. Fights would break out over a bottle of water. Now people, good people, try to keep to themselves. Everyone is scared, rightly so that's for certain.

My parents gave me a fair warning and supplied me with everything I would need to survive the initial fallout. They knew that I could handle the truth. They got me out of the Dome months in advance. I was one of the lucky ones. I knew this was coming. I was mentally and physically prepared. They got me out of the Dome by putting me on a train and secured my passage by bribing our family doctor. My work absence had to be explained somehow, and greasing the palm of our doctor was the easiest way. Money talked, and since he had no idea what was to come, he had no problem in saying I was ill and unable to work for an extended time frame. Sickness or death, those were your only options for getting out of a government placed job.

I had chosen not to go the college route, and, after my year of self-reflection, I was placed directly into work by the Dome. Once you are placed into work, you do not miss a job. Six days a week you are expected to show up and do your designated duty. You've got to put in 45 years before you can enjoy a leisure life, if you even make it that long. The poor go into the work life as they have no other choice. They sign the contract and usually get one bonus of some kind. Usually, it's secured housing for their family or something else they request. It just depends on the Dome and what they're willing to give in return for their labor.

My parents were shocked when I chose the work contract. Their high placement in the Dome would have cemented an easy life for me. I didn't want that. I didn't want to go to a boring party after party pretending to care about the Dome's agenda. I didn't want forced servants waiting on me day in and day out, staring at me with their blank faces. I wanted to earn my way in life. I didn't want to live my parents' lives. I wanted to work, and I wanted to be my own man. Well, now I'm definitely earning my own. And I've got a long night ahead of me.

Traveling at night is dangerous, but this far out from any major city should be safe. I can't handle the heat of the sun. Those first few weeks the sun was shrouded by clouds and ash dropping from the sky. Once the overcast gray was gone, the sun bore down hard with constant heat like no summer I'd ever felt before. It made traveling in the day nearly impossible. At first, I couldn't get out of the town my parents had sent me to in Indiana. The roads were destroyed, and I had to bide my time. I packed all of my pills that my parents supplied me with and re-read their instructions. I know from their instructions that I needed to get to Antelope Island on the north western side of Salt Lake City. I've covered a few hundred miles, and, with tonight's progress, I should almost be to Denver.

The heat has drained my energy, and I have to sit down for a rest. I find a tree and prop my back up against it. I open my pack and pull out the black envelope containing the letter my parents gave me. I read it for the first time on the day of the disaster as I was instructed to. I've read it every day since. It's my only connection to my parents. It provides the small amount of strength that I need in times of despair. My instructions were clear, and I can even hear my mother's tone as I read it.

Jesse,

You are prepared for today. In your pack you will find everything needed to help you succeed. We have given you enough pills to last six months, a compass and the maps you will need to get across the country. You must get to Antelope Island outside of Salt Lake City. There you will find someone who can be a great asset. She is the key to building a better world and can give you many answers. Do not let anything happen to her. Keep her far away from the Dome, and only return to the city when you receive notice. You must not let her know how important she is and, most of all you, must not let her know you were sent to find her. Keep her safe. Do whatever it takes.

Love, Mom and Dad.

I fold the letter and put it back in the envelope. I pull out the enclosed photograph and stare at her face. The girl I am to find. No name, no age and no address. She is my mystery girl. Why is she so important? Now, as I look at the photo, she looks plain to me. I can't see her body in the photo so it's hard to determine her age. She looks young, somewhere near my age. All I have to focus on is her face. Her pale skin looks almost translucent with her dark hair pulled up. Her green eyes stare back at me, taunting me to come find her. The only things I know about her are what my parents told me in the letter. I wonder, is she expecting me, waiting for me to come get her? Was she prepared, ready for the world to fall apart? All of these questions run through my mind. I didn't even know she was going to be my responsibility after the disaster. I should have known my parents had an ulterior motive for getting me out of the city. I'll always wonder what they got out of it.

I slide the photo back in the envelope and shove it into my bag. I get back up on my feet and continue to walk. The light from the moon is now shining, helping me find my way. I listen for noises around me. The looters have started making their way out of the city to set up camp in the woods. I know I'm far enough out, but I remain cautious. I keep heading west, always heading west. It's all I know to do. I stop a few times to drink water and rest, but I keep making my way. I have to get to my mystery girl.

Hours pass. The night drags on and finally the beginning of daylight is starting to creep up on the horizon. The trees are growing farther apart, and the overhead brush is becoming thinner. I need to find shelter to rest and stay out of the sun's blaze. I scan my surroundings for suitable shelter. Sunrise is almost complete, and I can see further ahead of me now. The woods are clearing around me, and a road is visible in the distance. The heat from the sun is starting to grow stronger every minute, and it's glaring off something ahead. I walk a few more minutes, and, once I'm upon it, I can see what the sun is reflecting off of. It's a large metal sign hanging on by a lone chain. It's faded, and I have to tilt my head to one side to make it out. It reads...**Welcome to Denver**

CHAPTER 5

Asmita

MY FEET ARE KILLING ME. *Literally,* killing me. They could be the death of me. If I can't keep walking, I don't know what I'll do. At this point, my feet are still covered in blisters, and one toe has lost its nail. I've had to walk the last eleven miles into town. I'm thirsty, dirty and sweating so badly that I don't know how I have a drop of moisture left in my body. I had to flirt, con, beg and barter my way for the last 500 miles and couldn't find anyone to get me these last few.

Now, I'm hiding from the sun and the crazies who go out into it. No one, and I mean no one, goes out into the sun unless they have no choice. That, or they're just plain crazy. I'm in the remnants of what used to be a gas station and convenience store. There are about fifteen other people hiding out here. I normally wouldn't bide my daylight hours around this many people. but I was desperate and had to get out of the sun. I remember those first few days when the sun came out blazing, and I shudder. I had never had a sunburn so bad in my life.

Right now, I'm so thirsty that all I can think about is taking a drink of water, but I've learned not to take my water out in front of anyone. I find a spot by the old milk coolers and throw my backpack down in front of me, locking it onto my arms. I slide my back down the glass until my butt hits the floor. I look around the large open space at the others around me. It took me two diamonds to learn about this place. I lost another two to the men guarding the front door. Once I paid, they lowered their weapons and let me into this paradise. Places like this have kept me alive.

What I assume is a mother and daughter sit across from me. The mother, holding the scared younger girl, is trying to comfort her. They had to have some help to find this place, so they are luckier than most. I wonder what the others had to pay to get in here. I scan the room, avoiding eye contact with the others. There is a restroom sign pointing toward an unlit hallway. I get up from the floor slowly and make my way over to it. I try to make as little noise as possible since people have started to fall asleep. The two men at the front door look back at me for a brief second but turn their eyes and attention back to the outside. They'll watch for trouble as everyone else sleeps the day away.

I reach the bathroom and turn the knob to find a dark room. The room is empty, and I step inside. The smell hits me, and it's a mixture of barf, piss and feces. I reflexively gag and start to breathe through my mouth. I lock the door behind me. I've gotten used to doing a lot in the dark. I take the water out of my backpack as fast as I can and swig the liquid into my body. The smell and the heat in the room start to make me feel sick so I know I have to go back out. I hide my water back in my bag, unlock the door and step back into the hallway. I breathe fresher air and wipe the sweat from my forehead.

I make my way back into the store and find a place to sit down in an aisle. I can't stare at the mom and daughter duo all day. I have things to do that I don't want others to see, but I must do this in daylight hours. I sit in my aisle and wait for the others to fall asleep. When I can't hear any movement or talking, I take the map out of my bag and carefully unfold it to the section I need. I'm careful not to make much noise because this item is almost as valuable as water. When I bartered for it outside of Reno, it cost me the high price of 10 diamonds. Not many people had paper maps available before the disaster, so they became a high-demand item.

People with cash couldn't even trade for them. What does anyone have use for paper money? Paper money is useless now. I've literally wiped my ass with it in the woods. It's all about bartering for goods, food and clean water now. My parents were right about that in their letter. They knew that money would do no good; they knew that people would want items. They knew that giving me a giant sack of diamonds would get me things I needed and hopefully, keep me safe at the same time.

I look around the room to make sure no one can see me in the aisle. If my math is correct, I'm about 45 miles from the border and another 100 miles from my destination. I quickly fold the map back up and get it into my backpack before anyone sees. My diamond supply is getting low, and I can't risk having nothing to trade. I'm going to have to walk the rest of the way there or at least a large portion. I divide the miles into days and try to decide how many miles I can cover in a day.

The most I've ever been able to cover before sunrise is twenty-eight. I've heard talk of others walking up to fifty which is insane to me. I don't know how they can do it or if it's even true. If I can keep the pace up of my personal record, I'll be there in five days. I don't know if I can do it, but I'm going to have to try. I've got to mentally psych myself up. I'm really going to have to walk it. I'm going to have to get a lot of rest during the days to be up for 10 hours in the darkness each night. I loop my arms through the straps of my backpack and hold it on my chest. I curl up on the dirty, white tile floor and close my eyes in the hopes of getting some rest. I have no idea when I'll have a roof over my head again.

CHAPTER 6

Asmita

A LOUD NOISE startles me awake. I sit up and look around the room. I don't know how long I've been asleep, but darkness has fallen, and my aisle in the store is empty. My shirt clings to my body from sweat. I rub my eyes, trying to get the sleep out of them. I stand up and can see the two men at the front door letting people out. It hasn't been dark for long then, so I haven't lost too much time. When I walk, I try to start moving as dusk is falling.

I can overhear the two guards talking about the town I'm in and try not to get caught ear hustling as I get my bag together. I take a better look at my surroundings, and it looks like I'm one of the last people inside. I hear the guards again talking about a gas leak and a countdown but can't make out the whole conversation. I wonder what they know, how they know and what it means. I try to pick up everything, but with the noise inside and outside it's hard to make out what they are saying.

I move my sleeve and check the time; it's 7:30 p.m. That means I've got about ten hours to move. I flip my backpack to my back and head for the doors. I take one last look around me and notice the mother and daughter duo have left. I don't know why, but the sight of them earlier stirred an emotion I didn't want to identify. I think about my own mother and wonder if she's alive, safe and thinking about me too. I wonder if I'll see her again. I have to hang on to the dream that she's okay and that I'll see her one day again soon. If not, I don't know what else I would do because I don't have too much else to live for in the world.

As I walk out the door, one of the guards reaches out for me. He grabs my arm, stopping me in my tracks. His grip on my arm is firm and tight. I have no doubt I'll have a bruise there from his fingers. He looks me straight in the eye and says, "If you want to see past sunrise, you'll need to get off flat land."

I take his warning as a threat and get out the door as fast as I can once he releases my arm. I've heard warnings before in other towns and whispers of things going on in other parts of the country. I've heard of towns testing weapons and odd occurrences. No one has gotten any confirmed information, so it could all be lies. I keep my mouth shut but always listen to what they have to say. When I was making my way out of California, I kept hearing news that the Dome was destroyed, no one survived and it's miles and miles of flat wasteland now.

If there's one thing I know, knowledge is power. One rumor I heard is that it wasn't a natural disaster but an attack, and that's why the power has never come back on. Not many people from the Dome travelled to the west coast before the disaster, so it's not like there's a ton of people around to ask. Dome residents weren't popular before the disaster, and now even less so. I never let anyone know the Dome is where I was born and raised. I'd be in even more danger if that information ever got out. When people randomly ask, I tell them I was traveling from the east when the disaster happened and was on the west coast. Luckily, not many have asked.

Now that the sun is down, it feels much cooler outside. The wind blows, and it causes a chill to run through me from my damp clothes. I comb my hair with my hands and adjust my ponytail. I take in the surroundings and realize the gas station is completely exposed with no nearby buildings or trees. It makes it an ideal place in the daylight but a sitting duck at night. I walk as fast as I can toward trees in the distance that appear to follow the mountain range out of town. The plus to being on such flat land at the moment is being able to see ahead so far, even in the dark. The negative is that I'm exposed. Getting to the trees will help hide me from trouble. I haven't had to walk in a while, and my feet are still aching from last night. I haven't been alone for a few weeks, and silence has become unfamiliar. There's usually been someone chatting or at least the noises of their breathing to lay a layer of comfort to walking at night. Tonight, I won't get any such comfort and probably not any night moving forward.

I check my watch, and the time tells me that I've been walking for 4 hours. My feet are throbbing now, but I've made it to the trees. They feel like two bloody stumps inside my shoes. I find a large rock to sit on outside the tree line to my feet. I have about 6 more hours before sunrise... before the odd threat from the locals becomes a reality. I untie the laces around my right foot to give it some relief. My foot is covered in blisters, and I can feel my pulse in it. Where's a horse or a large animal when you need one, or better, a microbus like the one that I paid ten diamonds to ride on to get me out of California and into Nevada? Knowing that I have to get up, I tie my shoe back up, take a drink of water and plunge into the trees. I've got to get through this tree line and up to the summit of the mountain before sunlight.

Hours pass, and I've made it deep enough into the tree line that I'm protected from trouble. I should make it far enough away to avoid the local threat. It's been a steep climb, and my hands are aching from holding on to tree branches and rocks while trying to climb. I pause to look at the sky and catch my breath. A tree branch snaps a few feet away from me, and I freeze in place. The sound came from behind me. I'm paralyzed with fear and don't know if I should turn around to see what caused the noise or run.

I don't have to wait long to find out what made the noise because when I turn around, I can see it was a person who broke the tree branch. They've acted quickly and made up their mind... they are racing toward me. Fight or flight takes hold of me, and I'm now running up the steep terrain. My feet slide on the dry leaves, and I curse myself in my mind to stay upright. I dare to look back, to get a glimpse of the person chasing me, and what I see makes me run harder.

The guy running behind me is literally a beast. He's got to be at least six feet tall and all muscle. He's practically foaming at the mouth he's so enraged. His large size is the only thing keeping the distance between us. He can't run as fast as I can. He's breathing heavy and from the look of his disheveled clothes, he's been tracking me in the woods for some time. He must have been hiding out, and I stumbled into his area. My legs are starting to ache, and I'm slowing down. My lungs are burning as I suck in the cool air. I scramble trying to see if there's anywhere to hide. It's all thick trees, fallen leaves and dried pinecones. Knowing I can't keep this uphill chase going forever, I start to panic. This is the first real immediate threat I've faced all alone. I see a tree ahead that's large enough for me to hide behind. I've got enough distance from the beast that he might just pass me by.

I duck behind the tree and try to get my breathing under control. I'm sucking in air so hard that people miles away can probably hear me. The fear I feel when I hear him getting closer stops me from making any noise. I can hear every step he takes as he's making no effort to hide his presence. The noise of crushing pinecones and leaves rustling gets louder and louder as he approaches. I only have a few seconds before he'll be right up on me. I look around for anything that I can use to defend myself.

My eyes hone in on a large rock, and I try to reach it without coming into his line of sight. The rock is heavy to lift from the ground, and I have to hold it with both hands. My arms strain to hold the rock above my head as I lean back against the tree, perched and waiting to strike.

When I see him out of the corner of my eye, he's about two steps in front of me beside the tree. I know this is the best shot I've got at surprising him. I leap out and hit him on the head with the rock I'm holding. With a giant thud, his body hits the ground, and a silver knife falls from his grip beside his hand. I drop the rock to the ground. My emotions get the best of me, and I start to sob, I've got tears streaming down my face and I'm shaking uncontrollably like a leaf. I bend down to check his pulse at the neck to see if he's still alive. He definitely is. I don't know how long he'll be knocked out, but I have no plans of being here when he wakes up.

I pick up his silver knife and see that its handle is carved with the Dome symbol. I haven't seen one of these since I was living in the Dome. I close the knife and place it in my backpack. It may come in handy later in more ways than one. I can use it for protection and for bartering. I shove my hand into his jeans pocket to see if he's carrying an identification card or anything else worth taking for trading. If this man was willing to kill me, then I'm willing to rob him and not have a guilty conscience about it.

The way his body is laying makes it hard for me to get the wallet out of his pocket. I open it, and a piece of paper falls to the ground. I bend down, pick it up and flip it over. Much to my surprise and bewilderment, my own face is staring back at me. His wallet holds a photo of me. *What the hell?* I look at the photo of myself, and a sinking feeling begins to set in. He knows who I am, and this encounter isn't a coincidence. I look at the photo of myself and remember the day it was taken. It was for my adult identification card taken only a few days before I left for San Francisco. I remember my mom was so proud she even started crying at one point.

Now, when I look back at days like that one, I wonder if my mom and dad's actions were genuine for being in the moment of their daughter growing up or because they knew what was to come. Some days when I think about certain memories, I feel angry. I feel lied to... like a fool. Was everyone in on it except me? Maybe I'll never know, but looking back at this photo of myself sends a chill down my spine.

I search the rest of the wallet, and he isn't carrying any identification for himself. I take the photograph and throw his wallet to the ground. I check his other pockets, but they all turn out empty. I take one last look at the man's face and commit it to memory. When he wakes up, I want to make sure I'm long gone. I quickly start to run away. I want as much distance between us as I can get.

Once I'm far enough away, I slow down to my walking pace and try to make sense of it all. *None of it makes sense.* Why would this man, a man I've never met have my photo in his wallet? Is he from the Dome? Is that why he had a Dome knife? Maybe it was just an item that got traded and ended up in his hands? How would he know where to find me and why would he want to harm me? I can't make sense of it, and I'm more scared than I've ever been. The unanswered questions swirl around my brain, and all I can do is keep walking. Walking and thinking. Paranoid, I am now constantly looking over my shoulder.

Darkness is turning to light, and the sun will rise quickly. I've made it to the top of the mountain range and, at the next nightfall, I'll make my way down the other side which will put me in Utah. From this vantage point, I can see above all the treetops and the town that I walked out of. As I'm looking at the town, a large beam of light bursts out from the center and spreads out in a circle around the town. The light is so bright it makes me close my eyes. It takes a few more seconds before I hear a rumbling sound that accompanies the flash of light.

The ground beneath my feet slightly shakes. I don't know what that was, but it was nothing good. It looked like some kind of explosion. The mother and daughter duo from the gas station come to mind. I wonder if they are down there and if they are safe. I shake the thought out of my head. I need to focus. I keep walking and start looking for shelter. I've got to look out for myself. I can't be exposed to the daylight for an entire day.

I start making my way down the other side of the mountain and notice a cluster of large boulders. A massive bolder is perched on top of two others. There is a large gap of space underneath that should provide me shade. I crawl under the boulder and my body can fit in between them. This is the best I'm going to find, and my skin will be shielded from direct sunlight. Sunrise is in full swing, and I can see the light hitting the ground all around the boulder. Here I'll be protected from the sun, but the heat will be intense. I drink my water and know that tomorrow I'll need to find more. I close my eyes and try to find peace to sleep. I'm not going anywhere for the next ten hours. Hopefully, the man I left behind isn't moving anywhere either.

CHAPTER 7

Jesse

THE SUN IS DISAPPEARING QUICKLY over the Colorado horizon in front of me. I can't help but gaze into the orange mass as I change into a cleaner t-shirt. I've made my way through this week and with tonight's travel, I should make it into Utah. I have another week of traveling to go but getting closer to finding the girl in the picture fills me with anxiety and fear. I've been going all of these months with the sole purpose of finding her. I've followed my parent's instructions exactly. I know it will be my job to keep her safe once I find her, but what else? I'm relying on her to have the answers as to what to do next.

The real unknown is what truly scares me. As I get closer to Utah, and the larger city of Salt Lake, I feel the anxiety creeping up in my chest. It makes me feel confused. I know I'm walking on foot, but I feel like I'm on a speeding train headed straight into a wall. I think about speeding up my travel and as I close the distance to Salt Lake, I think I should be able to find transportation.

When I passed through Denver, I heard rumors that a few major cities were starting to become more civilized. Salt Lake City was rumored to be the leader of this movement. I heard that they have started a free trading system for goods, have clean water and food readily available at a price. I couldn't help but smile to myself at the thought of a good meal. I'm really tired of eating nuts and berries and killing small animals that I randomly come across in the woods. I regret not rationing the food my parents supplied me with in those first few weeks. They had given me a two-month supply, and I blew through it in a month. Hopefully those rumors are true because I've got my hopes up on finding some good chow. Besides my mystery girl, food is always the other thing on my mind. Oh... water. Of course. Water is always on my mind.

I've got my gear packed and loaded up on my back. The last remnants of the sun have faded out, and the stars are visible in the sky. I dampen the fire I had for my food and make sure that it's completely out. It's time for me to start moving and make my way into Utah. I found out about this trail right outside of

Denver after some major haggling. I had to give up some flashlight batteries to find out the easiest way through this rocky, mountainous region. I must have gone back and forth with the local guy for half an hour. I had to dig through my bag until we found something he would trade the information for. I didn't have a choice though. I'm no expert at climbing, and the terrain in this area is almost all rough rock and canyons. If I wasn't in the position that I am, I'd stay here longer. The days have been extremely hot but dry, and the nights have been cooler to walk through. The land seems peaceful, and that's been in a nice change since this whole mess began.

I've started down the path that I paid for, and it's taking my full concentration. When my mind starts to wander, I find myself being startled back into reality with my feet slipping on the rocks beneath them. It's a steep climb down and as I take my time with my foot holds, I begin to lose track of the time. It's taking me a long time to climb down. I don't realize how much time has passed until I make it to the bottom of my descent, and I'm on flat land again. I realize only then that it's taken me almost all night to make it down the mountain and inside the border of Utah. If that was the easiest path, then my trade was a good one. I'm covered in dirt sticking to my arms from the sweat. For an inexperienced rock climber, it sure has been hard. Thankfully, I'm in excellent physical condition.

The color of the ground below my feet surprises me since I've only ever seen it in photos. I reach down and touch the orange dirt and quickly brush it off my hands. It's almost clay-like and smears in my hand to leave a stain. I keep walking forward and realize that I've climbed straight down into a canyon, and the only way to continue on this path is to climb up and out on the other side. I walk for a few minutes and reach the far side of the canyon. I start to look for places that I can grip with my hands and feet to make my way up. I've just placed my right foot on the rock and go to push myself up when a man's voice booms out behind me.

The echo bounces off the canyon walls and stills me. I slowly take my foot down off the rock and turn around to face the man. When I turn around, there isn't just one man standing with me in the canyon, there are four standing about 300 feet away from me. The men are holding weapons pointed and drawn directly at me. This can't be anything good.

I stand still with my hands up in the air. I try to remain calm as they walk toward me. My heart is beating so hard, it fills my ears with the blood pumping through me. They are the hunters, and I am their prey. As they approach me, I recognize one of the men. He's the guy I made the trade with back outside of Denver. I gave him the batteries for the path information. That's when it hits me - this was all one big trap. The friendly guy, the haggling of the supply for the route... the guy knew exactly what he was doing. My eyes scan the canyon looking for any way out. I am completely trapped with only one escape, which is up the rocks behind me. They've baited me, and now I'm at their mercy. What they don't realize is I'm not a sheep in a lion's den. I am the lion.

The men are within a few feet of me when they stop and the tradesman I recognize speaks up. "That's him alright," he says while he nods toward me. "He's the one who wanted to know how to get out of town so fast," he tells his friends.

"He traded me some fancy batteries to find the easiest way out. I got a good look in his bag too". He points his finger at my bag.

The older, heavy-set man of the group, who is clearly their leader, looks me up and down. He spits nonchalantly on the ground, and I can see he's only got about five teeth in his head. His thick, gray beard holds drops of the spit he just released from his mouth. I look at him with disgust, and he gauges my reaction. Before I can speak, he racks his shotgun and says, "The bag." He advances forward and stops in front of me.

His men move closer to me and nudge the straps of my backpack with one of their guns. I slowly take the bag off my back and put it on the ground at my feet. One of his men with dirty hands snatches my bag up and starts digging through it. I stand there, staring at their fat leader. He never takes his eyes or his gun off me. I keep my face calm and silently pray that this idiot going through my bag doesn't feel around on the bag itself. My parents didn't raise a fool, and I've got my orange water pills hidden in the lining of the bag. I've also got my maps hidden there too.

"All he's got in here are some dirty clothes, a few batteries, a flashlight and some old wrinkled letter," one of the men says disgustedly as he pokes through my bag. He looks back at the guy I had done the trade with a few days ago with pure hatred. "You drug us out all this way for a few batteries and a flashlight! It's almost light out, and you've wasted our night!" he screams. "We could have been a part of the gas leak."

"Quiet." the leader tells them calmly. "Search him for anything he may have on him," he tells his men. They come closer and start patting my body down. They pull the ID tag out from under my shirt and rip it from my neck. The pain from the metal cutting my neck hurts, and I instinctively put my hand to my neck that's slightly bleeding. One of the men takes the tag over to their leader. He shines his light onto my tag and reads my information aloud.

"Jesse Foxworth. Dome citizen. 21 years old." His group of men laugh, and he asks, "You're a long way from the Dome kid. What are you doing out this way?"

I stare him straight in the eye and reply with a lie, "I haven't lived in the Dome since I turned 18. I was in Indiana when the disaster happened, and I'm working my way west to start a life in this new world."

He holds my gaze, and after a few seconds of silence his face tells me he's pleased with my answer. He shrugs and says, "I guess some people can start over now. Not in this town though. We're going to take your valuables, but we'll leave you the clothes and bag. Crawl up the canyon wall and keep going straight. Don't come back here. Ever! Or we will kill you." He never once loses my gaze.

The man searching my bag throws it to the ground. He stuffs the batteries and flashlight into his own bag. The black envelope falls out of my bag, spilling the photo of the mystery girl onto the dirt. He reaches down and pulls the photo off the ground. His smile is so disgusting and perverted that I have to hold in my urge to rip his throat open. He looks up at me and asks, "Who's this one, your girlfriend? I'd like a go at her. Where are you hiding her?" He holds up the photo for the others to see. They're all laughing and having a good time. I just stare at him and don't answer. Their leader quiets them down which is almost a punish-ment for them. The pervert throws the photo back to the ground like a playing card and starts to walk away. Their leader continues to eye me and point his gun at me as they retreat.

I hold my hands up in the air as the men walk away from me. I wait until I can't see them in the canyon anymore before I reach down and begin to pick up my things. I feel my backpack first, and the pills are still in the lining. These idiots think they stole everything valuable to me, but they have no idea. I am more than the average loner passing through their dirt town. I pick up my clothing and shove it back into the bag. I bend down and dust off the photo of the girl. The thought of someone hurting her enrages me. Maybe she's beginning to grow on me more than I realized. What did they mean about a gas leak? The only one in that group with any brains is their fat leader. Those idiots would probably accidently kill each other playing with gas. Nonetheless, now I'm curious. Is there a person out there letting off gas?

CHAPTER 8

Asmita

My mother once told me as a little girl that nothing ever turns out as you plan. Well she was right about that. I've been in Utah a few days now and it's nothing like what I thought it would be. When I crossed the border into Utah, I found water that I could use my pills on. That got my hopes up for getting into Salt Lake easily and then on to Antelope Island. The first night in Utah, I climbed over rocks and canyons to make it into a town. My legs got so scratched up, it looks like I've been in a cage fighting with animals. I had to barter in town for a new pair of pants to stop the people from staring at my scratched-up legs. Here, people are more civilized than what I've experienced these past few months. I was able to pay my passage with one of my diamonds on a wagon cart that brought me into Salt Lake City. The wagon travelled during daylight hours; thankfully it was covered. As it was, I probably lost three pounds in sweat alone.

Today is my first day in Salt Lake City; I arrived just as it was getting dark. This is the most put-back-together city that I've seen since the disaster happened. The wagon cart carries us straight into downtown. The streets are lined with signs and stores. They've got everything for a price. Hot meals, clean water, clothing, transportation, lodging... the list could go on and on. I think I can be safe here for a day or two to rest. I want a real shower and some real food. I saw a sign for a lodging house above a drink spot as we passed. I'll go there first to see about a roof over my head for when the next daylight comes. The cart finally stops, and the handful of people I've traveled with scatter off the cart. I pull my backpack onto my back and begin to walk the bustling streets that we've just passed.

I can't get over how organized this town is. It makes me really believe that something good awaits me at Antelope Island. I'm so close to where I need to be. I wonder what's waiting for me there. Before I can let my mind daydream too much about my destination, I snap back to reality and remember that I have to take it one day at a time. As I'm looking in one of the shop windows, I catch my reflection. My face is covered with specks of dirt from the ride into town. My hair has grown at least four inches and desperately needs a cut. My classic pony-tail grows heavier by the day. I've let all my cosmetic appearances go since the disaster, not that I was too into that sort of stuff anyways. Maybe I'll find someone to cut my hair while I'm here or at least a pair of scissors to do it myself.

My good mood is quickly soured when I catch a young man in the glass eyeing me on the other side of the street. I turn around to glare at him, but he's disappeared as fast as I can turn. It makes me think of the man in the woods. He's filled my dreams and turned them into nightmares. I leave the shopfront and continue my walk along the street. I glance at the faces of the men who pass by me. Will I see him again? I push the question out of my mind. I remind myself that I need to stop being so paranoid. I'm sure it was just a coincidence that our eyes met. He was probably waiting for someone and left. It's still dark outside, and there isn't much light spilling out onto the street so I can't be sure. I shrug my shoulders, trying to forget the moment. I tighten my grip on my back-pack straps and keep my head down as I walk the next few blocks.

I stop outside the drink spot and look inside the windows. They have thick, green curtains pushed to the sides allowing people to see inside during the night hours. The place is full of people laughing and having a good time. They all appear to have a drink in their hands. It looks like alcohol in some, but many are holding waters. They've got gas lamps going around the room to keep it bright enough. It looks like a safe place to go into. I start at the door and stop to read the sign hanging above the entrance.

NO FREE STAYS. EVERYONE PAYS. INQUIRE WITHIN

I open the door and walk through the entryway. The lighting is vastly improved from anything I've experienced since the disaster. It's been so long since I've been indoors at night that I didn't really know what to expect. The gas lamps are evenly spread throughout the long room to allow people to see where they are walking and who they are interacting with. I move my bag to one shoulder and put it in front of my body to maneuver through the crowd easily. I make my way to the bar and wait while the bartender pours drinks for some men on the other side. There is nowhere to sit in the entire place, and everyone is standing around with their drinks in hand. When he's finished with his customers, I try to get his attention, but the noise of everyone talking drowns out my voice. He starts serving another customer with his back still to me.

"It's a shame a lady can't get a drink around here," a man says as he walks up and stands beside me. He startles me as he appears so fast.

I try to be polite and just smile. I nod my head to acknowledge his comment. I keep my eyes on the bartender, and I can see out of the corner of my eye the man beside me is still looking at me. I turn my head and look directly at him. I don't recognize him so that gives me a wave of relief. I eye the door behind him, and my exit is still clear. The bartender has finished up and makes his way back to this side. Before I can get his attention, the man beside me yells over the crowd to him.

"I'd like a large glass of water, and get this lady anything she'd like," he says to the bartender as he motions to me.

"That won't be necessary," I say, trying to be polite to the man. I don't want the bartender to think that I'm with this stranger. I turn my attention back to the bartender and ask him for more information about the rooms mentioned on the sign outside. The bartender looks at me for a minute and makes the decision that I'm serious and I must have some way to pay him. He tells me that the rooms are located above the bar. It also includes a shower and my safety till the end of the next daylight. He also makes a point to say, "We don't want any trouble around here, and I try to keep it out of my rooms. If you've got yourself in a bind, keep moving."

I assure the bartender that I won't cause a problem and that I'm just here for a day or two until I pass through. He motions for me to come around to the end of the long bar, and I can see the man who was beside me trying to pay attention to our movements without being obvious. When I get to the end of the bar, he asks me how I'll be paying. I ask him what items he needs for payment. He mentions water pills, but I know those are too hard to come by so I tell him I have none. I ask him if he'll take a map, and I can tell by the look in his eyes that it will do. I don't need it being this close to Antelope Island.

"A map will buy you two nights upstairs and a cold glass of water," he tells me as he smiles. His smile reveals a gold tooth. "Let's not do the trade out in the open. Maps are hard to come by, and I don't want to start a trading war," he says.

"That's fine. Just get me to the room, and I'll give it to you," I tell him. I want out of the bar and into the shower. The bar is growing hotter by the minute with more people filing in and out its door. I've been up for almost 24 hours with my day travelling, and my eyes are growing heavier by the minute. I take one last look toward the man that was at the bar beside me, but he appears to have lost interest. Good, I don't need another person in my dreams tonight.

The bartender takes me through a door behind the bar, and it opens to a long wooden stairway lit by a gas lamp. The stairs are so narrow we go up single file. At the top of the stairs, it opens into a well-lit hallway. He guides me down it, and I count six doors which can mean only six rooms. We stop at the end of the hallway and outside the last door. He puts the key in the door and pushes it open to reveal the room. Before I can step inside he says, "The map."

I take the map out of the front pocket of my bag and give it to him. He looks it over and seems pleased. He motions that I can go into the room. He tells me that he'll bring up my water before the sun rises and something for me to eat. He tells me the shower is located down at the other end of the hall and that it's a shared shower with the other rooms. He also tells me that the building locks down at sunrise. If I'm not back inside before then, I'll be locked out for the day. He stresses payment or not, there are no exceptions to this rule. I thank him for his kindness and go into the room. I lock the door behind me and look through the peephole. I walk further into the room and sit my bag down.

The room is small and only holds the necessities. It has a gas lamp on the wall that is spreading light throughout the room. There is a bed with clean sheets, a mirror and a small table. The table holds one folded towel and a wash-cloth. My room has a window on the far side of the bed, and I move the curtains to look out. They match the dark green curtains downstairs in the bar. From this vantage point, I can see the main street that the cart drove down. The room isn't a lot, but it will get me through the next two days and nights. It's the nicest place I've been since the disaster. Here, I can rest and build my strength up before making the final day's journey to the island.

I feel safe here. I might actually sleep through the night. I'll take a shower when I wake up, and tomorrow night will bring a new dawn... or dusk. I'll need to get some directions to Antelope, but it shouldn't be too hard. I can also get some supplies I need here. I can feel it. Tomorrow is going to be a good day.

CHAPTER 9

Asmita

I WAKE up to the hot sun trying to penetrate through the heavy curtains of my room. I roll over in the bed and can see the sunlight flooding the floor at the bottom of the curtains. The carpet has clearly faded from the constant days of unforgiving sun. I sit up and try to orientate myself. I'm thankful for the fresh glass of water sitting on the table beside me. I drink it greedily until the glass is empty. I check my watch, and there are still a few hours left before nightfall.

I get out of bed and pick up my backpack. I unpack it, count my supplies and take stock of the items that I can still use for trade. I have a handful of diamonds but not as many as I'd like. My water pills are dwindling, but I can always trade some of the jewelry for those. When I'm done counting, I repack my bag leaving some clothes out to change into. I shove my backpack under the bed to hide it. I want to shower before nightfall comes so I grab the towel and washcloth that was left for me and look out the peephole of my door. From my limited view, the hallway looks clear. Since the bartender didn't leave me a key to the door, I have to leave the room unlocked to get back in. I quickly walk to the other end of the hall and open the bathroom door.

The bathroom has two shower stalls. They also have a stack of clean towels and wrapped bars of soap. I pick up the soap and read the label: *The Peach Tree Inn*. These have been brought in or traded to get here because I've seen no mention of a name on this place. I sit my clothes down on the sink, quickly undress and get in the shower. The showers have no curtains so I'm hoping no one will walk in on me naked. When the clean water caresses my skin, it hits me like a wave of relief. I haven't had a real shower since before the disaster. I can feel the dirt and grime coming off of me, and the water becomes darker as it pools around my feet. I take my time in the shower. This isn't my water, and the sensation of showering again feels amazing to me.

When my hands start to become shriveled, I get out of the shower and dry off. I put on my fresh clothes and throw the wet towel into their designated bin.

I don't know why, but I keep the soap label and take it with me. The sun has begun to set, and someone has dimly lit the hallway with the gas lamps. I make it back to my room and before I step inside, I notice the door is slightly cracked. I immediately panic about my bag. Before I can even think about someone being in my room, I push the door open and rush in. My room is empty. Someone has come in to light the gas lamp on the wall. I bend down and pull my bag out from under the bed. I open it and check its contents. Everything is exactly as I left it. I exhale a sigh of relief.

I realize I'm still holding the soap label, so I stick in my bag along with my dirty clothing and zip it up. I put my backpack on and leave the room, shutting the door behind me. I make my way down the narrow hallway that leads into the bar. As I come down, the bar is just opening its doors to the outside. It's not overly crowded with people looking for a clean drink, but I assume when I return it will be. I nod a hello to the bartender. He reciprocates and lets me know that I've got one more daytime stay. I assure him I'll be back before sunrise and request he reserves my room for me. Once I'm outside, I walk around aimlessly looking at the different storefronts, trying to figure out what I'll need to take with me. The first thing that I need to get is directions to the island, then I can figure out what I may need.

I walk into a store set up with various items of trade. I notice they have a large collection of maps, and I quickly spot the map that I traded for my stay above the bar. This is the tradesman who can give me directions at least to the island. I wait until the other people looking at his items leave to approach him. "Excuse me, sir. Do you know the way to Antelope Island?"

The tradesman looks at me like I've just spoken a foreign language he doesn't understand. I continue and say, "I'm willing to pay for the information. It's very important that I get there." Again, he doesn't give me a reply. He simply looks at me with this face of confusion. When I begin to think he isn't going to answer me, and I start to walk away, he responds, "Don't you know? The Island has been shut off from everyone since the disaster."

Now it's my turn to look at him like I don't understand. I'm trying not to get myself worked up. I don't want him asking me too many questions in return. "No. What do you mean shut off?" I ask.

"It's closed off. No one has been in or out of there since the disaster. Besides, no one lives there. It was mainly just animals that roamed the land. People would go there to camp, but no one stayed for more than a few nights," he tells me. He stands there looking me over. I'm sure the look on my face conveys exactly how I feel: confused, lost and a little hopeless. As I start to walk away from the man, he begins telling me more information. I stop and listen to him.

"Funny thing about it though. Right after the disaster, when people were trying to figure out what to do to get the town up and going again, a group of men got together and started to go out there. When they got out there, they couldn't even get in the entrance. It had large rocks and debris blocking the way in," he says.

"I don't get it. What's so funny about that?" I ask him while shrugging my shoulders.

"Well for one thing, there aren't any big rocks or boulders out there to fall that could cause the entrance to get blocked," he says. He motions for me to come closer and when I do, he drops his voice to a whisper. He gets right by my ear and says, "People say that something was going on out there before the disaster and that the road was blocked for a reason. I don't know if they're right, but it's really odd." He nods his head up and down to convey his belief of it to me. I can tell this is all the information he's willing to give me. I thank him for his help and walk away.

The man has given me a lot to think about. It could just be more idle gossip but I have a feeling deep down that he's right. This town is so much more restored than any I've seen. The idea that they don't know what's going on around them seems impossible. Maybe they've made up that story because they don't want anyone going there. People could be living the life out there, having a great time with amazing food, clean water and tons of other perks. There is only one way to find out though, and that's to go there myself. That's what I'll do; it's what my mom was trying to tell me.

It takes me the rest of the night to walk around to various trade stores to find all the supplies I'll need in my bag. One by one, I gather the essentials to make the walk to the island. I've learned from people along the night that the path to and from the island doesn't offer many spots to hide from the sunlight. I'll have to head to the island as the sun is setting and get there before it can rise again. I should have enough time to make it there. I have a feeling once I arrive, everything will be okay. The more I've thought about it tonight, the rocks blocking the path just sound like a way to keep people in the city. This night has passed by quickly.

I start making my way back to the bar. I want to make sure I'm inside before the sun comes up. I'm carrying several brown sacks and have to push my way inside the bar's front doors as the crowd is being told to vacate. When the barman sees me, he motions for me to go around to the back. I walk the half block around the building, and he's waiting to let me in.

"I had just about given up on you coming back," he says. He eyes the brown sacks I'm holding in my hands and inquires, "Have you been shopping? Looks like a lot for one person." He shuts and locks the door behind me once I'm safely inside.

It's none of his business, but since he's been so kind to me I respond, "It's just some necessities." He seems like a nice enough man, but I don't want to share too much. He walks back to the front of the bar, and I follow him through the hall. "Can I ask you a question?"

"Sure," he says as he goes about his business. He locks the front door and bolts it shut for the daylight hours. He closes the curtains on the windows and has his back to me. I ask him, "What do you know about Antelope Island?"

He stops what he's doing and turns to look at me. "I know a great deal about it. This is my hometown, and I've never left the state. What do you want to know about it?" he asks me.

I decided that if I'm going to learn anything new about the island, I'm going to have to give a little information out myself. "I'm trying to go there. I want to travel there and see what it's like." He doesn't need the whole story, but I need him to know that I want to go there. I tell him, "I'm hoping you can tell me some about it and what to expect."

He thinks about it for a second and sits down at one of the tables near the window. He motions for me to join him, and I slide onto the bench seat across from him. "Antelope Island was always a place to go and hang out for the day. My family would go there often year-round to camp, have some fun and see the wildlife. That's what lived there. People would come from all over to see it before the disaster. Now it's a wasteland or at least that's what I hear," he says to me. I nod my head listening to his story. I dare not interrupt him. I want all the information I can get.

"Ever since the disaster, no one has been seen going in or out of there. They say that when the disaster happened huge boulders came crashing down from the mountains and blocked the entrance into the island. The wildlife is trapped in and we are trapped out. If people were in there when it happened, they are probably long dead. There wouldn't be any way for them to get out for food or clean water." He sits there silently for a minute, looking down at the table between us.

"Has anyone been out there since the rumors started?" I ask him, hoping to hear a yes. When he tells me a simple no, I don't press him on it. "Thank you for taking the time to tell me about it. When sunlight comes up tomorrow and your doors open, I'll be out of your way".

He quickly asks me, "Where are you headed next?"

I decide he doesn't need to know the truth, so I lie. "I don't really know. I figure I'll move east. See what I can find." I try to keep my voice and attitude casual.

"Well, I've heard that the east isn't as advanced as we are here. If you change your mind and decide to stay in town, I could always use a hand around here," he says as he offers me a job.

I smile at him and genuinely feel grateful. No one has shown me this much kindness. "I'll keep that in mind. I really appreciate you being so nice to me." Now I feel a little guilty about lying to him. I get up from the table and start to head up the stairs to my room. I realize that I never asked his name. I turn around, and he's still sitting at the table. "Hey, one more question for you, one I should have asked yesterday. What's your name?"

"I'm George. George McLeanon," he tells me. "What's yours? He asks.

"I'm Asmita. Asmita Billick," I say in reply. I wave goodnight and head back up the narrow stairs to my room. I get inside my room and lock the door behind me. I feel lightheaded, and I don't know if it's from my busy night or something else. I sit on the floor and pack my new items into my backpack, but my head feels fuzzy. Once I'm done, I settle in my bed for the day's sleep. The sun is already up, and I need all the rest I can get. When I wake up at nightfall, I'm headed to the island.

CHAPTER 10

Jesse

I TAKE back my earlier idea of ever wanting to live in Utah. The orange clay dirt sticks to everything I own. The days are hot and dry, so dry that you don't even realize how hot it is until you're beyond hydrated and baked. I made that mistake the first day in Utah. The sun was blazing brightly, but I didn't feel overly hot, so I kept moving. I had little choice after those guys in the canyon jumped me. I needed to get distance from them and find a safe place to spend the day. I walked for half of the daytime, something I hadn't done since the disaster first happened when the sun was shrouded by ash.

I missed my one opportunity to catch a ride into Salt Lake. I stumbled into a small town with a man taking a group in on a covered wagon. I was so nervous about opening my bag in front of a group to trade that I missed out. I haven't seen any other modes of transportation besides my own two feet since then. I'd even trade some of my water pills at this point to give my feet a little rest, but I don't have the luxury of time to just sit around and waste it. I think about my mystery girl constantly. I wonder what and how she's doing. I wonder if she's in some ivory tower eating fat meals and drinking all the clean water.

The only thing that stands between me and the city is ten hours of walking. By sunrise I should be in Salt Lake, plotting my next move to Antelope Island. One good thing about being in Utah is the gossip in the small towns that I've passed through. I keep hearing increasing news about the city, and I've even heard some things about the island. I've heard they have fresh water which interests me most since I'm down to half my supply of pills.

I've also heard rumors that there is only one way in and one way out of the island. I figure that should make my walk there pretty simple. I've plotted out my walk as much as I can, but Antelope is only a tiny dot on the many different maps that I have. If the rumor of one way in is true, it should make it easier to find her if she's there. Of course, I haven't been able to confirm any of the rumors yet. I don't trust anyone enough that I meet to ask. I'm more suspicious of people than ever before.

I keep my mind on mystery girl as I walk. It seems to make my walking go by faster. I play out scenarios in my mind of how things will go when I finally meet her. I'll need to earn her trust. The way my parents' message reads, she doesn't know I'm looking for her, and I can't tell her. I wonder if we'll get along and if we'll have anything in common. We need to have something in common if I'm going to be able to stay around her continuously. In my imaginings, I can never decide if we hit it off or not. My dreams have even increasingly been filled with her.

I've walked for a few solid hours on a trail that is now used as the road to get into the city, when a noise finally startles me out of my daydreaming. It is coming from behind me and getting louder by the second. I get to the side of the trail, ready to run into the thick foliage if needed. It's a cloudy night with hardly any moonlight, and I have to squint to make out the dark shapes coming down the trail. As the shapes get closer, my eyes adjust and begin to make sense of it.

Thank the universe it's a pull cart! It's not covered, but I couldn't care less about that. It's nighttime, and at this point, I'd get on it no matter what! As the cart gets closer to me, I step out onto the trail and wave my arms like an idiot to get the driver's attention. The driver eyes me suspiciously but slows down to a crawl to speak to me. He's refusing to come to a complete stop, so he's smart enough not to put everyone on the cart in danger. I have to yell over the noise of his horses and the noise the metal pull cart is making for the driver to hear me.

"Do you have room for another person?" I yell up at the driver. "I can pay you in goods or trade for the space." I try to hide my desperation as I wait for him to reply.

The driver pulls the horses to a stop and asks me what I've got to trade for the ride. I want this ride into town more than I'm willing to admit, so I pull four water pills out of my bag and hold them in my hand where only he can see them. It should be more than enough, but in these parts I don't know. I want to be sure that he'll give me a spot, but I don't want to insult him. Luckily, the four pills do the trick. He takes them from me without a word and nods for me to get on. I quickly walk to the back of the cart and pull myself up into the back.

There are no benches in the cart, so I have to sit down on the floor. I put my bag on my legs and squeeze into the space. There are five other people sitting in the cart, three men and two women. The women are avoiding eye contact, but the men stare directly at me. They watch me until I'm situated and once I'm seated, the driver starts the cart moving again. I'm overjoyed that I'm not walking, but I hide my elation so the others don't stare at me any more than they already have.

The cart is moving faster than I could ever walk. At this rate, I'll be into the city well before sunrise. I lean my head back onto the metal siding of the cart and look up into the clouds. I'm so excited I can't sit still. I fidget in my seat and try to not bring myself any more unwanted attention. I stare at the sky for what feels like eternity. The slow bumps from the road beneath the cart and the silence calm my anxiety. I can feel my body finally falling into a rest. I hold my bag tightly to my legs.

Before I realize it, I'm fast asleep on the cart. There she is... mystery girl is sitting across from me on the cart. How could I not recognize her as soon as I got on? She's smiling at me and eying me. Is she looking for me too? Is that why she's smiling? My pulse quickens when I realize we are this close to each other. She sees that I'm awake and waves at me shyly, almost seemingly coy. I smile back at her, and she says hello. Her voice is soft and feminine with a Dome accent. It's exactly what I imagined it to be. I tell her hello and find myself feeling shy. We stare at each other, smiling, not knowing what to do next. I tell her my name and she opens her mouth to tell me hers. As she starts to speak to me... BAM!

I'm jolted awake on the cart. My heart is racing out of my chest. I rub my eyes and look around me. Everyone on the cart is looking at me. I look at the woman sitting across from me, and it's clear from her expression that she thinks I'm crazy. The woman beside her tells me, "We hit a bump in the road," trying to explain what woke me. I think she's trying to calm me down.

My shirt is soaked from sweat, and I realize that it was only a dream. I can feel my face flushing with embarrassment. I look up at the sky again to escape the looks of everyone on the cart. What is this mystery girl doing to me? She's turning me into a jumpy mess. I need to get a grip. I've never even met the girl. The dream makes me wonder though, what if she's looking for me too. I think about it for a few minutes, but there's no way. My parents explicitly told me in my letter that she mustn't know how I was sent to find her. What if though... what if she really was out there looking for me too? Maybe we were sent to find each other. I would need some real answers for that.

Once I find her, I resolve to get all my questions answered. My parents said she was the key to the future. She has to know something that can help us; surely they wouldn't pin all their hopes and dreams on a young adult who didn't have a clue. My parents are reasonable people... they wouldn't do that to me. I have to stop thinking about it. Time passes as I stare at the sky again. I'm pulled out of my own thoughts when the women start giggling and whispering with excitement. I look around to see what is causing their delight. Even the men are sitting up on their knees looking excitingly around.

A few feet ahead of the cart is a large wooden sign. Even in the dark it is clear to see, and it reads: Welcome to the New Salt Lake City. A part of me is overjoyed to finally reach the city. My parents would be so proud. I've followed their instructions, and I've gotten this far all on my own. The other part of me has some reservations. I'm excited to have made it to the city, but I'm scared. The lingering questions and unknowns crawl up into my throat and make me feel like I'm going to be sick from anxiety. I'm dying to see which rumors I've heard are true and which are false.

As the cart gets further into the city, the streets begin overflowing with people. For as far as the eye can see, people are spilling in and out of buildings. The cart moves slower now that people are walking all around it. I look around, trying to take it all in. I take notice that all of these people look well dressed, well fed and in good spirits. The buildings aren't run down either, and everyone seems to be behaving in an orderly fashion.

They have gas lamps along the street allowing people to see more clearly at night. They have shops and trading areas, places to get something hot to eat, and I even saw a sign for a place to spend your daylight hours. The city is more than I ever expected it to be. The rumors of the city are true; I for one am delighted. I can't wait to get off this cart and get something hot to eat. As much as I want to find my mystery girl, my stomach needs food more. I got a whiff of something as the cart passed a food place, and it was the best smell I've smelled since the disaster. I'll need to eat a real meal to keep my strength up.

I've got more traveling ahead of me and besides, it's not like I'm going to make it to Antelope Island tonight. The sky is becoming lighter nearing daylight. We drive through the city and to a stable when the cart finally stops to let us off. I'm the first one off the cart, and I thank the man for the ride. I've got a little bit of time before I'll need to find shelter from the sun. First on the list of things to do... eat a hot meal.

CHAPTER 11

Jesse

I WALK DOWN the streets bumping into people who say excuse me. They are all so pleasant and proper. It gives me a creepy feeling of the Dome which was very civilized and very controlled. Maybe it's because I've been on my own for so long, but their kindness makes me even wearier about trusting any of them. Granted, I didn't trust that many people before the disaster and now even fewer after. Smile to their face and cross them behind their back; that's one thing my social-climbing parents taught me early on in life.

As I make my way through the city, I try to take everything in. I walk into makeshift shops to see what goods I might be able to trade for and buy. I won't be buying anything tonight, but tomorrow I can get started. I'm running low on food supplies, and I'll need to stock up on those before I head out to Antelope. I walk a little bit further and find someone making hot food. I go inside and wait my turn. I have to trade for a bowl of hot soup mixed in with meat. I have no idea what the meat is, and I don't ask. It tastes delicious, and that's all I care about.

When I'm done eating, I feel like my energy is renewed. From the way the sky is beginning to lighten, I can tell that I'm under an hour away from sunlight. I need to find a place to rest and spend my sunlight hours. I ask the woman who served me my soup if there's anywhere to stay in town, and she informs me about a lodging house further down the street. I thank her for the information and praise her cooking skills. The woman could have asked me for something in return for the information, but she gave it freely. I leave her area and head back outside.

The thick crowds on the streets are thinning as daylight begins to creep up. I try to quickly walk the few blocks to where the woman instructed. As I walk, I notice that heavy muscle men holding guns begin standing in front of door fronts that will be shaded from the sun. I haven't seen this in other towns, but

I've heard about it. People who are well off or establishments hire them to stand guard all day in the sunlight.

The most crime happening after the disaster was during the daylight hours. People weren't used to the oppressive heat. They would go indoors to avoid it and stay shut up till nightfall. The looters started banging up doors, breaking in windows and terrorizing people who were seeking shelter from the sun. It still happens in some places, but not as often. I guess one way to guarantee it's not happening is to have security.

It makes sense, and in a town like this I should expect to finally see it in action. I make it to the outside of the boarding house, and the door is closed. I look into the windows and can see a man cleaning things up inside. I knock on the door and test out the knob. It's unlocked, so I turn the knob and let myself inside. The bar man is standing a few feet out from the bar and walks toward me as I enter.

"You'll need to turn around and go right back out the door. We're closed up for daylight. Come back when it's nightfall," he harshly informs me.

I hold up my hands to show that they're empty. I don't want to scare him since I did just let myself into his place. He seems startled, so I nod my head, acknowledging what he's just told me. "I was hoping to acquire a room for the daylight. A nice lady serving soup down the street told me this was the place to come." I pause because I can see he's ready to cut me off. He's a no-nonsense kind of man. I change my tactics and just come right out with, "I need a room, and I can pay you in trade. I have maps and water pills."

That information perks the bartender right up. He smiles at me, and the beginning sunlight hits a gold tooth he's sporting in the front of his mouth. "Deal! We'll figure out the trade in a minute, Right now, I'm running behind in my schedule. Help me get these windows covered with the curtains and the door bolted," he says as he rushes around the room. We spend the next few minutes closing off the place from the sun and securing the windows and door. When we've finished, he goes behind the bar and pours two glasses of water. He sits one glass in front of me on the bar and takes the other one for himself. "You said you've got some maps and water pills?"

"Yes, let me get them for you," I say. I take my backpack off and sit it on top of the bar. I open it up and pull out several water pills and a few east coast maps that I'm willing to trade. He picks up the maps and begins inspecting them.

"You can put the water pills away. I'm in no short supply of them. These maps however, they will do. How many day stays are you looking to get out of them?" he asks.

"I just need one day, maybe two at the most. I'm not looking to stay around here. I'm just passing through," I tell him.

"Ah, like so many others. Eager to leave our fair city. This town is one of the best ones in the country. We've got clean water, places to stay, food, and most importantly, security," he proudly tells me as he stands there and sips his water. He turns around and points to a door on the other side of the bar. "Through that door is a stairwell, and it leads to the bedrooms. You'll have to share a bathroom with other guests but during the daylight hours, I guarantee your safety. I'll take all four maps for two nights. If you don't stay the second night, I still keep the maps," he says.

"Sounds fair enough," I say in agreement. "I'm pretty tired so if it's okay, I'd like to be shown to my room." Suddenly, I'm so tired I can barely hold my eyes open. Maybe it's the fact that my stomach is full of food, and I've travelled for so long. Days spent away from the sun are a luxury, and they've been few and far between for me since the disaster took place.

The bartender comes out from behind the bar and begins to lead me to the door. "I'm George. I own the place. If you need anything, just look for me," he informs me.

"I'm Jesse," I say. George holds out his hand and we shake.

We start toward the door, and he asks, "Where are you headed to next, young man? You know, a person used to be eager to leave here but once the city started getting rebuilt, everyone wanted to stay."

I don't see any harm in telling him where I'm going next. He's been kind to me so far, and this might be an easy way to get some tips out of him on how to get there quickly. I did overpay for my stay, so it's worth the risk. "I'm headed to Antelope Island. I've heard great things about the land, so I wanted to see it for myself."

The bartender stops climbing the stairs and turns to look at me. I can't place his expression, but he seems to be thinking. I don't press him and for a moment, we are standing on the steps just staring at each other. His expression turns odd and he shrugs his shoulder. Finally, he starts climbing the stairs again without a word. I can tell he wants to say something but he's holding his tongue.

"Did I say something to upset you?" I ask him. The last thing I need is to get kicked out of this place during the daylight.

"No, it's just we don't get a lot of people going to the island or asking about it, and you're the second person I've had in a week," he says.

We come to the top of the stairs, and he leads me down the hall to the right. George stops at the door across from the bathroom, takes out a key and unlocks it. He takes the key out of the lock and hands it to me. "You got a lucky room. This one has a working lock. Some of these rooms will only lock from the inside, but you'll be able to lock up while you're gone," he tells me.

I get a strange feeling from what he's told me about the island, so I decide to just ask him. "George, what do you mean someone was asking about the island recently? Is it not common for people coming through this area to go there?"

George leans against the wall beside my door in the hallway and folds his arms. He studies me for a few seconds before answering, "Not really, mate. I hate to break it to you if you don't already know, but it's been closed off since the disaster. I had to tell a young girl the same thing just a week ago. If you could have seen the look on her face, I think it about broke her heart," he says.

My pulse quickens, and I can't get the words out of my mouth fast enough, "A young girl was asking about Antelope Island?" I ask him.

He nods and looks at me like I'm an idiot. "Yeah, that's what I just said. She showed up about a week ago. Told me she was passing through town and had a whole bunch of questions about the island. Wouldn't stop until she got as many answers as she could."

My curiosity is more than peaked right now, but I try to keep my voice even and calm. I don't want to give off any indication that I'm seriously interested in this girl and who she could really be, but I have to know. "I'm curious. What did this girl look like?" I ask him.

Furrowing his brow, he unfolds his arms and points his finger at my chest while he talks, "Listen, this girl is a nice girl. I don't want to cause any trouble for her. Why are you so curious about her?"

"I swear she's not in any trouble. I just want to know what she looks like. She might be someone I know," I lie. I can't tell him the truth. I can't let him know my real reasons for wanting to find her. Each second that I stand there waiting for him to respond makes me feel like I'm bursting out of my skin. Could this be her? Could she have been here only a week ago? If the Island is closed off, I'll have to find out where she's gone. This could be even harder than I imagined, finding her.

"Alright... but you swear you won't be making any trouble for her?" he asks me.

"I swear, George. I'm just hoping she's a friend of mine." I try to convincingly tell him.

"Well, she has dark hair, and wore it up on her head the whole time. Dome accent, but I never asked her about it. Short. Looks about 18 or 19 years old. That's all I can really think of," he says, trying to remember.

I don't believe my ears. My luck might actually be changing. I can't let myself get too excited. It could be someone else... but it could be her. I know she's from the Dome originally, so that would explain the accent. I know she has dark hair, and I know her age is around what George has said from staring at her photo for months. I try to hide the excitement on my face. If he was the last person to see her before she left town then I'll need to find out everything I can from him. He's been nice so far, but something about him gives me a bad vibe.

"Too bad you don't know where she is now. It sounds like it's my friend," I try to say casually and work it from that angle.

"I know exactly where she is." George smiles with pride.

My heart beats so hard I can hear it in my ears. I'm losing my attempt to contain my excitement "Where is she George?"

"She got sick with the flu, at least that's what we think it was. It was the night she was heading out to leave. She's been in bed for a week. Been bringing up food and water myself. She's only four doors down from you."

All I can think is that he's kidding me! This must be some kind of a joke. We are in the same building. My stomach instantly goes into knots. I'm scared and excited all rolled into one. I can't believe it. I've finally found her.

CHAPTER 12

Asmita

It's taken me six days to finally start feeling normal again. I have found the strength to get out of bed. Now, I just have to wait for the sun to go down. My sleeping has been thrown off from laying down so much. I get up and walk to the curtain to peek outside. The sun is shining brightly, and it'll be a few hours before it's completely dark out. George has been so kind to me. I don't know how to repay him. I paid for the extra days for my room and food, but without him, I wouldn't have made it. I think I'll offer to help him with his business tonight. It will give me a chance to test out my strength level.

Once I'm fully healthy, which I'm hoping will only be another day or two, I'll continue my trip to the island. The setback in time has dampened my spirits, but I'm trying not to let it get me down. The time in bed has also given me time to think about all that I've learned about the island. George gave me a ton of information the night before I was going to leave, and so did the tradesman. I'm going with my gut, and I feel like I'll find something out there. I just know there has to be something there that my mother wanted me to see.

I lie back down on my bed and rest for a little while longer. Before the sun begins to set, I get my items for the bathroom and make my way down the hall. I'm going to take a shower tonight since I haven't for the last few days. This could be the last real shower I have for a while if I head out to the island tomorrow night. I make my way down the hall and get to the bathroom door. As always, I knock and wait to see if anyone comes out. I get this weird feeling someone is watching me.

I turn around and look up and down the hall. No one is there, but I can't shake the feeling I'm being watched. I turn the knob and go inside the bathroom. I quickly get undressed and shower. I take note of the soap again and see it's from the same hotel as before, *The Peach Tree Inn.* This time, I throw the label in the trash but make a mental note to ask George if he traded for the soap.

Maybe this place used to be known as that. Once I'm dressed, I slip down the hall and get back into my room.

The sun is finally beginning to set outside. I move my curtains open and look at the street below. People are starting to slowly go outside and are coming out from the canvas that provided them shade. I keep the curtains open and tidy up my bed. I take my backpack out from under the bed and throw it on my shoulder. I'm going to see if George needs any help tonight and thank him again for everything that he's done.

I walk down the hallway and head down the stairs. I don't know if it's because I've been sick, but my backpack feels so much heavier than before. That's when I remember, duh! It's got all of my supplies inside it ready for the island. When I get into the tavern, George is already behind the bar smiling, and the door is open with people already drifting inside. I smile back at him and slide my backpack off my shoulder.

"George, can I sit this behind the bar? I didn't want to leave it in my room because the door won't lock properly," I tell him.

"Course you can! If you want, you can take the key and lock your door from the outside. You'll just need to come get the key again to get back in," he tells me. He reaches up under the bar and extends the key to me.

I thank him and take the key from him. I pick my heavy backpack up off the floor and head towards the stairs. As I go up the stairs and turn to the left of the staircase, a man comes out of a room on the right. In this narrow hallway almost all of the doors are visible from the top of the stairs. I can see him stop outside of his door, and he just stands there staring at me. When our eyes meet, I put my head down and quickly walk straight to my room. I open up my door,

and I can see out of the corner of my eye he's still standing in front of his. In the week that I've been here, I haven't seen any of George's other guests. He's the first one and rather handsome, but he seems like an odd one with all the gawking.

I wait a few minutes in my room before I go back downstairs. I don't want to take a chance on running into anyone in the hall. I lock my room and leave my bag safely inside. I get downstairs and the tavern is now packed with people. I have to wedge my way across the room to get to the bar. George is so busy that he doesn't even notice when I put the key back under the bar. I stand behind the bar not knowing what to do. People are shouting orders over one another, holding items for trade in their hands, waving them in the air for attention.

When George realizes I'm behind the bar, he stops serving and comes over to me. He's out of breath from working so hard. "What are you doing? You should still be lying down," he stresses to me.

"George, I'm fine. I want to help you. Please let me repay you in some way. I know you need help. Look at this place," I tell him as I look at the people getting more frantic by the minute.

George looks around the room and knows I'm right. This is too much for one person to handle day in and day out. Besides, before I got sick he was even offering me a job. "Okay, fine. You can help, but just for tonight. I know you have other plans." He looks me in the eye. "Don't take anything you can't tell is real for trade. Don't take food or water pills, only stuff you know will trade on the streets for other items. Got it?" he asks me.

"Got it! I'm good at trading," I assure him. I don't tell him that the majority of my items I've traded have only been water pills, maps and, more importantly, diamonds. He has no idea what's in my bag, and that's a good thing. But I dive right in and start taking items for beverages. The majority of the crowd wants water, and a few people here and there want hard liquor. I spend the next few hours serving. It takes half the night before the crowd starts to die down.

Now that it's calmed down, I start to pick up items that fell on the floor during the rush. That's when I notice a man sitting at the other end of the bar. I can see him in my peripheral vision. He's looking at me, watching me closely. I look over at him, and our eyes meet. It's the same man I saw earlier upstairs. When he sees me look his way, he drops his eyes back down to the bar top. His cheeks flush with embarrassment. He busies himself with the drink he's holding. I go to walk over to him, but George crosses my path, stopping me in my tracks.

"You were great Asmita! Thank you so much. I forgot what it's like to have help around here," he tells me. He reaches out and gives me a giant hug. It's unexpected and honestly, makes me feel a little uncomfortable. I haven't had another person hug me since I said goodbye to my parents when I left for California. When he can see my face, he realizes my discomfort and releases me immediately. "Sorry... got carried away," he says apologetically. "Remember, my offer still stands on the job. Just say the word. You can have your room for free," he offers.

"No, I can't stay," I tell him. I try to stress this fact to him. "I really have to make it to the island. I'm planning on leaving after tomorrow's sunlight." I sneak a look at the man from upstairs. George is blocking his view of me, but I can slightly see him. He's leaning toward us, trying to hear our conversation.

"I understand." He nods sadly. "Besides, you've got a friend waiting to see you."

"A friend? Who are you talking about?" I ask him, feeling left out of the loop.

"He came in late this morning just as the sun was coming up. Asked to rent out a room. We got to talking about how he was also trying to go to the island and then you came up. He said you sound like a friend he knows," he tells me. He throws his head in the direction of the guy sitting at the end of the bar. It's the same guy I saw upstairs earlier.

"Did he mention me by name?" I ask him.

"Nope, just said you sounded like a friend of his."

I don't know this guy, and we are definitely not friends. It could just be a coincidence that he's passing through to the island, but I'm not sold. The fact that I got brought into his conversation makes me even more suspicious. My mother's words ring into my ears, *Don't trust anyone*. My mother's advice has kept me safe, and I don't see any reason not to follow it now. I need to find out if it's me he's interested in or if it was just a fluke him saying I could be his friend. There's only one way to find out, and that's to talk to him.

I walk over to the end of the bar and stand in front of this stranger. He looks up from his drink, and his dark brown eyes look directly into mine. I feel like we are suspended in time. The way he looks at me is like he knows me, but this is impossible. We are complete strangers. I look at his features, and he is handsome. He's not as old as I first assumed, younger, around my age. His dark hair falls onto his forehead, and he brushes it back with hand. I think he's going to speak to me, but he just continues to hold my gaze.

I break the gaze between us and speak first. "George told me you thought we might be friends."

"Ah, you're the girl he told me about this morning," he says. His voice is calm, but it's all Dome accent. He sounds exactly like me, and he can't hide that any better than I can. I can't quite put my finger on it, but something about him bothers me. I find myself getting annoyed.

I give him a reply. "That would be me. Sorry to disappoint you that I didn't turn out to be your friend." I need to keep him talking to see if this was just a coincidence. I can't take any chances with my safety.

"I'm not sorry at all. From what George told me, you seem like a nice girl. Besides, I haven't seen that friend since before the disaster. So, what's taking you to Antelope Island? I heard that's where you were headed before you became ill. That's where I'm headed too," he says.

He dives right in with a question. Hmm... I don't know what to make of him. I can't tell him the truth and frankly, it's none of his business. "I was heading there before George told me the news about it. Did he tell you? It's closed off. Now I don't know if I'll go. I'd like to though, just to see it. That was my original reason for going anyway. I had heard how nice it was; or used to be that is."

"Yes, me too. I had been travelling for a while to get out here. I came all the way from Indiana"

I decided to call his bluff. "Really? Your accent sounds like you're from the Dome. The only other person I've met from the Dome since the disaster wasn't very friendly toward me."

He smirks at me and takes a drink of his water. He knows that I'm upset. He sits his glass down on the bar and stands up. He takes his large backpack off the floor and puts it on his back. He goes to leave but turns around and says to me, "I'm from there but from the sound of *your* accent, it sounds like you are too." He walks out the door of the bar with me standing there looking at him like an idiot.

CHAPTER 13

Jesse

Dammit! I'm so mad at myself. I've overplayed my hand. I wasn't sure if George would tell her about our conversation, but he did. Now I'm walking out of the bar with my mystery girl behind me. I still don't even know her name. What an idiot I am! I had the perfect opportunity to ask her and make conversation, and all I could do was sit there and gawk at her. She clearly has her guard up and doesn't take kindly to people from the Dome.

I've got to figure out a way to go back in there and talk to her. I can't scare her off, and the vibe she was giving me tells me she's very scared and untrusting. I just don't know what to say. Maybe I should apologize. I don't even know what for. She was rude to me! You don't call out a stranger on where they are from and definitely not when you're from the Dome yourself. I keep walking while I think. I can't go back in there until I know what to say.

I keep trying to focus on what she said to me, but all I can think about is her appearance. She's far prettier than her photograph. Her lips were so plump, I had to resist the urge to reach out and touch them. She opened her mouth and that Dome accent rang out with its venom and slapped me back into reality. She's young, but not as young as I thought. I'm guessing she's 18 or 19 max. I need to relate to her. I need to figure out how to walk back into that bar.

I keep walking further away from the bar, my head filled with its own thoughts. When someone puts their hand on my shoulder, I'm startled and spin around to face them. I'm even more surprised that it's her who's startled me. She came outside and found me walking. The look on her face tells me that she's embarrassed, either from startling me or from her attitude in the bar. I soften my approach with her.

"I'm sorry if I said something that upset you back there. It wasn't my intention. I just thought we might have something in common with going to the island," I try to explain to her.

She looks down at her feet and fidgets with both of her hands. She doesn't look up at me as she responds, "No, I'm the one who's sorry. I was rude to you earlier."

I wait a second to see if she's going to look up from the ground and when she doesn't, I let her know it's okay. "Hey! How about we start over? I'm Jesse and, yes, I'm originally from the Dome, but I haven't lived there since months before the disaster." I stick my hand out to shake her hand.

She looks up from the ground and shakes my hand. "I'm Asmita." She looks around us and waits till no one is within earshot before continuing. "I was living in San Francisco when the disaster happened, but I'm also from the Dome"

Finally, I know my mystery girl's name... it's Asmita. I smile back at her, and the innocent look on her face makes me want to tell her everything I know; It feels as if I have to internally hold the information in my body. I have to start slowly with her. She isn't ready for my truth, but I do need to get close to her. I need to find out why she's so valuable and that could cause my parents to place all their faith, and their only son, on the line. "So, Asmita, how long do you plan on staying in town for? I only plan on stopping through."

I can't just start asking her questions without giving her some information. I can't keep her suspicious of me. If I tell her my plans, then maybe she'll realize I'm not someone she needs to fear. I can see on her face that she seems less suspicious of my intentions now.

"Well... I was just passing through town when I originally got here. I was preparing to leave town, and the next day when I woke up after sunlight, I was sick as can be. I couldn't even get out of bed. George, he came up and took one look at me and told me I had the flu. I was in bed every day for a week and tonight was the first night I felt almost back to normal," she tells me.

Wow! It sounds like she's lucky to make it through it. "Modern medicine isn't readily available out here, so I'm glad you're feeling better. You look good," I say and realize that it came out wrong. Her cheeks are flushed, and her eyes are cast on the ground again. I can feel my own cheeks heating up. I try to backtrack. "That didn't come out right. I'm sorry! You don't look nice. Shit! I mean you don't look sick. You look healthy."

Now the look on her face is hurt. I'm so confused. Maybe she wants me to think she looks good? I don't know. I give up. The only woman I've ever really socialized with is my mother, and she's nothing like Asmita, so I have no idea what to say to her. My parents should have given me lessons on this if they wanted me to get close to her. I give up and try to change the subject. "So, George seems like a decent guy."

"Yes, he's been very kind to me," she gives a little laugh and raises her eyes to look at me.

"He told me about the island being closed off. I'm still going to go there and see it for myself. I plan on leaving after tomorrow's daylight ends." This catches her off guard.

"I hadn't planned on leaving till the day after tomorrow. I told George that I would stay to help him out one more night. It's the least I can do. He'd like me to stay longer," she informs me.

I'm sure he would. I can see the way he looks at her. Something isn't right. He seems overprotective, and not in a good way. I can't tell her though because she clearly trusts and knows him better than I do. That would only push her further away from me. I've only got one more day to figure out how to keep us together. So far I'm not doing too well, but at least we've got a dialogue going between us now. We start to walk down the street together and before I realize it, we are in easy conversation. We haven't talked about anything that would lead to me finding out why she's so important, but it's a start.

"We're getting pretty far away from the bar. We should turn back before it starts getting daylight," she says. I look up at the sky and realize it's becoming lighter, so we turn around and start walking back. She's opening up more and asking me personal questions . I slow our walking pace down to prolong our conversation. It's her way of trying to figure out if I can be trusted. I can tell. I would do the exact same thing to her if she wasn't already doing it to me.

"How old are you? You seem around my age," she asks me.

"I'm twenty-one. How old are you?" I ask her in return.

"I just turned nineteen. I was halfway through my year of self-reflection when the disaster happened. Were you away at school when it happened?"

"No." My answer comes out harder than I mean it to. "I chose work. I didn't continue into school after my year was over." I can see the information sinking in. I try to gauge her reaction to this, and I instantly feel like she thinks less of me now. My anger gets the best of me. "Typical Dome brat!" I mumble the words before I even think about it. She hears me and gives me a sharp look. She folds her arms and continues to walk forward in silence. We continue to walk in silence, once again getting closer to the bar.

The bar is in sight when she finally speaks up. "You know, I don't think there's anything wrong with choosing the work program. That just wasn't going to be an option for me. I commend you for the choice, but now it's a moot point, right?"

In spite of myself I laugh, because she's right. The disaster changed everything, and it doesn't matter what we did before. Now it only matters what we do from here on out. I smile at her, and she knows that I'm not mad. We are within a block of the bar when I notice a group of men going into George's bar. We stop in our tracks and hide behind the end of a building on the end of the block. We peek around the edge to see them. The men are wearing all black, holding large guns, and they have more muscles than they know what to do with. A flash of an orange emblem on their sleeve catches my eye. These aren't your typical day guards. These guys are from the Dome. I look to Asmita, and she's seen the same thing.

"Have you ever seen them before?"

"No, never, not while I've been here. George doesn't have any guards of his own. The guy across the street keeps an eye on the place in the day, but he's not George's man."

I don't like the look of this, and I have a bad feeling about going back into the bar. I've got my bag on my back and can cut all ties with this place, but Asmita is another story. If she's like me then her entire life is in her backpack. I don't know where it's at, but it's not on her back.

"Where's your bag?" I quickly asked her.

"It's inside, up in my room. Why?" She gives me a quizzical look.

"You can't go back inside the bar," I tell her. This is alarming. These men aren't here by accident. I haven't seen a Dome guard since leaving there. If they're out here, it's for one reason and one reason alone... Asmita. My parents told me she was important, and they warned me not to take her to the Dome.

"I have to go back in there. I have to get my bag!" she screams at me.

"You don't get it do you? Those men are from the Dome. They aren't here to just say hi and chat about your day. They want something, and they're looking for it in that bar. Have you forgotten what the Dome is like? Whatever it is they want, they won't stop until they get it." I have to stop and take a deep breath before I can continue. "You do not cross these people!" I stress the words to her. We stand there in silence, watching the front of the bar together.

I take my eyes off the bar and look at her face. She has tears in her eyes, but she's fighting to hold them in. The tears start to fall, and she tells me about a man who had chased her. At first, I think the man was probably out to rob her, but when she tells me that he was holding a photo of her, I feel chills spread across my body. I ask her to describe the photo that she found on the man, and it matches the one I carry. It doesn't make sense that he was trying to harm her when I was given the same one to protect her. Then it hits me. Could it be George?

CHAPTER 14

Asmita

I TRY TO STOP CRYING, but the tears keep coming. I wipe them from my cheeks as quickly as I can. They make me feel weak in front of him and since we've just met, it's also embarrassing. I pull myself together and tell him again.

"I have to get my bag. It has all of my things inside it. I don't think George would let them hurt me," I tell him.

He spins around and looks at me. He's looking at me like I've grown a second head. He tries to keep his voice low, but he's seething, "Are you crazy?" he asks me. "You can't go in there! I think George is probably the one who told them you were here! He's the one who sent for them! Wake up and realize that, and you actually might survive through the next day."

I feel his words hit me like a ton of bricks to my chest. It makes perfect sense. I trusted George from that first night he took me in. I even trusted him enough to consume the food and water he was giving me without question. The more I look back at the past week, the more I realize Jesse's words are right. I never even questioned George or his motives for being so nice to me. I bet he poisoned me to keep me there. He knew I was planning on leaving town, and that's how he got me to stay. He had to do something drastic to keep me under his watch.

"We have to find a way to get my bag. It has everything I own in it, and I need those items to make it to the island," I tell him as I erase the tears from my face using my shirt.

"You really are crazy, aren't you? George knows we both want to get to the island. If we don't show up at the bar, he's going to know that's where we both went. And if he knows anything about that bag of yours then it's probably already gone or will be soon with those Dome goons showing up."

He turns his back on me, and I rest my head against his backpack. I was so stupid to leave my bag behind. I always have it with me. I can't leave it behind. I just can't. I must have those items. The diamonds can buy my way into places I need to survive, and I'm so close to the island that it'll take everything I've got to make it inside and survive there even if it's blocked off. Wait... I bet George was lying about that too. Then I remember the conversation I had with the tradesman; he wouldn't have any reason to lie, and he didn't know that I was staying in George's inn when I met him.

"Hey, do you think George was lying about the island being closed off. trying to keep me here and just telling me that?" I ask Jesse.

"Maybe, I don't know. I've never been there, but I'm willing to take the chance and find out for myself. Let's blow off your bag and just get out of here. We can go to the island together and see for ourselves. If it's closed off, I'll help you get back out of the woods and into safety," he tells me more calmly. He puts his hand on my arm, and I feel a shiver inside me.

How many times do I have to stress this to him? "I'm not leaving here without my backpack."

"Tell me something inside it that would make it okay to risk going in there and being caught just to get a backpack," he says as he stares at me.

I'm just going to have to tell him. "A bag of diamonds!" The look on his face instantly tells me what I need to know. He's going to help me get my bag. He understands now that it can't be left behind. I'm going to have to trust someone, and I'm placing it in him. I hope I'm not wrong this time. I can't afford to be. I trust him with my entire life. That bag holds everything for me to get to the island and survive. If he's serious about going to the island, then I'll go with him. There is safety in numbers but first, we must get my bag.

Jesse stands beside me and takes off his backpack. He tells me to hold out my arms to the side, and I do. He puts my arms into the straps and gently lays the bag on to my back. It's much heavier than mine, but I pull the straps tight and adjust it on my back. The straps are worn and frayed from overuse. He sees me struggling with the weight of the bag and smiles. He smiles as he tells me, "Don't worry you won't have to carry it for long. Now I'm the one trusting you with my entire life. That bag has everything I own in it. If something happens, and you have to get out of here quickly, and you can't make it with the bag then hide it. I'll come back for it."

"Where's your bag inside?" he asks me.

I knew I shouldn't have left it, but I got comfortable. It's going to be hard to get. "It's inside my room upstairs. I'm the last room to the left of the stairs, but there's one more problem."

He rolls his eyes at me. "What would that be?" he sarcastically asks.

"My door is locked, and I don't have the key. George does. It's hanging on a hook under the bar. He offered to let me leave it behind and lock it up for the night."

"Geez! I can't get a break here. Okay...let me think. That was probably another way to keep you tethered to the place, a guarantee for him to know you wouldn't leave it behind. You're sure he doesn't know anything else about you or what's inside your bag?"

"I'm sure. Only what you already know. He knows that I was passing through town and that I was going to the island. He's never seen inside my bag. When I paid for the room, I did it in trade and got the items out of a pocket. I never opened it up in front of him."

"Okay, here's what is going to happen. I want you to stay here. Stay out of sight. If I'm not out in five minutes, I want you to start making your way north toward the island. I'll catch up with you, and we'll trade backpacks. Stay off the main path and stay out of the sunlight as much as you can. I'm going to go in there and get that bag. If something goes south and I don't show up, don't come back for me."

"How do I know you aren't just taking my bag and ditching me?"

He looks me straight in the eye and with a serious face says, "I wouldn't do that to you. If I don't show up then I'm dead."

This is such a selfless act, and I've never had someone behave like this for me besides my parents. I have to ask him, "Why are you doing this for me? We barely know each other."

"Trust me on this one. I feel like I've known you a lot longer." With that, he leaves the safety of our hiding spot and starts making his way toward the bar. I look at my watch. He's got five minutes and then I'm following his instructions. I'm nervous and sweating. The sun is almost completely up, and I don't have any cover where I'm standing. I'm hidden out of view from others, but the sun finds me. If I have to spend the day outside, I don't want to do it alone. It's going to be hot, and it's been a long time since I've been without cover.

I peek around the corner, and I can see Jesse approaching the door of the bar. The Dome guard standing at the door looks him over. They talk for a few seconds, and he lets him past and into the bar. Time starts ticking now. The fear I feel for him surprises me. I care for this complete stranger, not only because I know what the Dome guards are capable of but because I actually like him.

CHAPTER 15

Jesse

IT KILLS me to have to walk away from her. I travelled for so long to get to her and now, here I am walking away from her and into a situation that I don't know how it will end. George completely set her up. He either knows who she really is, or he's got some other reason for calling the Dome into town. I didn't even know any of the Dome guards were alive and still out there, but it doesn't surprise me. My parents warned me to never trust anyone, and I don't. I trust Asmita now, and that's it. I don't even fully trust my parents.

I make the short walk from the alley to the front door of the bar. I need to be quick but not noticeably quick. I have no doubt that Asmita will leave me if I'm not back to her in the five minutes. At the front door of the bar, one of the large Dome guards stands at attention holding his weapon. He sees me and turns toward me. He points his gun at me and if I hadn't grown up as a Dome kid, I would have pissed my pants. I hold up my hands to show him I mean him no harm. I tell him my name and that I'm staying upstairs in one of the rooms. He relays the message to someone on the inside of the door. Once he gets a response, he steps aside to let me through the front door.

George is calmly standing behind the bar cleaning a glass. The curtains have been drawn, and everything has been put away. The door is quickly shut behind me and bolted by the guard. He looks up at me and smiles. "You almost missed your opportunity to get back in during sunlight."

"I guess so. What's with the guards? Do you have those during all the daylight hours?" I don't know what he's up to, but I have to get upstairs. I can't waste time standing here talking. He finishes polishing the glass and sets it under the bar top. "No, they're in town looking for a special someone. They'll protect us during the day. That's another thing you get when you pay to stay here… safety."

I'm not buying his story one bit. I need to find the key under the bar. I walk to the edge and fake a yawn. "George, would you mind pouring me a glass of water before I get upstairs?" I need to get his attention away from this side for a minute to look for the key.

"Sure. No problem at all," he says as he turns around to fill the empty glass he just put away.

I lean over the edge of the bar and look for the key. I see the hook where the key should be hanging, and it's empty. George has the key. I'll have to figure out another way into her room. George turns back around and walks down to the edge of the bar. He hands me the glass of water, and I take it from his hand. He stands there for a second just looking at me. I feel awkward and compelled to say something to him. I want to punch him in the face, but I resist. My calm face masks the hate I have for him.

He breaks the silence first. "I'm headed to bed. It's been a long night. The bar was hopping with thirsty people. Now that everyone is in, I'll see you at dusk."

I nod my head to him and stand there as he walks through a door beside the one leading upstairs. As soon as he's out of my sight, I head for the steps. I take the steps two at a time being as quiet as I can. When I get to the top of the steps, I look down both sides of the dimly lit hallway. I stand still and close my eyes, listening for any little noise. I can't hear a peep. I move as quietly as I can toward Asmita's room. I reach the door of the room and bend down to get eye level with the lock.

I put my eye up to the lock and try to look into the room. The room is either too dark or something is blocking the opening causing zero visibility. I stand back up and put my hand on the knob of the door. I figure I might as well try the door before I make the noise of breaking it down. I turn the knob slowly, and the door opens. I know for a fact this door was locked. Asmita was adamant about the fact that she locked it. George or one of the Dome guards must have come into the room.

I open the door slowly and take a few steps into the room. I leave the door open to shed some light from the hall lamps into the room. I can see a backpack lying on top of the comforter of the bed. It's open with some of the contents spread out on the bed. I need to be quick about grabbing it because someone may come back for it at any minute. I dash all of the way into the room and scoop all of the items back into the bag. I've got the bag zipped up and on my back and ready to leave when I hear the noise of the door close behind me.

I whirl around in the darkness of the room. Thankfully, I'm closer to the curtains, and the sunlight is coming in strong from underneath them. This light provides me with an advantage over the massive Dome guard that is now advancing toward me from the darker part of the room. The light catches the blade of a knife in his hand, and I lunge to miss it. His long swing manages to catch my t-shirt and tears open a small piece.

The guard's lunge was too far out for him to keep his balance, and I used his momentary stumble to aid my efforts. I ball my fists and punch him in the face. He may be stronger than me, but he wasn't ready for a fight. He thought I would go easily but now realizes how wrong he was to think that. I hit him a second time as he tries to get up from falling on to the bed. His heavy gear keeps him down as he loses the fight. I don't know what comes over me, but I'm so enraged that I hit him again. It's people like him who have caused nothing but pain and suffering to good, hard working people. I stop hitting him when I've realized I've knocked him out. He won't be calling for help, and I have no doubt others have heard this commotion.

I need to get out of the bar. I get around to the other side of the bed and move the curtains. The sun is so bright I have to shield my eyes. I look down at the streets and can see several other paid guards out in front of buildings. These are not the Dome guards. I press my face to the hot windowpane to see as far as I can down the street. I can't see any other Dome guards from this vantage point. I'm going to have to take my chances. It's the fastest way out of here, and it might be my only way.

I brace my hands on both sides of the window, and it slowly begins to rise. It creaks under the pressure, but it rises just enough for me to crawl out. I get my feet onto the ledge of the window. The awning hanging from the building is about three feet below. I can see the threadbare fabric moving slowly from the hot breeze. The sun is already up and in full force. My palms are sweating from the exertion. I take a deep breath and jump onto the awning. It gives way underneath me, and I crash onto the pavement underneath.

The guards standing at attention under the awning across the street gawk at me, unsure what to make of this. I've got one thing on my side though... Everyone hates Dome guards and this far away from the Dome, no one will go out of their way to help them. Luckily, my fall was broken by a Dome guard that was standing watch at the front door of the bar. It was probably the same jerk I encountered a few minutes ago. I get to my feet and run as quickly as I can away from the bar. It will be only seconds before more guards from the Dome are out in the street. I can't run to the alley because if the guards are on my tail, I don't want to lead them straight to Asmita.

I run the opposite direction of the alley and cross the street to get off the main road. The sun is fully up, and my clothes are sticking to my body from sweat. My eyes want to close from the brightness, and keeping them open is a struggle. I weave in between buildings, trying to shield myself from the eyes of paid guards watching over doors. The side streets have far fewer guards, so I make my way north quickly.

I try to think where Asmita could be hiding out. If she's smart, and I know that she is, then she's still on the move. I head north toward the island, taking care, making sure I'm not followed. The sun is strong, and after walking a while, I'm dying of thirst. I hate to stop, but I have to rest. The sun is zapping my energy faster than I thought it would. The road to the island is to my left, but I stick to a trail that is partially covered by trees. The tree line helps shield me from the harsh sun.

I wipe my forehead with my shirt. I can't stop myself from thinking of Asmita. I don't know if she's ever travelled during the daylight, and I'm worried about her. When I really can't walk anymore, I sit down on the dirt and rest my body. I have to get water. I wonder if she has any in her backpack. I hate to invade her privacy, but I have to open her bag to see. I'm too thirsty to rule it out, so I pull the bag off my back and pull the zippers down to open it.

I push her belongings around in the bag, looking and hoping for a full water bottle. At the bottom, I find a half-empty bottle and drink it until it's dry. The water is like heaven in my mouth. That's the only water in the bag, but she has a ton of the orange pills. If I can find a source of water, then I can use the pills till I find her with my own bag. Then I'll be okay. I start to close the backpack, and a familiar black envelope catches my eye. It looks identical to the one my parents gave me when I left. I can't resist the temptation, and I open the envelope and read the contents. I read the letter as fast as I can and when I've finished, I realize my mouth has fallen open in surprise. I read the letter a second time.

I know very little about Asmita, but this letter leads me to believe that she had no idea what was coming. My parents at least gave me the knowledge and the tools to help save my life. I sit on the ground and think about everything that I've just found out. This girl has no idea what's going on. Unless there's some hidden message that I don't understand, then I've travelled across the country to find a girl who is as clueless as I am. I don't know how long I sit there thinking but I realize I have to figure this out.

I stand up and brush the dirt off my butt. I'm determined, now more than ever, to find Asmita before it gets dark. I'm so mad I could punch the next person I see in the face. I don't know if it's because I just lost the only hope I was holding on to or if I feel more confused than ever. I do know though, that I'm her only hope of surviving if she has no training or skills. I have to find her before darkness comes. People will be out in full force then, and I have no idea how long I have before Dome guards make their way toward us. That realization propels me to keep moving forward.

CHAPTER 16

Asmita

I CHECK my watch one more time. It's been ten minutes, and I've given him double what he told me. I can't wait any longer. I have to get moving. He'll find me on the way to the island, and we will switch our bags. I have to trust that he'll show up. He needs me right now as much as I need him. I haven't travelled a lot during the daylight, and it makes me nervous. The fact that guards for the Dome are here makes me even more nervous.

The one thing I've learned while making my way to Utah, is that the Dome is hated by everyone in the west. People aren't willing to go out of their way to help them unless it benefits them. If anybody sees me that is not paid by them, they aren't going to give me up easily. I make my way out of the city streets being careful to stay out of the sunlight and out of the eyes of the guards. If I'm going to have any shot of making it out of here without getting caught, I've got to be slow and make wise movements. The heat slows me down even more.

As I make my way out of the city, I keep thinking about Jesse. I think about how it was so selfless of him to help me. He went into that bar knowing that Dome guards were there and knowing that he might not get back out. I silently pray as I walk that he's made it out. It would be awful for him to get hurt just to help me. I keep looking for him as I walk, hoping that the next corner I turn he'll be standing there waiting on me. I want him to be safe. He doesn't deserve to get into my mess, a mess that I didn't even know I had. I can't understand why people from the Dome would be looking for me.

I try to remember every detail of the last few days. Why would George have sold me out to the Dome, and what does the Dome even want with me? It doesn't make any sense. I keep walking, trying to get as far away as I can from the city center.

I'm weak from being sick, and the sun is making me feel worse. I'm dehydrated, and I feel like I'm going to pass out. I make it to the tree line beside the main road going to the island. I can't go any further. I have to sit down and rest.

The heat has literally worn me down. I take Jesse's backpack off and set it beside me on the ground. I need to see if he has anything to drink or eat.. If not, I'll have to keep moving until I find water. I'm sure at this point if he's made it out, and is out in this miserable heat, he's done the same with my bag.

I rest my back up against a tree and close my eyes. I listen to the sounds around me, hoping to hear Jesse's footsteps. All I can hear is the wind. I feel like crying. I'm just so exhausted, and I keep thinking about how I trusted George. I pull the backpack closer and pull the zipper tab to open it. I feel bad for opening his bag, but he'd understand. If he's out there with mine he's welcome to open it.

I go through his bag, taking each item out so I can get through all of it. I find a few things to eat and one bottle of water. I take the lid off and smell the water. It has a hint of orange to it, so it looks like it's already been given one of the pills. I take my chances and drink from the bottle. It's so refreshing that I greedily drink more, knowing that I should save some of it for later. I even put some of the water on my face. I can tell my forehead is sunburned. As I sit there cooling off and eating one of the snacks, I absentmindedly start looking through the stuff I took out of the bag.

What catches my eye is the tattered black envelope tucked in between his clothing. I know those envelopes, having grown up with them. It makes me feel like I'm invading his privacy just seeing it. I think of the one my parents gave me that's in my own bag. I leave the stack of clothes on the ground and repack the rest of the bag. Once I've got the rest of the contents back in the bag, I pull the envelope out from the clothing. I stare at the envelope, torn between wanting to open it and not wanting to invade his privacy. That's the least I could do for him considering the danger he's gone through for me.

My curiosity wins, however, and I pull the letter from the envelope and unfold it. I read the first few lines and stopped. His parents, just like mine, knew this was going to happen. They were prepared for it and apparently, they had prepared Jesse for it as well. I look up from the paper and scan the woods around me. I have this feeling I'm being watched. Maybe it's because I'm reading his letter, and I know I shouldn't be. I look back down at the letter and continue to read. The next few sentences send chills down my spine.

He was sent to protect a woman at Antelope Island. My mind scans everything I've learned about the island and what Jesse has said to me in the short time I've known him. I have so many questions and no answers to go with them. I know that my gut reaction is right about the island. It'll be confirmed shortly once I get there. My parents and his parents wouldn't have sent us out there in the middle of a disaster on a wild goose chase. There's a reason for it, and I'm so close to finding it out. I read the letter one more time, then fold it up. I pick up the envelope, and a small square of paper falls out onto my lap.

I turn the blank square over, and my face is now staring back at me. It's my ID photo, the same that the man in the woods was carrying. My heart is racing in my chest and my mind is reeling. Am I the girl his parents mention in the letter? Why does he have my photograph? Does he know who I am then? In a panic, I shove the letter and photograph back in the envelope and back into the backpack. I scramble to my feet and clean up the tracks I've made in the dirt. I have to get out of here. I need to get to the island.

My head is spinning. I feel as if I'm standing on the outside looking in through the glass at my own life. It all comes to me as I'm running through the brush beside the road. I don't care how much noise I'm making. I have to get out of here. I'm the girl he came across the country looking for. I'm the girl that his parents told him to find. I'm the girl that is labeled important. As I run through the brush with these thoughts in my mind, I can feel the sting of tears creeping into my eyes.

I'm exhausted, and to find out this information with no real answers doesn't help me in any way. I'm tired of running. I'm tired of fighting to survive each day. I'm so close but so far away from the island. It might as well be on the other side of the country. I stop running and try to catch my breath. I bend forward and place my hands on my knees, trying to take deep calming breaths. I suck the air through my lungs and can't get myself to calm down. I think I'm having a panic attack.

I fall to the ground and lay with my face on the dirt. As I slip into unconsciousness, my thoughts drift, wondering how my parents could do this to me. How could they send me out into the world, knowing this was going to happen, and leave me all alone? I think of Jesse and know he's out there... he has to be. He doesn't seem like a guy who gives up. I think of his face and the look he gave me when we first met. Then it all goes black.

CHAPTER 17

Jesse

THE SUN IS on the horizon, and the air around me is becoming easier to breathe as the sky begins to grow darker. I've searched about half of this side of the woods and have had no luck. My estimate of her having a lead on me has brought me further out into the brush. I'm exhausted from not getting any rest. I haven't slept now in 24 hours, and my adrenaline has worn off. My throat is parched, but I'm still moving. With every new step that I take, my faith in finding her fades a little bit more.

I don't even know if she got out of the city, but I'm clinging to the fact that she had made it this far on her own. That's even despite the fact that her parents gave her no real warning. At least my shit parents did that much. They at least gave me the skills to try to survive. I keep walking, looking for her. I stop every few yards and listen for any noises. Now that the sky is getting dark, more people will be out. If the Dome is still on the hunt for us, then they'll be out here sooner rather than later.

I know that by covering the brush looking for Asmita, I'm also getting closer to the island. I don't even want to think about what may await us there. I continue to walk for what feels like hours and as I go, the sky becomes black and speckled with white lights to guide me. It's falling into darkness, and I've almost given up hope of finding her when I spot an awkward shape on the ground. The lump on the ground is about fifty feet in front of me. My heart skips a beat, and my palms begin to sweat. I think I've finally found her, and I feel dreadful thinking that she's just lying on the ground.

I look around in the darkness then close my eyes, listening again for any sounds around me. It's almost impossible not to just run to her, but I need to be cautious. This could be a trap. If any of the Dome has followed either one of us, we're done for. There won't be any second chances on escaping from them. I take a few seconds and open my ears. I can't hear any noises and begin to move forward. As I get closer to the shape, I realize it is Asmita, and she's lying face down on the dirt in an unnatural pose. A rush of overwhelming terror fills my chest as I instantly think the worst. I rush to her side, reach down and feel for a pulse at her neck. She's alive and breathing! I feel a little relief. I would never forgive myself if something happened to her while she was out of my sight.

I put my hand on her shoulder and gently try to nudge her awake. It takes a few tries until she begins to stir. I take what little water I have and splash some on her face. She seems in a fog, and I begin to wonder if George was drugging her to keep easier tabs on her until he could get the Dome into town. I help her sit up, and it takes a minute for her to open her eyes. She looks around at her surroundings like she's momentarily forgotten where she is. When our eyes meet, she smacks my hand off her shoulder.

My reaction is to grab my stinging hand and rub it. I wasn't expecting that. She pushes back away from me on the ground and scrambles to get to her feet. I can see the dust falling back to the ground with what little light is left. Her face is pale white, and she's looking at me with eyes as big as saucers. I try to reassure her and when that doesn't work, I change my tone. I stand up so we will be face to face.

"What's wrong? Did someone hurt you? Are you okay?" I ask, confused. Standing there waiting for a response, I continue to rub my hand. It's no longer feeling the instant sting of the hit, but it gives me something to do with my hands. I'm frustrated and confused, and I know my tone of voice gives away exactly how I'm feeling.

Asmita doesn't move from where she's standing, and she isn't speaking. Quickly, she takes off my backpack and throws it at my feet. The dust rises and makes me cough. I have to wave it out of my face. I ask her another question, "What's wrong with you?"

She echoes me with, "What's wrong with me?" She gives a shrill laugh. She's filled with anger. Apparently, we've both had a very bad day. "I'll tell you what's wrong with me!" she yells. "You know exactly who I am, and I only know the lies you've told me."

My heart sinks. I thought she was going to tell me something awful. We've committed the same sin and gone through each other's bags. She knows my secrets and knows that I've been looking for her. I've failed in my mission to my parents and myself. The only thing I can do to keep her near me is come clean. I'll have to tell her everything that I know. It's the only way.

"Asmita, I'm sorry." As I speak the words, she's already turning and walking from me. "I mean it! You read the letter. I was instructed not to let you know. I'm not here to harm you. I'm here to do nothing but help you!" She continues walking away from me. "Why do you think I just risked my life getting your bag? I wouldn't do that for just anyone. You're special. My parents told me so!"

It does no good. She just keeps walking. I plead with her, something that I'm not accustomed to doing for anything or anyone. "Please! Just listen to me. Don't walk away from me!" That does the trick because she stops walking and slowly turns around to look at me.

The face that stares back at me is hard and filled with anguish. I know I've lost any trust that she may have given me for going back and getting her bag. To my surprise, she walks back toward me. We stare at each other and never lose eye contact. I dare not to break the connection with her. She stops beside me and drops the bag she was holding at my feet. It's my bag. She reaches up and takes the strap of the bag on my shoulder, her bag, and pulls it off of me. She does all of this without speaking. I can feel the anger rolling off of her like waves from the ocean. I start to think about what the ocean may really look like but snap back to my miserable reality.

Once she has her bag, she turns around and starts to walk toward the island and away from me again. I quickly pick up my own bag and follow her. I leave a little bit of distance between us. I try to give her space, but I won't leave her alone out here. I won't do it, not after it took me so long to find her. In the end, it was luck that I found her when I did. A part of me even thinks it was meant to be. This was the mission my parents sent me out on. I didn't know it at the time, but it was my destiny to find her. It's my job to keep her safe and watch over her. I may have screwed up the part where I was supposed to do it in secret, but I won't blow the whole thing.

I let her walk in front of me in silence for about an hour. We are in total darkness now and I'm exhausted. I don't know how much I've got left in me to keep walking. If I stay awake the whole night, I'll have been up and moving for two days straight. The only thing propelling me forward is her. I break our silence.

"Asmita, please" I beg her. "Please, stop walking."

I get no response from her. I try again. "Asmita. Please. I'm really asking you to stop walking. I'm not going to leave you. I'm tired. You're tired. Let's just take a break."

She stops in her tracks. I silently thank the heavens above us. She hasn't turned around to face me, and I take the few steps that separate us. I walk in front of her and sit down a few feet from her to keep her in my sights.

Asmita just sits down on the ground in the place she was standing. After what feels like forever, she finally opens her mouth to speak. "I just have one question," she says.

CHAPTER 18

Asmita

"Why me? Why am I so special? I read it in the letter. My mom told me that I was special in mine. What makes me so special that they'd send you across the country to find me?" I ask. I'm so mad. I don't think I've ever been this angry. A part of me wants to punch Jesse in the face. The other part of me wants to punch him in the face but let him keep following me around. I feel like I've been left in the dark about my own life.

Jesse runs his hand over his head and exhales. He shakes his head and says, "I don't know. What you read in my letter is what I knew about you after the disaster. I didn't even know your name until I got to Salt Lake." He shrugs his shoulders as if he's exasperated.

My mind fills with questions for him. He holds so many answers to my unknowns. "Did you leave before the disaster or after?" I ask him. I volunteer my information about leaving San Francisco after the disaster occurred in hopes of getting him to answer.

"Before," he responds.

"Did you know it was going to happen?" I ask him.

He pauses again, waiting to answer. He drops his eyes back down from the sky and looks me in the eyes and answers, "Yes." It's as if he has his own internal debate going on to decide if he's going to answer. We sit there in silence together and let some time pass. He stands to his feet, and I do the same.

"I'm feeling better. I can continue walking if you're ready," he tells me. I nod my head and turn around. I wait for him to be by my side before I take a step. I put my hand on his arm and wasted no time in asking him one more question. "Do you know what it was that happened?"

He doesn't waste a second before telling me, "No. I knew that something was going to happen, but my parents never shared that information with me. Honestly, I don't know if they knew exactly what was going to happen themselves. We just knew that *something* was going to happen, it wasn't going to be good and that I had to get far away from the Dome. They helped me learn certain skills and gave me things that would help me in my journey, and that's all. I really didn't even know about you until I opened the letter after the disaster happened. I swear."

I absorb what he says to me, and we keep walking. We walk and walk and walk till I'm so tired that I can't go on any longer. I stop, and we look at each other. We are both exhausted and emotionally drained. We've kept the silence between us since he answered my last question. I take a deep breath, and he speaks before I can.

"I don't think we're going to make it to the island tonight. I think we should stop and rest. We can rest here, find some water and shelter for the day then tomorrow, when darkness starts to fall, we can go the rest of the way to the island. What do you think?" he says.

I don't know why I say it, but it comes out of my mouth before I can stop it. "Are they going to kill me?" In the darkness, I can still see his eyes shining at me.

"If you're referring to the Dome then the answer is no. They haven't succeeded, and they won't. Not with me in the way," he tells me. He's so matter-of-fact as he says it. He puts down his bag, and I do the same. He starts giving me directions for what to go find. We can't light a fire because we don't want to draw any attention to us. I shiver in the coldness of the night air, and a few seconds later he's handing me a lightweight jacket out of his pack. I thank him and zip it up to my neck. I start looking for tree branches that have fallen. This far out into the woods we won't find anywhere to hide from the sun. We are going to have to improvise.

We spend the rest of the darkness working on our shelter for the hot daylight that's quickly approaching. There's very little chit chat as we go about our work. We've got our makeshift shelter of tree branches for the daylight complete. And while it might not be the greatest thing, we'll at least be somewhat protected from the direct sunlight. I get under the branches and lay down with my head resting on my backpack. Jesse takes his water bottle out and asks for mine. Our bottles are completely empty, and I'm thirsty now that I think about it.

"I'm going to go look and see if there's any water around here. I want you to stay here and rest. I won't be gone long. If you have any trouble, I want you to yell as loud as you can, and I'll come back," he tells me.

"Are you sure it's safe to split up?" I ask him. I feel uneasy knowing he'll be out there alone.

"We've made a lot of noise dragging these branches around and getting everything together. If the Dome guards are out there near us, they would have found us by now. I think we're safe for the moment." He smiles at me as he talks. I wonder what he really thinks our odds are of making it to the island tomorrow, but I don't ask. He walks away in search of water, and I watch him until I can't see him any longer.

Daylight starts to creep up, and I can feel the heat intensifying. Sweat beads form along my hairline and I fight them away with the back of my hand. I'm starting to get nervous that Jesse hasn't returned. I try to lay my head back down on my pack, but it's too sticky hot to lie against the fabric. I sit there thinking about the last 24 hours and how so much has changed. I absentmindedly chew my fingernails and look through the trees for any movement.

I realize I've been holding my breath when I see Jesse come into my view. His shirt is drenched in sweat, and I notice how it clings to his body. Thankfully, he's still too far away from me to notice that I'm admiring his muscles. When he gets close enough for me to see his face, I can see his wide grin. Maybe he wasn't too far away after all. He holds up two full water bottles to show me that he's found water. No, he's smiling because he's proud of himself not because I'm ogling over his toned body.

When he gets to the tent, I'm more than grateful to take one of the bottles off his hands. I open it up and begin to drink thirstily from it.

"Hey! Slow down, you'll want to save some for later. The water supply I found seems to be the only one around here, and it's too far to walk to again during the daylight. It's out of the way, and we won't be hitting it before we head out again at nightfall," he chastises.

I nod my understanding and stop drinking the water. I close my bottle and put it safely into my bag. I yawn and feel overwhelmed with how sleepy I suddenly feel. Jesse catches me yawn and says, "It's okay. You can go to sleep. I'm going to watch for a little bit longer and then try to get some rest myself."

I don't really want to fall asleep because a part of me feels like I should stay awake for as long as I can. The other part of me is screaming and begging for rest. This has been the longest day of my life, and I'm spent. After a few minutes, my struggle becomes useless, and I fall asleep under our makeshift shelter. The oppressive heat doesn't even bother me. I'm completely out to the world.

My subconscious takes over, and I begin to weave in and out of dreams. I dream of my parents on the day that I left them. I'm boarding my flight and I turn to wave goodbye to them. They stand there and wave back to me, my mother fighting tears trying to keep them in her eyes. She blows me a kiss and mouths I'll see you again soon. The memory of the day vanishes, and I'm running in the woods. This is the nightmare that won't leave me alone. This time in my nightmare, I recognize it's just that... a nightmare. At the end of it, I keep running and running and finally Jesse is running beside me. He's screaming at me to get closer. I look over my shoulder and the guards of the Dome are chasing us. Their weapons are drawn and aimed at us, but we keep running away. The noise from their guns rings out into the air, and I begin to scream.

I wake with a jolt, and Jesse has his hand over my mouth. My eyes come into focus, and I can see that he's leaning over me. His eyes are as big as saucers; something has scared him. When he realizes I'm awake, he slowly moves his hand away from my mouth.

"Are you alright?" he asks me in a whispered tone.

In the same tone, I answered him back, "It was a nightmare. Why are we whispering?"

He looks around before answering, "Because you were scaring me. You started screaming so loud, people for miles could probably hear you."

I sit up and rub my eyes. My throat is dry, and my clothes are soaked in sweat. The hottest part of the day has passed, and the sky has taken on that glow of many colors as the sun begins to go into hiding for the night. I look at Jesse, and he seems like he's managed some rest. He goes about what he was doing before I scared him. He's got all of his bag unpacked, and he's counting his supplies. I sit there and watch him do his work. I break the comfortable silence between us. "Will we start moving once it gets dark?" I ask.

"He takes his eyes off of his task and looks at me. "We'll leave before it gets completely dark. If the rest of the path is like what we've experienced, we'll do good to start out with a little light," he informs me.

I watch him pack the rest of his bag up and start to get myself together to leave our tiny spot. Much to my surprise, Jesse takes off his shirt and stands with his bare chest right in front of me. I know my face blushes because I've never seen a man's bare chest in person. I feel embarrassed and look away. When he sees my embarrassment, he quickly tells me, "I wouldn't do this otherwise, but I scratched my back on something yesterday, and it's been bleeding. Can you look at it for me? I need you to look and see if anything is in the cut."

He turns around, and I can see that the scratch isn't just a scratch; it's a large cut at least an inch deep and three inches long. Dirt is caked around it, and the dirt might be the only thing stopping it from oozing blood everywhere. From the little I know from schooling, it needs to be cleaned and stitched up.

I tell him what I think. "This is bad. It needs to be cleaned out, and you need stitches. It's going to get infected if you leave it like that."

"We don't have anything to stitch it up with. Try to clean it with some of my water, but don't use a lot"

I start to clean the wound and as I'm doing so, it begins to bleed. Jesse takes the shirt he's just removed and cuts it open on both sides. He's turned it into one long piece of fabric. He turns around and hands me the fabric. "Help me get this folded over and wrap it around me. We'll tie it on to me and use the pressure to help keep it closed. When we get to the island, we'll see how it's doing then."

The island. I can't wait to get there and apparently, neither can he.

<hr>

CHAPTER 19

<hr>

Jesse

THE CUT on my back is killing me. I could hardly get any rest with the heat. I could feel my heart beating in my back. I refuse to let Asmita know how much pain I'm in. I try not to think about it as we scatter our makeshift camp. I want to make sure that we leave no trace of our stay. We dismantle our camp and scatter the branches far enough apart to look natural. By the time we finish that task, the air has become cooler with the sun setting. We still have enough light to see our steps in the woods for a while.

I put my backpack on, and it scrapes the cut on my back. I wince in pain and Asmita eyes me instantly with a worried look. "I'm fine," I say, trying to reassure her but the shirt tied around me just isn't enough to dull the pain. I shift my bag, trying to find a more comfortable way to carry it, but it's no use. I'll just have to let it rub against the wound. I try to hide the pain on my face. I wait for Asmita to get her bag on her shoulder and then we set out.

I stare up at the fading light from the sky as we walk. I'm hoping that we can make it to the island before the sun comes back up. With each step that we take, I feel like we are getting closer to answers. It's hard to describe, but it's just a feeling that I have deep inside me. We take it slow at first, walking side by side. As the light fades from the sky, we go even slower, attempting to make as little noise as possible in the brush. We've gone a while without speaking, and the silence begins to weigh on me.

"Is it my turn to ask you some questions?" I ask her casually as we continue forward. She looks at me in surprise and nods her head yes in response.

I try to keep my manners casual and my voice low. Inside, I feel anything but casual. I've thought of these questions for months as I've travelled across the country, wanting to ask them as soon as I met her. To finally ask them out loud to her feels like an enormous relief.

"How did you know to go to the Island?" I ask her.

Asmita takes her time stepping over a large branch that has fallen recently.

Once she gets over it, she looks at me, stops and takes a breath. "I didn't at first. I mean, I wasn't told directly to go there."

"What does that mean?" I ask her. I sure as hell don't know.

"I just mean that my parents didn't tell me directly to go there. After the disaster and after I found my letter, which was a complete surprise to me by the way, I started thinking about what to do and where to go. I remembered a recent conversation I had had with my mom, and she mentioned this place out of the blue. It was odd, and it stuck out to me. I think it was her way of telling me where to go." She shrugs her shoulders to convey her bemusement.

"What if we get there and there's nothing? What will be next?" I ask her in all seriousness. I have no idea what we'll do next if that's the case.

She stops walking and looks at me. "You want the truth? I don't know. I'm hoping we don't have to make that decision." She starts walking again, and I wonder what she's thinking about. Did I stir something inside of her mind? Is she second-guessing herself? I've risked my life coming all this way to get to her. My parents risked their lives to get me on that train. Yeah, they may have had a secret agenda, but they may have given their lives for it. I still don't know if my parents are okay.

I haven't been able to get any messages from home. I haven't risked trying to send one either. Maybe it's the same with my parents. Maybe it's too dangerous for them to reach out. It's not as if they know where I'm at. I've been traveling for months. I never stay in the same place for long and for good reason. They wouldn't even know where to send a message. With my recent brush with the Dome, I'm glad I haven't sent any messages to them; they could be monitoring everyone's mail.

Until they came to George's boarding house and bar, I thought they were just a myth. I didn't even know for sure that they still existed. "Did you know the Dome guards were still functioning before we saw them in town?"

"No. I haven't seen any of them until they were at George's. If I did, I wouldn't have just walked up to them and said, '*Oh, hey, what are you doing here? How's it going on the other side of the continent? What happened that day?*' I don't think they would take too kindly to that." She smirks at me.

Sass. I'm getting sassed now. Clearly, her nerves are starting to fray. Maybe I just rub her the wrong way. Either way, I decide to stop asking her any more questions. As time goes on, daylight begins to creep up on us. If we don't make it before the sun is completely up and out, we will have to find another spot to weather the heat. I suggest to Asmita that we leave the dense brush and go closer to the main path. This will allow us to possibly see if anyone is around us and how far we have to the island. It should be getting very close.

We make our way out of the brush and onto what was once the main road. Like all the other main roads, debris is everywhere. Cars are parked in random places, and loose articles of clothing and items deemed as junk by scavengers, who have undoubtedly searched this area combing for treasures to trade and sell are scattered everywhere. I motion for Asmita to stay low, and we both crouch down between the abandoned cars. We have to be cautious and try to remain unseen. This could easily be a trap.

We slowly make our way up the road, weaving between the cars. The ground is mostly even, and our feet walk silently on the pavement. I slow our pace down by taking the lead and whisper instructions to Asmita.

"Start looking in cars for anything we can use over time. Who knows how long we might have to be out here," I tell her. She nods in response and whispers back to me.

"It's too quiet out here. It's unnerving," she says.

"Yeah, well, hopefully it's just us out here, and that's why it's so quiet."

The only good thing about being on the road is that after a few minutes of making our way up the path between the cars, a mangled sign up ahead comes into view. It reads: *Antelope Island, Great Salt Lake State Park*. It's up in the distance, and we can see it now. Asmita and I look at each other, and I give her my best smile. She doesn't return it. She looks deep in thought and scared. Really scared. The smile drops off my face and we keep walking forward.

The sun is starting to make its way up into the sky, and we begin to make out smaller objects in the light. We've made it to the mangled sign. From far away we couldn't see any of the smaller warnings written on it. The sign has seen major damage. It's bent in places with large grooves, and I'm guessing it's from rocks since there's large rocks laying everywhere around the sign. Spray painted at the bottom in red paint someone has left us a warning: *Turn Away. Do Not Enter.*

I look at Asmita's face, and she's taking in the sign. She looks over at me with the same weary look.

"I wonder how long this has been here. Was it written just for us?" she asks as she looks around.

"I don't know," I tell her as I scan the trees and brush on both sides of the road. I can't see any movement.

Further behind the sign is a barbed wire fence. It looks much newer than the sign. It seems in good condition, and it's blocking the actual entrance to the island. If I had to guess, I'd say it's at least twelve feet tall, and it's spanning as far across as my eyes can see. It's a mesh fence, and we just couldn't see it in the dark. It looks like it even cuts through the woods and brush. I don't know why, but it makes the hair on my neck and arms stand straight up.

If we're going to go for it, I think it has to be now. Anything could happen if we try to make camp out here during the daylight. I'm about to tell her my thoughts when she whispers to me, "I think we should take cover in one of those cars we passed further back and watch for any signs of life."

I have to physically restrain myself from rolling my eyes and laughing at her. Is she crazy? I'm not waiting out here for daylight to pass. I could die in this heat or from this gaping wound on my back or the big question, who knows how many Dome guards are out looking for us right now. I'm moving forward now, not later.

"Are you kidding me? We have to go now. This is the best chance we are going to have. We go in there now, at the beginning of daylight, and we see if anyone is in there. If we stay out here, the Dome Guards could catch up to us anytime," I say, trying to hold back my agitation.

"I'm just scared, okay! What if I'm wrong? What if we go in there and there's nothing or worse, we go in there and the Dome is already waiting for us," she says.

I see real fear in Asmita's eyes. She's deeply afraid of what's behind that fence. I'm going to have to push her to move forward. Doesn't she realize I wouldn't do anything to directly hurt her? I would put myself in front of the danger before letting her get hurt. The next words out of my mouth are going to sound harsh to her, but I have to say them.

"Asmita, you need to muster up all the courage you can find because we are not waiting for it to get dark again. We won't survive. One of us won't survive, and it will probably be me, and I need to keep living a little longer to get you inside."

She just stares at me for a second and then, like a light bulb has gone off in her head, she looks at me and says, "If you came all this way to die, you're going to have to wait a little while longer."

I am completely shocked by her words. Apparently, my authoritative tone helped knock some sense into her. Does that mean she's coming with me or staying though? "You understand we need to go right now, right? You get that? This is serious. We have to move, and we're wasting time standing here arguing about it."

She bends down and undoes the ties in her shoes. She re-ties them and stands back up. "Let's go!" she says and starts walking toward the fence.

It's like she didn't even hear the words come out of my mouth. A little acknowledgement would be nice. I'm only trying to help her stay alive and keep myself alive at the same time. I hope whatever is inside this fence brings us good news and real answers. If not, I'm at my wits end. I've got a lot of thinking to do about what's next for Asmita and me. The first thing is to keep surviving. I need some major stitches in my back to close up this wound or I won't be doing anything. I have to keep mopping the sweat off my face. I feel like I'm burning up from the inside. This only tells me one thing... it's infected.

CHAPTER 20

Asmita

I KEEP my face toward the fence and refuse to look at Jesse as I walk. How dare he speak to me like I'm some idiot! Clearly, I have made it this far and most of it on my own. Where was he when I was trying to get out of San Francisco or getting attacked in the woods? I made it through those situations; I can make it through this one. It's clear to me, when I do look back at him, that he's having a rough time. He's sweating profusely and his face has taken on an ashen color. He catches up to me, and I let him get a few steps in front of me. I can see the back of his clothing, and it's obvious to see that he's lost a lot of blood. His shirt is soaked through with sweat and blood and the darkest is over the spot of his wound.

We've made it to the fence and are now standing directly in front it. Jesse puts his hand up in the air to signal me to stop. He scans the length of the fence and then the height. He takes his backpack off of his back and opens it. He pulls out a shirt and hands it to me.

"What do I need this for?" I ask him, puzzled.

"I'm going to help you climb up first. When we get near the top, you'll swing this up and lay it over the wire so your skin won't get cut as we cross over it. That wire looks razor sharp, so don't let any of your skin come into contact with it. If you do, you'll be in the same boat as me with my back, and that's the last thing we need."

I instantly feel guilty for my previous thoughts. He's just trying to look out for me, of course. That's all he's tried to do since we met. I don't know why, but I instantly think the worst of him when really, when I think about it, he's been nothing but kind to me. When I've snapped at him, he's tried his best to not retaliate but explain himself to me and his actions. I resolve to do better.

"What about you? I don't want you to get in any worse shape" I smile weakly at him, trying to convey that I really am worried about the way he's looking.

"I'll be fine. I'll use this," he says as he holds up another shirt since the first is almost shredded.

"Good!" I tell him with a little too much enthusiasm. "I'm exhausted. Let's get this party started."

He looks at me a little funny, but once he gets his bag closed and on his shoulders again, we start to climb the fence. It's a chain link fence, but it's got to be a minimum of twenty feet tall with another foot of wire curling at the top. We take our time climbing up the fence. It sways some under our weight and our close proximity to each other. As we climb, I have to keep repositioning my hands. The heat from the sun is quickly making the metal too hot to touch. I look down at the ground getting further away from us, and I can see heat waves rising off the road we walked down to get to the fence.

Jesse makes it to the barbed wire quicker than I do. He holds on with both hands to the fence and waits for me to reach him. He doesn't complain once about his hands touching the hot metal. I try to push myself faster up to him and succeed. My feet are aching from trying to squeeze them into the chain link to steady myself, and my hands feel like I've juggled hot pans. I can see that Jesse has already got his shirt over the wire, but he's placed it on the wire in front of me so I can go over first. He reaches down and takes the shirt I have draped over my shoulder.

"Start climbing over the fence. Be very careful not to touch any of the wire that isn't covered by the shirt," he stresses to me.

"Why don't you go ahead over first so I can see how it's done?" I ask him.

He shakes his head to indicate no. "Because I don't want to be on the other side if something happens and you fall back onto this side. I want to keep us on the same side of the fence," he says, and his jaw tightens. This clearly isn't up for discussion.

He's concentrating to get the shirt to lay just right on the wires. I start making my way up the little area of the fence I have left before the wire. I don't want to screw this up.

"You can do this Asmita. You're stronger than you think."

He's trying to encourage me. I stare at him warily but continue to make my way up to the wire. Once I'm at the wire, and have no room to move any further up or beside it without crossing it, I realize how big the loops are. I'm instantly filled with fear that my skin is going to get ripped open. He can sense my hesitation about not knowing what to do.

"Asmita, put your hands on the wire through the shirt. You have to touch it. Try to touch it with one hand and get your leg over. If you don't press too hard with your hand it might not puncture through the shirt."

"What! You never said that the wire was going to go through the shirt."

"It's not thick material. You're going to feel some sensation even if it's on your legs. Trust me, it'll be better than the barbed wire touching your bare skin. Just go slowly if you have to, but don't make contact with any of the wire not under the shirt."

I touch the wire and in my mind I'm so on edge, I expect it to shock me. I touch it, and I can feel the thickness of the wire through the shirt. I'm able to get my leg up and over the wire, and I'm straddling the coils. The next thing I know, my body's momentum from swinging my leg up has made the fence sway. I've lost my balance and grip. I try to correct my position and catch the fence with my bare hand. It connects with the barbed wire. The movement instantly shoots pain up my left forearm and I'm screaming out in pain.

In the panic and pain, I lose my grip all together and begin to fall into the wire. Before I know it, Jesse climbs up the rest of the fence and flings his shirt on the wire next to me. He puts his upper body onto the shirt and uses his arms to help free me from the tangle of wire. He doesn't take the time to reassure me; he just gets me free from the wire.

"Can you keep climbing down?"

"Yes, I think so," I tell him. "My hand is bleeding, but I can make it."

I start to climb down, and Jesse does the same. He makes it over the barbed wire and joins me on the fence. He goes slowly with me and stays by my side as we climb down. I'm much slower than him, but he doesn't seem to mind. My hand is throbbing, and the sun is just continuing to heat the fence up. When I plant my feet on solid ground, I'm thrilled to be off the fence.

Jesse jumps off the fence with about five feet remaining. He has one of the shirts in his hands and begins ripping one side of it. He rips a long strip of fabric off. He takes my bleeding hand and gives it a look over.

"This is the best I've got at the moment," he says to me as he holds up the strip. "Put your hand out, and I'll wrap it."

I hold my hand up and he begins wrapping the cloth strip around my hand. It'll help stop the bleeding, but my hand won't be very useful. If I'm not careful, it'll get infected, and I'll die. I'll need to get water over it and clean it once we find a place to make camp, if we make camp, that is. We may just power through. I don't know what to expect now that we're over the fence and on the island. We could see through the chain link fence and as far as the eye can see the land all around us. Now, we'll have to get past the hills and see what's behind them.

CHAPTER 21

Jesse

ASMITA'S HAND will heal over time; I'm certain of it. What matters is she got herself over the wall, and we have made it to the island. A part of me is relieved to have made it this far. The low hills of sand that stretch out in front of our view won't take long to cross. Once we get past those, we should be able to see more of the landscape. We may have to look around the island to see if anything or anyone is out here. It's getting so hot outside and with no coverage in sight, we are going to have to keep moving forward.

Everything is barren as we walk toward the low hills. I feel completely exposed out in the open like this. My back is slowing me down, but I keep putting one foot in front of the other. I have to get us over that hill. I can tell that Asmita is slowing down too. The fact that we've been up for so long isn't helping. The sun is draining what little energy we have left. When we make it to the low sand hills, we have to pause for some rest.

I lay down on the sand and it sticks to my body from the sweat. My palms are covered, and I rub them onto my pant legs to clean them off. Asmita is just as weary. She drinks greedily from the bottle she pulled out of her backpack. I want to tell her to save it, but I don't have the energy or the heart to chastise her. When we get up, we start the slow and arduous climb over the hills. What feels like hours but is really only a few minutes later, we crest the top and can see into the valley of what must be the island's center. It takes my breath away.

Here, in the middle of the island, is a crystal blue lake, small in size but blue. Blue as a sapphire and sparkling, it almost blinds us from the reflection of the sun. Asmita and I look at each other in awe. A slow smile rises on her face, and I can feel the same coming across mine. When she goes to step forward, I put my hand out to stop her.

"We have to be careful. It could be some kind of trick," I warn her.

Asmita stands stoically beside me and turns her eyes back to the lake. "This is where I'm meant to be. I can feel it."

We make our way down the hill and toward the lake. I scan the landscape, looking for anything moving, anything that could harm us. I see nothing, and we continue moving forward. When we make it off the hill and back onto flat ground, we are only about 200 yards from the edge of the lake. The sand is so soft it makes it hard to walk on. Asmita gets past me on the sand and is about ten steps ahead of me when I hear the change in her steps.

The soft noise of our feet in the sand has been transformed into knocks on metal. I scream out to her, "Stop!" but it's too late. I run toward her in the sand, and my feet move faster the closer I get to her. My feet don't fall deep into the sand as before but stay level. I reach my arms out to Asmita, and my fingers grasp the shoulder straps of her backpack. I can see the silver metal through the sand below our feet.

I only get a glimpse of the metal before it gives way, and we are falling downward with the loose sand sprinkling us as we go. For the first time in my life, I truly feel terrified because this is a real unknown. As we fall down into the darkness, my hands never let go of the bag strapped to Asmita. If I have to sacrifice myself for her, I will. That is my last thought as everything goes pitch black.

CHAPTER 22

Asmita

I CAN'T CATCH my breath. We are falling into the darkness, and all I can hear are my own screams. Jesse holds on to me tightly as we fall deeper and deeper. I close my eyes as the sand slowly rains down upon us. I stop screaming because there is no use; it only wastes my energy and won't help us. Suddenly, light begins shining in and brightness surrounds us. I timidly open my eyes, and the light is so bright that I'm forced to squint. I try to open my eyes, but the light is bright and only getting brighter as we fall. Before I know it, we've stopped falling.

When we hit the ground, I expect to feel pain, but I feel nothing. It feels like clouds have caught me. I open my eyes against the brightness and slowly look around me. I take Jesse in, and he's laying only a few feet from me. When we hit the ground, he lost his grip and landed a few feet away. He's got his eyes wide open, trying to find his balance to stand up. I don't know what the look on his face means. It looks like he's bewildered.

I take my eyes off Jesse just long enough to take in our surroundings. A stark white room meets my gaze and as I look around us, I notice *everything* is white. There's no furniture in the room, no windows and no sign of an exit. There's a long mirror on one wall and as I look at it, I see my reflection. I see Jesse standing now taking in the room as well. I feel like my throat is closing up. The idea of being trapped in this room sets off a panic deep inside of me.

I circle the room and can't find any seams along the walls that would indicate a door or a way to escape. The panic in me is threatening to come to the surface the longer I'm in this room. My eyes go back to the mirror on the wall. I look at Jesse and his eyes meet mine in the mirror. We run toward the mirror and start looking over it and around it, and we cup our hands to try to see through the mirrored glass.

A loud buzzing sound startles us both, making me jump. The voice we hear sounds electronic, almost computerized, and the words that come out next terrify us both.

"Welcome Asmita. We've been waiting for you."

Those seven words are enough to knock all of the air out of my lungs. Whoever is here, possibly behind that mirrored glass wall, knows who I am. And it all comes crashing down on me... will I ever see my parents again? Will I ever be happy... grow old with someone who cares about me? Will I know the truth about my life, after being clueless for all those years?

I don't know the answers, and the panic rising in me has reached a boiling point. I start to see black. The bright lights of the room fade to black and that's all I know now. Black.

EPILOGUE

Jesse

Five days later

I haven't seen Asmita for five days. They've been keeping us separated. I don't know if she's okay, and the last memory I have of her was falling to the ground in shock and completely blacking out. I think about her hand in mine... the last smile she gave me. How she cared for me. It makes it all worth it to me to know that the fight is still not over. I'll keep fighting every day to try to get back to her. To see her smile, to see her look at me like she trusts me with her life, and that she trusts me with her heart.

If I never get an answer about anything else, I have to know that she's okay. I have to know that everything I did wasn't a waste of time and effort. I've asked to see her, and they answer me in singular words of *No* or *Later.* You'd think they'd show some gratitude to the person that delivered her to them. Now that I've been here for days, questioned for hours and walked around the underground compound, I have a better understanding. At least I think so. All my thoughts go back to Asmita. I've got to get back to her. I will. If it kills me then that's the price I'll pay, because she's worth it.

THE MILE HIGH MEET-CUTE

S.E. Rose

CHAPTER ONE

PARIS

I HATE FLYING. I hate flying almost as much as I hate the thought of having to spend the next two weeks at my father and stepmother's home before I can move into my new apartment. I sigh as I look out the window at the plane that I'll be boarding in just a few minutes. The only plus to being my father's daughter is that I, at least, get to fly first class.

Growing up on the Upper East Side, I was surrounded by kids whose parents owned private jets and houses on at least two continents. I used to wish my father would buy one, but that all changed when Alec's plane went down. It had only been three years since my boyfriend piloted his small plane and never came home. I've just recently felt ready to date again.

"Attention, passengers, flight four-thirty-seven with nonstop service to New York will begin boarding in ten minutes," a woman says over a loudspeaker.

"Excuse me, ma'am," a man with a Southern accent says. I roll my eyes at his super-American-sounding voice. I hadn't heard another American speaking English in at least three weeks since class ended, and I stayed to spend some time in Paris before having to return home to start my new job.

I glance over the top of my book at him. My gaze travels up and then up some more. This man is tall with broad shoulders and arm muscles that stretch his tailored jacket sleeves. Damn, he's super attractive. He's at least ten years older than me, but he is impeccably dressed in a designer suit. If he hadn't spoken, I would have mistaken him for a European man. His five o'clock shadow has a few gray hairs. His neatly combed hair also sports some gray at his temples, but his face is free of wrinkles, telling me he's older but not as old as my father. He looks vaguely familiar. It takes me a minute, but I realize he looks like the asshat who got me and my friend kicked out of the VIP lounge at my favorite nightclub last week. So, naturally, I already hate him.

"Oui, monsieur," the woman says. "How may I help you?"

"Is there a way to see if I have a row to myself?" he asks. "I'd prefer the legroom."

I bet he would, I think to myself.

"I'm not sure. One moment," she says as she clicks some buttons on a keyboard while glancing at what I assume is the boarding pass he's showing her on his phone.

"I'm sorry. There are no seats left in first class that allow for two seats to be occupied by one person," she explains.

"Can I speak to a supervisor?" the man says, annoyance clear in his voice.

"I'm sorry, monsieur. We could book you on a later flight, perhaps we can find two available seats on the next flight," she says as she types on the computer.

"When is that?" he asks in a clipped voice. What an asshole!

"Let me see…six hours from now if you want to fly into JFK," she states.

"Unacceptable," he retorts.

"I can get you on a flight to Newark in two hours," she offers.

"No, it's too far away. There's nothing on any other sister airlines that I can switch to?" he asks.

I raise an eyebrow. Clearly, this man is familiar with flying.

"No. You'd be flying standby if you did that," she says.

He huffs. "Fine," he says rudely and walks away, typing ferociously on his phone.

Damn, I hope I'm not sitting by him.

CHAPTER TWO

RIVER

I send my partner a text to have the notes for our meeting tomorrow sent to my email so I can prep on the flight. I had tried to push back this meeting, but with no luck. We've been working on this particular contract for too long and I need this deal done.

I get a thumbs-up reply.

"We'll now begin boarding flight four-thirty-seven nonstop service to John F. Kennedy International Airport. First class passengers and anyone needing assistance may begin boarding now," the woman who was of no help earlier says over the intercom.

I walk up to the podium and hold up my phone, she scans it.

"Have a nice flight," she says in a way that I know is meant as a sarcastic version of "I hope your flight sucks."

"Thanks," I mutter, making my way down the narrow hallways to the plane. At least I have an aisle seat. I stop at row five and put my bag in the overhead compartment. I'll take my laptop out later. I need a drink and a nap. The seats are large and turn into partial beds. The row is partly hidden and there's even a curtain for privacy. It would be perfect if I had it to myself.

"Excuse me," a voice comes from behind me.

I turn and my gaze travels down and lands on a petite blonde with her hair piled up on top of her head. Fuck, she looks young. Great, now I have to share my seating area with a college student. And one that looks like the young woman I asked to be removed from the VIP lounge last weekend after she and her friends were acting like drunk college kids. What the fuck? Someone is using daddy's money.

I step to the side, and she slides into her window seat and places her bag under the seat in front of her.

I take my seat and motion for the flight attendant. "Can I get a scotch on the rocks, please?"

She nods politely and looks over at the young woman. "And for you, miss?"

"Oh, uh, I'll have a Chardonnay," she says. Her voice. Damn, her voice doesn't sound like she's a college student. It's low and sexy as fuck. I glance at her quickly. She's pretty in a natural, no-plastic-surgery way. Her cheeks are rosy and dotted with freckles. Her long eyelashes don't even look fake. She has a cute little nose and plump lips with gloss on them. I wonder for a brief moment how they might look wrapped around my cock. I could use the distraction. This week has been...horrible.

A mother with two kids bumps into me while walking down the aisle, pulling me away from thoughts of my seatmate. She takes no notice and continues. I hear her yelling at the little boy who stops to look at every person already seated. I glare at him, and he runs forward.

I'm not in the mood for children. Hell, I'm not in the mood for anyone.

"Here you go," the flight attendant says as she sets our drinks down.

The woman next to me raises her glass to those sultry lips and I watch her drink. She glances out the window, ignoring me. Well, at least she won't bother me.

I drink my beverage. It's not exactly top-shelf liquor, but it works. I just want to get home and shower. I need to clean off this week physically and mentally.

My phone pings, and I glance down at it.

Mom: Did your father even come by the apartment?

I groan. I can hear her saying that in her Southern accent. An accent that I share, having spent most of my childhood in the South.

My grandfather died a week ago. My father should have come to clear out his apartment and attend the funeral, but instead, I got stuck doing it. My sister is eight months pregnant and couldn't make the trip. I seldom speak to my father since my parents divorced twenty years ago. He's an asshole. But his father was a great man. He would fly over to visit us every year and pay for us to come to visit him in the summers. I had so many good memories in Paris.

Me: No, Mom. Yvette is going to get the rest of the apartment cleaned out. I shipped the important stuff home, and the estate buyer came by yesterday and will get the expensive items picked up next week.

Yvette was my grandfather's caregiver for the past five years. I tried to offer her many items from my grandfather's home, but she wouldn't accept anything except an old typewriter that my grandfather liked to use when writing his books. Pierre Dumont, the famous mystery author, was no more. And more importantly, the only man I ever truly looked up to is now gone, nothing more than a distant memory. It still doesn't feel real.

"Good evening, ladies and gentlemen, this is your captain, Mark Tennison. We'll be pushing back from the gate shortly," the captain says.

"Can I take your glasses, please?" the flight attendant says.

"I'm not done yet," I state, not handing over the last of my drink.

"Sir, I can bring you another once we are in the air," she explains.

I glare at her before downing my drink and handing it to her.

I hear the woman next to me mutter something under her breath.

"Excuse me?" I ask turning to her.

"Nothing," she mutters and looks away from me. Oh, it's going to be like that. I sigh. I don't need this. Not now. Maybe I can find another seat once we're in the air. I look around, but there isn't one available seat. What the hell? Why are so many people wanting to go to New York of all places?

The flight crew secures the cabin and goes about the safety spiel as we start moving toward the runway. They dim the cabin lights, and we take off.

I watch France grow fainter as we climb into the sky. The woman next to me also looks out the window. I watch her throat constrict as she swallows. Her hand trembles slightly where she grips the armrest. She's nervous. I wonder why for a half second. It doesn't matter. What matters is figuring out a way to keep my mind from wandering for the next eight hours and thirty minutes. I wonder if they have any good movies available. I should have downloaded something onto my laptop. I glance down and freeze. In the woman's bag, sticking out of the side pocket is a book. *Lies, Suspicions, and Haunted Truths* by Pierre Dumont. Fuck. What are the odds? The *fasten seat belt* signs turn off and I watch as the flight attendants start working on getting things situated for what I assume is our soon-to-be-served meal.

"Good afternoon, again. Our expected flight time is eight hours and thirty minutes. We expect a smooth flight. So, sit back and enjoy," the captain says.

"Another drink?" the flight attendant asks.

I nod. "Same," I say. She nods and looks at the woman next to me.

"Yes, please," the woman says. "Can I have a Merlot?"

"Of course," the flight attendant states.

She leaves and the woman looks over at me. "Uh, do you mind if I...I need to use the restroom," she explains. I look over at her. Her cheeks are flushed.

I don't respond but pull my legs back to allow her to pass. She gets up, and as she stands, I catch a whiff of her perfume. Fuck. She smells good, really good. I lean into the aisle and watch her ass sway as she walks to the small corridor reserved for the first-class passengers' restrooms.

She opens a door and disappears. I use the opportunity to grab my laptop from the bag in the overhead compartment. I might as well get some work done. Maybe that can distract me for a hot minute from thinking about this shitty week, and from thinking inappropriate thoughts about my seatmate.

I'm just about to sit back down when she's standing in front of me. I motion for her to enter. She slides in and takes her seat. I sit and pull out my tray table, setting up my laptop as the flight attendant sets down our drinks.

"Would like chicken cordon bleu or steak for your meal?" she asks.

"I'll have the chicken," I state.

The woman next to me nods. "Same, please," she says.

I watch as she sips her Merlot and then reaches for the book, my grandfather's book. I return to reviewing my meeting notes for a while, until my eyes tire.

The plane shakes with some turbulence and I watch her clench her wineglass in one hand and the armrest with her other as she lets the book fall to her lap. Well, well, it appears that my irritating little seatmate is not a fan of flying. Something about that brings me a little joy.

I glance at her face, and I suddenly feel slightly guilty. She looks petrified. With another sigh, I decide to put my pain aside for a moment. My grandfather would want me to speak to a fan. I'll do this for him, but only for him.

"Is it a good book?" I ask.

The woman turns to me, wide-eyed, a look of shock on her face as if my speaking to her was more surprising than the existence of aliens or monsters.

"Oh, uh, yes. It is," she answers and looks away from me toward the window. There's nothing to look at now, just clouds, so I know she's ignoring me. But I also notice her hand isn't as clenched until the plane bounces a bit. All of a sudden, she grabs my arm that's lying on the armrest between us.

"Sorry, folks, we seem to have hit a pocket of air. I'm going to turn on the *fasten seat belt* sign for a minute if you can return to your seats," the captain says.

The woman's face pales.

"What's it about?" I ask, trying to distract her because quite frankly she looks green, and I don't want projectile vomit on this suit.

"Huh?" she asks, glancing at me with those big eyes again.

"The book," I say, motioning to it on her lap.

"Oh, it's a mystery. The author actually just passed away a few weeks ago. It's very sad. He was an amazing writer," she says. Her words hit me like a sucker punch. I nod as I try to focus on anything other than my grandfather's death.

I glance down at my arm where her hand grips it. Her gaze follows mine and she realizes she's gripping my arm. Mortification rolls over her features, and I have to fight the smirk that threatens my face.

"I'm sorry," she mutters, pulling her hand away as if my arm is suddenly made of lava.

I brush the fabric and look down at her. "It's fine. Not a fan of flying?"

She shrugs. "No," she finally admits.

"Bad flying experience?" I ask.

She swallows and shakes her head, looking around as if afraid someone else might hear her. I raise an inquisitive eyebrow. I watch as she considers her answer, but eventually, she speaks.

"My boyfriend was killed in a plane crash three years ago," she says.

Now, I'm the shocked one. Maybe there's more to this woman than I thought.

"I'm sorry to hear that," I say because I truly am. What a terrible way to go, I think.

She nods. "Thank you," she whispers so softly that I barely hear her.

"I take it you don't fly often, then?" I ask.

"No," she replies, her knuckles still gripping the armrest. This is going to be a long flight, but maybe distracting this slightly irritating beauty will be a good distraction from the thoughts I'd rather not have.

CHAPTER THREE

Is it him? Is that the same guy from the nightclub? I keep stealing glances at him as we interact. Trying to study his features without looking like I'm ogling him. The way he's acting, he probably thinks he's God's gift to women. I fight the overwhelming urge to roll my eyes.

"You should watch a movie," he suggests, pointing to the screens in front of us. The first class on this flight is nicer than other commercial flights I've taken. Our seats are cocooned by a wall, creating an element of privacy. Oddly, instead of a giant armrest table between our seats, there's an armrest that looks like it pushes down. I guess it's for if a couple wants to sleep side by side. The outside armrests have little tabletops where you can set a drink or phone. If Mr. High-and-Mighty stands up a bit and looks over the side wall toward the back, he can see the plane, but where I am, the wall behind us and in front of us keeps me out of view.

It's nice, except for my seatmate. Why couldn't I be stuck with the nice, normal-looking businesswoman two rows in front of us or the younger man who was a little cute but was still in college based on his dormitory identification card hanging from his wallet that he shoved into his bag while we waited to board the aircraft?

Nope. Lucky me gets Mr. Charmer here.

"I might just take a nap," I state, deciding sleep is the best route to forgetting I'm inside a pressurized tube sailing through the sky at an altitude that rivals Mount Everest.

"Well, then, I'll leave you to it," he says, his Southern drawl peeking through again.

Under normal circumstances, I might find that accent charming, but with him, I find it annoying. And I swear he lays it on thicker just to piss me off even more.

I grunt a response and put my book away. I take the blanket and semi-awful pillow offered to me by the flight attendant and turn away from the man.

The seat belt signs turn off and I lower my seat into a bed position and turn on my side, attempting to ignore my seatmate and also to try to avoid breathing in his cologne. It's like the universe has a sense of humor or something. Let's have Paris, the woman who hates flying, be forced to sit next to a total dick, but let's make that asshole super-hot, sort of nice in an asshole sort of way, oh, and make sure he smells good! I groan and pull the blanket up higher as if it will shield me from him.

I try to sleep. I count sheep. I replay in my mind the most boring show I watched on television recently. I try to figure out if I should paint my bedroom wall grass green, mint green, or hunter green. I remember nice moments from grad school...followed immediately by Mr. Asswipe's doppelganger getting me kicked out of the club last week. Ugh! I'm never going to get any sleep.

"Nightcap?" the flight attendant practically purrs. I know she's speaking to Mr. Hottie Asshat. I sit up and turn toward her.

"Can I have a vodka, straight up?" I ask, frowning as I wonder if that's a thing.

"Sure, miss," she says, giving me a small smile before turning back to my nameless seatmate.

"Scotch, neat," he says.

"Of course, Mr. Dumont," she says and walks away. Dumont...Dumont...wait, just like Pierre Dumont. What a strange coincidence! I guess it's not an unpopular last name. I begin to wonder if his family's French. Maybe he was visiting them from...Baton Rouge? Nashville? I'm horrible at placing Southern accents.

I give up on my sleep idea and reach back for my book. I might as well read for a while, that usually calms me down.

I feel him watching me and I turn toward the window. I pull out a small clip-on book light for reading and place it on the book since the aircraft's overhead lights have been dimmed.

I read for a while, and finally, after drinking the vodka and finishing five chapters, I feel a little groggy. I'm just about to lay my head down to go to sleep when the plane rattles again, listing a little from one side to the other and then bouncing violently up and down.

Mr. Dumont places a hand over my hip, pressing me to the now horizontal chair as if to keep me from moving. His other hand calmly holds his scotch. I glance over my shoulder at him.

"It's fine. Just a little turbulence," he assures me. The seat belt sign turns back on, and its bright red beacon might as well be the morning sun because I've lost any will to sleep. My nerves are frayed once again.

"How's the book?" he asks, motioning to where it still sits on the reclined chair.

"It's good," I say with a sigh.

"Just good?"

I turn and push my seat back up a little so I'm not lying down any longer. He releases his hand from my hip. "It's very good."

I pause biting my tongue, but my curiosity gets the better of me. "You have the same last name as the author."

He nods. "That I do," he states as if I'm an idiot for not knowing it.

"Have we met before?" I ask.

He looks at me. "Maybe?" He shrugs.

"You just look like some guy who was being an asshole to me at this club last week," I say.

His eyebrows rise and I see a knowing look.

"It was you," I state.

He shrugs. "I was wondering the same about you. To be fair, you shouldn't have been in the VIP section."

He's not wrong, but that's beside the point. I glare at him. He looks unfazed by this information. Wait until I tell Megan. Megan is one of my sorority sisters from college who happened to be visiting when we got kicked out of the VIP section. She was not a fan of my new acquaintance. I decide not to mention all the names she called him.

I don't continue with this discussion because I feel like I'm going to make a fool of myself. I'd never admit my friend dared me to get into the VIP section to find some celebrity we saw in there.

"So...business or pleasure?" I ask and immediately press my lips together. Why did I even ask that? Why do I care? This guy's an idiot. I shouldn't give a shit about him. No, it's fine. I can ask questions. If I'm asking questions about him, he won't be able to ask me questions because he'll be too busy being a pompous asshole and talking about himself, plus it'll distract me from my current life predicament of having to spend time with my father.

"Neither," he answers, taking another sip of scotch.

"Oh," I reply. Neither. What's the third option? Alien abduction?

"What about you?" he says.

"Uh, well, I guess sort of business...school," I reply.

"You're in college?" he asks, almost as if I said I was a clown on the weekends.

"No. I *was* in grad school. I graduated," I state dryly.

"Oh, uh, congratulations," he says.

I try to stop the eye roll, I really do, but it happens involuntarily, or at least that's what I tell myself.

"What?" he asks, narrowing his eyes.

"You're not very nice," I state.

His eyebrows shoot up in surprise. "I'm sorry, what?"

OK. Pissing him off makes him a little hotter for some weird-ass reason, but also, this is entertaining. Maybe I can spend the next six hours pushing all his buttons.

"You were rude to the woman at the gate. And you treat the flight attendant like a servant. I thought people from the South had manners."

At my last comment, his lips twitch as if he's fighting a smile. "I thought grad students had common sense," he retorts.

"I do," I say.

"So, picking fights with strangers seems a safe option for you?"

I glare at him. "It's an entertaining option," I reply. I lick my lips and his eyes drop to watch my tongue dart out.

He laughs and I hate that I like the sound of it. He has a nice voice, but his laugh is like a warm fire on a cold day. I feel myself relax a little, even though his responses should have me anything but relaxed.

"Do you have a job lined up?" he asks, switching the topic.

"I do," I reply.

"What's that?"

"I'm working with an editor at a publishing house," I state.

"Oh? Which one?" he asks.

"A big one," I reply, deciding that I'm not telling this man any details. What if he's some crazy stalker? Or maybe he hates me so much he'd pull his rich-guy strings to get me fired.

His lips twitch again. "Very well. We'll keep this casual. The spring semester ended a while ago for schools in Paris. Why were you staying there?" he asks.

Damn. He's smart.

"I had some items to check off on my bucket list," I explain.

"Is that so?"

"It is."

He leans forward. "Tell me about this bucket list, fougueuse."

Did he just call me a "feisty one"?

CHAPTER FOUR

RIVER

SHE'S GIVING me a look that says, why are you talking to me? Why *am* I talking to her? I have no idea but she's intriguing to me, and I'm essentially being held captive next to her for six more hours.

"*You* want to hear about my bucket list?" she asks with a little air of attitude in her voice that makes me want to do dirty things to her. Dirty things? Fuck. I clearly need to get laid. It's been months.

"Yes," I reply. I bring the glass of scotch back to my lips and she watches my throat as I swallow. I smirk, she's just as affected by me. Interesting.

She cocks her head to one side as she adjusts herself in her seat as if she's considering whether she'll humor me or not. She reaches up and pulls her hair out of the messy bun on top of her head. Long wavy locks cascade over her shoulders. Holy fuck! My hands itch to touch it, to rub strands of it between my fingers, to take some in my hand and yank her head back, giving me access to that slender neck of hers. I squirm in my seat as I feel my cock coming to attention. These are going to be a long six hours.

She runs her hands through her hair and pulls it back up into a new messy bun on top of her head. It doesn't help things because she only looks more like a sexy librarian, or at least what I envision a sexy librarian to look like.

"I still have about eight things to do," she admits with a shrug.

"How many things did you have on this list?" I ask as I lean back in my seat. The flight attendant sets down our meals which took fucking forever to bring.

I nod and Miss Smartypants here thanks her.

She grabs a carrot from her dinner tray and dips it in a sauce, bringing it to her plump lips and biting into it. It's like my own cabaret show, only she doesn't realize how sexy each and every movement she makes is.

"Fifteen," she says.

"What's left on the list?"

She takes a bite of her chicken and then looks back toward me. "Stuff."

I give her a pointed look and she sighs. Then it's like a lightbulb goes off and she looks at me in a way that I can't read. Is she going to tell me or leave me hanging?

"There are a few places left in the world that I'd like to see," she says.

"Such as?"

"The Taj Mahal. Angel Falls. Antarctica...for the penguins mostly. And I want to snorkel with whale sharks in New Caledonia," she begins.

"You'll like Antarctica," I state.

Her eyes widen. "You've been there?"

I nod. "I have. I went a few years ago," I say. Sadness washes over me. It was my grandfather's last big trip. He'd wanted to go his entire life, and five years ago he called me and said he had booked us an adventure. I was hesitant to go, but it ended up being the best week we'd ever had together. And now...I'm so glad I went. Those are memories I can never replace.

"Did you see lots of penguins?" she asks. It's like her entire body language has morphed into something else. Her excitement is adorable.

"Yes. Adélie, gentoo, and chinstrap," I say.

Her eyes gleam with curiosity. "That's so cool!" she squeals in delight. "Did you get to go right up to them?"

I shake my head. "You have to stay fifteen feet away. Although on one island I did have one come up to me. I had to wait thirty minutes for it to leave before I could continue my hike," I explain.

She smiles and it transforms her entire face. She's back to being sexy as fuck. We both eat in silence for a few moments.

"What else is on this list?" I ask, breaking the pause in our conversation.

She pulls her blanket up around her and I wonder if she's cold. I had placed my blanket over my lap, and I hold up the edge toward her. "You want some of mine?" I ask.

She looks surprised by my offer. "Uh, sure. It's very cold in here," she says as I take half of my blanket and place it over her lap.

"Better?" I ask once she's covered.

She nods. "So, what else?"

"I want to be an extra in a movie," she says.

I raise an eyebrow.

"I know it's silly, but I think it would be fun to experience it," she admits. "And it'd be cool to be watching a movie with my friends and then be like, oh, look, there I am." She giggles.

"You wouldn't tell anyone if you did it?" I ask.

She shrugs. "I don't think so. Maybe."

She pauses and finishes the last of her veggies and some of her chicken as the flight attendant comes by to collect them. The flight attendant refers to us by our names. Ms. Garrison is apparently the name of my seatmate.

When we are alone, I ask the obvious question.

"I'm River, by the way. River Dumont. And you are?"

"Paris Garrison," she says. She looks at me and gives a small laugh as she glances back at my grandfather's book. "I still think it's funny you share the same name."

I shrug, deciding I don't want to divulge that secret. Not yet anyhow.

"I think it's funny that you're named after our departure city," I counter.

She giggles. "Apparently...that's where I was made," she says, her voice lowering at the last part. I smile at her, and she grins back at me. Fuck, she's adorable.

I give her another look to urge her to continue.

"I want to go sleep under the stars somewhere where you can see the northern lights," she says. "Like, an impromptu night where I just get in my car with a friend, and we head out toward Maine or Canada or something and lie in the back of an old pickup truck and watch the sky erupt in greens."

There are two more items. So far, her list seems pretty straightforward. No big surprises. I'm guessing she's maybe twenty-three or twenty-four. It's a list of a young adult. Someone who is just starting to experience the world on their own. I probably had a similar list at her age but I'm a solid fourteen-plus years older than her. I've seen a lot more of the world and my list is much more fine-tuned. There are very specific places I want to visit now, specific restaurants I want to dine at, and the only experience I have left is to meet the one. I'd never admit that to my friends, who all applaud me for my wealthy bachelor lifestyle, but secretly, I'd like to settle down. I've built a massive marketing firm that specializes in book and movie launches. I've seen all the major things I want to see. I've done all the major things I want to do. And all before I turn forty. But the perfect woman...she's been elusive.

She curls up in her seat, tucking her legs beneath her. "I want to go skydiving," she says.

"It's exhilarating," I state.

"What haven't you done?" she asks with a laugh.

"I think I have a few more years on me than you do, so I've made the most of my time," I explain.

"Good for you. Carpe diem," she says.

There's one thing left on the list and I'm dying to know what it is. Does she want to meet a famous person? Does she want to go deep sea diving? Maybe she's interested in being on one of those private flights to space.

"Last one," I say quietly.

She blushes and now my curiosity is piqued.

"Uh-huh," she whispers.

"Don't leave me hanging. What's this last item?" I ask.

Her blush deepens.

I lean forward. "Don't lie. I'll know if you're lying."

She rolls her eyes. "How? You don't even know me."

I reach out and just barely touch her cheek. "Your skin gives you away."

She huffs. "Fine, but don't laugh."

I nod and she takes a deep breath. "Swear you won't laugh?"

I hold up my fingers in a Boy Scout salute. "I promise."

She giggles. "Fine. Mile high club."

My eyebrows shoot up. "What?" I say a little loudly.

She reaches out and clamps a hand over my mouth. "Shhhh," she hushes me.

I peel her hand away from my mouth when really, I want to lick it. I want to lick her everywhere. My little feisty one also has a dirty mind. I'm beginning to like her. Much more than I should.

"As in *the* mile high club?" I confirm.

Nodding, she blushes again. "Yes."

"Why haven't you done that before?" I glance at her designer clothes and expensive bag. She's clearly someone who has access to money. I bet she's been on a private jet before.

She shrugs. "I've only flown with family and friends before now. And none of those times were situations where it was possible...so..." She trails off.

"What would this mile high club entail?" I coax because she has one hundred percent of my attention now, my attention and my cock's attention.

"You're not going to laugh at me?" she inquires.

"Paris, I promise not to laugh," I state.

"I...I mean the ultimate would be a private jet with a bedroom, but otherwise...I have this uh, fantasy," she starts.

I motion for her to keep going.

"I meet a stranger." Check. "And we end up seated together on a flight." Check. "And he turns out to be really wonderful." Maybe check. "And a few hours into the flight when everyone is sleeping, and the cabin lights are off... he..." She blushes and I lean forward.

"He what?" I whisper close enough to smell her perfume again. I note that we are over two hours into our flight now and they just turned down the lights to allow passengers to sleep.

"He places his hand on my thigh," she whispers back.

"Like this?" I ask as I place my hand on her thigh, my pinky finger dangerously close to the heat of her sex.

"Uh-huh," she breathes.

"And then what?"

"Then we keep talking, but his fingers...start massaging me..." She sucks in a breath as I begin rubbing circles with my fingers.

"And then?"

"And then he moves his hand under the blanket I have over my lap." I comply and move my hand under the blanket while pulling closed the privacy curtain next to me. This flight just got a whole lot more interesting.

She whimpers a little as my hand moves closer to the apex of her thighs. She's so warm here and my cock does a little twitch at the mere thought of being buried between her legs. Fuck, if only she knew the things, she was doing to me right now.

"And?" I coax.

"And then slowly, he plays with the hem of my pants," she goes on, her eyelids drifting closed as I run a finger along the top hem of her yoga pants. They are loose and could be easily pushed down her legs.

This time she goes on. "And then he slides them inside my panties and...you know," she says as her face heats once more.

I lean forward. "No, feisty one, I don't know. But I think I'm going to like what you say next," I reply as I whisper against her face that's only inches from mine. "I think I'm going to like it very much."

CHAPTER FIVE

WHAT AM I DOING? I hated this man two hours ago. I loathed him. He was the embodiment of everything I hate. Arrogant. Entitled. Cruel.

And now? Now, I'm about to tell him to do something so intimate that only two men have ever done it to me. One of them was Alec. The memories of Alec's skin against mine still seem fresh in my mind even though it's been years. I shouldn't remember how it feels to be touched. I shouldn't remember how it feels to be kissed. But the memories seem to linger as if they are some cruel form of punishment. I had thought maybe Alec was the one. He had whispered sweet promises of giving me a life I wish I had. He had said those three little words I craved to hear. And then he'd taken up his Cessna. A gift from his father. He'd taken me for countless rides. I'd never once been afraid of planes until that day. The investigators on the crash site said it was a microburst. The winds had shifted suddenly. The turbulence had been strong. The plane had been low. And the mountain range had been high. The perfect storm, quite literally. A pilot friend who had tried to comfort me at the funeral said it was a one-in-a-million chance of hitting a storm like that right as he was climbing in altitude to go over the Appalachian Mountains. His small plane didn't stand a chance against Mother Nature's volatile force.

Since then, flying had become nearly unbearable. Private jets were better because there wasn't a chance of screaming babies or yelling passengers, but no plane felt safe...not anymore.

So here I was, struggling to ignore my current location by distracting myself with the man next to me. I wouldn't have so much as given him the time of day normally, but perhaps, for a few minutes or hours, I could use him to keep my mind off things I'd rather not think about.

"Paris," River whispers. He makes a tsking noise as if scolding me for taking so long and something about that thrills me. The fact is that it does feel wrong, yet I crave more of it. He slides two fingers back and forth over the joining of my skin and panties, teasing me, and taunting me.

I swallow. "He...he slides his hand between my belly and panties," I whisper in a barely audible voice.

He takes a single finger and presses it beneath the waistband of my underwear. I lean my chair back a little, my body nearly horizontal now, my legs raised slightly in the leg rest that pops up from beneath the seat. His finger pauses, waiting for my instruction and another thrill zaps through me. I like this power. He's like my own personal sex toy, doing what I say, how I say.

"And he slowly slides his fingers down between my legs," I continue.

River's fingers slide down and cup my sex. I blush. He has to feel how wet I am, but he doesn't make a sound or facial expression to let on.

"And then...he takes a single finger and slides it between my folds."

I feel one long, thick finger slide back and forth, separating my folds.

The only tell he has indicating that he's affected by me is his clenching jaw.

"He circles my...my clit," I say in a hushed voice, so low that I'm not sure he heard it until he follows my direction. My eyelids fall shut again for a long second as I feel his finger, slick with need, circling my clit, over and over.

"Then, he runs it down to my entrance," I continue.

His finger pauses over my vagina and slowly moves farther back toward a place that has not been touched before. My eyelids fly open.

He smirks. "You'll need to be more specific," he jests.

I narrow my eyes and his eyes light up with amusement. What. A. Dick.

"The vaginal one...you jackass," I hiss.

His smirk stays as he pulls his finger back toward the correct opening. He sinks it slowly inside me, but only up to the first knuckle.

"He pushes it all the way inside me," I demand.

River's finger pulls out a little and then painfully slowly pushes inside me until it can't go any farther.

"He...he starts fucking me with his finger."

River's smirk dissipates as he follows the order, his large digit moving in and out of me. I let my legs fall open. River pauses and gets his chair in a reclining position. He uses his free hand to move my right leg onto his leg rest, spreading me farther open for him. Then he goes back to fucking me with his finger.

"He adds a second finger," I state. River pulls his single finger and runs two fingers back and forth through my wet folds before sinking them both inside me. Shit! He's stretching me to the point of burning but it feels so good.

"He curls his fingers and finds my G-spot," I say as my cheeks heat once more. He complies and I let my eyes drift closed again. Fuck, he's good at this. So good. Like he's done this a million times. Hell, maybe he has. But I guess that's in my favor because if he keeps this up, I'm going to come like a freight train in a matter of seconds.

"He presses his thumb to my clit, and starts circling it," I say through gritted teeth. He does as I say, and I feel myself climbing.

My breaths are coming fast.

"He tells me to come for him," I whisper.

River leans toward me. His lips against my ear. I feel his hot breath on my skin. "Come for me, Paris. Right fucking now," he commands. And that's all it takes. I splinter into a million freaking pieces. My mouth falls open on a silent cry as my body trembles, my inner muscles clamping down on his fingers in rhythmic, fluttering clenches.

He doesn't stop and only slows after I feel my body relax.

"Now what, feisty one?" he asks. His breath is ragged. His body is tense.

I consider the logistics of how we are lying. I have a single condom in my bag. My "just in case" condom that I never use. With his fingers still buried in my pussy, I eye my bag pocket and squirm to reach it. I manage to get it open and pull out the small foil square, dropping it on the blanket. His eyes widen a bit in surprise, but then in the dim light, I swear they darken.

"He pulls his fingers from me, licking them before he takes my hand and places it over his dick, showing me how hard he is for me," I challenge. River doesn't miss a beat. He pulls his fingers from me, and he brings them to his mouth and sucks my juices from them. His eyes close for a long moment as if savoring it.

"Holy shit, that was hot," I whisper. He takes my hand and places it on his cock, and I know my eyes must widen because he's back to smirking. This man is huge. How's this possibly going to work? I run my hand up and down his erection, feeling him through the fabric of his pants.

His eyelids flicker for a moment and I know he likes it.

"Then he pushes my pants down and turns me to my side, away from him," I instruct.

He follows suit.

"Then he pulls out his dick and puts the condom on," I continue. I don't even hear his zipper. He's in stealth mode. The only way I know he's done it is the feel of his erection against my bare ass cheeks under the blanket. It's a little awkward since our chairs don't touch flush against each other. But somehow, he manages.

"What's next, feisty one?" he asks.

"He runs his cock between my wet folds before slowly pushing inside me," I whisper. River pushes my top leg forward a bit, reaching for his pillow and tucking it beneath my leg so it's propped up a bit. Then he takes his time running his cock through my wet heat before the enlarged head catches at my opening. He nudges forward just a little, giving me hope that maybe it won't burn. That only lasts a moment as he pushes all the way inside me.

The breath leaves my lungs in a whoosh. My last coherent thought is asking myself what the hell am I doing? I'm literally having sex on a commercial plane with a complete stranger.

"Does he fuck you fast or slow?" he whispers against my ear.

"Slow," I say, afraid of what this man could do if he went fast.

He complies and begins moving slowly. He's so big that he fills every inch of me. The ridge of his cock feels so good as he pushes in and out of me. We both still when we hear movement from someone seated near us. His cock twitches inside me and I stifle a groan. His hand clamps around my mouth to keep me quiet, and after a moment, he starts again, but he keeps his hand on my lips. He takes his time building my next climax, but when it comes, it hits like a tsunami. My whole body convulses and shakes and I feel his cock begin to twitch inside me, his strokes become uneven, and then as I fall over the edge, I feel him slam home once more and stay there, the only sign he's coming is the spams of his cock in my pussy and the way his hand goes from clamping over my mouth to squeezing my breast as his muscles strain against me.

There is no way a stranger-slash-asshole of a man just gave me the best orgasm of my life while indoctrinating me into the mile high club.

CHAPTER SIX

IT PHYSICALLY PAINS me to pull out of her. I feel a little guilty as I do. I hear her wince and something inside me wants to soothe her. I wish we had rooms with locks on them. I wish I could properly do all the things my mouth and hands are itching to do, but there's no space for that here.

I grab a napkin I stuck in the seat pocket and dispose of the used condom before quietly zipping up my pants. I reach back under her blanket and help her pull her panties and yoga pants back up her legs. I can't help myself as I slip my hand between her legs once more, feeling how wet she is makes me wish we had more condoms and more time.

She places her hand over mine, keeping it where she wants it. I slide two of my fingers inside her and slowly bring her to orgasm one last time. She grips my hand, riding it with small movements and then clenching when she comes.

When she releases me, I pull away and suck her juices off my digits. She rolls over to face me.

"Was the mile high club everything you hoped it would be, feisty one?" I ask as I brush a lock of hair away from her face.

She smiles shyly before answering. "Yes," she says in a low raspy voice that has my cock wishing to be back inside of her.

"I need to use the bathroom," she says. We raise our seats, and she climbs over me and pushes back the curtain. She looks over her shoulder at me as she stands in the aisle. The only lights on in the cabin, illuminating her silhouette. She looks like an angel, and I know I'll remember this moment for the rest of my life. She turns and heads to the bathroom. I adjust myself in my pants and grab the bottle of water I placed in my bag. Taking a sip of it, I realize I know nothing about this woman I just fucked. What's her story? Do I want to know? A part of me wants to just let it go. Leave this as a great story I tell the guys when we have drinks. Another part of me wants to not tell a soul and just let it be my little secret, one memory just for me. But a third part of me wants to continue what I started here. This woman is stubborn and irritating, but she's also interesting and funny. She has wit and beauty. She's a rare breed of human and I find that fascinating as fuck.

A movement draws my attention. She's standing by the curtain. She has the bottom of her shirt rolled up oddly. She lifts a leg over me and closes the curtain. I pull her down onto my lap so she's straddling me.

"What have we got here?" I ask.

She grins and unrolls her shirt to reveal six little bottles of alcohol.

"I didn't know which type you might like, besides scotch, of course," she says with a shrug.

"How'd you get these?" I ask.

She shrugs and then smirks.

I tickle her a little and she squirms on my lap. "You naughty woman," I scold.

She giggles. She takes the vodka one and opens it, handing me its twin bottle. I open mine and she clinks our bottles together. "To popping mile high cherries," she says quietly.

"To meeting gorgeous, interesting seatmates," I offer.

She raises an eyebrow. "What? Not irritating seatmates?" she asks.

I lean up and nuzzle my nose alongside hers. "That too," I breathe.

I pull back a little to bring the bottle to my lips. She mirrors me and we both toss back the drinks.

She slides off my lap and I miss her immediately. She plops into her seat and buckles up, pulling the blanket back over her legs.

She grabs the tequila bottles next, handing one to me.

"Let's play a game," she suggests.

"What game are we playing?" I ask.

"Never have I ever," she states.

"Explain it," I demand.

"I'll start. You're smart, you'll figure it out."

I glare at her.

"Never have I ever had sex on a plane," she says.

She takes a drink and motions for me to drink.

"So you drink if you have done something?" I confirm.

She nods.

"Never have I ever come from being given oral sex," I state, drinking my drink. She doesn't drink hers.

"Really?" I ask.

She shakes her head.

"Maybe we'll need to resolve that issue," I insist, licking my lips.

"River...no way. There's no room," she hisses as she looks around us.

I frown. "You're ruining all my fun."

She rolls her eyes.

"Never have I ever had a threesome," she says, not bringing the bottle to her mouth.

I take another shot.

"What? Seriously?" she asks.

I nod and shrug. "It was college. I was bored and...the ladies liked me."

"Figures," she says as she glares at me.

"Never have I ever met a movie star," I state.

We both drink. I'm not shocked at all. She looks like she comes from money. And in the States, that probably means she's run in circles with at least one celebrity.

"Never have I ever dated a famous person," she says.

She takes a sip and I raise an eyebrow.

"My high school boyfriend was in a band that's pretty well known. My dad hated it and him," she explains.

I laugh. "How old are you?"

"Twenty-four."

"How old are you?"

"Thirty-eight," I say.

Her eyes widen. "Damn, maybe I should be calling *you* Daddy," she says with a smirk.

My cock jumps to attention. "Cute. How long have you had daddy issues?" I ask.

This time she blushes and looks away. Well, damn, didn't mean to hit that nail on the head quite so hard.

I place my hand on her leg. "Hey, sorry, I didn't mean to...is he alive?" I ask.

She nods and I see her wipe a tear. Fuck. I hate that I made her cry. "He's just a dick," she explains.

I tighten my squeeze on her leg and then loosen it when I realize what I'm doing. "He doesn't...hurt you, does he?" I hiss through gritted teeth as I feel my anger boiling.

She shakes her head. "No, not physically. He's just a jerk," she clarifies.

I visibly relax. "Good. I was worried I might have to go home and beat the shit out of him for you," I state.

She grins. "Feel free. But it's more my mean stepmom that could use an ass kicking."

"Sorry. Do you live with them?"

"No, not really. I just am staying there for a few weeks until my apartment is ready," she explains and then yawns.

I take her little bottle and place it with the others in my bag's pocket. "I think we should try to sleep a little," I say.

She frowns. "But we only have like a few hours left," she whines as she fights another yawn. My feisty one is tired, and quite frankly, so am I.

I place a hand on her leg again. "I know. Come on," I encourage.

She sighs and leans her chair back again, rolling to her side. I do the same, spooning her, my hand on her hip as we fall asleep.

"WE'RE ON OUR FINAL DESCENT INTO NEW YORK." THE FLIGHT ATTENDANT'S voice wakes me.

"Please bring your seatbacks up to their full upright position. We'll be coming around the cabin one last time to hand out customs forms. And to collect any trash."

Paris stirs and sits up, raising her arms in the air, she stretches like a cat.

"Did you get some sleep?" I ask.

She nods and rubs her eyes. "Did we miss the food?" she asks as she looks around.

"I think so," I state. I reach into my bag and offer her one of the granola bars I'd grabbed at the airport. She accepts it and we eat in silence while filling out our customs cards.

As the plane lists a little to one side, she reaches out and grabs my hand. I hold hers tightly, giving it a reassuring squeeze. After placing my wrapper and card into my bag's pocket, I take my other hand and place it over our joined hands, rubbing small circles on the back of hers. I feel her relax a little. The flight attendant comes through and pulls back our curtain, eyeing our joined hands before moving on. I honestly don't care what the woman thinks.

The plane descends and the tires hit the tarmac. She gives a little jump and tightens her grip as the pilot applies the brakes.

When we make it to the gate, I wait for her to walk in front of me. She takes my hand again as we make our way to customs. We grab our bags. When we get there, I look at the Global Entry line and the other line where she's walking. Cursing, I decide to wait with her. I'll get at least thirty more minutes with her. We don't speak as we inch closer to the front of the line. Her grip stays strong on mine. My thumb continues drawing little circles on her hand.

When we finally get to the front, I look down at her and release her hand. "This is where I leave you, feisty one," I say.

She gives me a sad smile.

"Next in line," a TSA agent says.

I turn to her. "Go ahead." She steps away from me, but as she looks back, I smile.

"Pierre was my grandfather," I state.

Her eyes widen. "Seriously? You're telling me that now?"

I laugh and shrug. She rolls her eyes but pauses as realization washes over her. She realizes why I was in Paris. She gives me a sad smile and waves to me as she shuffles toward the open window and the passport-control agent waiting on her.

I get called next, and by the time I finish, I don't see her. I walk to a waiting car, feeling a little sad that I only got that one night with her. But it was definitely a night that I'll never forget.

PARIS

"PARIS, how's everything going? Are you settling in alright?" my new boss, Heidi Mason, asks.

"Yes. It's been a great week," I reply as I follow her toward a conference room where we're meeting with the team working on this new book her favorite client is releasing in six months. I barely survived the two weeks at Dad's house. Bridgit, his wife, was nearly murdered by me no less than a dozen times. I practically sprinted to the city when my apartment was ready.

Now that I'm working though, everything is better. I'm no longer in his house. I'm so busy that I haven't had time to think about River. Fine, that's a lie. I've thought about him every night as I fall asleep, wishing his hand was on my hip and his warm chest against my back. I've been so tempted to search for him online, but I feel like we made some sort of silent agreement, an agreement to keep that night to ourselves and never look back. Easier said than done. Tomorrow I'm going clubbing with some friends, so maybe I can meet someone and forget about Mr. Mile High Club.

"You're going to love the team. I gathered all our best people for this book launch. We have all the best line and content editors and wait till you meet our marketing team. They are seriously amazing. I've worked with them on my last six big launches, and they all hit the top ten," Heidi says as her heels click on the tile floor.

"Wow. That's great," I say enthusiastically. Internally, I'm just hoping they aren't jerks. Because I know as Heidi's assistant, I'm going to be the one stuck working with them the most.

"Oh, can you grab that poster? I left it on my side table," Heidi says as she looks through the items in her arms.

"Sure," I state, spinning on my heels and walking briskly back to the far end of the floor to her office. I find the poster in record time and power walk back through cubicles and corridors to the conference room. This place is giant. It takes up three whole floors of this high-rise building. I swear I've gotten lost at least five times this week.

My fingers itch again to search for River online as I wonder if he works somewhere like this or if he's a doctor or a lawyer or maybe a professor. I'm stewing over the options as I rearrange the items in my arms and push the door open to the conference room. My heel gets caught in the small divot in the floor likely caused by the locking mechanism and I go sailing onto my knees, the poster and my laptop skidding across the floor.

"Crap," I hiss as I reach for my laptop, hoping I didn't break it on day six at the office.

"Are you alright?" I hear Heidi say. A few people ask the same thing.

"I'm fine. Just my pride," I mutter as I continue to pick up the items. But as I reach for the poster, a hand closes over mine. My body goes rigid. I know that hand. I'd know that hand anywhere. I've dreamt about it for a solid month now.

"Are you alright, Paris?" his deep voice asks. I finally gather the courage to look up and I'm greeted by a very concerned-looking River.

"Uh, y-yeah," I stammer.

He gets to his feet and holds out his hand to help me up. I accept it, and the moment our hands join, I swear I feel an electric current. Was that there before?

"You sure?" he asks as he pulls up a chair for me.

"I'm sure," I squeak.

"Good," he replies, taking the seat next to mine.

"Oh. Do you know each other?" Heidi asks, giving me a surprised look.

I feel the color rushing to my cheeks.

"We met on a flight back from Paris a few weeks ago," River says, giving me a wink.

"Wow, what a small world!" Heidi exclaims.

"Well, this will make things so much easier since you two are already acquainted," she says.

Oh, Heidi, you have no idea how much we are acquainted, I think. I glance over and River raises an eyebrow as if he can read my mind.

"Let's get this meeting started," Cameron, Heidi's boss, says, and all our attention goes to the end of the table as the discussion begins.

I glance over periodically to find River watching me. Each time, I blush and look away quickly as if I was caught doing something naughty. When the meeting ends, Heidi comes over to me with River next to her.

"River's firm keeps an office here for late nights. I'll have River show you where, so you'll know where to find him," she says.

"Oh, uh, great," I say. River holds out a hand, motioning for me to walk in front of him. I step into the hall, and he steers me down some corridors and up a flight of stairs. When we get to the door to the next floor, he places a hand on it to keep me from opening it. He leans in so his front is against my back.

"I've been thinking of you nonstop for four weeks, Paris," he admits, his breath hot against my ear.

"Same," I admit, not looking back because I know I'm blushing.

I know he's grinning without looking at him. He's such a cocky asshole. But damn it if that doesn't make me want him even more. He leans closer, brushing my hair over my shoulder. "Is office sex on your bucket list?" he asks.

I laugh and spin around to face him. "It is now, Mr. Dumont. It is now."

The End

YOU CAN READ MORE ABOUT PARIS'S FRIEND, MEGAN, IN RELUCTANTLY Perfect. Check out the link on the next page for more details.

ABOUT THE AUTHOR

USA Today & International Bestselling romance author, S.E. Rose lives near Washington D.C. with her family.

When she's not wrangling her cats or keeping up with her kids, she's plotting her next story.

She loves all things wine, coffee, and cats.

In her non-existent free time, she enjoys traveling, going to concerts, binging on her favorite shows, and reading, especially if it's a good mystery or comedy.

Check out more books by S.E.Rose and sign-up for her newsletter to hear about her next release and the crazy antics of her cats and family.

https://www.seroseauthor.com

HEARTTHROB

S.M. West

$$\overline{}$$

JANE

$$\overline{}$$

A JARRING CACKLE of laughter that sounds like a pack of nipping toy dogs rushes into the elevator with me. Three chattering women follow, lanyards around two of their necks, all their gaits off-kilter.

Great, the women are drunk or well on their way. I back up and try to put as much distance as possible between us. My back hits the elevator wall as the doors slide together, shutting out the hotel lobby. Undeterred or oblivious to my presence, the women yammer on about alpha males and their favorite fictional heroes. This is the last thing I need. Can't a girl catch a break and wallow alone?

Huddling in the corner of the elevator, I cling to my oversized bag and try to ignore what they're talking about. Involuntarily, I flinch whenever a woman sighs blissfully while another waxes poetically about abs, orgasms, and romance.

Kill me now.

I swipe at the corner of my eye and a black smudge of mascara now coats my finger. It's too late to salvage my make-up, my dignity, and at this point, my life.

The mirrored walls taunt me. There's no getting around the feral raccoon staring back at me. My dark hair is a tangled disaster and the remains of my red lipstick bleed beyond the edges of my mouth. At least my dress still looks amazing, but it isn't enough to cover the scars left by the night's events.

I'm a literal mess.

My reflection makes me want to revive my crying marathon. The very one I'd just had to choke back before approaching the front desk of the Vivaldi, a ritzy hotel in Houston.

There's nothing more humbling than begging for a room at nearly midnight on a Friday with only the clothes on your back. A life in pieces.

Unfortunately, the super attentive hotel clerk, Manuel, remembered me from when we checked in only days ago.

Lucky me.

He knew I already had a room and said as much. How did I explain that I'd rather eat glass than stay in that room?

Manuel vehemently impressed upon me that the hotel was fully booked, and he couldn't help me. The Vivaldi is abuzz this first week in November, one of their busiest months, with a romance authors' conference—I'm pretty sure the women in the elevator are here for that—a wedding, and final championship game in baseball.

That's why I was here. I'm with the out of town team, the Philadelphia Flashes, and we're all staying at the hotel. To think, I was beyond excited to come this weekend. On top of the world, even.

Ugh. The fall was long and bumpy, and I'll definitely have bruises.

Despite all that, the clerk came through and put me in one of the presidential suites. We were both surprised it was available, and I didn't even want to know how much it would cost, but that wasn't my problem.

Monty will think of me when he gets his hefty credit card statement.

Choke on that, asshole. Though it hardly scratches the surface of all the bullshit and heartache he's put me through over the years, and I'm only twenty.

How pathetic is that?

I suppose things can't get any worse, can they?

A hoot from the blonde woman only feet away causes me to snap out of my pity party. Enough. It all worked out. I have a room.

The elevator dings as the doors slide open, the women amble out, and one of them glances back at me, smiling. "Have a good night."

I should keep my mouth shut—my predicament has nothing to do with them—but I can't help myself.

"Good luck, ladies. You've got your work cut out for you." My finger hovers over the button to close the doors as they spin to face me. "Romance is dead."

One woman gasps and another sputters and the bright, blushing joy falls from their faces. They look at me like I just killed their dog, and the elevator doors close.

Regret pinches at my chest, and I rest my head against the cool glass wall. I'm not usually rude to strangers unless they have it coming, and these women didn't. They were minding their own business, but my bitterness got the better of me. Yet I feel like someone had to tell them like it is or maybe I was stupidly trying to make myself feel better.

Romance books are a beautiful thing, no doubt. I love them—devour them—but they're a means of escape. In reality, I've never met a man who makes me weak in the knees or is so selfless that my pleasure drives his sole purpose.

I've never had a man give me multiple orgasms, or more to the point, the only man I've ever been with has never been able to give me one. I consider myself blessed if I come while having sex with him, and more times than not, it isn't intentional on his part.

My pleasure was merely an offshoot of his climax. And forget about having an orgasm that scrambles my brains.

Yeah, all fictional.

My hand dives into my large pool bag and fumbles for the key card that I need to use to select the top floor. A hairbrush, sunglasses, sunscreen, an Elizabeth O'Roark book—now there's a devilish hero I wish were real—lip gloss, a T-shirt, and hair tie. Where is the key card?

Why did I grab this bag instead of my still semi-packed suitcase or my purse?

Because I wasn't thinking straight.

Monty was only a minute or so behind me, and I didn't want to talk to him. I couldn't talk to him. The tears wouldn't stop, and although they weren't over him, I didn't want him to see me like that.

I was crying for me, for my stupidity, for wasting most of my youth on him. I'm still young, but those carefree days of high school were all spent with him. And what for? So I could wind up at a fancy hotel soon to be homeless and penniless?

Bastard.

Finally, I find the smooth cardboard sleeve with the key card tucked inside. The elevator doors open on the top floor of the hotel, and if I were in a better frame of mind, I'd be squealing at this kind of luxury.

All of this kind of life is so far removed from what I'm used to and the way I grew up. Who knew a girl from a small town in the Florida Keys would end up here? Staying in the presidential suite, no less.

Monty's goofy grin and honey-colored eyes flash before me. As much as I hate to admit it, I'm here because of him. I should be livid, wishing I were working my ass off in some part-time job while attending community college. At least then, I'd be working on my future, on me.

But I'm grateful despite everything else. Without him, I wouldn't have left home, seen parts of this country I'd only ever read about. No matter the chaos I'm in now, or how far beyond repair our relationship is, getting out of Marathon is something I appreciate, and while small, it helps me make peace with everything.

Outside the presidential suite, I tap the key card and a green light flashes. I open the door and step into a foyer. The lights are off, and it takes a few seconds for my eyes to adjust.

A glow from the next room provides enough illumination for me to take in the sleek wood and marble surfaces as well as the powder room to one side. From there, I amble into the living and dining area, with a hallway to my right.

Three floor-to-ceiling windows run across one wall and with the curtains open, Houston's city lights spill into the room. Directly in front of me are two large statues. One looks like a pony and the other is some kind of plant or small tree, and adjacent to that is a bookshelf.

The living room boasts a long, deep-cushioned sectional with a leather ottoman-type extension that perches in front of a gas fireplace. A modern, multi-layered glass coffee table and two tub chairs complete the look.

Across from the furniture, running the length of that wall, is the biggest flat-screen TV I've ever seen, and at the far end of the room sits a modern, expensive-looking dining table for eight.

There's even a piano. It may be a grand though I wouldn't know. Opposite the piano is a kitchen and an open-concept office with another, albeit more modest, flat-screen TV.

Holy cow. The suite is gigantic, and I haven't even seen half of it, I'm sure.

I spin on my heel and head down the hallway to where I'm guessing the bedroom must be. At the end, on my left, I spy a room with a treadmill, elliptical, and stationary bike. Wow.

I turn in the opposite direction, since I'm not exercising, and pass a closet bigger than my childhood bedroom. Across the hall is another room, and I blink at the blinding bright lights when I flick them on.

It's the bathroom though calling it that feels wrong. This is more a mini spa than anything else. Again, every surface is marble or glass, and everything is top of the line. There are double sinks, a private sauna, an all-glass shower in the middle of the room, and a freestanding bathtub so long and deep I could easily sleep in it. Maybe I will since I can't find the bed.

I need a shower, if only to wash off the filth and depravity of tonight. Out of habit, I close the bathroom door, then drop my bag onto the floor and strip. On the countertop, there's a small tube of toothpaste and a disposable toothbrush in plastic wrap, both provided by the hotel.

Sweet. Thank you very much.

I brush my teeth and finger comb some of the knots out of my hair but quickly give up. I hope I can tame the medusa look under the water. If I have to use loads of conditioner, so be it.

The shower is heavenly, and it almost makes up for the fact that I have no clean underwear or anything but my dress to wear. Screw it. I'll sleep naked and deal with my clothing situation in the morning.

Monty always tried to get me to come to bed naked, but for some reason, I never could with him. I wasn't comfortable though I could never say why.

With my hair wrapped in a towel and my body cocooned in one of the hotel's plush white robes, I stroll toward the workout room. The bedroom has to be that way.

Sure enough, there's a door slightly ajar inside the exercise room. I gently push it open and can make out a bed. It's much darker in here, dungeon-like with not a peep of light slicing through the drawn curtains.

Now I wish I hadn't left my phone along with everything else in the bathroom. I could really use something to light my way. Carefully, I shuffle into the room and my feet soon hit carpet right before my hand reaches out and touches a mattress. I shove off my robe, letting it pool at my feet, and slide under the cool, soft blankets. *Ah, yes.*

My head hits the pillow and I release a long, contented sigh. At the same time, the mattress ripples and there's rustling on the other side of the bed. Oh my God, what's happening?

I slowly turn in the direction of the noise and movement. Something clatters to the floor and a bedside lamp flicks on.

A dark, riotous stare drills into me. "What the fuck?"

A very muscled, familiar, and definitely pissed-off man springs from the bed. I'm both alarmed and speechless.

He has inky black hair, wavy and mussed from sleep, dark fiery eyes, and there's no missing the way his skin tightens over his flexing jaw. He's shocked, maybe even enraged.

And his body. Like slabs of granite, solid and smooth, I'm consumed by the chiseled muscles of his bare chest. He has those muscles on the sides of his hips. What are they called again?

The sinful twin ridges of his...Adonis belt, that's it. The infamously mouth-watering V some guys have.

My gaze shamelessly trails the muscles as they disappear into his low slung boxers. Not stopping to daydream about what's underneath all that cotton, my eyes drift lower and land on his thighs.

Another thing of wonder. They are the most sinewy and cut thighs I've ever seen. Hard, chiseled, and lean like super-sized bricks.

The man growls and curls one of his hands into a fist, and my eyes flash up to his. Suddenly, reality sinks in. My tongue sticks to the roof of my mouth and my fingers clutch the bedsheet to my chest.

I'm naked, and this isn't just any man.

Holy shit.

It's Roman Kingsley.

"Who the fuck are you? And what are you doing in my room?" Never taking his eyes off me, he bends to pick up whatever fell on the floor. His phone. He holds it like a weapon and bellows, "Answer me."

"Sorry, um, this is my room. The front desk gave me a key." I spin to look around and suddenly remember everything I own is scattered across the bathroom.

"Bullshit. I don't know who the fuck you are or what fucking game you're playing, but I'm calling hotel security. I'm not your husband, and we aren't fated to be together. I'm also calling the cops." He lunges for the bed before I have a chance to react and whips back the covers. "Get out."

I scream and jump off the mattress, hands and arms trying to hide my breasts and between my legs. Nothing about him softens as I scramble for the robe on the floor, trembling as I firmly tie the sash around my waist.

Only then do I let go of the breath I was holding. His odd words slide into place, suddenly making sense. He thinks I'm a stalker.

He glowers, nostrils flaring, as he dials what I'm guessing is the front desk.

My arms wildly gesture as if that will somehow convince him of my innocence. "Look, I don't know what happened, but I'm not crazy. I'm not some psycho fan."

He pauses in dialing to eye me skeptically. "But you know who I am."

It isn't a question. He says it in a way that somehow proves he's right about me. I'm dangerous and snuck into his room to see him.

My arms flap like a pelican taking off for flight. "I didn't even know you were in the hotel." The towel tumbles from my head.

Thwack. The damp cloth smacks onto the wooden floor, he jolts, and my wet hair slaps my face, some sticking to my eyelashes.

My fingers claw at the strands to clear my sight. I gawk at him as he puts the phone to his ear.

"This is Roman Kingsley. There's a situation. I need hotel security and for you to call the police. Now."

$$\rule{3cm}{0.4pt}$$

ROMAN

$$\rule{3cm}{0.4pt}$$

Pinching the bridge of my nose, I grind my teeth to stop from losing my shit. The hotel suite is crawling with people, most talking over one another. This is one of those rare instances where I wish I had my people with me—and usually I want the opposite.

I fucking pay people to deal with this crap. But of course, I had to sneak out of Hollywood, didn't tell a soul, and now there's no one here to handle this mess except me.

Alone. That's what I wanted—to block out the media bullshit and get my head on straight before Monday's meeting. My dreams are coming true, and I should be on top of the world.

This trip to Houston is my chance to make a good impression and prove them all wrong. This is my chance to prove to the media and the haters that my new position as top movie producer at AK Studios and heir to my father's dynasty isn't just another example of nepotism at its best.

Despite being only twenty-three, almost twenty-four, I earned this position and I'll be damn good at it. But public opinion says otherwise. Most think I'm just a mediocre actor despite the awards and accolades, a player, and I'm only where I am because my parents are Hollywood royalty.

Fuck 'em.

And fuck tonight.

So much for solitude. It's past midnight and I'm waist deep in this cluster-fuck. As if my life can't get any more complicated.

The hotel manager, security guards, and two more of the hotel staff are all kissing my ass. No one is listening to what anyone else has to say. Well, that isn't entirely true.

She's listening. The woman I found in my bed. Or maybe she isn't, but at the very least, she's quiet. Not uttering a fucking peep.

Like a mouse, she trembles in the corner of the living room, wedged between one of the statues and a bookcase. Arms wrapped around her middle, chin tucked into her chest, her long, dark hair wet and wild.

Dammit.

She is gorgeous.

I shouldn't be noticing her beauty or thinking about her in any other way than as a stranger. Just like everyone else in this suite.

Despite the circus as the group of men try to figure out how this happened, one thing is clear—she isn't an obsessed fan who broke into my room. I've had my fair share of fanatics, and that's why I freaked out when I found her lying next to me.

At the sight of her, I was catapulted back to Casey Jones, the fan who broke into my Pacific Palisades home when I was sixteen. I found her in my shower.

I was scared shitless and shell-shocked. That was the first time I'd ever come face-to-face with someone obsessed with me. No, not me. JJ Springs, the character I played for nearly ten years in the hit series *Laguna Beach*.

The hugely popular streaming show not only made me a household name, but it opened doors to a comic franchise and several blockbuster movies. There were many Caseys after that night, but she was the only one who'd ever gotten close to me. That is, until tonight.

But I got it wrong tonight. I'd overreacted without asking questions. This woman, whoever she is, isn't a stalker. The hotel simply, inextricably, fucked up.

Now at my breaking point, I harshly clap my hands together. "Everyone, get out."

All of them shut their mouths—*ah, silence*—and their heads swivel to stare at me. Even the woman in the corner snaps to attention, eyes widening, and I think she's holding her breath.

I watch her, and naturally, everyone follows my gaze. "What did you say your name was?"

She burrows into the wall, hands clutching at the robe. "Jane Hastings."

"Jane, go to the bathroom. Get dressed."

She tried to do so earlier, when everyone descended on the suite, but I wasn't about to let her out of my sight. I had too many questions and didn't know who she was.

In retrospect, I could have let her go to the restroom. Hotel security was here and we were going to call the police, though we never did.

Now I wish I had let her get changed. Jane is in a room with only men, in a bathrobe, naked underneath.

Shit.

No wonder she's terrified.

Jane stares, hesitant and hopeful, but unmoving, and I can't really blame her. I've been nothing but a tyrant.

"It's okay." I soften my tone and features. "Go. We'll talk when you come back."

The manager, an attractive middle-aged man, a little too slick for my liking, steps closer. "Mr. Kingsley, I wouldn't—"

I hold up a hand to stop him from saying any more and nod encouragingly at Jane. Without waiting for another word, she races down the hallway, and within seconds the living room echoes with her slamming of the bathroom door.

"Mr. Kingsley." The manager tries again. What doesn't this guy understand about shutting the fuck up? "Let us make this right. My sincere—"

"Enough. You've already explained, and damn straight, you're going to make this right. You fucked up. To confirm, you don't have any available rooms; is that correct?"

All three of the hotel staff nod, each of them anxious and fidgety, but none of them dare say anything. They hang on my every word. Whatever I decree will be. It's heady shit and also exhausting at times.

"Okay. So, here's what you're going to do." I pull out a business card from my pants pocket and thrust it at him. "This is my assistant's information. In the morning, you're going to call her, explain what happened, and together, you'll figure out how to make this right. My team's flying in on Sunday, and we'll be here for a couple of days. I'm sure something can be worked out."

I rest my hand heavily on his shoulder and steer him toward the door. Wordlessly, the others follow.

"In the meantime, get out." I pull the door open. "Goodnight, gentlemen."

They mutter more apologies and sentiments of regret as I shut the door in their faces. At last, I can hear myself think.

I saunter into the living room and drop down onto the sofa. Not long after, Jane appears from the hallway in high heels and a strapless, slinky dress that falls to midthigh.

The shiny blue material, the same color as her eyes, makes them seem bigger and brighter, more stunning than before. Her hair is gathered on top of her head in a bun, and she grips a large handbag—practically the same size as her—to her petite frame as if her life depends on it.

"Mr. Kingsley, I'm—"

"Call me Roman." I stand and cautiously approach. "Mr. Kingsley's my father."

Her lips don't so much as twitch at my poor attempt at humor. "I still don't understand what happened tonight, and while I'm not sure if I'm at fault, I am sorry."

"You have nothing to apologize for. The hotel has a special system for reservations and checking in celebrities, and whether it glitched or someone screwed up—I don't know nor do I care—you're not at fault. This mix-up is on them."

"Okay." Her shoulders relax a little, showing her relief that I'm not blaming her. "I'm going to leave now." She starts for the door and falters at the sound of my voice.

"Jane, where will you go? The hotel's fully booked, and clearly, I have enough space. Stay."

I'm not sure why I suggest this when it goes against my reasons for coming to Houston earlier than planned. It's just that she seems lost and...scared? No, not scared. Maybe anxious or restless.

"What?" She spins around so quickly that the strap of her bag slides from her shoulder, sending the bag flying through the air until it hits the floor with a thunk.

Stunned, she freezes, gaze flitting from the bag to me and back again. "I couldn't. You're...you're you." Her hands gesture at me as if that explains everything.

"True and you're you, but I insist." I grab her bag and deposit it on one of the chairs.

She rushes over to rummage through it, pulling out her phone. "I could call a friend who's staying in the hotel. Maybe I can stay with her." There isn't any conviction to her suggestion. She clearly doesn't want to call her friend, or perhaps, staying with her friend really isn't an option. She presses a button on the side of the phone to turn it on. "That is, if she answers."

Curious, I arch a brow and saunter across the room, taking a seat in the other chair. "Why didn't you call her in the first place?"

Suddenly, her phone pings continuously, at least twenty or thirty times, and it reminds me of someone incessantly slapping their hand on the little bell you sometimes find at the front desk of a hotel.

She drops her phone into the bag, abandoning the idea of calling anyone. With each chime, my eyebrow inches nearer to my hairline. What is her story?

"Wow, you're a popular woman. Someone—or more than one person—is clearly trying to get ahold of you. Is that why you turned off your phone?"

Swallowing hard, her gaze dips to her feet. "Um, yeah." She slumps into the chair next to me and pulls her bag onto her lap on a sigh. "I've had a shit night, and you're right, I don't have a place to stay. I actually came here with my fiancé. He's here to play in the final championship game."

"No shit. What's his name?"

"Montgomery Fisher." Her head rests on the cushion and she kicks off her heels. "Actually, he's now my ex-fiancé." She's matter-of-fact and I nod, holding back any commentary even if I want to know more.

Monty Fisher. I know the name. I like sports, watch what I can, and keep up with the players and team scores through the news. This is Fisher's first year in the major leagues, and boy, did he get lucky out of the gate. His stats are great, the press loves him, and if they win the championship, he'll go places.

Jane closes her eyes, and something about her—the flutter of her lashes or the soft pink hue to her cheeks; I'm not sure which—brings an odd sense of familiarity. Like a bolt of lightning, I'm struck by something else I recall about Fisher.

He just proposed to his high school sweetheart on national television at their final home game. That's why she looks familiar.

An image of Fisher with his blond hair, tall, and lanky, down on one knee and this petite beauty, laughing, as he slips a ring on her finger, dashes through my mind. The proposal was a ten-second blip among the headline clips from the past week that I'd watched on the flight from LA to Houston.

Shit, that was only a couple of days ago, and he's now her ex? Her left ring finger is bare. What the hell happened?

I clear my throat, not wanting to be rude and barrage her with questions, but also interested in knowing more. Her eyes open and she twists in the chair to face me, pulling her legs under her.

"After practice, some of the guys were wired for tomorrow's game, not ready to call it a night. So a bunch of us got together. The wives, girlfriends, and players. We were at the hotel restaurant in a private room. Most people were drinking—not the players and obviously, not me."

Her fingers work quickly and unravel her bun. Long, wild black hair falls in waves around her oval face.

"Monty went to the restroom... He was gone for a while, and I went to look for him. And guess what? I found him." Her breath stutters and cheeks darken to an angry shade of red. "I walked in on him with two women in the bathroom."

"Fuck." A knot of tension settles between my shoulder blades. "Jane—"

She plows over me. "You know, the weirdest part is, I knew. Deep down, I did. There'd been rumors, things people whispered behind my back, but I shut it all out. Then, tonight, there was this strange sense of relief when I caught him red-handed. Or more like bare-assed, his dick thrusting into some woman's mouth, and his face in another woman's tits."

Sarcasm drips from her words before she releases a harsh, watery laugh. "I think that's what it was. I needed to see it with my own eyes. But more than anything else, I was so angry. Humiliated, even. How could he do this to me? Cheat on me. Have a threesome when his teammates and our friends were only feet away. Anyone could have walked in on them. I've been with him since my first year of high school. I'm such an idiot."

"Why did you stay with him if you knew he was a cheater?" The question is automatic, out of my mouth before my tone hits me, incredulous and maybe even a touch accusing.

"Because I'm a coward. I don't know who I am without Monty-fucking-Fisher." Her sharp, rueful smile is further emphasized by the toss of her bag onto the floor.

Its contents scatter, and the diamond solitaire, easily a carat, catches my attention. The ring skips across the wooden floor, and she scoffs and puts her head in her hands when she sees it.

"I should have left him a long time ago."

Something snaps inside of me, and I drop to my knees in front of her. Witnessing her anguish, though I don't know her, feels like someone's wrenching my heart from my chest.

I've never had any kind of serious relationship, and contrary to the gossip sites, I'm not a heartless player. I have younger sisters and can't imagine what I'd do if someone hurt Marin or Fallon like this.

My hands pry hers away from her face, and I gently pinch the tip of her chin, lifting it to make her look at me. "Jane, don't beat yourself up over that asshole. This isn't your fault, and it sounds like he did you a favor."

She tilts her head to the side, brow knitting. "What?"

"He showed you what a douchebag he is. Be grateful you found out now and not after you married him."

"Oh, God, yes. Now that would be something to cry about."

A single tear slides down her cheek, and without much thought for any consequence, my thumb wipes it away. She shudders, and I give in to the mounting ache to touch her some more.

My hand takes hers, our fingers interlacing. Against mine, hers is so much smaller. I shouldn't be surprised—she's easily a full foot shorter than my six-one and tiny next to me.

She stares at where we're joined, and once more, I think she's forgotten to breathe.

I gently squeeze her hand. "Is this okay?"

Nodding, her blue eyes darken and heat by the second. "I'm flying home on Sunday afternoon. I'll find somewhere to stay tomorrow night."

Taken aback by her comment, I study her carefully, uncertain why she's chosen this moment to mention it. Her gaze slowly rakes down my chest and back up to meet my eyes, and she doesn't bother to hide her appreciation. The spark of desire smolders in her deep blues.

She feels it, too.

This irrepressible attraction.

Heat flares low in my stomach and shoots straight for my groin.

Dammit, if she keeps looking at me like that, I don't stand a chance of being a gentleman.

I clear my throat and look away for a blink. "You mean tonight, not tomorrow. It's already Saturday. And you don't have to go anywhere. Stay until your flight."

"I don't know. I've got to figure out how to get my things from...from his room. I don't want to face..." Her words trail off and the moment's gone.

She stiffens, expression tense and troubled, as if mentally preparing for the inevitable run-in with her ex. Unexpectedly, I'm overcome with the urge to protect her and maybe something more, something I don't want to think about. For sure, I'm consumed with the desire to hunt down Fisher and pound his flesh till he bleeds out.

Standing to my full height, I scoop her into my arms, and she releases a gasp as I sit back into the chair with her soft, warm body now on my lap. A wild strawberry and faint flowery scent fills my nose.

Shivering, she angles her head to look up at me. "Mr. King—um, Roman, what are you doing?"

I tighten my hold, not really sure how to answer. I don't know what I'm doing, only that I can't tear my eyes away from her and don't want to let go. Sure, some of what I'm feeling is lust, but I've been attracted to women before and never acted on it.

This is more. I'm driven by a deep-seated need to protect her or more like, to help her. I've got all this space and it costs me nothing to share it with her.

My cock pulses under the heat of her tight, little body with a fierce need to be inside her. While I hope she doesn't notice my growing desire, I'm not strong enough, gentleman enough, to get up and put distance between us.

She shudders again and I point my chin toward the fireplace. "Do you want that on?"

"No, thank you." A pink flush blooms on her cheeks.

"Are you tired?" Through the silky material of her dress, my thumb rubs small, slow circles along her hip bone, and she slowly settles, releasing the tension she's holding and sinking into me.

"I was but not anymore. Tonight's been..."

The unspoken ending to her thought hangs between us. There are so many things she could say, and I wonder what she wants, how I could make tonight end on a better note.

"You can take the bed, and I'll sleep out here." My comment contradicts my thoughts. I don't know why I'm encouraging we separate, but it's for the best.

As much as I'm enjoying how close we are, how one round, perky tit presses into me, and how well we fit together, if we stay like this much longer, I will lose all self-control.

Her hand lightly grazes my jaw, a tentative yet keen exploration, and that's it. Something breaks free inside me. One hand cradles the back of her head, my fingers threading through her mass of hair, and the other pulls her to me.

This may be the dumbest thing I've done in a long time. We barely know each other, and I should keep a low profile, not invite any chance of scandal or risk an entanglement with someone who could potentially become infatuated. More importantly, I should be focusing on business. But at this moment, I don't give a fuck.

My mouth crashes onto hers. Surprisingly, Jane doesn't miss a beat. Her mouth opens, and I hungrily accept the invitation, stroking my tongue against hers, devouring the taste of her and feel of her and becoming more intoxicated with her by the second.

THIS CAN'T POSSIBLY BE real, but I don't want it to stop.

I'm kissing Roman Kingsley.

Or more like, he's kissing me.

This may be an alternate universe where I imagined the glint of heat and craving in his furtive gaze. Those mesmerizing eyes of his—a deep mahogany framed by thick, coal-black lashes.

Or maybe I'm hallucinating how he kisses the life out of me. How his more-than-day-old stubble, not quite a beard, gratifyingly abrades my face.

Or who knows, this entire evening could all just be one fantastical dream.

He's one of the hottest Hollywood celebrities and my teenage crush, though I never did outgrow my affection for him. For adult me, he's my hall pass—a stupid notion that Monty brought into our relationship.

One night, many moons ago in the bed of his pickup truck, Monty told me Jenna Ortega was his dream girl. If ever he had the chance to sleep with her, he'd take it. She was his hall pass, the "freebie" that wouldn't hurt our monogamous relationship.

At the time, I was shocked and a little upset, even if it was extremely unlikely that it would ever happen. We'd just had sex, and he was talking about sleeping with another woman, celebrity or not.

God, I was such a fool. Even back then he showed me who he really was. But I buried any misgivings and played along, something I became a pro at although I'm only now realizing that.

I even flirted and laughed with him that night, and come to think of it, he never asked me who my hall pass was. I doubt he cared, yet I was quick to offer it up, wanting him to know there was someone I'd definitely jump at the chance to be with, even if it was only a dream.

Monty was my first. The only guy I'd ever slept with, made out with, kissed.

Until now.

Roman pulls back. "Hey, is this okay?"

I nod, not wanting to talk, and lean in for another kiss, but he stops me. Looking into his eyes, though dark and stormy, is a lot like looking into the sun. Arresting and unforgettable.

"Are you sure?" His thumb sweeps across the crest of my cheek, and every time he does it I shiver. "Where'd you go?"

"What?" Shit, I'd gotten lost in my head, reminded of the silly conversation about hall passes, and Roman must have sensed it. "Nowhere. I can hardly believe you're kissing me. You're a famous actor, and I'm—"

"You're sexy as fuck." His lips press against my forehead.

While it's sweet and comforting, I sense the embers of his desire waning, threatening to die out. I've messed this up. I can tell by how he slides backward, putting distance between us.

"Hey, I should let you get some sleep. You've been through a lot and…"

The way his words trail off make my lungs constrict like someone's dropped a Mack truck on my chest.

"Roman, what are we doing?" I sound like a child, clueless as to where this could lead.

But his gaze is warm and kind as the corners of his lips tip upward into a soft smile. "Whatever you want, Jane. We can stop right here or keep going. I'll only do whatever you're comfortable with."

Never have I been in a situation like this. I'm on the verge of the unthinkable. A one-night stand. If someone would've told me I'd find myself here, I'd have vehemently insisted that nothing would happen.

I'd never pursue this man. That isn't who I am. Still, Roman isn't just any man.

There is no chance of a future with him or, better yet, of getting my heart broken. I know what this is. My eyes are wide open. This would be just sex and nothing more.

And the idea of letting tonight slip away without grabbing this chance pricks at my chest. I was a colossal fool, blind and witless about Monty, and sure, there are a litany of reasons or excuses, depending on how you look at it, as to why I turned a blind eye.

But tonight is different. I won't make another critical misstep. And that realization is all I need to fuel my courage. I will not let this opportunity to be with Roman Kingsley pass me by.

No. Fucking. Way.

"I want you."

Raw and anxious, I open my body and mind to the possibilities of tonight. To whatever is to come. My skin's too tight, and adrenaline punches at my insides, looking for a way out.

But I'm not stopping now.

The worst he can say is no.

I can do this.

"Roman, if you want me…please don't stop."

"Jane, you fucking slay me. Of course I want you. Let me erase everything else that's happened tonight. Make us your only memory." His lips capture mine, and he kisses me again.

This time with no finesse or foreplay, there's only dominance in the way his tongue takes, possessively stroking and playing with mine. It's as if he's making sure I'm fully present, feeling every bit of him without giving me a chance to let my mind wander.

He tastes of cinnamon—I'm guessing it's his toothpaste—with a hint of musky spice. His mouth slips from mine to trail open-mouthed kisses down to where my neck meets my collarbone.

Butterfly wings batter at my insides, and heat flares along my spine. A moan spills from my parted lips when one of his hands pinches at my hardened nipple through my dress.

"Bedroom." The one word is hot and muffled against my flesh as he pushes to standing.

Since my dress is short and form-fitting, it rides up and bunches at my waist and I wrap my legs around him, sliding down to settle around his narrow hips. My arms slide around his neck and I feel just how big and hard his desire is for me.

He pulls me tighter against his arousal. The pure bliss of being this close to him slices through me like a hot knife through butter.

He strides down the dark hallway, lips still on my skin, and my hips twist and squirm at the burning friction mounting low in my core. His calloused fingers dig into my ass. Since I'm wearing a thong, we're more flesh on flesh than anything else, and I wonder if he feels how wet I am for him.

"Jane, hold on." His guttural command sends a shiver of delight through me, and his grip tightens, holding me against his erection as we enter the bedroom.

He slides back a curtain, and the city lights stream into the room before he drops me onto the mattress. His hand pulls at the bodice of my dress, and one breast springs free the second the fabric rips.

"Jesus Christ, Jane." Head dipping low, he draws a nipple into his mouth, and I shudder and whimper as his wet, hot tongue and sharp, greedy teeth nip and suck at me.

My fingers dive into the waves of hair on the top of his head. "God, Roman."

He chuckles against my breast and looks up at me. "I like it when you say my name, especially when you call me a deity."

I snort and guide his head back to my breast where he plants a wet kiss.

"I'm gonna fuck you hard. So hard you'll only know my name."

His lips press to mine and as much as I want what he promises as his head bobs against me and his tongue licks at my bottom lip, a hint of uncertainty ripples through me.

"I, uh, I've only ever been with one person." He stiffens like I've struck him, and I inwardly wince at my blunder. "I don't want you to stop. I still want this; I only wanted you to know."

"Are you sure?" Hovering above me, he scrutinizes my features, and though it's plain to see he's contemplating something—maybe even having second thoughts, I can't be sure—his expression is unreadable.

"Jane, you know what this is, right?" He drops onto the bed beside me, and I roll to face him, ignoring the sting at the corner of my eyes.

If I have messed this up by opening my big mouth, I'll bite my tongue.

I force the words past the lump that's formed in my throat. "Yes. I do."

He tucks some of my hair behind my ear, staring at me, his eyes dark and hooded. "What we're doing is only for this weekend. Fun."

His words cause a sharp sensation, knife-like, to twist my stomach, and it shouldn't. This is a fling. I suspect any misgivings or regret on my part is more about Monty. Since the hotel staff left the room, I've felt more respected and cared for by this man than I did during all the years with the man I planned to spend the rest of my life with.

"Fun. Yes." I straddle him and smile. "And I'm going to hold you to that."

When his gaze drops to my bare breasts, his apprehension shifts to a dark, unleashed hunger quicker than the flick of a light switch. He grips my waist and flips me onto my back while ordering me to remove my dress.

I do as he commands, fingers fumbling for the side zipper while he yanks my thong from my body, spreads my legs wide apart, and drops to his knees at the end of the bed.

His hands curl around my calves and he yanks me down until the lower half of my body hangs from the edge of the mattress. He places both my feet on his shoulders.

Holy hell.

Roman watches me for a few beats, stormy dark eyes locked with mine, and my legs quiver in anticipation.

Monty never went down on me, claiming it wasn't his thing, and though logically I knew it had nothing to do with me, I couldn't help but wonder.

None of that matters now.

All self-doubt vanishes at the way Roman stares at me and then my exposed pussy. It's like he's starving for me, and I'm the only taste he craves.

I stare down at him, this gorgeous heartthrob of a man, as his thumb strokes the bundle of nerves above my entrance. A whimper surges from deep within as he pushes a finger inside me.

"Fuck, Jane. You're so wet. So fucking tight." His finger pumps in and out a few more times before he adds another, and at first, it's almost a painful stretch. His long, thick digits strain against me.

"Roman..." His name releases on a sob, and he stops moving.

"Relax," he says, a quiet and gentle command.

My head flops back onto the bed, still sensing the solid pressure of his fingers until he sharply removes them. Then his mouth latches on to my sex and I gasp, eyes blinking rapidly.

Oh, my God. It's Roman's lips on me.

His tongue swirls and teases, and he slowly starts to thrust his fingers inside me once more. This time, there is no pain. I squeeze my eyes shut, overwhelmed by the sensations and needing to block everything else out, allowing the pleasure to wash over and through me.

"Oh, Roman. Roman. Oh, Roman." I can't stop chanting his name as if to remind myself this is real.

Roman is going down on me, and if ever there was an award equivalent to an Oscar for sex, hands down it would be his for this performance.

He mouth-fucks me the way he kisses, claiming and conquering, like he's enjoying every goddamn lick and suck. Like this is just as much about his pleasure as it is about mine.

My toes curl into his flexing shoulders and as if in response, the fingers of his free hand dig into my thigh to keep me still.

I'm on sensory overload.

I've never experienced anything like this, and that's why I don't realize what's happening. I come harder than I ever have before. My body convulses, and shocks of electricity spark and shoot throughout me as I come hard and fast with his mouth, tongue, and fingers still on and in me.

He's unrelenting, and I arch my back off the mattress, sobbing his name as my orgasm goes on and on and on.

When the tremors finally subside, I exhale a shuddering breath, and Roman slides his fingers out of me, kisses my inner thigh, and gently places my feet onto the floor.

Still off-balance, I don't fully notice when he pulls me with him higher onto the bed. It's only when he wraps his arms around me, strong and warm, do I feel more like myself.

He threads his hand through my hair and kisses my forehead, and absurdly, the women from the elevator and their conversation flickers to life.

Damn, this is what they were talking about. Maybe mind-blowing sex is more than fiction.

With my face to his chest, I laugh. "Oh, my God, that was the most fun I've ever had."

"I couldn't agree more."

"What?" I cock my head to see him. "But you didn't come."

"Don't have to get off. And trust me, Jane, seeing you come undone was a beautiful thing."

"Are you for real?"

"What?" His dark brows draw together.

"Nothing. It's just I've never had an orgasm like that. God, I wish I could bottle it. I'd need to steal your tongue and fingers."

A bark of laughter erupts from him and the vibrations echo through my chest as I nuzzle into him. "Maybe I missed my calling. Forget movies."

Feeling bold or maybe it's because I'm loose-limbed and carefree, my hand skates down between us to palm his hot, still hard, and very big erection.

He rests his hand on mine. "Jane, we don't have to."

"I want to."

"Hang on a sec." He jumps from the bed and drops his pants, and I've never been more grateful for something so simple as the opened curtains.

I shamelessly admire his magnificent backside as he strides from the room and barely have a chance to miss him. Seconds later, he's back with a box of condoms and falters as he nears the bed, likely at the stunned expression on my face.

"A box?" I choke out. "What were you planning on having, like, an orgy or something?" Even as I ask, I don't want to know.

He pulls two condoms out, tosses them onto the mattress, and drops the box on the side table. Then he's in bed next to me.

"They came with the suite. This place is fully stocked." He smirks. "Jane, I didn't plan on having sex this weekend. You're a gift from the gods."

Done with talking, he pulls me to him and captures my lips again, kissing me deeply and fervently while his fingers slip between my folds. I don't need any more foreplay. I am beyond ready.

I reach for a condom on the mattress and sit back to open the wrapper.

His thumb glides across my cheek and he smirks. "Someone's eager."

"I already told you. I want you."

I take him, hot, thick, and rigid, in my hand. Roman hisses at my touch, hands curling into the sheets, as he lets me lead. My palm barely wraps around him, and I feel his blistering stare as I roll the condom onto his shaft.

Then I lift a leg over his to straddle him, and I'm throbbing and pulsing with a raw, urgent need for him. I've also never done this before—taken control while having sex—but Roman seems to like it. His gaze is filled with an intense hunger, and that boosts my confidence.

I slide onto him, stalling and sucking in a breath when pain shoots up my spine. Good God, he's big.

"Hey, easy." He rolls me onto the bed and settles between my thighs. "For the first time, this might be better. On top can get intense."

I feel my cheeks redden that he knows this and I'm clueless. I don't want to think about why or how he knows this, but I immediately appreciate our new position. He's right—less pressure and more pleasure.

He slowly, patiently slides into me, stopping when he senses my discomfort. "Fuck, Jane." His breath stutters and his ab muscles tighten and tense with every thrust deeper inside me. "Woman, you're going to be the death of me. You feel fucking amazing."

I bask in his praise, though I struggle to register his words and more so when he starts to move.

"Jesus Christ, Jane." He leans down and crushes my lips in a kiss that's definitely ravenous, almost frenetic.

His teeth gently dig into the tender spot where my neck and collarbone meet while one hand grabs my breast, pinching my nipple. Sweet agony barrels through me. Sex with Roman is unparalleled, and while I don't have much to compare it to, I fear he's ruining me for all other men.

He lifts my leg and hooks it over his shoulder, deepening his strokes, and I moan to let him know I like it, that I don't want him to let up. I love how he makes me come alive, and I match him thrust for thrust as my heel digs into his back.

Like before, my orgasm sneaks up on me, stealing all the air from my lungs and seizing my muscles. I'm flying and breaking into a million little pieces all at the same time, and like before, Roman's name is all I utter. The only thing I know.

In turn, he snarls my name, and I cry out when he stiffens and jerks, spilling into me before collapsing next to me. Once his breathing slows, he leaves the room and returns with a damp washcloth for me.

I clean up, and then he snakes an arm around me, pulling me close. "Do you want a shower or sleep?"

My mouth opens, response at the ready, when his throaty voice sends a warm prickle down my spine. "Before you answer that, you should know that we're not done. So maybe you might want to hold off on the shower."

ROMAN

JANE STROLLS into the living room in a hotel robe, her long hair down and damp from her shower. The midday sun, vivid and extraordinary, much like the woman its rays dance around, envelops her lithe body in a warm, buttery glow.

Damn, I fucking want her again.

We didn't get much sleep last night. When we woke—minutes before ten—I figured she needed a break and we needed food more than I needed to fuck right away.

While I have a healthy sex drive, last night was a first. Maybe it was because the end of our time together is fast approaching, or maybe it's that I know this is it—I can't have her again. Whatever the reason, I wasn't able to stop myself or the insatiable longing for more of her.

At least we still have tonight. As with anything pleasurable—especially if it comes with an expiration date—it's far too easy to get sucked in and lose myself. Jane could easily become a dangerous habit.

That can't be what this is.

Shaking off those thoughts, I run a hand through my nearly dry hair and pour a cup of coffee for her.

While she slept, I had a quick shower, and then while she showered, I ordered room service.

I place my cup onto the saucer as she approaches the dining table. "Hungry?"

She leans over the table to pinch a piece of bacon from the breakfast spread. "Yes. This looks delicious, but it's way too much food for just the two of us."

"I wasn't sure what you liked or wanted."

Sliding into the chair next to me, she crunches on the crispy strip. "Thank you."

Somewhere close by, a phone pings and it isn't mine. Mine sits on the dining table, facedown and off, and has been that way for most of the time since I left Los Angeles.

Before the food arrived, I briefly checked messages, and as expected, my assistant and my father both want to know where I am. Once I fired off a response letting them know there was nothing to worry about, I promptly shut it off again.

She pulls her phone from the pocket of her robe and warily glances down at the screen. An edgy, almost apprehensive expression pollutes her striking features.

I lean forward. "Everything okay?"

"Sort of. It's nothing. Just Monty. He's sorry and wants to talk. He says he's worried about me." She deposits the phone on the table and wrinkles her nose in disgust before grabbing the coffee carafe. Her hand trembles as she pours the hot liquid into a cup.

"Jane, are—"

"It's fine. I don't plan on talking to him. Not now, anyway, and I don't want to talk about it." She selects a plate of fruit and a croissant. "I've been thinking. I need to get my stuff from Monty's room before my flight tomorrow, but I want to do it when he isn't there. The best time would be tonight during the game. The room will be empty."

Something, maybe a sense of relief or lingering satisfaction, bathes her expression and lessens the tension on her face. Before I can say anything, she forces a smile and changes the topic.

"What do you want to do today? We could get out of the hotel. I could use some fresh air, or will that be too tricky for you? I never did ask you why you're here. Is it for a movie?"

Finally, she pauses to take a breath, her jitters palpable and fraught between us. Since I don't know her all that well, I can't quite put my finger on what's causing the odd behavior, maybe it's the reality of last night. The magnitude of what Fisher did might finally be hitting her full force or maybe even what we did.

Though we haven't talked about it, and I don't have any personal experience with this, I imagine breaking off an engagement to someone you've been with for many years would disrupt your life in more ways than one. And with that, I bring us back to the topic of her ex.

"I'll come with you tonight." I hold up a hand as she opens her mouth to protest, wanting to reassure her that if only for this weekend, she isn't alone. "As for today, I'm supposed to be lying low, and I'm not here for a movie or anything to do with acting. I'm producing now and have a meeting with a screenwriter on Monday. I'm hoping to buy the option to the script."

"Oh. What does that mean?" She laughs and settles into the chair, coffee cup clasped in front of her.

"The script is written for a feature film entitled *Pinwheel*, and the screenwriter shopped it around to a few production companies. AKS, Alexander Kingsley Studios, my family's company, was one of them. We want to make it into a movie, and an option agreement basically means AKS wants to purchase the rights to the script."

"Okay, and your Monday meeting will make that happen?"

"Um, sort of. It's a little more complicated than that though I wish it was that easy. There's another production company interested in buying the option, and the screenwriter is undecided. There's a family connection or something with that company so it's a bit messy. I'm hoping to persuade the writer to choose us."

I don't want to bore her with all the details—how each production company has a different strategy and deal points, which makes the decision not so straightforward for the screenwriter—or let on her how huge this would be for my career.

"Wow, this sounds exciting." She tears off a piece of a pastry. "What does this mean for you and acting?"

"I'm not going to be doing that anymore. I've always wanted to produce and follow in my father's footsteps." I pause at how much I sound like a privileged asshole, getting to do what I've always dreamed of doing, and in some ways, there's no denying I am.

Though, like most things in life, nothing is ever as easy as it looks from the outside. While there was a press release and subsequent news articles about my addition to AKS my father has made it clear, in no uncertain terms, this is a trial run. None of my achievements so far matter, and our familial connection bears no weight, not that I'd ever use it.

Of course, this isn't public knowledge, but the possibility of him changing his mind hangs over my head. He doesn't think I'm serious enough to run AKS, and to his credit, I do have a stellar track record at making headlines for all the wrong reasons.

Being young, single, and one of Hollywood's most sought-after bachelors kind of guarantees I'll make waves and cause rumors. But the majority of the news stories about me aren't true.

All I have to do is walk by a nightclub or some questionable joint in any given city, and suddenly I'm debauched and wasted with my flock of models and young actresses.

Jane's response slices through the tsunami churning inside me at the thought of everything I'm up against. I must persuade my father that I'm the best person for the job. "This sounds like a big opportunity, Roman. I'm happy for you."

"Thanks. It is big, and that's why I came to Houston early. The rest of the team arrives tomorrow night, but I wanted to get my head on straight."

Scrutiny sparks in her gem-like blue eyes. "What aren't you telling me?"

Awkwardly, I dip my head, as if avoiding eye contact will make me feel any less exposed. "What do you mean?"

"I'm sensing a 'but' in all this. You're holding back." She pushes away her almost empty plate. "What is it?"

Incredulous at how astute she is, I barely contain my laughter. "This screenplay is really good. With the right director and cast, *Pinwheel* has Oscar written all over it. I could make that happen."

I let out a sigh, reality pressing down on my chest like an elephant. "But..." Our gazes lock and I can't remember the last time someone was so fully invested in something I had to say. Jane's interest and caring are so blindingly obvious that it causes a strange pang of uncertainty—or is it fear—to sear my insides.

"Go on." Her soft fingers caress the back of my hand, causing a feverish sensation to race up my spine.

"It doesn't help that a lot of people in Hollywood want nothing more than to see me fail."

The only way I'll change their minds is by showing them what I'm capable of. That's why *Pinwheel* matters so much.

"Fail?" She straightens. "Why?"

"Because I'm succeeding. I managed to make it big with my breakout role in *Laguna Beach* and from there, things have been good."

Again, there isn't any point in telling her about all the lows in my career and the shitty things and even shittier people I've had to deal with to get where I am. There's little sympathy—or more importantly, empathy—to be had for someone rich and successful, especially at my age.

"But you're an amazing actor. You earned the recognition and success you have. I don't get it."

"Every industry is competitive and AKS is a significant player. I'd have a lot of power in Hollywood as the head of AKS. Not everyone has been good to me. Some people, people in positions of power, don't want to see me rise. They don't want me as competition, or they view me as a threat."

"Shit, Roman."

"Yeah, and to make things even more complicated, my father isn't fully committed to the idea of me taking over AKS, though I think that has more to do with controlling me than anything else."

I push back my chair and cross my arms over my chest, resigned more than anything else.

"He's winding down his workload, and he's talked about selling off parts of the business as one option. I've tried to impress upon him that I'm the best person to carry on his legacy. Our entire family is in the business. I've got brothers and sisters, and most of them are actors. But apart from Marin, none of them want to produce. My sister and I have talked about joining forces one day, running AKS together, but that's someday. Right now, Mare's still in school."

"And your dad? He doesn't like this idea?"

I force a jubilant boom to my voice as if performing. "Sure, on the record, if any reporter or someone in the industry were to ask him, he'd say 'I love the idea. My kids running AKS, what more could a father want?'"

A wry laugh rumbles out of me, and Jane furrows her brow, mouth grim. "But that's not true?"

"No. He wants me to jump through hoops, and that's why the *Pinwheel* script is critical. If AKS gets the option to the screenplay, it will make my job of convincing him that much easier."

She slumps in her chair and pushes it away from the table. Her eyes are hazy as if digesting my woes. "That sucks, Roman. But I think you'll succeed. You'll get *Pinwheel*."

Once more, I chuckle but this time with more mirth. "From your lips to God's ears."

She leans forward, placing her elbows on her thighs, and peers up at me. In a more solemn tone she starts, "On a more serious note, I'm bummed that you won't be acting anymore. It's kind of a tragedy." Her lips twitch as if she's trying not to smile. "I'm not really sure how you could do this to your adoring fans. All those people you're depriving. They'll never get to see you on the screen again. I never thought you were heartless."

—

ROMAN

—

AMUSED, I lean forward, inching closer to where she is, and lower my voice. "Heartless? How can you say such a thing when, last night, I was so giving? Some might even say selfless."

The apples of her cheeks instantly pinken, and she bats her lashes, gaze fluttering down to the small space between us.

She's too adorable, all demure now, when her unabashed whimpers and moans from last night—begging for more, for me not to stop, to drive deeper inside her—still ring in my head. I've definitely committed all of it, all of her, to memory.

The vein in her neck throbs and her breath quickens as she steals a look at me. She's only teasing, and I plan to do more of my own teasing.

Moving closer still, I sweep her hair back from her face, and my lips graze the shell of her ear. "While some parts of your body might have forgotten last night, I'm sure your pussy remembers."

She sucks in a breath and we're so close, I sense her internal quake as her body vibrates at the mere memory of us, and I love her reaction. Jane's back there with me last night, in a tangle of lips and limbs.

"Roman." She bites her bottom lip, eyes shiny with desire. "Can I tell you a secret?"

"Yes, please." My mouth drops to her neck for a kiss. "I love secrets."

She shudders. "I had the biggest crush on you when I was younger."

Pulling back to face her, I twist my features, bemused. "*Had?* Is that a thing of the past?"

"Funny." A dimple appears on one cheek as she fights her smile, and something squeezes my chest at how much I like this.

Our conversations.

The fucking unparalleled sex.

Jane.

She brushes a quick kiss against my mouth. "Like you need me to answer that."

"Well, Jane Hastings, I *have* the biggest crush on you." I'm showering her with kisses, each one longer and wetter than the last, when a loud knock startles me.

Dark brows draw together over her ocean eyes. "Who could that be?"

"Oh, shit, I almost forgot. I arranged for us to have massages." I spring from the table and tighten my robe while mentally reciting the periodic table of elements—I'm no scientist, but as an easily excited teenager, I quickly discovered that shit would kill any boner.

Jane follows me. "What? Massages? Now?"

"Yup. They'll set up in here." I motion to the living room. "Why don't you go into the bedroom, and I'll join you in a minute."

She giggles, clearly excited, and sprints away as I swing the door open to greet the two massage therapists standing in the hallway.

The man and woman get to work, moving around furniture and setting up their tables, and as promised, I venture to the bedroom where I find a nervous Jane.

"I've never had a massage before." She bats her arms around. "What do I wear?"

"Nothing."

Both her eyes and mouth widen. "What? Naked? No way."

"Well, a massage is best naked. They use oils, and if you want, you can keep your underwear on, but you don't need to. They cover you with a sheet."

"I don't have any underwear on," she whisper-shouts, and it's cute to see how flustered she's getting over something that's supposed to be calming.

"Hey, relax. Just go out in the robe. I'm going like this." My hand waves down the robe I'm in and my bare feet.

"I don't know." She nibbles on her bottom lip, and my thumb tugs the tender flesh from her teeth.

"Jane, I promise you'll enjoy this. I'll be right beside you and afterward—" I gather her into my arms. "—we'll get into the sauna, then slide into that great big tub together. I've been dying to get you in there. I want you to ride me hard."

She gasps at the same time one of the therapists calls out to let us know they are ready for us.

Over the next hour and a half, Jane utters heavenly groans and mewls while the female therapist works on her limbs.

When we'd first appeared from the bedroom, the male masseuse had instructed Jane onto his table. *Uh-uh, no fucking way.*

I put a stop to that and we switched therapists. I wasn't about to let another man touch her body.

Once the massage is over and we're both loose-limbed and worry-free, I order a light snack while the two therapists pack up. We linger in the living room as they maneuver their tables and supplies out of the suite. As they are exiting, our food arrives. Room service waits in the hallway until the doorway is clear.

"You thirsty?" I hand her a bottle of water I'd taken from the hotel fridge before our massages, and she takes it, smiling her thanks.

Soon, we're alone and take a few minutes to eat. Then, as promised, Jane and I continue our hedonistic pursuits in the sauna and bathtub without any thoughts of leaving the hotel, getting fresh air, or much else.

Much later, perched on the ottoman, she shifts closer toward the fire. "I feel like the world's laziest person."

Absentmindedly, I turn on my phone, reluctant to see what's waiting for me but knowing I should check in again and maybe one more time later tonight.

As much as I want to shut out the outside world, I also want to be taken seriously. If I'm to be the head of a major production company, I can't disappear whenever I like.

The phone vibrates incessantly the second it springs to life. There are more than texts this time; there are also three missed calls. I check the call log, not wanting to dial in and listen to the messages. No surprise; one is from my father and the other, my assistant. I'm sure neither of them liked my vague, noncommittal response earlier.

But the other missed call is from Hilary Montrose, the head of the public relations firm that my family employs, and there's also a text from her.

I don't open any of the texts. "Shit."

The bone-melting sensation from the massage suddenly evaporates even though I don't know what's happened or why she's reaching out. At this point, the details don't matter; it's never a good sign when Hilary contacts you.

"Everything okay?" Jane sweeps her legs over the ottoman to face me.

I shrug. "Maybe. Just checking messages." Head still down, I opt for starting with Lainey, my assistant. While only five years older than I am, she's a straight-shooter and wise. She'll tell me like it is and prepare me for what Hilary wants.

I click on her name and a string of text messages pop up.

Lainey: WTF Roman?

Why couldn't you tell me you're in Houston?

She can't be ticked off because I didn't tell her where I am. She works for me. I keep reading.

Lainey: I've got your father breathing down my neck. He's out for blood. And he's finally sicced Hilary on me.

Who the fuck are you with?

This doesn't look good.

Call me.

I have no idea what she's talking about, but she includes a link with her texts. From the URL, I can tell it's to a media outlet. My stomach muscles clench, and I hold my breath and click.

This is why I left LA, to get away from all of this crap. If only for a few days.

"Holy shit."

Jane's voice barely registers as I stare at my phone. Splashed across the main page are pictures of the two of us.

Jane and me.

From this afternoon.

In my suite.

We're in hotel robes, and given the angle, whoever took the picture stood in the hallway. Who did this? Was it one of the therapists? I doubt it; they had their hands full, hauling things out of the room.

Was it the room service guy? From our position in the images, it's plausible, but we had eyes on him. Well, not all the time, but I've had far too many years of this shit to miss the guy pulling out his phone.

Dammit, for all I know, some lucky bastard may have been strolling by the room and took the picture. The door was wide open for some time.

Why didn't I think of the risk at the time?

But the pictures are innocent enough. Jane's hair is up and her head is at an angle where her face isn't in full view, but there's no mistaking it's me. One of the shots is of me handing her a bottle of water.

While Jane may not be a celebrity, which is fortunate, the kicker is the accompanying article.

My chest spasms.

Lainey's right. This doesn't look good for me.

In big bold letters at the top of the page, the headline reads:

Roman Kingsley not fit to be King

The captions under the photos aren't much better. One says, "Kingsley at it again. So much for mature and dedicated."

Another still, "If nothing else, Kingsley's consistent at having a good time."

And finally, "Who's the mystery woman Kingsley's shacking up with?"

My phone rings and a text from my father flashes on the screen. Fuck, he must have seen the news. There's no way he's going to let me run AKS now.

$$\text{———}$$

JANE

$$\text{———}$$

"WHAT'S WRONG?" A sharp twinge of anxiety shoots through my chest.

The way Roman's face pales then hardens strikes me in the stomach. He stares down at the ringing phone in his hand, silences it, and lets out a roar.

I jump and release a terrified squeak. "Roman, what is it?"

His expression shifts into something more conciliatory though still upset. At the same time, my phone chimes, startling me. A quick glimpse at the screen confirms it's Monty.

Why the hell is he calling me now? He should be preparing for the game.

I send the call to voicemail but before I can turn it off an alert pops up at the top of the screen. Roman's name catches my eye.

Though I'm not proud to admit it, when in the bathroom after the massage, I set up media monitoring on Roman Kingsley. This means I get an alert with any online mention of his name.

I was fascinated by his news of going into movie production, his family's company, and also the sad fact that he was leaving acting altogether.

What's happening between us this weekend may be a onetime thing, but I have no less interest in his new career path. I want to watch him succeed because I've no doubt that he will.

Before I can hit the alert and sneak a peek at the news on Roman, his voice pulls me out of my musings.

"There's no easy way to tell you. Have a look for yourself." He shoves his phone at me, and while I take his, I drop mine back into the pocket of my robe.

Pictures. The screen is a barrage of pictures, and at first, I'm not processing what I'm looking at. But only a few beats later all the images merge into one clear picture.

My stomach plummets to my toes like a rock dropping to the bottom of a lake. *Thud.*

Images of us. These are pictures from only hours ago, in this very suite.

"What on earth…" My blood cools, my internal temperature dropping fast, until I'm chilled to the bone.

Pictures of me in a bathrobe are on the Internet. I read the article, needing to understand how this happened and more importantly, what's being said.

With each word I digest, a prickly sensation gathers at the back of my eyes, and the sensation grows stronger as I click on the related links within the article. Panic, maybe something more like anger, hot and unwieldy, robs me of all common sense.

The words jumble and I force myself to look at Roman.

Too tight and tingly, my body doesn't feel like my own, and this foreign sensation zips through me when I stare at him, his expression flat and unreadable.

What have I done?

Bile rises up my throat.

Who is this man?

"Oh, no. Roman. Oh, my God. This can't be—"

He inches closer, and his expression of concern and determination, as if he means to placate or soothe me, sends alarm bells clanging through my brain.

I jump away from him. "You're seeing Palmira Lamont. You're a…you're a cheater just like Monty." I vibrate with rage. "You're no different, and to make matters worse, you made me an accomplice to your infidelity."

Palmira Lamont is a Hollywood darling, like Julia Roberts or Jennifer Aniston, only younger. I think she's a few years older than I am and a rising star. The daughter of an American tycoon and Italian mother, she has been linked to Roman in the past, if memory serves me right.

"Jane, no." He lunges for me, but I'm just as quick and sidestep his hold. "I'm not in a relationship with Palmira."

"Then what do you call this?" I shove the device at him and point to the words, the paragraphs about these stupid photos.

Not long into the story enters the mention of the beautiful, talented actress, and of course, not to miss the chance to hint at a scandal because everyone loves a good scandal, the reporter goes on to speculate what this mystery woman—that would be me—in a bathrobe in what looks to be a hotel suite with Roman Kingsley could mean for his relationship with his girlfriend, Palmira.

I click on a related article about the happy couple. My finger furiously flicks through the countless images of Roman and the actress over the past many months. The myriad of photos are a mixture of formal, regal almost, some on the red carpet, and casual and cozy, but all insinuate one thing—Roman and Palmira are an item.

"God, I'm such a fool. You're an actor. Of course, I never stood a chance at catching you in a lie. Monty was one thing. I'd given him the benefit of the doubt because of my misguided belief that he was a good guy. I mean, I've known him for most of my life. He'd never hurt me. Yeah, right."

My sarcasm and scathing bitterness cause both of us to tense, but he quickly rolls over any shock and resumes his quest to close the gap between us.

Muscles tight, stomach roiling, I hold up a hand to stop him. "You must be one hell of a liar. I can't wait to hear how you explain all this."

The scathing words spewing from me do as I intend. Roman stops advancing on me, and the way his face hardens at my comment punches me in the gut. I can't feel sorry for him, or feel anything at all where he's concerned.

He's a liar and a cheat.

God, what am I? Some kind of magnet for a certain kind of human garbage?

"Jane, it isn't what it looks like, and if you'll calm the fuck down and give me a chance to explain, I will."

In a jerky nod, my chin points at him, encouraging him to go on. I don't want his lies, but in a bizarre, can't-turn-away-from-the-train-wreck kind of way, I've got to see this through.

I ran from Monty only a day ago and what did that do? Only delay the inevitable. Delay the pain and anguish.

"All those pictures of Pal and me, they aren't real." Harshly, he rakes a hand through his hair. "They were planned, orchestrated for the media."

"Pal? Well, it sure sounds like you know her well. Go on. I'll admit, I'm curious to see just how creative you're gonna get with this made-up story of yours." I cross my arms over my chest, less as a barricade and more out of fear that I might crumble if I don't hold myself tight.

Why did I let myself get swept off my feet?

I fell for all of this. The suite. The movie star. His swoony smirks and wicked tongue.

Gah, I really need to give up on men and sex altogether. I have the shittiest taste in men.

His cheek muscle tics, and it's plain to see how tightly he's clenching his jaw. His dark eyes are almost incendiary, locked on me, and threatening to burn me to ash. There's no doubt he's determined to make me see things his way.

Why, I don't know. This was never meant to last past the weekend. It doesn't make a difference anyway. That's why I don't understand why it hurts the way it does.

We stand off, both of us tense, when the ringing of his phone cuts through the silence. Roman looks down at it, hits the screen, and groans.

Frustrated and wanting this over, I snap at him, "What now? Who is it?"

"My father. He's probably calling about this. He's already texted. Fuck."

He paces, and my heart pinches, somewhat sympathetic to his situation after what he's shared about his father.

No. No. No.

His problems shouldn't matter to me. I shouldn't care.

I steel my spine. "You know, you're going to have to face him eventually."

"I will. I want to see if he leaves a message." His phone chimes, and on a long exhale, he taps the screen and follows the prompts to enter his passcode.

"You're playing his message on speaker phone?" This surprises me.

"Yeah. It isn't going to be pretty, maybe even embarrassing because my father can be an asshole, but Jane,"—he pauses in hitting the number to play his new message and captures my gaze—"I don't have any secrets from you. I'm not lying to you about Palmira. Those pictures—they were just for the media. At first, it started as a way to generate buzz for our upcoming movie. The lead actors getting involved is so cliché but great for the press and to get people wanting to see the movie."

His tone and gaze are both so sincere and something else, something raw and imploring, that they stoke the barely flickering flame of hope low in my belly. Hope that this time with him won't be tainted with lies and infidelity.

My silly heart knots and flips, and despite no more proof than his word, I nod and he presses the screen.

Do I believe him? I want to.

A deep, booming voice, loud and insistent like the beating of drums, blares from the phone. "Roman, what the fuck is this? I'm so goddamn tired of this bullshit."

Alexander Kingsley's voice is velvety conviction, and despite how upset he is, I can tell where Roman gets his commanding confidence from. "I told you not to make me regret bringing you into AKS. Fucking call me. You said you were serious—"

Roman taps the screen and ends the call. "He's going to kick me out of AKS before I even have a chance to show him what I'm capable of. Shit, I wouldn't put it past him to get on a plane today and come to Houston."

Spinning away from me, he tosses the phone onto the sofa and marches toward a window. "I fucked this up. Goddammit."

At a loss for how to comfort him, I pull up the latest Roman media notification on my phone and stare down at the same article that was on his, or more specifically, the pictures.

The two of us in bathrobes, standing close. They are grainy, poor quality images but loaded with sexual overtones and innuendo. I recall the instant the shot was taken, and the irony is that nothing was going on.

An innocent moment.

We were only talking. We weren't even alone, though whoever took the picture was smart enough not to get the massage therapists in the picture.

Like he said about all the shots with Palmira, so much can be misinterpreted and easily give the wrong impression.

With his back still to me, his fingers interlace and lock behind his neck, every fiber of his being rigid. When I glance down at the pictures again, I'm instantly knocked back on my heels.

The solution is obvious.

Suddenly fizzing with hope, I venture closer to him. "So this arrangement you have with Palmira, does that mean you know her well?"

He peers over his shoulder at me, skeptical and intrigued. "Yeah. Why?"

Still unsure if we can pull off my idea but growing more confident as the seconds tick by, I take another step toward him.

"I think I know how to fix this."

Once more, I flip the phone around and show him the pictures of us. If he's like me, he doesn't need to see them—they are emblazoned on the inside of my eyelids—but it's important for him to be looking at them when I say this next bit.

"This could be you and Palmira."

"What?" He takes the phone from me and further examines the pictures.

"Look at them. The quality is shit, which works to our advantage, and though Palmira's a little taller than I am, I think you could say it's her. Tell the media that whatever hacks wrote this story should do their homework before publishing because they got it wrong."

Slowly, he raises his head to me, eyes sparkling, and a slow, triumphant—even a little dirty—grin skates across his face.

"The only thing is, you'd have to talk to Palmira. Make sure she would back you up. Do you think this is something she'd go along with?"

His body jolts to life, humming with an energy that wasn't there a beat before. "Holy shit, yes."

Closing the gap between us, his steps are self-assured and his gaze never strays from mine, bright and marvelous. "Fuck, you're a genius. This might work."

Cupping my face in his big palms, Roman plants a quick hot kiss on my lips, hands me my phone, and grabs his from the couch. "Pal would go for this, but first, let me get Hilary Montrose on the line."

"Who?"

"Hil owns the Montrose PR agency. I'm a client. Well, the entire Kingsley family is, actually."

Busily, he punches on his screen, and I swallow back the rising panic, not comprehending what he's doing. "Roman. I don't—"

"One sec." He holds up a finger, and in the next breath, a ringing emanates from the phone only to end when someone answers.

"Roman, thank you for calling." A pragmatic female voice fills the room. "We need to talk."

"Hilary, before you rip me a new one, I'm way ahead of you and have a solution. A way to fix all of this."

"Roman, we've talked about this before. It's my job to deal with things like this." Her placating tone, polished and even, suggests she's used to handling clients like him, the ones who think they've got it covered and don't need a publicist or crisis manager.

He chuckles as if he hasn't a care in the world, and while my idea is a good one, it isn't without flaws, and anything could go wrong.

"Seriously, I'm on it and have a solution, or actually I should say Jane Hastings does."

"Jane? Who? What are you talking about?" While Hilary Montrose is just a name, given the way she fires her questions, she doesn't have the time or patience for whatever she thinks this is.

This makes me wonder just how many phone calls her office must have received from the media because of those photos.

"Jane's the woman in the pictures."

A long sigh precedes her voice. "With all due respect, unless you're going to tell me she's now your wife and you're on your honeymoon or better yet, she's your future wife and you're engaged—that I can work with. I could easily sell it as the Hollywood wedding of the year. Roman Kingsley finally settles down. Other than that, I doubt you have a solution."

"Funny, but no. Hear me out, Hil. I've got Jane with me, and I want her to take you through this."

"What?" The one word flies clear from my throat like a squeak, and he smiles and nods like that's enough encouragement to get me to talk to this stranger.

Nerves aside, I clear my throat and ignore my shaking hands. "Uh, hi, Hilary."

There's no answer from her end of the line, and my nerves ratchet up, twitching and burning throughout me. He rolls his hand quickly, in a go on motion.

Somehow, with way too many *ums* and *ahs*, and sadly a few cringe-inducing stutters, I manage to lay out my thinking for her.

She doesn't need to know me or what I look like. She's seen the photos online, and hopefully, now that I've pointed out my resemblance to Palmira, she's able to fully grasp the possibility of this wild idea.

Silence ensues, and with every breath and every beat that passes without a word from the PR guru on the line, hundreds of miles away in Los Angeles, I slowly shrink. It's annoying because I don't know this woman and shouldn't care what she thinks, and I don't. This is more about Roman. Helping him.

He's as on edge as I am, tapping his foot, until eventually he can't take the waiting any longer. "Hilary, you there? Before you say it won't work, I think it will."

Finally, she breaks her silence. "Hang on." But that's it. Another round of beats of nothing pass, and I'm about to throw up. We look at each other, not sure what to make of it.

"This is brilliant. Jane, that's your name, right?"

"Um, yes."

"This is an excellent idea, and we can work with this. Roman, you call Palmira and float this by her. If she isn't on board with our plan, call me stat."

"Hil, we won't have a problem there."

"If we do, remind her of *Pinwheel*."

I raise my eyebrows, surprised by the insinuation or is it more a threat? And who is Hilary to suggest such a thing when it's Roman's project? Yet he seems unfazed and nods even though she can't see him.

The woman barrels on, "We'll need to get her to Houston ASAP. I'll get someone on my team talking to her assistant. I want the two of you seen out tonight. Dinner, fancy, romantic, then maybe a club. I'll call the hack who covered the initial story to express our outrage. What kind of journalism is this? Don't they do research? They'll apologize and grovel by the time I'm through with them. Then we'll also reach out to a few media in Houston, only reputable outlets, and let it drop where the two of you will be tonight. We'll squash this outrageous idea of a mystery woman and today's story will become a distant memory."

Her words are rapid-fire and said with such confidence that I now believe Palmira is in the pictures and feel somewhat sorry for the poor schmuck who wrote the story.

"Sounds good." Roman looks less stressed, relaxed even.

"Roman, there's also the matter of your father."

Immediately, tension jumps on his back, now rigid and ironing-board straight. "I'll call him." He rakes a hand through his hair and readies to end the call when Hilary says, "And Jane? What do you do for a living?"

The question punches me in the throat.

It's straightforward and shouldn't be hard to answer, but it's my ultimate humiliation.

"Um, I-ah, I'm not..." I can't think fast enough to make myself sound impressive, and I hate lying. "I don't do anything. I mean, I'm a waitress but I wouldn't call it my career or anything."

My lips smack shut as I force myself to stop talking. My cheeks redden. Again, my response doesn't pull a negative reaction from her.

"You might want to think about a career change. PR sounds like your calling. You're a natural. Roman, text me once you've spoken to Pal. Talk later."

Then she's gone and he mutters something about being right back as he marches toward the bedroom with his phone. I guess he's calling the actress, but funny how he doesn't want me to hear that conversation.

All doubts and worries are shoved to the back of my mind. I can't begin to understand Hollywood and though I desperately want to believe that there's nothing going on with him and Palmira, there may very well be.

And truthfully, as much as it sickens me to think he may have been unfaithful, that I may be the other woman, I don't know what kind of relationship they have. It could be an open one, and Roman does this kind of thing all the time.

Oh, God, I can't think like that, or I'll vomit for sure.

We never promised each other anything beyond this weekend, and I agreed to this. I wanted it, even.

Although, the idea of being just one woman among many doesn't sit right with me. In fact, I feel downright dirty. I guess I'm not cut out for this kind of thing.

He enters the living room in under fifteen minutes, beaming. "Jane Hastings, get your ass over here."

He rubs his hands together, and his easy grin, the one that's all for me, brings a sweet flutter deep in my chest. Before I can say a word or even get off the couch, he's on me.

His lean, muscled body crowds me, fills my nostrils with his heady, masculine scent, and the feral, possessive gleam in his stare sets my insides on fire.

I giggle, anticipation fizzing through my veins, and his mouth crashes onto mine. His hands undo my robe and his lips trail kisses from my face to between the valley of my breasts, down to my belly button.

My head swims, sensations squashing all thought and reason. Yet I have too many questions and I need to know what happened. Reluctantly, I push at his shoulders as his mouth presses into my pelvic bone. I can't believe I'm stopping Roman Kingsley from eating me out. This man is a master at it.

"Wait." I brush my hair out of my eyes. "What happened?"

He chuckles against my flesh, hot breath skating over my nether regions and causing me to quiver.

"Really? That's what you want right now?" He arches a brow.

Maybe it's the way he asks, or truth be told it's simply him—this man—that snaps some sense into me. "No. No." My fingers weave into his thick hair as I push his head down to my sex. "Tell me later."

And later he does.

We lie entwined on the couch, Roman at my back when he breaks our blissful silence. "So Palmira's on a flight from New Orleans and should be here within the next hour or so."

"Just like that? You call her and she shows up."

"She was flying in tomorrow anyway, so it's a little easier than asking her to drop everything."

"She was supposed to be in Houston tomorrow?"

He plays with my hair. "Yeah."

"What did I miss? You expect me to believe there's nothing between the two of you, but she was always going to be here with you." I try to get off the couch.

Lightning quick, he grabs the ends of the ties to my robe and twists them around his hand, drawing me closer.

"Jane, come on. I thought we were past that. She's my secret weapon for the *Pinwheel* meeting. The writer had an actress in mind for the lead role when she was writing the script."

He pauses and it takes me a bit to put two and two together. I'm too focused on how close we are and if I should be pushing him away or falling into his arms.

Then it clicks and the fog lifts from my mind.

"Oh...I see."

To be sure I'm following, his voice rumbles, "I've already secured Pal for the role, but only if AKS produces."

"That's—" I nervously laugh, suddenly feeling silly for jumping to the worst case scenario."—brilliant."

"No, you are, and like Hil said, you really should think about it. PR might be your thing. That's a rare compliment. She doesn't give out many of those and for her to give you kudos, you should take it to heart."

"Not a chance." I snort and will the heat creeping into my cheeks to evaporate. "I'd have to go to college, and I can't afford it. Now that things are over with Monty, I have to go home."

I don't want to think about going home. There's nothing there for me. My mother died when I was in high school, and my father remarried within the year. His new wife didn't care much for me and wanted me gone. I was the cause of many an argument between her and my dad. Luckily, I had Monty, and when he got drafted into the major league, I left with him.

Now my father's older, needs more care, and he's in no position to fight with her if I were to ask to stay with them. Even if I go back to Marathon, I'm not staying with them.

There was one time when Monty said he'd help with college, but it never came to pass. Whenever I brought it up, he'd say he wanted me with him. That I didn't need a job. Against his wishes, I got the waitressing job so I'd have my own money and something to do.

Roman's question pulls me back to the hotel suite. "Where's home?"

"The Florida Keys. Marathon."

He nods. "Money aside, you should give it some thought. You're young. You could still do college, and there's always scholarships or grants."

"I don't know. There's a lot to think about, and I'm not sure I could stomach all the underhandedness around PR."

"It's like anything—you don't have to conduct yourself that way. I mean, look at what we're doing now with the pictures. We aren't hurting anyone and this situation wasn't our doing. Someone else wanted to make a buck, and we're trying to lessen the fallout from that."

"What about your father? Did you talk to him?"

He nods, lips pressing into a grim line. "Yeah, it's fine."

"That's all you're giving me."

"You're not going to like what I said to him."

"Tell me."

"I told him what we're telling the media. I'm with Pal."

My heart hurts, and it shouldn't. It isn't true. Roman is here with me. But even so, he felt the need to lie to his father in order to make things right. That saddens me—mostly for him, as I get the sense he's been trying to please his father for most of his life and continually falls short.

I'm also disheartened to think that while I'm never going to meet Alexander Kingsley, something tells me that I'd fall short, too.

As soon as Roman leaves for dinner with Palmira, I head to Monty's room to gather my things. When Roman guessed I was going to do this while he was gone, he almost canceled tonight's plan. He wanted me to wait until he came back so we could go together.

I didn't want to wait. Besides, going later would only increase our chances of running into Monty.

So we compromised. If I was going without him, then I had to text him once I left Monty's room. But that wasn't enough. Roman also made me promise to call him if my ex showed up or if I simply needed him for anything at all.

Overwhelmed by his genuine concern for me, I almost lost it in front of him and broke down and cried. He was sweet and as much as I needed to know he was there for me, I wouldn't jeopardize his dinner. And fortunately, there was no need for him to be worried. Nothing happened.

Once back in the suite, I call Gail, a friend from work in Philly. I need a place to stay once I get back, and she's the only one I'm close enough with to ask. It also helps that she isn't Monty's friend.

The conversation isn't long. It's hard enough admitting to myself what Monty did and how much of a jerkwad he is, but it's another kind of difficult to share it with Gail or any of my friends. Fortunately, she readily invites me to stay as long as I want, and this eases some of the dread about leaving Houston.

Not long after that, news notifications about Roman start to appear on my phone, and quickly mushroom to the point that I'm forced to turn it off.

Deliberately, I don't click on any of them, and instead fill my time repacking my suitcase, picking out what to wear home tomorrow, and soaking in the bath for a long time.

But I have only so much willpower and don't know what to do with this sudden abundance of time. It's as if time has stopped, if only to torture me, and eventually I cave.

As promised by Hilary, dozens of media sites cover their romantic dinner with headlines that set the record straight. Palmira Lamont and Roman Kingsley are on a weekend getaway and madly in love.

My insides are at war. My heart races with lightness and joy. It's as if the photo debacle never existed, and I hope this means Alexander Kingsley is happy. Yet at the same time, my chest feels like it's imploding.

It's hard not to linger on the pictures of the two of them, even if they're fake. Both of them are stunning and flawless. It's plain to see they belong together.

By the time eleven rolls around, I'm on the couch, restless and nowhere near ready to sleep. I want to wait up for Roman. This is our last night together.

$$\text{---}$$

ROMAN

$$\text{---}$$

"Now this is the best kind of treat to come home to." I stare down at Jane curled into a ball on the couch and bend to nuzzle my face in her neck. "Wake up, Jane."

I kiss her warm, soft skin, and she stirs. Her sun-kissed legs lengthen and she unfurls her arms from her chest as she turns to face me.

She blinks up at me. "Roman? What time is it?"

"It's a little after midnight." My lips brush hers. "I hate to wake you." Another kiss. "Kind of. I should let you sleep, but I'm a selfish bastard and want you."

The rest of my thought, the words, lodge in my throat. I don't want to think about how little time we have left together.

Still sleepy and eyes half-closed, she yawns. "Did everything go okay?"

"Better than okay, but I don't want to talk about that. What are you wearing?" She's in a T-shirt I haven't seen before and a clean pair of what looks like my boxers.

Her cheeks heat and she turns her face into the cushion, bashful. "I figured you wouldn't mind. I can change into the robe if it's a problem."

"I'm not talking about my boxers. I like you in my clothes. Would love it more if you were out of them." My teeth nip at her bottom lip. "I mean the shirt."

We both stare at the words printed on the front of her shirt. It reads, "I have a good heart, but this mouth."

The corners of her lips twitch. "It's mine. I got my things from Monty's room. I'm all set for my flight."

Not wanting to dwell on her ex or her upcoming departure, I ask, "Are you saying you have a sassy mouth, Jane?"

"Um, yeah."

"Do you want to know what I want to do with that mouth of yours?"

She wets her lips with a quick swipe of her tongue, and I swear it's deliberate. She's torturing me as images of her lush, pouty lips and her hot, pink tongue around my cock flood my mind.

Her gaze dips to my crotch, and she quirks a brow. "I can guess."

"Can you now?" Hovering above her on the couch, I push back onto my knees. "Then why don't you show me."

She shivers, her fingers quickly undoing my belt, button, and zipper as she shimmies to sitting. Big blue eyes look up at me, and her slender hand wraps around my hardening length. *God, what a sight.*

Jane's perfect, and if I didn't know better, I'd say she was made for me.

The tip of her tongue darts from her mouth to touch the head of my cock, and the muscles in my thighs quake as she swirls it around like I'm a goddamn ice cream cone and I'm her favorite flavor.

Holy shit.

Her fiery gaze dances with delight and something else, something possessive. She's fucking enjoying this, and that thought only makes me swell more.

My cock hits the back of her throat, and I hiss at how tight-fisted she sucks. Squeezing me. I thrust into her mouth, and my fingers burrow into her thick hair. She slowly bobs her head up and down, each time taking as much of me as she can.

Motherfucker.

Something shifts or snaps, and suddenly Jane's no longer teasing. Her hot slippery mouth pulls faster, lips suctioning my shaft as one hand tugs gently on my balls. Normally, it wouldn't be enough. Too light, too insignificant, but fuck, not this time. Jane's touch electrifies me.

"Fuck, Jane." My head tips back as black dots and silvery lines swim behind my eyelids.

Just like that, I lose the quickly unraveling grasp on my control. The burgeoning pressure burns down my spine and my balls pull up, taut and heavy, in an eruption of ecstasy.

She slows at drawing me in, her mouth easing its grip, as I come so fucking hard I lose my sight and spill deep into her mouth. I pull back, and before she can do or say anything, I sheath myself with a condom from my pants pocket and slide my hands around her waist.

"Roman. What the..." She giggles as I carry her to the dining room table. The perfect height for me.

In one quick motion, I pull off the boxers, and thank fuck she doesn't have any panties on. Two fingers slide through her soft, slippery folds, and like a good girl, she spreads her legs wide, inviting me.

With my other hand, I yank my pants and boxers down to my knees and sink into her.

The back of her head thumps lightly onto the wood, and in a high-pitched voice she moans, "Oh, my God."

Though I only came moments ago, I'm still semi-hard, and with a few deep thrusts inside her, I'm rock solid once more.

My fingers circle her clit as I drive into her, and a near animalistic sound tears from Jane's throat as she arches her back clear off the table. Her pussy spasms around me, muscles rigid, toes curling into the wood, and fingernails digging into my flesh. And then she comes.

Growling and clenching my teeth, I ride out her orgasm, almost there but wanting to make sure she finishes completely before I come again.

Face flushed and lips parted, pure bliss eclipses her features. Watching her come undone causes me to fly over the edge. Blistering tingles fire through me, scoring my veins, and my climax crescendos and bulldozes over me so suddenly that my knees nearly give out.

One hand flies from Jane to clutch the edge of the table in an effort to stay upright. The other tightens my grasp on her hip, pinning her there as I bury myself inside her, until there is no end to her or beginning to me.

"Jane." My head spins and I lean forward to kiss her.

Limp and mind-blown, I hover over her until I catch my breath. Wordlessly, we move to clean up in the powder room.

Freshly fucked and glowing, she follows me to the kitchen where I get us each a bottle of water.

Sheepishly, she leans against the doorjamb between the kitchen and dining room. "Tell me more about dinner. Tonight. I saw the photos. It looks like everyone's buying it."

Nodding, I stalk toward her, not wanting to taint this moment, our final few hours together, with talk of spin-doctoring, Palmira, or any of that shit.

"It did. But I wanted to be here with you. Only one thing on my mind." My head bends toward her mouth and stops at the knock on the door. "What the hell?"

We silently go to the door and I check the peephole, immediately recognizing the asshole.

"Fuck, it's Fisher." I clench my fists at my side, and Jane wheezes and stiffens. "We don't have to open the door."

Monty pounds on the door. "Jane, I know you're in there. Open up. I'm not going anywhere."

"Let him in." She motions for me to step back.

"You don't have to talk to him." I try again to impress upon her that she doesn't have to do this. Not now. Not ever.

"I have to talk to him eventually, and now might be better. I don't want to run into him at our place tomorrow."

Before I can say anything else, she turns the knob and swings the door open. Montgomery Fisher looms in the doorway, light, shaggy hair falling over his forehead.

His sharp, angular features appear more haggard than I recall from seeing him on TV, and I suppose it could have something to do with his team losing the championship. His bloodshot eyes and grim expression are signs of a loser, and I can't help but think it suits him.

"I fucking knew it was you." He jabs his finger at her and pushes his way into the suite.

As much as I don't want him here, it's a necessary evil. We only just cleaned up the mess of the photos; we don't need another opportunist getting wind of this conversation and taking more pics for the Internet.

"What are you talking about?" She worries her bottom lip, but apart from that, her expression is unreadable. I can't tell what seeing her ex is doing to her.

"You fuck him?" His question stuns me, and it takes me a second to process the meaning, and Jane gasps.

In that time, Fisher gets in her face, features pointed and menacing. "You said you fucking would. Did you do this to get back at me, or did you plan this? I mean, fuck." He stands tall, hand brushing his hair back from his forehead, and his features pinch in agony. "Janie, I get that I hurt you, but I never thought you were this vindictive."

"What are you talking about? And how did you find me?"

He's on a different track, ignoring or not comprehending what Jane says. "Did you fucking know he'd be here in this hotel?"

"Monty, I don't—"

He grabs her by the bicep, and seeing his hand on her does something to me. I fly at him, rip his hand off her, and push him up against the wall.

"Get the fuck out, asshole."

Unexpectedly, he belts out a laugh and sways under my grip, not in the least bit afraid. He's drunk, maybe even high.

"You fucked him, didn't you." He pushes out of my grasp, and I let him go.

The fool is harmless and heartbroken. He's had time to come to grips with what he's lost, or more like, who. It serves him right.

"Janie, you're a whore." His vitriolic slur causes me to see red.

I toss him across the foyer. "You fucking piece of shit."

Monty lands on his ass, head lightly bumping into the door.

"Roman, no." Jane grabs at my arm, trying to stop me from advancing on him.

Reluctantly, I stop and glance over my shoulder at her. "I'm going to make him bleed for talking to you like that."

"Please. No. He may deserve it, and if this were last night, right after I found him in the bathroom, I'd have helped you." She nears me, and I turn to face her.

Jane places her hands on each of my biceps. "He isn't worth the trouble he could cause." She lowers her voice and her stare intensifies, penetrates into my soul. "This time with you has made me see that none of that matters. I'm better off without him, and I don't care about him. But I need to talk to him. Can you please give us a minute?"

"Alone?" Fuck, no way.

"Yes." She tugs me toward the hallway to the bedroom. "I'll be fine. He won't hurt me, even if he says nasty things. If I need you, I promise to holler."

My gut clenches at the thought, and though every fiber of my being wants to argue with her and plant my ass on the sofa, I nod.

From the corner of my eye, I see Fisher stumble to get up, blinking several times as if he's unable to focus on us.

It's childish and uncalled for, but I can't help myself. My hands cradle her face and I kiss her long and hard. Fisher groans obscenities but doesn't make a move toward us.

I stab a finger at him and glare. "You fucking step out of line and mine'll be the last face you see tonight."

He snorts but doesn't utter a comeback, and I leave. Once in the bedroom, I sag and press my forehead against the wall.

Fuck, I gotta respect her wishes even if it's killing me not to go out there. To not declare to him and the rest of the world that Jane and I are together.

If only.

AT THE END of the hallway the bedroom door snicks closed, and some of the tension pinching at the back of my neck and shoulders scatters. Roman and Monty together, in the same room, isn't a good thing. My nerves can't take it, let alone my heart.

I run a hand through my tousled hair and face my ex. "How did you find me?"

He slumps against the wall, hands clutching the sides of his head as if to hold himself together. "I'm not stupid."

He's been drinking and may be in pain. The loss of the championship—the Flashes killed it this season, and I so wanted them to win—is a huge hit. Monty had a lot riding on tonight, and despite how he's hurt me, empathy pinches at my heart.

Not wanting to dignify his words with a response, I choose kindness. What anyone would deserve when a dream has been dashed or they've suffered a setback. "I'm sorry about tonight. The game."

Exhaling, he drops his hands and looks up at me with his puppy dog eyes. "You watched it?"

I nod and swallow, not wanting to give him an inch to worm his way into my heart again. It isn't going to work. Not this time. "Yeah. Monty, tell me, how did you know I was here?"

Straightening, he squares his shoulders and tightens his jaw. "After you told me you had a crush on that actor, that he was your hall pass, I set up an alert on him."

His eyes shut and I stare, watching him breathe. He breathes so deeply and for so long, I wonder if he's going to continue or what he's doing.

With a blink, his gaze slices to me, pointed. "I'd get shit on him all the time, and I barely looked at it before. Deleted it as it came in. I mean, what were the chances of you two..." He scoffs and curls his upper lip at the irony. "Then this afternoon, I don't know why, but something made me click on the article...

maybe because of the headline. Maybe because you were gone and it reminded me of you or made me feel connected to you."

Another grunt as he shakes his head ruefully. "Fuck. When I saw that picture of you in a bathrobe with him..."

How is this even possible? Of all things. A lump forms in my throat, and though difficult to swallow or even talk, I have to know.

"You saw that? What makes you think it was me?"

He throws me the side-eye. "Jane, I'd know you anywhere, but the hair clip erased any doubt that it was anyone else but you."

The hair clip. The one I'd handmade during one of my mom's workshops for the tourists back in the summer between sixth and seventh grade.

She and I used to collect local items like seashells, flowers, leaves, even frayed rope, anything really. We'd prime and prep them for a kind of arts and crafts class she would offer to the tourists.

Create a keepsake to remember your stay. Make new memories of this special trip. My mom's voice rings loud and clear in my head as if she's here right now, trying to get people to sign up for the class.

The hairclip was my favorite, more because I'd made it with Mom than for any other reason, and I never went anywhere without it. My hair was up in the picture and for the massage.

Monty had been paying attention, even though more than half the time he didn't act like it. I'm not surprised he recognized the clip but more that he was attempting to keep tabs on Roman.

Until this weekend, I'd have laughed in his face and maybe even called him a little unhinged for online stalking my celebrity crush. Never in a million years would I have imagined I'd actually sleep with Roman Kingsley.

But realizing this about my ex doesn't change anything.

So what if he was more aware than I thought?

The real concern is if Monty knowing the truth could ruin all the work done by Hilary Montrose, Roman, and Palmira?

Shit.

Yeah, he could if he knew it was important, and soon enough, if he reads the news, he'll realize we've covered up the fact that it was me.

I've got to get him to keep his mouth shut.

"It was a hotel mix-up and they double-booked this room. The place is fully booked and since it's big, there's enough room for both of us to stay here. But you can't tell anyone I was here. Got that?"

I hate having to spell this out for him and wish I could act like this isn't a big deal. But I can't. Monty has a big mouth.

He loves to hear himself talk, and this story, even if it makes him look like a jackass, isn't one he'd ever pass on sharing. Although, he'd most probably change the details to make me look like the cheater and him, brokenhearted and faithful.

"If nothing happened and you're just sharing a room, what's the big deal? Why, because he's a celebrity?" His mocking tone on the word celebrity grates on my nerves, and I want to rant and rave, make him understand how important this is.

"Yes." I decide to appeal to his supposed love for me. "But it's more about me than him or anything else. Imagine the media frenzy even if this is a room mix-up. You know me; I don't like it when the reporters follow us."

Monty loves the attention, and anytime a reporter sticks a mic in his face, the boy's in his element. Not me.

"You've fucked him, haven't you?"

My heart lurches, and I narrow my eyes on him, incensed at how crass and disrespectful he is.

"That's none of your goddamn business."

"Christ, you have." His fingers grab at his hair and he bangs the back of his head against the wall. "Jane, you are my business. You're going to be my wife."

"Uh-uh. The engagement's off. We're over. I left the ring in the room in case you missed it."

He pulls the damn thing out of his pocket as if the sight of it will change my mind. And as if the ring wasn't enough to remind me what a cheating bastard he is, I haven't missed the smeared lipstick on his neck, or that in addition to the stench of booze and cigarettes, he reeks of sex.

"How did you find me? Even if you saw the photo and figured out the hotel." I hold my tongue, though I want to add, "and that's a big leap for you," but my sarcasm and lowly jab isn't going to help right now. "How did you know I was in this room?"

And there it is.

His complexion pales, eyes flying around the suite to look at anything but me. That's all the confirmation I need.

"Oh, I see. You whipped out the Monty charm, didn't you?" My word choice is deliberate, conjuring a sexual image because, in all likelihood, that's what we're talking about here. He had sex with someone to get the room information.

"Who was it? A woman at the front desk? No, wait..." I prance around the foyer, a finger tapping on my lips like I'm in deep contemplation, but I already have it all figured out. "You picked someone cleaning a room, right? Or was it room service? Did you sleep with her?"

"Shit, Jane. I didn't sleep with her. I may have flirted, but it was only to get the info I needed. I needed to find you. And baby, if this bothers you, let's face it, you're jealous, and that tells me you still care about me. We still have something."

"Oh, no." I chuckle and shake my head. "I'm not jealous. I just couldn't figure out how you found me. This makes sense."

It irks me to think how easily someone violated my privacy and Roman's for what? A make-out session or sex with Monty Fisher.

"Jane, none of that matters. I don't care if you've had sex with him, baby. I deserve it. I've been a shit, and I just want you back."

Baby. Ick.

Even now, he insists on calling me that stupid, childish nickname. From day one, I told him I didn't like it, but my opinion didn't count. He said I was too sensitive and it was his way of showing me how he felt about me.

I wasn't a fucking baby, and know what? If I was, then who the hell was he? My daddy? Fuck that.

There were so many signs from early on in our relationship that we weren't a good match. That Monty was a jerk. And little ol' Jane ignored it all. I was just so happy that a popular boy, a jock even, noticed me. I blew past all the warning signals telling me to get the hell away from Montgomery Fisher.

His insensitive words sever my rambling thoughts. "Maybe one day, like you, I'll get lucky with my hall pass. Who knew it was a thing?" He chortles, obtuse to how off-putting and heartless his comment is.

My stomach turns.

I'd rather have a root canal than touch him again, let alone marry him.

"We're over, and I'm not arguing with you about this. It's my life, and I'm done with you." I cross my arms over my chest and square my shoulders. "I'm going home tomorrow and clearing out my things. I'm taking an earlier flight than the one you're on."

He opens his mouth to say something, likely to protest, but I keep going. I'm calling the shots.

"While I'm going to be quick and take as much as I can—I only want my clothes and the things I brought with me from Marathon—you might get there before I'm done. I'd appreciate it if you stayed away for maybe an hour after your flight gets in."

"Fuck, Jane, why are you doing this? I messed up. I'm not perfect, but I'm not letting you go after all we've been through. You're the love of my life. I'm sorry, baby."

He starts toward me, arms outstretched, but my bark of laughter stops him in his tracks.

"You see, the thing is, Monty, this isn't your first time. Back in high school, some of my friends tried to tell me they'd seen you with other girls. I didn't wanna believe it, even though deep down, I knew it was true. And the time when you went off to spring training and I called you...remember that? There were women in the background, and I knew then, too. I may be foolish, but I am not stupid."

I shake my head, more in disgust with my naivete and how much time I wasted on this man than anything else.

"You did me a solid by not being able to keep your dick in your pants. I had to see it with my own eyes, so in some ways, I should thank you for it. But I won't because you don't deserve it."

His cheeks turn red and his fingers curl into fists. "Jane. Really? After all the years together, you're just going to end it. How am I going to explain this to the media? Or did you forget about that?"

He's talking about his very public proposal. Who does that? Especially with a partner that hates the spotlight. Thanks a lot, jerk-off.

Suddenly, I find myself in crisis mode, thinking the way I did earlier, when Roman was faced with the dilemma of the pictures and his father.

"You don't have to say anything right away. I won't talk to the media, and I won't tell anyone that the engagement's off. When you're ready, you can say it was your decision. I'd appreciate you telling me when and what you're going to say, but it's totally up to you. I promise to go along."

"You'd do that?" There's now a twinkle of hope in his bloodshot eyes, and I don't like it.

He's missing the point. This is another lie, not a chance at a reconciliation, and I need to make that very clear.

"Yes, I will. But you have to keep your mouth shut about this weekend. About me staying in this room. I mean it. If you so much as utter a word to anyone, I'll spill everything. I'm not just talking about reporters, but your team, our friends, anyone. I have people willing to talk about how much of a shit you are. A cheater and all."

I don't have anyone lined up at this moment but now I plan to. Two of the restaurant staff helped me get out of there unseen after I ran into the threesome in the bathroom.

His nostrils flare and his usually relaxed features pinch and sharpen. He opens his mouth, but once again, I don't give him a chance.

"And before you even think you can spin this so I'm the cheater, the people I'm talking about aren't friends from back home that you can easily throw doubt on. You don't think people saw you in the restaurant the other night? Or what about tonight? What you did to get the room number. I'm willing to bet your fangirl will be just as easily lured by a payout, maybe more so than your dick because it'll be a *big* payout." He chokes on my words but I'm not done. "Your image as the all-around American golden boy will be ruined. I'll make sure of it."

He clutches at his chest, features ashen. "Shit, Jane. That's harsh. I never thought you were like that."

"Yeah, well, once upon a time, I'd never have believed that you'd turn out to be such an asshole."

Jane zips up her suitcase and places it on the floor while I watch her from the doorway.

"You all set?" I squirm from one foot to the other in an attempt to overlook the mounting pang of melancholy taking up residence in my chest.

The sound of my voice startles her. She spins in one smooth move to face me. Her tight, shocked, expression smooths out at the sight of me, and she offers me a small smile.

"Yup." She wheels her luggage past me, and I follow her toward the door of the suite.

We only have a few more minutes before she has to go, and as much as I wish to walk her all the way down to the front entrance, I can't. All it would take is a photo of the two of us and everything we've achieved in the past twenty-four hours would be for nothing.

"Before you leave, I have something to tell you." I tug on her wrist.

"What is it?"

Sliding in front of her, I take both of her hands in mine. "Okay, I've been thinking a lot about what Hil said."

She cocks her head to one side, puzzled. "What are you talking about? Did something happen?"

"No. Everything's fine. I've been thinking about what she said about you and how good you were yesterday. Pal could really be your doppelgänger." I flash a flirty smile, hoping to lessen the mounting worry furrowing her brow. "Not to mention what you said to Monty last night."

I can't help the smile, huge and cocky, as I relive what she threatened him with in the early hours of the morning. Waiting things out in the bedroom had been rough, but her recount of their conversation when she came to bed was priceless.

"Hil's right. You're a natural, and before you say anything, I want you to hear me out. All of it. I have a friend in senior administration at the University of Southern California, Marty Cantrell. I told her about you. Hilary also gave her a call. She wants you to call her."

Jane gasps, eyes widening in what looks a lot like terror, and it forces me to keep talking, needing to settle her nerves and make her see this is a good thing.

"Listen, I explained you're going through some stuff right now and it might take a few weeks, so she isn't expecting a call tomorrow, but I'd say call her in a few weeks."

"Um, thank you, but you didn't need to and shouldn't have done that. I can't afford USC. I told you yesterday, college isn't for me." She tries to pull away from me, but I tighten my grip on her hands. "While I have some savings, it isn't much. Certainly not enough for USC. I'm most probably going home to Marathon after I give notice at work."

"Hey, you promised to hear me out. I'm not done and you haven't heard the best part. They have scholarships, and Marty thinks you have a good shot. Nothing's guaranteed, of course, but you've got a leg up with a recommendation from the head of the Montrose PR Agency."

My fingers squeeze hers and her eyes dip to the floor. "You most probably don't know it, but Hil's a big deal in LA. She's one of the two top PR agencies in Hollywood. If she's raving about you, people listen."

She releases a long sigh and her shoulders drop from where they'd risen to her ears. "Thank you, but no. I'm going back to Florida."

I slide a finger under her chin and tip her head up to lock eyes with hers. "What's there for you? You told me about your father and his wife. It doesn't sound like they'll welcome you into their home. This is a chance at a fresh start. I could give you some money."

She yanks her hand violently from my grasp. "No. I don't need a handout."

I hold up a hand in surrender. "Shit, I didn't mean it as a handout. I just would hate for you not to take this chance. I think you have a much bigger and better life ahead of you than both Monty and Florida."

Her body doesn't soften; nor does her expression. "Don't you see, this is no different from what I did with Monty."

"How so?"

"Everything I have is Monty's. The condo, the car I drive. All I have are my clothes and the little I've managed to put away from my job. You talking to this woman feels like all of that. I have to stop living my life this way. I'm no mooch."

I slap my lips together to hold back a laugh. This is funny. Not her, but how skewed and inaccurate her description is of herself.

"Jane, you're the furthest thing from a mooch. And this opportunity isn't being handed to you. You still have to do the work, prove yourself. I've merely made an introduction. This kind of thing happens every day and yeah, for some, this is huge, and others would say it's my privilege showing. All that may be true, but I'm not doing anything you wouldn't do for someone you cared about."

Her gaze softens and she nibbles on her bottom lip, studying me, nothing more. And as much as I want to continue to show her the countless ways that she deserves this chance, I keep my mouth shut and wait.

Jane finally blinks, and whatever she was thinking is now gone. She straightens and angles her chin just so. "Roman, I have to go."

"I know." I rest my hand on her arm and pull her close. "All I'm asking is don't throw this away. It's only a conversation. What could it hurt? And if you decide you don't want to do anything with it, well, I can't make you."

My hands slide around her neck and upward so my palms cup her face, and she shivers. "Don't get mad, but I may have given her your phone number. Marty's going to call you if she hasn't heard from you in about a month."

She groans and her eyes bug out at me. "You are the worst."

Playfully, she bats at my bicep then rests her forehead on my chest and slides her arms around my waist.

"Please do this for me."

"Okay, you big bully." Her splayed hands glide up my back. "Thank you. I wish you hadn't done this, but I can't say it isn't appreciated."

I capture her lips and kiss her deeply, fervently. This is the last time I will kiss her.

Somehow, some way, this weekend became about a whole lot more than two strangers sharing a hotel suite. The sex was unexpected and magnificent, but the greatest surprise of all was Jane. I enjoyed getting to know her and yet, I've only scratched the surface. I want more.

How we got here, to the point where I don't want to let her go, is one big blur and something I wish I could control.

I wish I could stop time and keep us in the here and now for forever.

I've had weekend flings before, though Jane doesn't need to know that, but none like this. None that have left a mark not only on my heart, but also my fucking soul.

How is it possible to like someone so much after only two days?

How is it possible that for the past few hours, I've been running through the ways in which we could make this work?

A relationship.

It's crazy.

Forget that Jane and I don't live in the same state and our lives are vastly different, there's also the very important fact that I need to completely focus, one hundred percent, on my new position with AKS.

Jane would be more than a distraction; she'd be my undoing. I can't have that.

And I wish this were all my dick talking, but if I'm honest with myself, it isn't.

Jane's a special kind of someone.

She breaks our kiss and looks away from me as she mashes her lips together. Then she's pulling away from me...one step, then two.

Her hand wraps around the handle of her suitcase, and when she looks back at me, she's smiling. Big and bright. But it's all too much of everything. Too forced. Too painful.

"Goodbye, Roman." She leans in and pecks me on the cheek. "I'll be watching from afar as you take AKS to new heights."

I grab for her and she puts up a hand to stop me. In my unraveled state, I snatch her hand instead, anything of hers to hold on to for that much longer.

My head bends and lips gently kiss the soft tips of her fingers. "Jane Hastings, it has been an utter fucking pleasure to know you."

Dropping her hand, I swallow with difficulty. She wheels her suitcase to the door and sniffles, but she doesn't look back as she opens and closes the door behind her.

Instinctually, I eat the small space to the door and hesitate, desperately wanting to open it and stop her. But that's foolish.

We had this weekend and that's it. There isn't anything more to be had, and in time, I'll be okay with that.

I have to be.

My forehead leans against the door, and I sink all my weight into the wood and rest my hands flat against the cool surface. Closing my eyes, I utter final words of goodbye in my head.

JANE

THE DOOR TO ROMAN'S SUITE CLICKS SHUT BEHIND ME, AND I TURN TO FACE the door. Silent tears now flow freely down my face.

How is it possible to miss someone I only met two days ago more than my ex-boyfriend of seven years? To miss them wholly and undeniably as if I've lost a limb, a part of me?

It's silly, really, and I can't begin to understand it.

I wipe at my tears and splay a palm against the door. As if in response, an echo to my deed, I sense a weight pressing in from the other side. Large and solid. Almost as if there's someone doing something similar from inside the hotel suite.

Roman? No. That's wishful thinking, but the heavy mass draws me in. Keeps me there.

I push my hand harder against the flat surface and hold still, inhaling deeply. Each breath. The still air. The wood. All of it helps soothe and ground me, helps me pull the broken pieces of myself back together.

The future may be unknown, but I'll be okay.

Only seconds pass, yet the longer I stand there, I seize, hoard, and commit to memory every single, glorious moment of this past weekend.

And the man...

Roman Kingsley moves right on in as if he belongs there, taking hold of a special place in my heart.

TEN YEARS LATER, PR MAVEN JANE HASTINGS IS SUMMONED TO A CLIENT MEETING where she unexpectedly comes face-to-face with the one and only Roman Kingsley, the one man she never got over.

*Sign up for a pre-order alert on **Mogul**, the first book in the all new Starstruck series.*

ABOUT S.M. WEST

S.M. West is a USA TODAY bestselling and award-winning author of sexy, angsty romances about brave hearts, wild love with a few heart-pounding twists along the way.

www.smwestauthor.com

HOME IS US

Tara Conrad

CHAPTER ONE

Scott

I WAS thirteen years old when I realized that the way I looked at other boys wasn't the same way my friends did. It wasn't some grand revelation, no sudden moment of clarity, that hit me all at once. It was quiet. A knowing that sat deep in my chest, growing roots before I even had the words to describe it.

I remember watching my friends talk about girls, the way they nudged each other in the ribs, and laughed when someone's crush walked by. I mimicked them. I nodded along and played my part. I even made up crushes of my own when the questions got too pointed. But it always felt like I was wearing a mask. Something that didn't quite fit.

No one ever suspected. Not once. I was too good at pretending, too good at blending in.

I had my first real crush on a boy named Brian when I was fifteen. He was in my biology class. Brian sat two seats ahead of me and was always twirling his pencil between his fingers when he was thinking. I remember the way my stomach twisted whenever he laughed. The way my face heated when he looked at me. It was the first time I felt something real, something undeniable. And it terrified me.

So, I shoved it down. Buried it beneath layers of denial and practiced smiles.

I even tried dating girls. It was easy enough. I liked them well enough. I liked their company, their laughter, and their kindness. But there was always something missing, something I could never quite grasp. I went to my senior prom with Melanie Williams. I put my arm around her shoulders and smiled for the pictures. She kissed me at the end of the night, and I kissed her back, waiting for the spark, the rush, anything. But it never came.

I told myself it was just because I didn't meet the right one. That when I did, everything would fall into place. That what I was feeling, or more accurately, what I wasn't feeling, was normal. That I just had to wait.

By the time I left for college, I knew better. I met people who lived freely, who didn't flinch when they said the word gay. People who talked about love the way I had always wanted to. And for the first time in my life, I let myself breathe. I kissed a boy at a party my sophomore year, and it was everything I'd spent my life convincing myself I didn't need.

I stopped pretending after that.

But I never told my parents.

I wanted so badly to be *normal*, to fit the mold they'd unknowingly built for me. I wished I could be the son they dreamed of, the one who would marry a beautiful woman, settle down in a house with a white picket fence, and raise children who would call them Grandma and Grandpa. I wanted to give them all the things they had dreamt of for my future. I wanted to be the son they envisioned in their hearts. I hated that I couldn't.

Every time I thought about telling them, my throat closed up, and my stomach turned to lead, fearing that if I told them my truth, I would disappoint them and shatter the expectations they had held onto for so long. I wondered if they'd look at me the same way or if their love had conditions.

So, I waited. And waited.

Until waiting started to feel like lying. Until I met Harrison.

In the beginning, I told myself it wasn't real. That whatever this was would fade as quickly as it sparked to life. But the more I tried to convince myself, the more I realized—some things aren't meant to be fleeting.

The night I told Harrison I love you while I held him in my arms changed everything. The lies began to feel suffocating. I no longer wanted to hide in the shadows hoping to not be found out. I wanted to share the man I love with my family.

Now, as I sit in my car outside my parents' home, I wonder if I should've waited longer. If I should've kept pretending. Kept the mask in place just a little while more.

But then I think of Harrison, of his laugh, his touch, the way he looks at me like I'm something worth holding onto. And I know I can't wait anymore.

Today, I tell the truth.

CHAPTER TWO

Scott

I GRIP MY KEYS, my fingers tightening around the cool metal as I look out the window at my childhood home.

The two-story colonial stands just as it always has, with its white siding and navy-blue shutters, a place frozen in time. The wraparound porch, where I spent countless summers watching fireflies dance in the twilight, still boasts the same wooden rocking chairs my mother insists are "too comfortable to replace."

The front yard is perfectly manicured. It's always been my father's pride and joy. The trimmed hedges line the cobblestone path leading up to the navy-blue door, the one that's been repainted more times than I can count but never strays from the same shade. A wreath hangs on it, simple but elegant, a touch of my mother's love for seasonal decor.

Growing up, this house was my sanctuary. My safe place. Within these walls, I learned the meaning of home—not just in the physical sense but in the warmth of shared laughter, the comfort of routine, and the unwavering presence of family.

I remember curling up in the bay window with a book, my mother's voice drifting in from the kitchen as she hummed along to the radio while kneading dough. She baked when she was happy, when she was stressed, and when she didn't know what else to do. The scent of cinnamon and vanilla was as much a part of my childhood as bedtime stories and Saturday morning cartoons.

This was the house where my father taught me how to ride a bike, steady hands gripping the back of the seat as he ran beside me down the driveway, shouting encouragement until I finally wobbled forward on my own. I can still hear the sound of my scraped knees being patched up in the bathroom, my mother's soft reassurances, and my father's gruff but comforting, "Toughen up, kid. You'll be fine."

On stormy nights, when thunder rattled the windows, and the power flickered, I would race downstairs to find my parents lighting candles. We'd huddle together in the living room, my mother pulling out an old deck of cards while my father told stories about the past, filling the darkness with the warmth of his deep, steady voice.

Even as I grew older, when teenage arguments flared and doors were slammed in frustration, this house was still my refuge. No matter how many times I left in anger, I always came back to find my mother waiting with a quiet understanding, a cup of tea, and my father's silent nod that told me all was forgiven.

This was home.

But will it still be after today?

The thought gnaws at my chest as I grip my keys a little tighter. A lump rises in my throat, thick with uncertainty. My parents have always been my anchor, my foundation. But I know that today, I'm going to test the strength of that foundation. What if it isn't strong enough, and today's the day it crumbles, and they let me go?

Taking a slow, unsteady breath, I step out of the car and swallow the lump in my throat. My pulse hammers as I walk up the familiar pathway and reach for the door handle. The weight of what I'm about to do settles heavily on my chest, but there's no turning back now.

My father sits in his favorite worn green recliner. His focus is on the Sunday afternoon football game.

The thought creeps in, insidious and tempting. My pulse pounds in my ears as I stand frozen in the entryway, my body screaming at me to turn around, to leave before I unravel everything. But I can't. I won't.

I swallow and push past the urge to retreat. "Hey, Dad."

My father glances over. "We weren't expecting you today, son."

My fingers tighten around my keys before I shove them into my pocket. "Yeah, I just thought I'd stop by." My voice comes out stilted, unsure, so I clear my throat and move further into the living room. "How's the game?"

Dad leans back in his chair, glancing at the now-muted television. "Third quarter. The defense is struggling. They need to stop playing soft."

I force a small chuckle as I lower myself onto the sofa. "Same story every season."

He snorts, shaking his head. "Damn right. You'd think they'd learn."

I nod along, letting the conversation settle over me like a well-worn blanket. The rhythm of normalcy, of safe topics, is almost comforting. For a fleeting second, I let myself pretend that this is just another visit. That I'm not about to drop something that will change everything.

But the moment is fragile, a bubble that's bound to pop.

I clasp my hands together to keep them steady, my gaze flickering to the hallway. "Where's Mom?"

"She's in the kitchen." Dad gestures. "She'll be thrilled to see you."

Thrilled. For now.

I swallow, my throat dry. "I have something I want to talk to you and Mom about."

Dad's attention shifts from the game entirely now. His brows draw together, and I can tell he's picking up on my unease. "Is everything okay?"

CHAPTER THREE

Scott

It all started over a year ago when I bought a cottage at Savannah Lake It was supposed to be my fresh start. A chance to carve out a life on my own terms, away from the expectations that had followed me since childhood.

I chose Hampstead because it's small. Quaint in a way that feels untouched by time. Tree-lined streets, mom-and-pop stores, a town square with a clock that chimes at every hour. It's the kind of place where people wave when you pass and where shopkeepers recognize their regulars.

It's quiet. Safe. And most of all, open-minded.

I've never felt more certain about who I was or where I belonged.

It's late afternoon, and I'm restless.

The kind of restlessness that settles deep in my bones, making it impossible to sit still, impossible to focus. I've spent the last few days unpacking, trying to make my new cottage feel like home, but the silence presses in on me. The empty rooms echo with a loneliness I can't quite shake.

I need to get out. To do something.

So, I head into town, letting my feet carry me down its cozy streets. It's my first time exploring on my own, really taking in the place I now call home. It's quieter than the city I left behind, slower, as if life here moves at its own pace. There's comfort in that. A sense of peace I'm still learning to fully embrace.

When I spot the historic theater, I don't hesitate. The old-fashioned marquee above the entrance reads Lincoln – 2:30 pm Matinee. Perfect. I could use the distraction.

I buy a ticket and step inside, the scent of buttered popcorn thick in the air. The lobby is small but charming, lined with vintage posters from films that came out decades before I was born. The floors creak underfoot, worn down by time, by the footsteps of generations who have passed through these doors.

I settle into a seat near the middle of the theater, exhaling slowly as the lights dim.

History fascinates me. It's steady. Permanent. No matter how much time passes, history remains, its stories preserved, its truths unchangeable.

Maybe that's why I cling to it. Because my own story feels anything but steady.

The opening credits roll and I let myself sink into the past, into a world where decisions have already been made and where fates are sealed. Where there's no uncertainty. Only the echoes of what was.

For a little while, I let it consume me.

Allow it to be enough.

Even if I know, deep down, that the real world is still waiting for me when the lights come back on.

And sure enough, as the final credits roll and the screen fades to black, reality rushes back in. The quiet hum of conversation, the rustling of jackets as people gather their things. The faint scent of buttered popcorn lingers in the air as I make my way toward the exit, stepping out into the late afternoon sun.

I blink against the brightness, my eyes adjusting as I take in the street before me. Across the street, the bakery window is lined with fresh pastries, the golden crusts glistening beneath the light. The smell of warm bread and sugar drifts toward me, mingling with the crisp autumn breeze. Next to the bakery, a small bookstore stands with a chalkboard sign propped outside:

New Arrivals: Small-Town Romances & Murder Mysteries

I huff out a small laugh. Oddly fitting.

And nestled between them, half-hidden in the shadow of a towering oak, is a grocery store.

I don't need much. Just a few essentials to make the cottage feel a little more like home. Milk. Coffee. Bread. Maybe something quick for dinner. I hadn't planned on stopping, but the thought of an empty fridge waiting for me and the lack of take-out restaurants is enough to make up my mind.

Pushing my hands into my pockets, I cross the street and step inside.

The scent of fresh produce greets me, familiar and comforting. The store is smaller than the ones I'm used to, but it has its charm. Warm lighting, tidy shelves, and hand-written labels mark the local goods. I grab a small cart and start down the first aisle, scanning the shelves and getting a feel for the layout.

I'm focused on my mental list, moving on autopilot until I turn down another aisle.

And that's when I see him.

He's standing on a step stool, restocking a shelf, his back to me. His wavy, shoulder-length brown hair shifts slightly as he moves, and for a brief second, I wonder what it would feel like to run my fingers through it.

The thought catches me off guard.

And then he turns.

Warm cinnamon-brown eyes meet mine, and my stomach does something I can't quite explain. It's like a jolt. An awareness, a pull.

He offers a polite smile. "Hey, how's it going?"

His voice is deeper than I expect, smooth and easy, with just a hint of amusement, like he's in on some inside joke the rest of the world doesn't know.

I blink, realizing I've been staring a second too long. "Uh...good. Thanks."

I take a step past him, my brain scrambling for something else to say, something casual. Something that doesn't make me seem like I've forgotten how normal human interaction works.

"How about you?" I ask.

He huffs out a short laugh. "No use complaining. Nobody listens anyway."

I smile and murmur, "I would."

But he doesn't hear me.

He's already turning, already walking away, leaving me standing there, feeling something I can't quite place. The only thing I know is that I want to feel it again.

I shake off the moment, forcing myself to focus. I grab a few essentials, but my mind is still stuck on him.

I don't even know his name, but something about him lingers in my mind.

By the time I make it to the checkout, I spot him again.

He's at the end of the register, bagging groceries with effortless ease, moving like he's done this a hundred times before. There's a certain rhythm to it. He places heavier items at the bottom and lighter ones on top, twisting the bags just right so nothing spills.

And he's talking.

Joking, actually.

The elderly woman ahead of me narrows her eyes at him as he studies the ingredients she's placing on the belt. A block of mozzarella, a container of ricotta, fresh basil, a jar of tomato sauce, and a box of pasta.

"Let me guess," he says, glancing up. "Lasagna?"

She lifts her chin, clearly pleased. "That's right."

He lets out a dramatic sigh. "Miss Margaret, that's cruel. You know I get off work late. Now, I have to go home thinking about the best lasagna I'll never get to taste."

She scoffs, waving a hand. "Oh, don't start. I might bring some leftovers by tomorrow."

He smiles, and his eyes light up. "Seriously? Margaret, I think I love you."

She laughs, shaking her head as she hands over a few bills to the cashier. "Don't get ahead of yourself, sweetheart. I said *might*."

"I'll take my chances," he says, expertly tying up the last bag before placing it in her cart. "Drive safe, alright?"

"I will," she says as she pushes her cart away.

Then it's my turn.

He glances up as I place my items on the conveyor belt, his gaze flickering over me in brief recognition.

"So," he says, tilting his head slightly. "Are you new in town or just passing through?"

My stomach clenches, and for a ridiculous second, I feel like I'm sixteen again, trying not to be awkward in front of someone I secretly have a crush on.

"I just moved here," I manage.

He hums in approval, packing my items neatly into bags. "Nice. What brought you to Hampstead?"

I shrug, suddenly hyper-aware of the way his fingers brush against the plastic as he folds the bag handles. "Just looking for a change, I guess."

He nods as if he understands. As if he's heard that answer before.

When I pull out my wallet, I catch him watching me, his expression unreadable.

"Do you need help getting these out to your car?" he asks, lifting one of the bags.

It's an innocent enough question, probably something he asks a dozen customers a day, but for some reason, my pulse jumps at the offer.

"I... uh, sure," I say, mentally cursing myself for how uncertain I sound.

He grins like he expected that answer. I pay, and we step out of the store together.

The late afternoon air is crisp, the sun hanging low in the sky. My car is parked just a few spots away, and as we walk, I glance at him from the corner of my eye.

He moves with the same relaxed confidence as before, like nothing ever rushes him, like he's completely at ease in his own skin. I envy that.

When we reach my car, I pop the trunk, and he sets the bags inside with care.

"There," he says, dusting off his hands. "All set."

I hesitate for a second, then stick out my hand. "Scott."

He glances at my hand, then takes it in a firm, warm grip. "Harrison."

There's a brief pause, something unspoken hanging between us as he lets go. I rub the back of my neck, suddenly feeling like an idiot just standing there.

I clear my throat. "So, do you ever take breaks?"

His lips twitch like he's trying not to laugh. "Usually. Why?"

I backpedal. "I mean, if you do, and if you ever want to, I don't know... maybe we can grab a coffee or something. Sometime. Maybe."

Harrison's smile grows, and my heart slams against my ribs.

"Well," he says, handing me my last bag, "I get off in half an hour. If you don't mind waiting."

I grip the handle, my palm slightly sweaty. "I don't mind."

Harrison nods, his smile lingering for a beat longer. Then, before turning to leave, he jerks his thumb toward the side of the building. "There's a coffee shop just around the corner. I'll meet you there."

My chest tightens. This is really happening. I nod, trying to play it cool after my earlier stumbling. "Yeah, sounds good."

"Perfect," he says, stepping backward toward the store, his gaze holding mine for just a second longer before he finally turns and disappears inside.

I watch him go, exhaling slowly as I close the trunk. My pulse is still racing, but for the first time in a long time, it's not from uncertainty.

It's anticipation.

Sitting in my parents' kitchen, I force myself to keep my voice steady as I tell the story. I keep it light and casual as if this is just another tale from my life, something easy to digest.

Mom rests her chin on her hands, eyes bright with interest. "Was it love at first sight?"

A short chuckle escapes me. "Something like that."

Dad leans forward, listening. "And then what?"

I glance at the coffee in my hands, feeling its warmth seep into my skin, grounding me. I swallow, letting the memories settle before I continue.

"We met at the coffee shop," I say, my voice steady but softer now. "It was this tiny place tucked around the corner, the kind with mismatched furniture and an old piano in the corner no one ever played. I got there first and grabbed a table by the window. I was nervous, trying not to overthink things, but the second they walked in, it was," I pause, searching for the right word. "Easy."

My mind drifts back to the moment Harrison strolled in like he belonged everywhere, the way he spotted me right away and smiled like we were already in on something together.

"We ordered coffee, and we just talked," I continue. "About everything and nothing at the same time. Movies, books, places we wanted to visit. Harrison told me about growing up a couple of towns over. I shared about how I just moved there and was still figuring things out. The hours just disappeared."

A small, nostalgic smile tugs at the corner of my mouth.

"The barista had to come over twice to remind us they were closing," I say with a quiet chuckle. "Neither of us wanted to leave."

Mom shifts slightly, listening intently, but she doesn't say anything.

"We walked out together," I go on, my fingers curling around my mug. "The streets were empty by then, just the streetlights and the sound of our footsteps. We exchanged phone numbers."

I exhale slowly, the memory settling in my chest.

"We talked all night," I finish. "Literally until sunrise."

Mom sighs like fate itself played a role in this. "Destiny."

Dad nods approvingly. "Sounds like a good woman."

The warmth drains from my body, and for a moment, I don't speak. My fingers tighten around the coffee cup, the weight of what comes next pressing down on me.

I could stop here. Let them believe what they want. Let the moment stretch a little longer. Let them stay happy—stay comfortable.

But I won't.

I can't.

"Mom, Dad," I inhale and force myself to meet their eyes. "Harrison isn't a woman."

The air shifts.

Mom blinks. "What do you mean?"

I swallow hard. "Harrison is a man."

Silence.

It stretches and stretches, suffocating.

My father pushes back from the table, his chair scraping against the floor as he stands. His face is unreadable. He doesn't speak, doesn't yell. He just turns and walks out of the room.

Mom stays seated, her eyes filled with something raw and unreadable.

"Why, Scott?" Her voice cracks. "How could you be in love with a man?"

I reach for her hand, but she pulls away.

"I know this is a shock," I say gently. "I didn't want to hurt you, but I love him. Please try to understand."

She wipes at her tears. "I don't know how to be okay with this."

My throat tightens. "Harrison asked me to marry him."

She gasps, shaking her head.

"I won't keep us a secret anymore," I whisper.

Her head drops into her hands, and something inside me splinters. I stand, unable to watch her break down.

From the living room, my father's voice cuts through the silence. "Get out."

The words land like a punch to the gut, knocking the air from my lungs. For a moment, I can't move. Can't breathe.

I turn to face him, but he won't look at me. He stands near the wall where our family photos hang, his back rigid, hands clenched at his sides. His shoulders rise and fall with deep, controlled breaths, but he doesn't turn around.

"Dad." My voice cracks.

"I said, get out."

Mom makes a small sound in the back of her throat, something caught between a sob and a protest, but she doesn't say anything. She doesn't stop him. The rejection wraps around my chest, tight and suffocating. I want to plead with him. To beg him to see that I'm still his son. That nothing really changed.

But I don't beg. I don't argue.

Because I know that right now, it wouldn't matter.

With a shaky breath, I push back my chair and stand. I take one last look at my mother, searching for something—hope, understanding, a promise that this isn't permanent. Tears shimmer in her eyes, but she stays rooted to her seat, her hands curled into tight fists on the table. She refuses to meet my gaze.

And that hurts more than the words my father just threw at me.

Swallowing hard, I turn and walk out of the kitchen. My footsteps echo in the quiet house, past the framed memories lining the hallway, past my father and the television that's still on mute, past the place where I once felt safe.

I reach the front door and pause, my hand on the knob. I wait.

For my father to call me back.

For my mother to tell me that she loves me anyway.

For something, anything, that tells me I haven't lost them completely.

But the only sound is the tick of the grandfather clock in the hall. I close my eyes for a second, letting the harsh reality sink in. Then, I open the door and step outside.

The cool evening air hits me as I walk down the path and cross the street to my car. By the time I slide into the driver's seat and shut the door, my hands are shaking. The weight of it all crashes over me, and I drop my forehead against the steering wheel. My breath comes in uneven gasps as my father's voice echoes in my head, over and over, like a wound that won't stop bleeding.

I fumble for my phone with trembling fingers and dial the only number I need.

Harrison answers on the first ring. "How did it go?"

I try to speak, but nothing comes out.

"Oh, babe," he says softly. "I'm so sorry."

I swallow hard, forcing the words through the tightness in my throat. "My father kicked me out."

Harrison is quiet for a beat, but when he speaks again, his voice is steady, warm, and safe. "Are you still there? I'll come get you."

I shake my head, even though he can't see me. "No, I'll be okay. I'm coming home."

Home.

Not my parents' house. Not anymore.

I start the car, gripping the wheel like it's the only thing keeping me grounded. The streetlights blur as I pull away from the curb, but I blink hard and focus on the road ahead.

I don't know if my parents will ever accept this part of me. But I do know one thing. I'm done hiding who I am. I'm done hiding my relationship with Harrison.

He deserves more—I deserve more.

CHAPTER FOUR

Harrison

I HEAR the car before I see it.

The low hum of the engine cuts through the quiet night, gravel crunching beneath the tires as Scott pulls into the driveway. I'm already on my feet before he even parks, stepping off the porch and moving toward him. My pulse is steady, but there's a heaviness in my chest that hasn't eased since he left for his parents' house.

And then he's here.

The second he opens the door, I close the distance between us, grabbing him and pulling him into my arms. He's trembling. Not shivering from the cold, not shaking from exhaustion. The kind of tremble that comes from heartbreak, from having your foundation ripped out from under you.

I tighten my grip, one hand pressing into the back of his head, the other around his waist, holding him as close as I can.

"I'm so sorry, babe," I murmur against his hair, pressing a kiss to the top of his head. "We'll get through this together."

His arms circle my back, clinging to me like I'm the only thing holding him upright. Maybe I am.

A few long, silent moments pass before he pulls back just enough to look at me. His blue eyes are red-rimmed, glistening with the weight of what he's just lost. But beneath the heartbreak, there's something else. Something raw and determined.

His voice is barely above a whisper when he asks, "Do you still want to marry me?"

I don't hesitate. Not for a second. "I do."

His breath catches, and something shifts in his expression. The hurt is still there, lingering at the edges, but relief settles in too.

Scott exhales a shaky breath, his fingers curling into my shirt. "Then my answer is yes."

Something inside me snaps. Not in a bad way. Not in a way that feels like breaking. This is something else entirely.

Because no matter what happened tonight, no matter what his father said or what his mother couldn't, Scott chose us. And that's all I need.

I tilt my head, capturing his lips in a slow, deliberate kiss. His breath stutters against my mouth before he melts into it, his fingers tightening in my shirt. I guide him backward toward the house, never breaking the kiss, needing him to feel everything I can't put into words.

We barely make it inside before I kick the door shut and press him against it.

His breath is warm, uneven. "Harrison—"

"I've got you," I whisper, brushing my lips against his jaw, his throat, the spot just below his ear that makes him shudder.

He needs this. He needs something to anchor him and remind him he's not alone. And God, I need this too.

I slide my hands down his back, gripping the hem of his shirt and lifting it over his head. He shivers at the loss of fabric, but I cover him with my hands, my mouth, as I trail kisses along his collarbone, down the center of his chest.

Scott exhales sharply, his head falling back against the door. "Bedroom," he murmurs, his fingers threading through my hair, tugging lightly.

I don't argue. Instead, I grab his wrist and guide him toward the bedroom. Our steps are hurried, driven by something neither of us can name but both of us need.

The second we reach the room, Scott tugs me forward, his hands fisting in my shirt as he crashes his mouth against mine. It's desperate now. Raw, messy, all-consuming. I push him back until his legs hit the bed, and he sits heavily, pulling me down with him.

I follow, pressing him down against the mattress, bracing myself over him. His breath is hot against my lips, his fingers threading into my hair, pulling me closer.

I kiss him again, deeper this time, my tongue sweeping against his, swallowing the soft sounds he makes. Scott arches beneath me, his hands dragging over my back and my shoulders. He pulls at my own shirt until I strip it off and toss it aside. His touch is urgent now, desperate, his breath coming in short bursts as he pushes his hips up, seeking friction.

I give him what he wants. Sliding my hands down his sides, I pop the button on his jeans, dragging the zipper down slowly just to hear the way his breath hitches. I tug them down, along with his boxers, and he lets out a shaky groan as I wrap my hand around him, stroking him slowly.

"Harrison." His voice is already wrecked, his fingers digging into my arms.

I kiss him again, swallowing every sound, every gasp, until he's pulling at my jeans. His desperation mirroring my own. Clothes hit the floor in quick succession.

And then it's just us. Skin against skin, warmth against warmth.

I press my forehead against his, slowing for just a second, giving him a chance to pull back if he wants to. But he doesn't. His hands slide down my back, his legs parting beneath me, a silent plea.

"I love you," I whisper against his lips, my hand sliding between us, wrapping around him. I stroke him slowly, savoring the way his breath hitches, his body arching into my touch.

Scott lets out a shaky exhale, his fingers tightening against my shoulders as I keep up the rhythm, dragging my thumb over his tip, coaxing more of those quiet, desperate sounds from him. His hips jerk slightly, his body fully attuned to mine, every reaction fueling the heat curling low in my stomach.

When I can't wait any longer, I position myself, kissing him softly as I push in, filling him inch by inch. Scott lets out a sharp breath, his body tensing before softening around me. His arms wind around my neck, pulling me down until our bodies are flush, our foreheads pressed together.

I move slowly at first, savoring every inch of him, the way he fits so perfectly against me. His breath is hot against my neck, his fingers digging into my back, his quiet moans sending heat straight to my core. My hand never leaves him, stroking him in time with my thrusts, drawing him closer, pushing him higher.

Then, I pick up the pace, rolling my hips in deeper strokes, and his nails scrape over my skin as he comes undone, gasping my name. I kiss him through it, whispering against his lips, telling him how perfect he is, how much I love him, how I'll never let him go. I follow right after, pressing my forehead to his as we both tremble through the aftershocks.

For a long time, neither of us moves. We lay there, tangled together, our breaths evening out, warmth still lingering between us.

Scott exhales softly, his fingers tracing lazy circles on my back. "So, you still wanna marry me?"

I huff out a quiet laugh, pressing a kiss to his shoulder. "Pretty sure I answered that already."

He smiles against my temple. "Just checking."

I pull back just enough to look at him, my thumb brushing over his cheek. "We're gonna be okay, babe."

His expression softens, his hand settling over mine. "Yeah," he whispers. "We are."

I kiss him again, slower this time, softer. He's lost so much tonight. But I'll make damn sure he never loses me.

CHAPTER FIVE

Scott

THE LAKE IS CALM this morning. Sunlight glistens on the surface, flickering through the trees like golden threads woven into the soft ripples of water. A light breeze stirs the air, carrying the scent of spring—fresh grass, damp earth, the faint sweetness of wildflowers growing along the edge of the cottage.

It's not extravagant or grand, but it's ours, and it's perfect.

A small gathering of friends stands in a loose circle near the water's edge, murmuring quietly as they wait. The wooden arch we built last week, now wrapped in white lilies and ivy, stands beneath the towering oak tree in the backyard. Strings of fairy lights hang between the branches, unlit for now but waiting to glow when the sun dips below the horizon.

I exhale slowly, my hands tightening at my sides. I never thought I'd be here. Never imagined I'd have this. This moment, this man, this life.

Yet in a few short minutes, Harrison will stand in front of me, and we'll make the kind of promises that don't break.

A hand claps my shoulder. "You ready?"

I turn to see Aiden, one of the few friends who's been by my side through everything. He's grinning, looking far too smug, like he knew this was coming before I ever did.

"I've been ready," I admit.

He lets out a low chuckle, adjusting his tie. "Good. Because I'd hate to have to wrestle Harrison to keep him from tackling you at the altar. You know he has zero patience."

I smirk, shaking my head. "Yeah, I know."

And I do.

Harrison isn't a man who hesitates. He's steady, sure. When he wants something, he goes for it—no second-guessing, no doubts. And months ago, when he asked me to marry him, I realized I wanted to be the same way.

Because if Harrison is sure about me, then I sure as hell am not letting him go.

A soft hush falls over the group, and my pulse jumps.

He's here.

I turn, and there he is, walking toward me.

Harrison doesn't take his eyes off me as he crosses the yard, his dark suit crisp, his hands relaxed at his sides. The breeze tugs at his tie, and for a moment, he looks like something out of a dream. Untouchable and unreal.

But then he smiles, and I remember—he's mine. And I'm his.

When he reaches me, he exhales slowly, his hands sliding into mine. His fingers are warm and familiar. He's steady as he laces them through mine.

The officiant clears her throat, giving us a moment before beginning.

"Scott and Harrison have chosen to stand before us today, not just to declare their love, but to promise each other forever." My heart pounds, and I barely hear the rest of what she's saying because all I see is him.

And then it's time for our vows.

Harrison goes first. He takes a deep breath, his thumb brushing over my knuckles as he looks at me. "Scott," he starts, his lips curving at the corners, "you walked into that tiny grocery store and turned my whole damn world upside down. I didn't know it at the time, but that was the day my life changed forever."

A lump forms in my throat.

"I didn't just fall in love with you," he continues, voice thick with emotion. "I chose you. And I'll keep choosing you—every day, every hour, every second. When things are easy. When things are difficult. When you're laughing so hard you can't breathe, and when you're quiet, lost in that head of yours."

He squeezes my hands gently. "You are my home. My heart. And I promise to love you fiercely, protect you endlessly, and stand beside you no matter what."

My chest tightens, a sharp ache spreading through me. Because this man, this incredible, stubborn, fiercely loyal man, is mine.

I swallow past the lump, gripping his hands tighter as I speak.

"Harrison," I say, my voice quieter but unwavering. "You once told me that life is too short to hide from the things we want. That if something matters, you hold onto it." His brows lift slightly, recognition flickering in his eyes.

I smile. "You matter. More than anything. You are the best thing that has ever happened to me. And every time I look at you, I know I made the right choice."

Harrison blinks rapidly, his grip tightening.

"I promise to love you without limits, without conditions, and without fear. To stand by your side through every storm, every quiet moment, and every stupid argument about whether pineapple belongs on pizza."

A soft laugh ripples through our friends, but Harrison just shakes his head, biting back a grin.

"I vow," I finish, my voice cracking with emotion, "to spend the rest of my life making sure you never have to question how much I love you."

Harrison lets out a slow breath, his thumb brushing under my eye, catching the tear I hadn't even realized had slipped free.

The officiant smiles. "Harrison and Scott, by the power vested in me, I now pronounce you—"

Harrison doesn't wait. He pulls me in, crashing his lips against mine, and I sink into him, wrapping my arms around his neck as the cheers and applause blur into nothing but background noise.

I don't need to hear the words. I already know how this ends.

It ends with him.

With us.

And for the first time in my life, I know—

This is forever.

BOSS VIBES

Tracie Delaney

ROWAN

A HIGH-PITCHED SCREECH rang out across the shopping center as I dug my heels into the slippery tiles. Several passersby shot irritated glances my way, as if I'd made a dire transgression. Ignoring them, I turned my attention to my best friend, Claire, who wore a determined expression mingled with too much mischief for my liking.

"I've told you. I'm not going in there. I mean it."

Claire wrapped her fingers around my wrist, and tugged, almost dislocating my shoulder. Okay, a bit of an exaggeration, but I enjoyed a little embellishment from time to time.

I drove my heels in further and yanked my shoulder up and back, dislodging her grip.

Claire pouted and folded her arms across her ample chest. I'd give anything for a rack like Claire's. Sadly, when the day for handing out tits arrived, my creator didn't get the memo.

"Oh, don't be a daft mare, Row. It'll be fun."

"No, it won't," I insisted. "I've hardly seen you these past few weeks, and this isn't how I planned to spend a rare early finish at work."

"You should ask that boss of yours for a raise. I know you fancy him, but that doesn't mean you should let him take advantage of you."

"He doesn't take advantage," I muttered. "Besides, I'm still on probation for another month, which means I have to work my backside off to prove my worth. You know this job was a step up for me, and I'm determined to make it work. My personal feelings for Grayson have nothing to do with how much effort I put into my career."

"I just hope he knows how lucky he is to have you. Now come on. Like you said, you don't get a lot of free time, so let's not waste it."

"What if someone I know sees me?"

"So?" Claire shrugged. "It's not illegal to browse a sex shop."

"Maybe it should be." I glanced over my shoulder. It'd be just my luck for someone from work to amble by the second I walked through the doors. If that bastard, Dave, from IT spotted me, he'd snap a picture and load the evidence onto the home page of the intranet in seconds, completing my mortification.

"Look." Claire planted both hands on her hips. "If your vajayjay doesn't get some action—battery operated or otherwise—in the not too distant future, you're going to need surgery to open you back up again."

"Claire, for fuck's sake," I hissed. "Keep your bloody voice down."

"No one cares."

"*I* care."

"And that's your problem. If you cared less and fucked more, you might finally jettison that pole shoved up your backside."

"Thanks a bunch, *mate*." I loaded a hefty dose of sarcasm into my tone.

"Babes, you know I love you to death. Tough love. That's what this is. Candles, a bubble bath, and a few orgasms, and you'll feel a lot better. Trust me."

"Fine," I mumbled with another surreptitious sweep of the mall. "Let's get it over with."

Claire grinned triumphantly. She linked her arm through mine—probably to make sure I didn't run—and hauled me through the door.

A couple of mannequins dressed in skimpy black-and-red lingerie stood like sentries on either side of the entranceway. Claire stopped to check out the barely there underwear. I hustled farther inside and away from the floor-to-ceiling glass windows where anyone could peer in. Why Claire and I were friends was beyond me. Opposites really did attract, I guess.

"Can I help you?"

Heat rushed to my face. The assistant, a homely-looking woman in her mid-forties with salt and pepper hair pinned into a neat bun, tilted her head to the side, waiting for my response. She appeared almost as out of place as me. Still, a job was a job. Everyone had bills to pay.

"First time, dear?"

Kill me. Kill me right this second.

I nodded. Christ, she must think I was mute. Or an idiot. Maybe both.

"Are you after anything in particular?"

Yeah. An escape route.

"Um... I... I'm—"

"That's okay." Claire nudged me in the shoulder, smiling at the woman. "I can take it from here. I'm a pro."

She led me deeper inside the store. Worked for me. Anything that hid me from view got a vote in my book.

"This is a terrible idea," I mumbled as Claire stopped in front of the rows and rows of vibrators and dildos.

"Nonsense," Claire replied. "Which one do you like?"

"Erm, that would be none of them."

"Oh, Row, stop. You're here now. And just think. The sooner you pick one, the faster you get out of here."

I like that. "Fine." I snatched up the first one I saw. "How about this?"

Claire gave it a thorough once-over, then picked up a sealed box and read its 'features.'

"Yeah, that's not a bad pick for your first one. It's got several speeds, and a clit stimulator. I'd advise starting on the slowest speed." Claire snorted with laughter. "Or your head will blow off."

"Jesus Christ." I grabbed it from her, then marched over to the checkout and shoved it across the counter. "Can you put this in a bag, please?"

The same woman who'd greeted me earlier winked. "Of course. Excellent choice. You'll have a lot of fun with this."

I prayed for a sinkhole to open right in the middle of the shop and swallow me. I handed over my credit card, winced at the price—damn, they were some expensive orgasms—grabbed the bag, then dashed out of the shop. I made a run for it, only breathing properly when I'd put a good hundred feet between me and the store.

Claire caught up to me, panting.

"Hold up, Usain Bolt. You entering for the next Olympics or something?"

"That was the most embarrassing experience of my entire life."

"Oh, please," Claire scoffed. "Everyone goes to sex shops. Everyone masturbates. It's no big deal. Just chill, Row."

She wrestled the bag from my hands and dove inside. The next thing I knew, she had the vibrator out of its packaging.

"What the hell are you doing?"

"Checking it's got the plug thingy to recharge it. It was missing from the last one I bought. Pissed me off no end, I can tell you."

"For God's sake, Claire." I yanked the bag back.

The next ten seconds unfolded into a nightmare of epic proportions.

The bag split. The vibrator hit the floor and rolled away, coming to rest in front of a pair of highly polished black dress shoes.

I dragged my gaze up. Smart trousers, single-breasted dark gray suit jacket with one button fastened, a crisp white shirt adorned with silver monochrome cufflinks, and a navy-and-white-striped tie. My eyes traveled farther, meeting a sharp, angular jaw enhanced by a dusting of stubble, an aristocratic nose, wide, intelligent brow, glacial-blue eyes, and a head of dark hair styled to perfection. He raised a single eyebrow in query.

"Oops." Claire giggled, bending to pick up the offending item. "Sorry about that, handsome. You got a runaway vibe, Row."

More giggles erupted while I stood there with horror splattered all over my face.

No. Please God, no. Don't do this to me.

"Good evening, Rowan."

Claire's head swiveled to him, then me, then back to him.

"Oh, crap. Do you two know each other?"

If I lived to be a hundred, I'd never know how I found my voice, but somehow, I uttered the awful truth.

"This is my boss."

GRABBING the stupid vibrator out of Claire's hand, I shoved it into the bag and fled. My face burned with shame as I stormed through the crowds, vaguely aware of Claire hollering at me to stop. She caught up to me at the east entrance, but instead of looking remotely apologetic, her face stretched into a shit-eating grin that did nothing to calm the rage warring with sheer humiliation coursing through me.

"This is all your fault," I snapped. "If you hadn't made me come here and buy this stupid thing, then I wouldn't have to find another job."

Claire's eyebrows kissed her hairline. "Another job? Don't be silly. You love that job."

"Didn't you hear me back there? That was Grayson Brent, my boss. You know, the guy I've spent the last six months swooning over. The same guy who barely notices me other than how well I manage his calendar, how fast I bring him his lunch, and how efficiently I guard him from unwanted visitors."

"Look on the positive side." Claire's beaming smile almost split her face in two. "He's noticed you now."

"Not helping, Claire." I yanked on the door and spilled out into the underground parking garage with my soon-to-be ex friend hot on my heels.

"Row, stop." She grabbed my elbow and hauled me to a stop. "Where's your sense of humor? You own a vibrator. So what? You honestly think he isn't whacking off on a regular basis?"

"I don't have a clue what he gets up to in his spare time." I ground the words out through clenched teeth.

Claire gave me a playful nudge. "Your most embarrassing moment didn't spend long at number one. Buying a vibrator isn't embarrassing, anyway. Having it spill out of a bag and land at the feet of Mr. Gorgeous, who you've dreamt about banging for six months... now *that's* a feat worthy of the number one spot. I can see why you drool over him, though. Talk about boss vibes. I'd do him." She burst into laughter, pointing at the bag containing the offending item. "Boss vibes. Haha. I crack myself up."

I fisted my hands on my hips. "We are no longer friends."

Claire chuckled. "Liar. You'd miss me if I wasn't around. I perk up your life, and you provide some balance in mine. You're stuck with me forever, and you know it."

"Bitch," I muttered.

"Uptight arse."

My lips twitched in the barest hint of a smile that I tried to stop. Too late.

"Aha!" Claire pronounced. "See, you love me." She set off toward the car, throwing a casual. "Dinner's on me," over her shoulder.

"After that disaster, caused by you and your grabby hands, *all* the dinners for the rest of eternity should be on you."

She threw her arms in the air. "Steady on."

Claire spent the next hour trying to steer the conversation toward Grayson, and coming up with ridiculous schemes of how I might use 'vibrator-gate' as she'd termed it, to my advantage. I tried to head her off, but when diverting her attention proved hopeless, I tuned her out.

Death was suddenly looking an attractive proposition.

How would I face Grayson in the office tomorrow?

GRAYSON

*W*ELL, *that was unexpected.*

I'd only stopped by the shopping center to pick up a birthday present for my sister. I despised shopping, but gift for a family member was the one thing I refused to palm off on my assistant. It occurred to me I should go after Rowan, reassure her that there was no need for embarrassment, but she scarpered so fast, I lost her in the crowds.

Rowan. I almost sighed her name. Five months since she'd started working for me, and in that time, my obsession with her had grown like a weed fed the perfect amount of sun and rain. Initially, I'd dealt with my attraction to her like a complete jerk. Cold, offhand, pushing her harder than I did with many of my other employees. Early starts, late finishes, demanding, overbearing. Downright rude on occasion, almost as if I subconsciously wanted her to quit as a way to solve my little fixation problem. When my unreasonable behavior didn't quash the burn inside me, I'd changed tactics, dating multiple women, all of whom made me feel hollow inside and proved how special Rowan was.

The issue I had was that I needed her to make the first move. As CEO and owner of the company, for me to make a pass at my executive assistant was a dumb fuck thing to do. The power imbalance alone is tantamount to coercion. Although I was pretty damn sure she had the hots for me—her covert shy glances and slight tremble whenever our arms or fingers brushed had showed as much—it wasn't beyond the realm of possibility to have read the signs wrong. If I went for it and I was mistaken about a mutual attraction, she could hit me with a sexual harassment suit, and my reputation, as well as that of my company, would lay in tatters.

I'd worked too damn hard to allow that to happen over a woman, no matter how much I wanted her. And by God, I wanted her. More than I'd ever wanted any woman in the thirty-two years I'd spent on this planet. I still remembered her interview, and how I'd struggled to concentrate with a dick as stiff as a cricket bat. I prided myself on my professionalism, and I took employee hiring seriously. Recruit someone unsuitable, and with employee rights as tight as they were in the UK, you were in for a whole world of pain.

Yet with Rowan, I'd spectacularly failed to pay proper attention to her answers, and in the end, I'd asked my COO, Charlotte, to interview her as well. To say Charlotte had thought my request an odd one was an understatement, but luckily, she'd given Rowan the thumbs-up, and two weeks later, the object of my obsession had joined the company on a six-month probationary period.

Turned out she was the best damn assistant I'd ever had. Hard-working, conscientious, great attention to detail. A real asset to my company, which was another reason I was reticent to ask her out. What if she quit? I'd found a rare gem in her, and I didn't want to lose her.

And just think of the fun we could have with that vibrator.

A tremor ricocheted up my spine. Good God. I couldn't carry on like this. The time had come to drop a few carefully placed hints and hope she found the courage to act first.

ROWAN

Not a word.

Grayson hadn't said a single word about what happened last night. All day I'd been on pins, waiting for him to bring up the single most embarrassing moment of my life, but other than work talk, it was as if the unfortunate incident hadn't happened.

If only...

The door behind me opened, and Grayson appeared with his visitors in tow. Our eyes met over the top of my computer screen, and my heart did a little flip.

"Rowan, would you mind escorting Mr. Devereaux and his colleagues down to reception?"

I stood. "Of course. No problem."

Grayson shook Mr. Devereaux's hand. "Good to see you, Sebastian. I'll have Rowan call your assistant and organize a follow-up meeting in a week. Do you want me to extend that invitation to the rest of the ROGUES board?"

ROGUES was the company that Sebastian Devereaux co-headed with five others. Grayson had been working on a joint venture with them for some time, and the negotiations were nearing the end.

"No." Sebastian paused. "On second thought, I'll ask Ryker if he wants to come. I'll forward him the details if he decides to attend the next meeting."

"Very well."

Sebastian made small talk with me as we rode the elevator to the ground floor. I waited until their car pulled away before returning to my office where I found Emma, the Chief Operating Officer's assistant, standing by my desk, coat on, handbag over her shoulder.

"A group of us are going for a drink. Fancy it?"

"Oh." I glanced at Grayson's closed door. "I'll have to check with Grayson."

"It's six p.m., Rowan. You don't have to ask Grayson's permission to go home when your workday has finished."

"That's easy for you to say. You're not on probation."

Emma inclined her head. "You work harder than most people here, apart from the board members. You'll sail through your probation."

"I hope so. It's busy, that's all. What with the ROGUES deal close to being signed." I shot another look at Grayson's door. "I'll give it a miss if it's all the same to you."

She shrugged. "Your call. Just don't burn out."

"I won't. Have fun." I sat at my computer and started work on updates to a commercial contract. Grayson's notes were specific, but there was a lot to get through, and concentration was key to ensuring I didn't make any mistakes. The last stragglers left the office, and an eerie silence descended. Grayson's door remained closed, and only then did it occur to me that he might have left while I was escorting his visitors down to reception. Rising from my chair, I stretched out my back and then rapped lightly on his office door.

"Come in."

So he is still here. I poked my head inside. "I wasn't sure if you'd left already."

He rubbed his eyes, then checked his watch. "I hadn't realized it was so late. What are you still doing here? I'm sure you have somewhere else you'd rather be."

I'd rather be sitting astride your lap and kissing you until I ran out of breath. "It's fine. I enjoy being here." I bit down on my bottom lip. "Grayson, about last night. I'm sorry. I'm so embarrassed."

He smiled, pointing his Mont Blanc pen at the chair opposite his desk in an invitation to sit. Willing the heat in my face to vanish, I took him up on his invitation.

"There really is no need for the embarrassment or an apology."

"I really like working here and I don't want things to be awkward between us."

He leveled me with a stare, his gaze intense. I fidgeted under the weight of his attention. "I like you working here, too," he said, voice smooth as velvet. "And there's no awkwardness from my perspective."

Nerve endings in my fingertips tingled, and electricity snapped through the air as silence descended. Maybe it was my imagination, but something between us shifted. I didn't dare move in case I broke the spell.

Instead, Grayson broke it. He pushed back his chair and walked to the corner of his office where he kept a decanter of whiskey and a tray of crystal glasses. I took a few deep breaths to slow my thundering heart. I'd been alone with Grayson inside his office many times, but the lack of hustle and bustle on the other side of the door lent itself to a far more intimate and thrilling affair.

Grayson poured two small measures of whiskey and returned, handing one over to me. Our fingers brushed, and as much as I tried to hide it, I shivered in pleasure. He perched on the edge of his desk, so close I could smell his after-shave and the hint of maleness underneath. I pressed my thighs together, but the pressure did nothing to relieve the growing ache between my legs.

"You're five months into your probation now, Rowan. How do you think it's going?"

"Great. At least I think so. I really enjoy working here." I lowered my gaze, then lifted it again. "Working for you."

He tugged on his bottom lip. *Damn, I'd love to do that with my teeth.*

"Are you happy with my performance?" My voice came out husky. I cleared my throat.

His gaze lowered to my mouth. "Very."

Oh God. I need a change of underwear. Kiss me. Go on, do it.

He brought the glass to his lips and sipped. I swallowed my disappointment that he'd chosen to put his mouth on the glass instead of me and took a sip of my own. The whiskey burned on its way down my throat, and while I wasn't a fan of hard liquor, it went some way to calming the storm of fiery need turning my insides to ash.

"Do you own a cocktail dress, Rowan?"

His out-of-the-blue question surprised me. I frowned. "I—um—do I own... own a dress?"

"A cocktail dress," he reiterated.

"I'm not sure. I have a black dress that falls just below my knees, but I wouldn't know whether it fits the description of a cocktail dress."

"I have an account at Harrods." He set his glass on his desk and reached into the inside pocket of his jacket. Opening his wallet, he removed a black business card with gold lettering and handed it to me. "Take tomorrow morning off and go to the ladies' department. Ask for Carina, give her this, and tell her I sent you. She'll make sure you get something suitable."

"But... I..." I smoothed my eyebrow. "Suitable for what?"

A veil of anticipation washed over his face. "I need a companion for a dinner tomorrow night, and you're it."

I STOOD BACK and scrutinized my appearance in my bedroom mirror. Not bad, Rowan. Acceptable. The emerald green number that the woman at Harrods had picked out for me—because I didn't know a cocktail dress from any other kind—accentuated my curves and clung in all the right places. She'd even picked out a pair of heels, a clutch bag, and accessories to complete the ensemble. And Grayson had paid for everything. Just as well. Given London's skyrocketing cost of living, I couldn't afford a coffee and a slice of cake at Harrods, let alone an entire outfit. My salary didn't stretch far, even though Grayson paid generously.

He'd blindsided me with the unexpected invitation. I'd been so consumed by desire, so lost in the moment, it hadn't occurred to me to berate him for assuming I was free to attend a dinner at such short notice.

That I had an empty calendar was neither here nor there.

Oh, who are you kidding, Row? I'd have cancelled dinner with the King for a chance to spend an evening with Grayson. Not that I'd ever get an invitation to the palace. Even so, it worked as a solid example of just how under Grayson Brent's spell I was.

The question of why he'd invited me ran on a constant loop inside my mind. Why would a man like him—gorgeous, rich, successful—need his executive assistant to attend a dinner as his plus-one? There were tons of women he could have called upon at a moment's notice, yet tonight, I was the female he'd picked to accompany him. I hoped it wasn't to win a bet or something equally awful. As soon as the thought crept into my mind, I discarded it. Grayson wasn't the kind of man to take part in locker room games. If I had to take a guess, it'd be along the lines of a last-minute change of plans, or the person he'd intended to take had a family emergency and he'd seen me and thought *she'll do*.

I winced. *Time to stop overthinking shit, Row.*

I checked my watch, a gift from my parents for my eighteenth birthday. Fifteen minutes before my ride came to pick me up. More than enough time for panic to set in. What if I ran out of conversation? Or what if I drank too much wine, tried to straddle him in the car on the way home, and made a huge fool of myself?

Oh God. This was a mistake. Maybe I should call and tell him I was sick, or I'd won the lottery, or aliens had whipped me off to their spaceship to do unspeakable things, or—

The doorbell rang. I cursed. Whoever Grayson had sent to pick me up, they were early. Crap. Stuffing my phone in my clutch bag, I grabbed my keys and went to answer the door. Except it wasn't my ride waiting on the other side.

"Jesus, Claire, what the hell are you doing here?"

My best friend gave me the once-over and whistled. "You look gorg, babes. I thought I'd pop by and make sure everything is okay before the big date."

"Everything is fine. And it's *not* a date."

She cocked her head to the side. "Well, what would you call it?"

"A convenience."

She snorted. "Whatever. I reckon you have the vibrator to thank for his impromptu and, frankly, overdue invitation."

"Really? How do you figure that?"

She grinned. "It got him to notice you as a sexual being rather than just his overworked assistant."

"You're so full of shit." I gripped her arm and turned her around. "Time to go. I'm being picked up soon."

"Ooh, can I hang around? Wouldn't mind copping another eyeful of Mr. Sexy."

"No, you can't. And you're out of luck, anyway. He's sending someone to pick me up."

"You're kidding? He can't be bothered to pick you up himself? What a jerk."

"He's not a jerk. He's a busy man. And like I said, this isn't a date. It's a business arrangement. Now will you just go?"

I shoved her again, and this time, she headed off, hand in the air as she waved to me.

"Call me tomorrow. I want all the gossip."

She disappeared into the stairwell. Grinning at my madcap friend, I returned inside. Seconds later, the bell rang for the second time. If this was Claire again, I'd kill her. I opened the door and sucked in a breath. Instead of the driver I'd expected, Grayson stood in front of me dressed in an impeccable suit, one hand shoved into his trouser pocket.

He ran his gaze over me. My heart stuttered inside my chest. It better not stop. My building didn't have a defibrillator.

"Breathe, Rowan." Another sweep of that gorgeous azure stare followed. "I must send Carina my personal thanks for that dress. She knows how to... accentuate a woman's best assets."

I searched for an appropriate response. When I came up empty, I wet my lips and swallowed. "Shall we go?" Fumbling with my keys, I dropped the damn things, and as I crouched to pick them up, so did Grayson. Our heads clashed.

"Ow."

Grayson chuckled and rubbed his head. "Ow indeed." He wrestled the keys from my grip, helped me to stand, and locked the door, then handed my keys to me. "Let's head off before there are any more mishaps."

Heat rushed to my face. "Sorry, I'm such a klutz."

"It's not often I'm headbutted by my date for the evening." He chuckled.

Date. *He said date.* He also said headbutted, so I'd better not get ahead of myself. He stuck out his elbow and, after a moment's hesitation, I slipped my hand inside.

A sleek, black SUV idled at the curb, and as we approached, a uniformed driver sprang to attention, opening the rear door. Grayson motioned for me to go first. As I climbed inside, I could have sworn he hissed through his teeth. Maybe he had a stone in his shoe, or my dress had split wide open as I bent over, giving him a flash of butt crack. I checked for an alfresco situation with a quick swipe over my backside. Phew. All clear.

The driver steered the car into the busy London traffic. Grayson shifted his body toward me, his eyes locked on my face. I took up fiddling with the clasp on my clutch bag and struggled to come up with a conversation opener. "Where are we going?" I groaned. Talk about lame, Row.

"The Dorchester."

"Oh." I chewed the inside of my cheek. "What's the event?"

"A fundraiser for a charity."

"That's nice."

As he opened his mouth to reply, his phone rang. Muttering something I couldn't make out under his breath, he reached into his inside pocket, frowning at the screen. "Sorry, Rowan, I need to take this."

He put the handset to his ear and spoke in low, rapid tones to the caller. Whoever it was, he clearly didn't want me to overhear their conversation. My stomach hardened, a wave of jealousy that I had absolutely no right to sweeping through me. What if the person on the other end was his original date, and they'd decided they could make it after all? Would he ask the driver to pull over and leave me on the side of the road, or take me home first?

"Sorry about that."

Grayson's apology yanked me from the dark thoughts racing through my mind. I forced a smile.

"No problem."

"I'd switch it off, but unfortunately, a man in my position needs to be contactable."

Oh, so maybe it was a work call after all. I sagged with relief.

"You work too hard. Even CEOs need a break now and then."

He leaned in, his gaze steady. "I solemnly promise that for the rest of the night, you have my undivided attention."

A tremor of desire trickled down my spine, and warmth settled in my stom-ach. The idea of being the subject of Grayson's undivided attention was right up there with my most prevalent fantasies.

The car drew to a halt outside The Dorchester. I'd never been lucky enough to visit this hotel, but from what I understood, it was the epitome of elegance and luxury. Grayson's driver opened the door, and I got out. Grayson joined me and gave me his arm again. As we were swept along with the other guests, all of whom looked so comfortable in these sumptuous surroundings, my nerves made an unwelcome return.

Several times on the way to the event room, people stopped us, and on each occasion, Grayson introduced me as Rowan.

Not his assistant. Rowan.

I took heart from that. It allowed me to be me, rather than his employee, and I told him as much the first chance I got.

"Tonight, you're definitely not my employee," he replied in a tone that oozed sex.

I suppressed a shiver of delight, but when he slid his palm across the back of my neck and squeezed, my legs almost buckled. God, his touch did things to me that should be illegal.

A smartly dressed man seated us at a large table with ten other guests. The room itself must house at least two hundred people. Ornate chandeliers hung overhead, and expensive art adorned the walls. Dinner was an elaborate affair with seven courses. I didn't know what half of them were, but I devoured every one. Damn, rich people ate well. From now on, my signature spag bol dish wouldn't taste half as good.

Grayson checked in with me now and then, but the other guests monopolized most of his attention. The conversation centered on bonds and yields and a bunch of other things I didn't have enough knowledge to contribute to, leaving little time for small talk.

Solved the problem of running out of things to say, at least.

As the wait staff collected the last of the dinner things, Grayson pushed back his chair.

"Ladies, gentlemen, if you'll excuse us. I promised my date my undivided attention, and with all the business talk this evening, I've let her down badly." He held out his hand to me. "Dance with me, Rowan."

How I stopped my chin from hitting the floor, I'd never know. Somehow, I rose to my feet without stumbling and folded my palm inside Grayson's. Was I dreaming? Had I fallen into one of those cheesy princess movies and any second, I'd wake up and plunge right back into the drudgery of everyday life?

He slipped one arm around my waist, his palm low on my back, his fingertips dangerously close to my arse.

"I'm sorry I've been such a dreadful companion this evening. Forgive me?"

I tilted my head back and met his gaze. Sincerity swam in his eyes. Grayson's sharp blue irises were warm and inviting, and a wave of daring came over me.

"Can I ask you a question?" I blurted before I lost my nerve.

"Of course."

"Why did you invite me to come here with you tonight? A successful, handsome man like you isn't short of female company."

"What makes you think that?"

I raised my eyebrows. "Really? Grayson, I'm your assistant. I know you're not short of suitable dates. I'm the one who buys the flowers and the jewelry and sends the Dear John notes to your latest victim."

My lungs flattened, and horror filled my chest. *Shut the hell up, Rowan. Jesus, you'll lose your job.*

"I'm sorry. That came out wrong."

"No, it didn't." Grayson's lips lifted, and his eyes glimmered, but not with irritation. With amusement. And something else, too. Awe, maybe. No, that couldn't be right.

"It came out exactly as you intended. The only reason you apologized was because you're still thinking of me as your boss, and you're worried I might fire you for insubordination."

He leaned in, trailing the tip of his nose down mine.

"I already told you, Rowan. You're not my employee this evening."

I swallowed past throat narrow as a flimsy straw and licked my dry lips. "Then what am I?"

He traced his tongue along the underside of his top teeth and skimmed his eyes over me. "What do you want to be?"

Your lover. Your girlfriend. Hell, I'd settle for your fuck buddy.

"You talk in riddles, you know that?"

A chuckle rumbled through his chest. "And you're a straight shooter. Except, at work, you hold back. You're the consummate professional, if a little... jittery sometimes." He pressed me closer to him, and his lips went to my ear. "So shoot straight, Rowan. And tell me what you want."

My forehead fell onto his shoulder and, with my stomach tied in knots, I gathered my courage and hoped like hell this didn't blow up in my face.

"You, Grayson. I want you."

GRAYSON

FIVE MONTHS. Five long, torturous months I'd waited for Rowan Saunders to tell me how she felt. And finally, *finally* she had. *Now* I could make my move.

I gently cupped her chin and eased her head back, giving her no choice other than to look at me. "It's about goddamn time."

She blinked, opened her mouth to say something, closed it, and blinked again. "Excuse me?"

"You took your time, sweet Rowan." I brushed my lips over hers, wanting to deepen the kiss but forcing restraint. This wasn't the time or the place for our first proper kiss. "I've wanted to tell you how I felt about you for months, but in my position, I couldn't risk it in case you didn't feel the same."

"Wait." She placed the flat of her hand on my chest and shook her head. "I'm confused. You... you... like me?"

"No. I don't like you. I'm crazy about you. Every day I've had to sit there in my office knowing you're on the other side of the wall. I'd have given anything to call you in on some pretext, lock my office door, bend you over my desk, and fuck you until neither of us could see straight." I grinned at her stunned expression. "So 'like' isn't nearly a strong enough word in my book. Blind lust is closer, adoration closer still."

"Oh God." She slipped out of my arms and braced her hands on her knees. "I need a minute."

"Take all the time you need."

She slowly straightened. A delicious blush stole over her cheeks as she spotted a few people at a nearby table had taken an unhealthy interest in us. She moved into my body and tucked her head underneath my chin.

"Tell me when they've stopped staring."

I chuckled. "You really need to learn to care less. I have a speech to make shortly, then what do you say we get the hell out of here?"

She smiled, and I fell, hard. "Sounds like a wonderful idea."

We saw out the rest of the dance and, I was ashamed to admit, I gave an abridged version of my speech, too eager for the real evening to begin. No one seemed to notice, and after the obligatory—and far too long—farewells, we slid into the back of my car.

"Where to, Mr. Brent?" my driver asked.

"Home, please." I pressed the button, activating the privacy screen. Waiting to get my hands on Rowan wasn't in the plan.

"You're taking me to your home?"

I arched a brow. "Well, I guess I could ask him to circle the block while I fucked you on the back seat of my car if you'd rather."

She narrowed her eyes. "Are you teasing me?"

"Would I?" I chuckled, reaching for her. "I can wait until we get home. I'd rather a large bed than a narrow car seat, anyway. Kissing, on the other hand…"

I cupped her face, angled her exactly how I needed, and closed my mouth over hers. The brief stroke of her lips earlier didn't count. *This,* this right here, was our first kiss, and it stole the air from my lungs. I pushed her onto her back, my hands roving over her hips, her waist, and the swell of her tits.

We kissed and touched and explored each other's bodies. By the time we stepped inside my private elevator, I was clinging to the edge of my sanity. Years had passed since I'd last dry-humped a girl up against a wall, but with Rowan, I couldn't resist. Months of stifled frustration spilled out in a haze of desire and need and want. We staggered into my bedroom, falling onto the bed in a tangle of arms and legs.

I rolled onto my back, taking Rowan with me. I tugged on the zipper that ran the length of her dress. When it caught on the runner, I grabbed the two pieces of material and yanked. The dress split wide open.

Rowan gasped. "It's ruined."

"Who cares? It's only a dress."

I wrestled it off of her, tossing it on the floor beside the bed. And then I stared and stared. And stared some more.

"Grayson?" Rowan frowned. "Is everything okay?"

"Christ, Rowan," I croaked. "You're fucking beautiful."

Her cheeks, neck, and chest flushed pink, and she lowered her chin. "I think you had too much wine with dinner."

"It wouldn't matter how much wine I drank, you, Rowan Saunders, are perfect."

I sat up, nose to nose, and kissed her, my mouth and hers moving together perfectly. Flipping her bra clasp, I slid the straps down her arms and threw it on top of her ruined dress, then removed her lace underwear.

"I need inside you," I mumbled against her lips.

She giggled. "Maybe take your clothes off first."

"Good point." I leaped off the bed and undressed in less than five seconds. Her eyes tracked my every move, and as I peeled off my boxers, she dropped her gaze.

"Do you have protection?"

I reached into the drawer beside my bed and withdrew a ream of condoms. Tearing one off the strip, I tossed the rest of them on the bed beside her.

"You might need permission from your boss to arrive late to work tomorrow."

"Oh, that's a shame." She shot me an impish grin. "He's such a stickler for punctuality."

I ripped open the packet and rolled the condom onto my dick.

"He sounds like a jerk."

Dampening her lips, she fixed her eyes on my groin. "He can be, sometimes." She propped herself up onto her elbows and reached for me. "But don't worry, I can handle him."

"Yeah," I rasped. "You can."

ROWAN

I PICKED up Grayson's arm where he'd wrapped it around my waist, and slipped out of bed. Padding across the room to what I hoped was the bathroom, I pushed on the door.

Result. Found it.

On a bad day, it'd be just my luck to stumble into the closet, trip over a stray shoe, and knock myself out on the clothes rail.

I used the toilet and closed the lid to muffle the flushing sound. Planting my hands on either side of the sink, I checked out my reflection, searching for signs I'd changed. The same old me stared back, but while I might look the same on the outside, everything on the inside had shifted.

Grayson. I'd slept with Grayson. My boss, Grayson Brent. Not just once or twice, but three times.

Three.

And he'd given me six orgasms.

See, who needed a vibrator to get their kicks? Not me.

I wrapped my arms over my chest and hugged myself. Not even in my wildest fantasies had I expected the night to end like this when Grayson picked me up from my apartment. If I thought about all the wasted months, I could crack both our heads together. I hadn't shown my hand, too scared of cocking up and failing my probation—and he'd been too afraid of a sexual harassment lawsuit to make a move on me.

Pair of dickheads. That described us perfectly.

And then it hit me. *Fuck.* What if the change in our relationship status meant he didn't want me working for him any longer? I had to work. I needed the money. And I refused to scrounge off Grayson. I paid my own way. My parents had drilled the importance of being financially independent into me, and I agreed with them wholeheartedly. I'd seen too many of my friends rely on a man for money only to see their entire lives wrecked when the relationship ended and they found themselves homeless and penniless.

Maybe he could transfer me to another department? Or use his network to find me a new job. He had a lot of contacts. One of them had to have an opening for an assistant. Perhaps Sebastian Devereaux from ROGUES was hiring.

"Why are you talking to yourself?"

I clasped a hand to my chest, my heart thumping against my ribcage. I hadn't even heard him get up. "Jesus, Grayson, you scared the hell out of me."

He moved behind me and wrapped his arms around my waist, nestling his chin on my shoulder. "Do you often talk out loud to yourself?"

"Sometimes, when I'm trying to figure things out."

His hands crept up until they cupped my boobs. He rolled my nipples between his thumb and forefinger, and my stomach lurched. I groaned, twisting my head to steal a kiss.

"What are you figuring out?"

"If I still have a job."

He spun me around so fast, I almost lost my balance. Only Grayson's firm hands at my waist kept me upright.

"Why wouldn't you have a job?"

"Well." I shrugged and chewed the inside of my cheek, a habit I often turned to when I felt uncomfortable. "After this. You and me. I thought it might be... awkward to work together."

Grayson's lips curved in a crooked smile. "I can think of at least ten benefits right off the bat to having you directly outside my office door." He bent down and sucked on my bottom lip. "And besides, you're the best assistant I've ever had. If you think I'm losing a perfectly good assistant just because we're fucking, you're wrong."

I almost sagged in relief, but it was short-lived. "What will everyone say?"

Grayson snorted. "You think I care about idle office gossip?"

"*I* care," I whispered.

Grayson lifted me onto the bathroom counter and eased my thighs apart. Dropping to his knees, he circled my clit with his tongue. "I already told you that you need to learn to care less. Now shut up, woman, and lie back. I have plans for you."

I groaned, heat rushing through me. Burying my fingers in his thick hair, I held him right where I needed him. It took an embarrassingly short twenty seconds of tongue action before I came, his name spilling from my lips over and over.

When I opened my eyes, he already had a condom on. He lifted me off the counter and spun me around.

"Hold on, baby."

Lifting my hips, he speared me in one smooth thrust. His hand cradled my throat, but when I closed my eyes, he bit my shoulder. "Eyes open. I want you to watch me fucking you."

My skin flushed hot. I'd never watched myself have sex before. Our eyes locked in the mirror. Grayson didn't break eye contact for a second. This was more than sex, more than fucking. It was a deep connection between two people who'd hidden from their attraction, but weren't hiding any longer.

His fingers swirled over my clit, pinching and rubbing. I wasn't sure I had another orgasm in me, but that familiar swell started in my stomach.

"Tel me you're close," Grayson muttered.

"I'm there."

I shattered, my muscles rippling along his cock. Grayson thrust into me twice more, then stilled, bliss etched across his face. I'd never seen anything so beautiful in my life. I was transfixed, unable to look away even if he'd asked me to.

He pulled out of me. I winced, sore after so much sex in a few short hours. Wouldn't change a thing.

Not a single fucking thing.

THE FOLLOWING MORNING, I AWOKE TO THE SOUND OF THE SHOWER running. I rolled over in bed and tucked the covers under my chin. Grayson had the most comfortable bed. His mattress made me feel as if I was lying on the softest, fluffiest cloud, and returning to my lumpy old thing didn't appeal. I thought about jumping into the shower with Grayson, but I didn't feel quite brave enough yet. So much had changed so fast, and my brain was struggling to process it all.

Maybe next time.

Lying here on my own gave me far too much time to think, and the swirl of anxiety I'd felt last night made an unwelcome return. Everyone at Grayson Enterprises knew I had the hots for Grayson. Well, okay, maybe not *everyone*, but enough. Mostly women, too. And one thing women loved was a good old gossip. Except, when you were the subject, it wasn't so much fun anymore. Not that I planned to go bleating to the world and his wife that I'd spent the night in Grayson's bed and, according to him, I'd spend plenty more nights here, too. But office workers could sniff out a story better than most journalists. I'd give it two days before *I* was the story.

I groaned. Whatever Grayson said, I might have to look for another job. It was okay for him, being the boss and all. No one dared giggle behind his back or make fun of him. But me? I was fair game.

Now if Claire was in my shoes, she'd waltz into the office swinging her handbag and announce to everyone that she could "barely walk straight". So many times over the course of our long friendship I'd wished I was more like her, but we were complete opposites. It was one of the things that worked so well for us. She was yin to my yang. I sighed. If it came down to it, I'd have to marshal my inner Claire and front it out.

"You're talking to yourself again."

I raised my eyes to find Grayson, a white towel hanging low on his hips and water trickling between his pecs, standing in the doorway to the bathroom. He rubbed another towel over his wet hair, then tossed it behind him and strolled over to me. As he approached, I reached out and tugged at the towel. It unraveled easily, and I dropped it on the floor.

Hmm, maybe that bravery gene was rallying?

I propped myself up on one elbow. "Want to play hooky?"

His smile came slowly, and his eyes shimmered with devious intent. "I thought you'd never ask."

ROWAN

OVER THE NEXT FEW WEEKS, my fears that I'd become the story of the moment turned out to be unfounded. Grayson and I didn't exactly broadcast our change of status from 'single' to 'in a relationship,' but everyone knew we were seeing each other. Apart from one or two individuals who couldn't help making a snide comment, nearly everyone else told me they were happy for us. Quite a few had mentioned that Grayson appeared less fearsome and slightly more approachable since we'd hooked up.

Amazing what sex on the regular did for a man. And a woman. I'd never been happier.

At work, we kept things largely professional, although we'd given in to an odd fumble here and there. And Grayson had been knee-deep in the latter stages of his joint business venture with ROGUES, which had taken up most of his time. Rarely an hour went by when he wasn't in some meeting or other, ironing out the finer details for what appeared to be a lucrative deal for all parties involved.

Claire had drilled for "all the deets" until I'd capitulated and shared enough to satisfy her unrelenting curiosity. If Claire ever told Grayson I'd given her a fair few tidbits that'd make the readers of *Playboy* blush, I'd beat her with that damned vibrator she'd forced on me.

I never had used it. Hadn't needed to. Grayson *never* ran out of batteries or needed a recharge. Maybe I should wrap it up for Claire's birthday. I chuckled to myself. It'd save me a chunk of cash, and it'd be funny as fuck to watch her face when she tore open the gift wrap.

The intercom on my desk buzzed, and my belly fluttered. I wondered how long that feeling would last. The newness, the insane urge to rip each other's clothes off, to spend lazy Sunday mornings in bed having copious amounts of sex. Hopefully, for a while longer yet.

"Yes, Grayson."

"Come into my office, please, Rowan."

He sounded so formal that a sliver of anxiety trickled down my spine. I stood, smoothed my skirt, and tapped on his door once before entering.

On his desk was a large bottle of champagne, two glasses, and a bowl of strawberries. He gave me a smile that turned my insides to mush, reaching me in two strides. Taking my face in his hands, he kissed me.

"What's this in aid of?" I asked when he let me go.

"I just had confirmation from my lawyer that ROGUES have signed the deal." An enormous grin etched across his face "This is going to be huge for Grayson Enterprises."

I threw my arms around his neck and hugged him. "Oh, Grayson. I'm so thrilled for you. It's what you deserve."

"Thank you for putting up with me these last few weeks," he murmured against my lips.

"Well, you can be pretty tough to take," I teased.

He opened the champagne and poured two glasses, handing one to me. "To success... and more time for sex."

I widened my eyes. "*More* time? Jesus, Grayson, I'm going to need a rubber ring to sit on."

He pressed a strawberry to my lips, and I bit down on the juicy fruit.

"Let's finish this glass of champagne and then head back to my place."

I frowned, glancing up at the clock on the far wall of his office. "It's only three-thirty."

He gave me a crooked grin. "Benefits of being the boss."

"You might set a bad example to your team."

"That's why we'll sneak out the back way."

Ten minutes later, Grayson and I slipped into the backseat of his car, giggling like a couple of teenagers. We kissed the entire way home, half undressed in the private elevator, and virtually ran to his bedroom, discarding the rest of our clothes on the way.

Lightheaded from the champagne and Grayson's searing kisses, I closed my eyes, angled my hips, and sighed as he slid home.

With smooth strokes, he drove me higher, touching me in just the right way to send me soaring. As I tumbled down into a mind-boggling orgasm that curled my toes and set off fireworks behind my closed lids, Grayson groaned and found his own release.

Rolling to the side, he reached for my hand and knitted our fingers together. Equally breathless, we both stared at the ceiling and waited for our hearts to slow.

"You and me, Rowan, we're perfect together." He shifted onto his side and caressed my cheek. "I wish we hadn't wasted all that time."

I turned to meet him, nose to nose. "You were too busy with all those other women."

He shook his head. "Since the day you walked into my office, I haven't wanted anyone else."

I frowned. "But the flowers, and the jewelry, and the 'see ya, sweet cheeks' notes you made me send to the women you dated. Are you saying they were fake?"

"No. The women were real. I dated to try to get you out of my head. They were all perfectly nice women, but they did nothing for me. The flowers and gifts were my way of apologizing for wasting their time." He captured my bottom lip and tugged it between his teeth. "You're the only one for me."

"Oh, Grayson."

"Talking of gifts." He reached into his bedside table drawer and fished out a rectangular box. "This is for you. Well, for us, really."

His mischievous grin had me narrowing my eyes in response.

"You're up to no good."

"Just open it." He thrust the package at me.

I sat up in bed, tugged on the silky black ribbon, and opened the box. My mouth dropped open. I gaped, and then I laughed.

"Are you kidding me? How did you get hold of this?" I removed the bright-pink vibrator, the one Claire made me buy all those weeks ago, and brandished it at him.

Snickering, he ducked to avoid a whack on the head.

"It seemed such a shame to let it go to waste. Just think of the fun we can have playing with this."

I started it up, and it buzzed. "You charged it?"

"Hell, yeah, I did." He snatched it out of my hands and straddled me.

"Tell me, Grayson." I gasped as he ran the tip of the vibrator around my nipple, causing it to harden. "Did you break into my home?"

He tapped his nose. "Not sharing. It's good for a relationship to have a little mystery."

"You're a bad, bad man."

"Only the beginning, gorgeous. Only the beginning."

ABOUT THE AUTHOR

Tracie Delaney writes billionaire romance where the men fall hard and the women make them work for it.

She's published more than 35 novels over several series although still considers herself a reader first and foremost.

She loves nothing more than discovering a new author with a huge backlist, although her husband doesn't appreciate the high pitched squeal when this happens.

At night she likes to curl up on the sofa with her two Westies, Murphy & Cooper, and binge-watch shows on Netflix. There may be wine involved..

Visit her website at www.authortraciedelaney.com

CHRISTMAS WITH MRS. ROBINSON

Whitley Cox

CHAPTER ONE

I GLANCED over at my twelve-year-old daughter while her knee bounced wildly as we drove through the busy Seattle streets toward the pool. Her reflection in the window—since it was already dark out—showed a scrunched brow and small frown.

Reaching over, I rested my hand on her thigh. "You okay?"

Kira pivoted to face me. "What if I suck?"

"At swimming?" I exclaimed. "You?" Then I gave her a 'you've gotta do better than that' look. "What's really eating you, kiddo? You're a champion swimmer. You're not going to suck."

"Okay, but what if I'm *too* good and all the other kids hate me because I'm the new kid who joins halfway through the season and shows them all up?"

"Still not buying it that's what's eating you. Try again."

She let out a long, dramatic sigh. "I just hate that we had to move halfway through the year. The school year *and* the swimming year. Why couldn't we wait until June?"

Nodding, I took a left on the advanced green light and pulled into the parking lot for the rec center. "Neither your dad nor I could afford to buy the other person out of the house. He moved to LA, and ... I—*we*—moved back here to be closer to family."

She scoffed. "Yeah, and that entire family decided to take a vacation to Mexico for Christmas, leaving us all on our own. *Great* family you've got there, Mom." She ran her tongue over the braces that covered her front teeth. She'd only had them for a couple of months and was still getting used to them.

She also wasn't wrong about my family. It was a big kick in the teeth when I told my parents, brother, and sister-in-law that Kira and I were moving back to Seattle. Only for them to one week later tell me about their family vacation in Mexico. And no, they didn't invite Kira and I. My divorce cost me an arm and a leg, not to mention my recent townhouse purchase and the ridiculous Seattle real estate market, so I couldn't just drop a few grand on a trip to Cancun.

Releasing a sigh of my own, I frowned and squeezed her thigh. "We'll make this Christmas really special, just the two of us. I promise."

"Dad hasn't returned my texts."

"Is that what's really bugging you?"

"Everything's bugging me."

Been there.

Kira didn't have her period yet, but she was due for it any day. I was twelve and a half when I first got mine, and I made sure she always had pads, period panties and extra pants in her school and swim bag just in case I wasn't there when she got it. We had discussed tampons at length too, because if she planned on sticking with swimming, she would need to use them.

I found a parking spot and put my Toyota RAV into park. "Bundle up, sugarplum, it's frosty out there."

Rolling her eyes, but not objecting, my temperamental teenager-to-be reached into the backseat for her sky-blue down-filled winter jacket and shrugged into it. I did the same.

"Ready?" I asked after we were both zipped up.

"No. But I need to go in anyway," she said sullenly.

"Good enough."

We both opened our doors, and she reached into the backseat for her swim bag, then we high-tailed to the front door, wrestling with the sleet and wind that threatened to freeze off our faces.

My cheeks stung from the icy pellets as we emerged into the warm rec center lobby. "I'll meet you out there," I said, taking the door that led to the pool while she needed to go to the change room first.

All I got in reply was a grunt and another eye roll.

My heart ached for my kid.

Her entire world was just flipped on its axis.

This time last year, Kira had a perfectly wonderful life. Her parents were married and seemingly happy. She had a lot of friends, and just won her tenth gold medal of her swimming "career" at the swim meet. She was living the preteen dream.

Then, around Easter, Damien, Kira's father, unveiled that he'd been having an affair with his student—his *male* student—and was leaving me for Paul.

I had no problem with the LGBTQAI2+ community, but I did have a problem with the fact that rather than come to me with his crisis of sexual orientation *before* he cheated, Damien dropped the mother of all bombs on me—on my birthday.

Not only that, but he'd been sleeping with Paul for nearly six months—*and* sleeping with me. And anytime during our divorce proceedings when I brought up his infidelity and dishonesty, he would call me a homophobe. That wasn't the issue at all. I would have been *just* as mad if he'd cheated on me with a woman.

What gutted me the most, though, was how he made it all about him. He didn't think that Kira had any reason to be mad at him. He figured she needed to celebrate that after thirty-six years, he was finally living his truth.

So of course, when the judge asked Kira who she wanted to live with, she said, me. Damien didn't even fight for custody. He did, however, fight over how much child support he figured he should pay. The judge hated him by the end and gave me everything I asked for.

That didn't mean I wasn't up to my eyeballs in lawyer fees, though. Damien fought with all his might when I tried to get him to cover my lawyer fees—and he won that battle.

I found a seat on the bleachers and pulled out my phone, bringing up the contact name: Fuckwad McShitstain AKA Damien Robinson. His avatar was also a squid, because squids were dicks.

*Y*OUR DAUGHTER HAS TEXTED YOU, AND YOU'VE IGNORED HER.

N*O* PLEASANTRIES, BECAUSE FUCK PLEASANTRIES. H*E* DIDN'T DESERVE THEM after what he did to us. Straight to the point, and that was it.

Three little dots appeared, bouncing on the screen. Taunting me.

Then they disappeared.

I growled.

Then they reappeared.

Then they disappeared again.

Then nothing.

Motherfucker.

He chose *Paul* over his own daughter. *Paul*, his student, who got accepted to UCLA for his PhD, so Damien just followed. He gave up his tenure at the college he worked at in Eugene, and moved into the private sector, becoming a consultant rather than a professor—which had always been his dream.

We met during my sophomore year of college and Damien's senior year. I was pregnant with Kira by the end of my junior year and had to quit with just a semester of school to go to complete my bachelor's. Damien, however, went on to get his masters, and PhD while I stayed home with Kira. I eventually finished my last semester, but the hope of going on to get a master's in computer science myself was a pipe dream. So I took more coding classes online and eventually became a freelance website developer. I was able to work while Kira napped, then eventually when she went to preschool and school, and after she went to bed in the evenings.

It was impossible to live in the Pacific Northwest on one income, so I needed to figure out a way to bring money into our family somehow.

No matter what, though, it'd always been about Damien. About his career. About his schooling. He had ample opportunity to take a sabbatical for a semester and spend time with his daughter, but he never did. He was in the tenure rat-race. He treated my career like a joke, saying that anybody could create a website now with companies like WordPress and Wix out there. Who needed the likes of me anymore?

Well, given that I was currently turning away clients and turning down projects daily, apparently a lot of people needed *the likes of me*.

What I couldn't understand, however, was who needed the *likes of him*. He was a fucking medieval literature professor. His work was derivative. It wasn't uncovering anything new. It wasn't changing the landscape of society, science, technology or anything. It was literally unpacking and dissecting work that had already been done and proving you were a fucking expert at understanding it. The only option for a useless degree like that was becoming a professor.

And yet, he thought he was contributing to the culture of the world and preserving important works. If he and others didn't study this historic shit, eventually it would be lost and gone forever.

Rage still burned like a thousand fires in my belly at how selfish my husband turned out to be. Thirteen years of marriage down the drain. All of it—a lie.

The only good thing to come out of that was Kira.

And right now, my poor child hated the world, and there was only so much I could do for her.

"Mrs. Robinson?" came a deep, yet also vaguely familiar voice, pulling me out of my rage fog and my eyes away from my phone. I was still staring at my unanswered text message to Damien, silently hoping the man had lost all of his fingers in a horrific logging accident. Not that he logged, but one could dream.

I lifted my head to find a god-like creature staring at me, wearing an enormous smile. A smile of familiarity, like he knew me. I narrowed my gaze, trying to place him. I'd never met anybody in my life this handsome. Clearly, he was a figment of my imagination.

He must have picked up on my not recognizing him, and grinned even wider. "Picture me without the facial hair and about six inches shorter."

I did my best, and holy shit! My mouth dropped open. "Deacon!"

That made him laugh, and his laugh made my panties damp. Before I knew it, I was being hauled to a standing and wrapped up in a big hug.

Holy mama, he smelled good. He was also hard as a freaking rock. Did this kid have even an ounce of body fat? He could certainly have some of mine. I had body fat to spare.

He let go of me, his green eyes glittering under the horrific fluorescent lights above. "I thought that was you. What are you doing here?" He glanced around. "Is Kira here swimming?"

Still a little flustered, I swallowed and told my belly to tame those butterflies. This *man* could not be older than twenty-two. He was barely a man.

And yet, he looked *all* man.

"I uh ... she is!" Why was I yelling?

His easygoing smile did absolutely nothing to calm me.

"W-we've moved back to Seattle. She's rejoined the swim league here, and today is her first day."

His smile was absolutely infectious, and before I knew it, my cheeks were in pain because I was trying to match his grin. "That's amazing," he said.

"A-are you still coaching?" I asked. I was stammering as if I had a stutter. Dear god, what must he think of me?

"I am," he said. "It's one of my *many* jobs, actually. I coach, I lifeguard, I teach guitar, I work part time at the lab. Anything to pay for school, right?"

"You're in school?"

The kids filed out of the change rooms, gathering behind him. Other coaches and parents joined the mix as well, but it was impossible not to feel the other moms watching our conversation with keen interest.

"I am. Getting my master's in biology with a focus on earth and ocean science. So I work a few days a week in the lab with my professor."

The word *professor* was clearly a trigger for me because my pulse immediately picked up and bile coated the back of my tongue.

Deacon is not Paul. Deacon is not Damien. Deacon is not YOURS!

"Mom?" Kira approached, her cheeks instantly going bright pink when she took in the redwood that was Deacon George.

Deacon smiled warmly at her. "Do you remember me, Kira?"

She shook her head. "This is Coach Deacon," I said. "He coached you for a couple of years before we moved."

All she did was nod, then turn back to me. "Can you braid my hair, please?"

I was relieved to be given a task; otherwise, I would have just stared inappropriately at the coach. Nodding, I accepted the hair elastic she gave me and gathered her long, dark curly hair—the exact same as mine—into three strands and effortlessly put it into a tight French braid. "There," I said, tossing the fastened end over her left shoulder.

"Thanks," she murmured. "Can you help me with my cap, please?"

I accepted the chartreuse-green swim cap from her and held it open so she could duck her head and hold it at her forehead. Then, with one hard yank over her head, I tugged it to the nape of her neck.

We'd probably done this nearly a thousand times, so we had a system that worked.

"Thanks," she murmured, swiping her tongue over her braces again.

"All right, guys, let's go over our drills for the warm-up today," Deacon announced before flashing me one more smile, and, fucking hell, a wink. "We've also got a new swimmer here with us today. I'd like everybody to welcome Kira Robinson to the team. I promise, Kira, we're all really nice and supportive. I'm sure you'll fit right in."

Kira glanced back at me, chewing on her bottom lip.

I gave her an encouraging thumbs up, but that was only met with another eye roll.

"How old's your daughter?" asked the blonde woman beside me. Her smile was friendly, and from what I could tell, she didn't have any judgement in her tone or hazel eyes.

"Twelve and a half going on twenty," I said with a sigh. "I'm sure I put my own mother through the wringer when I was that age, but yeesh, the pre-teen angst and hormones are ... they're a lot."

The woman nodded. "I hear that. My son is thirteen and a stinky, moody monster. I'm Jeanie." She held out her hand, and I shook it.

"Greta. Nice to meet you. Which one is yours?"

She pointed to the cute little redhead girl in the royal blue suit and matching goggles. "Maria. She's ten. My son Holden isn't into swimming. He's at lacrosse practice over at the field across the parking lot." She pointed west to indicate the field that was part of the enormous sports and recreation complex. "I feel you on the angst and hormones. My husband and I just separated, and both kids are acting out more than ever. So much fighting."

Relief swamped me. "I'm going through the same thing. Kira's dad and I just split, and he moved to California to be with his new boyfriend."

Jeanie's eyes nearly met her hairline. "Shit. That sucks. I'm really sorry."

"Thanks. Yeah. So navigating that, moving back to Seattle from Eugene, Oregon, and just her age and all the trials and tribulations that come with that have been a lot."

"We should get wine one night. Or, hell, bring a flask to the next practice. I feel like we are destined to commiserate and throw darts at our ex's faces together." Jeanie's smile was the exact balm I needed for the rash Damien left around my heart.

Grinning, I nodded. "Sounds like a perfect way to spend an evening. But when you say throw darts at our ex's faces, you mean *pictures* of them, right?"

Jeanie laughed. "Unless you have yours tied up in your basement like I do mine?"

CHAPTER TWO

I ABSOLUTELY WAS NOT EXPECTING to find my teenage crush sitting in the bleachers when I walked into the pool. My day had been totally shit. My bike tire was flat when I woke up that morning, and I was late for class. Then, I dropped my phone, and the screen cracked, and I heard that after January, life-guarding hours were going to get slashed because of city-wide budget cuts. I'd already lost two guitar lesson clients this month, too.

I thought moving home for my master's was going to save me money, and it was—a little—but life and school were really fucking expensive.

My mood was low when I walked into the pool, already worried about the paper I had to write when I got home, but when I saw Mrs. Robinson—Greta— sitting on the bleachers by herself, frowning at her phone, I forgot about my entire crappy day.

I'd loved this woman since the moment I met her when I was fifteen and covered in acne and patchy body hair. Now, I was twenty-two, had figured out a good skincare regimen, and my body hair was no longer playing favorites with random parts of my body and ignoring others. I'd also sprouted at least six inches and was six-foot-four. Maybe my prefrontal cortex wasn't completely developed just yet, but that didn't mean I wasn't someone who didn't know what he wanted.

And even after all these years since she moved away, I still wanted Greta Robinson.

She'd been off-limits before. For various reasons. I was a child, and she was an adult, and she was also married.

Before I even said hello, I zeroed in on her ring finger. Empty.

Did this mean she wasn't with that dingdong dipshit Damien anymore? I'd never liked that guy. She could do so much better.

I knew a ring didn't always mean single, but it gave me hope. It gave me something to think about besides my paper, for the two-hour swim practice.

However, Greta sitting there was also a massive distraction. I kept looking up at her, animatedly chatting away with Maria's mom, Jeanie. Then Greta would laugh, and my heart would do a heavy *thud* in my chest.

I've had plenty of girlfriends over the years and there was even one I said, "I love you," to, but always in the back of my mind, deep in the dark, private recesses of my heart, I still held a flame for Mrs. Robinson.

"All right, team, that was a great practice. Out of the water and head to the hot tub for five minutes to warm up," I said, the kids all heaving with spent efforts as they stared up at me with their goggle eyes.

One by one, they swam over to the ladder and hoisted themselves out of the water, walking their exhausted bodies to the hot tub. Their sighs of relief as they sunk into the hot water were heard all the way where their parents sat on the bleachers, prompting many parents to laugh.

"You worked them hard today, Deacon," one dad said. "Genevieve is going to sleep well."

"They worked themselves hard," I replied. "I'm just here to encourage them to do their best."

The dad smiled at me and stood up, heading over with a towel to the hot tub, along with several other parents.

Greta and Jeanie were still chatting on the bench. I didn't want to interrupt, but also I really did.

She caught me staring and smiled shyly.

That was enough of an opening for me.

I strutted over. "So, what brought you guys back to Seattle?" I asked. "Mr. Robinson get a job at U-Dub?"

Greta's cheeks flushed with color. "Damien and I are no longer together. He's moved to LA. So Kira and I moved back to Seattle to be near family. We didn't have anybody in Eugene, so there was no reason to stay."

I resisted the urge to fist-pump the air.

"I-I'm sorry to hear about you and Mr. Robinson," I said, hoping I sounded sincere, but in reality, I absolutely fucking wasn't. I was elated. I was cannonball-off-the-highest-platform celebratory.

"Thanks," she murmured, standing up along with Jeanie.

"Kira's a fantastic swimmer," I said, not ready to see her go. "I definitely think she'll do well at the meet in two weeks."

"There's a meet in two weeks?" Greta asked, with a look of surprise in her blue eyes. Eyes I'd more than once fantasized staring up at me as she took me in her mouth. My cock twitched in my neoprene swim shorts.

"Yeah, but it's here, so we don't have to travel," Jeanie said. "Thankfully."

"It's December twentieth," I added. "Then there's a team party afterward."

"I'm sure Kira will have lots of friends and want to attend by then," Jeanie said. "See," she pointed to the hot tub, "she's already chatting with Maria."

Jeanie's gaze was pulled to the left where her son, Holden, approached, decked out in all his lacrosse gear. I'd known the Newcombe family for a while now, but apparently Jeanie and her husband Rich were separating. I knew first-hand how tough that could be, so I gave Maria a bit more grace.

How recent was Greta and Damien's divorce? Was Kira going through a lot too?

"Hey sweetie," Jeanie said, running her hand over the back of Holden's dark red head. His cheeks were flushed and his nose dripped a little. The weather outside was nasty for lacrosse practice. Once again, making me really happy that I chose an indoor sport, despite the early morning practices.

Holden looked dead on his feet.

"Your sister is just in the hot tub. I was thinking we'd just stop and grab a pizza on the way home. I don't feel like cooking."

Holden merely nodded.

Jeanie turned to Greta. "Actually, would you and Kira like to come over for pizza? We don't live very far from here."

Greta's eyes widened in surprise. Why did my cock twitch at that? Probably because I had the filthiest mind imaginable when it came to this woman. And now I was standing there like an idiot while these two mothers planned dinner for their children. I could not be anymore of an awkward interloping outsider.

"Let me see how Kira's feeling," Greta said. "Thank you, though. That sounds wonderful."

Jeanie smiled and headed off with Holden to the hot tub. Thankfully, Greta hung back with me.

"The divorce is very recent," she said, turning to face me. "Kira is going through a lot. If she gives you any kind of attitude, let me know. Moving back and away from her school, friends and swimming team mid-year hasn't been easy. But it was ultimately the best choice for us."

I frowned in sympathy. "I'm really sorry to hear she's struggling. I know a bit about divorced parents. It's not easy for anybody."

Her eyes turned sad. "Oh no! Your parents aren't together anymore?"

I huffed a humorless laugh. "I know. I was as surprised as you are now. They were literally relationship and marriage goals. The day after my high school graduation, they sat my brother and me down and told us they hadn't been happy for some time. They said they stayed together for us, but now that we were both out of high school, it was time for them to go their separate ways."

"Oh, Deacon, I'm really sorry."

"Yeah, Cameron and I were blindsided. Now holidays are split, and dad's new girlfriend is a ..." I raked my fingers through my hair. "She's a piece of work. That's all I'll say about that."

Her frown deepened. "It's never easy for anybody."

I hadn't talked about their divorce like this with anybody, and yet, Greta Robinson had a way about her that made me want to just roll over onto my back and show her my sensitive underbelly. Lay out all my vulnerabilities and never kept a single secret from her.

"Where are you this year for Christmas?" she asked.

Another humorless laugh exploded from my chest. "Well, Mom's on a cruise with her sister, Dad's girlfriend—Brandi—convinced him to take her to Thailand, and Cameron is in Boston with his girlfriend's family."

Her mouth dropped open. "So you're alone?"

I shrugged. "I've got papers to write, so I'll probably just go into the lab. It'll be quiet. I'll be able to get some work done. I'll buy myself a really nice steak."

She shook her head. "Deacon ..."

"It's fine," I said quickly. "Grandparents are all dead. Aunts and uncles aren't in town. It's fine."

If I said it enough times, it would be true, right?

"Mom?" Kira sidled up to Greta, giving us a curious back-and-forth ping-pong look.

"Hey, sweetie," Greta said, wrapping the big fluffy towel around her daughter. "Ready to go?"

Kira nodded. "Yeah."

"Listen, Maria's mom invited us over to their house for pizza for dinner. What do you think?"

Kira glanced behind her where Maria, Jeanie, and Holden stood, and Jeanie was chatting with Maria's coach. "Is that Maria's brother?"

"Yeah, Holden," I said. "He's great. Really nice kid."

Kira's cheeks turned pink, and she traced her braces with her tongue. "Yeah ..." she said slowly, "I guess we could go over to their house for pizza."

Greta met my gaze and smiled. Was she picking up on Kira's little crush like I was? Was my crush as obvious? Hopefully not.

"Go shower and get changed, sugarplum, and I'll meet you in the lobby," Greta said.

Kira nodded and took off toward the changing rooms.

Greta faced me again. "I'm really glad you're her coach. A familiar face—for both of us—is going to help the transition a lot." She rested her hand on my arm. "Take care, Deacon. I'll see you next week."

Then she removed her hand, and it was all I could do not to grab the hood of her coat, haul her back and take her mouth.

CHAPTER THREE

With just one week until Christmas, I finally had the townhouse unpacked and all the Christmas decorations up—including the tree.

It wasn't easy with my demanding work schedule and Kira's even more demanding swim practice schedule, but late nights, wine and my super-supportive new friend Jeanie helped.

With just a splash of Carolans Irish Cream in my decaf Early Grey tea to-go mug, I climbed on to the bleachers—which were only six benches high—just before swim practice started and sat down, my back to the wall behind me. I was usually the first parent there, which I didn't mind. It allowed me to pick the best seat—the top bleacher row with the back support.

I peeled off my jacket and set it beside me to save a spot for Jeanie.

My phone vibrated in the back pocket of my jeans, and I pulled it out, but not before taking a sip of my spiked tea. A simmering ire filled my veins when I saw it was a message from Damien.

Teach your daughter some manners. See the text she just sent me.

He followed that message up with a screenshot of an exchange between Kira and Damien.

In any other circumstance, I would have agreed with him that Kira's message was rude and disrespectful, but considering how little respect he'd shown *our* daughter over the last half of the year, he deserved all the attitude—and more.

First of all, she's OUR daughter. Second of all, maybe if you showed her some respect AND love, she'd show you some in return. You go weeks without texting her,

Damien. You haven't called her in over a month, and when she sent you a picture of the Christmas-themed elastics on her braces, you reacted with an angry-face emoji. So her calling you a selfish asshole of a father who prioritizes his boy toy over his own child is pretty damn accurate.

I STARED AT THE MESSAGE. I KNEW BETTER THAN TO REACT IN HASTE AND LET my immediate feelings do the talking. I was thirty-four years old. I'd learned not to be so reactionary. Not to be so impulsive. It'd served me well over the years, walking away and taking a breather before responding to someone I'd sooner just punch in the throat.

But did Damien deserve my taking a deep breath?

"Uh-oh," came the smooth, deep and sexy voice of Coach Deacon. "That's an angry-mom face. What happened?"

I lifted my gaze away from my phone to his chiseled handsomeness. It had to be illegal to be that gorgeous. It really did. I'd heard more than once over the last two weeks that most of the young girls—and their mothers—had secret crushes on Coach Deacon. Fair enough. The man was absolutely gorgeous. He'd yet to take off his shirt, which was probably a good thing. More than one woman in the bleachers would surely faint—myself included.

"What's got you making that face?" he asked, climbing the bleachers and, surprisingly, taking a seat beside me.

At this point, I didn't give a shit anymore. I handed him my phone.

He read Damien's message, along with the screenshot and my unsent message. "Fuck," he breathed, glancing at me. "He left you for a dude?"

Releasing a long, slow breath, I nodded. "Yep. A *dude* not much older than you, actually. Not that age really matters. But he was his student. Which was a huge no-no. Damien left the college and followed Paul down to LA, where Paul is working on his PhD and Damien moved into consulting at a museum or some shit."

"Jesus."

"Is my response too harsh?"

"*Too* harsh? I'd say it's not harsh enough. You know I used to refer to him—in my head, of course—as Dingdong Dipshit. I always thought you could do better than him."

That comment warmed me more than I thought it would. "Really?"

He regarded me as if I were crazy for even asking. "Absolutely. Not only is he like a huge narcissist—and I know what those are because my dad's girlfriend is one—but you're *way* hotter than he is. He married *way* up." His finger hovered over the little arrow to send the message. "I say, send it. Unless you want me to add a bit more to it to really drive home how terrible a human being he is? Because I can."

That made me laugh. "I dunno ..."

"It's perfect the way it is. It's blunt, but it's not too harsh or over-the-top."

"Send it," I said before I could back down and delete it. I covered my eyes, peeking through parted fingers.

"Done," he said with a big grin, handing me back my phone. Then his smile dropped. "I'm really sorry he did that to you, and is doing that to Kira. Neither of you deserves such awful treatment."

My smile kicked up on one side more than the other. "Thanks. I can handle things myself. It's just Kira that my heart aches for. She doesn't deserve any of this. It's almost like he's punishing her for choosing to live with me rather than him. Which I honestly don't think is the case, because he's loving this free and easy childless life down in LA. You should see his Instagram." I gagged a little and pulled it up. I didn't follow Damien for obvious reasons, but his profile also wasn't private, so anybody could see what my midlife crisis ex-husband was up to.

Damien's green eyes bugged out, and his jaw went slack. "He's really going all out embracing the gay life, huh?" He was obviously referring to the pics of Damien and Paul at various gay nightclubs where they were dressed in neon Speedos, wearing glow stick necklaces and black-light body paint. He was living his best new life and probably loving that he didn't have a child at home that he needed to be responsible for.

"I don't care that he's gay," I said quickly. "I care that he lied. That he deceived us. That he cheated. And how he's treating Kira now. As if she's nothing but a burden. If he'd been a shitty dad when we were together, it wouldn't be such a blow, but he wasn't. He was a doting father. He loved her. And now ..."

"It doesn't seem that way," he said, finishing my sentence for me.

Emotion hung thick in my throat, so all I could do was nod.

"Does Kira have Instagram?" he asked.

I nodded again.

"So she can see all of his?"

I continued to nod.

He sucked in a deep breath through his nose and breathed it out like a heavy puff from his mouth. "That's rough. She's seeing her dad living it up, partying and whatever, meanwhile he can't even be bothered to message her back." He wrinkled his nose up in a cute way. "Why'd he respond to her braces picture with an angry face?"

"Probably because he's pissed off with how much the braces are costing us. We don't have an insurance plan since I'm freelance and self-employed, and he left the university and went private, so he doesn't have coverage either. And yeah, they aren't cheap, but she needs them, so ..."

Deacon shook his head. "Talk about selfish."

"His picture's right beside the word in the dictionary." I shook my head. "I'm also worried about what's going to happen when Paul eventually ends things with him. What do a twenty-five-year-old and a thirty-six-year-old have in common? How does that relationship even work? It doesn't. It's all about the sex. And Paul introduced Damien to all his gay friends. Will Damien *then* decide he wants to be part of Kira's life when Paul kicks him to the curb? Talk about fucking with your kid's head."

I didn't notice at first, but Deacon squirmed a little beside me, almost as if he was uncomfortable.

I cocked my head at him, squinting my eyes. "What's wrong?"

"I dunno ..." he started, breaking eye contact, "age-gap relationships can work. If the younger person is mature for their age, maybe? And the older person is open-minded and young-at-heart? They're not all doomed to fail." He shrugged. "I mean these two ..." he pointed to Damien and Paul on my phone in a picture on Instagram. They were at a nightclub, half-naked, with their arms around each other. Damien was kissing Paul on the cheek, and Paul was smiling with his mouth open while wearing those stupid sunglasses with all the lines across the lenses. "They're doomed to fail. But it's not because of their age. Damien is a narcissist, and Paul will eventually see that—if he isn't one himself."

I went to open my mouth, though I wasn't sure what exactly I was going to say, but the arrival of Jeanie saved the day. "What's in your mug today?" my friend asked, climbing the bleachers and sitting down on the other side of me. "I've got Bailey's in my decaf coffee."

Damien smirked and stood up. "Oh, these moms are here to party!"

Snorting, I rolled my eyes and shook my head at him. "Hardly. Just a little nip to add some extra flavor, that's all. And I've gone with Carolans Irish Cream today in decaf Earl Grey."

"Ooh, let me try." Jeanie took my to-go mug from my hand and had a sip. "Mmm. That's delicious," she replied. "I'm going to do that next time."

Deacon bobbed his brows at me before climbing down the bleachers just as all the kids, other coaches and parents started to file in. "Don't send anything else until I get to read it and you get my approval," he said, mostly in jest, but there was a thread of truth to his tone too.

"All right," I replied. "You're creating a lot of extra work for yourself, though, you know?"

"Don't care. Assholes need to be dealt with accordingly." Then he flashed me his biggest, brightest smile before turning around to address the swim team gathering behind him like eager little ducklings.

"What's going on with you two?" Jeanie asked, her gaze swiveling between Deacon's back and me a few times. "What does he mean, *don't send anything?*"

With a sigh, I showed her the message from Deacon, along with my reply. I'd yet to hear anything back from Dingdong Dipshit. I stifled a laugh at Deacon's secret nickname for Damien. It was fitting.

"That motherfucker," Jeanie breathed. "Pardon me, that *father*fucker. Either way, what a fucker. So what, Deacon wrote that message for you?"

I shook my head. "No, he saw me glaring at my phone in a rage fugue, asked what was wrong and since the fucks I have left to give about any of it have disappeared, I showed him. Then I asked him if the response was too harsh—I hadn't sent it yet—and he said no, that it wasn't harsh enough. But we didn't change it. I sent it."

"Definitely not harsh enough. All it is is a reality check. You're telling him the truth about how shitty of a dad he is and that he deserves every bit of disrespect she throws at him."

I needed that reassurance. More times than not, through this total nightmare, I caught myself wondering if I was being too harsh with Damien. Not understanding enough with regards to his later-in-life crisis. But when he treated our daughter this way ... I didn't care how he was struggling or *if* he was struggling. There was no excuse for his behavior toward Kira. None.

"Thanks," I murmured, hating every bit of all of this and reflecting on the last thirteen years of our marriage. He claimed he always "kind of" knew he was gay. He thought he just "needed" to be straight because life and work in his field were easier for straight men. So instead, he just "pretended" with me for years. Pretended to love me. Pretended to want me. He faked every part of himself. I was a beard to him. The doting wife, playing a role when I didn't even know I was in a fucking play.

If he cared for me at all, he would have been honest with me. He wouldn't have wasted the last fourteen-plus years of my life. I should have known something was up when he said he didn't want anymore children. That one was enough. He kept saying that we shouldn't contribute anymore to an already overpopulated world?

A tear slipped down my cheek before I could stop it. Jeanie noticed and wrapped an arm around me. "Oh, honey." She tugged me close. "He's a shitty dad. A shitty man. You and Kira deserve so much better."

"I just feel like the best years of my life are gone." I faced her. "I wanted more kids, you know? I wanted two kids. So Kira wouldn't be alone. But Damien only wanted one. So much so that he went and got a vasectomy without telling me"

"Fucking hell," Jeanie breathed.

"And now, I'm thirty-four, and although I technically *could* still have kids, I'd need a man for that because no way do I want to be a single mom to a teenager and an infant. Hormones and colic? Kill me now. Not that I am counting down the days until Kira is eighteen and independent-*ish*. They say one of the perks of having kids younger is freedom in your forties, but if I had another kid, I'd be nearly fifty before I was free."

"Hell no, you don't want anymore kids!" Jeanie said emphatically. "As someone who is *in* her forties, the best years of your life are *not* gone. They're right in front of you. Maybe the most *fertile* years are behind you, and you have perimenopause to look forward to—"

That made me laugh.

"But trust me, your best years are *not* behind you. You've shed the deadweight. Embrace the lightness. Embrace the new life ahead of you." She gave me a squeeze. "And all the hot, casual sex you get to have now."

"I'm not even thinking about that right now."

"Well, you should. Dating apps are a cesspool. Don't marry a man from a dating app, but they're great for hookups."

I glanced at her. "Are you hooking up?"

She shrugged and bit her lip, letting go of me. "I mean ... when the kids are with their dad, I'm going on some dates. Mind you, those dates usually involve the guy coming to my house, me tearing his clothes off and getting an orgasm or two before I tell him to hit the bricks, but yeah."

Chuckling, I shook my head. "I don't think I could do that. I've *never* been one for hookups or casual dating or casual sex. I've been Miss Monogamy since high school. One man, one penis," I said that last bit as a whisper, "forever."

"Give me your phone." Jeanie held out her hand.

"What? Why?"

"We're going to make you a dating profile."

I shook my head. "No. No way. I'm not ready for that. I can't."

"You are. And you will. Hand it over."

The woman was not taking no for an answer. Rolling my eyes, I handed her my phone. She grabbed my hand and used my thumbprint to unlock it. "We'll set you up on one where *you* have to make the first point of contact. Not one of those sleezy ones where the guys can send unsolicited dick pics straight off the bat." She cringed. "And if you get a dick pic, just send a different dick pic right back. I keep a collage of them hidden on my phone in a file labeled *Eggplant Parmesan Recipes*."

I'd just taken a sip of my tea, but nearly spat it out in an abrupt laugh that drew some attention from other parents.

"Damien just makes me so mad. Every time he texts—which isn't very often, but it's often enough—it's usually when I'm in a good mood, and *poof*, that good mood goes up in smoke. Just like my marriage."

"It's like he has a sixth-sense about when you're in a good mood."

"Exactly!"

"Well, fuck him," she said, scrolling through my photos. "Ooh, this is a nice one of you. You're on a hike, I take it? Shows you're outdoorsy and fun."

"And I'm sweaty. Look at the sweaty pit stains."

"Doesn't matter. I'm using it." Then she held up the phone. "Smile."

"What? Why?"

"Because that color red looks smoking hot on you, and your makeup is perfect. You're looking real fine today, Mrs. Robinson. Now smile."

I did as I was told, and she took a few shots before saying, "That's the one."

"See the difference here, though, is that you don't have full custody of your kids. You share them with your ex so you have days off. I have Kira full time, and I'm definitely not going to be bringing random app men into my house when she's asleep."

"You work from home. Have them over on your lunch hour."

I gaped at her, but she just grinned.

"There. Read that."

Reluctantly, I leaned over to read what she wrote for my profile.

Name: *Greta*

Age: *34*

Kids: *Single mom. One child.*

Occupation: *Web designer. Self-employed.*

Hobbies: *hiking, reading, cooking, swimming, gardening and listening to hardcore gangster rap when I run.*

Personal Statement: *I like Irish cream in my tea and honesty in my men. Also, squids are assholes.*

That last bit about hard-core gangster rap, and my personal statement made me burst out laughing. Jeanie asked a while ago why I had

Damien's avatar as a squid, and when I told her it was because squids were assholes, she found that hilarious. She, too, enjoyed listening to filthy hardcore gangster rap when she worked out. It was just another thing we bonded over.

"Anything you'd change?" she asked.

"You mean, except for the fact that I'd rather not do this at all?"

"Not an option. I mean, do I need a comma somewhere or do you want to add something to your personal statement?"

I let out a long sigh. "No. It's perfect."

She hit *submit*. "And done. No turning back now, lady. You're going to be getting all your overdue orgasms in no-time."

I leaned toward her. "I do have an entire drawer of vibrators. Orgasms are not the issue. It's killing spiders and reaching stuff on tall shelves. That's the problem."

CHAPTER FOUR

WHAT WERE they talking about over there?

Why was Jeanie Newcombe taking a picture of Greta?

I could barely focus on the swimmers. My attention kept getting diverted to the laughing women in the bleachers. Not to mention the fact that Greta looked more gorgeous that even in that top of hers. The red brought out the blue in her eyes and the way her dark curls cascaded over her shoulders and hung just above her breasts—I'd be using this as new spank bank material for fucking sure.

"Coach Deacon?" My attention was once again pulled away from the beauty in the stands and back to my job.

"Hmm?" I asked, hoping the kid hadn't said my name too many times, and I'd just ignored them. I glanced down to find Samuel, a shy kid who was an okay swimmer but very eager to get better, staring up at me from the pool, blood pouring down his face. "Oh shit!"

"Marty and I uh ... we bumped heads. I think my nose is bleeding."

"Fuck. Yeah, buddy, it's bleeding. Come on, up you get. I reached down and hooked my hands under his arms and hoisted him out of the pool. His mother was already rushing toward us.

"What happened?" she asked.

"Marty and I bonked heads in the pool," Samuel said again. "Is it bad?"

It probably wasn't *that* bad, but all the blood made it *look* bad. I caught the attention of one of the other coaches and asked them to watch my team while I escorted Samuel and his mother over to the first aid room where another life-guard would help him.

"Why weren't you watching them?" his mother—Cynthia—scolded me as we shuffled across the wet pool deck.

"I ... I lifted my head up for a second," I stammered. "I swear."

"It wasn't Coach Deacon's fault," Samuel said, accepting the towel from his mother and holding it under his nose. "Marty swerved and bonked me. He entered my lane."

"Even so," Cynthia huffed. "It's the coach's job to catch this stuff and pay attention."

She wasn't wrong. However, the kids had their faces and ears under the water. How the hell was I supposed to yell at them and warn them when they were in the middle of the pool and I was on the deck?

I was, admittedly, distracted by Greta being in the stands, however.

I needed to get a handle on my crush. It was getting worse. I saw the woman three days a week, two hours a day. She was all I thought about. I woke up thinking about her and went to bed thinking about her. I didn't even have it *this* bad for her when I was fifteen. Back then, I didn't even know what love was, and now that I knew, I knew beyond any doubt that I was madly in love with Mrs. Robinson.

"You're going to be okay, buddy," I said to Samuel, getting him seated on the bench inside the first aid room. "Eddie here is going to take good care of you." I slapped Eddie kindly on the back and smiled at him, then turned to Samuel's angry mother. "Probably best to call it a day for practice. Having his head down in the water, along with the blood rush from exercise, could cause the bleeding to start again."

Cynthia huffed at me. "So now he misses practice because of you?"

"I'm very sorry, Mrs. Weaver. If you'd like to schedule a time outside today where I meet Samuel for some one-on-one coaching to make up for it, we can over the holidays. You can email me."

The change in her expression was pretty hilarious. "Oh! Well ... thank you. That would be very nice."

It wasn't something I *had* to offer. Injuries and illnesses happened. It was just part of life and sports. But this mom sat on the board for the swimming club and could very easily make my life a living hell. She was also one of those parents who were clearly living vicariously through her child, convinced he was going to be the next multi-medal Olympian. Samuel was a good swimmer, but he wasn't the next Michael Phelps. I smiled and nodded. "Just shoot me an email and we'll make it work."

I ruffled Samuel's already-drying short hair. "Take it easy, buddy. Feel better."

"Thanks, Coach Deacon. I will." He gave me a thumbs up, and I gave him one back before taking my leave of them and returning to the deck.

I tried so hard for the rest of practice *not* to let my gaze drift to Greta, but as hard as I tried, I failed so fucking miserably. It was ridiculous.

Practice ended, and the kids all climbed out of the water, making their way to the hot tub. "How's the little guy with the nosebleed?" Jeanie asked, Greta beside her as they gathered all of their stuff to follow the kids to the hot tub.

"He'll live to swim another day," I said.

"We watched it happen, and it was brutal," Greta said. "That other little guy, the one in the blue suit, veered into the nosebleed kid's lane and *crash*. Practically heard the cartilage crunch from up in the stands."

That made me chuckle, but also feel guilty that I'd been watching Greta and not my swim team when it happened.

"Kids are tough," Jeanie said. "Now he's got a cool story to tell his friends."

Greta and I met each other's gazes and smiled, her eyes glittering like blue gems beneath the lighting. "What are your plans for the holiday?" I asked, making sure both women thought I was asking them.

"My parents have a cabin in the Snoqualmie Pass that we go to every year," Jeanie said. "So we're heading there. Their dad has them for New Year's, though."

"Quiet party of two this year," Greta said. "But it'll be nice. I told Kira we could just stay in our pajamas all day, and I'd even let her have some Irish cream in her morning tea."

"What about you?" Jeanie asked me.

Greta's eyes turned sad because she already knew the answer to that.

I shrugged as if it was no big deal. "I've got a couple of papers to write. I'll probably spend a lot of time in the lab, too."

"Yeah, but where are your parents? Your family?" Jeanie pressed.

I shrugged again. "They've got their own lives, just like I've got mine. Dad's already in Thailand with Brandi, and Mom and her sister are going on a cruise. And my brother is heading to Boston to be with his girlfriend and her family."

Jeanie's mouth dipped into a frown. "You mean you're all alone?"

"I happen to like my own company."

"Yeah, but on Christmas?" Then she swatted Greta on the arm. "You should invite him over to your house for dinner."

Greta's mouth dropped open. "Uh."

I quickly shook my head. "No. No. It's fine. I will be perfectly fine on my own. I've had twenty-one family-filled Christmases. It's okay. I will survive." I focused on Greta now. "Don't let her bully you into inviting an unwanted guest into your home out of pity."

That made Greta smirk. "It wouldn't be pity."

"Of course not," Jeanie said. "And you wouldn't be unwanted. You're the most well-liked coach, by kids and parents." She dropped her voice to a whisper on that last bit to not to offend the other nearby coaches. "Just bring a side dish. You can cook, can't you?"

"I can," I said slowly.

"Then it's settled. You're going to go over to Greta and Kira's for Christmas dinner. Bring a ... what?" She turned to Greta, who looked even more railroaded than I felt. "What can he bring?"

"Uh ... mashed potatoes?" Greta finally said.

"Perfect. Deacon, you bring the mashed potatoes. You can find her address on the team roster." Jeanie grinned at both of us, so proud of herself. "I just hate to hear of people being alone on Christmas. I mean, seriously, if I knew my ex wasn't already going to spend it with his parents, I'd have probably invited him up to my parents' cabin because as much as that man drives me nuts, nobody should be alone on Christmas." Then, before we could say another word, she flashed us both a giant smile and took off to go gather her child, leaving Greta and me standing there, shanghaied, speechless and extremely uncomfortable.

School was over for the semester now. I wrote my last exam, then hopped on my bike and raced through the city to the rec center for the swim meet. Thankfully, one of the other coaches was going to help my team until I arrived a little late. By the looks of the schedule, the team I coached would have only competed once while I was gone; the rest they would race while I was there.

Locking my bike up, I dodged the icy raindrops that had already attempted to shred my face on the ride, and ran inside the rec center, not even bothering to stop in at the change room to drop off my stuff first. I booked it onto the pool deck to the raucous cheering of parents and spectators as a race was just about over. It was the younger kids racing, not my crew.

Ditching my bag, coat, shoes and helmet in the pile of other coaches' gear, I shook my hair clean of the raindrops, and visually sought out my team. They were all sitting in a corner wrapped in their terry cloth swim covers and towels, silicone caps on their heads, goggles on their foreheads, watching their team-mates compete. Kira was in the mix, so without even thinking about it, my gaze slid to the bleachers to seek out Greta. She was there with Jeanie, both of them cheering on Maria as she swam the last few meters of her breaststroke. She would not win, but she had a solid hold on third place. Fourth place was way back.

The winner reached the end, followed by second place—neither of them from our team or town—and then it was Maria. Jeanie and Greta both stood up and cheered even louder, which prompted the little redhead in the water to turn toward her mom and go absolutely scarlet in the cheeks, but she was smiling and that was what mattered.

I turned back to face my team. "Sorry I'm late, guys."

"How was your exam, Coach Deacon?" one of the kids asked.

"Tough, but I think I did okay," I said. "How was your first race?"

They all kind of grumbled that none of them did as well as they had hoped. All of them except Kira, who remained suspiciously quiet. Was she being quiet because she actually did well and didn't want to stand out from her peers? I understood that. I'd been the best swimmer on my swim team for as long as I could remember, but I was never braggy about it. I didn't want to lose friends over being good at something, or have them think I thought I was better than them.

"Kira placed first, but none of the rest of us placed," another girl said.

I glanced at Kira, whose cheeks were turning pink. "Well done, Kira. Are you proud?" She ran her tongue over her teeth and shrugged. "I guess."

"Next up, the two-hundred-meter fly. Girls, ages eleven to thirteen," the announcer said.

"All right, team, that's us. Let's get ready."

Kira, along with two other girls who were racing, stood up, unzipping their swimsuit covers and stashing them against the wall. They walked single file toward the platforms, pulling their goggles over their eyes before climbing up.

Kira turned to me. "Maybe Winnie or Shante should win one this time?"

Oh shit.

I shook my head. "No. If they're meant to win, they will. But I want you to give it your all, Kira. Don't *give away* the gold because you think someone else should have it this time. If you're meant to get gold in every single race you swim today, then so be it. Do you think Michael Phelps slowed down so Ryan Lochte could get a gold?"

She shook her head.

"That's right. No, he didn't. He won that gold medal. He took it for himself. He *earned* it by being the best."

"Okay," she whispered.

"Kick some ass, kiddo. You've got this."

She slid her tongue over her teeth, then smiled. "Okay. Thanks, Coach Deacon."

I gave Winnie and Shante some words of encouragement too. Then, Kira wished her teammates good luck, and they all took their starting positions. The buzzer went, then the gun fired, and they dove into the water.

My gaze flew up to the stands where Greta and Jeanie stood cheering wildly for Kira, who swam her heart out. Not everybody could do the butterfly stroke. It involved a lot of upper-body strength. It was personally my favorite, but so far, we didn't have a lot of girls in particular, come through able to do the stroke well enough they wanted to compete.

Until Kira.

The kid was a star.

By the time she was on her length back, she was already half a pool length ahead of the rest, and she wasn't slowing down. The pool was wild with loud, enthusiastic cheers for the swimmers, but it was impossible not to see the awe on some people's faces with how fast Kira really was.

She reached the end of her second lap, did an underwater somersault and pushed off from the wall only to fly up like a flying fish, arms coming forward, propelling her.

A girl from another team was gaining on her, but it was questionable whether she would gain enough to overtake Kira. I didn't think so.

Kira reached the end, flipped and pushed off once more. The girl was on fire. She was giving it her all, just like I told her to. Literally sprinting to the end to finish the final fifty meters and win herself that gold.

The volume level of the crowd intensified, and I found myself cheering just as loudly. Ten meters to go. Then five. Then three. Then two. Then one. And ... she won!

I leaped into the air, fist pumping as Kira glanced up at me, an enormous smile on her face.

Winnie came third, and Shante came fourth. Still very good and nothing to be upset about.

With their chests heaving, they climbed out of the water and the whole team ran up to Kira, embracing her and congratulating her on another win. Her smile was wide.

I hedged a glance up at Greta in the stands. She was grinning as wide as her daughter, and my heart did a happy little thump in my chest.

Kira raced twice more that day, coming in first in both the 100-meter freestyle and the 100-meter backstroke. They would all be back tomorrow to compete in the relay, and for the boys to compete as well. It was expected that even if it wasn't your race day; you showed up to cheer on your teammates. There was nothing worse than looking up into the stands and not seeing anybody there because it wasn't their time to race, so they didn't bother to show up.

I didn't have a lot of rules as a coach, but that was one of them.

"Well done, everyone. I hope you're proud of yourselves. I'm certainly proud of all of you."

They all looked exhausted. Like pre-teen drowned rats.

"Can we hit the hot tub quick, Coach?" Winnie asked. "I'm freezing."

"For sure," I said, jerking my chin in the direction of the hot tub. "Go for it. Just tell your parents."

She and Shante gave me a thumbs up, then took off in the direction of the hot tub, shivering a little as they went. Kira had already taken off to the change room, but Greta was just gathering her stuff and climbing down the bleachers. We hadn't spoken since that awkward moment when Jeanie forced Greta to host me for Christmas dinner. Jeanie was already off with Maria somewhere, so I took the opportunity of having Greta alone to give her an out.

"You've got a future Olympian on your hands," I said, breaking the ice. "I know the early morning extra practices can't be easy on either of you. Do you at least have a garage, or do you have to scrape your window at five in the morning?"

Her smile was sweet, but small. Tired. "I have a garage, thankfully. And I wish I could be one of those parents who stick around for the morning practices, but I just can't. We live only ten minutes away, so I go home and crash on the couch."

Chuckling, I shoved my hands into my pockets and nodded. "Fair enough. The early mornings are a bitch for me to ride my bike here. I don't blame you."

"You ride your bike?" she exclaimed.

"Cars are expensive, and so is a graduate degree. Had to make a choice. I take the bus when it's particularly gross out, but it doesn't run on a very friendly schedule for the early practice schedule."

"Okay, I'll stop complaining then."

Smiling, I glanced at the ground. "Listen, Mrs. Robinson—"

"Ohhh, Deacon, you need to call me Greta. Please."

Chuckling awkwardly, I nodded. "Listen, *Greta*, I'm really sorry for Jeanie forcing you to invite me to Christmas dinner the other day. I swear I didn't put her up to it."

"I know you didn't. I love Jeanie, but she can be very pushy. She forced me to start an online dating profile. That has been ..." she shook her head in disbelief, "a lot, to say the least."

Flickers of jealous heat sparked in my belly. A dating profile? I could guarantee that not a douche she met on there would be worthy of her.

I cleared my throat. "Anyway, don't think you need to actually host me. Jeanie's not the boss of either of us. I don't want to intrude on your time with your daughter. I will survive Christmas alone. I'm not going to off myself if that's what Jeanie is worried about."

Another sweet, small smile curled at her mouth. "You should come. I don't like the idea of your being on your own, either. She's pushy, but she's got a good heart."

"You're sure?" I asked. "I really don't want to impose."

"Bring a bottle of wine with those mashed potatoes, and it won't be an imposition at all." She flashed me a bigger smile and stepped down onto the pool deck.

"Deal." I beamed.

"See you tomorrow, Deacon."

"See you tomorrow, Mrs. Rob—Greta."

CHAPTER FIVE

EVEN THOUGH WE weren't supposed to tell our children we were proud of them because that put the focus on "our" feelings, fuck that nonsense.

I hugged Kira when she finished her last race, winning yet another gold. "I'm so freaking proud of you, kiddo! Are you proud of yourself?"

She was still out of breath, but the enormous smile on her face was all the answer I needed.

Her teammates running up to congratulate her on her win essentially pushed me out of the way, but I didn't care. She was making friends. She was smiling, and that meant the absolute world to me.

Yesterday, Winnie's mom texted me to ask if Kira would like to have a sleepover with Winnie after the meet and year-end party. I honestly didn't think Kira would want to go, but when I asked her, she was all over it. So her sleepover stuff was in the car. It'd been ages since I'd had a night alone. I wasn't sure what I was going to do with myself.

Once everybody got changed, they headed to the podiums to accept their medals. My daughter was humble, yet also super smiley. Joy filled my chest to near bursting.

I'd questioned more than once if this was the right move for us, if I did the right thing leaving Eugene. But seeing her now, with friends and that gorgeous grin, just reassured me that it was the right thing to do.

With her neck weighted down from the medals, and faint goggle lines around her eyes, she approached me, bowing her head so I could remove all her medals.

"Meet you in the party room, Kira," Winnie and Shante said with waves and smiles as they headed with their parents off the pool deck to the rented rec room across the center.

"See you there," Kira replied.

"You're sure you want to go to Winnie's for a sleepover?" I asked once her friends were out of earshot.

Kira nodded. "Yeah, Mom. I'll be fine."

"Well, I'm only going to have one glass of wine, just in case you want me to come and get you."

She rolled her pretty blue eyes—the same shade as mine. "I'll be fine. Have some wine. You deserve it."

It was my turn to roll my eyes. "You saying *you're* the reason I need to drink?" I tossed her a smirk and tugged playfully on the end of her damp braid.

"No. Not me." She wrinkled her nose. "Well, not *just* me. Dad too."

I didn't have to ask if she'd heard from her father. I already knew she hadn't. Damien also didn't bother to reply to my text message yesterday. The yellow-bellied coward.

"Come on, you," I said, looping my arm around her neck and kissing the side of her head, "let's go celebrate."

THE PARTY WASN'T ANYTHING CRAZY. IT WAS JUST PIZZA, VEGGIE PLATTERS, flavored sparkling water, juice boxes, and ice cream sandwiches for dessert. Deacon connected music from his phone to a Bluetooth portable speaker, and everyone just relaxed after a busy and exhausting first half of the swim season.

"Do you have your guitar, Coach Deacon?" one of the kids asked, after everyone had stuffed themselves silly with food and were just lounging around chatting.

"I don't," Deacon said with a pout. "But I'll bring it to the end-of-year party in the spring. I promise." His gaze flitted over to me, and heat instantly flooded my body—and I'm sure made my face bloom with color. I was never one to easily steel my emotions and hide them from people. This man flustered me to no end. I kept a mental tally of how much attention he paid to the other parents, and it sure as hell wasn't as much as he paid to me. Did they all notice? Did they all think something more than just parent-coach friendliness was going on?

The last thing I wanted was to give the new batch of swim team parents any fodder to hate me, or even worse, Kira. Yes, Kira was a tremendous swimmer and earned every gold medal she won, but if they thought Deacon was giving her any kind of preferential treatment because of some underlying *something* between us, I'd be mortified.

I averted my gaze without returning his smile, sipping my can of strawberry-flavored sparkling water while gently bobbing my head and tapping my foot to the music. I was ready to head home, and even though Kira was sleeping over at Winnie's, I still had her sleepover stuff in the car, and I didn't want to leave until she did, just in case she got cold feet.

Slowly, and I mean *very* slowly, families began to leave the party. I was yawning like crazy by the time Kira and Winnie came up to me to let me know that Winnie's parents were ready to.

Many of us helped tidy up the party room so that the coaches didn't have to do it all themselves. I went in to grab an empty pizza box at the same time Deacon did, and our hands touched. I was the first to pull away, like his fingers were made of flames. "Oh, sorry!" I said, laughing awkwardly, reaching for a different box.

"All good," he said smoothly.

I moved over to another table and gathered up all the leftover juice boxes. They'd probably just be used for the next party. "Is there somewhere we can put all of this leftover stuff?" I asked.

"We have a bin in this storage closet here that the rec center lets us use," one of the other coaches said, opening up the closet and leading me through, then unlocking the big bin. I unloaded my heavily weighed-down arms into the bin, spun around and ran smack dab into the titanium-hard chest of non-other than Coach Deacon himself.

Dammit.

"Oh, sorry!" I exclaimed—again.

"All good," he repeated, this time with a chuckle.

Dear god, I needed to get the hell out of there. The smell of him alone was making my brain short-circuit and my panties way too freaking damp. They would probably freeze to my skin when I went outside in that nasty weather. It was calling for snow and lots of it over the next few days. We'd have a white Christmas at least, but I wasn't looking forward to having to shovel my driveway or venture out onto the roads with all the idiots who couldn't be bothered to get snow tires.

Without saying another word—or at least anything coherent—I shuffled past him and inhaled deeply when I emerged into the main room. But his scent still lingered in my nostrils, and those butterflies in my belly woke up and were ready to party.

I avoided him for the rest of the time we were in there cleaning up, even though I knew he was trying to catch my eye. Every time I felt his gaze on me, I pivoted away.

Did I encourage this by chatting with him, and showing him my phone, telling him about Damien and ... oh shit! He was coming over for Christmas dinner. How did I not see how freaking bad that looked?

I needed to figure out a way to cancel.

"Come on, Mom," Kira said. "I need my bag out of your car."

Nodding, I made sure I wasn't abandoning the coaches with more cleanup—though plenty of parents didn't lift a fucking finger—and headed toward Kira, Winnie, and Winnie's parents. "Put your hood up," I said to my child as we approached the front doors. "Your hair is still wet, and it's freezing outside."

"That's an old wives' tale, Mrs. Robinson," Winnie said. "You can't catch a cold from going outside with wet hair.

I smirked. "Well, I'm an old wife, so ..." I tugged my hood over my head as well and thanked Winnie's dad for holding open the door. Then we all ran to our vehicles. Luckily, Winnie's parents weren't parked too far from me, so it wasn't an icy hike across the parking lot for Kira.

"Call me if you want to come home," I said. "I know you told me to get shit-faced drunk, but I'm not going to."

She smirked at my exaggeration. "Just be kind to yourself, Mom. You're going through a lot, too." Then we hugged. I kissed her cold, rosy cheek and watched my daughter climb into someone else's car and drive away from me.

She would be fine. She was strong, resilient, and I needed to start giving her more credit.

Piling into my RAV, I sat there for a while, waiting for it to warm up. I pulled on my leather driving gloves, my fingers icy and stiff at first before they defrosted. My butt was the first thing to thaw, thanks to the seat warmers, then the windshield.

I took a mental inventory of whether I had wine at home or not, and decided it wouldn't be the worst idea in the world to hit up the liquor store on my way home.

Pulling out of the parking lot, I headed in the opposite direction of home, since the better liquor store with a more diverse wine selection was five minutes south.

I wasn't even a quarter of a mile away from the rec center when I nearly drove off the road because of who I saw walking on the sidewalk, already half frozen. Signaling to pull over to the right, I threw on my hazard lights and climbed out of my car. "What are you doing?" I yelled at Deacon over the wild wind. It wasn't raining at the moment, but the wind was nasty.

"My bike was stollen," he said, looking nearly hypothermic and incredibly sad.

"Get in," I demanded.

He shook his head. "No, I'll be fine. The bus stop is only another half mile."

"Get. In," I said again, using my stern mom-voice.

Nodding and shivering, he didn't argue and headed to the passenger side, opening the door.

I ran back around and climbed in behind the steering wheel, throwing the heat on full-blast. I also had to remove my jacket, though, otherwise, I'd boil.

"Someone stole your bike?" I don't know why I was asking a redundant question, but it was the only thing that came to mind.

He nodded. "Yeah, they used bolt-cutters to cut the lock."

"Fuck," I breathed. "I'm so sorry."

He shrugged. "It's okay."

"No, it's not. Do you want to go report it to the police?"

Shaking his head, he held his hands out in front of the vent to thaw them. "It won't do any good."

"It might. If the bike shows up at a pawnshop or something?"

More head shaking. More shivering. "It was stupid to ride it in this weather, anyway. My mom said I could use her car while she's on her cruise, so I'll just do that."

"And then what will you do when she's back?" I asked.

More shrugging. "I'll figure something out."

"Deacon ..."

"You can just drop me off at the bus stop. I'll be fine."

"I won't. I'll take you home. Just tell me where to go."

He tossed me a sideways glance as I turned off my hazard lights and pulled back out into traffic when it was safe to do so. "Are you mad at me or something?"

"Mad at you?"

"Yeah. All of a sudden today, ever since the party, you've been acting weird around me. Like you can't get away from me fast enough. You won't even look at me or smile. What did I do?"

Exhaling, I tightened my grip on the steering wheel. "You need to give me directions, remember?"

"I know. Keep going straight. But we can have a conversation while you drive, and I give you directions."

Dammit.

"I'm just worried about what the other parents might think."

"About what?"

"You're not as friendly with the other parents as you are with me."

"Because I've known you longer. I still chat with the other parents, though. I'm not rude or mean to them."

Pulling a deep breath in through my nose, I kept my gaze focused forward. It was just easier than looking at his handsome face and those impossible green eyes. "I know you're not. But the length of our acquaintance is not enough to rationalize how *much* extra attention you give to me. And maybe I've encouraged it, but it has to stop. People are going to start talking. They're going to think something is up between us."

"So?"

I couldn't not pivot to gape at him. Luckily, we were at a red light. "SO? So, I don't want the other parents thinking we're *something*. I'm like twelve years older than you. And we just moved here. Kira is adjusting and making friends. The last thing I want is for her friends or those friends' parents to think you're giving her preferential treatment because there's *something* going on between us. You're flirty with me, Deacon, admit it."

"The light's green," he said, his expression alarmingly blank.

I hit the accelerator and faced forward again, moving with the traffic. My body was an inferno. And goddammit, his wonderful, woodsy scent was filling my car and making my head a little fuzzy.

His silence, however, made me nervous.

"Are you going to say anything?" I finally asked.

More silence.

Oh fuck.

"Kira gets treated no differently than any of the other kids. I can't *give* her more medals or anything. She's earned those all by herself."

"I'm aware of that. But that's not going to stop other parents from making accusations based on observations. You didn't disagree with me when I said you were flirty."

"So what if I am?"

"It's inappropriate."

"Why? You're single. I'm single. You're an adult. I'm an adult. There's nothing *illegal* about it. And besides, what if it was a parent coaching the team? That's happened before. Remember when I was fifteen and Coach Fiona and

Coach Stu had kids who competed and were part of the team? Nobody accused them of anything. If anything, they were tougher on their own kids."

"It's different, and you know it."

I slowed down at another red light. "Maybe I was encouraging it at first. The attention was nice. But I was wrong to encourage it. To tell you about my divorce and all of that. So I accept responsibility for this too. But come the new year, it has to be different. You have to treat me like any other parent. We can't screw this up for Kira."

His expression turned stony, but it was a terrible mask for what was really beneath—and that was pain.

My heart hurt.

"What about what I want?" he whispered.

That made me face him fast enough to cause whiplash.

He lifted his brows. "I've ..." His chest heaved.

"You've what?"

Muscles ticked at the corners of his jaw, and he shook his head. "Never mind. The light's green. Take a right at the next set."

I waited for the car in front of me to move before I hit the accelerator again, facing forward, but unable to stop my gaze from drifting sideways to where he sat there looking like a thoroughly kicked puppy.

I took a right where he told me to.

"Next left, then right, then into the cul-de-sac."

Nodding, I did as I was told.

"Green house up there." He pointed.

I pulled into his driveway and put the car in park.

"So I take it I'm uninvited to Christmas dinner then, huh?"

Fuck.

Deacon was a good kid. But that was the thing. He was a *kid*. He was my daughter's swim coach. I wanted to tell him that, yeah, maybe it was a good idea he didn't come over for dinner, only the words refused to come out of my mouth.

I faced him. "Come for dinner. I couldn't bear the thought of your being here alone. We need to keep it platonic, though. No flirting. No ... whatever *this* is." I pointed back and forth between the two of us. "Kira will be there, and even though she's only twelve, she's very observant."

"Does she know that I was invited?"

I nodded. "She does. I don't keep anything from my child. She was fine with it."

His head bobbed stiffly. "Okay."

"You're going to drive, right? I don't want to find out you walked to my house carrying a pot of mashed potatoes."

That made him snort, though it came out mirthlessly. "I'll drive over, yeah."

"Good."

Our eyes locked, and he swallowed, a deep pain in his green gaze. "Thanks for the ride."

"Please consider reporting your bike stollen."

His hand fell to the door handle. "I'll think about it." Then he opened the door and stepped out onto his driveway, giving me a half-hearted wave before he headed inside.

I sat there in his driveway probably for too long, my head against the steering wheel as I berated myself for ... what? I wasn't sure. I should have told him not to come for dinner. Why didn't I?

Because you like him and he likes you. You're broken, and attention from a younger, hotter-than-the-sun man is exactly what you need to heal.

Right. That was why. I was thinking with my vagina, not my brain.

Great. I was no better than a freaking man.

CHAPTER SIX

I GOT into my house and threw my bag down on the couch with angry force.

Then, for good measure, I belted out a loud "FUCK!" to the ceiling.

She was right.

Of course she was.

This was bigger than any "crush" I may have on her.

We had to think about Kira. We had to think about the bigger picture.

She also never confirmed whether she felt the same way. All she did was tell me that the way we were acting and my flirting had to stop.

I needed to make things right on Christmas. I needed to go there, grateful for the invite, but with nothing more than gratitude in my mind and heart.

I had three days to shake my feelings for Greta.

You've been in love with her since you were fifteen. You really think you'll be able to quit in three days?

No, but I had to try.

Peeling off my wet clothes, I headed to my bathroom.

Since moving back home, my mom gave me basically the entire basement to myself. I had my own bathroom, my own living room, and even a mini-fridge. I kept weird hours and was barely home, so it was just easier than constantly waking her up or disturbing her when I came and went.

I turned on the shower, giving it a moment to heat up, and stared at myself in the vanity mirror. "Get your shit together, George. She's off-limits."

As if liking the challenge and taboo nature of it all, my dick started to thicken.

Fucking hell.

Of course it did. Because the idea of sneaking around with Greta, when the odds were monstrously stacked against us, did nothing but turn me on.

Fuck.

I stepped under the warm spray and let the water sluice down my body and over my face.

"I'm twelve years older than you." Her words echoed in my mind.

I didn't fucking care if we were forty years apart. I still wanted her. I was still madly attracted to her. With age came wisdom. With age came experience. With age came knowing what the fuck you wanted, and not being all wishy-washy.

Not that they had to have their lives all figured out, but girls my age just didn't do it for me. They were flighty and flaky, and a lot of them were vain and obsessed with their number of followers. I couldn't give two shits about any of that stuff.

Taking my cock in my hand, I began to stroke myself. I closed my eyes and pictured Greta pushing open the glass shower door and stepping into the steam with me. Her wild, dark, curly hair piled high on her head, and her blue eyes hooded with lust. A small, playful smile curled her lips, and she ate up the distance between us, pressing her breasts to my chest and reaching lower to take my shaft in her hand and continue stroking me.

She bit my chin, and I growled, grabbing her by the back of the neck and pushing her up against the tile wall, claiming her mouth as mine. Her moan made my cock grow even harder in her palm, and I thrust forward, revelling in her strokes, in the way I fit perfectly into her palm.

Reaching up with one hand, I cupped her breast, rolling the peaked tip between my thumb and forefinger until she gasped. Smiling, I deepened the kiss, sweeping my tongue into her mouth, exploring.

She met my tongue with her own, tangling and massaging. Another moan vibrated through her, pulling out one from me as well. She rode my thigh now, stroking me with her hand while using my leg to pleasure herself. If there weren't such a height disparity between us, I'd reach my hand between her legs and get her off myself. But I was also A-okay with her using my leg. I'd take care of her in a minute.

She picked up momentum, squeezing the crown just a little, bringing all the blood to the head. I was already close. So fucking close. I couldn't wait until she let me come down her throat. I'd take a mental screenshot of her on her knees with my cock in her mouth, and hold on to it forever.

"Deacon," she moaned, breaking the kiss. I trailed my mouth across her cheek, jaw and neck, biting her shoulder.

"Greta," I murmured.

"Oh, Deacon." Her hand picked up speed again.

I was going to come.

I was going to come so fucking hard.

"Deacon!" She rode my thigh harder and faster, using me like a ride 'em bull in a country bar. I fucking loved it.

Heat built in my lower belly, my balls cinched up tight against my taint, my brain went all fuzzy and ... I fucking exploded.

All over the shower wall, her belly, the glass door and the tile floor, my cum spurted out thick and ropey, painting everything in its path.

I exhaled in relief, the echoes of my release making me shudder a little and slump against the wall. I opened my eyes and ... I was alone.

Of course, I was alone.

It'd all been a fucking fantasy.

A really vivid, really sexy fantasy. One I'd had some iterations of many times before. And yet, tonight felt more realistic than ever. A small part of me really thought she was here. I could feel her heat on my thigh from where she rode me. But it was all just a mind-fuck.

How did I ever expect to fall out of love with Greta Robinson in three days?

I guess I'd just have to pretend and hope for the best.

Worst-case scenario, I sit at home on Christmas and eat a massive pot of mashed potatoes and steak and beat off to my fantasy of her, while she sits mashed potato-less at home with Kira.

Yeah ... nobody deserved to go without mashed potatoes on Christmas.

I guess I needed to just suck it up and pretend.

Not that I'd ever been very good at it, but I'd try. For Kira, for Greta, I'd try.

"Mom! Deacon's here!" Kira shouted when I showed up on their doorstep the evening of December twenty-fifth.

Greta came scuffing in her slippers around the corner to the front door, wearing a cute—but also sexy—holly berry-covered apron. "Merry Christmas, Deacon. We're glad you could join us."

I smiled at her, hoping it was warm enough she didn't think I was being weird or awkward. "Thank you for having me."

"Of course, of course," she said, waving her hand in dismissal of my gratitude, like hosting me was no big deal and wasn't going to be weird at all. "Kira, can you grab the mashed potatoes from Deacon so he can remove his coat and boots, please?"

Kira nodded and retrieved my mother's big orange Le Creuset cast-iron pot from me, making a little grunt of a noise when she realized how heavy it was. "What's in this? Rocks?"

"Yes," I said. "It's an old family recipe."

She snorted and stuck her tongue out at me before taking the pot into the kitchen.

"Uh, this is for you," I said, handing Greta the bottle of wine. "As requested."

Smiling, she accepted it from me. "Thank you. I trust you drove here?"

"I did. I do as I'm told. No walking or bussing for me today. Promise."

She nodded. "Good. How are the roads?"

"Not great, I'll admit," I said. "It was getting pretty dicey when I left the liquor store—because of course I left getting the wine to the last minute." I rolled my eyes at my own procrastination and followed her into the kitchen, where the action was happening. The table was set for three with festive place-mats, candles and cloth napkins. There were three wine glasses out as well. The mouth-watering scent of turkey filled the air, and my belly rumbled.

"Did you at least chat with your parents and brother today?" Greta asked, pulling a foil-covered dish out of the oven and checking under the foil to see if it was cooked.

"I video chatted with my brother earlier today, and with my mom. I spoke with my dad last night, since it was already Christmas in Thailand. Brandi says *hello* by the way."

Greta snorted. "Hi Brandi." She opened up a cupboard and pointed to the top shelf. "You're not here just as company. We needed a giraffe to grab stuff, too. Reach that decanter up there, will you, please?"

Chuckling, I stepped forward, but not until Greta made sure she was well out of the way. No risk of us touching or being in the same breathing space. I reached up and pulled down the crystal decanter from the shelf, placing it on the counter. "How'd you get it up there?"

"Stepladder," she said. "I figure a nice bottle of wine like the one you brought needs to breathe. This stuff I buy from the store—"

"She nearly drinks straight from the bottle," Kira interjected, earning a shocked look from her mother. The twelve-year-old cheeky child started laughing. "Just kidding!"

"Just for that, young lady, you can have grape juice," Greta retorted.

Kira snickered. "You already gave me Carolans in my tea this morning."

Greta rolled her eyes. "Yeah, there's no prohibition in this house."

She opened the wine and emptied it into the decanter. "Where is the cruise your mom and aunt are on?"

"Caribbean," I answered. "She's never been, so this was a pretty big and exciting trip for her. They've got like eight different port stops."

"Oh, that'll be fun. I got my scuba diving certification in St. Lucia back in the day when life was simpler."

"You mean before you had the responsibility of a child?" Kira added.

"Yeah," Greta said simply. "Life was simpler before I had you. Not gonna lie about that."

Kira made a pretend and playful sneer at her mother before popping an olive into her mouth from the pickle and olive tray on the counter.

Even though they were sort of arguing, I could tell it was all in jest. They said it all with love in their eyes and smiles on their faces. There was a strong mother-daughter bond here that I appreciated, and certainly didn't want to come between. Greta was doing her very best to give her daughter a good life after the bombshell Damien dropped on them. And from what I could see, Kira was thriving. Greta was an incredibly strong, capable and caring mother.

"How long do we need to let it breathe?" Greta asked, eyeing the wine.

I chuckled. "You're asking the wrong person. I usually drink beer if I drink anything."

"Oh shit! I should have picked up some beer. I'm sorry."

I held up my hand in protest. "Don't worry about it. I also like wine. I'm not picky at all. I just have no idea how long you're supposed to let wine *breathe*."

"If only there was a thing we could look up such questions," Kira said with a teenage eye roll before picking up her phone from the counter. "Google, how long should you let red wine breathe in a decanter?"

Google kicked alive and her robotic voice filled the room. *"Zealously swirl the wine and let it rest for twenty minutes in the wineglass. This is sufficient time to open up any tannic red wine. If you plan on drinking more thane glass, pour the wine into a decanter and let it breathe for roughly two hours. The longer aeration period will soften the wine's strong tannin flavor."*

"Two hours!" Greta exclaimed.

I laughed. "I think it's just a suggestion. And I mean, *technically*, you're having one glass, I'm having one glass, and Kira's having one glass—"

"Half a glass," Greta corrected.

"Either way, it said twenty minutes for one glass. So we can give it another ten minutes or so then we should be good."

She picked up the decanter and handed it to me. "Swirl it. It can't hurt, right?"

That made me laugh, but I did as I was told and swirled the wine in the decanter while she puttered in the kitchen. The turkey was already resting on top of the stove under foil, but it looked like she was the kind of cook who made her stuffing in a casserole dish. Not actually inside the turkey—which was how I preferred it, anyway.

I loved the crispy edges, and it also guaranteed that the stuffing would actually be cooked through. One year—the first year after my parents split—my dad decided he was going to cook a turkey for the first time. My dad, Cameron and I all got horrendous food poisoning because my dad didn't cook the turkey all the way through and the stuffing had raw turkey juice all through it.

She also had homemade cranberry sauce, roasted Brussels sprouts, roasted yams and what looked like a green bean casserole. It was a lot of food for three people. Good thing I hadn't eaten anything all day in preparation.

Or maybe that was because of the nerves I felt leading up to this evening, and having to be so close to Greta, in her home, and burning an unsnuffable flame for the woman.

"Is your mashed potato recipe an old family recipe or did you just go with what had the most and best reviews on Google?" she asked, poking a fork into a halved brussels sprout after opening the oven and pulling out the pan. Apparently, it needed a few more minutes.

"Well, I've tried Anthony Bourdain's recipe—"

"May he rest in peace," she said quickly.

I placed my hand over my heart and nodded. "May he rest in peace." Goddammit, she was just making herself more irresistible. *Fuck.* "Anyway," I cleared my throat and told my dick to calm the hell down, "but it was just too much freaking butter. I also like roasted garlic in my mashed potatoes. My mom uses Boursin in hers, which is great, but I went with the tried-and-true butter, whipping cream, roasted garlic, salt, pepper and parsley—for garnish the way my nan used to do."

She smiled at me. "My gran always sprinkled dried parsley on top of her mashed potatoes too. I do it as well as in homage to her. I thought I was the only one."

Oh, for fuck's sake. I couldn't catch a break.

"I think the wine has been *zealously* swirled enough," Kira said, having been busy washing dishes at the sink, quietly listening to our exchange.

"Right." I put the decanter down on the island.

"Glasses are already at the table," Greta said, lifting her chin in the direction of the table. Her hands were covered in turkey as she'd started to carve it.

I made myself useful and filled up two glasses, then poured a little bit into a third, setting it by Kira.

"Thank you," Greta said, her hands shiny with turkey juice. "Are you a white meat or dark meat person?"

"I'm not picky."

"Gun to your head though," Kira said, "which would you choose?"

"What kind of weird interrogation is this?" I asked, prompting them both to giggle.

"The most serious kind," Greta shot back.

"Fine, I'm a white-meat guy. But I'm honestly good with whatever."

"I like white meat for the proper turkey dinner, but then the dark meat for potpies. It adds more flavor and moisture."

I nodded. "Yeah, that makes sense."

Before I thought too hard about what I was doing and why, I brought Greta's wineglass up to her lips so she could take a sip. Her blue gaze met mine with wide-eyed surprise at first, but she took a sip, anyway. "Thank you."

"No problem."

Kira finished the dishes and came to stand between her mother and me, holding her wineglass. She was as tall as her mother, with the same hair and the same eyes. She had a different nose from Greta, though—probably from her father. Both women wore red and green striped socks in their matching slippers, and when I looked down, they also had on matching flannel tartan pajama pants.

"Nobody told me this was a pajama party," I said, glancing down at my dress slacks and gray sweater. "I've got some awesome flannel pants I could have rocked up in. I feel severely overdressed."

Kira beamed. "Mom said we could stay in our PJs all day. Dad always made us dress up as if we were going to church or a funeral or something. Even when we never went anywhere."

"We're creating our own new traditions," Greta said. "And I say, if we don't have anywhere to be, then wear whatever the hell you want. Be comfortable. Be you."

"So, should I go home and get my PJs?" I asked, hooking a thumb over my shoulder.

"Not in this weather," Greta said. "I don't want you driving in this."

Our eyes locked when she realized what she just said. If she didn't want me driving in this, how was I supposed to get home?

Leave it to Kira to say what the rest of us were thinking. "Then how is he supposed to get home, Mom?"

"Well, hopefully, the plows come through, or the snow lets up," she finally said. "We'll cross that bridge later tonight. He's not leaving until his belly is full. That's all I know right now." She gave a curt nod, as if to shut us all down once and for all from arguing with her. But the creep of pink into her cheeks said she was already worried about how this was going to look, and what the sleeping arrangements would be if I couldn't make it home.

CHAPTER SEVEN

I was trying my absolute best not to let that moment in my car three days ago affect Christmas dinner. I was basically pretending it never happened. Like I didn't shoot Deacon down and tell him to stop looking at me, talking to me, and flirting with me.

I drove home, cursing myself out for handling things the way I did.

Yet, no matter how I tackled it, I couldn't come up with a different way—a way I *should* have dealt with it better. I was as gentle with him as possible. I didn't *want* to hurt him. However, I knew I did. The pain in his eyes gutted me to the bone.

It was beyond the point now where his attraction to me was all in my head. Even though he didn't actually confirm his feelings, I knew they were there. He didn't deny them either. I gave him every opportunity to be like, "Sorry, Greta, if I gave you the wrong impression, but I don't see you that way." He didn't, though.

My bruised divorcee ego liked the attention, but my smarter mom-brain knew better. She knew that this was a slippery slope and, ultimately, Kira would be the one to get hurt. I needed to stop thinking with my vagina. I'd already connected with a few men on the dating app Jeanie set up for me, and so far, the conversations were going well. I set my age preference as thirty-two to forty-five. That was reasonable, right? Not too much younger than me, and not old enough to be my dad.

I wasn't ready to go on any dates yet, but the flirtatious chatting was nice.

Things had been going smoothly since Deacon arrived. Light and friendly banter, with Kira as a safe buffer in the middle. But then I went and opened my damn mouth regarding him driving—or more accurately, *not* driving home—in this weather. The look in his eyes said it all.

It would be foolish to send him home in this weather; it really would. But we were also in a two-bedroom townhouse. He could sleep on the couch, but even upstairs in my bedroom, I'd know he was just a closed door away, probably sleeping in boxer shorts with his eight-pack abs, zero percent body fat, and winning personality.

Thankfully, Kira—still none the wiser about what was going on in the surrounding air—saved the awkward moment, and made it all the more awkward. "We have a couch Coach Deacon can sleep on. And I just got a new toothbrush from the dentist I haven't opened yet that he can have."

Deacon's and my eyes met, but neither of us said anything.

"Let's just get through dinner first, sugarplum," I said, laying out the turkey meat on the platter. "Will you poke a fork into the Brussels sprouts, please? I think they're done."

Kira nodded and did as I asked. "They're done," she said.

"Okay. Pull them out, cover them with foil and move them to a heat pad. Deacon, do your potatoes need to be warmed up?"

"Couldn't hurt to plunk them in the oven for a few minutes to warm them," he replied.

Kira did that while I cleaned my hands and the knife, then covered the uncarved half of the turkey.

"You know, one thing I'll never understand is on television and in movies how they bring the entire, massive, uncarved turkey to the table," Deacon started. "I don't know anybody who does that. Everyone I know, every Thanksgiving and Christmas dinner I've been to, the turkey is carved in the kitchen, then the platter of meat is brought to the table."

He understood the assignment and was actively trying to soften the tension that had strung itself tight in the room a moment ago. I smiled at him. "I have thought the same thing several times. Kira and I were even talking about that when we watched a Christmas movie last night, how they brought the massive bird, all brown and beautiful, to the table."

"Mom was like, 'That's way too messy of a job to do there. What game are they playing?'"

Chuckling, I removed the foil from the stuffing and scooped half of it from the casserole dish into a bowl. "I swear sometimes that television and movies make a point of making things as *unrealistic* as possible, just to get people talking."

"You might be on to something," he mused, taking the bowl of stuffing from my hand—our fingers only brushing for a moment—and bringing it over to the table. "My mom constantly fusses about how unrealistic they make pregnancy and childbirth on television."

I nodded emphatically. "Yup. Babies come out looking three months old and clean as a whistle." I glanced at Kira. "Your face was smooshed as hell, and you were covered in gunk."

"Lovely," Kira said blandly, taking the green bean casserole over to the table.

"Still thought you were the most beautiful baby alive, but you weren't clean by any means."

How the hell did we segue into talking about babies and birth? Did I do that? Why? Why did I do that?

Luckily, Deacon didn't look too uncomfortable. He accepted the pan of roasted yams from Kira and took it to the table. I moved all the Brussels sprouts to a smaller bowl, and last but not least, the mashed potatoes came out of the oven. The cast-iron pot was hot, so I had to carry it with two hands in oven mitts over to the table, plunking it on a hot pad.

"All right, let's wash up, then we can eat," I said, catching myself from calling them both *kiddos* before even half a syllable was uttered.

I ditched the apron, so now Kira and I really were twins in our matching pajama pants, socks, slippers, and black fuzzy sweaters. I wasn't sure she'd want to match her mom. Twelve-year-olds were so hard to predict. But she seemed tickled pink when she opened up her matching outfit to mine this morning, and promptly changed into it right there in the living room.

"This all looks amazing, Greta," Deacon said, taking a seat across from me. "Thank you again for inviting me." He scrunched his nose. "Or I guess ... letting Jeanie talk you into hosting me."

"Jeanie's a pushy one, that's for sure. But her heart's in the right place." I took a sip of my wine and moaned. "Oh, that's good."

"It was the *zealous* swirling," he teased. "Had to be."

My lips twitched against the rim of my glass as I took another sip. "Dig in, everyone. Don't let it get cold."

We filled our plates and ate our fill until nobody could take another bite.

"I didn't bake pies," I said. "I hope you weren't pining for pie."

"I can't even think about pie without throwing up a little in my mouth," Kira said. "I'm so full."

"There are gingerbread cookies in the tin on the counter, but that's all I have in the way of dessert, I'm afraid."

Deacon shook his head. "Honestly, I'm not here for the cookies. Stuffing will always be my first choice. And yours is delicious."

"Thank you." I probably had three or four more bites left on my plate, but I couldn't fathom finishing them. Besides, didn't a lady always leave something on her plate?

Deacon stood up and started clearing the table.

"Oh, leave that," I said. "You're the guest. I don't expect you to clear the table."

"You cooked the entire meal. Just relax." He set a few bowls on the counter, then came back for his and Kira's plates. "Are you finished?" he asked me, his hand covering next to my plate.

I nodded, unable to argue with him. The turkey yawns were fast-approaching. "I am. Thank you." I took another sip of my wine and closed my eyes.

Kira's father had yet to send a gift, text, or call. It was as if his daughter didn't even exist, let alone matter to him anymore. Was he seriously punishing her for her text message to him? The one where I called him out and said that he didn't deserve respect since he didn't respect her?

A small part of me thought he'd do some stupid, grandiose gesture like fly up and knock on our door unexpectedly. That was a very Damien thing to do. Make it all about him while pretending it was all about someone else. So the snow-storm eased that tendril of fear that he might do that, because he was scared shitless of flying in bad weather, so he'd never step foot on a plane or drive in this.

Kira got up from the table, and she and Deacon finished putting the dishes away, and moving the leftovers to smaller containers for the fridge. "Do you want me to finish carving the turkey?" he asked, pulling me from my tryptophan coma.

I popped open my eyes and spun around to face him, marveling at the tidy kitchen. "No, no, you don't have to do that. I'm sorry. I must have dozed off for a second."

"You were full on snoring, Mom," Kira said with a giggle.

"I don't snore."

Deacon grinned.

"Sure," was all my child said.

"I don't mind carving it," Deacon replied. "I've carved a few turkeys in my day. Been told they weren't hack-jobs, either."

I was very comfortable in my seat. The turkey and wine had created a cocktail of drowsiness I wasn't altogether hating. So I nodded and smiled. "If you want to." Then, I closed my eyes again.

When I woke up, the kitchen was completely clean, the turkey was carved and put away, and the sound of Deacon and Kira in the living room laughing pulled me out of my chair and down the hallway to the living room. They had the movie Elf on in the background while they played a game of cribbage. I didn't even know Kira knew how to play cribbage.

"Hey Mom, good nap?" Kira asked with just a hint of cheekiness in her voice.

I yawned and ran my hand over the back of her head. "Who taught you to play cribbage?"

"Deacon just did," she said, glancing up at me with a smile. "There's a math component to it, and I love math."

"Where'd you find my old board?"

"In the cupboard with all the other board games. You don't mind, do you?"

I sat down next to her on the couch. "Not at all."

"You can play the next round with us if you want," Deacon offered, smiling at me with nothing hidden or flirty behind his eyes.

I nodded and stayed, watching the game play out. Deacon beat Kira, but not by much. It was pretty neck-and-neck for a while.

I joined in on the next round, and we played until nearly eleven o'clock.

"I'm exhausted," Kira said after finally beating Deacon and I and doing a small victory dance—which we all agreed she earned. "I'm going to head to bed." She came over and gave me a hug. "Thanks for a great Christmas, Mom. I can tell you really tried to make it special. You did a great job."

Well, if that didn't hit me hard in the feels, I wasn't sure what would. I hugged her back, my throat tight, and the backs of my eyes burning. "Merry Christmas, sugarplum. I'm glad you had a nice day. I love you." I kissed her cheek.

"I love you too, Mom."

"Goodnight, Coach," she said, offering him a friendly smile and wave. "Thanks for bringing those awesome potatoes."

"It's all about the roasted garlic," he said with a big smile of his own.

We waited until we heard her finish up in the bathroom—I had my own en suite bathroom—and her bedroom door closed.

"Listen," Deacon started, his eyes turning pleading, "I'm really sorry about the other night in your car."

I shook my head. "I should be apologizing to you. I ... I handled that terribly." I knew that I didn't handle it terribly, but somehow it felt like the right thing to say.

It was his turn to shake his head. "No. You're right. We can't jeopardize Kira's future on the team. And some of the parents can be ... intense."

"You're being kind," I said with a scoff. "I've known them for three weeks and already I can tell the Karens and Chads from the rest."

He nodded. "Yeah. And the last thing I'd ever want to do is hurt you or Kira."

"I appreciate that." My gaze shifted awkwardly around the room before I stood up and peeled back the drapes. It was a complete and utter whiteout.

"Yeah, I checked a little while ago," he said, remorse in his voice. "Plow hasn't come through, and it's really piled up."

"I'll go get some sheets from the linen closet upstairs," I replied, closing the drapes and heading to the stairs.

I'd only made it to the bottom of the stairs when I stopped and looked up.

Mistletoe hung from the ceiling. That absolutely was not there earlier today.

And there was only one person in this house who was tall enough to put it there.

The giraffe.

I stomped out to the living room, tossing my hands on my hips and glaring at him as he tidied up the cards and cribbage board. "Is that some kind of a joke?"

Deacon blinked at me in confusion. "Is what?"

"The mistletoe."

"What mistletoe?" He still pretended he had no idea.

Squinting at him, I shook my head. "Don't play games, Deacon." Then I stomped away, back to the scene of the crime. He was smart enough to follow me. I pointed to the hanging symbol of love. "I'm not tall enough to put that there, and neither is Kira, so that leaves one person in this house tall enough to fasten that to the ceiling."

He lifted his eyebrows as he studied the plastic fake foliage. "Climb the stairs," he said, his voice even.

I scoffed.

"Climb the stairs, Greta," he said, with an edge to his tone now.

Reluctantly, and still very pissed off, I hiked up the stairs the eight steps before he told me to stop.

"Lean forward and see if you can touch the ceiling from there," he said. "There's a significant slope to the ceiling."

Glaring at him, but humoring his experiment just to prove him wrong, I did as he instructed. And, fuck, I could touch the ceiling and the mistletoe. Heat flooded my face.

His brows rose. "I didn't put it there."

"Well, neither did I," I said, climbing down a few steps, but remaining under the decoration. Deacon and I were the same height.

"Kira?" he asked, though we both knew it was a rhetorical question.

"Why?" I shook my head in disbelief.

He shrugged. "Maybe she wants to see her mom happy?"

"This doesn't make any sense," I whispered. "You have your whole life ahead of you. I'm ... I've got a kid."

"A *great* kid."

"Who is almost a teenager."

"So?"

"I don't think I want anymore kids. I did ... once, but raising a teenager and a baby? I don't think that's the way my life is meant to go."

"Who said anything about more kids? About a baby?" His gaze roamed my face. "Greta, we haven't even kissed yet and you're already talking about kids."

"Because I *have* a kid. Because this is what grownups talk about. You're going to want kids one day, right? So this would never work ... not long-term, anyway. And what would your parents say?"

"Who said I wanted kids?"

"You don't?"

He shrugged again. "Just because I *work* with kids and am great with them doesn't mean I *need* my own. I've never been one of those people who feel like I *have* to have kids to make an impact. They're not a make-or-break deal for me. And as for my parents? Who gives a shit?"

"Deacon ..."

"You're coming up with a million excuses, Greta, but what you haven't said is that you *don't* want this. That you're not attracted to me."

I nibbled on my lip, studying his chiseled, angular features. "I ..."

"I've been in love with you since I was fifteen. Since the moment you brought Kira to her first swim practice and you had a big coffee stain on your cream-colored sweater."

My mouth dropped open.

"I thought my infatuation would go away. And I've had girlfriends who I tried to put above you, but ..." he shook his head, "no one ever has." His large Adam's apple bobbed on a swallow. "If you don't feel even remotely the same, then I will back off. I will respect the boundary you've set and treat you like any other parent. But if there's even a small part of you that wonders ... that has thought about me as more than that pimply-faced, squeaky-voiced teenager, then ..."

Where was my voice? Why wasn't I able to say anything?

"I'm in love with you. I want you, and I'm incredibly attracted to you. I'm putting all my cards on the table here." He glanced up at the mistletoe. "And maybe Kira wouldn't be as traumatized by the idea as we once thought?"

My gaze followed his to the mistletoe, and I blinked several times, processing his words and trying to make sense of everything he had just said.

Deacon George was quite possibly, the sexiest man alive, and he wanted me. Me.

"Deacon ..." Want, hope, and need *zealously* swirled together inside of me, creating an intoxicating cocktail far more potent than the wine. He took a step toward me, but he couldn't come any closer without having to climb the stairs. Our eyes locked. Heat filled every crevice around my heart, and those turkey-comatose butterflies woke up with a second-wind. Then his hand came up, and he cupped my jaw, his pinky resting against my neck, against my raging pulse. "Can't waste the mistletoe," he said, keeping his eyes locked on mine as he slowly moved in, pulling me forward just a little.

I moved in too, my eyes fluttering shut just before our lips met.

And holy father, son and spirit, this man could kiss. The way his tongue so effortlessly slipped inside my mouth, not forcefully, not aggressively, but just … perfectly. And it didn't stay there. He'd push it in for a bit, then pull it out and kiss me without tongue, nibble my bottom lip a little, then slide that tongue back in again. I let him lead it entirely and guide my body to how he needed it, tilting my head a little more and taking possession, taking control.

It'd been ages since I had handed over the reins to someone else—for anything—and I only found myself hesitating for a second. The next thing I knew, I was being swept into his arms and carried upstairs to my bedroom.

"Tell me you don't want me," he said, lying me down on the bed.

I shook my head. "I can't."

That pulled a cocky smirk to his mouth. "You can't tell me you don't want me?"

I did the double-negative math in my head, and then nodded. "Yeah."

"Because you do want me?"

I nodded again. "Yeah."

"I don't want to do anything to jeopardize Kira's life on the team. Or your life."

There was so much to work out, but at the moment, after that kiss, that was for future Greta to figure out. Right now, *this* Greta wanted him to take off his shirt and kiss me again.

I sat up and reached for the hem of his shirt. "We'll sort it out later."

He allowed me to peel off his sweater, and I was unable to control the gasp that came out of my mouth about as well as I was able to control the weather. "That shouldn't be legal," I whispered, hesitantly reaching up and trailing my hands over the sculpted ridges of his torso.

"Why do you think I never take my shirt off at practice?"

Snorting, I smiled and shook my head. "Afraid of being hauled away by the Handsome Police?"

"They exist. I've done time before."

I swatted his hard chest and rolled my eyes.

"Your turn," he said, his voice smooth like honey.

"M-my turn?"

"You've seen me without my shirt. Fair is fair." His fingers came to the hem of my fuzzy black sweater, and I lifted my arms so he could remove the fabric from my body. I ran on the treadmill in my garage almost daily, but I wasn't ripped like Mr. Universe here. Instinctively, I went to cover my stomach when he tossed the sweater to the floor, but he quickly took my hands, lacing his fingers through mine. "Don't."

I swallowed and met his eyes. "I don't get it," I whispered.

"Don't get what?"

"What … what do you see in me?"

Surprise filled his gaze. "I don't get it," he finally said, echoing me. My eyes narrowed in confusion as he lowered himself over top of me on the bed, cradling my face in his hands, our gazes locked. "I don't get what you don't see in yourself."

Lust flooded my veins, and I wrapped my arms around his neck and pulled his mouth down to mine, wrapping my legs around his torso and grinding my pelvis into his. Even if that was a line from a movie or something, it was a good line, and I was a hungry minnow with no qualms about biting.

We might only have tonight, but Deacon George wanted me, and it was high time I gave myself a Christmas present. Santa had been extra stingy with me this year ... or maybe he just delivered me Deacon George rather than anything in my stocking. I'd be sure to write the fat, bearded man a thank-you letter.

After the orgasms, of course.

FINALLY, having her in my arms, beneath me was more than I ever could have hoped for. It was the best Christmas present anybody could ever give me, and nothing would ever top it.

There was a lot to work out, and the future for us seemed bleak. But we had tonight.

And I intended to make the most of it.

Mindful that there was an impressionable twelve-year-old across the hall, I tried not to moan or groan too loudly, and I could tell Greta was taking the same kind of care.

It was tough, though. The feel of her, the taste of her—it was better than any of the thousand fantasies I conjured in my mind over the years to relieve the tension in my trousers.

She rocked her hips against my cock and ground down against her, with the layers of our pants still between us. We were shirtless, but we both wanted more. Kneeling up, then standing up, my chest heaving, I stared down at her. "You okay?"

She nodded, her eyes all sparkly, cheeks flushed and lips puffy. She'd never looked more gorgeous in all my life. Using her elbows to prop herself up, she sat up and reached for the belt at my waist. I swallowed and watched as she unfastened it, then unbuttoned and unzipped my navy-blue dress slacks. Licking her bottom lip, she fished my cock out of my Christmas-red boxer briefs—with the damp patch at the front—and swirled her thumb over the crown, coating the purple tip with my own precum.

I swallowed again, mesmerized by this goddess.

Tipping her gaze up to mine and keeping it locked there, she slowly fed me into her mouth, past her lips and into the wet heat I'd only ever dreamed about.

My eyes wanted to roll back and close, but I forced them to stay open. I forced myself to watch her, in awe of how deep she could take me without gagging, of how she kept her eyes on me. Her hand worked in tandem with her mouth, but she was able to take me nearly to the base.

I groaned when the crown knocked her tonsils and she did a little swallowing motion, squeezing the head of my cock with the back of her throat. She brought me all the way out again and flicked her tongue back and forth over the slit at the top, pulling another deep rumble from my chest. If she kept this up, I wasn't going to last long. But, fuck me, I also never wanted it to end. I wanted to come down her throat so fucking badly. I wanted to watch her neck undulate with each swallow of my load, knowing a part of me was going to sit in her belly for hours.

Was I a sick, perverted fucker? Maybe. But I didn't fucking care.

I let her deep-throat me a few more times before cupping her face in my hands and gently pulling her free with a wet *pop*. Her eyes were hooded and as glittery as ever as I dropped to a crouch and removed her slippers and socks. Slowly, trailing my hands up the outsides of her thighs, I hooked my fingers into the waistband over her tartan flannel pajama pants, along with the waistband of her panties and pulled both down at the same time, chucking them to the side with her sweater.

My eyes widened at the bareness of her pussy. I wasn't expecting her to be bare—not that I cared. Meeting her worried gaze, I hovered over her, taking her mouth again and allowing my kisses to travel down across her jaw and neck, and over the swell of each breast, pulling her nipples free one at a time and sucking them until she inhaled sharply and arched her back.

I continued on my journey south, swirling my tongue around her navel—not zealously though—until I reached her mound where I pressed my nose and pulled in a deep breath.

She wriggled against me a little, almost like she was trying to cross her legs, which was insane.

I sank to the floor on my knees, and gripped her by the ankles, yanking her across the bed so that her perfect, bare pussy was right in front of my mouth. Shouldering her legs apart a little more, I settled in, absolutely starved for a taste of her.

"I've been waiting for this for a long time," I murmured, using my fingers to gently spread her lips a little before flicking her clit with my tongue. "To finally taste you." I flicked her clit again, and she moaned, sinking into the bed."

With a long, slow inhale, I encircled her sensitive nub with my mouth and sucked hard at the same time two fingers navigated toward her already slick center. I slid one in and then the other, curling them just so until she rode them with vigor, setting her own pace for what she needed.

Her clit swelled hard against my tongue as I continued to suck, and from the way her hip movements grew erratic, I could tell she was close. So I backed off, edging her a little and stopped pressing on her G-spot so hard. I twiddled my tongue over her clit, rather than continue sucking on it, but that too seemed to bring her back to the brink.

This wasn't a one-orgasm, and the night is over kind of deal. If we only had tonight, we were going to make it last all fucking night.

She seemed to prefer sucking, so I went back to that while pressing my two fingers up against her G-spot. Her hips rose and dropped, and her breathing grew more ragged. Both hands came down, and her fingers curled into my hair, practically snatching me bald.

I fucking loved it.

Her clit swelled even more, her pussy gushed, all her muscles tightened, she sucked in a deep breath, paused and ...

Detonated.

Her pussy walls throbbed against my fingers, and her clit pulsed in the vice of my lips as her arousal gushed and coated my hand. But it was the way she kept her back arched and her fingers tight in my hair, holding my face against her like that, that did it for me. Yes, fucking, please. All day, every day.

Merry Christmas to me.

Her orgasm was intense, and it lasted a while. But I was anything if not thorough and patient, so I kept my fingers there, I kept my mouth there, even when things cramped, until she was finished and collapsed back onto the bed in a sigh. She released my hair, and I gently pulled my fingers free from inside her, standing up and wiping my mouth with the back of my hand. I quietly retreated to the bathroom to wash my hands and mouth, shucking the rest of my clothes as I returned.

She gaped at me from where she lay on the bed, in the exact position I had left her in. "Hand me my phone," she croaked. "I need to call the Handsome Police."

Smirking, I placed one knee, then the other, into the bed and climbed over her. "Condoms?" I asked.

"Nightstand drawer."

Nodding, I pressed a quick kiss to her lips and stood back up, opening up the drawer. "Oh my!" Reaching inside, I pulled out not one, not two, not three, not four, but *five* different silicone vibrating pleasure toys. Some were long and phallic, but a couple were just little balls. One was shaped like a red rose with a small, shallow hole. "What's this one do?" I held it up.

She was going pinker in the cheeks by the second. "That was is a clit sucker. It's almost too intense for me, though. The first setting is enough."

That made my brows spike on my forehead. I picked up the pink one shaped like lips with a tongue sticking out. "I think I can guess what this one does."

She nodded. "Yeah ... It gets the job done."

The ones I was most curious about though were the ones vaguely shaped like *C*s. "And what do these do?"

"Double stimulation. In and out," she said.

"Ah, so this part goes in—obviously—and this part—"

"Sits over the clit and sucks, yes."

"Does it work?"

"I'm walking funny afterward."

That made me snort.

Her eyes fell on mine. "Damien never went down on me. Not in the fourteen years we were together."

Holy shit. I wasn't expecting her to say that.

"My high school boyfriend did, and my freshman boyfriend. I don't know why I didn't see it as a ..."

"Red flag?"

"Is it though?"

"I mean ... it can be. Did he expect blowjobs?"

She nodded.

"So then, if he's not willing to reciprocate, then it's a red flag."

She nibbled her lips nervously. "I just made so many excuses for him. But over time, I started to think that maybe there was something wrong or gross about me."

I shook my head emphatically. "There's nothing wrong *or* gross about you. That was not the only time I'm dining on you tonight, just so you know. I'm going back for seconds and thirds."

Fresh color filled her cheeks, and she pointed to the drawer. "Put on the condom, Deacon."

Smiling, I reached into the box, tore open the wrapper and rolled it on. Then I climbed onto the bed, but rather than join her where she lay across it, with her feet dangling almost to the floor, I encouraged her to join me up with our heads on the pillows.

"I haven't been with anybody else in fourteen years."

"So?"

"So ... I'm not even sure if I'm any good at sex."

"Well, you're fantastic at giving blowjobs," I replied, dragging the pad of my thumb over her bottom lip. "That's been a fantasy of mine for a long time. And you did *not* disappoint."

She huffed. "I feel like I'm ruining the mood with all this ... talk."

"If you need to talk to get it off your chest or out of your head, we can. I don't want you to do this if you're not in the right headspace. I waited seven years for this. I can wait a little longer." I offered her an encouraging smile and wrapped my arm around her.

"Damien liked blowjobs, but I wonder if it's because he could close his eyes and pretend it was a man giving it to him. The same reason why he preferred doggy style and anal. He didn't want to see me."

Fresh anger flashed through me at what this incredible woman had to endure for so long.

I cupped her chin so that she would look at me. "I want to see you the entire time. I want to look into your eyes. You're the one I want; you're the one I've wanted forever. I don't want to waste a moment of not being able to see your beautiful face."

Swallowing, she sat up tall and reached behind her, unhooking her bra so her perfect tits tumbled free. My cock was already hard as granite, but it twitched and leaked a little more at the sight of more skin.

She lifted her leg and draped it over my waist, straddling me, then she reached between us, took my cock in her hand, lifted and notched me at her core.

Keeping our gazes locked, she slowly sank down, taking me inside her all the way to the hilt. I'd never felt such pleasure in all my life.

When she reached the bottom, we just stayed there for a moment, our eyes only on each other. My hands fell to her hipbones, then slid around to cup her incredible ass. Wrapping her arms around my neck, she brought her mouth forward to mine, taking my bottom lip between her teeth and tugging as she slowly began to lift and drop, riding me like she rode my fingers earlier.

I was in rapture. Utter heaven.

I could die right now, and it'd be as a happy and fulfilled man.

Encouraging her to rock harder so her clit grazed my lower stomach, I cupped one breast and brought the nipple to my mouth, laving at it with my tongue and scissoring my teeth over it. She gasped when I sucked on it hard, making it harder and tighter than ever. Her pussy squeezed my cock with every lift of her hips, then she'd do a not-too *zealous* little hip swirl at the top when just the crown of my cock remained in her heat, only to squeeze her muscles around me on the way down too.

I was so fucking close. So. Fucking. Close.

"Deacon," she breathed, lifting her head to meet my gaze.

I dropped my hand from her breast and cupped her jaw, holding her face just inches from mine. "Fuck, you're gorgeous," I gritted out. "Fucking you ... god, there's nothing better in this world."

"I'm going to come again, Deacon. It feels ... it feels too good."

"That's right, baby. I want you to come all over my dick. Fucking use me, Greta. Ride me as hard as you need to."

As if she was just waiting for me to give her permission, she gripped the headboard behind her, and like a filly set free from the paddock, she started to bob up and down on my cock faster and harder than ever. She wasn't squeezing as much anymore, but I didn't much care. It still felt incredible.

Her tits bounced against my chin, and the faint *slap-slap* of her ass against my thighs filled the room, competing with her muffled moans.

"Oh god," she mewled. "I can't ... I can't hang on."

"Don't hang on."

"I'm going to come."

"Fucking come for me, Greta. Come all over my cock, baby. It's hard just for you."

Her mouth parted, but barely a sound came out as she stilled, my cock buried as deep as it could be inside of her, and she let go—again.

Her pussy walls pulsed and squeezed my dick as her chest heaved and her sexy little whimpers filled the room. The constant, rhythmic dick squeezing was what did it for me, and I finally gave over to the fantasy and let go. I came inside Greta Robinson. My entire body was a maelstrom, a zealous swirling tornado of heat and pleasure, starting out in my lower belly and spreading into my limbs. My balls cinched up tight and pulsed with each spurt as my cock twitched.

My orgasm was winding down before hers was—which is how it should be—and we sat there, in our post-orgasmic fog for a moment, breathless, boneless and completely uncaring about anything beyond that bedroom door.

The world was beyond that door. And right now, the world could fucking wait.

After several long heartbeats, she gracefully slung her leg off me and slid off the bed, skittering to the bathroom where she closed the door. I lay there in the bed, the covers up to my waist, reliving the last hour and how I had absolutely not expected any of that to happen.

The door reopened, and she shyly came out, naked and beautiful as ever. Biting her bottom lip, she slid beneath the covers. I went to the bathroom to remove and dispose of the condom, hoping that when I returned to the bedroom, she wasn't going to kick me out.

I gave my wrist a quick pinch as I washed my hands in the sink. This wasn't a dream, right? I didn't get into a horrible car accident on the way to Christmas dinner and was currently lying in a hospital bed in a medically induced coma?

I opened the bedroom door, where she sat up in bed, smiling at me.

Nope. Not a coma dream.

Was she going to kick me out?

Carefully gauging her, I pulled back the covers and climbed under, tilting my head to the side to ask a wordless question.

"What's that you were saying about going back for seconds and thirds?" she asked, sliding down so her head was nestled among the pillows.

A massive grin curled my mouth like the Grinch when he got the idea to raid Whoville.

I dove under the covers. "Right. Good thing Mrs. Robinson always serves up the best, because baby, I'm starving."

JUST IN CASE KIRA WOKE UP BEFORE WE DID, AFTER AS MANY ORGASMS AS WE could stay awake for, I did retire down to the couch to sleep. Didn't stop me from waking up with a massive hard-on and nearly coming all over Greta's sheets after the filthy dream I had. But it was not so much a dream anymore as it was me simply re-living what actually happened.

I woke to the smell of coffee being brewed along with someone trying to be quiet in the kitchen. Tugging on my pants and the sweater over my head, I shoved my fingers through my hair and yawned before padding barefoot into the kitchen.

It was Greta, not Kira, though, so I quickly walked up behind her and cupped her ass while also sliding my teeth over the shell of her ear.

She moaned and pressed her ass into my still-hard cock.

"Careful, Mrs. Robinson, or I'll have my breakfast between your legs right here on this counter."

She spun around and looped her arms around my neck. I bent my head and kissed her. "A part of me thought it was all a dream when I woke up this morning."

"Me too."

"But then I got up to use the bathroom and the ache between my legs told me it was *very* much real."

That made me smile like a cocky asshole. But I didn't care.

"How do you want to handle things?" I asked.

She shrugged. "I have no clue."

The sound of footsteps on the stairs had us *zealously* breaking apart.

A sleepy-eyed twelve-year-old with a wild, messy topknot blinked at us. She frowned. "It didn't work?"

"What didn't work?" Greta asked, pouring two cups of coffee, then adding a healthy splash of Irish Cream to both.

Kira pointed to the mistletoe. "I hung it before I went to bed thinking maybe ..." She pouted. "I guess we don't always get what we want for Christmas, hmm?"

My brows flew nearly to my hairline, and I spun to face Greta, whose gob was equally smacked.

"Did you hang that with the hopes of Coach Deacon and me kissing?" Greta asked.

A rush of color filled Kira's pale cheeks. "Maybe?"

"Why, honey?"

"I dunno. You've just been so unhappy."

"I have not."

Kira rolled her pretty green eyes. "Okay, not unhappy, but like ... you're still young, Mom. You can still get married again and have more kids or whatever. And Coach Deacon is so nice. I've seen the way he looks at you. I figured you liked him anyway since you invited him to Christmas dinner."

"*Jeanie* invited him," Greta pointed out.

"You could have said no," I argued, which earned me a glare from Greta.

"It's fine, whatever," Kira said, taking a seat on a barstool next to the kitchen island.

"Say Coach Deacon and I *did* kiss," Greta asked cautiously, "how would you see it all going? Because I don't think it'd be easy for you at swimming. The other kids might make fun of you. The other parents might get upset and think he's playing favorites, even if he's not. There is quite a big age gap between us."

"Paul is eleven years younger than Dad. You're twelve years older than Deacon. It's not *that* much."

I couldn't stop myself from shooting Greta a look that said, "See, I told you!"

"And Winnie's dad is almost twenty years older than her mom. He's *really* old. He's like sixty and she's like forty."

"Winnie's dad does not look sixty," Greta said.

I nodded, agreeing with her. Wayne did not look sixty. I hoped I aged as well as he did.

"Anyway," Kira said, "I wouldn't care. I just want you to be happy."

Tears welled up in Greta's eyes, and she went to her daughter, wrapping her up in a big hug. She slid one hand across the island toward me, though, and snagged my gaze. I laced my fingers through hers, and when Kira pulled away from her mother, she gasped.

"Wait! Did you guys kiss last night? Did the mistletoe work?"

"It's very early," Greta said, her voice wobbling a little. "So we're going to keep it *very* quiet. Coach Deacon—"

"I think she can just call me Deacon when we're not at the pool," I interjected.

"*Deacon* is going to treat me like any other parent, and you like any other swimmer when we're not here, okay? We're taking this slow. There's still a lot to figure out. But you're right, honey. I want to be happy too." She smiled at me. "And Deacon makes me happy."

Kira squealed. "This is so exciting. I knew there was something going on between the two of you. I could just feel it."

"Well, let's hope you're the only one who could feel it," Greta said. "Can we trust you to keep this a secret?"

Kira nodded, beaming. "Absolutely. Nobody will know." She pretended to zip her mouth and throw away the key.

I squeezed Greta's fingers in mine, my heart so fucking full I wanted to go run around the snowy streets and shout my love for her.

Kira's eyes gleamed, and she mischievously rubbed her hands together. "I'm so good at this, I need to figure out who to se up next."

"Jeanie," Greta and I both said at the same time, which prompted all of us to start laughing.

My gaze met Greta's, and she smiled beautifully, because she was beautiful. Inside and out. And she was also worth the wait. I was just glad the wait was over and we could finally, at long last, start our life together. Which promised to be really, really amazing.

EPILOGUE

Six years later ...

STANDING IN THE CROWD ON THE SCHOOL FIELD, CELEBRATING WITH ALL THE other parents as their children got up on stage and accepted their diplomas, was as emotional as I expected it to be.

Doing it with Deacon George at my side, whooping and hollering and cheering louder than anybody for our valedictorian daughter, was way more wonderful than I ever expected it to be, let alone what me six years ago thought I deserved.

But there we were. And there she was, ready to address her fellow graduates and wish them well in the next chapter of their lives.

I'd always been an incredibly proud mother, but today I had no words for how I felt about Kira and her success. With a full swimming scholarship to Princeton, she was headed back east in the fall, and although I was sad to see her go, I was so excited for what the future held in store for my bright, beautiful, hardworking daughter.

"Okay," I said, tugging on Deacon's shirt to get him to sit down. "You realize you're the only parent still standing, right?"

"Don't care," he said, sitting down. "I'm a proud stepdad, what can I say?"

My brother and father snorted down the row, but they both really liked Deacon, so it was all done in jest.

I was surprised, but also relieved with how accepting my family was of Deacon and my relationship. I received only a little bit of teasing about the age-gap. But when they all saw how happy he made me, and how doting he was on Kira and me, the teasing stopped and they welcomed him with open arms.

Deacon's mom, thankfully, was the same way toward Kira and me. There wasn't any teasing, though. She seemed cautious, worried about her baby boy falling for an older woman. But just as quickly, I seemed to win her over, and now I considered my mother-in-law one of my dearest friends. She adored Kira, which was why she was also in the audience today.

Where was Damien?

Who the fuck knew?

He sent a card to Kira once in a while, and the court-ordered child-support, but he rarely reached out. He hadn't seen her in years, and it was probably for the better. She had the right kind of father figure in her life in Deacon. He was there for her in ways that Damien never was. He'd even been there for her when she got her first period. And he handled it like a champ.

He laced his fingers through mine on his thigh as our daughter gave her speech to the crowd. I would be surprised if by the end there was a dry eye in the crowd. I was certainly a sobbing mess at the end.

The applause from her peers that followed was thunderous and lasted ages. Kira's face was a bright, rosy little apple on the stage. Her cheeks probably hurt from how big she was smiling with those expensive, straight white teeth. Worth every penny.

Eventually, the applause and cheering died down, and before we knew it, we were trying our best to find her among the sea of caps and gowns.

"Now I know how penguins must feel," Deacon muttered. He let out a loud, "Caw, caw!" Cupping his hands over his mouth.

I gaped at him.

A distant "Caw, caw!" replied.

"This way," he said, ushering us through the crowd, only to pause again, and do the call again.

Another echoed reply.

They did that a few more times before we finally found Kira, swarmed by her friends.

"Did the two of you plan that?" I asked.

"It's how we always communicate with each other when we can't find the other person," Deacon said. "In the grocery store, in IKEA."

"Not the library, though," Kira said, pretending to give him a stern warning.

One-by-one we hugged our graduate. But of course, that just prompted more tears. Luckily, I had her robe to help mop up my mess.

"Totally up to you, sugarplum, but do you want to come out for dinner with all of us, or do you have plans with your friends?"

She scowled at me. "I'm coming for dinner with my family, duh!"

"I didn't want to assume," I said, holding my hands up in innocence.

"I'm going out with them later tonight once you old people are in bed. But I wouldn't be here without all of you, so of course I'm going to let you buy me an expensive celebration dinner."

My dad, brother and Deacon all tossed their heads back and laughed. I shook my head and smirked at my daughter's cheekiness.

"All right, well, bird-call Deacon when you're ready to go with us. We're going to get some air away from this crowd and go find some shade."

More friends were already approaching her for hugs. She was one of the most popular kids in the school, but it was for the absolute best reason. Because she was kind—to everyone.

Linking my fingers through Deacon's, I let him expertly navigate us to the shade of a big tree on the edge of the field. My parents and Deacon's mom were ahead of us, chatting with my brother and his wife.

I leaned into Deacon. "Still okay that we didn't have kids?"

He leaned down and kissed the top of my head. "More than okay. And I have a kid. And she's the best kid. Just because she's not mine by blood doesn't mean I wouldn't kill for that child."

His words warmed me like they always did when he spoke about how much he loved Kira.

"Besides. I get you all to myself in a few months. Naked Sundays, here we come."

"You've kept the eight-pack. I am absolutely on board with Naked Sundays."

He shot me a wink.

"Thank you," I said, glancing up at him and leaning my cheek against his arm, "for showing me that age really is just a number. I could have missed out on something—on *someone*—truly amazing if I had let what others thought and society's stigmas control me."

"All it took was a little mistletoe, a lot of patience, and this super-skilled tongue to convince you, huh?"

That made heat fill my cheeks. I bit my lip and made sure my parents weren't within earshot. "Once Kira is out for the night, I plan on putting that super-skilled tongue of yours to work."

He stopped me and gripped my chin, forcing me to look up into his fathomless green eyes. "Love what you do and you'll never work a day in your life." Then he dropped his mouth to mine, and the whole world melted away.

Whitley Cox is an English Major turned Psych Major, who after all was said and done came out with a B.A. in Psychology, and then subsequently moved to Indonesia to teach English. But after finding out that the school was not on the up and up (when Immigration came to scope out the teachers she was forced to hide in a closet because the school had not actually purchased a work permit for her), she broke her contract and took off traveling. Only to then return home and start working with children on the Autism spectrum as an intervention therapist, and begin writing her first book.

A Canadian West Coast baby born and raised, Whitley is married to her high school sweetheart, and together they have two beautiful daughters and a fluffy dog. She spends her days making food that gets thrown on the floor, vacuuming Cheerios out from under the couch and making sure that the dog food doesn't end up in the air conditioner. But when the kids are at school, and it's not quite wine o'clock, Whitley sits down, avoids the pile of laundry on the couch, and writes.

A lover of all things decadent; wine, cheese, chocolate and spicy erotic romance, Whitley brings the humorous side of sex, the ridiculous side of relationships and the suspense of everyday life into her stories. With single dads, firefighters, Navy SEALs, mommy wars, body issues, threesomes, bondage and role-playing, Whitley's books have all the funny and fabulously filthy words you could hope for.

Check out my online store: https://whitleycoxbookshop.com

THE KISS

Xavier Neal

CHAPTER ONE

Kolby

ALL I WANT for Christmas is my teammate's ex-wife under the mistletoe.

Why?

Because she's the fucking definition of meant for me.

Hell, her name is *Destiny* for crying out loud.

Destiny McKenzie.

We've crossed paths twice – with this being the second – and both times I forgot my name.

My. Own. Fucking. Name.

Thank the lord, I was wearing my practice jersey when we first met.

And thank that big bench boss in the sky again that *she* remembered it this sesh.

I – yet again – didn't.

Or couldn't.

There's something about just being around her that melts my very basic ability to think, which isn't fucking handy, considering I need to be able to do that to have an actual conversation with her.

One that consists of more than goofy grins and weird gurgling noises.

Fuck, she probably thinks I don't know how to speak anymore given the amount of times I've crashed headfirst into the boards.

Truth?

The number of concussions I've suffered is really low on paper but probably a lot higher off.

Pretty sure she's a doctor.

Wonder if she can just...*tell* that by looking at me?

I give the back of my light beige colored neck a bashful squeeze at the same time I open my mouth to say something – fuck *anything* at this point will do – when her attention snaps away to someone sprinting past me.

"*Stop!*" Destiny shouts prior to taking off. "*Stop him! Stop him! That's my son!*"

Oh yeah.

Now, is *definitely* not the time to try to finagle her into inching two steps to the left to get my holiday wish.

"*Stop him!*" she continues to scream, long, light brown sugar toned legs covered by candy cane covered tights, rapidly moving in pursuit. "*Security! Security!*" Following after her thoughtlessly occurs. "*Anyone! Help! Help!*"

Me.

I'm anyone!

I can save him!

All of a sudden, my older half-brother, Slater steps away from the checkout counter that's around the corner we're passing, just in time to see as much as hear the commotion.

"*Stop him!*" Destiny pleads with the random onlookers who are simply watching the scene unfold. "*That man has my son!*"

Unlike me – who always hesitates when it comes to decision making off the ice – Slater goes from bench sitting to full fucking PK – penalty kill – mode. "I'm on it!" His bags dramatically hitting the ground precedes his commands by just a couple of seconds. "*Kolby, get her ass somewhere safe!*" The kidnapper dips around another display hoping to hide the direction he's taking. "*Somewhere with lots of witnesses!*"

Why?

Why witnesses?

They're clearly not trying to kidnap her.

Of course there's no real time to ask that question or any question for that matter.

"*Now!*" He bellows oversized, 6'2 frame in motion. "*I'll get the kid!*"

I nod despite the fact he's not looking in my direction and call out to the breathtaking woman ahead of me, "Destiny, stop!

"I'm not fucking stopping!" She barks back, voice quivering and panting, painting a perfect picture of a different kind at a very unperfect time. "I can catch him! I have to! That's my son!"

Sprinting a bit ahead to cut her off is easily done; however, managing to imprison her in my arms is not. She flails around, fuzzy white sweater covered arms desperately extending past one side of my face. The other. Tiny kicks are followed by an attempt to shove me away, and once her hands are in a better position for seizing, I don't waste a second to do so. Her small, balled up, trapped fists furiously pound on the gingerbread man that's plastered on the front of my sweater – my brother *claims* my twin nieces, Allaira and Alura aka Lair Bear and Lu, picked this out for me last year – doing their best to pulverize everything in their path. While the hits themselves don't hurt – not even stub a toe level of pain – I can't deny the ache spreading through my chest.

The puck sized pang plummeting to the pit of my stomach.

I don't want her mad.

Or sad.

Or scared.

And I damn sure don't want her thinking I'm the type of prick to just stand ideally by when she needs him the most.

"*Letmego! Letmego!*" Her entire frame wildly whips around, dark brown wavy strands working their way loose from the bun pinned to the top of her head. "*Letmefuckinggo!*"

"No."

"*IsaidletmegoWahl! I can still get to him!*"

"No."

"*Letmefuckinggo!*" Destiny's movements not only increase in frenzy but in violence. She hastily lifts her knee to nail me in the nuts at the same time she commands, "*Now!*"

Dodging the strike takes some impressive maneuvering from my lower half, once more working off the entire batch of *Galletitas De Nuez* the girls and I ate during my babysitting duty last night. The same duty that led to me guilt tripping their father into joining me for some not so casual shopping.

It turns out, I don't know that part of my home team as well as I thought.

Then again, that may have just been the casual lie I convinced myself to be the truth to avoid having to deal with shopping rather than focusing on helping my hockey team, The Dalvegan Dragons, keep up our win-streak this season.

"*Wahl-*"

"*Enough.*" Flexing my arms tighter is attached to capturing her light brown glare with my blue. "*I'm not about to let somethin' happen to you too.*"

Destiny's jaw trembles along with her words, "But-"

"My brother's got this."

"But-"

"He *literally* does this for a livin'."

"But-"

"Alright, he *used* to." My grip shifts to one that's slightly softer. Warmer. "Now, he trains other people on how to do it." I let my head casually bounce side to side. "*Mostly.* If his wife asks, *only.* I'm honestly not sure if she knows he lets himself get roped into an actual assignment every now and again."

Huh.

Does this shit count as one of those times?

"*But-*"

"Nope. The only butt we're gonna be talkin' about is mine, and how amazin' it is 'cause we all know, hockey players have the most amazin' asses. Hands down."

At that, Destiny's shoulders finally peal themselves away from her ears. "What?"

"We all know-"

"Who is we?"

"Uh...society?"

"So, you speak for *all* of society now?"

"Yes." Seeing her dark eyebrows twitch has me quickly recanting my statement. "No." Another amused flicker pushes me to change my mind yet again. "Maybe? Some of it?" Verbally floundering can't be stopped. "The sports society?"

"You mean the store in the Locker District?"

"No, I meant – Well, I *mean* – Okay, but I thought-" tripping over myself abruptly comes to an end at the sight of her beginning to smirk. "You're fuckin' with me, aren't ya?"

"Absolutely." Seeing the edges of her lips completely curl upward ceases any ability to breathe. "And I'm trusting you, Wahl. I'm trusting that you're the great guy everyone on the team says you are, and that your brother is going to save Oakley."

"He is. And while he does that, I'm gonna do what a good d man on the same line does." My hands glide just a little lower to rest on the small of her back. *"Protect the most important player on the ice."*

CHAPTER TWO

Destiny

I HAVE to be the *worst* parent on the entire planet.

Like do a survey.

Ask people about where I rank after telling them that instead of running around the mall like a crazy mama bear on a rampage, roaring from department store to department store, turning over display tables and ripping off mannequin heads in search of my son who some asshole managed to Houdini mid pursuit, I'm sitting on an outdoor picnic bench, near the ice skating rink, having one of my ex-husband's latest teammates try to convince me to decorate a Christmas cookie and see if every person doesn't say the exact same shit.

I've failed.

Fuck, I am *failing.*

But what more can I do?

I flagged down a DPD officer who happened to be on the premises – apparently Christmas Eve brings out all sorts of criminals from the woodwork – told him about the situation, and right as he went to call it in, Wahl mentioned who his big brother is, which not only stopped the cop's actions, it had him echoing what the well sculpted, 6'o defenseman across from me already said.

Slater – although he too is known as Wahl in his own circles it seems – will rescue Oakley.

This is literally what he does for a living.

What he's more or less always done for a living.

And according to both men, he's one of the best in the whole world at it.

That fact alone should bring me comfort.

After all, who wouldn't want someone like that saving their child from possibly being sold or trafficked or black market harvested for his organs?

I mean I should feel *relief* knowing that a man who used to swoop down behind enemy lines to bring fellow soldiers home is out there, right now, hunting for my son like it's his own. Tracking and trailing and trapping the sonofabitch who snatched my reason for existing literally out of my hand.

Yet it doesn't.

I actually feel even shittier.

Like my ex is right.

Like I *am* a terrible mother.

Like I really don't deserve the bundle of wonderful our adorable four-year-old is.

Maybe I fucking don't.

I swear, it's like I never get anything right when it comes to him, which is something my mom claims all mothers feel at least six times in their life.

"Want one of my balls?" Wahl impishly offers at the same time he pushes his paper plate at me. "It's white."

Tearing my gaze away from the distance I was staring out into is followed by lifting a curious eyebrow.

"Not white," he immediately stumbles over his words, southern drawl damn near impossible to ignore. "Well, not *white, white*. Not like rink white. But like dry erase board white."

Against my own volition, I mirthfully beam. "You mean blank?"

"Yeah!" His blue frosting tipped fingertips go to give the back of his neck an uncomfortable scratch. "That's the uh...the word...that um...yeah."

It's impossible not to snicker at the streak of blue his action leaves behind. "And now your neck's not blank."

"Huh?"

Rather than verbally explain, I lift one set of fingers and wiggle them.

He drops his attention down to his, smacks himself in the middle of his forehead, and grunts, "*Fuck.*"

"And now neither is your face."

"*Double fuck,*" Wahl murmurs right before grabbing the napkin holder. "I'm such a fuckin' goof."

"Yeah, but at least you have an amazing ass."

The flirty compliment causes him to fumble the object right out of his grip onto the concrete where it cracks open, unleashing the thin brown items into a fresh gust of wind.

Another round of mumbles is attached to a slow, shameful headshake, "*Thiscantreallybehappenintome...*"

Funny how we're both in that mindset at the moment.

Big difference being I'm missing a literal piece of myself while he's slightly embarrassed, he's a bit clumsy.

Which is honestly not that surprising.

Most of the hockey players I've known throughout my entire life are graceful on the ice and graceless off.

My ex being no exception.

Unfortunately for Oakley, he inherited that klutziness, but not his dad's skating skills.

He got mine.

Put a pair of blades on him and the poor little guy looks like a drunk baby ostrich.

It's precious…you know unless you ask his father who says it's humiliating that they share genetics.

He says the same monstrous shit whenever he finds out about our latest ER visits too.

See, our sweet baby boy is all butterfingers, *all the time*.

He somehow manages to hurt himself simply restacking the pillows on his bed.

It's why I'm personally on a first name basis with one of the ER doctors at Dalvegan Memorial Hospital after only three months of being back here, although, I wish it were for other reasons.

Too bad that dating isn't exactly something I have time for right now.

And even if I did, his asshole father would go out of his way to make my life a living hell while I tried.

Trust me.

He's done it before.

I have no doubt he'll do it again.

Completely losing me isn't something he's quite accepted yet and part of me, deep down is terrified he never will.

Rather than sit by and watch the situation get worse, I get up to assist. Collecting as many crumpled-up napkins as possible is smoothly followed by a round of dumping them in the nearest trashcan along with grabbing a full holder from an empty table.

Stationing myself beside him is attached to suggesting, "Why don't we start this whole accidentally running into each other thing over?" I retrieve the to-go package of wet wipes from my waist purse and offer him one. "Clean slate? Both literally and figuratively?"

"Yeah. I'd like that." Wahl flashes me his crooked, knee wobbling grin again. "I'm a fan of fresh ice."

It's impossible not to tease, "And hockey metaphors?"

"Comes with the territory." He nonchalantly starts scrubbing away frosting. "But you know that. You married one of us."

"And divorced one of you."

Hurt appears and disappears in a single blink. ""Cause of the jock talk?"

"No, because of the narcissism and constant cheating."

Unmistakable disdain grows in his expression. "Stastney fucked around on you?"

"Come on, Wahl. *All* hockey players fuck around."

"No, not *all* of us," he firmly argues on a discarding of the wet wipe to the other side of the table. "And it's Kolby."

Being totally taken by surprise results in me leaning slightly away. "What?"

"Call me *Kolby*." He lets his crystal gaze carve itself in places it doesn't belong. "Please and thank you."

Additional shock leads to a mashup of incomplete thoughts, "But you – and I thought – Don't you – Everyone else–"

"That shit's cute when you do it," the sandy blond-haired defenseman lightly chuckles. "Me? Not so much."

"I'd argue otherwise," thoughtlessly rushes past my parted lips.

Shit.

I shouldn't have said that out loud.

I didn't *intend* to say that out loud.

Especially not to him.

Flirting – which I'm *not* openly admitting to doing – is the last thing that should be happening right now.

I should be fully focused on creative new ways to track my son's location at all times.

Perhaps installing a tracking chip in his shoes?

Socks?

Directly into his foot or is *that* overcorrecting?

Heat flushes my cold cheeks encouraging him to resume speaking instead of me. "When you're a free agent, yeah. Fuckin' around is the shit you *should* be doin'. You earned that. Every night you go out there and put your blood, sweat, tears, and even teeth on that ice, you *deserve* whatever sexy little snipe *wants* to hop on your stick for a ride. That's called a warrior's welcome."

"Not sure that it is."

"*But*–"

"Oh, there's a but to this little STD lesson?"

"*But*," he lightly laughs, body slightly angling itself in my direction, "when you've signed that contract with someone else...when you've put your signature on that shit...your name on their jersey...their name on your Stanley Cup...then it's done." Seriousness shifts into place. "Fuckin' around *stops*. You *commit* to that shit. You show up for warmies. You show up for pracky. You show up for two a days and three a days in playoff season. You show up early. You stay late. You fight for the logo that you agreed to wear and never give up on them. Not even when you're bein' dragged off the ice on a stretcher."

For the first time in my life, I'm left completely speechless.

I haven't heard anyone talk about marriage like that other than my parents who have been married for fifty years. And while they obviously didn't use hockey metaphors, the message was still the same. Relationships require work from *two* people at all times.

Not just one.

"You sayin' Statsney never gave you that?"

"*No one has ever given me that*," I quietly confess, attention cascading to the messy contents of my waist purse, needing something to distract myself with. "*Doubt anyone ever will.*"

Hell, just the idea of it feels like an unfathomable fairytale concept at this point in my life.

"Can't count it as a loss 'til that final buzzer, peppermint."

Whether it's the phrasing or the attempted nickname that returns my stare to his is unknown. "Peppermint?"

"'Cause of the uh...um...the pant drawings?" He flounders, pointed finger oscillating between gesturing at my lap and the table. "Your line stripes–"

"Isn't that redundant?"

"Ref stripes?"

"Those are black and white."

"Festive ref stripes?"

"Not a thing."

"Should be a thing, though," he loudly chuckles once more. "Those zebs could use color in their lives."

Letting myself get lost in the warmth of his laughter feels equally right and wrong.

On one hand, I have no business engaging in any emotion that's not fear or panic or some flavor of the two fused together, but on the other? Those things seem a lot harder to succumb to when I'm around him.

Next to him.

In his arms.

Ohmygod, earlier, when he held me tight and promised to protect me, I damn near melted like a snowman in the middle of a Texas summer.

Rationally?

Rationally, I know that I should've stomped on his foot, punched him in his light scruff covered face, and informed him that I've been taking care of me as well as Oakley basically all on my own for the past four years – Jake didn't even bother trying to get home to see his only son be born – so I don't need anyone else's help to save him or myself.

Irrationally?

We're talking Santa please grant me my asinine Christmas wish of starring in a Halmark movie featuring an exhausted single mom medical examiner who finally finds love in the mall – of all places – after walking in on her ex-husband fucking his neighbor's wife because he *begged* her to bring his son by for a couple hours to open gifts.

I knew I didn't belong trapped in Kolby's arms and yet...for just a micro-scopic snowflake moment...I didn't wanna be trapped anywhere else.

All of a sudden, the most heartwarming voice I could ever hear calls out, "Mommmm!"

Leaning slightly forward to look past Kolby reveals to me a much better Christmas miracle than the made for TV one I dreamt about for thirty seconds earlier. "Oakley!!!!!" There's no hesitation to scramble off the bench and sprint the short stretch over to where he's being carried by Slater. The instant I'm within reach, he stops playing with the Play-Doh in his hands to wordlessly request I hold him instead. *"Ohmygod,"* is mumbled in breathless repetition during the transfer; however, as soon as his tiny navy-blue sweater covered arms wrap around my neck I tearily croak out, *"I'm so glad you're okay!"*

"Your new friend saved me!" Oakley cheerfully declares prior to pulling back to show me the contents of his hand. "And look what he gave me!"

I sniffle away the remaining tears to enthusiastically say, "Play-Doh!"

"Sparkly hockey green Play-Doh, Mom!"

Cutting my watery gaze over to Slater is done at the same time he offhand-edly shrugs. *"Tis the season and all..."*

"Big bro," Kolby cautiously begins upon his approach, "do you really jus' walk around with Play Doh in your pocket?"

"Yup." The man who kept his word lets his attention transition over to the male who is now standing beside me. "Part of always bein' prepared."

"I must've missed that lesson at Scouts."

"You weren't in the Scouts."

"Neither were you."

"I know some PJs that might disagree," Slater jokingly scolds with a small grin.

Well...would you look at that.

If the two were a little closer in age, they could probably pass for fraternal twins.

Slater redirects his gaze back to me and takes a more professional tone, "The man who attempted to apprehend your son is currently bein' handled. To my understandin' – courtesy of a mild interrogation that occurred while Oakley was buildin' a Christmas tree with his Play-Doh – this was not a traffickin' related incident."

Adjusting my hold is done in tandem with me asking, "Then what the hell was it?"

"All I could get out of him was that someone paid him to take the kid."

"Who would wanna pay someone to kidnap my son!?"

"Speakin' from experience?" Slater folds his bulky arms across his rustic-colored flannel shirt. "Usually exes. Or family members *of* exes. Or once in a while the new spouse of the aforementioned ex. 'Ish like this – someone hired for a particular child – is usually jus' custody case related. One parent goin' to extreme lengths to prove the other isn't fit or isn't capable of completely mana-gin' the child on their own. There are also times when one parent forcefully acquires custody of said child and relocates them to another country where the other parent can't find them or even if they can, they can't legally gain guardian-ship or get them sent back to their rightful country due to said country's international abduction laws, which is then when the men that I train get hired to handle things."

My jaw cracks open, yet not a single word flutters free.

No.

That's not...that's not what was about to happen here, was it?

Jake is an asshole, yes.

But the spineless type.

The one who circles around the block again and again while blowing up your phone because he sees a car he doesn't recognize in your driveway and feels he has a right to know who it belongs to.

He's not *the other kind* of monster.

At least...I don't think he is.

Perhaps hope might be a better word until I get more definitive answers.

"I need to fill out a bit of paperwork," Slater politely announces after allowing my silence to carry on for too long. "Make a couple calls. Swing by the store and pick up those gifts I dropped. But you two have a very merry Christ-mas, alright?"

Rapid nodding precedes a quiet, heartfelt, "Thank you again, Slater."

"No thanks needed." He softly beams and locks eyes with Kolby for a second time. "Why don't you walk 'em to their car? Make sure they get settled safely?"

"Already ahead of ya," the man lingering at my side insists.

"Can we paint cookies first?!" Oakley pushes up his falling glasses. "Please, Mom?"

The request is instantly met with reluctance. "I don't think that's a good idea."

"But Mom…" he unhappily whines. "You said we could. You said we could paint cookies for Santa."

That was *before* he was momentarily kidnapped.

And definitely before having to entertain the idea it might've been his father who had it arranged.

"Mom," Kolby casually interjects, collecting my attention along with a furrowed brow, "what if the *three of us* decorate cookies and *then* I walk you to your car? I think it's a good play. It might even be the best play I make all season."

"Don't you have somewhere to be?" I cautiously investigate. "I mean it *is* Christmas Eve."

"Sounds like Big Bro is gonna be a min," his hands are innocently thrown in the air, "so I've got some time to kill." They find their way to his jean pockets. "And of all the people I could crush a couple appies with on Christmas Eve, I wouldn't mind it bein' you…"

Despite doing everything I can not to blush, I do. "Should we really consider Christmas cookies as an appetizer?"

"They are for Santa."

"They're a dessert."

"Let's meet in the neutral zone and say snack."

Snickering is accompanied by a good-natured headshake. "You're lucky I speak your lingo."

"And I'm even luckier this little guy is *wearin'* my lingo." Kolby kicks his chin in a parting nature to his brother before pointing to the design on Oakley's sweater. "Is that Claus usin' a candy cane like a hockey stick, bud?"

"Yeah!" He proudly states and thrusts his chest forward. "He's using an ornament ball for a puck!"

"Maybe we should go paint him ornament ball cookies then? Help him celly all the ginos he's gonna be puttin' on the scoreboard when he finishes deliverin' all the presents?"

"Yeah!" My son joyfully tosses his curled fists into the air, Play-Doh pieces flying everywhere. "Celly!"

"Yeah, bud!" Kolby echoes in both excitement and movement. "Celly!"

Their infectious attitude is impossible to deny, which is what prompts me to lovingly cave. "Alright boys, let's go paint Santa some cookies for his big, delivered all the presents around the world, celebration."

CHAPTER THREE

Kolby

I ALWAYS THOUGHT the best sounds in the world were a body crashing into the boards – particularly one I put there – and hearing the buzzer go off for that game winning gino – or *goal* to those that aren't hockey fluent.

But now?

Now, I know the truth.

Nothing could ever be better than hearing Destiny and Oakley laugh.

Doesn't matter if it's *at* me or *with* me as long as it's *around me.*

I swear to the bench boss upstairs it's that type of shit that gets you hyped at warmies. And focused in between the hard miles. And that you pump through the speakers in celly on your way home from earning *The Fucking Cup.*

It's the most perfect sound in the world.

And now that I've heard it?

I'm gonna do everything I can to never let it go.

"Kolby!" screeches the woman on the other end of my phone.

However...on the glover?

One of my *least* favorite sounds – aside from a shitty timed whistle blow – is my sister-in-law shouting.

It's like being yelled at by Princess Unikitty.

Slater may never admit it out loud, but he agrees.

It was written all over his face the first time I pointed that shit out.

"Kolby!" Arley Wahl shrieks for a second time. *"Answer me!"*

"What uh..." I move up in the cookie line at the same time I search for clarification, "what was the question again?"

"Forfuckssake," she unhappily huffs. *"Where. Is. Slater?!"*

"Slater?"

"My. Husband."

The word alone has me glancing over my shoulder to the woman I wouldn't mind calling me that someday and wistfully sighing, "Yeah..."

"Your. Big. Brother."

"Oh, right!" Angling my body to keep a more permanent watchful eye over the pair at the picnic table – who seem to be in the process of picking out a Band-Aid to apply to Oakley's forehead – is done in between answering. "Workin'."

"What?!" An unexpected shuffling sound has me momentarily leaning the device away from my ear. "What do you mean he's working!? You two said you were going shopping!"

"We were!"

"What do mean you *were*, Kolby?!"

Not sure I should be the one to explain the situation – even if it was *my fault* he got involved – leads to me rushing to end the call before I fuck around and say something else I shouldn't. "I kinda need to go…" The woman in front of me steps to the side to receive her order. "It's my turn in line."

"Line for what exactly?"

"Cookies."

"What?!"

"We'll be home in the next hour or two."

"Hour or two?!"

"Three tops."

"Wh-"

"See ya then." Abruptly hanging up acts as the perfect segue to placing what I'm going to go ahead and label is a bar down type of order. "Lots of everything. And I mean *lots.*"

The young, cute, big tittied redhead flops her hands on her hips in a flirty fashion. "Did you really go through your first order already, or are you just looking for an excuse to come and see me again?"

Six hours ago?

I would've been open to the idea of giving her a white Christmas.

Too bad for her my heavenly coach above had other, bigger, brighter, *better* plans for me this holiday.

"My cookie team grew in size," kicking my thumb over my shoulder encourages her to get a better idea of my single yet not so single situation, "so, naturally, I need more gear."

"*Ah,*" states the young woman, disappointment poorly kept out of her tone and gaze. "He's cute."

"Agreed."

"Bet you're a great dad."

I wanna be…is right on the tip of my tongue, but I swap that reply for a simple grin.

"Let's see what we can fit in the biggest container we have…" she sweetly announces prior to summoning over another volunteer for the assist.

One giant tray of overflowing cookies, toppings, and hot chocolates later, I'm proving just how silky my mitts are – aka my hand skills – by not spilling a single thing in the transferring process. The instant Destiny sets eyes on me, she gets up in preparation to score herself an apple – an assist – only to be met by a polite headshake of denial.

Gently placing everything down is done just as she asks, "What do I owe you?"

"Nothin', *Peppermint.*"

"Not nothing." Her head tilts slightly in disapproval. "This had to be expensive."

"It wasn't."

"You *know* it was."

"What I know is that the booth operates on donations and volunteers only, so *technically*, this was all *free*."

And the five-hundred-dollar donation along with a promise to swing by the youth sports center was just me showing my gratitude.

"Wahl-"

"*Kolby*," I firmly correct and gingerly place the smallest mug in front of her son. "Careful, bud. It's still pretty hot."

"Thank you!" Oakley happily exclaims.

"Anytime, kiddo."

To my surprise, his expression immediately falls. "*Bud.*"

"Huh?"

"I like *bud*," he confidently informs on an adjustment of his crooked glasses. "Not kiddo."

"I can co-sign on that." After placing the plate of Christmas shaped treats on the table, I meet Destiny's stare, revealing the mirth swimming in mine. "And Mom-"

"Stop calling me Mom."

"But you *are* Mom," Oakley insists, basically putting an invisible A – for Alternate Captain – on his sweater to let me know he has my back.

She presses her lips together to prevent herself from mouthing off.

"Yeah," I continue to tease while placing the bowls of various candies on display, "you *are* Mom especially around Bud."

Destiny does her best to resist letting her demeanor soften.

"Mom, he wants me to call him Bud, and I want you to call me Kolby."

"What about when I see you at the barn?" She inquires prior to pulling her mug over to her.

"What about it?"

"That's when everyone else calls you Wahl."

"You'll still call me Kolby."

"Actually, to be more accurate, the team calls you *Wonder Wahl*."

"Dad says your job is to protect him like a brick wall," Oakley innocently announces.

Yeah, well, if he had *anything* to do with this little dude briefly getting kidnapped, I'm gonna be putting his ass *through* a brick wall instead.

"It's one of my jobs," I state and settle into the space on the opposite side of the table from them. "It's also to protect the tendy who protects the house."

"I wanna be a tendy!" he gleefully announces, smile stretching from ear to ear. "I even asked Santa for *allllll* the gear!"

There's no use in fighting the wide mouth grin his excitement instills. "Is that right?"

"Yeah! And a special painted bucket too! Dad says it's never gonna happen..." The drop in his tone digs the earlier ache back up. "That I'm never gonna be a good goalie or any kinda goalie or hockey player...'cause I don't skate good..." His entire frame begins to sink lower to the ground. "He says that I should just give up...And like...do...space stuff or something else."

Oh...

I'm gonna check his ass. *So. Fucking. Hard.* At our next practice.

"But Mom says I can be anything I wanna be!" Oakley unexpectedly pops back up. "And that she believes in me! And that I gotta believe in me too!"

"Moms are the greatest coaches of all time, Bud." I push a paper plate in front of him and wink. *"Never forget that."* Giving Destiny an eyebrow wiggle is executed before declaring, "Time to get to work, team!"

Oakley and I grab ornament shaped cookies from the pile while his mother snatches up a present. Plastic spoons are passed around by Destiny next. Unlike Oakley who seems to be playing a round of glop and go with all the colors, I struggle to spread the thick globs across the tiny pallet in the form of stripes. Each stroke builds frustration and frustration is immediately fought by shoving an untouched spare cookie into my mouth on an announcement about needing to carbo load. Playful comments from Destiny about the mess I'm making on myself as much as my plate are easily laughed off.

Met with a M&M throw.

And once she learns the ornament is being painted to look like a peppermint – a not so subtle ode to the nickname I think she likes – the food flirting increases.

Whip cream less than cleverly brushed on the back of my hand by her.

Me keeping my eyes locked on hers while licking it off.

Forcefully swallowing moans from watching her seductively put marshmallows in her mouth two at a time.

Eventually, the filthy food fighting shifts away from sexual to silly to include the little guy who has been welcoming me into his world nonstop since we met.

"Ot oh," I dramatically claim on a poke to his nose, "now, you look like Rudolph."

Oakley laughs louder, exposing the half chewed gummy bear in his mouth, before copying my action of lightly smearing frosting on Destiny's nose. "You too, Mom! You too!"

"Hey!" She giggles yet swiftly sticks her fingers in the green frosting, leans across the table, and dabs one dollop on each of my ears. "Well, now *you* look like Santa's favorite elf."

"Had to give me the short end of the stick, yeah?"

More snickers slip free, spinning my whole world around faster. *So. Much. Fucking. Faster.* "Pun intended?"

"Accidental," I effortlessly chuckle, "but enjoyable."

"Far from top cheddar," she sassily counters causing a mixture of laughter and groaning to crawl out.

Fuck, I don't know if there's anything sexier than a woman who not only understands my language but can speak it too.

We spend the next half an hour finishing up our designs, chugging back lukewarm hot chocolate, and letting Oakley lead the conversation in every direction that hits him. Switching from hockey to superheroes to books, back to hockey and then space – the kid really does know a lot about it – not only keeps me on my toes but has me wanting to do this again and again and again.

I don't care if we're decorating cookies or his bucket or a homemade rocket ship for a mission to Saturn – because according to him by the time he grows up we'll already be on Mars.

The activity doesn't matter.

Just...doing something *together* does.

Having...*this* type of fun.

This type of bond.

I want it.

I want it more than any championship I've ever dreamt of.

Escorting Destiny and Oakley to their vehicle isn't a timely task; however, it seems like we all do whatever we can to stretch it. Clean up is slow due specifically to allowing Oakley to show off how his speed skills of running from the table to the trashcan and back – nearly face planting four times – while wrapping up the cookies is even slower because of the buffering protection "needed" not to have the cookies crashing into one another, messing up the designs for Santa. We take the longest route away from the rink to the parking lot, which has us wandering through the decorated area, closeness a requirement as opposed to an option, courtesy of the overcrowded paths. After our earlier encounter, Destiny decides to cradle Oakley to her chest rather than let him walk on his own and her protectiveness of him instantly prompts my protectiveness of her.

Pushes me to gently place my hand in the middle of her back to wordlessly announce I got her.

Them.

Convinces me to tuck myself in a little closer so that he can see I'm a real d man.

That I'll protect a tendy no matter his size.

By the time we make it to her SUV, my new pal is passed out on her shoulder, creating a tiny rink of drool near her neck. She mouths the request to grab the keys from her fanny pack and carefully shifts him upward to grant me easier access. I hit the unlock button, open the door behind the driver's side, and hover defensively close during the buckling of Oakley into his car seat. Afterward, I hand her the plate of cookies to place in the empty area beside him and step back to give her enough space to shut him safely inside.

The second Destiny's fingers begin to reach for her handle, I slyly intervene on a shake of the head. "No, ma'am. That's a gentleman's job."

She hits me with her signature playful smile, giving me another dose of what is sticks down the best present of all time. "Is that what you are?"

"Among other things," smoothly leaves my lips at the same time I pull open the door. "Smart choice parkin' under the streetlight, by the way."

"Yeah, contrary to the way this evening went, I don't really make a habit of putting my son in danger."

"Can't promise I won't make a habit of helpin' him stay *out* of it in the future."

A beautiful, bright crimson shade colors her complexion on a whispered, "Thanks again for helping me get him back, Kolby. And keeping me calm. And buying us cookies. And telling him he can play hockey. And be a tendy. And just being the best but weirdest, unexpected date ever."

This time it's my face that's reddening. "Was this – I mean *is this* – No. Wait. Does this count – *Should* this count – No. Wait. Wait. Wait. What just happened – You're sayin' that we just…" The words trip so hastily over one another I swear it makes my eyes cross. "Does that mean…you'll…That we can…" struggling to find the correct words exponentially increases in difficulty. "Should I-"

Destiny's mouth suddenly crashes against mine to end the faceoff over words, and the second they're there, my hands possessively cup her warm cheeks, wanting and needing to anchor onto the moment, unsure of when as much as if I'll ever get another chance. Quickly parting her lips grants me access to the flavors lingering on her tongue, turning every swipe into the only tasty holiday treat I ever wanna indulge in. Greed collides into anxiousness while anxiousness skates straight into obsession pushing me to roll the slippery wet muscle around and around and around, doing effortless laps in the new rink I'm determined to never leave.

Pretty sure this is it for me.

This kiss is much more than just my Christmas wish come true.

It's the beginning of a new season in my personal life.

And that season will most certainly include a teammate's ex-wife as well as his almost kidnapped son.

Thank you for reading *The Kiss (A Dalvegan Dragons Christmas Novella)*! I hope you loved this forced proximity, holiday romance novella and are excited to read more from me! Make sure to subscribe to my newsletter and enjoy NEW as well as FREE reads from me.

https://www.xavierneal.com/newsletter